Gripping Yarns

GRIPPING
YARNS

Selection by
ROSEMARY GRAY

Wordsworth Editions

In loving memory of
MICHAEL TRAYLER
the founder of Wordsworth Editions

I

Readers who are interested in other titles from
Wordsworth Editions are invited to visit our website at
www.wordsworth-editions.com

For our latest list and a full mail-order service, contact
Bibliophile Books, 5 Datapoint, South Crescent, London E16 4TL
TEL: +44 (0)20 7474 2474 FAX: +44 (0)20 7474 8589
ORDERS: orders@bibliophilebooks.com
WEBSITE: www.bibliophilebooks.com

This edition published in 2008 by Wordsworth Editions Limited
8B East Street, Ware, Hertfordshire SG12 9HJ

ISBN: 978 1 84022 080 3

Text © Wordsworth Editions Limited 2008

Wordsworth® is a registered trademark of
Wordsworth Editions Limited

Typeset by Antony Gray and Erica Sail
Printed and bound by Clays Ltd, St Ives plc

Contents

ANONYMOUS

One Night of Horror

I was but nineteen years of age when the incident occurred which has thrown a shadow over my life; and, ah me! how many and many a weary year has dragged by since then! Young, happy and beloved I was in those long-departed days. They said that I was beautiful. The mirror now reflects a haggard old woman, with ashen lips and face of deadly pallor. But do not fancy that you are listening to a mere puling lament. It is not the flight of years that has brought me to be this wreck of my former self: had it been so I could have borne the loss cheerfully, patiently, as the common lot of all; but it was no natural progress of decay which has robbed me of bloom, of youth, of the hopes and joys that belong to youth, snapped the link that bound my heart to another's and doomed me to a lone old age. I try to be patient, but my cross has been heavy, and my heart is empty and weary and I long for the death that comes so slowly to those who pray to die.

I will try and relate, exactly as it happened, the event which blighted my life. Though it occurred many years ago, there is no fear that I should have forgotten any of the minutest circumstances: they were stamped on my brain too clearly and burningly, like the brand of a red-hot iron. I see them written in the wrinkles of my brow, in the dead whiteness of my hair, which was a glossy brown once, and has known no gradual change from dark to grey, from grey to white, as with those happy ones who were the companions of my girlhood, and whose honoured age is soothed by the love of children and grandchildren. But I must not envy them. I only meant to say that the difficulty of my task has no connection with want of memory – I remember but too well. But as I take my pen my hand trembles, my head swims, the old rushing faintness and horror comes over me again, and the well-remembered fear is upon me. Yet I will go on.

This, briefly, is my story: I was a great heiress, I believe, though I cared little for the fact; but so it was. My father had great possessions, and no son to inherit after him. His three daughters, of whom I was the youngest, were to share the broad acres among them. I have said, and truly, that I cared little for the circumstance; and, indeed, I was so rich then in health and youth and love that I felt myself quite indifferent to all else. The possession of all the treasures of earth could never have made up for what I then had – and lost, as I am about to relate. Of course, we girls knew that we were heiresses, but I do not think Lucy and Minnie were any the prouder or the happier on that account. I know I was not. Reginald did not court me for my money. Of *that*

I felt assured. He proved it, heaven be praised! when he shrank from my side after the change. Yes, in all my lonely age, I can still be thankful that he did not keep his word, as some would have done – did not clasp at the altar a hand he had learned to loathe and shudder at, because it was full of gold – much gold! At least he spared me that. And I know that I was loved, and the knowledge has kept me from going mad through many a weary day and restless night, when my hot eyeballs had not a tear to shed, and even to weep was a luxury denied me.

Our house was an old Tudor mansion. My father was very particular in keeping the smallest peculiarities of his home unaltered. Thus the many peaks and gables, the numerous turrets and the mullioned windows, with their quaint lozenge panes set in lead, remained very nearly as they had been three centuries back. Over and above the quaint melancholy of our dwelling, with the deep woods of its park and the sullen waters of the mere, our neighbourhood was thinly peopled and primitive, and the people round us were ignorant, and tenacious of ancient ideas and traditions. Thus it was a superstitious atmosphere that we children were reared in, and we heard, from our infancy, countless tales of horror, some mere fables doubtless, others legends of dark deeds of the olden time, exaggerated by credulity and the love of the marvellous. Our mother had died when we were young, and our other parent being, though a kind father, much absorbed in affairs of various kinds, as an active magistrate and landlord, there was no one to check the unwholesome stream of tradition with which our plastic minds were inundated in the company of nurses and servants. As years went on, however, the old ghostly tales partially lost their effects, and our un-disciplined minds were turned more towards balls, dress and partners, and other matters airy and trivial, more welcome to our riper age. It was at a county assembly that Reginald and I first met – met and loved. Yes, I am sure that he loved me with all his heart. It was not as deep a heart as some, I have thought in my grief and anger; but I never doubted its truth and honesty. Reginald's father and mine approved of our growing attachment; and as for myself, I know I was so happy then that I look back upon those fleeting moments as on some delicious dream. I now come to the change. I have lingered on my childish reminiscences, my bright and happy youth, and now I must tell the rest – the blight and the sorrow.

It was Christmas, always a joyful and a hospitable time in the country, especially in such an old hall as our home, where quaint customs and frolics were much clung to, as part and parcel of the very dwelling itself. The hall was full of guests – so full, indeed, that there was great difficulty in providing sleeping accommodation for all. Several narrow and dark chambers in the turrets – mere pigeon-holes, as we irreverently called what had been thought good enough for the stately gentlemen of Elizabeth's reign – were now allotted to bachelor visitors, after having been empty for a century. All the spare rooms in the body and wings of the hall were occupied, of course; and the servants who had been brought down were lodged at the farm and at the keeper's, so great was the demand for space. At last the unexpected arrival of an elderly relative, who had been asked months before, but scarcely expected, caused great commotion. My aunts went about wringing their hands distractedly. Lady Speldhurst was a personage of some consequence; she was a distant cousin, and had been for years on cool terms with us all, on account of some fancied affront or slight when she had paid her *last* visit, about the time of my christening. She was seventy years old; she was infirm, rich and testy; moreover, she was my godmother, though I had forgotten the fact; but it seems that though I had formed no expectations of a legacy in my favour, my aunts had done so for me. Aunt Margaret was especially eloquent on the subject. 'There isn't a room left,' she said; 'was ever anything so unfortunate! We cannot put Lady Speldhurst into the turrets, and yet where *is* she to sleep? And Rosa's godmother, too! Poor, dear child, how dreadful! After all these years of estrangement, and with a hundred thousand in the funds, and no comfortable, warm room at her own unlimited disposal – and at Christmas, of all times in the year!' What *was* to be done? My aunts could not resign their own chambers to Lady Speldhurst, because they had already given them up to some of the married guests. My father was the most hospitable of men, but he was rheumatic, gouty and methodical. His sisters-in-law dared not propose to shift his quarters; and, indeed, he would have far sooner dined on prison fare than have been translated to a strange bed. The matter ended in my giving up my room. I had a strange reluctance to making the offer, which surprised myself. Was it a boding of evil to come? I cannot say. We are strangely and wonderfully made. It *may* have been. At any rate, I do not think it was any selfish unwillingness to make an old and infirm lady comfortable by a trifling sacrifice. I was perfectly healthy and strong. The weather was not cold for the time of the year. It was a dark, moist yule – not a snowy one, though snow brooded overhead in the darkling clouds. I *did* make the offer, which became me, I said with a laugh, as the youngest. My sisters laughed too, and made a jest of my evident wish to propitiate my godmother. 'She is a fairy godmother, Rosa,' said Minnie; 'and you know she was affronted at your christening, and went away muttering vengeance. Here she is coming back to see you; I hope she brings golden gifts with her.'

I thought little of Lady Speldhurst and her possible golden gifts. I cared nothing for the wonderful fortune in the funds that my aunts whispered and nodded about so mysteriously. But since then I have wondered whether, had I then showed myself peevish or obstinate – had I refused to give up my room for the expected kinswoman – it would not have altered the whole of my life? But then Lucy or Minnie would have offered in my stead, and been sacrificed – what do I say? – better that the blow should have fallen as it did than on those dear ones.

The chamber to which I removed was a dim little triangular room in the western wing, and was only to be reached by traversing the picture-gallery, or by mounting a little flight of stone stairs which led directly upwards from the low-browed arch of a door that opened into the garden. There was one more room on the same landing-place, and this was a mere receptacle for broken furniture, shattered toys, and all the lumber that *will* accumulate in a country house. The room I was to inhabit for a few nights was a tapestry-hung apartment, with faded green curtains of some costly stuff, contrasting oddly with a new carpet and the bright, fresh hangings of the bed, which had been hurriedly erected. The furniture was half old, half new; and on the dressing-table stood a very quaint oval mirror, in a frame of black wood – unpolished ebony, I think. I can remember the very pattern of the carpet, the number of chairs, the situation of the bed, the figures on the tapestry. Nay, I can recollect not only the colour of the dress I wore on that fated evening, but the arrangement of every scrap of lace and ribbon, of every flower, every jewel, with a memory but too perfect.

Scarcely had my maid finished spreading out my various articles of attire for the evening (when there was to be a great dinner-party) when the rumble of a carriage announced that Lady Speldhurst had arrived. The short winter's day drew to a close, and a large number of guests were gathered together in the ample drawing-room, around the blaze of the wood-fire, after dinner. My father, I recollect, was not with us at first. There were some squires of the old hard-riding, hard-drinking stamp still lingering over their port in the dining-room, and the host, of course, could not leave them. But the ladies and all the younger gentlemen – both those who slept under our roof, and those who would have a dozen miles of fog and mire to encounter on their road home – were all together. Need I say that Reginald was there? He sat near me – my accepted lover, my plighted future husband. We were to be married in the spring. My sisters were not far off; they, too, had found eyes that sparkled and softened in meeting theirs, had found hearts that beat responsive to their own. And, in their cases, no rude frost nipped the blossom ere it became the fruit; there was no canker in their flowerets of young hope, no cloud in their sky. Innocent and loving, they were beloved by men worthy of their esteem.

The room – a large and lofty one, with an arched roof – had somewhat of a sombre character from being wainscoted and ceiled with polished black oak of a great age. There were mirrors, and there were pictures on the walls, and handsome furniture, and marble chimney-pieces, and a gay Tournay carpet; but these merely appeared as bright spots on the dark background of the Elizabethan woodwork. Many lights were burning, but the blackness of the walls and roof seemed absolutely to swallow up their rays, like the mouth of a cavern. A hundred candles could not have given that apartment the cheerful lightness of a modern drawing room. But the gloomy richness of the panels matched well with the ruddy gleam from the enormous wood-fire, in which, crackling and glowing, now lay the mighty yule log. Quite a blood-red lustre poured forth from the fire, and quivered on the walls and the groined roof. We had gathered round the vast antique hearth in a wide circle. The quivering light of the fire and candles fell upon us all, but not equally, for some were in shadow. I remember still how tall and manly and handsome Reginald looked that night, taller by the head than any there, and full of high spirits and gaiety. I, too, was in the highest spirits; never had my bosom felt lighter, and I believe it was my mirth that gradually gained the rest, for I recollect what a blithe, joyous company we seemed. All save one. Lady Speldhurst, dressed in grey silk and wearing a quaint headdress, sat in her armchair, facing the fire, very silent, with her hands and her sharp chin propped on a sort of ivory-handled crutch that she walked with (for she was lame), peering at me with half-shut eyes. She was a little, spare old woman, with very keen, delicate features of the French type. Her grey silk dress, her spotless lace, old-fashioned jewels and prim neatness of array were well suited to the intelligence of her face, with its thin lips and eyes of a piercing black, undimmed by age. Those eyes made me uncomfortable, in spite of my gaiety, as they followed my every movement with curious scrutiny. Still I was very merry and blithe; my sisters even wondered at my ever-ready mirth, which was almost wild in its excess. I have heard since then of the Scottish belief that those doomed to some great calamity become fey, and are never so disposed for merriment and laughter as just before the blow falls. If ever mortal was fey, then I was so on that evening. Still, though I strove to shake it off, the pertinacious observation of old Lady Speldhurst's eyes *did* make an impression on me of a vaguely disagreeable nature. Others, too, noticed her scrutiny of me, but set it down as the mere eccentricity of a person always reputed whimsical, to say the least of it.

However, this disagreeable sensation lasted but a few moments. After a short pause my aunt took her part in the conversation, and we found ourselves listening to a weird legend, which the old lady told exceedingly well. One tale led to another. Everyone was called on in turn to contribute to the public entertainment, and story after story, always relating to demon-ology and witchcraft, succeeded. It was Christmas, the season for such tales; and the old room, with its dusky walls and pictures, and vaulted roof, drinking up the light so greedily, seemed just fitted to give effect to such legendary lore. The huge logs crackled and burned with glowing warmth; the blood-red glare of the yule log flashed on the faces of the listeners and narrator, on the portraits, and the holly wreathed about their frames, and the upright old dame, in her antiquated dress and trinkets, like one of the originals of the pictures, stepped from the canvas to join our circle. It threw a shimmering lustre of an ominously ruddy hue upon the oaken panels. No wonder that the ghost and goblin stories had a new zest. No wonder that the blood of the more timid grew chill and curdled, that their flesh crept, that their hearts beat irregularly, and the girls peeped fearfully over their shoulders, and huddled close together like frightened sheep, and half fancied they beheld some impish and malignant face gibbering at them from the darkling corners of the old room. By degrees my high spirits died out, and I felt the childish tremors, long latent, long forgotten, coming over me. I followed each story with painful interest; I did not ask myself if I believed the dismal tales. I listened, and fear grew upon me – the blind, irrational fear of our nursery days. I am sure most of the other ladies present, young or middle-aged, were affected by the circumstances under which these traditions were heard, no less than by the wild and fantastic character of them. But with them the impression would die out next morning, when the bright sun should shine on the frosted boughs, and the rime on the grass, and the scarlet berries and green spikelets of the holly; and with me – but, ah! what was to happen ere another day dawn? Before we had made an end of this talk my father and the other squires came in, and we ceased our ghost stories, ashamed to speak of such matters before these newcomers – hard-headed, unimaginative men, who had no sympathy with idle legends. There was now a stir and bustle.

Servants were handing round tea and coffee, and other refreshments. Then there was a little music and singing. I sang a duet with Reginald, who had a fine voice and good musical skill. I remember that my singing was much praised, and indeed I was surprised at the power and pathos of my own voice, doubtless due to my excited nerves and mind. Then I heard someone say to another that I was by far the cleverest of the squire's daughters, as well as the prettiest. It did not make me vain. I had no rivalry with Lucy and Minnie. But Reginald whispered some soft, fond words in my ear a little before he mounted his horse to set off homeward, which *did* make me happy and proud. And to think that the next time we met – but I forgave him long ago. Poor Reginald! And now shawls and cloaks were in request, and carriages rolled up to the porch, and the guests gradually departed. At last no one was left but those visitors staying in the house. Then my father, who had been called out to speak with the bailiff of the estate, came back with a look of annoyance on his face.

'A strange story I have just been told,' said he; 'here has been my bailiff to inform me of the loss of four of the choicest ewes out of that little flock of Southdowns I set such store by, and which arrived in the north but two months since. And the poor creatures have been destroyed in so strange a manner, for their carcasses are horribly mangled.'

Most of us uttered some expression of pity or surprise, and some suggested that a vicious dog was probably the culprit.

'It would seem so,' said my father; 'it certainly seems the work of a dog; and yet all the men agree that no dog of such habits exists near us, where, indeed, dogs are scarce, excepting the shepherds' collies and the sporting dogs secured in yards. Yet the sheep are gnawed and bitten, for they show the marks of teeth. Something has done this, and has torn their bodies wolfishly; but apparently it has been only to suck the blood, for little or no flesh is gone.'

'How strange!' cried several voices. Then some of the gentlemen remembered to have heard of cases when dogs addicted to sheep-killing had destroyed whole flocks, as if in sheer wantonness, scarcely deigning to taste a morsel of each slain wether.

My father shook his head. 'I have heard of such cases, too,' he said; 'but in this instance I am tempted to think the malice of some unknown enemy has been at work. The teeth of a dog have been busy, no doubt, but the poor sheep have been mutilated in a fantastic manner, as strange as it is horrible; their hearts, in especial, have been torn out, and left at some paces off, half-gnawed. Also, the men persist that they found the print of a naked human foot in the soft mud of the ditch, and near it – this.' And he held up what seemed a broken link of a rusted iron chain.

Many were the ejaculations of wonder and alarm, and many and shrewd the conjectures, but none seemed exactly to suit the bearings of the case. And when my father went on to say that two lambs of the same valuable breed had perished in the same singular manner three days previously, and that they also were found mangled and gore-stained, the amazement reached a higher pitch. Old Lady Speldhurst listened with calm, intelligent attention, but joined in none of our exclamations. At length she said to my father, 'Try and recollect – have you no enemy among your neighbours?' My father started, and knit his brows. 'Not one that I know of,' he replied; and indeed he was a popular man and a kind landlord. 'The more lucky you,' said the old dame, with one of her grim smiles. It was now late, and we retired to rest before long. One by one the guests dropped off. I was the member of the family selected to escort old Lady Speldhurst to her room – the room I had vacated in her favour. I did not much like the office. I felt a remarkable repugnance for my godmother, but my worthy aunts insisted so earnestly that I should ingratiate myself with one who had so much to leave that I could not but comply. The visitor hobbled up the broad oaken stairs actively enough, propped on my arm and her ivory crutch. The room never had looked more congenial and pretty, with its brisk fire, modern furniture and the gay French paper on the walls. 'A nice room, my dear, and I ought to be much obliged to you for it, since my maid tells me it is yours,' said her ladyship; 'but I am pretty sure you repent your generosity to me, after all those ghost stories, and tremble to think of a strange bed and chamber, eh?' I made some commonplace reply. The old lady arched her eyebrows. 'Where have they put you, child?' she asked; 'in some cock-loft of the turrets, eh? or in a lumber-room – a regular ghost-trap? I can hear your heart beating with fear this moment. You are not fit to be alone.' I tried to call up my pride, and laugh off the accusation against my courage, all the more, perhaps, because I felt its truth. 'Do you want anything more that I can get you, Lady Speldhurst?' I asked, trying to feign a yawn of sleepiness. The old dame's keen eyes were upon me. 'I rather like you, my dear,' she said, 'and I liked your mamma well enough before she treated me so shamefully about the christening dinner. Now, I know you are frightened and fearful, and if an owl should but flap your window tonight, it might drive you into fits. There is a nice little sofa-bed in this dressing closet – call your maid to arrange it for you, and you can sleep there snugly, under the old witch's protection, and then no goblin dare harm you, and nobody will be a bit the wiser, or quiz you for being afraid.' How little I knew what hung in the balance of my refusal or acceptance of that trivial proffer! Had the veil of the future been lifted for one instant! – but that veil is impenetrable to our gaze.

I left her door. As I crossed the landing a bright gleam came from another room, whose door was left ajar; it (the light) fell like a bar of golden sheen across my path. As I approached the door opened and my sister Lucy, who had been watching for me, came out. She was already in a white cashmere wrapper, over which her loosened hair hung darkly and heavily, like tangles of silk. 'Rosa, love,' she whispered, 'Minnie and I can't bear the idea of your sleeping out there, all alone, in that solitary room – the very room too Nurse Sherrard used to talk about! As you know Minnie has given up her room and come to sleep in mine, and we do so wish you would stop with us tonight instead. I could make up a bed on the sofa for myself or you – and – ' I stopped Lucy's mouth with a kiss. I declined her offer. I would not listen to it. In fact, my pride was up in arms, and I felt I would rather pass the night in the churchyard itself than accept a proposal dictated, I felt sure, by the notion that my nerves were shaken by the ghostly lore we had been raking up and that I was a weak, superstitious creature, unable to pass a night in a strange chamber. So I would not listen to Lucy, but kissed her, bade her good-night, and went on my way laughing, to show my light heart. Yet, as I looked back in the dark corridor, and saw the friendly door still ajar, the yellow bar of light still crossing from wall to wall, the sweet, kind face still peering after me from amidst its clustering curls, I felt a thrill of sympathy, a wish to return, a yearning after human love and companionship. False shame was strongest, and conquered. I waved a brave adieu. I turned the corner, and peeping over my shoulder, I saw the door close; the bar of yellow light was there no longer in the darkness of the passage. I thought at that instant that I heard a heavy sigh. I looked sharply round. No one was there. No door was open, yet I fancied, and fancied with a wonderful vividness, that I did hear an actual sigh breathed not far off, and plainly distinguishable from the groan of the sycamore branches as the wind tossed them to and fro in the outer blackness. If ever a mortal's good angel had cause to sigh for sorrow, not sin, mine had cause to mourn that night. But imagination plays us strange tricks and my nervous system was not over-composed or very fitted for judicial analysis. I had to go through the picture-gallery. I had never entered this apartment by candlelight before and I was struck by the gloomy array of the tall portraits, gazing moodily from the canvas on the lozenge-paned or painted windows, which rattled to the blast as it swept howling by. Many of the faces looked stern, and very different from their daylight expression. In others a furtive, flickering smile seemed to mock me as my candle illumined them; and in all, the eyes, as usual with artistic portraits, seemed to follow my motions with a scrutiny and an interest the more marked for the apathetic immovability of the other features. I felt ill at ease under this collective gaze, though conscious how absurd were my apprehensions; and I called up a smile and an air of mirth, more as if acting a part under the eyes of human beings than of their mere likenesses on the wall. I even laughed as I confronted them. No echo had my short-lived laughter but from the hollow armour and arching roof, and I continued on my way in silence.

By a sudden and not uncommon revulsion of feeling I shook off my aimless terrors, blushed at my weakness, and sought my chamber only too glad that I had been the only witness of my late tremors. As I entered my chamber I thought I heard something stir in the neglected lumber-room, which was the only neighbouring apartment. But I was determined to have no more panics, and resolutely shut my mind to this slight and transient noise, which had nothing unnatural in it; for surely, between rats and wind, an old manor house on a stormy night needs no sprites to disturb it. So I entered my room, and rang for my maid. As I did so I looked around me, and a most unaccountable repugnance for my temporary abode came over me, in spite of my efforts. It was no more to be shaken off than a chill is to be shaken off when we enter some damp cave. And, rely upon it, the feeling of dislike and apprehension with which we regard, at first sight, certain places and people, is not implanted in us without some wholesome purpose. I grant it is irrational – mere animal instinct – but is not instinct God's gift, and is it for us to despise it? It is by instinct that children know their friends from their enemies – that they distinguish with such unerring accuracy between those who like them and those who only flatter and hate them. Dogs do the same: they will fawn on one person, then slink snarling from another. Show me a man whom children and dogs shrink from, and I will show you a false, bad man – lies on his lips, and murder at his heart. No; let none despise the heaven-sent gift of innate antipathy, which makes the horse quail when the lion crouches in the thicket – which makes the cattle scent the shambles from afar, and low in terror and disgust as their nostrils snuff the blood-polluted air. I felt this antipathy strongly as I looked around me in my new sleeping-room, and yet I could find no reasonable pretext for my dislike. A very good room it was, after all, now that the green damask curtains were drawn, the fire burning bright and clear, candles burning on the mantelpiece, and the various familiar articles of toilet arranged as usual. The bed, too, looked peaceful and inviting – a pretty little white bed, not at all the gaunt funereal sort of couch which haunted apartments generally contain.

My maid entered, and assisted me to lay aside the dress and ornaments I had worn, and arranged my hair, as usual, prattling the while in Abigail fashion. I seldom cared to converse with servants; but on that night a sort of dread of being left alone – a longing to keep some human being near me – possessed me, and I encouraged the girl to gossip, so that her duties took her half an hour longer to get through than usual. At last, however, she had done all that could be done, and all my questions were answered, and my orders for the morrow reiterated and vowed obedience to, and the clock on the turret struck one. Then Mary, yawning a little, asked if I wanted anything more, and I was obliged to answer no, for very shame's sake; and she went. The shutting of the door, gently as it was closed, affected me unpleasantly. I took a dislike to the curtains, the tapestry, the dingy pictures – everything. I hated the room. I felt a temptation to put on a cloak, run, half-dressed, to my sisters' chamber, and say I had changed my mind and come for shelter. But they must be asleep, I thought, and I could not be so unkind as to wake them. I said my prayers with unusual earnestness and a heavy heart. I extinguished the candles, and was just about to lay my head on my pillow, when the idea seized me that I would fasten the door. The candles were extinguished, but the firelight was amply sufficient to guide me. I gained the door. There was a lock, but it was rusty or hampered; my utmost strength could not turn the key. The bolt was broken and worthless. Balked of my intention, I consoled myself by remembering that I had never had need of fastenings yet, and returned to my bed. I lay awake for a good while, watching the red glow of the burning coals in the grate. I was quiet now, and more composed. Even the light gossip of the maid, full of petty human cares and joys, had done me good – diverted my thoughts from brooding. I was on the point of dropping asleep, when I was twice disturbed. Once, by an owl, hooting in the ivy outside – no unaccustomed sound, but harsh and melancholy; once, by a long and mournful howling set up by the mastiff, chained in the yard beyond the wing I occupied. A long-drawn, lugubrious howling was this latter, and on just such a note as the vulgar declare to herald a death in the family. This was a fancy I had never shared; but yet I could not help feeling that the dog's mournful moans were sad, and expressive of terror, not at all like his fierce, honest bark of anger, but rather as if something evil and unwonted were abroad. But soon I fell asleep.

How long I slept I never knew. I awoke at once with that abrupt start which we all know well, and which carries us in a second from utter unconsciousness to the full use of our faculties. The fire was still burning, but was very low, and half the room or more was in deep shadow. I knew, I felt, that some person or thing was in the room, although nothing unusual was to be seen by the feeble light. Yet it was a sense of danger that had aroused me from slumber. I experienced, while yet asleep, the chill and shock of sudden alarm, and I knew, even in the act of throwing off sleep like a mantle, *why* I awoke, and that some intruder was present. Yet, though I listened intently, no sound was audible, except the faint murmur of the fire – the dropping of a cinder from the bars – the loud, irregular beatings of my own heart. Notwithstanding this silence, by some intuition I knew that I had not been deceived by a dream, and felt certain that I was not alone. I waited. My heart beat on; quicker, more sudden grew its pulsations, as a bird in a cage might flutter in presence of the hawk. And then I heard a sound, faint but quite distinct, the clank of iron, the rattling of a chain! I ventured to lift my head from the pillow. Dim and uncertain as the light was, I saw the curtains of my bed shake, and caught a glimpse of something beyond, a darker spot in the darkness. This confirmation of my fears did not surprise me so much as it shocked me. I strove to cry aloud, but could not utter a word. The chain rattled again, and this time the noise was louder and clearer. But though I strained my eyes, they could not penetrate the obscurity that shrouded the other end of the chamber whence came the sullen clanking. In a moment several distinct trains of thought, like many coloured strands of thread twining into one, became palpable to my mental vision. Was it a robber? Could it be a supernatural visitant? Or was I the victim of a cruel trick, such as I had heard of, and which some thoughtless persons love to practise on the timid, reckless of its dangerous results? And then a new idea, with some ray of comfort in it, suggested itself. There was a fine young dog of the Newfoundland breed, a favourite of my father's, which was usually chained by night in an outhouse. Neptune might have broken loose, found his way to my room, and, finding the door imperfectly closed, have pushed it open and entered. I breathed more freely as this harmless interpretation of the noise forced itself upon me. It was – it must be – the dog, and I was distressing myself uselessly. I resolved to call to him; I strove to utter his name – 'Neptune, Neptune,' but a secret apprehension restrained me, and I was mute.

Then the chain clanked nearer and nearer to the bed, and presently I saw a dusky, shapeless mass appear between the curtains on the opposite side to where I was lying. How I longed to hear the whine of the poor animal that I hoped might be the cause of my alarm. But no; I heard no sound save the rustle of the curtains and the clash of the iron chains. Just then the dying flame of the fire leaped up, and with one sweeping, hurried glance I saw that the door was shut, and, horror! it is not the dog! it is the semblance of a human form that now throws itself heavily on the bed, outside the clothes, and lies there, huge and swart, in the red gleam that treacherously dies away after showing so much to affright and sinks into dull darkness. There was now no light left, though the red cinders yet glowed with a ruddy gleam like the eyes of wild beasts. The chain rattled no more. I tried to speak, to scream wildly for help; my mouth was parched, my tongue refused to obey. I could not utter a cry, and, indeed, who could have heard me, alone as I was in that solitary chamber, with no living neighbour, and the picture-gallery between me and any aid that even the loudest, most piercing shriek could summon. And the storm that howled without would have drowned my voice, even if help had been at hand. To call aloud – to demand who was there – alas! how useless, how perilous! If the intruder were a robber, my outcries would but goad him to fury; but what robber would act thus? As for a trick, that seemed impossible. And yet, *what* lay by my side, now wholly unseen? I strove to pray aloud as there rushed on my memory a flood of weird legends – the dreaded yet fascinating lore of my childhood. I had heard and read of the spirits of the wicked men forced to revisit the scenes of their earthly crimes – of demons that lurked in certain accursed spots – of the ghouls and vampires of the East, stealing amidst the graves they rifled for their ghostly banquets; and then I shuddered as I gazed on the blank darkness where I knew it lay. It stirred – it moaned hoarsely; and again I heard the chain clank close beside me – so close that it must almost have touched me. I drew myself from it, shrinking away in loathing and terror of the evil thing – what, I knew not, but I felt that something malignant was near.

And yet, in the extremity of my fear, I dared not speak; I was strangely cautious to be silent, even in moving farther off; for I had a wild hope that it – the phantom, the creature, whichever it was – had not discovered my presence in the room. And then I remembered all the events of the night – Lady Speldhurst's ill-omened vaticinations, her half-warnings, her singular look as we parted, my sister's persuasions, my terror in the gallery, the remark that this was 'the room Nurse Sherrard used to talk of'. And then memory, stimulated by fear, recalled the long-forgotten past, the ill-repute of this disused chamber, the sins it had witnessed, the blood spilled, the poison administered by unnatural hate within its walls and the tradition which called it haunted. The green room – I remembered now how fearfully the servants avoided it – how it was mentioned rarely, and in whispers, when we were children, and how we had regarded it as a mysterious region, unfit for mortal habitation. Was It – the dark form with the chain – a creature of this world, or a spectre? And again – more dreadful still – could it be that the corpses of wicked men were forced to rise and haunt in the body the places where they had wrought their evil deeds? And was such as these my grisly neighbour? The chain faintly rattled. My hair bristled; my eyeballs seemed starting from their sockets; the damps of a great anguish were on my brow. My heart laboured as if I were crushed beneath some vast weight. Sometimes it appeared to stop its frenzied beatings, sometimes its pulsations were fierce and hurried; my breath came short and with extreme difficulty, and I shivered as if with cold; yet I feared to stir. It moved, it moaned, its fetters clanked dismally, the couch creaked and shook. This was no phantom, then – no air-drawn spectre. But its very solidity, its palpable presence, were a thousand times more terrible. I felt that I was in the very grasp of what could not only affright but harm; of something whose contact sickened the soul with deathly fear. I made a desperate resolve: I glided from the bed, I seized a warm wrapper, threw it around me, and tried to grope, with extended hands, my way to the door. My heart beat high at the hope of escape. But I had scarcely taken one step before the moaning was renewed – it changed into a threatening growl that would have suited a wolf's throat, and a hand clutched at my sleeve. I stood motionless. The muttering growl sank to a moan again, the chain sounded no more, but still the hand held its gripe of my garment and I feared to move. It knew of my presence, then. My brain reeled, the blood boiled in my ears and my knees lost all strength, while my heart panted like that of a deer in the wolf's jaws. I sank back, and the benumbing influence of excessive terror reduced me to a state of stupor.

When my full consciousness returned I was sitting on the edge of the bed, shivering with cold, and barefooted. All was silent, but I felt that my sleeve was still clutched by my unearthly visitant. The silence lasted a long time. Then followed a chuckling laugh that froze my very marrow, and the gnashing of teeth as in demoniac frenzy; and then a wailing moan, and this was succeeded by silence. Hours may have passed – nay, though the tumult of my own heart prevented my hearing the clock strike, must have passed – but they seemed ages to me. And how were they passed? Hideous visions passed before the aching eyes that I dared not close, but which gazed ever into the dumb darkness where It lay – my dread companion through the watches of the night. I pictured It in every abhorrent form which an excited fancy could summon up: now as a skeleton, with hollow eye holes and grinning, fleshless jaws; now as a vampire, with livid face and bloated form, and dripping mouth wet with blood. Would it never be light! And yet, when day should dawn I would be forced to see It face to face. I had heard that spectre and fiend were compelled to fade as morning brightened, but this creature was too real, too foul a thing of earth, to vanish at cockcrow. No! I should see it – the Horror – face to face! And then the cold prevailed, and my teeth chattered, and shiverings ran through me, and yet there was the damp of agony on my bursting brow. Some instinct made me snatch at a shawl or cloak that lay on a chair within reach, and wrap it round me. The moan was renewed, and the chain just stirred. Then I sank into apathy, like an Indian at the stake, in the intervals of torture. Hours fled by, and I remained like a statue of ice, rigid and mute. I even slept, for I remember that I started to find the cold grey light of an early winter's day was on my face and stealing around the room from between the heavy curtains of the window.

Shuddering, but urged by the impulse that rivets the gaze of the bird upon the snake, I turned to see the Horror of the night. Yes, it was no fevered dream, no hallucination of sickness, no airy phantom unable to face the dawn. In the sickly light I saw it lying on the bed, with its grim head on the pillow. A man? Or a corpse arisen from its unhallowed grave, and awaiting the demon that animated it? There it lay – a gaunt, gigantic form, wasted to a skeleton, half-clad, foul with dust and clotted gore, its huge limbs flung upon the couch as if at random, its shaggy hair streaming over the pillows like a lion's mane. His face was toward me. Oh, the wild hideousness of that face, even in sleep! In features it was human, even through its horrid mask of mud and half-dried bloody gouts, but the expression was brutish and savagely fierce; the white teeth were visible between the parted lips, in a malignant grin; the tangled hair and beard were mixed in leonine confusion, and there were scars disfiguring the brow. Round the creature's waist was a ring of iron, to which was attached a heavy but broken chain – the chain I had heard clanking. With a second glance I noted that part of the chain was wrapped in straw to prevent its galling the wearer. The creature – I cannot call it a man – had the marks of fetters on its wrists, the bony arm that protruded through one tattered sleeve was scarred and bruised; the feet were bare, and lacerated by pebbles and briers, and one of them was wounded, and wrapped in a morsel of rag. And the lean hands, one of which held my sleeve, were armed with talons like an eagle's. In an instant the horrid truth flashed upon me – I was in the grasp of a madman. Better the phantom that scares the sight than the wild beast that rends and tears the quivering flesh – the pitiless human brute that has no heart to be softened, no reason at whose bar to plead, no compassion, naught of man save the form and the cunning. I gasped in terror. Ah! the mystery of those ensanguined fingers, those gory, wolfish jaws, that face, all besmeared with blackening blood, is revealed!

The slain sheep, so mangled and rent – the fantastic butchery – the print of the naked foot – all, all were explained; and the chain, the broken link of which was found near the slaughtered animals – it came from his broken chain – the chain he had snapped, doubtless, in his escape from the asylum where his raging frenzy had been fettered and bound, in vain! in vain! Ah me! how had this grisly Samson broken manacles and prison bars – how had he eluded guardian and keeper and a hostile world, and come hither on his wild way, hunted like a beast of prey and snatching his hideous banquet like a beast of prey, too! Yes, through the tatters of his mean and ragged garb I could see the marks of the severities, cruel and foolish, with which men in that time tried to tame the might of madness. The scourge – its marks were there; and the scars of the hard iron fetters, and many a cicatrice and welt, that told a dismal tale of hard usage. But now he was loose, free to play the brute – the baited, tortured brute that they had made him – now without the cage, and ready to gloat over the victims his strength should overpower. Horror! horror! I was the prey – the victim – already in the tiger's clutch; and a deadly sickness came over me, and the iron entered into my soul, and I longed to scream – and was dumb! I died a thousand deaths as that morning wore on. I *dared not* faint. But words cannot paint what I suffered as I waited – waited till the moment when he should open his eyes and be aware of my presence; for I was assured he knew it not. He had entered the chamber as a lair, when weary and gorged with his horrid orgy; and he had flung himself down to sleep without a suspicion that he was not alone. Even his grasping my sleeve was doubtless an act done betwixt sleeping and waking, like his unconscious moans and laughter, in some frightful dream.

Hours went on; then I trembled as I thought that soon the house would be astir, that my maid would come to call me as usual, and awake that ghastly sleeper. And might he not have time to tear me, as he tore the sheep, before any aid could arrive? At last what I dreaded came to pass – a light footstep on the landing – a tap at the door. A pause succeeded, and then the tapping was renewed, and this time more loudly. Then the madman stretched his limbs, and uttered his moaning cry, and his eyes slowly opened – very slowly opened and met mine. The girl waited a while ere she knocked for the third time. I trembled lest she should open the door unbidden – see that grim thing, and bring about the worst.

I saw the wondering surprise in his haggard, bloodshot eyes; I saw him stare at me half vacantly, then with a crafty yet wondering look; and then I saw the devil of murder begin to peep forth from those hideous eyes, and the lips to part as in a sneer, and the wolfish teeth to bare themselves. But I was not what I had been. Fear gave me a new and a desperate composure – a courage foreign to my nature. I had heard of the best method of managing the insane; I could but try; I *did* try. Calmly, wondering at my own feigned calm, I fronted the glare of those terrible eyes. Steady and undaunted was my gaze – motionless my attitude. I marvelled at myself, but in that agony of sickening terror I was *outwardly* firm. They sink, they quail, abashed, those dreadful eyes, before the gaze of a helpless girl; and the shame that is never absent from insanity bears down the pride of strength, the bloody cravings of the wild beast. The lunatic moaned and drooped his shaggy head between his gaunt, squalid hands.

I lost not an instant. I rose, and with one spring reached the door, tore it open and, with a shriek, rushed through, caught the wondering girl by the arm and, crying to her to run for her life, rushed like the wind along the gallery, down the corridor, down the stairs. Mary's screams filled the house as she fled beside me. I heard a long-drawn, raging cry, the roar of a wild animal cheated of its prey, and I knew what was behind me. I never turned my head – I flew rather than ran. I was in the hall already; there was a rush of many feet, an outcry of many voices, a sound of scuffling feet and brutal yells and oaths and heavy blows, and I fell to the ground crying, 'Save me!' and lay in a swoon. I awoke from a delirious trance. Kind faces were around my bed, loving looks were bent on me by all, by my dear father and dear sisters; but I scarcely saw them before I swooned again.

When I recovered from that long illness, through which I had been nursed so tenderly, the pitying looks I met made me tremble. I asked for a looking-glass. It was long denied me, but my importunity prevailed at last – a mirror was brought. My youth was gone at one fell swoop. The glass showed me a livid and haggard face, blanched and bloodless as of one who sees a spectre; and in the ashen lips, and wrinkled brow, and dim eyes, I could trace nothing of my old self. The hair, too, jetty and rich before, was now as white as snow; and in one night the ravages of half a century had passed over my face. Nor have my nerves ever recovered their tone after that dire shock. Can you wonder that my life was blighted, that my lover shrank from me, so sad a wreck was I?

I am old now – old and alone. My sisters would have had me to live with them, but I chose not to sadden their genial homes with my phantom face and dead eyes. Reginald married another. He has been dead many years. I never ceased to pray for him, though he left me when I was bereft of all. The sad journey is nearly over now. I am old, and near the end, and wishful for it. I have not been bitter or hard, but I cannot bear to see many people, and am best alone. I tried to do what good I could with the worthless wealth Lady Speldhurst left me, for, at my wish, my portion was shared between my sisters. What need had I of inheritance? – I, the shattered wreck made by that one night of horror!

The Pipe

ONE

Randolph Crescent, London

MY DEAR PUGH – I hope you will like the pipe which I send with this. It is rather a curious example of a certain school of Indian carving. And is a present from

Yours truly,   JOSEPH TRESS

It was really very handsome of Tress – very handsome! The more especially as I was aware that to give presents was not exactly in Tress's line. The truth is that when I saw what manner of pipe it was I was amazed. It was contained in a sandalwood box, which was itself illustrated with some remarkable specimens of carving. I use the word 'remarkable' advisedly, because, although the workmanship was undoubtedly, in its way, artistic, the result could not be described as beautiful. The carver had thought proper to ornament the box with some of the ugliest figures I remember to have seen. They appeared to me to be devils. Or perhaps they were intended to represent deities appertaining to some mythological system with which, thank goodness, I am unacquainted. The pipe itself was worthy of the case in which it was contained. It was of meerschaum, with an amber mouthpiece. It was rather too large for ordinary smoking. But then, of course, one doesn't smoke a pipe like that. There are pipes in my collection which I should as soon think of smoking as I should of eating. Ask a china maniac to let you have afternoon tea out of his Old Chelsea, and you will learn some home truths as to the durability of human friendships. The glory of the pipe, as Tress had suggested, lay in its carving. Not that I claim that it was beautiful, any more than I make such a claim for the carving on the box, but, as Tress said in his note, it was curious.

The stem and the bowl were quite plain, but on the edge of the bowl was perched some kind of lizard. I told myself it was an octopus when I first saw it, but I have since had reason to believe that it was some almost unique member of the lizard tribe. The creature was represented as climbing over the edge of the bowl down towards the stem, and its legs, or feelers, or tentacula, or whatever the things are called, were, if I may use a vulgarism, sprawling about 'all over the place'. For instance, two or three of them were twined about the bowl, two or three of them were twisted round the stem, and one, a particularly horrible one, was uplifted in the air, so that if you put the pipe in your mouth the thing was pointing straight at your nose.

Not the least agreeable feature about the creature was that it was hideously lifelike. It appeared to have been carved in amber, but some colouring matter must have been introduced, for inside the amber the creature was of a peculiarly ghastly green. The more I examined the pipe the more amazed I was at Tress's generosity. He and I are rival collectors. I am not going to say, in so many words, that his collection of pipes contains nothing but rubbish, because, as a matter of fact, he has two or three rather decent specimens. But to compare his collection to mine would be absurd. Tress is conscious of this, and he resents it. He resents it to such an extent that he has been known, at least on one occasion, to declare that one single pipe of his – I believe he alluded to the Brummagem relic preposterously attributed to Sir Walter Raleigh – was worth the whole of my collection put together. Although I have forgiven this, as I hope I always shall forgive remarks made when envious passions get the better of our nobler nature, even of a Joseph Tress, it is not to be supposed that I have forgotten it. He was, therefore, not at all the sort of person from whom I expected to receive a present. And such a present! I do not believe that he himself had a finer pipe in his collection. And to have given it to me! I had misjudged the man. I wondered where he had got it from. I had seen his pipes; I knew them off by heart – and some nice trumpery he has among them, too! but I had never seen *that* pipe before. The more I looked at it, the more my amazement grew. The beast perched upon the edge of the bowl was so lifelike. Its two bead-like eyes seemed to gleam at me with positively human intelligence. The pipe fascinated me to such an extent that I actually resolved to – smoke it!

I filled it with Perique. Ordinarily I use bird's-eye, but on those very rare occasions on which I use a specimen I smoke Perique. I lit up with quite a small sensation of excitement. As I did so I kept my eyes perforce fixed upon the beast. The beast pointed its upraised tentacle directly at me. As I inhaled the pungent tobacco that tentacle impressed me with a feeling of actual uncanniness. It was broad daylight, and I was smoking in front of the window, yet to such an extent was I affected that it seemed to me that the tentacle was not only vibrating, which, owing to the peculiarity of its position, was quite within the range of probability, but actually moving, elongating – stretching forward, that is, farther towards me, and towards the tip of my nose. So impressed was I by this idea that I took the pipe out of my mouth and minutely examined the beast. Really, the delusion was excusable. So cunningly had the artist wrought that he succeeded in producing a creature which, such was its uncanniness, I could only hope had no original in nature.

Replacing the pipe between my lips I took several whiffs. Never had smoking had such an effect on me before. Either the pipe, or the creature on it, exercised some singular fascination. I seemed, without an instant's warning, to be passing into some land of dreams. I saw the beast, which was perched upon the bowl, writhe and twist. I saw it lift itself bodily from the meerschaum.

TWO

'Feeling better now?'

I looked up. Joseph Tress was speaking.

'What's the matter? Have I been ill?'

'You appear to have been in some kind of swoon.' Tress's tone was peculiar, even a little dry.

'Swoon! I never was guilty of such a thing in my life.'

'Nor was I, until I smoked that pipe.'

I sat up. The act of sitting up made me conscious of the fact that I had been lying down. Conscious, too, that I was feeling more than a little dazed. It seemed as though I was waking out of some strange, lethargic sleep – a kind of feeling which I have read of and heard about, but never before experienced.

'Where am I?'

'You're on the couch in your own room. You *were* on the floor; but I thought it would be better to pick you up and place you on the couch – though no one performed the same kind office to me when I was on the floor.' Again Tress's tone was distinctly dry.

'How came *you* here?'

'Ah, that's the question.' He rubbed his chin – a habit of his which has annoyed me more than once before. 'Do you think you're sufficiently recovered to enable you to understand a little simple explanation?' I stared at him, amazed. He went on stroking his chin. 'The truth is that when I sent you the pipe I made a slight omission.'

'An omission?'

'I omitted to advise you not to smoke it.'

'And why?'

'Because – well, I've reason to believe the thing is drugged.'

'Drugged!'

'Or poisoned.'

'Poisoned!' I was wide awake enough then. I jumped off the couch with a celerity which proved it.

'It is this way. I became its owner in rather a singular manner.' He paused, as if for me to make a remark; but I was silent. 'It is not often that I smoke a specimen, but, for some reason, I did smoke this. I commenced to smoke it, that is. How long I continued to smoke it is more than I can say. It had on me the same peculiar effect which it appears to have had on you. When I recovered consciousness I was lying on the floor.'

'On the floor?'

'On the floor. In about as uncomfortable a position as you can easily conceive. I was lying face downward, with my legs bent under me. I was never so surprised in my life as I was when I found myself *where* I was. At first I supposed that I had had a stroke. But by degrees it dawned upon me that I didn't *feel* as though I had had a stroke.' Tress, by the way, has been an army surgeon. 'I was conscious of distinct nausea. Looking about, I saw the pipe. With me it had fallen on to the floor. I took it for granted, considering the delicacy of the carving, that the fall had broken it. But when I picked it up I found it quite uninjured. While I was examining it a thought flashed through my brain. Might it not be answerable for what had happened to me? Suppose, for instance, it was drugged? I had heard of such things. Besides, in my case were present all the symptoms of drug poisoning, though what drug had been used I couldn't in the least conceive. I resolved that I would give the pipe another trial.'

'On yourself? or on another party, meaning me?'

'On myself, my dear Pugh – on myself! At that point of my investigations I had not begun to think of you. I lit up and had another smoke.'

'With what result?'

'Well, that depends on the standpoint from which you regard the thing. From one point of view the result was wholly satisfactory – I proved that the thing was drugged, and more.'

'Did you have another fall?'

'I did. And something else besides.'

'On that account, I presume, you resolved to pass the treasure on to me?'

'Partly on that account, and partly on another.'

'On my word, I appreciate your generosity. You might have labelled the thing as poison.'

'Exactly. But then you must remember how often you have told me that you *never* smoke your specimens.'

'That was no reason why you shouldn't have given me a hint that the thing was more dangerous than dynamite.'

'That did occur to me afterwards. Therefore I called to supply the slight omission.'

'*Slight* omission, you call it! I wonder what you would have called it if you had found me dead.'

'If I had known that you *intended* smoking it I should not have been at all surprised if I had.'

'Really, Tress, I appreciate your kindness more and more! And where is this example of your splendid benevolence? Have you pocketed it, regretting your lapse into the unaccustomed paths of generosity? Or is it smashed to atoms?'

'Neither the one nor the other. You will find the pipe upon the table. I neither desire its restoration nor is it in any way injured. It is merely an expression of personal opinion when I say that I don't believe that it *could* be injured. Of course, having discovered its deleterious properties, you will not want to smoke it again. You will therefore be able to enjoy the consciousness of being the possessor of what I honestly believe to be the most remarkable pipe in existence. Good-day, Pugh.'

He was gone before I could say a word. I immediately concluded, from the precipitancy of his flight, that the pipe *was* injured. But when I subjected it to close examination I could discover no signs of damage. While I was still eying it with jealous scrutiny the door reopened, and Tress came in again.

'By the way, Pugh, there is one thing I might mention, especially as I know it won't make any difference to you.'

'That depends on what it is. If you have changed your mind, and want the pipe back again, I tell you frankly that it won't. In my opinion, a thing once given is given for good.'

'Quite so; I don't want it back again. You may make your mind easy on that point. I merely wanted to tell you *why* I gave it you.'

'You have told me that already.'

'Only partly, my dear Pugh – only partly. You don't suppose I should have given you such a pipe as that merely because it happened to be drugged? Scarcely! I gave it you because I discovered from indisputable evidence, and to my cost, that it was haunted.'

'Haunted?'

'Yes, haunted. Good-day.'

He was gone again. I ran out of the room, and shouted after him down the stairs. He was already at the bottom of the flight.

'Tress! Come back! What do you mean by talking such nonsense?'

'Of course it's only nonsense. We know that that sort of thing always is nonsense. But if you should have reason to suppose that there is something in it besides nonsense, you may think it worth your while to make enquiries of me. But I won't have that pipe back again in my possession on any terms – mind that!'

The bang of the front door told me that he had gone out into the street. I let him go. I laughed to myself as I re-entered the room. Haunted! That was not a bad idea of his. I saw the whole position at a glance. The truth of the matter was that he did regret his generosity, and he was ready to go any lengths if he could only succeed in cajoling me into restoring his gift. He was aware that I have views upon certain matters which are not wholly in accordance with those which are popularly supposed to be the views of the day, and particularly that on the question of what are commonly called supernatural visitations I have a standpoint of my own. Therefore, it was not a bad move on his part to try to make me believe that about the pipe on which he knew I had set my heart there was something which could not be accounted for by ordinary laws. Yet, as his own sense would have told him it would do, if he had only allowed himself to reflect for a moment, the move failed. Because I am not yet so far gone as to suppose that a pipe, a thing of meerschaum and of amber, in the sense in which I understand the word, *could* be haunted – a pipe, a mere pipe.

'Hallo! I thought the creature's legs were twined right round the bowl!'

I was holding the pipe in my hand, regarding it with the affectionate eyes with which a connoisseur does regard a curio, when I was induced to make this exclamation. I was certainly under the impression that, when I first took the pipe out of the box, two, if not three of the feelers had been twined about the bowl – twined tightly, so that you could not see daylight between them and it. Now they were almost entirely detached, only the tips touching the meerschaum, and those particular feelers were gathered up as though the creature were in the act of taking a spring. Of course I was under a misapprehension: the feelers *couldn't* have been twined; a moment before I should have been ready to bet a thousand to one that they were. Still, one does make mistakes, and very egregious mistakes, at times. At the same time, I confess that when I saw that dreadful-looking animal poised on the extreme edge of the bowl, for all the world as though it were just going to spring at me, I was a little startled. I remembered that when I was smoking the pipe I did think I saw the uplifted tentacle moving, as though it were reaching out to me. And I had a clear recollection that just as I had been sinking into that strange state of unconsciousness, I had been under the impression that the creature was writhing and twisting, as though it had suddenly become instinct with life. Under the circumstances, these reflections were not pleasant. I wished Tress had not talked that nonsense about the thing being haunted. It was surely sufficient to know that it was drugged and poisonous, without anything else.

I replaced it in the sandalwood box. I locked the box in a cabinet. Quite apart from the question as to whether that pipe was or was not haunted, I know it haunted me. It was with me in a figurative – which was worse than actual – sense all the day. Still worse, it was with me all the night. It was with me in my dreams. Such dreams! Possibly I had not yet wholly recovered from the effects of that insidious drug, but, whether or no, it was very wrong of Tress to set my thoughts into such a channel. He knows that I am of a highly imaginative temperament, and that it is easier to get morbid thoughts into my mind than to get them out again. Before that night was through I wished very heartily that I had never seen the pipe! I woke from one nightmare to fall into another. One dreadful dream was with me all the time – of a hideous, green reptile which advanced towards me out of some awful darkness, slowly, inch by inch, until it clutched me round the neck, and, gluing its lips to mine, sucked the life's blood out of my veins as it embraced me with a slimy kiss. Such dreams are not restful. I woke anything but refreshed when the morning came. And when I got up and dressed I felt that, on the whole, it would perhaps have been better if I never had gone to bed. My nerves were unstrung, and I had that generally tremulous feeling which is, I believe, an inseparable companion of the more advanced stages of dipsomania. I ate no breakfast. I am no breakfast eater as a rule, but that morning I ate absolutely nothing.

'If this sort of thing is to continue, I will let Tress have his pipe again. He may have the laugh of me, but anything is better than this.'

It was with almost funereal forebodings that I went to the cabinet in which I had placed the sandalwood box. But when I opened it my feelings of gloom partially vanished. Of what phantasies had I been guilty! It must have been an entire delusion on my part to have supposed that those tentacula had ever been twined about the bowl. The creature was in exactly the same position in which I had left it the day before – as, of course, I knew it would be – poised, as if about to spring. I was telling myself how foolish I had been to allow myself to dwell for a moment on Tress's words, when Martin Brasher was shown in.

Brasher is an old friend of mine. We have a common ground – ghosts. Only we approach them from different points of view. He takes the scientific – psychological – enquiry side. He is always anxious to hear of a ghost, so that he may have an opportunity of 'showing it up'.

'I've something in your line here,' I observed, as he came in.

'In my line? How so? *I'm* not pipe mad.'

'No; but you're ghost mad. And this is a haunted pipe.'

'A haunted pipe! I think you're rather more mad about ghosts, my dear Pugh, than I am.'

Then I told him all about it. He was deeply interested, especially when I told him that the pipe was drugged. But when I repeated Tress's words about its being haunted, and mentioned my own delusion about the creature moving, he took a more serious view of the case than I had expected he would do.

'I propose that we act on Tress's suggestion, and go and make enquiries of him.'

'But you don't really think that there is anything in it?'

'On these subjects I never allow myself to think at all. There are Tress's words, and there is your story. It is agreed on all hands that the pipe has peculiar properties. It seems to me that there is a sufficient case here to merit enquiry.'

He persuaded me. I went with him. The pipe, in the sandalwood box, went too. Tress received us with a grin – a grin which was accentuated when I placed the sandalwood box on the table.

'You understand,' he said, 'that a gift is a gift. On no terms will I consent to receive that pipe back in my possession.'

I was rather nettled by his tone.

'You need be under no alarm. I have no intention of suggesting anything of the kind.'

'Our business here,' began Brasher – I must own that his manner is a little ponderous – 'is of a scientific, and I may say also, at the same time, of a judicial nature. Our object is the Pursuit of Truth and the Advancement of Enquiry.'

'Have you been trying another smoke?' enquired Tress, nodding his head towards me.

Before I had time to answer, Brasher went droning on: 'Our friend here tells me that you say this pipe is haunted.'

'I say it is haunted because it *is* haunted.'

I looked at Tress. I half suspected that he was poking fun at us. But he appeared to be serious enough.

'In these matters,' remarked Brasher, as though he were giving utterance to a new and important truth, 'there is a scientific and a non-scientific method of enquiry. The scientific method is to begin at the beginning. May I ask how this pipe came into your possession?'

Tress paused before he answered.

'You may ask.' He paused again. 'Oh, you certainly may ask. But it doesn't follow that I shall tell you.'

'Surely your object, like ours, can be but the Spreading About of the Truth?'

'I don't see it at all. It is possible to imagine a case in which the spreading about of the truth might make me look a little awkward.'

'Indeed!' Brasher pursed up his lips. 'Your words would almost lead one to suppose that there was something about your method of acquiring the pipe which you have good and weighty reasons for concealing.'

'I don't know why I should conceal the thing from you. I don't suppose either of you is any better than I am. I don't mind telling you how I got the pipe. I stole it.'

'Stole it!'

Brasher seemed both amazed and shocked. But I, who had previous experience of Tress's methods of adding to his collection, was not at all surprised. Some of the pipes which he calls his, if only the whole truth about them were publicly known, would send him to jail.

'That's nothing!' he continued. 'All collectors steal! The eighth commandment was not intended to apply to them. Why, Pugh there has "conveyed" three fourths of the pipes which he flatters himself are his.'

I was so dumfoundered by the charge that it took my breath away. I sat in astounded silence.

Tress went raving on: 'I was so shy of this particular pipe when I had obtained it, that I put it away for quite three months. When I took it out to have a look at it something about the thing so tickled me that I resolved to smoke it. Owing to peculiar circumstances attending the manner in which the thing came into my possession, and on which I need not dwell – you don't like to dwell on those sort of things, do you, Pugh? – I knew really nothing about the pipe. As was the case with Pugh, one peculiarity I learned from actual experience. It was also from actual experience that I learned that the thing was – well, I said haunted, but you may use any other word you like.'

'Tell us, as briefly as possible, what it was you really did discover.'

'Take the pipe out of the box!' Brasher took the pipe out of the box and held it in his hand. 'You see that creature on it. Well, when I first had it it was underneath the pipe.'

'How do you mean that it was underneath the pipe?'

'It was bunched together underneath the stem, just at the end of the mouthpiece, in the same way in which a fly might be suspended from the ceiling. When I began to smoke the pipe I saw the creature move.'

'But I thought that unconsciousness immediately followed.'

'It did follow, but not before I saw that the thing was moving. It was because I thought that I had been, in a way, a victim of delirium that I tried the second smoke. Suspecting that the thing was drugged I swallowed what I believed would prove a powerful antidote. It enabled me to resist the influence of the narcotic much longer than before, and while I still retained my senses I saw the creature crawl along under the stem and over the bowl. It was that sight, I believe, as much as anything else, which sent me silly. When I came to, I then and there decided to present the pipe to Pugh. There is one more thing I would remark. When the pipe left me the creature's legs were twined about the bowl. Now they are withdrawn. Possibly you, Pugh, are able to cap my story with a little one which is all your own.'

'I certainly did imagine that I saw the creature move. But I supposed that while I was under the influence of the drug imagination had played me a trick.'

'Not a bit of it! Depend upon it, the beast is bewitched. Even to my eye it looks as though it were, and to a trained eye like yours, Pugh! You've been looking for the devil a long time, and you've got him at last.'

'I – I wish you wouldn't make those remarks, Tress. They jar on me.'

'I confess,' interpolated Brasher – I noticed that he had put the pipe down on the table as though he were tired of holding it – 'that, to *my* thinking, such remarks are not appropriate. At the same time what you have told us is, I am bound to allow, a little curious. But of course what I require is ocular demonstration. I haven't seen the movement myself.'

'No, but you very soon will do if you care to have a pull at the pipe on your own account. Do, Brasher, to oblige me! There's a dear!'

'It appears, then, that the movement is only observable when the pipe is smoked. We have at least arrived at step No. 1.'

'Here's a match, Brasher! Light up, and we shall have arrived at step No. 2.'

Tress lit a match and held it out to Brasher. Brasher retreated from its neighbourhood.

'Thank you, Mr Tress, I am no smoker, as you are aware. And I have no desire to acquire the art of smoking by means of a poisoned pipe.'

Tress laughed. He blew out the match and threw it into the grate.

'Then I tell you what I'll do – I'll have up Bob.'

'Bob – why Bob?'

Bob – whose full name was Robert Haines, though I should think he must have forgotten the fact, so seldom was he addressed by it – was Tress's servant. He had been an old soldier, and had accompanied his master when he left the service. He was as depraved a character as Tress himself. I am not sure even that he was not worse than his master. I shall never forget how he once behaved toward myself. He actually had the assurance to accuse me of attempting to steal the Wardour Street relic which Tress fondly deludes himself was once the property of Sir Walter Raleigh. The truth is that I had slipped it with my handkerchief into my pocket in a fit of absence of mind. A man who could accuse *me* of such a thing would be guilty of anything. I was therefore quite at one with Brasher when he asked what Bob could possibly be wanted for. Tress explained.

'I'll get him to smoke the pipe,' he said.

Brasher and I exchanged glances, but we refrained from speech.

'It won't do him any harm,' said Tress.

'What – not a poisoned pipe?' asked Brasher.

'It's not poisoned – it's only drugged.'

'*Only* drugged!'

'Nothing hurts Bob. He is like an ostrich. He has digestive organs which are peculiarly his own. It will only serve him as it served me – and Pugh – it will knock him over. It is all done in the Pursuit of Truth and for the Advancement of Enquiry.'

I could see that Brasher did not altogether like the tone in which Tress repeated his words. As for me, it was not to be supposed that I should put myself out in a matter which in no way concerned me. If Tress chose to poison the man, it was his affair, not mine. He went to the door and shouted:

'Bob! Come here, you scoundrel!'

That is the way in which he speaks to him. No really decent servant would stand it. I shouldn't care to address Nalder, my servant, in such a way. He would give me notice on the spot. Bob came in. He is a great hulking fellow who is always on the grin. Tress had a decanter of brandy in his hand. He filled a tumbler with the neat spirit.

'Bob, what would you say to a glassful of brandy – the real thing – my boy?'

'Thank you, sir.'

'And what would you say to a pull at a pipe when the brandy is drunk!'

'A pipe?' The fellow is sharp enough when he likes. I saw him look at the pipe upon the table, and then at us, and then a gleam of intelligence came into his eyes. 'I'd do it for a dollar, sir.'

'A dollar, you thief?'

'I meant ten shillings, sir.'

'Ten shillings, you brazen vagabond?'

'I should have said a pound.'

'A pound! Was ever the like of that! Do I understand you to ask a pound for taking a pull at your master's pipe?'

'I'm thinking that I'll have to make it two.'

'The deuce you are! Here, Pugh, lend me a pound.'

'I'm afraid I've left my purse behind.'

'Then lend me ten shillings – Ananias!'

'I doubt if I have more than five.'

'Then give me the five. And, Brasher, lend me the other fifteen.'

Brasher lent him the fifteen. I doubt if we shall either of us ever see our money again. He handed the pound to Bob.

'Here's the brandy – drink it up!' Bob drank it without a word, draining the glass of every drop. 'And here's the pipe.'

'Is it poisoned, sir?'

'Poisoned, you villain! What do you mean?'

'It isn't the first time I've seen your tricks, sir – is it now? And you're not the one to give a pound for nothing at all. If it kills me you'll send my body to my mother – she'd like to know that I was dead.'

'Send your body to your grandmother! You idiot, sit down and smoke!'

Bob sat down. Tress had filled the pipe, and handed it, with a lighted match, to Bob. The fellow declined the match. He handled the pipe very gingerly, turning it over and over, eying it with all his eyes.

'Thank you, sir – I'll light up myself if it's the same to you. I carry matches of my own. It's a beautiful pipe, entirely. I never see the like of it for ugliness. And what's the slimy-looking varmint that looks as though it would like to have my life? Is it living, or is it dead?'

'Come, we don't want to sit here all day, my man!'

'Well, sir, the look of this here pipe has quite upset my stomach. I'd like another drop of liquor, if it's the same to you.'

'Another drop! Why, you've had a tumblerful already! Here's another tumblerful to put on top of that. You won't want the pipe to kill you – you'll be killed before you get to it.'

'And isn't it better to die a natural death?'

Bob emptied the second tumbler of brandy as though it were water. I believe he would empty a hogshead without turning a hair! Then he gave another look at the pipe. Then, taking a match from his waistcoat pocket, he drew a long breath, as though he were resigning himself to fate. Striking the match on the seat of his trousers, while, shaded by his hand, the flame was gathering strength, he looked at each of us in turn. When he looked at Tress I distinctly saw him wink his eye. What my feelings would have been if a servant of mine had winked his eye at me I am unable to imagine! The match was applied to the tobacco, a puff of smoke came through his lips – the pipe was alight!

During this process of lighting the pipe we had sat – I do not wish to use exaggerated language, but we had sat and watched that alcoholic scamp's proceedings as though we were witnessing an action which would leave its mark upon the age. When we saw the pipe was lighted we gave a simultaneous start. Brasher put his hands under his coat-tails and gave a kind of hop. I raised myself a good six inches from my chair, and Tress rubbed his palms together with a chuckle. Bob alone was calm.

'Now,' cried Tress, 'you'll see the devil moving.'

Bob took the pipe from between his lips.

'See what?' he said.

'Bob, you rascal, put that pipe back into your mouth, and smoke it for your life!'

Bob was eying the pipe askance.

'I dare say, but what I want to know is whether this here varmint's dead or whether he isn't. I don't want to have him flying at my nose – and he looks vicious enough for anything.'

'Give me back that pound, you thief, and get out of my house, and bundle.'

'I ain't going to give you back no pound.'

'Then smoke that pipe!'

'I am smoking it, ain't I?'

With the utmost deliberation Bob returned the pipe to his mouth. He emitted another whiff or two of smoke.

'Now – now!' cried Tress, all excitement, and wagging his hand in the air.

We gathered round. As we did so Bob again withdrew the pipe.

'What is the meaning of all this here? I ain't going to have you playing none of your larks on me. I know there's something up, but I ain't going to throw my life away for twenty shillings – not quite I ain't.'

Tress, whose temper is not at any time one of the best, was seized with quite a spasm of rage.

'As I live, my lad, if you try to cheat me by taking that pipe from between your lips until I tell you, you leave this room that instant, never again to be a servant of mine.'

I presume the fellow knew from long experience when his master meant what he said, and when he didn't. Without an attempt at remonstrance he replaced the pipe. He continued stolidly to puff away. Tress caught me by the arm.

'What did I tell you? There – there! That tentacle is moving.'

The uplifted tentacle *was* moving. It was doing what I had seen it do, as I supposed, in my distorted imagination – it was reaching forward. Undoubtedly Bob saw what it was doing; but, whether in obedience to his master's commands, or whether because the drug was already beginning to take effect, he made no movement to withdraw the pipe. He watched the slowly advancing tentacle, coming closer and closer towards his nose, with an expression of such intense horror on his countenance that it became quite shocking. Farther and farther the creature reached forward, until on a sudden, with a sort of jerk, the movement assumed a downward direction, and the tentacle was slowly lowered until the tip rested on the stem of the pipe. For a moment the creature remained motionless. I was quieting my nerves with the reflection that this thing was but some trick of the carver's art, and that what we had seen we had seen in a sort of nightmare, when the whole hideous reptile was seized with what seemed to be a fit of convulsive shuddering. It seemed to be in agony. It trembled so violently that I expected to see it loosen its hold of the stem and fall to the ground. I was sufficiently master of myself to steal a glance at Bob. We had had an inkling of what might happen. He was wholly unprepared. As he saw that dreadful, human-looking creature, coming to life, as it seemed, within an inch or two of his nose, his pupils dilated to twice their usual size. I hoped, for his sake, that unconsciousness would supervene, through the action of the drug, before through sheer fright his senses left him. Perhaps mechanically he puffed steadily on.

The creature's shuddering became more violent. It appeared to swell before our eyes. Then, just as suddenly as it began, the shuddering ceased. There was another instant of quiescence. Then the creature began to crawl along the stem of the pipe! It moved with marvellous caution, the merest fraction of an inch at a time. But still it moved! Our eyes were riveted on it with a fascination which was absolutely nauseous. I am unpleasantly affected even as I think of it now. My dreams of the night before had been nothing to this.

Slowly, slowly, it went, nearer and nearer to the smoker's nose. Its mode of progression was in the highest degree unsightly. It glided, never, so far as I could see, removing its tentacles from the stem of the pipe. It slipped its hindmost feelers onward until they came up to those which were in advance. Then, in their turn, it advanced those which were in front. It seemed, too, to move with the utmost labour, shuddering as though it were in pain.

We were all, for our parts, speechless. I was momentarily hoping that the drug would take effect on Bob. Either his constitution enabled him to offer a strong resistance to narcotics, or else the large quantity of neat spirit which he had drunk acted – as Tress had malevolently intended that it should – as an antidote. It seemed to me that he would *never* succumb. On went the creature – on, and on, in its infinitesimal progression. I was spellbound. I would have given the world to scream, to have been able to utter a sound. I could do nothing else but watch.

The creature had reached the end of the stem. It had gained the amber mouthpiece. It was within an inch of the smoker's nose. Still on it went. It seemed to move with greater freedom on the amber. It increased its rate of progress. It was actually touching the foremost feature on the smoker's countenance. I expected to see it grip the wretched Bob, when it began to oscillate from side to side. Its oscillations increased in violence. It fell to the floor. That same instant the narcotic prevailed. Bob slipped sideways from the chair, the pipe still held tightly between his rigid jaws.

We were silent. There lay Bob. Close beside him lay the creature. A few more inches to the left, and he would have fallen on it and squashed it flat. It had fallen on its back. Its feelers were extended upwards. They were writhing and twisting and turning in the air.

Tress was the first to speak.

'I think a little brandy won't be amiss.' Emptying the remainder of the brandy into a glass, he swallowed it at a draught. 'Now for a closer examination of our friend.' Taking a pair of tongs from the grate he nipped the creature between them. He deposited it upon the table. 'I rather fancy that this is a case for dissection.'

He took a penknife from his waistcoat pocket. Opening the large blade, he thrust its point into the object on the table. Little or no resistance seemed to be offered to the passage of the blade, but as it was inserted the tentacula simultaneously began to writhe and twist. Tress withdrew the knife.

'I thought so!' He held the blade out for our inspection. The point was covered with some viscid-looking matter. 'That's blood! The thing's alive!'

'Alive!'

'Alive! That's the secret of the whole performance!'

'But – '

'But me no buts, my Pugh! The mystery's exploded! One more ghost is lost to the world! The person from whom I *obtained* that pipe was an Indian juggler – up to many tricks of the trade. He, or someone for him, got hold of this sweet thing in reptiles – and a sweeter thing would, I imagine, be hard to find – and covered it with some preparation of, possibly, gum arabic. He allowed this to harden. Then he stuck the thing – still living, for those sort of gentry are hard to kill – to the pipe. The consequence was that when anyone lit up, the warmth was communicated to the adhesive agent – again some preparation of gum, no doubt – it moistened it, and the creature, with infinite difficulty, was able to move. But I am open to lay odds with any gentleman of sporting tastes that *this* time the creature's travelling days *are* done. It has given me rather a larger taste of the horrors than is good for my digestion.'

With the aid of the tongs he removed the creature from the table. He placed it on the hearth. Before Brasher or I had a notion of what it was he intended to do he covered it with a heavy marble paperweight. Then he stood upon the weight, and between the marble and the hearth he ground the creature flat.

While the execution was still proceeding, Bob sat up upon the floor.

'Hallo!' he asked, 'what's happened?'

'We've emptied the bottle, Bob,' said Tress. 'But there's another where that came from. Perhaps you could drink another tumblerful, my boy?'

Bob drank it!

Footnote

'Those gentry are hard to kill.' Here is fact, not fantasy. Lizard yarns no less sensational than this mystery story can be found between the covers of solemn, zoological textbooks.

Reptiles, indeed, are far from finicky in the matters of air, space and especially warmth. Frogs and other such sluggish-blooded creatures have lived after being frozen fast in ice. Their blood is little warmer than air or water, enjoying no extra casing of fur or feathers.

Air and food seem held in light esteem by lizards. Their blood need not be highly oxygenated; it nourishes just as well when impure. In temperate climes lizards lie torpid and buried all winter; some species of the tropic deserts sleep peacefully all summer. Their anatomy includes no means for the continuous introduction and expulsion of air; reptilian lungs are little more than closed sacs, without cell structure.

If any further zoological fact were needed to verify the denouement of 'The Pipe', it might be the general statement that lizards are abnormal brutes anyhow. Consider the chameleons of unsettled hue. And what is one to think of an animal which, when captured by the tail, is able to make its escape by willfully shuffling off that appendage? – EDITOR

The Puzzle

ONE

Pugh came into my room holding something wrapped in a piece of brown paper. 'Tress, I have brought you something on which you may exercise your ingenuity.' He began, with exasperating deliberation, to untie the string which bound his parcel; he is one of those persons who would not cut a knot to save their lives. The process occupied him the better part of a quarter of an hour. Then he held out the contents of the paper.

'What do you think of that?' he asked. I thought nothing of it, and I told him so. 'I was prepared for that confession. I have noticed, Tress, that you generally do think nothing of an article which really deserves the attention of a truly thoughtful mind. Possibly, as you think so little of it, you will be able to solve the puzzle.'

I took what he held out to me. It was an oblong box, perhaps seven inches long by three inches broad.

'Where's the puzzle?' I asked.

'If you will examine the lid of the box, you will see.'

I turned it over and over; it was difficult to see which was the lid. Then I perceived that on one side were printed these words: 'Puzzle: To open the Box.'

The words were so faintly printed that it was not surprising that I had not noticed them at first. Pugh explained.

'I observed that box on a tray outside a second-hand furniture shop. It struck my eye. I took it up. I examined it. I enquired of the proprietor of the shop in what the puzzle lay. He replied that that was more than he could tell me. He himself had made several attempts to open the box, and all of them had failed. I purchased it. I took it home. I have tried, and I have failed. I am aware, Tress, of how you pride yourself upon your ingenuity. I cannot doubt that, if you try, you will not fail.'

While Pugh was prosing, I was examining the box. It was at least well made. It weighed certainly under two ounces. I struck it with my knuckles; it sounded hollow. There was no hinge; nothing of any kind to show that it ever had been opened, or, for the matter of that, that it ever could be opened. The more I examined the thing, the more it whetted my curiosity. That it could be opened, and in some ingenious manner, I made no doubt – but how?

The box was not a new one. At a rough guess I should say that it had been a box for a good half century; there were certain signs of age about it which could not escape a practised eye. Had it remained unopened all that time? When opened, what would be found inside? It *sounded* hollow; probably nothing at all – who could tell?

It was formed of small pieces of inlaid wood. Several woods had been used; some of them were strange to me. They were of different colours; it was pretty obvious that they must all of them have been hard woods. The pieces were of various shapes – hexagonal, octagonal, triangular, square, oblong and even circular. The process of inlaying them had been beautifully done. So nicely had the parts been joined that the lines of meeting were difficult to discover with the naked eye; they had been joined solid, so to speak. It was an excellent example of marquetry. I had been over-hasty in my deprecation; I owned as much to Pugh.

'This box of yours is better worth looking at than I first supposed. Is it to be sold?'

'No, it is not to be sold. Nor' – he fixed me with his spectacles – 'is it to be given away. I have brought it to you for the simple purpose of ascertaining if you have ingenuity enough to open it.'

'I will engage to open it in two seconds – with a hammer.'

'I dare say. *I* will open it with a hammer. The thing is to open it without.'

'Let me see.' I began, with the aid of a microscope, to examine the box more closely. 'I will give you one piece of information, Pugh. Unless I am mistaken, the secret lies in one of these little pieces of inlaid wood. You push it, or you press it, or something, and the whole affair flies open.'

'Such was my own first conviction. I am not so sure of it now. I have pressed every separate piece of wood; I have tried to move each piece in every direction. No result has followed. My theory was a hidden spring.'

'But there must be a hidden spring of some sort, unless you are to open it by a mere exercise of force. I suppose the box is empty.'

'I thought it was at first, but now I am not so sure of that either. It all depends on the position in which you hold it. Hold it in this position – like this – close to your ear. Have you a small hammer?' I took a small hammer. 'Tap it softly, with the hammer. Don't you notice a sort of reverberation within?'

Pugh was right, there certainly was something within; something which seemed to echo back my tapping, almost as if it were a living thing. I mentioned this to Pugh.

'But you don't think that there is something alive inside the box? There can't be. The box must be airtight, probably as much airtight as an exhausted receiver.'

'How do we know that? How can we tell that no minute interstices have been left for the express purpose of ventilation?' I continued tapping with the hammer. I noticed one peculiarity, that it was only when I held the box in a particular position, and tapped at a certain spot, that there came the answering taps from within. 'I tell you what it is, Pugh, what I hear is the reverberation of some machinery.'

'Do you think so?'

'I'm sure of it.'

'Give the box to me.' Pugh put the box to his ear. He tapped. 'It sounds to me like the echoing tick, tick of some great beetle; like the sort of noise which a deathwatch makes, you know.'

Trust Pugh to find a remarkable explanation for a simple fact; if the explanation leans towards the supernatural, so much the more satisfactory to Pugh. I knew better.

'The sound which you hear is merely the throbbing or the trembling of the mechanism with which it is intended that the box should be opened. The mechanism is placed just where you are tapping it with the hammer. Every tap causes it to jar.'

'It sounds to me like the ticking of a deathwatch. However, on such subjects, Tress, I know what you are.'

'My dear Pugh, give it an extra hard tap, and you will see.'

He gave it an extra hard tap. The moment he had done so, he started.

'I've done it now.'

'What have you done?'

'Broken something, I fancy.' He listened intently, with his ear to the box. 'No – it seems all right. And yet I could have sworn I had damaged something; I heard it smash.'

'Give me the box.' He gave it me. In my turn, I listened. I shook the box. Pugh must have been mistaken. Nothing rattled; there was not a sound; the box was as empty as before. I gave a smart tap with the hammer, as Pugh had done. Then there certainly was a curious sound. To my ear, it sounded like the smashing of glass. 'I wonder if there is anything fragile inside your precious puzzle, Pugh, and, if so, if we are shivering it by degrees!'

TWO

'What *is* that noise?'

I lay in bed in that curious condition which is between sleep and waking. When, at last, I *knew* that I was awake, I asked myself what it was that had woken me. Suddenly I became conscious that something was making itself audible in the silence of the night. For some seconds I lay and listened. Then I sat up in bed.

'What *is* that noise?'

It was like the tick, tick of some large and unusually clear-toned clock. It might have been a clock, had it not been that the sound was varied, every half dozen ticks or so, by a sort of stifled screech, such as might have been uttered by some small creature in an extremity of anguish. I got out of bed; it was ridiculous to think of sleep during the continuation of that uncanny shrieking. I struck a light. The sound seemed to come from the neighbour-hood of my dressing-table. I went to the dressing-table, the lighted match in my hand, and, as I did so, my eyes fell on Pugh's mysterious box. That same instant there issued, from the bowels of the box, a more uncomfortable screech than any I had previously heard. It took me so completely by surprise that I let the match fall from my hand to the floor. The room was in darkness. I stood, I will not say trembling, listening – considering their volume – to the *eeriest* shrieks I ever heard. All at once they ceased. Then came the tick, tick, tick again. I struck another match and lit the gas.

Pugh had left his puzzle box behind him. We had done all we could, together, to solve the puzzle. He had left it behind to see what I could do with it alone. So much had it engrossed my attention that I had even brought it into my bedroom, in order that I might, before retiring to rest, make a final attempt at the solution of the mystery. *Now* what possessed the thing?

As I stood, and looked, and listened, one thing began to be clear to me – some sort of machinery had been set in motion inside the box. How it had been set in motion was another matter. But the box had been subjected to so much handling, to such pressing and such hammering, that it was not strange if, after all, Pugh or I had unconsciously hit upon the spring which set the whole thing going. Possibly the mechanism had got so rusty that it had refused to act at once. It had hung fire, and only after some hours had something or other set the imprisoned motive power free.

But what about the screeching? Could there be some living creature concealed within the box? Was I listening to the cries of some small animal in agony? Momentary reflection suggested that the explanation of the one thing was the explanation of the other. Rust! – there was the mystery. The same rust which had prevented the mechanism from acting at once was causing the screeching now. The uncanny sounds were caused by nothing more nor less than the want of a drop or two of oil. Such an explanation would not have satisfied Pugh, it satisfied me.

Picking up the box, I placed it to my ear.

'I wonder how long this little performance is going to continue. And what is going to happen when it is good enough to cease? I hope' – an uncomfortable thought occurred to me – 'I hope Pugh hasn't picked up some pleasant little novelty in the way of an infernal machine. It would be a first-rate joke if he and I had been endeavoring to solve the puzzle of how to set it going.'

I don't mind owning that as this reflection crossed my mind I replaced Pugh's puzzle on the dressing-table. The idea did not commend itself to me at all. The box evidently contained some curious mechanism. It might be more curious than comfortable. Possibly some agreeable little device in clockwork. The tick, tick, tick suggested clockwork which had been planned to go a certain time, and then – then, for all I knew, ignite an explosive, and – blow up. It would be a charming solution to the puzzle if it were to explode while I stood there, in my nightshirt, looking on. It is true that the box weighed very little. Probably, as I have said, the whole affair would not have turned the scale at a couple of ounces. But then its very lightness might have been part of the ingenious inventor's little game. There are explosives with which one can work a very satisfactory amount of damage with considerably less than a couple of ounces.

While I was hesitating – I own it! – whether I had not better immerse Pugh's puzzle in a can of water, or throw it out of the window, or call down Bob with a request to remove it at once to his apartment, both the tick, tick, tick, and the screeching ceased, and all within the box was still. If it *was* going to explode, it was now or never. Instinctively I moved in the direction of the door.

I waited with a certain sense of anxiety. I waited in vain. Nothing happened, not even a renewal of the sound.

'I wish Pugh had kept his precious puzzle at home. This sort of thing tries one's nerves.'

When I thought that I perceived that nothing seemed likely to happen, I returned to the neighbourhood of the table. I looked at the box askance. I took it up gingerly. Something might go off at any moment for all I knew. It would be too much of a joke if Pugh's precious puzzle exploded in my hand. I shook it doubtfully; nothing rattled. I held it to my ear. There was not a sound. What had taken place? Had the clockwork run down, and was the machine arranged with such a diabolical ingenuity that a certain interval was required, after the clockwork had run down, before an explosion could occur? Or had rust caused the mechanism again to hang fire?

'After making all that commotion the thing might at least come open.' I banged the box viciously against the corner of the table. I felt that I would almost rather that an explosion should take place than that nothing should occur. One does not care to be disturbed from one's sound slumber in the small hours of the morning for a trifle.

'I've half a mind to get a hammer, and try, as they say in the cookery books, another way.'

Unfortunately I had promised Pugh to abstain from using force. I might have shivered the box open with my hammer, and then explained that it had fallen, or got trod upon, or sat upon, or something, and so got shattered, only I was afraid that Pugh would not believe me. The man is himself such an untruthful man that he is in a chronic state of suspicion about the truthfulness of others.

'Well, if you're not going to blow up, or open, or something, I'll say good-night.'

I gave the box a final rap with my knuckles and a final shake, replaced it on the table, put out the gas and returned to bed.

I was just sinking again into slumber when that box began again. It was true that Pugh had purchased the puzzle, but it was evident that the whole enjoyment of the purchase was destined to be mine. It was useless to think of sleep while that performance was going on. I sat up in bed once more.

'It strikes me that the puzzle consists in finding out how it is possible to go to sleep with Pugh's purchase in your bedroom. This is far better than the old-fashioned prescription of cats on the tiles.'

It struck me the noise was distinctly louder than before; this applied both to the tick, tick, tick, and the screeching.

'Possibly,' I told myself, as I relighted the gas, 'the explosion is to come off this time.'

I turned to look at the box. There could be no doubt about it; the noise was louder. And, if I could trust my eyes, the box was moving – giving a series of little jumps. This might have been an optical delusion, but it seemed to me that at each tick the box gave a little bound. During the screeches – which sounded more like the cries of an animal in an agony of pain even than before – if it did not tilt itself first on one end, and then on another, I shall never be willing to trust the evidence of my own eyes again. And surely the box had increased in size; I could have sworn not only that it had increased, but that it was increasing, even as I stood there looking on. It had grown, and still was growing, both broader, and longer, and deeper. Pugh, of course, would have attributed it to supernatural agency; there never was a man with such a nose for a ghost. I could picture him, occupying my position, shivering in his nightshirt as he beheld that miracle taking place before his eyes. The solution which at once suggested itself to me – and which would *never* have suggested itself to Pugh! – was that the box was fashioned, as it were, in layers, and that the ingenious mechanism it contained was forcing the sides at once both upwards and outwards. I took it in my hand. I could feel something striking against the bottom of the box, like the tap, tap, tapping of a tiny hammer.

'This is a pretty puzzle of Pugh's. He would say that that is the tapping of a deathwatch. For my part I have not much faith in deathwatches, *et hoc genus omne*, but it certainly is a curious tapping; I wonder what is going to happen next?'

Apparently nothing, except a continuation of those mysterious sounds. That the box had increased in size I had, and have, no doubt whatever. I should say that it had increased a good inch in every direction, at least half an inch while I had been looking on. But while I stood looking its growth was suddenly and perceptibly stayed; it ceased to move. Only the noise continued.

'I wonder how long it will be before anything worth happening does happen! I suppose something is going to happen; there can't be all this to-do for nothing. If it is anything in the infernal machine line, and there is going to be an explosion, I might as well be here to see it. I think I'll have a pipe.'

I put on my dressing-gown. I lit my pipe. I sat and stared at the box. I dare say I sat there for quite twenty minutes when, as before, without any sort of warning, the sound was stilled. Its sudden cessation rather startled me.

'Has the mechanism again hung fire? Or, this time, is the explosion coming off?' It did not come off; nothing came off. 'Isn't the box even going to open?' It did not open. There was simply silence all at once, and that was all. I sat there in expectation for some moments longer. But I sat for nothing. I rose. I took the box in my hand. I shook it.

'This puzzle *is* a puzzle.' I held the box first to one ear, then to the other. I gave it several sharp raps with my knuckles. There was not an answering sound, not even the sort of reverberation which Pugh and I had noticed at first. It seemed hollower than ever. It was as though the soul of the box was dead. 'I suppose if I put you down and extinguish the gas and return to bed, in about half an hour or so, just as I am dropping off to sleep, the performance will be recommenced. Perhaps the third time will be lucky.'

But I was mistaken – there was no third time. When I returned to bed that time I returned to sleep, and I was allowed to sleep; there was no continuation of the performance, at least so far as I know. For no sooner was I once more between the sheets than I was seized with an irresistible drowsiness, a drowsiness which so mastered me that I – I imagine it must have been instantly – sank into slumber which lasted till long after day had dawned. Whether or not any more mysterious sounds issued from the bowels of Pugh's puzzle is more than I can tell. If they did, they did not succeed in rousing me.

And yet, when at last I did awake, I had a sort of consciousness that my waking had been caused by something strange. What it was I could not surmise. My own impression was that I had been awakened by the touch of a person's hand. But that impression must have been a mistaken one, because, as I could easily see by looking round the room, there was no one in the room to touch me.

It was broad daylight. I looked at my watch; it was nearly eleven o'clock. I am a pretty late sleeper as a rule, but I do not usually sleep as late as that. That scoundrel Bob would let me sleep all day without thinking it necessary to call me. I was just about to spring out of bed with the intention of ringing the bell so that I might give Bob a piece of my mind for allowing me to sleep so late, when my glance fell on the dressing-table on which, the night before, I had placed Pugh's puzzle. It had gone!

Its absence so took me by surprise that I ran to the table. It *had* gone. But it had not gone far; it had gone to pieces! There were the pieces lying where the box had been. The puzzle had solved itself. The box was open, open with a vengeance, one might say. Like that unfortunate Humpty Dumpty, who, so the chroniclers tell us, sat on a wall, surely 'all the king's horses and all the king's men' never could put Pugh's puzzle together again!

The marquetry had resolved itself into its component parts. How those parts had ever been joined was a mystery. They had been laid upon no foundation, as is the case with ordinary inlaid work. The several pieces of wood were not only of different shapes and sizes, but they were as thin as the thinnest veneer; yet the box had been formed by simply joining them together. The man who made that box must have been possessed of ingenuity worthy of a better cause.

I perceived how the puzzle had been worked. The box had contained an arrangement of springs, which, on being released, had expanded themselves in different directions until their mere expansion had rent the box to pieces. There were the springs, lying amid the ruin they had caused.

There was something else amid that ruin besides those springs; there was a small piece of writing paper. I took it up. On the reverse side of it was written in a minute, crabbed hand: 'A Present For You'. What was a present for me? I looked, and, not for the first time since I had caught sight of Pugh's precious puzzle, could scarcely believe my eyes.

There, poised between two upright wires, the bent ends of which held it aloft in the air, was either a piece of glass or – a crystal. The scrap of writing paper had exactly covered it. I understood what it was that, when Pugh and I had tapped with the hammer, had caused the answering taps to proceed from within. Our taps caused the wires to oscillate, and in these oscillations the crystal, which they held suspended, had touched the side of the box.

I looked again at the piece of paper. 'A Present For You'. Was *this* the present – this crystal? I regarded it intently.

'It *can't* be a diamond.'

The idea was ridiculous, absurd. No man in his senses would place a diamond inside a twopenny-halfpenny puzzle box. The thing was as big as a walnut! And yet – I am a pretty good judge of precious stones – if it was not an uncut diamond it was the best imitation I had seen. I took it up. I examined it closely. The more closely I examined it, the more my wonder grew.

'It *is* a diamond!'

And yet the idea was too preposterous for credence. Who would present a diamond as big as a walnut with a trumpery puzzle? Besides, all the diamonds which the world contains of that size are almost as well known as the Koh-i-noor.

'If it is a diamond, it is worth – it is worth – heaven only knows what it isn't worth if it's a diamond.'

I regarded it through a strong pocket lens. As I did so I could not restrain an exclamation.

'The world to a China orange, it *is* a diamond!'

The words had scarcely escaped my lips when there came a tapping at the door.

'Come in!' I cried, supposing it was Bob. It was not Bob, it was Pugh. Instinctively I put the lens and the crystal behind my back. At sight of me in my nightshirt Pugh began to shake his head.

'What hours, Tress, what hours! Why, my dear Tress, I've breakfasted, read the papers and my letters, come all the way from my house here, and you're not up!'

'Don't I look as though I were up?'

'Ah, Tress! Tress!' He approached the dressing-table. His eye fell upon the ruins. 'What's this?'

'That's the solution to the puzzle.'

'Have you – have you solved it fairly, Tress?'

'It has solved itself. Our handling, and tapping, and hammering must have freed the springs which the box contained, and during the night, while I slept, they have caused it to come open.'

'While you slept? Dear me! How strange! And – what are these?'

He had discovered the two upright wires on which the crystal had been poised.

'I suppose they're part of the puzzle.'

'And was there anything in the box? What's this?' He picked up the scrap of paper; I had left it on the table. He read what was written on it: 'A Present For You'. What's it mean? Tress, was this in the box?'

'It was.'

'What's it mean about a present? Was there anything in the box besides?'

'Pugh, if you will leave the room I shall be able to dress; I am not in the habit of beng paid quite such early calls, or I should have been prepared to receive you. If you will wait in the next room, I will be with you as soon as I'm dressed. There is a little subject in connection with the box which I wish to discuss with you.'

'A subject in connection with the box? What is the subject?'

'I will tell you, Pugh, when I have performed my toilet.'

'Why can't you tell me now?'

'Do you propose, then, that I should stand here shivering in my shirt

while you are prosing at your ease? Thank you; I am obliged, but I decline.
May I ask you once more, Pugh, to wait for me in the adjoining apartment?'

He moved towards the door. When he had taken a couple of steps, he
halted.

'I – I hope, Tress, that you're – you're going to play no tricks on me?'

'Tricks on you! Is it likely that I am going to play tricks upon my oldest
friend?'

When he had gone – he vanished, it seemed to me, with a somewhat
doubtful visage – I took the crystal to the window. I drew the blind. I let the
sunshine fall on it. I examined it again, closely and minutely, with the aid of
my pocket lens. It *was* a diamond; there could not be a doubt of it. If, with
my knowledge of stones, I was deceived, then I was deceived as never man
had been deceived before. My heart beat faster as I recognised the fact that I
was holding in my hand what was, in all probability, a fortune for a man of
moderate desires. Of course, Pugh knew nothing of what I had discovered,
and there was no reason why he should know. Not the least! The only
difficulty was that if I kept my own counsel, and sold the stone and utilised
the proceeds of the sale, I should have to invent a story which would account
for my sudden accession to fortune. Pugh knows almost as much of my
affairs as I do myself. That is the worst of these old friends!

When I joined Pugh I found him dancing up and down the floor like a
bear upon hot plates. He scarcely allowed me to put my nose inside the door
before attacking me.

'Tress, give me what was in the box.'

'My dear Pugh, how do you know that there was something in the box to
give you?'

'I know there was!'

'Indeed! If you know that there was something in the box, perhaps you
will tell me what that something was.'

He eyed me doubtfully. Then, advancing, he laid upon my arm a hand
which positively trembled.

'Tress, you – you wouldn't play tricks on an old friend.'

'You are right, Pugh, I wouldn't, though I believe there have been
occasions on which you have had doubts upon the subject. By the way,
Pugh, I believe that I am the oldest friend you have.'

'I – I don't know about that. There's – there's Brasher.'

'Brasher! Who's Brasher? You wouldn't compare my friendship to the
friendship of such a man as Brasher? Think of the tastes we have in common,
you and I. We're both collectors.'

'Ye–es, we're both collectors.'

'I make my interests yours, and you make your interests mine. Isn't that
so, Pugh?'

'Tress, what – what was in the box?'

'I will be frank with you, Pugh. If there had been something in the box, would you have been willing to go halves with me in my discovery?'

'Go halves! In your discovery, Tress! Give me what is mine!'

'With pleasure, Pugh, if you will tell me what is yours.'

'If – if you don't give me what was in the box I'll – I'll send for the police.'

'Do! Then I shall be able to hand to them what was in the box in order that it may be restored to its proper owner.'

'Its proper owner! I'm its proper owner!'

'Excuse me, but I don't understand how that can be; at least, until the police have made enquiries. I should say that the proper owner was the person from whom you purchased the box, or, more probably, the person from whom he purchased it, and by whom, doubtless, it was sold in ignorance, or by mistake. Thus, Pugh, if you will only send for the police, we shall earn the gratitude of a person of whom we never heard in our lives – I for discovering the contents of the box, and you for returning them.'

As I said this, Pugh's face was a study. He gasped for breath. He actually took out his handkerchief to wipe his brow.

'Tress, I – I don't think you need to use a tone like that to me. It isn't friendly. What – what was in the box?'

'Let us understand each other, Pugh. If you don't hand over what was in the box to the police, I go halves.'

Pugh began to dance about the floor.

'What a fool I was to trust you with the box! I knew I couldn't trust you.' I said nothing. I turned and rang the bell. 'What's that for?'

'That, my dear Pugh, is for breakfast, and, if you desire it, for the police. You know, although you have breakfasted, I haven't. Perhaps while I am breaking my fast, you would like to summon the representatives of law and order.' Bob came in. I ordered breakfast. Then I turned to Pugh. 'Is there anything you would like?'

'No, I – I've breakfasted.'

'It wasn't of breakfast I was thinking. It was of – something else. Bob is at your service, if, for instance, you wish to send him on an errand.'

'No, I want nothing. Bob can go.' Bob went. Directly he was gone, Pugh turned to me. 'You shall have half. What was in the box?'

'I shall have half?'

'You shall!'

'I don't think it is necessary that the terms of our little understanding should be expressly embodied in black and white. I fancy that, under the circumstance, I can trust you, Pugh. I believe that I am capable of seeing that, in this matter, you don't do me. That was in the box.'

I held out the crystal between my finger and thumb.

'What is it?'

'That is what I desire to learn.'

'Let me look at it.'

'You are welcome to look at it where it is. Look at it as long as you like, and as closely.'

Pugh leaned over my hand. His eyes began to gleam. He is himself not a bad judge of precious stones, is Pugh.

'It's – it's – Tress! – is it a diamond?'

'That question I have already asked myself.'

'Let me look at it! It will be safe with me! It's mine!'

I immediately put the thing behind my back.

'Pardon me, it belongs neither to you nor to me. It belongs, in all probability, to the person who sold that puzzle to the man from whom you bought it – perhaps some weeping widow, Pugh, or hopeless orphan – think of it. Let us have no further misunderstanding upon that point, my dear old friend. Still, because you are my dear old friend, I am willing to trust you with this discovery of mine, on condition that you don't attempt to remove it from my sight, and that you return it to me the moment I require you to.'

'You're – you're very hard on me.' I made a movement towards my waistcoat pocket. 'I'll return it to you!'

I handed him the crystal, and with it I handed him my pocket lens.

'With the aid of that glass I imagine that you will be able to subject it to a more acute examination, Pugh.'

He began to examine it through the lens. Directly he did so, he gave an exclamation. In a few moments he looked up at me. His eyes were glistening behind his spectacles. I could see he trembled.

'Tress, it's – it's a diamond, a Brazil diamond. It's worth a fortune!'

'I'm glad you think so.'

'Glad I think so! Don't you think that it's a diamond?'

'It appears to be a diamond. Under ordinary conditions I should say, without hesitation, that it was a diamond. But when I consider the circumstances of its discovery, I am driven to doubts. How much did you give for that puzzle, Pugh?'

'Ninepence; the fellow wanted a shilling, but I gave him ninepence. He seemed content.'

'Ninepence! Does it seem reasonable that we should find a diamond, which, if it is a diamond, is the finest stone I ever saw and handled, in a ninepenny puzzle? It is not as though it had got into the thing by accident; it had evidently been placed there to be found, and, apparently, by anyone who chanced to solve the puzzle; witness the writing on the scrap of paper.'

Pugh reexamined the crystal.

'It is a diamond! I'll stake my life that it's a diamond!'

'Still, though it be a diamond, I smell a rat!'

'What do you mean?'

'I strongly suspect that the person who placed that diamond inside that puzzle intended to have a joke at the expense of the person who discovered it. What was to be the nature of the joke is more than I can say at present, but I should like to have a bet with you that the man who compounded that puzzle was an ingenious practical joker. I may be wrong, Pugh; we shall see. But, until I have proved the contrary, I don't believe that the maddest man that ever lived would throw away a diamond worth, apparently, shall we say a thousand pounds?'

'A thousand pounds! This diamond is worth a good deal more than a thousand pounds.'

'Well, that only makes my case the stronger; I don't believe that the maddest man that ever lived would throw away a diamond worth more than a thousand pounds with such utter wantonness as seems to have characterised the action of the original owner of the stone which I found in your ninepenny puzzle, Pugh.'

'There have been some eccentric characters in the world, some very eccentric characters. However, as you say, we shall see. I fancy that I know somebody who would be quite willing to have such a diamond as this, and who, moreover, would be willing to pay a fair price for its possession; I will take it to him and see what he says.'

'Pugh, hand me back that diamond.'

'My dear Tress, I was only going – '

Bob came in with the breakfast tray.

'Pugh, you will either hand me that at once, or Bob shall summon the representatives of law and order.'

He handed me the diamond. I sat down to breakfast with a hearty appetite. Pugh stood and scowled at me.

'Joseph Tress, it is my solemn conviction, and I have no hesitation in saying so in plain English, that you're a thief.'

'My dear Pugh, it seems to me that we show every promise of becoming a couple of thieves.'

'Don't bracket me with you!'

'Not at all, you are worse than I. It is you who decline to return the contents of the box to its proper owner. Put it to yourself, you have *some* common sense, my dear old friend! – do you suppose that a diamond worth more than a thousand pounds is to be *honestly* bought for ninepence?'

He resumed his old trick of dancing about the room.

'I was a fool ever to let you have the box! I ought to have known better than to have trusted you; goodness knows you have given me sufficient cause to mistrust you! Over and over again! Your character is only too notorious!

You have plundered friend and foe alike – friend and foe alike! As for the rubbish which you call your collection, nine tenths of it, I know as a positive fact, you have stolen out and out.'

'Who stole my Sir Walter Raleigh pipe? Wasn't it a man named Pugh?'

'Look here, Joseph Tress!'

'I'm looking.'

'Oh, it's no good talking to you, not the least! You're – you're dead to all the promptings of conscience! May I enquire, Mr Tress, what it is you propose to do?'

'I *propose* to do nothing, except summon the representatives of law and order. Failing that, my dear Pugh, I had some faint, vague, very vague idea of taking the contents of your ninepenny puzzle to a certain firm in Hatton Garden, who are dealers in precious stones, and to learn from them if they are disposed to give anything for it, and if so, what.'

'I shall come with you.'

'With pleasure, on condition that you pay the cab.'

'I pay the cab! I will pay half.'

'Not at all. You will either pay the whole fare, or else I will have one cab and you shall have another. It is a three-shilling cab fare from here to Hatton Garden. If you propose to share my cab, you will be so good as to hand over that three shillings before we start.'

He gasped, but he handed over the three shillings. There are few things I enjoy so much as getting money out of Pugh!

On the road to Hatton Garden we wrangled nearly all the way. I own that I feel a certain satisfaction in irritating Pugh, he is such an irritable man. He wanted to know what I thought we should get for the diamond.

'You can't expect to get much for the contents of a ninepenny puzzle, not even the price of a cab fare, Pugh.'

He eyed me, but for some minutes he was silent. Then he began again.

'Tress, I don't think we ought to let it go for less than – than five thousand pounds.'

'Seriously, Pugh, I doubt whether, when the whole affair is ended, we shall get five thousand pence for it, or, for the matter of that, five thousand farthings.'

'But why not? Why not? It's a magnificent stone – magnificent! I'll stake my life on it.'

I tapped my breast with the tips of my fingers.

'There's a warning voice within my breast that ought to be in yours, Pugh! Something tells me, perhaps it is the unusually strong vein of common sense which I possess, that the contents of your ninepenny puzzle will be found to be a magnificent do – an ingenious practical joke, my friend.'

'I don't believe it.'

But I think he did; at any rate, I had unsettled the foundations of his faith.

We entered the Hatton Garden office side by side; in his anxiety not to let me get before him, Pugh actually clung to my arm. The office was divided into two parts by a counter which ran from wall to wall. I advanced to a man who stood on the other side of this counter.

'I want to sell you a diamond.'

'*We* want to sell you a diamond,' interpolated Pugh.

I turned to Pugh. I fixed him with my glance. '*I* want to sell you a diamond. Here it is. What will you give me for it?'

Taking the crystal from my waistcoat pocket I handed it to the man on the other side of the counter. Directly, he got it between his fingers, and saw what it was that he had got, I noticed a sudden gleam come into his eyes.

'This is – this is rather a fine stone.'

Pugh nudged my arm. 'I told you so.'

I paid no attention to Pugh. 'What will you give me for it?'

'Do you mean, what will I give you for it cash down upon the nail?'

'Just so – what will you give me for it cash down upon the nail?'

The man turned the crystal over and over in his fingers.

'Well, that's rather a large order. We don't often get a chance of buying such a stone as this across the counter. What do you say to – well – to ten thousand pounds?'

Ten thousand pounds! It was beyond my wildest imaginings. Pugh gasped. He lurched against the counter.

'Ten thousand pounds!' he echoed.

The man on the other side glanced at him, I thought, a little curiously.

'If you can give me references, or satisfy me in any way as to your *bona fides*, I am prepared to give you for this diamond an open check for ten thousand pounds, or if you prefer it, the cash instead.'

I stared; I was not accustomed to see business transacted on quite such lines as those.

'We'll take it,' murmured Pugh; I believe he was too much overcome by his feelings to do more than murmur.

I interposed. 'My dear sir, you will excuse my saying that you arrive very rapidly at your conclusions. In the first place, how can you make sure that it is a diamond?'

The man behind the counter smiled.

'I should be very ill-fitted for the position which I hold if I could not tell a diamond directly I get a sight of it, especially such a stone as this.'

'But have you no tests you can apply?'

'We have tests which we apply in cases in which doubt exists, but in this case there is no doubt whatever. I am as sure that this is a diamond as I am sure that it is air I breathe. However, here is a test.'

There was a wheel close by the speaker. It was worked by a treadle. It was more like a superior sort of travelling-tinker's grindstone than anything else. The man behind the counter put his foot upon the treadle. The wheel began to revolve. He brought the crystal into contact with the swiftly revolving wheel. There was a s–s–sh! And, in an instant, his hand was empty; the crystal had vanished into air.

'Good heavens!' he gasped. I never saw such a look of amazement on a human countenance before. 'It's splintered!'

Postscript

It *was* a diamond, although it *had* splintered. In that fact lay the point of the joke. The man behind the counter had not been wrong; examination of such dust as could be collected proved that fact beyond a doubt. It was declared by experts that the diamond, at some period of its history, had been subjected to intense and continuing heat. The result had been to make it as brittle as glass.

There could be no doubt that its original owner had been an expert too. He knew where he got it from, and he probably knew what it had endured. He was aware that, from a mercantile point of view, it was worthless; it could never have been cut. So, having a turn for humour of a peculiar kind, he had devoted days, and weeks, and possibly months, to the construction of that puzzle. He had placed the diamond inside, and he had enjoyed, in anticipation and in imagination, the Alnaschar visions of the lucky finder.

Pugh blamed me for the catastrophe. He said, and still says, that if I had not, in a measure, and quite gratuitously, insisted on a test, the man behind the counter would have been satisfied with the evidence of his organs of vision, and we should have been richer by ten thousand pounds. But I satisfy my conscience with the reflection that what I did at any rate was honest, though, at the same time, I am perfectly well aware that such a reflection gives Pugh no sort of satisfaction.

The Closed Cabinet

ONE

It was with a little alarm and a good deal of pleasurable excitement that I looked forward to my first grown-up visit to Mervyn Grange. I had been there several times as a child, but never since I was twelve years old, and now I was over eighteen. We were all of us very proud of our cousins the Mervyns: it is not everybody that can claim kinship with a family who are in full and admitted possession of a secret, a curse and a mysterious cabinet, in addition to the usual surplusage of horrors supplied in such cases by popular imagination. Some declared that a Mervyn of the days of Henry VIII had been cursed by an injured abbot from the foot of the gallows. Others affirmed that a dissipated Mervyn of the Georgian era was still playing cards for his soul in some remote region of the Grange. There were stories of white ladies and black imps, of bloodstained passages and magic stones. We, proud of our more intimate acquaintance with the family, naturally gave no credence to these wild inventions. The Mervyns, indeed, followed the accepted precedent in such cases, and greatly disliked any reference to the reputed mystery being made in their presence; with the inevitable result that there was no subject so pertinaciously discussed by their friends in their absence. My father's sister had married the late Baronet, Sir Henry Mervyn, and we always felt that she ought to have been the means of imparting to us a very complete knowledge of the family secret. But in this connection she undoubtedly failed of her duty. We knew that there had been a terrible tragedy in the family some two or three hundred years ago – that a peculiarly wicked owner of Mervyn, who flourished in the latter part of the sixteenth century, had been murdered by his wife who subsequently committed suicide. We knew that the mysterious curse had some connection with this crime, but what the curse exactly was we had never been able to discover. The history of the family since that time had indeed in one sense been full of misfortune. Not in every sense. A coal mine had been discovered in one part of the estate, and a populous city had grown over the corner of another part; and the Mervyns of today, in spite of the usual percentage of extravagant heirs and political mistakes, were three times as rich as their ancestors had been. But still their story was full of bloodshed and shame, of tales of duels and suicides, broken hearts and broken honour. Only these calamities seemed to have little or no relation to each other, and what the precise curse was that was supposed to connect or account for them we could not learn. When she first married, my aunt was told nothing about it. Later on in life, when my father asked her for the story, she begged him to talk upon a pleasanter subject; and being unluckily a man of much courtesy and little curiosity, he complied with her request. This, however, was the only part of the ghostly traditions of her husband's home upon which she was so reticent. The haunted chamber, for instance – which, of course, existed at the Grange – she treated with the greatest contempt. Various friends and relations had slept in it at different times, and no approach to any kind of authenticated ghost-story, even of the most trivial description, had they been able to supply. Its only claim to respect, indeed, was that it contained the famous Mervyn cabinet, a fascinating puzzle of which I will speak later, but which certainly had nothing haunting or horrible about its appearance.

My uncle's family consisted of three sons. The eldest, George, the present baronet, was now in his thirties, married, and with children of his own. The second, Jack, was the black-sheep of the family. He had been in the Guards, but, about five years back, had got into some very disgraceful scrape, and had been obliged to leave the country. The sorrow and the shame of this had killed his unhappy mother, and her husband had not long afterwards followed her to the grave. Alan, the youngest son, probably because he was the nearest to us in age, had been our special favourite in earlier years. George was grown up before I had well left the nursery, and his hot, quick temper had always kept us youngsters somewhat in awe of him. Jack was four years older than Alan, and, besides, his profession had, in a way, cut his boyhood short. When my uncle and aunt were abroad, as they frequently were for months together on account of her health, it was Alan, chiefly, who had to spend his holidays with us, both as schoolboy and as undergraduate. And a brighter, sweeter-tempered comrade, or one possessed of more diversified talents for the invention of games or the telling of stories, it would have been difficult to find.

For five years together now our ancient custom of an annual visit to Mervyn had been broken. First there had been the seclusion of mourning for my aunt, and a year later for my uncle; then George and his wife, Lucy – she was a connection of our own on our mother's side, and very intimate with us all – had been away for nearly two years on a voyage round the world; and since then sickness in our own family had kept us in our turn a good deal abroad. So that I had not seen my cousins since all the calamities which had befallen them in the interval, and as I steamed northwards I wondered a good deal as to the changes I should find. I was to have come out that year in London, but ill-health had prevented me; and as a sort of consolation Lucy had kindly asked me to spend a fortnight at Mervyn, and be present at a shooting-party, which was to assemble there in the first week of October.

I had started early, and there was still an hour of the short autumn day left when I descended at the little wayside station, from which a six-mile drive brought me to the Grange. A dreary drive I found it – the round, grey, treeless outline of the fells stretching around me on every side beneath the leaden, changeless sky. The night had nearly fallen as we drove along the narrow valley in which the Grange stood: it was too dark to see the autumn tints of the woods which clothed and brightened its sides, almost too dark to distinguish the old tower – Dame Alice's tower as it was called – which stood some half a mile farther on at its head. But the light shone brightly from the Grange windows, and all feeling of dreariness departed as I drove up to the door. Leaving maid and boxes to their fate, I ran up the steps into the old, well-remembered hall, and was informed by the dignified manservant that her ladyship and the tea were awaiting me in the morning-room.

I found that there was nobody staying in the house except Alan, who was finishing the long vacation there: he had been called to the Bar a couple of years before. The guests were not to arrive for another week, so that I had plenty of opportunity in the interval to make up for lost time with my cousins. I began my observations that evening as we sat down to dinner, a cosy party of four. Lucy was quite unchanged – pretty, foolish and gentle as ever. George showed the full five years' increase of age, and seemed to have acquired a somewhat painful control of his temper. Instead of the old petulant outbursts, there was at times an air of nervous, irritable self-restraint, which I found the less pleasant of the two. But it was in Alan that the most striking alteration appeared. I felt it the moment I shook hands with him, and the impression deepened that evening with every hour. I told myself that it was only the natural difference between boy and man, between twenty and twenty-five, but I don't think that I believed it. Superficially the change was not great. The slight-built, graceful figure; the deep grey eyes, too small for beauty; the clear-cut features, the delicate, sensitive lips, close shaven now, as they had been hairless then – all were as I remembered them. But the face was paler and thinner than it had been, and there were lines round the eyes and at the corners of the mouth which were no more natural to twenty-five than they would have been to twenty. The old charm indeed – the sweet friendliness of manner, which was his own peculiar possession – was still there. He talked and laughed almost as much as formerly, but the talk was manufactured for our entertainment, and the laughter came from his head and not from his heart. And it was when he was taking no part in the conversation that the change showed most. Then the face, on which in the old time every passing emotion had expressed itself in a constant, living current, became cold and impassive – without interest, and without desire. It was at such times that I knew most certainly that here was something which had been living and was dead. Was it only his boyhood? This question I was unable to answer.

Still, in spite of all, that week was one of the happiest in my life. The brothers were both men of enough ability and cultivation to be pleasant talkers, and Lucy could perform adequately the part of conversational accompanist, which, socially speaking, is all that is required of a woman. The meals and evenings passed quickly and agreeably; the mornings I spent in unending gossips with Lucy, or in games with the children, two bright boys of five and six years old. But the afternoons were the best part of the day. George was a thorough squire in all his tastes and habits, and every afternoon his wife dutifully accompanied him round farms and coverts, inspecting new buildings, trudging along half-made roads or marking unoffending trees for destruction. Then Alan and I would ride by the hour together over moor and meadowland, often picking our way homewards down the glen-side long after the autumn evenings had closed in. During these rides I had glimpses many a time into depths in Alan's nature of which I doubt whether in the old days he had himself been aware. To me certainly they were as a revelation. A prevailing sadness, occasionally a painful tone of bitterness, characterised these more serious moods of his, but I do not think that, at the end of that week, I would, if I could, have changed the man, whom I was learning to revere and to pity, for the light-hearted playmate whom I felt was lost to me for ever.

TWO

The only feature of the family life which jarred on me was the attitude of the two brothers towards the children. I did not notice this much at first, and at all times it was a thing to be felt rather than to be seen. George himself never seemed quite at ease with them. The boys were strong and well grown, healthy in mind and body; and one would have thought that the existence of two such representatives to carry on his name and inherit his fortune would have been the very crown of pride and happiness to their father. But it was not so. Lucy indeed was devoted to them, and in all practical matters no one could have been kinder to them than was George. They were free of the whole house, and every indulgence that money could buy for them they had. I never heard him give them a harsh word. But there was something wrong. A constraint in their presence, a relief in their absence, an evident dislike of discussing them and their affairs, a total want of that enjoyment of love and possession which in such a case one might have expected to find. Alan's state of mind was even more marked. Never did I hear him willingly address his nephews, or in any way allude to their existence. I should have said that he simply ignored it, but for the heavy gloom which always overspread his spirits in their company, and for the glances which he would now and again cast in their direction – glances full of some hidden painful emotion, though of what nature it would have been hard to define. Indeed, Alan's attitude towards her children I soon found to be the only source of friction between Lucy and this otherwise much-loved member of her husband's family. I asked her one day why the boys never appeared at luncheon.

'Oh, they come when Alan is away,' she answered; 'but they seem to annoy him so much that George thinks it is better to keep them out of sight when he is here. It is very tiresome. I know that it is the fashion to say that George has got the temper of the family; but I assure you that Alan's nervous moods and fancies are much more difficult to live with.'

That was on the morning – a Friday it was – of the last day which we were to spend alone. The guests were to arrive soon after tea; and I think that with the knowledge of their approach Alan and I prolonged our ride that afternoon beyond its usual limits. We were on our way home, and it was already dusk, when a turn of the path brought us face to face with the old ruined tower, of which I have already spoken as standing at the head of the valley. I had not been close up to it yet during this visit at Mervyn. It had been a very favourite haunt of ours as children, and partly on that account, partly perhaps in order to defer the dreaded close of our ride to the last possible moment, I proposed an inspection of it. The only portion of the old building left standing in any kind of entirety was two rooms, one above the other. The lower room, level with the bottom of the moat, was dark and damp, and it was the upper one, reached by a little outside staircase, which had been our rendezvous of old. Alan showed no disposition to enter, and said that he would stay outside and hold my horse, so I dismounted and ran up alone.

The room seemed in no way changed. A mere stone shell, littered with fragments of wood and mortar. There was the rough wooden block on which Alan used to sit while he first frightened us with bogey-stories, and then calmed our excited nerves by rapid sallies of wild nonsense. There was the plank from behind which, erected as a barrier across the doorway, he would defend the castle against our united assault, pelting us with fir-cones and sods of earth. This and many a bygone scene thronged on me as I stood there, and the room filled again with the memories of childish mirth. And following close came those of childish terrors. Horrors which had oppressed me then, wholly imagined or dimly apprehended from half-heard traditions, and never thought of since, flitted around me in the gathering dusk. And with them it seemed to me as if there came other memories too – memories which had never been my own, of scenes whose actors had long been with the dead, but which, immortal as the spirit before whose eyes they had dwelt, still lingered in the spot where their victim had first learnt to shudder at their presence. Once the ghastly notion came to me, it seized on my imagination with irresistible force. It seemed as if from the darkened corners of the room vague, ill-defined shapes were actually peering out at me. When night came they would show themselves in that form, livid and terrible, in which they had been burnt into the brain and heart of the long ago dead.

I turned and glanced towards where I had left Alan. I could see his figure framed by the window, a black shadow against the grey twilight of the sky behind. Erect and perfectly motionless he sat, so motionless as to look almost lifeless, gazing before him down the valley into the illimitable distance beyond. There was something in that stern immobility of look and attitude which struck me with a curious sense of congruity. It was right that he should be thus – right that he should be no longer the laughing boy who a moment before had been in my memory. The haunting horrors of that place seemed to demand it, and for the first time I felt that I understood the change. With an effort I shook myself free from these fancies, and turned to go. As I did so, my eye fell upon a queer-shaped painted board, leaning up against the wall, which I well recollected in old times. Many a discussion had we had about the legend inscribed upon it, which in our wisdom we had finally pronounced to be German, chiefly because it was illegible. Though I had loudly professed my faith in this theory at the time, I had always had uneasy doubts on the subject, and now half smiling I bent down to verify or remove them. The language was English, not German; but the badly painted, faded Gothic letters in which it was written made the mistake excusable. In the dim light I had difficulty even now in deciphering the words, and felt when I had done so that neither the information conveyed nor the style of the composition was sufficient reward for the trouble I had taken. This is what I read:

> Where the woman sinned the maid shall win;
> But God help the maid that sleeps within.

What the lines could refer to I neither had any notion nor did I pause then even in my own mind to enquire. I only remember vaguely wondering whether they were intended for a tombstone or for a doorway. Then, continuing my way, I rapidly descended the steps and remounted my horse, glad to find myself once again in the open air and by my cousin's side.

The train of thought into which he had sunk during my absence was apparently an absorbing one, for to my first question as to the painted board he could hardly rouse himself to answer.

A board with a legend written on it? Yes, he remembered something of the kind there. It had always been there, he thought. He knew nothing about it – and so the subject was not continued.

The weird feelings which had haunted me in the tower still oppressed me, and I proceeded to ask Alan about that old Dame Alice whom the traditions of my childhood represented as the last occupant of the ruined building. Alan roused himself now, but did not seem anxious to impart information on the subject. She had lived there, he admitted, and no one had lived there since. 'Had she not,' I enquired, 'something to do with the mysterious cabinet at the house? I remember hearing it spoken of as "Dame Alice's cabinet".'

'So they say,' he assented; 'she and an Italian artificer who was in her service, and who, chiefly I imagine on account of his skill, shared with her the honour of reputed witchcraft.'

'She was the mother of Hugh Mervyn, the man who was murdered by his wife, was she not?' I asked.

'Yes,' said Alan, briefly.

'And had she not something to do with the curse?' I enquired after a short pause, and nervously I remembered my father's experience on that subject. I had never before dared to allude to it in the presence of any member of the family. My nervousness was fully warranted. The gloom on Alan's brow deepened, and after a very short, 'They say so,' he turned full upon me, and enquired with some asperity why on earth I had developed this sudden curiosity about his ancestress.

I hesitated a moment, for I was a little ashamed of my fancies; but the darkness gave me courage, and besides I was not afraid of telling Alan – he would understand. I told him of the strange sensations I had had while in the tower – sensations which had struck me with all that force and clearness which we usually associate with a direct experience of fact. 'Of course it was a trick of imagination,' I commented; 'but I could not get rid of the feeling that the person who had dwelt there last must have had terrible thoughts for the companions of her life.'

Alan listened in silence, and the silence continued for some time after I had ceased speaking.

'It is strange,' he said at last; 'instincts which we do not understand form the motive-power of most of our life's actions, and yet we refuse to admit them as evidence of any external truth. I suppose it is because we *must* act somehow, rightly or wrongly; and there are a great many things which we need not believe unless we choose. As for this old lady, she lived long – long enough, like most of us, to do evil; unlike most of us, long enough to witness some of the results of that evil. To say that, is to say that the last years of her life must have been weighted heavily enough with tragic thought.'

I gave a little shudder of repulsion.

'That is a depressing view of life, Alan,' I said. 'Does our peace of mind depend only upon death coming early enough to hide from us the truth?

And, after all, can it? Our spirits do not die. From another world they may witness the fruits of our lives in this one.'

'If they do,' he answered with sudden violence, 'it is absurd to doubt the existence of a purgatory. There must in such a case be a terrible one in store for the best among us.'

I was silent. The shadow that lay on his soul did not penetrate to mine, but it hung round me nevertheless, a cloud which I felt powerless to disperse.

After a moment he went on – 'Provided that they are distant enough, how little, after all, do we think of the results of our actions! There are few men who would deliberately instil into a child a love of drink, or wilfully deprive him of his reason; and yet a man with drunkenness or madness in his blood thinks nothing of bringing children into the world tainted as deeply with the curse as if he had inoculated them with it directly. There is no responsibility so completely ignored as this one of marriage and fatherhood, and yet how heavy it is and far-reaching.'

'Well,' I said, smiling, 'let us console ourselves with the thought that we are not all lunatics and drunkards.'

'No,' he answered; 'but there are other evils besides these, moral taints as well as physical, curses which have their roots in worlds beyond our own – sins of the fathers which are visited upon the children.'

He had lost all violence and bitterness of tone now; but the weary dejection which had taken their place communicated itself to my spirit with more subtle power than his previous mood had owned.

'That is why,' he went on, and his manner seemed to give more purpose to his speech than hitherto – 'that is why, so far as I am concerned, I mean to shirk the responsibility and remain unmarried.'

I was hardly surprised at his words. I felt that I had expected them, but their utterance seemed to intensify the gloom which rested upon us. Alan was the first to arouse himself from its influence.

'After all,' he said, turning round to me and speaking lightly, 'without looking so far and so deep, I think my resolve is a prudent one. Above all things, let us take life easily, and you know what St Paul says about "trouble in the flesh" – a remark which I am sure is specially applicable to briefless barristers, even though possessed of a modest competence of their own. Perhaps one of these days, when I am a fat old judge, I shall give my cook a chance if she is satisfactory in her clear soups; but till then I shall expect you, Evie, to work me one pair of carpet-slippers per annum, as tribute due to a bachelor cousin.'

I don't quite know what I answered – my heart was heavy and aching – but I tried with true feminine docility to follow the lead he had set me. He continued for some time in the same vein; but as we approached the house the effort seemed to become too much for him, and we relapsed again into silence.

This time I was the first to break it. 'I suppose,' I said, drearily, 'all those horrid people will have come by now.'

'Horrid people,' he repeated, with rather an uncertain laugh, and through the darkness I saw his figure bend forward as he stretched out his hand to caress my horse's neck. 'Why, Evie, I thought you were pining for gaiety, and that it was, in fact, for the purpose of meeting these "horrid people" that you came here.'

'Yes, I know,' I said, wistfully; 'but somehow the last week has been so pleasant that I cannot believe that anything will ever be quite so nice again.'

We had arrived at the house as I spoke, and the groom was standing at our horses' heads. Alan got off and came round to help me to dismount; but instead of putting up his arm as usual as a support for me to spring from, he laid his hand on mine. 'Yes, Evie,' he said, 'it has been indeed a pleasant time. God bless you for it.' For an instant he stood there looking up at me, his face full in the light which streamed from the open door, his grey eyes shining with a radiance which was not wholly from thence. Then he straightened his arm, I sprang to the ground, and as if to preclude the possibility of any answer on my part, he turned sharply on his heel, and began giving some orders to the groom. I went on alone into the house, feeling, I knew not and cared not to know why, that the gloom had fled from my spirit, and that the last ride had not after all been such a melancholy failure as it had bid fair at one time to become.

THREE

In the hall I was met by the housekeeper, who informed me that, owing to a misunderstanding about dates, a gentleman had arrived whom Lucy had not expected at that time, and that in consequence my room had been changed. My things had been put into the East Room – the haunted room – the room of the Closed Cabinet, as I remembered with a certain sense of pleased importance, though without any surprise. It stood apart from the other guest-rooms, at the end of the passage from which opened George and Lucy's private apartment; and as it was consequently disagreeable to have a stranger there, it was always used when the house was full for a member of the family. My father and mother had often slept there: there was a little room next to it, though not communicating with it, which served for a dressing-room. Though I had never passed the night there myself, I knew it as well as any room in the house. I went there at once, and found Lucy superintending the last arrangements for my comfort.

She was full of apologies for the trouble she was giving me. I told her that the apologies were due to my maid and to her own servants rather than to me;

'and besides,' I added, glancing round, 'I am distinctly a gainer by the change.'

'You know, of course,' she said, lightly, 'that this is the haunted room of the house, and that you have no right to be here?'

'I know it is the haunted room,' I answered; 'but why have I no right to be here?'

'Oh, I don't know,' she said. 'There is one of those tiresome Mervyn traditions against allowing unmarried girls to sleep in this room. I believe two girls died in it a hundred and fifty years ago, or something of that sort.'

'But I should think that people, married or unmarried, must have died in nearly every room in the house,' I objected.

'Oh, yes, of course they have,' said Lucy; 'but once you come across a bit of superstition in this family, it is of no use to ask for reasons. However, this particular bit is too ridiculous even for George. Owing to Mr Leslie having come today, we must use every room in the house: it is intolerable having a stranger here, and you are the only relation staying with us. I pointed all that out to George, and he agreed that, under the circumstances, it would be absurd not to put you here.'

'I am quite agreeable,' I answered; 'and, indeed, I think I am rather favoured in having a room where the last recorded death appears to have taken place a hundred and fifty years ago, particularly as I should think that there can be scarcely anything now left in it which was here then, except, of course, the cabinet.'

The room had, in fact, been entirely done up and refurnished by my uncle, and was as bright and modern-looking an apartment as you could wish to see. It was large, and the walls were covered with one of those white and gold papers which were fashionable thirty years ago. Opposite us, as we stood warming our backs before the fire, was the bed – a large double one, hung with a pretty shade of pale blue. Material of the same colour covered the comfortable modern furniture, and hung from gilded cornices before the two windows which pierced the side of the room on our left. Between them stood the toilet-table, all muslin, blue ribbons, and silver. The carpet was a grey and blue Brussels one. The whole effect was cheerful, though I fear inartistic, and sadly out of keeping with the character of the house. The exception to these remarks was, as I had observed, the famous closed cabinet, to which I have more than once alluded. It stood against the same wall of the room as that in which the fireplace was, and on our right – that is, on that side of the fireplace which was farthest from the windows. As I spoke, I turned to go and look at it, and Lucy followed me. Many an hour as a child had I passed in front of it, fingering the seven carved brass handles, or rather buttons, which were ranged down its centre. They all slid, twisted or screwed with the greatest ease, and apparently like many another ingeniously contrived lock; but neither I nor anyone else had ever yet succeeded in sliding, twisting or screwing them after such a fashion as to open the closed doors of the cabinet. No one yet had robbed them of their secret since first it was placed there three hundred years ago by the old lady and her faithful Italian. It was a beautiful piece of workmanship, was this tantalising cabinet. Carved out of some dark foreign wood, the doors and panels were richly inlaid with lapis lazuli, ivory and mother-of-pearl, among which were twisted delicately chased threads of gold and silver. Above the doors, between them and the cornice, lay another mystery, fully as tormenting as was the first. In a smooth strip of wood about an inch wide, and extending along the whole breadth of the cabinet, was inlaid a fine pattern in gold wire. This at first sight seemed to consist of a legend or motto. On looking closer, however, though the pattern still looked as if it was formed out of characters of the alphabet curiously entwined together, you found yourself unable to fix upon any definite word, or even letter. You looked again and again, and the longer that you looked the more certain became your belief that you were on the verge of discovery. If you could approach the mysterious legend from a slightly different point of view, or look at it from another distance, the clue to the puzzle would be seized, and the words would stand forth clear and legible in your sight. But the clue never had been discovered, and the motto, if there was one, remained unread.

For a few minutes we stood looking at the cabinet in silence, and then Lucy gave a discontented little sigh. 'There's another tiresome piece of superstition!' she exclaimed; 'by far the handsomest piece of furniture in the house stuck away here in a bedroom which is hardly ever used. Again and again have I asked George to let me have it moved downstairs, but he won't hear of it.'

'Was it not placed here by Dame Alice herself?' I enquired a little reproachfully, for I felt that Lucy was not treating the cabinet with the respect which it really deserved.

'Yes, so they say,' she answered; and the tone of light contempt in which she spoke was now pierced by a not unnatural pride in the romantic mysteries of her husband's family. 'She placed it here, and it is said, you know, that when the closed cabinet is opened, and the mysterious motto is read, the curse will depart from the Mervyn family.'

'But why don't they break it open?' I asked, impatiently. 'I am sure that I would never have remained all my life in a house with a thing like that, and not found out in some way or another what was inside it.'

'Oh, but that would be quite fatal,' answered she. 'The curse can only be removed when the cabinet is opened as Dame Alice intended it to be, in an orthodox fashion. If you were to force it open, that could never happen, and the curse would therefore remain for ever.'

'And what is the curse?' I asked, with very different feelings from those with which I had timidly approached the same subject with Alan. Lucy was not a Mervyn, and not a person to inspire awe under any circumstances. My instincts were right again, for she turned away with a slight shrug of her shoulders.

'I have no idea,' she said. 'George and Alan always look portentously solemn and gloomy whenever one mentions the subject, so I don't. If you ask me for the truth, I believe it to be a pure invention, devised by the Mervyns for the purpose of delicately accounting for some of the disreputable actions of their ancestors. For you know, Evie,' she added, with a little laugh, 'the less said about the character of the family into which your aunt and I have married the better.'

The remark made me angry, I don't know why, and I answered stiffly that as far as I was acquainted with them, I at least saw nothing to complain of.

'Oh, as regards the present generation, no – except for that poor, wretched Jack,' acquiesced Lucy, with her usual imperturbable good-humour.

'And as regards the next?' I suggested, smiling, and already ashamed of my little temper.

'The next is perfect, of course – poor dear boys.' She sighed as she spoke, and I wondered whether she was really as unconscious as she generally appeared to be of the strange dissatisfaction with which her husband seemed to regard his children. Anyhow the mention of them had evidently changed her mood, and almost directly afterwards, with the remark that she must go and look after her guests, who had all arrived by now, she left me to myself.

For some minutes I sat by the bright fire, lost in aimless, wandering thought, which began with Dame Alice and her cabinet, and which ended somehow with Alan's face, as I had last seen it looking up at me in front of the hall-door. When I had reached that point, I roused myself to decide that I had dreamt long enough, and that it was quite time to go down to the guests and to tea. I accordingly donned my best teagown, arranged my hair, and proceeded towards the drawing-room. My way there lay through the great central hall. This apartment was approached from most of the bed-rooms in the house through a large, arched doorway at one end of it, which communicated directly with the great staircase. My bedroom, however, which, as I have said, lay among the private apartments of the house, opened into a passage which led into a broad gallery, or upper chamber, stretching right across the end of the hall. From this you descended by means of a small staircase in oak, whose carved balustrade, bending round the corner of the hall, formed one of the prettiest features of the picturesque old room. The barrier which ran along the front of the gallery was in solid oak, and of such a height that, unless standing close up to it, you could neither see nor be seen by the occupants of the room below. On approaching this gallery I heard voices in the hall. They were George's and Alan's, evidently in hot discussion. As I issued from the passage, George was speaking, and his voice had that exasperated tone in which an angry man tries to bring to a close an argument in which he has lost his temper. 'For heaven's sake leave it alone, Alan; I neither can nor will interfere. We have enough to bear from these cursed traditions as it is, without adding one which has no foundation whatever to justify it – a mere contemptible piece of superstition.'

'No member of our family has a right to call any tradition contemptible which is connected with that place, and you know it,' answered Alan; and though he spoke low, his voice trembled with some strong emotion. A first impulse of hesitation which I had had I checked, feeling that as I had heard so much it was fairer to go on, and I advanced to the top of the staircase. Alan stood by the fireplace facing me, but far too occupied to see me. His last speech had seemingly aroused George to fury, for the latter turned on him now with savage passion.

'Damn it all, Alan!' he cried, 'can't you be quiet? I will be master in my own house. Take care, I tell you; the curse may not be quite fulfilled yet after all.'

As George uttered these words, Alan lifted his eyes to him with a glance of awful horror: his face turned ghastly white; his lips trembled for a moment; and then he answered back with one half-whispered word of supreme appeal – 'George!' There was a long-drawn, unutterable anguish in his tone, and his voice, though scarcely audible, penetrated to every corner of the room, and seemed to hang quivering in the air around one after the sound had ceased. Then there was a terrible stillness. Alan stood trembling in every limb, incapable apparently of speech or action, and George faced him, as silent and motionless as he was. For an instant they remained thus, while I looked breathlessly on. Then George, with a muttered imprecation, turned on his heel and left the room. Alan followed him as he went with dull lifeless eyes; and as the door closed he breathed deeply, with a breath that was almost a groan.

Taking my courage in both hands, I now descended the stairs, and at the sound of my footfall he glanced up, started, and then came rapidly to meet me.

'Evie! you here,' he said; 'I did not notice you. How long have you been here?' He was still quite white, and I noticed that he panted for breath as he spoke.

'Not long,' I answered, timidly and rather spasmodically; 'I only heard a sentence or two. You wanted George to do something about some tradition or other – and he was angry – and he said something about the curse.'

While I spoke Alan kept his eyes fixed on mine, reading through them, as

I knew, into my mind. When I had finished he turned his gaze away satisfied, and answered very quietly, 'Yes, that was it.' Then he went back to the fireplace, rested his arm against the high mantelpiece above it, and leaning his forehead on his arm, remained silently looking into the fire. I could see by his bent brow and compressed lips that he was engaged upon some earnest train of thought or reasoning, and I stood waiting – worried, puzzled, curious, but above all things, pitiful, and oh! longing so intensely to help him if I could. Presently he straightened himself a little, and addressed me more in his ordinary tone of voice, though without looking round. 'So I hear they have changed your room.'

'Yes,' I answered. And then, flushing rather, 'Is that what you and George have been quarrelling about?' I received no reply, and taking this silence for assent, I went on deprecatingly, 'Because you know, if it was, I think you are rather foolish, Alan. As I understand, two girls are said to have died in that room more than a hundred years ago, and for that reason there is a prejudice against putting a girl to sleep there. That is all. Merely a vague, unreasonable tradition.'

Alan took a moment to answer.

'Yes,' he said at length, speaking slowly, and as if replying to arguments in his own mind as much as to those which I had uttered. 'Yes, it is nothing but a tradition after all, and that of the very vaguest and most unsupported kind.'

'Is there even any proof that girls have not slept there since those two died?' I asked. I think that the suggestion conveyed in this question was a relief to him, for after a moment's pause, as if to search his memory, he turned round.

'No,' he answered, 'I don't think that there is any such proof; and I have no doubt that you are right, and that it is a mere prejudice that makes me dislike your sleeping there.'

'Then,' I said, with a little assumption of sisterly superiority, 'I think George was right, and that you were wrong.'

Alan smiled – a smile which sat oddly on the still pale face, and in the wearied, worn-looking eyes. 'Very likely,' he said; 'I dare say that I am superstitious. I have had things to make me so.' Then coming nearer to me, and laying his hands on my shoulders, he went on, smiling more brightly, 'We are a queer-tempered, bad-nerved race, we Mervyns, and you must not take us too seriously, Evie. The best thing that you can do with our odd ways is to ignore them.'

'Oh, I don't mind,' I answered, laughing, too glad to have won him back to even temporary brightness, 'as long as you and George don't come to blows over the question of where I am to sleep; which after all is chiefly my concern – and Lucy's.'

'Well, perhaps it is,' he replied, in the same tone; 'and now be off to the drawing-room, where Lucy is defending the tea-table single-handed all this time.'

I obeyed, and should have gone more cheerfully had I not turned at the doorway to look back at him, and caught one glimpse of his face as he sank heavily down into the large armchair by the fireside.

However, by dinner-time he appeared to have dismissed all painful reflections from his mind, or to have buried them too deep for discovery. The people staying in the house were, in spite of my sense of grievance at their arrival, individually pleasant, and after dinner I discovered them to be socially well assorted. For the first hour or two, indeed, after their arrival, each glared at the other across those triple lines of moral fortification behind which every well-bred Briton takes refuge on appearing at a friend's country house. But flags of truce were interchanged over the soup, an armistice was agreed upon during the roast, and the terms of a treaty of peace and amity were finally ratified under the sympathetic influence of George's best champagne. For the achievement of this happy result Alan certainly worked hard, and received therefore many a grateful glance from his sister-in-law. He was more excited than I had ever seen him before, and talked brilliantly and well – though perhaps not as exclusively to his neighbours as they may have wished. His eyes and his attention seemed everywhere at once: one moment he was throwing remarks across to some despairing couple opposite, and the next he was breaking an embarrassing pause in the conversation by some rapid sally of nonsense addressed to the table in general. He formed a great contrast to his brother, who sat gloomy and dejected, making little or no response to the advances of the two dowagers between whom he was placed. After dinner the younger members of the party spent the evening by Alan's initiative, and chiefly under his direction, in a series of lively and rather riotous games such as my nursery days had delighted in, and my schoolroom ones had disdained. It was a great and happy surprise to discover that, grown up, I might again enjoy them. I did so, hugely, and when bedtime came all memories more serious than those of 'musical chairs' or 'follow my leader' had vanished from my mind. I think, from Alan's glance as he handed me my bed candle, that the pleasure and excitement must have improved my looks.

'I hope you have enjoyed your first evening of gaiety, Evie,' he said.

'I have,' I answered, with happy conviction; 'and really I believe that it is chiefly owing to you, Alan.' He met my smile by another; but I think that there must have been something in his look which recalled other thoughts, for as I started up the stairs I threw a mischievous glance back at him and whispered, 'Now for the horrors of the haunted chamber.'

He laughed rather loudly, and saying, 'Good-night, and good-luck,' turned to attend to the other ladies.

His wishes were certainly fulfilled. I got to bed quickly, and – as soon as my happy excitement was sufficiently calmed to admit of it – to sleep. The only thing which disturbed me was the wind, which blew fiercely and loudly all the earlier portion of the night, half arousing me more than once. I spoke of it at breakfast the next morning; but the rest of the world seemed to have slept too heavily to have been aware of it.

FOUR

The men went out shooting directly after breakfast, and we women passed the day in orthodox country-house fashion – working and eating; walking and riding; driving and playing croquet; and above, beyond and through all things, chattering. Beyond a passing sigh while I was washing my hands, or a moment of mournful remembrance while I changed my dress, I had scarcely time even to regret the quiet happiness of the week that was past. In the evening we danced in the great hall. I had two waltzes with Alan. During a pause for breath, I found that we were standing near the fireplace, on the very spot where he and George had stood on the previous afternoon. The recollection made me involuntarily glance up at his face. It looked sad and worried, and the thought suddenly struck me that his extravagant spirits of the night before, and even his quieter, careful cheerfulness of tonight, had been but artificial moods at best. He turned, and finding my eyes fixed on him, at once plunged into conversation, discussed the peculiarities of one of the guests, good-humouredly enough, but with so much fun as to make me laugh in spite of myself. Then we danced again. The plaintive music, the smooth floor and the partner were all alike perfect, and I experienced that entire delight of physical enjoyment which I believe nothing but a waltz under such circumstances can give. When it was over I turned to Alan, and exclaimed with impulsive appeal, 'Oh, I am so happy – you must be happy too!' He smiled rather uncertainly, and answered, 'Don't bother yourself about me, Evie, I am all right. I told you that we Mervyns had bad nerves; and I am rather tired. That's all.' I was too passionately determined just then upon happiness, and his was too necessary to mine for me not to believe that he was speaking the truth.

We kept up the dancing till Lucy discovered with a shock that midnight had struck, and that Sunday had begun, and we were all sent off to bed. I was not long in making my nightly preparations, and had scarcely inserted myself between the sheets when, with a few long moans, the wind began again, more violently even than the night before. It had been a calm, fine day, and I made wise reflections as I listened upon the uncertainty of the north-country climate. What a tempest it was! How it moaned, and howled, and shrieked! Where had I heard the superstition which now came to my mind, that borne upon the wind come the spirits of the drowned, wailing and crying for the sepulture which had been denied them? But there were other sounds in that wind, too. Evil, murderous thoughts, perhaps, which had never taken body in deeds, but which, caught up in the air, now hurled themselves in impotent fury through the world. How I wished the wind would stop. It seemed full of horrible fancies, and it kept knocking them into my head, and it wouldn't leave off. Fancies, or memories – which? – and my mind reverted with a flash to the fearful thoughts which had haunted it in Dame Alice's tower. It was dark now. Those ghastly intangible shapes must have taken full form and colour, peopling the old ruin with their ageless hideousness. And the storm had found them there and borne them along with it as it blew through the creviced walls. That was why the wind's sound struck so strangely on my brain. Ah! I could hear them now, those still living memories of dead horror. Through the window crannies they came shrieking and wailing. They filled the chimney with spirit sobs, and now they were pressing on, crowding through the room – eager, eager to reach their prey. Nearer they came – nearer still! They were round my bed now! Through my closed eyelids I could almost see their dreadful shapes; in all my quivering flesh I felt their terrors as they bent over me – lower, lower . . .

With a start I aroused myself and sat up. Was I asleep or awake? I was trembling all over still, and it required the greatest effort of courage I had ever made to enable me to spring from my bed and strike a light. What a state my nerves or my digestion must be in! From my childhood the wind had always affected me strangely, and I blamed myself now for allowing my imagination to run away with me at the first. I found a novel which I had brought up to my room with me, one of the modern, Chinese-American school, where human nature is analysed with the patient, industrious in-difference of the true Celestial. I took the book to bed with me, and soon under its soothing influences fell asleep. I dreamt a good deal – nightmares, the definite recollection of which, as is so often the case, vanished from my mind as soon as I awoke, leaving only a vague impression of horror. They had been connected with the wind, of that alone I was conscious, and I went down to breakfast, maliciously hoping that others' rest had been as much disturbed as my own.

To my surprise, however, I found that I had again been the only sufferer. Indeed, so impressed were most of the party with the quiet in which their night had been passed, that they boldly declared my storm to have been the creature of my dreams. There is nothing more annoying when you feel yourself aggrieved by fate than to be told that your troubles have originated in your own fancy; so I dropped the subject. Though the discussion spread for a few minutes round the whole table, Alan took no part in it. Neither did George, except for what I thought a rather unnecessarily rough expression of his disbelief in the cause of my night's disturbance. As we rose from breakfast I saw Alan glance towards his brother, and make a movement, evidently with the purpose of speaking to him. Whether or not George was aware of the look or action, I cannot say; but at the same moment he made rapidly across the room to where one of his principal guests was standing, and at once engaged him in conversation. So earnestly and so volubly was he borne on, that they were still talking together when we ladies appeared again some minutes later, prepared for our walk to church. That was not the only occasion during the day on which I witnessed as I thought the same by-play going on. Again and again Alan appeared to be making efforts to engage George in private conversation, and again and again the latter successfully eluded him.

The church was about a mile away from the house, and as Lucy did not like having the carriages out on a Sunday, one service a week as a rule contented the household. In the afternoon we took the usual Sunday walk. On returning from it, I had just taken off my outdoor things, and was issuing from my bedroom, when I found myself face to face with Alan. He was coming out of George's study, and had succeeded apparently in obtaining that interview for which he had been all day seeking. One glance at his face told me what its nature had been. We paused opposite each other for a moment, and he looked at me earnestly.

'Are you going to church?' he enquired at last, abruptly.

'No,' I answered, with some surprise. 'I did not know that anyone was going this evening.'

'Will you come with me?'

'Yes, certainly; if you don't mind waiting a moment for me to put my things on.'

'There's plenty of time,' he answered; 'meet me in the hall.'

A few minutes later we started.

It was a calm, cloudless night, and although the moon was not yet half-full, and already past her meridian, she filled the clear air with gentle light. Not a word broke our silence. Alan walked hurriedly, looking straight before him, his head upright, his lips twitching nervously, while every now and then a half-uttered moan escaped unconsciously from between them. At last I could bear it no longer, and burst forth with the first remark which occurred to me. We were passing a big, black, queer-shaped stone standing in rather a lonely uncultivated spot at one end of the garden. It was an old acquaintance of my childhood; but my thoughts had been turned towards it now from the fact that I could see it from my bedroom window, and had been struck afresh by its uncouth, incongruous appearance.

'Isn't there some story connected with that stone?' I asked. 'I remember that we always called it the Dead Stone as children.'

Alan cast a quick, sidelong glance in that direction, and his brows contracted in an irritable frown. 'I don't know,' he answered shortly; 'they say that there is a woman buried beneath it, I believe.'

'A woman buried there!' I exclaimed in surprise; 'but who?'

'How should I know? They know nothing whatever about it. The place is full of stupid traditions of that kind.' Then, looking suspiciously round at me, 'Why do you ask?'

'I don't know; it was just something to say,' I answered plaintively. His strange mood so worked upon my nerves that it was all that I could do to restrain my tears. I think that my tone struck his conscience, for he made a few feverish attempts at conversation after that. But they were so entirely abortive that he soon abandoned the effort, and we finished our walk to church as speechlessly as we had begun it.

The service was bright, and the sermon perhaps a little commonplace, but sensible as it seemed to me in matter, and adequate in style. The peaceful evening hymn which followed the short solemn pause of silent prayer at the end soothed and refreshed my spirit. A hasty glance at my companion's face as he stood waiting for me in the porch, with the full light from the church streaming round him, assured me that the same influence had touched him too. Haggard and sad he still looked, it is true; but his features were composed, and the expression of actual pain had left his eyes.

Silent as we had come we started homeward through the waning moonlight, but this silence was of a very different nature from the other, and after a minute or two I did not hesitate to break it.

'It was a good sermon?' I observed, interrogatively.

'Yes,' he assented, 'I suppose you would call it so; but I confess that I should have found the text more impressive without its exposition.'

'Poor man!'

'But don't you often find it so?' he asked. 'Do you not often wish, to take this evening's instance, that clergymen would infuse themselves with something of St Paul's own spirit? Then perhaps they would not water all the strength out of his words in their efforts to explain them.'

'That is rather a large demand to make upon them, is it not?'

'Is it?' he questioned. 'I don't ask them to be inspired saints. I don't expect St Paul's breadth and depth of thought. But could they not have something of his vigorous completeness, something of the intensity of his feeling and belief? Look at the text of tonight. Did not the preacher's examples and applications take something from its awful unqualified strength?'

'Awful!' I exclaimed, in surprise; 'that is hardly the expression I should have used in connection with those words.'

'Why not?'

'Oh, I don't know. The text is very beautiful, of course, and at times, when people are tiresome and one ought to be nice to them, it is very difficult to act up to. But – '

'But you think that "awful" is rather a big adjective to use for so small a duty,' interposed Alan, and the moonlight showed the flicker of a smile upon his face. Then he continued, gravely, 'I doubt whether you yourself realise the full import of the words. The precept of charity is not merely a code of rules by which to order our conduct to our neighbours; it is the picture of a spiritual condition, and such, where it exists in us, must by its very nature be roused into activity by anything that affects us. So with this particular injunction, every circumstance in our lives is a challenge to it, and in presence of all alike it admits of one attitude only: "Beareth all things, endureth all things." I hope it will be long before that "all" sticks in your gizzard, Evie – before you come face to face with things which nature cannot bear, and yet which must be borne.'

He stopped, his voice quivering; and then after a pause went on again more calmly, 'And throughout it is the same. Moral precepts everywhere, which will admit of no compromise, no limitation, and yet which are at war with our strongest passions. If one could only interpose some "unless", some "except", even an "until", which should be short of the grave. But we cannot. The law is infinite, universal, eternal; there is no escape, no repose. Resist, strive, endure, that is the recurring cry; that is existence.'

'And peace,' I exclaimed, appealingly. 'Where is there room for peace, if that be true?'

He sighed for answer, and then in a changed and lower tone added, 'However thickly the clouds mass, however vainly we search for a coming glimmer in their midst, we never doubt that the sky *is* still beyond – beyond and around us, infinite and infinitely restful.'

He raised his eyes as he spoke, and mine followed his. We had entered the wooded glen. Through the scanty autumn foliage we could see the stars shining faintly in the dim moonlight, and beyond them the deep illimitable blue. A dark world it looked, distant and mysterious, and my young spirit rebelled at the consolation offered me.

'Peace seems a long way off,' I whispered.

'It is for me,' he answered, gently; 'not necessarily for you.'

'Oh, but I am worse and weaker than you are. If life is to be all warfare, I must be beaten. I cannot always be fighting.'

'Cannot you? Evie, what I have been saying is true of every moral law worth having, of every ideal of life worth striving after, that men have yet conceived. But it is only half the truth of Christianity. You know that. We must strive, for the promise is to him that overcometh; but though our aim be even higher than is that of others, we cannot in the end fail to reach it. The victory of the Cross is ours. You know that? You believe that?'

'Yes,' I answered, softly, too surprised to say more. In speaking of religion he, as a rule, showed to the full the reserve which is characteristic of his class and country, and this sudden outburst was in itself astonishing; but the eager anxiety with which he emphasised the last words of appeal impressed and bewildered me still further. We walked on for some minutes in silence. Then suddenly Alan stopped, and turning, took my hand in his. In what direction his mind had been working in the interval I could not divine; but the moment he began to speak I felt that he was now for the first time giving utterance to what had been really at the bottom of his thoughts the whole evening. Even in that dim light I could see the anxious look upon his face, and his voice shook with restrained emotion.

'Evie,' he said, 'have you ever thought of the world in which our spirits dwell, as our bodies do in this one of matter and sense, and of how it may be peopled? I know,' he went on hurriedly, 'that it is the fashion nowadays to laugh at such ideas. I envy those who have never had cause to be convinced of their reality, and I hope that you may long remain among the number. But should that not be so, should those unseen influences ever touch your life, I want you to remember then that, as one of the race for whom Christ died, you have as high a citizenship in that spirit land as any creature there: that you are your own soul's warden, and that neither principalities nor powers can rob you of that your birthright.'

I think my face must have shown my bewilderment, for he dropped my hand, and walked on with an impatient sigh.

'You don't understand me. Why should you? I daresay that I am talking nonsense – only – only – '

His voice expressed such an agony of doubt and hesitation that I burst out – 'I think that I do understand you a little, Alan. You mean that even from unearthly enemies there is nothing that we need really fear – at least, that is, I suppose, nothing worse than death. But that is surely enough!'

'Why should you fear death?' he said, abruptly; 'your soul will live.'

'Yes, I know that, but still – ' I stopped with a shudder.

'What is life after all but one long death?' he went on, with sudden violence. 'Our pleasures, our hopes, our youth are all dying; ambition dies, and even desire at last; our passions and tastes will die, or will live only to mourn their dead opportunity. The happiness of love dies with the loss of the loved, and, worst of all, love itself grows old in our hearts and dies. Why should we shrink only from the one death which can free us from all the others?'

'It is not true, Alan!' I cried, hotly. 'What you say is not true. There are many things even here which are living and shall live; and if it were otherwise, in everything, life that ends in death is better than no life at all.'

'You say that,' he answered, 'because for you these things are yet living. To leave life now, therefore, while it is full and sweet, untainted by death, surely that is not a fate to fear. Better, a thousand times better, to see the cord cut with one blow while it is still whole and strong, and to launch out straight into the great ocean, than to sit watching through the slow years, while strand after strand, thread by thread, loosens and unwinds itself – each with its own separate pang breaking, bringing the bitterness of death without its release.

His manner, the despairing ring in his voice, alarmed me even more than his words. Clinging to his arm with both hands, while the tears sprang to my eyes – 'Alan,' I cried, 'don't say such things – don't talk like that. You are making me miserable.'

He stopped short at my words, with bent head, his features hidden in the shadow thus cast upon them – nothing in his motionless form to show what was passing within him. Then he looked up, and turned his face to the moonlight and to me, laying his hand on one of mine.

'Don't be afraid,' he said; 'it is all right, my little David. You have driven the evil spirit away.' And lifting my hand, he pressed it gently to his lips. Then drawing it within his arm, he went on, as he walked forward, 'And even when it was on me at its worst, I was not meditating suicide, as I think you imagine. I am a very average specimen of humanity – neither brave enough to defy the possibilities of eternity nor cowardly enough to shirk those of time. No, I was only trying idiotically to persuade a girl of eighteen that life was not worth living; and more futilely still, myself that I did not wish her to live. I am afraid that in my mind philosophy and fact have but small connection with each other; and though my theorising for your welfare may be true enough, yet – I cannot help it, Evie – it would go terribly hard with me if anything were to happen to you.'

His voice trembled as he finished. My fear had gone with his return to his natural manner, but my bewilderment remained.

'Why *should* anything happen to me?' I asked.

'That is just it,' he answered, after a pause, looking straight in front of him and drawing his hand wearily over his brow. 'I know of no reason why it should.' Then giving a sigh, as if finally to dismiss from his mind a worrying subject – 'I have acted for the best,' he said, 'and may God forgive me if I have done wrong.'

There was a little silence after that, and then he began to talk again, steadily and quietly. The subject was deep enough still, as deep as any that we had touched upon, but both voice and sentiment were calm, bringing peace to my spirit, and soon making me forget the wonder and fear of a few moments before. Very openly did he talk as we passed on across the long trunk shadows and through the glades of silver light; and I saw further then into the most sacred recesses of his soul than I have ever done before or since.

When we reached home the moon had already set; but some of her beams seemed to have been left behind within my heart, so pure and peaceful was the light which filled it.

The same feeling continued with me all through that evening. After dinner some of the party played and sang. As it was Sunday, and Lucy was rigid in her views, the music was of a sacred character. I sat in a low armchair in a dark corner of the room, my mind too dreamy to think, and too passive to dream. I hardly interchanged three words with Alan, who remained in a still darker spot, invisible and silent the whole time. Only as we left the room to go to bed, I heard Lucy ask him if he had a headache. I did not hear his answer, and before I could see his face he had turned back again into the drawing-room.

FIVE

It was early, and when first I got to my room I felt little inclined for sleep. I wandered to the window, and drawing aside the curtains, looked out upon the still, starlit sky. At least I should rest quiet tonight. The air was very clear, and the sky seemed full of stars. As I stood there scraps of schoolroom learning came back to my mind. That the stars were all suns, surrounded perhaps in their turn by worlds as large or larger than our own. Worlds beyond worlds, and others farther still, which no man might number or even descry. And about the distance of those wonderful suns too – that one, for instance, at which I was looking – what was it that I had been told? That our world was not yet peopled, perhaps not yet formed, when the actual spot of light which now struck my sight first started from the star's surface! While it flashed along, itself the very symbol of speed, the whole of mankind had had time to be born, and live, and die!

My gaze dropped, and fell upon the dim, half-seen outline of the Dead Stone. That woman too. While that one ray speeded towards me her life had been lived and ended, and her body had rotted away into the ground. How close together we all were! Her life and mine; our joys, sufferings, deaths – all crowded together into the space of one flash of light! And yet there was nothing there but a horrible skeleton of dead bones, while I – !

I stopped with a shudder and turned back into the room. I wished that Alan had not told me what lay under the stone; I wished that I had never asked him. It was a ghastly thing to think about, and spoilt all the beauty of the night for me.

I got quickly into bed, and soon dropped asleep. I do not know how long I slept; but when I woke it was with the consciousness again of that haunting wind.

It was worse than ever. The world seemed filled with its din. Hurling itself passionately against the house, it gathered strength with every gust, till it seemed as if the old walls must soon crash in ruins round me. Gust upon gust; blow upon blow; swelling, lessening, never ceasing. The noise surrounded me; it penetrated my inmost being, as all-pervading as silence itself, and wrapping me in a solitude even more complete. There was nothing left in the world but the wind and I, and then a weird intangible doubt as to my own identity seized me. The wind was real, the wind with its echoes of passion and misery from the eternal abyss; but was there anything else? What was, and what had been, the world of sense and of knowledge, my own consciousness, my very self – all seemed gathered up and swept away in that one sole-existent fury of sound.

I pulled myself together, and getting out of bed, groped my way to the table which stood between the bed and the fireplace. The matches were there, and my half-burnt candle, which I lit. The wind penetrating the rattling casement circled round the room, and the flame of my candle bent and flared and shrank before it, throwing strange moving lights and shadows in every corner. I stood there shivering in my thin nightdress, half stunned by the cataract of noise beating on the walls outside, and peered anxiously around me. The room was not the same. Something was changed. What was it? How the shadows leaped and fell, dancing in time to the wind's music. Everything seemed alive. I turned my head slowly to the left, and then to the right, and then round – and stopped with a sudden gasp of fear.

The cabinet was open!

I looked away, and back, and away again. There was no room for doubt. The doors were thrown back, and were waving gently in the draught. One of the lower drawers was pulled out, and in a sudden flare of the candlelight I could see something glistening at its bottom. Then the light dwindled again, the candle was almost out, and the cabinet showed a dim black mass in the darkness. Up and down went the flame, and each returning brightness flashed back at me from the thing inside the drawer. I stood fascinated, my eyes fixed upon the spot, waiting for the fitful glitter as it came and went. What was there there? I knew that I must go and see, but I did not want to. If only the cabinet would close again before I looked, before I knew what was inside it. But it stood open, and the glittering thing lay there, dragging me towards itself.

Slowly at last, and with infinite reluctance, I went. The drawer was lined with soft white satin, and upon the satin lay a long, slender knife, hilted and sheathed in antique silver, richly set with jewels. I took it up and turned back to the table to examine it. It was Italian in workmanship, and I knew that the carving and chasing of the silver were more precious even than the jewels which studded it, and whose rough setting gave so firm a grasp to my hand. Was the blade as fair as the covering, I wondered? A little resistance at first, and then the long thin steel slid easily out. Sharp, and bright, and finely tempered it looked with its deadly, tapering point. Stains, dull and irregular, crossed the fine engraving on its surface and dimmed its polish. I bent to examine them more closely, and as I did so a sudden stronger gust of wind blew out the candle. I shuddered a little at the darkness and looked up. But it did not matter: the curtain was still drawn away from the window opposite my bedside, and through it a flood of moonlight was pouring in upon floor and bed.

Putting the sheath down upon the table, I walked to the window to examine the knife more closely by that pale light. How gloriously brilliant it was! darkened now and again by the quickly passing shadows of wind-driven clouds. At least so I thought, and I glanced up and out of the window to see them. A black world met my gaze. Neither moon was there nor moonlight: the broad silver beam in which I stood stretched no farther than the window. I caught my breath, and my limbs stiffened as I looked. No moon, no cloud, no movement in the clear, calm, starlit sky; while still the ghastly light stretched round me, and the spectral shadows drifted across the room.

But it was not all dark outside: one spot caught my eye, bright with a livid unearthly brightness – the Dead Stone shining out into the night like an ember from hell's furnace! There was a horrid semblance of life in the light – a palpitating, breathing glow – and my pulses beat in time to it, till I seemed to be drawing it into my veins. It had no warmth, and as it entered my blood my heart grew colder, and my muscles more rigid. My fingers clutched the dagger-hilt till its jewelled roughness pressed painfully into my palm. All the strength of my strained powers seemed gathered in that grasp, and the more tightly I held the more vividly did the rock gleam and quiver with infernal life. The dead woman! The dead woman! What had I to do with her? Let her bones rest in the filth of their own decay – out there under the accursed stone.

And now the noise of the wind lessens in my ears. Let it go on – yes, louder and wilder, drowning my senses in its tumult. What is there with me in the room – the great empty room behind me? Nothing; only the cabinet with its waving doors. They are waving to and fro, to and fro – I know it. But there is no other life in the room but that – no, no; no other life in the room but that.

Oh! don't let the wind stop. I can't hear anything while it goes on – but if it stops! Ah! the gusts grow weaker, struggling, forced into rest. Now – now – they have ceased.

Silence!

A fearful pause.

What is that that I hear? There, behind me in the room?

Do I hear it? Is there anything?

The throbbing of my own blood in my ears.

No, no! There is something as well – something outside myself.

What is it?

Low; heavy; regular.

God! it is – it is the breath of a living creature! A living creature! here – close to me – alone with me!

The numbness of terror conquers me. I can neither stir nor speak. Only my whole soul strains at my ears to listen.

Where does the sound come from?

Close behind me – close.

Ah–h!

It is from there – from the bed where I was lying a moment ago! . . .

I try to shriek, but the sound gurgles unuttered in my throat. I clutch the stone mullions of the window, and press myself against the panes. If I could but throw myself out! – anywhere, anywhere – away from that dreadful sound – from that thing close behind me in the bed! But I can do nothing. The wind has broken forth again now; the storm crashes round me. And still through it all I hear the ghastly breathing – even, low, scarcely audible – but I hear it. I shall hear it as long as I live! . . .

Is the thing moving?

Is it coming nearer?

No, no; not that – that was but a fancy to freeze me dead.

But to stand here, with that creature behind me, listening, waiting for the warm horror of its breath to touch my neck! Ah! I cannot. I will look. I will see it face to face. Better any agony than this one.

Slowly, with held breath, and eyes aching in their stretched fixity, I turn. There it is! Clear in the moonlight I see the monstrous form within the bed – the dark coverlet rises and falls with its heaving breath . . . Ah! heaven have mercy! Is there none to help, none to save me from this awful presence? . . .

And the knife-hilt draws my fingers round it, while my flesh quivers, and my soul grows sick with loathing. The wind howls, the shadows chase through the room, hunting with fearful darkness more fearful light; and I stand looking . . . listening . . .

* * *

I must not stand here for ever; I must be up and doing. What a noise the wind makes, and the rattling of the windows and the doors. If he sleeps through this he will sleep through all. Noiselessly my bare feet tread the carpet as I approach the bed; noiselessly my left arm raises the heavy curtain. What does it hide? Do I not know? The bestial features, half-hidden in coarse, black growth; the muddy, blotched skin, oozing foulness at every pore. Oh, I know them too well! What a monster it is! How the rank breath gurgles through his throat in his drunken sleep. The eyes are closed now, but I know them too; their odious leer, and the venomous hatred with which they can glare at me from their bloodshot setting. But the time has come at last. Never again shall their passion insult me or their fury degrade me in slavish terror. There he lies; there at my mercy, the man who for fifteen years has made God's light a shame to me, and His darkness a terror. The end has come at last – the only end possible, the only end left me. On his head be the blood and the crime! God almighty, I am not guilty! The end has come; I can bear my burden no farther.

'Beareth all things, endureth all things.'

Where have I heard those words? They are in the Bible; the precept of charity. What has that to do with me? Nothing. I heard the words in my dreams somewhere. A white-faced man said them, a white-faced man with pure eyes. To me? – no, no, not to me; to a girl it was – an ignorant, innocent girl, and she accepted them as an eternal, unqualified law. Let her bear but half that I have borne, let her endure but one-tenth of what I have endured, and then if she dare let her speak in judgement against me.

Softly now; I must draw the heavy coverings away, and bare his breast to the stroke – the stroke that shall free me. I know well where to plant it; I have learned that from the old lady's Italian. Did he guess why I questioned him so closely of the surest, straightest road to a man's heart? No matter, he cannot hinder me now. Gently! Ah! I have disturbed him. He moves, mutters in his sleep, throws out his arm. Down; down; crouching behind the curtain. Heavens! if he wakes and sees me, he will kill me. No! alas! if only he would. I would kiss the hand that he struck me with; but he is too cruel for that. He will imagine some new and more hellish torture to punish me with. But the knife! I have got that; he shall never touch me living again . . . He is quieter now. I hear his breath, hoarse and heavy as a wild beast's panting. He draws it more evenly, more deeply. The danger is past. Thank God!

God! What have I to do with Him? A God of Judgement. Ha, ha! Hell cannot frighten me; it will not be worse than earth. Only he will be there too. Not with him, not with him – send me to the lowest circle of torment, but not with him. There, his breast is bare now. Is the knife sharp? Yes; and the blade is strong enough. Now let me strike – myself afterwards if need be, but him first. Is it the devil that prompts me? Then the devil is my friend, and the friend of the world. No. God is a God of love. He cannot wish such a man to live. He made him, but the devil spoilt him; and let the devil have his handiwork back again. It has served him long enough here; and its last service shall be to make me a murderess.

How the moonlight gleams from the blade as my arm swings up and back:

in how close a grasp the rough hilt draws my fingers round it. Now.

A murderess?

Wait a moment. A moment may make me free; a moment may make me – that! Wait.

Hand and dagger droop again. His life has dragged its slime over my soul; shall his death poison it with a fouler corruption still?

'My own soul's warden.'

What was that? Dream memories again.

'Resist, strive, endure.'

Easy words. What do they mean for me? To creep back now to bed by his side, and to begin living again tomorrow the life which I have lived today? No, no; I cannot do it. Heaven cannot ask it of me. And there is no other way. That or this; this or that. Which shall it be? Ah! I have striven, God knows. I have endured so long that I hoped even to do so to the end. But today! Oh! the torment and the outrage: body and soul still bear the stain of it. I thought that my heart and my pride were dead together, but he has stung them again into aching, shameful life. Yesterday I might have spared him, to save my own cold soul from sin; but now it is cold no longer. It burns, it burns and the fire must be slaked.

Ay, I will kill him, and have done with it. Why should I pause any longer? The knife drags my hand back for the stroke. Only the dream surrounds me; the pure man's face is there, white, beseeching, and God's voice rings in my heart – 'To him that overcometh.'

But I cannot overcome. Evil has governed my life, and evil is stronger than I am. What shall I do? what shall I do? God, if Thou art stronger than evil, fight for me.

'The victory of the Cross is ours.'

Yes, I know it. It is true, it is true. But the knife? I cannot loose the knife if I would. How to wrench it from my own hold? Thou God of Victory, be with me! Christ, help me!

I seize the blade with my left hand; the two-edged steel slides through my grasp; a sharp pain in fingers and palm; and then – nothing . . .

SIX

When I again became conscious, I found myself half kneeling, half lying across the bed, my arms stretched out in front of me, my face buried in the clothes. Body and mind were alike numbed. A smarting pain in my left hand, a dreadful terror in my heart, were at first the only sensations of which I was aware. Slowly, very slowly, sense and memory returned to me, and with them a more vivid intensity of mental anguish, as detail by detail I recalled the weird horror of the night. Had it really happened – was the thing still there – or was it all a ghastly nightmare? It was some minutes before I dared either to move or look up, and then fearfully I raised my head. Before me stretched the smooth white coverlet, faintly bright with yellow sunshine. Weak and giddy, I struggled to my feet, and, steadying myself against the foot of the bed, with clenched teeth and bursting heart, forced my gaze round to the other end. The pillow lay there, bare and unmarked save for what might well have been the pressure of my own head. My breath came more freely, and I turned to the window. The sun had just risen, the golden tree-tops were touched with light, faint threads of mist hung here and there across the sky, and the twittering of birds sounded clearly through the crisp autumn air.

It was nothing but a bad dream then, after all, this horror which still hung round me, leaving me incapable of effort, almost of thought. I remembered the cabinet, and looked swiftly in that direction. There it stood, closed as usual, closed as it had been the evening before, as it had been for the last three hundred years, except in my dreams.

Yes, that was it; nothing but a dream – a gruesome, haunting dream. With an instinct of wiping out the dreadful memory, I raised my hand wearily to my forehead. As I did so, I became conscious again of how it hurt me. I looked at it. It was covered with half-dried blood, and two straight clean cuts appeared, one across the palm and one across the inside of the fingers just below the knuckles. I looked again towards the bed, and, in the place where my hand had rested during my faint, a small patch of red blood was to be seen.

Then it was true! Then it had all happened! With a low shuddering sob I threw myself down upon the couch at the foot of the bed, and lay there for some minutes, my limbs trembling and my soul shrinking within me. A mist of evil, fearful and loathsome, had descended upon my girlhood's life, sullying its ignorant innocence, saddening its brightness, as I felt, for ever. I lay there till my teeth began to chatter, and I realised that I was bitterly cold. To return to that accursed bed was impossible, so I pulled a rug which hung at one end of the sofa over me, and, utterly worn out in mind and body, fell uneasily asleep.

I was roused by the entrance of my maid. I stopped her exclamations and questions by shortly stating that I had had a bad night, had been unable to rest in bed, and had had an accident with my hand – without further specifying of what description.

'I didn't know that you had been feeling unwell when you went to bed last night, miss,' she said.

'When I went to bed last night? Unwell? What do you mean?'

'Only Mr Alan has just asked me to let him know how you find yourself this morning,' she answered.

Then he expected something, dreaded something. Ah! why had he yielded and allowed me to sleep here, I asked myself bitterly, as the incidents of the day before flashed through my mind.

'Tell him,' I said, 'what I have told you; and say that I wish to speak to him directly after breakfast.' I could not confide my story to anyone else, but speak of it I must to someone or go mad.

Every moment passed in that place was an added misery. Much to my maid's surprise I said that I would dress in her room – the little one which, as I have said, was close to my own. I felt better there; but my utter fatigue and my wounded hand combined to make my toilet slow, and I found that most of the party had finished breakfast when I reached the dining-room. I was glad of this, for even as it was I found it difficult enough to give coherent answers to the questions which my white face and bandaged hand called forth. Alan helped me by giving a resolute turn to the conversation. Once only our eyes met across the table. He looked as haggard and worn as I did: I learned afterwards that he had passed most of that fearful night pacing the passage outside my door, though he listened in vain for any indication of what was going on within the room.

The moment I had finished breakfast he was by my side. 'You wish to speak to me? Now?' he asked in a low tone.

'Yes; now,' I answered, breathlessly, and without raising my eyes from the ground.

'Where shall we go? Outside? It is a bright day, and we shall be freer there from interruption.'

I assented; and then looking up at him appealingly, 'Will you fetch my things for me? *I cannot* go up to that room again.'

He seemed to understand me, nodded, and was gone. A few minutes later we left the house, and made our way in silence towards a grassy spot on the side of the ravine where we had already indulged in more than one friendly talk.

As we went, the Dead Stone came for a moment into view. I seized Alan's arm in an almost convulsive grip. 'Tell me,' I whispered – 'you refused to tell me yesterday, but you must now – who is buried beneath that rock?'

There was now neither timidity nor embarrassment in my tone. The horrors of that house had become part of my life for ever, and their secrets were mine by right. Alan, after a moment's pause, a questioning glance at my face, tacitly accepted the position.

'I told you the truth,' he replied, 'when I said that I did not know; but I can tell you the popular tradition on the subject, if you like. They say that

Margaret Mervyn, the woman who murdered her husband, is buried there, and that Dame Alice had the rock placed over her grave – whether to save it from insult or to mark it out for opprobrium, I never heard. The poor people about here do not care to go near the place after dark, and among the older ones there are still some, I believe, who spit at the suicide's grave as they pass.'

'Poor woman, poor woman!' I exclaimed, in a burst of uncontrollable compassion.

'Why should you pity her?' demanded he with sudden sternness; 'she *was* a suicide and a murderess too. It would be better for the public conscience, I believe, if such were still hung in chains, or buried at the crossroads with a stake through their bodies.'

'Hush, Alan, hush!' I cried hysterically, as I clung to him; 'don't speak harshly of her: you do not know, you cannot tell, how terribly she was tempted. How can you?'

He looked down at me in bewildered surprise. 'How can I?' he repeated. 'You speak as if *you* could. What do you mean?'

'Don't ask me,' I answered, turning towards him my face – white, quivering, tear-stained. 'Don't ask me. Not now. You must answer my questions first, and after that I will tell you. But I cannot talk of it now. Not yet.'

We had reached the place we were in search of as I spoke. There, where the spreading roots of a great beech tree formed a natural resting place upon the steep side of the ravine, I took my seat, and Alan stretched himself upon the grass beside me. Then looking up at me – 'I do not know what questions you would ask,' he said, quietly; 'but I will answer them, whatever they may be.'

But I did not ask them yet. I sat instead with my hands clasping my knee, looking opposite at the glory of harmonious colour, or down the glen at the vista of far-off, dreamlike loveliness on which it opened out. The yellow autumn sunshine made everything golden, the fresh autumn breezes filled the air with life; but to me a loathsome shadow seemed to rest upon all, and to stretch itself out far beyond where my eyes could reach, befouling the beauty of the whole wide world. At last I spoke. 'You have known of it all, I suppose; of this curse that is in the world – sin and suffering, and what such words mean.'

'Yes,' he said, looking at me with wondering pity, 'I am afraid so.'

'But have you known them as they are known to some – agonised, hopeless suffering, and sin that is all but inevitable? Sometime in your life probably you have realised that such things are: it has come home to you, and to everyone else, no doubt, except a few ignorant girls such as I was yesterday. But there are some – yes, thousands and thousands – who even now, at this moment, are feeling sorrow like that, are sinking deep, deeper into the bottomless pit of their soul's degradation. And yet men who know this, who have seen it, laugh, talk, are happy, amuse themselves – how can they, how can they?' I stopped with a catch in my voice, and then stretching out my arms in front of me – 'And it is not only men. Look how beautiful the earth is, and God has made it, and lets the sun crown it every day with a new glory, while this horror of evil broods over and poisons it all. Oh, why is it so? I cannot understand it.'

My arms drooped again as I finished, and my eyes sought Alan's. His were full of tears, but there was almost a smile quivering at the corners of his lips as he replied: 'When you have found an answer to that question, Evie, come and tell me and mankind at large: it will be news to us all.' Then he continued – 'But, after all, the earth is beautiful, and the sun does shine: we have our own happiness to rejoice in, our own sorrows to bear, the suffering that is near to us to grapple with. For the rest, for this blackness of evil which surrounds us, and which we can do nothing to lighten, it will soon, thank God, become as vague and far off to you as it is to others: your feeling of it will be dulled, and, except at moments, you too will forget.'

'But that is horrible,' I exclaimed, passionately; 'the evil will be there all the same, whether I feel it or not. Men and women will be struggling in their misery and sin, only I shall be too selfish to care.'

'We cannot go outside the limits of our own nature,' he replied; 'our knowledge is shallow and our spiritual insight dark, and God in His mercy has made our hearts shallow too and our imagination dull. If, knowing and trusting only as men do, we were to feel as angels feel, earth would be hell indeed.'

It was cold comfort, but at that moment anything warmer or brighter would have been unreal and utterly repellent to me. I hardly took in the meaning of his words, but it was as if a hand had been stretched out to me, struggling in the deep mire, by one who himself felt solid ground beneath him. Where he stood I also might someday stand, and that thought seemed to make patience possible.

It was he who first broke the silence which followed. 'You were saying that you had questions to ask me. I am impatient to put mine in return, so please go on.'

It had been a relief to me to turn even to generalisations of despair from the actual horror which had inspired them, and to which my mind was thus recalled. With an effort I replied, 'Yes, I want to ask you about that room – the room in which I slept, and – and about the murder which was committed there.' In spite of all that I could do, my voice sank almost to a whisper as I concluded, and I was trembling from head to foot.

'Who told you that a murder was committed there?' Something in my face as he asked the question made him add quickly, 'Never mind. You are right. That is the room in which Hugh Mervyn was murdered by his wife. I was surprised at your question, for I did not know that anyone but my brothers and myself were aware of the fact. The subject is never mentioned: it is closely connected with one intensely painful to our family, and besides, if spoken of, there would be inconveniences arising from the superstitious terrors of servants, and the natural dislike of guests to sleep in a room where such a thing had happened. Indeed it was largely with the view of wiping out the last memory of the crime's locality, that my father renewed the interior of the room some twenty years ago. The only tradition which has been adhered to in connection with it is the one which has now been violated in your person – the one which precludes any unmarried woman from sleeping there. Except for that, the room has, as you know, lost all sinister reputation, and its title of "haunted" has become purely conventional. Nevertheless, as I said, you are right – that is undoubtedly the room in which the murder was committed.'

He stopped and looked up at me, waiting for more.

'Go on; tell me about it, and what followed.' My lips formed the words; my heart beat too faintly for my breath to utter them.

'About the murder itself there is not much to tell. The man, I believe, was an inhuman scoundrel, and the woman first killed him in desperation, and afterwards herself in despair. The only detail connected with the actual crime of which I have ever heard was the gale that was blowing that night – the fiercest known to this countryside in that generation; and it has always been said since that any misfortune to the Mervyns – especially any misfortune connected with the curse – comes with a storm of wind. That was why I so disliked your story of the imaginary tempests which have disturbed your nights since you slept there. As to what followed' – he gave a sigh – 'that story is long enough and full of incident. On the morning after the murder, so runs the tale, Dame Alice came down to the Grange from the tower to which she had retired when her son's wickednesses had driven her from his house, and there in the presence of the two corpses she foretold the curse which should rest upon their descendants for generations to come. A clergyman who was present, horrified, it is said at her words, adjured her by the mercy of heaven to place some term to the doom which she had pronounced. She replied that no mortal might reckon the fruit of a plant which drew its life from hell; that a term there should be, but as it passed the wisdom of man to fix it, so it should pass the wit of man to discover it. She then placed in the room this cabinet, constructed by herself and her Italian follower, and said that the curse should not depart from the family until the day when its doors were unlocked and its legend read.

'Such is the story. I tell it to you as it was told to me. One thing only is certain, that the doom thus traditionally foretold has been only too amply fulfilled.'

'And what was the doom?'

Alan hesitated a little, and when he spoke his voice was almost awful in its passionless sternness, in its despairing finality; it seemed to echo the irrevocable judgement which his words pronounced: 'That the crimes against God and each other which had destroyed the parents' life should enter into the children's blood, and that never thereafter should there fail a Mervyn to bring shame or death upon one generation of his father's house.

'There were two sons of that ill-fated marriage,' he went on after a pause, 'boys at the time of their parents' death. When they grew up they both fell in love with the same woman, and one killed the other in a duel. The story of the next generation was a peculiarly sad one. Two brothers took opposite sides during the civil troubles; but so fearful were they of the curse which lay upon the family, that they chiefly made use of their mutual position in order to protect and guard each other. After the wars were over, the younger brother, while travelling upon some Parliamentary commission, stopped a night at the Grange. There, through a mistake, he exchanged the report which he was bringing to London for a packet of papers implicating his brother and several besides in a Royalist plot. He only discovered his error as he handed the papers to his superior, and was but just able to warn his brother in time for him to save his life by flight. The other men involved were taken and executed, and as it was known by what means information had reached the government, the elder Mervyn was universally charged with the vilest treachery. It is said that when after the Restoration his return home was rumoured the neighbouring gentry assembled, armed with riding whips, to flog him out of the country if he should dare to show his face there. He died abroad, shame-stricken and broken-hearted. It was his son, brought up by his uncle in the sternest tenets of Puritanism, who, coming home after a lengthened journey, found that during his absence his sister had been shamefully seduced. He turned her out of doors, then and there, in the midst of a bitter January night, and the next morning her dead body and that of her newborn infant were found half buried in the fresh-fallen snow on the top of the wolds. The "white lady" is still supposed by the villagers to haunt that side of the glen. And so it went on. A beautiful, heartless Mervyn in Queen Anne's time enticed away the affections of her sister's betrothed, and on the day of her own wedding with him, her forsaken sister was found drowned by her own act in the pond at the bottom of the garden. Two brothers were soldiers together in some Continental war, and one was involuntarily the means of discovering and exposing the treason of the other. A girl was betrayed into a false marriage, and her life ruined by a man who came into the house as her brother's friend, and whose infamous designs were forwarded and finally accomplished by that same brother's active though unsuspecting assistance. Generation after generation, men or women, guilty or innocent, through the action of their own will or in spite of it, the curse has never yet failed of its victims.'

'Never yet? But surely in our own time – your father?' I did not dare to put the question which was burning my lips.

'Have you never heard of the tragic end of my poor young uncles?' he replied. 'They were several years older than my father. When boys of fourteen and fifteen they were sent out with the keeper for their first shooting lesson, and the elder shot his brother through the heart. He himself was delicate, and they say that he never entirely recovered from the shock. He died before he was twenty, and my father, then a child of seven years old, became the heir. It was partly, no doubt, owing to this calamity having thus occurred before he was old enough to feel it, that his comparative scepticism on the whole subject was due. To that I suppose, and to the fact that he grew up in an age of railways and liberal culture.'

'He didn't believe, then, in the curse?'

'Well, rather, he thought nothing about it. Until, that is, the time came when it took effect, to break his heart and end his life.'

'How do you mean?'

There was silence for a little. Alan had turned away his head, so that I could not see his face. Then –

'I suppose you have never been told the true story of why Jack left the country?'

'No. Was he – is he – ?'

'He is one victim of the curse in this generation, and I, God help me, am the other and perhaps more wretched one.'

His voice trembled and broke, and for the first time that day I almost forgot the mysterious horror of the night before in my pity for the actual, tangible suffering before me. I stretched out my hand to his, and his fingers closed on mine with a sudden, painful grip. Then quietly – 'I will tell you the story,' he said, 'though since that miserable time I have spoken of it to no one.'

There was a pause before he began. He lay there by my side, his gaze turned across me up the sunbright, autumn-tinted glen, but his eyes shadowed by the memories which he was striving to recall and arrange in due order in his mind. And when he did speak it was not directly to begin the promised recital.

'You never knew Jack,' he said, abruptly.

'Hardly,' I acquiesced. 'I remember thinking him very handsome.'

'There could not be two opinions as to that,' he answered. 'And a man who could have done anything he liked with life, had things gone differently.

His abilities were fine, but his strength lay above all in his character: he was strong – strong in his likes and in his dislikes, resolute, fearless, incapable of half measures – a man, every inch of him. He was not generally popular – stiff, hard, unsympathetic, people called him. From one point of view, and one only, he perhaps deserved the epithets. If a woman lost his respect she seemed to lose his pity too. Like a medieval monk, he looked upon such rather as the cause than the result of male depravity, and his contempt for them mingled with anger, almost, as I sometimes thought, with hatred. And this attitude was, I have no doubt, resented by the men of his own class and set, who shared neither his faults nor his virtues. But in other ways he was not hard. He could love; I, at least, have cause to know it. If you would hear his story rightly from my lips, Evie, you must try and see him with my eyes. The friend who loved me, and whom I loved with the passion which, if not the strongest, is certainly, I believe, the most enduring of which men are capable – that perfect brother's love, which so grows into our being that when it is at peace we are scarcely conscious of its existence, and when it is wounded our very life-blood seems to flow at the stroke. Brothers do not always love like that: I can only wish that we had not done so.

SEVEN

'Well, about five years ago, before I had taken my degree, I became acquainted with a woman whom I will call "Delia" – it is near enough to the name by which she went. She was a few years older than myself, very beautiful, and I believed her to be what she described herself – the innocent victim of circumstance and false appearance, a helpless prey to the vile calumnies of worldlings. In sober fact, I am afraid that, whatever her life may have been actually at the time that I knew her – a subject which I have never cared to investigate – her past had been not only bad enough irretrievably to fix her position in society, but bad enough to leave her without an ideal in the world, though still retaining within her heart the possibilities of a passion which, from the moment that it came to life, was strong enough to turn her whole existence into one desperate reckless straining after an object hopelessly beyond her reach. That was the woman with whom, at the age of twenty, I fancied myself in love. She wanted to get a husband, and she thought me – rightly – ass enough to accept the post. I was very young then even for my years – a student, an idealist, with an imagination highly developed, and no knowledge whatever of the world as it actually is. Anyhow, before I had known her a month, I had determined to make her my wife. My parents were abroad at the time, George and Lucy here, so that it was to Jack that I imparted the news of my resolve. As you may imagine, he did all that he could to shake it. But I was immovable. I disbelieved his facts, and despised his contempt from the standpoint of my own superior morality. This state of things continued for several weeks, during the greater part of which time I was at Oxford. I only knew that while I was there, Jack had made Delia's acquaintance, and was apparently cultivating it assiduously.

'One day, during the Easter vacation, I got a note from her asking me to supper at her house. Jack was invited too: we lodged together while my people were away.

'There is no need to dwell upon that supper. There were two or three women there of her own sort, or worse, and a dozen men from among the most profligate in London. The conversation was, I should think, bad even for that class; and she, the goddess of my idolatry, outstripped them all by the foul, coarse shamelessness of her language and behaviour. Before the entertainment was half over, I rose and took my leave, accompanied by Jack and another man – Legard was his name – who I presume was bored. Just as we had passed through into the ante-room, which lay beyond the room in which we had been eating, Delia caught up with us, and laying her hand on Jack's arm, said that she must speak with him. Legard and I went into the outer hall, and we had not been there more than a minute when the door from the ante-room opened, and we heard Delia's voice. I remember the words well – that was not the only occasion on which I was to hear them. "I will keep the ring as a record of my love," she said, "and understand that though you may forget, I never shall." Jack came through, the door closed, and as we went out I glanced towards his left hand, and saw, as I expected to see, the absence of the ring which he usually wore there. It contained a gem which my mother had picked up in the East, and I knew that he valued it quite peculiarly. We always called it Jack's talisman.

'A miserable time followed, a time for me of agonising wonder and doubt, during which regret for my dead illusion was entirely swallowed up in the terrible dread of my brother's degradation. Then came the announcement of his engagement to Lady Sylvia Grey; and a week later, the very day after I had finally returned to London from Oxford, I received a summons from Delia to come and see her. Curiosity, and the haunting fear about Jack, which still hung round me, induced me to consent to what otherwise would have been intolerably repellent to me, and I went. I found her in a mad passion of fury. Jack had refused to see her or to answer her letters, and she had sent for me that I might give him her message – tell him that he belonged to her and her only, and that he never should marry another woman. Angry at my interference, Jack disdained even to repudiate her claims, only sending back a threat of appealing to the police if she ventured upon any further annoyance. I wrote as she told me, and she emphasised my silence on the subject by writing back to me a more definite and explicit assertion of her rights. Beyond that for some weeks she made no sign. I have no doubt that she had means of keeping watch upon both his movements and mine; and during that time, as she relinquished gradually all hopes of inducing him to abandon his purpose, she was being driven to her last despairing resolve.

'Later, when all was over, Jack told me the story of that spring and summer. He told me how, when he found me immovable on the subject, he had resolved to stop the marriage somehow through Delia herself. He had made her acquaintance, and sought her society frequently. She had taken a fancy to him, and he admitted that he had availed himself of this fact to increase his intimacy with her, and, as he hoped ultimately, his power over her. But he was not conscious of ever having varied in his manner towards her of contemptuous indifference. This contradictory behaviour – his being constantly near her, yet always beyond her reach – was probably the very thing which excited her fancy into passion, the one strong passion of the poor woman's life. Then came his deliberate demand that she should by her own act unmask herself in my sight. The unfortunate woman tried to bargain for some proof of affection in return, and on this occasion had first openly declared her feelings towards him. He did not believe her; he refused her terms; but when as her payment she asked for the ring which was so especially associated with himself, he agreed to give it to her. Otherwise, hoping, no doubt against hope, dreading above all things a quarrel and final separation, she submitted unconditionally. And from the time of that evening, when Legard and I had overheard her parting words, Jack never saw her again until the last and final catastrophe.

'It was in July. My parents had returned to England, but had come straight on here. Jack and I were dining together with Lady Sylvia at her father's house – her brother, young Grey, making the fourth at dinner. I had arranged to go to a party with your mother, and I told the servants that a lady would call for me early in the evening. The house stood in Park Lane, and after dinner we all went out on to the broad balcony which opened from the drawing-room. There was a strong wind blowing that night, and I remember well the vague, disquieted feeling of unreality that possessed me – sweeping through me, as it were, with each gust of wind. Then, suddenly, a servant stood behind me, saying that the lady had come for me, and was in the drawing-room. Shocked that my aunt should have troubled herself to come so far, I turned quickly, stepped back into the room, and found myself face to face with Delia. She was fully dressed for the evening, with a long silk opera-cloak over her shoulders, her face as white as her gown, her splendid eyes strangely wide open and shining. I don't know what I said or did; I tried to get her away, but it was too late. The others had heard us, and appeared at the open window. Jack came forward at once, speaking rapidly, fiercely; telling her to leave the house at once; promising desperately that he would see her in his own rooms on the morrow. Well I remember how her answer rang out: "Neither tomorrow nor another day: I will never leave you again while I live."

'At the same instant she drew something swiftly from under her cloak, there was the sound of a pistol shot and she lay dead at our feet, her blood splashing upon Jack's shirt and hands as she fell.'

Alan paused in his recital. He was trembling from head to foot; but he kept his eyes turned steadily downwards, and both face and voice were cold – almost expressionless.

'Of course there was an inquest,' he resumed, 'which, as usual, exercised its very ill-defined powers in enquiring into all possible motives for the suicide. Young Grey, who had stepped into the room just before the shot had been fired, swore to the last words Delia had uttered; Legard to those he had overheard the night of that dreadful supper; there were scores of men to bear witness to the intimate relations which had existed between her and Jack during the whole of the previous spring. I had to give evidence. A skilful lawyer had been retained by one of her sisters, and had been instructed by her on points which no doubt she had originally learnt from Delia herself. In his hands, I had not only to corroborate Grey and Legard, and to give full details of that last interview, but also to swear to the peculiar value which Jack attached to the talisman ring which he had given Delia; to the language she had used when I saw her after my return from Oxford; to her subsequent letter, and Jack's fatal silence on the occasion. The story by which Jack and I strove to account for the facts was laughed at as a clumsy invention, and my undisguised reluctance in giving evidence added greatly to its weight against my brother's character.

'The jury returned a verdict of suicide while of unsound mind, the result of desertion by her lover. You may imagine how that verdict was commented upon by every radical newspaper in the kingdom, and for once society more than corroborated the opinions of the press. The larger public regarded the story as an extreme case of the innocent victim and the cowardly society villain. It was only among a comparatively small set that Delia's reputation was known, and there, in view of Jack's notorious and peculiar intimacy, his repudiation of all relations with her was received with contemptuous incredulity. That he should have first entered upon such relations at the very time when he was already courting Lady Sylvia was regarded even in those circles as a "strong order", and they looked upon his present attitude with great indignation, as a cowardly attempt to save his own character by casting upon the dead woman's memory all the odium of a false accusation. With an entire absence of logic, too, he was made responsible for the suicide having taken place in Lady Sylvia's presence. She had broken off the engagement the day after the catastrophe, and her family, a clan powerful in the London world, furious at the mud through which her name had been dragged, did all that they could to intensify the feeling already existing against Jack.

'Not a voice was raised in his defence. He was advised to leave the army; he was requested to withdraw from some of his clubs, turned out of others, avoided by his fast acquaintances, cut by his respectable ones. It was enough to kill a weaker man.

'He showed no resentment at the measure thus dealt out to him. Indeed, at the first, except for Sylvia's desertion of him, he seemed dully indifferent to it all. It was as if his soul had been stunned, from the moment that that wretched woman's blood had splashed upon his fingers, and her dead eyes had looked up into his own.

'But it was not long before he realised the full extent of the social damnation which had been inflicted upon him, and he then resolved to leave the country and go to America. The night before he started he came down here to take leave. I was here looking after my parents – George, whose mind was almost unhinged by the family disgrace, having gone abroad with his wife. My mother at the first news of what had happened had taken to her bed, never to leave it again; and thus it was in my presence alone, up there in my father's little study, that Jack gave him that night the whole story. He told it quietly enough; but when he had finished, with a sudden outburst of feeling he turned upon me. It was I who had been the cause of it all. My insensate folly had induced him to make the unhappy woman's acquaintance, to allow and even encourage her fatal love, to commit all the blunders and sins which had brought about her miserable ending and his final overthrow. It was by means of me that she had obtained access to him on that dreadful night; my evidence which most utterly damned him in public opinion; through me he had lost his reputation, his friends, his career, his country, the woman he loved, his hopes for the future; through me, above all, that the burden of that horrible death would lie for ever on his soul. He was lashing himself to fury with his own words as he spoke; and I stood leaning against the wall opposite to him, cold, dumb, unresisting, when suddenly my father interrupted. I think that both Jack and I had forgotten his presence; but at the sound of his voice, changed out of recognition, we turned to him, and I then for the first time saw in his face the death-look which never afterwards quitted it.

' "Stop, Jack," he said; "Alan is not to blame; and if it had not been in this way, it would have been in some other. I only am guilty, who brought you both into existence with my own hell-stained blood in your veins. If you wish to curse anyone, curse your family, your name, me if you will, and may God forgive me that you were ever born into the world!" '

Alan stopped with a shudder, and then continued, dully, 'It was when I heard those words, the most terrible that a father could have uttered, that I first understood all that that old sixteenth-century tale might mean to me and mine – I have realised it vividly enough since. Early the next morning, when the dawn was just breaking, Jack came to the door of my room to bid me goodbye. All his passion was gone. His looks and tones seemed part and parcel of the dim grey morning light. He freely withdrew all the charges he had made against me the night before; forgave me all the share that I had had in his misfortunes; and then begged that I would never come near him, or let him hear from me again. "The curse is heavy upon us both," he said, "and it is the only favour which you can do me." I have never seen him since.'

'But you have heard of him!' I exclaimed; 'what has become of him?'

Alan raised himself to a sitting posture. 'The last that I heard,' he said, with a catch in his voice, 'was that in his misery and hopelessness he was taking to drink. George writes to him, and does what he can; but I – I dare not say a word, for fear it should turn to poison on my lips – I dare not lift a hand to help him, for fear it should have power to strike him to the ground. The worst may be yet to come; I am still living, still living: there are depths of shame to which he has not sunk. And oh, Evie, Evie, he is my own, my best-loved brother!'

All his composure was gone now. His voice rose to a kind of wail with the last words, and folding his arms on his raised knee, he let his head fall upon them, while his figure quivered with scarcely restrained emotion. There was a silence for some moments while he sat thus, I looking on in wretched helplessness beside him. Then he raised his head, and, without looking round at me, went on in a low tone: 'And what is in the future? I pray that death instead of shame may be the portion of the next generation, and I look at George's boys only to wonder which of them is the happy one who shall some day lie dead at his brother's feet. Are you surprised at my resolution never to marry? The fatal prophecy is rich in its fulfilment; none of our name and blood are safe; and the day might come when I too should have to call upon my children to curse me for their birth – should have to watch while the burden which I could no longer bear alone pressed the life from their mother's heart.'

Through the tragedy of this speech I was conscious of a faint suggestion of comfort, a far-off glimmer, as of unseen home-lights on a midnight sky. I was in no mood then to understand, or to seek to understand, what it was; but I know now that his words had removed the weight of helpless banishment from my spirit – that his heart, speaking through them to my own, had made me for life the sharer of his grief.

EIGHT

Presently he drew his shoulders together with a slight determined jerk, threw himself back upon the grass, and turning to me, with that tremulous, haggard smile upon his lips which I knew so well, but which had never before struck me with such infinite pathos, 'Luckily,' he said, 'there are other things to do in life besides be happy. Only perhaps you understand now what I meant last night when I spoke of things which flesh and blood cannot bear, and yet which must be borne.'

Suddenly and sharply his words roused again into activity the loathsome memory which my interest in his story had partially deadened. He noticed the quick involuntary contraction of my muscles, and read it aright. 'That reminds me,' he went on; 'I must claim your promise. I have told you my story. Now, tell me yours.'

I told him; not as I have set it down here, though perhaps even in greater detail, but incoherently, bit by bit, while he helped me out with gentle questions, quickly comprehending gestures, and patient waiting during the pauses of exhaustion which perforce interposed themselves. As my story approached its climax, his agitation grew almost equal to my own, and he listened to the close, his teeth clenched, his brows bent, as if passing again with me through that awful conflict. When I had finished, it was some moments before either of us could speak; and then he burst forth into bitter self-reproach for having so far yielded to his brother's angry obstinacy in allowing me to sleep the third night in that fatal room.

'It was cowardice,' he said, 'sheer cowardice! After all that has happened, I dared not have a quarrel with one of my own blood. And yet if I had not hardened my heart, I had reason to know what I was risking.'

'How do you mean?' I asked.

'Those other two girls who slept there,' he said, breathlessly; 'it was in each case after the third night there that they were found dead – dead, Evie, so runs the story, with a mark upon their necks similar in shape and position to the death-wound which Margaret Mervyn inflicted upon herself.'

I could not speak, but I clutched his hand with an almost convulsive grip.

'And I knew the story – I knew it!' he cried. 'As boys we were not allowed to hear much of our family traditions, but this one I knew. When my father redid the interior of the east room, he removed at the same time a board from above the doorway outside, on which had been written – it is said by Dame Alice herself – a warning upon this very subject. I happened to be present when our old housekeeper, who had been his nurse, remonstrated with him warmly upon this act; and I asked her afterwards what the board was, and why she cared about it so much. In her excitement she told me the story of those unhappy girls, repeating again and again that, if the warning were taken away, evil would come of it.'

'And she was right,' I said, dully. 'Oh, if only your father had left it there!'

'I suppose,' he answered, speaking more quietly, 'that he was impatient of traditions which, as I told you, he at that time more than half despised. Indeed he altered the shape of the doorway, raising it, and making it flat and square, so that the old inscription could not have been replaced, even had it been wished. I remember it was fitted round the low Tudor arch which was previously there.'

My mind, too worn with many emotions for deliberate thought, wandered on languidly, and dwelt, as it were mechanically, upon these last trivial words. The doorway presented itself to my view as it had originally stood, with the discarded warning above it; and then, by a spontaneous comparison of mental vision, I recalled the painted board which I had noticed three days before in Dame Alice's tower. I suggested to Alan that it might have been the identical one – its shape was as he described. 'Very likely,' he answered, absently. 'Do you remember what the words were?'

'Yes, I think so,' I replied. 'Let me see.' And I repeated them slowly, dragging them out as it were one by one from my memory:

> Where the woman sinned the maid shall win;
> But God help the maid that sleeps within.

'You see,' I said, turning towards him slowly, 'the last line is a warning such as you spoke of.'

But to my surprise Alan had sprung to his feet, and was looking down at me, his whole body quivering with excitement. 'Yes, Evie,' he cried, 'and the first line is a prophecy – where the woman sinned the maid *has* won.' He seized the hand which I instinctively reached out to him. 'We have not seen the end of this yet,' he went on, speaking rapidly, and as if articulation had become difficult to him. 'Come, Evie, we must go back to the house and look at the cabinet – now, at once.'

I had risen to my feet by this time, but I shrank away at those words. 'To that room? Oh, Alan – no, I cannot.'

He had hold of my hand still, and he tightened his grasp upon it. 'I shall be with you; you will not be afraid with me,' he said. 'Come.' His eyes were burning, his face flushed and paled in rapid alternation, and his hand held mine like a vice of iron.

I turned with him, and we walked back to the Grange, Alan quickening his pace as he went, till I almost had to run by his side. As we approached the dreaded room my sense of repulsion became almost unbearable; but I was now infected by his excitement, though I but dimly comprehended its cause.

We met no one on our way, and in a moment he had hurried me into the house, up the stairs, and along the narrow passage, and I was once more in the east room, and in the presence of all the memories of that accursed night. For an instant I stood strengthless, helpless, on the threshold, my gaze fixed panic-stricken on the spot where I had taken such awful part in that phantom tragedy of evil; then Alan threw his arm round me, and drew me hastily on in front of the cabinet. Without a pause, giving himself time neither to speak nor think, he stretched out his left hand and moved the buttons one after another. How or in what direction he moved them I know not; but as the last turned with a click, the doors, which no mortal hand had unclosed for three hundred years, flew back, and the cabinet stood open. I gave a little gasp of fear. Alan pressed his lips closely together, and turned to me with eager questioning in his eyes. I pointed in answer tremblingly at the drawer which I had seen open the night before. He drew it out, and there on its satin bed lay the dagger in its silver sheath. Still without a word he took it up, and reaching his right hand round me, for I could not now have stood had he withdrawn his support, with a swift strong jerk he unsheathed the blade. There in the clear autumn sunshine I could see the same dull stains I had marked in the flickering candlelight, and over them, still ruddy and moist, were the drops of my own half-dried blood. I grasped the lapel of his coat with both my hands, and clung to him like a child in terror, while the eyes of both of us remained fixed as if fascinated upon the knife-blade. Then, with a sudden start of memory, Alan raised his to the cornice of the cabinet, and mine followed. No change that I could detect had taken place in that twisted goldwork; but there, clear in the sight of us both, stood forth the words of the magic motto:

> Pure blood shed by the blood-stained knife
> Ends Mervyn shame, heals Mervyn strife.

In low steady tones Alan read out the lines, and then there was silence – on my part of stunned bewilderment, the bewilderment of a spirit overwhelmed beyond the power of comprehension by rushing, conflicting emotions. Alan pressed me closer to him, while the silence seemed to throb with the beating of his heart and the panting of his breath. But except for that he remained motionless, gazing at the golden message before him. At length I felt a movement, and looking up saw his face turned down towards mine, the lips quivering, the cheeks flushed, the eyes soft with passionate feeling. 'We are saved, my darling,' he whispered; 'saved, and through you.' Then he bent his head lower, and there in that room of horror, I received the first long lover's kiss from my own dear husband's lips.

*   *   *

My husband, yes; but not till some time after that. Alan's first act, when he had once fully realised that the curse was indeed removed, was – throwing his budding practice to the winds – to set sail for America. There he sought out Jack, and laboured hard to impart to him some of his own new-found hope. It was slow work, but he succeeded at last; and only left him when, two years later, he had handed him over to the charge of a bright-eyed Western girl, to whom the whole story had been told, and who showed herself ready and anxious to help in building up again the broken life of her English lover. To judge from the letters that we have since received, she has shown herself well fitted for the task. Among other things she has money, and Jack's worldly affairs have so prospered that George declares that he can well afford now to waste some of his superfluous cash upon farming a few of his elder brother's acres. The idea seems to smile upon Jack, and I have every hope this winter of being able to institute an actual comparison between our small boy, his namesake, and his own three-year-old Alan. The comparison, by the way, will have to be conditional, for Jacket – the name by which my son and heir is familiarly known – is but a little more than two.

I turn my eyes for a moment, and they fall upon the northern corner of the east room, which shows round the edge of the house. Then the skeleton leaps from the cupboard of my memory; the icy hand which lies ever near my soul grips it suddenly with a chill shudder. Not for nothing was that wretched woman's life interwoven with my own, if only for an hour; not for nothing did my spirit harbour a conflict and an agony, which, thank God, are far from its own story. Though Margaret Mervyn's dagger failed to pierce my flesh, the wound in my soul may never wholly be healed. I know that that is so; and yet as I turn to start through the sunshine to the cedar shade and its laughing occupants, I whisper to myself with fervent conviction, 'It was worth it.'

The Alibi

I wholly disbelieve in spirit-rapping, table-turning, and all supernatural eccentricities of that nature. I refuse credence to the best authenticated ghost story. I can sleep in the gloomiest haunted room in the gloomiest haunted house without the slightest fear of a nocturnal visit from the other world. But, although I scoff at white ladies and bleeding nuns, there is a species of supernatural occurrence in which I am, I confess, an unwilling and hesitating believer.

The circumstances I am about to relate are of this nature, and were told me by an intimate friend of mine, as having lately occurred to a relation of his own. I give the story as he gave it to me, namely, in the words as nearly as possible of the principal actor in it.

Two years ago, towards the end of the London season, weary of the noise and bustle that for the last three months had been ceaselessly going on around me, I determined upon seeking a few days' rest and quiet in the country. The next evening saw me comfortably installed in a pretty farmhouse about two miles from a cathedral town. The little cottage in which I had taken up my quarters belonged to an old servant of my father's, and had long been a favourite resort of mine when wishing for quiet and fresh air.

The evening of the second day after my arrival was unusually close and sultry, even for the time of year. Weary with the heat, and somewhat sated with the two days' experience I had enjoyed of a quiet country life, I went up to my bedroom about half-past ten, with the intention of taking refuge from the *ennui* which was growing on me in a good long night's sleep. Finding, however, the heat an insuperable obstacle to closing my eyes, I got up, put on my dressing-gown, and, lighting a cigar, sat down at the open window, and dreamily gazed out on the garden in front of the cottage.

Before me several low, flat meadows stretched down to the river which separated us from the town. In the distance the massive towers of the cathedral appeared in strong and bright relief against the sky. The whole landscape, indeed, was bathed in a flood of light from the clear summer moon.

I was gradually getting sleepy, and beginning to think of turning in, when I heard a soft, clear voice, proceeding apparently from someone just beneath my window, saying: 'George, George, be quick! You are wanted in the town.'

I immediately looked from the window, and although the moon still shone most brilliantly, somewhat to my surprise I could see no one. Thinking, however, that it was some friend of my landlord's who was begging him to come into the town upon business, I turned from the window, and, getting into bed, in a few minutes was fast asleep.

I must have slept about three hours, when I awoke with a sudden start, and with a shivering 'goose-skin' feeling all over me. Fancying that this was caused by the morning air from the open window, I was getting out of bed to close it, when I heard the same voice proceeding from the very window itself. 'George, be quick! You are wanted in the town.'

These words produced an indescribable effect upon me. I trembled from head to foot, and, with a curious creeping about the roots of the hair, stood and listened. Hearing nothing more, I walked quickly to the window, and looked out. As before, nothing was to be seen. I stood in the shade of the curtain for some minutes, watching for the speaker to show himself, and then, laughing at my own nervousness, closed the window and returned to bed.

The grey morning light was now gradually overspreading the heavens, and daylight is antagonistic to all those fears which under cover of the darkness will steal at times over the boldest. In spite of this, I could not shake off the uncomfortable feeling produced by that voice. Vainly I tried to close my eyes. Eyes remained obstinately open; ears sensitively alive to the smallest sound.

Some half-hour had elapsed when again I felt the same chill stealing over me. With the perspiration standing on my forehead, I started up in bed, and listened with all my might. An instant of dead silence, and the mysterious voice followed: 'George, be quick! You *must* go into the town.'

The voice was in the room – nay, more, by my very bedside. The miserable fear that came over me I cannot attempt to describe. I felt that the words were addressed to me, and by no human mouth.

Hearing nothing more, I slowly got out of bed, and by every means in my power convinced myself that I was wide awake and not dreaming. Looking at myself in the glass on the dressing-table, I was at first shocked, and then, in spite of myself, somewhat amused by the pallid hue and scared expression of my countenance.

I grinned a ghastly grin at myself, whistled a bit of a polka, and got into bed again.

I had a horrible sort of notion that someone was looking at me, and that it would never do to let them see that I was the least uneasy.

I soon found out, however, that bed, in the circumstances, was a mistake, and I determined to get up and calm my nerves in the fresh morning air.

I dressed hurriedly, with many a look over my shoulder, keeping as much as possible to one corner of the room, where nobody could get behind me.

The grass in front of my window was glistening with the heavy morning dew, on which no foot could press without leaving a visible trace.

I searched the whole garden thoroughly, but no sign could I see of any person having been there.

Pondering over the events of the night, which, in spite of broad daylight and common sense, persisted in assuming a somewhat supernatural aspect, I wandered across the meadows towards the river by a footpath which led to the ferry. As I drew near to the boatman's cottage I saw him standing at his door, looking up the path by which I was approaching. As soon as he saw me, he turned and walked down to his boat, where he waited my arrival. 'You are early on foot, my friend, this morning,' said I, as I joined him.

'Early, sir,' answered he, in a somewhat grumbling tone. 'Yes, it is early, sir, and I have been waiting here for you these two hours or more.'

'Waiting for me, my friend – how so?'

'Yes, sir, I have; for they seemed so very anxious that you should not be kept waiting; they have been down from the farm twice this blessed night telling me that you would want to cross the ferry very early this morning.'

I answered the man not a word, and, getting into his boat, was quickly put across the water. As I walked rapidly up towards the town, I endeavoured to persuade myself that somebody was attempting to play a silly hoax upon me. At last, stopping at a gate through which I had to pass, I determined upon proceeding no further. As I turned to retrace my steps, suddenly the same shivering sensation passed over me – I can only describe it as a cold damp blast of air meeting me in the face, and then, stealing round and behind me, enveloping me in its icy folds.

I distinctly heard the words, 'George, George,' uttered in my very ear, in a somewhat plaintive and entreating tone.

I shuddered with a craven fear, and, turning hastily round, hurried on towards the town.

A few minutes' walking brought me into the marketplace. It was evidently market day, for, in spite of the early hour, there was already a considerable bustle going on. Shops were being opened, and the country people were exposing their butter, poultry and eggs for sale, and for about two hours I wandered among the busy and constantly increasing crowd, listening to every scrap of conversation that reached my ear, and vainly endeavouring to connect them with the strange summons that had roused me from my bed, and led me to the town.

I could hear nothing that interested me in any way, and, feeling tired and hungry, I decided on breakfasting at the hotel, which overlooked the marketplace, and then taking myself back to the cottage, in spite of the mysterious voice.

The cheerful and noisy bustle of the market had indeed partly dissipated the morbid turn which my fancies had taken.

After I had breakfasted I lit my cigar, and strolled into the bar, where I talked for ten minutes with the landlord without elucidating anything of greater moment than that it was his (the landlord's) opinion that things were bad – very; that Squire Thornbury was going to give a great ball on the occasion of his daughter's approaching marriage; and that Mr Weston's ox was certain to carry off the prize at the next agricultural meeting.

I bade him good-morning, and turned my steps homeward. I was checked on my way down the High Street by a considerable crowd, and upon enquiring what was the matter, was informed that the assizes were being held and that an 'interesting murder case' was going on. My curiosity was roused, I turned into the courthouse, and, meeting an acquaintance who fortunately happened to be a man in authority, was introduced into the court and accommodated with a seat.

The prisoner at the bar, who was accused of robbing and murdering a poor country girl, was a man of low, slight stature, with a coarse, brutal cast of features, rendered peculiarly striking by their strangely sinister expression.

As his small bright eyes wandered furtively round the court they met mine, and for an instant rested upon me. I shrank involuntarily from his gaze, as I would from that of some loathsome reptile, and kept my eyes steadily averted from him till the end of the trial, which had been nearly concluded the previous evening. The evidence, as summed up by the judge, was principally circumstantial, though apparently overwhelming in its nature. In spite of his counsel's really excellent defence, the jury unhesitatingly found him guilty.

The judge, before passing sentence, asked the prisoner, as usual, if he had anything further to urge why sentence of death should not be passed upon him.

The unfortunate prisoner, in an eager, excited manner, emphatically denied his guilt – declared that he was an honest, hard-working, travelling glazier, that he was in Bristol, many miles from the scene of the murder, on the day of its commission, and that he knew no more about it than a babe unborn. When asked why he had not brought forward this line of defence during the trial, he declared that he had wished it, but that the gentleman who had conducted his defence had refused to do so.

His counsel, in a few words of explanation, stated that, although he had every reason to believe the story told by the prisoner, he had been forced to confine his endeavours in his behalf to breaking down the circumstantial evidence for the prosecution – that most minute and searching enquiries had been made in Bristol, but that from the short time the prisoner had passed in that town (some three or four hours), and from the lengthened period which had elapsed since the murder, he had been unable to find witnesses who could satisfactorily have proved an alibi, and had therefore been forced to rely upon the weakness of the evidence produced by the prosecution. Sentence of death was passed upon the prisoner, who was removed from the bar loudly and persistently declaring his innocence.

I left the court painfully impressed with the conviction that he was innocent. The passionate earnestness with which he had pleaded his own cause, the fearless, haughty expression that crossed his ill-omened features, when, finding his assertions entirely valueless, he exclaimed with an imprecation, 'Well, then, do your worst, but I am *innocent!* I never saw the poor girl in my life, much less murdered her,' caused the whole court, at least the unprofessional part of it, to feel that there was some doubt about the case, and that circumstantial evidence, however strong, should rarely be permitted to carry a verdict of guilty. I am sure that the fervent though unsupported assertions made by the prisoner affected the jury far more than the florid defence made for him by his counsel.

The painful scene that I had just witnessed entirely put the events of the morning out of my head, and I walked home with my thoughts fully occupied with the trial. The earnest protestations of the unfortunate man rang in my ears, and his face, distorted with anxiety and passion, rose ever before me.

I passed the afternoon writing answers to several business letters, which had found me out in my retreat, and soon after dinner retired to my room, weary with want of sleep the previous night and with the excitement of the day.

It had been my habit for many years to make every night short notes of the events of the day, and this evening, as usual, I sat down to write my journal. I had hardly opened the book when, to my horror, the deadly chill that I had experienced in the morning again crept round me.

I listened eagerly for the voice that had hitherto followed, but this time in vain; not a sound could I hear but the ticking of my watch upon the table, and, I fear I must add, the beating of my own coward heart.

I got up and walked about, endeavouring to shake off my fears. The cold shadow, however, followed me about, impeding, as it seemed, my very respiration. I hesitated for a moment at the door, longing to call up the servant upon some pretext, but, checking myself, I turned to the table, and resolutely sitting down, again opened my journal.

As I turned over the leaves of the book, the word Bristol caught my eye. One glance at the page, and in an instant the following circumstances flashed across my memory.

I had been in Bristol on that very day – the day on which this dreadful murder had been committed!

Anonymous

On my way to a friend's house I had missed at Bristol the train I had expected to catch, and having a couple of hours to spare, I had wandered into the town, and entering the first hotel I came to, had called for some luncheon. The annoyance I felt at having some hours to wait was aggravated by the noise a workman was making in replacing a pane of glass in one of the coffee-room windows. I spoke to him once or twice, and finding my remonstrances of no avail, walked to the window and, with the assistance of the waiter, forced the man to discontinue his work.

In an instant I recalled the features of the workman. It was the very man I had seen in the felon's dock that morning. There was no doubt about it. That hideous face as it peered through the broken pane had fixed itself indelibly in my memory, and now identified itself beyond the possibility of doubt with the sinister countenance that had impressed me so painfully in the morning.

I have little more to add. I immediately hurried back to the town and laid these facts before the judge. On his communicating with the landlady of the hotel at Bristol, she was able to prove the payment of a small sum on that day to a travelling glazier. She came to the town, and from among a crowd of felons unhesitatingly picked out the convicted man as the person to whom she had paid the money.

The poor fellow, being a stranger at Bristol and having only passed two or three hours there, was utterly unable to remember at what houses he had been employed. I myself had forgotten the fact of my having ever been in that town.

A week later the man was at liberty. Some matter-of-fact people may endeavour to divest these circumstances of their, to me, mysterious nature by ascribing them to a disordered imagination and the fortuitous recognition of a prisoner condemned to die. Nothing will ever efface from my mind the conviction that providence in this case chose to work out its ends by extraordinary and supernatural means.

Here ended his story. I give it you without addition or embellishment as he told it to me. It is second-hand, I confess, but hitherto I have never been fortunate enough to hear a story with anything supernatural in it that was not open to the same objection.

STACY AUMONIER

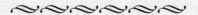

Stacy Aumonier (1887–1928), son of a sculptor, was educated at Cranleigh, and began his career as a designer and a landscape painter, frequently exhibiting at the Royal Academy and various London galleries. He served as a private in the First World War, and died in Switzerland at the age of forty-one. Although he wrote a number of successful novels, he was more popular as a writer of short stories, some of which won for him prestigious literary prizes.

Miss Bracegirdle Does her Duty

'This is the room, madame.'

'Ah, thank you . . . thank you.'

'Does it appear satisfactory to madame?'

'Oh, yes, thank you . . . quite.'

'Does madame require anything further?'

'Er – if not too late, may I have a hot bath?'

'*Parfaitement*, madame. The bathroom is at the end of the passage on the left. I will go and prepare it for madame.'

'There is one thing more . . . I have had a very long journey. I am very tired. Will you please see that I am not disturbed in the morning until I ring.'

'Certainly, madame.'

Millicent Bracegirdle was speaking the truth – she *was* tired. In the sleepy cathedral town of Easingstroke, from which she came, it was customary for everyone to speak the truth. It was customary, moreover, for everyone to lead simple, self-denying lives – to give up their time to good works and elevating thoughts. One had only to glance at little Miss Bracegirdle to see that in her were epitomised all the virtues and ideals of Easingstoke. Indeed, it was the pursuit of duty which had brought her to the Hôtel de l'Ouest at Bordeaux on this summer's night. She had travelled from Easingstoke to London, then without a break to Dover, crossed that horrid stretch of sea to Calais, entrained for Paris, where she of necessity had to spend four hours – a terrifying experience – and then had come on to Bordeaux, arriving at midnight. The reason for this journey being that someone had to come to Bordeaux to meet her young sister-in-law, who was arriving the next day from South America. The sister-in-law was married to a missionary brother in Paraguay, but the climate not agreeing with her, she was returning to England. Her dear brother, the dean, would have come himself, but the claims on his time were so extensive, the parishioners would miss him so . . . it was clearly Millicent's duty to go.

She had never been out of England before, and she had a horror of travel, and an ingrained distrust of foreigners. She spoke a little French – sufficient for the purposes of travel and for obtaining any modest necessities, but not sufficient for carrying on any kind of conversation. She did not deplore this latter fact, for she was of the opinion that French people were not the kind of people that one would naturally want to have conversation with; broadly speaking, they were not quite 'nice', in spite of their ingratiating manners.

The dear dean had given her endless advice, warning her earnestly not to enter into conversation with strangers, to obtain all information from the police, railway officials – in fact, anyone in an official uniform. He deeply regretted to say that he was afraid that France was not a country for a woman to travel about in *alone*. There were loose, bad people about, always on the lookout . . . He really thought perhaps he ought not to let her go. It was only by the utmost persuasion, in which she rather exaggerated her knowledge of the French language and character, her courage, and indifference to discomfort, that she managed to carry the day.

She unpacked her valise, placed her things about the room, tried to thrust back the little stabs of homesickness as she visualised her darling room at the deanery. How strange and hard and unfriendly seemed these foreign hotel bedrooms – heavy and depressing, no chintz and lavender and photographs of . . . all the dear family, the dean, the nephews and nieces, the interior of the cathedral during harvest festival, no samplers and needle-work or coloured reproductions of the paintings by Marcus Stone. Oh dear, how foolish she was! What did she expect?

She disrobed and donned a dressing-gown; then, armed with a sponge-bag and towel, she crept timidly down the passage to the bathroom, after closing her bedroom door and turning out the light. The gay bathroom cheered her. She wallowed luxuriously in the hot water, regarding her slim legs with quiet satisfaction. And for the first time since leaving home there came to her a pleasant moment – a sense of enjoyment in her adventure. After all, it *was* rather an adventure, and her life had been peculiarly devoid of it. What queer lives some people must live, travelling about, having experiences! How old was she? Not really old – not by any means. Forty-two? Forty-three? She had shut herself up so. She hardly ever regarded the potentialities of age. As the world went, she was a well-preserved woman for her age. A life of self-abnegation, simple living, healthy walking and fresh air, had kept her younger than these hurrying, pampered city people.

Love? yes, once when she was a young girl . . . he was a schoolmaster, a most estimable kind gentleman. They were never engaged – not actually, but it was a kind of understood thing. For three years it went on, this pleasant understanding and friendship. He was so gentle, so distinguished and considerate. She would have been happy to have continued in this strain for ever. But there was something lacking. Stephen had curious restless lapses. From the physical aspect of marriage she shrank – yes, even with Stephen, who was gentleness and kindness itself. And then one day . . . one day he went away – vanished, and never returned. They told her he had married one of the country girls – a girl who used to work in Mrs Forbes's dairy – not a very nice girl, she feared, one of these fast, pretty, foolish women. Heigho! well, she had lived that down, destructive as the blow appeared at the time. One lives everything down in time. There is always work, living for others, faith, duty . . . At the same time she could sympathise with people who found satisfaction in unusual experiences.

There would be lots to tell the dear dean when she wrote to him on the morrow; nearly losing her spectacles in the restaurant car; the amusing remarks of an American child on the train to Paris; the curious food every-where, nothing simple and plain; the two English ladies at the hotel in Paris who told her about the death of their uncle – the poor man being taken ill on Friday and dying on Sunday afternoon, just before teatime; the kindness of the hotel proprietor who had sat up for her; the prettiness of the chamber-maid. Oh, yes, everyone was really very kind. The French people, after all, were very nice. She had seen nothing – nothing but was quite nice and decorous. There would be lots to tell the dean tomorrow.

Her body glowed with the friction of the towel. She again donned her night attire and her thick, woollen dressing-gown. She tidied up the bath-room carefully in exactly the same way she was accustomed to do at home, then once more gripping her sponge-bag and towel, and turning out the light, she crept down the passage to her room. Entering the room she switched on the light and shut the door quickly. Then one of those ridiculous things happened – just the kind of thing you would expect to happen in a foreign hotel. The handle of the door came off in her hand.

She ejaculated a quiet 'Bother!' and sought to replace it with one hand, the other being occupied with the towel and sponge-bag. In doing this she behaved foolishly, for thrusting the knob carelessly against the steel pin – without properly securing it – she only succeeded in pushing the pin farther into the door and the knob was not adjusted. She uttered another little 'Bother!' and put her sponge-bag and towel down on the floor. She then tried to recover the pin with her left hand, but it had gone in too far.

'How very foolish!' she thought. 'I shall have to ring for the chamber-maid – and perhaps the poor girl has gone to bed.'

She turned and faced the room, and suddenly the awful horror was upon her. *There was a man asleep in her bed!*

The sight of that swarthy face on the pillow, with its black tousled hair and heavy moustache, produced in her the most terrible moment of her life. Her heart nearly stopped. For some seconds she could neither think nor scream, and her first thought was: 'I mustn't scream!'

She stood there like one paralysed, staring at the man's head and the great curved hunch of his body under the clothes. When she began to think she thought very quickly, and all her thoughts worked together. The first vivid realisation was that it wasn't the man's fault; it was *her* fault. *She was in the wrong room*. It was the man's room. The rooms were identical, but there were all his things about, his clothes thrown carelessly over chairs, his collar and tie on the wardrobe, his great heavy boots and the strange yellow trunk. She must get out somehow, anyhow.

She clutched once more at the door, feverishly driving her fingernails into the hole where the elusive pin had vanished. She tried to force her fingers in the crack and open the door that way, but it was of no avail. She was to all intents and purposes locked in – locked in a bedroom in a strange hotel alone with a man . . . a foreigner . . . *a Frenchman*! She must think. She must think . . . She switched off the light. If the light was off he might not wake up. It might give her time to think how to act. It was surprising that he had not awakened. If he *did* wake up, what would he do? How could she explain herself? He wouldn't believe her. No one would believe her. In an English hotel it would be difficult enough, but here where she wasn't known, where they were all foreigners and consequently antagonistic . . . merciful heavens!

She *must* get out. Should she wake the man? No, she couldn't do that. He might murder her. He might . . . Oh, it was too awful to contemplate! Should she scream? ring for the chambermaid? But no, it would be the same thing. People would come rushing. They would find her there in the strange man's bedroom after midnight – she, Millicent Bracegirdle, sister of the Dean of Easingstoke! Easingstoke!

Visions of Easingstoke flashed through her alarmed mind. Visions of the news arriving, women whispering around tea-tables: 'Have you heard, my dear? . . . Really no one would have imagined! Her poor brother! He will of course have to resign, you know, my dear. Have a little more cream, my love.'

Would they put her in prison? She might be in the room for the purpose of stealing or . . . She might be in the room for the purpose of breaking every one of the ten commandments. There was no explaining it away. She was a ruined woman, suddenly and irretrievably, unless she could open the door. The chimney? Should she climb up the chimney? But where would that lead to? And then she visualised the man pulling her down by her legs when she was already smothered in soot. Any moment he might wake up . . .

She thought she heard the chambermaid going along the passage. If she had wanted to scream, she ought to have screamed before. The maid would know she had left the bathroom some minutes ago. Was she going to her room? Suddenly she remembered that she had told the chambermaid that she was not to be disturbed until she rang the next morning. That was something. Nobody would be going to her room to find out that she was not there.

An abrupt and desperate plan formed in her mind. It was already getting on for one o'clock. The man was probably a quite harmless commercial traveller or businessman. He would probably get up about seven or eight o'clock, dress quickly, and go out. She would hide under his bed until he went. Only a matter of a few hours. Men don't look under their beds, although she made a religious practice of doing so herself. When he went he would be sure to open the door all right. The handle would be lying on the floor as though it had dropped off in the night. He would probably ring for the chambermaid or open it with a penknife. Men were so clever at those things. When he had gone she would creep out and steal back to her room, and then there would be no necessity to give any explanation to anyone. But heavens! What an experience! Once under the white frill of that bed she would be safe till the morning. In daylight nothing seemed so terrifying.

With feline precaution she went down on her hands and knees and crept towards the bed. What a lucky thing there was that broad white frill! She lifted it at the foot of the bed and crept under. There was just sufficient depth to take her slim body. The floor was fortunately carpeted all over, but it seemed very close and dusty. Suppose she coughed or sneezed! Anything might happen. Of course . . . it would be much more difficult to explain her presence under the bed than to explain her presence just inside the door. She held her breath in suspense. No sound came from above, but under this frill it was difficult to hear anything. It was almost more nerve-racking than hearing everything . . . listening for signs and portents. This temporary escape in any case would give her time to regard the predicament detachedly. Up to the present she had not been able to visualise the full significance of her action. She had in truth lost her head. She had been like a wild animal, consumed with the sole idea of escape . . . a mouse or a cat would do this kind of thing – take cover and lie low. If only it hadn't all happened *abroad*! She tried to frame sentences of explanation in French, but French escaped her. And then – they talked so rapidly, these people. They didn't listen. The situation was intolerable. Would she be able to endure a night of it?

At present she was not altogether uncomfortable, only stuffy and . . . very, very frightened. But she had to face six or seven or eight hours of it – perhaps even then discovery in the end! The minutes flashed by as she turned the matter over and over in her head. There was no solution. She began to wish she had screamed or awakened the man. She saw now that that would have been the wisest and most politic thing to do; but she had allowed ten minutes or a quarter of an hour to elapse from the moment when the chambermaid would know that she had left the bathroom. They would want an explanation of what she had been doing in the man's bedroom all that time. Why hadn't she screamed before?

She lifted the frill an inch or two and listened. She thought she heard the man breathing but she couldn't be sure. In any case it gave her more air. She became a little bolder, and thrust her face partly through the frill so that she could breathe freely. She tried to steady her nerves by concentrating on the fact that – well, there it was. She had done it. She must make the best of it. Perhaps it would be all right after all.

'Of course I shan't sleep,' she kept on thinking, 'I shan't be able to. In any case it will be safer not to sleep. I must be on the watch.'

She set her teeth and waited grimly. Now that she had made up her mind to see the thing through in this manner she felt a little calmer. She almost smiled as she reflected that there would certainly be something to tell the dear dean when she wrote to him tomorrow. How would he take it? Of course he would believe it – he had never doubted a single word that she had uttered in her life – but the story would sound so . . . preposterous. In Easingstoke it would be almost impossible to envisage such an experience. She, Millicent Bracegirdle, spending a night under a strange man's bed in a foreign hotel! What would those women think? Fanny Shields and that garrulous old Mrs Rusbridger? Perhaps . . . yes, perhaps it would be advisable to tell the dear dean to let the story go no further. One could hardly expect Mrs Rushbridger to . . . not make implications . . . exaggerate.

Oh, dear! What were they all doing now? They would be all asleep, everyone in Easingstoke. Her dear brother always retired at ten-fifteen. He would be sleeping calmly and placidly, the sleep of the just . . . breathing the clear sweet air of Sussex, not this – oh, it *was* stuffy! She felt a great desire to cough. She mustn't do that. Yes, at nine-thirty all the servants summoned to the library – a short service – never more than fifteen minutes, her brother didn't believe in a great deal of ritual – then at ten o'clock cocoa for everyone. At ten-fifteen bed for everyone. The dear sweet bedroom with the narrow white bed, by the side of which she had knelt every night as long as she could remember – even in her dear mother's day – and said her prayers.

Prayers! Yes, that was a curious thing. This was the first night in her life's experience that she had not said her prayers on retiring. The situation was certainly very peculiar . . . exceptional, one might call it. God would understand and forgive such a lapse. And yet after all, why . . . what was to prevent her saying her prayers? Of course she couldn't kneel in the proper devotional attitude, that would be a physical impossibility; nevertheless, perhaps her prayers might be just as efficacious . . . if they came from the heart. So little Miss Bracegirdle curved her body and placed her hands in a devout attitude in front of her face and quite inaudibly murmured her prayers under the strange man's bed.

'Our Father which art in heaven, Hallowed be Thy name. Thy kingdom come. Thy will be done in earth as it is in heaven. Give us this day our daily bread. And forgive us our trespasses . . .'

Trespasses! Yes, surely she was trespassing on this occasion, but God would understand. She had not wanted to trespass. She was an unwitting sinner. Without uttering a sound she went through her usual prayers in her heart. At the end she added fervently: 'Please God protect me from the dangers and perils of this night.'

Then she lay silent and inert, strangely soothed by the effort of praying. 'After all,' she thought, 'it isn't the attitude which matters – it is that which occurs deep down in us.'

For the first time she began to meditate – almost to question – church forms and dogma. If an attitude was not indispensable, why a building, a ritual, a church at all? Of course her dear brother couldn't be wrong, the church was so old, so very old, its root deep buried in the story of human life; it was only that . . . well, outward forms *could* be misleading. Her own present position for instance. In the eyes of the world she had, by one silly careless little action, convicted herself of being the breaker of every single one of the ten commandments.

She tried to think of one of which she could not be accused. But no – even to dishonouring her father and mother, bearing false witness, stealing, coveting her neighbour's . . . husband! That was the worst thing of all. Poor man! He might be a very pleasant honourable married gentleman with children and she – she was in a position to compromise him! Why hadn't she screamed? Too late! Too late!

It began to get very uncomfortable, stuffy, but at the same time draughty, and the floor was getting harder every minute. She changed her position stealthily and controlled her desire to cough. Her heart was beating rapidly. Over and over again recurred the vivid impression of every little incident and argument that had occurred to her from the moment she left the bathroom. This must, of course, be the room next to her own. So confusing, with perhaps twenty bedrooms all exactly alike on one side of a passage – how was one to remember whether one's number was 115 or 116?

Her mind began to wander idly off into her schooldays. She was always very bad at figures. She disliked Euclid and all those subjects about angles and equations – so unimportant, not leading anywhere. History she liked, and botany, and reading about strange foreign lands, although she had always been too timid to visit them. And the lives of great people, *most* fascinating – Oliver Cromwell, Lord Beaconsfield, Lincoln, Grace Darling – *there* was a heroine for you – General Booth, a great, good man, even if a little vulgar. She remembered dear old Miss Trimming talking about him one afternoon at the vicar of St Bride's garden party. She was *so* amusing. She . . . *Good heavens!*

Almost unwittingly, Millicent Bracegirdle had emitted a violent sneeze!

It was finished! For the second time that night she was conscious of her heart nearly stopping. For the second time that night she was so paralysed with fear that her mentality went to pieces. Now she would hear the man get out of bed. He would walk across to the door, switch on the light, and then lift up the frill. She could almost see that fierce moustached face glaring at her and growling something in French. Then he would thrust out an arm and drag her out. And then? O God in heaven! What then? . . .

'I shall scream before he does it. Perhaps I had better scream now. If he drags me out he will clap his hand over my mouth. Perhaps chloroform . . . '

But somehow she could not scream. She was too frightened even for that. She lifted the frill and listened. Was he moving stealthily across the carpet? She thought – no, she couldn't be sure. Anything might be happening. He might strike her from above – with one of those heavy boots perhaps. Nothing seemed to be happening, but the suspense was intolerable. She realised now that she hadn't the power to endure a night of it. Anything would be better than this – disgrace, imprisonment, even death. She would crawl out, wake the man, and try and explain as best she could.

She would switch on the light, cough, and say: '*Monsieur!*'

Then he would start up and stare at her.

Then she would say – what should she say?

'*Pardon, monsieur, mais je* – ' What on earth was the French for 'I have made a mistake'.

'*J'ai tort. C'est la chambre* – er – incorrect. *Voulez-vous* – er –'

What was the French for 'doorknob', 'let me go'?

It didn't matter. She would turn on the light, cough and trust to luck. If he got out of bed, and came towards her, she would scream the hotel down . . .

The resolution formed, she crawled deliberately out at the foot of the bed. She scrambled hastily towards the door – a perilous journey. In a few seconds the room was flooded with light. She turned towards the bed, coughed, and cried out boldly: '*Monsieur!*'

Then, for the third time that night, little Miss Bracegirdle's heart all but stopped. In this case the climax of the horror took longer to develop, but when it was reached, it clouded the other two experiences into insignificance.

The man on the bed was dead!

She had never beheld death before, but one does not mistake death.

She stared at him bewildered, and repeated almost in a whisper: '*Monsieur! . . . Monsieur!*'

Then she tiptoed towards the bed. The hair and moustache looked extraordinarily black in that grey, wax- like setting. The mouth was slightly open, and the face, which in life might have been vicious and sensual, looked incredibly peaceful and far away. It was as though she were regarding the features of a man across some vast passage of time, a being who had always been completely remote from mundane preoccupations.

When the full truth came home to her, little Miss Bracegirdle buried her face in her hands and murmured: 'Poor fellow . . . poor fellow!'

For the moment her own position seemed an affair of small consequence. She was in the presence of something greater and more all-pervading. Almost instinctively she knelt by the bed and prayed.

For a few moments she seemed to be possessed by an extraordinary calmness and detachment. The burden of her hotel predicament was a gossamer trouble – a silly, trivial, almost comic episode, something that could be explained away.

But this man – he had lived his life, whatever it was like, and now he was in the presence of his Maker. What kind of man had he been?

Her meditations were broken by an abrupt sound. It was that of a pair of heavy boots being thrown down by the door outside. She started, thinking at first it was someone knocking or trying to get in. She heard the 'boots', however, stumping away down the corridor, and the realisation stabbed her with the truth of her own position. She mustn't stop there. The necessity to get out was even more urgent.

To be found in a strange man's bedroom in the night is bad enough, but to be found in a dead man's bedroom was even worse. They could accuse her of murder, perhaps. Yes, that would be it – how could she possibly explain to these foreigners? Good God! they would hang her. No, guillotine her, that's what they do in France. They would chop her head off with a great steel knife. Merciful heavens! She envisaged herself standing blindfold, by a priest and an executioner in a red cap, like that man in the Dickens story – what was his name? . . . Sydney Carton, that was it, and before he went on the scaffold he said: 'It is a far, far better thing that I do than I have ever done.'

But no, she couldn't say that. It would be a far, far worse thing that she did. What about the dear dean? Her sister-in-law arriving alone from Paraguay tomorrow? All her dear people and friends in Easingstoke? Her darling Tony, the large grey tabby cat? It was her duty not to have her head chopped off if it could possibly be avoided. She could do no good in the room. She could not recall the dead to life. Her only mission was to escape. Any minute people might arrive. The chambermaid, the boots, the manager, the gendarmes . . . Visions of gendarmes arriving armed with swords and notebooks vitalised her almost exhausted energies. She was a desperate woman. Fortunately now she had not to worry about the light. She sprang once more at the door and tried to force it open with her fingers. The result hurt her and gave her pause. If she was to escape she must *think*, and think intensely. She mustn't do anything rash and silly, she must just think and plan calmly.

She examined the lock carefully. There was no keyhole, but there was a slip-bolt, so that the hotel guest could lock the door on the inside, but it couldn't be locked on the outside. Oh, why didn't this poor dear dead man lock his door last night? Then this trouble could not have happened. She could see the end of the steel pin. It was about half an inch down the hole. If anyone was passing they must surely notice the handle sticking out on the other side! She drew a hairpin out of her hair and tried to coax the pin back, but she only succeeded in pushing it a little farther in. She felt the colour leaving her face and a strange feeling of faintness come over her.

She was fighting for her life, she mustn't give way. She darted round the room like an animal in a trap, her mind alert for the slightest crevice of escape. The window had no balcony and there was a drop of five storeys to the street below. Dawn was breaking. Soon the activities of the hotel and the city would begin. The thing must be accomplished before then.

She went back once more and stared at the lock. She stared at the dead man's property, his razors, and brushes, and writing materials, pens and pencils and rubber and sealing-wax . . . Sealing-wax!

Necessity is truly the mother of invention. It is in any case quite certain that Millicent Bracegirdle, who had never invented a thing in her life, would never have evolved the ingenious little device she did, had she not believed that her position was utterly desperate. For in the end this is what she did. She got together a box of matches, a candle, a bar of sealing-wax and a hairpin. She made a little pool of hot sealing-wax, into which she dipped the end of the hairpin. Collecting a small blob on the end of it she thrust it into the hole, and let it adhere to the end of the steel pin. At the seventh attempt she got the thing to move. It took her just an hour and ten minutes to get that steel pin back into the room, and when at length it came far enough through for her to grip it with her fingernails, she burst into tears through the sheer physical tension of the strain. Very, very carefully she pulled it farther, and holding it firmly with her left hand she fixed the knob with her right, then slowly turned it. The door opened!

The temptation to dash out into the corridor and scream with relief was almost irresistible, but she forbore. She listened; she peeped out. No one was about. With beating heart, she went out, closing the door inaudibly. She crept like a little mouse to the room next door, stole in and flung herself on her bed. Immediately she did so it flashed through her mind that *she had left her sponge-bag and towel in the dead man's room*!

In looking back upon her experience she always considered that that second expedition was the worst of all. She might have left the sponge-bag and towel there, only that the towel – she never used hotel towels – had neatly inscribed in the corner 'M.B'.

With furtive caution she managed to retrace her steps. She re-entered the dead man's room, reclaimed her property, and returned to her own. When this mission was accomplished she was indeed wellnigh spent. She lay on her bed and groaned feebly. At last she fell into a fevered sleep . . .

It was eleven o'clock when she awoke and no one had been to disturb her.

The sun was shining, and the experiences of the night appeared a dubious nightmare. Surely she had dreamt it all?

With dread still burning in her heart she rang the bell. After a short interval of time the chambermaid appeared. The girl's eyes were bright with some uncontrollable excitement. No, she had not been dreaming. This girl had heard something.

'Will you bring me some tea, please?'

'Certainly, madame.'

The maid drew back the curtains and fussed about the room. She was under a pledge of secrecy, but she could contain herself no longer. Suddenly she approached the bed and whispered excitedly: 'Oh, madame, I have promised not to tell . . . but a terrible thing has happened. A man, a dead man, has been found in Room 117 – a guest. Please not to say I tell you. But they have all been there, the gendarmes, the doctors, the inspectors. Oh, it is terrible . . . terrible.'

The little lady in the bed said nothing. There was indeed nothing to say. But Marie Louise Lancret was too full of emotional excitement to spare her.

'But the terrible thing is – Do you know who he is, madame? They say it is Boldhu, the man wanted for the murder of Jeanne Carreton in the barn at Vincennes. They say he strangled her, and then cut her up in pieces and hid her in two barrels which he threw into the river . . . Oh, but he was a bad man, madame, a terrible bad man . . . and he died in the room next door . . . suicide, they think; or was it an attack of the heart? . . . Remorse, some shock perhaps . . . Did you say a *café complet*, madame?'

'No, thank you, my dear . . . just a cup of tea . . . strong tea . . . '

'*Parfaitement*, madame.'

The girl retired, and a little later a waiter entered the room with a tray of tea. She could never get over her surprise at this. It seemed so – well, indecorous for a man – although only a waiter – to enter a lady's bedroom. There was no doubt a great deal in what the dear dean said. They were certainly very peculiar, these French people – they had most peculiar notions. It was not the way they behaved at Easingstoke. She got farther under the sheets, but the waiter appeared quite indifferent to the situation. He put the tray down and retired.

When he had gone she sat up and sipped her tea, which gradually warmed her. She was glad the sun was shining. She would have to get up soon. They said that her sister-in-law's boat was due to berth at one o'clock. That would give her time to dress comfortably, write to her brother, and then go down to the docks. Poor man! So he had been a murderer, a man who cut up the bodies of his victims . . . and she had spent the night in his bedroom! They were certainly a most – how could she describe it? – people. Nevertheless she felt a little glad that at the end she had been there to kneel and pray by his bedside. Probably nobody else had ever done that. It was very difficult to judge people . . . Something at some time might have gone wrong. He might not have murdered the woman after all. People were often wrongly convicted. She herself . . . If the police had found her in that room at three o'clock that morning . . . It is that which takes place in the heart which counts. One learns and learns. Had she not learnt that one can pray just as effectively lying under a bed as kneeling beside it? . . . Poor man!

She washed and dressed herself and walked calmly down to the writing-room. There was no evidence of excitement among the other hotel guests. Probably none of them knew about the tragedy except herself. She went to a writing-table, and after profound meditation wrote as follows:

My dear Brother – I arrived late last night after a very pleasant journey. Everyone was very kind and attentive, the manager was sitting up for me. I nearly lost my spectacle case in the restaurant car! But a kind old gentleman found it and returned it to me. There was a most amusing American child on the train. I will tell you about her on my return. The people are very pleasant, but the food is peculiar, nothing *plain and wholesome*. I am going down to meet Annie at one o'clock. How have you been keeping, my dear? I hope you have not had any further return of the bronchial attacks.

'Please tell Lizzie that I remembered in the train on the way here that that large stone jar of marmalade that Mrs Hunt made is behind those empty tins in the top shelf of the cupboard next to the coach-house. I wonder whether Mrs Butler was able to come to evensong after all? This is a nice hotel, but I think Annie and I will stay at the Grand tonight, as the bedrooms here are rather noisy. Well, my dear, nothing more till I return. Do take care of yourself.

Your loving sister,

Millicent

Yes, she couldn't tell Peter about it, neither in the letter nor when she went back to him. It was her duty not to tell him. It would only distress him; she felt convinced of it. In this curious foreign atmosphere the thing appeared possible, but in Easingstoke the mere recounting of the fantastic situations would be positively . . . indelicate. There was no escaping that broad general fact – she had spent a night in a strange man's bedroom. Whether he was a gentleman or a criminal, even whether he was dead or alive, did not seem to mitigate the jar upon her sensibilities, or rather it would not mitigate the jar upon the peculiarly sensitive relationship between her brother and herself. To say that she had been to the bathroom, the knob of the door-handle came off in her hand, she was too frightened to awaken the sleeper or scream, she got under the bed – well, it was all perfectly true.

Peter would believe her, but – one simply could not conceive such a situation in Easingstoke deanery. It would create a curious little barrier between them, as though she had been dipped in some mysterious solution which alienated her. It was her duty not to tell.

She put on her hat and went out to post the letter. She distrusted an hotel letter-box. One never knew who handled these letters. It was not a proper official way of treating them. She walked to the head post office in Bordeaux.

The sun was shining. It was very pleasant walking about amongst these queer excitable people, so foreign and different-looking – and the cafés already crowded with chattering men and women, and the flower stalls, and the strange odour of – what was it? Salt? Brine? Charcoal? . . . A military band was playing in the square . . . very gay and moving. It was all life, and movement, and bustle . . . thrilling rather.

'I spent a night in a strange man's bedroom.'

Little Miss Bracegirdle hunched her shoulders, murmured to herself, and walked faster. She reached the post office and found the large metal plate with the slot for letters and 'R.F.' stamped above it. Something official at last! Her face was a little flushed – was it the warmth of the day or the contact of movement and life? – as she put her letter into the slot. After posting it she put her hand into the slot and flicked it round to see that there were no foreign contraptions to impede its safe delivery. No, the letter had dropped safely in. She sighed contentedly and walked off in the direction of the docks to meet her sister- in-law from Paraguay.

A Source of Irritation

To look at old Sam Gates you would never suspect him of having nerves. His sixty-nine years of close application to the needs of the soil had given him a certain earthy stolidity. To observe him hoeing, or thinning out a broad field of turnips, hardly attracted one's attention, he seemed so much part and parcel of the whole scheme. He blended into the soil like a glorified swede. Nevertheless, the half-dozen people who claimed his acquaintance knew him to be a man who suffered from little moods of irritability.

And on this glorious morning a little incident annoyed him unreasonably. It concerned his niece Aggie. She was a plump girl with clear, blue eyes, and a face as round and inexpressive as the dumplings for which the county was famous. She came slowly across the long sweep of the downland and, putting down the bundle wrapped in a red handkerchief which contained his breakfast and dinner, she said: 'Well, uncle, is there any noos?'

Now, this may not appear to the casual reader to be a remark likely to cause irritation, but it affected old Sam Gates as a very silly and unnecessary question. It was, moreover, the constant repetition of it which was beginning to anger him. He met his niece twice a day. In the morning she brought his bundle of food at seven, and when he passed his sister's cottage on the way home to tea at five she was invariably hanging about the gate, and she always said in the same voice: 'Well, uncle, is there any noos?'

Noos! What noos should there be? For sixty-nine years he had never lived farther than five miles from Halvesham. For nearly sixty of those years he had bent his back above the soil. There were, indeed, historic occasions. Once, for instance, when he had married Annie Hachet. And there was the birth of his daughter. There was also a famous occasion when he had visited London. Once he had been to a flower-show at Market Roughborough. He either went or didn't go to church on Sundays. He had had many interesting chats with Mr James at the Cowman, and three years ago had sold a pig to Mrs Way. But he couldn't always have interesting noos of this sort up his sleeve. Didn't the silly zany know that for the last three weeks he had been hoeing and thinning out turnips for Mr Hodge on this very same field? What noos could there be?

He blinked at his niece, and didn't answer. She undid the parcel and said: 'Mrs Goping's fowl got out again last night.'

'Ah,' he replied in a noncommittal manner and began to munch his bread and bacon. His niece picked up the handkerchief and, humming to herself, walked back across the field.

It was a glorious morning, and a white sea mist added to the promise of a hot day. He sat there munching, thinking of nothing in particular, but gradually subsiding into a mood of placid content. He noticed the back of Aggie disappear in the distance. It was a mile to the cottage and a mile and a half to Halvesham. Silly things, girls. They were all alike. One had to make allowances. He dismissed her from his thoughts, and took a long swig of tea out of a bottle. Insects buzzed lazily. He tapped his pocket to assure himself that his pouch of shag was there, and then he continued munching. When he had finished, he lighted his pipe and stretched himself comfortably. He looked along the line of turnips he had thinned and then across the adjoining field of swedes. Silver streaks appeared on the sea below the mist. In some dim way he felt happy in his solitude amidst this sweeping immensity of earth and sea and sky.

And then something else came to irritate him: it was one of 'these dratted airyplanes'. 'Airyplanes' were his pet aversion. He could find nothing to be said in their favour. Nasty, noisy, disfiguring things that seared the heavens and made the earth dangerous. And every day there seemed to be more and more of them. Of course 'this old war' was responsible for a lot of them, he knew. The war was a 'plaguy noosance'. They were short-handed on the farm, beer and tobacco were dear, and Mrs Steven's nephew had been and got wounded in the foot.

He turned his attention once more to the turnips; but an 'airyplane' has an annoying genius for gripping one's attention. When it appears on the scene, however much we dislike it, it has a way of taking the stage-centre. We cannot help constantly looking at it. And so it was with old Sam Gates. He spat on his hands and blinked up at the sky. And suddenly the aeroplane behaved in a very extraordinary manner. It was well over the sea when it seemed to lurch drunkenly and skimmed the water. Then it shot up at a dangerous angle and zigzagged. It started to go farther out, and then turned and made for the land. The engines were making a curious grating noise. It rose once more, and then suddenly dived downwards, and came plump down right in the middle of Mr Hodge's field of swedes.

And then, as if not content with this desecration, it ran along the ground, ripping and tearing twenty-five yards of good swedes, before it came to a stop.

Old Sam Gates was in a terrible state. The aeroplane was more than a hundred yards away, but he waved his arms and called out: 'Hi, you there, you mustn't land in they swedes! They're Mr Hodge's.'

The instant the aeroplane stopped, a man leaped out and gazed quickly round. He glanced at Sam Gates, and seemed uncertain whether to address him or whether to concentrate his attention on the flying-machine. The latter arrangement appeared to be his ultimate decision. He dived under the engine and became frantically busy. Sam had never seen anyone work with such furious energy; but all the same it was not to be tolerated. It was disgraceful. Sam started out across the field, almost hurrying in his indignation. When he appeared within earshot of the aviator he cried out again: 'Hi! you mustn't rest your old airyplane here! You've kicked up all Mr Hodge's swedes. A noice thing you've done!'

He was within five yards when suddenly the aviator turned and covered him with a revolver! And speaking in a sharp, staccato voice, he said: 'Old grandfather, you must sit down. I am very much occupied. If you interfere or attempt to go away, I shoot you. So!'

Sam gazed at the horrid, glittering little barrel and gasped. Well, he never! To be threatened with murder when you're doing your duty on your employer's private property! But, still, perhaps the man was mad. A man must be more or less mad to go up in one of those crazy things. And life was very sweet on that summer morning despite sixty-nine years. He sat down among the swedes.

The aviator was so busy with his cranks and machinery that he hardly deigned to pay him any attention except to keep the revolver handy. He worked feverishly, and Sam sat watching him. At the end of ten minutes he appeared to have solved his troubles with the machine, but he still seemed very scared. He kept on glancing round and out to sea. When his repairs were complete he straightened his back and wiped the perspiration from his brow. He was apparently on the point of springing back into the machine and going off when a sudden mood of facetiousness, caused by relief from the strain he had endured, came to him. He turned to old Sam and smiled, at the same time remarking: 'Well, old grandfather, and now we shall be all right, isn't it?'

He came close up to Sam, and suddenly started back. '*Gott!*' he cried, 'Paul Jouperts!'

Bewildered, Sam gazed at him, and the madman started talking to him in some foreign tongue. Sam shook his head.

'You've no roight,' he remarked, 'to come bargin' through they swedes of Mr Hodge's.'

And then the aviator behaved in a most peculiar manner. He came up and examined Sam's face very closely, and gave a sudden tug at his beard and hair, as if to see whether they were real or false.

'What is your name, old man?' he said.

'Sam Gates.'

The aviator muttered some words that sounded something like 'mare vudish', and then turned to his machine. He appeared to be dazed and in a great state of doubt. He fumbled with some cranks, but kept glancing at old Sam. At last he got into the cockpit and strapped himself in. Then he stopped, and sat there deep in thought. At last he suddenly unstrapped himself and sprang out again and, approaching Sam, said very deliberately: 'Old grandfather, I shall require you to accompany me.'

Sam gasped.

'Eh?' he said. 'What be 'ee talkin' about? 'Company? I got these 'ere loines o' turnips – I be already behoind – '

The disgusting little revolver once more flashed before his eyes.

'There must be no discussion,' came the voice. 'It is necessary that you climb in without delay. Otherwise I shoot you like the dog you are. So!'

Old Sam was hale and hearty. He had no desire to die so ignominiously. The pleasant smell of the Norfolk downland was in his nostrils; his foot was on his native heath. He got into the passenger seat, contenting himself with a mutter: 'Well, that be a noice thing, I must say! Flyin' about the country with all they turnips on'y half thinned!'

He found himself strapped in. The aviator was in a fever of anxiety to get away. The engines made a ghastly splutter and noise. The thing started running along the ground. Suddenly it shot upward, giving the swedes a last contemptuous kick. At twenty minutes to eight that morning old Sam found himself being borne right up above his fields and out to sea! His breath came quickly. He was a little frightened.

'God forgive me!' he murmured.

The thing was so fantastic and sudden that his mind could not grasp it. He only felt in some vague way that he was going to die, and he struggled to attune his mind to the change. He offered up a mild prayer to God, Who, he felt, must be very near, somewhere up in these clouds. Automatically he thought of the vicar at Halvesham, and a certain sense of comfort came to him at the reflection that on the previous day he had taken a 'cooking of runner beans' to God's representative in that village. He felt calmer after that, but the horrid machine seemed to go higher and higher. He could not turn in his seat and he could see nothing but sea and sky. Of course the man was mad, mad as a March hare. Of what earthly use could *he* be to anyone? Besides, he had talked pure gibberish, and called him Paul something, when he had already told him that his name was Sam. The thing would fall down into the sea soon, and they would both be drowned. Well, well, he had almost reached three-score years and ten. He was protected by a screen, but it seemed very cold. What on earth would Mr Hodge say? There was no one left to work the land but a fool of a boy named Billy Whitehead at Dene's Cross. On, on, on they went at a furious pace. His thoughts danced disconnectedly from incidents of his youth, conversations with the vicar, hearty meals in the open, a frock his sister wore on the day of the postman's wedding, the drone of a psalm, the illness of some ewes belonging to Mr Hodge. Everything seemed to be moving very rapidly, upsetting his sense of time. He felt outraged, and yet at moments there was something entrancing in the wild experience. He seemed to be living at an incredible pace. Perhaps he was really dead and on his way to the kingdom of God. Perhaps this was the way they took people.

After some indefinite period he suddenly caught sight of a long strip of land. Was this a foreign country, or were they returning? He had by this time lost all feeling of fear. He became interested and almost disappointed. The 'airyplane' was not such a fool as it looked. It was very wonderful to be right up in the sky like this. His dreams were suddenly disturbed by a fearful noise. He thought the machine was blown to pieces. It dived and ducked through the air, and things were bursting all round it and making an awful din, and then it went up higher and higher. After a while these noises ceased, and he felt the machine gliding downward. They were really right above solid land – trees, fields, streams and white villages. Down, down, down they glided. This was a foreign country. There were straight avenues of poplars and canals. This was not Halvesham. He felt the thing glide gently and bump into a field. Some men ran forward and approached them, and the mad aviator called out to them. They were mostly fat men in grey uniforms, and they all spoke this foreign gibberish. Someone came and unstrapped him. He was very stiff and could hardly move. An exceptionally gross-looking man punched him in the ribs and roared with laughter. They all stood round and laughed at him, while the mad aviator talked to them and kept pointing at him. Then he said: 'Old grandfather, you must come with me.'

He was led to an iron-roofed building and shut in a little room. There were guards outside with fixed bayonets. After a while the mad aviator appeared again, accompanied by two soldiers. He beckoned him to follow. They marched through a quadrangle and entered another building. They went straight into an office where a very important-looking man, covered with medals, sat in an easy-chair. There was a lot of saluting and clicking of heels. The aviator pointed at Sam and said something, and the man with the medals started at sight of him, and then came up and spoke to him in English.

'What is your name? Where do you come from? Your age? The name and birthplace of your parents?

He seemed intensely interested, and also pulled his hair and beard to see if they came off. So well and naturally did he and the aviator speak English that after a voluble examination they drew apart, and continued the conversation in that language. And the extraordinary conversation was of this nature: 'It is a most remarkable resemblance,' said the man with medals. '*Unglaublich!* But what do you want me to do with him, Hausemann?'

'The idea came to me suddenly, excellency,' replied the aviator, 'and you may consider it worthless. It is just this. The resemblance is so amazing. Paul Jouperts has given us more valuable information than anyone at present in our service, and the English know that. There is an award of five thousand francs on his head. Twice they have captured him, and each time he escaped. All the company commanders and their staff have his photograph. He is a serious thorn in their flesh.'

'Well?' replied the man with the medals.

The aviator whispered confidentially: 'Suppose, your excellency, that they found the dead body of Paul Jouperts?'

'Well?' replied the big man.

'My suggestion is this. Tomorrow, as you know, the English are attacking Hill 701, which for tactical reasons we have decided to evacuate. If after the attack they find the dead body of Paul Jouperts in, say, the second line, they will take no further trouble in the matter. You know their lack of thoroughness. Pardon me, I was two years at Oxford University. And consequently Paul Jouperts will be able to prosecute his labours undisturbed.'

The man with the medals twirled his mustache and looked thoughtfully at his colleague.

'Where is Paul at the moment?' he asked.

'He is acting as a gardener at the Convent of St Eloïse, at Mailleton-en-haut, which, as you know, is one hundred meters from the headquarters of the British central army staff.'

The man with the medals took two or three rapid turns up and down the room, then he said: 'Your plan is excellent, Hausemann. The only point of difficulty is that the attack started this morning.'

'This morning?' exclaimed the other.

'Yes; the English attacked unexpectedly at dawn. We have already evacuated the first line. We shall evacuate the second line at eleven-fifty. It is now ten-fifteen. There may be just time.'

He looked suddenly at old Sam in the way that a butcher might look at a prize heifer at an agricultural show and remarked casually: 'Yes, it is a remarkable resemblance. It seems a pity not to – do something with it.'

Then, speaking in German, he added: 'It is worth trying. And if it succeeds, the higher authorities shall hear of your lucky accident and inspiration, Herr Hausemann. Instruct Ober-leutnant Schultz to send the old fool by two orderlies to the east extremity of Trench 38. Keep him there till the order of evacuation is given, then shoot him, but don't disfigure him, and lay him out face upwards.'

The aviator saluted and withdrew, accompanied by his victim. Old Sam had not understood the latter part of the conversation, and he did not catch quite all that was said in English; but he felt that somehow things were not becoming too promising, and it was time to assert himself. So he remarked when they got outside: 'Now, look 'ee 'ere, mister, when am I goin' to get back to my turnips?'

And the aviator replied, with a pleasant smile: 'Do not be disturbed, old grandfather. You shall get back to the soil quite soon.'

In a few moments he found himself in a large grey car, accompanied by four soldiers. The aviator left him. The country was barren and horrible, full of great pits and rents, and he could hear the roar of artillery and the shriek of shells. Overhead, aeroplanes were buzzing angrily. He seemed to be suddenly transported from the kingdom of God to the pit of darkness. He wondered whether the vicar had enjoyed the runner beans. He could not imagine runner beans growing here; runner beans, aye, or anything else. If this was a foreign country, give him dear old England!

Gr–r–r! bang! Something exploded just at the rear of the car. The soldiers ducked, and one of them pushed him in the stomach and swore.

'An ugly-looking lout,' he thought. 'If I wor twenty years younger, I'd give him a punch in the eye that 'u'd make him sit up.'

The car came to a halt by a broken wall. The party hurried out and dived behind a mound. He was pulled down a kind of shaft, and found himself in a room buried right underground, where three officers were drinking and smoking. The soldiers saluted and handed them a typewritten dispatch. The officers looked at him drunkenly, and one came up and pulled his beard and spat in his face and called him 'an old English swine'. He then shouted out some instructions to the soldiers, and they led him out into the narrow trench One walked behind him, and occasionally prodded him with the butt-end of a gun. The trenches were half full of water and reeked of gases, powder and decaying matter. Shells were constantly bursting overhead, and in places the trenches had crumbled and were nearly blocked up. They stumbled on, sometimes falling, sometimes dodging moving masses, and occasionally crawling over the dead bodies of men. At last they reached a deserted-looking trench, and one of the soldiers pushed him into the corner of it and growled something, and then disappeared round the angle. Old Sam was exhausted. He leaned panting against the mud wall, expecting every minute to be blown to pieces by one of those infernal things that seemed to be getting more and more insistent. The din went on for nearly twenty minutes, and he was alone in the trench. He fancied he heard a whistle amidst the din. Suddenly one of the soldiers who had accompanied him came stealthily round the corner, and there was a look in his eye old Sam did not like. When he was within five yards the soldier raised his rifle and pointed it at Sam's body. Some instinct impelled the old man at that instant to throw himself forward on his face. As he did so he was aware of a terrible explosion, and he had just time to observe the soldier falling in a heap near him, and then he lost consciousness.

His consciousness appeared to return to him with a snap. He was lying on a plank in a building, and he heard someone say: 'I believe the old boy's English.'

He looked round. There were a lot of men lying there, and others in khaki and white overalls were busy among them. He sat up, rubbed his head, and said: 'Hi, mister, where be I now?'

Someone laughed, and a young man came up and said: 'Well, old man, you were very nearly in hell. Who the devil are you?'

Someone came up, and two of them were discussing him. One of them said: 'He's quite all right. He was only knocked out. Better take him into the colonel. He may be a spy.'

The other came up, touched his shoulder, and remarked: 'Can you walk, uncle?'

He replied: 'Aye, I can walk all roight.'

'That's an old sport!'

The young man took his arm and helped him out of the room into a courtyard. They entered another room, where an elderly, kind-faced officer was seated at a desk. The officer looked up and exclaimed: 'Good God! Bradshaw, do you know who you've got there?'

The younger one said: 'No. Who, sir?'

'It's Paul Jouperts!' exclaimed the colonel.

'Paul Jouperts! Great Scott!'

The older officer addressed himself to Sam. He said: 'Well, we've got you once more, Paul. We shall have to be a little more careful this time.'

The young officer said: 'Shall I detail a squad, sir?'

'We can't shoot him without a court martial,' replied the kind-faced senior.

Then Sam interpolated: 'Look 'ee 'ere, sir, I'm fair' sick of all this. My name bean't Paul. My name's Sam. I was a-thinnin' a loine o' turnips – '

Both officers burst out laughing, and the younger one said: 'Good! damn good! Isn't it amazing, sir, the way they not only learn the language, but even take the trouble to learn a dialect!'

The older man busied himself with some papers.

'Well, Sam,' he remarked, 'you shall be given a chance to prove your identity. Our methods are less drastic than those of your Boche masters. What part of England are you supposed to come from? Let's see how much you can bluff us with your topographical knowledge.'

'I was a-thinnin' a loine o' turnips this mornin' at 'alf-past seven on Mr. Hodge's farm at Halvesham when one o' these 'ere airyplanes come down among the swedes. I tells 'e to get clear o' that, when the feller what gets out o' the car 'e trains a revolver and 'e says, 'You must 'company I – '

'Yes, yes,' interrupted the senior officer; 'that's all very good. Now tell me – where is Halvesham? What is the name of the local vicar? I'm sure you'd know that.'

Old Sam rubbed his chin.

'I sits under the Reverend David Pryce, mister, and a good, God-fearin' man he be. I took him a cookin' o' runner beans on'y yesterday. I works for Mr Hodge, what owns Greenway Manor and 'as a stud-farm at Newmarket, they say.'

'Charles Hodge?' asked the young officer.

'Aye, Charlie Hodge. You write and ask un if he knows old Sam Gates.'

The two officers looked at each other, and the older one looked at Sam more closely. 'It's very extraordinary,' he remarked.

'Everybody knows Charlie Hodge,' added the younger officer.

It was at that moment that a wave of genius swept over old Sam. He put his hand to his head and suddenly jerked out: 'What's more, I can tell 'ee where this yere Paul is. He's actin' a gardener in a convent at —' He puckered up his brows, fumbled with his hat, and then got out, 'Mighteno.'

The older officer gasped.

'Mailleton-en-haut! Good God! what makes you say that, old man?'

Sam tried to give an account of his experience and the things he had heard said by the German officers; but he was getting tired, and he broke off in the middle to say: 'Ye haven't a bite o' somethin' to eat, I suppose, mister; or a glass o' beer? I usually 'as my dinner at twelve o'clock.'

Both the officers laughed, and the older said: 'Get him some food, Bradshaw, and a bottle of beer from the mess. We'll keep this old man here. He interests me.'

While the younger man was doing this, the chief pressed a button and summoned another junior officer.

'Gateshead,' he remarked, 'ring up the GHQ and instruct them to arrest the gardener in that convent at the top of the hill and then to report.'

The officer saluted and went out, and in a few minutes a tray of hot food and a large bottle of beer were brought to the old man, and he was left alone in the corner of the room to negotiate this welcome compensation And in the execution he did himself and his county credit. In the meanwhile the officers were very busy. People were coming and going and examining maps, and telephone bells were ringing furiously. They did not disturb old Sam's gastric operations. He cleaned up the mess tins and finished the last drop of beer. The senior officer found time to offer him a cigarette, but he replied: 'Thank 'ee kindly, sir, but I'd rather smoke my pipe.'

The colonel smiled and said: 'Oh, all right; smoke away.'

He lighted up, and the fumes of the shag permeated the room. Some one opened another window, and the young officer who had addressed him at first suddenly looked at him and exclaimed: 'Innocent, by God! You couldn't get shag like that anywhere but in Norfolk.'

It must have been an hour later when another officer entered and saluted.

'Message from the GHQ, sir,' he said.

'Well?'

'They have arrested the gardener at the convert of St Eloïse, and they have every reason to believe that he is the notorious Paul Jouperts.'

The colonel stood up, and his eyes beamed. He came over to old Sam and shook his hand.

'Mr Gates,' he said, 'you are an old brick. You will probably hear more of this. You have probably been the means of delivering something very useful into our hands. Your own honour is vindicated. A loving government will probably award you five shillings or a Victoria Cross or something of that sort. In the meantime, what can I do for you?'

Old Sam scratched his chin.

'I want to get back 'ome,' he said.

'Well, even that might be arranged.'

'I want to get back 'ome in toime for tea.'

'What time do you have tea?'

'Foive o'clock or thereabouts.'

'I see.'

A kindly smile came into the eyes of the colonel. He turned to another officer standing by the table and said:

'Raikes, is anyone going across this afternoon with dispatches?'

'Yes, sir,' replied the other officer. 'Commander Jennings is leaving at three o'clock.'

'You might ask him if he could see me.'

Within ten minutes a young man in a flight-commander's uniform entered.

'Ah, Jennings,' said the colonel, 'here is a little affair which concerns the honour of the British army. My friend here, Sam Gates, has come over from Halvesham, in Norfolk, in order to give us valuable information. I have promised him that he shall get home for tea at five o'clock. Can you take a passenger?'

The young man threw back his head and laughed.

'Lord!' he exclaimed, 'what an old sport! Yes, I expect I can manage it. Where is the God-forsaken place?'

A large ordnance-map of Norfolk (which had been captured from a German officer) was produced, and the young man studied it closely.

At three o'clock precisely old Sam, finding himself something of a hero and quite glad to escape from the embarrassment which this position entailed upon him, once more sped skyward in a 'dratted airyplane'.

At twenty minutes to five he landed once more among Mr Hodge's swedes. The breezy young airman shook hands with him and departed inland. Old Sam sat down and surveyed the familiar field of turnips.

'A noice thing, I must say!' he muttered to himself as he looked along the lines of unthinned turnips. He still had twenty minutes, and so he went slowly along and completed a line which he had begun in the morning. He then deliberately packed up his dinner things and his tools and started out for home.

As he came round the corner of Stillway's meadow and the cottage came in view, his niece stepped out of the copse with a basket on her arm.

'Well, uncle,' she said, 'is there any noos?'

It was then that old Sam really lost his temper.

'Noos!' he said. 'Noos! Drat the girl! What noos should there be? Sixty-nine year' I live in these 'ere parts, hoein' and weedin' and thinnin', and mindin' Charlie Hodge's sheep. Am I one o' these 'ere storybook folk havin' noos 'appen to 'em all the time? Ain't it enough, ye silly, dab-faced zany, to earn enough to buy a bite o' some' to eat and a glass o' beer and a place to rest a's head o'night without always wantin' noos, noos, noos! I tell 'ee it's this that leads 'ee to 'alf the troubles in the world. Devil take the noos!'

And turning his back on her, he went fuming up the hill.

Where was Wych Street?

In the public bar of the Wagtail, in Wapping, four men and a woman were drinking beer and discussing diseases. It was not a pretty subject, and the company was certainly not a handsome one. It was a dark November evening, and the dingy lighting of the bar seemed but to emphasise the bleak exterior. Drifts of fog and damp from without mingled with the smoke of shag. The sanded floor was kicked into a muddy morass not unlike the surface of the pavement. An old lady down the street had died from pneumonia the previous evening, and the event supplied a fruitful topic of conversation. The things that one could get! Everywhere were germs eager to destroy one. At any minute the symptoms might break out. And so – one foregathered in a cheerful spot amidst friends, and drank forgetfulness.

Prominent in this little group was Baldwin Meadows, a sallow-faced villain with battered features and prominent cheekbones, his face cut and scarred by a hundred fights. Ex-seaman, ex-boxer, ex-fish-porter – indeed, to everyone's knowledge, ex-everything. No one knew how he lived. By his side lurched an enormous coloured man who went by the name of Harry Jones. Grinning above a tankard sat a pimply-faced young man who was known as the Agent. Silver rings adorned his fingers. He had no other name, and most emphatically no address, but he 'arranged things' for people, and appeared to thrive upon it in a scrambling, fugitive manner.

Then, at one point, the conversation suddenly took a peculiar turn. It came about through Mrs Dawes mentioning that her aunt, who died from eating tinned lobster, used to work in a corset shop in Wych Street.

When she said that, the Agent, whose right eye appeared to survey the ceiling, whilst his left eye looked over the other side of his tankard, remarked: 'Where was Wych Street, ma?'

'Lord!' exclaimed Mrs Dawes. 'Don't you know, dearie? You must be a young 'un, you must. Why, when I was a gal everyone knew Wych Street. It was just down there where they built the Kingsway, like.'

Baldwin Meadows cleared his throat, and said: 'Wych Street used to be a turnin' runnin' from Long Acre into Wellington Street.'

'Oh, no, old boy,' chipped in Mr Dawes, who always treated the ex-fighter with great deference. 'If you'll excuse me, Wych Street was a narrow lane at the back of the old Globe Theatre, that used to pass by the church.'

'I know what I'm talkin' about,' growled Meadows.

Mrs Dawes's high nasal whine broke in: 'Hi, Mr Booth, you used ter know yer wye abaht. Where was Wych Street?'

Mr Booth, the proprietor, was polishing a tap. He looked up.

'Wych Street? Yus, of course I knoo Wych Street. Used to go there with some of the boys – when I was Covent Garden way. It was at right angles to the Strand, just east of Wellington Street.'

'No, it warn't. It were alongside the Strand, before yer come to Wellington Street.'

The coloured man took no part in the discussion, one street and one city being alike to him, provided he could obtain the material comforts dear to his heart; but the others carried it on with a certain amount of acerbity.

Before any agreement had been arrived at three other men entered the bar. The quick eye of Meadows recognised them at once as three of what was known at that time as the Gallows Ring. Every member of the Gallows Ring had done time, but they still carried on a lucrative industry devoted to blackmail, intimidation, shoplifting, and some of the clumsier recreations. Their leader, Ben Orming, had served seven years for bashing a Chinaman down at Rotherhithe.

The Gallows Ring was not popular in Wapping, for the reason that many of their depredations had been inflicted upon their own class. When Meadows and Harry Jones took it into their heads to do a little wild prancing they took the trouble to go up into the West End. They considered the Gallows Ring an ungentlemanly set; nevertheless, they always treated them with a certain external deference – an unpleasant crowd to quarrel with.

Ben Orming ordered beer for the three of them, and they leant against the bar and whispered in sullen accents. Something had evidently miscarried with the Ring.

Mrs Dawes continued to whine above the general drone of the bar. Suddenly she said: 'Ben, you're a hot old devil, you are. We was just 'aving a discussion like. Where was Wych Street?' Ben scowled at her, but she continued: 'Some sez it was one place, some sez it was another. I *know* where it was, 'cors my aunt what died from blood p'ison, after eatin' tinned lobster, used to work at a corset shop – '

'Yus,' barked Ben, emphatically. 'I know where Wych Street was – it was just sarth of the river, afore yer come to Waterloo Station.'

It was then that the coloured man, who up to that point had taken no part in the discussion, thought fit to intervene.

'Nope. You's all wrong, cap'n. Wych Street were alongside de church, way over where the Strand takes a side-line up west.'

Ben turned on him fiercely. 'What the blazes do *you* know know abaht it? I've told yer where Wych Street was.'

'Yus, and I know where it was,' interposed Meadows. 'Yer both wrong.

Wych Street was a turning running from Long Acre into Wellington Street.'

'I didn't ask yer what *you* thought,' growled Ben.

'Well, I suppose I've a right to an opinion?'

'You always think you know everything, you do.'

'You can just keep yer mouth shut.'

'It 'ud take more'n you to shut it.'

Mr Booth thought it advisable at this juncture to bawl across the bar: 'Now, gentlemen, no quarrelling – please.'

The affair might have subsided at that point, but for Mrs Dawes. Her emotions over the death of the old lady in the street had been so stirred that she had been, almost unconsciously, drinking too much gin. She suddenly screamed out: 'Don't you take no lip from 'im, Mr Medders. The dirty, thieving devil, 'e always thinks 'e's goin' to come it over everyone.'

She stood up threateningly, and one of Ben's supporters gave her a gentle push backwards. In three minutes the bar was in a complete state of pandemonium. The three members of the Gallows Ring fought two men and a woman, for Mr Dawes merely stood in a corner and screamed out: 'Don't! Don't!'

Mrs Dawes stabbed the man who had pushed her through the wrist with a hatpin. Meadows and Ben Orming closed on each other and fought savagely with naked fists. A lucky blow early in the encounter sent Meadows reeling against the wall, with blood streaming down his temple. Then the coloured man hurled a pewter tankard straight at Ben and it hit him on the knuckles. The pain maddened him to a frenzy. His other supporter had immediately got to grips with Harry Jones, and picked up one of the high stools and, seizing an opportunity, brought it down crash on to the coloured man's skull.

The whole affair was over in a matter of minutes. Mr Booth was bawling out in the street. A whistle sounded. People were running in all directions.

'Beat it! Beat it for God's sake!' called the man who had been stabbed through the wrist. His face was very white, and he was obviously about to faint.

Ben and the other man, whose name was Toller, dashed to the door. On the pavement there was a confused scramble. Blows were struck indiscriminately. Two policemen appeared. One was laid *hors de combat* by a kick on the knee-cap from Toller. The two men fled into the darkness, followed by a hue-and-cry. Born and bred in the locality, they took every advantage of their knowledge. They tacked through alleys and raced down dark mews, and clambered over walls. Fortunately for them, the people they passed, who might have tripped them up or aided in the pursuit, merely fled indoors. The people in Wapping are not always on the side of the pursuer. But the police held on. At last Ben and Toller slipped through the door of an empty house in Aztec Street barely ten yards ahead of their nearest pursuer. Blows rained on the door, but they slid the bolts, and then fell panting to the floor.

When Ben could speak, he said: 'If they cop us, it means swinging.'

'Was the black feller done in?'

'I think so. But even if 'e wasn't, there was that other affair the night before last. The game's up.'

The ground-floor rooms were shuttered and bolted, but they knew that the police would probably force the front door. At the back there was no escape, only a narrow stable yard, where lanterns were already flashing. The roof only extended thirty yards either way and the police would probably take possession of it. They made a round of the house, which was sketchily furnished. There was a loaf, a small piece of mutton and a bottle of pickles, and – the most precious possession – three bottles of whisky. Each man drank half a glass of neat whisky; then Ben said: 'We'll be able to keep 'em quiet for a bit, anyway,' and he went and fetched an old twelve-bore gun and a case of cartridges. Toller was opposed to this last desperate resort, but Ben continued to murmur, 'It means swinging, anyway.'

And thus began the notorious siege of Aztec Street. It lasted three days and four nights. You may remember that, on forcing a panel of the front door, Sub-Inspector Wraithe, of V Division, was shot through the chest. The police then tried other methods. A hose was brought into play without effect. Two policemen were killed and four wounded. The military was requisitioned. The street was picketed. Snipers occupied windows of the houses opposite. A distinguished member of the Cabinet drove down in a motor car, and directed operations in a top-hat. It was the introduction of poison-gas which was the ultimate cause of the downfall of the citadel. The body of Ben Orming was never found, but that of Toller was discovered near the front door with a bullet through his heart. The medical officer to the court pronounced that the man had been dead three days, but whether killed by a chance bullet from a sniper or whether killed deliberately by his fellow-criminal was never revealed. For when the end came Orming had apparently planned a final act of venom. It was known that in the basement a considerable quantity of petrol had been stored. The contents had probably been carefully distributed over the most inflammable materials in the top rooms. The fire broke out, as one witness described it, 'almost like an explosion'. Orming must have perished in this. The roof blazed up, and the sparks carried across the yard and started a stack of light timber in the annexe of Messrs Morrel's piano-factory. The factory and two blocks of tenement buildings were burnt to the ground. The estimated cost of the destruction was one hundred and eighty thousand pounds. The casualties amounted to seven killed and fifteen wounded.

At the inquiry held under Chief Justice Pengammon various odd interesting facts were revealed. Mr Lowes-Parlby, the brilliant young KC, distinguished himself by his searching cross-examination of many witnesses. At one point a certain Mrs Dawes was put in the box.

'Now,' said Mr Lowes-Parlby, 'I understand that on the evening in question, Mrs Dawes, you, and the victims, and these other people who have been mentioned, were all seated in the public bar of the Wagtail, enjoying its no doubt excellent hospitality and indulging in a friendly discussion. Is that so?'

'Yes, sir.'

'Now, will you tell his lordship what you were discussing?'

'Diseases, sir.'

'Diseases! And did the argument become acrimonious?'

'Pardon?'

'Was there a serious dispute about diseases?'

'No, sir.'

'Well, what was the subject of the dispute?'

'We was arguin' as to where Wych Street was, sir.'

'What's that?' said his lordship.

'The witness states, my lord, that they were arguing as to where Wych Street was.'

'Wych Street? Do you mean W–Y–C–H?'

'Yes, sir.'

'You mean the narrow old street that used to run across the site of what is now the Gaiety Theatre?'

Mr Lowes-Parlby smiled in his most charming manner.

'Yes, my lord, I believe the witness refers to the same street you mention, though, if I may be allowed to qualify your lordship's description of the locality, may I suggest that it was a little farther east – at the side of the old Globe Theatre, which was adjacent to St Martin's in the Strand? That is the street you were all arguing about, isn't it, Mrs Dawes?'

'Well, sir, my aunt who died from eating tinned lobster used to work at a corset-shop. I ought to know.'

His lordship ignored the witness. He turned to the counsel rather peevishly.

'Mr Lowes-Parlby, when I was your age I used to pass through Wych Street every day of my life. I did so for nearly twelve years. I think it hardly necessary for you to contradict me.'

The counsel bowed. It was not his place to dispute with a chief justice, although that chief justice be a hopeless old fool; but another eminent KC, an elderly man with a tawny beard, rose in the body of the court, and said: 'If I may be allowed to interpose, your lordship, I also spent a great deal of my youth passing through Wych Street. I have gone into the matter, comparing past and present ordnance survey maps. If I am not mistaken, the street the witness was referring to began near the hoarding at the entrance to Kingsway and ended at the back of what is now the Aldwych Theatre.'

'Oh, no, Mr Backer!' exclaimed Lowes-Parlby.

His lordship removed his glasses and snapped out: 'The matter is entirely irrelevant to the case.'

It certainly was, but the brief passage-of-arms left an unpleasant tang of bitterness behind. It was observed that Mr Lowes-Parlby never again quite got the prehensile grip upon his cross-examination that he had shown in his treatment of the earlier witnesses. The coloured man, Harry Jones, had died in hospital, but Mr Booth, the proprietor of the Wagtail, Baldwin Meadows, Mr Dawes, and the man who was stabbed in the wrist, all gave evidence of a rather nugatory character. Lowes-Parlby could do nothing with it. The findings of this Special Inquiry do not concern us. It is sufficient to say that the witnesses already mentioned all returned to Wapping. The man who had received the thrust of a hatpin through his wrist did not think it advisable to take any action against Mrs Dawes. He was pleasantly relieved to find that he was only required as a witness of an abortive discussion.

In a few weeks' time the great Aztec Street siege remained only a romantic memory to the majority of Londoners. To Lowes-Parlby the little dispute with Chief Justice Pengammon rankled unreasonably. It is annoying to be publicly snubbed for making a statement which you know to be absolutely true, and which you have even taken pains to verify. And Lowes-Parlby was a young man accustomed to score. He made a point of looking everything up, of being prepared for an adversary thoroughly. He liked to give the appearance of knowing everything. The brilliant career just ahead of him at times dazzled him. He was one of the darlings of the gods. Everything came to Lowes-Parlby. His father had distinguished himself at the bar before him, and had amassed a modest fortune. He was an only son. At Oxford he had carried off every possible degree. He was already being spoken of for very high political honours. But the most sparkling jewel in the crown of his successes was Lady Adela Charters, the daughter of Lord Vermeer, the Minister for Foreign Affairs. She was his fiancée, and it was considered the most brilliant match of the season. She was young and almost pretty, and Lord Vermeer was immensely wealthy and one of the most influential men in Great Britain. Such a combination was irresistible. There seemed to be nothing missing in the life of Francis Lowes-Parlby, KC.

One of the most regular and absorbed spectators at the Aztec Street inquiry was old Stephen Garrit. Stephen Garrit held a unique but quite inconspicuous position in the legal world at that time. He was a friend of judges, a specialist at various abstruse legal rulings, a man of remarkable memory, and yet – an amateur. He had never taken silk, never eaten the requisite dinners, never passed an examination in his life; but the law of evidence was meat and drink to him. He passed his life in the Temple, where he had chambers. Some of the most eminent counsel in the world would take his opinion, or come to him for advice. He was very old, very silent, and very absorbed. He attended every meeting of the Aztec Street inquiry, but from beginning to end he never volunteered an opinion.

After the inquiry was over he went and visited an old friend at the London Survey Office. He spent two mornings examining maps. After that he spent two mornings pottering about the Strand and Aldwych; then he worked out some careful calculations on a ruled chart. He entered the particulars in a little book which he kept for purposes of that kind, and then retired to his chambers to study other matters. But before doing so, he entered a little apophthegm in another book. It was apparently a book in which he intended to compile a summary of his legal experiences. The sentence ran: 'The basic trouble is that people make statements without sufficient data.'

Old Stephen need not have appeared in this story at all, except for the fact that he was present at the dinner at Lord Vermeer's, where a rather deplorable incident occurred.

And you must acknowledge that in the circumstances it is useful to have such a valuable and efficient witness.

Lord Vermeer was a competent, forceful man, a little quick-tempered and autocratic. He came from Lancashire, and before entering politics had made an enormous fortune out of borax, artificial manure and starch.

It was a small dinner-party, with a motive behind it. His principal guest was Mr Sandeman, the London agent of the Amir of Bakkan. Lord Vermeer was very anxious to impress Mr Sandeman and to be very friendly with him: the reasons will appear later. Mr Sandeman was a self-confessed cosmo-politan. He spoke seven languages and professed to be equally at home in any capital in Europe. London had been his headquarters for over twenty years. Lord Vermeer also invited Mr Arthur Toombs, a colleague in the Cabinet, his prospective son-in-law Lowes-Parlby, James Trolley, a very tame Socialist MP, and Sir Henry and Lady Breyd, the two latter being invited, not because Sir Henry was of any use, but because Lady Breyd was a pretty and brilliant woman who might amuse his principal guest. The sixth guest was Stephen Garrit.

The dinner was a great success. When the succession of courses eventually came to a stop, and the ladies had retired, Lord Vermeer conducted his male guests into another room for a ten minutes' smoke before rejoining them. It was then that the unfortunate incident occurred. There was no love lost between Lowes-Parlby and Mr Sandeman. It is difficult to ascribe the real reason of their mutual animosity, but on the several occasions when they had met there had invariably passed a certain sardonic byplay. They were both clever, both comparatively young, each a little suspect and jealous of the other; moreover, it was said in some quarters that Mr Sandeman had had intentions himself with regard to Lord Vermeer's daughter, that he had been on the point of a proposal when Lowes-Parlby had butted in and forestalled him. Mr Sandeman had dined well, and he was in the mood to dazzle with a display of his varied knowledge and experiences. The conversation drifted from a discussion of the rival claims of great cities to the slow, inevitable removal of old landmarks. There had been a slightly acrimonious disagreement between Lowes-Parlby and Mr Sandeman as to the claims of Budapest and Lisbon, and Mr Sandeman had scored because he extracted from his rival a confession that, though he had spent two months in Budapest, he had only spent two days in Lisbon. Mr Sandeman had lived for four years in either city. Lowes-Parlby changed the subject abruptly.

'Talking of landmarks,' he said, 'we had a queer point arise in that Aztec Street inquiry. The original dispute arose owing to a discussion between a crowd of people in a pub as to where Wych Street was.'

'I remember,' said Lord Vermeer. 'A perfectly absurd discussion. Why, I should have thought that any man over forty would remember exactly where it was.'

'Where would you say it was, sir?' asked Lowes-Parlby.

'Why to be sure, it ran from the corner of Chancery Lane and ended at the second turning after the Law Courts, going west.'

Lowes-Parlby was about to reply, when Mr Sandeman cleared his throat and said, in his supercilious, oily voice: 'Excuse me, my lord. I know my Paris, and Vienna, and Lisbon, every brick and stone, but I look upon London as my home. I know my London even better. I have a perfectly clear recollection of Wych Street. When I was a student I used to visit there to buy books. It ran parallel to New Oxford Street on the south side, just between it and Lincoln's Inn Fields.'

There was something about this assertion that infuriated Lowes-Parlby. In the first place, it was so hopelessly wrong and so insufferably asserted. In the second place, he was already smarting under the indignity of being shown up about Lisbon. And then there suddenly flashed through his mind the wretched incident when he had been publicly snubbed by Justice Pengammon about the very same point; and he knew that he was right each time. Damn Wych Street! He turned on Mr Sandeman.

'Oh, nonsense! You may know something about these – eastern cities; you certainly know nothing about London if you make a statement like that. Wych Street was a little farther east of what is now the Gaiety Theatre. It used to run by the side of the old Globe Theatre, parallel to the Strand.'

The dark moustache of Mr Sandeman shot upwards, revealing a narrow line of yellow teeth. He uttered a sound that was a mingling of contempt and derision; then he drawled out: 'Really? How wonderful – to have such comprehensive knowledge!'

He laughed, and his small eyes fixed his rival. Lowes-Parlby flushed a deep red. He gulped down half a glass of port and muttered just above a whisper: 'Damned impudence!' Then, in the rudest manner he could display, he turned his back deliberately on Sandeman and walked out of the room.

In the company of Adela he tried to forget the little contretemps. The whole thing was so absurd – so utterly undignified. As though *he* didn't know! It was the little accumulation of pin-pricks all arising out of that one argument. The result had suddenly goaded him to – well, being rude, to say the least of it. It wasn't that Sandeman mattered. To the devil with Sandeman! But what would his future father-in-law think? He had never before given way to any show of ill-temper before him. He forced himself into a mood of rather fatuous jocularity. Adela was at her best in those moods. They would have lots of fun together in the days to come. Her almost pretty, not too clever face was dimpled with kittenish glee. Life was a tremendous rag to her. They were expecting La Toccata, the famous opera-singer. She had been engaged at a very high fee to come on from Covent Garden. Mr Sandeman was very fond of music. Adela was laughing, and discussing which was the most honourable position for the great Sandeman to occupy. There came to Lowes-Parlby a sudden abrupt misgiving. What sort of wife would she be to him when they were not just fooling? He immediately dismissed the curious, furtive little stab of doubt. The splendid proportions of the room calmed his senses. A huge bowl of dark red roses quickened his perceptions. His career . . . The door opened. But it was not La Toccata. It was one of the household flunkies. Lowes-Parlby turned again to his inamorata.

'Excuse me, sir. His lordship says will you kindly go and see him in the library?'

Lowes-Parlby regarded the messenger, and his heart beat quickly. An uncontrollable presage of evil racked his nerve-centres. Something had gone wrong; and yet the whole thing was so absurd, trivial. In a crisis – well, he could always apologise. He smiled confidently at Adela, and said: 'Why, of course; with pleasure. Please excuse me, dear.'

He followed the impressive servant out of the room. His foot had barely touched the carpet of the library when he realised that his worst apprehensions were to be plumbed to the depths. For a moment he thought Lord Vermeer was alone, then he observed old Stephen Garrit, lying in an easy-chair in the corner like a piece of crumpled parchment. Lord Vermeer did not beat about the bush. When the door was closed, he bawled out, savagely: 'What the devil have you done?'

'Excuse me, sir. I'm afraid I don't understand. Is it Sandeman – ?'

'Sandeman has gone.'

'Oh, I'm sorry.'

'Sorry! By God, I should think you might be sorry! You insulted him. My prospective son-in-law insulted him in my own house!'

'I'm awfully sorry. I didn't realise – '

'Realise! Sit down, and don't assume for one moment that you continue to be my prospective son-in-law. Your insult was a most intolerable piece of effrontery, not only to him, but to me.'

'But I – '

'Listen to me. Do you know that the government were on the verge of concluding a most far-reaching treaty with that man? Do you know that the position was just touch-and-go? The concessions we were prepared to make would have cost the State thirty million pounds, and it would have been cheap. Do you hear that? It would have been cheap! Bakkan is one of the most vulnerable outposts of the Empire. It is a terrible danger-zone. If certain powers can usurp our authority – and, mark you, the whole blamed place is already riddled with this new pernicious doctrine – you know what I mean – before we know where we are the whole East will be in a blaze. India! My God! This contract we were negotiating would have countered this outward thrust. And you, you blockhead, you come here and insult the man upon whose word the whole thing depends.'

'I really can't see, sir, how I should know all this.'

'You can't see it! But, you fool, you seemed to go out of your way. You insulted him about the merest quibble – in my house!'

'He said he knew where Wych Street was. He was quite wrong. I corrected him.'

'Wych Street! Wych Street be damned! If he said Wych Street was on the moon, you should have agreed with him. There was no call to act in the way you did. And you – you think of going into politics!'

The somewhat cynical inference of this remark went unnoticed. Lowes-Parlby was too unnerved. He mumbled: 'I'm very sorry.'

'I don't want your sorrow. I want something more practical.'

'What's that, sir?'

'You will drive straight to Mr Sandeman's, find him, and apologise. Tell him you agree that he was right about Wych Street after all. If you can't find him tonight, you must find him tomorrow morning. I give you till midday tomorrow. If by that time you have not offered a handsome apology to Mr Sandeman, you do not enter this house again, you do not see my daughter again. Moreover, all the power I possess will be devoted to hounding you out of that profession you have dishonoured. Now you can go.'

Dazed and shaken, Lowes-Parlby drove back to his flat at Knightsbridge.

Before acting he must have time to think. Lord Vermeer had given him till tomorrow midday. Any apologising that was done should be done after a night's reflection. The fundamental purposes of his being were to be tested. He knew that. He was at a great crossing. Some deep instinct within him was grossly outraged. Is it that a point comes when success demands that a man shall sell his soul? It was all so absurdly trivial – a mere argument about the position of a street that had ceased to exist. As Lord Vermeer said, what did it matter about Wych Street?

Of course he should apologise. It would hurt horribly to do so, but would a man sacrifice everything on account of some footling argument about a street?

In his own rooms, Lowes-Parlby put on a dressing-gown, and, lighting a pipe, he sat before the fire. He would have given anything for companionship at such a moment – the right companionship. How lovely it would be to have – a woman, just the right woman, to talk this all over with; someone who understood and sympathised. A sudden vision came to him of Adela's face grinning about the prospective visit of La Toccata, and again the low voice of misgiving whispered in his ears. Would Adela be – just the right woman? In very truth, did he really love Adela? Or was it all – a rag? Was life a rag – a game played by lawyers, politicians, and people?

The fire burned low, but still he continued to sit thinking, his mind principally occupied with the dazzling visions of the future. It was past midnight when he suddenly muttered a low 'Damn!' and walked to the bureau. He took up a pen and wrote:

DEAR MR SANDEMAN – I must apologise for acting so rudely to you last night. It was quite unpardonable of me, especially as I since find, on going into the matter, that you were quite right about the position of Wych Street. I can't think how I made the mistake. Please forgive me. Yours cordially,

FRANCIS LOWES-PARLBY

Having written this, he sighed and went to bed. One might have imagined at that point that the matter was finished. But there are certain little greedy demons of conscience that require a lot of stilling, and they kept Lowes-Parlby awake more than half the night. He kept on repeating to himself, 'It's all positively absurd!' But the little greedy demons pranced around the bed, and they began to group things into two definite issues. On the one side, the great appearances; on the other, something at the back of it all, something deep, fundamental, something that could only be expressed by one word – truth. If he had *really* loved Adela – if he weren't so absolutely certain that Sandeman was wrong and he was right – why should he have to say that Wych Street was where it wasn't? 'Isn't there, after all,' said one of the little demons, 'something which makes for greater happiness than success? Confess this, and we'll let you sleep.'

Perhaps that is one of the most potent weapons the little demons possess. However full our lives may be, we ever long for moments of tranquillity. And conscience holds before our eyes some mirror of an ultimate tranquillity. Lowes-Parlby was certainly not himself. The gay, debonair, and brilliant egoist was tortured, and tortured almost beyond control; and it had all apparently risen through the ridiculous discussion about a street. At a quarter past three in the morning he arose from his bed with a groan, and, going into the other room, he tore the letter to Mr Sandeman to pieces.

Three weeks later old Stephen Garrit was lunching with the Lord Chief Justice. They were old friends, and they never found it incumbent to be very conversational. The lunch was an excellent, but frugal, meal. They both ate slowly and thoughtfully, and their drink was water. It was not till they reached the dessert stage that his lordship indulged in any very informative comment, and then he recounted to Stephen the details of a recent case in which he considered that the presiding judge had, by an unprecedented paralogy, misinterpreted the law of evidence. Stephen listened with absorbed attention. He took two cob-nuts from the silver dish, and turned them over meditatively, without cracking them.

When his lordship had completely stated his opinion and peeled a pear, Stephen mumbled: 'I have been impressed, very impressed indeed. Even in my own field of – limited observation – the opinion of an outsider, you may say – so often it happens – the trouble caused by an affirmation without sufficiently established data. I have seen lives lost, ruin brought about, endless suffering. Only last week, a young man – a brilliant career – almost shattered. People make statements without – '

He put the nuts back on the dish, and then, in an apparently irrelevant manner, he said abruptly: 'Do you remember Wych Street, my lord?'

The Lord Chief Justice grunted. 'Wych Street! Of course I do.'

'Where would you say it was, my lord?'

'Why, here, of course.'

His lordship took a pencil from his pocket and sketched a plan on the tablecloth.

'It used to run from there to here.'

Stephen adjusted his glasses and carefully examined the plan. He took a long time to do this, and when he had finished his hand instinctively went towards a breast pocket where he kept a note-book with little squared pages. Then he stopped and sighed. After all, why argue with the law? The law was like that – an excellent thing, not infallible, of course (even the plan of the Lord Chief Justice was a quarter of a mile out), but still an excellent, a wonderful thing. He examined the bony knuckles of his hands and yawned slightly.

'Do you remember it?' said the Lord Chief Justice.

Stephen nodded sagely, and his voice seemed to come from a long way off: 'Yes, I remember it, my lord. It was a melancholy little street.'

HAROLD AUTEN

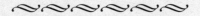

One of the most important parts played by the navy during the early days of the blockade of Germany was the creation of the sinister Q-boats or mystery ships. Every type of vessel was enlisted, and while appearing to be harmless fishing-craft, tramp steamers, etc., they were in reality equipped with guns and men ready to deal with enemy submarines. Lieutenant-Commander Auten, vc, was one of the first officers appointed to these ships in 1915.

The *Stock Force* was an ordinary coastal collier commandeered by Auten as she lay at Cardiff waiting to take coal to St Malo. Three months were spent in fitting her out and she served her country valiantly until in 1918, following an encounter off the Devonshire coast, she sank within eight miles of the shore.

A Fight to a Finish

On 30 July 1918, the *Stock Force* had an opportunity of showing her mettle. Early in the morning we were making our way up channel along the northern coast of France. Nothing was anywhere visible, and everything seemed peaceful and quiet. There was hardly a ripple on the water, and somewhere about 8 a.m. the Island of Guernsey became visible, through the morning mist. A little later the sun's rays played on the many glasshouses of the island. These were plainly visible from the passing collier, and the day seemed as if it were going to be absolutely ideal.

About 8.15 a signal was intercepted by our concealed wireless, stating that an enemy submarine was working roughly on the line between Casquets to twenty miles south of Start Point (South Devon). Everything seemed to point to this being a good day for an encounter with Fritz. We were in a position where we could alter our course without much suspicion being caused by any watching craft. I accordingly ordered that we steer so as to pass five miles south of Lizard Point, thus assuring that we pass right through the area in which the submarine had been reported. The new course tallied with that of a ship bound from Havre to Cardiff.

About 10 a.m. two French seaplanes came upon the peaceful scene and started to fly about over the ship. First they went ahead, then astern, and finally dropped two messages, which we picked up by our boat. After we had got them on board they turned out to be little red buoys with a tally attached advising us that there was a submarine in the vicinity, and that we had better clear out at once.

Nothing suited us better and we continued to stand on our course, but the two seaplanes were a trouble. They spoilt our game, and we wanted to get rid of them; but there seemed no way to communicate with them without giving ourselves away, so all we could do was to grin and bear it, and pray that they would clear off. That day there was a lot said on the lower deck about seaplanes.

They went ahead and then on the bows. Suddenly several loud explosions occurred. The seaplanes had dropped some bombs on what was evidently an oil slack, but with no apparent result. They hung around and appeared to be convoying the ship. During all this time everybody on board was cursing the seaplanes for all they were worth. 'Why don't they buzz off?' was the remark heard on all sides. The seaplanes, however, thinking that they were doing us a good service, continued to escort us through the danger zone. This went on for some time, the ship steering her course, the two French seaplanes escorting us.

At noon one of the seaplanes alighted on the water. By this time I was thoroughly fed up with them and wished them gone. The day was ideal for the work in which we were engaged, and all we wanted was to be left to ourselves. The Frenchmen, however, were apparently worked up to such a state of excitement that they would have dropped a.bomb on a sprat had it appeared.

The seaplane that had alighted on the water appeared to have something wrong with it, so I altered my course to render any assistance I could, and also to tell him to clear out. Before we could reach her, however, she had risen again, and then, the pair of them, after a valedictory circling around the ship, made off for the coast of France, satisfied in their own minds that they had saved a very stupid and dull-witted, not to say dirty, little craft from her fate.

The ship continued to plough her way on towards the supposed destination, and all through the afternoon a specially good lookout was kept. The first dog-watch keepers relieved the afternoon watch from their trying duties, and these continued to keep a good lookout, realising that anywhere on this peaceful scene might lurk a U-boat.

The officer on watch was walking up and down the bridge, giving a keen glance round when he came to each wing. Suddenly, when looking over the starboard side, he saw a commotion in the water some considerable distance away. After gazing at it intently for a second, wondering if it were a school of porpoises, he saw that it was the track of a torpedo coming direct for the ship. He instantly struck the alarm, at the same time ordering the helm to be put hard over and the engines full speed astern. At this moment the majority of those on board were having tea, the officers being seated in the saloon discussing the events of the morning.

One and all quickly and quietly got to our stations. I reached the bridge just in time to see the torpedo, then about fifty yards off, coming direct for the ship. She was coming very slowly in the end, having been fired at a long range and appearing to have very nearly run her distance. It looked to everybody on the bridge as if the torpedo would pass ahead; but suddenly, to my amazement, it took a turn in towards the ship and struck us abreast of No. 1 hatch.

The damage done was indescribable. The ship was only 161 feet over all, with a beam of 29 feet, and the torpedo had hit direct on the second watertight bulkhead, forcing it clean through the other side of the ship. The forward end of the bridge went entirely, and all I recollected was going up in the air, and coming down to find myself underneath the chart-table. Probably, if I had been a light weight, the chart-table would have won.

The whole fore-deck was bent, the derricks were blown overboard, and up went an awful shower of flotation planks, unexploded 12-pounder shells and debris caused by the explosion. This lot came down again with an awful, clatter, wounding all the people on the bridge except myself, by virtue of having won the race with the chart-table.

Immediately after this came down a huge deluge of water that had been thrown up by the explosion. This drenched us all to the skin and, combined with the explosion, caused many who were in the vicinity to become violently sick.

I asked one of the men on the bridge afterwards what he really thought had happened at that moment.

'Well, sir,' he said, 'if you really want to know, I thought the end of the world had come.'

As soon as we had recovered ourselves, the officers and the crew on the bridge hurriedly went to their stations, while I went down to find out the number of our casualties. To my intense surprise I discovered that there had been nobody killed, which was marvellous, considering that some of the men were going to their stations right alongside where the torpedo had exploded; somehow they had escaped with their lives.

A number were wounded, and these were quickly got down on to the 'tween deck. On looking round I found one poor fellow, an officers' steward named Starling, pinned in a mass of wreckage underneath a 12-pounder gun. It would have taken a working party an hour to get him out, and time was valuable.

The ship was settling down by the head, and I wondered how long she was going to float, so I told him that he would have to remain where he was for the present, and we would get him out at the first possible opportunity. On my telling him this he said quite cheerfully: 'All right, sir, I'll lay quiet until you let me know.'

I asked him some time afterwards what he recollected of this event.

'Well, sir,' he said, 'I lay quiet there after you had left and the "abandon-ship party" had gone, and the first thing that I remember was the black cat making her way forward.'

The cat, it appeared, had been blown up in the explosion, and had ended up by being buried beneath some debris under the rising water. She had managed to extricate herself from this, and the steward watched her get up on the top of a plank, very carefully shake herself like a dog, and then, with her hair all standing on end, her tail up, start to pick her way gingerly and carefully over the debris to a dry spot.

After having got the wounded down on the 'tween deck, which by this time was also filling rapidly with water, we manned the two after 4-inch guns; they were luckily all right, except that the tremendous column of water had smashed in the roof of the foremost one. The guns' crews, however, immediately got up some oars as props, so that everything from the outward appearance appeared quite natural.

The 'panic party', who had been carrying out their theatrical perform-ance, were then ordered to shove off. The wounded were now locked down in the 'tween deck, where the surgeon, above his knees in water, worked and attended to their injuries. They were shut down like rats in a trap, and could not possibly have escaped had the ship foundered.

The steward was lying pinned in the range end of the fore-gun, the two after guns' crews were lying on their stomachs waiting for what was to happen, while the engine-room staff remained at their posts. The ship was settling rapidly by the head, and at one time I felt she would not last much longer, but the wood which had been so splendidly stowed kept us up.

The 'abandon-ship party' pulled off on to the port bow, where they lay waiting for what would happen. The fore-end of the ship having been entirely shattered, voice-pipes and wire-reel control gone, the only place left from which to control the ship was the after gun-house, from which I could see nearly all round except right ahead.

Luckily the voice-pipes between the two guns remained intact, so that I was able to communicate with the others.

Everybody lay quiet on board the poor little ship, which by this time had practically her forecastle submerged. Everywhere the water was rising rapidly except in the engine room, which, being in the stern, remained comparatively dry. We were all keyed up to a state of high tension. We knew the submarine was hanging about watching our every movement through her periscope. If anyone had made the slightest mistake, betraying the fact that there was anyone on board, it would have meant another torpedo, and then goodbye to us all.

After having carefully surveyed the ship through her periscope, the sub-marine came to the surface about half a mile off and lay there. Two men appeared on the conning tower intently watching the ship for any suspicious movement. After they had scrutinised us for some fifteen minutes, they were evidently almost satisfied, and started to go slowly towards the boat. The 'abandon-ship party' then pulled slowly down the port side of the *Stock Force* about three hundred yards off.

The submarine was still carefully surveying the ship. When she got down on to the port bow, about four hundred yards distant, she stopped again and watched the ship. She was a very shy bird.

Now was coming the critical moment. Everybody on board lay absolutely quiet, hardly daring to breathe. After this scrutiny the submarine appeared to be quite satisfied, and came very slowly down the port bow of the ship, following the boat, which by this time had got in a position where, if the submarine approached her, she would be in the range of both guns.

The submarine came on slowly, awfully slowly. It seemed ages before she got on the beam where both the 4-inch guns could bear. Time after time the after-gunner and myself peeped through the little crack we were using as an observation position, but, no, the submarine was not yet in a satisfactory position to open fire on her. At last she reached the fatal spot.

'Submarine bearing, red ninety, range three hundred yards, stand by,' I whispered through the voice-pipes; then, a second or so later, 'Let go!'

Down fell the shutters of both guns with a crash. I started violently at the noise. It must have been the surprise of her life for the submarine. The after 4-inch gun, being stowed on the port beam, was right on the bearing when the flaps went down, and her first shot passed over the top of the conning tower, bringing down the periscope and wireless. The second shot hit the conning tower, and from reports afterwards received from the 'abandon-ship party', who were about seventy yards ahead of the submarine, shifted this bodily on one side and blew one man, evidently the commanding officer, into the air.

By this time the forward 4-inch gun had trained round, and her first shot hit on the hull of the submarine, just below the conning tower. After this shot the submarine seemed to shake herself and she sank a little by the stern, the bows coming up to a corresponding angle. A lot of loose smoke, and what appeared to be steam, began to pour out of her. The first shot from the forward gun had evidently exploded inside the submarine. She now presented a large immobile target into which shell after shell was poured. Gradually she sank by the stern, her bows coming right up out of the water.

During this time the 'abandon-ship party' were in a splendid position to see the effect of the ship's firing, being at the most only about seventy yards ahead of the submarine. When the flaps went down, the white ensign went up and the first gun fired, they got up in the boat and yelled themselves hoarse, waving their caps and cheering time after time until the Hun sank.

The effect of the firing had evidently disturbed the trim of the *Stock Force*. After the submarine had sunk she started to take a big list to starboard, and it became apparent that she saw no reason to keep afloat much longer now her work was accomplished. The 'abandon-ship party' was recalled, and after they had been picked up, we started to get under way to try and reach the land and, if possible, beach her.

All the compasses had gone in the explosion. We were also in a critical condition. There were a number of wounded on board the ship, the wireless had gone, and there were no means of getting into communication with anyone, or of steering except by sun and wind.

Our first task after the submarine had sunk was the rescuing of the rating who had been lying pinned underneath the forward gun. He uttered no word of complaint during the awful period of waiting for the submarine to be lured into the position where the *Stock Force*'s guns could bear.

All hands turned to with a will, for the water had crept nearly up to him. However, we got him safely out, but in an unconscious condition.

Immediately after this the rest of the wounded, who had been put down on the 'tween deck, which by now had nearly three feet of water on it, were got up on the main hatch, so that they could be better attended to by the doctor.

After this, every man who was able to started with hand pumps, buckets – in fact, anything that would hold water – to bail. The boat accommodation was not sufficient for all of us, so another small party started to construct rafts. Despite our efforts, the water gained rapidly, which taking into consideration that there was a forty-foot hole in the little ship, was hardly to be wondered at. It was the timber which had been so tightly packed in her that had kept her afloat so long, and had so materially helped to gain the victory over the Hun.

The bulkhead between the stoke-hold and the engine room had started, and despite every effort made to shore it up and stop the leaks, it continued to make water fast.

A little later on, to everyone's intense relief, a smudge of smoke was sighted on the port bow. Presently two little trawlers came on the scene, their attention having been drawn by the sound of our gunfire. One was immediately ordered alongside, and to her were transferred the wounded and part of the ship's company. Two of the officers and myself stayed on board with a small volunteer crew to attempt if possible to save the ship.

The stoke-hold and the engine-room staff worked on down below until the fires were put out by the rapidly rising water, and then the chief engineer secured the boilers and came on deck.

The ship now started to heel over to starboard, until she floated the starboard lifeboat at the davit head. It became obvious that her last moments were coming. Accordingly, the rest of the crew, with the exception of the first lieutenant and myself, were got away in the lifeboat.

A little previous to this two small torpedo boats had come upon the scene. One of them put down a small boat and sent over to rescue us both. The first lieutenant and myself got out on to the port side and sat on the rubbing streak, not liking to leave the ship that we had fitted out and for which we entertained such an affection. It was no good, however. She was going, and was now practically lying on her side. We therefore got into the dinghy and were put on board the torpedo boat.

A minute or so afterwards the poor little *Stock Force* sank to her last home. She had been torpedoed twenty-seven miles from the shore, and it was particularly hard to have got her almost within sight of land – the shore was only eight miles away – and then to lose her.

We all landed at Devonport early the next morning. The wounded were carted away to the hospital, where they were carefully attended to. The remainder of the crew, many of them suffering from shock, were accommodated in the barracks.

I should like to say a few words about the behaviour of my officers and crew. It was beyond all praise. Their coolness and courage throughout the action were worthy of the best traditions of the British Navy. Although many of them were suffering from wounds, and others from the tremendous shock sustained through the torpedo striking so small a ship, everyone went about their duties, which included lying doggo for a full forty minutes on the part of the gun crews, and later stoking in a stoke-hold fast filling with water; all this was done as if exercising their quarters. The success of this action was due to their splendid behaviour.

The following extracts from the Commander-in-Chief's covering letter and the Secretary of the Admiralty's reply will be of interest.

ADMIRAL TO ADMIRALTY – This is one of the best examples of coolness, discipline and good organisation that I have ever come across. Number one hold was a huge gash in a little ship, and yet everybody went to their stations as usual. None gave the ship away by a careless or stupid movement or action. When the smallness of the ship and the force of the explosion are considered, it is hard to understand how the officers and men could have stood the shock so well.

SECRETARY OF THE ADMIRALTY TO ADMIRAL – I am to acquaint you that their Lordships concur in your high opinion of the coolness, discipline and good organisation in this action, and I am to request that an expression of their appreciation may be conveyed to all concerned. I am further to inform you that the King has been pleased to approve of the following honours to officers and men for their services on this occasion.

This list included the awarding of a Conspicuous Gallantry Medal to the rating who had lain under the gun, and no one more richly deserved it.

ETIENNE BARSONY

The Dancing Bear

Fife and drum were heard from the big marketplace. People went running towards it. In a village the slightest unusual bustle makes a riot. Everybody is curious to know the cause of the alarm, and whether the wheels of the world are running out of their orbit. In the middle of the great dusty marketplace some stunted locust trees were hanging their faint, dried foliage, and from far off one could already see that underneath these miserable trees a tall, handsome young man and a huge, plump dark-brown, growling bear were hugging each other.

Joco, the bear-tamer, was giving a performance. His voice rang like a bugle-horn, and, singing his melancholy songs, he from time to time interrupted himself and hurrahed, whereupon the bear began to spring and roar angrily. The two stamped their feet, holding close together, like two tipsy comrades. But the iron-weighted stick in the young man's hand made it evident that the gigantic beast was quite capable of causing trouble, and was only restrained from doing so because it had learnt from experience that the least outbreak never failed to bring down vengeance upon its back. The bear was a very powerful specimen from Bosnia, with thick brown fur and a head as broad as a bull's. When he lifted himself up on his hind legs he was half a head taller than Joco, his master.

The villagers stood round them with anxious delight, and animated the bear with shouts of, 'Jump, Ibrahim! Hop, Ibrahim!' but nobody ventured to go near. Joco was no stranger to these people. After every harvest he visited the rich villages of Banat with his bear. They knew that he was a native of the frontier of Slavonia, and they were not particularly keen to know anything else about him. A man who leads such a vagrant life does not stay long in any one place, and has neither friends nor foes anywhere. They supposed that he spent part of the year in Bosnia, perhaps the winter, visiting, one after the other, the Serbian monasteries. Now, in midsummer, when he was least to be expected, they suddenly heard his fife and drum.

Ibrahim, the big old bear, roused the whole village in less than a quarter of an hour with his far-reaching growls. The dogs crouched horror-struck, their hair standing on end, barking at him in fear and trembling.

When Joco stopped at some street corner, or in the marketplace, and began to beat his rattling drum, the bear lifted himself with heavy groans on his hind legs, and then the great play began, the cruel amusement, the uncanny, fearful embracings which one could never be sure would not end fatally. For Joco is not satisfied to let Ibrahim jump and dance, but, whistling and singing, grasps the wild beast's skin, and squeezes his paws; and so the two dance together, the one roaring and groaning, the other singing with monotonous voice a melancholy song.

The company of soldiers stationed in the village was just returning from drill, and Captain Winter, Ritter von Wallishausen, turned in curiosity his horse's head towards the crowd, and made a sign to Lieutenant Vig to lead the men on. His fiery half-blood Graditz horse snuffed the disgusting odour of the wild beast, and would go no nearer.

The captain called a hussar from the last line that passed him, and confided the stubborn horse to his charge. Then he bent his steps towards the swaying crowd. The villagers opened out a way for him, and soon the captain stood close behind the bear-tamer. But before he could fix his eyes on Ibrahim they were taken captive by something else.

A few steps away from Joco a young girl sat upon the ground, gently stroking a light-coloured little bear. They were both so huddled up together that the villagers scarcely noticed them, and the captain was therefore all the better able to observe the young woman, who appeared to be withdrawing herself as much as possible from public gaze. And really she seemed to be an admirable young creature. She was slight of build, perhaps not yet fully developed, with the early ripeness of Eastern beauty expressed in face and figure – a black cherry, at sight of which the mouth of such a gourmand as the Ritter von Wallishausen would naturally water! Her fine face seemed meant only to be the setting of her two black eyes. She wore a shirt of coarse linen, a frock of many-coloured material, and a belt around her waist. Her beautifully formed bosom covered only by the shirt, rose and fell in goddesslike shamelessness. A string of glass beads hung round her neck, and two long earrings tapped her cheeks at every movement. She made no effort to hide her bare feet, but now and then put back her untidy but beautiful black hair from her forehead and eyes; for it was so thick that if she did not do so she could not see.

The girl felt that the captain's fiery gaze was meant for her and not for the little bear. She became embarrassed, and instinctively turned her head away. Just at this moment Joco turned round with Ibrahim. The tall Serbian peasant let the whistle fall from his hand, and the wild dance came to an end. Ibrahim understood that the performance was over, and, putting down his front paws on the ground, licked, as he panted, the strong iron bars of his muzzle.

The captain and Joco looked at each other. The powerful young bear-tamer was as pale as death. He trembled as if something terrible had befallen him. Captain Winter looked at him searchingly. Where, he asked himself, had he met this man?

The villagers did not understand what was going on, and began to shout, 'Zorka! Now, Zorka, it is your turn with Mariska.' The cries of the villagers brought Joco to himself, and with a motion worthy of a player he roused the little bear to its feet. Then he made signs to the girl. Being too excited to blow his whistle, he started singing and beating the drum; but his voice trembled so much that by and by he left off singing and let the girl go through her performance alone.

Then the captain saw something that wrought him up to ecstasy. Zorka was singing a sad Bosnian song in her tender, crooning voice, and dancing with graceful steps round the little bear, who, to tell the truth, also danced more lightly than the heavy Ibrahim, and was very amusing when he lifted his paw to his head as Hungarians do when they are in high spirits and break forth in hurrahs.

Captain Winter, however, saw nothing but the fair maid, whose pearly white teeth shone out from between her red lips. He felt he would like to slip a silk ribbon round her waist, which swayed as lightly as a reed waving to and fro in the wind, and lead her off as if she were a beautiful coloured butterfly.

Zorka grew tired of the sad, melancholy song, and began to dance wildly and passionately. Perhaps her natural feminine vanity was roused within her, and she wanted to show off at her best before the handsome soldier. Her eyes sparkled; a flush spread from time to time over her face; with her sweet voice she animated the little bear, crying, 'Mariska, Mariska, jump!' But after a while she seemed to forget the growling little creature altogether, and went on dancing a kind of graceful fandango of her own invention. As she swayed, it seemed as if the motion and excitement caused every fibre of her body to flash out a sort of electric glow. By the time the girl flung herself, quite exhausted, in the dust at his feet, Captain Winter was absolutely beside himself. Such a morsel of heavenly daintiness did not often drop in his path now that he was fasting in this purgatory of a village. His stay there had been one long Lent, during which joys and pleasures had been rare indeed.

*   *   *

It began to grow dark. At the other end of the marketplace several officers were on their way to supper at the village inn where they always messed. The captain turned to the man and woman in possession of the bears and ordered them in no friendly tone to go with him to the inn as his guests. Joco bowed humbly like a culprit, and gloomily led on his comrade Ibrahim. Zorka, on the contrary, looked gay as she walked along beside the light-coloured bear.

The captain looked again and again at the bear-tamer walking in front of him. 'Where have I seen this fellow before?' he kept asking himself. His uncertainty did not last long. His face brightened. 'Oh, yes; I remember!' he inwardly exclaimed. Now he felt sure that this black cherry of Bosnia, this girl with the waist of a dragonfly, was his.

The inn, once a gentleman's country-house, was built of stone. The bears were lodged in a little room which used to serve the former owner of the house as pantry, and were chained to the strong iron lattice of the window. In one corner of this little room the landlord ordered one of his servants to make a good bed of straw. 'The captain will pay for it,' he said.

When everything was ready in the little room, the captain called Joco to him. He knew that what he was going to do was not chivalrous; but he had already worked himself up to a blaze of excitement over the game he meant to play, and this fellow was too stupid to understand what a hazardous piece of play it was. When they were alone he stood erect before the bear-tamer and looked fixedly into his eyes.

'You are Joco Hics,' he said; 'two years ago you deserted from my regiment.'

The strong, tall young peasant began to tremble so that his knees knocked together, but could not answer a single word. Fritz Winter, Ritter von Wallishausen, whispered into Joco's ear, his speech agitated and stuttering: 'You have a woman with you,' he said, 'who surely is not your wife. Set her free. I will buy her from you for any price you ask. You can go away with your bears and pluck yourself another such flower where you found this one.'

Joco stood motionless for a while as if turned into stone. He did not tremble any longer: the crisis was over. He had only been frightened as long as he was uncertain whether or not he would be instantly hanged if he were found out.

'In all Bosnia,' he answered gloomily, 'there was only one such flower and her I stole.'

Before a man who was willing to share his guilt, he dared acknowledge his crime. In truth, this man was no better than himself. He only wore finer clothes.

The captain became impatient. 'Are you going to give her up, or not?' he asked. 'I do not want to harm you; but I could put you in prison and in chains, and what would become of your sweetheart then?'

Joco answered proudly: 'She would cry her eyes out for me; otherwise she would not have run away from her rich father's house for my sake.'

Ah! thought the captain, if it were only that! By degrees I could win her to me.

But it was not advisable to make a fuss, either for the sake of his position or because of his wife, who lived in the town.

'Joco, I tell you what,' said the captain, suddenly becoming calm. 'I am going away now for a short time. I shall be gone about an hour. By that time everybody will be in bed. The officers who sup with me, and the innkeeper and his servants, will all be sound asleep. I give you this time to think it over. When I come back you will either hold out your hand to be chained or to receive a pile of gold in it. In the meantime I shall lock you in this room, because I know how very apt you are to disappear.' He went out, and turned the key twice in the lock. Joco was left alone.

When the hour had expired, Captain Winter noisily opened the door. His eyes sparkled from the strong wine he had taken during supper, as well as from the exquisite expectation which made his pulse race.

Joco stood smiling submissively before him. 'I have thought it over, sir,' he said. 'I will speak with the little Zorka about it.'

Ritter Winter now forgot that he was speaking with a deserter, whom it was his duty to arrest. He held out his hand joyfully to the Bosnian peasant, and said encouragingly: 'Go speak with her; but make haste. Go instantly.'

They crept together to the pantry where the girl slept near the chained bears. Joco opened the door without making a sound, and slipped in. It seemed to the captain that he heard whispering inside. These few moments seemed an eternity to him. At last the bear-tamer reappeared and, nodding to the captain, said: 'Sir, you are expected.'

Captain Winter had undoubtedly taken too much wine. He staggered as he entered the pantry, the door of which the bear-tamer shut and locked directly he had entered. He then listened with such an expression on his face as belongs only to a born bandit. Almost immediately a growling was heard, and directly afterwards some terrible swearing and a fall. The growling grew stronger and stronger. At last it ended in a wild roar. A desperate cry disturbed the stillness of the night: 'Help! help!'

In the yard and round about it the dogs woke up, and with terrible yelping ran towards the pantry, where the roaring of the bear grew ever wilder and more powerful. The rattling of the chain and the cries of the girl mingled with Ibrahim's growling. The neighbours began to wake up. Human voices, confused questionings, were heard. The innkeeper and his servants appeared on the scene in their night clothes, but, hearing the terrible roaring, fled again into security. The captain's cries for help became weaker and weaker. And now Joco took his iron stake, which he always kept by him, opened the door, and at one bound was at the side of the wild beast. His voice sounded again like thunder, and the iron stick fell with a thud on the bear's back. Ibrahim had smelt blood. Beneath his paws a man's mangled body was writhing. The beast could hardly be made to let go his prey. In the light that came through the small window, Joco soon found the chain from which not long before he had freed Ibrahim, and with a swift turn he put the muzzle over the beast's jaws. It was done in a twinkling. During this time Zorka had been running up and down the empty yard, crying in vain for help. Nobody had dared come near.

The following day Captain Fritz Winter, Ritter von Wallishausen, was lying between burning wax candles upon his bier. Nobody could be made responsible for the terrible accident. Why did he go to the bears when he was not sober?

But that very day the siren of Bosnia danced her wild dance again in the next village, and with her sweet, melodious voice urged the light-coloured little bear: 'Mariska, jump, jump!'

JORGEN WILHELM BERGSOE

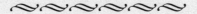

The Amputated Arms

It happened when I was about eighteen or nineteen years old. I was studying at the university, and being coached in anatomy by my old friend Solling. He was an amusing fellow, this Solling. Full of jokes and whimsical ideas, and equally merry, whether he was working at the dissecting table or brewing a punch for a jovial crowd.

He had but one fault – if one might call it so – and that was his exaggerated idea of punctuality. He grumbled if you were late two minutes; any longer delay would spoil the entire evening for him. He himself was never known to be late. At least not during the entire years of my studying.

One Wednesday evening our little circle of friends met as usual in my room at seven o'clock. I had made the customary preparations for the meeting, had borrowed three chairs – I had but one myself – had cleaned all my pipes, and had persuaded Hans to take the breakfast dishes from the sofa and carry them downstairs. One by one my friends arrived, the clock struck seven, and to our great astonishment, Solling had not yet appeared. One, two, even five minutes passed before we heard him run upstairs and knock at the door with his characteristic short blows.

When he entered the room he looked so angry and at the same time so upset that I cried out: 'What's the matter, Solling? You look as if you had been robbed.'

'That's exactly what has happened,' replied Solling angrily. 'But it was no ordinary sneak thief,' he added, hanging his overcoat behind the door.

'What have you lost?' asked my neighbour Nansen.

'Both arms from the new skeleton I've just recently received from the hospital,' said Solling, with an expression as if his last cent had been taken from him. 'It's vandalism!'

We burst out into loud laughter at this remarkable answer, but Solling continued: 'Can you imagine it? Both arms are gone, cut off at the shoulder joint; and the strangest part of it is that the same thing has been done to my shabby old skeleton which stands in my bedroom. There wasn't an arm on either of them.'

'That's too bad,' I remarked. 'For we were just going to study the anatomy of the arm tonight.'

'Osteology,' corrected Solling gravely. 'Get out your skeleton, little Simsen. It isn't as good as mine, but it will do for this evening.'

I went to the corner where my anatomical treasures were hidden behind a green curtain – 'the museum', was what Solling called it – but my astonishment was great when I found my skeleton in its accustomed place and wearing as usual my student's uniform – but without arms.

'The devil!' cried Solling. 'That was done by the same person who robbed me; the arms are taken off at the shoulder joint in exactly the same manner. You did it, Simsen!'

I declared my innocence, very angry at the abuse of my fine skeleton, while Nansen cried: 'Wait a moment, I'll bring in mine. There hasn't been a soul in my room since this morning, I can swear to that. I'll be back in an instant.'

He hurried into his room, but returned in a few moments greatly depressed and somewhat ashamed. The skeleton was in its usual place, but the arms were gone, cut off at the shoulder in exactly the same manner as mine.

The affair, mysterious in itself, had now come to be a serious matter. We lost ourselves in suggestions and explanations, none of which seemed to throw any light on the subject. Finally we sent a messenger to the other side of the house where, as I happened to know, was a new skeleton which the young student Ravn had recently received from the janitor of the hospital.

Ravn had gone out and taken the key with him. The messenger whom we had sent to the rooms of the Iceland students returned with the information that one of them had used the only skeleton they possessed to pummel the other with, and that consequently only the thigh bones were left unbroken.

What were we to do? We couldn't understand the matter at all. Solling scolded and cursed and the company was about to break up when we heard someone coming noisily upstairs. The door was thrown open and a tall, thin figure appeared on the threshold – our good friend Niels Daae.

He was a strange chap, this Niels Daae, the true type of a species seldom found nowadays. He was no longer young, and by reason of a queer chain of circumstances, as he expressed it, he had been through nearly all the professions and could produce papers proving that he had been on the point of passing not one but three examinations.

He had begun with theology; but the story of the quarrel between Jacob and Esau had led him to take up the study of law. As a law student he had come across an interesting poisoning case, which had proved to him that a study of medicine was extremely necessary for lawyers; and he had taken up the study of medicine with such energy that he had forgotten all his law and was about to take his last examinations at the age of forty.

Niels Daae took the story of our troubles very seriously. 'Every pot has two handles,' he began. 'Every sausage two ends, every question two sides, except this one – this has three.' (Applause.) 'When we look at it from the legal point of view there can be no doubt that it belongs in the category of ordinary theft. But from the fact that the thief took only the arms when he might have taken the entire skeleton, we must conclude that he is not in a responsible condition of mind, which therefore introduces a medical side to the affair. From a legal point of view, the thief must be convicted for robbery, or at least for the illegal appropriation of the property of others; but from the medical point of view, we must acquit him, because he is not responsible for his acts. Here we have two professions quarrelling with one another, and who shall say which is right? But now I will introduce the theological point of view, and raise the entire affair up to a higher plane. Providence, in the material shape of a patron of mine in the country, whose children I have inoculated with the juice of wisdom, has sent me two fat geese and two first-class ducks. These animals are to be cooked and eaten this evening in Mathiesen's establishment, and I invite this honoured company to join me there. Personally I look upon the disappearance of these arms as an all-wise intervention of providence, which sets its own inscrutable wisdom up against the wisdom which we would otherwise have heard from the lips of my venerable friend Solling.'

Daae's confused speech was received with laughter and applause, and Solling's weak protests were lost in the general delight at the invitation. I have often noticed that such improvised festivities are usually the most enjoyable, and so it was for us that evening. Niels Daae treated us to his ducks and to his most amusing jokes, Solling sang his best songs, our jovial host Mathiesen told his wittiest stories, and the merriment was in full swing when we heard cries in the street, and then a rush of confused noises broken by screams of pain.

'There's been an accident,' cried Solling, running out to the door.

We all followed him and discovered that a pair of runaway horses had thrown a carriage against a tree, hurling the driver from his box, under the wheels. His right arm had been broken near the shoulder. In the twinkling of an eye the hall of festivities was transformed into an emergency hospital. Solling shook his head as he examined the injury, and ordered the transport of the patient to the city hospital. It was his belief that the arm would have to be amputated, cut off at the shoulder joint, just as had been the case with our skeleton. 'Damned odd coincidence, isn't it?' he remarked to me.

Our merry mood had vanished and we took our way, quiet and depressed, through the old avenues towards our home. For the first time in its existence possibly, our venerable 'barracks', as we called the dormitory, saw its occupants returning home from an evening's bout just as the night watchman intoned his eleven o'clock verse.

'Just eleven,' exclaimed Solling. 'It's too early to go to bed, and too late to go anywhere else. We'll go up to your room, little Simsen, and see if we can't have some sort of a lesson this evening. You have your coloured plates and we'll try to get along with them. It's a nuisance that we should have lost those arms just this evening.'

'The doctor can have all the arms and legs he wants,' grinned Hans, who came out of the doorway just in time to hear Solling's last word.

'What do you mean, Hans?' asked Solling in astonishment.

'It'll be easy enough to get them,' said Hans. 'They've torn down the planking around Holy Trinity churchyard, and dug up the earth to build a new wall. I saw it myself, as I came past the church. Lord, what a lot of bones they've dug out there! There's arms and legs and heads, many more than the doctor could possibly need.'

'Much good that does us,' answered Solling. 'They shut the gates at seven o'clock and it's after eleven already.'

'Oh, yes, they shut them,' grinned Hans again. 'But there's another way to get in. If you go through the gate of the porcelain factory and over the courtyard, and through the mill in the fourth courtyard that leads out into Spring Street, there you will see where the planking is torn down, and you can get into the churchyard easily.'

'Hans, you're a genius!' exclaimed Solling in delight. 'Here, Simsen, you know that factory inside and out, you're so friendly with that fellow Outzen who lives there. Run along to him and let him give you the key of the mill. It will be easy to find an arm that isn't too much decayed. Hurry along, now; the rest of us will wait for you upstairs.'

To be quite candid I must confess that I was not particularly eager to fulfil Solling's command. I was at an age to have still a sufficient amount of reverence for death and the grave, and the mysterious occurrence of the stolen arms still ran through my mind. But I was still more afraid of Solling's irony and of the laughter of my comrades, so I trotted off as carelessly as if I had been sent to buy a package of cigarettes.

It was some time before I could arouse the old janitor of the factory from his peaceful slumbers. I told him that I had an important message for Outzen, and hurried upstairs to the latter's room. Outzen was a strictly moral character; knowing this, I was prepared to have him refuse me the key which would let me into the fourth courtyard and from there into the cemetery. As I expected, Outzen took the matter very seriously. He closed the Hebrew Bible which he had been studying as I entered, turned up his lamp and looked at me in astonishment as I made my request.

'Why, my dear Simsen, it is a most sinful deed that you are about to do,' he said gravely. 'Take my advice and desist. You will get no key from me for any such cause. The peace of the grave is sacred. No man dare disturb it.'

'And how about the gravedigger? He puts the newly dead down beside the old corpses, and lives as peacefully as anyone else.'

'He is doing his duty,' answered Outzen calmly. 'But to disturb the peace of the grave from sheer daring, with the fumes of the punch still in your head – that is a different matter – that will surely be punished!'

His words irritated me. It is not very flattering, particularly if one is not yet twenty, to be told that you are about to perform a daring deed simply because you are drunk. Without any further reply to his protests I took the key from its place on the wall and ran downstairs two steps at a time, vowing to myself that I would take home an arm let it cost what it would. I would show Outzen, and Solling, and all the rest, what a devil of a fellow I was.

My heart beat rapidly as I stole through the long dark corridor, past the ruins of the old convent of St Clara, into the so-called third courtyard. Here I took a lantern from the hall, lit it and crossed to the mill where the clay was prepared for the factory. The tall wheels and cylinders, with their straps and bolts, looked like weird creatures of the night in the dim light of my tallow candle. I felt my courage sinking even here, but I pulled myself together, opened the last door with my key and stepped out into the fourth courtyard. A moment later I stood on the dividing line between the cemetery and the factory.

The entire length of the tall blackened planking had been torn down. The pieces of it lay about, and the earth had been dug up to a considerable depth to make a foundation for a new wall between Life and Death. The uncanny emptiness of the place seized upon me. I halted involuntarily as if to harden myself against it. It was a raw, cold, stormy evening. The clouds flew past the moon in jagged fragments, so that the churchyard, with its white crosses and stones, lay now in full light, now in dim shadow. Now and then a rush of wind rattled over the graves, roared through the leafless trees, bent the complaining bushes, and caught itself in the little eddy at the corner of the church, only to escape again over the roofs, turning the old weather vane with a sharp scream of the rusty iron.

I looked towards the left – there I saw several weird white shapes moving gently in the moonlight. 'White sheets,' I said to myself, 'it's nothing but white sheets! This drying of linen in the churchyard ought to be stopped.'

I turned in the opposite direction and saw a heap of bones scarce two paces distant from me. Holding my lantern lower, I approached them and stretched out my hand – there was a rattling in the heap; something warm and soft touched my fingers.

I started and shivered. Then I exclaimed: 'The rats! nothing but the rats in the churchyard! I must not get frightened. It will be so foolish – they would laugh at me. Where the devil is that arm? I can't find one that isn't broken!'

With trembling knees and in feverish haste I examined one heap after another. The light in my lantern flickered in the wind and suddenly went out. The foul smell of the smoking wick rose to my face and I felt as if I were about to faint, it took all my energy to recover my control. I walked two or three steps ahead, and saw at a little distance a coffin which had been still in good shape when taken out of the earth.

I approached it and saw that it was of old-fashioned shape, made of heavy oaken boards that were slowly rotting. On its cover was a metal plate with an illegible inscription. The old wood was so brittle that it would have been very easy for me to open the coffin with any sort of a tool. I looked about me and saw a hatchet and a couple of spades lying near the fence. I took one of the latter, put its flat end between the boards – the old coffin fell apart with a dull crackling protest.

I turned my head aside, put my hand in through the opening, felt about, and taking a firm hold on one arm of the skeleton, I loosened it from the body with a quick jerk. The movement loosened the head as well, and it rolled out through the opening right to my very feet. I took up the skull to lay it in the coffin again – and then I saw a greenish phosphorescent glimmer in its empty eye sockets, a glimmer which came and went. Mad terror shook me at the sight. I looked up at the houses in the distance, then back again to the skull; the empty sockets shone more brightly than before. I felt that I must have some natural explanation for this appearance or I would go mad. I took up the head again – and never in my life have I had so overpowering an impression of the might of death and decay than in this moment. Myriads of disgusting clammy insects poured out of every opening of the skull, and a couple of shining, wormlike centipedes – *Geophila* the scientists call them – crawled about in the eye sockets. I threw the skull back into the coffin, sprang over the heaps of bones without even taking time to pick up my lantern, and ran like a hunted thing through the dark mill, over the factory courtyards, until I reached the outer gate. Here I washed the arm at the fountain and smoothed my disarranged clothing. I hid my booty under my overcoat, nodded to the sleepy old janitor as he opened the door to me, and a few moments later I entered my own room with an expression which I had attempted to make quite calm and careless.

'What the devil is the matter with you, Simsen?' cried Solling as he saw me. 'Have you seen a ghost? Or is the punch wearing off already? We thought you'd never come; why, it's nearly twelve o'clock!'

Without a word I drew back my overcoat and laid my booty on the table.

'By all the devils,' exclaimed Solling in anatomical enthusiasm, 'where did you find that superb arm? Simsen knows what he's about all right. It's a girl's arm; isn't it beautiful? Just look at the hand – how fine and delicate it is! Must have worn a No. 6 glove. There's a pretty hand to caress and kiss!'

The arm passed from one to the other amid general admiration. Every word that was said increased my disgust for myself and for what I had done. It was a woman's arm, then – what sort of a woman might she have been? Young and beautiful possibly – her brothers' pride, her parents' joy. She had faded away in her youth, cared for by loving hands and tender thoughts. She had fallen asleep gently, and those who loved her had desired to give her in death the peace she had enjoyed throughout her lifetime. For this they had made her coffin of thick, heavy oaken boards. And this hand, loved and missed by so many – it lay there now on an anatomical table, encircled by clouds of tobacco smoke, stared at by curious glances, and made the object of coarse jokes. O God! how terrible it was!

'I must have that arm,' exclaimed Solling, when the first burst of admiration had passed. 'When I bleach it and touch it up with varnish, it wild be a superb specimen. I'll take it home with me.'

'No,' I exclaimed, 'I can't permit it. It was wrong of me to bring it away from the churchyard. I'm going right back to put the arm in its place.'

'Well, will you listen to that?' cried Solling, amid the hearty laughter of the others. 'Simsen's so lyric, he certainly must be drunk. I must have that arm at any cost.'

'Not much,' cut in Niels Daae; 'you have no right to it. It was buried in the earth and dug out again; it is a find, and all the rest of us have just as much right to it as you have.'

'Yes, every one of us has some share in it,' said someone else.

'But what are you going to do about it?' remarked Solling. 'It would be vandalism to break up that arm. What God has joined together let no man put asunder,' he concluded with pathos.

'Let's auction it off,' exclaimed Daae. 'I will be the auctioneer, and this key to the graveyard will serve me for a hammer.'

The laughter broke out anew as Daae took his place solemnly at the head of the table and began to whine out the following announcement: 'I hereby notify all present that on the 25th of November, at twelve o'clock at midnight, in corridor No. 5 of the student barracks, a lady's arm in excellent condition, with all its appurtenances of wrist bones, joints and fingertips, is to be offered at public auction. The buyer can have possession of his purchase immediately after the auction, and a credit of six weeks will be given to any reliable customer. I bid a Danish shilling.'

'One mark,' cried Solling mockingly.

'Two,' cried somebody else.

'Four,' exclaimed Solling. 'It's worth it. Why don't you join in, Simsen? You look as if you were sitting in a hornet's nest.'

I bid one mark more, and Solling raised me a thaler. There were no more bids, the hammer fell, and the arm belonged to Solling.

'Here, take this,' he said, handing me a mark piece; 'it's part of your commission as grave robber. You shall have the rest later, unless you prefer that I should turn it over to the drinking fund.' With these words Solling wrapped the arm in a newspaper, and the merry crowd ran noisily down the stairs and through the streets, until their singing and laughter were lost in the distance.

I stood alone, still dazed and bewildered, staring at the piece of money in my hand. My thoughts were far too much excited to allow me to sleep. I turned up my lamp and took out one of my books to try and study myself into a quieter mood. But without success.

Suddenly I heard a sound like that of a swinging pendulum. I raised my head and listened attentively. There was no clock either in my room or in the neighbouring ones – but I could still hear the sound. At the same moment my lamp began to flicker. The oil was apparently exhausted. I was about to rise to fill it again, when my eyes fell upon the door, and I saw the graveyard key, which I had hung there, moving slowly back and forth with a rhythmic swing. Just as its motion seemed about to die away, it would receive a gentle push as from an unseen hand, and would swing back and forth more than ever. I stood there with open mouth and staring eyes, ice-cold chills ran down my back, and drops of perspiration stood out on my forehead. Finally, I could endure it no longer. I sprang to the door, seized the key with both hands and put it on my desk under a pile of heavy books. Then I breathed a sigh of relief.

My lamp was about to go out and I discovered that I had no more oil. With feverish haste I threw my clothes off, blew out the light and sprang into bed as if to smother my fears.

But once I was alone in the darkness the fears grew worse than ever. They grew into dreams and visions. It seemed to me as if I were out in the graveyard again, and heard the screaming of the rusty weather vane as the wind turned it. Then I was in the mill again; the wheels were turning and stretching out ghostly hands to draw me into the yawning maw of the machine. Then again, I found myself in a long, low, pitch-black corridor, followed by Something I could not see – Something that drove me to the mouth of a bottomless abyss. I would start up out of my half sleep, listen and look about me, then fall back again into an uneasy slumber.

Suddenly something fell from the ceiling on to the bed, and 'buzz – buzz – buzz' sounded about my head. It was a huge fly which had been sleeping in a corner of my room and had been roused by the heat of the stove. It flew about in great circles, now around the bed, now in all four corners of the chamber – 'buzz – buzz – buzz' – it was unendurable! At last I heard it creep into a bag of sugar which had been left on the window sill. I sprang up and closed the bag tight. The fly buzzed worse than ever, but I went back to bed and attempted to sleep again, feeling that I had conquered the enemy.

I began to count: I counted slowly to one hundred, two hundred, finally up to one thousand, and then at last I experienced that pleasant weakness which is the forerunner of true sleep. I seemed to be in a beautiful garden, bright with many flowers and odorous with all the perfumes of spring. At my side walked a beautiful young girl. I seemed to know her well, and yet it was not possible for me to remember her name, or even to know how we came to be wandering there together. As we walked slowly through the paths she would stop to pick a flower or to admire a brilliant butterfly swaying in the air. Suddenly a cold wind blew through the garden. The young girl trembled and her cheeks grew pale. 'I am cold,' she said to me, 'do you not see? It is Death who is approaching us.'

I would have answered, but in the same moment another stronger and still more icy gust roared through the garden. The leaves turned pale on the trees, the flowerets bent their heads, and the bees and butterflies fell lifeless to the earth. 'That is Death,' whispered my companion, trembling.

A third icy gust blew the last leaves from the bushes, white crosses and gravestones appeared between the bare twigs – and I was in the churchyard again and heard the screaming of the rusty weather vane. Beside me stood a heavy brass-bound coffin with a metal plate on the cover. I bent down to read the inscription, the cover rolled off suddenly, and from out the coffin rose the form of the young girl who had been with me in the garden. I stretched out my arms to clasp her to my breast – then, oh horror! I saw the greenish-gleaming, empty eye sockets of the skull. I felt bony arms around me, dragging me back into the coffin. I screamed aloud for help and woke up.

My room seemed unusually light; but I remembered that it was a moon-light night and thought no more of it. I tried to explain the visions of my dream with various natural noises about me. The imprisoned fly buzzed as loudly as a whole swarm of bees; one half of my window had blown open, and the cold night air rushed in gusts into my room.

I sprang up to close the window, and then I saw that the strong white light that filled my room did not come from the moon, but seemed to shine out from the church opposite. I heard the chiming of the bells, soft at first, as if in far distance, then stronger and stronger until, mingled with the rolling notes of the organ, a mighty rush of sound struck against my windows. I stared out into the street and could scarcely believe my eyes. The houses in the market place just beyond were all little one-storey buildings with bow windows and wooden eave troughs ending in carved dragon heads from a bygone age. Most of them had balconies of carved woodwork, and high stone stoops with gleaming brass rails.

But it was the church most of all that aroused my astonishment. Its position was completely changed. Its front turned towards our house where usually the side had stood. The church was brilliantly lighted, and now I perceived that it was this light which filled my room. I stood speechless amid the chiming of the bells and the roaring of the organ, and I saw a long wedding procession moving slowly up the centre aisle of the church towards the altar. The light was so brilliant that I could distinguish each one of the figures. They were all in strange old-time costumes; the ladies in brocades and satins with strings of pearls in their powdered hair, the gentlemen in uniform with knee breeches, swords, and cocked hats held under their arms. But it was the bride who drew my attention most strongly. She was clothed in white satin, and a faded myrtle wreath was twisted through the powdered locks beneath her sweeping veil. The bridegroom at her side wore a red uniform and many decorations. Slowly they approached the altar, where an old man in black vestments and a heavy white wig was awaiting them. They stood before him, and I could see that he was reading the ritual from a gold-lettered book.

One of the train stepped forward and unbuckled the bridegroom's sword, that his right hand might be free to take that of the bride. She seemed about to raise her own hand to his, when she suddenly sank fainting at his feet. The guests hurried towards the altar, the lights went out, the music stopped, and the figures floated together like pale white mists.

But outside in the square it was still brighter than before, and I suddenly saw the side portal of the church burst open and the wedding procession move out across the market place.

I turned as if to flee, but could not move a muscle. Quiet, as if turned to stone, I stood and watched the ghostly figures that came nearer and nearer. The clergyman led the train, then came the bridegroom and the bride, and as the latter raised her eyes to me I saw that it was the young girl of the garden. Her eyes were so full of pain, so full of sad entreaty that I could scarce endure them; but how shall I explain the feeling that shot through me as I suddenly discovered that the right sleeve of her white satin gown hung empty at her side? The train disappeared, and the tone of the church bells changed to a strange, dry, creaking sound, and the gate below me complained as it turned on its rusty hinges. I faced towards my own door. I knew that it was shut and locked, but I knew that the ghostly procession were coming to call me to account, and I felt that no walls could keep them out. My door flew open, there was a rustling as of silken gowns, but the figures seemed to float in in the changing forms of swaying white mists. Closer and closer they gathered around me, robbing me of breath, robbing me of the power to move. There was a silence as of the grave – and then I saw before me the old priest with his gold-lettered book. He raised his hand and spoke with a soft, deep voice: 'The grave is sacred! Let no one dare to disturb the peace of the dead.'

'The grave is sacred!' an echo rolled through the room as the swaying figures moved like reeds in the wind.

'What do you want? What do you demand?' I gasped in the grip of a deathly fear.

'Give back to the grave that which belongs to it,' said the deep voice again.

'Give back to the grave that which belongs to it,' repeated the echo as the swaying forms pressed closer to me.

'But it's impossible – I can't – I have sold it – sold it at auction!' I screamed in despair. 'It was buried and found in the earth – and sold for five marks eight shillings – '

A hideous scream came from the ghostly ranks. They threw themselves upon me as the white fog rolls in from the sea, they pressed upon me until I could no longer breathe. Beside myself, I threw open the window and attempted to spring out, screaming aloud: 'Help! help! murder! they are murdering me!'

The sound of my own voice awoke me. I found myself in my night clothes on the window sill, one leg already out of the window and both hands clutching at the centre post. On the street below me stood the night-watchman, staring up at me in astonishment, while faint white clouds of mist rolled out of my window like smoke. All around outside lay the November fog, grey and moist, and as the fresh air of the early dawn blew cool on my face I felt my senses returning to me. I looked down at the night-watchman – God bless him! He was a big, strong, comfortably fat fellow made of real flesh and blood, and no ghost shape of the night. I looked at the round tower of the church – how massive and venerable it stood there, grey in the grey of the morning mists. I looked over at the market place. There was a light in the baker's shop and a farmer stood before it, tying his horse to a post. Back in my own room everything was in its usual place. Even the little paper bag with the sugar lay there on the window sill, and the imprisoned fly buzzed louder than ever. I knew that I was really awake and that the day was coming. I sprang back hastily from the window and was about to jump into bed, when my foot touched something hard and sharp.

I stooped to see what it was, felt about on the floor in the half light, and touched a long, dry, skeleton arm which held a tiny roll of paper in its bony fingers. I felt about again, and found still another arm, also holding a roll of paper. Then I began to think that my reason must be going. What I had seen thus far was only an unusually vivid dream – a vision of my heated imagination. But I knew that I was awake now, and yet here lay two – no, three (for there was still another arm) – hard, undeniable, material proofs that what I had thought was hallucination might have been reality. Trembling in the thought that madness was threatening me, I tore open the first roll of paper. On it was written the name: 'Solling'. I caught at the second and opened it. There stood the word: 'Nansen'. I had just strength enough left to catch the third paper and open it – there was my own name: 'Simsen'.

Then I sank fainting to the floor.

When I came to myself again, Niels Daae stood beside me with an empty water bottle, the contents of which were dripping off my person and off the sofa upon which I was lying. 'Here, drink this,' he said in a soothing tone. 'It will make you feel better.'

I looked about me wildly, as I sipped at the glass of brandy which put new life into me once more. 'What has happened?' I asked weakly.

'Oh, nothing of importance,' answered Niels. 'You were just about to commit suicide by means of charcoal gas. Those are mighty bad ventilators on your old stove there. The wind must have blown them shut, unless you were fool enough to close them yourself before you went to bed. If you had not opened the window, you would have already been too far along the path to paradise to be called back by a glass of brandy. Take another.'

'How did you get up here?' I asked, sitting upright on the sofa.

'Through the door in the usual simple manner,' answered Niels Daae. 'I was on watch last night in the hospital; but Mathiesen's punch is heavy and my watching was more like sleeping, so I thought it better to come away in the early morning. As I passed your barracks here, I saw you sitting in the window in your nightshirt and calling down to the night-watchman that someone was murdering you. I managed to wake up Jansen down below you, and got into the house through his window. Do you usually sleep on the bare floor?'

'But where did the arms come from?' I asked, still half bewildered.

'Oh, the devil take those arms,' cried Niels. 'Just see if you can stand up all right now. Oh, those arms there? Why, those are the arms I cut off your skeletons. Clever idea, wasn't it? You know how grumpy Solling gets if anything interferes with his tutoring. You see, I'd had the geese sent me, and I wanted you all to come with me to Mathiesen's place. I knew you were going to read the osteology of the arm, so I went up into Solling's room, opened it with his own keys and took the arms from his skeleton. I did the same here while you were downstairs in the reading room. Have you been stupid enough to take them down off their frames, and take away their tickets? I had marked them so carefully, that each man should get his own again.'

I dressed hastily and went out with Niels into the fresh, cool morning air. A few minutes later we separated, and I turned towards the street where Solling lived. Without heeding the protest of his old landlady, I entered the room where he still slept the sleep of the just. The arm, still wrapped in newspaper, lay on his desk. I took it up, put the mark piece in its place and hastened with all speed to the churchyard.

How different it looked in the early dawn! The fog had risen and shining frost pearls hung in the bare twigs of the tall trees where the sparrows were already twittering their morning song. There was no one to be seen. The churchyard lay quiet and peaceful. I stepped over the heaps of bones to where the heavy oaken coffin lay under a tree. Cautiously I pushed the arm back into its interior, and hammered the rusty nails into their places again, just as the first rays of the pale November sun touched a gleam of light from the metal plate on the cover. Then the weight was lifted from my soul.

AMBROSE BIERCE

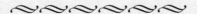

Born in 1842, Ambrose Bierce was the author of supernatural stories that have secured his place in both the weird tradition and in the wider world of American letters. He is also noted for his tales of the Civil War, which drew on his own experience as a Union cartographer and officer. His first job in journalism was as editor for the *San Francisco News-Letter* and *California Advertiser* (1868–72). In time, Bierce established himself as a kind of literary dictator of the West Coast and was so respected and feared as a critic that his judgement could 'make or break' an aspiring author's reputation. Well known by his mere initials, A. G. B., he was called by his enemies and detractors 'Almighty God Bierce'. He was also nicknamed 'Bitter Bierce' and his nihilistic motto was, 'Nothing matters.' Bierce is best remembered for his cynical but humorous *Devil's Dictionary*. In 1913, at the age of seventy-one, Bierce disappeared into revolution-torn Mexico to fight alongside the bandit Pancho Villa. Although a popular theory is that Bierce argued with Villa over military strategy and was subsequently shot, he probably perished in the battle of Ojinaga on 11 January 1914.

The Moonlit Road

ONE

Statement of Joel Hetman Jr

I am the most unfortunate of men. Rich, respected, fairly well educated and of sound health – with many other advantages usually valued by those having them and coveted by those who have them not – I sometimes think that I should be less unhappy if they had been denied me, for then the contrast between my outer and my inner life would not be continually demanding a painful attention. In the stress of privation and the need of effort I might sometimes forget the sombre secret ever baffling the conjecture that it compels.

I am the only child of Joel and Julia Hetman. The one was a well-to-do country gentleman, the other a beautiful and accomplished woman to whom he was passionately attached with what I now know to have been a jealous and exacting devotion. The family home was a few miles from Nashville, Tennessee, a large, irregularly built dwelling of no particular order of architecture, a little way off the road, in a park of trees and shrubbery.

At the time of which I write I was nineteen years old, a student at Yale. One day I received a telegram from my father of such urgency that in compliance with its unexplained demand I left at once for home. At the railway station in Nashville a distant relative awaited me to apprise me of the reason for my recall: my mother had been barbarously murdered – why and by whom none could conjecture, but the circumstances were these:

My father had gone to Nashville, intending to return the next afternoon. Something prevented his accomplishing the business in hand, so he returned on the same night, arriving just before the dawn. In his testimony before the coroner he explained that having no latchkey and not caring to disturb the sleeping servants, he had, with no clearly defined intention, gone round to the rear of the house. As he turned an angle of the building, he heard a sound as of a door being gently closed, and saw in the darkness, indistinctly, the figure of a man, which instantly disappeared among the trees of the lawn. A hasty pursuit and brief search of the grounds in the belief that the trespasser was someone secretly visiting a servant proving fruitless, he entered at the unlocked door and mounted the stairs to my mother's chamber. Its door was open, and stepping into black darkness he fell headlong over some heavy object on the floor. I may spare myself the details; it was my poor mother, dead of strangulation by human hands!

Nothing had been taken from the house, the servants had heard no sound, and excepting those terrible fingermarks upon the dead woman's throat – dear God! that I might forget them! – no trace of the assassin was ever found.

I gave up my studies and remained with my father, who, naturally, was greatly changed. Always of a sedate, taciturn disposition, he now fell into so deep a dejection that nothing could hold his attention, yet anything – a footfall, the sudden closing of a door – aroused in him a fitful interest; one might have called it an apprehension. At any small surprise of the senses he would start visibly and sometimes turn pale, then relapse into a melancholy apathy deeper than before. I suppose he was what is called a 'nervous wreck'. As to me, I was younger then than now – there is much in that. Youth is Gilead, in which is balm for every wound. Ah, that I might again dwell in that enchanted land! Unacquainted with grief, I knew not how to appraise my bereavement; I could not rightly estimate the strength of the stroke.

One night, a few months after the dreadful event, my father and I walked home from the city. The full moon was about three hours above the eastern horizon; the entire countryside had the solemn stillness of a summer night; our footfalls and the ceaseless song of the katydids were the only sound, aloof. Black shadows of bordering trees lay athwart the road, which, in the short reaches between, gleamed a ghostly white. As we approached the gate to our dwelling, whose front was in shadow, and in which no light shone, my father suddenly stopped and clutched my arm, saying, hardly above his breath: 'God! God! what is that?'

'I hear nothing,' I replied.

'But see – see!' he said, pointing along the road, directly ahead.

I said: 'Nothing is there. Come, father, let us go in – you are ill.'

He had released my arm and was standing rigid and motionless in the centre of the illuminated roadway, staring like one bereft of sense. His face in the moonlight showed a pallor and fixity inexpressibly distressing. I pulled gently at his sleeve, but he had forgotten my existence. Presently he began to retire backward, step by step, never for an instant removing his eyes from what he saw, or thought he saw. I turned half round to follow, but stood irresolute. I do not recall any feeling of fear, unless a sudden chill was its physical manifestation. It seemed as if an icy wind had touched my face and enfolded my body from head to foot; I could feel the stir of it in my hair.

At that moment my attention was drawn to a light that suddenly streamed from an upper window of the house: one of the servants, awakened by what mysterious premonition of evil who can say, and in obedience to an impulse that she was never able to name, had lit a lamp. When I turned to look for my father he was gone, and in all the years that have passed no whisper of his fate has come across the borderland of conjecture from the realm of the unknown.

TWO

Statement of Caspar Grattan

Today I am said to live; tomorrow, here in this room, will lie a senseless shape of clay that all too long was I. If anyone lift the cloth from the face of that unpleasant thing it will be in gratification of a mere morbid curiosity. Some, doubtless, will go further and enquire, 'Who was he?' In this writing I supply the only answer that I am able to make – Caspar Grattan. Surely, that should be enough. The name has served my small need for more than twenty years of a life of unknown length. True, I gave it to myself, but lacking another I had the right. In this world one must have a name; it prevents confusion, even when it does not establish identity. Some, though, are known by numbers, which also seem inadequate distinctions.

One day, for illustration, I was passing along a street of a city, far from here, when I met two men in uniform, one of whom, half pausing and looking curiously into my face, said to his companion, 'That man looks like 767.' Something in the number seemed familiar and horrible. Moved by an uncontrollable impulse, I sprang into a side street and ran until I fell exhausted in a country lane.

I have never forgotten that number, and always it comes to memory attended by gibbering obscenity, peals of joyless laughter, the clang of iron doors. So I say a name, even if self-bestowed, is better than a number. In the register of the potter's field I shall soon have both. What wealth!

Of him who shall find this paper I must beg a little consideration. It is not the history of my life; the knowledge to write that is denied me. This is only a record of broken and apparently unrelated memories, some of them as distinct and sequent as brilliant beads upon a thread, others remote and strange, having the character of crimson dreams with interspaces blank and black – witch-fires glowing still and red in a great desolation.

Standing upon the shore of eternity, I turn for a last look landward over the course by which I came. There are twenty years of footprints fairly distinct, the impressions of bleeding feet. They lead through poverty and pain, devious and unsure, as of one staggering beneath a burden – 'remote, unfriended, melancholy, slow'.

Ah, the poet's prophecy of Me – how admirable, how dreadfully admirable!

Backward beyond the beginning of this *via dolorosa* – this epic of suffering with episodes of sin – I see nothing clearly; it comes out of a cloud. I know that it spans only twenty years, yet I am an old man.

One does not remember one's birth – one has to be told. But with me it was different; life came to me full-handed and dowered me with all my faculties and powers. Of a previous existence I know no more than others, for all have stammering intimations that may be memories and may be dreams. I know only that my first consciousness was of maturity in body and mind – a consciousness accepted without surprise or conjecture. I merely found myself walking in a forest, half-clad, footsore, unutterably weary and hungry. Seeing a farmhouse, I approached and asked for food, which was given me by one who enquired my name. I did not know, yet knew that all had names. Greatly embarrassed, I retreated, and night coming on, lay down in the forest and slept.

The next day I entered a large town which I shall not name. Nor shall I recount further incidents of the life that is now to end – a life of wandering, always and everywhere haunted by an overmastering sense of crime in punishment of wrong and of terror in punishment of crime. Let me see if I can reduce it to narrative.

I seem once to have lived near a great city, a prosperous planter, married to a woman whom I loved and distrusted. We had, it sometimes seems, one child, a youth of brilliant parts and promise. He is at all times a vague figure, never clearly drawn, frequently altogether out of the picture.

One luckless evening it occurred to me to test my wife's fidelity in a vulgar, commonplace way familiar to everyone who has acquaintance with the literature of fact and fiction. I went to the city, telling my wife that I should be absent until the following afternoon. But I returned before day-break and went to the rear of the house, purposing to enter by a door with which I had secretly so tampered that it would seem to lock, yet not actually fasten. As I approached it, I heard it gently open and close, and saw a man steal away into the darkness. With murder in my heart, I sprang after him, but he had vanished without even the bad luck of identification. Sometimes now I cannot even persuade myself that it was a human being.

Crazed with jealousy and rage, blind and bestial with all the elemental passions of insulted manhood, I entered the house and sprang up the stairs to the door of my wife's chamber. It was closed, but having tampered with its lock also, I easily entered, and despite the black darkness soon stood by the side of her bed. My groping hands told me that although disarranged it was unoccupied. 'She is below,' I thought, 'and terrified by my entrance has evaded me in the darkness of the hall.'

With the purpose of seeking her I turned to leave the room, but took a wrong direction – the right one! My foot struck her, cowering in a corner of the room. Instantly my hands were at her throat, stifling a shriek; my knees were upon her struggling body; and there in the darkness, without a word of accusation or reproach, I strangled her till she died!

There ends the dream. I have related it in the past tense, but the present would be the fitter form, for again and again the sombre tragedy re-enacts itself in my consciousness – over and over I lay the plan, I suffer the confirmation, I redress the wrong. Then all is blank; and afterwards the rains beat against the grimy window-panes, or the snows fall upon my scant attire, the wheels rattle in the squalid streets where my life lies in poverty and mean employment. If there is ever sunshine I do not recall it; if there are birds they do not sing.

There is another dream, another vision of the night. I stand among the shadows in a moonlit road. I am aware of another presence, but whose I cannot rightly determine. In the shadow of a great dwelling I catch the gleam of white garments; then the figure of a woman confronts me in the road – my murdered wife! There is death in the face; there are marks upon the throat. The eyes are fixed on mine with an infinite gravity which is not reproach, nor hate, nor menace, nor anything less terrible than recognition. Before this awful apparition I retreat in terror – a terror that is upon me as I write. I can no longer rightly shape the words. See! they –

Now I am calm, but truly there is no more to tell: the incident ends where it began – in darkness and in doubt.

Yes, I am again in control of myself: 'the captain of my soul'. But that is not respite; it is another stage and phase of expiation. My penance, constant in degree, is mutable in kind: one of its variants is tranquillity. After all, it is only a life-sentence. 'To Hell for life' – that is a foolish penalty: the culprit chooses the duration of his punishment. Today my term expires.

To each and all, the peace that was not mine.

THREE

Statement of the Late Julia Hetman, through the Medium Bayrolles

I had retired early and fallen almost immediately into a peaceful sleep, from which I awoke with that indefinable sense of peril which is, I think, a common experience in that other, earlier life. Of its unmeaning character, too, I was entirely persuaded, yet that did not banish it. My husband, Joel Hetman, was away from home; the servants slept in another part of the house. But these were familiar conditions; they had never before distressed me. Nevertheless, the strange terror grew so insupportable that conquering my reluctance to move I sat up and lit the lamp at my bedside. Contrary to my expectation this gave me no relief; the light seemed rather an added danger, for I reflected that it would shine out under the door, disclosing my presence to whatever evil thing might lurk outside. You that are still in the flesh, subject to horrors of the imagination, think what a monstrous fear that must be which seeks in darkness security from malevolent existences of the night. That is to spring to close quarters with an unseen enemy – the strategy of despair!

Extinguishing the lamp I pulled the bedclothing about my head and lay trembling and silent, unable to shriek, forgetful to pray. In this pitiable state I must have lain for what you call hours – with us there are no hours, there is no time.

At last it came – a soft, irregular sound of footfalls on the stairs! They were slow, hesitant, uncertain, as of something that did not see its way; to my disordered reason all the more terrifying for that, as the approach of some blind and mindless malevolence to which is no appeal. I even thought that I must have left the hall lamp burning and the groping of this creature proved it a monster of the night. This was foolish and inconsistent with my previous dread of the light, but what would you have? Fear has no brains; it is an idiot. The dismal witness that it bears and the cowardly counsel that it whispers are unrelated. We know this well, we who have passed into the Realm of Terror, who skulk in eternal dusk among the scenes of our former lives, invisible even to ourselves, and one another, yet hiding forlorn in lonely places; yearning for speech with our loved ones, yet dumb, and as fearful of them as they of us. Sometimes the disability is removed, the law suspended: by the deathless power of love or hate we break the spell – we are seen by those whom we would warn, console or punish. What form we seem to them to bear we know not; we know only that we terrify even those whom we most wish to comfort, and from whom we most crave tenderness and sympathy.

Forgive, I pray you, this inconsequent digression by what was once a woman. You who consult us in this imperfect way – you do not understand. You ask foolish questions about things unknown and things forbidden. Much that we know and could impart in our speech is meaningless in yours. We must communicate with you through a stammering intelligence in that small fraction of our language that you yourselves can speak. You think that we are of another world. No, we have knowledge of no world but yours, though for us it holds no sunlight, no warmth, no music, no laughter, no song of birds, nor any companionship. O God! what a thing it is to be a ghost, cowering and shivering in an altered world, a prey to apprehension and despair!

No, I did not die of fright: the Thing turned and went away. I heard it go down the stairs, hurriedly, I thought, as if itself in sudden fear. Then I rose to call for help. Hardly had my shaking hand found the doorknob when – merciful heaven! – I heard it returning. Its footfalls as it remounted the stairs were rapid, heavy and loud; they shook the house. I fled to an angle of the wall and crouched upon the floor. I tried to pray. I tried to call the name of my dear husband. Then I heard the door thrown open. There was an interval of unconsciousness, and when I revived I felt a strangling clutch upon my throat – felt my arms feebly beating against something that bore me backward – felt my tongue thrusting itself from between my teeth! And then I passed into this life.

No, I have no knowledge of what it was. The sum of what we knew at death is the measure of what we know afterwards of all that went before. Of this existence we know many things, but no new light falls upon any page of that; in memory is written all of it that we can read. Here are no heights of truth overlooking the confused landscape of that dubitable domain. We still dwell in the Valley of the Shadow, lurk in its desolate places, peering from brambles and thickets at its mad, malign inhabitants. How should we have new knowledge of that fading past?

What I am about to relate happened on a night. We know when it is night, for then you retire to your houses and we can venture from our places of concealment to move unafraid about our old homes, to look in at the windows, even to enter and gaze upon your faces as you sleep. I had lingered long near the dwelling where I had been so cruelly changed to what I am, as we do while any that we love or hate remain. Vainly I had sought some method of manifestation, some way to make my continued existence and my great love and poignant pity understood by my husband and son. Always if they slept they would wake, or if in my desperation I dared approach them when they were awake, would turn towards me the terrible eyes of the living, frightening me by the glances that I sought from the purpose that I held.

On this night I had searched for them without success, fearing to find them; they were nowhere in the house, nor about the moonlit dawn. For, although the sun is lost to us for ever, the moon, full-orbed or slender, remains to us. Sometimes it shines by night, sometimes by day, but always it rises and sets, as in that other life.

I left the lawn and moved in the white light and silence along the road, aimless and sorrowing. Suddenly I heard the voice of my poor husband in exclamations of astonishment, with that of my son in reassurance and dissuasion; and there by the shadow of a group of trees they stood – near, so near! Their faces were towards me, the eyes of the elder man fixed upon mine. He saw me – at last, at last, he saw me! In the consciousness of that, my terror fled as a cruel dream. The death-spell was broken: Love had conquered Law! Mad with exultation I shouted – I *must* have shouted, 'He sees, he sees: he will understand!' Then, controlling myself, I moved forward, smiling and consciously beautiful, to offer myself to his arms, to comfort him with endearments, and, with my son's hand in mine, to speak words that should restore the broken bonds between the living and the dead.

Alas! alas! his face went white with fear, his eyes were as those of a hunted animal. He backed away from me, as I advanced, and at last turned and fled into the wood – whither, it is not given to me to know.

To my poor boy, left doubly desolate, I have never been able to impart a sense of my presence. Soon he, too, must pass to this Life Invisible and be lost to me for ever.

A Tough Tussle

One night in the autumn of 1861 a man sat alone in the heart of a forest in western Virginia. The region was one of the wildest on the continent – the Cheat Mountain country. There was no lack of people close at hand, however; within a mile of where the man sat was the now silent camp of a whole Federal brigade. Somewhere about – it might be still nearer – was a force of the enemy, the numbers unknown. It was this uncertainty as to its numbers and position that accounted for the man's presence in that lonely spot; he was a young officer of a Federal infantry regiment and his business there was to guard his sleeping comrades in the camp against a surprise. He was in command of a detachment of men constituting a picket-guard. These men he had stationed just at nightfall in an irregular line, determined by the nature of the ground, several hundred yards in front of where he now sat. The line ran through the forest, among the rocks and laurel thickets, the men fifteen or twenty paces apart, all in concealment and under injunction of strict silence and unremitting vigilance. In four hours, if nothing occurred, they would be relieved by a fresh detachment from the reserve now resting in care of its captain some distance away to the left and rear. Before stationing his men the young officer of whom we are writing had pointed out to his two sergeants the spot at which he would be found if it should be necessary to consult him, or if his presence at the front line should be required.

It was a quiet enough spot – the fork of an old wood road, on the two branches of which, prolonging themselves deviously forward in the dim moonlight, the sergeants were themselves stationed, a few paces in rear of the line. If driven sharply back by a sudden onset of the enemy – and pickets are not expected to make a stand after firing – the men would come into the converging roads and naturally following them to their point of intersection could be rallied and 'formed'. In his small way the author of these dispositions was something of a strategist; if Napoleon had planned as intelligently at Waterloo he would have won that memorable battle and been overthrown later.

Second-Lieutenant Brainerd Byring was a brave and efficient officer, young and comparatively inexperienced as he was in the business of killing his fellow-men. He had enlisted in the very first days of the war as a private, with no military knowledge whatever, had been made first-sergeant of his company on account of his education and engaging manner, and had been lucky enough to lose his captain by a Confederate bullet; in the resulting

promotions he had gained a commission. He had been in several engagements, such as they were – at Philippi, Rich Mountain, Carrick's Ford and
Green-Brier – and had borne himself with such gallantry as not to attract the
attention of his superior officers. The exhilaration of battle was agreeable to
him, but the sight of the dead, with their clay faces, blank eyes and stiff
bodies, which when not unnaturally shrunken were unnaturally swollen, had
always intolerably affected him. He felt toward them a kind of reasonless
antipathy that was something more than the physical and spiritual repugnance
common to us all. Doubtless this feeling was due to his unusually acute
sensibilities – his keen sense of the beautiful, which these hideous things
outraged. Whatever may have been the cause, he could not look upon a dead
body without a loathing which had in it an element of resentment. What
others have respected as the dignity of death had to him no existence – was
altogether unthinkable. Death was a thing to be hated. It was not picturesque,
it had no tender and solemn side – a dismal thing, hideous in all its manifestations and suggestions. Lieutenant Byring was a braver man than anybody
knew, for nobody knew his horror of that which he was ever ready to incur.

Having posted his men, instructed his sergeants and retired to his station,
he seated himself on a log, and with senses all alert began his vigil. For greater
ease he loosened his sword-belt and taking his heavy revolver from his holster
laid it on the log beside him. He felt very comfortable, though he hardly gave
the fact a thought, so intently did he listen for any sound from the front which
might have a menacing significance – a shout, a shot, or the footfall of one of
his sergeants coming to apprise him of something worth knowing. From the
vast, invisible ocean of moonlight overhead fell, here and there, a slender,
broken stream that seemed to splash against the intercepting branches and
trickle to earth, forming small white pools among the clumps of laurel. But
these leaks were few and served only to accentuate the blackness of his
environment, which his imagination found it easy to people with all manner of
unfamiliar shapes, menacing, uncanny or merely grotesque.

He to whom the portentous conspiracy of night and solitude and silence in
the heart of a great forest is not an unknown experience needs not to be told
what another world it all is – how even the most commonplace and familiar
objects take on another character. The trees group themselves differently;
they draw closer together, as if in fear. The very silence has another quality
than the silence of the day. And it is full of half-heard whispers – whispers
that startle – ghosts of sounds long dead. There are living sounds, too, such as
are never heard under other conditions: notes of strange night-birds, the
cries of small animals in sudden encounters with stealthy foes or in their
dreams, a rustling in the dead leaves – it may be the leap of a wood-rat, it may
be the footfall of a panther. What caused the breaking of that twig? – what
the low, alarmed twittering in that bushful of birds? There are sounds

without a name, forms without substance, translations in space of objects which have not been seen to move, movements wherein nothing is observed to change its place. Ah, children of the sunlight and the gaslight, how little you know of the world in which you live!

Surrounded at a little distance by armed and watchful friends, Byring felt utterly alone. Yielding himself to the solemn and mysterious spirit of the time and place, he had forgotten the nature of his connection with the visible and audible aspects and phases of the night. The forest was boundless; men and the habitations of men did not exist. The universe was one primeval mystery of darkness, without form and void, himself the sole, dumb questioner of its eternal secret. Absorbed in thoughts born of this mood, he suffered the time to slip away unnoted. Meantime the infrequent patches of white light lying amongst the tree-trunks had undergone changes of size, form and place. In one of them nearby, just at the roadside, his eye fell upon an object that he had not previously observed. It was almost before his face as he sat; he could have sworn that it had not before been there. It was partly covered in shadow, but he could see that it was a human figure. Instinctively he adjusted the clasp of his sword-belt and laid hold of his pistol – again he was in a world of war, by occupation an assassin.

The figure did not move. Rising, pistol in hand, he approached. The figure lay upon its back, its upper part in shadow, but standing above it and looking down upon the face, he saw that it was a dead body. He shuddered and turned from it with a feeling of sickness and disgust, resumed his seat upon the log and forgetting military prudence struck a match and lit a cigar. In the sudden blackness that followed the extinction of the flame he felt a sense of relief; he could no longer see the object of his aversion. Nevertheless, he kept his eyes in that direction until it appeared again with growing distinctness. It seemed to have moved a trifle nearer.

'Damn the thing!' he muttered. 'What does it want?'

It did not appear to be in need of anything but a soul.

Byring turned away his eyes and began humming a tune, but he broke off in the middle of a bar and looked at the dead body. Its presence annoyed him, though he could hardly have had a quieter neighbour. He was conscious, too, of a vague, indefinable feeling that was new to him. It was not fear, but rather a sense of the supernatural – in which he did not at all believe.

'I have inherited it,' he said to himself. 'I suppose it will require a thousand ages – perhaps ten thousand – for humanity to outgrow this feeling. Where and when did it originate? Away back, probably, in what is called the cradle of the human race – the plains of Central Asia. What we inherit as a superstition our barbarous ancestors must have held as a reasonable conviction. Doubtless they believed themselves justified by facts whose nature we cannot even conjecture in thinking a dead body a malign thing endowed with some strange power of mischief, with perhaps a will and a purpose to exert it. Possibly they had some awful form of religion of which that was one of the chief doctrines, sedulously taught by their priesthood, as ours teach the immortality of the soul. As the Aryans moved slowly on, to and through the Caucasus passes, and spread over Europe, new conditions of life must have resulted in the formulation of new religions. The old belief in the malevolence of the dead body was lost from the creeds and even perished from tradition, but it left its heritage of terror, which is transmitted from generation to generation – is as much a part of us as are our blood and bones.'

In following out his thought he had forgotten that which suggested it; but now his eye fell again upon the corpse. The shadow had now altogether uncovered it. He saw the sharp profile, the chin in the air, the whole face, ghastly white in the moonlight. The clothing was grey, the uniform of a Confederate soldier. The coat and waistcoat, unbuttoned, had fallen away on each side, exposing the white shirt. The chest seemed unnaturally prominent, but the abdomen had sunk in, leaving a sharp projection at the line of the lower ribs. The arms were extended, the left knee was thrust upward. The whole posture impressed Byring as having been studied with a view to the horrible.

'Bah!' he exclaimed; 'he was an actor – he knows how to be dead.'

He drew away his eyes, directing them resolutely along one of the roads leading to the front, and resumed his philosophising where he had left off.

'It may be that our Central Asian ancestors had not the custom of burial. In that case it is easy to understand their fear of the dead, who really were a menace and an evil. They bred pestilences. Children were taught to avoid the places where they lay, and to run away if by inadvertence they came near a corpse. I think, indeed, I'd better go away from this chap.'

He half rose to do so, then remembered that he had told his men in front and the officer in the rear who was to relieve him that he could at any time be found at that spot. It was a matter of pride, too. If he abandoned his post he feared they would think he feared the corpse. He was no coward and he was unwilling to incur anybody's ridicule. So he again seated himself, and to prove his courage looked boldly at the body. The right arm – the one farthest from him – was now in shadow. He could hardly see the hand which, he had before observed, lay at the root of a clump of laurel. There had been no change, a fact which gave him a certain comfort, he could not have said why. He did not at once remove his eyes; that which we do not wish to see has a strange fascination, sometimes irresistible. Of the woman who covers her eyes with her hands and looks between the fingers let it be said that the wits have dealt with her not altogether justly.

Byring suddenly became conscious of a pain in his right hand. He withdrew his eyes from his enemy and looked at it. He was grasping the hilt of his drawn sword so tightly that it hurt him. He observed, too, that he was leaning forward in a strained attitude – crouching like a gladiator ready to spring at the throat of an antagonist. His teeth were clenched and he was breathing hard. This matter was soon set right, and as his muscles relaxed and he drew a long breath he felt keenly enough the ludicrousness of the incident. It affected him to laughter. Heavens! what sound was that? What mindless devil was uttering an unholy glee in mockery of human merriment? He sprang to his feet and looked about him, not recognising his own laugh.

He could no longer conceal from himself the horrible fact of his cowardice; he was thoroughly frightened! He would have run from the spot, but his legs refused their office; they gave way beneath him and he sat again upon the log, violently trembling. His face was wet, his whole body bathed in a chill perspiration. He could not even cry out. Distinctly he heard behind him a stealthy tread, as of some wild animal, and dared not look over his shoulder. Had the soulless living joined forces with the soulless dead? – was it an animal? Ah, if he could but be assured of that! But by no effort of will could he now unfix his gaze from the face of the dead man.

I repeat that Lieutenant Byring was a brave and intelligent man. But what would you have? Shall a man cope, single-handed, with so monstrous an alliance as that of night and solitude and silence and the dead, while an incalculable host of his own ancestors shriek into the ear of his spirit their coward counsel, sing their doleful death-songs in his heart, and disarm his very blood of all its iron? The odds are too great – courage was not made for so rough use as that.

One sole conviction now had the man in possession: that the body had moved. It lay nearer to the edge of its plot of light – there could be no doubt of it. It had also moved its arms, for, look, they are both in the shadow! A breath of cold air struck Byring full in the face; the boughs of trees above him stirred and moaned. A strongly defined shadow passed across the face of the dead, left it luminous, passed back upon it and left it half obscured. The horrible thing was visibly moving! At that moment a single shot rang out upon the picket-line – a lonelier and louder, though more distant, shot than ever had been heard by mortal ear! It broke the spell of that enchanted man; it slew the silence and the solitude, dispersed the hindering host from Central Asia and released his modern manhood. With a cry like that of some great bird pouncing upon its prey he sprang forward, hot-hearted for action!

Shot after shot now came from the front. There were shoutings and confusion, hoof-beats and desultory cheers. Away to the rear, in the sleeping camp, were a singing of bugles and grumble of drums. Pushing through the thickets on either side the roads came the Federal pickets, in full retreat, firing backward at random as they ran. A straggling group that had followed back one of the roads, as instructed, suddenly sprang away into the bushes as half a hundred horsemen thundered by them, striking wildly with their sabres as they passed. At headlong speed these mounted madmen shot past the spot where Byring had sat, and vanished round an angle of the road, shouting and firing their pistols. A moment later there was a roar of musketry, followed by dropping shots – they had encountered the reserve-guard in line; and back they came in dire confusion, with here and there an empty saddle and many a maddened horse, bullet-stung, snorting and plunging with pain. It was all over – 'an affair of outposts'.

The line was re-established with fresh men, the roll called, the stragglers were reformed. The Federal commander, with a part of his staff, imperfectly clad, appeared upon the scene, asked a few questions, looked exceedingly wise and retired. After standing at arms for an hour the brigade in camp 'swore a prayer or two' and went to bed.

Early the next morning a fatigue-party, commanded by a captain and accompanied by a surgeon, searched the ground for dead and wounded. At the fork of the road, a little to one side, they found two bodies lying close together – that of a Federal officer and that of a Confederate private. The officer had died of a sword-thrust through the heart, but not, apparently, until he had inflicted upon his enemy no fewer than five dreadful wounds. The dead officer lay on his face in a pool of blood, the weapon still in his heart. They turned him on his back and the surgeon removed it.

'Gad!' said the captain – 'It is Byring!' – adding, with a glance at the other, 'They had a tough tussle.'

The surgeon was examining the sword. It was that of a line officer of Federal infantry – exactly like the one worn by the captain. It was, in fact, Byring's own. The only other weapon discovered was an undischarged revolver in the dead officer's belt.

The surgeon laid down the sword and approached the other body. It was frightfully gashed and stabbed, but there was no blood. He took hold of the left foot and tried to straighten the leg. In the effort the body was displaced. The dead do not wish to be moved – it protested with a faint, sickening odour. Where it had lain were a few maggots, manifesting an imbecile activity.

The surgeon looked at the captain. The captain looked at the surgeon.

A Jug of Syrup

This narrative begins with the death of its hero. Silas Deemer died on the 16th day of July 1874, and two days later his remains were buried. As he had been personally known to every man, woman and well-grown child in the village, the funeral, as the local newspaper phrased it, 'was largely attended'. In accordance with a custom of the time and place, the coffin was opened at the graveside and the entire assembly of friends and neighbours filed past, taking a last look at the face of the dead. And then, before the eyes of all, Silas Deemer was put into the ground. Some of the eyes were a trifle dim, but in a general way it may be said that at that interment there was lack of neither observance nor observation; Silas was indubitably dead, and none could have pointed out any ritual delinquency that would have justified him in coming back from the grave. Yet if human testimony is good for anything (and certainly it once put an end to witchcraft in and about Salem) he came back.

I forgot to state that the death and burial of Silas Deemer occurred in the little village of Hillbrook, where he had lived for thirty-one years. He had been what is known in some parts of the Union (which is admittedly a free country) as a 'merchant'; that is to to say, he kept a retail shop for the sale of such things as are commonly sold in shops of that character. His honesty had never been questioned, so far as is known, and he was held in high esteem by all. The only thing that could be urged against him by the most censorious was a too close attention to business. It was not urged against him, though many another, who manifested it in no greater degree, was less leniently judged. The business to which Silas was devoted was mostly his own – that, possibly, may have made a difference.

At the time of Deemer's death nobody could recollect a single day, Sundays excepted, that he had not passed in his 'store', since he had opened it more than a quarter-century before. His health having been perfect during all that time, he had been unable to discern any validity in whatever may or might have been urged to lure him astray from his counter; and it is related that once when he was summoned to the county seat as a witness in an important law case and did not attend, the lawyer who had the hardihood to move that he be 'admonished' was solemnly informed that the court regarded the proposal with 'surprise'. Judicial surprise being an emotion that attorneys are not commonly ambitious to arouse, the motion was hastily withdrawn and an agreement with the other side effected as to what Mr Deemer would have said if he had been there – the other side pushing its advantage to the extreme and making the supposititious testimony distinctly damaging to the interests of its proponents. In brief, it was the general feeling in all that region that Silas Deemer was the one immobile verity of Hillbrook, and that his translation in space would precipitate some dismal public ill or strenuous calamity.

Mrs Deemer and two grown daughters occupied the upper rooms of the building, but Silas had never been known to sleep elsewhere than on a cot behind the counter of the store. And there, quite by accident, he was found one night, dying, and passed away just before the time for taking down the shutters. Though speechless, he appeared conscious, and it was thought by those who knew him best that if the end had unfortunately been delayed beyond the usual hour for opening the store the effect upon him would have been deplorable.

Such had been Silas Deemer – such the fixity and invariety of his life and habit – that the village humorist (who had once attended college) was moved to bestow upon him the sobriquet of 'Old Ibidem', and, in the first issue of the local newspaper after the death, to explain without offence that Silas had taken 'a day off'. It was more than a day, but from the record it appears that well within a month Mr Deemer made it plain that he had not the leisure to be dead.

One of Hillbrook's most respected citizens was Alvan Creede, a banker. He lived in the finest house in town, kept a carriage and was a most estimable man variously. He knew something of the advantages of travel, too, having been frequently in Boston, and once, it was thought, in New York, though he modestly disclaimed that glittering distinction. The matter is mentioned here merely as a contribution to an understanding of Mr Creede's worth, for either way it is creditable to him – to his intelligence if he had put himself, even temporarily, into contact with metropolitan culture; to his candour if he had not.

One pleasant summer evening at about the hour of ten Mr Creede, entering at his garden gate, passed up the gravel walk, which looked very white in the moonlight, mounted the stone steps of his fine house and pausing a moment inserted his latchkey in the door. As he pushed this open he met his wife, who was crossing the passage from the parlour to the library. She greeted him pleasantly and pulling the door farther back held it for him to enter. Instead he turned and, looking about his feet in front of the threshold, uttered an exclamation of surprise.

'Why! – what the devil,' he said, 'has become of that jug?'

'What jug, Alvan?' his wife enquired, not very sympathetically.

'A jug of maple syrup – I brought it along from the store and set it down here to open the door. What the –'

'There, there, Alvan, please don't swear again,' said the lady, interrupting.

Hillbrook, by the way, is not the only place in Christendom where a vestigial polytheism forbids the taking in vain of the Evil One's name.

The jug of maple syrup which the easy ways of village life had permitted Hillbrook's foremost citizen to carry home from the store was not there.

'Are you quite sure, Alvan?'

'My dear, do you suppose a man does not know when he is carrying a jug? I bought that syrup at Deemer's as I was passing. Deemer himself drew it and lent me the jug, and I – '

The sentence remains to this day unfinished. Mr Creede staggered into the house, entered the parlour and dropped into an armchair, trembling in every limb. He had suddenly remembered that Silas Deemer was three weeks dead.

Mrs Creede stood by her husband, regarding him with surprise and anxiety.

'For heaven's sake,' she said, 'what ails you?'

Mr Creede's ailment having no obvious relation to the interests of the better land he did not apparently deem it necessary to expound it on that demand; he said nothing – merely stared. There were long moments of silence broken by nothing but the measured ticking of the clock, which seemed somewhat slower than usual, as if it were civilly granting them an extension of time in which to recover their wits.

'Jane, I have gone mad – that is it.' He spoke thickly and hurriedly. 'You should have told me; you must have observed my symptoms before they became so pronounced that I have observed them myself. I thought I was passing Deemer's store; it was open and lit up – that is what I thought; of course it is never open now. Silas Deemer stood at his desk behind the counter. My God, Jane, I saw him as distinctly as I see you. Remembering that you had said you wanted some maple syrup, I went in and bought some – that is all – I bought two quarts of maple syrup from Silas Deemer, who is dead and underground, but nevertheless drew that syrup from a cask and handed it to me in a jug. He talked with me, too, rather gravely, I remember, even more so than was his way, but not a word of what he said can I now recall. But I saw him – good Lord, I saw and talked with him – and he is dead! So I thought, but I'm mad, Jane, I'm as crazy as a beetle; and you have kept it from me.'

This monologue gave the woman time to collect what faculties she had.

'Alvan,' she said, 'you have given no evidence of insanity, believe me. This was undoubtedly an illusion – how should it be anything else? That would be too terrible! But there is no insanity; you are working too hard at the bank. You should not have attended the meeting of directors this evening; anyone could see that you were ill; I knew something would occur.'

It may have seemed to him that the prophecy had lagged a bit, awaiting the event, but he said nothing of that, being concerned with his own condition. He was calm now, and could think coherently.

'Doubtless the phenomenon was subjective,' he said, with a somewhat ludicrous transition to the slang of science. 'Granting the possibility of spiritual apparition and even materialisation, yet the apparition and material-isation of a half-gallon brown clay jug – a piece of coarse, heavy pottery evolved from nothing – that is hardly thinkable.'

As he finished speaking, a child ran into the room – his little daughter. She was clad in a bedgown. Hastening to her father she threw her arms about his neck, saying: 'You naughty papa, you forgot to come in and kiss me. We heard you open the gate and got up and looked out. And, papa dear, Eddy says mayn't he have the little jug when it is empty?'

As the full import of that revelation imparted itself to Alvan Creede's understanding he visibly shuddered. For the child could not have heard a word of the conversation.

The estate of Silas Deemer being in the hands of an administrator who had thought it best to dispose of the 'business', the store had been closed ever since the owner's death, the goods having been removed by another 'merchant' who had purchased them *en bloc*. The rooms above were vacant as well, for the widow and daughters had gone to another town.

On the evening immediately after Alvan Creede's adventure (which had somehow 'got out') a crowd of men, women and children thronged the sidewalk opposite the store. That the place was haunted by the spirit of the late Silas Deemer was now well known to every resident of Hillbrook, though many affected disbelief. Of these the hardiest, and in a general way the youngest, threw stones against the front of the building, the only part accessible, but carefully missed the unshuttered windows. Incredulity had not grown to malice. A few venturesome souls crossed the street and rattled the door in its frame; struck matches and held them near the window; attempted to view the black interior. Some of the spectators invited attention to their wit by shouting and groaning and challenging the ghost to a foot-race.

After a considerable time had elapsed without any manifestation, and many of the crowd had gone away, all those remaining began to observe that the interior of the store was suffused with a dim, yellow light. At this all demonstrations ceased; the intrepid souls about the door and windows fell back to the opposite side of the street and were merged in the crowd; the small boys ceased throwing stones. Nobody spoke above his breath; all whispered excitedly and pointed to the now steadily growing light. How long a time had passed since the first faint glow had been observed none could have guessed, but eventually the illumination was bright enough to reveal the whole interior of the store; and there, standing at his desk behind the counter Silas Deemer was distinctly visible!

The effect upon the crowd was marvellous. It began rapidly to melt away at both flanks, as the timid left the place. Many ran as fast as their legs would let them; others moved off with greater dignity, turning occasionally to look backward over the shoulder. At last a score or more, mostly men, remained where they were, speechless, staring, excited. The apparition inside gave them no attention; it was apparently occupied with a book of accounts.

Presently three men left the crowd on the sidewalk as if by a common impulse and crossed the street. One of them, a heavy man, was about to set his shoulder against the door when it opened, apparently without human agency, and the courageous investigators passed in. No sooner had they crossed the threshold than they were seen by the awed observers outside to be acting in the most unaccountable way. They thrust out their hands before them, pursued devious courses, came into violent collision with the counter, with boxes and barrels on the floor, and with one another. They turned awkwardly hither and thither and seemed trying to escape, but unable to retrace their steps. Their voices were heard in exclamations and curses. But in no way did the apparition of Silas Deemer manifest an interest in what was going on.

By what impulse the crowd was moved none ever recollected, but the entire mass – men, women, children, dogs – made a simultaneous and tumultuous rush for the entrance. They congested the doorway, pushing for precedence – resolving themselves at length into a line and moving up step by step. By some subtle spiritual or physical alchemy observation had been transmuted into action – the sightseers had become participants in the spectacle – the audience had usurped the stage.

To the only spectator remaining on the other side of the street – Alvan Creede, the banker – the interior of the store with its inpouring crowd continued in full illumination; all the strange things going on there were clearly visible. To those inside all was black darkness. It was as if each person as he was thrust in at the door had been stricken blind, and was maddened by the mischance. They groped with aimless imprecision, tried to force their way out against the current, pushed and elbowed, struck at random, fell and were trampled, rose and trampled in their turn. They seized one another by the garments, the hair, the beard – fought like animals, cursed, shouted, called one another opprobrious and obscene names. When, finally, Alvan Creede had seen the last person of the line pass into that awful tumult the light that had illuminated it was suddenly quenched and all was as black to him as to those within. He turned away and left he place.

In the early morning a curious crowd had gathered about 'Deemer's'. It was composed partly of those who had run away the night before, but now had the courage of sunshine, partly of honest folk going to their daily toil. The door of the store stood open; the place was vacant, but on the walls, the floor, the furniture, were shreds of clothing and tangles of hair. Hillbrook militant had managed somehow to pull itself out and had gone home to medicine its hurts and swear that it had been all night in bed. On the dusty desk, behind the counter, was the sales book. The entries in it, in Deemer's handwriting, had ceased on the 16th day of July, the last of his life. There was no record of a later sale to Alvan Creede.

That is the entire story – except that men's passions having subsided and reason having resumed its immemorial sway, it was confessed in Hillbrook that, considering the harmless and honourable character of his first commercial transaction under the new conditions, Silas Deemer, deceased, might properly have been suffered to resume business at the old stand without mobbing. In that judgement the local historian from whose unpublished work these facts are compiled had the thoughtfulness to signify his concurrence.

The Middle Toe of the Right Foot

ONE

It is well known that the old Manton house is haunted. In all the rural district near about, and even in the town of Marshall, a mile away, not one person of unbiased mind entertains a doubt of it; incredulity is confined to those opinionated persons who will be called 'cranks' as soon as the useful word shall have penetrated the intellectual demesne of the Marshall *Advance*. The evidence that the house is haunted is of two kinds: the testimony of disinterested witnesses who have had ocular proof, and that of the house itself. The former may be disregarded and ruled out on any of the various grounds of objection which may be urged against it by the ingenious; but facts within the observation of all are material and controlling.

In the first place, the Manton house has been unoccupied by mortals for more than ten years, and with its outbuildings is slowly falling into decay – a circumstance which in itself the judicious will hardly venture to ignore. It stands a little way off the loneliest reach of the Marshall and Harriston road, in an opening which was once a farm and is still disfigured with strips of rotting fence and half covered with brambles overrunning a stony and sterile soil long unacquainted with the plough. The house itself is in tolerably good condition, though badly weather-stained and in dire need of attention from the glazier, the smaller male population of the region having attested in the manner of its kind its disapproval of a dwelling without dwellers. It is two storeys in height, nearly square, its front pierced by a single doorway flanked on each side by a window boarded up to the very top. Corresponding windows above, not protected, serve to admit light and rain to the rooms of the upper floor. Grass and weeds grow pretty rankly all about, and a few shade trees, somewhat the worse for wind, and leaning all in one direction, seem to be making a concerted effort to run away. In short, as the Marshall town humorist explained in the columns of the *Advance*, 'the proposition that the Manton house is badly haunted is the only logical conclusion from the premises'. The fact that in this dwelling Mr Manton thought it expedient one night some ten years ago to rise and cut the throats of his wife and two small children, removing at once to another part of the country, has no doubt done its share in directing public attention to the fitness of the place for supernatural phenomena.

To this house, one summer evening, came four men in a wagon. Three of them promptly alighted, and the one who had been driving hitched the team to the only remaining post of what had been a fence. The fourth remained seated in the wagon. 'Come,' said one of his companions, approaching him, while the others moved away in the direction of the dwelling – 'this is the place.'

The man addressed did not move. 'By God!' he said harshly, 'this is a trick, and it looks to me as if you were in it.'

'Perhaps I am,' the other said, looking him straight in the face and speaking in a tone which had something of contempt in it. 'You will remember, however, that the choice of place was with your own assent left to the other side. Of course, if you are afraid of spooks – '

'I am afraid of nothing,' the man interrupted with another oath, and sprang to the ground. The two then joined the others at the door, which one of them had already opened with some difficulty, caused by rust of lock and hinge. All entered. Inside it was dark, but the man who had unlocked the door produced a candle and matches and made a light. He then unlocked a door on their right as they stood in the passage. This gave them entrance to a large, square room that the candle but dimly lighted. The floor had a thick carpeting of dust, which partly muffled their footfalls. Cobwebs were in the angles of the walls and depended from the ceiling like strips of rotting lace, making undulatory movements in the disturbed air. The room had two windows in adjoining sides, but from neither could anything be seen except the rough inner surfaces of boards a few inches from the glass. There was no fireplace, no furniture; there was nothing: besides the cobwebs and the dust, the four men were the only objects there which were not a part of the structure.

Strange enough they looked in the yellow light of the candle. The one who had so reluctantly alighted was especially spectacular – he might have been called sensational. He was of middle age, heavily built, deep chested and broad shouldered. Looking at his figure, one would have said that he had a giant's strength; at his features, that he would use it like a giant. He was clean shaven, his hair rather closely cropped and grey. His low forehead was seamed with wrinkles above the eyes, and over the nose these became vertical. The heavy black brows followed the same law, saved from meeting only by an upward turn at what would otherwise have been the point of contact. Deeply sunken beneath these, glowed in the obscure light a pair of eyes of uncertain colour, but obviously enough too small. There was something forbidding in their expression, which was not bettered by the cruel mouth and wide jaw. The nose was well enough, as noses go; one does not expect much of noses. All that was sinister in the man's face seemed accentuated by an unnatural pallor – he appeared altogether bloodless.

The appearance of the other men was sufficiently commonplace: they were such persons as one meets and forgets that he has met. All were younger than the man described, between whom and the eldest of the others, who stood apart, there was apparently no kindly feeling. They avoided looking at each other.

'Gentlemen,' said the man holding the candle and keys, 'I believe everything is right. Are you ready, Mr Rosser?'

The man standing apart from the group bowed and smiled.

'And you, Mr Grossmith?'

The heavy man bowed and scowled.

'You will be pleased to remove your outer clothing.'

Their hats, coats, waistcoats and neckwear were soon removed and thrown outside the door, in the passage. The man with the candle now nodded, and the fourth man – he who had urged Grossmith to leave the wagon – produced from the pocket of his overcoat two long, murderous-looking bowie-knives, which he drew now from their leather scabbards.

'They are exactly alike,' he said, presenting one to each of the two principals – for by this time the dullest observer would have understood the nature of this meeting. It was to be a duel to the death.

Each combatant took a knife, examined it critically near the candle and tested the strength of blade and handle across his lifted knee. Their persons were then searched in turn, each by the second of the other.

'If it is agreeable to you, Mr Grossmith,' said the man holding the light, 'you will place yourself in that corner.'

He indicated the angle of the room farthest from the door, whither Grossmith retired, his second parting from him with a grasp of the hand which had nothing of cordiality in it. In the angle nearest the door Mr Rosser stationed himself, and after a whispered consultation his second left him, joining the other near the door. At that moment the candle was suddenly extinguished, leaving all in profound darkness. This may have been done by a draught from the opened door; whatever the cause, the effect was startling.

'Gentlemen,' said a voice which sounded strangely unfamiliar in the altered condition affecting the relations of the senses – 'gentlemen, you will not move until you hear the closing of the outer door.'

A sound of trampling ensued, then the closing of the inner door; and finally the outer one closed with a concussion which shook the entire building.

A few minutes afterwards a belated farmer's boy met a light wagon which was being driven furiously towards the town of Marshall. He declared that behind the two figures on the front seat stood a third, with its hands upon the bowed shoulders of the others, who appeared to struggle vainly to free themselves from its grasp. This figure, unlike the others, was clad in white, and had undoubtedly boarded the wagon as it passed the haunted house. As the lad could boast a considerable former experience with the supernatural thereabouts his word had the weight justly due to the testimony of an expert. The story (in connection with the next day's events) eventually appeared in the *Advance*, with some slight literary embellishments and a concluding intimation that the gentlemen referred to would be allowed the use of the paper's columns for their version of the night's adventure. But the privilege remained without a claimant.

TWO

The events that led up to this 'duel in the dark' were simple enough. One evening three young men of the town of Marshall were sitting in a quiet corner of the porch of the village hotel, smoking and discussing such matters as three educated young men of a Southern village would naturally find interesting. Their names were King, Sancher and Rosser. At a little distance, within easy hearing, but taking no part in the conversation, sat a fourth. He was a stranger to the others. They merely knew that on his arrival by the stagecoach that afternoon he had written in the hotel register the name Robert Grossmith. He had not been observed to speak to anyone except the hotel clerk. He seemed, indeed, singularly fond of his own company – or, as the *personnel* of the *Advance* expressed it, 'grossly addicted to evil associations'. But then it should be said in justice to the stranger that the *personnel* was himself of a too convivial disposition fairly to judge one differently gifted, and had, moreover, experienced a slight rebuff in an effort at an 'interview'.

'I hate any kind of deformity in a woman,' said King, 'whether natural or acquired. I have a theory that any physical defect has its correlative mental and moral defect.'

'I infer, then,' said Rosser gravely, 'that a lady lacking the moral advantage of a nose would find the struggle to become Mrs King an arduous enterprise.'

'Of course you may put it that way,' was the reply; 'but, seriously, I once threw over a most charming girl on learning quite accidentally that she had suffered the amputation of a toe. My conduct was brutal if you like, but if I had married that girl I should have been miserable for life and should have made her so.'

'Whereas,' said Sancher, with a light laugh, 'by marrying a gentleman of more liberal views she escaped with a parted throat.'

'Ah, you know to whom I refer. Yes, she married Manton, but I don't know about his liberality; I'm not sure but he cut her throat because he discovered that she lacked that excellent thing in woman, the middle toe of the right foot.'

'Look at that chap!' said Rosser in a low voice, his eyes fixed upon the stranger.

'That chap' was obviously listening intently to the conversation.

'Damn his impudence!' muttered King – 'what ought we to do?'

'That's an easy one,' Rosser replied, rising. 'Sir,' he continued, addressing the stranger, 'I think it would be better if you would remove your chair to the other end of the veranda. The presence of gentlemen is evidently an unfamiliar situation to you.'

The man sprang to his feet and strode forward with clenched hands, his face white with rage. All were now standing. Sancher stepped between the belligerents.

'You are hasty and unjust,' he said to Rosser; 'this gentleman has done nothing to deserve such language.'

But Rosser would not withdraw a word. By the custom of the country and the time there could be but one outcome to the quarrel.

'I demand the satisfaction due to a gentleman,' said the stranger, who had become more calm. 'I have not an acquaintance in this region. Perhaps you, sir,' bowing to Sancher, 'will be kind enough to represent me in this matter.'

Sancher accepted the trust – somewhat reluctantly it must be confessed, for the man's appearance and manner were not at all to his liking. King, who during the colloquy had hardly removed his eyes from the stranger's face and had not spoken a word, consented with a nod to act for Rosser, and the upshot of it was that, the principals having retired, a meeting was arranged for the next evening. The nature of the arrangements has been already disclosed. The duel with knives in a dark room was once a commoner feature of south-western life than it is likely to be again. How thin a veneering of 'chivalry' covered the essential brutality of the code under which such encounters were possible we shall see.

THREE

In the blaze of a midsummer noonday the old Manton house was hardly true to its traditions. It was of the earth, earthy. The sunshine caressed it warmly and affectionately, with evident disregard of its bad reputation. The grass greening all the expanse in its front seemed to grow, not rankly, but with a natural and joyous exuberance, and the weeds blossomed quite like plants. Full of charming lights and shadows and populous with pleasant-voiced birds, the neglected shade trees no longer struggled to run away, but bent reverently beneath their burden of sun and song. Even in the glassless upper windows was an expression of peace and contentment, due to the light within. Over the stony fields the visible heat danced with a lively tremor incompatible with the gravity which is an attribute of the supernatural.

Such was the aspect under which the place presented itself to Sheriff Adams and two other men who had come out from Marshall to look at it. One of these men was Mr King, the sheriff's deputy; the other, whose name was Brewer, was a brother of the late Mrs Manton. Under a beneficent law of the state relating to property which had been for a certain period abandoned by an owner whose residence cannot be ascertained, the sheriff was legal custodian of the Manton farm and appurtenances thereunto belonging. His present visit was in mere perfunctory compliance with some order of a court in which Mr Brewer had an action to get possession of the property as heir to his deceased sister. By a mere coincidence, the visit was made on the day after the night that Deputy King had unlocked the house for another and very different purpose. His presence now was not of his own choosing: he had been ordered to accompany his superior, and at the moment could think of nothing more prudent than simulated alacrity in obedience to the command.

Carelessly opening the front door, which to his surprise was not locked, the sheriff was amazed to see, lying on the floor of the passage into which it opened, a confused heap of men's apparel. Examination showed it to consist of two hats, and the same number of coats, waistcoats and scarves, all in a remarkably good state of preservation, albeit somewhat defiled by the dust in which they lay. Mr Brewer was equally astonished, but Mr King's emotion is not on record. With a new and lively interest in his own actions the sheriff now unlatched and pushed open the door on the right, and the three entered. The room was apparently vacant – no; as their eyes became accustomed to the dimmer light something was visible in the farthest angle of the wall. It was a human figure – that of a man crouching close in the corner. Something in the attitude made the intruders halt when they had barely passed the threshold. The figure more and more clearly defined itself. The man was upon one knee, his back in the angle of the wall, his shoulders elevated to the level of his ears, his hands before his face, palms outward, the fingers spread and crooked like claws; the white face turned upward on the retracted neck had an expression of unutterable fright, the mouth half open, the eyes incredibly expanded. He was stone dead. Yet, with the exception of a bowie-knife, which had evidently fallen from his own hand, not another object was in the room.

In the thick dust that covered the floor were some confused footprints near the door and along the wall through which it opened. Along one of the adjoining walls, too, past the boarded-up windows, was the trail made by the man himself in reaching his corner. Instinctively in approaching the body the three men followed that trail. The sheriff grasped one of the out-thrown arms; it was as rigid as iron, and the application of a gentle force rocked the entire body without altering the relation of its parts. Brewer, pale with excitement, gazed intently into the distorted face. 'God of mercy!' he suddenly cried, 'it is Manton!'

'You are right,' said King, with an evident attempt at calmness: 'I knew Manton. He then wore a full beard and his hair long, but this is he.'

He might have added: 'I recognised him when he challenged Rosser. I told Rosser and Sancher who he was before we played him this horrible trick. When Rosser left this dark room at our heels, forgetting his outer clothing in the excitement, and driving away with us in his shirt sleeves – all through the discreditable proceedings we knew whom we were dealing with, murderer and coward that he was!'

But nothing of this did Mr King say. With his better light he was trying to penetrate the mystery of the man's death. That he had not once moved from the corner where he had been stationed; that his posture was that of neither attack nor defence; that he had dropped his weapon; that he had obviously perished of sheer horror of something that he *saw* – these were circumstances which Mr King's disturbed intelligence could not rightly comprehend.

Groping in intellectual darkness for a clue to his maze of doubt, his gaze, directed mechanically downward in the way of one who ponders momentous matters, fell upon something which there, in the light of day and in the presence of living companions, affected him with terror. In the dust of years that lay thick upon the floor – leading from the door by which they had entered, straight across the room to within a yard of Manton's crouching corpse – were three parallel lines of footprints – light but definite impressions of bare feet, the outer ones those of small children, the inner a woman's. From the point at which they ended they did not return; they pointed all one way. Brewer, who had observed them at the same moment, was leaning forward in an attitude of rapt attention, horribly pale.

'Look at that!' he cried, pointing with both hands at the nearest print of the woman's right foot, where she had apparently stopped and stood. 'The middle toe is missing – it was Gertrude!'

Gertrude was the late Mrs Manton, sister of Mr Brewer.

John Bartine's Watch

A Story by a Physician

'The exact time? Good God! my friend, why do you insist? One would think – but what does it matter; it is easily bedtime – isn't that near enough? But, here, if you must set your watch, take mine and see for yourself.'

With that he detached his watch – a tremendously heavy, old-fashioned one – from the chain, and handed it to me; then turned away, and walking across the room to a shelf of books, began an examination of their backs. His agitation and evident distress surprised me; they appeared reasonless. Having set my watch by his I stepped over to where he stood and said, 'Thank you.'

As he took his timepiece and reattached it to the guard I observed that his hands were unsteady. With a tact upon which I greatly prided myself, I sauntered carelessly to the sideboard and took some brandy and water; then, begging his pardon for my thoughtlessness, asked him to have some and went back to my seat by the fire, leaving him to help himself, as was our custom. He did so and presently joined me at the hearth, as tranquil as ever.

This odd little incident occurred in my apartment, where John Bartine was passing an evening. We had dined together at the club, had come home in a cab and – in short, everything had been done in the most prosaic way; and why John Bartine should break in upon the natural and established order of things to make himself spectacular with a display of emotion, apparently for his own entertainment, I could nowise understand. The more I thought of it, while his brilliant conversational gifts were commending themselves to my inattention, the more curious I grew, and of course had no difficulty in persuading myself that my curiosity was friendly solicitude. That is the disguise that curiosity usually assumes to evade resentment. So I ruined one of the finest sentences of his disregarded monologue by cutting it short without ceremony.

'John Bartine,' I said, 'you must try to forgive me if I am wrong, but with the light that I have at present I cannot concede your right to go all to pieces when asked the time o' night. I cannot admit that it is proper to experience a mysterious reluctance to look your own watch in the face and to cherish in my presence, without explanation, painful emotions which are denied to me, and which are none of my business.'

To this ridiculous speech Bartine made no immediate reply, but sat looking gravely into the fire. Fearing that I had offended him I was about to apologise and beg him to think no more about the matter, when looking me calmly in the eyes he said: 'My dear fellow, the levity of your manner does not at all disguise the hideous impudence of your demand; but happily I had already decided to tell you what you wish to know, and no manifestation of your unworthiness to hear it shall alter my decision. Be good enough to give me your attention and you shall hear all about the matter.

'This watch,' he said, 'had been in my family for three generations before it fell to me. Its original owner, for whom it was made, was my great-grandfather, Bramwell Olcott Bartine, a wealthy planter of colonial Virginia, and as staunch a Tory as ever lay awake nights contriving new kinds of maledictions for the head of Mr Washington, and new methods of aiding and abetting good King George. One day this worthy gentleman had the deep misfortune to perform for his cause a service of capital importance which was not recognised as legitimate by those who suffered its disadvantages. It does not matter what it was, but among its minor consequences was my excellent ancestor's arrest one night in his own house by a party of Mr Washington's rebels. He was permitted to say farewell to his weeping family, and was then marched away into the darkness which swallowed him up for ever. Not the slenderest clue to his fate was ever found. After the war the most diligent enquiry and the offer of large rewards failed to turn up any of his captors or any fact concerning his disappearance. He had disappeared, and that was all.'

Something in Bartine's manner that was not in his words – I hardly knew what it was – prompted me to ask: 'What is your view of the matter – of the justice of it?'

'My view of it,' he flamed out, bringing his clenched hand down upon the table as if he had been in a public-house dicing with blackguards – 'my view of it is that it was a characteristically dastardly assassination by that damned traitor Washington and his ragamuffin rebels!'

For some minutes nothing was said: Bartine was recovering his temper, and I waited. Then I said: 'Was that all?'

'No – there was something else. A few weeks after my great-grandfather's arrest his watch was found lying on the porch at the front door of his dwelling. It was wrapped in a sheet of letter paper bearing the name of Rupert Bartine, his only son, my grandfather. I am wearing that watch.'

Bartine paused. His usually restless black eyes were staring fixedly into the grate, a point of red light in each, reflected from the glowing coals. He seemed to have forgotten me. A sudden threshing of the branches of a tree outside one of the windows, and almost at the same instant a rattle of rain against the glass, recalled him to a sense of his surroundings. A storm had risen, heralded by a single gust of wind, and in a few moments the steady plash of the water on the pavement was distinctly heard. I hardly know why I relate this incident; it seemed somehow to have a certain significance and relevancy which I am unable now to discern. It at least added an element of seriousness, almost solemnity.

Bartine resumed: 'I have a singular feeling towards this watch – a kind of affection for it; I like to have it about me, though partly from its weight, and partly for a reason I shall now explain, I seldom carry it. The reason is this: Every evening when I have it with me I feel an unaccountable desire to open and consult it, even if I can think of no reason for wishing to know the time. But if I yield to it, the moment my eyes rest upon the dial I am filled with a mysterious apprehension – a sense of imminent calamity. And this is the more insupportable the nearer it is to eleven o'clock – by this watch, no matter what the actual hour may be. After the hands have registered eleven the desire to look is gone; I am entirely indifferent. Then I can consult the thing as often as I like, with no more emotion than you feel in looking at your own. Naturally I have trained myself not to look at the watch in the evening before eleven; nothing could induce me. Your insistence this evening upset me a trifle. I felt very much as I suppose an opium-eater might feel if his yearning for his special and particular kind of hell were reinforced by opportunity and advice.

'Now that is my story, and I have told it in the interest of your trumpery science; but if on any evening hereafter you observe me wearing this damnable watch, and you have the thoughtfulness to ask me the hour, I shall beg leave to put you to the inconvenience of being knocked down.'

His humour did not amuse me. I could see that in relating his delusion he was again somewhat disturbed. His concluding smile was positively ghastly, and his eyes had resumed something more than their old restlessness; they shifted hither and thither about the room with apparent aimlessness and I fancied had taken on a wild expression, such as is sometimes observed in cases of dementia. Perhaps this was my own imagination, but at any rate I was now persuaded that my friend was afflicted with a most singular and interesting monomania. Without, I trust, any abatement of my affectionate solicitude for him as a friend, I began to regard him as a patient, rich in possibilities of profitable study. Why not? Had he not described his delusion in the interests of science? Ah, poor fellow, he was doing more for science than he knew: not only his story but he himself was in evidence. I should cure him if I could, of course, but first I should make a little experiment in psychology – nay, the experiment itself might be a step in his restoration.

'That is very frank and friendly of you, Bartine,' I said cordially, 'and I'm rather proud of your confidence. It is all very odd, certainly. Do you mind showing me the watch?'

He detached it from his waistcoat, chain and all, and passed it to me without a word. The case was of gold, very thick and strong, and singularly engraved. After closely examining the dial and observing that it was nearly twelve o'clock, I opened it at the back and was interested to observe an inner case of ivory, upon which was painted a miniature portrait in that exquisite and delicate manner which was in vogue during the eighteenth century.

'Why, bless my soul!' I exclaimed, feeling a sharp artistic delight – 'how under the sun did you get that done? I thought miniature painting on ivory was a lost art.'

'That,' he replied, gravely smiling, 'is not I; it is my excellent great-grandfather, the late Bramwell Olcott Bartine Esquire of Virginia. He was younger then than later – about my age, in fact. It is said to resemble me; do you think so?'

'Resemble you? I should say so! Barring the costume, which I supposed you to have assumed out of compliment to the art – or for *vraisemblance*, so to say – and the no moustache, that portrait is you in every feature, line and expression.'

No more was said at that time. Bartine took a book from the table and began reading. I heard outside the incessant plash of the rain in the street. There were occasional hurried footfalls on the sidewalks; and once a slower, heavier tread seemed to cease at my door – a policeman, I thought, seeking shelter in the doorway. The boughs of the trees tapped significantly on the window panes, as if asking for admittance. I remember it all through these years and years of a wiser, graver life.

Seeing myself unobserved, I took the old-fashioned key that dangled from the chain and quickly turned back the hands of the watch a full hour; then, closing the case, I handed Bartine his property and saw him replace it on his person.

'I think you said,' I began, with assumed carelessness, 'that after eleven the sight of the dial no longer affects you. As it is now nearly twelve' – looking at my own timepiece – 'perhaps, if you don't resent my pursuit of proof, you will look at it now.'

He smiled good-humouredly, pulled out the watch again, opened it, and instantly sprang to his feet with a cry that heaven has not had the mercy to permit me to forget! His eyes, their blackness strikingly intensified by the pallor of his face, were fixed upon the watch, which he clutched in both hands. For some time he remained in that attitude without uttering another sound; then, in a voice that I should not have recognised as his, he said: 'Damn you! it is two minutes to eleven!'

I was not unprepared for some such outbreak, and without rising replied, calmly enough: 'I beg your pardon; I must have misread your watch in setting my own by it.'

He shut the case with a sharp snap and put the watch in his pocket. He looked at me and made an attempt to smile, but his lower lip quivered and he seemed unable to close his mouth. His hands, also, were shaking, and he thrust them, clenched, into the pockets of his sackcoat. The courageous spirit was manifestly endeavouring to subdue the coward body. The effort was too great; he began to sway from side to side, as from vertigo, and before I could spring from my chair to support him his knees gave way and he pitched awkwardly forward and fell upon his face. I sprang to assist him to rise; but when John Bartine rises we shall all rise. The post-mortem examination disclosed nothing; every organ was normal and sound. But when the body had been prepared for burial a faint dark circle was seen to have developed around the neck; at least I was so assured by several persons who said they saw it, but of my own knowledge I cannot say if that was true.

Nor can I set limitations to the law of heredity. I do not know that in the spiritual world a sentiment or emotion may not survive the heart that held it, and seek expression in a kindred life, ages removed. Surely, if I were to guess at the fate of Bramwell Olcott Bartine, I should guess that he was hanged at eleven o'clock in the evening, and that he had been allowed several hours in which to prepare for the change.

As to John Bartine, my friend, my patient for five minutes, and – heaven forgive me! – my victim for eternity, there is no more to say. He is buried, and his watch with him – I saw to that. May God rest his soul in paradise, and the soul of his Virginian ancestor, if, indeed, they are two souls.

ALGERNON BLACKWOOD

Algernon Henry Blackwood (1869–1951), novelist, born in Kent, son of Sir Arthur Blackwood and Sidney, Duchess of Manchester, was educated at Wellington College and Edinburgh University. At the age of twenty he went to Canada, where he was successively journalist, dairy-farmer, hotel-keeper, prospector, artist's model, actor and private secretary. He had a great interest in the occult and has been called 'the ghost man' because of his subjects. After two volumes of short stories, *The Empty House* (1906) and *The Listener* (1907), he made his reputation with the weird *John Silence* (1908). Other novels were *The Human Chord* (1910), *The Wave* (1916) and *Dudley and Gilderoy* (1929). *Incredible Adventures* (1914), *Tongues of Fire* (1924) and *Tales of the Uncanny and Supernatural* (1949) are collections of short stories. *Sambo and Snitch* (1927) and *Mr Cupboard* (1928) are children's books, and *Episodes Before Thirty* (1923) tells of his early roving life. He was made a CBE in 1949.

A Silent Visitation

The following events occurred on a small island of isolated position in a large Canadian lake, to whose cool waters the inhabitants of Montreal and Toronto flee for rest and recreation in the hot months. It is only to be regretted that events of such peculiar interest to the genuine student of the psychical should be entirely uncorroborated. Such unfortunately, however, is the case.

Our own party of nearly twenty had returned to Montreal that very day, and I was left in solitary possession for a week or two longer, in order to accomplish some important 'reading' for the law which I had foolishly neglected during the summer.

It was late in September, and the big trout and maskinonge were stirring themselves in the depths of the lake, and beginning slowly to move up to the surface waters as the north winds and early frosts lowered their temperature. Already the maples were crimson and gold, and the wild laughter of the loons echoed in sheltered bays that never knew their strange cry in the summer.

With a whole island to oneself, a two-storey cottage, a canoe, and only the chipmunks and the farmer's weekly visit with eggs and bread to disturb one, the opportunities for hard reading might be very great. It all depends!

The rest of the party had gone off – with many warnings to beware of Indians and not to stay late enough to be the victim of a frost that thinks nothing of forty below zero. After they had gone, the loneliness of the situation made itself unpleasantly felt. There were no other islands within six or seven miles, and though the mainland forests lay a couple of miles behind me, they stretched for a very great distance unbroken by any signs of human habitation. But, though the island was completely deserted and silent, the rocks and trees that had echoed human laughter and voices almost every hour of the day for two months could not fail to retain some memories of it all; and I was not surprised to fancy I heard a shout or a cry as I passed from rock to rock, and more than once to imagine that I heard my own name called aloud.

In the cottage there were six tiny little bedrooms divided from one another by plain unvarnished partitions of pine. A wooden bedstead, a mattress and a chair stood in each room, but I only found two mirrors, and one of these was broken.

The boards creaked a good deal as I moved about, and the signs of occupation were so recent that I could hardly believe I was alone. I half expected to find someone left behind, still trying to crowd into a box more than it would hold. The door of one room was stiff, and refused for a moment to open, and it required very little persuasion to imagine someone was holding the handle on the inside and that when it opened I should meet a pair of human eyes.

A thorough search of the floor led me to select as my own sleeping quarters a little room with a diminutive balcony over the verandah roof. The room was very small, but the bed was large, and had the best mattress of them all. It was situated directly over the sitting-room where I should live and do my 'reading', and the miniature window looked out to the rising sun. With the exception of a narrow path which led from the front door and verandah through the trees to the boat-landing, the island was densely covered with maples, hemlocks and cedars. The trees gathered in round the cottage so closely that the slightest wind made the branches scrape the roof and tap the wooden walls. A few moments after sunset the darkness became impenetrable, and ten yards beyond the glare of the lamps that shone through the sitting-room windows – of which there were four – you could not see an inch before your nose, nor move a step without running up against a tree.

The rest of that day I spent moving my belongings from my tent to the sitting-room, taking stock of the contents of the larder and chopping enough wood for the stove to last me for a week. After that, just before sunset, I went round the island a couple of times in my canoe for precaution's sake. I had never dreamed of doing this before, but when a man is alone he does things that never occur to him when he is one of a large party.

How lonely the island seemed when I landed again! The sun was down, and twilight is unknown in these northern regions. The darkness comes up at once. The canoe safely pulled up and turned over on her face, I groped my way up the little narrow pathway to the verandah. The six lamps were soon burning merrily in the front room; but in the kitchen, where I 'dined', the shadows were so gloomy, and the lamplight was so inadequate, that the stars could be seen peeping through the cracks between the rafters.

I turned in early that night. Though it was calm and there was no wind, the creaking of my bedstead and the musical gurgle of the water over the rocks below were not the only sounds that reached my ears. As I lay awake, the appalling emptiness of the house grew upon me. The corridors and vacant rooms seemed to echo innumerable footsteps, shufflings, the rustle of skirts and a constant undertone of whispering. When sleep at length over-took me, the breathings and noises, however, passed gently to mingle with the voices of my dreams.

A week passed by, and the 'reading' progressed favourably. On the tenth day of my solitude, a strange thing happened. I awoke after a good night's sleep to find myself possessed with a marked repugnance for my room. The air seemed to stifle me. The more I tried to define the cause of this dislike, the more unreasonable it appeared. There was something about the room that made me afraid. Absurd as it seems, this feeling clung to me obstinately while dressing, and more than once I caught myself shivering, and conscious of an inclination to get out of the room as quickly as possible. The more I tried to laugh it away, the more real it became; and when at last I was dressed and went out into the passage and downstairs into the kitchen, it was with feelings of relief such as I might imagine would accompany one's escape from the presence of a dangerous contagious disease.

While cooking my breakfast, I carefully recalled every night spent in the room, in the hope that I might in some way connect the dislike I now felt with some disagreeable incident that had occurred in it. But the only thing I could recall was one stormy night when I suddenly awoke and heard the boards creaking so loudly in the corridor that I was convinced there were people in the house. So certain was I of this that I had descended the stairs, gun in hand, only to find the doors and windows securely fastened, and the mice and black-beetles in sole possession of the floor. This was certainly not sufficient to account for the strength of my feelings.

The morning hours I spent in steady reading; and when I broke off in the middle of the day for a swim and luncheon, I was very much surprised, if not a little alarmed, to find that my dislike for the room had, if anything, grown stronger. Going upstairs to get a book, I experienced the most marked aversion to entering the room, and while within I was conscious all the time of an uncomfortable feeling that was half uneasiness and half apprehension. The result of it was that, instead of reading, I spent the afternoon on the water paddling and fishing, and when I got home about sundown, brought with me half a dozen delicious black bass for the supper-table and the larder.

As sleep was an important matter to me at this time, I had decided that if my aversion to the room was so strongly marked on my return as it had been before, I would move my bed down into the sitting-room, and sleep there. This was, I argued, in no sense a concession to an absurd and fanciful fear, but simply a precaution to ensure a good night's sleep. A bad night involved the loss of the next day's reading – a loss I was not prepared to incur.

I accordingly moved my bed downstairs into a corner of the sitting-room facing the door, and was moreover uncommonly glad when the operation was completed, and the door of the bedroom closed finally upon the shadows, the silence and the strange *fear* that shared the room with them.

The croaking stroke of the kitchen clock sounded the hour of eight as I finished washing up my few dishes and, closing the kitchen door behind me, passed into the front room. All the lamps were lit, and their reflectors, which I had polished up during the day, threw a blaze of light into the room.

Outside the night was still and warm. Not a breath of air was stirring; the waves were silent, the trees motionless and heavy clouds hung like an oppressive curtain over the heavens. The darkness seemed to have rolled up with unusual swiftness and not the faintest glow of colour remained to show where the sun had set. There was present in the atmosphere that ominous and overwhelming silence which so often precedes the most violent storms.

I sat down to my books with my brain unusually clear, and in my heart the pleasant satisfaction of knowing that five black bass were lying in the ice-house, and that tomorrow morning the old farmer would arrive with fresh bread and eggs. I was soon absorbed in my books.

As the night wore on the silence deepened. Even the chipmunks were still; and the boards of the floors and walls ceased creaking. I read on steadily till from the gloomy shadows of the kitchen came the hoarse sound of the clock striking nine. How loud the strokes sounded! They were like blows of a big hammer. I closed one book and opened another, feeling that I was just warming up to my work.

This, however, did not last long. I presently found that I was reading the same paragraphs over twice, simple paragraphs that did not require such effort. Then I noticed that my mind began to wander to other things, and the effort to recall my thoughts became harder with each digression. Concentration was growing momentarily more difficult. Presently I discovered that I had turned over two pages instead of one, and had not noticed my mistake until I was well down the page. This was becoming serious. What was the disturbing influence? It could not be physical fatigue. On the contrary, my mind was unusually alert, and in a more receptive condition than usual. I made a new and determined effort to read, and for a short time succeeded in giving my whole attention to my subject. But in a very few moments again I found myself leaning back in my chair, staring vacantly into space.

Something was evidently at work in my subconsciousness. There was something I had neglected to do. Perhaps the kitchen door and windows were not fastened. I accordingly went to see, and found that they were! The fire perhaps needed attention. I went in to see, and found that it was all right! I looked at the lamps, went upstairs into every bedroom in turn, and then went round the house, and even into the ice-house. Nothing was wrong; everything was in its place. Yet something *was* wrong! The conviction grew stronger and stronger within me.

When I at length settled down to my books again and tried to read, I became aware, for the first time, that the room seemed growing cold. Yet the day had been oppressively warm, and evening had brought no relief. The six big lamps, moreover, gave out heat enough to warm the room pleasantly. But a chilliness, that perhaps crept up from the lake, made itself felt in the room, and caused me to get up to close the glass door opening on to the verandah.

For a brief moment I stood looking out at the shaft of light that fell from the windows and shone some little distance down the pathway, and out for a few feet into the lake.

As I looked, I saw a canoe glide into the pathway of light and, immediately crossing it, pass out of sight again into the darkness. It was perhaps a hundred feet from the shore, and it moved swiftly.

I was surprised that a canoe should pass the island at that time of night, for all the summer visitors from the other side of the lake had gone home weeks before, and the island was a long way out of any line of water traffic.

My reading from this moment did not make very good progress, for somehow the picture of that canoe, gliding so dimly and swiftly across the narrow track of light on the black waters, silhouetted itself against the background of my mind with singular vividness. It kept coming between my eyes and the printed page. The more I thought about it the more surprised I became. It was of larger build than any I had seen during the past summer months, and was more like the old Indian war canoes with the high curving bows and stern and wide beam. The more I tried to read, the less success attended my efforts; and finally I closed my books and went out on the verandah to walk up and down a bit and shake the chilliness out of my bones.

The night was perfectly still, and as dark as imaginable. I stumbled down the path to the little landing wharf, where the water made the very faintest of gurgling under the timbers. The sound of a big tree falling in the mainland forest, far across the lake, stirred echoes in the heavy air, like the first guns of a distant night attack. No other sound disturbed the stillness that reigned supreme.

As I stood upon the wharf in the broad splash of light that followed me from the sitting-room windows, I saw another canoe cross the pathway of uncertain light upon the water, and disappear at once into the impenetrable gloom that lay beyond. This time I saw more distinctly than before. It was like the former canoe, a big birch-bark, with high-crested bows and stern and broad beam. It was paddled by two Indians, of whom the one in the stern – the steerer – appeared to be a very large man. I could see this very plainly; and though the second canoe was much nearer the island than the first, I judged that they were both on their way home to the Government Reservation, which was situated some fifteen miles away upon the mainland.

I was wondering in my mind what could possibly bring any Indians down to this part of the lake at such an hour of the night, when a third canoe, of precisely similar build, and also occupied by two Indians, passed silently round the end of the wharf. This time the canoe was very much nearer shore, and it suddenly flashed into my mind that the three canoes were in reality one and the same, and that only one canoe was circling the island!

This was by no means a pleasant reflection, because, if it were the correct solution of the unusual appearance of the three canoes in this lonely part of the lake at so late an hour, the purpose of the two men could only reasonably be considered to be in some way connected with myself. I had never known of the Indians attempting any violence upon the settlers who shared the wild, inhospitable country with them; at the same time, it was not beyond the region of possibility to suppose . . . But then I did not care even to think of such hideous possibilities, and my imagination immediately sought relief in all manner of other solutions to the problem, which indeed came readily enough to my mind but did not succeed in recommending themselves to my reason.

Meanwhile, by a sort of instinct, I stepped back out of the bright light in which I had hitherto been standing and waited in the deep shadow of a rock to see if the canoe would again make its appearance. Here I could see, without being seen, and the precaution seemed a wise one.

After less than five minutes the canoe, as I had anticipated, made its fourth appearance. This time it was not twenty yards from the wharf, and I saw that the Indians meant to land. I recognised the two men as those who had passed before, and the steerer was certainly an immense fellow. It was unquestionably the same canoe. There could be no longer any doubt that for some purpose of their own the men had been going round and round the island for some time, waiting for an opportunity to land. I strained my eyes to follow them in the darkness, but the night had completely swallowed them up, and not even the faintest swish of the paddles reached my ears as the Indians plied their long and powerful strokes. The canoe would be round again in a few moments, and this time it was possible that the men might land. It was well to be prepared. I knew nothing of their intentions, and two to one (when the two are big Indians!) late at night on a lonely island was not exactly my idea of pleasant intercourse.

In a corner of the sitting-room, leaning up against the back wall, stood my Marlin rifle, with ten cartridges in the magazine and one lying snugly in the greased breech. There was just time to get up to the house and take up a position of defence in that corner. Without an instant's hesitation I ran up to the verandah, carefully picking my way among the trees, so as to avoid being seen in the light. Entering the room, I shut the door leading to the verandah, and as quickly as possible turned out every one of the six lamps. To be in a room so brilliantly lighted, where my every movement could be observed from outside, while I could see nothing but impenetrable darkness at every window, was by all laws of warfare an unnecessary concession to the enemy. And this enemy, if enemy it was to be, was far too wily and dangerous to be granted any such advantages.

I stood in the corner of the room with my back against the wall, and my hand on the cold rifle-barrel. The table, covered with my books, lay between me and the door, but for the first few minutes after the lights were out the darkness was so intense that nothing could be discerned at all. Then, very gradually, the outline of the room became visible, and the framework of the windows began to shape itself dimly before my eyes.

After a few minutes the door (its upper half of glass), and the two windows that looked out upon the front verandah, became specially distinct; and I was glad that this was so, because if the Indians came up to the house I should be able to see their approach, and gather something of their plans. Nor was I mistaken, for there presently came to my ears the peculiar hollow sound of a canoe landing and being carefully dragged up over the rocks. The paddles I distinctly heard being placed underneath, and the silence that ensued thereupon I rightly interpreted to mean that the Indians were stealthily approaching the house . . .

While it would be absurd to claim that I was not alarmed – even frightened – at the gravity of the situation and its possible outcome, I speak the whole truth when I say that I was not overwhelmingly afraid for myself. I was conscious that even at this stage of the night I was passing into a psychical condition in which my sensations seemed no longer normal. Physical fear at no time entered into the nature of my feelings; and though I kept my hand upon my rifle the greater part of the night, I was all the time conscious that its assistance could be of little avail against the terrors that I had to face. More than once I seemed to feel most curiously that I was in no real sense a part of the proceedings, nor actually involved in them, but that I was playing the part of a spectator – a spectator, moreover, on a psychic rather than on a material plane. Many of my sensations that night were too vague for definite description and analysis, but the main feeling that will stay with me to the end of my days is the awful horror of it all, and the miserable sensation that if the strain had lasted a little longer than was actually the case my mind must inevitably have given way.

Meanwhile I stood still in my corner, and waited patiently for what was to come. The house was as still as the grave, but the inarticulate voices of the night sang in my ears, and I seemed to hear the blood running in my veins and dancing in my pulses.

If the Indians came to the back of the house, they would find the kitchen door and window securely fastened. They could not get in there without making considerable noise, which I was bound to hear. The only mode of getting in was by means of the door that faced me, and I kept my eyes glued on that door without taking them off for the smallest fraction of a second.

My sight adapted itself every minute better to the darkness. I saw the table that nearly filled the room and left only a narrow passage on each side. I could also make out the straight backs of the wooden chairs pressed up against it, and could even distinguish my papers and inkstand lying on the white oilcloth covering. I thought of the gay faces that had gathered round that table during the summer, and I longed for the sunlight as I had never longed for it before.

Less than three feet to my left the passageway led to the kitchen, and the stairs leading to the bedrooms above commenced in this passageway, but almost in the sitting-room itself. Through the windows I could see the dim motionless outlines of the trees: not a leaf stirred, not a branch moved.

A few moments of this awful silence, and then I was aware of a soft tread on the boards of the verandah, so stealthy that it seemed an impression directly on my brain rather than upon the nerves of hearing. Immediately afterwards a black figure darkened the glass door, and I perceived that a face was pressed against the upper panes. A shiver ran down my back, and my hair was conscious of a tendency to rise and stand at right angles to my head.

It was the figure of an Indian, broad-shouldered and immense; indeed, the largest figure of a man I have ever seen outside of a circus hall. By some power of light that seemed to generate itself in the brain, I saw the strong dark face with the aquiline nose and high cheekbones flattened against the glass. The direction of the gaze I could not determine; but faint gleams of light as the big eyes rolled round and showed their whites, told me plainly that no corner of the room escaped their searching.

For what seemed fully five minutes the dark figure stood there, with the huge shoulders bent forward so as to bring the head down to the level of the glass; while behind him, though not nearly so large, the shadowy form of the other Indian swayed to and fro like a bent tree. While I waited in an agony of suspense and agitation for their next movement little currents of icy sensation ran up and down my spine and my heart seemed alternately to stop beating and then start off again with terrifying rapidity. They must have heard its thumping and the singing of the blood in my head! Moreover, I was conscious, as I felt a cold stream of perspiration trickle down my face, of a desire to scream, to shout, to bang the walls like a child, to make a noise, or do anything that would relieve the suspense and bring things to a speedy climax.

It was probably this inclination that led me to another discovery, for when I tried to bring my rifle from behind my back to raise it and have it pointed at the door ready to fire, I found that I was powerless to move. The muscles, paralysed by this strange fear, refused to obey the will. Here indeed was a terrifying complication!

There was a faint sound of rattling at the brass knob, and the door was pushed open a couple of inches. A pause of a few seconds, and it was pushed open still further. Without a sound of footsteps that was appreciable to my ears, the two figures glided into the room, and the man behind gently closed the door after him.

They were alone with me between the four walls. Could they see me standing there, so still and straight in my corner? Had they, perhaps, already seen me? My blood surged and sang like the roll of drums in an orchestra; and though I did my best to suppress my breathing, it sounded like the rushing of wind through a pneumatic tube.

My suspense as to the next move was soon at an end – only, however, to give place to a new and keener alarm. The men had hitherto exchanged no words and no signs, but there were general indications of a movement across the room, and whichever way they went they would have to pass round the table. If they came my way they would have to pass within six inches of my person. While I was considering this very disagreeable possibility, I perceived that the smaller Indian (smaller by comparison) suddenly raised his arm and pointed to the ceiling. The other fellow raised his head and followed the direction of his companion's arm. I began to understand at last. They were going upstairs, and the room directly overhead to which they pointed had been until this night my bedroom. It was the room in which I had experienced that very morning so strange a sensation of fear, and in which, but for that, I should then have been lying asleep in the narrow bed against the window.

The Indians then began to move silently around the room; they were going upstairs, and they were coming round my side of the table. So stealthy were their movements that, but for the abnormally sensitive state of my nerves, I should never have heard them. As it was, their catlike tread was distinctly audible. Like two monstrous black cats they came round the table towards me, and for the first time I perceived that the smaller of the two dragged something along the floor behind him. As it trailed along over the floor with a soft, sweeping sound, I somehow got the impression that it was a large dead thing with outstretched wings, or a large, spreading cedar branch. Whatever it was, I was unable to see it even in outline, and I was too terrified, even had I possessed the power over my muscles, to move my neck forward in the effort to determine its nature.

Nearer and nearer they came. The leader rested a giant hand upon the table as he moved. My lips were glued together, and the air seemed to burn in my nostrils. I tried to close my eyes, so that I might not see as they passed me; but my eyelids had stiffened, and refused to obey. Would they never get by me? Sensation seemed also to have left my legs, and it was as if I were standing on mere supports of wood or stone. Worse still, I was conscious that I was losing the power of balance, the power to stand upright, or even to lean backwards against the wall. Some force was drawing me forward, and a dizzy terror seized me that I should lose my balance and topple forward against the Indians just as they were in the act of passing me.

Even moments drawn out into hours must come to an end sometime, and almost before I knew it the figures had passed me and had their feet upon the lower step of the stairs leading to the upper bedrooms. There could not have been six inches between us, and yet I was conscious only of a current of cold air that followed them. They had not touched me, and I was convinced that they had not seen me. Even the trailing thing on the floor behind them had not touched my feet, as I had dreaded it would, and on such an occasion as this I was grateful even for the smallest mercies.

The absence of the Indians from my immediate neighbourhood brought little sense of relief. I stood shivering and shuddering in my corner, and, beyond being able to breathe more freely, I felt no whit less uncomfortable. Also, I was aware that a certain light, which, without apparent source or rays, had enabled me to follow their every gesture and movement, had gone out of the room with their departure. An unnatural darkness now filled the room and pervaded its every corner so that I could barely make out the positions of the windows and the glass door.

As I said before, my condition was evidently an abnormal one. The capacity for feeling surprise seemed, as in dreams, to be wholly absent. My senses recorded with unusual accuracy every smallest occurrence, but I was able to draw only the simplest deductions.

The Indians soon reached the top of the stairs, and there they halted for a moment. I had not the faintest clue as to their next movement. They appeared to hesitate. They were listening attentively. Then I heard one of them, who by the weight of his soft tread must have been the giant, cross the narrow corridor and enter the room directly overhead – my own little bedroom. But for the insistence of that unaccountable dread I had experienced there in the morning, I should at that very moment have been lying in the bed with the big Indian in the room standing beside me.

For the space of a hundred seconds there was silence, such as might have existed before the birth of sound. It was followed by a long quivering shriek of terror, which rang out into the night and ended in a short gulp before it had run its full course. At the same moment the other Indian left his place at the head of the stairs, and joined his companion in the bedroom. I heard the 'thing' trailing behind him along the floor. A thud followed, as of something heavy falling, and then all became as still and silent as before.

It was at this point that the atmosphere, surcharged all day with the electricity of a fierce storm, found relief in a dancing flash of brilliant lightning, simultaneously with a crash of loudest thunder. For five seconds every article in the room was visible to me with amazing distinctness, and through the windows I saw the tree trunks standing in solemn rows. The thunder pealed and echoed across the lake and among the distant islands, and the floodgates of heaven then opened and let out their rain in streaming torrents.

The drops fell with a swift rushing sound upon the still waters of the lake, which leaped up to meet them, and pattered with the rattle of shot on the leaves of the maples and the roof of the cottage. A moment later, and another flash, even more brilliant and of longer duration than the first, lit up the sky from zenith to horizon, and bathed the room momentarily in dazzling whiteness. I could see the rain glistening on the leaves and branches outside. The wind rose suddenly, and in less than a minute the storm that had been gathering all day burst forth in its full fury.

Above all the noisy voices of the elements, the slightest sounds in the room overhead made themselves heard, and in the few seconds of deep silence that followed the shriek of terror and pain I was aware that the movements had commenced again. The men were leaving the room and approaching the top of the stairs. A short pause, and they began to descend. Behind them, tumbling from step to step, I could hear that trailing 'thing' being dragged along. It had become ponderous!

I awaited their approach with a degree of calmness, almost of apathy, which was only explicable on the ground that after a certain point nature applies her own anaesthetic, and a merciful condition of numbness supervenes. On they came, step by step, nearer and nearer, with the shuffling sound of the burden behind growing louder as they approached.

They were already halfway down the stairs when I was galvanised afresh into a condition of terror by the consideration of a new and horrible possibility. It was the reflection that if another vivid flash of lightning were to come when the shadowy procession was in the room, perhaps when it was actually passing in front of me, I should see everything in detail, and worse, be seen myself! I could only hold my breath and wait – wait while the minutes lengthened into hours, and the procession made its slow progress round the room.

The Indians had reached the foot of the staircase. The form of the huge leader loomed in the doorway of the passage, and the burden with an ominous thud had dropped from the last step to the floor. There was a moment's pause while I saw the Indian turn and stoop to assist his companion. Then the procession moved forward again, entered the room close on my left, and began to move slowly round my side of the table. The leader was already beyond me, and his companion, dragging on the floor behind him the burden, whose confused outline I could dimly make out, was exactly in front of me, when the cavalcade came to a dead halt. At the same moment, with the strange suddenness of thunderstorms, the splash of the rain ceased altogether and the wind died away into utter silence.

For the space of five seconds my heart seemed to stop beating, and then the worst came. A double flash of lightning lit up the room and its contents with merciless vividness.

The huge Indian leader stood a few feet past me on my right. One leg was stretched forward in the act of taking a step. His immense shoulders were turned towards his companion, and in all their magnificent fierceness I saw the outline of his features. His gaze was directed upon the burden his companion was dragging along the floor; but his profile, with the big aquiline nose, high cheekbone, straight black hair and bold chin, burnt itself in that brief instant into my brain, never again to fade.

Dwarfish, compared with this gigantic figure, appeared the proportions of the other Indian, who, within twelve inches of my face, was stooping over the thing he was dragging in a position that lent to his person the additional horror of deformity. And the burden, lying upon a sweeping cedar branch which he held and dragged by a long stem, was the body of a white man. The scalp had been neatly lifted, and blood lay in a broad smear upon the cheeks and forehead.

Then, for the first time that night, the terror that had paralysed my muscles and my will lifted its unholy spell from my soul. With a loud cry I stretched out my arms to seize the big Indian by the throat, and, grasping only air, tumbled forward unconscious upon the ground.

I had recognised the body, and *the face was my own*! . . .

It was bright daylight when a man's voice recalled me to consciousness. I was lying where I had fallen, and the farmer was standing in the room with the loaves of bread in his hands. The horror of the night was still in my heart, and as the bluff settler helped me to my feet and picked up the rifle which had fallen with me, with many questions and expressions of condolence, I imagine my brief replies were neither self-explanatory nor even intelligible.

That day, after a thorough and fruitless search of the house, I left the island, and went over to spend my last ten days with the farmer; and when the time came for me to leave, the necessary reading had been accomplished, and my nerves had completely recovered their balance.

On the day of my departure the farmer started early in his big boat with my belongings to row to the point, twelve miles distant, where a little steamer ran twice a week for the accommodation of hunters. Late in the afternoon I went off in another direction in my canoe, wishing to see the place once again where I had been the victim of so strange an experience.

In due course I arrived there, and made a tour of the island. I also made a search of the little house and it was not without a curious sensation in my heart that I entered the little upstairs bedroom. There seemed nothing unusual.

Just after I re-embarked, I saw a canoe gliding ahead of me around the curve of the island. A canoe was an unusual sight at this time of the year, and this one seemed to have sprung from nowhere. Altering my course a little, I watched it disappear around the next projecting point of rock. It had high curving bows, and there were two Indians in it. I lingered with some excitement, to see if it would appear again round the other side of the island; and in less than five minutes it came into view. There were less than two hundred yards between us, and the Indians, sitting on their haunches, were paddling swiftly in my direction.

I never paddled faster in my life than I did in those next few minutes. When I turned to look again, the Indians had altered their course, and were again circling the island.

The sun was sinking behind the forests on the mainland, and the crimson-coloured clouds of sunset were reflected in the waters of the lake, when I looked round for the last time, and saw the big bark canoe and its two dusky occupants still going round the island. Then the shadows deepened rapidly; the lake grew black; and the night wind blew its first breath in my face as I turned a corner and a projecting bluff of rock hid from my view both island and canoe.

The Wood of the Dead

One summer, in my wanderings with a knapsack, I was at luncheon in the room of a wayside inn in the West Country, when the door opened and there entered an old rustic, who crossed close to my end of the table and sat himself down very quietly in the seat by the bow window. We exchanged glances, or, properly speaking, nods, for at the moment I did not actually raise my eyes to his face, so concerned was I with the important business of satisfying an appetite gained by tramping twelve miles over difficult country.

The fine warm rain of seven o'clock, which had since risen in a kind of luminous mist about the treetops, now floated far overhead in a deep blue sky, and the day was settling down into a blaze of golden light. It was one of those days peculiar to Somerset and North Devon, when the orchards shine and the meadows seem to add a radiance of their own, so brilliantly soft are the colourings of grass and foliage.

The innkeeper's daughter, a little maiden with a simple country loveliness, presently entered with a foaming pewter mug, enquired after my welfare, and went out again. Apparently she had not noticed the old man sitting in the settle by the bow window, nor had he, for his part, so much as once turned his head in our direction.

Under ordinary circumstances I should probably have given no thought to this other occupant of the room; but the fact that it was supposed to be reserved for my private use, and the singular thing that he sat looking aimlessly out of the window, with no attempt to engage me in conversation, drew my eyes more than once somewhat curiously upon him, and I soon caught myself wondering why he sat there so silently, and always with averted head.

He was, I saw, a rather bent old man in rustic dress, and the skin of his face was wrinkled like that of an apple; his corduroy trousers were caught up with a string below the knee, and he wore a sort of brown fustian jacket that was very much faded. His thin hand rested upon a stoutish stick. He wore no hat and carried none, and I noticed that his head, covered with silvery hair, was finely shaped and gave the impression of something noble.

Though rather piqued by his studied disregard of my presence, I came to the conclusion that he probably had something to do with the little hostel and had a perfect right to use this room with freedom, and I finished my luncheon without breaking the silence and then took the settle opposite to smoke a pipe before going on my way.

Through the open window came the scents of the blossoming fruit trees; the orchard was drenched in sunshine and the branches danced lazily in the breeze; the grass below fairly shone with white and yellow daisies, and the red roses climbing in profusion over the casement mingled their perfume with the sweetly penetrating odour of the sea.

It was a place to dawdle in, to lie and dream away a whole afternoon, watching the sleepy butterflies and listening to the chorus of birds which seemed to fill every corner of the sky. Indeed, I was already debating in my mind whether to linger and enjoy it all instead of taking the strenuous pathway over the hills, when the old rustic in the settle opposite suddenly turned his face towards me for the first time and began to speak.

His voice had a quiet dreamy note in it that was quite in harmony with the day and the scene, but it sounded far away, I thought, almost as though it came to me from outside, where the shadows were weaving their eternal tissue of dreams upon the garden floor. Moreover, there was no trace in it of the rough quality one might naturally have expected, and, now that I saw the full face of the speaker for the first time, I noted with something like a start that the deep, gentle eyes seemed far more in keeping with the timbre of the voice than with the rough and very countrified appearance of the clothes and manner. His voice set pleasant waves of sound in motion towards me, and the actual words, if I remember rightly, were, 'You are a stranger in these parts?' or, 'Is not this part of the country strange to you?'

There was no 'sir', nor any outward and visible sign of the deference usually paid by real country folk to the town-bred visitor, but in its place a gentleness, almost a sweetness, of polite sympathy that was far more of a compliment than either.

I answered that I was wandering on foot through a part of the country that was wholly new to me, and that I was surprised not to find a place of such idyllic loveliness marked upon my map.

'I have lived here all my life,' he said, with a sigh, 'and am never tired of coming back to it again.'

'Then you no longer live in the immediate neighbourhood?'

'I have moved,' he answered briefly, adding after a pause in which his eyes seemed to wander wistfully to the wealth of blossoms beyond the window; 'but I am almost sorry, for nowhere else have I found the sunshine lie so warmly, the flowers smell so sweetly, or the winds and streams make such tender music . . . '

His voice died away into a thin stream of sound that lost itself in the rustle of the rose-leaves climbing in at the window, for he turned his head away from me as he spoke and looked out into the garden. But it was impossible to conceal my surprise, and I raised my eyes in frank astonishment on hearing so poetic an utterance from such a figure of a man, though at the same time realising that it was not in the least inappropriate, and that, in fact, no other sort of expression could have properly been expected from him.

'I am sure you are right,' I answered at length, when it was clear he had ceased speaking; 'for there is something of enchantment here – of real fairylike enchantment – that makes me think of the visions of childhood days, before one knew anything of – of – '

I had been oddly drawn into his vein of speech, some inner force compelling me. But here the spell passed and I could not catch the thoughts that had a moment before opened a long vista before my inner vision.

'To tell you the truth,' I concluded lamely, 'the place fascinates me and I am in two minds about going farther – '

Even at this stage I remember thinking it odd that I should be talking like this with a stranger whom I met in a country inn, for it has always been one of my failings that to strangers my manner is brief to surliness. It was as though we were figures meeting in a dream, speaking without sound, obeying laws not operative in the everyday working world, and about to play with a new scale of space and time perhaps. But my astonishment passed quickly into an entirely different feeling when I became aware that the old man opposite had turned his head from the window again, and was regarding me with eyes so bright they seemed almost to shine with an inner flame. His gaze was fixed upon my face with an intense ardour, and his whole manner had suddenly become alert and concentrated. There was something about him I now felt for the first time that made little thrills of excitement run up and down my back. I met his look squarely, but with an inward tremor.

'Stay, then, a little while longer,' he said in a much lower and deeper voice than before; 'stay, and I will teach you something of the purpose of my coming.'

He stopped abruptly. I was conscious of a decided shiver.

'You have a special purpose then – in coming back?' I asked, hardly knowing what I was saying.

'To call away someone,' he went on in the same thrilling voice, 'someone who is not quite ready to come, but who is needed elsewhere for a worthier purpose.' There was a sadness in his manner that mystified me more than ever.

'You mean – ?' I began, with an unaccountable access of trembling.

'I have come for someone who must soon move, even as I have moved.'

He looked me through and through with a dreadfully piercing gaze, but I met his eyes with a full straight stare, trembling though I was, and I was aware that something stirred within me that had never stirred before, though for the life of me I could not have put a name to it, or have analysed its nature. Something lifted and rolled away. For one single second I understood clearly that the past and the future exist actually side by side in one immense present; that it was *I* who moved to and fro among shifting, protean appearances.

The old man dropped his eyes from my face, and the momentary glimpse of a mightier universe passed utterly away. Reason regained its sway over a dull, limited kingdom.

'Come tonight,' I heard the old man say, 'come to me tonight into the Wood of the Dead. Come at midnight – '

Involuntarily I clutched the arm of the settle for support, for I then felt that I was speaking with someone who knew more of the real things that are and will be, than I could ever know while in the body, working through the ordinary channels of sense – and this curious half-promise of a partial lifting of the veil had its undeniable effect upon me.

The breeze from the sea had died away outside, and the blossoms were still. A yellow butterfly floated lazily past the window. The song of the birds hushed – I smelt the sea – I smelt the perfume of heated summer air rising from fields and flowers, the ineffable scents of June and of the long days of the year – and with it, from countless green meadows beyond, came the hum of myriad summer life, children's voices, sweet pipings and the sound of water falling.

I knew myself to be on the threshold of a new order of experience – of an ecstasy. Something drew me forth with a sense of inexpressible yearning towards the being of this strange old man in the window seat, and for a moment I knew what it was to taste a mighty and wonderful sensation, and to touch the highest pinnacle of joy I have ever known. It lasted for less than a second, and was gone; but in that brief instant of time the same terrible lucidity came to me that had already shown me how the past and future exist in the present, and I realised and understood that pleasure and pain are one and the same force, for the joy I had just experienced included also all the pain I ever had felt, or ever could feel . . .

The sunshine grew to dazzling radiance, faded, passed away. The shadows paused in their dance upon the grass, deepened a moment, and then melted into air. The flowers of the fruit trees laughed with their little silvery laughter as the wind sighed over their radiant eyes the old, old tale of its personal love. Once or twice a voice called my name. A wonderful sensation of lightness and power began to steal over me.

Suddenly the door opened and the innkeeper's daughter came in. By all ordinary standards, her's was a charming country loveliness, born of the stars and wild-flowers, of moonlight shining through autumn mists upon the river and the fields; yet, by contrast with the higher order of beauty I had just momentarily been in touch with, she seemed almost ugly. How dull her eyes, how thin her voice, how vapid her smile and insipid her whole presentment.

For a moment she stood between me and the occupant of the window seat while I counted out the small change for my meal and for her services; but when, an instant later, she moved aside, I saw that the settle was empty and that there was no longer anyone in the room but our two selves.

This discovery was no shock to me; indeed, I had almost expected it, and the man had gone just as a figure goes out of a dream, causing no surprise and leaving me as part and parcel of the same dream without breaking the continuity. But, as soon as I had paid my bill and thus resumed in very practical fashion the thread of my normal consciousness, I turned to the girl and asked her if she knew the old man who had been sitting in the window seat, and what he had meant by the Wood of the Dead.

The maiden started visibly, glancing quickly round the empty room, but answering simply that she had seen no one. I described him in great detail, and then, as the description grew clearer, she turned a little pale under her pretty sunborn and said very gravely that it must have been the ghost.

'Ghost! What ghost?'

'Oh, the village ghost,' she said quietly, coming closer to my chair with a little nervous movement of genuine alarm, and adding in a lower voice, 'He comes before a death, they say!'

It was not difficult to induce the girl to talk, and the story she told me, shorn of the superstition that had obviously gathered with the years round the memory of a strangely picturesque figure, was interesting and peculiar.

The inn, she said, was originally a farmhouse, occupied by a yeoman farmer, evidently of a superior, if rather eccentric, character, who had been very poor until he reached old age, when a son died suddenly in the colonies and left him an unexpected amount of money, almost a fortune.

The old man thereupon altered no whit his simple manner of living, but devoted his income entirely to the improvement of the village and to the assistance of its inhabitants; he did this quite regardless of his personal likes and dislikes, as if one and all were absolutely alike to him, objects of a genuine and impersonal benevolence. People had always been a little afraid of the man, not understanding his eccentricities, but the simple force of this love for humanity changed all that in a very short space of time; and before he died he came to be known as Father of the Village and was held in great love and veneration by all.

A short time before his end, however, he began to act queerly. He spent his money just as usefully and wisely, but the shock of sudden wealth after a life of poverty, people said, had unsettled his mind. He claimed to see things that others did not see, to hear voices and to have visions. Evidently, he was not of the harmless, foolish, visionary order, but a man of character and of great personal force, for the people became divided in their opinions, and the vicar, good man, regarded and treated him as a 'special case'. For many, his name and atmosphere became charged almost with a spiritual influence that was not of the best. People quoted texts about him; kept when possible out of his way, and avoided his house after dark. None understood him, but though the majority loved him, an element of dread and mystery became associated with his name, chiefly owing to the ignorant gossip of the few.

A grove of pine trees behind the farm – the girl pointed them out to me on the slope of the hill – he said was the Wood of the Dead, because just before anyone died in the village he saw them walk into that wood, singing. None who went in ever came out again. He often mentioned the names to his wife, who usually published them to all the inhabitants within an hour of her husband's confidence; and it was found that the people he had seen enter the wood – died. On warm summer nights he would sometimes take an old stick and wander out, hatless, under the pines, for he loved this wood, and used to say he met all his old friends there, and would one day walk in there never to return. His wife tried to break him gently off this habit, but he always had his own way; and once, when she followed and found him standing under a great pine in the thickest portion of the grove, talking earnestly to someone she could not see, he turned and rebuked her very gently, but in such a way that she never repeated the experiment: 'You should never interrupt me, Mary, when I am talking with the others; for they teach me, remember, wonderful things, and I must learn all I can before I go to join them.'

This story went like wildfire through the village, increasing with every repetition, until at length everyone was able to give an accurate description of the great veiled figures the woman declared she had seen moving among the trees where her husband stood. The innocent pine-grove now became positively haunted, and the title of 'Wood of the Dead' clung naturally as if it had been applied to it in the ordinary course of events by the compilers of the Ordnance Survey.

On the evening of his ninetieth birthday the old man went up to his wife and kissed her. His manner was loving, and very gentle, and there was something about him besides, she declared afterwards, that made her slightly in awe of him and feel that he was almost more of a spirit than a man.

He kissed her tenderly on both cheeks, but his eyes seemed to look right through her as he spoke.

'Dearest wife,' he said, 'I am saying goodbye to you, for I am now going into the Wood of the Dead, and I shall not return. Do not follow me, or send to search, but be ready soon to come upon the same journey yourself.'

The good woman burst into tears and tried to hold him, but he easily slipped from her hands, and she was afraid to follow him. Slowly she saw him cross the field in the sunshine, and then enter the cool shadows of the grove, where he disappeared from her sight.

That same night, much later, she woke to find him lying peacefully by her side in bed, with one arm stretched out towards her, *dead*. Her story was half believed, half doubted at the time, but in a very few years afterwards it evidently came to be accepted by all the countryside. A funeral service was held to which the people flocked in great numbers, and everyone approved of the sentiment which led the widow to add the words 'Father of the Village' after the usual texts which appeared upon the stone over his grave.

This, then, was the story I pieced together of the village ghost as the little innkeeper's daughter told it to me that afternoon in the parlour of the inn.

'But you're not the first to say you've seen him,' the girl concluded; 'and your description is just what we've always heard, and that window, they say, was just where he used to sit and think, and think, when he was alive, and sometimes, they say, to cry for hours together.'

'And would you feel afraid if you had seen him?' I asked, for the girl seemed strangely moved and interested in the whole story.

'I think so,' she answered timidly. 'Surely, if he spoke to me. He did speak to *you*, didn't he, sir?' she asked after a slight pause.

'He said he had come for someone.'

'Come for someone,' she repeated. 'Did he say – ' she went on falteringly.

'No, he did not say for whom,' I said quickly, noticing the sudden shadow on her face and the tremulous voice.

'Are you really sure, sir?'

'Oh, quite sure,' I answered cheerfully. 'I did not even ask him.' The girl looked at me steadily for nearly a whole minute as though there were many things she wished to tell me or to ask. But she said nothing, and presently picked up her tray from the table and walked slowly out of the room.

Instead of keeping to my original purpose and pushing on to the next village over the hills, I ordered a room to be prepared for me at the inn, and that afternoon I spent wandering about the fields and lying under the fruit trees, watching the white clouds sailing out over the sea. The Wood of the Dead I surveyed only from a distance, but in the village I visited the stone erected to the memory of the 'Father of the Village' – who was thus, evidently, no mythical personage – and saw also the monuments of his fine unselfish spirit: the schoolhouse he built, the library, the home for the aged poor and the tiny hospital.

That night, as the clock in the church tower was striking half-past eleven, I stealthily left the inn and crept through the dark orchard and over the hayfield in the direction of the hill whose southern slope was clothed with the Wood of the Dead. A genuine interest impelled me to the adventure, but I also was obliged to confess to a certain sinking in my heart as I stumbled along over the field in the darkness, for I was approaching what might prove to be the birthplace of a real country myth, and a spot already lifted by the imaginative thoughts of a considerable number of people into the region of the haunted and ill-omened.

The inn lay below me, and all round it the village clustered in a soft black shadow unrelieved by a single light. The night was moonless, yet distinctly luminous, for the stars crowded the sky. The silence of deep slumber was everywhere; so still, indeed, that every time my foot kicked against a stone I thought the sound must be heard below in the village and waken the sleepers.

I climbed the hill slowly, thinking chiefly of the strange story of the noble old man who had seized the opportunity to do good to his fellows the moment it came his way, and wondering why the causes that operate ceaselessly behind human life did not always select such admirable instruments. Once or twice a night-bird circled swiftly over my head, but the bats had long since gone to rest, and there was no other sign of life stirring.

Then, suddenly, with a singular thrill of emotion, I saw the first trees of the Wood of the Dead rise in front of me in a high black wall. Their crests stood up like giant spears against the starry sky; and though there was no perceptible movement of the air on my cheek I heard a faint, rushing sound among their branches as the night breeze passed to and fro over their countless little needles. A remote, hushed murmur rose overhead and died away again almost immediately; for in these trees the wind seems to be never absolutely at rest, and on the calmest day there is always a sort of whispering music among their branches.

For a moment I hesitated on the edge of this dark wood, and listened intently. Delicate perfumes of earth and bark stole out to meet me. Impenetrable darkness faced me. Only the consciousness that I was obeying an order, strangely given, and including a mighty privilege, enabled me to find the courage to go forward and step in boldly under the trees.

Instantly the shadows closed in upon me and 'something' came forward to meet me from the centre of the darkness. It would be easy enough to meet my imagination halfway with fact, and say that a cold hand grasped my own and led me by invisible paths into the unknown depths of the grove; but at any rate, without stumbling, and always with the positive knowledge that I was going straight towards the desired object, I pressed on confidently and securely into the wood. So dark was it that, at first, not a single star-beam pierced the roof of branches overhead; and, as we moved forward side by side, the trees shifted silently past us in long lines, row upon row, squadron upon squadron, like the units of a vast, soundless army.

And, at length, we came to a comparatively open space where the trees halted upon us for a while, and, looking up, I saw the white river of the sky beginning to yield to the influence of a new light that now seemed spreading swiftly across the heavens.

'It is the dawn coming,' said the voice at my side that I certainly recognised, but which seemed almost like a whispering from the trees, 'and we are now in the heart of the Wood of the Dead.'

We seated ourselves on a moss-covered boulder and waited the coming of the sun. With marvellous swiftness, it seemed to me, the light in the east passed into the radiance of early morning, and when the wind awoke and began to whisper in the treetops, the first rays of the risen sun fell between the trunks and rested in a circle of gold at our feet.

'Now, come with me,' whispered my companion in the same deep voice, 'for time has no existence here, and that which I would show you is already *there!*'

We trod gently and silently over the soft pine needles. Already the sun was high over our heads, and the shadows of the trees coiled closely about their feet. The wood became denser again, but occasionally we passed through little open bits where we could smell the hot sunshine and the dry, baked pine needles. Then, presently, we came to the edge of the grove, and I saw a hayfield lying in the blaze of day, and two horses basking lazily with switching tails in the shafts of a laden hay-waggon.

So complete and vivid was the sense of reality, that I remember the grateful realisation of the cool shade where we sat and looked out upon the hot world beyond.

The last pitchfork had tossed up its fragrant burden, and the great horses were already straining in the shafts after the driver, as he walked slowly in front with one hand upon their bridles. He was a stalwart fellow, with sun-burned neck and hands. Then, for the first time, I noticed, perched aloft upon the trembling throne of hay, the figure of a slim young girl. I could not see her face, but her brown hair escaped in disorder from a white sun-bonnet, and her still browner hands held a well-worn hay rake. She was laughing and talking with the driver, and he, from time to time, cast up at her ardent glances of admiration – glances that won instant smiles and soft blushes in response.

The cart presently turned into the roadway that skirted the edge of the wood where we were sitting. I watched the scene with intense interest and became so much absorbed in it that I quite forgot the manifold, strange steps by which I had been permitted to become a spectator.

'Come down and walk with me,' cried the young fellow, stopping a moment in front of the horses and opening wide his arms. 'Jump! and I'll catch you!'

'Oh, oh,' she laughed, and her voice sounded to me as the happiest, merriest laughter I had ever heard from a girl's throat. 'Oh, oh! that's all very well. But remember I'm Queen of the Hay, and I must ride!'

'Then I must come and ride beside you,' he cried, and began at once to climb up by way of the driver's seat. But, with a peal of silvery laughter, she slipped down easily over the back of the hay to escape him, and ran a little way along the road. I could see her quite clearly, and noticed the charming, natural grace of her movements, and the loving expression in her eyes as she looked over her shoulder to make sure he was following. Evidently, she did not wish to escape for long, certainly not for ever.

In two strides the big, brown swain was after her, leaving the horses to do as they pleased. Another second and his arms would have caught the slender waist and pressed the little body to his heart. But, just at that instant, the old man beside me uttered a peculiar cry. It was low and thrilling, and it went through me like a sharp sword. He had called her name – and she had heard. For a second she halted, glancing back with frightened eyes. Then, with a brief cry, the girl swerved aside and dived in swiftly among the shadows of the trees.

But the young man saw the sudden movement and cried to her passionately: 'Not that way, my love! Not that way! It's the Wood of the Dead!'

She threw a laughing glance over her shoulder at him, and the wind caught her hair and drew it out in a brown cloud under the sun. But the next minute she was close beside me, lying on the breast of my companion, and I was certain I heard the words repeatedly uttered with many sighs: 'Father, you called, and I have come. And I come willingly, for I am very, very tired.'

At any rate, so the words sounded to me, and mingled with them I seemed to catch the answer in that deep, thrilling whisper I already knew: 'And you shall sleep, my child, sleep for a long, long time, until it is time for you to begin the journey again.'

In that brief second of time I had recognised the face and voice of the innkeeper's daughter, but the next minute a dreadful wail broke from the lips of the young man, and the sky grew suddenly as dark as night, the wind rose and began to toss the branches about us, and the whole scene was swallowed up in a wave of utter blackness.

Again the chill fingers seemed to seize my hand, and I was guided by the way I had come to the edge of the wood, and crossing the hayfield still slumbering in the starlight, I crept back to the inn and went to bed.

A year later I happened to be in the same part of the country, and the memory of the strange summer vision returned to me with the added softness of distance. I went to the old village and had tea under the same orchard trees at the same inn. But the little maid of the inn did not show her face, and I took occasion to enquire of her father as to her welfare and her whereabouts.

'Married, no doubt,' I laughed, but with a strange feeling that clutched at my heart.

'No, sir,' replied the innkeeper sadly, 'not married – though she was just going to be – but dead. She got a sunstroke in the hayfields, just a few days after you were here, if I remember rightly, and she was gone from us in less than a week.'

A Suspicious Gift

Blake had been in very low water for months – almost underwater part of the time – due to circumstances he was fond of saying were no fault of his own; and as he sat writing in the 'third-floor back' of a New York boarding-house, part of his mind was busily occupied in wondering when his luck was going to turn again.

It was his room only in the sense that he paid the rent. Two friends, one a little Frenchman and the other a big Dane, shared it with him, both hoping eventually to contribute something towards expenses, but so far not having accomplished this result. They had two beds only, the third being a mattress they slept upon in turns, a week at a time. A good deal of their irregular 'feeding' consisted of oatmeal, potatoes, and sometimes eggs, all of which they cooked on a strange utensil they had contrived to fix into the gas jet. Occasionally, when dinner failed them altogether, they swallowed a little raw rice and drank hot water from the bathroom on the top of it, and then made a wild race for bed so as to get to sleep while the sensation of false repletion was still there. For sleep and hunger are slight acquaintances as they well knew. Fortunately all New York houses are supplied with hot air, and they only had to open a grating in the wall to get a plentiful if not a wholesome amount of heat.

Though loneliness in a big city is a real punishment, as they had severally learnt to their cost, their experiences, three in a small room for several months, had revealed to them horrors of quite another kind, and their nerves had suffered according to the temperament of each. But, on this particular evening, as Blake sat scribbling by the only window that was not cracked, the Dane and the Frenchman, his companions in adversity, were in wonderful luck. They had both been asked out to a restaurant to dine with a friend who also held out to one of them a chance of work and remuneration. They would not be back till late, and when they did come they were pretty sure to bring in supplies of one kind or another. For the Frenchman never could resist the offer of a glass of absinthe, and this meant that he would be able to help himself plentifully from the free-lunch counters, with which all New York bars are furnished, and to which any purchaser of a drink is entitled to help himself and devour on the spot or carry away casually in his hand for consumption elsewhere. Thousands of unfortunate men get their sole subsistence in this way in New York, and experience soon teaches where, for the price of a single drink, a man can take away almost a meal of chip potatoes, sausage, bits of bread and even eggs. The Frenchman and the Dane knew their way about, and Blake looked forward to a supper more or less substantial before pulling his mattress out of the cupboard and turning in upon the floor for the night.

Meanwhile he could enjoy a quiet and lonely evening with the room all to himself.

In the daytime he was a reporter on an evening newspaper of sensational and lying habits. His work was chiefly in the police courts; and in his spare hours at night, when not too tired or too empty, he wrote sketches and stories for the magazines that very rarely saw the light of day on their printed and paid-for sentences. On this particular occasion he was deep in a most involved tale of a psychological character, and had just worked his way into a sentence, or set of sentences, that completely baffled and muddled him.

He was fairly out of his depth, and his brain was too poorly supplied with blood to invent a way out again. The story would have been interesting had he written it simply, keeping to facts and feelings, and not diving into difficult analysis of motive and character which was quite beyond him. For it was largely autobiographical, and was meant to describe the adventures of a young Englishman who had come to grief in the usual manner on a Canadian farm, had then subsequently become bar-keeper, sub-editor on a Methodist magazine, a teacher of French and German to clerks at twenty-five cents per hour, a model for artists, a super on the stage, and, finally, a wanderer to the goldfields.

Blake scratched his head, dipped the pen in the inkpot, stared out through the blindless windows and sighed deeply. His thoughts kept wandering to food, to beefsteak and steaming vegetables. The smell of cooking that came from a lower floor through the broken windows was a constant torment to him. He pulled himself together and again attacked the problem.

' . . . for with some people,' he wrote, 'the imagination is so vivid as to be almost an extension of consciousness . . . ' But here he stuck absolutely. He was not quite sure what he meant by the words, and how to finish the sentence puzzled him into blank inaction. It was a difficult point to decide, for it seemed to come in appropriately at this point in his story, and he did not know whether to leave it as it stood, change it round a bit or take it out altogether. It might just spoil its chances of being accepted: editors were such clever men. But, to rewrite the sentence was a grind, and he was so tired and sleepy. After all, what did it matter? People who were clever would force a meaning into it; people who were not clever would pretend – he knew of no other classes of readers. He would let it stay, and go on with the action of the story. He put his head in his hands and began to think hard.

His mind soon passed from thought to reverie. He fell to wondering when his friends would find work and relieve him of the burden – he acknowledged it as such – of keeping them, and of letting another man wear his best clothes on alternate Sundays. He wondered when his 'luck' would turn. There were one or two influential people in New York whom he could go and see if he had a dress suit and the other conventional uniforms. His thoughts ran on far ahead, and at the same time, by a sort of double process, far behind as well. His home in the 'old country' rose up before him; he saw the lawn and the cedars in sunshine; he looked through the familiar windows and saw the clean, swept rooms. His story began to suffer; the psychological masterpiece would not make much progress unless he pulled up and dragged his thoughts back to the treadmill. But he no longer cared; once he had got as far as that cedar with the sunshine on it, he never could get back again. For all he cared, the troublesome sentence might run away and get into someone else's pages, or be snuffed out altogether.

There came a gentle knock at the door, and Blake started. The knock was repeated louder. Who in the world could it be at this late hour of the night? On the floor above, he remembered, there lived another Englishman, a foolish, second-rate creature, who sometimes came in and made himself objectionable with endless and silly chatter. But he was an Englishman for all that, and Blake always tried to treat him with politeness, realising that he was lonely in a strange land. But tonight, of all people in the world, he did not want to be bored with Perry's cackle, as he called it, and the 'Come in' he gave in answer to the second knock had no very cordial sound of welcome in it.

However, the door opened in response, and the man came in. Blake did not turn round at once, and the other advanced to the centre of the room, but without speaking. At once Blake knew it was not his enemy, Perry, and turned round. He saw a man of about forty standing in the middle of the carpet, but standing sideways so that he did not present a full face. He wore an overcoat buttoned up to the neck, and on the felt hat which he held in front of him fresh raindrops glistened. In his other hand he carried a small black bag. Blake gave him a good look, and came to the conclusion that he might be a secretary, or a chief clerk, or a confidential man of sorts. He was a shabby-respectable-looking person. This was the sum-total of the first impression, gained the moment his eyes took in that it was not Perry; the second impression was less pleasant, and reported at once that something was wrong.

Though otherwise young and inexperienced, Blake – thanks, or curses, to the police-court training – knew more about common criminal black-guardism than most men of fifty, and he recognised that there was some-where a suggestion of this undesirable world about the man. But there was more than this. There was something singular about him, something far out of the common, though for the life of him Blake could not say wherein it lay. The fellow was out of the ordinary, and in some very undesirable manner.

All this, that takes so long to describe, Blake saw with the first and second glance. The man at once began to speak in a quiet and respectful voice.

'Are you Mr Blake?' he asked.

'I am.'

'Mr Arthur Blake?'

'Yes.'

'Mr Arthur *Herbert* Blake?' persisted the other, with emphasis on the middle name.

'That is my full name,' Blake answered simply, adding, as he remembered his manners; 'but won't you sit down, first, please?'

The man advanced with a curious sideways motion like a crab and took a seat on the edge of the sofa. He put his hat on the floor at his feet, but still kept the bag in his hand.

'I come to you from a well-wisher,' he went on in oily tones, without lifting his eyes. Blake, in his mind, ran quickly over all the people he knew in New York who might possibly have sent such a man, while waiting for him to supply the name. But the man had come to a full stop and was waiting too.

'A well-wisher of *mine*?' repeated Blake, not knowing quite what else to say.

'Just so,' replied the other, still with his eyes on the floor. 'A well-wisher of yours.'

'A man or – ' he felt himself blushing, 'or a woman?'

'That,' said the man shortly, 'I cannot tell you.'

'You can't tell me!' exclaimed the other, wondering what was coming next, and who in the world this mysterious well-wisher could be who sent so discreet and mysterious a messenger.

'I cannot tell you the name,' replied the man firmly. 'Those are my instructions. But I bring you something from this person, and I am to give it to you, to take a receipt for it, and then to go away without answering any questions.'

Blake stared very hard. The man, however, never raised his eyes above the level of the second china knob on the chest of drawers opposite. The giving of a receipt sounded like money. Could it be that some of his influential friends had heard of his plight? There were possibilities that made his heart beat. At length, however, he found his tongue, for this strange creature was determined apparently to say nothing more until he had heard from him.

'Then, what have you got for me, please?' he asked bluntly.

By way of answer the man proceeded to open the bag. He took out a parcel wrapped loosely in brown paper, and about the size of a large book. It was tied with string, and the man seemed unnecessarily long in untying the knot. When at last the string was off and the paper unfolded, there appeared a series of smaller packages inside. The man took them out very carefully, almost as if they had been alive, Blake thought, and set them in a row upon his knees. They were slender wads of dollar bills. Blake, all in a flutter, craned his neck forward a little to try and make out their denomination. He read plainly the figures 100.

'There are ten thousand dollars here,' said the man quietly.

The other could not suppress a little cry.

'And they are for you.'

Blake simply gasped. 'Ten thousand dollars!' he repeated, a queer feeling growing up in his throat. '*Ten thousand*. Are you sure? I mean – you mean they are for *me*?' he stammered. He felt quite silly with excitement, and grew more so with every minute, as the man maintained a perfect silence. Was it not a dream? Wouldn't the man put them back in the bag presently and say it was a mistake, and they were meant for somebody else? He could not believe his eyes or his ears. Yet, in a sense, it was possible. He had read of such things in books, and even come across them in his experience of the courts – the erratic and generous philanthropist who is determined to do his good deed and to get no thanks or acknowledgment for it. Still, it seemed almost incredible. His troubles began to melt away like bubbles in the sun; he thought of the other fellows when they came in, and what he would have to tell them; he thought of the German landlady and the arrears of rent, of regular food and clean linen, and books and music, of the chance of getting into some respectable business, of – well, of as many things as it is possible to think of when excitement and surprise fling wide open the gates of the imagination.

The man, meanwhile, began quietly to count over the packages aloud from one to ten, and then to count the bills in each separate packet, also from one to ten. Yes, there were ten little heaps, each containing ten bills of a hundred-dollar denomination. That made ten thousand dollars. Blake had never seen so much money in a single lump in his life before; and for many months of privation and discomfort he had not known the 'feel' of a twenty-dollar note, much less of a hundred-dollar one. He heard them crackle under the man's fingers, and it was like crisp laughter in his ears. The bills were evidently new and unused.

But, side by side with the excitement caused by the shock of such an event, Blake's caution, acquired by a year of vivid New York experience, was meanwhile beginning to assert itself. It all seemed just a little too much out of the likely order of things to be quite right. The police courts had taught him the amazing ingenuity of the criminal mind, as well as something of the plots and devices by which the unwary are beguiled into the dark places where blackmail may be levied with impunity. New York, as a matter of fact, just at that time was literally undermined with the secret ways of the blackmailers, the green-goods men and other police-protected abominations; and the only weak point in the supposition that this was part of some such proceeding was the selection of himself – a poor newspaper reporter – as a victim. It did seem absurd, but then the whole thing was so out of the ordinary, and the thought once having entered his mind, was not so easily got rid of. Blake resolved to be very cautious.

The man meanwhile, though he never appeared to raise his eyes from the carpet, had been watching him closely all the time.

'If you will give me a receipt I'll leave the money at once,' he said, with just a vestige of impatience in his tone, as if he were anxious to bring the matter to a conclusion as soon as possible.

'But you say it is quite impossible for you to tell me the name of my well-wisher, or why *she* sends me such a large sum of money in this extraordinary way?'

'The money is sent to you because you are in need of it,' returned the other; 'and it is a present without conditions of any sort attached. You have to give me a receipt only to satisfy the sender that it has reached your hands. The money will never be asked of you again.'

Blake noticed two things from this answer: first, that the man was not to be caught into betraying the sex of the well-wisher; and secondly, that he was in some hurry to complete the transaction. For he was now giving reasons, attractive reasons, why he should accept the money and make out the receipt.

Suddenly it flashed across his mind that if he took the money and gave the receipt *before a witness*, nothing very disastrous could come of the affair. It would protect him against blackmail, if this was, after all, a plot of some sort with blackmail in it; whereas, if the man were a madman, or a criminal who was getting rid of a portion of his ill-gotten gains to divert suspicion, or if any other improbable explanation turned out to be the true one, there was no great harm done, and he could hold the money till it was claimed, or advertised for in the newspapers. His mind rapidly ran over these possibilities, though, of course, under the stress of excitement, he was unable to weigh any of them properly; then he turned to his strange visitor again and said quietly –

'I will take the money, although I must say it seems to me a very unusual transaction, and I will give you for it such a receipt as I think proper under the circumstances.'

'A proper receipt is all I want,' was the answer.

'I mean by that a receipt before a proper witness – '

'Perfectly satisfactory,' interrupted the man, his eyes still on the carpet. 'Only, it must be dated, and headed with your address here in the correct way.'

Blake could see no possible objection to this, and he at once proceeded to obtain his witness. The person he had in his mind was a Mr Barclay, who occupied the room above his own; an old gentleman who had retired from business and who, the landlady always said, was a miser, and kept large sums secreted in his room. He was, at any rate, a perfectly respectable man and would make an admirable witness to a transaction of this sort. Blake made an apology and rose to fetch him, crossing the room in front of the sofa where the man sat, in order to reach the door. As he did so, he saw for the first time the *other side* of his visitor's face, the side that had been always so carefully turned away from him.

There was a broad smear of blood down the skin from the ear to the neck. It glistened in the gaslight.

Blake never knew how he managed to smother the cry that sprang to his lips, but smother it he did. In a second he was at the door, his knees trembling, his mind in a sudden and dreadful turmoil.

His main object, so far as he could recollect afterwards, was to escape from the room as if he had noticed nothing, so as not to arouse the other's suspicions. The man's eyes were always on the carpet, and probably, Blake hoped, he had not noticed the consternation that must have been written plainly on his face. At any rate he had uttered no cry.

In another second he would have been in the passage, when suddenly he met a pair of wicked, staring eyes fixed intently and with a cunning smile upon his own. It was the other's face in the mirror calmly watching his every movement.

Instantly, all his powers of reflection flew to the winds, and he thought only upon the desirability of getting help at once. He tore upstairs, his heart in his mouth. Barclay must come to his aid. This matter was serious – perhaps horribly serious. Taking the money, or giving a receipt, or having anything at all to do with it became an impossibility. Here was crime. He felt certain of it.

In three bounds he reached the next landing and began to hammer at the old miser's door as if his very life depended on it. For a long time he could get no answer. His fists seemed to make no noise. He might have been knocking on cotton wool, and the thought dashed through his brain that it was all just like the terror of a nightmare.

Barclay, evidently, was still out, or else sound asleep. But the other simply could not wait a minute longer in suspense. He turned the handle and walked into the room. At first he saw nothing for the darkness, and made sure the owner of the room was out; but the moment the light from the passage began a little to disperse the gloom, he saw the old man, to his immense relief, lying asleep on the bed.

Blake opened the door to its widest to get more light and then walked quickly up to the bed. He now saw the figure more plainly, and noted that it was dressed and lay only upon the outside of the bed. It struck him, too, that he was sleeping in a very odd, almost an unnatural, position.

Something clutched at his heart as he looked closer. He stumbled over a chair and found the matches. Calling upon Barclay the whole time to wake up and come downstairs with him, he blundered across the floor, a dreadful thought in his mind, and lit the gas over the table. It seemed strange that there was no movement or reply to his shouting. But it no longer seemed strange when at length he turned, in the full glare of the gas, and saw the old man lying huddled up into a ghastly heap on the bed, his throat cut across from ear to ear.

And all over the carpet lay new dollar bills, crisp and clean like those he had left downstairs, here strewn about in little heaps.

For a moment Blake stood stock-still, bereft of all power of movement. The next, his courage returned, and he fled from the room and dashed downstairs, taking five steps at a time. He reached the bottom and tore along the passage to his room, determined at any rate to seize the man and prevent his escape till help came.

But when he got to the end of the little landing he found that his door had been closed. He seized the handle, fumbling with it in his violence. It felt slippery and kept turning under his fingers without opening the door, and fully half a minute passed before it yielded and let him in headlong.

At the first glance he saw the room was empty, and the man gone!

Scattered upon the carpet lay a number of the bills, and beside them, half hidden under the sofa where the man had sat, he saw a pair of gloves – thick, leather gloves – and a butcher's knife. Even from the distance where he stood the bloodstains on both were easily visible.

Dazed and confused by the terrible discoveries of the last few minutes, Blake stood in the middle of the room, overwhelmed and unable to think or move. Unconsciously he must have passed his hand over his forehead in the natural gesture of perplexity, for he noticed that the skin felt wet and sticky. His hand was covered with blood! And when he rushed in terror to the looking-glass, he saw that there was a broad red smear across his face and forehead. Then he remembered the slippery handle of the door and knew that it had been carefully moistened!

In an instant the whole plot became clear as daylight, and he was so spellbound with horror that a sort of numbness came over him and he came very near to fainting. He was in a condition of utter helplessness, and had anyone come into the room at that minute and called him by name he would simply have dropped to the floor in a heap.

'If the police were to come in now!' The thought crashed through his brain like thunder, and at the same moment, almost before he had time to appreciate a quarter of its significance, there came a loud knocking at the front door below. The bell rang with a dreadful clamour; men's voices were heard talking excitedly, and presently heavy steps began to come up the stairs in the direction of his room.

It *was* the police!

And all Blake could do was to laugh foolishly to himself – and wait till they were upon him. He could not move nor speak. He stood face to face with the evidence of his horrid crime, his hands and face smeared with the blood of his victim, and there he was standing when the police burst open the door and came noisily into the room.

'Here it is!' cried a voice he knew. 'Third-floor back! And the fellow caught red-handed!'

It was the man with the bag leading in the two policemen.

Hardly knowing what he was doing in the fearful stress of conflicting emotions, he made a step forward. But before he had time to make a second one, he felt the heavy hand of the law descend upon both shoulders at once as the two policemen moved up to seize him. At the same moment a voice of thunder cried in his ear –

'Wake up, man! Wake up! Here's the supper, and good news too!'

Blake turned with a start in his chair and saw the Dane, very red in the face, standing beside him, a hand on each shoulder, and a little farther back he saw the Frenchman leering happily at him over the end of the bed, a bottle of beer in one hand and a paper package in the other.

He rubbed his eyes, glancing from one to the other, and then got up sleepily to fix the wire arrangement on the gas jet to boil water for cooking the eggs which the Frenchman was in momentary danger of letting drop upon the floor.

Skeleton Lake: An Episode in Camp

The utter loneliness of our moose-camp on Skeleton Lake had impressed us from the beginning – in the Quebec backwoods, five days by trail and canoe from civilisation – and perhaps the singular name contributed a little to the sensation of eeriness that made itself felt in the camp circle when once the sun was down and the late October mists began rising from the lake and winding their way in among the tree trunks.

For, in these regions, all names of lakes and hills and islands have their origin in some actual event, taking either the name of a chief participant, such as Smith's Ridge, or claiming a place in the map by perpetuating some special feature of the journey or the scenery, such as Long Island, Deep Rapids or Rainy Lake.

All names thus have their meaning and are usually pretty recently acquired, while the majority are self-explanatory and suggest human and pioneer relations. Skeleton Lake, therefore, was a name full of suggestion, and though none of us knew the origin or the story of its birth, we all were conscious of a certain lugubrious atmosphere that haunted its shores and islands, and but for the evidence of recent moose tracks in its neigh-bourhood we should probably have pitched our tents elsewhere.

For several hundred miles in any direction we knew of only one other party of whites. They had journeyed up on the train with us, getting in at North Bay, and hailing from Boston way. A common goal and object had served by way of introduction. But the acquaintance had made little progress. The noisy, aggressive Yankee did not suit our fancy much as a possible neighbour, and it was only a slight intimacy between his chief guide, Jake the Swede, and one of our men that kept the thing going at all. They went on to camp on Beaver Creek, fifty miles and more to the west of us.

But that was six weeks ago, and seemed as many months, for days and nights pass slowly in these solitudes and the scale of time changes wonderfully. Our men always seemed to know by instinct pretty well 'whar them other fellows was movin' ', but in the interval no one had come across their trails, or once so much as heard their rifle shots.

Our little camp consisted of the professor, his wife, a splendid shot and keen woodswoman, and myself. We had a guide apiece, and hunted daily in pairs from before sunrise till dark.

It was our last evening in the woods, and the professor was lying in my little wedge tent, discussing the dangers of hunting alone in couples in this way. The flap of the tent hung back and let in fragrant odours of cooking over an open wood fire; everywhere there were bustle and preparation, and one canoe already lay packed with moose horns, her nose pointing southwards.

'If an accident happened to one of them,' he was saying, 'the survivor's story when he returned to camp would be entirely unsupported evidence, wouldn't it? Because, you see – '

And he went on laying down the law after the manner of professors, until I became so bored that my attention began to wander to pictures and memories of the scenes we were just about to leave: Garden Lake, with its hundred islands; the rapids out of Round Pond; the countless vistas of forest, crimson and gold in the autumn sunshine; and the starlit nights we had spent watching in cold, cramped positions for the wary moose on lonely lakes among the hills. The hum of the professor's voice in time grew more soothing. A nod or a grunt was all the reply he looked for. Fortunately, he loathed interruptions. I think I could almost have gone to sleep under his very nose; perhaps I did sleep for a brief interval.

Then it all came about so quickly, and the tragedy of it was so unexpected and painful, throwing our peaceful camp into momentary confusion, that now it all seems to have happened with the uncanny swiftness of a dream.

First, there was the abrupt ceasing of the droning voice, and then the running of quick little steps over the pine needles, and the confusion of men's voices; and the next instant the professor's wife was at the tent door, hatless, her face white, her hunting bloomers bagging at the wrong places, a rifle in her hand, and her words running into one another anyhow.

'Quick, Harry! It's Rushton. I was asleep and it woke me. Something's happened. You must deal with it!'

In a second we were outside the tent with our rifles.

'My God!' I heard the professor exclaim, as if he had first made the discovery. 'It *is* Rushton!'

I saw the guides helping – dragging – a man out of a canoe. A brief space of deep silence followed in which I heard only the waves from the canoe washing up on the sand; and then, immediately after, came the voice of a man talking with amazing rapidity and with odd gaps between his words. It was Rushton telling his story, and the tones of his voice, now whispering, now almost shouting, mixed with sobs and solemn oaths and frequent appeals to the Deity, somehow or other struck the false note at the very start, and before any of us guessed or knew anything at all. Something moved secretly between his words, a shadow veiling the stars, destroying the peace of our little camp and touching us all personally with an indefinable sense of horror and distrust.

I can see that group to this day, with all the detail of a good photograph: standing halfway between the firelight and the darkness, a slight mist rising from the lake, the frosty stars, and our men, in silence that was all sympathy, dragging Rushton across the rocks towards the camp fire. Their moccasins crunched on the sand and slipped several times on the stones beneath the weight of the limp, exhausted body, and I can still see every inch of the pared cedar branch he had used for a paddle on that lonely and dreadful journey.

But what struck me most, as it struck us all, was the limp exhaustion of his body compared to the strength of his utterance and the tearing rush of his words. A vigorous driving-power was there at work, forcing out the tale, red-hot and throbbing, full of discrepancies and the strangest contradictions; and the nature of this driving-power I first began to appreciate when they had lifted him into the circle of firelight and I saw his face, grey under the tan, terror in the eyes, tears too, hair and beard awry, and listened to the wild stream of words pouring forth without ceasing.

I think we all understood then, but it was only after many years that anyone dared to confess what he thought.

There was Matt Morris, my guide; Silver Fizz, whose real name was unknown, and who bore the title of his favourite drink; and huge Hank Milligan – all ears and kind intention; and there was Rushton, pouring out his ready-made tale, with ever-shifting eyes, turning from face to face, seeking confirmation of details none had witnessed but himself – and *one other*.

Silver Fizz was the first to recover from the shock of the thing, and to realise, with the natural sense of chivalry common to most genuine back-woodsmen, that the man was at a terrible disadvantage. At any rate, he was the first to start putting the matter to rights.

'Never mind telling it just now,' he said in a gruff voice, but with real gentleness; 'get a bite t'eat first and then let her go afterwards. Better have a horn of whisky too. It ain't all packed yet, I guess.'

'Couldn't eat or drink a thing,' cried the other. 'Good Lord, don't you see, man, I want to *talk* to someone first? I want to get it out of me to someone who can answer – answer. I've had nothing but trees to talk with for three days, and I can't carry it alone any longer. Those cursed, silent trees – I've told it 'em a thousand times. Now, just see here, it was this way. When we started out from camp – '

He looked fearfully about him, and we realised it was useless to stop him. The story was bound to come, and come it did.

Now, the story itself was nothing out of the way; such tales are told by the dozen round any campfire where men who have knocked about in the woods are in the circle. It was the way he told it that made our flesh creep. He was near the truth all along, but he was skimming it, and the skimming took off the cream that might have saved his soul.

Of course, he smothered it in words – odd words, too – melodramatic, poetic, out-of-the-way words that lie just on the edge of frenzy. Of course, too, he kept asking us each in turn, scanning our faces with those restless, frightened eyes of his, 'What would *you* have done?' 'What else could I do?' and, 'Was that *my* fault?' But that was nothing, for he was no milk-and-water fellow who dealt in hints and suggestions; he told his story boldly, forcing his conclusions upon us as if we had been so many wax cylinders of a phonograph that would repeat accurately what had been told us, and these questions I have mentioned he used to emphasise any special point that he seemed to think required such emphasis.

The fact was, however, the picture of what had actually happened was so vivid still in his own mind that it reached ours by a process of telepathy which he could not control or prevent. All through his true-false words this picture stood forth in fearful detail against the shadows behind him. He could not veil, much less obliterate, it. We knew; and, I always thought, *he knew that we knew*.

The story itself, as I have said, was sufficiently ordinary. Jake and himself, in a nine-foot canoe, had upset in the middle of a lake, and had held hands across the upturned craft for several hours, eventually cutting holes in her ribs to stick their arms through and grasp hands lest the numbness of the cold water should overcome them. They were miles from shore, and the wind was drifting them down upon a little island. But when they got within a few hundred yards of the island, they realised to their horror that they would after all drift past it.

It was then the quarrel began. Jake was for leaving the canoe and swimming. Rushton believed in waiting till they actually had passed the island and were sheltered from the wind. Then they could make the island easily by swimming, canoe and all. But Jake refused to give in, and after a short struggle – Rushton admitted there was a struggle – got free from the canoe – and disappeared *without a single cry*.

Rushton held on and proved the correctness of his theory, finally making the island, canoe and all, after being in the water over five hours. He described to us how he crawled up on to the shore and fainted at once, with his feet lying half in the water; how lost and terrified he felt upon regaining consciousness in the dark; how the canoe had drifted away and his extra-ordinary luck in finding it caught again at the end of the island by a projecting cedar branch. He told us that the little axe – another bit of real luck – had caught in the thwart when the canoe turned over, and how the little bottle in his pocket holding the emergency matches was whole and dry. He made a blazing fire and searched the island from end to end, calling upon Jake in the darkness, but getting no answer; till, finally, so many half-drowned men seemed to come crawling out of the water on to the rocks, and vanish among the shadows when he came up with them, that he lost his nerve completely and returned to lie down by the fire till the daylight came.

He then cut a bough to replace the lost paddles, and after one more useless search for his lost companion, he got into the canoe, fearing every moment he would upset again, and crossed over to the mainland. He knew roughly the position of our camping place, and after paddling day and night, and making many weary portages, without food or covering, he reached us two days later.

This, more or less, was the story, and we, knowing whereof he spoke, knew that every word was literally true, and at the same time went to the building up of a hideous and prodigious lie.

Once the recital was over, he collapsed, and Silver Fizz, after a general expression of sympathy from the rest of us, came again to the rescue.

'But now, mister, you jest *got* to eat and drink whether you've a mind to or no.'

And Matt Morris, cook that night, soon had the fried trout and bacon, and the wheat cakes and hot coffee passing round a rather silent and oppressed circle. So we ate round the fire, ravenously, as we had eaten every night for the past six weeks, but with this difference: that there was one among us who was more than ravenous – and he gorged.

In spite of all our devices he somehow kept himself the centre of observation. When his tin mug was empty, Morris instantly passed the tea-pail; when he began to mop up the bacon grease with the dough on his fork, Hank reached out for the frying pan; and the can of steaming boiled potatoes was always by his side. And there was another difference as well: he was sick, terribly sick before the meal was over, and this sudden nausea after food was more eloquent than words of what the man had passed through on his dreadful, foodless, ghost-haunted journey of forty miles to our camp. In the darkness he thought he would go crazy, he said. There were voices in the trees, and figures were always lifting themselves out of the water, or from behind boulders, to look at him and make awful signs. Jake constantly peered at him through the underbrush, and everywhere the shadows were moving, with eyes, footsteps and following shapes.

We tried hard to talk of other things, but it was no use, for he was bursting with the rehearsal of his story and refused to allow himself the chances we were so willing and anxious to grant him. After a good night's rest he might have had more self-control and better judgement, and would probably have acted differently. But, as it was, we found it impossible to help him.

Once the pipes were lit, and the dishes cleared away, it was useless to pretend any longer. The sparks from the burning logs zigzagged upwards into a sky brilliant with stars. It was all wonderfully still and peaceful, and the forest odours floated to us on the sharp autumn air. The cedar fire smelt sweet and we could just hear the gentle wash of tiny waves along the shore. All was calm, beautiful and remote from the world of men and passion. It was, indeed, a night to touch the soul, and yet, I think, none of us heeded these things. A bull-moose might almost have thrust his great head over our shoulders and have escaped unnoticed. The death of Jake the Swede, with its sinister setting, was the real presence that held the centre of the stage and compelled attention.

'You won't p'raps care to come along, mister,' said Morris, by way of a beginning; 'but I guess I'll go with one of the boys here and have a hunt for it.'

'Sure,' said Hank. 'Jake an' I done some biggish trips together in the old days, and I'll do that much for 'm.'

'It's deep water, they tell me, round them islands,' added Silver Fizz; 'but we'll find it, sure pop – if it's thar.'

They all spoke of the body as 'it'.

There was a minute or two of heavy silence, and then Rushton again burst out with his story in almost the identical words he had used before. It was almost as if he had learned it by heart. He wholly failed to appreciate the efforts of the others to let him off.

Silver Fizz rushed in, hoping to stop him, Morris and Hank closely following his lead.

'I once knew another travellin' partner of his,' he began quickly; 'used to live down Moosejaw Rapids way – '

'Is that so?' said Hank.

'Kind o' useful sort er feller,' chimed in Morris.

All the idea the men had was to stop the tongue wagging before the discrepancies became so glaring that we should be forced to take notice of them, and ask questions. But just as well try to stop an angry bull-moose on the run, or prevent Beaver Creek freezing in midwinter by throwing in pebbles near the shore. Out it came! And, though the discrepancy this time was insignificant, it somehow brought us all in a second face to face with the inevitable and dreaded climax.

'And so I tramped all over that little bit of an island, hoping he might somehow have gotten in without my knowing it, and always thinking I heard *that awful last cry of his* in the darkness – and then the night dropped down impenetrably, like a damn thick blanket out of the sky, and – '

All eyes fell away from his face. Hank poked up the logs with his boot, and Morris seized an ember in his bare fingers to light his pipe, although it was already emitting clouds of smoke. But the professor caught the ball flying.

'I thought you said he sank without a cry,' he remarked quietly, looking straight up into the frightened face opposite, and then riddling mercilessly the confused explanation that followed.

The cumulative effect of all these forces, hitherto so rigorously repressed, now made itself felt, and the circle spontaneously broke up, everybody moving at once by a common instinct. The professor's wife left the party abruptly, with excuses about an early start next morning. She first shook hands with Rushton, mumbling something about his comfort in the night.

The question of his comfort, however, devolved by force of circumstances upon myself, and he shared my tent. Just before wrapping up in my double blankets – for the night was bitterly cold – he turned and began to explain that he had a habit of talking in his sleep and hoped I would wake him if he disturbed me by doing so.

Well, he did talk in his sleep – and it disturbed me very much indeed. The anger and violence of his words remain with me to this day, and it was clear in a minute that he was living over again some portion of the scene upon the lake. I listened, horror-struck, for a moment or two, and then understood that I was face to face with one of two alternatives: I must continue an unwilling eavesdropper, or I must waken him. The former was impossible for me, yet I shrank from the latter with the greatest repugnance; and in my dilemma I saw the only way out of the difficulty and at once accepted it.

Cold though it was, I crawled stealthily out of my warm sleeping-bag and left the tent, intending to keep the old fire alight under the stars and spend the remaining hours till daylight in the open.

As soon as I was out I noticed at once another figure moving silently along the shore. It was Hank Milligan, and it was plain enough what he was doing: he was examining the holes that had been cut in the upper ribs of the canoe. He looked half ashamed when I came up with him, and mumbled something about not being able to sleep for the cold. But, there, standing together beside the overturned canoe, we both saw that the holes were far too small for a man's hand and arm and could not possibly have been cut by two men hanging on for their lives in deep water. Those holes had been made afterwards.

Hank said nothing to me and I said nothing to Hank, and presently he moved off to collect logs for the fire, which needed replenishing, for it was a piercingly cold night and there were many degrees of frost.

Three days later Hank and Silver Fizz followed with stumbling footsteps the old Indian trail that leads from Beaver Creek to the southwards. A hammock was slung between them, and it weighed heavily. Yet neither of the men complained; and, indeed, speech between them was almost nothing. Their thoughts, however, were exceedingly busy, and the terrible secret of the woods which formed their burden weighed far more heavily than the uncouth, shifting mass that lay in the swinging hammock and tugged so severely at their shoulders.

They had found 'it' in four feet of water not more than a couple of yards from the lee shore of the island. And in the back of the head was a long, terrible wound which no man could possibly have inflicted upon himself.

GEORGE BRAME

Private George Brame joined up under the Derby Scheme in 1916. He was drafted to Colchester in the 2/5th Battalion East Lancashire (Territorial) Regiment, 66th Division. The Division arrived in France early in March 1917. They took over the line on the Givenchy and Festubert front. In April, Private Brame became attached to the Royal Engineers and served in the dump at Le Fresnoy; a few weeks afterwards he was transferred to Nieuport-Baines. He rejoined his battalion in the autumn of 1917 and went over the top with them in the Passchendaele attack, during which he was rather badly wounded. He remained in hospital until April 1918, having undergone two operations. Again in France, November 1918 found him in the 1/5th East Lancashires. After the Armistice he was billeted at Gilley, Charleroi, and worked in the demobilisation office until April 1919.

On the Belgian Coast

I had not been in France more than a few weeks before I was detailed off with a permanent working party. My friend Hal was also put into this section, and our acquaintance soon developed into the richest friendship. We were constantly together until he met his death.

About a dozen of us were eventually attached to the Royal Engineers' trench-stores dumps. Our activities began at Fresnoy. For the next three months we were kept fully occupied. No short time on this job. For the whole period I was there I had only one half-day holiday. It was easy to see where the money was going and why we were spending so many millions a day. The amount of hurdles, duckboards, barbed wire, etc., we turned out of that dump was enormous. I remember asking Sergeant Myers how much we went through in a week, and he put the sum at thirty thousand pounds. Taken on the whole, my sojourn at this 'park' was fairly pleasant. I had a good billet, good food and some good friends.

Orders at last arrived that we had to leave this place, and take over the dump right on the Belgian coast. We soon realised the difference between Le Fresnoy and Nieuport-Baines. Instead of being able to work in the daytime, we had now to rush things through at night.

Well do I remember one incident which occurred shortly after we had taken over. My duty was to get materials ready for the troops in the trenches. A runner would be sent from the trenches with a chit for duckboards, hurdles, barbed wire, etc. This particular afternoon an orderly had brought a chit asking for a certain number of feet of timber 7 inches by $2\frac{1}{2}$ inches to be called for later, and I set out to get it ready for the fatigue party which would call for it at night. This timber was kept in one of the shell-shattered villas on the front, in what had formerly been a bedroom. I measured the timber and, instead of carrying the lengths down the stairs, I thought it would be easier to throw them out of the bedroom window. After sending three or four lengths out, and just as I was in the act of throwing another, I was almost blinded by a blast of lightning. I knew it was the bursting of a shell.

I have often heard it said that the shell which was meant for you always went about it quietly.

As soon as I was able to pick myself up, I rushed from that unhealthy place like one possessed, and never stopped until I reached the safety of the subterranean passage running through the cellars of the house. I was certain that Jerry would follow the first up with another, but he did not.

When I was able to take my bearings, I noticed a man running towards me who seemed to be saying something, for his lips were moving as if in speech, but I could not hear a sound. The explosion had deafened me.

'Cannot hear,' I said.

He came towards me, making a megaphone of his hands, and shouted, 'I thought of picking you up in bits.'

'Not yet,' said I; 'but it's been a near thing.'

We went out together and found the nose-cap of the shell on the ground underneath the window. I went back to the sergeant and reported the incident, still trembling through the shock, and he advised me to rest a few minutes and then carry on. I carried on.

It was the intention to make a big advance here, and if possible to drive the German army out of Ostend. The enemy was not asleep, however, and just as we had got everything ready for the push, he opened out with a vengeance. I shall never forget that terrific bombardment. I never experienced anything like it before or since. The shells were flying in all directions, heavies, lights, high explosives, armour-piercing shells of all calibres, some whistling overhead, to burst as far away as La Panne, others dropping in the village with a roar that shook the foundations of the earth.

Our only refuge was our billet, a most horrible and loathsome place – a cellar alive with cockroaches and other vermin. And there we were, cooped up like rats in a trap, waiting for we knew not what.

Hour after hour the awful bombardment raged. To venture out was certain death, for the enemy aircraft were dropping bombs and training their machine guns on to the cellars. And we were without ammunition. Evening came, and still the shells were dropping as fiercely as ever. Midnight arrived without the slightest cessation in his devilish artillery fire. The cry rang out : 'Will it never end?'

One soldier cried : 'Can't we run for it?'

'Where can we run to?' asked Sergeant Myers. 'There must be no running or moving until we receive orders to that effect' – a thing that was impossible, for we learnt afterwards that all lines of communication had been cut.

The tempest raged all through the night. No one slept; every man was waiting to be captured or slaughtered by the foe.

The enemy now changed his tactics, and in place of his high explosives, he turned upon us his new and diabolical mustard gas. The order went through the dungeons, 'Gas! All men put on your masks.' For four hours we had to keep them on.

As day was beginning to dawn, the twenty-four hours' awful tornado ceased. What a transformation met my eyes when I went out for a breath of air. Houses, theatre, casino, the church were levelled to the ground. During the day we learnt that two thousand of our lads had been slaughtered or taken prisoner. In fact, every soldier on the other side of the Yser Canal excepting one or two was rendered *hors de combat*.

The result of Jerry's attack drove us out of the village, and we attempted to establish a dump at Laitre Royale.

Every night a train of five trucks, loaded up with trees, pit-props, hurdles, elephant shelters, etc., came to the dump.

It was whilst engaged on the task of unloading the train that I lost my pal Hal. We were carrying the pickets, etc., into the dump, a matter of some twenty or thirty yards, and were making good progress with the work, for so far there had been little shelling. We were congratulating ourselves that we were going to have a quiet night when Jerry opened out.

I heard a shell coming, and before I had time to fall, the shell burst with a terrifying crash. The concussion sent me headlong over the rails. In an instant I was on my feet, and rushed off to the gable end of Laitre Royale for cover. When I got there I found that Hal and a few more of the working party were already there.

The shelling soon became violent, and it was obvious that Jerry was after the dump, for the shells were gradually closing in upon us. I turned to Hal and told him that I was going to make for the covered communication trench, which was about a hundred yards away, as I thought it would be safer there than where we were.

'I think we are better here,' said Hal. 'He will have to blow this house over before he can get us.'

'If you think you are safer here you had better stay, but I'm off for the tunnel,' and, after waiting until the next shell burst, I made for the trench. I had just got about a third of the way when I heard another shell coming which exploded some yards distant. I flung myself to the ground before it burst. Thinking I might gain the trench before another arrived, I picked myself up and made a spurt, but before I reached that harbour of refuge another was on me, and such was the effect of the concussion that it lifted me clean off my feet and pitched me over a stack of wire some three feet from the ground. I again attempted to reach the tunnel, when I heard Hal calling me.

Retracing my steps, I found my friend lying on the ground in great pain.

'What's the matter, Hal?' I enquired.

'The square-headed blighter has got me this time, George.'

'Where are you hit?'

'Right in my back.'

'Do you think you can manage to get to the trench if I help you?'

'I'll try, George.'

Stooping down, I put his arm round my neck and assisted him into the trench. How we got there I never knew, for the shelling became intense, and the shells dropped round us like hailstones. Having got him under some semblance of cover, I asked him how he felt.

'George, I am done.'

I tried to comfort him by telling him they would soon put him right when he got to hospital.

'No, Jerry's done me this time.'

Stretching out his hand and placing it into mine, he said: 'George, you have been the best pal I've had. I want you to write to my wife and mother and tell them that I died doing my duty.'

'No, no,' said I. 'But I'll write and tell them that you are wounded and that you are in hospital. What's your address?'

He motioned me to feel in his tunic pocket. I did so and took some of the letters he had there.

I could see that he was mortally wounded. Every time he spoke blood spurted out of his mouth.

'One more thing I want you to do for me,' he said.

'What's that, Hal?'

'Pray for me now.'

'I am not much used to praying, Hal,' I replied, 'but I'll do my best.'

I knelt down and offered up a simple prayer, and I was conscious that the prayer was received. My friend again seized my hand and thanked and blessed me. The stretcher bearers arrived, placed him upon it, took him to the dressing station, and I saw him no more.

After three months there, with never a rest, I was ordered to rejoin my battalion, which was about to go over at Passchendaele. When I reported to the sergeant-major, he said: 'You'll see some soldiering now.' I smiled, for I considered I had received my baptism of fire. When we went over the top the sergeant-major was miles behind the line, soldiering at forming an echelon.

We had scarcely got there before we were making ready for the grand assault. Our officer came to make an inspection of us. In my section there were ten soldiers, differing in many respects; some were taking it as an adventure; one or two were developing nerves – none more so than the lance-corporal who was supposed to be in charge of us.

The officer asked us if there was anything we required.

I replied asking if we might be allowed to give our rifles a 'pull through'. We had constantly been falling into the mud during the twelve-hours' march, owing to the terrible state of the roads, with the result that our rifles were covered with dirt.

'Oh, no,' said he. 'You have no time to do that. You must be up and over at once,'

'But who's going to lead us?' asked one of the squad. 'Surely you do not expect us to go over with Walker in charge. Look at him; he's frightened to death.'

True, poor Walker was in a bad way; his face was the picture of death. I felt sorry for him, for it was evident that he was feeling his responsibility. In the section was a soldier who had recently been reduced from corporal. The officer turned to him and asked him if he would take charge of the section. He replied that he did not wish to go over the head of the lance-corporal.

And there we stood, arguing the point as to who should lead. The situation appeared so ludicrous to me that in spite of the awful carnage that was going on around, I burst out laughing. The ex-corporal noticed me, and immediately struck a dramatic pose. Brandishing his rifle in the air, he cried, 'Follow me, boys, I'll pull you through. This is no laughing matter – it's the real thing.'

The situation was so funny, I could not help laughing louder still. Here we were, in the midst of our own barrage, and the German barrage. Shells were falling round us and taking their toll of human lives. And we were being entreated to look upon it as the 'real thing'!

The officer came to us once more, and, taking the matter into his own hands, cried out in an heroic tone, 'Follow me.'

He rushed off, pointing his revolver into the air, shouting, 'There is your objective; take it.' He then began to fire into the clouds, and it struck me he must be trying to kill skylarks. Had it not been so tragical, it would have been a farce.

We followed as best we could. We had not gone far before we had to plunge into the sodden ground. Someone gave the alarm, 'Gas!' and we struggled into our gas masks. No sooner had we got them on than the officer ordered us to take them off, as there was no gas.

We advanced in rushes, and on looking round I found we were mixed up with men of another battalion. An officer approached me and asked who I belonged to. I told him the 5th East Lancs. 'Come on,' says he, 'follow this sergeant; you will be all right.'

I kept up with the sergeant until, passing over a shell hole, I felt something like a red hot needle go through my shin. It dropped me into that hole, one foot resting on the other, and I realised that I was wounded.

The sergeant asked me what was the matter. I told him I was hit, but advised him to go on as I thought I could manage.

It was not until I tried to liberate myself that I found out what a trap I was in. The shell hole was full of mud, slime and barbed wire, and for three hours I was held there as if in a vice. I felt myself gradually being sucked under. The slime was rising higher and higher, until I found it above my waist. My cries for help were unheeded. I suppose every man had as much as he could do to look after himself.

When I was giving myself up for lost, a lad from the 4th East Lancs saw the plight I was in, and came and rescued me from that awful death. If he did not win the vc that day, he won the eternal gratitude of the soldier he had liberated.

Whilst in that hole, I heard a heavy thud, and looking up I saw a soldier crouching on the top. I told him not to stay there, as Jerry had got me there. Then I noticed that he had been hit behind the ear. He must have been killed instantly.

This soldier, who was a sergeant wearing a green flash, was of the same battalion as the soldier who came to my rescue. I pointed him out to my friend, and told him that he was killed and fell like an ox. He looked up and recognised the sergeant, then turned to me and said : 'It's Sergeant Rogers. It serves the bugger right.' I knew what he meant. I had had some myself.

The wound which I had received got me back to Blighty, and, among thousands of others that day, I counted myself very fortunate.

JOHN BUCHAN

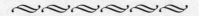

John Buchan, 1st Baron Tweedsmuir (1875–1940), Scottish author and statesman, was born in Perth, son of a minister, and educated at Glasgow University and Oxford, where be had a brilliant career and was President of the Union. In 1901 he was called to the Bar at the Middle Temple. As assistant private secretary to Lord Milner in South Africa from 1901 to 1903 he gained practical experience of statesmanship. Of his long list of adventure stories the best known are *The Watcher by the Threshold* (1902), *Prester John* (1910), *The Thirty-Nine Steps* (1915), *Greenmantle* (1916), *The Power House* (1916), *Mr Standfast* (1919), *Huntingtower* (1922) and *The Three Hostages* (1924). During the First World War he became Director of Information and wrote the history of the war in twenty-four volumes, which was later abridged. Among his other historical works were biographies of *Montrose* (1928), *Sir Walter Scott* (1932), *Cromwell* (1934) and *Augustus* (1937). His *Poems, Scots and English* appeared in 1917. From 1927 to 1935 he was Conservative MP for Scottish Universities, and in 1935, on his appointment as Governor-General of Canada, was given the GCMG and a peerage. He had already been made a Companion of Honour in 1932, and in 1938 he was Chancellor of Edinburgh University. His autobiography, *Memory Hold-the-Door*, appeared in 1940.

The Wind in the Portico

Henry Nightingale's Story

> A dry wind of the high places . . . not to fan, nor to cleanse,
> Even a full wind from those places shall come unto me.
>
> JEREMIAH 4:11-12

Nightingale was a hard man to draw. His doings with the Bedouin had become a legend, but he would as soon have talked about them as claimed to have won the war. He was a slim dark fellow about thirty-five years of age, very short-sighted, and wearing such high-powered double glasses that it was impossible to tell the colour of his eyes. This weakness made him stoop a little and peer, so that he was the strangest figure to picture in a burnous leading an army of desert tribesmen. I fancy his power came partly from his oddness, for his followers thought that the hand of Allah had been laid on him, and partly from his quick imagination and his flawless courage. After the war he had gone back to his Cambridge fellowship, declaring that, thank God, that chapter in his life was over.

As I say, he never mentioned the deeds which had made him famous. He knew his own business, and probably realised that to keep his mental balance he had to drop the curtain on what must have been the most nerve-racking four years ever spent by man. We respected his decision and kept off Arabia. It was a remark of Hannay's that drew from him the following story. Hannay was talking about his Cotswold house, which was on the Fosse Way, and saying that it always puzzled him how so elaborate a civilisation as Roman Britain could have been destroyed utterly and left no mark on the national history beyond a few roads and ruins and place-names. Peckwether, the historian, demurred, and had a good deal to say about how much the Roman tradition was woven into the Saxon culture. 'Rome only sleeps,' he said; 'she never dies.'

Nightingale nodded. 'Sometimes she dreams in her sleep and talks. Once she scared me out of my senses.'

After a good deal of pressing he produced this story. He was not much of a talker, so he wrote it out and read it to us.

There is a place in Shropshire which I do not propose to visit again. It lies between Ludlow and the hills, in a shallow valley full of woods. Its name is St

Sant, a village with a big house and park adjoining, on a stream called the Vaun, about five miles from the little town of Faxeter. They have queer names in those parts, and other things queerer than the names.

I was motoring from Wales to Cambridge at the close of the long vacation. All this happened before the war, when I had just got my fellowship and was settling down to academic work. It was a fine night in early October, with a full moon, and I intended to push on to Ludlow for supper and bed. The time was about half-past eight, the road was empty and good going, and I was trundling pleasantly along when something went wrong with my headlights. It was a small thing, and I stopped to remedy it beyond a village and just at the lodge-gates of a house.

On the opposite side of the road a carrier's cart had drawn up, and two men, who looked like indoor servants, were lifting some packages from it on to a big barrow. The moon was up, so I didn't need the feeble light of the carrier's lamp to see what they were doing. I suppose I wanted to stretch my legs for a moment, for when I had finished my job I strolled over to them. They did not hear me coming, and the carrier on his perch seemed to be asleep.

The packages were the ordinary consignments from some big shop in town. But I noticed that the two men handled them very gingerly, and that, as each was laid in the barrow, they clipped off the shop label and affixed one of their own. The new labels were odd things, large and square, with some address written on them in very black capital letters. There was nothing in that, but the men's faces puzzled me. For they seemed to do their job in a fever, longing to get it over and yet in a sweat lest they should make some mistake. Their commonplace task seemed to be for them a matter of tremendous importance. I moved so as to get a view of their faces, and I saw that they were white and strained. The two were of the butler or valet class, both elderly, and I could have sworn that they were labouring under something like fear.

I shuffled my feet to let them know of my presence and remarked that it was a fine night. They started as if they had been robbing a corpse. One of them mumbled something in reply, but the other caught a package which was slipping, and in a tone of violent alarm growled to his mate to be careful. I had a notion that they were handling explosives.

I had no time to waste, so I pushed on. That night, in my room at Ludlow, I had the curiosity to look up my map and identify the place where I had seen the men. The village was St Sant, and it appeared that the gate I had stopped at belonged to a considerable demesne called Vauncastle. That was my first visit.

At that time I was busy on a critical edition of Theocritus, for which I was making a new collation of the manuscripts. There was a variant of the

Medicean Codex in England, which nobody had seen since Gaisford, and after a good deal of trouble I found that it was in the library of a man called Dubellay. I wrote to him at his London club, and got a reply to my surprise from Vauncastle Hall, Faxeter. It was an odd letter, for you could see that he longed to tell me to go to the devil, but couldn't quite reconcile it with his conscience. We exchanged several letters, and the upshot was that he gave me permission to examine his manuscript. He did not ask me to stay, but mentioned that there was a comfortable little inn in St Sant.

My second visit began on the 27th of December, after I had been home for Christmas. We had had a week of severe frost, and then it had thawed a little; but it remained bitterly cold, with leaden skies that threatened snow. I drove from Faxeter, and as we ascended the valley I remember thinking that it was a curiously sad country. The hills were too low to be impressive, and their outlines were mostly blurred with woods; but the tops showed clear, funny little knolls of grey bent that suggested a volcanic origin. It might have been one of those backgrounds you find in Italian primitives, with all the light and colour left out. When I got a glimpse of the Vaun in the bleached meadows it looked like the 'wan water' of the Border ballads. The woods, too, had not the friendly bareness of English copses in wintertime. They remained dark and cloudy, as if they were hiding secrets. Before I reached St Sant, I decided that the landscape was not only sad, but ominous.

I was fortunate in my inn. In the single street of one-storied cottages it rose like a lighthouse, with a cheery glow from behind the red curtains of the bar parlour. The inside proved as good as the outside. I found a bedroom with a bright fire, and I dined in a wainscoted room full of preposterous old pictures of lanky hounds and hollow-backed horses. I had been rather depressed on my journey, but my spirits were raised by this comfort, and when the house produced a most respectable bottle of port I had the landlord in to drink a glass. He was an ancient man who had been a gamekeeper, with a much younger wife, who was responsible for the management. I was curious to hear something about the owner of my manuscript, but I got little from the landlord. He had been with the old squire, and had never served the present one. I heard of Dubellays in plenty – the landlord's master, who had hunted his own hounds for forty years, the Major his brother, who had fallen at Abu Klea; Parson Jack, who had had the living till he died, and of all kinds of collaterals. The 'Deblays' had been a high-spirited, open-handed stock, and much liked in the place. But of the present master of the Hall he could or would tell me nothing. The Squire was a 'great scholard', but I gathered that he followed no sport and was not a convivial soul like his predecessors. He had spent a mint of money on the house, but not many people went there. He, the landlord, had never been inside the grounds in the new master's time, though in the old days there had been hunt breakfasts on the lawn for the whole countryside, and mighty tenantry dinners. I went to bed with a clear picture in my mind of the man I was to interview on the morrow. A scholarly and autocratic recluse, who collected treasures and beautified his dwelling and probably lived in his library. I rather looked forward to meeting him, for the bonhomous sporting squire was not much in my line.

After breakfast next morning I made my way to the Hall. It was the same leaden weather, and when I entered the gates the air seemed to grow bitterer and the skies darker. The place was muffled in great trees which even in their winter bareness made a pall about it. There was a long avenue of ancient sycamores, through which one caught only rare glimpses of the frozen park. I took my bearings, and realised that I was walking nearly due south, and was gradually descending. The house must be in a hollow. Presently the trees thinned, I passed through an iron gate, came out on a big untended lawn, untidily studden with laurels and rhododendrons, and there before me was the house front.

I had expected something beautiful – an old Tudor or Queen Anne façade or a dignified Georgian portico. I was disappointed, for the front was simply mean. It was low and irregular, more like the back parts of a house, and I guessed that at some time or another the building had been turned round, and the old kitchen door made the chief entrance. I was confirmed in my conclusion by observing that the roofs rose in tiers, like one of those recessed New York skyscrapers, so that the present back parts of the building were of an impressive height.

The oddity of the place interested me, and still more its dilapidation. What on earth could the owner have spent his money on? Everything – lawn, flower-beds, paths – was neglected. There was a new stone doorway, but the walls badly needed pointing, the window woodwork had not been painted for ages, and there were several broken panes. The bell did not ring, so I was reduced to hammering on the knocker, and it must have been ten minutes before the door opened. A pale butler, one of the men I had seen at the carrier's cart the October before, stood blinking in the entrance.

He led me in without question, when I gave my name, so I was evidently expected. The hall was my second surprise. What had become of my picture of the collector? The place was small and poky, and furnished as barely as the lobby of a farmhouse. The only thing I approved was its warmth. Unlike most English country houses there seemed to be excellent heating arrangements.

I was taken into a little dark room with one window that looked out on a shrubbery, while the man went to fetch his master. My chief feeling was of gratitude that I had not been asked to stay, for the inn was paradise compared with this sepulchre. I was examining the prints on the wall, when I heard my name spoken and turned round to greet Mr Dubellay.

He was my third surprise. I had made a portrait in my mind of a fastidious old scholar, with eye-glasses on a black cord, and a finical *weltkind*-ish manner. Instead I found a man still in early middle age, a heavy fellow dressed in the roughest country tweeds. He was as untidy as his demesne, for he had not shaved that morning, his flannel collar was badly frayed, and his fingernails would have been the better for a scrubbing brush. His face was hard to describe. It was high-coloured, but the colour was not healthy; it was friendly, but it was also wary; above all, it was *unquiet*. He gave me the impression of a man whose nerves were all wrong, and who was perpetually on his guard.

He said a few civil words, and thrust a badly tied brown-paper parcel at me.

'That's your manuscript,' he said jauntily.

I was staggered. I had expected to be permitted to collate the codex in his library, and in the last few minutes had realised that the prospect was distasteful. But here was this casual owner offering me the priceless thing to take away.

I stammered my thanks, and added that it was very good of him to trust a stranger with such a treasure.

'Only as far as the inn,' he said. 'I wouldn't like to send it by post. But there's no harm in your working at it at the inn. There should be confidence among scholars.' And he gave an odd cackle of a laugh.

'I greatly prefer your plan,' I said. 'But I thought you would insist on my working at it here.'

'No, indeed,' he said earnestly. 'I shouldn't think of such a thing . . . Wouldn't do at all . . . An insult to our freemasonry . . . That's how I should regard it.'

We had a few minutes' further talk. I learned that he had inherited under the entail from a cousin, and had been just over ten years at Vauncastle. Before that he had been a London solicitor. He asked me a question or two about Cambridge – wished he had been at the University – much hampered in his work by a defective education. I was a Greek scholar? – Latin, too, he presumed. Wonderful people the Romans . . . He spoke quite freely, but all the time his queer restless eyes were darting about, and I had a strong impression that he would have liked to say something to me very different from these commonplaces – that he was longing to broach some subject but was held back by shyness or fear. He had such an odd appraising way of looking at me.

I left without his having asked me to a meal, for which I was not sorry, for I did not like the atmosphere of the place. I took a short cut over the ragged lawn, and turned at the top of the slope to look back. The house was in reality a huge pile, and I saw that I had been right and that the main building was all at the back. Was it, I wondered, like the Alhambra, which behind a front like a factory concealed a treasure-house? I saw, too, that the woodland hollow was more spacious than I had fancied. The house, as at present arranged, faced due north, and behind the south front was an open space in which I guessed that a lake might lie. Far beyond I could see in the December dimness the lift of high dark hills.

That evening the snow came in earnest, and fell continuously for the better part of two days. I banked up the fire in my bedroom and spent a happy time with the codex. I had brought only my working books with me and the inn boasted no library, so when I wanted to relax I went down to the tap-room, or gossiped with the landlady in the bar parlour. The yokels who congregated in the former were pleasant fellows, but, like all the folk on the Marches, they did not talk readily to a stranger and I heard little from them of the Hall. The old squire had reared every year three thousand pheasants, but the present squire would not allow a gun to be fired on his land and there were only a few wild birds left. For the same reason the woods were thick with vermin. This they told me when I professed an interest in shooting. But of Mr Dubellay they would not speak, declaring that they never saw him. I dare say they gossiped wildly about him, and their public reticence struck me as having in it a touch of fear.

The landlady, who came from a different part of the shire, was more communicative. She had not known the former Dubellays and so had no standard of comparison, but she was inclined to regard the present squire as not quite right in the head. 'They do say,' she would begin, but she, too, suffered from some inhibition, and what promised to be sensational would tail off into the commonplace. One thing apparently puzzled the neighbourhood above others, and that was his rearrangement of the house. 'They do say,' she said in an awed voice, 'that he have built a great church.' She had never visited it – no one in the parish had, for Squire Dubellay did not allow intruders – but from Lyne Hill you could see it through a gap in the woods. 'He's no good Christian,' she told me, 'and him and Vicar has quarrelled this many a day. But they do say as he worships summat there.' I learned that there were no women servants in the house, only the men he had brought from London. 'Poor benighted souls, they must live in a sad hobble,' and the buxom lady shrugged her shoulders and giggled.

On the last day of December I decided that I needed exercise and must go for a long stride. The snow had ceased that morning, and the dull skies had changed to a clear blue. It was still very cold, but the sun was shining, the snow was firm and crisp underfoot, and I proposed to survey the country. So after luncheon I put on thick boots and gaiters, and made for Lyne Hill. This meant a considerable circuit, for the place lay south of the Vauncastle park. From it I hoped to get a view of the other side of the house.

I was not disappointed. There was a rift in the thick woodlands, and below me, two miles off, I suddenly saw a strange building, like a classical temple. Only the entablature and the tops of the pillars showed above the trees, but they stood out vivid and dark against the background of snow. The spectacle in that lonely place was so startling that for a little I could only stare. I remember that I glanced behind me to the snowy line of the Welsh mountains, and felt that I might have been looking at a winter view of the Apennines two thousand years ago.

My curiosity was now alert, and I determined to get a nearer view of this marvel. I left the track and ploughed through the snowy fields down to the skirts of the woods. After that my troubles began. I found myself in a very good imitation of a primeval forest, where the undergrowth had been unchecked and the rides uncut for years. I sank into deep pits, I was savagely torn by briars and brambles, but I struggled on, keeping a line as best I could. At last the trees stopped. Before me was a flat expanse which I knew must be a lake, and beyond rose the temple.

It ran the whole length of the house, and from where I stood it was hard to believe that there were buildings at its back where men dwelt. It was a fine piece of work – the first glance told me that – admirably proportioned, classical, yet not following exactly any of the classical models. One could imagine a great echoing interior, dim with the smoke of sacrifice, and it was only by reflecting that I realised that the peristyle could not be continued down the two sides, that there was no interior, and that what I was looking at was only a portico.

The thing was at once impressive and preposterous. What madness had been in Dubellay when he embellished his house with such a grandiose garden front? The sun was setting and the shadow of the wooded hills darkened the interior, so I could not even make out the back wall of the porch. I wanted a nearer view, so I embarked on the frozen lake.

Then I had an odd experience. I was not tired, the snow lay level and firm, but I was conscious of extreme weariness. The biting air had become warm and oppressive. I had to drag boots that seemed to weigh tons across that lake. The place was utterly silent in the stricture of the frost, and from the pile in front no sign of life came.

I reached the other side at last and found myself in a frozen shallow of bulrushes and skeleton willow-herbs. They were taller than my head, and to see the house I had to look upward through their snowy traceries. It was perhaps eighty feet above me and a hundred yards distant, and, since I was below it, the delicate pillars seemed to spring to a great height. But it was still dusky, and the only detail I could see was on the ceiling, which seemed either to be carved or painted with deeply-shaded monochrome figures.

Suddenly the dying sun came slanting through the gap in the hills, and for an instant the whole portico to its farthest recesses was washed in clear gold and scarlet. That was wonderful enough, but there was something more. The air was utterly still with not the faintest breath of wind – so still that when I had lit a cigarette half an hour before the flame of the match had burned steadily upward like a candle in a room. As I stood among the sedges not a single frost crystal stirred . . . But there was a wind blowing in the portico.

I could see it lifting feathers of snow from the base of the pillars and fluffing the cornices. The floor had already been swept clean, but tiny flakes drifted on to it from the exposed edges. The interior was filled with a furious movement, though a yard from it was frozen peace. I felt nothing of the action of the wind, but I knew that it was hot, hot as the breath of a furnace.

I had only one thought, dread of being overtaken by night near that place. I turned and ran. Ran with labouring steps across the lake, panting and stifling with a deadly hot oppression, ran blindly by a sort of instinct in the direction of the village. I did not stop till I had wrestled through the big wood, and come out on some rough pasture above the highway. Then I dropped on the ground, and felt again the comforting chill of the December air.

The adventure left me in an uncomfortable mood. I was ashamed of myself for playing the fool, and at the same time hopelessly puzzled, for the oftener I went over in my mind the incidents of that afternoon the more I was at a loss for an explanation. One feeling was uppermost, that I did not like this place and wanted to be out of it. I had already broken the back of my task, and by shutting myself up for two days I completed it; that is to say, I made my collation as far as I had advanced myself in my commentary on the text. I did not want to go back to the Hall, so I wrote a civil note to Dubellay, expressing my gratitude and saying that I was sending up the manuscript by the landlord's son, as I scrupled to trouble him with another visit.

I got a reply at once, saying that Mr Dubellay would like to give himself the pleasure of dining with me at the inn before I went, and would receive the manuscript in person.

It was the last night of my stay in St Sant, so I ordered the best dinner the place could provide, and a magnum of claret, of which I discovered a bin in the cellar. Dubellay appeared promptly at eight o'clock, arriving to my surprise in a car. He had tidied himself up and put on a dinner jacket, and he looked exactly like the city solicitors you see dining in the Junior Carlton.

He was in excellent spirits, and his eyes had lost their air of being on guard. He seemed to have reached some conclusion about me, or decided that I was harmless. More, he seemed to be burning to talk to me. After my adventure I was prepared to find fear in him, the fear I had seen in the faces of the menservants. But there was none; instead there was excitement, overpowering excitement.

He neglected the courses in his verbosity. His coming to dinner had considerably startled the inn, and instead of a maid the landlady herself waited on us. She seemed to want to get the meal over, and hustled the biscuits and the port on to the table as soon as she decently could. Then Dubellay became confidential.

He was an enthusiast, it appeared, an enthusiast with a single hobby. All his life he had pottered among antiquities, and when he succeeded to Vauncastle he had the leisure and money to indulge himself. The place, it seemed, had been famous in Roman Britain – Vauni Castra – and Faxeter was a corruption of the same. 'Who was Vaunus?' I asked. He grinned, and told me to wait.

There had been an old temple up in the high woods. There had always been a local legend about it, and the place was supposed to be haunted. Well, he had had the site excavated and he had found – Here he became the cautious solicitor, and explained to me the law of treasure trove. As long as the objects found were not intrinsically valuable, not gold or jewels, the finder was entitled to keep them. He had done so – had not published the results of his excavations in the proceedings of any learned society – did not want to be bothered by tourists. I was different, for I was a scholar.

What had he found? It was really rather hard to follow his babbling talk, but I gathered that he had found certain carvings and sacrificial implements. And – he sunk his voice – most important of all, an altar, an altar of Vaunus, the tutelary deity of the vale. When he mentioned this word his face took on a new look – not of fear but of secrecy, a kind of secret excitement. I have seen the same look on the face of a street-preaching Salvationist.

Vaunus had been a British god of the hills, whom the Romans in their liberal way appear to have identified with Apollo. He gave me a long confused account of him, from which it appeared that Mr Dubellay was not an exact scholar. Some of his derivations of place-names were absurd – like St Sant from Sancta Sanctorum – and in quoting a line of Ausonius he made two false quantities. He seemed to hope that I could tell him something more about Vaunus, but I said that my subject was Greek, and that I was deeply ignorant about Roman Britain. I mentioned several books, and found that he had never heard of Haverfield.

One word he used, 'hypocaust', which suddenly gave me a clue. He must have heated the temple, as he heated his house, by some very efficient system of hot air. I know little about science, but I imagined that the artificial heat of the portico, as contrasted with the cold outside, might create an air current. At any rate that explanation satisfied me, and my afternoon's adventure lost its uncanniness. The reaction made me feel friendly towards him, and I listened to his talk with sympathy, but I decided not to mention that I had visited his temple.

He told me about it himself in the most open way. 'I couldn't leave the altar on the hillside,' he said. 'I had to make a place for it, so I turned the old front of the house into a sort of temple. I got the best advice, but architects are ignorant people, and I often wished I had been a better scholar. Still the place satisfies me.'

'I hope it satisfies Vaunus,' I said jocularly.

'I think so,' he replied quite seriously, and then his thoughts seemed to go wandering, and for a minute or so he looked through me with a queer abstraction in his eyes.

'What do you do with it now you've got it?' I asked.

He didn't reply, but smiled to himself.

'I don't know if you remember a passage in Sidonius Apollinaris,' I said, 'a formula for consecrating pagan altars to Christian uses. You begin by sacrificing a white cock or something suitable, and tell Apollo with all friendliness that the old dedication is off for the present. Then you have a Christian invocation – '

He nearly jumped out of his chair.

'That wouldn't do – wouldn't do at all! . . . Oh Lord, no! . . . Couldn't think of it for one moment!'

It was as if I had offended his ears by some horrid blasphemy, and the odd thing was that he never recovered his composure. He tried, for he had good manners, but his ease and friendliness had gone. We talked stiffly for another half-hour about trifles, and then he rose to leave. I returned him his manuscript neatly parcelled up, and expanded in thanks, but he scarcely seemed to heed me. He stuck the thing in his pocket, and departed with the same air of shocked absorption.

After he had gone I sat before the fire and reviewed the situation. I was satisfied with my hypocaust theory, and had no more perturbation in my memory about my afternoon's adventure. Yet a slight flavour of unpleasantness hung about it, and I felt that I did not quite like Dubellay. I set him down as a crank who had tangled himself up with a half-witted hobby, like an old maid with her cats, and I was not sorry to be leaving the place.

My third and last visit to St Sant was in the following June – the midsummer of 1914. I had all but finished my Theocritus, but I needed another day or two with the Vauncastle manuscript, and, as I wanted to clear the whole thing off before I went to Italy in July, I wrote to Dubellay and asked if I might have another sight of it. The thing was a bore, but it had to be faced, and I fancied that the valley would be a pleasant place in that hot summer.

I got a reply at once, inviting, almost begging me to come, and insisting that I should stay at the Hall. I couldn't very well refuse, though I would have preferred the inn. He wired about my train, and wired again saying he would meet me. This time I seemed to be a particularly welcome guest.

I reached Faxeter in the evening, and was met by a car from a Faxeter garage. The driver was a talkative young man, and, as the car was a closed one, I sat beside him for the sake of fresh air. The term had tired me, and I was glad to get out of stuffy Cambridge, but I cannot say that I found it much cooler as we ascended the Vaun valley. The woods were in their summer magnificence but a little dulled and tarnished by the heat, the river was shrunk to a trickle, and the curious hill-tops were so scorched by the sun that they seemed almost yellow above the green of the trees. Once again I had the feeling of a landscape fantastically un-English.

'Squire Dubellay's been in a great way about your coming, sir,' the driver informed me. 'Sent down three times to the boss to make sure it was all right. He's got a car of his own, too, a nice little Daimler, but he don't seem to use it much. Haven't seen him about in it for a month of Sundays.'

As we turned in at the Hall gates he looked curiously about him. 'Never been here before, though I've been in most gentlemen's parks for fifty miles round. Rum old-fashioned spot, isn't it, sir?'

If it had seemed a shuttered sanctuary in midwinter, in that June twilight it was more than ever a place enclosed and guarded. There was almost an autumn smell of decay, a dry decay like touchwood. We seemed to be descending through layers of ever-thickening woods. When at last we turned through the iron gate I saw that the lawns had reached a further stage of neglect, for they were as shaggy as a hayfield.

The white-faced butler let me in, and there, waiting at his back, was Dubellay. But he was not the man whom I had seen in December. He was dressed in an old baggy suit of flannels, and his unwholesome red face was painfully drawn and sunken. There were dark pouches under his eyes, and these eyes were no longer excited, but dull and pained. Yes, and there was more than pain in them – there was fear. I wondered if his hobby were becoming too much for him.

He greeted me like a long-lost brother. Considering that I scarcely knew him, I was a little embarrassed by his warmth. 'Bless you for coming, my dear fellow,' he cried. 'You want a wash and then we'll have dinner. Don't bother to change, unless you want to. I never do.' He led me to my bedroom, which was clean enough but small and shabby like a servant's room. I guessed that he had gutted the house to build his absurd temple.

We dined in a fair-sized room which was a kind of library. It was lined with old books, but they did not look as if they had been there long; rather it seemed like a lumber room in which a fine collection had been stored. Once no doubt they had lived in a dignified Georgian chamber. There was nothing else, none of the antiques which I had expected.

'You have come just in time,' he told me. 'I fairly jumped when I got your letter, for I had been thinking of running up to Cambridge to insist on your coming down here. I hope you're in no hurry to leave.'

'As it happens,' I said, 'I *am* rather pressed for time, for I hope to go abroad next week. I ought to finish my work here in a couple of days. I can't tell you how much I'm in your debt for your kindness.'

'Two days,' he said. 'That will get us over midsummer. That should be enough.' I hadn't a notion what he meant.

I told him that I was looking forward to examining his collection. He opened his eyes. 'Your discoveries, I mean,' I said; 'the altar of Vaunus . . .'

As I spoke the words his face suddenly contorted in a spasm of what looked like terror. He choked and then recovered himself. 'Yes, yes,' he said rapidly. 'You shall see it – you shall see everything – but not now – not tonight. Tomorrow – in broad daylight – that's the time.'

After that the evening became a bad dream. Small talk deserted him, and he could only reply with an effort to my commonplaces. I caught him often looking at me furtively, as if he were sizing me up and wondering how far he could go with me. The thing fairly got on my nerves, and to crown all it was abominably stuffy. The windows of the room gave on to a little paved court with a background of laurels, and I might have been in Seven Dials for all the air there was.

When coffee was served I could stand it no longer. 'What about smoking in the temple?' I said. 'It should be cool there with the air from the lake.'

I might have been proposing the assassination of his mother. He simply gibbered at me. 'No, no,' he stammered. 'My God, no!' It was half an hour before he could properly collect himself. A servant lit two oil lamps, and we sat on in the frowsty room.

'You said something when we last met,' he ventured at last, after many a sidelong glance at me, 'something about a ritual for rededicating an altar.'

I remembered my remark about Sidonius Apollinaris.

'Could you show me the passage? There is a good classical library here, collected by my great-grandfather. Unfortunately my scholarship is not equal to using it properly.'

I got up and hunted along the shelves, and presently found a copy of Sidonius, the Plantin edition of 1609. I turned up the passage, and roughly translated it for him. He listened hungrily and made me repeat it twice.

'He says a cock,' he hesitated. 'Is that essential?'

'I don't think so. I fancy any of the recognised ritual stuff would do.'

'I am glad,' he said simply. 'I am afraid of blood.'

'Good God, man,' I cried out, 'are you taking my nonsense seriously? I was only chaffing. Let old Vaunus stick to his altar!'

He looked at me like a puzzled and rather offended dog.

'Sidonius was in earnest . . .'

'Well, I'm not,' I said rudely. 'We're in the twentieth century and not in the third. Isn't it about time we went to bed?'

He made no objection, and found me a candle in the hall. As I undressed I wondered into what kind of lunatic asylum I had strayed. I felt the strongest distaste for the place, and longed to go straight off to the inn; only I couldn't make use of a man's manuscripts and insult his hospitality. It was fairly clear to me that Dubellay was mad. He had ridden his hobby to the death of his wits and was now in its bondage. Good Lord! he had talked of his precious Vaunus as a votary talks of a god. I believed he had come to worship some figment of his half-educated fancy.

I think I must have slept for a couple of hours. Then I woke dripping with perspiration, for the place was simply an oven. My window was as wide open as it would go, and, though it was a warm night, when I stuck my head out the air was fresh. The heat came from indoors. The room was on the first floor near the entrance and I was looking on to the overgrown lawns. The night was very dark and utterly still, but I could have sworn that I heard wind. The trees were as motionless as marble, but somewhere close at hand I heard a strong gust blowing. Also, though there was no moon, there was somewhere near me a steady glow of light; I could see the reflection of it round the end of the house. That meant that it came from the temple. What kind of saturnalia was Dubellay conducting at such an hour?

When I drew in my head I felt that if I was to get any sleep something must be done. There could be no question about it; some fool had turned on the steam heat, for the room was a furnace. My temper was rising. There was no bell to be found, so I lit my candle and set out to find a servant.

I tried a cast downstairs and discovered the room where we had dined. Then I explored a passage at right angles, which brought me up against a great oak door. The light showed me that it was a new door, and that there was no apparent way of opening it. I guessed that it led into the temple, and, though it fitted close and there seemed to be no keyhole, I could hear through it a sound like a rushing wind . . . Next I opened a door on my right and found myself in a big store cupboard. It had a funny, exotic, spicy smell, and arranged very neatly on the floor and shelves was a number of small sacks and coffers. Each bore a label, a square of stout paper with very black lettering. I read: 'Pro servitio Vauni.'

I had seen them before, for my memory betrayed me if they were not the very labels that Dubellay's servants had been attaching to the packages from the carrier's cart that evening in the past autumn. The discovery made my suspicions an unpleasant certainty. Dubellay evidently meant the labels to read: 'For the service of Vaunus.' He was no scholar, for it was an impossible use of the word *servitium*, but he was very patently a madman.

However, it was my immediate business to find some way to sleep, so I continued my quest for a servant. I followed another corridor, and discovered a second staircase. At the top of it I saw an open door and looked in. It must have been Dubellay's room, for his flannels were tumbled untidily on a chair, but Dubellay himself was not there and the bed had not been slept in.

I suppose my irritation was greater than my alarm – though I must say I was getting a little scared – for I still pursued the evasive servant. There was another stair which apparently led to attics, and in going up it I slipped and made a great clatter. When I looked up the butler in his nightgown was staring down at me, and if ever a mortal face held fear it was his. When he saw who it was he seemed to recover a little.

'Look here,' I said, 'for God's sake turn off that infernal hot air. I can't get a wink of sleep. What idiot set it going?'

He looked at me owlishly, but he managed to find his tongue.

'I beg your pardon, sir,' he said, 'but there is no heating apparatus in this house.'

There was nothing more to be said. I returned to my bedroom and it seemed to me that it had grown cooler. As I leaned out of the window, too, the mysterious wind seemed to have died away, and the glow no longer showed from beyond the corner of the house. I got into bed and slept heavily till I was roused by the appearance of my shaving water about half-past nine. There was no bathroom, so I bathed in a tin pannikin.

It was a hazy morning which promised a day of blistering heat. When I went down to breakfast I found Dubellay in the dining-room. In the daylight he looked a very sick man, but he seemed to have taken a pull on himself, for his manner was considerably less nervy than the night before. Indeed, he appeared almost normal, and I might have reconsidered my view but for the look in his eyes.

I told him that I proposed to sit tight all day over the manuscript, and get the thing finished. He nodded. 'That's all right. I've a lot to do myself, and I won't disturb you.'

'But first,' I said, 'you promised to show me your discoveries.'

He looked out of the window where the sun was shining on the laurels and on a segment of the paved court.

'The light is good,' he said – an odd remark. 'Let us go there now. There are times and seasons for the temple.'

He led me down the passage I had explored the previous night. The door opened not by a key but by some lever in the wall. I found myself looking suddenly at a bath of sunshine with the lake below as blue as a turquoise.

It is not easy to describe my impressions of that place. It was unbelievably light and airy, as brilliant as an Italian colonnade in midsummer. The proportions must have been good, for the columns soared and swam, and the roof (which looked like cedar) floated as delicately as a flower on its stalk. The stone was some local limestone, which on the floor took a polish like marble. All around was a vista of sparkling water and summer woods and far blue mountains. It should have been as wholesome as the top of a hill.

And yet I had scarcely entered before I knew that it was a prison. I am not an imaginative man, and I believe my nerves are fairly good, but I could scarcely put one foot before the other, so strong was my distaste. I felt shut off from the world, as if I were in a dungeon or on an ice-floe. And I felt, too, that though far enough from humanity, we were not alone.

On the inner wall there were three carvings. Two were imperfect friezes sculptured in low-relief, dealing apparently with the same subject. It was a ritual procession, priests bearing branches, the ordinary *dendrophori* business. The faces were only half-human, and that was from no lack of skill, for the artist had been a master. The striking thing was that the branches and the hair of the hierophants were being tossed by a violent wind, and the expression of each was of a being in the last stage of endurance, shaken to the core by terror and pain.

Between the friezes was a great roundel of a Gorgon's head. It was not a female head, such as you commonly find, but a male head, with the viperous hair sprouting from chin and lip. It had once been coloured, and fragments of a green pigment remained in the locks. It was an awful thing, the ultimate horror of fear, the last dementia of cruelty made manifest in stone. I hurriedly averted my eyes and looked at the altar.

That stood at the west end on a pediment with three steps. It was a beautiful piece of work, scarcely harmed by the centuries, with two words inscribed on its face – *Apoll. Vaun.* It was made of some foreign marble, and the hollow top was dark with ancient sacrifices. Not so ancient either, for I could have sworn that I saw there the mark of recent flame.

I do not suppose I was more than five minutes in the place. I wanted to get out, and Dubellay wanted to get me out. We did not speak a word till we were back in the library.

'For God's sake give it up!' I said. 'You're playing with fire, Mr Dubellay. You're driving yourself into Bedlam. Send these damned things to a museum and leave this place. Now, now, I tell you. You have no time to lose. Come down with me to the inn straight off and shut up this house.'

He looked at me with his lip quivering like a child about to cry.

'I will. I promise you I will . . . But not yet . . . After tonight . . . Tomorrow I'll do whatever you tell me . . . You won't leave me?'

'I won't leave you, but what earthly good am I to you if you won't take my advice?'

'Sidonius . . . ' he began.

'Oh, damn Sidonius! I wish I had never mentioned him. The whole thing is arrant nonsense, but it's killing you. You've got it on the brain. Don't you know you're a sick man?'

'I'm not feeling very grand. It's so warm today. I think I'll lie down.'

It was no good arguing with him, for he had the appalling obstinacy of very weak things. I went off to my work in a shocking bad temper.

The day was what it had promised to be, blisteringly hot. Before midday the sun was hidden by a coppery haze, and there was not the faintest stirring of wind. Dubellay did not appear at luncheon – it was not a meal he ever ate, the butler told me. I slogged away all the afternoon, and had pretty well finished my job by six o'clock. That would enable me to leave next morning, and I hoped to be able to persuade my host to come with me.

The conclusion of my task put me into a better humour, and I went for a walk before dinner. It was a very close evening, for the heat haze had not lifted; the woods were as silent as a grave, not a bird spoke, and when I came out of the cover to the burnt pastures the sheep seemed too languid to graze. During my walk I prospected the environs of the house, and saw that it would be very hard to get access to the temple except by a long circuit. On one side was a mass of outbuildings, and then a high wall, and on the other the very closest and highest quickset hedge I have ever seen, which ended in a wood with savage spikes on its containing wall. I returned to my room, had a cold bath in the exiguous tub, and changed.

Dubellay was not at dinner. The butler said that his master was feeling unwell and had gone to bed. The news pleased me, for bed was the best place for him. After that I settled myself down to a lonely evening in the library. I browsed among the shelves and found a number of rare editions which served to pass the time. I noticed that the copy of Sidonius was absent from its place.

I think it was about ten o'clock when I went to bed, for I was unaccountably tired. I remember wondering whether I oughtn't to go and visit Dubellay, but decided that it was better to leave him alone. I still reproach myself for that decision. I know now I ought to have taken him by force and haled him to the inn.

Suddenly I came out of heavy sleep with a start. A human cry seemed to be ringing in the corridors of my brain. I held my breath and listened. It came again, a horrid scream of panic and torture.

I was out of bed in a second, and only stopped to get my feet into slippers. The cry must have come from the temple. I tore downstairs expecting to hear the noise of an alarmed household. But there was no sound, and the awful cry was not repeated.

The door in the corridor was shut, as I expected. Behind it pandemonium seemed to be loose, for there was a howling like a tempest – and something more, a crackling like fire. I made for the front door, slipped off the chain, and found myself in the still, moonless night. Still, except for the rending gale that seemed to be raging in the house I had left.

From what I had seen on my evening's walk I knew that my one chance to get to the temple was by way of the quickset hedge. I thought I might manage to force a way between the end of it and the wall. I did it, at the cost of much of my raiment and my skin. Beyond was another rough lawn set with tangled shrubberies, and then a precipitous slope to the level of the lake. I scrambled along the sedgy margin, not daring to lift my eyes till I was on the temple steps.

The place was brighter than day with a roaring blast of fire. The very air seemed to be incandescent and to have become a flaming ether. And yet there were no flames – only a burning brightness. I could not enter, for the waft from it struck my face like a scorching hand and I felt my hair singe . . .

I am short-sighted, as you know, and I may have been mistaken, but this is what I think I saw. From the altar a great tongue of flame seemed to shoot upwards and lick the roof, and from its pediment ran flaming streams. In front of it lay a body – Dubellay's – a naked body, already charred and black. There was nothing else, except that the Gorgon's head in the wall seemed to glow like a sun in hell.

I suppose I must have tried to enter. All I know is that I found myself staggering back, rather badly burned. I covered my eyes, and as I looked through my fingers I seemed to see the flames flowing under the wall, where there may have been lockers, or possibly another entrance. Then the great oak door suddenly shrivelled like gauze, and with a roar the fiery river poured into the house.

I ducked myself in the lake to ease the pain, and then ran back as hard as I could by the way I had come. Dubellay, poor devil, was beyond my aid. After that I am not very clear what happened. I know that the house burned like a haystack. I found one of the menservants on the lawn, and I think I helped to get the other down from his room by one of the rain-pipes. By the time the neighbours arrived the house was ashes, and I was pretty well mother-naked. They took me to the inn and put me to bed, and I remained there till after the inquest. The coroner's jury were puzzled, but they found it simply death by misadventure; a lot of country houses were burned that summer. There was nothing found of Dubellay; nothing remained of the house except a few blackened pillars; the altar and the sculptures were so cracked and scarred that no museum wanted them. The place has not been rebuilt, and for all I know they are there today. I am not going back to look for them.

Nightingale finished his story and looked round his audience.

'Don't ask me for an explanation,' he said, 'for I haven't any. You may believe if you like that the god Vaunus inhabited the temple which Dubellay built for him, and, when his votary grew scared and tried Sidonius's receipt for shifting the dedication, became angry and slew him with his flaming wind. That wind seems to have been a perquisite of Vaunus. We know more about him now, for last year they dug up a temple of his in Wales.'

'Lightning,' someone suggested.

'It was a quiet night, with no thunderstorm,' said Nightingale.

'Isn't the countryside volcanic?' Peckwether asked. 'What about pockets of natural gas or something of the kind?'

'Possibly. You may please yourself in your explanation. I'm afraid I can't help you. All I know is that I don't propose to visit that valley again!'

'What became of your Theocritus?'

'Burned, like everything else. However, that didn't worry me much. Six weeks later came the war, and I had other things to think about.'

The Loathley Opposite

Oliver Pugh's Story

How loathly opposite I stood
To his unnatural purpose.

King Lear

Burminster had been to a Guildhall dinner the night before, which had been attended by many – to him – unfamiliar celebrities. He had seen for the first time in the flesh people whom he had long known by reputation, and he declared that in every case the picture he had formed of them had been cruelly shattered. An eminent poet, he said, had looked like a starting-price bookmaker, and a financier of world-wide fame had been exactly like the music-master at his preparatory school. Wherefore Burminster made the profound deduction that things were never what they seemed.

'That's only because you have a feeble imagination,' said Sandy Arbuthnot. 'If you had really understood Timson's poetry you would have realised that it went with close-cropped red hair and a fat body, and you should have known that Macintyre (this was the financier) had the music-and-metaphysics type of mind. That's why he puzzles the City so. If you understand a man's work well enough you can guess pretty accurately what he'll look like. I don't mean the colour of his eyes and his hair, but the general atmosphere of him.'

It was Sandy's agreeable habit to fling an occasional paradox at the table with the view of starting an argument. This time he stirred up Pugh, who had come to the War Office from the Indian Staff Corps. Pugh had been a great figure in Secret Service work in the East, but he did not look the part, for he had the air of a polo-playing cavalry subaltern. The skin was stretched as tight over his cheek-bones as over the knuckles of a clenched fist, and was so dark that it had the appearance of beaten bronze. He had black hair, rather beady black eyes, and the hooky nose which in the Celt often goes with that colouring. He was himself a very good refutation of Sandy's theory.

'I don't agree,' Pugh said. 'At least not as a general principle. One piece of humanity whose work I studied with the microscope for two aching years upset all my notions when I came to meet it.'

Then he told us this story.

'When I was brought to England in November 1917 and given a "hush" department on three floors of an eighteenth-century house in a back street, I had a good deal to learn about my business. That I learned it in reasonable time was due to the extraordinarily fine staff that I found provided for me. Not one of them was a regular soldier. They were all educated men – they had to be in that job – but they came out of every sort of environment. One of the best was a Shetland laird, another was an Admiralty Court KC, and I had besides a metallurgical chemist, a golf champion, a leader-writer, a popular dramatist, several actuaries and an East End curate. None of them thought of anything but his job, and at the end of the war, when some ass proposed to make them OBEs, there was a very fair imitation of a riot. A more loyal crowd never existed, and they accepted me as their chief as unquestioningly as if I had been with them since 1914.

'To the war in the ordinary sense they scarcely gave a thought. You found the same thing in a lot of other behind-the-lines departments, and I dare say it was a good thing – it kept their nerves quiet and their minds concentrated. After all our business was only to decode and decypher German messages; we had nothing to do with the use which was made of them. It was a curious little nest, and when the Armistice came my people were flabbergasted – they hadn't realised that their job was bound up with the war.

'The one who most interested me was my second-in-command, Philip Channell. He was a man of forty-three, about five-foot-four in height, weighing, I fancy, under nine stone, and almost as blind as an owl. He was good enough at papers with his double glasses, but he could hardly recognise you three yards off. He had been a professor at some Midland college – mathematics or physics, I think – and as soon as the war began he had tried to enlist. Of course they wouldn't have him – he was about E5 in any physical classification, besides being well over age – but he would take no refusal, and presently he worried his way into the government service. Fortunately he found a job which he could do superlatively well, for I do not believe there was a man alive with a more natural genius for cryptography.

'I don't know if any of you have ever given your mind to that heart-breaking subject. Anyhow you know that secret writing falls under two heads – codes and cyphers, and that codes are combinations of words and cyphers of numerals. I remember how one used to be told that no code or cypher which was practically useful was really undiscoverable, and in a sense that is true, especially of codes. A system of communication which is in constant use must obviously not be too intricate, and a working code, if you get long enough for the job, can generally be read. That is why a code is periodically changed by the users. There are rules in worrying out the permutations and combinations of letters in most codes, for human ingenuity seems to run in certain channels, and a man who has been a long time at the business gets surprisingly clever at it. You begin by finding out a little bit, and then empirically building up the rules of decoding, till in a week or two you get the whole thing. Then, when you are happily engaged in reading enemy messages, the code is changed suddenly, and you have to start again from the beginning . . . You can make a code, of course, that it is simply impossible to read except by accident – the key to which is a page of some book, for example – but fortunately that kind is not of much general use.

'Well, we got on pretty well with the codes, and read the intercepted enemy messages, cables and wireless, with considerable ease and precision. It was mostly diplomatic stuff, and not very important. The more valuable stuff was in cypher, and that was another pair of shoes. With a code you can build up the interpretation by degrees, but with a cypher you either know it or you don't – there are no halfway houses. A cypher, since it deals with numbers, is a horrible field for mathematical ingenuity. Once you have written out the letters of a message in numerals there are many means by which you can lock it and double-lock it. The two main devices, as you know, are transposition and substitution, and there is no limit to the ways one or other or both can be used. There is nothing to prevent a cypher having a double meaning, produced by two different methods, and, as a practical question, you have to decide which meaning is intended. By way of an extra complication, too, the message, when decyphered, may turn out to be itself in a difficult code. I can tell you our job wasn't exactly a rest cure.'

Burminster, looking puzzled, enquired as to the locking of cyphers.

'It would take too long to explain. Roughly, you write out a message horizontally in numerals; then you pour it into vertical columns, the number and order of which are determined by a keyword; then you write out the contents of the columns horizontally, following the lines across. To unlock it you have to have the key word, so as to put it back into the vertical columns, and then into the original horizontal form.'

Burminster cried out like one in pain. 'It can't be done. Don't tell me that any human brain could solve such an acrostic.'

'It was frequently done,' said Pugh.

'By you?'

'Lord bless you, not by me. I can't do a simple crossword puzzle. By my people.'

'Give me the trenches,' said Burminster in a hollow voice. 'Give me the trenches any day. Do you seriously mean to tell me that you could sit down before a muddle of numbers and travel back the way they had been muddled to an original that made sense?'

'I couldn't, but Channell could – in most cases. You see, we didn't begin entirely in the dark. We already knew the kind of intricacies that the enemy favoured, and the way we worked was by trying a variety of clues till we lit on the right one.'

'Well, I'm blessed! Go on about your man Channell.'

'This isn't Channell's story,' said Pugh. 'He only comes into it accidentally . . . There was one cypher which always defeated us, a cypher used between the German General Staff and their forces in the East. It was a locked cypher, and Channell had given more time to it than to any dozen of the others, for it put him on his mettle. But he confessed himself absolutely beaten. He wouldn't admit that it was insoluble, but he declared that he would need a bit of real luck to solve it. I asked him what kind of luck, and he said a mistake and a repetition. That, he said, might give him a chance of establishing equations.

'We called this particular cypher P.Y., and we hated it poisonously. We felt like pygmies battering at the base of a high stone tower. Dislike of the thing soon became dislike of the man who had conceived it. Channell and I used to – I won't say amuse, for it was too dashed serious – but torment ourselves by trying to picture the fellow who owned the brain that was responsible for P.Y. We had a pretty complete dossier of the German Intelligence Staff, but of course we couldn't know who was responsible for this particular cypher. We knew no more than his code name, Reinmar, with which he signed the simpler messages to the East, and Channell, who was a romantic little chap for all his science, had got it into his head that it was a woman. He used to describe her to me as if he had seen her – a she-devil, young, beautiful, with a much-painted white face, and eyes like a cobra's. I fancy he read a rather low class of novel in his off-time.

'My picture was different. At first I thought of the histrionic type of scientist, the "ruthless brain" type, with a high forehead and a jaw puckered like a chimpanzee. But that didn't seem to work, and I settled on a picture of a first-class *Generalstaboffizier*, as handsome as Falkenhayn, trained to the last decimal, absolutely passionless, with a mind that worked with the relentless precision of a fine machine. We all of us at the time suffered from the bogy of this kind of German, and, when things were going badly, as in March '18, I couldn't sleep for hating him. The infernal fellow was so water-tight and armour-plated, a Goliath who scorned the pebbles from our feeble slings.

'Well, to make a long story short, there came a moment in September '18 when P.Y. was about the most important thing in the world. It mattered enormously what Germany was doing in Syria, and we knew that it was all in P.Y. Every morning a pile of the intercepted German wireless messages lay on Channell's table, which were as meaningless to him as a child's scrawl. I was prodded by my chiefs and in turn I prodded Channell. We had a week to find the key to the cypher, after which things must go on without us, and if we had failed to make anything of it in eighteen months of quiet work, it didn't seem likely that we would succeed in seven feverish days. Channell nearly went off his head with overwork and anxiety. I used to visit his dingy little room and find him fairly grizzled and shrunken with fatigue.

'This isn't a story about him, though there is a good story which I may tell you another time. As a matter of fact we won on the post. P.Y. made a mistake. One morning we got a long message dated *en clair*, then a very short message, and then a third message almost the same as the first. The second must mean, "Your message of today's date unintelligible, please repeat," the regular formula. This gave us a translation of a bit of the cypher. Even that would not have brought it out, and for twelve hours Channell was on the verge of lunacy, till it occurred to him that Reinmar might have signed the long message with his name, as we used to do sometimes in cases of extreme urgency. He was right, and, within three hours of the last moment Operations could give us, we had the whole thing pat. As I have said, that is a story worth telling, but it is not this one.

'We both finished the war too tired to think of much except that the darned thing was over. But Reinmar had been so long our unseen but constantly pictured opponent that we kept up a certain interest in him. We would like to have seen how he took the licking, for he must have known that we had licked him. Mostly when you lick a man at a game you rather like him, but I didn't like Reinmar. In fact I made him a sort of compost of everything I had ever disliked in a German. Channell stuck to his she-devil theory, but I was pretty certain that he was a youngish man with an intellectual arrogance which his country's débâcle would in no way lessen. He would never acknowledge defeat. It was highly improbable that I should ever find out who he was, but I felt that if I did, and met him face to face, my dislike would be abundantly justified.

'As you know, for a year or two after the Armistice I was a pretty sick man. Most of us were. We hadn't the fillip of getting back to civilised comforts, like the men in the trenches. We had always been comfortable enough in body, but our minds were fagged out, and there is no easy cure for that. My digestion went nobly to pieces, and I endured a miserable space of lying in bed and living on milk and olive-oil. After that I went back to work, but the darned thing always returned, and every leech had a different regime to advise. I tried them all – dry meals, a snack every two hours, lemon juice, sour milk, starvation, knocking off tobacco – but nothing got me more than halfway out of the trough. I was a burden to myself and a nuisance to others, dragging my wing through life, with a constant pain in my tummy.

'More than one doctor advised an operation, but I was chary about that, for I had seen several of my friends operated on for the same mischief and left as sick as before. Then a man told me about a German fellow called

Christoph, who was said to be very good at handling my trouble. The best hand at diagnosis in the world, my informant said – no fads – treated every case on its merits – a really original mind. Dr Christoph had a modest *Kurhaus* at a place called Rosensee in the Holsteinische Schweiz. By this time I was getting pretty desperate, so I packed a bag and set off for Rosensee.

'It was a quiet little town at the mouth of a narrow valley, tucked in under wooded hills, a clean fresh place with open channels of running water in the streets. There was a big church with an onion spire, a Catholic seminary, and a small tanning industry. The *Kurhaus* was halfway up a hill, and I felt better as soon as I saw my bedroom, with its bare scrubbed floors and its wide verandah looking up into a forest glade. I felt still better when I saw Dr Christoph. He was a small man with a grizzled beard, a high forehead, and a limp, rather like what I imagine the Apostle Paul must have been. He looked wise, as wise as an old owl. His English was atrocious, but even when he found that I talked German fairly well he didn't expand in speech. He would deliver no opinion of any kind until he had had me at least a week under observation; but somehow I felt comforted, for I concluded that a first-class brain had got to work on me.

'The other patients were mostly Germans with a sprinkling of Spaniards, but to my delight I found Channell. He also had been having a thin time since we parted. Nerves were his trouble – general nervous debility and perpetual insomnia, and his college had given him six months' leave of absence to try to get well. The poor chap was as lean as a sparrow, and he had the large dull eyes and the dry lips of the sleepless. He had arrived a week before me, and like me was under observation. But his vetting was different from mine, for he was a mental case, and Dr Christoph used to devote hours to trying to unriddle his nervous tangles. "He is a good man for a German," said Channell, "but he is on the wrong tack. There's nothing wrong with my mind. I wish he'd stick to violet rays and massage, instead of asking me silly questions about my great-grandmother."

'Channell and I used to go for invalidish walks in the woods, and we naturally talked about the years we had worked together. He was living mainly in the past, for the war had been the great thing in his life, and his professorial duties seemed trivial by comparison. As we tramped among the withered bracken and heather his mind was always harking back to the dingy little room where he had smoked cheap cigarettes and worked fourteen hours out of the twenty-four. In particular he was as eagerly curious about our old antagonist, Reinmar, as he had been in 1918. He was more positive than ever that she was a woman, and I believe that one of the reasons that had induced him to try a cure in Germany was a vague hope that he might get on her track. I had almost forgotten about the thing, and I was amused by Channell in the part of the untiring sleuth-hound.

'"You won't find her in the *Kurhaus*," I said. "Perhaps she is in some old *Schloss* in the neighbourhood, waiting for you like the Sleeping Beauty."

'"I'm serious," he said plaintively. "It is purely a matter of intellectual curiosity, but I confess I would give a great deal to see her face to face. After I leave here, I thought of going to Berlin to make some enquiries. But I'm handicapped, for I know nobody and I have no credentials. Why don't you, who have a large acquaintance and far more authority, take the thing up?"

'I told him that my interest in the matter had flagged and that I wasn't keen on digging into the past, but I promised to give him a line to our military attaché if he thought of going to Berlin. I rather discouraged him from letting his mind dwell too much on events in the war. I said that he ought to try to bolt the door on all that had contributed to his present breakdown.

'"That is not Dr Christoph's opinion," he said emphatically. "He encourages me to talk about it. You see, with me it is a purely intellectual interest. I have no emotion in the matter. I feel quite friendly towards Reinmar, whoever she may be. It is, if you like, a piece of romance. I haven't had so many romantic events in my life that I want to forget this."

'"Have you told Dr Christoph about Reinmar?" I asked.

'"Yes," he said, "and he was mildly interested. You know the way he looks at you with his solemn grey eyes. I doubt if he quite understood what I meant, for a little provincial doctor, even though he is a genius in his own line, is not likely to know much about the ways of the Great General Staff . . . I had to tell him, for I have to tell him all my dreams, and lately I have taken to dreaming about Reinmar."

'"What's she like?" I asked.

'"Oh, a most remarkable figure. Very beautiful, but uncanny. She has long fair hair down to her knees."

'Of course I laughed. "You're mixing her up with the Valkyries," I said. "Lord, it would be an awkward business if you met that she-dragon in the flesh."

'But he was quite solemn about it, and declared that his waking picture of her was not in the least like his dreams. He rather agreed with my nonsense about the old *Schloss*. He thought that she was probably some penniless grandee, living solitary in a moated grange, with nothing now to exercise her marvellous brain on, and eating her heart out with regret and shame. He drew so attractive a character of her that I began to think that Channell was in love with a being of his own creation, till he ended with, "But all the same she's utterly damnable. She must be, you know."

'After a fortnight I began to feel a different man. Dr Christoph thought that he had got on the track of the mischief, and certainly, with his deep massage and a few simple drugs, I had more internal comfort than I had known for three years. He was so pleased with my progress that he refused to treat me as an invalid. He encouraged me to take long walks into the hills, and presently he arranged for me to go out roebuck-shooting with some of the local *Junkers*.

'I used to start before daybreak on the chilly November mornings and drive to the top of one of the ridges, where I would meet a collection of sportsmen and beaters, shepherded by a fellow in a green uniform. We lined out along the ridge, and the beaters, assisted by a marvellous collection of dogs, including the sporting dachshund, drove the roe towards us. It wasn't very cleverly managed, for the deer generally broke back, and it was chilly waiting in the first hours with a powdering of snow on the ground and the fir boughs heavy with frost crystals. But later, when the sun grew stronger, it was a very pleasant mode of spending a day. There was not much of a bag, but whenever a roe or a capercailzie fell all the guns would assemble and drink little glasses of kirschwasser. I had been lent a rifle, one of those appalling contraptions which are double-barrelled shot-guns and rifles in one, and to transpose from one form to the other requires a mathematical calculation. The rifle had a hair trigger too, and when I first used it I was nearly the death of a respectable Saxon peasant.

'We all ate our midday meal together and in the evening, before going home, we had coffee and cakes in one or other of the farms. The party was an odd mixture, big farmers and small squires, an hotel-keeper or two, a local doctor and a couple of lawyers from the town. At first they were a little shy of me, but presently they thawed, and after the first day we were good friends. They spoke quite frankly about the war, in which every one of them had had a share, and with a great deal of dignity and good sense.

'I learned to walk in Sikkim, and the little Saxon hills seemed to me inconsiderable. But they were too much for most of the guns, and instead of going straight up or down a slope they always chose a circuit, which gave them an easy gradient. One evening, when we were separating as usual, the beaters taking a short cut and the guns a circuit, I felt that I wanted exercise, so I raced the beaters downhill, beat them soundly, and had the better part of an hour to wait for my companions, before we adjourned to the farm for refreshment. The beaters must have talked about my pace, for as we walked away one of the guns, a lawyer called Meissen, asked me why I was visiting Rosensee at a time of year when few foreigners came. I said I was staying with Dr Christoph.

'"Is he then a private friend of yours?" he asked.

'I told him no, that I had come to his *Kurhaus* for treatment, being sick. His eyes expressed polite scepticism. He was not prepared to regard as an invalid a man who went down a hill like an avalanche.

'But, as we walked in the frosty dusk, he was led to speak of Dr Christoph, of whom he had no personal knowledge, and I learned how little honour a prophet may have in his own country. Rosensee scarcely knew him, except as a doctor who had an inexplicable attraction for foreign patients. Meissen was curious about his methods and the exact diseases in which he specialised. "Perhaps he may yet save me a journey to Hamburg?" he laughed. "It is well to have a skilled physician at one's doorstep. The doctor is something of a hermit, and except for his patients does not appear to welcome his kind. Yet he is a good man, beyond doubt, and there are those who say that in the war he was a hero."

'This surprised me, for I could not imagine Dr Christoph in any fighting capacity, apart from the fact that he must have been too old. I thought that Meissen might refer to work in the base hospitals. But he was positive; Dr Christoph had been in the trenches; the limping leg was a war wound.

'I had had very little talk with the doctor, owing to my case being free from nervous complications. He would say a word to me morning and evening about my diet, and pass the time of day when we met, but it was not till the very eve of my departure that we had anything like a real conversation. He sent a message that he wanted to see me for not less than one hour, and he arrived with a batch of notes from which he delivered a kind of lecture on my case. Then I realised what an immense amount of care and solid thought he had expended on me. He had decided that his diagnosis was right – my rapid improvement suggested that – but it was necessary for some time to observe a simple regime, and to keep an eye on certain symptoms. So he took a sheet of note-paper from the table and in his small precise hand wrote down for me a few plain commandments.

'There was something about him, the honest eyes, the mouth which looked as if it had been often compressed in suffering, the air of grave goodwill, which I found curiously attractive. I wished that I had been a mental case like Channell, and had had more of his society. I detained him in talk, and he seemed not unwilling. By and by we drifted to the war and it turned out that Meissen was right.

'Dr Christoph had gone as medical officer in November '14 to the Ypres Salient with a Saxon regiment, and had spent the winter there. In '15 he had been in Champagne, and in the early months of '16 at Verdun, till he was invalided with rheumatic fever. That is to say, he had had about seventeen months of consecutive fighting in the worst areas with scarcely a holiday. A pretty good record for a frail little middle-aged man!

'His family was then at Stuttgart, his wife and one little boy. He took a long time to recover from the fever, and after that was put on home duty. "Till the war was almost over," he said, "almost over, but not quite. There was just time for me to go back to the front and get my foolish leg hurt." I must tell you that whenever he mentioned his war experience it was with a comical deprecating smile, as if he agreed with anyone who might think that gravity like his should have remained in bed.

'I assumed that this home duty was medical, until he said something about getting rusty in his professional work. Then it appeared that it had been some job connected with Intelligence. "I am reputed to have a little talent for mathematics," he said. "No. I am no mathematical scholar, but, if you understand me, I have a certain mathematical aptitude. My mind has always moved happily among numbers. Therefore I was set to construct and to interpret cyphers, a strange interlude in the noise of war. I sat in a little room and excluded the world, and for a little I was happy."

'He went on to speak of the enclave of peace in which he had found himself, and as I listened to his gentle monotonous voice, I had a sudden inspiration.

'I took a sheet of note-paper from the stand, scribbled the word Reinmar on it, and shoved it towards him. I had a notion, you see, that I might surprise him into helping Channell's researches.

'But it was I who got the big surprise. He stopped thunderstruck, as soon as his eye caught the word, blushed scarlet over every inch of his face and bald forehead, seemed to have difficulty in swallowing, and then gasped, "How did you know?"

'I hadn't known, and now that I did, the knowledge left me speechless. This was the loathly opposite for which Channell and I had nursed our hatred. When I came out of my stupefaction I found that he had recovered his balance and was speaking slowly and distinctly, as if he were making a formal confession.

'"You were among my opponents? . . . that interests me deeply . . . I often wondered . . . You beat me in the end. You are aware of that?"

'I nodded. "Only because you made a slip," I said.

'"Yes, I made a slip. I was to blame – very gravely to blame, for I let my private grief cloud my mind."

'He seemed to hesitate, as if he were loath to stir something very tragic in his memory.

'"I think I will tell you," he said at last. "I have often wished – it is a childish wish – to justify my failure to those who profited by it. My chiefs understood, of course, but my opponents could not. In that month when I failed I was in deep sorrow. I had a little son – his name was Reinmar – you remember that I took that name for my code signature?"

'His eyes were looking beyond me into some vision of the past.

'"He was, as you say, my mascot. He was all my family, and I adored him. But in those days food was not plentiful. We were no worse off than many million Germans, but the child was frail. In the last summer of the war he developed phthisis due to malnutrition, and in September he died. Then I failed my country, for with him some virtue seemed to depart from my mind. You see, my work was, so to speak, his also, as my name was his, and when he left me he took my power with him . . . So I stumbled. The rest is known to you."

'He sat staring beyond me, so small and lonely that I could have howled. I remember putting my hand on his shoulder, and stammering some platitude about being sorry. We sat quite still for a minute or two, and then I remembered Channell. Channell must have poured his views of Reinmar into Dr Christoph's ear. I asked him if Channell knew.

'A flicker of a smile crossed his face.

'"Indeed no. And I will exact from you a promise never to breathe to him what I have told you. He is my patient, and I must first consider his case. At present he thinks that Reinmar is a wicked and beautiful lady whom he may someday meet. That is romance, and it is good for him to think so . . . If he were told the truth, he would be pitiful, and in Herr Channell's condition it is important that he should not be vexed with such emotions as pity." '

GEORGE WASHINGTON CABLE

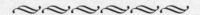

George Washington Cable (1844–1925), novelist, was born in New Orleans, though descended from an old Virginian family. After serving in the Civil War with the 4th Mississippi Cavalry he started as a newspaper reporter, then became an accountant and educated himself, learning French. Starting to write short stories, he found material in the old records of the Creoles, the French-speaking natives of Louisiana. The collection *Old Creole Days* (1879) was followed by the historical romances *Grandissimes* (1880), *The Creoles of Louisiana* (1884) and *Dr Sevier* (1885). He then moved to Northampton, Massachusetts. Later novels include *Bonaventure* (1888), *The Cavalier* (1901), *Kincaid's Battery* (1908), *Gideon's Band* (1914) and *Lovers of Louisiana* (1918). More serious works, dealing with the colour problem, were *The Silent South* (1885) and *The Negro Question* (1888).

The Young Aunt with White Hair

The date of this letter – I hold it in one hand as I write, and for the first time noticed that it has never in its hundred years been sealed or folded, but only doubled once, lightly, and rolled in the hand, just as the young Spanish officer might have carried it when he rode so hard to bear it to its destination – its date is the last year but one of our American Revolution. France, Spain and the thirteen colonies were at war with Great Britain, and the Indians were on both sides.

Galvez, the heroic young governor of Louisiana, had just been decorated by his king and made a count for taking the forts at Manchac, Baton Rouge, Natchez and Mobile, and besieging and capturing the stronghold of Pensacola, thus winning all west Florida, from the Mississippi to the Appalachicola, for Spain. But this vast wilderness was not made safe; Fort Panmure (Natchez) changed hands twice, and the land was full of Indians, partly hireling friends and partly enemies. The waters about the Bahamas and the Greater and Lesser Antilles were fields for the movements of hostile fleets, corsairs and privateers. Yet the writer of this letter was tempted to run the gauntlet of these perils, expecting, if all went well, to arrive in Louisiana in midsummer.

'How many times,' says the memorandum of her brother's now aged great-granddaughter – 'How many times during my childhood has been told me the story of my grand-aunt Louise. It was not until several years after the death of my grandmother that, on examining the contents of the basket which she had given me, I found at the bottom of a little black-silk bag the letter written by my grand-aunt to her brother, my own ancestor. Frankly, I doubt that my grandmother had intended to give it to me, so highly did she prize it, though it was very difficult to read. The orthography is perfect; the difficulty is all owing to the paper and, moreover, to the situation of the poor wounded sufferer.' It is in French:

> To my brother mister Pierre Bossier
> In the parish[3] of St James's Parish, Fort Latourette
> The 5 August, 1782

MY GOOD DEAR BROTHER – Ah! how shall I tell you the frightful position in which I am placed! I would that I were dead! I seem to be the prey of a horrible nightmare! O Pierre! my brother! hasten with all speed to me. When you left Germany, your little sister was a blooming girl, very beautiful in your eyes, very happy! and today! ah! today, my brother, come see for yourself.

After having received your letter, not only my husband and I decided to leave our village and go to join you, but twelve of our friends united with us, and on the 10 May, 1782, we quitted Strasbourg on the little vessel *North Star* [if this was an English ship – for her crew was English and her master's name seems to have been Andrews – she was probably not under British colours], which set sail for New Orleans, where you had promised to come to meet us. Let me tell you the names of my fellow-travellers. O brother! what courage I need to write this account: first my husband, Leonard Cheval, and my son Pierre, poor little angel who was not yet two years old! Fritz Newman, his wife Nina, and their three children; Irwin Vizey; William Hugo, his wife, and their little daughter; Jacques Lewis, his wife, and their son Henry. We were full of hope: We hoped to find fortune in this new country of which you spoke with so much enthusiasm. How in that moment did I bless my parents and you, my brother, for the education you had procured me. You know how good a musician my Leonard was, and our intention was on arriving to open a boarding-school in New Orleans; in your last letter you encouraged the project – all of us had our movables with us, all our savings, everything we owned in this world.

This paper is very bad, brother, but the captain of the fort says it is all he has; and I write lying down, I am so uncomfortable.

The earlier days of the voyage passed without accident, without disturbance, but often Leonard spoke to me of his fears. The vessel was old, small, and very poorly supplied. The captain was a drunkard [here the writer attempted to turn the sheet and write on the back of it], who often incapacitated himself with his first officers [word badly blotted]; and then the management of the vessel fell to the mate, who was densely ignorant. Moreover, we knew that the seas were infested with pirates. I must stop, the paper is too bad.

The captain has brought me another sheet.

Our uneasiness was great. Often we emigrants assembled on deck and told each other our anxieties. Living on the frontier of France, we spoke German and French equally well; and when the sailors heard us, they, who spoke only English, swore at us, accused us of plotting against them, and called us Sauerkrauts. At such times I pressed my child to my heart and drew nearer to Leonard, more dead than alive. A whole month passed in this constant anguish. At its close, fevers broke out among us, and we discovered, to our horror, there was not a drop of medicine on board. We had them lightly, some of us, but only a few; and [bad blot] Newman's son and William Hugo's little daughter died . . . and the poor mother soon followed her child. My God! but it was sad. And the provisions ran low, and the captain refused to turn back to get more.

One evening, when the captain, his lieutenant, and two other officers were shut in their cabin drinking, the mate, of whom I had always such fear, presented himself before us surrounded by six sailors armed, like himself, to the teeth, and ordered us to surrender all the money we had. To resist would have been madness; we had to yield. They searched our trunks and took away all that we possessed: they left us nothing, absolutely nothing. Ah! why am I not dead? Profiting by the absence of their chiefs they seized the [or some – the word is blotted] boats and abandoned us to our fate. When, the next day, the captain appeared on deck quite sober, and saw the cruelty of our plight, he told us, to console us, that we were very near the mouth of the Mississippi, and that within two days we should be at New Orleans. Alas! all that day passed without seeing any land [the treeless marshes of the Delta would be very slow coming into view], but towards evening the vessel, after incredible efforts, had just come to a stop – at what I supposed should be the mouth of the river. We were so happy to have arrived that we begged Captain Andrieux to sail all night. He replied that our men, who had worked all day in place of the sailors, were tired and did not understand at all sufficiently the handling of a vessel to sail by night. He wanted to get drunk again. As in fact our men were worn out, we went, all of us, to bed. O great God! give me strength to go on. All at once we were awakened by horrible cries, not human sounds: we thought ourselves surrounded by ferocious beasts. We poor women clasped our children to our breasts, while our husbands armed themselves with whatever came to hand and dashed forward to meet the danger. My God! my God! we saw ourselves hemmed in by a multitude of savages yelling and lifting over us their horrible arms, grasping hatchets, knives, and tomahawks. The first to fall was my husband, my dear Leonard; all, except Irwin Vizey, who had the fortune to jump into the water unseen, all were massacred by the monsters. One Indian tore my child from me while another fastened my arms behind my back. In response to my cries, to my prayers, the monster who held my son took him by one foot and, swinging him several times around, shattered his head against the wall. And I live to write these horrors! . . . I fainted, without doubt, for on opening my eyes I found I was on land [blot], firmly fastened to a stake. Nina Newman and Kate Lewis were fastened as I was: the latter was covered with blood and appeared to be dangerously wounded. About daylight three Indians came looking for them and took them God knows where! Alas! I have never since heard of either of them or their children.

I remained fastened to the stake in a state of delirium, which saved me doubtless from the horrors of my situation. I recall one thing: that is, having seen those savages eat human flesh, the members of a child – at least it seemed so. Ah! you see plainly I must have been mad to have seen all that without dying! They had stripped me of my clothing and I remained exposed, half naked, to a July sun and to clouds of mosquitoes. An Indian who spoke French informed me that, as I was young and fat, they were reserving me for the dinner of the chief, who was to arrive next day. In a moment I was dead with terror; in that instant I lost all feeling. I had become indifferent to all. I saw nothing, I heard nothing. Towards evening one of the sub-chiefs approached and gave me some water in a gourd. I drank without knowing what I did; thereupon he set himself to examine me as the butcher examines the lamb that he is about to kill; he seemed to find me worthy to be served on the table of the head-chief, but as he was hungry and did not wish to wait [blot], he drew from its sheath the knife that he carried at his belt and before I had had time to guess what he intended to do . . . [Enough to say, in place of literal translation, that the savage, from the outside of her right thigh, flayed off a large piece of her flesh.] It must be supposed that I again lost consciousness. When I came to myself, I was lying some paces away from the stake of torture on a heap of cloaks, and a soldier was kneeling beside me, while I was surrounded by about a hundred others. The ground was strewed with dead Indians. I learned later that Vizey had reached the woods and by chance had stumbled into Fort Latourette, full of troops. Without loss of time, the brave soldiers set out, and arrived just in time to save me. A physician dressed my wound, they put me into an ambulance and brought me away to Fort Latourette, where I still am. A fierce fever took possession of me. My generous protectors did not know to whom to write; they watched over me and showed every care imaginable.

Now that I am better, I write to you, my brother, and close with these words: I await you! make all haste!

Your sister,

LOUISE CHEVAL

'My grandmother,' resumes the memorandum of the Creole great-grandniece, 'had often read this letter, and had recounted to me the incidents that followed its reception. She was then but three years old, but as her aunt lived three years in her (i.e., the aunt's) brother's family, my grandmother had known her, and described her to me as a young woman with white hair and walking with a staff. It was with difficulty that she used her right leg. My great-grandfather used to tell his children that his sister Louise had been blooming and gay, and spoke especially of her beautiful blonde hair. A few hours had sufficed to change it to snow, and on the once charming countenance of the poor invalid to stamp an expression of grief and despair.

'It was Lieutenant Rosello, a young Spaniard, who came on horseback from Fort Latourette to carry to my great-grandfather his sister's letter . . . Not to lose a moment, he [the brother] began, like Lieutenant Rosello, the journey on horseback, procuring a large ambulance as he passed through New Orleans . . . He did all he could to lighten the despair of his poor sister . . . All the members of the family lavished upon her every possible care and attention; but alas! the blow she had received was too terrible. She lingered three years, and at the end of that time passed peaceably away in the arms of her brother, the last words on her lips being: 'Leonard! – my child!''

EGERTON CASTLE

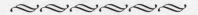

Egerton Castle (1858–1920), novelist, was born in London. His father, who was an intimate friend of Browning, George Sand, Verdi and Liszt, took the boy with him on walking tours on the Continent. He was educated at the universities of Paris, Glasgow and Cambridge; was entered at the Inner Temple; went to Sandhurst and served three years with the colours; and represented England as an international at fencing. From 1885 to 1894 he was on the staff of the *Saturday Review*. With his wife Agnes he produced a series of romantic novels which include *The Pride of Jennico* (1898), *The Bath Comedy* (1900), *The Secret Orchard* (1901), *The Star Dreamer* (1903), *The Incomparable Bellairs* (1904) and *If Youth But Knew* (1906). He also wrote a play, *Desperate Remedies*.

The Baron's Quarry

'Oh, no, I assure you, you are not boring Mr Marshfield,' said this personage himself in his gentle voice – that curious voice that could flow on for hours, promulgating profound and startling theories on every department of human knowledge or conducting paradoxical arguments without a single inflection or pause of hesitation. 'I am, on the contrary, much interested in your hunting talk. To paraphrase a well-worn quotation somewhat widely, *nihil humanum a me alienum est*. Even hunting stories may have their point of biological interest; the philologist sometimes pricks his ear to the jargon of the chase; moreover, I am not incapable of appreciating the subject matter itself. This seems to excite some derision. I admit I am not much of a sportsman to look at, nor, indeed, by instinct, yet I have had some out-of-the-way experiences in that line – generally when intent on other pursuits. I doubt, for instance, if even you, Major Travers, notwithstanding your well-known exploits against man and beast, notwithstanding that doubtful smile of yours, could match the strangeness of a certain hunting adventure in which I played an important part.'

The speaker's small, deep-set black eyes, that never warmed to anything more human than a purely speculative scientific interest in his surroundings, here wandered round the sceptical yet expectant circle with bland amusement. He stretched out his bloodless fingers for another of his host's superfine cigars and proceeded, with only such interruptions as were occasioned by the lighting and careful smoking of the latter.

'I was returning home after my prolonged stay in Petersburg, intending to linger on my way and test with mine own ears certain among the many dialects of Eastern Europe – anent which there is a symmetrical little cluster of philological knotty points it is my modest intention one day to unravel. However, that is neither here nor there. On the road to Hungary I bethought myself opportunely of proving the once pressingly offered hospitality of the Baron Kossowski.

'You may have met the man, Major Travers; he was a tremendous sportsman, if you like. I first came across him at McNeil's place in remote Ireland. Now, being in Bukowina, within measurable distance of his Carpathian abode, and curious to see a Polish lord at home, I remembered his invitation. It was already of long standing, but it had been warm, born in fact of a sudden fit of enthusiasm for me' – here a half-mocking smile quivered an instant under the speaker's black mustache – 'which, as it was characteristic, I may as well tell you about.

'It was on the day of, or, rather, to be accurate, on the day after my arrival, towards the small hours of the morning, in the smoking-room at Rathdrum. Our host was peacefully snoring over his empty pipe and his seventh glass of whisky, also empty. The rest of the men had slunk off to bed. The baron, who all unknown to himself had been a subject of most interesting observation to me the whole evening, being now practically alone with me, condescended to turn an eye, as wide awake as a fox's, albeit slightly bloodshot, upon the contemptible white-faced person who had preferred spending the raw hours over his papers, within the radius of a glorious fire's warmth, to creeping slyly over treacherous quagmires in the pursuit of timid bog creatures (snipe shooting had been the order of the day) – the baron, I say, became aware of my existence and entered into conversation with me.

'He would no doubt have been much surprised could he have known that he was already mapped out, craniologically and physiognomically, catalogued with care and neatly laid by in his proper ethnological box, in my private type museum; that, as I sat and examined him from my different coigns of vantage in library, in dining- and smoking-room that evening, not a look of his, not a gesture went forth but had significance for me.

'You, I had thought, with your broad shoulders and deep chest; your massive head that should have gone with a tall stature, not with those short sturdy limbs; with your thick red hair, that should have been black for that matter, as should your wide-set yellow eyes – you would be a real puzzle to one who did not recognise in you equal mixtures of the fair, stalwart and muscular Slav with the bilious-sanguine, thick-set, wiry Turanian. Your pedigree would no doubt bear me out: there is as much of the Magyar as of the Pole in your anatomy. Athlete, and yet a tangle of nerves; a ferocious brute at bottom, I dare say, for your broad forehead inclines to flatness; under your bristling beard your jaw must protrude, and the base of your skull is ominously thick. And, with all that, capable of ideal transports: when that girl played and sang tonight I saw the swelling of your eyelid veins, and how that small, tenacious, claw-like hand of yours twitched! You would be a fine leader of men – but God help the wretches in your power!

'So had I mused upon him. Yet I confess that when we came in closer contact with each other, even I was not proof against the singular courtesy of his manner and his unaccountable personal charm.

'Our conversation soon grew interesting; to me as a matter of course, and evidently to him also. A few general words led to interchange of remarks upon the country we were both visitors in and so to national characteristics – Pole and Irishman have not a few in common, both in their nature and history. An observation which he made, not without a certain flash in his light eyes and a transient uncovering of the teeth, on the Irish type of female beauty suddenly suggested to me a stanza of an ancient Polish ballad, very full of milk-and-blood imagery, of alternating ferocity and voluptuousness. This I quoted to the astounded foreigner in the vernacular, and this it was that metamorphosed his mere perfection of civility into sudden warmth, and, in fact, procured me the invitation in question.

'When I left Rathdrum the baron's last words to me were that if I ever thought of visiting his country otherwise than in books, he held me bound to make Yany, his Galician seat, my headquarters of study.

'From Czernowicz, therefore, where I stopped some time, I wrote, received in due time a few lines of prettily worded reply, and ultimately entered my sled in the nearest town to, yet at a most forbidding distance from, Yany, and started on my journey thither.

'The undertaking meant many long hours of undulation and skidding over the November snow, to the somniferous bell jangle of my dirty little horses, the only impression of interest being a weird gypsy concert I came in for at a miserable drinking-booth half buried in the snow where we halted for the refreshment of man and beast. Here, I remember, I discovered a very definite connection between the characteristic run of the tsimbol, the peculiar bite of the Zigeuner's bow on his fiddle-string and some distinctive points of Turanian tongues. In other countries, in Spain, for instance, your gypsy speaks differently on his instrument. But, oddly enough, when I later attempted to put this observation on paper I could find no word to express it.'

A few of our company evinced signs of sleepiness, but most of us who knew Marshfield, and that he could, unless he had something novel to say, be as silent and retiring as he now evinced signs of being copious, awaited further developments with patience. He has his own deliberate way of speaking, which he evidently enjoys greatly, though it be occasionally trying to his listeners.

'On the afternoon of my second day's drive, the snow, which till then had fallen fine and continuous, ceased, and my Jehu, suddenly interrupting himself in the midst of some exciting wolf story quite in keeping with the time of year and the wild surroundings, pointed to a distant spot against the grey sky to the north-west, between two wood-covered folds of ground – the first eastern spurs of the great Carpathian chain.

' "There stands Yany," said he. I looked at my far-off goal with interest. As we drew nearer, the sinking sun, just dipping behind the hills, tinged the now distinct frontage with a cold copper-like gleam, but it was only for a minute; the next the building became nothing more to the eye than a black irregular silhouette against the crimson sky.

'Before we entered the long, steep avenue of poplars, the early winter darkness was upon us, rendered all the more depressing by grey mists which gave a ghostly aspect to such objects as the sheen of the snow rendered visible. Once or twice there were feeble flashes of light looming in iridescent halos as we passed little clusters of hovels, but for which I should have been induced to fancy that the great Hof stood alone in the wilderness, such was the deathly stillness around. But even as the tall, square building rose before us above the vapour, yellow lighted in various storeys, and mighty in height and breadth, there broke upon my ear a deep-mouthed, menacing bay, which gave at once almost alarming reality to the eerie surroundings. "His lordship's boar- and wolf- hounds," quoth my charioteer calmly, unmindful of the regular pandemonium of howls and barks which ensued as he skilfully turned his horses through the gateway and flogged the tired beasts into a sort of shambling canter that we might land with glory before the house door: a weakness common, I believe, to drivers of all nations.

'I alighted in the court of honour, and while awaiting an answer to my tug at the bell, stood, broken with fatigue, depressed, chilled and aching, questioning the wisdom of my proceedings and the amount of comfort, physical and moral, that was likely to await me in a tête-à-tête visit with a well-mannered savage in his own home.

'The unkempt tribe of stable retainers who began to gather round me and my rough vehicle in the gloom, with their evil-smelling sheepskins and their resigned, battered visages, were not calculated to reassure me. Yet when the door opened, there stood a smart chasseur and a solemn major-domo who might but just have stepped out of Mayfair; and there was displayed a spreading vista of warm, deep-coloured halls, with here a statue and there a stuffed bear, and underfoot pile carpets strewn with rarest skins.

'Marvelling, yet comforted withal, I followed the solemn butler, who received me with the deference due to an expected guest and expressed the master's regret for his enforced absence till dinner time. I traversed vast rooms, each more sumptuous than the last, feeling the strangeness of the contrast between the outer desolation and this sybaritic excess of luxury growing ever more strongly upon me; caught a glimpse of a picture gallery, where peculiar yet admirably executed latter-day French pictures hung side by side with ferocious boar hunts of Snyder and such kin; and, at length, was ushered into a most cheerful room, modern to excess in its comfortable promise, where, in addition to the tall stove necessary for warmth, there burned on an open hearth a vastly pleasant fire of resinous logs, and where, on a low table, awaited me a dainty service of fragrant Russian tea.

'My impression of utter novelty seemed somehow enhanced by this unexpected refinement in the heart of the solitudes and in such a rugged shell, and yet, when I came to reflect, it was only characteristic of my cosmopolitan host. But another surprise was in store for me.

'When I had recovered bodily warmth and mental equilibrium in my downy armchair before the roaring logs, and during the delicious absorption of my second glass of tea, I turned my attention to the French valet, evidently the baron's own man, who was deftly unpacking my portmanteau, and who, unless my practiced eye deceived me, asked for nothing better than to entertain me with agreeable conversation the while.

' "Your master is out, then?" quoth I, knowing that the most trivial remark would suffice to start him.

'True, monseigneur was out; he was desolated in despair (this with the national amiable and imaginative instinct); but it was doubtless important business. M. le Baron had the visit of his factor during the midday meal; had left the table hurriedly, and had not been seen since. Madame la Baronne had been a little suffering, but she would receive monsieur!

' "Madame!" exclaimed I, astounded, "is your master then married? – since when?" – visions of a fair Tartar, fit mate for my baron, immediately springing somewhat alluringly before my mental vision. But the answer dispelled the picturesque fancy.

' "Oh, yes," said the man, with a somewhat peculiar expression. "Yes, monseigneur is married. Did monsieur not know? And yet it was from England that monseigneur brought back his wife."

' "An Englishwoman!"

'My first thought was one of pity; an Englishwoman alone in this wilderness – two days' drive from even a railway station – and at the mercy of Kossowski! But the next minute I reversed my judgement. Probably she adored her rufous lord, took his veneer of courtesy – a veneer of the most exquisite polish, I grant you, but perilously thin – for the very perfection of chivalry. Or perchance it was his inner savageness itself that charmed her; the most refined women often amaze one by the fascination which the preponderance of the brute in the opposite sex seems to have for them.

'I was anxious to hear more.

' "Is it not dull for the lady here at this time of the year?"

'The valet raised his shoulders with a gesture of despair that was almost passionate.

'Dull! Ah, monsieur could not conceive to himself the dullness of it. That poor Madame la Baronne! not even a little child to keep her company on the long, long days when there was nothing but snow in the heaven and on the earth and the howling of the wind and the dogs to cheer her. At the beginning, indeed, it had been different; when the master first brought home his bride the house was gay enough. It was all redecorated and refurnished to receive her (monsieur should have seen it before, a mere *rendezvous-de-chasse* – for the matter of that so were all the country houses in these parts). Ah, that was the good time! There were visits month after month; parties, sleighing, dancing, trips to St Petersburg and Vienna. But this year it seemed they were to have nothing but boars and wolves. How madame could stand it – well, it was not for him to speak – and heaving a deep sigh he delicately inserted my white tie round my collar, and with a flourish twisted it into an irreproachable bow beneath my chin. I did not think it right to cross-examine the willing talker any further, especially as, despite his last asseveration, there were evidently volumes he still wished to pour forth; but I confess that, as I made my way slowly out of my room along the noiseless length of passage, I was conscious of an unwonted, not to say vulgar, curiosity concerning the woman who had captivated such a man as the Baron Kossowski.

'In a fit of speculative abstraction I must have taken the wrong turning, for I presently found myself in a long, narrow passage I did not remember. I was retracing my steps when there came the sound of rapid footfalls upon stone flags; a little door flew open in the wall close to me, and a small, thick-set man, huddled in the rough sheepskin of the Galician peasant, with a mangy fur cap on his head, nearly ran headlong into my arms. I was about condescendingly to interpellate him in my best Polish, when I caught the gleam of an angry yellow eye and noted the bristle of a red beard – Kossowski!

'Amazed, I fell back a step in silence. With a growl like an uncouth animal disturbed, he drew his filthy cap over his brow with a savage gesture and pursued his way down the corridor at a sort of wild-boar trot.

'This first meeting between host and guest was so odd, so incongruous, that it afforded me plenty of food for a fresh line of conjecture as I traced my way back to the picture gallery, and from thence successfully to the drawing-room, which, as the door was ajar, I could not this time mistake.

'It was large and lofty and dimly lit by shaded lamps; through the rosy gloom I could at first only just make out a slender figure by the hearth; but as I advanced, this was resolved into a singularly graceful woman in clinging, fur-trimmed velvet gown, who, with one hand resting on the high mantel-piece, the other hanging listlessly by her side, stood gazing down at the crumbling wood fire as if in a dream.

'My friends are kind enough to say that I have a cat-like tread; I know not how that may be; at any rate the carpet I was walking upon was thick enough to smother a heavier footfall: not until I was quite close to her did my hostess become aware of my presence. Then she started violently and looked over her shoulder at me with dilating eyes. Evidently a nervous creature, I saw the pulse in her throat, strained by her attitude, flutter like a terrified bird.

'The next instant she had stretched out her hand with sweet English words of welcome, and the face, which I had been comparing in my mind to that of Guido's Cenci, became transformed by the arch and exquisite smile of a Greuse. For more than two years I had had no intercourse with any of my nationality. I could conceive the sound of his native tongue under such circumstances moving a man in a curious unexpected fashion.

'I babbled some commonplace reply, after which there was silence while we stood opposite each other, she looking at me expectantly. At length, with a sigh checked by a smile and an overtone of sadness in a voice that yet tried to be sprightly: "Am I then so changed, Mr Marshfield?" she asked. And all at once I knew her: the girl whose nightingale throat had redeemed the desolation of the evenings at Rathdrum, whose sunny beauty had seemed (even to my celebrated cold-blooded aestheticism) worthy to haunt a man's dreams. Yes, there was the subtle curve of the waist, the warm line of throat, the dainty foot, the slender tip-tilted fingers – witty fingers, as I had classified them – which I now shook like a true Briton, instead of availing myself of the privilege the country gave me and kissing her slender wrist.

'But she was changed; and I told her so with unconventional frankness, studying her closely as I spoke.

' "I am afraid," I said gravely, "that this place does not agree with you."

'She shrank from my scrutiny with a nervous movement and flushed to the roots of her red-brown hair. Then she answered coldly that I was wrong, that she was in excellent health, but that she could not expect any more than other people to preserve perennial youth (I rapidly calculated she might be two-and-twenty), though, indeed, with a little forced laugh, it was scarcely flattering to hear one had altered out of all recognition. Then, without allowing me time to reply, she plunged into a general topic of conversation which, as I should have been obtuse indeed not to take the hint, I did my best to keep up.

'But while she talked of Vienna and Warsaw, of her distant neighbours, and last year's visitors, it was evident that her mind was elsewhere; her eye wandered, she lost the thread of her discourse, answered me at random, and smiled her piteous smile incongruously.

'However lonely she might be in her solitary splendour, the company of a countryman was evidently no such welcome diversion.

'After a little while she seemed to feel herself that she was lacking in cordiality, and, bringing her absent gaze to bear upon me with a puzzled strained look: "I fear you will find it very dull," she said, "my husband is so wrapped up this winter in his country life and his sport. You are the first visitor we have had. There is nothing but guns and horses here, and you do not care for these things."

'The door creaked behind us; and the baron entered, in faultless evening dress. Before she turned towards him I was sharp enough to catch again the upleaping of a quick dread in her eyes, not even so much dread perhaps, I thought afterwards, as horror – the horror we notice in some animals at the nearing of a beast of prey. It was gone in a second, and she was smiling. But it was a revelation.

'Perhaps he beat her in Russian fashion, and she, as an Englishwoman, was narrow-minded enough to resent this; or perhaps, merely, I had the misfortune to arrive during a matrimonial misunderstanding.

'The baron would not give me leisure to reflect; he was so very effusive in his greeting – not a hint of our previous meeting – unlike my hostess, all in all to me; eager to listen, to reply; almost affectionate, full of references to old times and genial allusions. No doubt when he chose he could be the most charming of men; there were moments when, looking at him in his quiet smile and restrained gesture, the almost exaggerated politeness of his manner to his wife, whose fingers he had kissed with pretty, old-fashioned gallantry upon his entrance, I asked myself, Could that encounter in the passage have been a dream? Could that savage in the sheepskin be my courteous entertainer?

' "Just as I came in, did I hear my wife say there was nothing for you to do in this place?" he said presently to me. Then, turning to her: "You do not seem to know Mr Marshfield. Wherever he can open his eyes there is for him something to see which might not interest other men. He will find things in my library which I have no notion of. He will discover objects for scientific observation in all the members of my household, not only in the good-looking maids – though he could, I have no doubt, tell their points as I could those of a horse. We have maidens here of several distinct races, Marshfield. We have also witches, and Jew leeches, and holy daft people. In any case, Yany, with all its dependencies, material, male and female, are at your disposal, for what you can make out of them.

' "It is good," he went on gayly, "that you should happen to have this happy disposition, for I fear that, no later than tomorrow, I may have to absent myself from home. I have heard that there is news of wolves – they threaten to be a greater pest than usual this winter, but I am going to drive them on quite a new plan, and it will go hard with me if I don't come even with them. Well for you, by the way, Marshfield, that you did not pass within their scent today." Then, musingly: "I should not give much for the life of a traveller who happened to wander in these parts just now." Here he interrupted himself hastily and went over to his wife, who had sunk back on her chair, livid, seemingly on the point of swooning.

'His gaze was devouring; so might a man look at the woman he adored, in his anxiety.

' "What! faint, Violet? Do not be alarmed!" His voice was subdued, yet there was an unmistakable thrill of emotion in it.

' "Pshaw!" thought I to myself, "the man is a model husband."

'She clenched her hands, and by sheer force of will seemed to pull herself together. These nervous women have often an unexpected fund of strength.

' "Come, that is well," said the baron with a flickering smile; "Mr Marshfield will think you but badly acclimatised to Poland if a little wolf scare can upset you. My dear wife is so soft-hearted," he went on to me, "that she is capable of making herself quite ill over the sad fate that might have, but has not, overcome you. Or, perhaps," he added, in a still gentler voice, "her fear is that I may expose myself to danger for the public weal."

'She turned her head away, but I saw her set her teeth as if to choke a sob. The baron chuckled in his throat and seemed to luxuriate in the pleasant thought.

'At this moment folding doors were thrown open, and supper was announced. I offered my arm, she rose and took it in silence. This silence she maintained during the first part of the meal, despite her husband's brilliant conversation and almost uproarious spirits. But by and by a bright colour mounted to her cheeks and lustre to her eyes. I suppose you will think me horribly unpoetical if I add that she drank several glasses of champagne one after the other, a fact which perhaps may have accounted for the change.

'At any rate she spoke and laughed and looked lovely, and I did not wonder that the baron could hardly keep his eyes off her. But whether it was her wifely anxiety or not – it was evident her mind was not at ease through it all, and I fancied that her brightness was feverish, her merriment slightly hysterical.

'After supper – an exquisite one it was – we adjourned together, in foreign fashion, to the drawing-room; the baron threw himself into a chair and, somewhat with the air of a pasha, demanded music. He was flushed; the veins of his forehead were swollen and stood out like cords; the wine drunk at table was potent: even through my phlegmatic frame it ran hotly.

'She hesitated a moment or two, then docilely sat down to the piano. That she could sing I have already made clear: how she could sing, with what pathos, passion, as well as perfect art, I had never realised before.

'When the song was ended she remained for a while, with eyes lost in distance, very still, save for her quick breathing. It was clear she was moved by the music; indeed she must have thrown her whole soul into it.

'At first we, the audience, paid her the rare compliment of silence. Then the baron broke forth into loud applause. "Brava, brava! that was really said *con amore*. A delicious love song, delicious – but French! You must sing one of our Slav melodies for Marshfield before you allow us to go and smoke."

'She started from her reverie with a flush, and after a pause struck slowly a few simple chords, then began one of those strangely sweet, yet intensely pathetic Russian airs, which give one a curious revelation of the profound, endless melancholy lurking in the national mind.

' "What do you think of it?" asked the baron of me when it ceased.

' "What I have always thought of such music – it is that of a hopeless people; poetical, crushed and resigned."

'He gave a loud laugh. "Hear the analyst, the *psychologue* – why, man, it is a love song! Is it possible that we, uncivilised, are truer realists than our hypercultured Western neighbours? Have we gone to the root of the matter, in our simple way?"

'The baroness got up abruptly. She looked white and spent; there were bistre circles round her eyes.

' "I am tired," she said, with dry lips. "You will excuse me, Mr Marshfield, I must really go to bed."

' "Go to bed, go to bed," cried her husband gayly. Then, quoting in Russian from the song she had just sung: "Sleep, my little soft white dove: my little innocent tender lamb!" She hurried from the room. The baron laughed again, and, taking me familiarly by the arm, led me to his own set of apartments for the promised smoke. He ensconced me in an armchair, placed cigars of every description and a Turkish pipe ready to my hand, and a little table on which stood cut-glass flasks and beakers in tempting array.

'After I had selected my cigar with some precautions, I glanced at him over a careless remark, and was startled to see a sudden alteration in his whole look and attitude.

' "You will forgive me, Marshfield," he said, as he caught my eye, speaking with spasmodic politeness. 'It is more than probable that I shall have to set out upon this chase I spoke of tonight, and I must now go and change my clothes, that I may be ready to start at any moment. This is the hour when it is most likely these hell beasts are to be got at. You have all you want, I hope,' interrupting an outbreak of ferocity by an effort after his former courtesy.

'It was curious to watch the man of the world struggling with the primitive man.

' "But, baron," said I, "I do not at all see the fun of sticking at home like this. You know my passion for witnessing everything new, strange and outlandish. You will surely not refuse me such an opportunity for observation as a midnight wolf raid. I will do my best not to be in the way if you will take me with you."

'At first it seemed as if he had some difficulty in realising the drift of my words, he was so engrossed by some inner thought. But as I repeated them, he gave vent to a loud cachinnation.

' "By heaven! I like your spirit," he exclaimed, clapping me strongly on the shoulder. "Of course you shall come. You shall," he repeated, "and I promise you a sight, a hunt such as you never heard or dreamed of – you will be able to tell them in England the sort of thing we can do here in that line – such wolves are rare quarry," he added, looking slyly at me, "and I have a new plan for getting at them."

'There was a long pause, and then there rose in the stillness the unearthly howling of the baron's hounds, a cheerful sound which only their owner's somewhat loud converse of the evening had kept from becoming excessively obtrusive.

' "Hark at them – the beauties!" cried he, showing his short, strong teeth, pointed like a dog's in a wide grin of anticipative delight. "They have been kept on pretty short commons, poor things! They are hungry. By the way, Marshfield, you can sit tight to a horse, I trust? If you were to roll off, you know, these splendid fellows – they would chop you up in a second. They would chop you up," he repeated unctuously, "snap, crunch, gobble, and there would be an end of you!"

' "If I could not ride a decent horse without being thrown," I retorted, a little stung by his manner, "after my recent three months' torture with the Guard Cossacks, I should indeed be a hopeless subject. Do not think of frightening me from the exploit, but say frankly if my company would be displeasing.'

' "Tut!" he said, waving his hand impatiently, "it is your affair. I have warned you. Go and get ready if you want to come. Time presses."

'I was determined to be of the fray; my blood was up. I have hinted that the baron's Tokay had stirred it.

'I went to my room and hurriedly donned clothes more suitable for rough night work. My last care was to slip into my pockets a brace of double-barrelled pistols which formed part of my travelling kit. When I returned I found the baron already booted and spurred; this without metaphor. He was stretched full length on the divan, and did not speak as I came in, or even look at me. Chewing an unlit cigar, with eyes fixed on the ceiling, he was evidently following some absorbing train of ideas.

'The silence was profound; time went by; it grew oppressive; at length, wearied out, I fell, over my chibouk, into a doze filled with puzzling visions, out of which I was awakened with a start. My companion had sprung up, very lightly, to his feet. In his throat was an odd, half-suppressed cry, grewsome to hear. He stood on tiptoe, with eyes fixed, as though looking through the wall, and I distinctly saw his ears point in the intensity of his listening.

'After a moment, with hasty, noiseless energy, and without the slightest ceremony, he blew the lamps out, drew back the heavy curtains and threw the tall window wide open. A rush of icy air, and the bright rays of the moon – gibbous, I remember, in her third quarter – filled the room. Outside the mist had condensed, and the view was unrestricted over the white plains at the foot of the hill.

'The baron stood motionless in the open window, callous to the cold in which, after a minute, I could hardly keep my teeth from chattering, his head bent forward, still listening. I listened too, with "all my ears", but could not catch a sound; indeed the silence over the great expanse of snow might have been called awful; even the dogs were mute.

'Presently, far, far away, came a faint tinkle of bells; so faint, at first, that I thought it was but fancy, then distincter. It was even more eerie than the silence, I thought, though I knew it could come but from some passing sleigh. All at once that ceased, and again my duller senses could perceive nothing, though I saw by my host's craning neck that he was more on the alert than ever. But at last I too heard once more, this time not bells, but as it were the tread of horses muffled by the snow, intermittent and dull, yet drawing nearer. And then in the inner silence of the great house it seemed to me I caught the noise of closing doors; but here the hounds, as if suddenly becoming alive to some disturbance, raised the same fearsome concert of yells and barks with which they had greeted my arrival, and listening became useless.

'I had risen to my feet. My host, turning from the window, seized my shoulder with a fierce grip, and bade me "hold my noise"; for a second or two I stood motionless under his iron talons, then he released me with an exultant whisper: "Now for our chase!" and made for the door with a spring. Hastily gulping down a mouthful of arak from one of the bottles on the table, I followed him, and, guided by the sound of his footsteps before me, groped my way through passages as black as Erebus.

'After a time, which seemed a long one, a small door was flung open in front, and I saw Kossowski glide into the moonlit courtyard and cross the square. When I too came out he was disappearing into the gaping darkness of the open stable door, and there I overtook him.

'A man who seemed to have been sleeping in a corner jumped up at our entrance, and led out a horse ready saddled. In obedience to a gruff order from his master, as the latter mounted, he then brought forward another which he had evidently thought to ride himself and held the stirrup for me.

'We came delicately forth, and the Cossack hurriedly barred the great door behind us. I caught a glimpse of his worn, scarred face by the moonlight, as he peeped after us for a second before shutting himself in; it was stricken with terror.

'The baron trotted briskly towards the kennels, from whence there was now issuing a truly infernal clangour, and, as my steed followed suit of his own accord, I could see how he proceeded dexterously to unbolt the gates without dismounting, while the beasts within dashed themselves against them and tore the ground in their fury of impatience.

'He smiled, as he swung back the barriers at last, and his "beauties" came forth. Seven or eight monstrous brutes, hounds of a kind unknown to me: fulvous and sleek of coat, tall on their legs, square-headed, long-tailed, deep-chested; with terrible jaws slobbering in eagerness. They leaped around and up at us, much to our horses' distaste. Kossowski, still smiling, lashed at them unsparingly with his hunting whip, and they responded, not with yells of pain, but with snarls of fury.

'Managing his restless steed and his cruel whip with consummate ease, my host drove the unruly crew before him out of the precincts, then halted and bent down from his saddle to examine some slight prints in the snow which led, not the way I had come, but towards what seemed another avenue. In a second or two the hounds were gathered round this spot, their great snake-like tails quivering, noses to earth, yelping with excitement. I had some ado to manage my horse, and my eyesight was far from being as keen as the baron's, but I had then no doubt he had come already upon wolf tracks, and I shuddered mentally, thinking of the sleigh bells.

'Suddenly Kossowski raised himself from his strained position; under his low fur cap his face, with its fixed smile, looked scarcely human in the white light; and then we broke into a hand canter just as the hounds dashed, in a compact body, along the trail.

'But we had not gone more than a few hundred yards before they began to falter, then straggled, stopped and ran back and about with dismal cries. It was clear to me they had lost the scent. My companion reined in his horse, and mine, luckily a well-trained brute, halted of himself.

'We had reached a bend in a broad avenue of firs and larches, and just where we stood, and where the hounds ever returned and met nose to nose in frantic conclave, the snow was trampled and soiled, and a little farther on planed in a great sweep, as if by a turning sleigh. Beyond was a double-furrowed track of runners and regular hoofprints leading far away.

'Before I had time to reflect upon the bearing of this unexpected inter-ruption, Kossowski, as if suddenly possessed by a devil, fell upon the hounds with his whip, flogging them upon the new track, uttering the while the most savage cries I have ever heard issue from human throat. The dis-appointed beasts were nothing loath to seize upon another trail; after a second of hesitation they had understood, and were off upon it at a tearing pace, we after them at the best speed of our horses.

'Some unformed idea that we were going to escort, or rescue, benighted travellers flickered dimly in my mind as I galloped through the night air; but when I managed to approach my companion and called out to him for explanation, he only turned half round and grinned at me.

'Before us lay now the white plain, scintillating under the high moon's rays. That light is deceptive; I could be sure of nothing upon the wide expanse but of the dark, leaping figures of the hounds already spread out in a straggling line, some right ahead, others just in front of us. In a short time also the icy wind, cutting my face mercilessly as we increased our pace, well nigh blinded me with tears of cold.

'I can hardly realise how long this pursuit after an unseen prey lasted; I can only remember that I was getting rather faint with fatigue, and igno-miniously held on to my pommel, when all of a sudden the black outline of a sleigh merged into sight in front of us.

'I rubbed my smarting eyes with my benumbed hand; we were gaining upon it second by second; two of those hell hounds of the baron's were already within a few leaps of it.

'Soon I was able to make out two figures, one standing up and urging the horses on with whip and voice, the other clinging to the back seat and looking towards us in an attitude of terror. A great fear crept into my half-frozen brain – were we not bringing deadly danger instead of help to these travellers? Great God! did the baron mean to use them as a bait for his new method of wolf hunting?

'I would have turned upon Kossowski with a cry of expostulation or warning, but he, urging on his hounds as he galloped on their flank, howling and gesticulating like a veritable Hun, passed me by like a flash – and all at once I knew.'

Marshfield paused for a moment and sent his pale smile round upon his listeners, who now showed no signs of sleepiness; he knocked the ash from his cigar, twisted the latter round in his mouth, and added dryly: 'And I confess it seemed to me a little strong even for a baron in the Carpathians. The travellers were our quarry. But the reason why the lord of Yany had turned man-hunter I was yet to learn. Just then I had to direct my energies to frustrating his plans. I used my spurs mercilessly. While I drew up even with him I saw the two figures in the sleigh change places; he who had hitherto driven now faced back, while his companion took the reins, there was the pale blue sheen of a revolver barrel under the moonlight, followed by a yellow flash, and the nearest hound rolled over in the snow.

'With an oath the baron twisted round in his saddle to call up and urge on the remainder. My horse had taken fright at the report and dashed irresistibly forward, bringing me at once almost level with the fugitives, and the next instant the revolver was turned menacingly towards me. There was no time to explain; my pistol was already drawn, and as another of the brutes bounded up, almost under my horse's feet, I loosed it upon him. I must have let off both barrels at once, for the weapon flew out of my hand, but the hound's back was broken. I presume the traveller understood; at any rate, he did not fire at me.

'In moments of intense excitement like these, strangely enough, the mind is extraordinarily open to impressions. I shall never forget that man's countenance in the sledge, as he stood upright and defied us in his mortal danger; it was young, very handsome, the features not distorted, but set into a sort of desperate, stony calm, and I knew it, beyond all doubt, for that of an Englishman. And then I saw his companion – it was the baron's wife. And I understood why the bells had been removed.

'It takes a long time to say this; it only required an instant to see it. The loud explosion of my pistol had hardly ceased to ring before the baron, with a fearful imprecation, was upon me. First he lashed at me with his whip as we tore along side by side, and then I saw him wind the reins round his off arm and bend over, and I felt his angry fingers close tightly on my right foot. The next instant I should have been lifted out of my saddle, but there came another shot from the sledge. The baron's horse plunged and stumbled, and the baron, hanging on to my foot with a fierce grip, was wrenched from his seat. His horse, however, was up again immediately, and I was released, and then I caught a confused glimpse of the frightened and wounded animal galloping wildly away to the right, leaving a black track of blood behind him in the snow, his master, entangled in the reins, running with incredible swiftness by his side and endeavouring to vault back into the saddle.

'And now came to pass a terrible thing which, in his savage plans, my host had doubtless never anticipated.

'One of the hounds that had during this short check recovered lost ground, coming across this hot trail of blood, turned away from his course, and with a joyous yell darted after the running man. In another instant the remainder of the pack was upon the new scent.

'As soon as I could stop my horse, I tried to turn him in the direction the new chase had taken, but just then, through the night air, over the receding sound of the horse's scamper and the sobbing of the pack in full cry, there came a long scream, and after that a sickening silence. And I knew that somewhere yonder, under the beautiful moonlight, the Baron Kossowski was being devoured by his starving dogs.

'I looked round, with the sweat on my face, vaguely, for some human being to share the horror of the moment, and I saw, gliding away, far away in the white distance, the black silhouette of the sledge.'

'Well?' said we, in divers tones of impatience, curiosity or horror, according to our divers temperaments, as the speaker uncrossed his legs and gazed at us in mild triumph, with all the air of having said his say, and satisfactorily proved his point.

'Well,' repeated he, 'what more do you want to know? It will interest you but slightly, I am sure, to hear how I found my way back to the Hof; or how I told as much as I deemed prudent of the evening's gruesome work to the baron's servants, who, by the way, to my amazement, displayed the profoundest and most unmistakable sorrow at the tidings, and sallied forth (at their head the Cossack who had seen us depart) to seek for his remains. Excuse the unpleasantness of the remark: I fear the dogs must have left very little of him, he had dieted them so carefully. However, since it was to have been a case of "chop, crunch and gobble", as the baron had it, I preferred that that particular fate should have overtaken him rather than me – or, for that matter, either of those two countrypeople of ours in the sledge.

'Nor am I going to inflict upon you,' continued Marshfield, after draining his glass, 'a full account of my impressions when I found myself once more in that immense, deserted and stricken house, so luxuriously prepared for the mistress who had fled from it; how I philosophised over all this, according to my wont; the conjectures I made as to the first acts of the drama; the untold sufferings my countrywoman must have endured from the moment her husband first grew jealous till she determined on this desperate step; as to how and when she had met her lover, how they communicated, and how the baron had discovered the intended flitting in time to concoct his characteristic revenge.

'One thing you may be sure of, I had no mind to remain at Yany an hour longer than necessary. I even contrived to get well clear of the neighbourhood before the lady's absence was discovered. Luckily for me – or I might have been taxed with connivance, though indeed the simple household did not seem to know what suspicion was, and accepted my account with childlike credence – very typical, and very convenient to me at the same time.'

'But how do you know,' said one of us, 'that the man was her lover? He might have been her brother or some other relative.'

'That,' said Marshfield, with his little flat laugh, 'I happen to have ascertained – and, curiously enough, only a few weeks ago. It was at the play, between the acts, from my comfortable seat (the first row in the pit). I was looking leisurely round the house when I caught sight of a woman, in a box close by, whose head was turned from me, and who presented the somewhat unusual spectacle of a young neck and shoulders of the most exquisite contours – and perfectly grey hair; and not dull grey, but rather of a pleasing tint like frosted silver. This aroused my curiosity. I brought my glasses to a focus on her and waited patiently till she turned round. Then I recognised the Baroness Kassowski, and I no longer wondered at the young hair being white.

'Yet she looked placid and happy; strangely so, it seemed to me, under the sudden reviving in my memory of such scenes as I have now described. But presently I understood further: beside her, in close attendance, was the man of the sledge, a handsome fellow with much of a military air about him.

'During the course of the evening, as I watched, I saw a friend of mine come into the box, and at the end I slipped out into the passage to catch him as he came out.

' "Who is the woman with the white hair?" I asked. Then, in the fragmentary style approved of by ultra-fashionable young men – this earnest-languid mode of speech presents curious similarities in all languages – he told me: "Most charming couple in London – awfully pretty, wasn't she? – he had been in the Guards – attaché at Vienna once – they adored each other. White hair, devilish queer, wasn't it? Suited her, somehow. And then she had been married to a Russian, or something, somewhere in the wilds, and their names were – " But do you know,' said Marshfield, interrupting himself, 'I think I had better let you find that out for yourselves, if you care.'

WILKIE COLLINS

The eldest son of the landscape painter William Collins, Wilkie Collins was born in London in 1824. Educated for a few years at private schools in London, he moved with his family to Italy when he was thirteen and it was there that he gained his real education. Rebelling against his father's strict religious code and conservative values, Wilkie Collins refused to settle into life in either the tea business or as a barrister and remained adamant that he wanted to write. He went on to become one of the most popular novelists of his day. His reputation now rests on his novels *The Woman in White* and *The Moonstone*. Because in his work he explored the realms of mystery, suspense and crime, he is often regarded as the inventor of the detective story. Collins never married and his private life remains a mixture of the romantic and the raffish. Living with his mother until he was thirty-two, Collins then left to set up home with a young woman, Caroline Graves, and her daughter by another man. Remaining with Caroline on and off for the rest of his life, he also fathered three illegitimate children by Martha Rudd. This scandalous arrangement led to Collins being ostracised by smart Victorian society. Plagued by gout from his thirties, Collins was often in great pain, which he attempted to dull with increasing amounts of opium. He died in 1889.

The Dream Woman

A Mystery in Four Narratives

The First Narrative:
Introductory Statement of the Facts by Percy Fairbank

ONE

'Hallo, there! Ostler! Hallo–o–o!'

'My dear! why don't you look for the bell?'

'I have looked – there is no bell.'

'And nobody in the yard. How very extraordinary! Call again, dear.'

'Ostler! Hallo, there! Ostler–r–r!'

My second call echoes through empty space, and rouses nobody – produces, in short, no visible result. I am at the end of my resources – I don't know what to say or what to do next. Here I stand in the solitary inn yard of a strange town, with two horses to hold, and a lady to take care of. By way of adding to my responsibilities, it so happens that one of the horses is dead lame, and that the lady is my wife.

Who am I? – you will ask.

There is plenty of time to answer the question. Nothing happens; and nobody appears to receive us. Let me introduce myself and my wife.

I am Percy Fairbank – English gentleman – age (let us say) forty – no profession – moderate politics – middle height – fair complexion – easy character – plenty of money.

My wife is a French lady. She was Mademoiselle Clotilde Delorge – when I was first presented to her at her father's house in France. I fell in love with her – I really don't know why. It might have been because I was perfectly idle, and had nothing else to do at the time. Or it might have been because all my friends said she was the very last woman whom I ought to think of marrying. On the surface, I must own, there is nothing in common between Mrs Fairbank and me. She is tall; she is dark; she is nervous, excitable, romantic; in all her opinions she proceeds to extremes. What could such a woman see in me? what could I see in her? I know no more than you do. In some mysterious manner we exactly suit each other. We have been man and wife for ten years and our only regret is that we have no children. I don't know what you may think; I call that – upon the whole – a happy marriage.

So much for ourselves. The next question is – what has brought us into the inn yard? and why am I obliged to turn groom, and hold the horses?

We live for the most part in France – at the country house in which my wife and I first met. Occasionally, by way of variety, we pay visits to my friends in England. We are paying one of those visits now. Our host is an old college friend of mine, possessed of a fine estate in Somersetshire; and we have arrived at his house – called Farleigh Hall – towards the close of the hunting season.

On the day of which I am now writing – destined to be a memorable day in our calendar – the hounds meet at Farleigh Hall. Mrs Fairbank and I are mounted on two of the best horses in my friend's stables. We are quite unworthy of that distinction; for we know nothing and care nothing about hunting. On the other hand, we delight in riding, and we enjoy the breezy spring morning and the fair and fertile English landscape surrounding us on every side. While the hunt prospers, we follow the hunt. But when a check occurs – when time passes and patience is sorely tried; when the bewildered dogs run hither and thither, and strong language falls from the lips of exasperated sportsmen – we fail to take any further interest in the proceedings. We turn our horses' heads in the direction of a grassy lane, delightfully shaded by trees. We trot merrily along the lane, and find ourselves on an open common. We gallop across the common, and follow the windings of a second lane. We cross a brook, we pass through a village, we emerge into pastoral solitude among the hills. The horses toss their heads, and neigh to each other, and enjoy it as much as we do. The hunt is forgotten. We are as happy as a couple of children; we are actually singing a French song – when in one moment our merriment comes to an end. My wife's horse sets one of his forefeet on a loose stone, and stumbles. His rider's ready hand saves him from falling. But, at the first attempt he makes to go on, the sad truth shows itself – a tendon is strained; the horse is lame.

What is to be done? We are strangers in a lonely part of the country. Look where we may, we see no signs of human habitation. There is nothing for it but to take the bridle road up the hill, and try what we can discover on the other side. I transfer the saddles, and mount my wife on my own horse. He is not used to carry a lady; he misses the familiar pressure of a man's legs on either side of him; he fidgets, and starts, and kicks up the dust. I follow on foot, at a respectful distance from his heels, leading the lame horse. Is there a more miserable object on the face of creation than a lame horse? I have seen lame men and lame dogs who were cheerful creatures; but I never yet saw a lame horse who didn't look heartbroken over his own misfortune.

For half an hour my wife capers and curvets sideways along the bridle road. I trudge on behind her; and the heartbroken horse halts behind me.

Hard by the top of the hill, our melancholy procession passes a Somersetshire peasant at work in a field. I summon the man to approach us; and the man looks at me stolidly, from the middle of the field, without stirring a step. I ask at the top of my voice how far it is to Farleigh Hall.

The Somersetshire peasant answers at the top of *his* voice: 'Vourteen mile. Gi' oi a drap o' zyder.'

I translate (for my wife's benefit) from the Somersetshire language into the English language. We are fourteen miles from Farleigh Hall; and our friend in the field desires to be rewarded, for giving us that information, with a drop of cider. There is the peasant, painted by himself! Quite a bit of character, my dear! Quite a bit of character!

Mrs Fairbank doesn't view the study of agricultural human nature with my relish. Her fidgety horse will not allow her a moment's repose; she is beginning to lose her temper.

'We can't go fourteen miles in this way,' she says. 'Where is the nearest inn? Ask that brute in the field!'

I take a shilling from my pocket and hold it up in the sun. The shilling exercises magnetic virtues. The shilling draws the peasant slowly toward me from the middle of the field. I inform him that we want to put up the horses and to hire a carriage to take us back to Farleigh Hall. Where can we do that? The peasant answers (with his eye on the shilling):

'At Oonderbridge, to be zure.' (At Underbridge, to be sure.)

'Is it far to Underbridge?'

The peasant repeats, 'Var to Oonderbridge?' – and laughs at the question. 'Hoo-hoo-hoo!' (Underbridge is evidently close by – if we could only find it.)

'Will you show us the way, my man?'

'Will you gi' oi a drap of zyder?'

I courteously bend my head, and point to the shilling. The agricultural intelligence exerts itself. The peasant joins our melancholy procession. My wife is a fine woman, but he never once looks at my wife – and, more extraordinary still, he never even looks at the horses. His eyes are with his mind – and his mind is on the shilling.

We reach the top of the hill – and, behold on the other side, nestling in a valley, the shrine of our pilgrimage, the town of Underbridge! Here our guide claims his shilling, and leaves us to find out the inn for ourselves. I am constitutionally a polite man. I say 'Good-morning' at parting. The guide looks at me with the shilling between his teeth to make sure that it is a good one. 'Marnin!' he says savagely – and turns his back on us, as if we had offended him. A curious product, this, of the growth of civilisation. If I didn't see a church spire at Underbridge, I might suppose that we had lost ourselves on a savage island.

TWO

Arriving at the town, we had no difficulty in finding the inn. The town is composed of one desolate street; and midway in that street stands the inn – an ancient stone building sadly out of repair. The painting on the signboard is obliterated. The shutters over the long range of front windows are all closed. A cock and his hens are the only living creatures at the door. Plainly, this is one of the old inns of the stage-coach period, ruined by the railway. We pass through the open arched doorway, and find no one to welcome us. We advance into the stable yard behind; I assist my wife to dismount – and there we are in the position already disclosed to view at the opening of this narrative. No bell to ring. No human creature to answer when I call. I stand helpless, with the bridles of the horses in my hand. Mrs Fairbank saunters gracefully down the length of the yard and does – what all women do, when they find themselves in a strange place. She opens every door as she passes it, and peeps in. On my side, I have just recovered my breath, I am on the point of shouting for the ostler for the third and last time, when I hear Mrs Fairbank suddenly call to me: 'Percy! come here!'

Her voice is eager and agitated. She has opened a last door at the end of the yard, and has started back from some sight which has suddenly met her view. I hitch the horses' bridles on a rusty nail in the wall near me, and join my wife. She has turned pale, and catches me nervously by the arm.

'Good heavens!' she cries; 'look at that!'

I look – and what do I see? I see a dingy little stable, containing two stalls. In one stall a horse is munching his corn. In the other a man is lying asleep on the litter.

A worn, withered, woebegone man in a ostler's dress. His hollow wrinkled cheeks, his scanty grizzled hair, his dry yellow skin, tell their own tale of past sorrow or suffering. There is an ominous frown on his eyebrows – there is a painful nervous contraction on the side of his mouth. I hear him breathing convulsively when I first look in; he shudders and sighs in his sleep. It is not a pleasant sight to see, and I turn round instinctively to the bright sunlight in the yard. My wife turns me back again in the direction of the stable door.

'Wait!' she says. 'Wait! he may do it again.'

'Do what again?'

'He was talking in his sleep, Percy, when I first looked in. He was dreaming some dreadful dream. Hush! he's beginning again.'

I look and listen. The man stirs on his miserable bed. The man speaks in a quick, fierce whisper through his clenched teeth. 'Wake up! Wake up, there! Murder!'

There is an interval of silence. He moves one lean arm slowly until it rests over his throat; he shudders, and turns on his straw; he raises his arm from his throat, and feebly stretches it out; his hand clutches at the straw on the side towards which he has turned; he seems to fancy that he is grasping at the edge of something. I see his lips begin to move again; I step softly into the stable; my wife follows me, with her hand fast clasped in mine. We both bend over him. He is talking once more in his sleep – strange talk, mad talk, this time.

'Light grey eyes' (we hear him say), 'and a droop in the left eyelid – flaxen hair, with a gold-yellow streak in it – all right, mother! fair, white arms with a down on them – little, lady's hand, with a reddish look round the finger-nails – the knife – the cursed knife – first on one side, then on the other – aha, you she-devil! where is the knife?'

He stops and grows restless on a sudden. We see him writhing on the straw. He throws up both his hands and gasps hysterically for breath. His eyes open suddenly. For a moment they look at nothing, with a vacant glitter in them – then they close again in deeper sleep. Is he dreaming still? Yes; but the dream seems to have taken a new course. When he speaks next, the tone is altered; the words are few – sadly and imploringly repeated over and over again. 'Say you love me! I am so fond of *you*. Say you love me! say you love me!' He sinks into deeper and deeper sleep, faintly repeating those words. They die away on his lips. He speaks no more.

By this time Mrs Fairbank has got over her terror; she is devoured by curiosity now. The miserable creature on the straw has appealed to the imaginative side of her character. Her illimitable appetite for romance hungers and thirsts for more. She shakes me impatiently by the arm.

'Do you hear? There is a woman at the bottom of it, Percy! There is love and murder in it, Percy! Where are the people of the inn? Go into the yard, and call to them again.'

My wife belongs, on her mother's side, to the South of France. The South of France breeds fine women with hot tempers. I say no more. Married men will understand my position. Single men may need to be told that there are occasions when we must not only love and honour – we must also obey – our wives.

I turn to the door to obey my wife, and find myself confronted by a stranger who has stolen on us unawares. The stranger is a tiny, sleepy, rosy old man, with a vacant pudding-face and a shining bald head. He wears drab breeches and gaiters, and a respectable square-tailed ancient black coat. I feel instinctively that here is the landlord of the inn.

'Good-morning, sir,' says the rosy old man. 'I'm a little hard of hearing. Was it you that was a-calling just now in the yard?'

Before I can answer, my wife interposes. She insists (in a shrill voice, adapted to our host's hardness of hearing) on knowing who that unfortunate person is sleeping on the straw. 'Where does he come from? Why does he say such dreadful things in his sleep? Is he married or single? Did he ever fall in love with a murderess? What sort of a looking woman was she? Did she really stab him or not? In short, dear Mr Landlord, tell us the whole story!'

Dear Mr Landlord waits drowsily until Mrs Fairbank has quite done – then delivers himself of his reply as follows:

'His name's Francis Raven. He's an Independent Methodist. He was forty-five year old last birthday. And he's my ostler. That's his story.'

My wife's hot southern temper finds its way to her foot, and expresses itself by a stamp on the stable yard.

The landlord turns himself sleepily round, and looks at the horses. 'A fine pair of horses, them two in the yard. Do you want to put 'em in my stables?' I reply in the affirmative by a nod. The landlord, bent on making himself agreeable to my wife, addresses her once more. 'I'm a-going to wake Francis Raven. He's an Independent Methodist. He was forty-five year old last birthday. And he's my ostler. That's his story.'

Having issued this second edition of his interesting narrative, the landlord enters the stable. We follow him to see how he will wake Francis Raven, and what will happen upon that. The stable broom stands in a corner; the landlord takes it – advances toward the sleeping ostler – and coolly stirs the man up with a broom as if he was a wild beast in a cage. Francis Raven starts to his feet with a cry of terror – looks at us wildly, with a horrid glare of suspicion in his eyes – recovers himself the next moment – and suddenly changes into a decent, quiet, respectable serving-man.

'I beg your pardon, ma'am. I beg your pardon, sir.'

The tone and manner in which he makes his apologies are both above his apparent station in life. I begin to catch the infection of Mrs Fairbank's interest in this man. We both follow him out into the yard to see what he will do with the horses. The manner in which he lifts the injured leg of the lame horse tells me at once that he understands his business. Quickly and quietly, he leads the animal into an empty stable; quickly and quietly, he gets a bucket of hot water, and puts the lame horse's leg into it. 'The warm water will reduce the swelling, sir. I will bandage the leg afterwards.' All that he does is done intelligently; all that he says, he says to the purpose.

Nothing wild, nothing strange about him now. Is this the same man whom we heard talking in his sleep? – the same man who woke with that cry of terror and that horrid suspicion in his eyes? I determine to try him with one or two questions.

THREE

'Not much to do here,' I say to the ostler.

'Very little to do, sir,' the ostler replies.

'Anybody staying in the house?'

'The house is quite empty, sir.'

'I thought you were all dead. I could make nobody hear me.'

'The landlord is very deaf, sir, and the waiter is out on an errand.'

'Yes; and *you* were fast asleep in the stable. Do you often take a nap in the daytime?'

The worn face of the ostler faintly flushes. His eyes look away from my eyes for the first time. Mrs Fairbank furtively pinches my arm. Are we on the eve of a discovery at last? I repeat my question. The man has no civil alternative but to give me an answer. The answer is given in these words:

'I was tired out, sir. You wouldn't have found me asleep in the daytime but for that.'

'Tired out, eh? You had been hard at work, I suppose?'

'No, sir.'

'What was it, then?'

He hesitates again, and answers unwillingly, 'I was up all night.'

'Up all night? Anything going on in the town?'

'Nothing going on, sir.'

'Anybody ill?'

'Nobody ill, sir.'

That reply is the last. Try as I may, I can extract nothing more from him. He turns away and busies himself in attending to the horse's leg. I leave the stable to speak to the landlord about the carriage which is to take us back to Farleigh Hall. Mrs Fairbank remains with the ostler, and favours me with a look at parting. The look says plainly, '*I* mean to find out why he was up all night. Leave him to me.'

The ordering of the carriage is easily accomplished. The inn possesses one horse and one chaise. The landlord has a story to tell of the horse, and a story to tell of the chaise. They resemble the story of Francis Raven – with this exception, that the horse and chaise belong to no religious persuasion. 'The horse will be nine year old next birthday. I've had the shay for four-and-twenty year. Mr Max, of Underbridge, he bred the horse; and Mr Pooley, of Yeovil, he built the shay. It's my horse and my shay. And that's *their* story!' Having relieved his mind of these details, the landlord proceeds to put the harness on the horse. By way of assisting him, I drag the chaise into the yard. Just as our preparations are completed, Mrs Fairbank appears.

A moment or two later the ostler follows her out. He has bandaged the horse's leg, and is now ready to drive us to Farleigh Hall. I observe signs of agitation in his face and manner, which suggest that my wife has found her way into his confidence. I put the question to her privately in a corner of the yard. 'Well? Have you found out why Francis Raven was up all night?'

Mrs Fairbank has an eye to dramatic effect. Instead of answering plainly yes or no, she suspends the interest and excites the audience by putting a question on her side.

'What is the day of the month, dear?'

'The day of the month is the first of March.'

'The first of March, Percy, is Francis Raven's birthday.'

I try to look as if I was interested – and don't succeed.

'Francis was born,' Mrs Fairbank proceeds gravely, 'at two o'clock in the morning.'

I begin to wonder whether my wife's intellect is going the way of the landlord's intellect. 'Is that all?' I ask.

'It is *not* all,' Mrs Fairbank answers. 'Francis Raven sits up on the morning of his birthday because he is afraid to go to bed.'

'And why is he afraid to go to bed?'

'Because he is in peril of his life.'

'On his birthday?'

'On his birthday. At two o'clock in the morning. As regularly as the birthday comes round.'

There she stops. Has she discovered no more than that? No more thus far. I begin to feel really interested by this time. I ask eagerly what it means? Mrs Fairbank points mysteriously to the chaise – with Francis Raven (hitherto our ostler, now our coachman) waiting for us to get in. The chaise has a seat for two in front, and a seat for one behind. My wife casts a warning look at me, and places herself on the seat in front.

The necessary consequence of this arrangement is that Mrs Fairbank sits by the side of the driver during a journey of two hours and more. Need I state the result? It would be an insult to your intelligence to state the result. Let me offer you my place in the chaise. And let Francis Raven tell his terrible story in his own words.

The Second Narrative: The Ostler's Story – Told by Himself

FOUR

It is now ten years ago since I got my first warning of the great trouble of my life in a dream.

I shall be better able to tell you about it if you will please suppose yourselves to be drinking tea along with us in our little cottage in Cambridgeshire, ten years since.

The time was the close of day, and there were three of us at the table, namely, my mother, myself and my mother's sister, Mrs Chance. These two were Scotchwomen by birth, and both were widows. There was no other resemblance between them that I can call to mind. My mother had lived all her life in England, and had no more of the Scotch brogue on her tongue than I have. My Aunt Chance had never been out of Scotland until she came to keep house with my mother after her husband's death. And when *she* opened her lips you heard broad Scotch, I can tell you, if you ever heard it yet!

As it fell out, there was a matter of some consequence in debate among us that evening. It was this: whether I should do well or not to take a long journey on foot the next morning.

Now the next morning happened to be the day before my birthday; and the purpose of the journey was to offer myself for a situation as groom at a great house in the neighbouring county to ours. The place was reported as likely to fall vacant in about three weeks' time. I was as well fitted to fill it as any other man. In the prosperous days of our family, my father had been manager of a training stable, and he had kept me employed among the horses from my boyhood upwards. Please to excuse my troubling you with these small matters. They all fit into my story further on, as you will soon find out.

My poor mother was dead against my leaving home on the morrow. 'You can never walk all the way there and all the way back again by tomorrow night,' she says. 'The end of it will be that you will sleep away from home on your birthday. You have never done that yet, Francis, since your father's death, I don't like your doing it now. Wait a day longer, my son – only one day.'

For my own part, I was weary of being idle, and I couldn't abide the notion of delay. Even one day might make all the difference. Some other man might take time by the forelock and get the place.

'Consider how long I have been out of work,' I says, 'and don't ask me to put off the journey. I won't fail you, mother. I'll get back by tomorrow night, if I have to pay my last sixpence for a lift in a cart.

My mother shook her head. 'I don't like it, Francis – I don't like it!' There was no moving her from that view. We argued and argued, until we were both at a deadlock. It ended in our agreeing to refer the difference between us to my mother's sister, Mrs Chance.

While we were trying hard to convince each other, my Aunt Chance sat as dumb as a fish, stirring her tea and thinking her own thoughts. When we made our appeal to her, she seemed as it were to wake up. 'Ye baith refer it to my puir judgement?' she says, in her broad Scotch. We both answered yes. Upon that my Aunt Chance first cleared the tea-table, and then pulled out from the pocket of her gown a pack of cards.

Don't run away, if you please, with the notion that this was done lightly, with a view to amuse my mother and me. My Aunt Chance seriously believed that she could look into the future by telling fortunes with the cards. She did nothing herself without first consulting the cards. She could give no more serious proof of her interest in my welfare than the proof which she was offering now. I don't say it profanely; I only mention the fact – the cards had, in some incomprehensible way, got themselves jumbled up together with her religious convictions. You meet with people nowadays who believe in spirits working by way of tables and chairs. On the same principle (if there *is* any principle in it) my Aunt Chance believed in providence working by way of the cards.

'Whether *you* are right, Francie, or your mither – whether ye will do weel or ill, the morrow, to go or stay – the cairds will tell it. We are a' in the hands of proavidence. The cairds will tell it.'

Hearing this, my mother turned her head aside, with something of a sour look in her face. Her sister's notions about the cards were little better than flat blasphemy to her mind. But she kept her opinion to herself. My Aunt Chance, to own the truth, had inherited, through her late husband, a pension of thirty pounds a year. This was an important contribution to our housekeeping, and we poor relations were bound to treat her with a certain respect. As for myself, if my poor father never did anything else for me before he fell into difficulties, he gave me a good education, and raised me (thank God) above superstitions of all sorts. However, a very little amused me in those days; and I waited to have my fortune told, as patiently as if I believed in it too!

My aunt began her hocus pocus by throwing out all the cards in the pack under seven. She shuffled the rest with her left hand for luck; and then she gave them to me to cut. 'Wi' yer left hand, Francie. Mind that! Pet your trust in proavidence – but dinna forget that your luck's in yer left hand!' A long and roundabout shifting of the cards followed, reducing them in number until there were just fifteen of them left, laid out neatly before my aunt in a half circle. The card which happened to lie outermost, at the right-hand end of the circle, was, according to rule in such cases, the card chosen to represent Me. By way of being appropriate to my situation as a poor groom out of employment, the card was – the King of Diamonds.

'I tak' up the King o' Diamants,' says my aunt. 'I count seven cairds fra' richt to left; and I humbly ask a blessing on what follows.' My aunt shut her eyes as if she was saying grace before meat, and held up to me the seventh card. I called the seventh card – the Queen of Spades. My aunt opened her eyes again in a hurry, and cast a sly look my way. 'The Queen o' Spades means a dairk woman. Ye'll be thinking in secret, Francie, of a dairk woman?'

When a man has been out of work for more than three months, his mind isn't troubled much with thinking of women – light or dark. I was thinking of the groom's place at the great house, and I tried to say so. My Aunt Chance wouldn't listen. She treated my interpretation with contempt. 'Hoot-toot! there's the caird in your hand! If ye're no thinking of her the day, ye'll be thinking of her the morrow. Where's the harm of thinking of a dairk woman! I was ance a dairk woman myself, before my hair was grey. Haud yer peace, Francie, and watch the cairds.'

I watched the cards as I was told. There were seven left on the table. My aunt removed two from one end of the row and two from the other, and desired me to call the two outermost of the three cards now left on the table. I called the Ace of Clubs and the Ten of Diamonds. My Aunt Chance lifted her eyes to the ceiling with a look of devout gratitude which sorely tried my mother's patience. The Ace of Clubs and the Ten of Diamonds, taken together, signified – first, good news (evidently the news of the groom's place); secondly, a journey that lay before me (pointing plainly to my journey tomorrow!); thirdly and lastly, a sum of money (probably the groom's wages!) waiting to find its way into my pockets. Having told my fortune in these encouraging terms, my aunt declined to carry the experiment any further. 'Eh, lad! it's a clean tempting o' proavidence to ask mair o' the cairds than the cairds have tauld us noo. Gae yer ways tomorrow to the great hoose. A dairk woman will meet ye at the gate; and she'll have a hand in getting ye the groom's place, wi' a' the gratifications and pairquisites appertaining to the same. And, mebbe, when yer poaket's full o' money, ye'll no' be forgetting yer Aunt Chance, maintaining her ain unblemished widowhood – wi' proavidence assisting – on thratty punds a year!'

I promised to remember my Aunt Chance (who had the defect, by the way, of being a terribly greedy person after money) on the next happy occasion when my poor empty pockets were to be filled at last. This done, I looked at my mother. She had agreed to take her sister for umpire between us, and her sister had given it in my favour. She raised no more objections. Silently, she got on her feet, and kissed me, and sighed bitterly – and so left the room. My Aunt Chance shook her head. 'I doubt, Francie, yer puir mither has but a heathen notion of the vairtue of the cairds!'

By daylight the next morning I set forth on my journey. I looked back at the cottage as I opened the garden gate. At one window was my mother, with her handkerchief to her eyes. At the other stood my Aunt Chance, holding up the Queen of Spades by way of encouraging me at starting. I waved my hands to both of them in token of farewell, and stepped out briskly into the road. It was then the last day of February. Be pleased to remember, in connection with this, that the first of March was the day and two o'clock in the morning the hour of my birth.

FIVE

Now you know how I came to leave home. The next thing to tell is, what happened on the journey.

I reached the great house in reasonably good time considering the distance. At the very first trial of it, the prophecy of the cards turned out to be wrong. The person who met me at the lodge gate was not a dark woman – in fact, not a woman at all – but a boy. He directed me on the way to the servants' offices; and there again the cards were all wrong. I encountered, not one woman, but three – and not one of the three was dark. I have stated that I am not superstitious, and I have told the truth. But I must own that I did feel a certain fluttering at the heart when I made my bow to the steward, and told him what business had brought me to the house. His answer completed the discomfiture of Aunt Chance's fortune-telling. My ill-luck still pursued me. That very morning another man had applied for the groom's place, and had got it.

I swallowed my disappointment as well as I could, and thanked the steward, and went to the inn in the village to get the rest and food which I sorely needed by this time.

Before starting on my homeward walk I made some enquiries at the inn, and ascertained that I might save a few miles, on my return, by following a new road. Furnished with full instructions, several times repeated, as to the various turnings I was to take, I set forth, and walked on till the evening with only one stoppage for bread and cheese. Just as it was getting towards dark, the rain came on and the wind began to rise; and I found myself, to make matters worse, in a part of the country with which I was entirely unacquainted, though I guessed myself to be some fifteen miles from home. The first house I found to enquire at was a lonely roadside inn, standing on the outskirts of a thick wood. Solitary as the place looked, it was welcome to a lost man who was also hungry, thirsty, footsore and wet.

The landlord was civil and respectable-looking; and the price he asked for a bed was reasonable enough. I was grieved to disappoint my mother. But there was no conveyance to be had, and I could go no farther afoot that night. My weariness fairly forced me to stop at the inn.

I may say for myself that I am a temperate man. My supper simply consisted of some rashers of bacon, a slice of home-made bread, and a pint of ale. I did not go to bed immediately after this moderate meal, but sat up with the landlord, talking about my bad prospects and my long run of ill-luck, and diverging from these topics to the subjects of horse-flesh and racing. Nothing was said, either by myself, my host or the few labourers who strayed into the tap-room, which could, in the slightest degree, excite my mind, or set my fancy – which is only a small fancy at the best of times – playing tricks with my common sense.

At a little after eleven the house was closed. I went round with the landlord and held the candle while the doors and lower windows were being secured. I noticed with surprise the strength of the bolts, bars and iron-sheathed shutters.

'You see, we are rather lonely here,' said the landlord. 'We never have had any attempts to break in yet, but it's always as well to be on the safe side. When nobody is sleeping here, I am the only man in the house. My wife and daughter are timid, and the servant girl takes after her missuses. Another glass of ale, before you turn in? – No! – Well, how such a sober man as you comes to be out of a place is more than I can understand for one. – Here's where you're to sleep. You're the only lodger tonight, and I think you'll say my missus has done her best to make you comfortable. You're quite sure you won't have another glass of ale? – Very well. Good-night.'

It was half-past eleven by the clock in the passage as we went upstairs to the bedroom. The window looked out on the wood at the back of the house.

I locked my door, set my candle on the chest of drawers, and wearily got ready for bed. The bleak wind was still blowing, and the solemn, surging moan of it in the wood was very dreary to hear through the night silence. Feeling strangely wakeful, I resolved to keep the candle alight until I began to grow sleepy. The truth is, I was not quite myself. I was depressed in mind by my disappointment of the morning; and I was worn out in body by my long walk. Between the two, I own I couldn't face the prospect of lying awake in the darkness, listening to the dismal moan of the wind in the wood.

Sleep stole on me before I was aware of it; my eyes closed, and I fell off to rest, without having so much as thought of extinguishing the candle.

The next thing that I remember was a faint shivering that ran through me from head to foot, and a dreadful sinking pain at my heart, such as I had never felt before. The shivering only disturbed my slumbers – the pain woke me instantly. In one moment I passed from a state of sleep to a state of wakefulness – my eyes wide open – my mind clear on a sudden as if by a miracle. The candle had burned down nearly to the last morsel of tallow, but the unsnuffed wick had just fallen off, and the light was, for the moment, fair and full.

Between the foot of the bed and the closet door I saw a person in my room. The person was a woman, standing looking at me, with a knife in her hand. It does no credit to my courage to confess it – but the truth *is* the truth. I was struck speechless with terror. There I lay with my eyes on the woman; there the woman stood (with the knife in her hand) with *her* eyes on *me*.

She said not a word as we stared each other in the face; but she moved after a little – moved slowly towards the left-hand side of the bed.

The light fell full on her face. A fair, fine woman, with yellowish flaxen hair, and light grey eyes, with a droop in the left eyelid. I noticed these things and fixed them in my mind before she was quite round at the side of the bed. Without saying a word; without any change in the stony stillness of her face; without any noise following her footfall, she came closer and closer; stopped at the bed-head; and lifted the knife to stab me. I laid my arm over my throat to save it; but, as I saw the blow coming, I threw my hand across the bed to the right side, and jerked my body over that way, just as the knife came down, like lightning, within a hair's breadth of my shoulder.

My eyes fixed on her arm and her hand – she gave me time to look at them as she slowly drew the knife out of the bed. A white, well-shaped arm, with a pretty down lying lightly over the fair skin. A delicate lady's hand, with a pink flush round the fingernails.

She drew the knife out, and passed back again slowly to the foot of the bed; she stopped there for a moment looking at me; then she came on without saying a word; without any change in the stony stillness of her face; without any noise following her footfall – came on to the side of the bed where I now lay.

Getting near me, she lifted the knife again, and I drew myself away to the left side. She struck, as before right into the mattress, with a swift downward action of her arm; and she missed me, as before, by a hair's breadth. This time my eyes wandered from her to the knife. It was like the large clasp knives which labouring men use to cut their bread and bacon with. Her delicate little fingers did not hide more than two thirds of the handle; I noticed that it was made of buckhorn, clean and shining as the blade was, and looking like new.

For the second time she drew the knife out of the bed, and suddenly hid it away in the wide sleeve of her gown. That done, she stopped by the bedside watching me. For an instant I saw her standing in that position – then the wick of the spent candle fell over into the socket. The flame dwindled to a little blue point, and the room grew dark.

A moment, or less, if possible, passed so – and then the wick flared up, smokily, for the last time. My eyes were still looking for her over the right-hand side of the bed when the last flash of light came. Look as I might, I could see nothing. The woman with the knife was gone.

I began to get back to myself again. I could feel my heart beating; I could hear the woeful moaning of the wind in the wood; I could leap up in bed, and give the alarm before she escaped from the house. 'Murder! Wake up there! Murder!'

Nobody answered to the alarm. I rose and groped my way through the darkness to the door of the room. By that way she must have got in. By that way she must have gone out.

The door of the room was fast locked, exactly as I had left it on going to bed! I looked at the window. Fast locked too!

Hearing a voice outside, I opened the door. There was the landlord, coming towards me along the passage, with his burning candle in one hand, and his gun in the other.

'What is it?' he says, looking at me in no very friendly way.

I could only answer in a whisper, 'A woman, with a knife in her hand. In my room. A fair, yellow-haired woman. She jabbed at me with the knife, twice over.'

He lifted his candle and looked at me steadily from head to foot. 'She seems to have missed you – twice over.'

'I dodged the knife as it came down. It struck the bed each time. Go in, and see.'

The landlord took his candle into the bedroom immediately. In less than a minute he came out again into the passage in a violent passion.

'The devil fly away with you and your woman with the knife! There isn't a mark in the bedclothes anywhere. What do you mean by coming into a man's place and frightening his family out of their wits by a dream?'

A dream? The woman who had tried to stab me, not a living human being like myself? I began to shake and shiver. The horrors got hold of me at the bare thought of it.

'I'll leave the house,' I said. 'Better be out on the road in the rain and dark, than back in that room, after what I've seen in it. Lend me the light to get my clothes by, and tell me what I'm to pay.'

The landlord led the way back with his light into the bedroom. 'Pay?' says he. 'You'll find your score on the slate when you go downstairs. I wouldn't have taken you in for all the money you've got about you, if I had known your dreaming, screeching ways beforehand. Look at the bed – where's the cut of a knife in it? Look at the window – is the lock bursted? Look at the door (which I heard you fasten yourself) – is it broke in? A murdering woman with a knife in my house! You ought to be ashamed of yourself!'

My eyes followed his hand as it pointed first to the bed – then to the window – then to the door. There was no gainsaying it. The bed sheet was as sound as on the day it was made. The window was fast. The door hung on its hinges as steady as ever. I huddled my clothes on without speaking. We went downstairs together. I looked at the clock in the bar-room. The time was twenty minutes past two in the morning. I paid my bill, and the landlord let me out. The rain had ceased; but the night was dark, and the wind was bleaker than ever. Little did the darkness, or the cold, or the doubt about the way home matter to me. My mind was away from all these things. My mind was fixed on the vision in the bedroom. What had I seen trying to murder me? The creature of a dream? Or that other creature from the world beyond the grave, whom men call ghost? I could make nothing of it as I walked along in the night; I had made nothing by it by midday – when I stood at last, after many times missing my road, on the doorstep of home.

SIX

My mother came out alone to welcome me back. There were no secrets between us two. I told her all that had happened, just as I have told it to you. She kept silence till I had done. And then she put a question to me.

'What time was it, Francis, when you saw the woman in your dream?'

I had looked at the clock when I left the inn, and I had noticed that the hands pointed to twenty minutes past two. Allowing for the time consumed in speaking to the landlord, and in getting on my clothes, I answered that I must have first seen the woman at two o'clock in the morning. In other words, I had not only seen her on my birthday, but at the hour of my birth.

My mother still kept silence. Lost in her own thoughts, she took me by the hand, and led me into the parlour. Her writing-desk was on the table by the fireplace. She opened it, and signed to me to take a chair by her side.

'My son! your memory is a bad one, and mine is fast failing me. Tell me again what the woman looked like. I want her to be as well known to both of us, years hence, as she is now.'

I obeyed; wondering what strange fancy might be working in her mind. I spoke and she wrote the words as they fell from my lips:

'Light grey eyes, with a droop in the left eyelid. Flaxen hair, with a golden-yellow streak in it. White arms, with a down upon them. Little, lady's hands, with a rosy-red look about the fingernails.'

'Did you notice how she was dressed, Francis?'

'No, mother.'

'Did you notice the knife?'

'Yes. A large clasp knife, with a buckhorn handle, as good as new.'

My mother added the description of the knife. Also the year, month, day of the week and hour of the day when the dream-woman appeared to me at the inn. That done, she locked up the paper in her desk.

'Not a word, Francis, to your aunt. Not a word to any living soul. Keep your dream a secret between you and me.'

The weeks passed, and the months passed. My mother never returned to the subject again. As for me, time, which wears out all things, wore out my remembrance of the dream. Little by little, the image of the woman grew dimmer and dimmer. Little by little, she faded out of my mind.

SEVEN

The story of the warning is now told. Judge for yourself if it was a true warning or a false when you hear what happened to me on my next birthday.

In the summer time of the year, the wheel of fortune turned the right way for me at last. I was smoking my pipe one day, near an old stone quarry at the entrance to our village, when a carriage accident happened, which gave a new turn, as it were, to my lot in life. It was an accident of the commonest kind – not worth mentioning at any length. A lady driving herself; a runaway horse; a cowardly manservant in attendance, frightened out of his wits; and the stone quarry too near to be agreeable – that is what I saw, all in a few moments, between two whiffs of my pipe. I stopped the horse at the edge of the quarry, and got myself a little hurt by the shaft of the chaise. But that didn't matter. The lady declared I had saved her life; and her husband, coming with her to our cottage the next day, took me into his service then and there. The lady happened to be of a dark complexion; and it may amuse you to hear that my Aunt Chance instantly pitched on that circumstance as a means of saving the credit of the cards. Here was the promise of the Queen of Spades performed to the very letter, by means of 'a dark woman', just as my aunt had told me. 'In the time to come, Francis, beware o' pettin' yer ain blinded intairpretation on the cairds. Ye're ower ready, I trow, to murmur under dispensation of proavidence that ye canna fathom – like the Eesraelites of auld. I'll say nae mair to ye. Mebbe when the mony's powering into yer poakets, ye'll no forget yer Aunt Chance, left like a sparrow on the housetop, wi' a sma' annuitee o' thratty punds a year.'

I remained in my situation (in the West End of London) until the spring of the New Year. About that time, my master's health failed. The doctors ordered him away to foreign parts, and the establishment was broken up. But the turn in my luck still held good. When I left my place, I left it – thanks to the generosity of my kind master – with a yearly allowance granted to me, in remembrance of the day when I had saved my mistress's life. For the future, I could go back to service or not, as I pleased; my little income was enough to support my mother and myself.

My master and mistress left England toward the end of February. Certain matters of business to do for them detained me in London until the last day of the month. I was only able to leave for our village by the evening train, to keep my birthday with my mother as usual. It was bedtime when I got to the cottage; and I was sorry to find that she was far from well. To make matters worse, she had finished her bottle of medicine on the previous day, and had omitted to get it replenished, as the doctor had strictly directed. He dispensed his own medicines, and I offered to go and knock him up. She refused to let me do this; and, after giving me my supper, sent me away to my bed.

I fell asleep for a little, and woke again. My mother's bedchamber was next to mine. I heard my Aunt Chance's heavy footsteps going to and fro in the room, and, suspecting something wrong, knocked at the door. My mother's pains had returned upon her; there was a serious necessity for relieving her sufferings as speedily as possible; I put on my clothes and ran off, with the medicine bottle in my hand, to the other end of the village, where the doctor lived. The church clock chimed the quarter to two on my birthday just as I reached his house. One ring of the night bell brought him to his bedroom window to speak to me. He told me to wait and he would let me in at the surgery door. I noticed, while I was waiting, that the night was wonderfully fair and warm for the time of year. The old stone quarry where the carriage accident had happened was within view. The moon in the clear heavens lit it up almost as bright as day.

In a minute or two the doctor let me into the surgery. I closed the door, noticing that he had left his room very lightly clad. He kindly pardoned my mother's neglect of his directions, and set to work at once at compounding the medicine. We were both intent on the bottle, he filling it and I holding the light, when we heard the surgery door suddenly opened from the street.

EIGHT

Who could possibly be up and about in our quiet village at the second hour of the morning?

The person who opened the door appeared within range of the light of the candle. To complete our amazement, the person proved to be a woman! She walked up to the counter, and standing side by side with me, lifted her veil. At the moment when she showed her face, I heard the church clock strike two. She was a stranger to me, and a stranger to the doctor. She was also, beyond all comparison, the most beautiful woman I have ever seen in my life.

'I saw the light under the door,' she said. 'I want some medicine.' She spoke quite composedly, as if there was nothing at all extraordinary in her being out in the village at two in the morning and following me into the surgery to ask for medicine!

The doctor stared at her as if he suspected his own eyes of deceiving him. 'Who are you?' he asked. 'How do you come to be wandering about at this time in the morning?'

She paid no heed to his questions. She only told him coolly what she wanted. 'I have got a bad toothache. I want a bottle of laudanum.'

The doctor recovered himself when she asked for the laudanum. He was on his own ground, you know, when it came to a matter of laudanum; and he spoke to her smartly enough this time.

'Oh, you have got the toothache, have you? Let me look at the tooth.'

She shook her head, and laid a two-shilling piece on the counter. 'I won't trouble you to look at the tooth,' she said. 'There is the money. Let me have the laudanum, if you please.'

The doctor put the two-shilling piece back again in her hand. 'I don't sell laudanum to strangers,' he answered. 'If you are in any distress of body or mind, that is another matter. I shall be glad to help you.'

She put the money back in her pocket. '*You* can't help me,' she said, as quietly as ever. 'Good-morning.'

With that, she opened the surgery door to go out again into the street. So far, I had not spoken a word on my side. I had stood with the candle in my hand (not knowing I was holding it) – with my eyes fixed on her, with my mind fixed on her like a man bewitched. Her looks betrayed, even more plainly than her words, her resolution, in one way or another, to destroy herself. When she opened the door, in my alarm at what might happen I found the use of my tongue.

'Stop!' I cried out. 'Wait for me. I want to speak to you before you go away.' She lifted her eyes with a look of careless surprise and a mocking smile on her lips.

'What can *you* have to say to me?' She stopped, and laughed to herself. 'Why not?' she said. 'I have got nothing to do, and nowhere to go.' She turned back a step, and nodded to me. 'You're a strange man – I think I'll humour you – I'll wait outside.' The door of the surgery closed on her. She was gone.

I am ashamed to own what happened next. The only excuse for me is that I was really and truly a man bewitched. I turned round to follow her out, without once thinking of my mother. The doctor stopped me.

'Don't forget the medicine,' he said. 'And if you will take my advice, don't trouble yourself about that woman. Rouse up the constable. It's his business

345

to look after her – not yours.'

I held out my hand for the medicine in silence: I was afraid I should fail in respect if I trusted myself to answer him. He must have seen, as I saw, that she wanted the laudanum to poison herself. He had, to my mind, taken a very heartless view of the matter. I just thanked him when he gave me the medicine – and went out.

She was waiting for me as she had promised; walking slowly to and fro – a tall, graceful, solitary figure in the bright moonbeams. They shed over her fair complexion, her bright golden hair, her large grey eyes, just the light that suited them best. She looked hardly mortal when she first turned to speak to me.

'Well?' she said. 'And what do you want?'

In spite of my pride, or my shyness, or my better sense – whichever it might me – all my heart went out to her in a moment. I caught hold of her by the hands, and owned what was in my thoughts, as freely as if I had known her for half a lifetime.

'You mean to destroy yourself,' I said. 'And I mean to prevent you from doing it. If I follow you about all night, I'll prevent you from doing it.'

She laughed. 'You saw yourself that he wouldn't sell me the laudanum. Do you really care whether I live or die?' She squeezed my hands gently as she put the question: her eyes searched mine with a languid, lingering look in them that ran through me like fire. My voice died away on my lips; I couldn't answer her.

She understood, without my answering. 'You have given me a fancy for living by speaking kindly to me,' she said. 'Kindness has a wonderful effect on women, and dogs, and other domestic animals. It is only men who are superior to kindness. Make your mind easy – I promise to take as much care of myself as if I was the happiest woman living! Don't let me keep you here, out of your bed. Which way are you going?'

Miserable wretch that I was, I had forgotten my mother – with the medicine in my hand! 'I am going home,' I said. 'Where are you staying? At the inn?'

She laughed her bitter laugh, and pointed to the stone quarry. 'There is my inn for tonight,' she said. 'When I got tired of walking about, I rested there.'

We walked on together, on my way home. I took the liberty of asking her if she had any friends.

'I thought I had one friend left,' she said, 'or you would never have met me in this place. It turns out I was wrong. My friend's door was closed in my face some hours since; my friend's servants threatened me with the police. I had nowhere else to go, after trying my luck in your neighborhood; and nothing left but my two-shilling piece and these rags on my back. What respectable innkeeper would take *me* into his house? I walked about, wondering how I could find my way out of the world without disfiguring myself, and without suffering much pain. You have no river in these parts. I didn't see my way out of the world, till I heard you ringing at the doctor's house. I got a glimpse at the bottles in the surgery, when he let you in, and I thought of the laudanum directly. What were you doing there? Who is that medicine for? Your wife?'

'I am not married!'

She laughed again. 'Not married! If I was a little better dressed there might be a chance for *me*. Where do you live? Here?'

We had arrived, by this time, at my mother's door. She held out her hand to say goodbye. Houseless and homeless as she was, she never asked me to give her a shelter for the night. It was my proposal that she should rest under my roof, unknown to my mother and my aunt. Our kitchen was built out at the back of the cottage: she might remain there unseen and unheard until the household was astir in the morning. I led her into the kitchen, and set a chair for her by the dying embers of the fire. I dare say I was to blame – shamefully to blame, if you like. I only wonder what *you* would have done in my place. On your word of honour as a man, would *you* have let that beautiful creature wander back to the shelter of the stone quarry like a stray dog? God help the woman who is foolish enough to trust and love you, if you would have done that!

I left her by the fire, and went to my mother's room.

NINE

If you have ever felt the heartache, you will know what I suffered in secret when my mother took my hand, and said, 'I am sorry, Francis, that your night's rest has been disturbed through me.' I gave her the medicine; and I waited by her till the pains abated. My Aunt Chance went back to her bed and my mother and I were left alone. I noticed that her writing-desk, moved from its customary place, was on the bed by her side. She saw me looking at it. 'This is your birthday, Francis,' she said. 'Have you anything to tell me?' I had so completely forgotten my dream, that I had no notion of what was passing in her mind when she said those words. For a moment there was a guilty fear in me that she suspected something. I turned away my face, and said, 'No, mother; I have nothing to tell.' She signed to me to stoop down over the pillow and kiss her. 'God bless you, my love!' she said; 'and many happy returns of the day.' She patted my hand, and closed her weary eyes, and, little by little, fell off peaceably into sleep.

I stole downstairs again. I think the good influence of my mother must have followed me down. At any rate, this is true: I stopped with my hand on the closed kitchen door, and said to myself: 'Suppose I leave the house, and leave the village, without seeing her or speaking to her more?'

Should I really have fled from temptation in this way, if I had been left to myself to decide? Who can tell? As things were, I was not left to decide. While my doubt was in my mind, she heard me, and opened the kitchen door. My eyes and her eyes met. That ended it.

We were together, unsuspected and undisturbed, for the next two hours. Time enough for her to reveal the secret of her wasted life. Time enough for her to take possession of me as her own, to do with me as she liked. It is needless to dwell here on the misfortunes which had brought her low; they are misfortunes too common to interest anybody.

Her name was Alicia Warlock. She had been born and bred a lady. She had lost her station, her character and her friends. Virtue shuddered at the sight of her; and Vice had got her for the rest of her days. Shocking and common, as I told you. It made no difference to *me*. I have said it already – I say it again – I was a man bewitched. Is there anything so very wonderful in that? Just remember who I was. Among the honest women in my own station in life, where could I have found the like of *her*? Could *they* walk as she walked? and look as she looked? When *they* gave me a kiss, did their lips linger over it as hers did? Had *they* her skin, her laugh, her foot, her hand, her touch? *She* never had a speck of dirt on her: I tell you her flesh was a perfume. When she embraced me, her arms folded round me like the wings of angels; and her smile covered me softly with its light like the sun in heaven. I leave you to laugh at me, or to cry over me, just as your temper may incline. I am not trying to excuse myself – I am trying to explain. You are gentlefolk; what dazzled and maddened *me* is everyday experience to *you*. Fallen or not, angel or devil, it came to this – she was a lady; and I was a groom.

Before the house was astir, I got her away (by the workmen's train) to a large manufacturing town in our parts.

Here – with my savings in money to help her – she could get her outfit of decent clothes and her lodging among strangers who asked no questions so long as they were paid. Here – now on one pretence and now on another – I could visit her, and we could both plan together what our future lives were to be. I need not tell you that I stood pledged to make her my wife. A man in my station always marries a woman of her sort.

Do you wonder if I was happy at this time? I should have been perfectly happy but for one little drawback. It was this: I was never quite at my ease in the presence of my promised wife.

I don't mean that I was shy with her, or suspicious of her, or ashamed of her. The uneasiness I am speaking of was caused by a faint doubt in my mind whether I had not seen her somewhere before the morning when we met at the doctor's house. Over and over again, I found myself wondering whether her face did not remind me of some other face – *what* other I never could tell. This strange feeling, this one question that could never be answered, vexed me to a degree that you would hardly credit. It came between us at the strangest times – oftenest, however, at night, when the candles were lit. You have known what it is to try and remember a forgotten name – and to fail, search as you may, to find it in your mind. That was my case. I failed to find my lost face, just as you failed to find your lost name.

In three weeks we had talked matters over, and had arranged how I was to make a clean breast of it at home. By Alicia's advice, I was to describe her as having been one of my fellow servants during the time I was employed under my kind master and mistress in London. There was no fear now of my mother taking any harm from the shock of a great surprise. Her health had improved during the three weeks' interval. On the first evening when she was able to take her old place at teatime, I summoned my courage, and told her I was going to be married. The poor soul flung her arms round my neck, and burst out crying for joy. 'Oh, Francis!' she says, 'I am so glad you will have somebody to comfort you and care for you when I am gone!' As for my Aunt Chance, you can anticipate what *she* did, without being told. Ah, me! If there had really been any prophetic virtue in the cards, what a terrible warning they might have given us that night! It was arranged that I was to bring my promised wife to dinner at the cottage on the next day.

TEN

I own I was proud of Alicia when I led her into our little parlour at the appointed time. She had never, to my mind, looked so beautiful as she looked that day. I never noticed any other woman's dress – I noticed hers as carefully as if I had been a woman myself! She wore a black silk gown, with plain collar and cuffs, and a modest lavender-coloured bonnet, with one white rose in it placed at the side. My mother, dressed in her Sunday best, rose up, all in a flutter, to welcome her daughter-in-law that was to be. She walked forward a few steps, half smiling, half in tears – she looked Alicia full in the face – and suddenly stood still. Her cheeks turned white in an instant; her eyes stared in horror; her hands dropped helplessly at her sides. She staggered back, and fell into the arms of my aunt, standing behind her. It was no swoon – she kept her senses. Her eyes turned slowly from Alicia to me. 'Francis,' she said, 'does that woman's face remind you of nothing?'.

Before I could answer, she pointed to her writing-desk on the table at the fireside. 'Bring it!' she cried, 'bring it!'

At the same moment I felt Alicia's hand on my shoulder, and saw Alicia's face red with anger – and no wonder!

'What does this mean?' she asked. 'Does your mother want to insult me?'.

I said a few words to quiet her; what they were I don't remember – I was so confused and astonished at the time. Before I had done, I heard my mother behind me.

My aunt had fetched her desk. She had opened it; she had taken a paper from it. Step by step, helping herself along by the wall, she came nearer and nearer, with the paper in her hand. She looked at the paper – she looked in Alicia's face – she lifted the long, loose sleeve of her gown, and examined her hand and arm. I saw fear suddenly take the place of anger in Alicia's eyes. She shook herself free of my mother's grasp. 'Mad!' she said to herself, 'and Francis never told me!' With those words she ran out of the room.

I was hastening out after her, when my mother signed to me to stop. She read the words written on the paper. While they fell slowly, one by one, from her lips, she pointed towards the open door.

'Light grey eyes, with a droop in the left eyelid. Flaxen hair, with a gold-yellow streak in it. White arms, with a down upon them. Little, lady's hand, with a rosy-red look about the fingernails. The dream woman, Francis! The dream woman!'

Something darkened the parlour window as those words were spoken. I looked sidelong at the shadow. Alicia Warlock had come back! She was peering in at us over the low window blind. There was the fatal face which had first looked at me in the bedroom of the lonely inn. There, resting on the window blind, was the lovely little hand which had held the murderous knife. I *had* seen her before we met in the village. The dream woman! The dream woman!

ELEVEN

I expect nobody to approve of what I have next to tell of myself. In three weeks from the day when my mother had identified her with the woman of the dream, I took Alicia Warlock to church and made her my wife. I was a man bewitched. Again and again I say it – I was a man bewitched!

During the interval before my marriage, our little household at the cottage was broken up. My mother and my aunt quarrelled. My mother, believing in the dream, entreated me to break off my engagement. My aunt, believing in the cards, urged me to marry.

This difference of opinion produced a dispute between them, in the course of which my Aunt Chance – quite unconscious of having any superstitious feelings of her own – actually set out the cards which prophesied happiness to me in my married life, and asked my mother how anybody but 'a blinded heathen could be fule enough, after seeing those cairds, to believe in a dream!' This was, naturally, too much for my mother's patience; hard words followed on either side; Mrs Chance returned in dudgeon to her friends in Scotland. She left me a written statement of my future prospects, as revealed by the cards, and with it an address at which a post-office order would reach her. 'The day was not that far off,' she remarked, 'when Francie might remember what he owed to his Aunt Chance, maintaining her ain unbleemished widowhood on thratty punds a year.'

Having refused to give her sanction to my marriage, my mother also refused to be present at the wedding, or to visit Alicia afterwards. There was no anger at the bottom of this conduct on her part. Believing as she did in this dream, she was simply in mortal fear of my wife. I understood this, and I made allowances for her. Not a cross word passed between us. My one happy remembrance now – though I did disobey her in the matter of my marriage – is this: I loved and respected my good mother to the last.

As for my wife, she expressed no regret at the estrangement between her mother-in-law and herself. By common consent, we never spoke on that subject. We settled in the manufacturing town which I have already mentioned, and we kept a lodging-house. My kind master, at my request, granted me a lump sum in place of my annuity. This put us into a good house, decently furnished. For a while things went well enough. I may describe myself at this time of my life as a happy man.

My misfortunes began with a return of the complaint with which my mother had already suffered. The doctor confessed, when I asked him the question, that there was danger to be dreaded this time. Naturally, after hearing this, I was a good deal away at the cottage. Naturally also, I left the business of looking after the house, in my absence, to my wife. Little by little, I found her beginning to alter towards me. While my back was turned, she formed acquaintances with people of the doubtful and dissipated sort. One day, I observed something in her manner which forced the suspicion on me that she had been drinking. Before the week was out, my suspicion was a certainty. From keeping company with drunkards, she had grown to be a drunkard herself.

I did all a man could do to reclaim her. Quite useless! She had never really returned the love I felt for her: I had no influence; I could do nothing. My mother, hearing of this last worse trouble, resolved to try what her influence could do. Ill as she was, I found her one day dressed to go out.

'I am not long for this world, Francis,' she said. 'I shall not feel easy on my deathbed, unless I have done my best to the last to make you happy. I mean to put my own fears and my own feelings out of the question, and go with you to your wife, and try what I can do to reclaim her. Take me home with you, Francis. Let me do all I can to help my son, before it is too late.'

How could I disobey her? We took the railway to the town: it was only half an hour's ride. By one o'clock in the afternoon we reached my house. It was our dinner hour, and Alicia was in the kitchen. I was able to take my mother quietly into the parlour and then to prepare my wife for the visit. She had drunk but little at that early hour; and, luckily, the devil in her was tamed for the time.

She followed me into the parlour, and the meeting passed off better than I had ventured to forecast; with this one drawback, that my mother – though she tried hard to control herself – shrank from looking my wife in the face when she spoke to her. It was a relief to me when Alicia began to prepare the table for dinner.

She laid the cloth, brought in the bread tray, and cut some slices for us from the loaf. Then she returned to the kitchen. At that moment, while I was still anxiously watching my mother, I was startled by seeing the same ghastly change pass over her face which had altered it on the occasion when Alicia and she first met. Before I could say a word, she started up with a look of horror.

'Take me back! – home, home again, Francis! Come with me, and never go back more!'

I was afraid to ask for an explanation; I could only sign her to be silent, and help her quickly to the door. As we passed the bread tray on the table, she stopped and pointed to it.

'Did you see what your wife cut your bread with?' she asked.

'No, mother; I was not noticing. What was it?'

'Look!'

I did look. A new clasp knife, with a buckhorn handle, lay with the loaf in the bread tray. I stretched out my hand to possess myself of it. At the same moment, there was a noise in the kitchen, and my mother caught me by the arm.

'The knife of the dream! Francis, I'm faint with fear – take me away before she comes back!'

I couldn't speak to comfort or even to answer her. Superior as I was to superstition, the discovery of the knife staggered me. In silence, I helped my mother out of the house; and took her home.

I held out my hand to say goodbye. She tried to stop me.

'Don't go back, Francis! don't go back!'

'I must get the knife, mother. I must go back by the next train.' I held to that resolution. By the next train I went back.

TWELVE

My wife had, of course, discovered our secret departure from the house. She had been drinking. She was in a fury of passion. The dinner in the kitchen was flung under the grate; the cloth was off the parlour table. Where was the knife?

I was foolish enough to ask for it. She refused to give it to me. In the course of the dispute between us which followed, I discovered that there was a horrible story attached to the knife. It had been used in a murder – years since – and had been so skilfully hidden that the authorities had been unable to produce it at the trial. By help of some of her disreputable friends, my wife had been able to purchase this relic of a bygone crime. Her perverted nature set some horrid unacknowledged value on the knife. Seeing there was no hope of getting it by fair means, I determined to search for it, later in the day, in secret. The search was unsuccessful. Night came on, and I left the house to walk about the streets. You will understand what a broken man I was by this time, when I tell you I was afraid to sleep in the same room with her!

Three weeks passed. Still she refused to give up the knife; and still that fear of sleeping in the same room with her possessed me. I walked about at night, or dozed in the parlour, or sat watching by my mother's bedside. Before the end of the first week in the new month, the worst misfortune of all befell me – my mother died. It wanted then but a short time to my birthday. She had longed to live till that day. I was present at her death. Her last words in this world were addressed to me. 'Don't go back, my son – don't go back!'

I was obliged to go back, if it was only to watch my wife. In the last days of my mother's illness she had spitefully added a sting to my grief by declaring she would assert her right to attend the funeral. In spite of all that I could do or say, she held to her word. On the day appointed for the burial she forced herself, inflamed and shameless with drink, into my presence, and swore she would walk in the funeral procession to my mother's grave.

This last insult – after all I had gone through already – was more than I could endure. It maddened me. Try to make allowances for a man beside himself. I struck her.

The instant the blow was dealt, I repented it. She crouched down, silent, in a corner of the room, and eyed me steadily. It was a look that cooled my hot blood in an instant. There was no time now to think of making atonement. I could only risk the worst, and make sure of her till the funeral was over. I locked her into her bedroom.

When I came back, after laying my mother in the grave, I found her sitting by the bedside, very much altered in look and bearing, with a bundle on her lap. She faced me quietly; she spoke with a curious stillness in her voice – strangely and unnaturally composed in look and manner.

'No man has ever struck me yet,' she said. 'My husband shall have no second opportunity. Set the door open, and let me go.'

She passed me, and left the room. I saw her walk away up the street. Was she gone for good?

All that night I watched and waited. No footstep came near the house. The next night, overcome with fatigue, I lay down on the bed in my clothes, with the door locked, the key on the table, and the candle burning. My slumber was not disturbed. The third night, the fourth, the fifth, the sixth, passed, and nothing happened. I lay down on the seventh night, still suspicious of something happening; still in my clothes; still with the door locked, the key on the table, and the candle burning.

My rest was disturbed. I awoke twice, without any sensation of uneasiness. The third time, that horrid shivering of the night at the lonely inn, that awful sinking pain at the heart, came back again, and roused me in an instant. My eyes turned to the left-hand side of the bed. And there stood, looking at me –

The dream woman again? No! My wife. The living woman, with the face of the dream – in the attitude of the dream – the fair arm up; the knife clasped in the delicate white hand.

I sprang upon her on the instant; but not quickly enough to stop her from hiding the knife. Without a word from me, without a cry from her, I pinioned her in a chair. With one hand I felt up her sleeve; and there, where the dream woman had hidden the knife, my wife had hidden it – the knife with the buckhorn handle, that looked like new.

What I felt when I made that discovery I could not realise at the time, and I can't describe now. I took one steady look at her with the knife in my hand. 'You meant to kill me?' I said.

'Yes,' she answered; 'I meant to kill you.' She crossed her arms over her bosom, and stared me coolly in the face. 'I shall do it yet,' she said. 'With that knife.'

I don't know what possessed me – I swear to you I am no coward; and yet I acted like a coward. The horrors got hold of me. I couldn't look at her – I couldn't speak to her. I left her (with the knife in my hand), and went out into the night.

There was a bleak wind abroad, and the smell of rain was in the air. The church clocks chimed the quarter as I walked beyond the last house in the town. I asked the first policeman I met what hour that was, of which the quarter past had just struck.

The man looked at his watch, and answered, 'Two o'clock.' Two in the morning. What day of the month was this day that had just begun? I reckoned it up from the date of my mother's funeral. The horrid parallel between the dream and the reality was complete – it was my birthday!

Had I escaped the mortal peril which the dream foretold? or had I only received a second warning? As that doubt crossed my mind I stopped on my way out of the town. The air had revived me – I felt in some degree like my own self again. After a little thinking, I began to see plainly the mistake I had made in leaving my wife free to go where she liked and to do as she pleased.

I turned instantly, and made my way back to the house. It was still dark. I had left the candle burning in the bedchamber. When I looked up to the window of the room now, there was no light in it. I advanced to the house door. On going away, I remembered to have closed it; on trying it now, I found it open.

I waited outside, never losing sight of the house till daylight. Then I ventured indoors – listened, and heard nothing – looked into the kitchen, scullery, parlour, and found nothing – went up at last into the bedroom. It was empty.

A picklock lay on the floor, which told me how she had gained entrance in the night. And that was the one trace I could find of the dream woman.

THIRTEEN

I waited in the house till the town was astir for the day, and then I went to consult a lawyer. In the confused state of my mind at the time, I had one clear notion of what I meant to do: I was determined to sell my house and leave the neighbourhood. There were obstacles in the way which I had not counted on. I was told I had creditors to satisfy before I could leave – I, who had given my wife the money to pay my bills regularly every week! Enquiry showed that she had embezzled every farthing of the money I had intrusted to her. I had no choice but to pay over again.

Placed in this awkward position, my first duty was to set things right, with the help of my lawyer. During my forced sojourn in the town I did two foolish things. And, as a consequence that followed, I heard once more, and heard for the last time, of my wife.

In the first place, having got possession of the knife, I was rash enough to keep it in my pocket. In the second place, having something of importance to say to my lawyer, at a late hour of the evening, I went to his house after dark – alone and on foot. I got there safely enough. Returning, I was seized on from behind by two men, dragged down a passage and robbed – not only of the little money I had about me, but also of the knife. It was the lawyer's opinion (as it was mine) that the thieves were among the disreputable acquaintances formed by my wife, and that they had attacked me at her instigation. To confirm this view I received a letter the next day, without date or address, written in Alicia's hand. The first line informed me that the knife was back again in her possession. The second line reminded me of the day when I struck her. The third line warned me that she would wash out the stain of that blow in my blood, and repeated the words, 'I shall do it with the knife!'

The law laid hands on the men who had robbed me; but from that time to this, the law has failed completely to find a trace of my wife.

My story is told. When I had paid the creditors and paid the legal expenses, I had barely five pounds left out of the sale of my house; and I had the world to begin over again. Some months since – drifting here and there – I found my way to Underbridge. The landlord of the inn had known something of my father's family in times past. He gave me (all he had to give) my food, and shelter in the yard. Except on market days, there is nothing to do. In the coming winter the inn is to be shut up, and I shall have to shift for myself. My old master would help me if I applied to him – but I don't like to apply: he has done more for me already than I deserve. Besides, in another year who knows but my troubles may all be at an end? Next winter will bring me nigh to my next birthday, and my next birthday may be the day of my death. Yes! it's true I sat up all last night; and I heard two in the morning strike: and nothing happened. Still, allowing for that, the time to come is a time I don't trust. My wife has got the knife – my wife is looking for me. I am above superstition, mind! I don't say I believe in dreams; I only say, Alicia Warlock is looking for me. It is possible I may be wrong. It is possible I may be right. Who can tell?

The Third Narrative: The Story Continued by Percy Fairbank

FOURTEEN

We took leave of Francis Raven at the door of Farleigh Hall, with the understanding that he might expect to hear from us again.

The same night Mrs Fairbank and I had a discussion in the sanctuary of our own room. The topic was the ostler's story, and the question in dispute between us turned on the measure of charitable duty that we owed to the ostler himself.

The view I took of the man's narrative was of the purely matter-of-fact kind. Francis Raven had, in my opinion, brooded over the misty connection between his strange dream and his vile wife, until his mind was in a state of partial delusion on that subject. I was quite willing to help him with a trifle of money, and to recommend him to the kindness of my lawyer, if he was really in any danger and wanted advice. There my idea of my duty towards this afflicted person began and ended.

Confronted with this sensible view of the matter, Mrs Fairbank's romantic temperament rushed, as usual, into extremes. 'I should no more think of losing sight of Francis Raven when his next birthday comes round,' says my wife, 'than I should think of laying down a good story with the last chapters unread. I am positively determined, Percy, to take him back with us when we return to France, in the capacity of groom. What does one man more or less among the horses matter to people as rich as we are?' In this strain the partner of my joys and sorrows ran on, perfectly impenetrable to everything that I could say on the side of common sense. Need I tell my married brethren how it ended? Of course I allowed my wife to irritate me, and spoke to her sharply. Of course my wife turned her face away indignantly on the conjugal pillow, and burst into tears. Of course upon that, 'Mr' made his excuses, and 'Mrs' had her own way.

Before the week was out we rode over to Underbridge, and duly offered to Francis Raven a place in our service as supernumerary groom.

At first the poor fellow seemed hardly able to realise his own extra-ordinary good fortune. Recovering himself, he expressed his gratitude modestly and becomingly. Mrs Fairbank's ready sympathies overflowed, as usual, at her lips. She talked to him about our home in France, as if the worn, grey-headed ostler had been a child. 'Such a dear old house, Francis; and such pretty gardens! Stables! Stables ten times as big as your stables here – quite a choice of rooms for you. You must learn the name of our house – Maison Rouge. Our nearest town is Metz. We are within a walk of the beautiful River Moselle. And when we want a change we have only to take the railway to the frontier, and find ourselves in Germany.'

Listening, so far, with a very bewildered face, Francis started and changed colour when my wife reached the end of her last sentence. 'Germany?' he repeated.

'Yes. Does Germany remind you of anything?'

The ostler's eyes looked down sadly on the ground. 'Germany reminds me of my wife,' he replied.

'Indeed! How?'

'She once told me she had lived in Germany – long before I knew her – in the time when she was a young girl.'

'Was she living with relations or friends?'

'She was living as governess in a foreign family.'

'In what part of Germany?'

'I don't remember, ma'am. I doubt if she told me.'

'Did she tell you the name of the family?'

'Yes, ma'am. It was a foreign name, and it has slipped my memory long since. The head of the family was a wine grower in a large way of business – I remember that.'

'Did you hear what sort of wine he grew? There are wine growers in our neighborhood. Was it Moselle wine?'

'I couldn't say, ma'am, I doubt if I ever heard.'

There the conversation dropped. We engaged to communicate with Francis Raven before we left England, and took our leave. I had made arrangements to pay our round of visits to English friends, and to return to Maison Rouge in the summer. On the eve of departure, certain difficulties in connection with the management of some landed property of mine in Ireland obliged us to alter our plans. Instead of getting back to our house in France in the summer, we only returned a week or two before Christmas. Francis Raven accompanied us, and was duly established, in the nominal capacity of stable keeper, among the servants at Maison Rouge.

Before long, some of the objections to taking him into our employment, which I had foreseen and had vainly mentioned to my wife, forced themselves on our attention in no very agreeable form. Francis Raven failed (as I had feared he would) to get on smoothly with his fellow-servants. They were all French; and not one of them understood English. Francis, on his side, was equally ignorant of French. His reserved manners, his melancholy temperament, his solitary ways – all told against him. Our servants called him 'the English Bear'. He grew widely known in the neighborhood under his nickname. Quarrels took place, ending once or twice in blows. It became plain, even to Mrs Fairbank herself, that some wise change must be made.

While we were still considering what the change was to be, the unfortunate ostler was thrown on our hands for some time to come by an accident in the stables. Still pursued by his proverbial ill-luck, the poor wretch's leg was broken by a kick from a horse.

He was attended to by our own surgeon, in his comfortable bedroom at the stables. As the date of his birthday drew near, he was still confined to his bed.

Physically speaking, he was doing very well. Morally speaking, the surgeon was not satisfied. Francis Raven was suffering under some mysterious mental disturbance, which interfered seriously with his rest at night. Hearing this, I thought it my duty to tell the medical attendant what was preying on the patient's mind. As a practical man, he shared my opinion that the ostler was in a state of delusion on the subject of his wife and his dream. 'Curable delusion, in my opinion,' the surgeon added, 'if the experiment could be fairly tried.'

'How can it be tried?' I asked. Instead of replying, the surgeon put a question to me, on his side.

'Do you happen to know,' he said, 'that this year is a leap year?'

'Mrs Fairbank reminded me of it yesterday,' I answered. 'Otherwise I might *not* have known it.'

'Do you think Francis Raven knows that this year is a leap year?'

(I began to see dimly what my friend was driving at.)

'It depends,' I answered, 'on whether he has got an English almanac. Suppose he has *not* got the almanac – what then?'

'In that case,' pursued the surgeon, 'Francis Raven is innocent of all suspicion that there is a twenty-ninth day in February this year. As a necessary consequence – what will he do? He will anticipate the appearance of the woman with the knife at two in the morning of the twenty-ninth of February, instead of the first of March. Let him suffer all his superstitious terrors on the wrong day. Leave him, on the day that is really his birthday, to pass a perfectly quiet night, and to be as sound asleep as other people at two in the morning. And then, when he wakes comfortably in time for his breakfast, shame him out of his delusion by telling him the truth.'

I agreed to try the experiment. Leaving the surgeon to caution Mrs Fairbank on the subject of leap years, I went to the stables to see Mr Raven.

FIFTEEN

The poor fellow was full of forebodings of the fate in store for him on the ominous first of March. He eagerly entreated me to order one of the men-servants to sit up with him on the birthday morning. In granting his request, I asked him to tell me on which day of the week his birthday fell. He reckoned the days on his fingers and proved his innocence of all suspicion that it was a leap year by fixing on the twenty-ninth of February, in the full persuasion that it was the first of March. Pledged to try the surgeon's experiment, I left his error uncorrected, of course. In so doing, I took my first step blindfold towards the last act in the drama of the ostler's dream.

The next day brought with it a little domestic difficulty, which indirectly and strangely associated itself with the coming end.

My wife received a letter inviting us to assist in celebrating the silver wedding of two worthy German neighbours of ours – Mr and Mrs Beldheimer. Mr Beldheimer was a large wine grower on the banks of the Moselle. His house was situated on the frontier line of France and Germany; and the distance from our house was sufficiently considerable to make it necessary for us to sleep under our host's roof. Under these circumstances, if we accepted the invitation, a comparison of dates showed that we should be away from home on the morning of the first of March. Mrs Fairbank – holding to her absurd resolution to see with her own eyes what might, or might not, happen to Francis Raven on his birthday – flatly declined to leave Maison Rouge. 'It's easy to send an excuse,' she said, in her off-hand manner.

I failed, for my part, to see any easy way out of the difficulty. The celebration of a silver wedding in Germany is the celebration of twenty-five years of happy married life; and the host's claim upon the consideration of his friends on such an occasion is something in the nature of a royal command. After considerable discussion, finding my wife's obstinacy in-vincible, and feeling that the absence of both of us from the festival would certainly offend our friends, I left Mrs Fairbank to make her excuses for herself, and directed her to accept the invitation so far as I was concerned. In so doing, I took my second step, blindfold, towards the last act in the drama of the ostler's dream.

A week elapsed; the last days of February were at hand. Another domestic difficulty happened; and, again, this event also proved to be strangely associated with the coming end.

My head groom at the stables was one Joseph Rigobert. He was an ill-conditioned fellow, inordinately vain of his personal appearance, and by no means scrupulous in his conduct with women. His one virtue consisted of his fondness for horses, and in the care he took of the animals under his charge. In a word, he was too good a groom to be easily replaced, or he would have quitted my service long since. On the occasion of which I am now writing, he was reported to me by my steward as growing idle and disorderly in his habits. The principal offense alleged against him was that he had been seen that day in the city of Metz in the company of a woman (supposed to be an Englishwoman), whom he was entertaining at a tavern, when he ought to have been on his way back to Maison Rouge. The man's defence was that 'the lady' (as he called her) was an English stranger, unacquainted with the ways of the place, and that he had only shown her where she could obtain some refreshment at her own request. I administered the necessary reprimand, without troubling myself to enquire further into the matter. In failing to do this, I took my third step, blindfold, toward the last act in the drama of the ostler's dream.

On the evening of the twenty-eighth, I informed the servants at the stables that one of them must watch through the night by the Englishman's bedside. Joseph Rigobert immediately volunteered for the duty – as a means, no doubt, of winning his way back to my favour. I accepted his proposal.

That day the surgeon dined with us. Towards midnight he and I left the smoking-room, and repaired to Francis Raven's bedside. Rigobert was at his post, with no very agreeable expression on his face. The Frenchman and the Englishman had evidently not got on well together so far. Francis Raven lay helpless on his bed, waiting silently for two in the morning and the appearance of the dream woman.

'I have come, Francis, to bid you good-night,' I said, cheerfully. 'Tomorrow morning I shall look in at breakfast time, before I leave home on a journey.'

'Thank you for all your kindness, sir. You will not see me alive tomorrow morning. She will find me this time. Mark my words – she will find me this time.'

'My good fellow! she couldn't find you in England. How in the world is she to find you in France?'

'It's borne in on my mind, sir, that she will find me here. At two in the morning on my birthday I shall see her again, and see her for the last time.'

'Do you mean that she will kill you?'

'I mean that, sir, she will kill me – with the knife.'

'And with Rigobert in the room to protect you?'

'I am a doomed man. Fifty Rigoberts couldn't protect me.'

'And you wanted somebody to sit up with you?'

'Mere weakness, sir. I don't like to be left alone on my deathbed.'

I looked at the surgeon. If he had encouraged me, I should certainly, out of sheer compassion, have confessed to Francis Raven the trick that we were playing him. The surgeon held to his experiment; the surgeon's face plainly said – 'No.'

The next day (the twenty-ninth of February) was the day of the silver wedding. The first thing in the morning, I went to Francis Raven's room. Rigobert met me at the door.

'How has he passed the night?' I asked.

'Saying his prayers, and looking for ghosts,' Rigobert answered. 'A lunatic asylum is the only proper place for him.'

I approached the bedside. 'Well, Francis, here you are, safe and sound, in spite of what you said to me last night.'

His eyes rested on mine with a vacant, wondering look.

'I don't understand it,' he said.

'Did you see anything of your wife when the clock struck two?'

'No, sir.'

'Did anything happen?'

'Nothing happened, sir.'

'Doesn't *this* satisfy you that you were wrong?'

His eyes still kept their vacant, wondering look. He only repeated the words he had spoken already: 'I don't understand it.'

I made a last attempt to cheer him. 'Come, come, Francis! keep a good heart. You will be out of bed in a fortnight.'

He shook his head on the pillow. 'There's something wrong,' he said. 'I don't expect you to believe me, sir. I only say there's something wrong – and time will show it.'

I left the room. Half an hour later I started for Mr Beldheimer's house, leaving the arrangements for the morning of the first of March in the hands of the doctor and my wife.

SIXTEEN

The one thing which principally struck me when I joined the guests at the silver wedding is also the one thing which it is necessary to mention here. On this joyful occasion a noticeable lady present was out of spirits. That lady was no other than the heroine of the festival, the mistress of the house!

In the course of the evening I spoke to Mr Beldheimer's eldest son on the subject of his mother. As an old friend of the family, I had a claim on his confidence which the young man willingly recognised.

'We have had a very disagreeable matter to deal with,' he said; 'and my mother has not recovered from the painful impression left on her mind. Many years since, when my sisters were children, we had an English governess in the house. She left us, as we then understood, to be married. We heard no more of her until a week or ten days since, when my mother received a letter, in which our ex-governess described herself as being in a condition of great poverty and distress. After much hesitation she had ventured – at the suggestion of a lady who had been kind to her – to write to her former employers, and to appeal to their remembrance of old times. You know my mother: she is not only the most kind-hearted, but the most innocent of women – it is impossible to persuade her of the wickedness that there is in the world. She replied by return of post, inviting the governess to come here and see her, and enclosing the money for her travelling expenses. When my father came home, and heard what had been done, he wrote at once to his agent in London to make enquiries, enclosing the address on the governess's letter. Before he could receive the agent's reply the governess arrived. She produced the worst possible impression on his mind. The agent's letter, arriving a few days later, confirmed his suspicions. Since we had lost sight of her, the woman had led a most disreputable life. My father spoke to her privately: he offered – on condition of her leaving the house – a sum of money to take her back to England. If she refused, the alternative would be an appeal to the authorities and a public scandal. She accepted the money, and left the house. On her way back to England she appears to have stopped at Metz. You will understand what sort of woman she is when I tell you that she was seen the other day in a tavern, with your handsome groom, Joseph Rigobert.'

While my informant was relating these circumstances, my memory was at work. I recalled what Francis Raven had vaguely told us of his wife's experience in former days as governess in a German family. A suspicion of the truth suddenly flashed across my mind. 'What was the woman's name?' I asked.

Mr Beldheimer's son answered: 'Alicia Warlock.'

I had but one idea when I heard that reply – to get back to my house without a moment's needless delay. It was then ten o'clock at night – the last train to Metz had left long since. I arranged with my young friend – after duly informing him of the circumstances – that I should go by the first train in the morning, instead of staying to breakfast with the other guests who slept in the house.

At intervals during the night I wondered uneasily how things were going on at Maison Rouge. Again and again the same question occurred to me, on my journey home in the early morning – the morning of the first of March. As the event proved, but one person in my house knew what really happened at the stables on Francis Raven's birthday. Let Joseph Rigobert take my place as narrator, and tell the story of the end to you – as he told it, in times past, to his lawyer and to me.

The Fourth and Last Narrative: Statement of Joseph Rigobert –
addressed to the Advocate who Defended Him at His Trial

Respected Sir – On the twenty-seventh of February I was sent, on business connected with the stables at Maison Rouge, to the city of Metz. On the public promenade I met a magnificent woman. Complexion, blond. Nationality, English. We mutually admired each other; we fell into conversation. (She spoke French perfectly – with the English accent.) I offered refreshment; my proposal was accepted. We had a long and interesting interview – we discovered that we were made for each other. So far, who is to blame?

Is it my fault that I am a handsome man – universally agreeable as such to the fair sex? Is it a criminal offence to be accessible to the amiable weakness of love? I ask again, who is to blame? Clearly, nature. Not the beautiful lady – not my humble self.

To resume. The most hard-hearted person living will understand that two beings made for each other could not possibly part without an appointment to meet again.

I made arrangements for the accommodation of the lady in the village near Maison Rouge. She consented to honour me with her company at supper, in my apartment at the stables, on the night of the twenty-ninth. The time fixed on was the time when the other servants were accustomed to retire – eleven o'clock.

Among the grooms attached to the stables was an Englishman, laid up with a broken leg. His name was Francis. His manners were repulsive; he was ignorant of the French language. In the kitchen he went by the nickname of the 'English Bear'. Strange to say, he was a great favourite with my master and my mistress. They even humoured certain superstitious terrors to which this repulsive person was subject – terrors into the nature of which I, as an advanced freethinker, never thought it worth my while to enquire.

On the evening of the twenty-eighth the Englishman, being a prey to the terrors which I have mentioned, requested that one of his fellow servants might sit up with him for that night only. The wish that he expressed was backed by Mr Fairbank's authority. Having already incurred my master's displeasure – in what way, a proper sense of my own dignity forbids me to relate – I volunteered to watch by the bedside of the English Bear. My object was to satisfy Mr Fairbank that I bore no malice, on my side, after what had occurred between us. The wretched Englishman passed a night of delirium. Not understanding his barbarous language, I could only gather from his gestures that he was in deadly fear of some fancied apparition at his bedside. From time to time, when this madman disturbed my slumbers, I quieted him by swearing at him. This is the shortest and best way of dealing with persons in his condition.

On the morning of the twenty-ninth, Mr Fairbank left us on a journey. Later in the day, to my unspeakable disgust, I found that I had not done with the Englishman yet. In Mr Fairbank's absence, Mrs Fairbank took an incomprehensible interest in the question of my delirious fellow servant's repose at night. Again, one or the other of us was to watch at his bedside, and report it, if anything happened. Expecting my fair friend to supper, it was necessary to make sure that the other servants at the stables would be safe in their beds that night. Accordingly, I volunteered once more to be the man who kept watch. Mrs Fairbank complimented me on my humanity. I possess great command over my feelings. I accepted the compliment without a blush.

Twice, after nightfall, my mistress and the doctor (the last staying in the house in Mr Fairbank's absence) came to make enquiries. Once *before* the arrival of my fair friend – and once *after*. On the second occasion (my apartment being next door to the Englishman's) I was obliged to hide my charming guest in the harness room. She consented, with angelic resignation, to immolate her dignity to the servile necessities of my position. A more amiable woman (so far) I never met with!

After the second visit I was left free. It was then close on midnight. Up to that time there was nothing in the behavior of the mad Englishman to reward Mrs Fairbank and the doctor for presenting themselves at his bedside. He lay half awake, half asleep, with an odd wondering kind of look in his face. My mistress at parting warned me to be particularly watchful of him towards two in the morning. The doctor (in case anything happened) left me a large hand bell to ring, which could easily be heard at the house.

Restored to the society of my fair friend, I spread the supper table. A pâté, a sausage and a few bottles of generous Moselle wine composed our simple meal. When persons adore each other, the intoxicating illusion of Love transforms the simplest meal into a banquet. With immeasurable capacities for enjoyment, we sat down to table. At the very moment when I placed my fascinating companion in a chair, the infamous Englishman in the next room took that occasion, of all others, to become restless and noisy once more. He struck with his stick on the floor; he cried out, in a delirious access of terror, 'Rigobert! Rigobert!'

The sound of that lamentable voice, suddenly assailing our ears, terrified my fair friend. She lost all her charming colour in an instant. 'Good heavens!' she exclaimed. 'Who is that in the next room?'

'A mad Englishman.'

'An Englishman?'

'Compose yourself, my angel. I will quiet him.'

The lamentable voice called out on me again, 'Rigobert! Rigobert!'

My fair friend caught me by the arm. 'Who is he?' she cried. 'What is his name?'

Something in her face struck me as she put that question. A spasm of jealousy shook me to the soul. 'You know him?' I said.

'His name!' she vehemently repeated; 'his name!'

'Francis,' I answered.

'Francis – *what?*'

I shrugged my shoulders. I could neither remember nor pronounce the barbarous English surname. I could only tell her it began with an R.

She dropped back into the chair. Was she going to faint? No: she recovered, and more than recovered, her lost colour. Her eyes flashed superbly. What did it mean? Profoundly as I understand women in general, I was puzzled by *this* woman!

'You know him?' I repeated.

She laughed at me. 'What nonsense! How should I know him? Go and quiet the wretch.'

My looking-glass was near. One glance at it satisfied me that no woman in her senses could prefer the Englishman to me. I recovered my self-respect. I hastened to the Englishman's bedside.

The moment I appeared he pointed eagerly towards my room. He overwhelmed me with a torrent of words in his own language. I made out, from his gestures and his looks, that he had, in some incomprehensible manner, discovered the presence of my guest; and, stranger still, that he was scared by the idea of a person in my room. I endeavoured to compose him on the system which I have already mentioned – that is to say, I swore at him in *my* language. The result not proving satisfactory, I own I shook my fist in his face, and left the bedchamber.

Returning to my fair friend, I found her walking backwards and forwards in a state of excitement wonderful to behold. She had not waited for me to fill her glass – she had begun the generous Moselle in my absence. I prevailed on her with difficulty to place herself at the table. Nothing would induce her to eat. 'My appetite is gone,' she said. 'Give me wine.'

The generous Moselle deserves its name – delicate on the palate, with prodigious 'body'. The strength of this fine wine produced no stupefying effect on my remarkable guest. It appeared to strengthen and exhilarate her – nothing more. She always spoke in the same low tone, and always, turn the conversation as I might, brought it back with the same dexterity to the subject of the Englishman in the next room. In any other woman this persistency would have offended me. My lovely guest was irresistible; I answered her questions with the docility of a child. She possessed all the amusing eccentricity of her nation. When I told her of the accident which confined the Englishman to his bed, she sprang to her feet. An extraordinary smile irradiated her countenance. She said, 'Show me the horse who broke the Englishman's leg! I must see that horse!' I took her to the stables. She kissed the horse – on my word of honour, she kissed the horse! That struck me. I said. 'You *do* know the man; and he has wronged you in some way.' No! she would not admit it, even then. 'I kiss all beautiful animals,' she said. 'Haven't I kissed *you*?' With that charming explanation of her conduct, she ran back up the stairs. I only remained behind to lock the stable door again. When I rejoined her, I made a startling discovery. I caught her coming out of the Englishman's room.

'I was just going downstairs again to call you,' she said. 'The man in there is getting noisy once more.'

The mad Englishman's voice assailed our ears once again. 'Rigobert! Rigobert!'

He was a frightful object to look at when I saw him this time. His eyes were staring wildly; the perspiration was pouring over his face. In a panic of terror he clasped his hands; he pointed up to heaven. By every sign and gesture that a man can make, he entreated me not to leave him again. I really could not help smiling. The idea of my staying with *him*, and leaving my fair friend by herself in the next room!

I turned to the door. When the mad wretch saw me leaving him he burst out into a screech of despair – so shrill that I feared it might awaken the sleeping servants.

My presence of mind in emergencies is proverbial among those who know me. I tore open the cupboard in which he kept his linen – seized a handful of his handkerchiefs – gagged him with one of them, and secured his hands with the others. There was now no danger of his alarming the servants. After tying the last knot, I looked up.

The door between the Englishman's room and mine was open. My fair friend was standing on the threshold – watching *him* as he lay helpless on the bed; watching *me* as I tied the last knot.

'What are you doing there?' I asked. 'Why did you open the door?'

She stepped up to me, and whispered her answer in my ear, with her eyes all the time upon the man on the bed:

'I heard him scream.'

'Well?'

'I thought you had killed him.'

I drew back from her in horror. The suspicion of me which her words implied was sufficiently detestable in itself. But her manner when she uttered the words was more revolting still. It so powerfully affected me that I started back from that beautiful creature as I might have recoiled from a reptile crawling over my flesh.

Before I had recovered myself sufficiently to reply, my nerves were assailed by another shock. I suddenly heard my mistress's voice calling to me from the stable yard.

There was no time to think – there was only time to act. The one thing needed was to keep Mrs Fairbank from ascending the stairs, and discovering – not my lady guest only – but the Englishman also, gagged and bound on his bed. I instantly hurried to the yard. As I ran down the stairs I heard the stable clock strike the quarter to two in the morning.

My mistress was eager and agitated. The doctor (in attendance on her) was smiling to himself, like a man amused at his own thoughts.

'Is Francis awake or asleep?' Mrs Fairbank enquired.

'He has been a little restless, madam. But he is now quiet again. If he is not disturbed' (I added those words to prevent her from ascending the stairs), 'he will soon fall off into a quiet sleep.'

'Has nothing happened since I was here last?'

'Nothing, madam.'

The doctor lifted his eyebrows with a comical look of distress. 'Alas, alas, Mrs Fairbank!' he said. 'Nothing has happened! The days of romance are over!'

'It is not two o'clock yet,' my mistress answered, a little irritably.

The smell of the stables was strong on the morning air. She put her handkerchief to her nose and led the way out of the yard by the north entrance – the entrance communicating with the gardens and the house. I was ordered to follow her, along with the doctor. Once out of the smell of the stables she began to question me again. She was unwilling to believe that nothing had occurred in her absence. I invented the best answers I could think of on the spur of the moment; and the doctor stood by laughing. So the minutes passed till the clock struck two. Upon that, Mrs Fairbank announced her intention of personally visiting the Englishman in his room. To my great relief, the doctor interfered to stop her from doing this.

'You have heard that Francis is just falling asleep,' he said. 'If you enter his room you may disturb him. It is essential to the success of my experiment that he should have a good night's rest, and that he should own it himself, before I tell him the truth. I must request, madam, that you will not disturb the man. Rigobert will ring the alarm bell if anything happens.'

My mistress was unwilling to yield. For the next five minutes, at least, there was a warm discussion between the two. In the end Mrs Fairbank was obliged to give way – for the time. 'In half an hour,' she said, 'Francis will either be sound asleep, or awake again. In half an hour I shall come back.' She took the doctor's arm. They returned together to the house.

Left by myself, with half an hour before me, I resolved to take the Englishwoman back to the village – then, returning to the stables, to remove the gag and the bindings from Francis, and to let him screech to his heart's content. What would his alarming the whole establishment matter to me after I had got rid of the compromising presence of my guest?

Returning to the yard I heard a sound like the creaking of an open door on its hinges. The gate of the north entrance I had just closed with my own hand. I went round to the west entrance, at the back of the stables. It opened on a field crossed by two footpaths in Mr Fairbank's grounds. The nearest footpath led to the village. The other led to the highroad and the river.

Arriving at the west entrance I found the door open – swinging to and fro slowly in the fresh morning breeze. I had myself locked and bolted that door after admitting my fair friend at eleven o'clock. A vague dread of something wrong stole its way into my mind. I hurried back to the stables.

I looked into my own room. It was empty. I went to the harness room. Not a sign of the woman was there. I returned to my room, and approached the door of the Englishman's bedchamber. Was it possible that she had remained there during my absence? An unaccountable reluctance to open the door made me hesitate, with my hand on the lock. I listened. There was not a sound inside. I called softly. There was no answer. I drew back a step, still hesitating. I noticed something dark moving slowly in the crevice between the bottom of the door and the boarded floor. Snatching up the candle from the table, I held it low, and looked. The dark, slowly moving object was a stream of blood!

That horrid sight roused me. I opened the door. The Englishman lay on his bed – alone in the room. He was stabbed in two places – in the throat and in the heart. The weapon was left in the second wound. It was a knife of English manufacture, with a handle of buckhorn as good as new.

I instantly gave the alarm. Witnesses can speak to what followed. It is monstrous to suppose that I am guilty of the murder. I admit that I am capable of committing follies: but I shrink from the bare idea of a crime. Besides, I had no motive for killing the man. The woman murdered him in my absence. The woman escaped by the west entrance while I was talking to my mistress. I have no more to say. I swear to you what I have here written is a true statement of all that happened on the morning of the first of March.

Accept, sir, the assurance of my sentiments of profound gratitude and respect.

JOSEPH RIGOBERT

Last Lines added by Percy Fairbank

Tried for the murder of Francis Raven, Joseph Rigobert was found Not Guilty; the papers of the assassinated man presented ample evidence of the deadly animosity felt towards him by his wife.

The investigations pursued on the morning when the crime was committed showed that the murderess, after leaving the stable, had taken the footpath which led to the river. The river was dragged – without result. It remains doubtful to this day whether she died by drowning or not. The one thing certain is that Alicia Warlock was never seen again.

So – beginning in mystery, ending in mystery – the dream woman passes from your view. Ghost; demon; or living human creature – say for yourselves which she is. Or, knowing what unfathomed wonders are around you, what unfathomed wonders are *in* you, let the wise words of the greatest of all poets be explanation enough:

> We are such stuff
> As dreams are made on, and our little life
> Is rounded with a sleep.

JOSEPH CONRAD

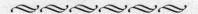

Joseph Conrad was born in the Ukraine to Polish parents in 1857 and orphaned as a child. He longed for a life at sea from an early age and in 1874 began a twenty-year career as a sailor. In 1886 he became a British subject and eight years later devoted himself to being a full-time writer. He married Jessie George – the mother of his two sons – in 1895. Publication of his first novel, *Almayer's Folly*, when he was thirty-eight, marked the beginning of a career as a novelist that was to produce such classics as *Lord Jim* (1900), *Nostromo* (1904) and *Under Western Eyes* (1911). Conrad died in 1924 at a point when his stature as a writer of considerable significance was firmly established.

The Secret Sharer

ONE

On my right hand there were lines of fishing-stakes resembling a mysterious system of half-submerged bamboo fences, incomprehensible in its division of the domain of tropical fishes, and crazy of aspect as if abandoned for ever by some nomad tribe of fishermen now gone to the other end of the ocean; for there was no sign of human habitation as far as the eye could reach. To the left a group of barren islets, suggesting ruins of stone walls, towers and blockhouses, had its foundations set in a blue sea that itself looked solid, so still and stable did it lie below my feet; even the track of light from the westering sun shone smoothly, without that animated glitter which tells of an imperceptible ripple. And when I turned my head to take a parting glance at the tug which had just left us anchored outside the bar, I saw the straight line of the flat shore joined to the stable sea, edge to edge, with a perfect and unmarked closeness, in one levelled floor half brown, half blue under the enormous dome of the sky. Corresponding in their insignificance to the islets of the sea, two small clumps of trees, one on each side of the only fault in the impeccable joint, marked the mouth of the River Meinam we had just left on the first preparatory stage of our homeward journey; and, far back on the inland level, a larger and loftier mass, the grove surrounding the great Paknam pagoda, was the only thing on which the eye could rest from the vain task of exploring the monotonous sweep of the horizon. Here and there gleams as of a few scattered pieces of silver marked the windings of the great river; and on the nearest of them, just within the bar, the tug steaming right into the land became lost to my sight, hull and funnel and masts, as though the impassive earth had swallowed her up without an effort, without a tremor. My eye followed the light cloud of her smoke, now here, now there, above the plain, according to the devious curves of the stream, but always fainter and farther away, till I lost it at last behind the mitre-shaped hill of the great pagoda. And then I was left alone with my ship, anchored at the head of the Gulf of Siam.

She floated at the starting-point of a long journey, very still in an immense stillness, the shadows of her spars flung far to the eastward by the setting sun. At that moment I was alone on her decks. There was not a sound in her – and around us nothing moved, nothing lived, not a canoe on the water, not a bird in the air, not a cloud in the sky. In this breathless pause at the threshold of a long passage we seemed to be measuring our fitness for a long and arduous enterprise, the appointed task of both our existences to be carried out, far from all human eyes, with only sky and sea for spectators and for judges.

There must have been some glare in the air to interfere with one's sight, because it was only just before the sun left us that my roaming eyes made out beyond the highest ridge of the principal islet of the group something which did away with the solemnity of perfect solitude. The tide of darkness flowed on swiftly; and with tropical suddenness a swarm of stars came out above the shadowy earth, while I lingered yet, my hand resting lightly on my ship's rail as if on the shoulder of a trusted friend. But, with all that multitude of celestial bodies staring down at one, the comfort of quiet communion with her was gone for good. And there were also disturbing sounds by this time – voices, footsteps forward; the steward flitted along the maindeck, a busily ministering spirit; a handbell tinkled urgently under the poop-deck . . .

I found my two officers waiting for me near the supper table, in the lighted cuddy. We sat down at once, and as I helped the chief mate, I said: 'Are you aware that there is a ship anchored inside the islands? I saw her mastheads above the ridge as the sun went down.'

He raised sharply his simple face, overcharged by a terrible growth of whisker, and emitted his usual ejaculations: 'Bless my soul, sir! You don't say so!'

My second mate was a round-cheeked, silent young man, grave beyond his years, I thought; but as our eyes happened to meet I detected a slight quiver on his lips. I looked down at once. It was not my part to encourage sneering on board my ship. It must be said, too, that I knew very little of my officers. In consequence of certain events of no particular significance, except to myself, I had been appointed to the command only a fortnight before. Neither did I know much of the hands forward. All these people had been together for eighteen months or so, and my position was that of the only stranger on board. I mention this because it has some bearing on what is to follow. But what I felt most was my being a stranger to the ship; and if all the truth must be told, I was somewhat of a stranger to myself. The youngest man on board (barring the second mate), and untried as yet by a position of the fullest responsibility, I was willing to take the adequacy of the others for granted. They had simply to be equal to their tasks; but I wondered how far I should turn out faithful to that ideal conception of one's own personality every man sets up for himself secretly.

Meantime the chief mate, with an almost visible effect of collaboration on the part of his round eyes and frightful whiskers, was trying to evolve a theory of the anchored ship. His dominant trait was to take all things into earnest consideration. He was of a painstaking turn of mind. As he used to say, he 'liked to account to himself' for practically everything that came in his way, down to a miserable scorpion he had found in his cabin a week before. The why and the wherefore of that scorpion – how it got on board and came to select his room rather than the pantry (which was a dark place and more what a scorpion would be partial to), and how on earth it managed to drown itself in the inkwell of his writing-desk – had exercised him infinitely. The ship within the islands was much more easily accounted for; and just as we were about to rise from table he made his pronouncement. She was, he doubted not, a ship from home lately arrived. Probably she drew too much water to cross the bar except at the top of spring tides. Therefore she went into that natural harbour to wait for a few days in preference to remaining in an open roadstead.

'That's so,' confirmed the second mate, suddenly, in his slightly hoarse voice. 'She draws over twenty feet. She's the Liverpool ship *Sephora* with a cargo of coal. Hundred and twenty-three days from Cardiff.'

We looked at him in surprise.

'The tugboat skipper told me when he came on board for your letters, sir,' explained the young man. 'He expects to take her up the river the day after tomorrow.'

After thus overwhelming us with the extent of his information he slipped out of the cabin. The mate observed regretfully that he 'could not account for that young fellow's whims'. What prevented him telling us all about it at once, he wanted to know.

I detained him as he was making a move. For the last two days the crew had had plenty of hard work, and the night before they had had very little sleep. I felt painfully that I – a stranger – was doing something unusual when I directed him to let all hands turn in without setting an anchor-watch. I proposed to keep on deck myself till one o'clock or thereabouts. I would get the second mate to relieve me at that hour.

'He will turn out the cook and the steward at four,' I concluded, 'and then give you a call. Of course at the slightest sign of any sort of wind we'll have the hands up and make a start at once.'

He concealed his astonishment. 'Very well, sir.' Outside the cuddy he put his head in the second mate's door to inform him of my unheard-of caprice to take a five hours' anchor-watch on myself. I heard the other raise his voice incredulously – 'What? The captain himself?' Then a few more murmurs, a door closed, then another. A few moments later I went on deck.

My strangeness, which had made me sleepless, had prompted that unconventional arrangement, as if I had expected in those solitary hours of the night to get on terms with the ship of which I knew nothing, manned by men of whom I knew very little more. Fast alongside a wharf, littered like any ship in port with a tangle of unrelated things, invaded by unrelated shore people, I had hardly seen her yet properly. Now, as she lay cleared for sea, the stretch of her maindeck seemed to me very fine under the stars. Very fine, very roomy for her size, and very inviting. I descended the poop and paced the waist, my mind picturing to myself the coming passage through the Malay Archipelago, down the Indian Ocean, and up the Atlantic. All its phases were familiar enough to me, every characteristic, all the alternatives which were likely to face me on the high seas – everything! . . . except the novel responsibility of command. But I took heart from the reasonable thought that the ship was like other ships, the men like other men, and that the sea was not likely to keep any special surprises expressly for my discomfiture.

Arrived at that comforting conclusion, I bethought myself of a cigar and went below to get it. All was still down there. Everybody at the after end of the ship was sleeping profoundly. I came out again on the quarterdeck, agreeably at ease in my sleeping-suit on that warm breathless night, bare-footed, a glowing cigar in my teeth, and, going forward, I was met by the profound silence of the fore-end of the ship. Only as I passed the door of the forecastle I heard a deep, quiet, trustful sigh of some sleeper inside. And suddenly I rejoiced in the great security of the sea as compared with the unrest of the land, in my choice of that untempted life presenting no disquieting problems, invested with an elementary moral beauty by the absolute straightforwardness of its appeal and by the singleness of its purpose.

The riding-light in the fore-rigging burned with a clear, untroubled, as if symbolic, flame, confident and bright in the mysterious shades of the night. Passing on my way aft along the other side of the ship, I observed that the rope side-ladder, put over, no doubt, for the master of the tug when he came to fetch away our letters, had not been hauled in as it should have been. I became annoyed at this, for exactitude in small matters is the very soul of discipline. Then I reflected that I had myself peremptorily dismissed my officers from duty, and by my own act had prevented the anchor-watch being formally set and things properly attended to. I asked myself whether it was wise ever to interfere with the established routine of duties even from the kindest of motives. My action might have made me appear eccentric. Goodness only knew how that absurdly whiskered mate would 'account' for my conduct, and what the whole ship thought of that informality of their new captain. I was vexed with myself.

Not from compunction certainly, but, as it were mechanically, I proceeded to get the ladder in myself. Now a side-ladder of that sort is a light affair and comes in easily, yet my vigorous tug, which should have brought it flying on board, merely recoiled upon my body in a totally unexpected jerk. What the devil! . . . I was so astounded by the immovableness of that ladder that I remained stock-still, trying to account for it to myself like that imbecile mate of mine. In the end, of course, I put my head over the rail.

The side of the ship made an opaque belt of shadow on the darkling glassy shimmer of the sea. But I saw at once something elongated and pale floating very close to the ladder. Before I could form a guess a faint flash of phosphorescent light, which seemed to issue suddenly from the naked body of a man, flickered in the sleeping water with the elusive, silent play of summer lightning in a night sky. With a gasp I saw revealed to my stare a pair of feet, the long legs, a broad livid back immersed right up to the neck in a greenish cadaverous glow. One hand, awash, clutched the bottom rung of the ladder. He was complete but for the head. A headless corpse! The cigar dropped out of my gaping mouth with a tiny plop and a short hiss quite audible in the absolute stillness of all things under heaven. At that I suppose he raised up his face, a dimly pale oval in the shadow of the ship's side. But even then I could only barely make out down there the shape of his black-haired head. However, it was enough for the horrid, frost-bound sensation which had gripped me about the chest to pass off. The moment of vain exclamations was past, too. I only climbed on the spare spar and leaned over the rail as far as I could, to bring my eyes nearer to that mystery floating alongside.

As he hung by the ladder, like a resting swimmer, the sea-lightning played about his limbs at every stir; and he appeared in it ghastly, silvery, fish-like. He remained as mute as a fish, too. He made no motion to get out of the water, either. It was inconceivable that he should not attempt to come on board, and strangely troubling to suspect that perhaps he did not want to. And my first words were prompted by just that troubled incertitude.

'What's the matter?' I asked in my ordinary tone, speaking down to the face upturned exactly under mine.

'Cramp,' it answered, no louder. Then slightly anxious, 'I say, no need to call anyone.'

'I was not going to,' I said.

'Are you alone on deck?'

'Yes.'

I had somehow the impression that he was on the point of letting go the ladder to swim away beyond my ken – mysterious as he came. But, for the moment, this being appearing as if he had risen from the bottom of the sea (it was certainly the nearest land to the ship) wanted only to know the time. I told him. And he, down there, tentatively: 'I suppose your captain's turned in?'

'I am sure he isn't,' I said.

He seemed to struggle with himself, for I heard something like the low, bitter murmur of doubt. 'What's the good?' His next words came out with a hesitating effort. 'Look here, my man. Could you call him out quietly?'

I thought the time had come to declare myself.

'*I* am the captain.'

I heard a 'By Jove!' whispered at the level of the water. The phosphorescence flashed in the swirl of the water all about his limbs, his other hand seized the ladder.

'My name's Leggatt.'

The voice was calm and resolute. A good voice. The self-possession of that man had somehow induced a corresponding state in myself. It was very quietly that I remarked: 'You must be a good swimmer.'

'Yes. I've been in the water practically since nine o'clock. The question for me now is whether I am to let go this ladder and go on swimming till I sink from exhaustion, or – to come on board here.'

I felt this was no mere formula of desperate speech, but a real alternative in the view of a strong soul. I should have gathered from this that he was young; indeed, it is only the young who are ever confronted by such clear issues. But at the time it was pure intuition on my part. A mysterious communication was established already between us two – in the face of that silent, darkened tropical sea. I was young, too; young enough to make no comment. The man in the water began suddenly to climb up the ladder, and I hastened away from the rail to fetch some clothes.

Before entering the cabin I stood still, listening in the lobby at the foot of the stairs. A faint snore came through the closed door of the chief mate's room. The second mate's door was on the hook, but the darkness in there was absolutely soundless. He, too, was young and could sleep like a stone. Remained the steward, but he was not likely to wake up before he was called. I got a sleeping-suit out of my room and, coming back on deck, saw the naked man from the sea sitting on the main-hatch, glimmering white in the darkness, his elbows on his knees and his head in his hands. In a moment he had concealed his damp body in a sleeping-suit of the same grey-stripe pattern as the one I was wearing and followed me like my double on the poop. Together we moved right aft, barefooted, silent.

'What is it?' I asked in a deadened voice, taking the lighted lamp out of the binnacle, and raising it to his face.

'An ugly business.'

He had rather regular features; a good mouth; light eyes under somewhat heavy, dark eyebrows; a smooth, square forehead; no growth on his cheeks; a small, brown moustache, and a well-shaped, round chin. His expression was concentrated, meditative, under the inspecting light of the lamp I held up to his face; such as a man thinking hard in solitude might wear. My sleeping-suit was just right for his size. A well-knit young fellow of twenty-five at most. He caught his lower lip with the edge of white, even teeth.

'Yes,' I said, replacing the lamp in the binnacle. The warm, heavy tropical night closed upon his head again.

'There's a ship over there,' he murmured.

'Yes, I know. The *Sephora*. Did you know of us?'

'Hadn't the slightest idea. I am the mate of her – ' He paused and corrected himself. 'I should say I *was*.'

'Aha! Something wrong?'

'Yes. Very wrong indeed. I've killed a man.'

'What do you mean? Just now?'

'No, on the passage. Weeks ago. Thirty-nine south. When I say a man – '

'Fit of temper,' I suggested, confidently.

The shadowy, dark head, like mine, seemed to nod imperceptibly above the ghostly grey of my sleeping-suit. It was, in the night, as though I had been faced by my own reflection in the depths of a sombre and immense mirror.

'A pretty thing to have to own up to for a *Conway* boy,' murmured my double, distinctly.

'You're a *Conway* boy?'

'I am,' he said, as if startled. Then, slowly . . . 'Perhaps you too – '

It was so; but being a couple of years older I had left before he joined. After a quick interchange of dates a silence fell; and I thought suddenly of my absurd mate with his terrific whiskers and the 'Bless my soul – you don't say so' type of intellect.

My double gave me an inkling of his thoughts by saying: 'My father's a parson in Norfolk. Do you see me before a judge and jury on that charge? For myself I can't see the necessity. There are fellows that an angel from heaven – And I am not that. He was one of those creatures that are just simmering all the time with a silly sort of wickedness. Miserable devils that have no business to live at all. He wouldn't do his duty and wouldn't let anybody else do theirs. But what's the good of talking! You know well enough the sort of ill-conditioned snarling cur – '

He appealed to me as if our experiences had been as identical as our clothes. And I knew well enough the pestiferous danger of such a character where there are no means of legal repression. And I knew well enough also that my double there was no homicidal ruffian. I did not think of asking him for details, and he told me the story roughly in brusque, disconnected sentences. I needed no more. I saw it all going on as though I were myself inside that other sleeping-suit.

'It happened while we were setting a reefed foresail, at dusk. Reefed foresail! You understand the sort of weather. The only sail we had left to keep the ship running; so you may guess what it had been like for days. Anxious sort of job, that. He gave me some of his cursed insolence at the sheet. I tell you I was overdone with this terrific weather that seemed to have no end to it. Terrific, I tell you – and a deep ship. I believe the fellow himself was half crazed with funk. It was no time for gentlemanly reproof, so I turned round and felled him like an ox. He up and at me. We closed just as an awful sea made for the ship. All hands saw it coming and took to the rigging, but I had him by the throat, and went on shaking him like a rat, the men above us yelling, "Look out! look out!" Then a crash as if the sky had fallen on my head. They say that for over ten minutes hardly anything was to be seen of the ship – just the three masts and a bit of the forecastle head and of the poop all awash driving along in a smother of foam. It was a miracle that they found us, jammed together behind the forebits. It's clear that I meant business, because I was holding him by the throat still when they picked us up. He was black in the face. It was too much for them. It seems they rushed us aft together, gripped as we were, screaming "Murder!" like a lot of lunatics, and broke into the cuddy. And the ship running for her life, touch and go all the time, any minute her last in a sea fit to turn your hair grey only a-looking at it. I understand that the skipper, too, started raving like the rest of them. The man had been deprived of sleep for more than a week, and to have this sprung on him at the height of a furious gale nearly drove him out of his mind. I wonder they didn't fling me overboard after getting the carcass of their precious shipmate out of my fingers. They had rather a job to separate us, I've been told. A sufficiently fierce story to make an old judge and a respectable jury sit up a bit. The first thing I heard when I came to myself was the maddening howling of that endless gale, and on that the voice of the old man. He was hanging on to my bunk, staring into my face out of his sou'wester.

' "Mr Leggatt, you have killed a man. You can act no longer as chief mate of this ship." '

His care to subdue his voice made it sound monotonous. He rested a hand on the end of the skylight to steady himself with, and all that time did not stir a limb, so far as I could see. 'Nice little tale for a quiet tea-party,' he concluded in the same tone.

One of my hands, too, rested on the end of the skylight; neither did I stir a limb, so far as I knew. We stood less than a foot from each other. It occurred to me that if old 'Bless my soul – you don't say so' were to put his head up the companion and catch sight of us, he would think he was seeing double, or imagine himself come upon a scene of weird witchcraft; the strange captain having a quiet confabulation by the wheel with his own grey ghost. I became very much concerned to prevent anything of the sort. I heard the other's soothing undertone.

'My father's a parson in Norfolk,' it said. Evidently he had forgotten he had told me this important fact before. Truly a nice little tale.

'You had better slip down into my stateroom now,' I said, moving off stealthily. My double followed my movements; our bare feet made no sound; I let him in, closed the door with care, and, after giving a call to the second mate, returned on deck for my relief.

'Not much sign of any wind yet,' I remarked when he approached.

'No, sir. Not much,' he assented, sleepily, in his hoarse voice, with just enough deference, no more, and barely suppressing a yawn.

'Well, that's all you have to look out for. You have got your orders.'

'Yes, sir.'

I paced a turn or two on the poop and saw him take up his position face forward with his elbow in the ratlines of the mizzen-rigging before I went below. The mate's faint snoring was still going on peacefully. The cuddy lamp was burning over the table on which stood a vase with flowers, a polite attention from the ship's provision merchant – the last flowers we should see for the next three months at the very least. Two bunches of bananas hung from the beam symmetrically, one on each side of the rudder-casing. Everything was as before in the ship – except that two of her captain's sleeping-suits were simultaneously in use, one motionless in the cuddy, the other keeping very still in the captain's stateroom.

It must be explained here that my cabin had the form of the capital letter L, the door being within the angle and opening into the short part of the letter. A couch was to the left, the bed-place to the right; my writing-desk and the chronometers' table faced the door. But anyone opening it, unless he stepped right inside, had no view of what I call the long (or vertical) part of the letter. It contained some lockers surmounted by a bookcase; and a few clothes, a thick jacket or two, caps, oilskin coat and suchlike, hung on hooks. There was at the bottom of that part a door opening into my bathroom, which could be entered also directly from the saloon. But that way was never used.

The mysterious arrival had discovered the advantage of this particular shape. Entering my room, lighted strongly by a big bulkhead lamp swung on gimbals above my writing-desk, I did not see him anywhere till he stepped out quietly from behind the coats hung in the recessed part.

'I heard somebody moving about, and went in there at once,' he whispered.

I, too, spoke under my breath. 'Nobody is likely to come in here without knocking and getting permission.'

He nodded. His face was thin and the sunburn faded, as though he had been ill. And no wonder. He had been, I heard presently, kept under arrest in his cabin for nearly nine weeks. But there was nothing sickly in his eyes or in his expression. He was not a bit like me, really; yet, as we stood leaning over my bed-place, whispering side by side, with our dark heads together and our backs to the door, anybody bold enough to open it stealthily would have been treated to the uncanny sight of a double captain busy talking in whispers with his other self.

'But all this doesn't tell me how you came to hang on to our side-ladder,' I enquired, in the hardly audible murmurs we used, after he had told me something more of the proceedings on board the *Sephora* once the bad weather was over.

'When we sighted Java Head I had had time to think all those matters out several times over. I had six weeks of doing nothing else, and with only an hour or so every evening for a tramp on the quarterdeck.'

He whispered, his arms folded on the side of my bed-place, staring through the open port. And I could imagine perfectly the manner of this thinking out – a stubborn if not a steadfast operation; something of which I should have been perfectly incapable.

'I reckoned it would be dark before we closed with the land,' he continued, so low that I had to strain my hearing, near as we were to each other, shoulder touching shoulder almost. 'So I asked to speak to the old man. He always seemed very sick when he came to see me – as if he could not look me in the face. You know, that foresail saved the ship. She was too deep to have run long under bare poles. And it was I that managed to set it for him. Anyway, he came. When I had him in my cabin – he stood by the door looking at me as if I had the halter round my neck already – I asked him right away to leave my cabin door unlocked at night while the ship was going through Sunda Straits. There would be the Java coast within two or three miles, off Angier Point. I wanted nothing more. I've had a prize for swimming – my second year in the *Conway*.'

'I can believe it,' I breathed out.

'God only knows why they locked me in every night. To see some of their faces you'd have thought they were afraid I'd go about at night strangling people. Am I a murdering brute? Do I look it? By Jove! if I had been he wouldn't have trusted himself like that into my room. You'll say I might have chucked him aside and bolted out, there and then – it was dark already. Well, no. And for the same reason I wouldn't think of trying to smash the door. There would have been a rush to stop me at the noise, and I did not mean to get into a confounded scrimmage. Somebody else might have got killed – for I would not have broken out only to get chucked back, and I did not want any more of that work. He refused, looking more sick than ever. He was afraid of the men, and also of that old second mate of his who had been sailing with him for years – a grey-headed old humbug; and his steward, too, had been with him devil knows how long – seventeen years or more – a dogmatic sort of loafer who hated me like poison, just because I was the chief mate. No chief mate ever made more than one voyage in the *Sephora*, you know. Those two old chaps ran the ship. Devil only knows what the skipper wasn't afraid of (all his nerve went to pieces altogether in that hellish spell of bad weather we had) – of what the law would do to him – of his wife, perhaps. Oh, yes! she's on board. Though I don't think she would have meddled. She would have been only too glad to have me out of the ship in any way. The "brand of Cain" business, don't you see. That's all right. I was ready enough to go off wandering on the face of the earth – and that was price enough to pay for an Abel of that sort. Anyhow, he wouldn't listen to me. "This thing must take its course. I represent the law here." He was shaking like a leaf. "So you won't?" "No!" "Then I hope you will be able to sleep on that," I said, and turned my back on him. "I wonder that *you* can," cries he, and locks the door.

'Well, after that, I couldn't. Not very well. That was three weeks ago. We have had a slow passage through the Java Sea; drifted about Carimata for ten days. When we anchored here they thought, I suppose, it was all right. The nearest land (and that's five miles) is the ship's destination; the consul would soon set about catching me; and there would have been no object in bolting to these islets there. I don't suppose there's a drop of water on them. I don't know how it was, but tonight that steward, after bringing me my supper, went out to let me eat it, and left the door unlocked. And I ate it – all there was, too. After I had finished I strolled out on the quarterdeck. I don't know that I meant to do anything. A breath of fresh air was all I wanted, I believe. Then a sudden temptation came over me. I kicked off my slippers and was in the water before I had made up my mind fairly. Somebody heard the splash and they raised an awful hullabaloo. "He's gone! Lower the boats! He's committed suicide! No, he's swimming." Certainly I was swimming. It's not so easy for a swimmer like me to commit suicide by drowning. I landed on the nearest islet before the boat left the ship's side. I heard them pulling about in the dark, hailing, and so on, but after a bit they gave up. Everything quieted down and the anchorage became as still as death. I sat down on a stone and began to think. I felt certain they would start searching for me at daylight. There was no place to hide on those stony things – and if there had been, what would have been the good? But now I was clear of that ship, I was not going back. So after a while I took off all my clothes, tied them up in a bundle with a stone inside, and dropped them in the deep water on the outer side of that islet. That was suicide enough for me. Let them think what they liked, but I didn't mean to drown myself. I meant to swim till I sank – but that's not the same thing. I struck out for another of these little islands, and it was from that one that I first saw your riding-light. Something to swim for. I went on easily, and on the way I came upon a flat rock a foot or two above water. In the daytime, I dare say, you might make it out with a glass from your poop. I scrambled up on it and rested myself for a bit. Then I made another start. That last spell must have been over a mile.'

His whisper was getting fainter and fainter, and all the time he stared straight out through the porthole, in which there was not even a star to be seen. I had not interrupted him. There was something that made comment impossible in his narrative, or perhaps in himself; a sort of feeling, a quality, which I can't find a name for. And when he ceased, all I found was a futile whisper: 'So you swam for our light?'

'Yes – straight for it. It was something to swim for. I couldn't see any stars low down because the coast was in the way, and I couldn't see the land, either. The water was like glass. One might have been swimming in a confounded thousand-feet-deep cistern with no place for scrambling out anywhere; but what I didn't like was the notion of swimming round and round like a crazed bullock before I gave out; and as I didn't mean to go back ... No. Do you see me being hauled back, stark naked, off one of these little islands by the scruff of the neck and fighting like a wild beast? Somebody would have got killed for certain, and I did not want any of that. So I went on. Then your ladder – '

'Why didn't you hail the ship?' I asked, a little louder.

He touched my shoulder lightly. Lazy footsteps came right over our heads and stopped. The second mate had crossed from the other side of the poop and might have been hanging over the rail, for all we knew.

'He couldn't hear us talking – could he?' My double breathed into my very ear, anxiously.

His anxiety was an answer, a sufficient answer, to the question I had put to him. An answer containing all the difficulty of that situation. I closed the porthole quietly, to make sure. A louder word might have been overheard.

'Who's that?' he whispered then.

'My second mate. But I don't know much more of the fellow than you do.'

And I told him a little about myself. I had been appointed to take charge while I least expected anything of the sort, not quite a fortnight ago. I didn't know either the ship or the people. Hadn't had the time in port to look about me or size anybody up. And as to the crew, all they knew was that I was appointed to take the ship home. For the rest, I was almost as much of a stranger on board as himself, I said. And at the moment I felt it most acutely. I felt that it would take very little to make me a suspect person in the eyes of the ship's company.

He had turned about meantime; and we, the two strangers in the ship, faced each other in identical attitudes.

'Your ladder – ' he murmured, after a silence. 'Who'd have thought of finding a ladder hanging over at night in a ship anchored out here! I felt just then a very unpleasant faintness. After the life I've been leading for nine weeks, anybody would have got out of condition. I wasn't capable of swimming round as far as your rudder-chains. And, lo and behold! there was a ladder to get hold of. After I gripped it I said to myself, 'What's the good?' When I saw a man's head looking over I thought I would swim away presently and leave him shouting – in whatever language it was. I didn't mind being looked at. I – I liked it. And then you speaking to me so quietly – as if you had expected me – made me hold on a little longer. It had been a confounded lonely time – I don't mean while swimming. I was glad to talk a little to somebody that didn't belong to the *Sephora*. As to asking for the captain, that was a mere impulse. It could have been no use, with all the ship knowing about me and the other people pretty certain to be round here in the morning. I don't know – I wanted to be seen, to talk with somebody, before I went on. I don't know what I would have said . . . "Fine night, isn't it?" or something of the sort.'

'Do you think they will be round here presently?' I asked with some incredulity.

'Quite likely,' he said, faintly.

He looked extremely haggard all of a sudden. His head rolled on his shoulders.

'H'm. We shall see then. Meantime get into that bed,' I whispered. 'Want help? There.'

It was a rather high bed-place with a set of drawers underneath. This amazing swimmer really needed the lift I gave him by seizing his leg. He tumbled in, rolled over on his back, and flung one arm across his eyes. And then, with his face nearly hidden, he must have looked exactly as I used to look in that bed. I gazed upon my other self for a while before drawing across carefully the two green serge curtains which ran on a brass rod. I thought for a moment of pinning them together for greater safety, but I sat down on the couch, and once there I felt unwilling to rise and hunt for a pin. I would do it in a moment. I was extremely tired, in a peculiarly intimate way, by the strain of stealthiness, by the effort of whispering and the general secrecy of this excitement. It was three o'clock by now and I had been on my feet since nine, but I was not sleepy; I could not have gone to sleep. I sat there, fagged out, looking at the curtains, trying to clear my mind of the confused sensation of being in two places at once, and greatly bothered by an exasperating knocking in my head. It was a relief to discover suddenly that it was not in my head at all, but on the outside of the door. Before I could collect myself the words 'Come in' were out of my mouth, and the steward entered with a tray, bringing in my morning coffee. I had slept, after all, and I was so frightened that I shouted, 'This way! I am here, steward,' as though he had been miles away. He put down the tray on the table next the couch and only then said, very quietly, 'I can see you are here, sir.' I felt him give me a keen look, but I dared not meet his eyes just then. He must have wondered why I had drawn the curtains of my bed before going to sleep on the couch. He went out, hooking the door open as usual.

I heard the crew washing decks above me. I knew I would have been told at once if there had been any wind. Calm, I thought, and I was doubly vexed. Indeed, I felt dual more than ever. The steward reappeared suddenly in the doorway. I jumped up from the couch so quickly that he gave a start.

'What do you want here?'

'Close your port, sir – they are washing decks.'

'It is closed,' I said, reddening.

'Very well, sir.' But he did not move from the doorway and returned my stare in an extraordinary, equivocal manner for a time. Then his eyes wavered, all his expression changed, and in a voice unusually gentle, almost coaxingly: 'May I come in to take the empty cup away, sir?'

'Of course!' I turned my back on him while he popped in and out. Then I unhooked and closed the door and even pushed the bolt. This sort of thing could not go on very long. The cabin was as hot as an oven, too. I took a peep at my double, and discovered that he had not moved, his arm was still over his eyes; but his chest heaved; his hair was wet; his chin glistened with perspiration. I reached over him and opened the port.

'I must show myself on deck,' I reflected.

Of course, theoretically, I could do what I liked, with no one to say nay to me within the whole circle of the horizon; but to lock my cabin door and take the key away I did not dare. Directly I put my head out of the companion I saw the group of my two officers, the second mate barefooted, the chief mate in long india-rubber boots, near the break of the poop, and the steward halfway down the poop-ladder talking to them eagerly. He happened to catch sight of me and dived, the second mate ran down on the main-deck shouting some order or other, and the chief mate came to meet me, touching his cap.

There was a sort of curiosity in his eye that I did not like. I don't know whether the steward had told them that I was 'queer' only, or downright drunk, but I know the man meant to have a good look at me. I watched him coming with a smile which, as he got into point-blank range, took effect and froze his very whiskers. I did not give him time to open his lips.

'Square the yards by lifts and braces before the hands go to breakfast.'

It was the first particular order I had given on board that ship; and I stayed on deck to see it executed, too. I had felt the need of asserting myself without loss of time. That sneering young cub got taken down a peg or two on that occasion, and I also seized the opportunity of having a good look at the face of every foremast man as they filed past me to go to the after braces. At breakfast time, eating nothing myself, I presided with such frigid dignity that the two mates were only too glad to escape from the cabin as soon as decency permitted; and all the time the dual working of my mind distracted me almost to the point of insanity. I was constantly watching myself, my secret self, as dependent on my actions as my own personality, sleeping in that bed, behind that door which faced me as I sat at the head of the table. It was very much like being mad, only it was worse because one was aware of it.

I had to shake him for a solid minute, but when at last he opened his eyes it was in the full possession of his senses, with an enquiring look.

'All's well so far,' I whispered. 'Now you must vanish into the bathroom.'

He did so, as noiseless as a ghost, and I then rang for the steward, and facing him boldly, directed him to tidy up my stateroom while I was having my bath – 'and be quick about it'. As my tone admitted of no excuses, he said, 'Yes, sir,' and ran off to fetch his dustpan and brushes. I took a bath and did most of my dressing, splashing, and whistling softly for the steward's edification, while the secret sharer of my life stood drawn up bolt upright in that little space, his face looking very sunken in daylight, his eyelids lowered under the stern, dark line of his eyebrows drawn together by a slight frown.

When I left him there to go back to my room the steward was finishing dusting. I sent for the mate and engaged him in some insignificant conversation. It was, as it were, trifling with the terrific character of his whiskers; but my object was to give him an opportunity for a good look at my cabin. And then I could at last shut, with a clear conscience, the door of my stateroom and get my double back into the recessed part. There was nothing else for it. He had to sit still on a small folding stool, half smothered by the heavy coats hanging there. We listened to the steward going into the bathroom out of the saloon filling the water-bottles there, scrubbing the bath, setting things to rights, whisk, bang, clatter – out again into the saloon – turn the key – click. Such was my scheme for keeping my second self invisible. Nothing better could be contrived under the circumstances. And there we sat; I at my writing-desk ready to appear busy with some papers, he behind me, out of sight of the door. It would not have been prudent to talk in daytime; and I could not have stood the excitement of that queer sense of whispering to myself. Now and then, glancing over my shoulder, I saw him far back there, sitting rigidly on the low stool, his bare feet close together, his arms folded, his head hanging on his breast – and perfectly still. Anybody would have taken him for me.

I was fascinated by it myself. Every moment I had to glance over my shoulder. I was looking at him when a voice outside the door said: 'Beg pardon, sir.'

'Well!' . . . I kept my eyes on him, and so, when the voice outside the door announced, 'There's a ship's boat coming our way, sir,' I saw him give a start – the first movement he had made for hours. But he did not raise his bowed head.

'All right. Get the ladder over.'

I hesitated. Should I whisper something to him? But what? His immobility seemed never to have been disturbed. What could I tell him he did not know already? . . . Finally I went on deck.

TWO

The skipper of the *Sephora* had a thin red whisker all round his face, and the sort of complexion that goes with hair of that colour; also the particular, rather smeary shade of blue in the eyes. He was not exactly a showy figure; his shoulders were high, his stature but middling – one leg slightly more bandy than the other. He shook hands, looking vaguely around. A spiritless tenacity was his main characteristic, I judged. I behaved with a politeness which seemed to disconcert him. Perhaps he was shy. He mumbled to me as if he were ashamed of what he was saying; gave his name (it was something like Archbold – but at this distance of years I am hardly sure), his ship's name, and a few other particulars of that sort, in the manner of a criminal making a reluctant and doleful confession. He had had terrible weather on the passage out – terrible – terrible – wife aboard, too.

By this time we were seated in the cabin and the steward brought in a tray with a bottle and glasses. 'Thanks! No.' Never took liquor. Would have some water, though. He drank two tumblerfuls. Terrible thirsty work. Ever since daylight had been exploring the islands round his ship.

'What was that for – fun?' I asked, with an appearance of polite interest.

'No!' He sighed. 'Painful duty.'

As he persisted in his mumbling and I wanted my double to hear every word, I hit upon the notion of informing him that I regretted to say I was hard of hearing.

'Such a young man, too!' he nodded, keeping his smeary blue, unintelligent eyes fastened upon me. 'What was the cause of it – some disease?' he enquired, without the least sympathy and as if he thought that, if so, I'd got no more than I deserved.

'Yes; disease,' I admitted in a cheerful tone which seemed to shock him. But my point was gained, because he had to raise his voice to give me his tale. It is not worth while to record that version. It was just over two months since all this had happened, and he had thought so much about it that he seemed completely muddled as to its bearings, but still immensely impressed.

'What would you think of such a thing happening on board your own ship? I've had the *Sephora* for these fifteen years. I am a well-known shipmaster.'

He was densely distressed – and perhaps I should have sympathised with him if I had been able to detach my mental vision from the unsuspected sharer of my cabin as though he were my second self. There he was on the other side of the bulkhead, four or five feet from us, no more, as we sat in the saloon. I looked politely at Captain Archbold (if that was his name), but it was the other I saw, in a grey sleeping-suit, seated on a low stool, his bare feet close together, his arms folded, and every word said between us falling into the ears of his dark head bowed on his chest.

'I have been at sea now, man and boy, for seven-and-thirty years, and I've never heard of such a thing happening in an English ship. And that it should be my ship. Wife on board, too.'

I was hardly listening to him.

'Don't you think,' I said, 'that the heavy sea which, you told me, came aboard just then might have killed the man? I have seen the sheer weight of a sea kill a man very neatly, by simply breaking his neck.'

'Good God!' he uttered, impressively, fixing his smeary blue eyes on me. 'The sea! No man killed by the sea ever looked like that.' He seemed positively scandalised at my suggestion. And as I gazed at him, certainly not prepared for anything original on his part, he advanced his head close to mine and thrust his tongue out at me so suddenly that I couldn't help starting back.

After scoring over my calmness in this graphic way he nodded wisely. If I had seen the sight, he assured me, I would never forget it as long as I lived. The weather was too bad to give the corpse a proper sea burial. So next day at dawn they took it up on the poop, covering its face with a bit of bunting; he read a short prayer, and then, just as it was, in its oilskins and long boots, they launched it amongst those mountainous seas that seemed ready every moment to swallow up the ship herself and the terrified lives on board of her.

'That reefed foresail saved you,' I threw in.

'Under God – it did,' he exclaimed fervently. 'It was by a special mercy, I firmly believe, that it stood some of those hurricane squalls.'

'It was the setting of that sail which – ' I began.

'God's own hand in it,' he interrupted me. 'Nothing less could have done it. I don't mind telling you that I hardly dared give the order. It seemed impossible that we could touch anything without losing it, and then our last hope would have been gone.'

The terror of that gale was on him yet. I let him go on for a bit, then said, casually – as if returning to a minor subject: 'You were very anxious to give up your mate to the shore people, I believe?'

He was. To the law. His obscure tenacity on that point had in it something incomprehensible and a little awful; something, as it were, mystical, quite apart from his anxiety that he should not be suspected of 'countenancing any doings of that sort'. Seven-and-thirty virtuous years at sea, of which over twenty of immaculate command, and the last fifteen in the *Sephora*, seemed to have laid him under some pitiless obligation.

'And you know,' he went on, groping shamefacedly amongst his feelings, 'I did not engage that young fellow. His people had some interest with my owners. I was in a way forced to take him on. He looked very smart, very gentlemanly, and all that. But do you know – I never liked him, somehow. I am a plain man. You see, he wasn't exactly the sort for the chief mate of a ship like the *Sephora*.'

I had become so connected in thoughts and impressions with the secret sharer of my cabin that I felt as if I, personally, were being given to understand that I, too, was not the sort that would have done for the chief mate of a ship like the *Sephora*. I had no doubt of it in my mind.

'Not at all the style of man. You understand,' he insisted, superfluously, looking hard at me.

I smiled urbanely. He seemed at a loss for a while.

'I suppose I must report a suicide.'

'Beg pardon?'

'Suicide! That's what I'll have to write to my owners directly I get in.'

'Unless you manage to recover him before tomorrow,' I assented, dispassionately . . . 'I mean, alive.'

He mumbled something which I really did not catch, and I turned my ear to him in a puzzled manner.

He fairly bawled: 'The land – I say, the mainland is at least seven miles off my anchorage.'

'About that.'

My lack of excitement, of curiosity, of surprise, of any sort of pronounced interest, began to arouse his distrust. But except for the felicitous pretence of deafness I had not tried to pretend anything. I had felt utterly incapable of playing the part of ignorance properly, and therefore was afraid to try. It is also certain that he had brought some ready-made suspicions with him, and that he viewed my politeness as a strange and unnatural phenomenon. And yet how else could I have received him? Not heartily! That was impossible for psychological reasons, which I need not state here. My only object was to keep off his enquiries. Surlily? Yes, but surliness might have provoked a point-blank question. From its novelty to him and from its nature, punctilious courtesy was the manner best calculated to restrain the man. But there was the danger of his breaking through my defence bluntly. I could not, I think, have met him by a direct lie, also for psychological (not moral) reasons. If he had only known how afraid I was of his putting my feeling of identity with the other to the test! But, strangely enough (I thought of it only afterwards), I believe that he was not a little disconcerted by the reverse side of that weird situation, by something in me that reminded him of the man he was seeking – suggested a mysterious similitude to the young fellow he had distrusted and disliked from the first.

However that might have been, the silence was not very prolonged. He took another oblique step.

'I reckon I had no more than a two-mile pull to your ship. Not a bit more.'

'And quite enough, too, in this awful heat,' I said.

Another pause full of mistrust followed. Necessity, they say, is mother of invention, but fear, too, is not barren of ingenious suggestions. And I was afraid he would ask me point-blank for news of my other self.

'Nice little saloon, isn't it?' I remarked, as if noticing for the first time the way his eyes roamed from one closed door to the other. 'And very well fitted out, too. Here, for instance,' I continued, reaching over the back of my seat negligently and flinging the door open, 'is my bathroom.'

He made an eager movement, but hardly gave it a glance. I got up, shut the door of the bathroom, and invited him to have a look round, as if I were very proud of my accommodation. He had to rise and be shown round, but he went through the business without any raptures whatever.

'And now we'll have a look at my stateroom,' I declared, in a voice as loud as I dared to make it, crossing the cabin to the starboard side with purposely heavy steps.

He followed me in and gazed around. My intelligent double had vanished. I played my part.

'Very convenient – isn't it?'

'Very nice. Very comf . . . ' He didn't finish, and went out brusquely as if to escape from some unrighteous wiles of mine. But it was not to be. I had been too frightened not to feel vengeful; I felt I had him on the run, and I meant to keep him on the run. My polite insistence must have had something menacing in it, because he gave in suddenly. And I did not let him off a single item: mate's room, pantry, storerooms, the very sail-locker which was also under the poop – he had to look into them all. When at last I showed him out on the quarterdeck he drew a long, spiritless sigh, and mumbled dismally that he must really be going back to his ship now. I desired my mate, who had joined us, to see to the captain's boat.

The man of whiskers gave a blast on the whistle which he used to wear hanging round his neck, and yelled, '*Sephora*'s away!' My double down there in my cabin must have heard, and certainly could not feel more relieved than I. Four fellows came running out from somewhere forward and went over the side, while my own men, appearing on deck too, lined the rail. I escorted my visitor to the gangway ceremoniously, and nearly overdid it. He was a tenacious beast. On the very ladder he lingered, and in that unique, guiltily conscientious manner of sticking to the point: 'I say . . . you . . . you don't think that – '

I covered his voice loudly: 'Certainly not . . . I am delighted. Goodbye.'

I had an idea of what he meant to say, and just saved myself by the privilege of defective hearing. He was too shaken generally to insist, but my mate, close witness of that parting, looked mystified and his face took on a thoughtful cast. As I did not want to appear as if I wished to avoid all communication with my officers, he had the opportunity to address me.

'Seems a very nice man. His boat's crew told our chaps a very extraordinary story, if what I am told by the steward is true. I suppose you had it from the captain, sir?'

'Yes. I had a story from the captain.'

'A very horrible affair – isn't it, sir?'

'It is.'

'Beats all these tales we hear about murders in Yankee ships.'

'I don't think it beats them. I don't think it resembles them in the least.'

'Bless my soul – you don't say so! But of course I've no acquaintance whatever with American ships, not I, so I couldn't go against your knowledge. It's horrible enough for me . . . But the queerest part is that those fellows seemed to have some idea the man was hidden aboard here. They had really. Did you ever hear of such a thing?'

'Preposterous – isn't it?'

We were walking to and fro athwart the quarterdeck. No one of the crew forward could be seen (the day was Sunday), and the mate pursued: 'There was some little dispute about it. Our chaps took offence. "As if we would harbour a thing like that," they said. "Wouldn't you like to look for him in our coal-hole?" Quite a tiff. But they made it up in the end. I suppose he did drown himself. Don't you, sir?'

'I don't suppose anything.'

'You have no doubt in the matter, sir?'

'None whatever.'

I left him suddenly. I felt I was producing a bad impression, but with my double down there it was most trying to be on deck. And it was almost as trying to be below. Altogether a nerve-trying situation. But on the whole I felt less torn in two when I was with him. There was no one in the whole ship whom I dared take into my confidence. Since the hands had got to know his story, it would have been impossible to pass him off for anyone else, and an accidental discovery was to be dreaded now more than ever . . .

The steward being engaged in laying the table for dinner, we could talk only with our eyes when I first went down. Later in the afternoon we had a cautious try at whispering. The Sunday quietness of the ship was against us;

the stillness of air and water around her was against us; the elements, the men were against us – everything was against us in our secret partnership; time itself – for this could not go on for ever. The very trust in providence was, I suppose, denied to his guilt. Shall I confess that this thought cast me down very much? And as to the chapter of accidents which counts for so much in the book of success, I could only hope that it was closed. For what favourable accident could be expected?

'Did you hear everything?' were my first words as soon as we took up our position side by side, leaning over my bed-place.

He had. And the proof of it was his earnest whisper, 'The man told you he hardly dared to give the order.'

I understood the reference to be to that saving foresail.

'Yes. He was afraid of it being lost in the setting.'

'I assure you he never gave the order. He may think he did, but he never gave it. He stood there with me on the break of the poop after the maintopsail blew away, and whimpered about our last hope – positively whimpered about it and nothing else – and the night coming on! To hear one's skipper go on like that in such weather was enough to drive any fellow out of his mind. It worked me up into a sort of desperation. I just took it into my own hands and went away from him, boiling, and – But what's the use telling you? *You* know! . . . Do you think that if I had not been pretty fierce with them I should have got the men to do anything? Not it! The bo's'n perhaps? Perhaps! It wasn't a heavy sea – it was a sea gone mad! I suppose the end of the world will be something like that; and a man may have the heart to see it coming once and be done with it – but to have to face it day after day I don't blame anybody. I was precious little better than the rest. Only – I was an officer of that old coal-wagon, anyhow – '

'I quite understand,' I conveyed that sincere assurance into his ear. He was out of breath with whispering; I could hear him pant slightly. It was all very simple. The same strung-up force which had given twenty-four men a chance, at least, for their lives, had, in a sort of recoil, crushed an unworthy mutinous existence.

But I had no leisure to weigh the merits of the matter – footsteps in the saloon, a heavy knock. 'There's enough wind to get under way with, sir.' Here was the call of a new claim upon my thoughts and even upon my feelings.

'Turn the hands up,' I cried through the door. 'I'll be on deck directly.'

I was going out to make the acquaintance of my ship. Before I left the cabin our eyes met – the eyes of the only two strangers on board. I pointed to the recessed part where the little camp-stool awaited him and laid my finger on my lips. He made a gesture – somewhat vague – a little mysterious, accompanied by a faint smile, as if of regret.

This is not the place to enlarge upon the sensations of a man who feels for the first time a ship move under his feet to his own independent word. In my case they were not unalloyed. I was not wholly alone with my command; for there was that stranger in my cabin. Or rather, I was not completely and wholly with her. Part of me was absent. That mental feeling of being in two places at once affected me physically as if the mood of secrecy had penetrated my very soul. Before an hour had elapsed since the ship had begun to move, having occasion to ask the mate (he stood by my side) to take a compass bearing of the Pagoda, I caught myself reaching up to his ear in whispers. I say I caught myself, but enough had escaped to startle the man. I can't describe it otherwise than by saying that he shied. A grave, preoccupied manner, as though he were in possession of some perplexing intelligence, did not leave him henceforth. A little later I moved away from the rail to look at the compass with such a stealthy gait that the helmsman noticed it – and I could not help noticing the unusual roundness of his eyes. These are trifling instances, though it's to no commander's advantage to be suspected of ludicrous eccentricities. But I was also more seriously affected. There are to a seaman certain words, gestures, that should in given conditions come as naturally, as instinctively as the winking of a menaced eye. A certain order should spring on to his lips without thinking; a certain sign should get itself made, so to speak, without reflection. But all unconscious alertness had abandoned me. I had to make an effort of will to recall myself back (from the cabin) to the conditions of the moment. I felt that I was appearing an irresolute commander to those people who were watching me more or less critically.

And, besides, there were the scares. On the second day out, for instance, coming off the deck in the afternoon (I had straw slippers on my bare feet) I stopped at the open pantry door and spoke to the steward. He was doing something there with his back to me. At the sound of my voice he nearly jumped out of his skin, as the saying is, and incidentally broke a cup.

'What on earth's the matter with you?' I asked, astonished.

He was extremely confused. 'Beg your pardon, sir. I made sure you were in your cabin.'

'You see I wasn't.'

'No, sir. I could have sworn I had heard you moving in there not a moment ago. It's most extraordinary . . . very sorry, sir.'

I passed on with an inward shudder. I was so identified with my secret double that I did not even mention the fact in those scanty, fearful whispers we exchanged. I suppose he had made some slight noise of some kind or other. It would have been miraculous if he hadn't at one time or another. And yet, haggard as he appeared, he looked always perfectly self-controlled, more than calm – almost invulnerable. On my suggestion he remained almost entirely in the bathroom, which, upon the whole, was the safest place. There could be really no shadow of an excuse for anyone ever wanting to go in there, once the steward had done with it. It was a very tiny place. Sometimes he reclined on the floor, his legs bent, his head sustained on one elbow. At others I would find him on the camp-stool, sitting in his grey sleeping-suit and with his cropped dark hair like a patient, unmoved convict. At night I would smuggle him into my bed-place, and we would whisper together, with the regular footfalls of the officer of the watch passing and repassing over our heads. It was an infinitely miserable time. It was lucky that some tins of fine preserves were stowed in a locker in my stateroom; hard bread I could always get hold of; and so he lived on stewed chicken, pâté de foie gras, asparagus, cooked oysters, sardines – on all sorts of abominable sham delicacies out of tins. My early-morning coffee he always drank; and it was all I dared do for him in that respect.

Every day there was the horrible manoeuvring to go through so that my room and then the bathroom should be done in the usual way. I came to hate the sight of the steward, to abhor the voice of that harmless man. I felt that it was he who would bring on the disaster of discovery. It hung like a sword over our heads.

The fourth day out, I think (we were then working down the east side of the Gulf of Siam, tack for tack, in light winds and smooth water) – the fourth day, I say, of this miserable juggling with the unavoidable, as we sat at our evening meal, that man, whose slightest movement I dreaded, after putting down the dishes ran up on deck busily. This could not be dangerous. Presently he came down again; and then it appeared that he had remembered a coat of mine which I had thrown over a rail to dry after having been wetted in a shower which had passed over the ship in the afternoon. Sitting stolidly at the head of the table I became terrified at the sight of the garment on his arm. Of course he made for my door. There was no time to lose.

'Steward,' I thundered. My nerves were so shaken that I could not govern my voice and conceal my agitation. This was the sort of thing that made my terrifically whiskered mate tap his forehead with his forefinger. I had detected him using that gesture while talking on deck with a confidential air to the carpenter. It was too far to hear a word, but I had no doubt that this pantomime could only refer to the strange new captain.

'Yes, sir,' the pale-faced steward turned resignedly to me. It was this maddening course of being shouted at, checked without rhyme or reason, arbitrarily chased out of my cabin, suddenly called into it, sent flying out of his pantry on incomprehensible errands, that accounted for the growing wretchedness of his expression.

'Where are you going with that coat?'

'To your room, sir.'

'Is there another shower coming?'

'I'm sure I don't know, sir. Shall I go up again and see, sir?'

'No! never mind.'

My object was attained, as of course my other self in there would have heard everything that passed. During this interlude my two officers never raised their eyes off their respective plates; but the lip of that confounded cub, the second mate, quivered visibly.

I expected the steward to hook my coat on and come out at once. He was very slow about it; but I dominated my nervousness sufficiently not to shout after him. Suddenly I became aware (it could be heard plainly enough) that the fellow for some reason or other was opening the door of the bathroom. It was the end. The place was literally not big enough to swing a cat in. My voice died in my throat and I went stony all over. I expected to hear a yell of surprise and terror, and made a movement, but had not the strength to get on my legs. Everything remained still. Had my second self taken the poor wretch by the throat? I don't know what I would have done next moment if I had not seen the steward come out of my room, close the door, and then stand quietly by the sideboard.

'Saved,' I thought. 'But, no! Lost! Gone! He was gone!'

I laid my knife and fork down and leaned back in my chair. My head swam. After a while, when sufficiently recovered to speak in a steady voice, I instructed my mate to put the ship round at eight o'clock himself.

'I won't come on deck,' I went on. 'I think I'll turn in, and unless the wind shifts I don't want to be disturbed before midnight. I feel a bit seedy.'

'You did look middling bad a little while ago,' the chief mate remarked without showing any great concern.

They both went out, and I stared at the steward clearing the table. There was nothing to be read on that wretched man's face. But why did he avoid my eyes, I asked myself. Then I thought I should like to hear the sound of his voice.

'Steward!'

'Sir!' Startled as usual.

'Where did you hang up that coat?'

'In the bathroom, sir.' The usual anxious tone. 'It's not quite dry yet, sir.'

For some time longer I sat in the cuddy. Had my double vanished as he had come? But of his coming there was an explanation, whereas his disappearance would be inexplicable . . . I went slowly into my dark room, shut the door, lighted the lamp, and for a time dared not turn round. When at last I did I saw him standing bolt-upright in the narrow recessed part. It would not be true to say I had a shock, but an irresistible doubt of his bodily existence flitted through my mind. Can it be, I asked myself, that he is not visible to other eyes than mine? It was like being haunted. Motionless, with a grave face, he raised his hands slightly at me in a gesture which meant clearly, 'Heavens! what a narrow escape!' Narrow indeed. I think I had come creeping quietly as near insanity as any man who has not actually gone over the border. That gesture restrained me, so to speak.

The mate with the terrific whiskers was now putting the ship on the other tack. In the moment of profound silence which follows upon the hands going to their stations I heard on the poop his raised voice: 'Hard alee!' and the distant shout of the order repeated on the maindeck. The sails, in that light breeze, made but a faint fluttering noise. It ceased. The ship was coming round slowly; I held my breath in the renewed stillness of expectation; one wouldn't have thought that there was a single living soul on her decks. A sudden brisk shout, 'Mainsail haul!' broke the spell, and in the noisy cries and rush overhead of the men running away with the main-brace we two, down in my cabin, came together in our usual position by the bed-place.

He did not wait for my question. 'I heard him fumbling here and just managed to squat myself down in the bath,' he whispered to me. 'The fellow only opened the door and put his arm in to hang the coat up. All the same –'

'I never thought of that,' I whispered back, even more appalled than before at the closeness of the shave, and marvelling at that something unyielding in his character which was carrying him through so finely. There was no agitation in his whisper. Whoever was being driven distracted, it was not he. He was sane. And the proof of his sanity was continued when he took up the whispering again.

'It would never do for me to come to life again.'

It was something that a ghost might have said. But what he was alluding to was his old captain's reluctant admission of the theory of suicide. It would obviously serve his turn – if I had understood at all the view which seemed to govern the unalterable purpose of his action.

'You must maroon me as soon as ever you can get amongst these islands off the Cambodje shore,' he went on.

'Maroon you! We are not living in a boy's adventure tale,' I protested. His scornful whispering took me up.

'We aren't indeed! There's nothing of a boy's tale in this. But there's nothing else for it. I want no more. You don't suppose I am afraid of what can be done to me? Prison or gallows or whatever they may please. But you don't see me coming back to explain such things to an old fellow in a wig and twelve respectable tradesmen, do you? What can they know whether I am guilty or not – or of *what* I am guilty, either? That's my affair. What does the Bible say? "Driven off the face of the earth." Very well. I am off the face of the earth now. As I came at night so I shall go.'

'Impossible!' I murmured. 'You can't.'

'Can't? . . . Not naked like a soul on the Day of Judgment. I shall freeze on to this sleeping-suit. The Last Day is not yet – and . . . you have understood thoroughly. Didn't you?'

I felt suddenly ashamed of myself. I may say truly that I understood – and my hesitation in letting that man swim away from my ship's side had been a mere sham sentiment, a sort of cowardice.

'It can't be done now till next night,' I breathed out. 'The ship is on the offshore tack and the wind may fail us.'

'As long as I know that you understand,' he whispered. 'But of course you do. It's a great satisfaction to have got somebody to understand. You seem to have been there on purpose.' And in the same whisper, as if we two whenever we talked had to say things to each other which were not fit for the world to hear, he added, 'It's very wonderful.'

We remained side by side talking in our secret way – but sometimes silent or just exchanging a whispered word or two at long intervals. And as usual he stared through the port. A breath of wind came now and again into our faces. The ship might have been moored in dock, so gently and on an even keel she slipped through the water, that did not murmur even at our passage, shadowy and silent like a phantom sea.

At midnight I went on deck, and to my mate's great surprise put the ship round on the other tack. His terrible whiskers flitted round me in silent criticism. I certainly should not have done it if it had been only a question of getting out of that sleepy gulf as quickly as possible. I believe he told the second mate, who relieved him, that it was a great want of judgement. The other only yawned. That intolerable cub shuffled about so sleepily and lolled against the rails in such a slack, improper fashion that I came down on him sharply.

'Aren't you properly awake yet?'

'Yes, sir! I am awake.'

'Well, then, be good enough to hold yourself as if you were. And keep a lookout. If there's any current we'll be closing with some islands before daylight.'

The east side of the gulf is fringed with islands, some solitary, others in groups. On the blue background of the high coast they seem to float on silvery patches of calm water, arid and grey, or dark green and rounded like clumps of evergreen bushes, with the larger ones, a mile or two long, showing the outlines of ridges, ribs of grey rock under the dank mantle of matted leafage. Unknown to trade, to travel, almost to geography, the manner of life they harbour is an unsolved secret. There must be villages – settlements of fishermen at least – on the largest of them, and some communication with the world is probably kept up by native craft. But all that forenoon, as we headed for them, fanned along by the faintest of breezes, I saw no sign of man or canoe in the field of the telescope I kept on pointing at the scattered group.

At noon I gave no orders for a change of course, and the mate's whiskers became much concerned and seemed to be offering themselves unduly to my notice.

At last I said: 'I am going to stand right in. Quite in – as far as I can take her.'

The stare of extreme surprise imparted an air of ferocity also to his eyes, and he looked truly terrific for a moment.

'We're not doing well in the middle of the gulf,' I continued, casually. 'I am going to look for the land breezes tonight.'

'Bless my soul! Do you mean, sir, in the dark amongst the lot of all them islands and reefs and shoals?'

'Well – if there are any regular land breezes at all on this coast one must get close inshore to find them, mustn't one?'

'Bless my soul!' he exclaimed again under his breath. All that afternoon he wore a dreamy, contemplative appearance which in him was a mark of perplexity. After dinner I went into my stateroom as if I meant to take some rest. There we two bent our dark heads over a half-unrolled chart lying on my bed.

'There,' I said. 'It's got to be Koh-ring. I've been looking at it ever since sunrise. It has got two hills and a low point. It must be inhabited. And on the coast opposite there is what looks like the mouth of a biggish river – with some town, no doubt, not far up. It's the best chance for you that I can see.'

'Anything. Koh-ring let it be.'

He looked thoughtfully at the chart as if surveying chances and distances from a lofty height – and following with his eyes his own figure wandering on the blank land of Cochin-China, and then passing off that piece of paper clean out of sight into uncharted regions. And it was as if the ship had two captains to plan her course for her. I had been so worried and restless running up and down that I had not had the patience to dress that day. I had remained in my sleeping-suit, with straw slippers and a soft floppy hat. The closeness of the heat in the gulf had been most oppressive, and the crew were used to see me wandering in that airy attire.

'She will clear the south point as she heads now,' I whispered into his ear. 'Goodness only knows when, though, but certainly after dark. I'll edge her in to half a mile, as far as I may be able to judge in the dark – '

'Be careful,' he murmured, warningly – and I realised suddenly that all my future, the only future for which I was fit, would perhaps go irretrievably to pieces in any mishap to my first command.

I could not stop a moment longer in the room. I motioned him to get out of sight and made my way up on to the poop. That unplayful cub had the watch. I walked up and down for a while thinking things out, then beckoned him over.

'Send a couple of hands to open the two quarterdeck ports,' I said, mildly.

He actually had the impudence, or else so forgot himself in his wonder at such an incomprehensible order, as to repeat: 'Open the quarterdeck ports! What for, sir?'

'The only reason you need concern yourself about is because I tell you to do so. Have them open wide and fastened properly.'

He reddened and went off, but I believe made some jeering remark to the carpenter as to the sensible practice of ventilating a ship's quarterdeck. I know he popped into the mate's cabin to impart the fact to him because the whiskers came on deck, as it were by chance, and stole glances at me from below – for signs of lunacy or drunkenness, I suppose.

A little before supper, feeling more restless than ever, I rejoined, for a moment, my second self. And to find him sitting so quietly was surprising, like something against nature, inhuman.

I developed my plan in a hurried whisper.

'I shall stand in as close as I dare and then put her round. I shall presently find means to smuggle you out of here into the sail-locker, which communicates with the lobby. But there is an opening, a sort of square for hauling the sails out, which gives straight on the quarterdeck and which is never closed in fine weather, so as to give air to the sails. When the ship's way is deadened in stays and all the hands are aft at the main-braces you shall have a clear road to slip out and get overboard through the open quarterdeck port. I've had them both fastened up. Use a rope's end to lower yourself into the water so as to avoid a splash – you know. It could be heard and cause some beastly complication.'

He kept silent for a while, then whispered, 'I understand.'

'I won't be there to see you go,' I began with an effort. 'The rest . . . I only hope I have understood, too.'

'You have. From first to last' – and for the first time there seemed to be a faltering, something strained in his whisper. He caught hold of my arm, but the ringing of the supper bell made me start. He didn't, though; he only released his grip.

After supper I didn't come below again till well past eight o'clock. The faint, steady breeze was loaded with dew; and the wet, darkened sails held all there was of propelling power in it. The night, clear and starry, sparkled darkly, and the opaque, lightless patches shifting slowly against the low stars were the drifting islets. On the port bow there was a big one more distant and shadowily imposing by the great space of sky it eclipsed.

On opening the door I had a back view of my very own self looking at a chart. He had come out of the recess and was standing near the table.

'Quite dark enough,' I whispered.

He stepped back and leaned against my bed with a level, quiet glance. I sat on the couch. We had nothing to say to each other. Over our heads the officer of the watch moved here and there. Then I heard him move quickly. I knew what that meant. He was making for the companion; and presently his voice was outside my door.

'We are drawing in pretty fast, sir. Land looks rather close.'

'Very well,' I answered. 'I am coming on deck directly.'

I waited till he was gone out of the cuddy, then rose. My double moved too. The time had come to exchange our last whispers, for neither of us was ever to hear each other's natural voice.

'Look here!' I opened a drawer and took out three sovereigns. 'Take this, anyhow. I've got six and I'd give you the lot, only I must keep a little money to buy some fruit and vegetables for the crew from native boats as we go through Sunda Straits.'

He shook his head.

'Take it,' I urged him, whispering desperately. 'No one can tell what – '

He smiled and slapped meaningly the only pocket of the sleeping-jacket. It was not safe, certainly. But I produced a large old silk handkerchief of mine, and tying the three pieces of gold in a corner, pressed it on him. He was touched, I suppose, because he took it at last and tied it quickly round his waist under the jacket, on his bare skin.

Our eyes met; several seconds elapsed till, our glances still mingled, I extended my hand and turned the lamp out. Then I passed through the cuddy, leaving the door of my room wide open. . . . 'Steward!'

He was still lingering in the pantry in the greatness of his zeal, giving a rub-up to a plated cruet stand the last thing before going to bed. Being careful not to wake up the mate, whose room was opposite, I spoke in an undertone.

He looked round anxiously. 'Sir!'

'Can you get me a little hot water from the galley?'

'I am afraid, sir, the galley fire's been out for some time now.'

'Go and see.'

He fled up the stairs.

'Now,' I whispered, loudly, into the saloon – too loudly, perhaps, but I was afraid I couldn't make a sound. He was by my side in an instant – the double captain slipped past the stairs – through a tiny dark passage . . . a sliding door. We were in the sail-locker, scrambling on our knees over the sails. A sudden thought struck me. I saw myself wandering barefooted, bareheaded, the sun beating on my dark poll. I snatched off my floppy hat and tried hurriedly in the dark to ram it on my other self. He dodged and fended off silently. I wonder what he thought had come to me before he understood and suddenly desisted. Our hands met gropingly, lingered united in a steady, motionless clasp for a second . . . No word was breathed by either of us when they separated.

I was standing quietly by the pantry door when the steward returned.

'Sorry, sir. Kettle barely warm. Shall I light the spirit-lamp?'

'Never mind.'

I came out on deck slowly. It was now a matter of conscience to shave the land as close as possible – for now he must go overboard whenever the ship was put in stays. Must! There could be no going back for him. After a moment I walked over to leeward and my heart flew into my mouth at the nearness of the land on the bow. Under any other circumstances I would not have held on a minute longer. The second mate had followed me anxiously.

I looked on till I felt I could command my voice.

'She will weather,' I said then in a quiet tone.

'Are you going to try that, sir?' he stammered out incredulously.

I took no notice of him and raised my tone just enough to be heard by the helmsman. 'Keep her good full.'

'Good full, sir.'

The wind fanned my cheek, the sails slept, the world was silent. The strain of watching the dark loom of the land grow bigger and denser was too much for me. I had shut my eyes – because the ship must go closer. She must! The stillness was intolerable. Were we standing still?

When I opened my eyes the second view started my heart with a thump. The black southern hill of Koh-ring seemed to hang right over the ship like a towering fragment of the everlasting night. On that enormous mass of blackness there was not a gleam to be seen, not a sound to be heard. It was gliding irresistibly towards us and yet seemed already within reach of the hand. I saw the vague figures of the watch grouped in the waist, gazing in awed silence.

'Are you going on, sir,' enquired an unsteady voice at my elbow.

I ignored it. I had to go on.

'Keep her full. Don't check her way. That won't do now,' I said, warningly.

'I can't see the sails very well,' the helmsman answered me, in strange, quavering tones.

Was she close enough? Already she was, I won't say in the shadow of the land, but in the very blackness of it, already swallowed up as it were, gone too close to be recalled, gone from me altogether.

'Give the mate a call,' I said to the young man who stood at my elbow as still as death. 'And turn all hands up.'

My tone had a borrowed loudness reverberated from the height of the land. Several voices cried out together: 'We are all on deck, sir.'

Then stillness again, with the great shadow gliding closer, towering higher, without a light, without a sound. Such a hush had fallen on the ship that she might have been a bark of the dead floating in slowly under the very gate of Erebus.

'My God! Where are we?'

It was the mate moaning at my elbow. He was thunderstruck, and as it were deprived of the moral support of his whiskers. He clapped his hands and absolutely cried out, 'Lost!'

'Be quiet,' I said, sternly.

He lowered his tone, but I saw the shadowy gesture of his despair. 'What are we doing here?'

'Looking for the land wind.'

He made as if to tear his hair, and addressed me recklessly.

'She will never get out. You have done it, sir. I knew it'd end in something like this. She will never weather, and you are too close now to stay. She'll drift ashore before she's round. O my God!'

I caught his arm as he was raising it to batter his poor devoted head, and shook it violently.

'She's ashore already,' he wailed, trying to tear himself away.

'Is she? . . . Keep good full there!'

'Good full, sir,' cried the helmsman in a frightened, thin, childlike voice.

I hadn't let go the mate's arm and went on shaking it. 'Ready about, do you hear? You go forward' – shake – 'and stop there' – shake – 'and hold your noise' – shake – 'and see these head-sheets properly overhauled' – shake, shake – shake.

And all the time I dared not look towards the land lest my heart should fail me. I released my grip at last and he ran forward as if fleeing for dear life.

I wondered what my double there in the sail-locker thought of this commotion. He was able to hear everything – and perhaps he was able to understand why, on my conscience, it had to be thus close – no less. My first order, 'Hard alee!' re-echoed ominously under the towering shadow of Koh-ring as if I had shouted in a mountain gorge. And then I watched the land intently. In that smooth water and light wind it was impossible to feel the ship coming-to. No! I could not feel her. And my second self was making now ready to slip out and lower himself overboard. Perhaps he was gone already . . . ?

The great black mass brooding over our very mastheads began to pivot away from the ship's side silently. And now I forgot the secret stranger ready to depart, and remembered only that I was a total stranger to the ship. I did not know her. Would she do it? How was she to be handled?

I swung the mainyard and waited helplessly. She was perhaps stopped, and her very fate hung in the balance, with the black mass of Koh-ring like the gate of the everlasting night towering over her taffrail. What would she do now? Had she way on her yet? I stepped to the side swiftly, and on the shadowy water I could see nothing except a faint phosphorescent flash revealing the glassy smoothness of the sleeping surface. It was impossible to tell – and I had not learned yet the feel of my ship. Was she moving? What I needed was something easily seen, a piece of paper, which I could throw overboard and watch. I had nothing on me. To run down for it I didn't dare. There was no time. All at once my strained, yearning stare distinguished a white object floating within a yard of the ship's side. White on the black water. A phosphorescent flash passed under it. What was that thing? . . . I recognised my own floppy hat. It must have fallen off his head . . . and he didn't bother. Now I had what I wanted – the saving mark for my eyes. But I hardly thought of my other self, now gone from the ship, to be hidden for ever from all friendly faces, to be a fugitive and a vagabond on the earth, with no brand of the curse on his sane forehead to stay a slaying hand . . . too proud to explain.

And I watched the hat – the expression of my sudden pity for his mere flesh. It had been meant to save his homeless head from the dangers of the sun. And now – behold – it was saving the ship, by serving me for a mark to help out the ignorance of my strangeness. Ha! It was drifting forward, warning me just in time that the ship had gathered sternway. 'Shift the helm,' I said in a low voice to the seaman standing still like a statue.

The man's eyes glistened wildly in the binnacle light as he jumped round to the other side and spun round the wheel.

I walked to the break of the poop. On the overshadowed deck all hands stood by the forebraces waiting for my order. The stars ahead seemed to be gliding from right to left. And all was so still in the world that I heard the quiet remark, 'She's round,' passed in a tone of intense relief between two seamen.

'Let go and haul.'

The foreyards ran round with a great noise, amidst cheery cries. And now the frightful whiskers made themselves heard giving various orders. Already the ship was drawing ahead. And I was alone with her. Nothing! no one in the world should stand now between us, throwing a shadow on the way of silent knowledge and mute affection, the perfect communion of a seaman with his first command.

Walking to the taffrail, I was in time to make out, on the very edge of a darkness thrown by a towering black mass like the very gateway of Erebus – yes, I was in time to catch an evanescent glimpse of my white hat left behind to mark the spot where the secret sharer of my cabin and of my thoughts, as though he were my second self, had lowered himself into the water to take his punishment: a free man, a proud swimmer striking out for a new destiny.

A Smile of Fortune

Ever since the sun rose I had been looking ahead. The ship glided gently in smooth water. After a sixty days' passage I was anxious to make my landfall, a fertile and beautiful island of the tropics. The more enthusiastic of its inhabitants delight in describing it as the 'Pearl of the Ocean'. Well, let us call it the 'Pearl'. It's a good name. A pearl distilling much sweetness upon the world.

This is only a way of telling you that first-rate sugar-cane is grown there. All the population of the Pearl lives for it and by it. Sugar is their daily bread, as it were. And I was coming to them for a cargo of sugar in the hope of the crop having been good and of the freights being high.

Mr Burns, my chief mate, made out the land first; and very soon I became entranced by this blue, pinnacled apparition, almost transparent against the light of the sky, a mere emanation, the astral body of an island risen to greet me from afar. It is a rare phenomenon, such a sight of the Pearl at sixty miles off. And I wondered half seriously whether it was a good omen, whether what would meet me in that island would be as luckily exceptional as this beautiful, dreamlike vision so very few seamen have been privileged to behold.

But horrid thoughts of business interfered with my enjoyment of an accomplished passage. I was anxious for success and I wished, too, to do justice to the flattering latitude of my owners' instructions contained in one noble phrase: 'We leave it to you to do the best you can with the ship . . . ' All the world being thus given me for a stage, my abilities appeared to me no bigger than a pinhead.

Meantime the wind dropped, and Mr Burns began to make disagreeable remarks about my usual bad luck. I believe it was his devotion to me which made him critically outspoken on every occasion. All the same, I would not have put up with his humours if it had not been my lot at one time to nurse him through a desperate illness at sea. After snatching him out of the jaws of death, so to speak, it would have been absurd to throw away such an efficient officer. But sometimes I wished he would dismiss himself.

We were late in closing in with the land, and had to anchor outside the harbour till next day. An unpleasant and unrestful night followed. In this roadstead, strange to us both, Burns and I remained on deck almost all the time. Clouds swirled down the porphyry crags under which we lay. The rising wind made a great bullying noise amongst the naked spars, with interludes of sad moaning. I remarked that we had been in luck to fetch the anchorage before dark. It would have been a nasty, anxious night to hang off a harbour under canvas. But my chief mate was uncompromising in his attitude.

'Luck, you call it, sir! Ay – our usual luck. The sort of luck to thank God it's no worse!'

And so he fretted through the dark hours, while I drew on my fund of philosophy. Ah, but it was an exasperating, weary, endless night, to be lying at anchor close under that black coast! The agitated water made snarling sounds all round the ship. At times a wild gust of wind out of a gully high up on the cliffs struck on our rigging a harsh and plaintive note like the wail of a forsaken soul.

ONE

By half-past seven in the morning, the ship being then inside the harbour at last and moored within a long stone's-throw from the quay, my stock of philosophy was nearly exhausted. I was dressing hurriedly in my cabin when the steward came tripping in with a morning suit over his arm.

Hungry, tired and depressed, with my head engaged inside a white shirt irritatingly stuck together by too much starch, I desired him peevishly to 'heave round with that breakfast'. I wanted to get ashore as soon as possible.

'Yes, sir. Ready at eight, sir. There's a gentleman from the shore waiting to speak to you, sir.'

This statement was curiously slurred over. I dragged the shirt violently over my head and emerged staring.

'So early!' I cried. 'Who is he? What does he want?'

On coming in from sea one has to pick up the conditions of an utterly unrelated existence. Every little event at first has the peculiar emphasis of novelty. I was greatly surprised by that early caller; but there was no reason for my steward to look so particularly foolish.

'Didn't you ask for the name?' I enquired in a stern tone.

'His name's Jacobus, I believe,' he mumbled shamefacedly.

'Mr Jacobus!' I exclaimed loudly, more surprised than ever, but with a total change of feeling. 'Why couldn't you say so at once?'

But the fellow had scuttled out of my room. Through the momentarily opened door I had a glimpse of a tall, stout man standing in the cuddy by the table on which the cloth was already laid; a 'harbour' tablecloth, stainless and dazzlingly white. So far good.

I shouted courteously through the closed door, that I was dressing and would be with him in a moment. In return the assurance that there was no hurry reached me in the visitor's deep, quiet undertone. His time was my own. He dared say I would give him a cup of coffee presently.

'I am afraid you will have a poor breakfast,' I cried apologetically. 'We have been sixty-one days at sea, you know.'

A quiet little laugh, with a, 'That'll be all right, captain,' was his answer. All this, words, intonation, the glimpsed attitude of the man in the cuddy, had an unexpected character, a something friendly in it – propitiatory. And my surprise was not diminished thereby. What did this call mean? Was it the sign of some dark design against my commercial innocence?

Ah! These commercial interests – spoiling the finest life under the sun. Why must the sea be used for trade – and for war as well? Why kill and traffic on it, pursuing selfish aims of no great importance after all? It would have been so much nicer just to sail about with here and there a port and a bit of land to stretch one's legs on, buy a few books and get a change of cooking for a while. But, living in a world more or less homicidal and desperately mercantile, it was plainly my duty to make the best of its opportunities.

My owners' letter had left it to me, as I have said before, to do my best for the ship, according to my own judgement. But it contained also a postscript worded somewhat as follows:

> Without meaning to interfere with your liberty of action we are writing by the outgoing mail to some of our business friends there who may be of assistance to you. We desire you particularly to call on Mr Jacobus, a prominent merchant and charterer. Should you hit it off with him he may be able to put you in the way of profitable employment for the ship.

Hit it off! Here was the prominent creature absolutely on board asking for the favour of a cup of coffee! And life not being a fairy-tale the im-probability of the event almost shocked me. Had I discovered an enchanted nook of the earth where wealthy merchants rush fasting on board ships before they are fairly moored? Was this white magic or merely some black trick of trade? I came in the end (while making the bow of my tie) to suspect that perhaps I did not get the name right. I had been thinking of the prominent Mr Jacobus pretty frequently during the passage and my hearing might have been deceived by some remote similarity of sound . . . The steward might have said Antrobus – or maybe Jackson.

But coming out of my stateroom with an interrogative, 'Mr Jacobus?' I was met by a quiet, 'Yes,' uttered with a gentle smile. The 'yes' was rather perfunctory. He did not seem to make much of the fact that he was Mr Jacobus. I took stock of a big, pale face, hair thin on the top, whiskers also thin, of a faded nondescript colour, heavy eyelids. The thick, smooth lips in repose looked as if glued together. The smile was faint. A heavy, tranquil man. I named my two officers, who just then came down to breakfast; but why Mr Burns's silent demeanour should suggest suppressed indignation I could not understand.

While we were taking our seats round the table some disconnected words of an altercation going on in the companionway reached my ear. A stranger apparently wanted to come down to interview me, and the steward was opposing him.

'You can't see him.'

'Why can't I?'

'The captain is at breakfast, I tell you. He'll be going on shore presently, and you can speak to him on deck.'

'That's not fair. You let – '

'I've had nothing to do with that.'

'Oh, yes, you have. Everybody ought to have the same chance. You let that fellow – '

The rest I lost. The person having been repulsed successfully, the steward came down. I can't say he looked flushed – he was a mulatto – but he looked flustered. After putting the dishes on the table he remained by the sideboard with that lackadaisical air of indifference he used to assume when he had done something too clever by half and was afraid of getting into a scrape over it. The contemptuous expression of Mr Burns's face as he looked from him to me was really extraordinary. I couldn't imagine what new bee had stung the mate now.

The captain being silent, nobody else cared to speak, as is the way in ships. And I was saying nothing simply because I had been made dumb by the splendour of the entertainment. I had expected the usual sea-breakfast, whereas I beheld spread before us a veritable feast of shore provisions: eggs, sausages, butter which plainly did not come from a Danish tin, cutlets, and even a dish of potatoes. It was three weeks since I had seen a real, live potato. I contemplated them with interest, and Mr Jacobus disclosed himself as a man of human, homely sympathies, and something of a thought-reader.

'Try them, captain,' he encouraged me in a friendly undertone. 'They are excellent.'

'They look that,' I admitted. 'Grown on the island, I suppose.'

'Oh, no, imported. Those grown here would be more expensive.'

I was grieved at the ineptitude of the conversation. Were these the topics for a prominent and wealthy merchant to discuss? I thought the simplicity with which he made himself at home rather attractive; but what is one to talk about to a man who comes on one suddenly, after sixty-one days at sea, out of a totally unknown little town in an island one has never seen before? What were (besides sugar) the interests of that crumb of the earth, its gossip, its topics of conversation? To draw him on business at once would have been almost indecent – or even worse: impolitic. All I could do at the moment was to keep on in the old groove.

'Are the provisions generally dear here?' I asked, fretting inwardly at my inanity.

'I wouldn't say that,' he answered placidly, with that appearance of saving his breath his restrained manner of speaking suggested.

He would not be more explicit, yet he did not evade the subject. Eyeing the table in a spirit of complete abstemiousness (he wouldn't let me help him to any eatables) he went into details of supply. The beef was for the most part imported from Madagascar; mutton of course was rare and somewhat expensive, but good goat's flesh –

'Are these goat's cutlets?' I exclaimed hastily, pointing at one of the dishes.

Posed sentimentally by the sideboard, the steward gave a start. 'Lor', no, sir! It's real mutton!'

Mr Burns got through his breakfast impatiently, as if exasperated by being made a party to some monstrous foolishness, muttered a curt excuse, and went on deck. Shortly afterwards the second mate took his smooth red countenance out of the cabin. With the appetite of a schoolboy, and after two months of sea-fare, he appreciated the generous spread. But I did not. It smacked of extravagance. All the same, it was a remarkable feat to have produced it so quickly, and I congratulated the steward on his smartness in a somewhat ominous tone. He gave me a deprecatory smile and, in a way I didn't know what to make of, blinked his fine dark eyes in the direction of the guest.

The latter asked under his breath for another cup of coffee, and nibbled ascetically at a piece of very hard ship's biscuit. I don't think he consumed a square inch in the end; but meantime he gave me, casually as it were, a complete account of the sugar crop, of the local business houses, of the state of the freight market. All that talk was interspersed with hints as to personalities, amounting to veiled warnings, but his pale, fleshy face remained equable, without a gleam, as if ignorant of his voice. As you may imagine I opened my ears very wide. Every word was precious. My ideas as to the value of business friendship were being favourably modified. He gave me the names of all the disponible ships together with their tonnage and the names of their commanders. From that, which was still commercial information, he condescended to mere harbour gossip.

The *Hilda* had unaccountably lost her figurehead in the Bay of Bengal, and her captain was greatly affected by this. He and the ship had been getting on in years together and the old gentleman imagined this strange event to be the forerunner of his own early dissolution. The *Stella* had experienced awful weather off the Cape – had her decks swept, and the chief officer washed overboard. And only a few hours before reaching port the baby died. Poor

Captain H— and his wife were terribly cut up. If they had only been able to bring it into port alive it could have been probably saved; but the wind failed them for the last week or so, light breezes, and . . . the baby was going to be buried this afternoon. He supposed I would attend –

'Do you think I ought to?' I asked, shrinkingly.

He thought so, decidedly. It would be greatly appreciated. All the captains in the harbour were going to attend. Poor Mrs H— was quite prostrated. Pretty hard on H— altogether.

'And you, captain – you are not married I suppose?'

'No, I am not married,' I said. 'Neither married nor even engaged.'

Mentally I thanked my stars; and while he smiled in a musing, dreamy fashion, I expressed my acknowledgements for his visit and for the interesting business information he had been good enough to impart to me. But I said nothing of my wonder thereat.

'Of course, I would have made a point of calling on you in a day or two,' I concluded.

He raised his eyelids distinctly at me, and somehow managed to look rather more sleepy than before.

'In accordance with my owners' instructions,' I explained. 'You have had their letter, of course?'

By that time he had raised his eyebrows too but without any particular emotion. On the contrary he struck me then as absolutely imperturbable.

'Oh! You must be thinking of my brother.'

It was for me, then, to say, 'Oh!' But I hope that no more than civil surprise appeared in my voice when I asked him to what, then, I owed the pleasure . . . He was reaching for an inside pocket leisurely.

'My brother's a very different person. But I am well known in this part of the world. You've probably heard – '

I took a card he extended to me. A thick business card, as I lived! Alfred Jacobus – the other was Ernest – dealer in every description of ship's stores! Provisions salt and fresh, oils, paints, rope, canvas, etc., etc. Ships in harbour victualled by contract on moderate terms –

'I've never heard of you,' I said brusquely.

His low-pitched assurance did not abandon him.

'You will be very well satisfied,' he breathed out quietly.

I was not placated. I had the sense of having been circumvented some-how. Yet I had deceived myself – if there was any deception. But the confounded cheek of inviting himself to breakfast was enough to deceive anyone. And the thought struck me: Why! The fellow had provided all these eatables himself in the way of business. I said: 'You must have got up mighty early this morning.'

He admitted with simplicity that he was on the quay before six o'clock waiting for my ship to come in. He gave me the impression that it would be impossible to get rid of him now.

'If you think we are going to live on that scale,' I said, looking at the table with an irritated eye, 'you are jolly well mistaken.'

'You'll find it all right, captain. I quite understand.'

Nothing could disturb his equanimity. I felt dissatisfied, but I could not very well fly out at him. He had told me many useful things – and besides he was the brother of that wealthy merchant. That seemed queer enough.

I rose and told him curtly that I must now go ashore. At once he offered the use of his boat for all the time of my stay in port.

'I only make a nominal charge,' he continued equably. 'My man remains all day at the landing-steps. You have only to blow a whistle when you want the boat.'

And, standing aside at every doorway to let me go through first, he carried me off in his custody after all. As we crossed the quarter-deck two shabby individuals stepped forward and in mournful silence offered me business cards which I took from them without a word under his heavy eye. It was a useless and gloomy ceremony. They were the touts of the other ship-chandlers, and he, placid at my back, ignored their existence.

We parted on the quay, after he had expressed quietly the hope of seeing me often 'at the store'. He had a smoking-room for captains there, with newspapers and a box of 'rather decent cigars'. I left him very unceremoniously.

My consignees received me with the usual business heartiness, but their account of the state of the freight-market was by no means so favourable as the talk of the wrong Jacobus had led me to expect. Naturally I became inclined now to put my trust in his version, rather. As I closed the door of the private office behind me I thought to myself: 'H'm. A lot of lies. Commercial diplomacy. That's the sort of thing a man coming from sea has got to expect. They would try to charter the ship under the market rate.'

In the big, outer room, full of desks, the chief clerk, a tall, lean, shaved person in immaculate white clothes and with a shiny, closely-cropped black head on which silvery gleams came and went, rose from his place and detained me affably. Anything they could do for me, they would be most happy. Was I likely to call again in the afternoon? What? Going to a funeral? Oh, yes, poor Captain H—.

He pulled a long, sympathetic face for a moment, then, dismissing from this workaday world the baby, which had got ill in a tempest and had died from too much calm at sea, he asked me with a dental, shark-like smile – if sharks had false teeth – whether I had yet made my little arrangements for the ship's stay in port.

'Yes, with Jacobus,' I answered carelessly. 'I understand he's the brother of Mr Ernest Jacobus to whom I have an introduction from my owners.'

I was not sorry to let him know I was not altogether helpless in the hands of his firm. He screwed his thin lips dubiously.

'Why,' I cried, 'isn't he the brother?'

'Oh, yes . . . They haven't spoken to each other for eighteen years,' he added impressively after a pause.

'Indeed! What's the quarrel about?'

'Oh, nothing! Nothing that one would care to mention,' he protested primly. 'He's got quite a large business. The best ship-chandler here, without a doubt. Business is all very well, but there is such a thing as personal character, too, isn't there? Good-morning, captain.'

He went away mincingly to his desk. He amused me. He resembled an old maid, a commercial old maid, shocked by some impropriety. Was it a commercial impropriety? Commercial impropriety is a serious matter, for it aims at one's pocket. Or was he only a purist in conduct who disapproved of Jacobus doing his own touting? It was certainly undignified. I wondered how the merchant brother liked it. But then different countries, different customs. In a community so isolated and so exclusively 'trading', social standards have their own scale.

TWO

I would have gladly dispensed with the mournful opportunity of becoming acquainted by sight with all my fellow-captains at once. However I found my way to the cemetery. We made a considerable group of bareheaded men in sombre garments. I noticed that those of our company most approaching to the now obsolete sea-dog type were the most moved – perhaps because they had less 'manner' than the new generation. The old sea-dog, away from his natural element, was a simple and sentimental animal. I noticed one – he was facing me across the grave – who was dropping tears. They trickled down his weather-beaten face like drops of rain on an old rugged wall. I learned afterwards that he was looked upon as the terror of sailors, a hard man; that he had never had wife or chick of his own, and that, engaged from his tenderest years in deep-sea voyages, he knew women and children merely by sight.

Perhaps he was dropping those tears over his lost opportunities, from sheer envy of paternity and in strange jealousy of a sorrow which he could never know. Man, and even the sea-man, is a capricious animal, the creature and the victim of lost opportunities. But he made me feel ashamed of my callousness. I had no tears.

I listened with horribly critical detachment to that service I had had to read myself, once or twice, over childlike men who had died at sea. The words of hope and defiance, the winged words so inspiring in the free immensity of water and sky, seemed to fall wearily into the little grave. What was the use of asking Death where its sting was, before that small, dark hole in the ground? And then my thoughts escaped me altogether – away into matters of life – and no very high matters at that – ships, freights, business. In the instability of his emotions man resembles deplorably a monkey. I was disgusted with my thoughts – and I thought: Shall I be able to get a charter soon? Time's money . . . Will that Jacobus really put good business in my way? I must go and see him in a day or two.

Don't imagine that I pursued these thoughts with any precision. They pursued me rather: vague, shadowy, restless, shamefaced. Theirs was a callous, abominable, almost revolting, pertinacity. And it was the presence of that pertinacious ship-chandler which had started them. He stood mournfully amongst our little band of men from the sea, and I was angry at his presence, which, suggesting his brother the merchant, had caused me to become outrageous to myself. For indeed I had preserved some decency of feeling. It was only the mind which –

It was over at last. The poor father – a man of forty with black, bushy side-whiskers and a pathetic gash on his freshly-shaved chin – thanked us all, swallowing his tears. But for some reason, either because I lingered at the gate of the cemetery being somewhat hazy as to my way back, or because I was the youngest, or ascribing my moodiness caused by remorse to some more worthy and appropriate sentiment, or simply because I was even more of a stranger to him than the others – he singled me out. Keeping at my side, he renewed his thanks, which I listened to in a gloomy, conscience-stricken silence. Suddenly he slipped one hand under my arm and waved the other after a tall, stout figure walking away by itself down a street in a flutter of thin, grey garments. 'That's a good fellow – a real good fellow' – he swallowed down a belated sob – 'this Jacobus.'

And he told me in a low voice that Jacobus was the first man to board his ship on arrival, and, learning of their misfortune, had taken charge of everything, volunteered to attend to all routine business, carried off the ship's papers on shore, arranged for the funeral –

'A good fellow. I was knocked over. I had been looking at my wife for ten days. And helpless. Just you think of that! The dear little chap died the very day we made the land. How I managed to take the ship in God alone knows! I couldn't see anything; I couldn't speak; I couldn't . . . You've heard, perhaps, that we lost our mate overboard on the passage? There was no one to do it for me. And the poor woman nearly crazy down below there all alone with the . . . By the Lord! It isn't fair.'

We walked in silence together. I did not know how to part from him. On the quay he let go my arm and struck fiercely his fist into the palm of his other hand. 'By God, it isn't fair!' he cried again. 'Don't you ever marry unless you can chuck the sea first . . . It isn't fair.'

I had no intention to 'chuck the sea', and when he left me to go aboard his ship I felt convinced that I would never marry. While I was waiting at the steps for Jacobus's boatman, who had gone off somewhere, the captain of the *Hilda* joined me, a slender silk umbrella in his hand and the sharp points of his archaic, Gladstonian shirt-collar framing a small, clean-shaved, ruddy face. It was wonderfully fresh for his age, beautifully modelled and lit up by remarkably clear blue eyes. A lot of white hair, glossy like spun glass, curled upwards slightly under the brim of his valuable, ancient, panama hat with a broad black ribbon. In the aspect of that vivacious, neat, little old man there was something quaintly angelic and also boyish.

He accosted me, as though he had been in the habit of seeing me every day of his life from my earliest childhood, with a whimsical remark on the appearance of a stout negro woman who was sitting upon a stool near the edge of the quay. Presently he observed amiably that I had a very pretty little barque.

I returned this civil speech by saying readily, 'Not so pretty as the *Hilda*.'

At once the corners of his clear-cut, sensitive mouth drooped dismally.

'Oh, dear! I can hardly bear to look at her now.'

Did I know, he asked anxiously, that he had lost the figurehead of his ship; a woman in a blue tunic edged with gold, the face perhaps not so very, very pretty, but her bare white arms beautifully shaped and extended as if she were swimming? Did I? Who would have expected such a thing? . . . After twenty years too!

Nobody could have guessed from his tone that the woman was made of wood; his trembling voice, his agitated manner gave to his lamentations a ludicrously scandalous flavour . . . Disappeared at night – a clear fine night with just a slight swell – in the gulf of Bengal. Went off without a splash; no one in the ship could tell why, how, at what hour – after twenty years last October . . . Did I ever hear! . . .

I assured him sympathetically that I had never heard – and he became very doleful. This meant no good he was sure. There was something in it which looked like a warning. But when I remarked that surely another figure of a woman could be procured I found myself being soundly rated for my levity. The old boy flushed pink under his clear tan as if I had proposed something improper. One could replace masts, I was told, or a lost rudder – any working part of a ship; but where was the use of sticking up a new figurehead? What satisfaction? How could one care for it? It was easy to see that I had never been shipmates with a figurehead for over twenty years.

'A new figurehead!' he scolded in unquenchable indignation. 'Why! I've been a widower now for eight-and-twenty years come next May and I would just as soon think of getting a new wife. You're as bad as that fellow Jacobus.'

I was highly amused.

'What has Jacobus done? Did he want you to marry again, captain?' I enquired in a deferential tone. But he was launched now and only grinned fiercely.

'Procure – indeed! He's the sort of chap to procure you anything you like for a price. I hadn't been moored here for an hour when he got on board and at once offered to sell me a figurehead he happens to have in his yard somewhere. He got Smith, my mate, to talk to me about it. "Mr Smith," says I, "don't you know me better than that? Am I the sort that would pick up with another man's cast-off figurehead?" And after all these years too! The way some of you young fellows talk – '

I affected great compunction, and as I stepped into the boat I said soberly, 'Then I see nothing for it but to fit in a neat fiddlehead – perhaps. You know, carved scrollwork, nicely gilt.'

He became very dejected after his outburst.

'Yes. Scrollwork. Maybe. Jacobus hinted at that too. He's never at a loss when there's any money to be extracted from a sailorman. He would make me pay through the nose for that carving. A gilt fiddlehead did you say – eh? I dare say it would do for you. You young fellows don't seem to have any feeling for what's proper.'

He made a convulsive gesture with his right arm.

'Never mind. Nothing can make much difference. I would just as soon let the old thing go about the world with a bare cutwater,' he cried sadly. Then as the boat got away from the steps he raised his voice on the edge of the quay with comical animosity 'I would! If only to spite that figurehead-procuring bloodsucker. I am an old bird here and don't you forget it. Come and see me on board some day!'

I spent my first evening in port quietly in my ship's cuddy; and glad enough was I to think that the shore life, which strikes one as so pettily complex, discordant and so full of new faces on first coming from sea, could be kept off for a few hours longer. I was however fated to hear the Jacobus note once more before I slept.

Mr Burns had gone ashore after the evening meal to have, as he said, 'a look round'. As it was quite dark when he announced his intention I didn't ask him what it was he expected to see. Sometime about midnight, while sitting with a book in the saloon, I heard cautious movements in the lobby and hailed him by name.

Burns came in, stick and hat in hand, incredibly vulgarised by his smart shore togs, with a jaunty air and an odious twinkle in his eye. Being asked to sit down he laid his hat and stick on the table and after we had talked of ship affairs for a little while, 'I've been hearing pretty tales on shore about that ship-chandler fellow who snatched the job from you so neatly, sir.'

I remonstrated with my late patient for his manner of expressing himself. But he only tossed his head disdainfully. A pretty dodge indeed: boarding a strange ship with breakfast in two baskets for all hands and calmly inviting himself to the captain's table! Never heard of anything so crafty and so impudent in his life!

I found myself defending Jacobus's unusual methods. 'He's the brother of one of the wealthiest merchants in the port.'

The mate's eyes fairly snapped green sparks. 'His grand brother hasn't spoken to him for eighteen or twenty years,' he declared triumphantly. 'So there!'

'I know all about that,' I interrupted loftily.

'Do you sir? H'm!' His mind was still running on the ethics of commercial competition. 'I don't like to see your good nature taken advantage of. He's bribed that steward of ours with a five-rupee note to let him come down – or ten for that matter. He don't care. He will shove that and more into the bill presently.'

'Is that one of the tales you have heard ashore?' I asked.

He assured me that his own sense could tell him that much. No; what he had heard on shore was that no respectable person in the whole town would come near Jacobus. He lived in a large old-fashioned house in one of the quiet streets with a big garden. After telling me this Burns put on a mysterious air. 'He keeps a girl shut up there who, they say – '

'I suppose you've heard all this gossip in some eminently respectable place?' I snapped at him in a most sarcastic tone.

The shaft told, because Mr Burns, like many other disagreeable people, was very sensitive himself. He remained as if thunderstruck, with his mouth open for some further communication, but I did not give him the chance. 'And, anyhow, what the deuce do I care?' I added, retiring into my room.

And this was a natural thing to say. Yet somehow I was not indifferent. I admit it is absurd to be concerned with the morals of one's ship-chandler, if ever so well connected; but his personality had stamped itself upon my first day in harbour, in the way you know.

After this initial exploit Jacobus showed himself anything but intrusive. He was out in a boat early every morning going round the ships he served, and occasionally remaining on board one of them for breakfast with the captain.

As I discovered that this practice was generally accepted, I just nodded to him familiarly when one morning, on coming out of my room, I found him in the cabin. Glancing over the table I saw that his place was already laid. He stood awaiting my appearance, very bulky and placid, holding a beautiful bunch of flowers in his thick hand. He offered them to my notice with a faint, sleepy smile. From his own garden; had a very fine old garden; picked them himself that morning before going out to business; thought I would like . . . He turned away. 'Steward, can you oblige me with some water in a large jar, please.'

I assured him jocularly, as I took my place at the table, that he made me feel as if I were a pretty girl, and that he mustn't be surprised if I blushed. But he was busy arranging his floral tribute at the sideboard. 'Stand it before the captain's plate, steward, please.' He made this request in his usual undertone.

The offering was so pointed that I could do no less than to raise it to my nose, and as he sat down noiselessly he breathed out the opinion that a few flowers improved notably the appearance of a ship's saloon. He wondered why I did not have a shelf fitted all round the skylight for flowers in pots to take with me to sea. He had a skilled workman able to fit up shelves in a day, and he could procure me two or three dozen good plants –

The tips of his thick, round fingers rested composedly on the edge of the table on each side of his cup of coffee. His face remained immovable. Mr Burns was smiling maliciously to himself. I declared that I hadn't the slightest intention of turning my skylight into a conservatory only to keep the cabin-table in a perpetual mess of mould and dead vegetable matter.

'Rear most beautiful flowers,' he insisted with an upward glance. 'It's no trouble really.'

'Oh, yes, it is. Lots of trouble,' I contradicted. 'And in the end some fool leaves the skylight open in a fresh breeze, a flick of salt water gets at them and the whole lot is dead in a week.'

Mr Burns snorted a contemptuous approval. Jacobus gave up the subject passively. After a time he unglued his thick lips to ask me if I had seen his brother yet. I was very curt in my answer.

'No, not yet.'

'A very different person,' he remarked dreamily and got up. His movements were particularly noiseless. 'Well – thank you, captain. If anything is not to your liking please mention it to your steward. I suppose you will be giving a dinner to the office-clerks presently.'

'What for?' I cried with some warmth. 'If I were a steady trader to the port I could understand it. But a complete stranger! . . . I may not turn up again here for years. I don't see why! . . . Do you mean to say it is customary?'

'It will be expected from a man like you,' he breathed out placidly. 'Eight of the principal clerks, the manager, that's nine, you three gentlemen, that's twelve. It needn't be very expensive. If you tell your steward to give me a day's notice –'

It will be expected of me! Why should it be expected of me? Is it because I look particularly soft – or what?

His immobility struck me as dignified suddenly, his imperturbable quality as dangerous. 'There's plenty of time to think about that,' I concluded weakly with a gesture that tried to wave him away. But before he departed he took time to mention regretfully that he had not yet had the pleasure of seeing me at his 'store' to sample those cigars. He had a parcel of six thousand to dispose of, very cheap.

'I think it would be worth your while to secure some,' he added with a fat, melancholy smile and left the cabin.

Mr Burns struck his fist on the table excitedly.

'Did you ever see such impudence! He's made up his mind to get something out of you one way or another, sir.'

At once feeling inclined to defend Jacobus, I observed philosophically that all this was business, I supposed. But my absurd mate, muttering broken disjointed sentences, such as: 'I cannot bear! . . . Mark my words! . . .' and so on, flung out of the cabin. If I hadn't nursed him through that deadly fever I wouldn't have suffered such manners for a single day.

THREE

Jacobus having put me in mind of his wealthy brother I concluded I would pay that business call at once. I had by that time heard a little more of him. He was a member of the Council, where he made himself objectionable to the authorities. He exercised a considerable influence on public opinion. Lots of people owed him money. He was an importer on a great scale of all sorts of goods. For instance, the whole supply of bags for sugar was practically in his hands. This last fact I did not learn till afterwards. The general impression conveyed to me was that of a local personage. He was a bachelor and gave weekly card-parties in his house out of town, which were attended by the best people in the colony.

The greater, then, was my surprise to discover his office in shabby surroundings, quite away from the business quarter, amongst a lot of hovels. Guided by a black board with white lettering, I climbed a narrow wooden staircase and entered a room with a bare floor of planks littered with bits of brown paper and wisps of packing straw. A great number of what looked like wine-cases were piled up against one of the walls. A lanky, inky, light-yellow, mulatto youth, miserably long-necked and generally recalling a sick chicken, got off a three-legged stool behind a cheap deal desk and faced me as if gone dumb with fright. I had some difficulty in persuading him to take in my name, though I could not get from him the nature of his objection. He did it at last with an almost agonised reluctance which ceased to be mysterious to me when I heard him being sworn at menacingly with savage, suppressed growls, then audibly cuffed and finally kicked out without any concealment whatever; because he came back flying head foremost through the door with a stifled shriek.

To say I was startled would not express it. I remained still, like a man lost in a dream. Clapping both his hands to that part of his frail anatomy which had received the shock, the poor wretch said to me simply, 'Will you go in, please.' His lamentable self-possession was wonderful; but it did not do away with the incredibility of the experience. A preposterous notion that I had seen this boy somewhere before, a thing obviously impossible, was like a delicate finishing touch of weirdness added to a scene fit to raise doubts as to one's sanity. I stared anxiously about me like an awakened somnambulist.

'I say,' I cried loudly, 'there isn't a mistake, is there? This is Mr Jacobus's office.'

The boy gazed at me with a pained expression – and somehow so familiar! A voice within growled offensively: 'Come in, come in, since you are there . . . I didn't know.'

I crossed the outer room as one approaches the den of some unknown wild beast; with intrepidity but in some excitement. Only no wild beast that ever lived would rouse one's indignation; the power to do that belongs to the odiousness of the human brute. And I was very indignant, which did not prevent me from being at once struck by the extraordinary resemblance of the two brothers.

This one was dark instead of being fair like the other; but he was as big. He was without his coat and waistcoat; he had been doubtless snoozing in the rocking-chair which stood in a corner farthest from the window. Above the great bulk of his crumpled white shirt, buttoned with three diamond studs, his round face looked swarthy. It was moist; his brown moustache hung limp and ragged. He pushed a common, cane-bottomed chair towards me with his foot.

'Sit down.'

I glanced at it casually, then, turning my indignant eyes full upon him, I declared in precise and incisive tones that I had called in obedience to my owners' instructions.

'Oh! Yes. H'm! I didn't understand what that fool was saying . . . But never mind! It will teach the scoundrel to disturb me at this time of the day,' he added, grinning at me with savage cynicism.

I looked at my watch. It was past three o'clock – quite the full swing of afternoon office work in the port. He snarled imperiously: 'Sit down, captain.'

I acknowledged the gracious invitation by saying deliberately: 'I can listen to all you may have to say without sitting down.'

Emitting a loud and vehement 'Pshaw!' he glared for a moment, very round-eyed and fierce. It was like a gigantic tomcat spitting at one suddenly.

'Look at him! . . . What do you fancy yourself to be? What did you come here for? If you won't sit down and talk business you had better go to the devil.'

'I don't know him personally,' I said. 'But after this I wouldn't mind calling on him. It would be refreshing to meet a gentleman.'

He followed me, growling behind my back: 'The impudence! I've a good mind to write to your owners what I think of you.'

I turned on him for a moment. 'As it happens I don't care. For my part I assure you I won't even take the trouble to mention you to them.'

He stopped at the door of his office while I traversed the littered ante-room. I think he was somewhat taken aback.

'I will break every bone in your body,' he roared suddenly at the miserable mulatto lad, 'if you ever dare to disturb me before half-past three for anybody. D'ye hear? For anybody! . . . Let alone any damned skipper,' he added, in a lower growl.

The frail youngster, swaying like a reed, made a low moaning sound. I stopped short and addressed this sufferer with advice. It was prompted by the sight of a hammer (used for opening the wine-cases, I suppose) which was lying on the floor.

'If I were you, my boy, I would have that thing up my sleeve when I went in next and at the first occasion I would – '

What was there so familiar in that lad's yellow face? Entrenched and quaking behind the flimsy desk, he never looked up. His heavy, lowered eyelids gave me suddenly the clue of the puzzle. He resembled – yes, those thick glued lips – he resembled the brothers Jacobus. He resembled both, the wealthy merchant and the pushing shopkeeper (who resembled each other); he resembled them as much as a thin, light-yellow mulatto lad may resemble a big, stout, middle-aged white man. It was the exotic complexion and the slightness of his build which had put me off so completely. Now I saw in him unmistakably the Jacobus strain, weakened, attenuated, diluted as it were in a bucket of water – and I refrained from finishing my speech. I had intended to say: 'Crack this brute's head for him.' I still felt the conclusion to be sound. But it is no trifling responsibility to counsel parricide to anyone, however deeply injured.

'Beggarly – cheeky – skippers.'

I despised the emphatic growl at my back; only, being much vexed and upset, I regret to say that I slammed the door behind me in a most undignified manner.

It may not appear altogether absurd if I say that I brought out from that interview a kindlier view of the other Jacobus. It was with a feeling resembling partisanship that, a few days later, I called at his 'store'. That long, cavern-like place of business, very dim at the back and stuffed full of all sorts of goods, was entered from the street by a lofty archway. At the far end I saw my Jacobus exerting himself in his shirt-sleeves among his assistants. The captains' room was a small, vaulted apartment with a stone floor and heavy iron bars in its windows like a dungeon converted to hospitable purposes. A couple of cheerful bottles and several gleaming glasses made a brilliant cluster round a tall, cool red earthenware pitcher on the centre table which was littered with newspapers from all parts of the world. A well-groomed stranger in a smart grey check suit, sitting with one leg flung over his knee, put down one of these sheets briskly and nodded to me.

I guessed him to be a steamer-captain. It was impossible to get to know these men. They came and went too quickly and their ships lay moored far out, at the very entrance of the harbour. Theirs was another life altogether. He yawned slightly.

'Dull hole, isn't it?'

I understood this to allude to the town.

'Do you find it so?' I murmured.

'Don't you? But I'm off tomorrow, thank goodness.'

He was a very gentlemanly person, good-natured and superior. I watched him draw the open box of cigars to his side of the table, take a big cigar-case out of his pocket and begin to fill it very methodically. Presently, on our eyes meeting, he winked like a common mortal and invited me to follow his example. 'They are really decent smokes.'

I shook my head. 'I am not off tomorrow.'

'What of that? Think I am abusing old Jacobus's hospitality? Heavens! It goes into the bill, of course. He spreads such little matters all over his account. He can take care of himself! Why, it's business – '

I noted a shadow fall over his well-satisfied expression, a momentary hesitation in closing his cigar-case. But he ended by putting it in his pocket jauntily. A placid voice uttered in the doorway: 'That's quite correct, captain.'

The large noiseless Jacobus advanced into the room. His quietness, in the circumstances, amounted to cordiality. He had put on his jacket before joining us, and he sat down in the chair vacated by the steamer-man, who nodded again to me and went out with a short, jarring laugh. A profound silence reigned. With his drowsy stare Jacobus seemed to be slumbering open-eyed. Yet, somehow, I was aware of being profoundly scrutinised by those heavy eyes. In the enormous cavern of the store somebody began to nail down a case, expertly: tap-tap . . . tap-tap-tap.

Two other experts, one slow and nasal, the other shrill and snappy, started checking an invoice.

'A half-coil of three-inch manilla rope.'

'Right!'

'Six assorted shackles.'

'Right!'

'Six tins assorted soups, three of pâté, two asparagus, fourteen pounds tobacco, cabin.'

'Right!'

'It's for the captain who was here just now,' breathed out the immovable Jacobus. 'These steamer orders are very small. They pick up what they want as they go along. That man will be in Samarang in less than a fortnight. Very small orders indeed.'

The calling over of the items went on in the shop – an extraordinary jumble of varied articles, paintbrushes, Yorkshire Relish, etc., etc. . . . 'Three sacks of best potatoes,' read out the nasal voice.

At this Jacobus blinked like a sleeping man roused by a shake, and displayed some animation. At his order, shouted into the shop, a smirking half-caste clerk with his ringlets much oiled and with a pen stuck behind his ear, brought in a sample of six potatoes which he paraded in a row on the table.

Being urged to look at their beauty I gave them a cold and hostile glance. Calmly, Jacobus proposed that I should order ten or fifteen tons – tons! I couldn't believe my ears. My crew could not have eaten such a lot in a year; and potatoes (excuse these practical remarks) are a highly perishable commodity. I thought he was joking – or else trying to find out whether I was an unutterable idiot. But his purpose was not so simple. I discovered that he meant me to buy them on my own account.

'I am proposing you a bit of business, captain. I wouldn't charge you a great price.'

I told him that I did not go in for trade. I even added grimly that I knew only too well how that sort of speculation generally ended.

He sighed and clasped his hands on his stomach with exemplary resignation. I admired the placidity of his impudence. Then, waking up somewhat, 'Won't you try a cigar, captain?'

'No, thanks. I don't smoke cigars.'

'For once!' he exclaimed, in a patient whisper. A melancholy silence ensued. You know how sometimes a person discloses a certain unsuspected depth and acuteness of thought; that is, in other words, utters something unexpected. It was unexpected enough to hear Jacobus say: 'The man who just went out was right enough. You might take one, captain. Here everything is bound to be in the way of business.'

I felt a little ashamed of myself. The remembrance of his horrid brother made him appear quite a decent sort of fellow. It was with some compunction that I said a few words to the effect that I could have no possible objection to his hospitality.

Before I was a minute older I saw where this admission was leading me. As if changing the subject, Jacobus mentioned that his private house was about ten minutes' walk away. It had a beautiful old walled garden. Something really remarkable. I ought to come round someday and have a look at it.

He seemed to be a lover of gardens. I too take extreme delight in them; but I did not mean my compunction to carry me as far as Jacobus's flower-beds, however beautiful and old. He added, with a certain homeliness of tone: 'There's only my girl there.'

It is difficult to set everything down in due order; so I must revert here to what happened a week or two before. The medical officer of the port had come on board my ship to have a look at one of my crew who was ailing, and naturally enough he was asked to step into the cabin. A fellow-shipmaster of mine was there too; and in the conversation, somehow or other, the name of Jacobus came to be mentioned. It was pronounced with no particular reverence by the other man, I believe. I don't remember now what I was going to say. The doctor – a pleasant, cultivated fellow, with an assured manner – prevented me by striking in, in a sour tone, 'Ah! You're talking about my respected papa-in-law.'

Of course, that sally silenced us at the time. But I remembered the episode, and at this juncture, pushed for something noncommittal to say, I enquired with polite surprise: 'You have your married daughter living with you, Mr Jacobus?'

He moved his big hand from right to left quietly. No! That was another of his girls, he stated, ponderously and under his breath as usual. She . . . He seemed in a pause to be ransacking his mind for some kind of descriptive phrase. But my hopes were disappointed. He merely produced his stereotyped definition.

'She's a very different sort of person.'

'Indeed . . . And by the by, Jacobus, I called on your brother the other day. It's no great compliment if I say that I found him a very different sort of person from you.'

He had an air of profound reflection, then remarked quaintly: 'He's a man of regular habits.'

He might have been alluding to the habit of a late siesta; but I mumbled something about 'beastly habits anyhow' – and left the store abruptly.

FOUR

My little passage with Jacobus the merchant became known generally. One or two of my acquaintances made distant allusions to it. Perhaps the mulatto boy had talked. I must confess that people appeared rather scandalised, but not with Jacobus's brutality. A man I knew remonstrated with me for my hastiness.

I gave him the whole story of my visit, not forgetting the tell-tale resemblance of the wretched mulatto boy to his tormentor. He was not surprised. No doubt, no doubt. What of that? In a jovial tone he assured me that there must be many of that sort. The elder Jacobus had been a bachelor all his life. A highly respectable bachelor. But there had never been open scandal in that connection. His life had been quite regular. It could cause no offence to anyone.

I said that I had been offended considerably. My interlocutor opened very wide eyes. Why? Because a mulatto lad got a few knocks? That was not a great affair, surely. I had no idea how insolent and untruthful these half-castes were. In fact he seemed to think Mr Jacobus rather kind than other–wise to employ that youth at all; a sort of amiable weakness which could be forgiven.

This acquaintance of mine belonged to one of the old French families, descendants of the old colonists; all noble, all impoverished, and living a narrow domestic life in dull, dignified decay. The men, as a rule, occupy inferior posts in government offices or in business houses. The girls are almost always pretty, ignorant of the world, kind and agreeable and generally bilingual; they prattle innocently both in French and English. The emptiness of their existence passes belief.

I obtained my entry into a couple of such households because some years before, in Bombay, I had occasion to be of use to a pleasant, ineffectual young man who was rather stranded there, not knowing what to do with himself or even how to get home to his island again. It was a matter of two hundred rupees or so, but, when I turned up, the family made a point of showing their gratitude by admitting me to their intimacy. My knowledge of the French language made me specially acceptable. They had meantime managed to marry the fellow to a woman nearly twice his age, comparatively well off: the only profession he was really fit for. But it was not all cakes and ale. The first time I called on the couple she spied a little spot of grease on the poor devil's pantaloons and made him a screaming scene of reproaches so full of sincere passion that I sat terrified as at a tragedy of Racine.

Of course there was never question of the money I had advanced him; but his sisters, Miss Angèle and Miss Mary, and the aunts of both families, who spoke quaint archaic French of pre-Revolution period, and a host of distant relations adopted me for a friend outright in a manner which was almost embarrassing.

It was with the eldest brother (he was employed at a desk in my consignee's office) that I was having this talk about the merchant Jacobus. He regretted my attitude and nodded his head sagely. An influential man. One never knew when one would need him. I expressed my immense preference for the shopkeeper of the two. At that my friend looked grave.

'What on earth are you pulling that long face about?' I cried impatiently. 'He asked me to see his garden and I have a good mind to go someday.'

'Don't do that,' he said, so earnestly that I burst into a fit of laughter; but he looked at me without a smile.

This was another matter altogether. At one time the public conscience of the island had been mightily troubled by my Jacobus. The two brothers had been partners for years in great harmony, when a wandering circus came to the island and my Jacobus became suddenly infatuated with one of the lady-riders. What made it worse was that he was married. He had not even the grace to conceal his passion. It must have been strong indeed to carry away such a large placid creature. His behaviour was perfectly scandalous. He followed that woman to the Cape, and apparently travelled at the tail of that beastly circus to other parts of the world, in a most degrading position. The woman soon ceased to care for him, and treated him worse than a dog. Most extraordinary stories of moral degradation were reaching the island at that time. He had not the strength of mind to shake himself free . . .

The grotesque image of a fat, pushing ship-chandler, enslaved by an unholy love-spell, fascinated me; and I listened rather open-mouthed to the tale as old as the world, a tale which had been the subject of legend, of moral fables, of poems, but which so ludicrously failed to fit the personality. What a strange victim for the gods!

Meantime his deserted wife had died. His daughter was taken care of by his brother, who married her as advantageously as was possible in the circumstances.

'Oh! The Mrs Doctor!' I exclaimed.

'You know that? Yes. A very able man. He wanted a lift in the world, and there was a good bit of money from her mother, besides the expectations. . . Of course, they don't know him,' he added. 'The doctor nods in the street, I believe, but he avoids speaking to him when they meet on board a ship, as must happen sometimes.'

I remarked that this surely was an old story by now.

My friend assented. But it was Jacobus's own fault that it was neither forgiven nor forgotten. He came back ultimately. But how? Not in a spirit of contrition, in a way to propitiate his scandalised fellow-citizens. He must needs drag along with him a child – a girl . . .

'He spoke to me of a daughter who lives with him,' I observed, very much interested.

'She's certainly the daughter of the circus-woman,' said my friend. 'She may be his daughter too; I am willing to admit that she is. In fact I have no doubt – '

But he did not see why she should have been brought into a respectable community to perpetuate the memory of the scandal. And that was not the worst. Presently something much more distressing happened. That abandoned woman turned up. Landed from a mail-boat . . .

'What! Here? To claim the child perhaps,' I suggested.

'Not she!' My friendly informant was very scornful. 'Imagine a painted, haggard, agitated, desperate hag. Been cast off in Mozambique by somebody who paid her passage here. She had been injured internally by a kick from a horse; she hadn't a cent on her when she got ashore; I don't think she even asked to see the child. At any rate, not till the last day of her life. Jacobus hired for her a bungalow to die in. He got a couple of Sisters from the hospital to nurse her through those few months. If he didn't marry her *in extremis* as the good Sisters tried to bring about, it's because she wouldn't even hear of it. As the nuns said: "The woman died impenitent." It was reported that she ordered Jacobus out of the room with her last breath. This may be the real reason why he didn't go into mourning himself; he only put the child into black. While she was little she was to be seen sometimes about the streets attended by a negro woman, but since she became of age to put her hair up I don't think she has set foot outside that garden once. She must be over eighteen now.'

Thus my friend, with some added details – such as, that he didn't think the girl had spoken to three people of any position in the island, and that an elderly female relative of the brothers Jacobus had been induced by extreme poverty to accept the position of *gouvernante* to the girl. As to Jacobus's business (which certainly annoyed his brother) it was a wise choice on his part. It brought him in contact only with strangers of passage; whereas any other would have given rise to all sorts of awkwardness with his social equals. The man was not wanting in a certain tact – only he was naturally shameless. For why did he want to keep that girl with him? It was most painful for everybody.

I thought suddenly (and with profound disgust) of the other Jacobus, and I could not refrain from saying slily: 'I suppose if he employed her, say, as a scullion in his household and occasionally pulled her hair or boxed her ears, the position would have been more regular – less shocking to the respectable class to which he belongs.'

He was not so stupid as to miss my intention, and shrugged his shoulders impatiently.

'You don't understand. To begin with, she's not a mulatto. And a scandal is a scandal. People should be given a chance to forget. I dare say it would have been better for her if she had been turned into a scullion or something of that kind. Of course he's trying to make money in every sort of petty way, but in such a business there'll never be enough for anybody to come forward.'

When my friend left me I had a conception of Jacobus and his daughter existing, a lonely pair of castaways, on a desert island; the girl sheltering in the house as if it were a cavern in a cliff, and Jacobus going out to pick up a living for both on the beach – exactly like two shipwrecked people who always hope for some rescuer to bring them back at last into touch with the rest of mankind.

But Jacobus's bodily reality did not fit in with this romantic view. When he turned up on board in the usual course, he sipped the cup of coffee placidly, asked me if I was satisfied – and I hardly listened to the harbour gossip he dropped slowly in his low, voice-saving enunciation. I had then troubles of my own. My ship chartered, my thoughts dwelling on the success of a quick round voyage, I had been suddenly confronted by a shortage of bags. A catastrophe! The stock of one especial kind, called pockets, seemed to be totally exhausted. A consignment was shortly expected – it was afloat, on its way, but, meantime, the loading of my ship stopped dead, I had enough to worry about. My consignees, who had received me with such heartiness on my arrival, now, in the character of my charterers, listened to my complaints with polite helplessness. Their manager, the old-maidish, thin man, who so prudishly didn't even like to speak about the impure Jacobus, gave me the correct commercial view of the position.

'My dear captain' – he was retracting his leathery cheeks into a condescending, shark-like smile – 'we were not morally obliged to tell you of a possible shortage before you signed the charter-party. It was for you to guard against the contingency of a delay – strictly speaking. But of course we shouldn't have taken any advantage. This is no one's fault really. We ourselves have been taken unawares,' he concluded primly, with an obvious lie.

This lecture I confess had made me thirsty. Suppressed rage generally produces that effect; and as I strolled on aimlessly I bethought myself of the tall earthenware pitcher in the captains' room of the Jacobus 'store'.

With no more than a nod to the men I found assembled there, I poured down a deep, cool draught on my indignation, then another, and then, becoming dejected, I sat plunged in cheerless reflections. The others read, talked, smoked, bandied over my head some unsubtle chaff. But my abstraction was respected. And it was without a word to anyone that I rose and went out, only to be quite unexpectedly accosted in the bustle of the store by Jacobus the outcast.

'Glad to see you, Captain. What? Going away? You haven't been looking so well these last few days, I notice. Run down, eh?'

He was in his shirt-sleeves, and his words were in the usual course of business, but they had a human note. It was commercial amenity, but I had been a stranger to amenity in that connection. I do verily believe (from the direction of his heavy glance towards a certain shelf) that he was going to suggest the purchase of Clarkson's Nerve Tonic, which he kept in stock, when I said impulsively: 'I am rather in trouble with my loading.'

Wide awake under his sleepy, broad mask with glued lips, he understood at once, had a movement of the head so appreciative that I relieved my exasperation by exclaiming: 'Surely there must be eleven hundred quarter-bags to be found in the colony. It's only a matter of looking for them.'

Again that slight movement of the big head, and in the noise and activity of the store that tranquil murmur: 'To be sure. But then people likely to have a reserve of quarter-bags wouldn't want to sell. They'd need that size themselves.'

'That's exactly what my consignees are telling me. Impossible to buy. Bosh! They don't want to. It suits them to have the ship hung up. But if I were to discover the lot they would have to – Look here, Jacobus! You are the man to have such a thing up your sleeve.'

He protested with a ponderous swing of his big head. I stood before him helplessly, being looked at by those heavy eyes with a veiled expression as of a man after some soul-shaking crisis. Then, suddenly: 'It's impossible to talk quietly here,' he whispered. 'I am very busy. But if you could go and wait for me in my house. It's less than ten minutes' walk. Oh, yes, you don't know the way.'

He called for his coat and offered to take me there himself. He would have to return to the store at once for an hour or so to finish his business, and then he would be at liberty to talk over with me that matter of quarter-bags. This programme was breathed out at me through slightly parted, still lips; his heavy, motionless glance rested upon me, placid as ever, the glance of a tired man – but I felt that it was searching, too. I could not imagine what he was looking for in me and kept silent, wondering.

'I am asking you to wait for me in my house till I am at liberty to talk this matter over. You will?'

'Why, of course!' I cried.

'But I cannot promise – '

'I dare say not,' I said. 'I don't expect a promise.'

'I mean I can't even promise to try the move I've in my mind. One must see first . . . h'm!'

'All right. I'll take the chance. I'll wait for you as long as you like. What else have I to do in this infernal hole of a port!'

Before I had uttered my last words we had set off at a swinging pace. We turned a couple of corners and entered a street completely empty of traffic, of semi-rural aspect, paved with cobblestones nestling in grass tufts. The house came to the line of the roadway; a single storey on an elevated basement of rough-stones, so that our heads were below the level of the windows as we went along. All the jalousies were tightly shut, like eyes, and the house seemed fast asleep in the afternoon sunshine. The entrance was at the side, in an alley even more grass-grown than the street: a small door, simply on the latch.

With a word of apology as to showing me the way, Jacobus preceded me up a dark passage and led me across the naked parquet floor of what I supposed to be the dining-room. It was lighted by three glass doors which stood wide open on to a verandah or rather loggia running its brick arches along the garden side of the house. It was really a magnificent garden: smooth green lawns and a gorgeous maze of flowerbeds in the foreground, displayed around a basin of dark water framed in a marble rim, and in the distance the massed foliage of varied trees concealing the roofs of other houses. The town might have been miles away. It was a brilliantly coloured solitude, drowsing in a warm, voluptuous silence. Where the long, still shadows fell across the beds, and in shady nooks, the massed colours of the flowers had an extraordinary magnificence of effect. I stood entranced. Jacobus grasped me delicately above the elbow, impelling me to a half-turn to the left.

I had not noticed the girl before. She occupied a low, deep, wickerwork armchair, and I saw her in exact profile like a figure in a tapestry, and as motionless. Jacobus released my arm.

'This is Alice,' he announced tranquilly; and his subdued manner of speaking made it sound so much like a confidential communication that I fancied myself nodding understandingly and whispering: 'I see, I see.' . . . Of course, I did nothing of the kind. Neither of us did anything; we stood side by side looking down at the girl. For quite a time she did not stir, staring straight before her as if watching the vision of some pageant passing through the garden in the deep, rich glow of light and the splendour of flowers.

Then, coming to the end of her reverie, she looked round and up. If I had not at first noticed her, I am certain that she too had been unaware of my presence till she actually perceived me by her father's side. The quickened upward movement of the heavy eyelids, the widening of the languid glance, passing into a fixed stare, put that beyond doubt.

Under her amazement there was a hint of fear, and then came a flash as of anger. Jacobus, after uttering my name fairly loud, said: 'Make yourself at home, captain – I won't be gone long,' and went away rapidly. Before I had time to make a bow I was left alone with the girl – who, I remembered suddenly, had not been seen by any man or woman of that town since she had found it necessary to put up her hair. It looked as though it had not been touched again since that distant time of first putting up; it was a mass of black, lustrous locks, twisted anyhow high on her head, with long, untidy wisps hanging down on each side of the clear sallow face; a mass so thick and strong and abundant that but to look at it gave you a sensation of heavy pressure on the top of your head and an impression of magnificently cynical untidiness. She leaned forward, hugging herself with crossed legs; a dingy, amber-coloured, flounced wrapper of some thin stuff revealed the young supple body drawn together tensely in the deep low seat as if crouching for a spring. I detected a slight, quivering start or two, which looked un-commonly like bounding away. They were followed by the most absolute immobility.

The absurd impulse to run out after Jacobus (for I had been startled, too) once repressed, I took a chair, placed it not very far from her, sat down deliberately, and began to talk about the garden, caring not what I said, but using a gentle caressing intonation as one talks to soothe a startled wild animal. I could not even be certain that she understood me. She never raised her face nor attempted to look my way. I kept on talking only to prevent her from taking flight. She had another of those quivering, repressed starts which made me catch my breath with apprehension.

Ultimately I formed a notion that what prevented her perhaps from going off in one great, nervous leap, was the scantiness of her attire. The wicker armchair was the most substantial thing about her person. What she had on under that dingy, loose, amber wrapper must have been of the most flimsy and airy character. One could not help being aware of it. It was obvious. I felt it actually embarrassing at first; but that sort of embarrassment is got over easily by a mind not enslaved by narrow prejudices. I did not avert my gaze from Alice. I went on talking with ingratiating softness, the recollection that, most likely, she had never before been spoken to by a strange man adding to my assurance. I don't know why an emotional tenseness should have crept into the situation. But it did. And just as I was becoming aware of it a slight scream cut short my flow of urbane speech.

The scream did not proceed from the girl. It was emitted behind me, and caused me to turn my head sharply. I understood at once that the apparition in the doorway was the elderly relation of Jacobus, the companion, the *gouvernante*. While she remained thunderstruck, I got up and made her a low bow.

The ladies of Jacobus's household evidently spent their days in light attire. This stumpy old woman, with a face like a large wrinkled lemon, beady eyes and a shock of iron-grey hair, was dressed in a garment of some ash-coloured, silky, light stuff. It fell from her thick neck down to her toes with the simplicity of an unadorned nightgown. It made her appear truly cylindrical. She exclaimed: 'How did you get here?'

Before I could say a word she vanished and presently I heard a confusion of shrill protestations in a distant part of the house. Obviously no one could tell her how I got there. In a moment, with great outcries from two negro women following her, she waddled back to the doorway, infuriated.

'What do you want here?'

I turned to the girl. She was sitting straight up now, her hands posed on the arms of the chair. I appealed to her.

'Surely, Miss Alice, you will not let them drive me out into the street?'

Her magnificent black eyes, narrowed, long in shape, swept over me with an indefinable expression, then in a harsh, contemptuous voice she let fall in French a sort of explanation: 'C'est papa.'

I made another low bow to the old woman.

She turned her back on me in order to drive away her black henchwomen, then surveying my person in a peculiar manner with one small eye nearly closed and her face all drawn up on that side as if with a twinge of toothache, she stepped out on the verandah, sat down in a rocking-chair some distance away, and took up her knitting from a little table. Before she started at it she plunged one of the needles into the mop of her grey hair and stirred it vigorously.

Her elementary nightgown-sort of frock clung to her ancient, stumpy and floating form. She wore white cotton stockings and flat brown velvet slippers. Her feet and ankles were obtrusively visible on the foot-rest. She began to rock herself slightly, while she knitted. I had resumed my seat and kept quiet, for I mistrusted that old woman. What if she ordered me to depart? She seemed capable of any outrage. She had snorted once or twice; she was knitting violently. Suddenly she piped at the young girl in French a question which I translate colloquially: 'What's your father up to, now?'

The young creature shrugged her shoulders so comprehensively that her whole body swayed within the loose wrapper; and in that unexpectedly harsh voice which yet had a seductive quality to the senses, like certain kinds of natural rough wines one drinks with pleasure, she said: 'It's some captain. Leave me alone – will you!'

The chair rocked quicker, the old, thin voice was like a whistle.

'You and your father make a pair. He would stick at nothing – that's well known. But I didn't expect this.'

I thought it high time to air some of my own French. I remarked modestly, but firmly, that this was business. I had some matters to talk over with Mr Jacobus.

At once she piped out a derisive: 'Poor innocent!' Then, with a change of tone: 'The shop's for business. Why don't you go to the shop to talk with him?' The furious speed of her fingers and knitting-needles made one dizzy; and with squeaky indignation: 'Sitting here staring at that girl – is that what you call business?'

'No,' I said suavely. 'I call this pleasure – an unexpected pleasure. And unless Miss Alice objects – '

I half turned to her. She flung at me an angry and contemptuous: 'Don't care!' and leaning her elbow on her knees took her chin in her hand – a Jacobus chin undoubtedly. And those heavy eyelids, this black irritated stare, reminded me of Jacobus, too – the wealthy merchant, the respected one. The design of her eyebrows also was the same, rigid and ill-omened. Yes! I traced in her a resemblance to both of them. It came to me as a sort of surprising remote inference that both these Jacobuses were rather handsome men after all. I said: 'Oh! Then I shall stare at you till you smile.'

She favoured me again with an even more viciously scornful: 'Don't care!'

The old woman broke in blunt and shrill: 'Hear his impudence! And you too! Don't care! Go at least and put some more clothes on. Sitting there like this before this sailor riff-raff.'

The sun was about to leave the Pearl of the Ocean for other seas, for other lands. The walled garden full of shadows blazed with colour as if the flowers were giving up the light absorbed during the day. The amazing old woman became very explicit. She suggested to the girl a corset and a petticoat with a cynical unreserve which humiliated me. Was I of no more account than a wooden dummy? The girl snapped out: 'Shan't!'

It was not the naughty retort of a vulgar child; it had a note of desperation. Clearly my intrusion had somehow upset the balance of their established relations. The old woman knitted with furious accuracy, her eyes fastened down on her work.

'Oh, you are the true child of your father! And *that* talks of entering a convent! Letting herself be stared at by a fellow.'

'Leave off.'

'Shameless thing!'

'Old sorceress,' the girl uttered distinctly, preserving her meditative pose, chin in hand, and a far-away stare over the garden.

It was like the quarrel of the kettle and the pot. The old woman flew out of the chair, banged down her work, and with a great play of thick limb perfectly visible in that weird, clinging garment of hers, strode at the girl – who never stirred. I was experiencing a sort of trepidation when, as if awed by that unconscious attitude, the aged relative of Jacobus turned short upon me.

She was, I perceived, armed with a knitting-needle; and as she raised her hand her intention seemed to be to throw it at me like a dart. But she only used it to scratch her head with, examining me the while at close range, one eye nearly shut and her face distorted by a whimsical, one-sided grimace.

'My dear man,' she asked abruptly, 'do you expect any good to come of this?'

'I do hope so indeed, Miss Jacobus.' I tried to speak in the easy tone of an afternoon caller. 'You see, I am here after some bags.'

'Bags! Look at that now! Didn't I hear you holding forth to that graceless wretch?'

'You would like to see me in my grave,' uttered the motionless girl hoarsely.

'Grave! What about me? Buried alive before I am dead for the sake of a thing blessed with such a pretty father!' she cried; and turning to me: 'You're one of these men he does business with. Well – why don't you leave us in peace, my good fellow?'

It was said in a tone – this 'leave us in peace!' There was a sort of ruffianly familiarity, a superiority, a scorn in it. I was to hear it more than once, for you would show an imperfect knowledge of human nature if you thought that this was my last visit to that house – where no respectable person had put foot for ever so many years. No, you would be very much mistaken if you imagined that this reception had scared me away. First of all I was not going to run before a grotesque and ruffianly old woman.

And then you mustn't forget these necessary bags. That first evening Jacobus made me stay to dinner; after, however, telling me loyally that he didn't know whether he could do anything at all for me. He had been thinking it over. It was too difficult, he feared . . . But he did not give it up in so many words.

We were only three at table; the girl by means of repeated, 'Won't!' 'Shan't!' and 'Don't care!' having conveyed and affirmed her intention not to come to the table, not to have any dinner, not to move from the verandah. The old relative hopped about in her flat slippers and piped indignantly; Jacobus towered over her and murmured placidly in his throat; I joined jocularly from a distance, throwing in a few words, for which under the cover of the night I received secretly a most vicious poke in the ribs from the old woman's elbow or perhaps her fist. I restrained a cry. And all the time the girl didn't even condescend to raise her head to look at any of us. All this may sound childish – and yet that stony, petulant sullenness had an obscurely tragic flavour.

And so we sat down to the food around the light of a good many candles while she remained crouching out there, staring in the dark as if feeding her bad temper on the heavily scented air of the admirable garden.

Before leaving I said to Jacobus that I would come next day to hear if the bag affair had made any progress. He shook his head slightly at that.

'I'll haunt your house daily till you pull it off. You'll be always finding me here.'

His faint, melancholy smile did not part his thick lips.

'That will be all right, Captain.'

Then seeing me to the door, very tranquil, he murmured earnestly the recommendation: 'Make yourself at home,' and also the hospitable hint about there being always 'a plate of soup'. It was only on my way to the quay, down the ill-lighted streets, that I remembered I had been engaged to dine that very evening with the S— family. Though vexed by my forgetfulness (it would be rather awkward to explain), I couldn't help thinking that it had procured me a more amusing evening. And besides – business. The sacred business –

In a barefooted negro who overtook me at a run and bolted down the landing-steps I recognised Jacobus's boatman, who must have been feeding in the kitchen. His usual 'Good-night, sah!' as I went up my ship's ladder had a more cordial sound than on previous occasions.

FIVE

I kept my word to Jacobus. I haunted his home. He was perpetually finding me there of an afternoon when he popped in for a moment from the 'store'. The sound of my voice talking to his Alice greeted him on his doorstep; and when he returned for good in the evening, ten to one he would hear it still going on in the verandah. I just nodded to him; he would sit down heavily and gently, and watch with a sort of approving anxiety my efforts to make his daughter smile.

I called her often 'Alice', right before him; sometimes I would address her as Miss 'Don't Care', and I exhausted myself in nonsensical chatter without succeeding once in taking her out of her peevish and tragic self. There were moments when I felt I must break out and start swearing at her till all was blue. And I fancied that had I done so Jacobus would not have moved a muscle. A sort of shady, intimate understanding seemed to have been established between us.

I must say the girl treated her father exactly in the same way she treated me.

And how could it have been otherwise? She treated me as she treated her father. She had never seen a visitor. She did not know how men behaved. I belonged to the low lot with whom her father did business at the port. I was of no account. So was her father. The only decent people in the world were the people of the island, who would have nothing to do with him because of something wicked he had done. This was apparently the explanation Miss Jacobus had given her of the household's isolated position. For she had to be told something! And I feel convinced that this version had been assented to by Jacobus. I must say the old woman was putting it forward with considerable gusto. It was on her lips the universal explanation, the universal allusion, the universal taunt.

One day Jacobus came in early and, beckoning me into the dining-room, wiped his brow with a weary gesture and told me that he had managed to unearth a supply of quarter-bags.

'It's fourteen hundred your ship wanted, did you say, captain?'

'Yes, yes!' I replied eagerly; but he remained calm. He looked more tired than I had ever seen him before.

'Well, captain, you may go and tell your people that they can get that lot from my brother.'

As I remained open-mouthed at this, he added his usual placid formula of assurance 'You'll find it correct, captain.'

'You spoke to your brother about it?' I was distinctly awed. 'And for me? Because he must have known that my ship's the only one hung up for bags. How on earth – '

He wiped his brow again. I noticed that he was dressed with unusual care, in clothes in which I had never seen him before. He avoided my eye.

'You've heard people talk, of course . . . That's true enough. He . . . I . . . We certainly. . . for several years . . .' His voice declined to a mere sleepy murmur. 'You see I had something to tell him of, something which – '

His murmur stopped. He was not going to tell me what this something was. And I didn't care. Anxious to carry the news to my charterers, I ran back on the verandah to get my hat.

At the bustle I made the girl turned her eyes slowly in my direction, and even the old woman was checked in her knitting. I stopped a moment to exclaim excitedly: 'Your father's a brick, Miss Don't Care. That's what he is.'

She beheld my elation in scornful surprise. Jacobus with unwonted familiarity seized my arm as I flew through the dining-room, and breathed heavily at me a proposal about 'a plate of soup' that evening. I answered distractedly: 'Eh? What? Oh, thanks! Certainly. With pleasure,' and tore myself away. Dine with him? Of course. The merest gratitude

But some three hours afterwards, in the dusky, silent street, paved with cobble-stones, I became aware that it was not mere gratitude which was guiding my steps towards the house with the old garden, where for years no guest other than myself had ever dined. Mere gratitude does not gnaw at one's interior economy in that particular way. Hunger might; but I was not feeling particularly hungry for Jacobus's food.

On that occasion, too, the girl refused to come to the table.

My exasperation grew. The old woman cast malicious glances at me. I said suddenly to Jacobus: 'Here! Put some chicken and salad on that plate.'

He obeyed without raising his eyes. I carried it with a knife and fork and a serviette out on the verandah. The garden was one mass of gloom, like a cemetery of flowers buried in the darkness, and she, in the chair, seemed to muse mournfully over the extinction of light and colour. Only whiffs of heavy scent passed like wandering, fragrant souls of that departed multitude of blossoms. I talked volubly, jocularly, persuasively, tenderly; I talked in a subdued tone. To a listener it would have sounded like the murmur of a pleading lover. Whenever I paused expectantly there was only a deep silence. It was like offering food to a seated statue.

'I haven't been able to swallow a single morsel thinking of you out here starving yourself in the dark. It's positively cruel to be so obstinate. Think of my sufferings.'

'Don't care.'

I felt as if I could have done her some violence – shaken her, beaten her maybe. I said: 'Your absurd behaviour will prevent me coming here any more.'

'What's that to me?'

'You like it.'

'It's false,' she snarled.

My hand fell on her shoulder; and if she had flinched I verily believe I would have shaken her. But there was no movement and this immobility disarmed my anger.

'You do. Or you wouldn't be found on the verandah every day. Why are you here, then? There are plenty of rooms in the house. You have your own room to stay in – if you did not want to see me. But you do. You know you do.'

I felt a slight shudder under my hand and released my grip as if frightened by that sign of animation in her body. The scented air of the garden came to us in a warm wave like a voluptuous and perfumed sigh.

'Go back to them,' she whispered, almost pitifully.

As I re-entered the dining-room I saw Jacobus cast down his eyes. I banged the plate on the table. At this demonstration of ill-humour he murmured something in an apologetic tone, and I turned on him viciously as if he were accountable to me for these 'abominable eccentricities', I believe I called them.

'But I dare say Miss Jacobus here is responsible for most of this offensive manner,' I added loftily.

She piped out at once in her brazen, ruffianly manner: 'Eh? Why don't you leave us in peace, my good fellow?'

I was astonished that she should dare before Jacobus. Yet what could he have done to repress her? He needed her too much. He raised a heavy, drowsy glance for an instant, then looked down again. She insisted with shrill finality: 'Haven't you done your business, you two? Well, then – '

She had the true Jacobus impudence, that old woman. Her mop of iron-grey hair was parted on the side like a man's, raffishly, and she made as if to plunge her fork into it, as she used to do with the knitting-needle, but refrained. Her little black eyes sparkled venomously. I turned to my host at the head of the table – menacingly as it were.

'Well, and what do you say to that, Jacobus? Am I to take it that we have done with each other?'

I had to wait a little. The answer when it came was rather unexpected, and in quite another spirit than the question.

'I certainly think we might do some business yet with those potatoes of mine, captain. You will find that – '

I cut him short.

'I've told you before that I don't trade.'

His broad chest heaved without a sound in a noiseless sigh.

'Think it over, captain,' he murmured, tenacious and tranquil; and I burst into a jarring laugh, remembering how he had stuck to the circus-rider woman – the depth of passion under that placid surface, which even cuts with a riding-whip (so the legend had it) could never ruffle into the semblance of a storm; something like the passion of a fish would be if one could imagine such a thing as a passionate fish.

That evening I experienced more distinctly than ever the sense of moral discomfort which always attended me in that house lying under the ban of all 'decent' people. I refused to stay on and smoke after dinner; and when I put my hand into the thickly-cushioned palm of Jacobus, I said to myself that it would be for the last time under his roof. I pressed his bulky paw heartily nevertheless. Hadn't he got me out of a serious difficulty? To the few words of acknowledgment I was bound, and indeed quite willing, to utter, he answered by stretching his closed lips in his melancholy, glued-together smile.

'That will be all right, I hope, captain,' he breathed out weightily.

'What do you mean?' I asked, alarmed. 'That your brother might yet – '

'Oh, no,' he reassured me. 'He . . . he's a man of his word, captain.'

My self-communion as I walked away from his door, trying to believe that this was for the last time, was not satisfactory. I was aware myself that I was not sincere in my reflections as to Jacobus's motives, and, of course, the very next day I went back again.

How weak, irrational and absurd we are! How easily carried away whenever our awakened imagination brings us the irritating hint of a desire! I cared for the girl in a particular way, seduced by the moody expression of her face, by her obstinate silences, her rare, scornful words; by the perpetual pout of her closed lips, the black depths of her fixed gaze turned slowly upon me as if in contemptuous provocation, only to be averted next moment with an exasperating indifference.

Of course the news of my assiduity had spread all over the little town. I noticed a change in the manner of my acquaintances and even something different in the nods of the other captains, when meeting them at the landing-steps or in the offices where business called me. The old-maidish head clerk treated me with distant punctiliousness and, as it were, gathered his skirts round him for fear of contamination. It seemed to me that the very niggers on the quays turned to look after me as I passed; and as to Jacobus's boatman, his 'Good-night, sah!' when he put me on board was no longer merely cordial – it had a familiar, confidential sound as though we had been partners in some villainy.

My friend S— the elder passed me on the other side of the street with a wave of the hand and an ironic smile. The younger brother, the one they had married to an elderly shrew, he, on the strength of an older friendship and as if paying a debt of gratitude, took the liberty to utter a word of warning.

'You're doing yourself no good by your choice of friends, my dear chap,' he said with infantile gravity.

As I knew that the meeting of the brothers Jacobus was the subject of excited comment in the whole of the sugary Pearl of the Ocean I wanted to know why I was blamed.

'I have been the occasion of a move which may end in a reconciliation surely desirable from the point of view of the proprieties – don't you know?'

'Of course, if that girl were disposed of it would certainly facilitate – ' he mused sagely, then, inconsequential creature, gave me a light tap on the lower part of my waistcoat. 'You old sinner,' he cried jovially, 'much you care for proprieties. But you had better look out for yourself, you know, with a personage like Jacobus who has no sort of reputation to lose.'

He had recovered his gravity of a respectable citizen by that time and added regretfully: 'All the women of our family are perfectly scandalised.'

But by that time I had given up visiting the S— family and the D— family. The elder ladies pulled such faces when I showed myself, and the multitude of related young ladies received me with such a variety of looks: wondering, awed, mocking (except Miss Mary, who spoke to me and looked at me with hushed, pained compassion as though I had been ill), that I had no difficulty in giving them all up. I would have given up the society of the whole town, for the sake of sitting near that girl, snarling and superb and barely clad in that flimsy, dingy, amber wrapper, open low at the throat. She looked, with the wild wisps of hair hanging down her tense face, as though she had just jumped out of bed in the panic of a fire.

She sat leaning on her elbow, looking at nothing. Why did she stay listening to my absurd chatter? And not only that; but why did she powder her face in preparation for my arrival? It seemed to be her idea of making a toilette, and in her untidy negligence a sign of great effort towards personal adornment.

But I might have been mistaken. The powdering might have been her daily practice and her presence in the verandah a sign of an indifference so complete as to take no account of my existence. Well, it was all one to me.

I loved to watch her slow changes of pose, to look at her long immobilities composed in the graceful lines of her body, to observe the mysterious narrow stare of her splendid black eyes, somewhat long in shape, half closed, contemplating the void. She was like a spellbound creature with the forehead of a goddess crowned by the dishevelled magnificent hair of a gypsy tramp. Even her indifference was seductive. I felt myself growing attached to her by the bond of an irrealisable desire, for I kept my head – quite. And I put up with the moral discomfort of Jacobus's sleepy watchfulness, tranquil and yet so expressive, as if there had been a tacit pact between us two. I put up with the insolence of the old woman's: 'Aren't you ever going to leave us in peace, my good fellow?'; with her taunts; with her brazen and sinister scolding. She was of the true Jacobus stock, and no mistake.

Directly I got away from the girl I called myself many hard names. What folly was this? I would ask myself. It was like being the slave of some depraved habit. And I returned to her with my head clear, my heart certainly free, not even moved by pity for that castaway (she was as much of a castaway as anyone ever wrecked on a desert island), but as if beguiled by some extraordinary promise. Nothing more unworthy could be imagined. The recollection of that tremulous whisper when I gripped her shoulder with one hand and held a plate of chicken with the other was enough to make me break all my good resolutions.

Her insulting taciturnity was enough sometimes to make one gnash one's teeth with rage. When she opened her mouth it was only to be abominably rude in harsh tones to the associate of her reprobate father; and the full approval of her aged relative was conveyed to her by offensive chuckles. If not that, then her remarks, always uttered in the tone of scathing contempt, were of the most appalling inanity.

How could it have been otherwise? That plump, ruffianly Jacobus old maid in the tight grey frock had never taught her any manners. Manners I suppose are not necessary for born castaways. No educational establishment could ever be induced to accept her as a pupil – on account of the proprieties, I imagine. And Jacobus had not been able to send her away anywhere. How could he have done it? Who with? Where to? He himself was not enough of an adventurer to think of settling down anywhere else. His passion had tossed him at the tail of a circus up and down strange coasts, but, the storm over, he had drifted back shamelessly where, social outcast as he was, he remained still a Jacobus – one of the oldest families on the island, older than the French even. There must have been a Jacobus in at the death of the last dodo . . . The girl had learned nothing, she had never listened to a general conversation, she knew nothing, she had heard of nothing. She could read certainly; but all the reading matter that ever came in her way were the newspapers provided for the captains' room of the 'store'. Jacobus had the habit of taking these sheets home now and then in a very stained and ragged condition.

As her mind could not grasp the meaning of any matters treated there except police-court reports and accounts of crimes, she had formed for herself a notion of the civilised world as a scene of murders, abductions, burglaries, stabbing affrays, and every sort of desperate violence. England and France, Paris and London (the only two towns of which she seemed to have heard), appeared to her sinks of abomination, reeking with blood, in contrast to her little island where petty larceny was about the standard of current misdeeds, with, now and then, some more pronounced crime – and that only amongst the imported coolie labourers on sugar estates or the negroes of the town. But in Europe these things were being done daily by a wicked population of white men amongst whom, as that ruffianly, aristocratic old Miss Jacobus pointed out, the wandering sailors, the associates of her precious papa, were the lowest of the low.

It was impossible to give her a sense of proportion. I suppose she figured England to herself as about the size of the Pearl of the Ocean; in which case it would certainly have been reeking with gore and a mere wreck of burgled houses from end to end. One could not make her understand that these horrors on which she fed her imagination were lost in the mass of orderly life like a few drops of blood in the ocean. She directed upon me for a moment the uncomprehending glance of her narrowed eyes and then would turn her scornful powdered face away without a word. She would not even take the trouble to shrug her shoulders.

At that time the batches of papers brought by the last mail reported a series of crimes in the East End of London, there was a sensational case of abduction in France and a fine display of armed robbery in Australia. One afternoon, crossing the dining-room, I heard Miss Jacobus piping in the verandah with venomous animosity: 'I don't know what your precious papa is plotting with that fellow. But he's just the sort of man who's capable of carrying you off far away somewhere and then cutting your throat someday for your money.'

There was a good half of the length of the verandah between their chairs. I came out and sat down fiercely midway between them.

'Yes, that's what we do with girls in Europe,' I began in a grimly matter-of-fact tone. I think Miss Jacobus was disconcerted by my sudden appearance. I turned upon her with cold ferocity: 'As to objectionable old women, they are first strangled quietly, then cut up into small pieces and thrown away, a bit here and a bit there. They vanish – '

I cannot go so far as to say I had terrified her. But she was troubled by my truculence, the more so because I had been always addressing her with a politeness she did not deserve. Her plump, knitting hands fell slowly on her knees. She said not a word while I fixed her with severe determination. Then as I turned away from her at last, she laid down her work gently and, with noiseless movements, retreated from the verandah. In fact, she vanished.

But I was not thinking of her. I was looking at the girl. It was what I was coming for daily; troubled, ashamed, eager; finding in my nearness to her a unique sensation which I indulged with dread, self-contempt and deep pleasure, as if it were a secret vice bound to end in my undoing, like the habit of some drug or other which ruins and degrades its slave.

I looked her over, from the top of her dishevelled head, down the lovely line of the shoulder, following the curve of the hip, the draped form of the long limb, right down to her fine ankle below a torn, soiled flounce and as far as the point of the shabby, high-heeled, blue slipper, dangling from her well-shaped foot, which she moved slightly, with quick, nervous jerks, as if impatient of my presence. And in the scent of the massed flowers I seemed to breathe her special and inexplicable charm, the heady perfume of the everlastingly irritated captive of the garden.

I looked at her rounded chin, the Jacobus chin; at the full, red lips pouting in the powdered, sallow face; at the firm modelling of the cheek, the grains of white in the hairs of the straight sombre eyebrows; at the long eyes, a narrowed gleam of liquid white and intense motionless black, with their gaze so empty of thought, and so absorbed in their fixity that she seemed to be staring at her own lonely image, in some far-off mirror hidden from my sight among the trees.

And suddenly, without looking at me, with the appearance of a person speaking to herself, she asked, in that voice slightly harsh yet mellow and always irritated: 'Why do you keep on coming here?'

'Why do I keep on coming here?' I repeated, taken by surprise. I could not have told her. I could not even tell myself with sincerity why I was coming there. 'What's the good of you asking a question like that?'

'Nothing is any good,' she observed scornfully to the empty air, her chin propped on her hand, that hand never extended to any man, that no one had ever grasped – for I had only grasped her shoulder once – that generous, fine, somewhat masculine hand. I knew well the peculiarly efficient shape – broad at the base, tapering at the fingers – of that hand, for which there was nothing in the world to lay hold of. I pretended to be playful.

'No! But do you really care to know?'

She shrugged indolently her magnificent shoulders, from which the dingy thin wrapper was slipping a little.

'Oh – never mind – never mind!'

There was something smouldering under those airs of lassitude. She exasperated me by the provocation of her nonchalance, by something elusive and defiant in her very form which I wanted to seize. I said roughly: 'Why? Don't you think I should tell you the truth?'

Her eyes glided my way for a sidelong look, and she murmured, moving only her full, pouting lips: 'I think you would not dare.'

'Do you imagine I am afraid of you? What on earth . . . Well, it's possible, after all, that *I* don't know exactly why I am coming here. Let us say, with Miss Jacobus, that it is for no good. You seem to believe the outrageous things she says, if you do have a row with her now and then.'

She snapped out viciously: 'Who else am I to believe?'

'I don't know,' I had to own, seeing her suddenly very helpless and condemned to moral solitude by the verdict of a respectable community. 'You might believe me, if you chose.'

She made a slight movement and asked me at once, with an effort as if making an experiment: 'What is the business between you and papa?'

'Don't you know the nature of your father's business? Come! He sells provisions to ships.'

She became rigid again in her crouching pose.

'Not that. What brings you here – to this house?'

'And suppose it's you? You would not call that business? Would you? And now let us drop the subject. It's no use. My ship will be ready for sea the day after tomorrow.'

She murmured a distinctly scared: 'So soon,' and getting up quickly, went to the little table and poured herself a glass of water. She walked with rapid steps and with an indolent swaying of her whole young figure above the hips; when she passed near me I felt with tenfold force the charm of the peculiar, promising sensation I had formed the habit to seek near her. I thought with sudden dismay that this was the end of it; that after one more day I would be no longer able to come into this verandah, sit on this chair, and taste perversely the flavour of contempt in her indolent poses, drink in the provocation of her scornful looks, and listen to the curt, insolent remarks uttered in that harsh and seductive voice. As if my innermost nature had been altered by the action of some moral poison, I felt an abject dread of going to sea.

I had to exercise a sudden self-control, as one puts on a brake, to prevent myself jumping up to stride about, shout, gesticulate, make her a scene. What for? What about? I had no idea. It was just the relief of violence that I wanted; and I lolled back in my chair, trying to keep my lips formed in a smile; that half-indulgent, half-mocking smile which was my shield against the shafts of her contempt and the insulting sallies flung at me by the old woman.

She drank the water at a draught, with the avidity of raging thirst, and let herself fall on the nearest chair, as if utterly overcome. Her attitude, like certain tones of her voice, had in it something masculine: the knees apart in the ample wrapper, the clasped hands hanging between them, her body leaning forward, with drooping head. I stared at the heavy black coil of twisted hair. It was enormous, crowning the bowed head with a crushing and disdained glory. The escaped wisps hung straight down. And suddenly I perceived that the girl was trembling from head to foot, as though that glass of iced water had chilled her to the bone.

'What's the matter now?' I said, startled, but in no very sympathetic mood.

She shook her bowed, overweighted head and cried in a stifled voice but with a rising inflection: 'Go away! Go away! Go away!'

I got up then and approached her, with a strange sort of anxiety. I looked down at her round, strong neck, then stooped low enough to peep at her face. And I began to tremble a little myself.

'What on earth are you gone wild about, Miss Don't Care?'

She flung herself backwards violently, her head going over the back of the chair. And now it was her smooth, full, palpitating throat that lay exposed to my bewildered stare. Her eyes were nearly closed, with only a horrible white gleam under the lids as if she were dead.

'What has come to you?' I asked in awe. 'What are you terrifying yourself with?'

She pulled herself together, her eyes open frightfully wide now. The tropical afternoon was lengthening the shadows on the hot, weary earth, the abode of obscure desires, of extravagant hopes, of unimaginable terrors.

'Never mind! Don't care!' Then, after a gasp, she spoke with such frightful rapidity that I could hardly make out the amazing words: 'For if you were to shut me up in an empty place as smooth all round as the palm of my hand, I could always strangle myself with my hair.'

For a moment, doubting my ears, I let this inconceivable declaration sink into me. It is ever impossible to guess at the wild thoughts that pass through the heads of our fellow-creatures. What monstrous imaginings of violence could have dwelt under the low forehead of that girl who had been taught to regard her father as 'capable of anything' more in the light of a misfortune than that of a disgrace; as, evidently, something to be resented and feared rather than to be ashamed of? She seemed, indeed, as unaware of shame as of anything else in the world; but in her ignorance, her resentment and fear took a childish and violent shape.

443

Of course she spoke without knowing the value of words. What could she know of death – she who knew nothing of life? It was merely as the proof of her being beside herself with some odious apprehension that this extraordinary speech had moved me, not to pity, but to a fascinated, horrified wonder. I had no idea what notion she had of her danger. Some sort of abduction? It was quite possible with the talk of that atrocious old woman. Perhaps she thought she could be carried off, bound hand and foot and even gagged. At that surmise I felt as if the door of a furnace had been opened in front of me.

'Upon my honour!' I cried. 'You shall end by going crazy if you listen to that abominable old aunt of yours – '

I studied her haggard expression, her trembling lips. Her cheeks even seemed sunk a little. But how I, the associate of her disreputable father, the 'lowest of the low' from the criminal Europe, could manage to reassure her I had no conception. She was exasperating.

'Heavens and earth! What do you think I can do?'

'I don't know.'

Her chin certainly trembled. And she was looking at me with extreme attention. I made a step nearer to her chair.

'I shall do nothing. I promise you that. Will that do? Do you understand? I shall do nothing whatever, of any kind; and the day after tomorrow I shall be gone.'

What else could I have said? She seemed to drink in my words with the thirsty avidity with which she had emptied the glass of water. She whispered tremulously, in that touching tone I had heard once before on her lips, and which thrilled me again with the same emotion: 'I would believe you. But what about papa – '

'He be hanged!' My emotion betrayed itself in the brutality of my tone. 'I've had enough of your papa. Are you so stupid as to imagine that I am frightened of him? He can't make me do anything.'

All that sounded feeble to me in the face of her ignorance. But I must conclude that the 'accent of sincerity' has, as some people say, a really irresistible power. The effect was far beyond my hopes – and even beyond my conception. To watch the change in the girl was like watching a miracle – the gradual but swift relaxation of her tense glance, of her stiffened muscles, of every fibre of her body. That black, fixed stare into which I had read a tragic meaning more than once, in which I had found a sombre seduction, was perfectly empty now, void of all consciousness whatever, and not even aware any longer of my presence; it had become a little sleepy, in the Jacobus fashion.

But, man being a perverse animal, instead of rejoicing at my complete success, I beheld it with astounded and indignant eyes. There was something cynical in that unconcealed alteration, the true Jacobus shamelessness. I felt as though I had been cheated in some rather complicated deal into which I had entered against my better judgement. Yes, cheated without any regard for, at least, the forms of decency.

With an easy, indolent, and in its indolence supple, feline movement, she rose from the chair, so provokingly ignoring me now that for very rage I held my ground within less than a foot of her. Leisurely and tranquil, behaving right before me with the ease of a person alone in a room, she extended her beautiful arms, with her hands clenched, her body swaying, her head thrown back a little, revelling contemptuously in a sense of relief, easing her limbs in freedom after all these days of crouching, motionless poses when she had been so furious and so afraid.

All this with supreme indifference, incredible, offensive, exasperating, like ingratitude doubled with treachery.

I ought to have been flattered, perhaps, but, on the contrary, my anger grew; her movement to pass by me as if I were a wooden post or a piece of furniture, that unconcerned movement brought it to a head.

I won't say I did not know what I was doing, but, certainly, cool reflection had nothing to do with the circumstance that next moment both my arms were round her waist. It was an impulsive action, as one snatches at something falling or escaping; and it had no hypocritical gentleness about it either. She had no time to make a sound, and the first kiss I planted on her closed lips was vicious enough to have been a bite.

She did not resist, and of course I did not stop at one. She let me go on, not as if she were inanimate – I felt her there, close against me, young, full of vigour, of life, a strong desirable creature – but as if she did not care in the least, in the absolute assurance of her safety, what I did or left undone. Our faces brought close together in this storm of haphazard caresses, her big, black, wide-open eyes looked into mine without the girl appearing either angry or pleased or moved in any way. In that steady gaze which seemed impersonally to watch my madness I could detect a slight surprise, perhaps – nothing more. I showered kisses upon her face and there did not seem to be any reason why this should not go on for ever.

That thought flashed through my head, and I was on the point of desisting, when, all at once, she began to struggle with a sudden violence which all but freed her instantly, which revived my exasperation with her, indeed a fierce desire never to let her go any more. I tightened my embrace in time, gasping out: 'No – you don't!' as if she were my mortal enemy. On her part not a word was said. Putting her hands against my chest, she pushed with all her might without succeeding to break the circle of my arms. Except that she seemed thoroughly awake now, her eyes gave me no clue whatever. To meet her black stare was like looking into a deep well, and I was totally unprepared for her change of tactics. Instead of trying to tear my hands apart, she flung herself upon my breast and with a downward, undulating, serpentine motion, a quick sliding dive, she got away from me smoothly. It was all very swift; I saw her pick up the tail of her wrapper and run for the door at the end of the verandah not very gracefully. She appeared to be limping a little – and then she vanished; the door swung behind her so noiselessly that I could not believe it was completely closed. I had a distinct suspicion of her black eye being at the crack to watch what I would do. I could not make up my mind whether to shake my fist in that direction or blow a kiss.

SIX

Either would have been perfectly consistent with my feelings. I gazed at the door, hesitating, but in the end I did neither. The monition of some sixth sense – the sense of guilt, maybe, that sense which always acts too late, alas! – warned me to look round; and at once I became aware that the conclusion of this tumultuous episode was likely to be a matter of lively anxiety. Jacobus was standing in the doorway of the dining-room. How long he had been there it was impossible to guess; and remembering my struggle with the girl I thought he must have been its mute witness from beginning to end. But this supposition seemed almost incredible. Perhaps that impenetrable girl had heard him come in and had got away in time.

He stepped on to the verandah in his usual manner, heavy-eyed, with glued lips. I marvelled at the girl's resemblance to this man. Those long, Egyptian eyes, that low forehead of a stupid goddess, she had found in the sawdust of the circus; but all the rest of the face, the design and the modelling, the rounded chin, the very lips – all that was Jacobus, fined down, more finished, more expressive.

His thick hand fell on and grasped with force the back of a light chair (there were several standing about) and I perceived the chance of a broken head at the end of all this – most likely. My mortification was extreme. The scandal would be horrible; that was unavoidable. But how to act so as to satisfy myself I did not know. I stood on my guard and at any rate faced him. There was nothing else for it. Of one thing I was certain – that, however brazen my attitude, it could never equal the characteristic Jacobus impudence.

He gave me his melancholy, glued smile and sat down. I own I was relieved. The perspective of passing from kisses to blows had nothing particularly attractive in it. Perhaps – perhaps he had seen nothing? He behaved as usual, but he had never before found me alone on the verandah.

If he had alluded to it, if he had asked: 'Where's Alice?' or something of the sort, I would have been able to judge from the tone. He would give me no opportunity. The striking peculiarity was that he had never looked up at me yet. 'He knows,' I said to myself confidently. And my contempt for him relieved my disgust with myself.

'You are early home,' I remarked.

'Things are very quiet; nothing doing at the store today,' he explained with a cast-down air.

'Oh, well, you know, I am off,' I said, feeling that this, perhaps, was the best thing to do.

'Yes,' he breathed out. 'Day after tomorrow.'

This was not what I had meant; but as he gazed persistently on the floor, I followed the direction of his glance. In the absolute stillness of the house we stared at the high-heeled slipper the girl had lost in her flight. We stared. It lay overturned.

After what seemed a very long time to me, Jacobus hitched his chair forward, stooped with extended arm and picked it up. It looked a slender thing in his big, thick hands. It was not really a slipper, but a low shoe of blue, glazed kid, rubbed and shabby. It had straps to go over the instep, but the girl only thrust her feet in, after her slovenly manner. Jacobus raised his eyes from the shoe to look at me.

'Sit down, captain,' he said at last, in his subdued tone.

As if the sight of that shoe had renewed the spell, I gave up suddenly the idea of leaving the house there and then. It had become impossible. I sat down, keeping my eyes on the fascinating object. Jacobus turned his daughter's shoe over and over in his cushioned paws as if studying the way the thing was made. He contemplated the thin sole for a time; then, glancing inside with an absorbed air: 'I am glad I found you here, captain.'

I answered this by some sort of grunt, watching him covertly. Then I added: 'You won't have much more of me now.'

He was still deep in the interior of that shoe on which my eyes too were resting.

'Have you thought any more of this deal in potatoes I spoke to you about the other day?'

'No, I haven't,' I answered curtly. He checked my movement to rise by an austere, commanding gesture of the hand holding that fatal shoe. I remained seated and glared at him. 'You know I don't trade.'

'You ought to, captain. You ought to.'

I reflected. If I left that house now I would never see the girl again. And I felt I must see her once more, if only for an instant. It was a need, not to be reasoned with, not to be disregarded. No, I did not want to go away. I wanted to stay for one more experience of that strange provoking sensation of indefinite desire the habit of which had made me – me of all people! – dread the prospect of going to sea.

'Mr Jacobus,' I pronounced slowly. 'Do you really think that upon the whole and taking various matters into consideration – I mean everything, do you understand? – it would be a good thing for me to trade, let us say, with you?'

I waited for a while. He went on looking at the shoe which he held now crushed in the middle, the worn point of the toe and the high heel protruding on each side of his heavy fist.

'That will be all right,' he said, facing me squarely at last.

'Are you sure?'

'You'll find it quite correct, captain.' He had uttered his habitual phrases in his usual placid, breath-saving voice and stood my hard, inquisitive stare sleepily without as much as a wink.

'Then let us trade,' I said, turning my shoulder to him. 'I see you are bent on it.'

I did not want an open scandal, but I thought that outward decency may be bought too dearly at times. I included Jacobus, myself, the whole population of the island, in the same contemptuous disgust as though we had been partners in an ignoble transaction. And the remembered vision at sea, diaphanous and blue, of the Pearl of the Ocean at sixty miles off; the unsubstantial, clear marvel of it as if evoked by the art of a beautiful and pure magic, turned into a thing of horrors too. Was this the fortune this vaporous and rare apparition had held for me in its hard heart, hidden within the shape as of fair dreams and mist? Was this my luck?

'I think' – Jacobus became suddenly audible after what seemed the silence of vile meditation – 'that you might conveniently take some thirty tons. That would be about the lot, captain.'

'Would it? The lot! I dare say it would be convenient, but I haven't got enough money for that.'

I had never seen him so animated.

'No!' he exclaimed with what I took for the accent of grim menace. 'That's a pity.' He paused, then, unrelenting: 'How much money have you got, captain?' he enquired with awful directness.

It was my turn to face him squarely. I did so and mentioned the amount I could dispose of. And I perceived that he was disappointed. He thought it over, his calculating gaze lost in mine, for quite a long time before he came out in a thoughtful tone with the rapacious suggestion: 'You could draw some more from your charterers. That would be quite easy, captain.'

'No, I couldn't,' I retorted brusquely. 'I've drawn my salary up to date, and besides, the ship's accounts are closed.' I was growing furious. I pursued: 'And I'll tell you what: if I *could* do it, I wouldn't.' Then throwing off all restraint, I added: 'You are a bit too much of a Jacobus, Mr Jacobus.'

The tone alone was insulting enough, but he remained tranquil, only a little puzzled, till something seemed to dawn upon him; but the unwonted light in his eyes died out instantly. As a Jacobus on his native heath, what a mere skipper chose to say could not touch him, outcast as he was. As a ship-chandler he could stand anything. All I caught of his mumble was a vague – 'quite correct', than which nothing could have been more egregiously false at bottom – to my view, at least. But I remembered – I had never forgotten – that I must see the girl. I did not mean to go. I meant to stay in the house till I had seen her once more.

'Look here!' I said finally. 'I'll tell you what I'll do. I'll take as many of your confounded potatoes as my money will buy, on condition that you go off at once down to the wharf to see them loaded in the lighter and sent alongside the ship straight away. Take the invoice and a signed receipt with you. Here's the key of my desk. Give it to Burns. He will pay you.

He got up from his chair before I had finished speaking, but he refused to take the key. Burns would never do it. He wouldn't like to ask him even.

'Well, then,' I said, eyeing him slightingly, 'there's nothing for it, Mr Jacobus, but you must wait on board till I come off to settle with you.'

'That will be all right, captain. I will go at once.'

He seemed at a loss what to do with the girl's shoe he was still holding in his fist. Finally, looking dully at me, he put it down on the chair from which he had risen.

'And you, captain? Won't you come along, too, just to see – '

'Don't bother about me. I'll take care of myself.'

He remained perplexed for a moment, as if trying to understand; and then his weighty: 'Certainly, certainly, captain,' seemed to be the outcome of some sudden thought. His big chest heaved. Was it a sigh? As he went out to hurry off those potatoes he never looked back at me.

I waited till the noise of his footsteps had died out of the dining-room, and I waited a little longer. Then turning towards the distant door I raised my voice along the verandah 'Alice!'

Nothing answered me, not even a stir behind the door. Jacobus's house might have been made empty for me to make myself at home in. I did not call again. I had become aware of a great discouragement. I was mentally jaded, morally dejected. I turned to the garden again, sitting down with my elbows spread on the low balustrade, and took my head in my hands.

The evening closed upon me. The shadows lengthened, deepened, mingled together into a pool of twilight in which the flowerbeds glowed like coloured embers; whiffs of heavy scent came to me as if the dusk of this hemisphere were but the dimness of a temple and the garden an enormous censer swinging before the altar of the stars. The colours of the blossoms deepened, losing their glow one by one.

The girl, when I turned my head at a slight noise, appeared to me very tall and slender, advancing with a swaying limp, a floating and uneven motion which ended in the sinking of her shadowy form into the deep low chair. And I don't know why or whence I received the impression that she had come too late. She ought to have appeared at my call. She ought to have . . . It was as if a supreme opportunity had been missed.

I rose and took a seat close to her, nearly opposite her armchair. Her ever discontented voice addressed me at once, contemptuously: 'You are still here.'

I pitched mine low.

'You have come out at last.'

'I came to look for my shoe – before they bring in the lights.'

It was her harsh, enticing whisper, subdued, not very steady, but its low tremulousness gave me no thrill now. I could only make out the oval of her face, her uncovered throat, the long, white gleam of her eyes. She was mysterious enough. Her hands were resting on the arms of the chair. But where was the mysterious and provoking sensation which was like the perfume of her flower-like youth? I said quietly: 'I have got your shoe here.' She made no sound and I continued: 'You had better give me your foot and I will put it on for you.'

She made no movement. I bent low down and groped for her foot under the flounces of the wrapper. She did not withdraw it and I put on the shoe, buttoning the instep-strap. It was an inanimate foot. I lowered it gently to the floor.

'If you buttoned the strap you would not be losing your shoe, Miss Don't Care,' I said, trying to be playful without conviction. I felt more like wailing over the lost illusion of vague desire, over the sudden conviction that I would never find again near her the strange, half-evil, half-tender sensation which had given its acrid flavour to so many days, which had made her appear tragic and promising, pitiful and provoking. That was all over.

'Your father picked it up,' I said, thinking she may just as well be told of the fact.

'I am not afraid of papa – by himself,' she declared scornfully.

'Oh! It's only in conjunction with his disreputable associates, strangers, the "riff-raff of Europe" as your charming aunt or great-aunt says – men like me, for instance – that you – '

'I am not afraid of you,' she snapped out.

'That's because you don't know that I am now doing business with your father. Yes, I am in fact doing exactly what he wants me to do. I've broken my promise to you. That's the sort of man I am. And now – aren't you afraid? If you believe what that dear, kind, truthful old lady says you ought to be.'

It was with unexpected modulated softness that she affirmed: 'No. I am not afraid.' She hesitated . . . 'Not now.'

'Quite right. You needn't be. I shall not see you again before I go to sea.' I rose and stood near her chair. 'But I shall often think of you in this old garden, passing under the trees over there, walking between these gorgeous flowerbeds. You must love this garden – '

'I love nothing.'

I heard in her sullen tone the faint echo of that resentfully tragic note which I had found once so provoking. But it left me unmoved except for a sudden and weary conviction of the emptiness of all things under heaven.

'Goodbye, Alice,' I said.

She did not answer, she did not move. Merely to take her hand, shake it, and go away seemed impossible, almost improper. I stooped without haste and pressed my lips to her smooth forehead. This was the moment when I realised clearly with a sort of terror my complete detachment from that unfortunate creature. And as I lingered in that cruel self-knowledge I felt the light touch of her arms falling languidly on my neck and received a hasty, awkward, haphazard kiss which missed my lips. No! She was not afraid; but I was no longer moved. Her arms slipped off my neck slowly, she made no sound, the deep wicker armchair creaked slightly; only a sense of my dignity prevented me fleeing headlong from that catastrophic revelation.

I traversed the dining-room slowly. I thought: She's listening to my footsteps; she can't help it; she'll hear me open and shut that door. And I closed it as gently behind me as if I had been a thief retreating with his ill-gotten booty. During that stealthy act I experienced the last touch of emotion in that house, at the thought of the girl I had left sitting there in the obscurity, with her heavy hair and empty eyes as black as the night itself, staring into the walled garden, silent, warm, odorous with the perfume of imprisoned flowers, which, like herself, were lost to sight in a world buried in darkness.

The narrow, ill-lighted, rustic streets I knew so well on my way to the harbour were extremely quiet. I felt in my heart that the further one ventures the better one understands how everything in our life is common, short and empty; that it is in seeking the unknown in our sensations that we discover how mediocre are our attempts and how soon defeated! Jacobus's boatman was waiting at the steps with an unusual air of readiness. He put me alongside the ship, but did not give me his confidential: 'Good-evening, sah,' and, instead of shoving off at once, remained holding by the ladder.

I was a thousand miles from commercial affairs, when on the dark quarter-deck Mr Burns positively rushed at me, stammering with excitement. He had been pacing the deck distractedly for hours awaiting my arrival. Just before sunset a lighter loaded with potatoes had come alongside with that fat ship-chandler himself sitting on the pile of sacks. He was now stuck immovable in the cabin. What was the meaning of it all? Surely I did not –

'Yes, Mr Burns, I did,' I cut him short. He was beginning to make gestures of despair when I stopped that, too, by giving him the key of my desk and desiring him, in a tone which admitted of no argument, to go below at once, pay Mr Jacobus's bill, and send him out of the ship.

'I don't want to see him,' I confessed frankly, climbing the poop-ladder. I felt extremely tired. Dropping on the seat of the skylight, I gave myself up to idle gazing at the lights about the quay and at the black mass of the mountain on the south side of the harbour. I never heard Jacobus leave the ship with every single sovereign of my ready cash in his pocket. I never heard anything till, a long time afterwards, Mr Burns, unable to contain himself any longer, intruded upon me with his ridiculously angry lamentations at my weakness and good nature.

'Of course, there's plenty of room in the after-hatch. But they are sure to go rotten down there. Well! I never heard . . . seventeen tons! I suppose I must hoist in that lot first thing tomorrow morning.'

'I suppose you must. Unless you drop them overboard. But I'm afraid you can't do that. I wouldn't mind myself, but it's forbidden to throw rubbish into the harbour, you know.'

'That is the truest word you have said for many a day, sir – rubbish. That's just what I expect they are. Nearly eighty good gold sovereigns gone; a perfectly clean sweep of your drawer, sir. Bless me if I understand!'

As it was impossible to throw the right light on this commercial transaction I left him to his lamentations and under the impression that I was a hopeless fool. Next day I did not go ashore. For one thing, I had no money to go ashore with – no, not enough to buy a cigarette. Jacobus had made a clean sweep. But that was not the only reason. The Pearl of the Ocean had in a few short hours grown odious to me. And I did not want to meet anyone. My reputation had suffered. I knew I was the object of unkind and sarcastic comments.

The following morning at sunrise, just as our stern-fasts had been let go and the tug plucked us out from between the buoys, I saw Jacobus standing up in his boat. The nigger was pulling hard; several baskets of provisions for ships were stowed between the thwarts. The father of Alice was going his morning round. His countenance was tranquil and friendly. He raised his arm and shouted something with great heartiness. But his voice was of the sort that doesn't carry any distance; all I could catch faintly, or rather guess at, were the words 'next time' and 'quite correct'. And it was only of these last that I was certain. Raising my arm perfunctorily for all response, I turned away. I rather resented the familiarity of the thing. Hadn't I settled accounts finally with him by means of that potato bargain?

This being a harbour story it is not my purpose to speak of our passage. I was glad enough to be at sea, but not with the gladness of old days. Formerly

I had no memories to take away with me. I shared in the blessed forget-fulness of sailors, that forgetfulness natural and invincible, which resembles innocence in so far that it prevents self-examination. Now however I remembered the girl. During the first few days I was forever questioning myself as to the nature of facts and sensations connected with her person and with my conduct.

And I must say also that Mr Burns's intolerable fussing with those potatoes was not calculated to make me forget the part which I had played. He looked upon it as a purely commercial transaction of a particularly foolish kind, and his devotion – if it was devotion and not the mere cussedness I came to regard it as before long – inspired him with a zeal to minimise my loss as much as possible. Oh, yes! He took care of those infamous potatoes with a vengeance, as the saying goes.

Everlastingly, there was a tackle over the after-hatch and everlastingly the watch on deck were pulling up, spreading out, picking over, rebagging, and lowering down again, some part of that lot of potatoes. My bargain with all its remotest associations, mental and visual – the garden of flowers and scents, the girl with her provoking contempt and her tragic loneliness of a hopeless castaway – was everlastingly dangled before my eyes, for thousands of miles along the open sea. And as if by a satanic refinement of irony it was accompanied by a most awful smell. Whiffs from decaying potatoes pursued me on the poop, they mingled with my thoughts, with my food, poisoned my very dreams. They made an atmosphere of corruption for the ship.

I remonstrated with Mr Burns about this excessive care. I would have been well content to batten the hatch down and let them perish under the deck.

That perhaps would have been unsafe. The horrid emanations might have flavoured the cargo of sugar. They seemed strong enough to taint the very ironwork. In addition Mr Burns made it a personal matter. He assured me he knew how to treat a cargo of potatoes at sea – had been in the trade as a boy, he said. He meant to make my loss as small as possible. What between his devotion – it must have been devotion – and his vanity, I positively dared not give him the order to throw my commercial-venture overboard. I believe he would have refused point blank to obey my lawful command. An unprecedented and comical situation would have been created with which I did not feel equal to deal.

I welcomed the coming of bad weather as no sailor had ever done. When at last I hove the ship to, to pick up the pilot outside Port Philip Heads, the after-hatch had not been opened for more than a week and I might have believed that no such thing as a potato had ever been on board.

It was an abominable day, raw, blustering, with great squalls of wind and rain; the pilot, a cheery person, looked after the ship and chatted to me, streaming from head to foot; and the heavier the lash of the downpour the more pleased with himself and everything around him he seemed to be. He rubbed his wet hands with a satisfaction, which to me, who had stood that kind of thing for several days and nights, seemed inconceivable in any non-aquatic creature.

'You seem to enjoy getting wet, pilot,' I remarked.

He had a bit of land round his house in the suburbs and it was of his garden he was thinking. At the sound of the word garden, unheard, un-spoken for so many days, I had a vision of gorgeous colour, of sweet scents, of a girlish figure crouching in a chair. Yes. That was a distinct emotion breaking into the peace I had found in the sleepless anxieties of my respon-sibility during a week of dangerous bad weather. The colony, the pilot explained, had suffered from unparalleled drought. This was the first decent drop of water they had had for seven months. The root crops were lost. And, trying to be casual, but with visible interest, he asked me if I had perchance any potatoes to spare.

Potatoes! I had managed to forget them. In a moment I felt plunged into corruption up to my neck. Mr Burns was making eyes at me behind the pilot's back.

Finally, he obtained a ton, and paid ten pounds for it. This was twice the price of my bargain with Jacobus. The spirit of covetousness woke up in me. That night, in harbour, before I slept, the custom-house galley came alongside. While his underlings were putting seals on the storerooms, the officer in charge took me aside confidentially. 'I say, captain, you don't happen to have any potatoes to sell.'

Clearly there was a potato famine in the land. I let him have a ton for twelve pounds and he went away joyfully. That night I dreamt of a pile of gold in the form of a grave in which a girl was buried, and woke up callous with greed. On my calling at my ship-broker's office, that man, after the usual business had been transacted, pushed his spectacles up on his forehead.

'I was thinking, captain, that coming from the Pearl of the Ocean you may have some potatoes to sell.'

I said negligently: 'Oh, yes, I could spare you a ton. Fifteen pounds.'

He exclaimed: 'I say!' But after studying my face for a while accepted my terms with a faint grimace. It seems that these people could not exist without potatoes. I could. I didn't want to see a potato as long as I lived; but the demon of lucre had taken possession of me. How the news got about I don't know, but, returning on board rather late, I found a small group of men of the coster type hanging about the waist, while Mr Burns walked to and fro the quarterdeck loftily, keeping a triumphant eye on them. They had come to buy potatoes.

'These chaps have been waiting here in the sun for hours,' Burns whispered to me excitedly. 'They have drunk the water-cask dry. Don't you throw away your chances, sir. You are too good-natured.'

I selected a man with thick legs and a man with a cast in his eye to negotiate with; simply because they were easily distinguishable from the rest. 'You have the money on you?' I enquired, before taking them down into the cabin.

'Yes, sir,' they answered in one voice, slapping their pockets. I liked their air of quiet determination. Long before the end of the day all the potatoes were sold at about three times the price I had paid for them. Mr Burns, feverish and exulting, congratulated himself on his skilful care of my commercial venture, but hinted plainly that I ought to have made more of it.

That night I did not sleep very well. I thought of Jacobus by fits and starts, between snatches of dreams concerned with castaways starving on a desert island covered with flowers. It was extremely unpleasant. In the morning, tired and unrefreshed, I sat down and wrote a long letter to my owners, giving them a carefully-thought-out scheme for the ship's employment in the East and about the China Seas for the next two years. I spent the day at that task and felt somewhat more at peace when it was done.

Their reply came in due course. They were greatly struck with my project; but considering that, notwithstanding the unfortunate difficulty with the bags (which they trusted I would know how to guard against in the future), the voyage showed a very fair profit, they thought it would be better to keep the ship in the sugar trade – at least for the present.

I turned over the page and read on:

We have had a letter from our good friend Mr Jacobus. We are pleased to see how well you have hit it off with him; for, not to speak of his assistance in the unfortunate matter of the bags, he writes us that should you, by using all possible dispatch, manage to bring the ship back early in the season, he would be able to give us a good rate of freight. We have no doubt that your best endeavours . . . etc., . . . etc.

I dropped the letter and sat motionless for a long time. Then I wrote my answer (it was a short one) and went ashore myself to post it. But I passed one letter-box, then another, and in the end found myself going up Collins Street with the letter still in my pocket – against my heart. Collins Street at four o'clock in the afternoon is not exactly a desert solitude; but I had never felt more isolated from the rest of mankind as when I walked that day its crowded pavement, battling desperately with my thoughts and feeling already vanquished.

There came a moment when the awful tenacity of Jacobus, the man of one passion and of one idea, appeared to me almost heroic. He had not given me up. He had gone again to his odious brother. And then he appeared to me odious himself. Was it for his own sake or for the sake of the poor girl? And on that last supposition the memory of the kiss which missed my lips appalled me; for whatever he had seen, or guessed at, or risked, he knew nothing of that. Unless the girl had told him. How could I go back to fan that fatal spark with my cold breath? No, no, that unexpected kiss had to be paid for at its full price.

At the first letter-box I came to I stopped and reaching into my breast-pocket I took out the letter – it was as if I were plucking out my very heart – and dropped it through the slit. Then I went straight on board.

I wondered what dreams I would have that night; but as it turned out I did not sleep at all. At breakfast I informed Mr Burns that I had resigned my command.

He dropped his knife and fork and looked at me with indignation.

'You have, sir! I thought you loved the ship.'

'So I do, Burns,' I said. 'But the fact is that the Indian Ocean and everything that is in it has lost its charm for me. I am going home as passenger by the Suez Canal.'

'Everything that is in it,' he repeated angrily. 'I've never heard anybody talk like this. And to tell you the truth, sir, all the time we have been together I've never quite made you out. What's one ocean more than another? Charm, indeed!'

He was really devoted to me, I believe. But he cheered up when I told him that I had recommended him for my successor.

'Anyhow,' he remarked, 'let people say what they like, this Jacobus has served your turn. I must admit that this potato business has paid extremely well. Of course, if only you had – '

'Yes, Mr Burns,' I interrupted. 'Quite a smile of fortune.'

But I could not tell him that it was driving me out of the ship I had learned to love. And as I sat heavy-hearted at that parting, seeing all my plans destroyed, my modest future endangered – for this command was like a foot in the stirrup for a young man – he gave up completely for the first time his critical attitude.

'A wonderful piece of luck!' he said.

The Black Mate

A good many years ago there were several ships loading at the Jetty, London Dock. I am speaking here of the 'eighties of the nineteenth century, of the time when London had plenty of fine ships in the docks, though not so many fine buildings in its streets.

The ships at the Jetty were fine enough; they lay one behind the other; and the *Sapphire*, third from the end, was as good as the rest of them, and nothing more. Each ship at the Jetty had, of course, her chief officer on board. So had every other ship in dock.

The policeman at the gates knew them all by sight, without being able to say at once, without thinking, to what ship any particular man belonged. As a matter of fact, the mates of the ships then lying in the London Dock were like the majority of officers in the Merchant Service – a steady, hard-working, staunch, unromantic-looking set of men, belonging to various classes of society, but with the professional stamp obliterating the personal characteristics, which were not very marked anyhow.

This last was true of them all, with the exception of the mate of the *Sapphire*. Of him the policemen could not be in doubt. This one had a presence.

He was noticeable to them in the street from a great distance; and when in the morning he strode down the Jetty to his ship, the lumpers and the dock labourers rolling the bales and trundling the cases of cargo on their hand-trucks would remark to each other: 'Here's the black mate coming along.'

That was the name they gave him, being a gross lot, who could have no appreciation of the man's dignified bearing. And to call him black was the superficial impressionism of the ignorant.

Of course, Mr Bunter, the mate of the *Sapphire*, was not black. He was no more black than you or I, and certainly as white as any chief mate of a ship in the whole of the Port of London. His complexion was of the sort that did not take the tan easily; and I happen to know that the poor fellow had had a month's illness just before he joined the *Sapphire*.

From this you will perceive that I knew Bunter. Of course I knew him. And, what's more, I knew his secret at the time, this secret which – never mind just now. Returning to Bunter's personal appearance, it was nothing but ignorant prejudice on the part of the foreman stevedore to say, as he did in my hearing: 'I bet he's a furriner of some sort.' A man may have black hair without being set down for a dago. I have known a West Country sailor, boatswain of a fine ship, who looked more Spanish than any Spaniard afloat I've ever met. He looked like a Spaniard in a picture.

Competent authorities tell us that this earth is to be finally the inheritance of men with dark hair and brown eyes. It seems that already the great majority of mankind is dark-haired in various shades. But it is only when you meet one that you notice how men with really black hair, black as ebony, are rare. Bunter's hair was absolutely black, black as a raven's wing. He wore, too, all his beard (clipped, but a good length all the same), and his eyebrows were thick and bushy. Add to this steely blue eyes, which in a fair-haired man would have been nothing so extraordinary, but in that sombre framing made a startling contrast, and you will easily understand that Bunter was noticeable enough.

If it had not been for the quietness of his movements, for the general soberness of his demeanour, one would have given him credit for a fiercely passionate nature.

Of course, he was not in his first youth; but if the expression 'in the force of his age' has any meaning, he realised it completely. He was a tall man, too, though rather spare. Seeing him from his poop indefatigably busy with his duties, Captain Ashton, of the clipper ship *Elsinore*, lying just ahead of the *Sapphire*, remarked once to a friend that: 'Johns has got somebody there to hustle his ship along for him.'

Captain Johns, master of the *Sapphire*, having commanded ships for many years, was well known without being much respected or liked. In the company of his fellows he was either neglected or chaffed. The chaffing was generally undertaken by Captain Ashton, a cynical and teasing sort of man. It was Captain Ashton who permitted himself the unpleasant joke of proclaiming once in company that: 'Johns is of the opinion that every sailor above forty years of age ought to be poisoned – shipmasters in actual command excepted.'

It was in a City restaurant, where several well-known shipmasters were having lunch together. There was Captain Ashton, florid and jovial, in a large white waistcoat and with a yellow rose in his buttonhole; Captain Sellers in a sack-coat, thin and pale-faced, with his iron-grey hair tucked behind his ears, and, but for the absence of spectacles, looking like an ascetical mild man of books; Captain Bell, a bluff sea-dog with hairy fingers, in blue serge and a black felt hat pushed far back off his crimson forehead. There was also a very young shipmaster, with a little fair moustache and serious eyes, who said nothing, and only smiled faintly from time to time.

Captain Johns, very much startled, raised his perplexed and credulous glance, which, together with a low and horizontally wrinkled brow, did not make a very intellectual *ensemble*. This impression was by no means mended by the slightly pointed form of his bald head.

Everybody laughed outright, and, thus guided, Captain Johns ended by smiling rather sourly, and attempted to defend himself. It was all very well to joke, but nowadays, when ships, to pay anything at all, had to be driven hard on the passage and in harbour, the sea was no place for elderly men. Only young men and men in their prime were equal to modern conditions of push and hurry. Look at the great firms: almost every single one of them was getting rid of men showing any signs of age. He, for one, didn't want any oldsters on board his ship.

And, indeed, in this opinion Captain Johns was not singular. There was at that time a lot of seamen, with nothing against them but that they were grizzled, wearing out the soles of their last pair of boots on the pavements of the City in the heart-breaking search for a berth.

Captain Johns added with a sort of ill-humoured innocence that from holding that opinion to thinking of poisoning people was a very long step.

This seemed final but Captain Ashton would not let go his joke.

'Oh, yes. I am sure you would. You said distinctly "of no use". What's to be done with men who are "of no use"? You are a kind-hearted fellow, Johns. I am sure that if only you thought it over carefully you would consent to have them poisoned in some painless manner.'

Captain Sellers twitched his thin, sinuous lips.

'Make ghosts of them,' he suggested, pointedly.

At the mention of ghosts Captain Johns became shy, in his perplexed, sly and unlovely manner.

Captain Ashton winked.

'Yes. And then perhaps you would get a chance to have a communication with the world of spirits. Surely the ghosts of seamen should haunt ships. Some of them would be sure to call on an old shipmate.'

Captain Sellers remarked drily: 'Don't raise his hopes like this. It's cruel. He won't see anything. You know, Johns, that nobody has ever seen a ghost.'

At this intolerable provocation Captain Johns came out of his reserve. With no perplexity whatever, but with a positive passion of credulity giving momentary lustre to his dull little eyes, he brought up a lot of authenticated instances. There were books and books full of instances. It was merest ignorance to deny supernatural apparitions. Cases were published every month in a special newspaper. Professor Cranks saw ghosts daily. And Professor Cranks was no small potatoes either. One of the biggest scientific men living. And there was that newspaper fellow – what's his name? – who had a girl-ghost visitor. He printed in his paper things she said to him. And to say there were no ghosts after that! 'Why, they have been photographed! What more proof do you want?'

Captain Johns was indignant. Captain Bell's lips twitched, but Captain Ashton protested now.

'For goodness' sake don't keep him going with that. And by the by, Johns, who's that hairy pirate you've got for your new mate? Nobody in the Dock seems to have seen him before.'

Captain Johns, pacified by the change of subject, answered simply that Willy, the tobacconist at the corner of Fenchurch Street, had sent him along.

Willy, his shop, and the very house in Fenchurch Street, I believe, are gone now. In his time, wearing a careworn, absent-minded look on his pasty face, Willy served with tobacco many southern-going ships out of the Port of London. At certain times of the day the shop would be full of shipmasters. They sat on casks, they lounged against the counter.

Many a youngster found his first lift in life there; many a man got a sorely needed berth by simply dropping in for four pennyworth of birds'-eye at an auspicious moment. Even Willy's assistant, a redheaded, uninterested, delicate-looking young fellow, would hand you across the counter sometimes a bit of valuable intelligence with your box of cigarettes, in a whisper, lips hardly moving, thus: 'The *Bellona*, South Dock. Second officer wanted. You may be in time for it if you hurry up.'

And didn't one just fly!

'Oh, Willy sent him,' said Captain Ashton. 'He's a very striking man. If you were to put a red sash round his waist and a red handkerchief round his head he would look exactly like one of them buccaneering chaps that made men walk the plank and carried women off into captivity. Look out, Johns, he don't cut your throat for you and run off with the *Sapphire*. What ship has he come out of last?'

Captain Johns, after looking up credulously as usual, wrinkled his brow, and said placidly that the man had seen better days. His name was Bunter. 'He's had command of a Liverpool ship, the *Samaria*, some years ago. He lost her in the Indian Ocean, and had his certificate suspended for a year. Ever since then he has not been able to get another command. He's been knocking about in the Western Ocean trade lately.'

'That accounts for him being a stranger to everybody about the Docks,' Captain Ashton concluded as they rose from table.

Captain Johns walked down to the Dock after lunch. He was short of stature and slightly bandy. His appearance did not inspire the generality of mankind with esteem; but it must have been otherwise with his employers. He had the reputation of being an uncomfortable commander, meticulous in trifles, always nursing a grievance of some sort and incessantly nagging. He was not a man to kick up a row with you and be done with it, but to say nasty things in a whining voice; a man capable of making one's life a perfect misery if he took a dislike to an officer.

That very evening I went to see Bunter on board, and sympathised with him on his prospects for the voyage. He was subdued. I suppose a man with a secret locked up in his breast loses his buoyancy. And there was another reason why I could not expect Bunter to show a great elasticity of spirits. For one thing he had been very seedy lately, and besides – but of that later.

Captain Johns had been on board that afternoon and had loitered and dodged about his chief mate in a manner which had annoyed Bunter exceedingly.

'What could he mean?' he asked with calm exasperation. 'One would think he suspected I had stolen something and tried to see in what pocket I had stowed it away; or that somebody told him I had a tail and he wanted to find out how I managed to conceal it. I don't like to be approached from behind several times in one afternoon in that creepy way and then to be looked up at suddenly in front from under my elbow. Is it a new sort of peep-bo game? It doesn't amuse me. I am no longer a baby.'

I assured him that if anyone were to tell Captain Johns that he – Bunter – had a tail, Johns would manage to get himself to believe the story in some mysterious manner. He would. He was suspicious and credulous to an inconceivable degree. He would believe any silly tale, suspect any man of anything, and crawl about with it and ruminate the stuff, and turn it over and over in his mind in the most miserable, inwardly whining perplexity. He would take the meanest possible view in the end, and discover the meanest possible course of action by a sort of natural genius for that sort of thing.

Bunter also told me that the mean creature had crept all over the ship on his little, bandy legs, taking him along to grumble and whine to about a lot of trifles. Crept about the decks like a wretched insect – like a cockroach, only not so lively.

Thus did the self-possessed Bunter express himself with great disgust. Then, going on with his usual stately deliberation, made sinister by the frown of his jet-black eyebrows: 'And the fellow is mad, too. He tried to be sociable for a bit, and could find nothing else but to make big eyes at me, and ask me if I believed "in communication beyond the grave". Communication beyond – I didn't know what he meant at first. I didn't know what to say. "A very solemn subject, Mr Bunter," says he. I've given a great deal of study to it.'

Had Johns lived on shore he would have been the predestined prey of fraudulent mediums; or even if he had had any decent opportunities between the voyages. Luckily for him, when in England, he lived somewhere far away in Leytonstone, with a maiden sister ten years older than himself, a fearsome virago twice his size, before whom he trembled. It was said she bullied him terribly in general; and in the particular instance of his spiritualistic leanings she had her own views.

These leanings were to her simply satanic. She was reported as having declared that, 'With God's help, she would prevent that fool from giving himself up to the Devil.' It was beyond doubt that Johns's secret ambition was to get into personal communication with the spirits of the dead – if only his sister would let him. But she was adamant. I was told that while in London he had to account to her for every penny of the money he took with him in the morning, and for every hour of his time. And she kept the bankbook, too.

Bunter (he had been a wild youngster, but he was well connected; had ancestors; there was a family tomb somewhere in the home counties) – Bunter was indignant, perhaps on account of his own dead. Those steely-blue eyes of his flashed with positive ferocity out of that black-bearded face. He impressed me – there was so much dark passion in his leisurely contempt.

'The cheek of the fellow! Enter into relations with . . . A mean little cad like this! It would be an impudent intrusion. He wants to enter! . . . What is it? A new sort of snobbishness or what?'

I laughed outright at this original view of spiritism – or whatever the ghost craze is called. Even Bunter himself condescended to smile. But it was an austere, quickly vanished smile. A man in his almost, I may say, tragic position couldn't be expected – you understand. He was really worried. He was ready eventually to put up with any dirty trick in the course of the voyage. A man could not expect much consideration should he find himself at the mercy of a fellow like Johns. A misfortune is a misfortune, and there's an end of it. But to be bored by mean, low-spirited, inane ghost stories in the Johns style, all the way out to Calcutta and back again, was an intolerable apprehension to be under. Spiritism was indeed a solemn subject to think about in that light. Dreadful, even!

Poor fellow! Little we both thought that before very long he himself . . . However, I could give him no comfort. I was rather appalled myself.

Bunter had also another annoyance that day. A confounded berthing master came on board on some pretence or other, but in reality, Bunter thought, simply impelled by an inconvenient curiosity – inconvenient to Bunter, that is. After some beating about the bush, that man suddenly said: 'I can't help thinking I've seen you before somewhere, Mr Mate. If I heard your name, perhaps – '

That's the worst of a life with a mystery in it – he was much alarmed. It was very likely that the man had seen him before – worse luck to his excellent memory. Bunter himself could not be expected to remember every casual dock walloper he might have had to do with. Bunter brazened it out by turning upon the man, making use of that impressive, black-as-night sternness of expression his unusual hair furnished him with. 'My name's Bunter, sir. Does that enlighten your inquisitive intellect? And I don't ask what your name may be. I don't want to know. I've no use for it, sir. An individual who calmly tells me to my face that he is *not sure* if he has seen me before, either means to be impudent or is no better than a worm, sir. Yes, I said a worm – a blind worm!'

Brave Bunter. That was the line to take. He fairly drove the beggar out of the ship, as if every word had been a blow. But the pertinacity of that brass-bound Paul Pry was astonishing. He cleared out of the ship, of course, before Bunter's ire, not saying anything, and only trying to cover up his retreat by a sickly smile. But once on the Jetty he turned deliberately round, and set himself to stare in dead earnest at the ship. He remained planted there like a mooring-post, absolutely motionless, and with his stupid eyes winking no more than a pair of cabin portholes.

What could Bunter do? It was awkward for him, you know. He could not go and put his head into the bread-locker. What he did was to take up a position abaft the mizzen-rigging, and stare back as unwinking as the other. So they remained, and I don't know which of them grew giddy first; but the man on the Jetty, not having the advantage of something to hold on to, got tired the soonest, flung his arm, giving the contest up, as it were, and went away at last.

Bunter told me he was glad the *Sapphire*, 'that gem amongst ships' as he alluded to her sarcastically, was going to sea next day. He had had enough of the Dock. I understood his impatience. He had steeled himself against any possible worry the voyage might bring, though it is clear enough now that he was not prepared for the extraordinary experience that was awaiting him already, and in no other part of the world than the Indian Ocean itself; the very part of the world where the poor fellow had lost his ship and had broken his luck, as it seemed for good and all, at the same time.

As to his remorse in regard to a certain secret action of his life, well, I understand that a man of Bunter's fine character would suffer not a little. Still, between ourselves, and without the slightest wish to be cynical, it cannot be denied that with the noblest of us the fear of being found out enters for some considerable part into the composition of remorse. I didn't say this in so many words to Bunter, but, as the poor fellow harped a bit on it, I told him that there were skeletons in a good many honest cupboards, and that, as to his own particular guilt, it wasn't writ large on his face for everybody to see – so he needn't worry as to that. And besides, he would be gone to sea in about twelve hours from now.

He said there was some comfort in that thought, and went off then to spend his last evening for many months with his wife. For all his wildness, Bunter had made no mistake in his marrying. He had married a lady. A perfect lady. She was a dear little woman, too. As to her pluck, I, who know what times they had to go through, I cannot admire her enough for it. Real, hard-wearing, everyday and day-after-day pluck that only a woman is capable of when she is of the right sort – the undismayed sort I would call it.

The black mate felt this parting with his wife more than any of the previous ones in all the years of bad luck. But she was of the undismayed kind, and showed less trouble in her gentle face than the black-haired, buccaneer-like, but dignified mate of the *Sapphire*. It may be that her conscience was less disturbed than her husband's. Of course, his life had no secret places for her; but a woman's conscience is somewhat more resourceful in finding good and valid excuses. It depends greatly on the person that needs them, too.

They had agreed that she should not come down to the Dock to see him off. 'I wonder you care to look at me at all,' said the sensitive man. And she did not laugh.

Bunter was very sensitive; he left her rather brusquely at the last. He got on board in good time, and produced the usual impression on the mud-pilot in the broken-down straw hat who took the *Sapphire* out of dock. The river-man was very polite to the dignified, striking-looking chief mate. 'The five-inch manilla for the check-rope, Mr – Bunter, thank you – Mr Bunter, please.' The sea-pilot who left the 'gem of ships' heading comfortably down Channel off Dover told some of his friends that, this voyage, the *Sapphire* had for chief mate a man who seemed a jolly sight too good for old Johns. 'Bunter's his name. I wonder where he's sprung from? Never seen him before in any ship I piloted in or out all these years. He's the sort of man you don't forget. You couldn't. A thorough good sailor, too. And won't old Johns just worry his head off! Unless the old fool should take fright at him – for he does not seem the sort of man that would let himself be put upon without letting you know what he thinks of you. And that's exactly what old Johns would be more afraid of than of anything else.'

As this is really meant to be the record of a spiritualistic experience which came, if not precisely to Captain Johns himself, at any rate to his ship, there is no use in recording the other events of the passage out. It was an ordinary passage, the crew was an ordinary crew, the weather was of the usual kind. The black mate's quiet, sedate method of going to work had given a sober tone to the life of the ship. Even in gales of wind everything went on quietly somehow.

There was only one severe blow which made things fairly lively for all hands for full four-and-twenty hours. That was off the coast of Africa, after passing the Cape of Good Hope. At the very height of it several heavy seas were shipped with no serious results, but there was a considerable smashing of breakable objects in the pantry and in the staterooms. Mr Bunter, who was so greatly respected on board, found himself treated scurvily by the Southern Ocean, which, bursting open the door of his room like a ruffianly burglar, carried off several useful things, and made all the others extremely wet.

Later, on the same day, the Southern Ocean caused the *Sapphire* to lurch over in such an unrestrained fashion that the two drawers fitted under Mr Bunter's sleeping-berth flew out altogether, spilling all their contents. They ought, of course, to have been locked, and Mr Bunter had only to thank himself for what had happened. He ought to have turned the key on each before going out on deck.

His consternation was very great. The steward, who was paddling about all the time with swabs, trying to dry out the flooded cuddy, heard him exclaim 'Hallo!' in a startled and dismayed tone. In the midst of his work the steward felt a sympathetic concern for the mate's distress.

Captain Johns was secretly glad when he heard of the damage. He was indeed afraid of his chief mate, as the sea-pilot had ventured to foretell, and afraid of him for the very reason the sea-pilot had put forward as likely.

Captain Johns, therefore, would have liked very much to hold that black mate of his at his mercy in some way or other. But the man was irreproachable, as near absolute perfection as could be. And Captain Johns was much annoyed, and at the same time congratulated himself on his chief officer's efficiency.

He made a great show of living sociably with him, on the principle that the more friendly you are with a man the more easily you may catch him tripping; and also for the reason that he wanted to have somebody who would listen to his stories of manifestations, apparitions, ghosts, and all the rest of the imbecile spook-lore. He had it all at his fingers' ends; and he spun those ghostly yarns in a persistent, colourless voice, giving them a futile turn peculiarly his own.

'I like to converse with my officers,' he used to say. 'There are masters that hardly ever open their mouths from beginning to end of a passage for fear of losing their dignity. What's that, after all – this bit of position a man holds!'

His sociability was most to be dreaded in the second dog-watch, because he was one of those men who grow lively towards the evening, and the officer on duty was unable then to find excuses for leaving the poop. Captain Johns would pop up the companion suddenly, and, sidling up in his creeping way to poor Bunter, as he walked up and down, would fire into him some spiritualistic proposition, such as: 'Spirits, male and female, show a good deal of refinement in a general way, don't they?'

To which Bunter, holding his black-whiskered head high, would mutter: 'I don't know.'

'Ah! that's because you don't want to. You are the most obstinate, prejudiced man I've ever met, Mr Bunter. I told you you may have any book out of my bookcase. You may just go into my stateroom and help yourself to any volume.'

And if Bunter protested that he was too tired in his watches below to spare any time for reading, Captain Johns would smile nastily behind his back, and remark that of course some people needed more sleep than others to keep themselves fit for their work. If Mr Bunter was afraid of not keeping properly awake when on duty at night, that was another matter.

'But I think you borrowed a novel to read from the second mate the other day – a trashy pack of lies,' Captain Johns sighed. 'I am afraid you are not a spiritually minded man, Mr Bunter. That's what's the matter.'

Sometimes he would appear on deck in the middle of the night, looking very grotesque and bandy-legged in his sleeping suit. At that sight the persecuted Bunter would wring his hands stealthily, and break out into moisture all over his forehead. After standing sleepily by the binnacle, scratching himself in an unpleasant manner, Captain Johns was sure to start on some aspect or other of his only topic.

He would, for instance, discourse on the improvement of morality to be expected from the establishment of general and close intercourse with the spirits of the departed. The spirits, Captain Johns thought, would consent to associate familiarly with the living if it were not for the unbelief of the great mass of mankind. He himself would not care to have anything to do with a crowd that would not believe in his – Captain Johns's – existence. Then why should a spirit? This was asking too much.

He went on breathing hard by the binnacle and trying to reach round his shoulder-blades; then, with a thick, drowsy severity, declared: 'Incredulity, sir, is the evil of the age!'

It rejected the evidence of Professor Cranks and of the journalist chap. It resisted the production of photographs.

For Captain Johns believed firmly that certain spirits had been photographed. He had read something of it in the papers. And the idea of it having been done had got a tremendous hold on him, because his mind was not critical. Bunter said afterwards that nothing could be more weird than this little man, swathed in a sleeping suit three sizes too large for him, shuffling with excitement in the moonlight near the wheel, and shaking his fist at the serene sea.

'Photographs! photographs!' he would repeat, in a voice as creaky as a rusty hinge.

The very helmsman just behind him got uneasy at that performance, not being capable of understanding exactly what the 'old man was kicking up a row with the mate about'.

Then Johns, after calming down a bit, would begin again.

'The sensitised plate can't lie. No, sir.'

Nothing could be more funny than this ridiculous little man's conviction – his dogmatic tone. Bunter would go on swinging up and down the poop like a deliberate, dignified pendulum. He said not a word. But the poor fellow had not a trifle on his conscience, as you know; and to have imbecile ghosts rammed down his throat like this on top of his own worry nearly drove him crazy. He knew that on many occasions he was on the verge of lunacy, because he could not help indulging in half-delirious visions of Captain Johns being picked up by the scruff of the neck and dropped over the taffrail into the ship's wake – the sort of thing no sane sailorman would think of doing to a cat or any other animal, anyhow. He imagined him bobbing up – a tiny black speck left far astern on the moonlit ocean.

I don't think that even at the worst moments Bunter really desired to drown Captain Johns. I fancy that all his disordered imagination longed for was merely to stop the ghostly inanity of the skipper's talk.

But, all the same, it was a dangerous form of self-indulgence. Just picture to yourself that ship in the Indian Ocean, on a clear, tropical night, with her sails full and still, the watch on deck stowed away out of sight; and on her poop, flooded with moonlight, the stately black mate walking up and down with measured, dignified steps, preserving an awful silence, and that grotesquely mean little figure in striped flannelette alternately creaking and droning of 'personal intercourse beyond the grave'.

It makes me creepy all over to think of. And sometimes the folly of Captain Johns would appear clothed in a sort of weird utilitarianism. How useful it would be if the spirits of the departed could be induced to take a practical interest in the affairs of the living! What a help, say, to the police, for instance, in the detection of crime! The number of murders, at any rate, would be considerably reduced, he guessed with an air of great sagacity. Then he would give way to grotesque discouragement.

Where was the use of trying to communicate with people that had no faith, and more likely than not would scorn the offered information? Spirits had their feelings. They were *all* feelings in a way. But he was surprised at the forbearance shown towards murderers by their victims. That was the sort of apparition that no guilty man would dare to pooh-pooh. And perhaps the undiscovered murderers – whether believing or not – were haunted. They wouldn't be likely to boast about it, would they?

'For myself,' he pursued, in a sort of vindictive, malevolent whine, 'if anybody murdered me I would not let him forget it. I would wither him up – I would terrify him to death.'

The idea of his skipper's ghost terrifying anyone was so ludicrous that the black mate, little disposed to mirth as he was, could not help giving vent to a weary laugh.

And this laugh, the only acknowledgment of a long and earnest discourse, offended Captain Johns.

'What's there to laugh at in this conceited manner, Mr Bunter?' he snarled. 'Supernatural visitations have terrified better men than you. Don't you allow me enough soul to make a ghost of?'

I think it was the nasty tone that caused Bunter to stop short and turn about.

'I shouldn't wonder,' went on the angry fanatic of spiritism, 'if you weren't one of them people that take no more account of a man than if he were a beast. You would be capable, I don't doubt, to deny the possession of an immortal soul to your own father.'

And then Bunter, being bored beyond endurance, and also exasperated by the private worry, lost his self-possession.

He walked up suddenly to Captain Johns, and, stooping a little to look close into his face, said, in a low, even tone: 'You don't know what a man like me is capable of.'

Captain Johns threw his head back, but was too astonished to budge. Bunter resumed his walk; and for a long time his measured footsteps and the low wash of the water alongside were the only sounds which troubled the silence brooding over the great waters. Then Captain Johns cleared his throat uneasily, and, after sidling away towards the companion for greater safety, plucked up enough courage to retreat under an act of authority: 'Raise the starboard clew of the mainsail, and lay the yards dead square, Mr Bunter. Don't you see the wind is nearly right aft?'

Bunter at once answered: 'Ay, ay, sir,' though there was not the slightest necessity to touch the yards, and the wind was well out on the quarter. While he was executing the order Captain Johns hung on the companion-steps, growling to himself: 'Walk this poop like an admiral and don't even notice when the yards want trimming!' – loud enough for the helmsman to overhear. Then he sank slowly backwards out of the man's sight; and when he reached the bottom of the stairs he stood still and thought.

'He's an awful ruffian, with all his gentlemanly airs. No more gentleman mates for me.'

Two nights afterwards he was slumbering peacefully in his berth, when a heavy thumping just above his head (a well-understood signal that he was wanted on deck) made him leap out of bed, broad awake in a moment.

'What's up?' he muttered, running out barefooted. On passing through the cabin he glanced at the clock. It was the middle watch. 'What on earth can the mate want me for?' he thought.

Bolting out of the companion, he found a clear, dewy moonlit night and a strong, steady breeze. He looked around wildly. There was no one on the poop except the helmsman, who addressed him at once.

'It was me, sir. I let go the wheel for a second to stamp over your head. I am afraid there's something wrong with the mate.'

'Where's he got to?' asked the captain sharply.

The man, who was obviously nervous, said 'The last I saw of him was as he fell down the port poop-ladder.'

'Fell down the poop-ladder! What did he do that for? What made him?'

'I don't know, sir. He was walking the port side. Then just as he turned towards me to come aft . . . '

'You saw him?' interrupted the captain.

'I did. I was looking at him. And I heard the crash, too – something awful. Like the mainmast going overboard. It was as if something had struck him.'

Captain Johns became very uneasy and alarmed. 'Come,' he said sharply. 'Did anybody strike him? What did you see?'

'Nothing, sir, so help me! There was nothing to see. He just gave a little sort of hallo! threw his hands before him, and over he went – crash. I couldn't hear anything more, so I just let go the wheel for a second to call you up.'

'You're scared!' said Captain Johns.

'I am, sir, straight!'

Captain Johns stared at him. The silence of his ship driving on her way seemed to contain a danger – a mystery. He was reluctant to go and look for his mate himself, in the shadows of the main-deck, so quiet, so still.

All he did was to advance to the break of the poop, and call for the watch. As the sleepy men came trooping aft, he shouted to them fiercely: 'Look at the foot of the port poop-ladder, some of you! See the mate lying there?'

Their startled exclamations told him immediately that they did see him. Somebody even screeched out emotionally: 'He's dead!'

Mr Bunter was laid in his bunk and when the lamp in his room was lit he looked indeed as if he were dead, but it was obvious also that he was breathing yet. The steward had been roused out, the second mate called and sent on deck to look after the ship, and for an hour or so Captain Johns devoted himself silently to the restoring of consciousness. Mr Bunter at last opened his eyes, but he could not speak. He was dazed and inert. The steward bandaged a nasty scalp-wound while Captain Johns held an additional light. They had to cut away a lot of Mr Bunter's jet-black hair to make a good dressing. This done, and after gazing for a while at their patient, the two left the cabin.

'A rum go, this, steward,' said Captain Johns in the passage.

'Yessir.'

'A sober man that's right in his head does not fall down a poop-ladder like a sack of potatoes. The ship's as steady as a church.'

'Yessir. Fit of some kind, I shouldn't wonder.'

'Well, I should. He doesn't look as if he were subject to fits and giddiness. Why, the man's in the prime of life. I wouldn't have another kind of mate – not if I knew it. You don't think he has a private store of liquor, do you, eh? He seemed to me a bit strange in his manner several times lately. Off his feed, too, a bit, I noticed.'

'Well, sir, if he ever had a bottle or two of grog in his cabin, that must have gone a long time ago. I saw him throw some broken glass overboard after the last gale we had; but that didn't amount to anything. Anyway, sir, you couldn't call Mr Bunter a drinking man.'

'No,' conceded the captain, reflectively. And the steward, locking the pantry door, tried to escape out of the passage, thinking he could manage to snatch another hour of sleep before it was time for him to turn out for the day.

Captain Johns shook his head.

'There's some mystery there.'

'There's special providence that he didn't crack his head like an eggshell on the quarter-deck mooring-bits, sir. The men tell me he couldn't have missed them by more than an inch.'

And the steward vanished skilfully.

Captain Johns spent the rest of the night and the whole of the ensuing day between his own room and that of the mate.

In his own room he sat with his open hands reposing on his knees, his lips pursed up, and the horizontal furrows on his forehead marked very heavily. Now and then raising his arm by a slow, as if cautious, movement, he scratched lightly the top of his bald head. In the mate's room he stood for long periods of time with his hand to his lips, gazing at the half-conscious man.

For three days Mr Bunter did not say a single word. He looked at people sensibly enough but did not seem to be able to hear any questions put to him. They cut off some more of his hair and swathed his head in wet cloths. He took some nourishment, and was made as comfortable as possible. At dinner on the third day the second mate remarked to the captain, in connection with the affair: 'These half-round brass plates on the steps of the poop-ladders are beastly dangerous things!'

'Are they?' retorted Captain Johns, sourly. 'It takes more than a brass plate to account for an able-bodied man crashing down in this fashion like a felled ox.'

The second mate was impressed by that view. There was something in that, he thought.

'And the weather fine, everything dry, and the ship going along as steady as a church!' pursued Captain Johns, gruffly.

As Captain Johns continued to look extremely sour, the second mate did not open his lips any more during the dinner. Captain Johns was annoyed and hurt by an innocent remark, because the fitting of the aforesaid brass plates had been done at his suggestion only the voyage before, in order to smarten up the appearance of the poop-ladders.

On the fourth day Mr Bunter looked decidedly better; very languid yet, of course, but he heard and understood what was said to him, and even could say a few words in a feeble voice.

Captain Johns, coming in, contemplated him attentively, without much visible sympathy.

'Well, can you give us your account of this accident, Mr Bunter?'

Bunter moved slightly his bandaged head, and fixed his cold blue stare on Captain Johns's face, as if taking stock and appraising the value of every feature: the perplexed forehead, the credulous eyes, the inane droop of the mouth. And he gazed so long that Captain Johns grew restive, and looked over his shoulder at the door.

'No accident,' breathed out Bunter, in a peculiar tone.

'You don't mean to say you've got the falling sickness,' said Captain Johns. 'How would you call it signing as chief mate of a clipper ship with a thing like that on you?'

Bunter answered him only by a sinister look.

The skipper shuffled his feet a little. 'Well, what made you have that tumble, then?'

Bunter raised himself a little, and looking straight into Captain Johns's eyes said, in a very distinct whisper: 'You – were – right!'

He fell back and closed his eyes. Not a word more could Captain Johns get out of him; and, the steward coming into the cabin, the skipper withdrew.

But that very night, unobserved, Captain Johns, opening the door cautiously, entered again the mate's cabin. He could wait no longer. The suppressed eagerness, the excitement expressed in all his mean, creeping little person, did not escape the chief mate, who was lying awake, looking frightfully pulled down and perfectly impassive.

'You are coming to gloat over me, I suppose,' said Bunter without moving, and yet making a palpable hit.

'Bless my soul!' exclaimed Captain Johns with a start, and assuming a sobered demeanour. 'There's a thing to say!'

'Well, gloat, then! You and your ghosts, you've managed to get over a live man.'

This was said by Bunter without stirring, in a low voice, and with not much expression.

'Do you mean to say,' enquired Captain Johns, in awe-struck whisper, 'that you had a supernatural experience that night? You saw an apparition, then, on board my ship?'

Reluctance, shame, disgust, would have been visible on poor Bunter's countenance if the great part of it had not been swathed up in cotton-wool and bandages. His ebony eyebrows, more sinister than ever amongst all that lot of white linen, came together in a frown as he made a mighty effort to say: 'Yes, I have seen one.'

The wretchedness in his eyes would have awakened the compassion of any other man than Captain Johns. But Captain Johns was all agog with triumphant excitement. He was just a little bit frightened, too. He looked at that unbelieving scoffer laid low, and did not even dimly guess at his profound, humiliating distress. He was not generally capable of taking much part in the anguish of his fellow-creatures. This time, moreover, he was excessively anxious to know what had happened. Fixing his credulous eyes on the bandaged head, he asked, trembling slightly: 'And did it – did it knock you down?'

'Come! am I the sort of man to be knocked down by a ghost?' protested Bunter in a little stronger tone. 'Don't you remember what you said yourself the other night? Better men than me – Ha! you'll have to look a long time before you find a better man for a mate of your ship.'

Captain Johns pointed a solemn finger at Bunter's bedplace.

'You've been terrified,' he said. 'That's what's the matter. You've been terrified. Why, even the man at the wheel was scared, though he couldn't see anything. He *felt* the supernatural. You are punished for your incredulity, Mr Bunter. You were terrified.'

'And suppose I was,' said Bunter. 'Do you know what I had seen? Can you conceive the sort of ghost that would haunt a man like me? Do you think it was a ladyish, afternoon-call, another-cup-of-tea-please apparition that visits your Professor Cranks and that journalist chap you are always talking about? No; I can't tell you what it was like. Every man has his own ghosts. You couldn't conceive . . .'

Bunter stopped, out of breath; and Captain Johns remarked, with the glow of inward satisfaction reflected in his tone: 'I've always thought you were the sort of man that was ready for anything; from pitch-and-toss to wilful murder, as the saying goes. Well, well! So you were terrified.'

'I stepped back,' said Bunter, curtly. 'I don't remember anything else.'

'The man at the wheel told me you went backwards as if something had hit you.'

'It was a sort of inward blow,' explained Bunter. 'Something too deep for you, Captain Johns, to understand. Your life and mine haven't been the same. Aren't you satisfied to see me converted?'

'And you can't tell me any more?' asked Captain Johns, anxiously.

'No, I can't. I wouldn't. It would be no use if I did. That sort of experience must be gone through. Say I am being punished. Well, I take my punishment, but talk of it I won't.'

'Very well,' said Captain Johns; 'you won't. But, mind, I can draw my own conclusions from that.'

'Draw what you like; but be careful what you say, sir. You don't terrify me. *You* aren't a ghost.'

'One word. Has it any connection with what you said to me on that last night, when we had a talk together on spiritualism?'

Bunter looked weary and puzzled.

'What did I say?'

'You told me that I couldn't know what a man like you was capable of.'

'Yes, yes. Enough!'

'Very good. I am fixed, then,' remarked Captain Johns. 'All I say is that I am jolly glad not to be you, though I would have given almost anything for the privilege of personal communication with the world of spirits. Yes, sir, but not in that way.'

Poor Bunter moaned pitifully. 'It has made me feel twenty years older.'

Captain Johns retired quietly. He was delighted to observe this over-bearing ruffian humbled to the dust by the moralising agency of the spirits. The whole occurrence was a source of pride and gratification; and he began to feel a sort of regard for his chief mate.

It is true that in further interviews Bunter showed himself very mild and deferential. He seemed to cling to his captain for spiritual protection. He used to send for him, and say, 'I feel so nervous,' and Captain Johns would stay patiently for hours in the hot little cabin, and feel proud of the call.

For Mr Bunter was ill, and could not leave his berth for a good many days. He became a convinced spiritualist, not enthusiastically – that could hardly have been expected from him – but in a grim, unshakable way. He could not be called exactly friendly to the disembodied inhabitants of our globe, as Captain Johns was. But he was now a firm, if gloomy, recruit of spiritualism.

One afternoon, as the ship was already well to the north in the Gulf of Bengal, the steward knocked at the door of the captain's cabin, and said, without opening it: 'The mate asks if you could spare him a moment, sir. He seems to be in a state in there.'

Captain Johns jumped up from the couch at once.

'Yes. Tell him I am coming.'

He thought: Could it be possible there had been another spiritual manifestation – in the daytime, too!

He revelled in the hope. It was not exactly that, however. Still, Bunter, whom he saw sitting collapsed in a chair – he had been up for several days, but not on deck as yet – poor Bunter had something startling enough to communicate. His hands covered his face. His legs were stretched straight out, dismally.

'What's the news now?' croaked Captain Johns, not unkindly, because in truth it always pleased him to see Bunter – as he expressed it – tamed.

'News!' exclaimed the crushed sceptic through his hands. 'Ay, news enough, Captain Johns. Who will be able to deny the awfulness, the genuineness? Another man would have dropped dead. You want to know what I had seen. All I can tell you is that since I've seen it my hair is turning white.'

Bunter detached his hands from his face, and they hung on each side of his chair as if dead. He looked broken in the dusky cabin.

'You don't say!' stammered out Captain Johns. 'Turned white! Hold on a bit! I'll light the lamp!'

When the lamp was lit, the startling phenomenon could be seen plainly enough. As if the dread, the horror, the anguish of the supernatural were being exhaled through the pores of his skin, a sort of silvery mist seemed to cling to the cheeks and the head of the mate. His short beard, his cropped hair, were growing, not black, but grey – almost white.

When Mr Bunter, thin-faced and shaky, came on deck for duty, he was clean-shaven, and his head was white. The hands were awe-struck. 'Another man,' they whispered to each other. It was generally and mysteriously agreed that the mate had 'seen something', with the exception of the man at the wheel at the time, who maintained that the mate was 'struck by something'.

This distinction hardly amounted to a difference. On the other hand, everybody admitted that, after he picked up his strength a bit, he seemed even smarter in his movements than before.

One day in Calcutta, Captain Johns, pointing out to a visitor his white-headed chief mate standing by the main-hatch, was heard to say oracularly: 'That man's in the prime of life.'

Of course, while Bunter was away, I called regularly on Mrs Bunter every Saturday, just to see whether she had any use for my services. It was understood I would do that. She had just his half-pay to live on – it amounted to about a pound a week. She had taken one room in a quiet little square in the East End.

And this was affluence to what I had heard that the couple were reduced to for a time after Bunter had to give up the Western Ocean trade – he used to go as mate of all sorts of hard packets after he lost his ship and his luck together – it was affluence to that time when Bunter would start at seven o'clock in the morning with but a glass of hot water and a crust of dry bread. It won't stand thinking about, especially for those who know Mrs Bunter. I had seen something of them, too, at that time; and it just makes me shudder to remember what that born lady had to put up with. Enough!

Dear Mrs Bunter used to worry a good deal after the *Sapphire* left for Calcutta. She would say to me: 'It must be so awful for poor Winston' – Winston is Bunter's name – and I tried to comfort her the best I could. Afterwards, she got some small children to teach in a family, and was half the day with them, and the occupation was good for her.

In the very first letter she had from Calcutta, Bunter told her he had had a fall down the poop-ladder, and cut his head, but no bones broken, thank God. That was all. Of course, she had other letters from him, but that vagabond Bunter never gave me a scratch of the pen the solid eleven months. I supposed, naturally, that everything was going on all right. Who could imagine what was happening?

Then one day dear Mrs Bunter got a letter from a legal firm in the City, advising her that her uncle was dead – her old curmudgeon of an uncle – a retired stockbroker, a heartless, petrified antiquity that had lasted on and on. He was nearly ninety, I believe; and if I were to meet his venerable ghost this minute, I would try to take him by the throat and strangle him.

The old beast would never forgive his niece for marrying Bunter; and years afterwards, when people made a point of letting him know that she was in London, pretty nearly starving at forty years of age, he only said: 'Serve the little fool right!' I believe he meant her to starve. And, lo and behold, the old cannibal died intestate, with no other relatives but that very identical little fool. The Bunters were wealthy people now.

Of course, Mrs Bunter wept as if her heart would break. In any other woman it would have been mere hypocrisy. Naturally, too, she wanted to cable the news to her Winston in Calcutta, but I showed her, *Gazette* in hand, that the ship had been on the homeward-bound list for more than a week already. So we sat down to wait, and talked meantime of dear old Winston every day. There were just one hundred such days before the *Sapphire* got reported 'All well' in the chops of the Channel by an incoming mailboat.

'I am going to Dunkirk to meet him,' says she. The *Sapphire* had a cargo of jute for Dunkirk. Of course, I had to escort the dear lady in the quality of her 'ingenious friend'. She calls me 'our ingenious friend' to this day; and I've observed some people – strangers – looking hard at me, for the signs of the ingenuity, I suppose.

After settling Mrs Bunter in a good hotel in Dunkirk, I walked down to the docks – late afternoon it was – and what was my surprise to see the ship actually fast alongside. Either Johns or Bunter, or both, must have been driving her hard up Channel. Anyway, she had been in since the day before last, and her crew was already paid off. I met two of her apprenticed boys going off home on leave with their dunnage on a Frenchman's barrow, as happy as larks, and I asked them if the mate was on board.

'There he is, on the quay, looking at the moorings,' says one of the youngsters as he skipped past me.

You may imagine the shock to my feelings when I beheld his white head. I could only manage to tell him that his wife was at a hotel in town. He left me at once, to go and get his hat on board. I was mightily surprised by the smartness of his movements as he hurried up the gangway.

Whereas the black mate struck people as deliberate and strangely stately in his gait for a man in the prime of life, this white-headed chap seemed the most wonderfully alert of old men. I don't suppose Bunter was any quicker on his pins than before. It was the colour of the hair that made all the difference in one's judgement.

The same with his eyes. Those eyes, that looked at you so steely, so fierce, and so fascinating out of a bush of a buccaneer's black hair, now had an innocent almost boyish expression in their good-humoured brightness under those white eyebrows.

I led him without any delay into Mrs Bunter's private sitting-room. After she had dropped a tear over the late cannibal, given a hug to her Winston, and told him that he must grow his moustache again, the dear lady tucked her feet upon the sofa, and I got out of Bunter's way.

He started at once to pace the room, waving his long arms. He worked himself into a regular frenzy, and tore Johns limb from limb many times over that evening.

'Fell down? Of course I fell down, by slipping backwards on that fool's patent brass plates. 'Pon my word, I had been walking that poop in charge of the ship, and I didn't know whether I was in the Indian Ocean or in the moon. I was crazy. My head spun round and round with sheer worry. I had made my last application of your chemist's wonderful stuff.' (This to me.) 'All the store of bottles you gave me got smashed when those drawers fell out in the last gale. I had been getting some dry things to change, when I heard the cry: "All hands on deck!" and made one jump of it, without even pushing them in properly. Ass! When I came back and saw the broken glass and the mess, I felt ready to faint.

'No; look here – deception is bad; but not to be able to keep it up after one has been forced into it. You know that since I've been squeezed out of the Western Ocean packets by younger men, just on account of my grizzled muzzle – you know how much chance I had ever to get a ship. And not a soul to turn to. We have been a lonely couple, we two – she threw away everything for me – and to see her want a piece of dry bread – '

He banged with his fist fit to split the Frenchman's table in two.

'I would have turned a sanguinary pirate for her, let alone cheating my way into a berth by dyeing my hair. So when you came to me with your chemist's wonderful stuff – '

He checked himself.

'By the way, that fellow's got a fortune when he likes to pick it up. It is a wonderful stuff – you tell him salt water can do nothing to it. It stays on as long as your hair will.'

'All right,' I said. 'Go on.'

Thereupon he went for Johns again with a fury that frightened his wife, and made me laugh till I cried.

'Just you try to think what it would have meant to be at the mercy of the meanest creature that ever commanded a ship! Just fancy what a life that crawling Johns would have led me! And I knew that in a week or so the white hair would begin to show. And the crew. Did you ever think of that? To be shown up as a low fraud before all hands. What a life for me till we got to Calcutta! And once there – kicked out, of course. Half-pay stopped. Annie here alone without a penny – starving; and I on the other side of the earth, ditto. You see?'

'I thought of shaving twice a day. But could I shave my head, too? No way – no way at all. Unless I dropped Johns overboard; and even then –

'Do you wonder now that with all these things boiling in my head I didn't know where I was putting down my foot that night? I just felt myself falling – then crash, and all dark.

'When I came to myself that bang on the head seemed to have steadied my wits somehow. I was so sick of everything that for two days I wouldn't speak to anyone. They thought it was a slight concussion of the brain. Then the idea dawned upon me as I was looking at that ghost-ridden, wretched fool. "Ah, you love ghosts," I thought. "Well, you shall have something from beyond the grave."

'I didn't even trouble to invent a story. I couldn't imagine a ghost if I wanted to. I wasn't fit to lie connectedly if I had tried. I just bulled him on to it. Do you know, he got, quite by himself, a notion that at some time or other I had done somebody to death in some way, and that – '

'Oh, the horrible man!' cried Mrs Bunter from the sofa. There was a silence.

'And didn't he bore my head off on the home passage!' began Bunter again in a weary voice. 'He loved me. He was proud of me. I was converted. I had had a manifestation. Do you know what he was after? He wanted me and him "to make a *seance*", in his own words, and to try to call up that ghost (the one that had turned my hair white – the ghost of my supposed victim), and, as he said, talk it over with him – the ghost – in a friendly way.

' "Or else, Bunter," he says, "you may get another manifestation when you least expect it, and tumble overboard perhaps, or something. You ain't really safe till we pacify the spirit-world in some way."

'Can you conceive a lunatic like that? No – say?'

I said nothing. But Mrs Bunter did, in a very decided tone.

'Winston, I don't want you to go on board that ship again any more.'

'My dear,' says he, 'I have all my things on board yet.'

'You don't want the things. Don't go near that ship at all.'

He stood still; then, dropping his eyes with a faint smile, said slowly, in a dreamy voice 'The haunted ship.'

'And your last,' I added.

We carried him off, as he stood, by the night train. He was very quiet; but crossing the Channel, as we two had a smoke on deck, he turned to me suddenly, and, grinding his teeth, whispered: 'He'll never know how near he was being dropped overboard!'

He meant Captain Johns. I said nothing.

But Captain Johns, I understand, made a great to-do about the disappearance of his chief mate. He set the French police scouring the country for the body. In the end, I fancy he got word from his owners' office to drop all this fuss – that it was all right. I don't suppose he ever understood anything of that mysterious occurrence.

To this day he tries at times (he's retired now, and his conversation is not very coherent) – he tries to tell the story of a black mate he once had, 'a murderous, gentlemanly ruffian, with raven-black hair which turned white all at once in consequence of a manifestation from beyond the grave'. An avenging apparition. What with reference to black and white hair, to poop-ladders, and to his own feelings and views, it is difficult to make head or tail of it. If his sister (she's very vigorous still) should be present she cuts all this short – peremptorily: 'Don't you mind what he says. He's got devils on the brain.'

A. R. COOPER

The author joined the French Foreign Legion in 1914 at the age of fifteen and a half, after an adventurous few years at sea. He enlisted at Algiers under the name of Cornélis Jean de Bruin and was sent to Fort St Thérèse at Oran and thence to Sidi Bel Abbès, the headquarters of the Legion in Algeria.

With the Foreign Legion in Gallipoli

ONE

At Sidi Bel Abbès we were met by a sergeant of the Legion, marched in through the great central gate and taken to the barracks.

On each side of a tree-bordered avenue are the four-storeyed buildings in which the men live; at the end of the avenue are the offices and beyond (a place very well known to every legionnaire!) the canteen, also the wash-house, stores and other buildings; on the right of the main building is the Salle d'Honneur, where all the trophies and flags of the Legion are kept, and beyond that the prison, all enclosed by a high wall.

We arrived at Sidi Bel Abbès on 14 October 1914. Everything was in a state of commotion. The 3rd Battalion had just received orders for active service. We recruits were sent right away to the stores to get our kit, rations, rifles and ammunition and then were told to fall in with the rest. A pretty raw and awkward bunch we must have been.

The kit issued to us in those days consisted of kepi, which was red with a blue band, blue tunic, red trousers and a short vest, which we called *veste de singe*, an overcoat and the blue woollen belt which it is compulsory to wear over our tunics as a precaution against dysentery. The *couvre nuque* (a shaped piece of white linen to be worn under the kepi to protect the neck from the sun) was also issued, but in spite of the fact that in films about the Legion the officers and men are always shown wearing it, day and night, this is not so in reality. It is never worn. The only use to which it is put by legionnaires is to strain their coffee or even water when it is very muddy! The epaulettes, which are also 'featured' in films and fiction, have not been worn since 1907. The only epaulette a Legion soldier wears is a little blue rosette of felt which he sews on his right shoulder in order to hitch his rifle over it. When we were in the Dardanelles in 1914–15 blue linen trousers called *salopettes* were issued to us to wear over our red ones. During the war, when the French troops got their *bleu horizon*, we were given khaki and since then all the French colonial troops have worn khaki. The French government bought up all the American uniforms at the end of the war.

Within a few hours of our arrival at Sidi Bel Abbès the battalion was entrained for Perrigaux. As we got there we heard firing and learned that the Arabs had attacked the town and that we had to push them back into the mountains. This attack on Perrigaux was the last Arab revolt in Algeria.

Our forces consisted of one battalion of the Legion, some French colonial troops and a few *Tirailleurs*.

We dug a trench. We could see the Arabs only about two hundred yards away and knew that there were a lot more that we could not see, among the rocks at the foot of the hills. The rifle that was issued to us in those days was the *fusil gras*, which had been in use since 1870. It was monstrously heavy and fired great big bullets. I had no idea how to use it but I lay down in the trench next to an old soldier and watched what he did. The first shot I fired there was a terrible kick which made my shoulder sore for days! I opened the bolt very carefully and slowly for fear of what would happen if that the ejector did not work and I had to poke the cartridge case out with a pencil!

The soldier next me laughed and showed me how to use the rifle and after that it was better and I began to enjoy firing it.

After an hour of this we were ordered to fix bayonets and charge. In a charge like this it is the old soldiers, who have experience of colonial warfare and know how to take cover and watch out for the Arabs, who get through. On that charge nearly all the recruits who came up with me were killed.

I was not at all afraid and to my own surprise I was not even excited. I seemed to feel quite cool; in those days I was unconscious of danger. I did not know what it meant. Everyone was all over the place. I found myself face to face with an Arab and plunged my bayonet into him, but in doing so I turned it, which meant I could not get it out again and had to leave it in his body. The Arabs do not like facing steel and they began to ran away towards the mountains with our troops after them in any sort of order.

I had already been told that for every enemy killed a legionnaire cuts a notch in his rifle and as I went on I got out my knife and started to make a notch on mine. It was very hot and I was dead tired with running over the rough ground and carrying the heavy rifle and kit, and so I sat down on a rock to rest. Suddenly I saw a party of Arabs quite near to me on the right. They closed round me and I realised that I was their prisoner but, not really knowing what that meant, I was not frightened and thought it best to be friendly so I offered them cigarettes. They took them and also took my cartridges away from me, but left me to carry the heavy rifle. I could not understand what they said but something in their faces and gestures alarmed me in an unexpected way, and when one of them started to put his hands on me in a nauseating, caressing way I upped with the butt of the rifle and smashed his head in. That ended all friendly relationship with my captors!

When they got me back to their camp I was handed over to the women. It is the women who do the torturing. On the way up to Perrigaux in the train an old soldier had been telling of his adventures and had talked of having been taken prisoner by the Arabs. I remembered his saying that if this should happen to a man the only thing to do to escape torture was to pretend to be mad, as the Arabs think that a madman is 'possessed' by a spirit and will not touch him. So I thought I had better do this and I started catching flies where there were none, catching at my own thumb and making any idiotic face and gesture I could think of. When I saw them draw back from me I wanted to laugh, but I managed not to do so.

They put some food near me which I was glad of by then and in the evening they brought me to the marabout (a sort of holy man or priest) who could speak French and he questioned me about the strength of the battalion. I don't think I even knew, but, anyway, I made up some tremendous number and all the time I was playing the fool to make him believe me mad.

The Arabs evidently did not think much of me as a prisoner for that night they took me down to the plain near where we had been fighting that day and signed to me to go back to our lines. But they had taken my rifle away from me and that bothered me very much. I did not want to go back without it. Already I had been made to understand that it was a terrible offence in the Legion to lose any part of your kit or equipment but also my rifle had that notch in it for my 'first man'. I went on for a few hundred yards towards Perrigaux and then I hid behind a bush and began wondering how on earth I could get my rifle back. The rest of the night I lay out there between the lines.

Early in the morning the Legion started to attack again and a lot of them came right past me. The Arabs were shooting from behind their boulders and bushes and the Arab marksmen are deadly sure. They appropriate any kind of rifle they can get hold of and they do not use the sights, but put two fingers on the barrel when they aim. A Legion soldier fell dead, shot through the head, within a yard of where I was hiding. Then I came out, made sure he was lifeless, picked up his rifle and joined in the attack.

When it was over I went to my captain and reported. I told him all that had happened. He seemed to find it amusing, as I did when I started to talk about it, and he laughed and said he was pleased with me, that I was a good soldier. I felt very proud of that. We quelled the Arab revolt in, I think, four or five days and then we went back to Sidi Bel Abbès.

TWO

When we were back in barracks I got in touch with an old soldier who promised to show me the ropes and put me wise to the ways of the legionnaires. He was a very nice fellow, a bugler from Brittany called Le Gonnec.

When a man joins the French Foreign Legion the first thing he has to learn is the *base de la discipline* – the Legion's code:

> Discipline being the principal strength of the Legion it is essential that all superiors receive from their subordinates absolute obedience and submission on all occasions. Orders must be executed instantly, without hesitation or complaint. The authorities who give them are responsible for them and an inferior is only permitted to make an objection after he has obeyed.

The second thing a legionnaire must learn is how to get drunk when he has no money to buy wine!

My company was the 9th of the 3rd Battalion of the 1st Regiment commanded by Captain Rousseau. He was a splendid officer and understood his men, having been a ranker himself. His old mother used to keep a canteen in Sidi Bel Abbès. Although there were the sergeants and corporals between them and the men, the good officers always studied their men and knew their characters, when to overlook their faults, when to punish and how to get the best out of them.

A second-class soldier is an ordinary private. First-class soldiers are rare and are not thought anything of as, in order to gain this nebulous distinction, a man must have no punishment, and that is practically impossible for a real legionnaire. The best soldiers in the fighting line spend a great deal of their time in prison when their battalion is in barracks.

I always hated parades and one morning when the sergeant who was drilling us had made us stand to attention and slope arms several dozen times, I began obeying slackly, just bending my knee and not moving my feet apart at the word *repos*, and when he went for me, I threw my rifle down on the ground. For this I was tied to a tree for the rest of the morning, with the woollen belt which, as I have said, we all wore, by orders, over our tunics. Afterwards I was reported to the captain.

When he asked me why I had behaved like that, I said: 'I am intelligent enough to know how to stand at attention and slope arms after doing it once; I don't need to go on doing it fifty times an hour.'

As a matter of fact, I was rather a favourite with Captain Rousseau. He knew my age, as indeed they all did (unofficially, of course), and he chose to overlook both my 'crime' and my cheek.

He cautioned me that to refuse to obey a command meant court martial and prison and told me not to do it again. But by his orders I was given a job in the store-room and so escaped those eternal and infernal parades.

In February 1915, it was posted in orders that any man who wished to do so could volunteer for active service. I think nearly the whole battalion wanted to. I was for rushing off to find the captain to put my name down then and there. Someone tried to stop me and explained that I must go to the corporal, who would forward my name to the sergeant and *he* would give it to the lieutenant for the captain.

'Not I!' I called to them, as I went off. 'I'm going straight to God, not to all his saints first!'

I found Captain Rousseau in the mess-room, saluted and said: 'If you please, sir, will you put my name down for active service?'

'That's all right, de Bruin' – he smiled – 'you're down already!'

THREE

The 1st Battalion of the Premier Régiment de Marche d'Orient was formed, with three companies of legionnaires, at Tiaret, the training centre in West Central Algeria.

From Tiaret we were sent to Oran where we camped in an old Roman arena which is surrounded by a very high wall, the idea being that this would make it difficult for us to break camp and go into the town to drink. As a matter of fact, the authorities are never very optimistic about the success of their expedients in this direction. They know the legionnaires too well. Those of us who were determined to get into the town that night fastened our leather belts together and so managed to scale those noble Roman walls.

Many are the ways in which a Legion soldier will earn drinks or the money to buy them. I used to go into the cafés and entertain people by blowing fire out of my mouth (a trick easily done with petrol) eating the red-hot end of my cigarette (the doctors say it is good for the stomach!) and piercing my cheeks with needles or pins. This does not hurt in the least if you do it quickly enough. The price of these edifying exhibitions was enough wine to keep me happy for the evening.

So well do the authorities know what is going on that they send out patrols to bring the truants back under arrest, sometimes unconscious. But there is no punishment on the eve of going into action.

The morning after we camped at Oran, half the battalion was missing, but legionnaires do not desert when they know they are going to fight and gradually they came in. Some turned up even without hats and other parts of their kit when we were on the quay ready to embark, but the battalion left Oran full strength.

We went on *La France* which had been a passenger boat plying between Marseilles and Tunis. She had been converted into a troopship. At Malta we had to stay on board and we were disembarked at Alexandria. There we were attached to the Régiment de Marche d'Afrique, composed of volunteers from regular French regiments, under General d'Amade. We camped at the back of the Victoria Hospital on English territory. We still did not know our destination.

We had been kept hanging about, on the boat and at Alexandria, for over two months. There was a shortage of cigarettes and wine and there was a faction in the battalion which began to be actively discontented and to discuss whether it would not be a good thing to desert. We were on English territory and the idea was that if we could get away we might join the English forces and see some of the fighting for which we had volunteered. I was young and easily led and anything that sounded like an adventure was in my line so I threw in my lot with about forty men who decided to get away. It was a very abortive effort at desertion and we were caught and brought back to camp under arrest.

Then orders came through that there was to be a review. Whether this was intended to occupy us or impress someone else, I don't know; but on account of it those under arrest were released and put back into the lines. When the review was over we were again put under arrest.

At last we were embarked on the *Bien Hoa*, one of the ships which had relieved Casablanca when the town was captured by the Arabs in 1907.

It was a relief to know that we were on our way somewhere, presumably to the fighting line, and once on board, those under arrest were released.

We landed at Mudros on the island of Lemnos and again camped. We had now been without tobacco for a month and so a right royal welcome was accorded to an old Greek who turned up with a whole cartload of cigarettes. Guided by his native knowledge of the laws of supply and demand and in blissful ignorance of the ways of the Legion and the *Système débrouillage* (the legionnaires' system of helping themselves to what they want), he expected to make his fortune. The price of the tobacco rose, so did the old Greek, who was lifted bodily and dropped splashingly into the harbour. The battalion enjoyed its first smoke for a month.

While we were in camp at Mudros, British troopships kept coming into the harbour and we learnt at last that we were going to the Dardanelles.

FOUR

On 28 April 1915, we landed at Gallipoli from the *Petite Savoie*. We were the first French troops to do so. We went ashore on V beach just beside the *River Clyde*, the ship from which the British had landed with rafts a few days before. The sea was full of dead bodies. The English had cleared the way and our landing was without incident, but very soon the Turks started shelling from Fort Chanak. It was my first experience of shellfire and I did not like it very much.

We started marching straight away. There was no camping; that night we rested on a hilltop. We had no idea where the enemy was. It was pitch dark and raining in torrents. The 12th Company was lost and Captain Rousseau detailed me, with four or five other men, to go out in different directions to find them and lead them back to the battalion.

I walked for about half an hour through the rain and darkness, stumbling over rocks and dead bodies, and, at last, scrambling up a hill, I saw a dim silhouette at the top. I was glad to see any living human being and went right up to him and spoke in French. With a yell the man dropped his rifle and fled, calling on Allah in Turkish. The best part of it was that I was so startled that I did the same thing; that is, I dropped my rifle and ran. When I was about a hundred yards down the hill bullets began to whistle over my head. I stopped and dropped down and then I realised that I must get back and retrieve my rifle at all costs; so I started crawling cautiously up the hill. Gradually the firing died down. But when I got near the spot where the sentry had been he was back there, or another man in his place. I lay out there behind a bush all night in the rain. I could just see my rifle lying on the ground. Eventually the sentry moved away. There was utter silence, except for the sound of the rain, and I crept forward an inch at a time until I could reach the rifle. Then I made off down the hill as fast as I knew how and got back to camp just before dawn.

That day we started marching and in the afternoon (the 29th) the real fighting began. We were holding the right of the line farthest from the sea with the British on our left. It was chiefly hand-to-hand bayonet fighting and we were up against what seemed to be an inexhaustible force of Turks. It was terrible to see the way our men were slaughtered. We lost about half the battalion and three-quarters of our officers were killed.

The fighting went on day after day, getting fiercer and fiercer. On May 1st, Captain Rousseau was wounded. He got a bullet through his arm. Although this might not have been very serious for another man, his constitution had been undermined by service in China where he had taken to opium smoking and he died of that wound.

We had now no officers left and the senior sergeant, Léon, was promoted lieutenant on the field and took charge of what was left of the battalion. He got the Légion d'honneur for his courage and efficiency that day and he deserved it. He was in command of the battalion for just over a month, until he was wounded himself on 4 June. He was a little, wiry man, incredibly brave, and had the respect of all the men who fought under him. Although only an NCO, his tactics were better than those of some of the superior officers, and the casualties were not so heavy while he was in command, although the fighting was fiercer than ever. Our officers, although excellent at their own job, which was desert fighting such as the Legion gets against the Arabs, had no practical experience of modern warfare.

On 4 May we got reinforcements and the fighting went on.

The Legion had been very upset because the flag of the Régiment de Marche was given to the 3rd Zouave Regiment to carry. But during the third day's fighting in the Dardanelles the Turks captured it from them. We were determined to get it back and we made a special, unauthorised, attack in order to recover it. We did so, but it was impossible, during the fighting, to get it back to our lines and so it was buried. It was a fortnight before we were able to return for it, then the flag of the regiment was unearthed and brought back in triumph by the soldiers of the Legion. Afterwards General d'Amade gave orders that the Legion should carry the regiment's colours.

We were holding a part of the line about eight kilometres from V Beach, the right wing of the British Expeditionary Force, north of Cap Hellès. I had got used to the shelling by this time and in the intervals between actual attacks I used to get across to the English lines and do a bit of 'scrounging'. We used to make deals over rations, exchanging our supplies for theirs. One of our greatest needs was cigarettes, and after a battle certain of us used to volunteer to creep out and search the dead Turks for tobacco, of which they seemed to have plenty. One night I found a nice big packet of tobacco in the coat pocket of a dead Turk. On the way back to our lines I rolled myself a cigarette but at the first puff I was nearly sick. God knows how long that Turk had lain out there but the tobacco had become tainted by his decaying body and was putrid. I rolled about twenty cigarettes and distributed them to the men in my company, who were duly grateful – until they tried to smoke them! Our jokes were a bit on the gruesome side, but then so were the conditions in which we were living and dying.

One of the worst jobs we had was to take a ravine called, officially, Kereves-Deré, but known to us as Le Ravin de la Mort. We were on one side of the ravine and the Turks on high ground the other side, commanding the only point at which we could enter it. To occupy it we had to jump down, across a kind of gully, and had orders to do this in single file; then, one by one, we had to run to the end of the place marked out for a trench and start digging. But as each man jumped he was picked off by a Turkish sniper and fell dead or wounded.

This happened ten times; one man after the other was shot down just as he jumped. I was the eleventh man to go. It was not exactly an enlivening job as it looked like certain death. But I had an idea. Instead of jumping I dived – threw myself down and the Turkish bullet whizzed above my body and I picked myself up and ran for the head of the trench, which was sheltered from their line of fire by the overhanging side of the ravine. The man who followed me did the same thing and got past, then the next, but the Turks were on to the trick by then and got him. I started shouting to them.

'Don't all do the same thing . . . Some jump, some dive . . .' They did so, and most of the rest of them got through and we dug our trench and were able to hold the ravine.

I suppose it was for my initiative (and for getting down alive!) that my officer recommended me for a medal, but it never came through . . .

While we were holding the ravine I got friendly with an Italian in my company. He had been gun-running in Morocco before he joined the Legion and was an adventurous sort of creature. He was also a very good swimmer and he told me that he was going to get out and swim the Dardanelles to Asia Minor. We were quite near to the water. He knew I spoke Turkish and Greek and I may have told him I had relations in Asia Minor, and he asked me if I would go with him. It sounded a bit hazardous but not more dangerous than sitting in that ravine with the Turks on the high ground above us and I thought I might as well have a shot at it.

So one night we got down to the water, took off our clothes and went in. About a hundred yards from the shore we were caught by a terrifically strong current and carried right downstream. I thought we would be swept out to sea, but as a matter of fact we managed to get ashore just near the foot of the peninsula, not far from where we landed originally. And there we were, stark naked, eight kilometres from, our company! We made those eight kilometres during the night and got back, our feet torn and bleeding and the spirit of adventure low in us!

I felt rather bad about this attempt to desert which I had really only agreed to on impulse and because we were all pretty fed up with what we had been through, and, to salve my own conscience, I determined to do all I could for the Legion, and afterwards I was always volunteering for any extra or dangerous mission.

FIVE

On 1 and 2 May orders came through from General d'Amade to attack the enemy with bayonets, although they were over a kilometre from our lines. Of course our losses were appalling. The official reason that General d'Amade was relieved of his command shortly afterwards was that he had had a nervous breakdown, but it was generally believed that his retirement from the Dardanelles was connected with these disastrous bayonet charges; also he was always at loggerheads with General Ian Hamilton and General Braithwaite, Chief of Staff.

On 5 May I was sent down to Cap Hellès to take over the job of telephone operator at headquarters. It was there I first met Mr Ashmead Bartlett, the English war correspondent. How it happened was that I saw that he was smoking an English cigarette. We were always short of tobacco at that time, and I followed him about in the hope that he would throw down the end of his cigarette and I could get it. He noticed me and called me up.

'Hallo, youngster, what d'you want?'

I told him what I was after and he gave me a cigarette and started talking to me. He was very interested in the Legion. He told me that he had been with them during the fighting at Casablanca in 1907 and had known General d'Amade there. He asked me about our landing in the Dardanelles on the 28th and I gave him what particulars I could.

Admiral Roger Keyes, General Ian Hamilton, General Braithwaite, Admiral Guàpratte and General d'Amade were having a conference in the next room. We could hear the sound of their raised voices; evidently some pretty heated arguments were in progress. Although Mr Ashmead Bartlett was questioning me I could see that he was, at the same time, trying to hear what was going on. As the generals came out after the conference I thought I heard General Hamilton say to General Braithwaite, with brusque emphasis, 'He's no damned good.'

Later in the day Turkish prisoners were brought in and I got into conversation with some of them. General d'Amade walked in and was obviously astonished to hear one of his soldiers talking fluent Turkish. He gave me a look of deepest suspicion, and turning to one of his officers, said: 'Have that man relieved at once.'

My work at headquarters lasted just fourteen hours!

General d'Amade's place was taken, shortly afterwards, by General Gouraud.

It was on 1 May that I was recommended for the Croix de Guerre, and later had permission to put it up, although I was not officially decorated until December when I got back to Sidi Bel Abbès. This was the first Croix de Guerre given in the Legion and it is entered in the *Livré d'Honneur* as such.

In the middle of May I was sent down to the island of Tenedos, with a fatigue party consisting of half a company, to get rations, clothing and so on. The *Askold* was lying there, the only Russian gunboat in the Dardanelles. She was called by the English soldiers 'the packet of Woodbines' because of her row of funnels.

While we were waiting, the ship was shelling, and I was watching the sailors firing when a shell from Fort Chanak burst and all the gunners were killed or wounded. The gun was untouched. I rushed forward impetuously and started turning the firing-handle as I had seen them do. The ship was turning and of course I did not and could not have turned the gun. In another moment I should have been firing on our own men and allies but luckily I was stopped in time. I expected to get court-martialled for that but I never heard any more about it.

Towards the end of May I was sent with a man called Dixon to Cap Hellès to pilot the Paymaster back to our ranks. Dixon was a Frenchman. He did not speak a word of English although he had joined the Legion as an Englishman. He was the champion 'scrounger' in the battalion. It was with him that I used to crawl out into no man's land at night in search of Turkish tobacco, only Dixon was not particular what it was he could find on the dead Turks and appropriated to his own uses anything he fancied.

On the way back from Cap Hellès a shell from a six-inch gun burst near us, killing the Paymaster and sending flying the attaché-case in which he was carrying the money for the battalion. Notes were scattered all over the place, five-franc notes, ten, twenty, fifty, hundred-franc notes . . . Dixon went after them. Shells were bursting all round and I took cover. But Dixon sat down and began calmly to count a pile of notes and shouted to me to come on out if I wanted some money and get it while there was still some to get. At that moment another shell burst and decapitated him; his head was thrown right on to my knees. I felt pretty sick and as soon as I could I got away, made for our lines and reported what had happened. A party was sent out to look for the money. It was stated that the amount the Paymaster was carrying was ten thousand francs (about four hundred pounds in those days). All that was recovered was five hundred and fifty francs. Some of the rest no doubt had found its way into the searchers' pockets and perhaps some poor blighters in the trenches literally had a 'windfall'!

Another imperturbable character in our company was an Austrian. He had joined the Legion as a Swiss. He was an excellent cook, in fact he had been a chef at the Hôtel Meurice in Paris. One day he was making soup when a shell killed a legionnaire named Keller. A great piece of his flesh was thrown into the stock pot. The Austrian simply cut it up and cooked it in the soup. Rations were neither plentiful nor palatable and we all ate that soup, which tasted of pork, with a relish. When, afterwards, he told us what he had done, many of the men were sick.

An incident which very nearly caused trouble with our men was connected with an Arab who was in our company. One of the officers, a lieutenant, had spotted him in hiding while we were in action. Afterwards the lieutenant made us form up in single file. He marched down the line with his revolver in his hand and when he came to the Arab he stopped and shot him dead. Then he took his body and flung it down the slope.

The men did not like this because he had waited until after the attack. They thought he ought to have killed him at the time or not at all, and grumbled a good deal.

But nevertheless the spirit of the Legion, especially when we were in action, remained the same.

STEPHEN CRANE

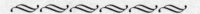

Stephen Crane was born in Newark, New Jersey, in 1871, the youngest son of a Methodist minister. After failing to settle at university, Crane moved to New York where he worked as a journalist and wrote his first novel *Maggie: A Girl of the Streets* in 1893. His second novel, *The Red Badge of Courage*, was far more successful, critically and commercially, and after its publication in 1895 he travelled as a newspaper correspondent to Mexico, to Cuba and to Greece. In 1897 he settled in England, where he met Joseph Conrad and Henry James. He died in Germany in 1900, aged twenty-eight.

Manacled

In the first act there had been a farm scene, wherein real horses had drunk real water out of real buckets, afterward dragging a real wagon off stage left. The audience was consumed with admiration of this play, and the great Theatre Nouveau rang to its roof with the crowd's plaudits.

The second act was now well advanced. The hero, cruelly victimised by his enemies, stood in prison garb, panting with rage, while two brutal warders fastened real handcuffs on his wrists and real anklets on his ankles. And the hovering villain sneered.

' 'Tis well, Aubrey Pettingill,' said the prisoner. 'You have so far succeeded; but, mark you, there will come a time – '

The villain retorted with a cutting allusion to the young lady whom the hero loved.

'Curse you,' cried the hero, and he made as if to spring upon this demon; but, as the pitying audience saw, he could only take steps four inches long.

Drowning the mocking laughter of the villain came cries from both the audience and the people back of the wings: 'Fire! Fire! Fire!' Throughout the great house resounded the roaring crashes of a throng of human beings moving in terror, and even above this noise could be heard the screams of women more shrill than whistles. The building hummed and shook; it was like a glade which holds some bellowing cataract of the mountains. Most of the people who were killed on the stairs still clutched their play-bills in their hands as if they had resolved to save them at all costs.

The Theatre Nouveau fronted upon a street which was not of the first importance, especially at night, when it only aroused when the people came to the theatre, and aroused again when they came out to go home. On the night of the fire, at the time of the scene between the enchained hero and his tormentor, the thoroughfare echoed with only the scraping shovels of some street-cleaners, who were loading carts with blackened snow and mud. The gleam of lights made the shadowed pavement deeply blue, save where lay some yellow plum-like reflection.

Suddenly a policeman came running frantically along the street. He charged upon the fire-box on a corner. Its red light touched with flame each of his brass buttons and the municipal shield. He pressed a lever. He had been standing in the entrance of the theatre chatting to the lonely man in the box-office. To send an alarm was a matter of seconds.

Out of the theatre poured the first hundreds of fortunate ones, and some were not altogether fortunate. Women, their bonnets flying, cried out tender names; men, white as death, scratched and bleeding, looked wildly from face to face. There were displays of horrible blind brutality by the strong. Weaker men clutched and clawed like cats. From the theatre itself came the howl of a gale.

The policeman's fingers had flashed into instant life and action the most perfect counter-attack to the fire. He listened for some seconds, and presently he heard the thunder of a charging engine. She swept around a corner, her three shining enthrilled horses leaping. Her consort, the hose-cart, roared behind her. There were the loud clicks of the steel-shod hoofs, hoarse shouts, men running, the flash of lights, while the crevice-like streets resounded with the charges of other engines.

At the first cry of fire, the two brutal warders had dropped the arms of the hero and run off the stage with the villain. The hero cried after them angrily: 'Where are you going? Here, Pete – Tom – you've left me chained up, damn you!'

The body of the theatre now resembled a mad surf amid rocks, but the hero did not look at it. He was filled with fury at the stupidity of the two brutal warders, in forgetting that they were leaving him manacled. Calling loudly, he hobbled off stage left, taking steps four inches long.

Behind the scenes he heard the hum of flames. Smoke, filled with sparks sweeping on spiral courses, rolled thickly upon him. Suddenly his face turned chalk-colour beneath his skin of manly bronze for the stage. His voice shrieked: 'Pete – Tom – damn you – come back – you've left me chained up.'

He had played in this theatre for seven years, and he could find his way without light through the intricate passages which mazed out behind the stage. He knew that it was a long way to the street door.

The heat was intense. From time to time masses of flaming wood sung down from above him. He began to jump. Each jump advanced him about three feet, but the effort soon became heartbreaking. Once he fell, and it took time to get upon his feet again.

There were stairs to descend. From the top of this flight he tried to fall feet first. He precipitated himself in a way that would have broken his hip under common conditions. But every step seemed covered with glue, and on almost every one he stuck for a moment. He could not even succeed in falling downstairs. Ultimately he reached the bottom, windless from the struggle.

There were stairs to climb. At the foot of the flight he lay for an instant with his mouth close to the floor trying to breathe. Then he tried to scale this frightful precipice up the face of which many an actress had gone at a canter.

Each succeeding step arose eight inches from its fellow. The hero dropped to a seat on the third step, and pulled his feet to the second step. From this position he lifted himself to a seat on the fourth step. He had not gone far in this manner before his frenzy caused him to lose his balance, and he rolled to the foot of the flight. After all, he could fall downstairs.

He lay there whispering. 'They all got out but I. All but I.' Beautiful flames flashed above him, some were crimson, some were orange, and here and there were tongues of purple, blue, green.

A curiously calm thought came into his head. 'What a fool I was not to foresee this! I shall have Rogers furnish manacles of papier-mâché tomorrow.'

The thunder of the fire-lions made the theatre have a palsy.

Suddenly the hero beat his handcuffs against the wall, cursing them in a loud wail. Blood started from under his fingernails. Soon he began to bite the hot steel, and blood fell from his blistered mouth. He raved like a wolf.

Peace came to him again. There were charming effects amid the flames . . . He felt very cool, delightfully cool . . . 'They've left me chained up.'

An Illusion in Red and White

Nights on the Cuban blockade were long, at times exciting, often dull. The men on the small leaping dispatch boats became as intimate as if they had all been buried in the same coffin. Correspondents, who in New York had passed as fairly good fellows, sometimes turned out to be perfect rogues of vanity and selfishness, but still more often the conceited chumps of Park Row became the kindly and thoughtful men of the Cuban blockade. Also each correspondent told all he knew, and sometimes more. For this gentle tale I am indebted to one of the brightening stars of New York journalism.

'Now, this is how I imagine it happened. I don't say it happened this way, but this is how I imagine it happened. And it always struck me as being a very interesting story. I hadn't been on the paper very long, but just about long enough to get a good show, when the city editor suddenly gave me this sparkling murder assignment.

'It seems that up in one of the back counties of New York State a farmer had taken a dislike to his wife; and so he went into the kitchen with an axe, and in the presence of their four little children he just casually rapped his wife on the nape of the neck with the head of this axe. It was early in the morning, but he told the children they had better go to bed. Then he took his wife's body out in the woods and buried it.

'This farmer's name was Jones. The widower's eldest child was named Freddy. A week after the murder, one of the long-distance neighbours was rattling past the house in his buckboard when he saw Freddy playing in the road. He pulled up, and asked the boy about the welfare of the Jones family.

' "Oh, we're all right," said Freddy, "only ma – she ain't – she's dead."

' "Why, when did she die?" cried the startled farmer. "What did she die of?"

' "Oh," answered Freddy, "last week a man with red hair and big white teeth and real white hands came into the kitchen, and killed ma with an axe."

'The farmer was indignant with the boy for telling him this strange childish nonsense, and drove off much disgruntled. But he recited the incident at a tavern that evening, and when people began to miss the familiar figure of Mrs Jones at the Methodist Church on Sunday mornings, they ended by having an investigation. The calm Jones was arrested for murder, and his wife's body was lifted from its grave in the woods and buried by her own family.

'The chief interest now centred upon the children. All four declared that they were in the kitchen at the time of the crime, and that the murderer had red hair. The hair of the virtuous Jones was grey. They said that the murderer's teeth were large and white. Jones only had about eight teeth, and these were small and brown. They said the murderer's hands were white. Jones's hands were the colour of black walnuts. They lifted their dazed, innocent faces, and crying, simply because the mysterious excitement and their new quarters frightened them, they repeated their heroic legend without important deviation, and without the parroty sameness which would excite suspicion.

'Women came to the jail and wept over them, and made little frocks for the girls, and little breeches for the boys, and idiotic detectives questioned them at length. Always they upheld the theory of the murderer with red hair, big white teeth and white hands. Jones sat in his cell, his chin sullenly on his first vest button. He knew nothing about any murder, he said. He thought his wife had gone on a visit to some relatives. He had had a quarrel with her, and she had said that she was going to leave him for a time, so that he might have proper opportunities for cooling down. Had he seen the blood on the floor? Yes, he had seen the blood on the floor. But he had been cleaning and skinning a rabbit at that spot on the day of his wife's disappearance. He had thought nothing of it. What had his children said when he returned from the fields? They had told him that their mother had been killed by an axe in the hands of a man with red hair, big white teeth and white hands. To questions as to why he had not informed the police of the county, he answered that he had not thought it a matter of sufficient importance. He had cordially hated his wife, anyhow, and he was glad to be rid of her. He decided afterwards that she had run off; and he had never credited the fantastic tale of the children.

'Of course, there was very little doubt in the minds of the majority that Jones was guilty, but there was a fairly strong following who insisted that Jones was a coarse and brutal man, and perhaps weak in his head – yes – but not a murderer. They pointed to the children and declared that children could never lie, and these kids, when asked, said that the murder had been committed by a man with red hair, large white teeth and white hands. I myself had a number of interviews with the children, and I was amazed at the convincing power of their little story. Shining in the depths of the limpid up-turned eyes, one could fairly see tiny mirrored images of men with red hair, big white teeth and white hands.

'Now, I'll tell you how it happened – how I imagine it was done. Some time after burying his wife in the woods Jones strolled back into the house. Seeing nobody, he called out in the familiar fashion, "Mother!" Then the kids came out whimpering. "Where is your mother?" said Jones. The children looked at him blankly. "Why, pa," said Freddy, "you came in here, and hit ma

499

with the axe; and then you sent us to bed." "Me?" cried Jones "I haven't been near the house since breakfast time."

'The children did not know how to reply. Their meagre little sense informed them that their father had been the man with the axe, but he denied it, and to their minds everything was a mere great puzzle with no meaning whatever, save that it was mysteriously sad and made them cry.

' "What kind of a looking man was it?" said Jones.

'Freddy hesitated. "Now – he looked a good deal like you, pa."

' "Like me?" said Jones. "Why, I thought you said he had red hair?"

' "No, I didn't," replied Freddy. "I thought he had grey hair, like yours."

' "Well," said Jones, "I saw a man with kind of red hair going along the road up yonder, and I thought maybe that might have been him."

'Little Lucy, the second child, here piped up with intense conviction. "His hair was a little teeny bit red. I saw it."

' "No," said Jones. "The man I saw had very red hair. And what did his teeth look like? Were they big and white?"

' "Yes," answered Lucy, "they were."

'Even Freddy seemed to incline to think it.

' "His teeth may have been big and white."

'Jones said little more at that time. Later he intimated to the children that their mother had gone off on a visit, and although they were full of wonder, and sometimes wept because of the oppression of an incomprehensible feeling in the air, they said nothing. Jones did his chores. Everything was smooth.

'The morning after the day of the murder, Jones and his children had a breakfast of hominy and milk.

' "Well, this man with red hair and big white teeth, Lucy," said Jones. "Did you notice anything else about him?"

'Lucy straightened in her chair, and showed the childish desire to come out with brilliant information which would gain her father's approval.

' "He had white hands – hands all white – "

' "How about you, Freddy?"

' "I didn't look at them much, but I think they were white," answered the boy.

' "And what did little Martha notice?" cried the tender parent. "Did she see the big bad man?"

'Martha, aged four, replied solemnly, "His hair was all yed, and his hand was white – all white."

' "That's the man I saw up the road," said Jones to Freddy.

' "Yes, sir, it seems like it must have been him," said the boy, his brain now completely muddled.

'Again Jones allowed the subject of his wife's murder to lapse. The children did not know that it was a murder, of course. Adults were always performing in a way to make children's heads swim. For instance, what could be more incomprehensible than that a man with two horses, dragging a queer thing, should walk all day, making the grass turn down and the earth turn up? And why did they cut the long grass and put it in a barn? And what was a cow for? Did the water in the well like to be there? All these actions and things were grand, because they were associated with the high estate of grown-up people, but they were deeply mysterious. If then, a man with red hair, big white teeth and white hands should hit their mother on the nape of the neck with an axe, it was merely a phenomenon of grown-up life. Little Henry, the baby, when he had a want, howled and pounded the table with his spoon. That was all of life to him. He was not concerned with the fact that his mother had been murdered.

'One day Jones said to his children suddenly, "Look here; I wonder if you could have made a mistake. Are you absolutely sure that the man you saw had red hair, big white teeth and white hands?"

'The children were indignant with their father. "Why, of course, pa, we ain't made no mistake. We saw him as plain as day."

'Later young Freddy's mind began to work like ketchup. His nights were haunted with terrible memories of the man with the red hair, big white teeth and white hands, and the prolonged absence of his mother made him wonder and wonder. Presently he quite gratuitously developed the theory that his mother was dead. He knew about death. He had once seen a dead dog; also dead chickens, rabbits and mice. One day he asked his father, "Pa, is ma ever coming back?"

'Jones said: "Well, no; I don't think she is." This answer confirmed the boy in his theory. He knew that dead people did not come back.

'The attitude of Jones towards this descriptive legend of the man with the axe was very peculiar. He came to be in opposition to it. He protested against the convictions of the children, but he could not move them. It was the one thing in their lives of which they were stonily and absolutely positive.

'Now that really ends the story. But I will continue for your amusement. The jury hung Jones as high as they could, and they were quite right: because Jones confessed before he died. Freddy is now a highly respected driver of a grocery wagon in Ogdensburg. When I was up there a good many years afterwards people told me that when he ever spoke of the tragedy at all he was certain to denounce the alleged confession as a lie. He considered his father a victim of the stupidity of juries, and someday he hopes to meet the man with the red hair, big white teeth and white hands, whose image still remains so distinct in his memory that he could pick him out in a crowd of ten thousand.'

Twelve o'Clock

Where were you at twelve o'clock, noon, on 9 June 1875?
Question on intelligent cross-examination

ONE

'Excuse *me*,' said Ben Roddle with graphic gestures to a group of citizens in Nantucket's store. 'Excuse *me*! When them fellers in leather pants an' six-shooters ride in, I go home an' set in th' cellar. That's what I do. When you see me pirooting through the streets at th' same time an' occasion as them punchers, you kin put me down fer bein' crazy. Excuse *me*!'

'Why, Ben,' drawled old Nantucket, 'you ain't never really seen 'em turned loose. Why, I kin remember – in th' old days – when – '

'Oh! damn yer old days!' retorted Roddle. Fixing Nantucket with the eye of scorn and contempt, he said, 'I suppose you'll be sayin' in a minute that in th' old days you used to kill Injuns, won't you?'

There was some laughter, and Roddle was left free to expand his ideas on the periodic visits of cowboys to the town. 'Mason Rickets, he had ten big punkins a-sittin' in front of his store, an' them fellers from the Upsidedown-P ranch shot 'em – shot em all – an' Rickets lyin' on his belly in th' store a-callin' fer 'em to quit it. An' what did they do! Why they *laughed* at 'im – just *laughed* at 'im! That don't do a town no good. Now, how would an eastern capiterlist' – (it was the town's humour to be always gassing of phantom investors who were likely to come any moment and pay a thousand prices for everything) – 'how would an eastern capiterlist like that? Why, you couldn't see 'im fer th' dust on his trail. Then he'd tell all his friends that "there town may be all right, but ther's too much loose-handed shootin' fer my money". An' he'd be right, too. Them rich fellers they don't make no bad breaks with their money. They watch it all th' time b'cause they know blame well there ain't hardly room fer their feet fer th' pikers an' tin-horns an' thimble-riggers what are layin' fer 'em. I tell you, one puncher racin' his cow-pony hell-bent-fer-election down Main Street an' yellin' an' shootin' an' nothin' at all done about it, would scare away a whole herd of capiterlists. An' it ain't right. It oughter be stopped.'

A pessimistic voice asked: 'How you goin' to stop it, Ben?'

'Organise,' replied Roddle pompously. 'Organise. That's the only way to make these fellers lay down. I – '

From the street sounded a quick scudding of pony hoofs, and a party of cowboys swept past the door. One man, however, was seen to draw rein and dismount. He came clanking into the store. 'Mornin', gentlemen,' he said civilly.

'Mornin',' they answered in subdued voices.

He stepped to the counter and said, 'Give me a paper of fine cut, please.' The group of citizens contemplated him in silence. He certainly did not look threatening. He appeared to be a young man of twenty-five years, with a tan from wind and such, with a remarkably clear eye from perhaps a period of enforced temperance, a quiet young man who wanted to buy some tobacco. A six-shooter swung low on his hip, but at the moment it looked more decorative than warlike; it seemed merely a part of his old gala dress – his sombrero with its band of rattlesnake skin, his great flaming neckerchief, his belt of embroidered Mexican leather, his high-heeled boots, his huge spurs. And, above all, his hair had been watered and brushed until it lay as close to his head as the fur lays to a wet cat. Paying for his tobacco, he withdrew.

Ben Roddle resumed his harangue. 'Well, there you are! Looks like a calm man now, but in less'n half an hour he'll be as drunk as three bucks an' a squaw, an' then . . . excuse *me!*'

TWO

On this day the men of two outfits had come into town, but Ben Roddle's ominous words were not justified at once. The punchers spent most of the morning in an attack on whiskey which was too earnest to be noisy.

At five minutes of eleven, a tall, lank, brick-coloured cowboy strode over to Placer's Hotel. Placer's Hotel was a notable place. It was the best hotel within two hundred miles. Its office was filled with armchairs and brown papier-mâché receptacles. At one end of the room was a wooden counter painted a bright pink, and on this morning a man was behind the counter writing in a ledger. He was the proprietor of the hotel, but his customary humour was so sullen that all strangers immediately wondered why in life he had chosen to play the part of mine host. Near his left hand, double doors opened into the dining-room, which in warm weather was always kept darkened in order to discourage the flies, which was not compassed at all.

Placer, writing in his ledger, did not look up when the tall cowboy entered.

'Mornin', mister,' said the latter. 'I've come to see if you kin grub-stake th' hull crowd of us fer dinner t'day.'

Placer did not then raise his eyes, but with a certain churlishness, as if it annoyed him that his hotel was patronised, he asked: 'How many?'

'Oh, about thirty,' replied the cowboy. 'An' we want th' best dinner you kin raise an' scrape. Everything th' best. We don't care what it costs s'long as we git a good square meal. We'll pay a dollar a head, by God, we will! We won't kick on nothin' in the bill if you do it up fine. If you ain't got it in the house, russle th' hull town fer it. That's our gait. So you just tear loose, an' we'll – '

At this moment the machinery of a cuckoo-clock on the wall began to whirr, little doors flew open, and a wooden bird appeared and cried, 'Cuckoo!' And this was repeated until eleven o'clock had been announced, while the cowboy, stupefied, glass-eyed, stood with his red throat gulping. At the end he wheeled upon Placer and demanded, *'What in hell is that?'*

Placer revealed by his manner that he had been asked this question too many times. 'It's a clock,' he answered shortly.

'I know it's a clock,' gasped the cowboy; 'but what *kind* of a clock?'

'A cuckoo-clock. Can't you see?'

The cowboy, recovering his self-possession by a violent effort, suddenly went shouting into the street. 'Boys! Say, boys! Com' 'ere a minute!'

His comrades, comfortably inhabiting a nearby saloon, heard his stentorian calls, but they merely said one to another: 'What's th' matter with Jake? – he's off his nut again.'

But Jake burst in upon them with violence. 'Boys,' he yelled, 'come over to th' hotel! They got a clock with a bird inside it, an' when it's eleven o'clock or anything like that, th' bird comes out and says, "*toot*-toot, *toot*-toot!" that way, as many times as whatever time of day it is. It's immense! Come on over!'

The roars of laughter which greeted his proclamation were of two qualities; some men laughing because they knew all about cuckoo-clocks, and other men laughing because they had concluded that the eccentric Jake had been victimised by some wise child of civilisation.

Old Man Crumford, a venerable ruffian who probably had been born in a corral, was particularly offensive with his loud guffaws of contempt. 'Bird a-comin' out of a clock an' a-tellin' ye th' time! Haw – haw – haw!' He swallowed his whisky. 'A bird! a-tellin' ye th' time! Haw-haw! Jake, you ben up agin some new drink. You ben drinkin' lonely an' got up agin some snake-medicine licker. A bird a-tellin' ye th' time! Haw-haw!'

The shrill voice of one of the younger cowboys piped from the background. 'Brace up, Jake. Don't let 'em laugh at ye. Bring 'em that salt codfish of yourn what kin pick out th' ace.'

'Oh, he's only kiddin' us. Don't pay no 'tention to 'im. He thinks he's smart.'

A cowboy whose mother had a cuckoo-clock in her house in Philadelphia spoke with solemnity. 'Jake's a liar. There's no such clock in the world. What? a bird inside a clock to tell the time? Change your drink, Jake.'

Jake was furious, but his fury took a very icy form. He bent a withering glance upon the last speaker. 'I don't mean a *live* bird,' he said, with terrible dignity. 'It's a wooden bird, an' – '

'A wooden bird!' shouted Old Man Crumford. 'Wooden bird a-tellin' ye th' time! Haw-haw!'

But Jake still paid his frigid attention to the Philadelphian. 'An' if yer sober enough to walk, it ain't such a blame long ways from here to th' hotel, an' I'll bet my pile agin yours if you only got two bits.'

'I don't want your money, Jake,' said the Philadelphian. 'Somebody's been stringin' you – that's all. I wouldn't take your money.' He cleverly appeared to pity the other's innocence.

'You couldn't *git* my money,' cried Jake, in sudden hot anger. 'You couldn't git it. Now – since yer so fresh – let's see how much you got.' He clattered some large gold pieces noisily upon the bar.

The Philadelphian shrugged his shoulders and walked away. Jake was triumphant. 'Any more bluffers 'round here?' he demanded. 'Any more? Any more bluffers? Where's all these here hot sports? Let 'em step up. Here's my money – come an' git it.'

But they had ended by being afraid. To some of them his tale was absurd, but still one must be circumspect when a man throws forty-five dollars in gold upon the bar and bids the world come and win it. The general feeling was expressed by Old Man Crumford, when with deference he asked: 'Well, this here bird, Jake – what kinder lookin' bird is it?'

'It's a little brown thing,' said Jake, briefly. Apparently he almost disdained to answer.

'Well – how does it work?' asked the old man, meekly.

'Why in blazes don't you go an' look at it?' yelled Jake. 'Want me to paint it in iles fer you? Go an' look!'

THREE

Placer was writing in his ledger. He heard a great trample of feet and clink of spurs on the porch, and there entered quietly the band of cowboys, some of them swaying a trifle, and these last being the most painfully decorous of all. Jake was in advance. He waved his hand towards the clock. 'There she is,' he said laconically. The cowboys drew up and stared. There was some giggling, but a serious voice said half-audibly, 'I don't see no bird.'

Jake politely addressed the landlord. 'Mister, I've fetched these here friends of mine in here to see yer clock – '

Placer looked up suddenly. 'Well, they can see it, can't they?' he asked in sarcasm. Jake, abashed, retreated to his fellows.

There was a period of silence. From time to time the men shifted their feet. Finally, Old Man Crumford leaned toward Jake, and in a penetrating whisper demanded, 'Where's th' bird?' Some frolicsome spirits on the outskirts began to call, 'Bird! Bird!' as men at a political meeting call for a particular speaker.

Jake removed his big hat and nervously mopped his brow.

The young cowboy with the shrill voice again spoke from the skirts of the crowd. 'Jake, is ther' sure 'nough a bird in that thing?'

'Yes. Didn't I tell you once?'

'Then,' said the shrill-voiced man, in a tone of conviction, 'it ain't a clock at all. It's a bird-cage.'

'I tell you it's a clock,' cried the maddened Jake, but his retort could hardly be heard above the howls of glee and derision which greeted the words of him of the shrill voice.

Old Man Crumford was again rampant. 'Wooden bird a-tellin' ye th' time! Haw-haw!'

Amid the confusion Jake went again to Placer. He spoke almost in supplication. 'Say, mister, what time does this here thing go off agin?'

Placer lifted his head, looked at the clock, and said, 'Noon.'

There was a stir near the door, and Big Watson of the Square-X outfit, and at this time very drunk indeed, came shouldering his way through the crowd and cursing everybody. The men gave him much room, for he was notorious as a quarrelsome person when drunk. He paused in front of Jake, and spoke as through a wet blanket. 'What's all this – monkeyin' about?'

Jake was already wild at being made a butt for everybody, and he did not give backward. 'None a' your dam business, Watson.'

'Huh?' growled Watson, with the surprise of a challenged bull.

'I said,' repeated Jake, distinctly, 'it's none a' your dam business.'

Watson whipped his revolver half out of its holster. 'I'll make it m' business, then, you – '

But Jake had backed a step away, and was holding his left-hand palm outward towards Watson, while in his right he held his six-shooter, its muzzle pointing at the floor. He was shouting in a frenzy, 'No – don't you try it, Watson! Don't you dare try it, or, by Gawd, I'll kill you, sure – *sure*!'

He was aware of a torment of cries about him from fearful men; from men who protested, from men who cried out because they cried out. But he kept his eyes on Watson, and those two glared murder at each other, neither seeming to breathe, fixed like two statues.

A loud new voice suddenly rang out: 'Hol' on a minute!' All spectators who had not stampeded turned quickly, and saw Placer standing behind his bright pink counter with an aimed revolver in each hand.

'Cheese it!' he said. 'I won't have no fightin' here. If you want to fight, git out in the street.'

Big Watson laughed, and speeding up his six-shooter like a flash of blue light, he shot Placer through the throat – shot the man as he stood behind his absurd pink counter with his two aimed revolvers in his incompetent hands. With a yell of rage and despair, Jake smote Watson on the pate with his heavy weapon, and knocked him sprawling and bloody. Somewhere a woman shrieked like windy, midnight death. Placer fell behind the counter, and down upon him came his ledger and his inkstand, so that one could not have told blood from ink.

The cowboys did not seem to hear, see nor feel, until they saw numbers of citizens with Winchesters running wildly upon them. Old Man Crumford threw high a passionate hand. 'Don't shoot! We'll not fight ye for 'im.'

Nevertheless two or three shots rang, and a cowboy who had been about to gallop off suddenly slumped over on his pony's neck, where he held for a moment like an old sack, and then slid to the ground, while his pony, with flapping rein, fled to the prairie.

'In God's name, don't shoot!' trumpeted Old Man Crumford. 'We'll not fight ye fer 'im!'

'It's murder,' bawled Ben Roddle.

In the chaotic street it seemed for a moment as if everybody would kill everybody. 'Where's the man what done it?' These hot cries seemed to declare a war which would result in an absolute annihilation of one side. But the cowboys were singing out against it. They would fight for nothing – yes – they often fought for nothing – but they would not fight for this dark something.

At last, when a flimsy truce had been made between the inflamed men, all parties went to the hotel. Placer, in some dying whim, had made his way out from behind the pink counter, and, leaving a horrible trail, had travelled to the centre of the room, where he had pitched headlong over the body of Big Watson.

The men lifted the corpse and laid it at the side.

'Who done it?' asked a white, stern man.

A cowboy pointed at Big Watson. 'That's him,' he said huskily.

There was a curious grim silence, and then suddenly, in the death-chamber, there sounded the loud whirring of the clock's works, little doors flew open, a tiny wooden bird appeared and cried, 'Cuckoo!' – twelve times.

F. MARION CRAWFORD

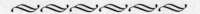

Francis Marion Crawford (1854–1909), novelist, son of an American sculptor and nephew of Julia Ward Howe, was born at Bagni di Lucca, Tuscany, and had a cosmopolitan education. He wrote in French as easily as in English; he studied German, Swedish and Spanish at Cambridge; he also studied Sanskrit at Rome and Harvard and knew many Eastern languages. His first novel, *Mr Isaacs* (1882), was a great success and was followed by over forty others, mainly historical romances, including *Dr Claudius* (1883), *A Roman Singer* (1884), *Zoroaster* (1885), *Saracinesca* (1887), *Sant' Ilario* (1889), *A Cigarette Maker's Romance* (1890) and *The White Sister* (1909). *The Novel – What Is It?* (1893) embodied his theory of fiction. His last years were spent at Sorrento.

By the Waters of Paradise

ONE

I remember my childhood very distinctly. I do not think that the fact argues a good memory, for I have never been clever at learning words by heart, in prose or rhyme; so that I believe my remembrance of events depends much more upon the events themselves than upon my possessing any special facility for recalling them. Perhaps I am too imaginative, and the earliest impressions I received were of a kind to stimulate the imagination abnormally. A long series of little misfortunes, so connected with each other as to suggest a sort of weird fatality, so worked upon my melancholy temperament when I was a boy that, before I was of age, I sincerely believed myself to be under a curse, and not only myself, but my whole family and every individual who bore my name.

I was born in the old place where my father, and his father, and all his predecessors had been born, beyond the memory of man. It is a very old house, and the greater part of it was originally a castle, strongly fortified, and surrounded by a deep moat supplied with abundant water from the hills by a hidden aqueduct. Many of the fortifications have been destroyed, and the moat has been filled up. The water from the aqueduct supplies great fountains, and runs down into huge oblong basins in the terraced gardens, one below the other, each surrounded by a broad pavement of marble between the water and the flower-beds. The waste surplus finally escapes through an artificial grotto, some thirty yards long, into a stream, flowing down through the park to the meadows beyond, and thence to the distant river. The buildings were extended a little and greatly altered more than two hundred years ago, in the time of Charles II, but since then little has been done to improve them, though they have been kept in fairly good repair, according to our fortunes.

In the gardens there are terraces and huge hedges of box and evergreen, some of which used to be clipped into shapes of animals, in the Italian style. I can remember when I was a lad how I used to try to make out what the trees were cut to represent, and how I used to appeal for explanations to Judith, my Welsh nurse. She dealt in a strange mythology of her own, and peopled the gardens with griffins, dragons, good genii and bad, and filled my mind with them at the same time. My nursery window afforded a view of the great fountains at the head of the upper basin, and on moonlight nights the Welshwoman would hold me up to the glass and bid me look at the mist and spray rising into mysterious shapes, moving mystically in the white light like living things.

'It's the Woman of the Water,' she used to say; and sometimes she would threaten that if I did not go to sleep the Woman of the Water would steal up to the high window and carry me away in her wet arms.

The place was gloomy. The broad basins of water and the tall evergreen hedges gave it a funereal look, and the damp-stained marble causeways by the pools might have been made of tombstones. The grey and weather-beaten walls and towers without, the dark and massively furnished rooms within, the deep, mysterious recesses and the heavy curtains, all affected my spirits. I was silent and sad from my childhood. There was a great clock tower above, from which the hours rang dismally during the day, and tolled like a knell in the dead of night. There was no light nor life in the house, for my mother was a helpless invalid, and my father had grown melancholy in his long task of caring for her. He was a thin, dark man, with sad eyes; kind, I think, but silent and unhappy. Next to my mother, I believe he loved me better than anything on earth, for he took immense pains and trouble in teaching me, and what he taught me I have never forgotten. Perhaps it was his only amusement, and that may be the reason why I had no nursery governess or teacher of any kind while he lived.

I used to be taken to see my mother every day, and sometimes twice a day, for an hour at a time. Then I sat upon a little stool near her feet, and she would ask me what I had been doing, and what I wanted to do. I dare say she saw already the seeds of a profound melancholy in my nature, for she looked at me always with a sad smile, and kissed me with a sigh when I was taken away.

One night, when I was just six years old, I lay awake in the nursery. The door was not quite shut, and the Welsh nurse was sitting sewing in the next room. Suddenly I heard her groan, and say in a strange voice, 'One – two – one – two!' I was frightened, and I jumped up and ran to the door, bare-footed as I was.

'What is it, Judith?' I cried, clinging to her skirts. I can remember the look in her strange dark eyes as she answered: 'One – two leaden coffins, fallen from the ceiling!' she crooned, working herself in her chair. 'One – two – a light coffin and a heavy coffin, falling to the floor!'

Then she seemed to notice me, and she took me back to bed and sang me to sleep with a queer old Welsh song.

I do not know how it was, but the impression got hold of me that she had meant that my father and mother were going to die very soon. They died in the very room where she had been sitting that night. It was a great room, my day nursery, full of sun when there was any; and when the days were dark it was the most cheerful place in the house. My mother grew rapidly worse, and I was transferred to another part of the building to make place for her. They thought my nursery was gayer for her, I suppose; but she could not live. She was beautiful when she was dead, and I cried bitterly.

'The light one, the light one – the heavy one to come,' crooned the Welshwoman. And she was right. My father took the room after my mother was gone, and day by day he grew thinner and paler and sadder.

'The heavy one, the heavy one – all of lead,' moaned my nurse, one night in December, standing still, just as she was going to take away the light after putting me to bed. Then she took me up again and wrapped me in a little gown, and led me away to my father's room. She knocked, but no one answered. She opened the door, and we found him in his easy chair before the fire, very white, quite dead.

So I was alone with the Welshwoman till strange people came, and relations whom I had never seen; and then I heard them saying that I must be taken away to some more cheerful place. They were kind people, and I will not believe that they were kind only because I was to be very rich when I grew to be a man. The world never seemed to be a very bad place to me, nor all the people to be miserable sinners, even when I was most melancholy. I do not remember that anyone ever did me any great injustice, nor that I was ever oppressed or ill treated in any way, even by the boys at school. I was sad, I suppose, because my childhood was so gloomy, and, later, because I was unlucky in everything I undertook, till I finally believed I was pursued by fate, and I used to dream that the old Welsh nurse and the Woman of the Water between them had vowed to pursue me to my end. But my natural disposition should have been cheerful, as I have often thought.

Among the lads of my age I was never last, or even among the last, in anything; but I was never first. If I trained for a race, I was sure to sprain my ankle on the day when I was to run. If I pulled an oar with others, my oar was sure to break. If I competed for a prize, some unforeseen accident prevented my winning it at the last moment. Nothing to which I put my hand succeeded, and I got the reputation of being unlucky, until my companions felt it was always safe to bet against me, no matter what the appearances might be. I became discouraged and listless in everything. I gave up the idea of competing for any distinction at the University, comforting myself with the thought that I could not fail in the examination for the ordinary degree. The day before the examination began I fell ill; and when at last I recovered, after a narrow escape from death, I turned my back upon Oxford, and went down alone to visit the old place where I had been born, feeble in health and profoundly disgusted and discouraged. I was twenty-one years of age, master of myself and of my fortune; but so deeply had the long chain of small unlucky circumstances affected me that I thought seriously of shutting myself up from the world to live the life of a hermit and to die as soon as possible. Death seemed the only cheerful possibility in my existence, and my thoughts soon dwelt upon it altogether.

I had never shown any wish to return to my own home since I had been taken away as a little boy, and no one had ever pressed me to do so. The place had been kept in order after a fashion, and did not seem to have suffered during the fifteen years or more of my absence. Nothing earthly could affect those old grey walls that had fought the elements for so many centuries. The garden was more wild than I remembered it; the marble causeways about the pools looked more yellow and damp than of old, and the whole place at first looked smaller. It was not until I had wandered about the house and grounds for many hours that I realised the huge size of the home where I was to live in solitude. Then I began to delight in it, and my resolution to live alone grew stronger.

The people had turned out to welcome me, of course, and I tried to recognise the changed faces of the old gardener and the old housekeeper, and to call them by name. My old nurse I knew at once. She had grown very grey since she heard the coffins fall in the nursery fifteen years before, but her strange eyes were the same, and the look in them woke all my old memories. She went over the house with me.

'And how is the Woman of the Water?' I asked, trying to laugh a little. 'Does she still play in the moonlight?'

'She is hungry,' answered the Welshwoman, in a low voice.

'Hungry? Then we will feed her.' I laughed. But old Judith turned very pale, and looked at me strangely.

'Feed her? Aye – you will feed her well,' she muttered, glancing behind her at the ancient housekeeper, who tottered after us with feeble steps through the halls and passages.

I did not think much of her words. She had always talked oddly, as Welshwomen will, and though I was very melancholy I am sure I was not superstitious, and I was certainly not timid. Only, as in a far-off dream, I seemed to see her standing with the light in her hand and muttering, 'The heavy one – all of lead,' and then leading a little boy through the long corridors to see his father lying dead in a great easy-chair before a smoldering fire. So we went over the house, and I chose the rooms where I would live; and the servants I had brought with me ordered and arranged everything, and I had no more trouble. I did not care what they did provided I was left in peace and was not expected to give directions; for I was more listless than ever, owing to the effects of my illness at college.

I dined in solitary state, and the melancholy grandeur of the vast old dining-room pleased me. Then I went to the room I had selected for my study, and sat down in a deep chair, under a bright light, to think, or to let my thoughts meander through labyrinths of their own choosing, utterly indifferent to the course they might take.

The tall windows of the room opened to the level of the ground upon the terrace at the head of the garden. It was at the end of July, and everything was open, for the weather was warm. As I sat alone I heard the unceasing splash of the great fountains, and I fell to thinking of the Woman of the Water. I rose and went out into the still night, and sat down upon a seat on the terrace, between two gigantic Italian flower pots. The air was deliciously soft and sweet with the smell of the flowers, and the garden was more congenial to me than the house. Sad people always like running water and the sound of it at night, though I cannot tell why. I sat and listened in the gloom, for it was dark below, and the pale moon had not yet climbed over the hills in front of me, though all the air above was light with her rising beams. Slowly the white halo in the eastern sky ascended in an arch above the wooded crests, making the outlines of the mountains more intensely black by contrast, as though the head of some great white saint were rising from behind a screen in a vast cathedral, throwing misty glories from below. I longed to see the moon herself, and I tried to reckon the seconds before she must appear. Then she sprang up quickly, and in a moment more hung round and perfect in the sky. I gazed at her, and then at the floating spray of the tall fountains, and down at the pools, where the water lilies were rocking softly in their sleep on the velvet surface of the moonlit water. Just then a great swan floated out silently into the midst of the basin, and wreathed his long neck, catching the water in his broad bill, and scattering showers of diamonds around him.

Suddenly, as I gazed, something came between me and the light. I looked up instantly. Between me and the round disk of the moon rose the luminous face of a woman, with great strange eyes, and a woman's mouth, full and soft, but not smiling, hooded in black, staring at me as I sat still upon my bench. She was close to me – so close that I could have touched her with my hand. But I was transfixed and helpless. She stood still for a moment, but her expression did not change. Then she passed swiftly away, and my hair stood up on my head, while the cold breeze from her white dress was wafted to my temples as she moved. The moonlight, shining through the tossing spray of the fountain, made traceries of shadow on the gleaming folds of her garments. In an instant she was gone and I was alone.

I was strangely shaken by the vision, and some time passed before I could rise to my feet, for I was still weak from my illness, and the sight I had seen would have startled anyone. I did not reason with myself, for I was certain that I had looked on the unearthly, and no argument could have destroyed that belief. At last I got up and stood unsteadily, gazing in the direction in which I thought the face had gone; but there was nothing to be seen – nothing but the broad paths, the tall, dark evergreen hedges, the tossing water of the fountains and the smooth pool below. I fell back upon the seat and recalled the face I had seen. Strange to say, now that the first impression had passed, there was nothing startling in the recollection; on the contrary, I felt that I was fascinated by the face, and would give anything to see it again. I could retrace the beautiful straight features, the long dark eyes, and the wonderful mouth most exactly in my mind, and when I had reconstructed every detail from memory I knew that the whole was beautiful, and that I should love a woman with such a face.

'I wonder whether she is the Woman of the Water!' I said to myself. Then rising once more, I wandered down the garden, descending one short flight of steps after another from terrace to terrace by the edge of the marble basins, through the shadow and through the moonlight; and I crossed the water by the rustic bridge above the artificial grotto, and climbed slowly up again to the highest terrace by the other side. The air seemed sweeter, and I was very calm, so that I think I smiled to myself as I walked, as though a new happiness had come to me. The woman's face seemed always before me, and the thought of it gave me an unwonted thrill of pleasure, unlike anything I had ever felt before.

I turned as I reached the house, and looked back upon the scene. It had certainly changed in the short hour since I had come out, and my mood had changed with it. Just like my luck, I thought, to fall in love with a ghost! But in old times I would have sighed, and gone to bed more sad than ever, at such a melancholy conclusion. Tonight I felt happy, almost for the first time in my life. The gloomy old study seemed cheerful when I went in. The old pictures on the walls smiled at me, and I sat down in my deep chair with a new and delightful sensation that I was not alone. The idea of having seen a ghost, and of feeling much the better for it, was so absurd that I laughed softly, as I took up one of the books I had brought with me and began to read.

That impression did not wear off. I slept peacefully, and in the morning I threw open my windows to the summer air and looked down at the garden, at the stretches of green and at the coloured flower-beds, at the circling swallows and at the bright water.

'A man might make a paradise of this place,' I exclaimed. 'A man and a woman together!'

From that day the old castle no longer seemed gloomy, and I think I ceased to be sad; for some time, too, I began to take an interest in the place, and to try and make it more alive. I avoided my old Welsh nurse, lest she should damp my humour with some dismal prophecy, and recall my old self by bringing back memories of my dismal childhood. But what I thought of most was the ghostly figure I had seen in the garden that first night after my arrival. I went out every evening and wandered through the walks and paths; but, try as I might, I did not see my vision again. At last, after many days, the memory grew more faint, and my old moody nature gradually overcame the temporary sense of lightness I had experienced. The summer turned to autumn, and I grew restless. It began to rain. The dampness pervaded the gardens, and the outer halls smelled musty, like tombs; the grey sky oppressed me intolerably. I left the place as it was and went abroad, determined to try anything which might possibly make a second break in the monotonous melancholy from which I suffered.

TWO

Most people would be struck by the utter insignificance of the small events which, after the death of my parents, influenced my life and made me unhappy. The gruesome forebodings of a Welsh nurse, which chanced to be realised by an odd coincidence of events, should not seem enough to change the nature of a child and to direct the bent of his character in after years. The little disappointments of schoolboy life, and the somewhat less childish ones of an uneventful and undistinguished academic career, should not have sufficed to turn me out at one-and-twenty years of age a melancholic, listless idler. Some weakness of my own character may have contributed to the result, but in a greater degree it was due to my having a reputation for bad luck. However, I will not try to analyse the causes of my state, for I should satisfy nobody, least of all myself. Still less will I attempt to explain why I felt a temporary revival of my spirits after my adventure in the garden. It is certain that I was in love with the face I had seen, and that I longed to see it again; that I gave up all hope of a second visitation, grew more sad than ever, packed up my traps, and finally went abroad. But in my dreams I went back to my home, and it always appeared to me sunny and bright, as it had looked on that summer's morning after I had seen the woman by the fountain.

I went to Paris. I went farther, and wandered about Germany. I tried to amuse myself, and I failed miserably. With the aimless whims of an idle and useless man come all sorts of suggestions for good resolutions. One day I made up my mind that I would go and bury myself in a German university for a time, and live simply like a poor student. I started with the intention of going to Leipzig, determined to stay there until some event should direct my life or change my humour, or make an end of me altogether. The express train stopped at some station of which I did not know the name. It was dusk on a winter's afternoon, and I peered through the thick glass from my seat. Suddenly another train came gliding in from the opposite direction, and stopped alongside of ours. I looked at the carriage which chanced to be abreast of mine, and idly read the black letters painted on a white board swinging from the brass handrail: BERLIN – COLOGNE – PARIS. Then I looked up at the window above. I started violently, and the cold perspiration broke out upon my forehead. In the dim light, not six feet from where I sat, I saw the face of a woman, the face I loved, the straight, fine features, the strange eyes, the wonderful mouth, the pale skin. Her headdress was a dark veil which seemed to be tied about her head and passed over the shoulders under her chin. As I threw down the window and knelt on the cushioned seat, leaning far out to get a better view, a long whistle screamed through the station, followed by a quick series of dull, clanking sounds; then there was a slight jerk, and my train moved on. Luckily the window was narrow, being the one over the seat, beside the door, or I believe I would have jumped out of it then and there. In an instant the speed increased, and I was being carried swiftly away in the opposite direction from the thing I loved.

For a quarter of an hour I lay back in my place, stunned by the suddenness of the apparition. At last one of the two other passengers, a large and gorgeous captain of the White Konigsberg Cuirassiers, civilly but firmly suggested that I might shut my window, as the evening was cold. I did so, with an apology, and relapsed into silence. The train ran swiftly on for a long time, and it was already beginning to slacken speed before entering another station, when I roused myself and made a sudden resolution. As the carriage stopped before the brilliantly lighted platform, I seized my belongings, saluted my fellow-passengers, and got out, determined to take the first express back to Paris.

This time the circumstances of the vision had been so natural that it did not strike me that there was anything unreal about the face, or about the woman to whom it belonged. I did not try to explain to myself how the face, and the woman, could be travelling by a fast train from Berlin to Paris on a winter's afternoon, when both were in my mind indelibly associated with the moonlight and the fountains in my own English home. I certainly would not have admitted that I had been mistaken in the dusk, attributing to what I had seen a resemblance to my former vision which did not really exist. There was not the slightest doubt in my mind, and I was positively sure that I had again seen the face I loved. I did not hesitate, and in a few hours I was on my way back to Paris. I could not help reflecting on my ill luck. Wandering as I had been for many months, it might as easily have chanced that I should be travelling in the same train with that woman, instead of going the other way. But my luck was destined to turn for a time.

I searched Paris for several days. I dined at the principal hotels; I went to the theatres; I rode in the Bois de Boulogne in the morning, and picked up an acquaintance, whom I forced to drive with me in the afternoon. I went to mass at the Madeleine, and I attended the services at the English Church. I hung about the Louvre and Notre Dame. I went to Versailles. I spent hours in parading the Rue de Rivoli, in the neighbourhood of Meurice's corner, where foreigners pass and repass from morning till night. At last I received an invitation to a reception at the English Embassy. I went, and I found what I had sought so long.

There she was, sitting by an old lady in grey satin and diamonds, who had a wrinkled but kindly face and keen grey eyes that seemed to take in everything they saw, with very little inclination to give much in return. But I did not notice the chaperon. I saw only the face that had haunted me for months, and in the excitement of the moment I walked quickly towards the pair, forgetting such a trifle as the necessity for an introduction.

She was far more beautiful than I had thought, but I never doubted that it was she herself and no other. Vision or no vision before, this was the reality, and I knew it. Twice her hair had been covered, now at last I saw it, and the added beauty of its magnificence glorified the whole woman. It was rich hair, fine and abundant, golden, with deep ruddy tints in it like red-bronze spun fine. There was no ornament in it, not a rose, not a thread of gold, and I felt that it needed nothing to enhance its splendour; nothing but her pale face, her dark strange eyes and her heavy eyebrows. I could see that she was slender too, but strong withal, as she sat there quietly gazing at the moving scene in the midst of the brilliant lights and the hum of perpetual conversation.

I recollected the detail of introduction in time, and turned aside to look for my host. I found him at last. I begged him to present me to the two ladies, pointing them out to him at the same time.

'Yes – uh – by all means – uh,' replied his excellency with a pleasant smile. He evidently had no idea of my name, which was not to be wondered at.

'I am Lord Cairngorm,' I observed.

'Oh – by all means,' answered the ambassador with the same hospitable smile. 'Yes – uh – the fact is, I must try and find out who they are; such lots of people, you know.'

'Oh, if you will present me, I will try and find out for you,' said I, laughing.

'Ah, yes – so kind of you – come along,' said my host. We threaded the crowd, and in a few minutes we stood before the two ladies.

' 'Lowmintrduce L'd Cairngorm,' he said; then, adding quickly to me, 'Come and dine tomorrow, won't you?' he glided away with his pleasant smile and disappeared in the crowd.

I sat down beside the beautiful girl, conscious that the eyes of the duenna were upon me.

'I think we have been very near meeting before,' I remarked, by way of opening the conversation.

My companion turned her eyes full upon me with an air of enquiry. She evidently did not recall my face, if she had ever seen me.

'Really – I cannot remember,' she observed, in a low and musical voice. 'When?'

'In the first place, you came down from Berlin by the express ten days ago. I was going the other way, and our carriages stopped opposite each other. I saw you at the window.'

'Yes – we came that way, but I do not remember – ' She hesitated.

'Secondly,' I continued, 'I was sitting alone in my garden last summer – near the end of July – do you remember? You must have wandered in there through the park; you came up to the house and looked at me – '

'Was that you?' she asked, in evident surprise. Then she broke into a laugh. 'I told everybody I had seen a ghost; there had never been any Cairngorms in the place since the memory of man. We left the next day, and never heard that you had come there; indeed, I did not know the castle belonged to you.'

'Where were you staying?' I asked.

'Where? Why, with my aunt, where I always stay. She is your neighbour, since it *is* you.'

'I – beg your pardon – but then – is your aunt Lady Bluebell? I did not quite catch – '

'Don't be afraid. She is amazingly deaf. Yes. She is the relict of my beloved uncle, the sixteenth or seventeenth Baron Bluebell – I forget exactly how many of them there have been. And I – do you know who I am?' She laughed, well knowing that I did not.

'No,' I answered frankly. 'I have not the least idea. I asked to be introduced because I recognised you. Perhaps – perhaps you are a Miss Bluebell?'

'Considering that you are a neighbour, I will tell you who I am,' she answered. 'No; I am of the tribe of Bluebells, but my name is Lammas, and I have been given to understand that I was christened Margaret. Being a floral family, they call me Daisy. A dreadful American man once told me that my aunt was a Bluebell and that I was a Harebell – with two l's and an e – because my hair is so thick. I warn you, so that you may avoid making such a bad pun.'

'Do I look like a man who makes puns?' I asked, being very conscious of my melancholy face and sad looks.

Miss Lammas eyed me critically.

'No; you have a mournful temperament. I think I can trust you,' she answered. 'Do you think you could communicate to my aunt the fact that you are a Cairngorm and a neighbour? I am sure she would like to know.'

I leaned toward the old lady, inflating my lungs for a yell. But Miss Lammas stopped me.

'That is not of the slightest use,' she remarked. 'You can write it on a bit of paper. She is utterly deaf.'

'I have a pencil,' I answered; 'but I have no paper. Would my cuff do, do you think?'

'Oh, yes!' replied Miss Lammas, with alacrity; 'men often do that.'

I wrote on my cuff: 'Miss Lammas wishes me to explain that I am your neighbour, Cairngorm.' Then I held out my arm before the old lady's nose. She seemed perfectly accustomed to the proceeding, put up her glasses, read the words, smiled, nodded, and addressed me in the unearthly voice peculiar to people who hear nothing.

'I knew your grandfather very well,' she said. Then she smiled and nodded to me again, and to her niece, and relapsed into silence.

'It is all right,' remarked Miss Lammas. 'Aunt Bluebell knows she is deaf, and does not say much, like the parrot. You see, she knew your grandfather. How odd that we should be neighbours! Why have we never met before?'

'If you had told me you knew my grandfather when you appeared in the garden, I should not have been in the least surprised,' I answered rather irrelevantly. 'I really thought you were the ghost of the old fountain. How in the world did you come there at that hour?'

'We were a large party and we went out for a walk. Then we thought we should like to see what your park was like in the moonlight, and so we trespassed. I got separated from the rest, and came upon you by accident, just as I was admiring the extremely ghostly look of your house, and wondering whether anybody would ever come and live there again. It looks like the castle of Macbeth, or a scene from the opera. Do you know anybody here?'

'Hardly a soul! Do you?'

'No. Aunt Bluebell said it was our duty to come. It is easy for her to go out; she does not bear the burden of the conversation.'

'I am sorry you find it a burden,' said I. 'Shall I go away?'

Miss Lammas looked at me with a sudden gravity in her beautiful eyes, and there was a sort of hesitation about the lines of her full, soft mouth.

'No,' she said at last, quite simply, 'don't go away. We may like each other, if you stay a little longer – and we ought to, because we are neighbours in the country.'

I suppose I ought to have thought Miss Lammas a very odd girl. There is, indeed, a sort of freemasonry between people who discover that they live near each other and that they ought to have known each other before. But there was a sort of unexpected frankness and simplicity in the girl's amusing manner which would have struck anyone else as being singular, to say the least of it. To me, however, it all seemed natural enough. I had dreamed of her face too long not to be utterly happy when I met her at last and could talk to her as much as I pleased. To me, the man of ill luck in everything, the whole meeting seemed too good to be true. I felt again that strange sensation of lightness which I had experienced after I had seen her face in the garden. The great rooms seemed brighter, life seemed worth living; my sluggish, melancholy blood ran faster, and filled me with a new sense of strength. I said to myself that without this woman I was but an imperfect being, but that with her I could accomplish everything to which I should set my hand. Like the great Doctor, when he thought he had cheated Mephistopheles at last, I could have cried aloud to the fleeting moment, *Verweile doch, du bist so schon!*

'Are you always gay?' I asked, suddenly. 'How happy you must be!'

'The days would sometimes seem very long if I were gloomy,' she answered, thoughtfully. 'Yes, I think I find life very pleasant, and I tell it so.'

'How can you "tell life" anything?' I enquired. 'If I could catch my life and talk to it, I would abuse it prodigiously, I assure you.'

'I dare say. You have a melancholy temper. You ought to live out of doors, dig potatoes, make hay, shoot, hunt, tumble into ditches and come home muddy and hungry for dinner. It would be much better for you than moping in your rook tower and hating everything.'

'It is rather lonely down there,' I murmured, apologetically, feeling that Miss Lammas was quite right.

'Then marry, and quarrel with your wife,' she laughed. 'Anything is better than being alone.'

'I am a very peaceable person. I never quarrel with anybody. You can try it. You will find it quite impossible.'

'Will you let me try?' she asked, still smiling.

'By all means – especially if it is to be only a preliminary canter,' I answered, rashly.

'What do you mean?' she enquired, turning quickly upon me.

'Oh – nothing. You might try my paces with a view to quarrelling in the future. I cannot imagine how you are going to do it. You will have to resort to immediate and direct abuse.'

'No. I will only say that if you do not like your life, it is your own fault. How can a man of your age talk of being melancholy, or of the hollowness of existence? Are you consumptive? Are you subject to hereditary insanity? Are you deaf, like Aunt Bluebell? Are you poor, like – lots of people? Have you been crossed in love? Have you lost the world for a woman, or any particular woman for the sake of the world? Are you feeble-minded, a cripple, an outcast? Are you – repulsively ugly?' She laughed again. 'Is there any reason in the world why you should not enjoy all you have got in life?'

'No. There is no reason whatever, except that I am dreadfully unlucky, especially in small things.'

By the Waters of Paradise

'Then try big things, just for a change,' suggested Miss Lammas. 'Try and get married, for instance, and see how it turns out.'

'If it turned out badly it would be rather serious.'

'Not half so serious as it is to abuse everything unreasonably. If abuse is your particular talent, abuse something that ought to be abused. Abuse the Conservatives – or the Liberals – it does not matter which, since they are always abusing each other. Make yourself felt by other people. You will like it, if they don't. It will make a man of you. Fill your mouth with pebbles, and howl at the sea, if you cannot do anything else. It did Demosthenes no end of good, you know. You will have the satisfaction of imitating a great man.'

'Really, Miss Lammas, I think the list of innocent exercises you propose – '

'Very well – if you don't care for that sort of thing, care for some other sort of thing. Care for something, or hate something. Don't be idle. Life is short, and though art may be long, plenty of noise answers nearly as well.'

'I do care for something – I mean, somebody,' I said.

'A woman? Then marry her. Don't hesitate.'

'I do not know whether she would marry me,' I said. 'I have never asked.'

'Then ask her at once,' answered Miss Lammas. 'I shall die happy if I feel I have persuaded a melancholy fellow creature to rouse himself to action. Ask her, by all means, and see what she says. If she does not accept you at once, she may take you the next time. Meanwhile, you will have entered for the race. If you lose, there are the All-Age Trial Stakes and the Consolation Race.'

'And plenty of selling races into the bargain. Shall I take you at your word, Miss Lammas?'

'I hope you will,' she answered.

'Since you yourself advise me, I will. Miss Lammas, will you do me the honour to marry me?'

For the first time in my life the blood rushed to my head and my sight swam. I cannot tell why I said it. It would be useless to try to explain the extraordinary fascination the girl exercised over me, or the still more extraordinary feeling of intimacy with her which had grown in me during that half-hour. Lonely, sad, unlucky as I had been all my life, I was certainly not timid, nor even shy. But to propose to marry a woman after half an hour's acquaintance was a piece of madness of which I never believed myself capable, and of which I should never be capable again, could I be placed in the same situation. It was as though my whole being had been changed in a moment by magic – by the white magic of her nature brought into contact with mine. The blood sank back to my heart, and a moment later I found myself staring at her with anxious eyes. To my amazement she was as calm as ever, but her beautiful mouth smiled, and there was a mischievous light in her dark-brown eyes.

'Fairly caught,' she answered. 'For an individual who pretends to be listless and sad you are not lacking in humour. I had really not the least idea what you were going to say. Wouldn't it be singularly awkward for you if I had said yes? I never saw anybody begin to practise so sharply what was preached to him – with so very little loss of time!'

'You probably never met a man who had dreamed of you for seven months before being introduced.'

'No, I never did,' she answered gayly. 'It smacks of the romantic. Perhaps you are a romantic character, after all. I should think you were if I believed you. Very well; you have taken my advice, entered for a Stranger's Race and lost it. Try the All-Age Trial Stakes. You have another cuff, and a pencil. Propose to Aunt Bluebell; she would dance with astonishment, and she might recover her hearing.'

THREE

That was how I first asked Margaret Lammas to be my wife, and I will agree with anyone who says I behaved very foolishly. But I have not repented of it, and I never shall. I have long ago understood that I was out of my mind that evening, but I think my temporary insanity on that occasion has had the effect of making me a saner man ever since. Her manner turned my head, for it was so different from what I had expected. To hear this lovely creature, who, in my imagination, was a heroine of romance, if not of tragedy, talking familiarly and laughing readily was more than my equanimity could bear, and I lost my head as well as my heart. But when I went back to England in the spring, I went to make certain arrangements at the castle – certain changes and improvements which would be absolutely necessary. I had won the race for which I had entered myself so rashly, and we were to be married in June.

Whether the change was due to the orders I had left with the gardener and the rest of the servants, or to my own state of mind, I cannot tell. At all events, the old place did not look the same to me when I opened my window on the morning after my arrival. There were the grey walls below me and the grey turrets flanking the huge building; there were the fountains, the marble causeways, the smooth basins, the tall box hedges, the water lilies and the swans, just as of old. But there was something else there, too – something in the air, in the water, and in the greenness that I did not recognise – a light over everything by which everything was transfigured. The clock in the tower struck seven, and the strokes of the ancient bell sounded like a wedding chime. The air sang with the thrilling treble of the songbirds, with the silvery music of the plashing water and the softer harmony of the leaves stirred by the fresh morning wind. There was a smell of new-mown hay from the distant meadows, and of blooming roses from the beds below, wafted up together to my window. I stood in the pure sunshine and drank the air and all the sounds and the odours that were in it; and I looked down at my garden and said: 'It is paradise, after all.' I think the men of old were right when they called heaven a garden, and Eden, a garden inhabited by one man and one woman, the earthly paradise.

I turned away, wondering what had become of the gloomy memories I had always associated with my home. I tried to recall the impression of my nurse's horrible prophecy before the death of my parents – an impression which hitherto had been vivid enough. I tried to remember my old self, my dejection, my listlessness, my bad luck, my petty disappointments. I endeavoured to force myself to think as I used to think, if only to satisfy myself that I had not lost my individuality. But I succeeded in none of these efforts. I was a different man, a changed being, incapable of sorrow, of ill luck, or of sadness. My life had been a dream, not evil, but infinitely gloomy and hopeless. It was now a reality, full of hope, gladness, and all manner of good. My home had been like a tomb; today it was paradise. My heart had been as though it had not existed; today it beat with strength and youth and the certainty of realised happiness. I revelled in the beauty of the world, and called loveliness out of the future to enjoy it before time should bring it to me, as a traveller in the plains looks up to the mountains, and already tastes the cool air through the dust of the road.

Here, I thought, we will live and live for years. There we will sit by the fountain towards evening and in the deep moonlight. Down those paths we will wander together. On those benches we will rest and talk. Among those eastern hills we will ride through the soft twilight, and in the old house we will tell tales on winter nights, when the logs burn high, and the holly berries are red, and the old clock tolls out the dying year. On these old steps, in these dark passages and stately rooms, there will one day be the sound of little pattering feet, and laughing child voices will ring up to the vaults of the ancient hall. Those tiny footsteps shall not be slow and sad as mine were, nor shall the childish words be spoken in an awed whisper. No gloomy Welsh-woman shall people the dusky corners with weird horrors, nor utter horrid prophecies of death and ghastly things. All shall be young, and fresh, and joyful, and happy, and we will turn the old luck again, and forget that there was ever any sadness.

So I thought, as I looked out of my window that morning and for many mornings after that, and every day it all seemed more real than ever before, and much nearer. But the old nurse looked at me askance, and muttered odd sayings about the Woman of the Water. I cared little what she said, for I was far too happy.

At last the time came near for the wedding. Lady Bluebell and all the tribe of Bluebells, as Margaret called them, were at Bluebell Grange, for we had determined to be married in the country, and to come straight to the castle afterwards. We cared little for travelling, and not at all for a crowded ceremony at St George's in Hanover Square, with all the tiresome formalities afterwards. I used to ride over to the Grange every day, and very often Margaret would come with her aunt and some of her cousins to the castle. I was suspicious of my own taste, and was only too glad to let her have her way about the alterations and improvements in our home.

We were to be married on the 30th of July, and on the evening of the 28th Margaret drove over with some of the Bluebell party. In the long summer twilight we all went out into the garden. Naturally enough, Margaret and I were left to ourselves, and we wandered down by the marble basins.

'It is an odd coincidence,' I said; 'it was on this very night last year that I first saw you.'

'Considering that it is the month of July,' answered Margaret with a laugh, 'and that we have been here almost every day, I don't think the coincidence is so extraordinary, after all.'

'No, dear,' said I, 'I suppose not. I don't know why it struck me. We shall very likely be here a year from today, and a year from that. The odd thing, when I think of it, is that you should be here at all. But my luck has turned. I ought not to think anything odd that happens now that I have you. It is all sure to be good.'

'A slight change in your ideas since that remarkable performance of yours in Paris,' said Margaret. 'Do you know, I thought you were the most extraordinary man I had ever met.'

'I thought you were the most charming woman I had ever seen. I naturally did not want to lose any time in frivolities. I took you at your word, I followed your advice, I asked you to marry me, and this is the delightful result – what's the matter?'

Margaret had started suddenly, and her hand tightened on my arm. An old woman was coming up the path, and was close to us before we saw her, for the moon had risen, and was shining full in our faces. The woman turned out to be my old nurse.

'It's only Judith, dear – don't be frightened,' I said. Then I spoke to the Welshwoman: 'What are you about, Judith? Have you been feeding the Woman of the Water?'

'Aye – when the clock strikes, Willie – my lord, I mean,' muttered the old creature, drawing aside to let us pass, and fixing her strange eyes on Margaret's face.

'What does she mean?' asked Margaret, when we had gone by.

'Nothing, darling. The old thing is mildly crazy, but she is a good soul.'

We went on in silence for a few moments, and came to the rustic bridge just above the artificial grotto through which the water ran out into the park, dark and swift in its narrow channel. We stopped, and leaned on the wooden rail. The moon was now behind us, and shone full upon the long vista of basins and on the huge walls and towers of the castle above.

'How proud you ought to be of such a grand old place!' said Margaret, softly.

'It is yours now, darling,' I answered. 'You have as good a right to love it as I – but I only love it because you are to live in it, dear.'

Her hand stole out and lay on mine, and we were both silent. Just then the clock began to strike far off in the tower. I counted – eight – nine – ten – eleven – I looked at my watch – twelve – thirteen – I laughed. The bell went on striking.

'The old clock has gone crazy, like Judith,' I exclaimed. Still it went on, note after note ringing out monotonously through the still air. We leaned over the rail, instinctively looking in the direction whence the sound came. On and on it went. I counted nearly a hundred, out of sheer curiosity, for I understood that something had broken and that the thing was running itself down.

Suddenly there was a crack as of breaking wood, a cry and a heavy splash, and I was alone, clinging to the broken end of the rail of the rustic bridge.

I do not think I hesitated while my pulse beat twice. I sprang clear of the bridge into the black rushing water, dived to the bottom, came up again with empty hands, turned and swam downward through the grotto in the thick darkness, plunging and diving at every stroke, striking my head and hands against jagged stones and sharp corners, clutching at last something in my fingers and dragging it up with all my might. I spoke, I cried aloud, but there was no answer. I was alone in the pitchy darkness with my burden, and the house was five hundred yards away. Struggling still, I felt the ground beneath my feet, I saw a ray of moonlight – the grotto widened, and the deep water became a broad and shallow brook as I stumbled over the stones and at last laid Margaret's body on the bank in the park beyond.

'Aye, Willie, as the clock struck!' said the voice of Judith, the Welsh nurse, as she bent down and looked at the white face. The old woman must have turned back and followed us, seen the accident, and slipped out by the lower gate of the garden. 'Aye,' she groaned, 'you have fed the Woman of the Water this night, Willie, while the clock was striking.'

I scarcely heard her as I knelt beside the lifeless body of the woman I loved, chafing the wet white temples and gazing wildly into the wide-staring eyes. I remember only the first returning look of consciousness, the first heaving breath, the first movement of those dear hands stretching out towards me.

*　　*　　*

That is not much of a story, you say. It is the story of my life. That is all. It does not pretend to be anything else. Old Judith says my luck turned on that summer's night when I was struggling in the water to save all that was worth living for. A month later there was a stone bridge above the grotto, and Margaret and I stood on it and looked up at the moonlit castle, as we had done once before, and as we have done many times since. For all those things happened ten years ago last summer, and this is the tenth Christmas Eve we have spent together by the roaring logs in the old hall, talking of old times; and every year there are more old times to talk of. There are curly-headed boys, too, with red-gold hair and dark-brown eyes like their mother's, and a little Margaret, with solemn black eyes like mine. Why could not she look like her mother, too, as well as the rest of them?

The world is very bright at this glorious Christmas time, and perhaps there is little use in calling up the sadness of long ago, unless it be to make the jolly firelight seem more cheerful, the good wife's face look gladder, and to give the children's laughter a merrier ring, by contrast with all that is gone. Perhaps, too, some sad-faced, listless, melancholy youth, who feels that the world is very hollow, and that life is like a perpetual funeral service, just as I used to feel myself, may take courage from my example, and having found the woman of his heart, ask her to marry him after half an hour's acquaintance. But, on the whole, I would not advise any man to marry, for the simple reason that no man will ever find a wife like mine, and being obliged to go farther, he will necessarily fare worse. My wife has done miracles, but I will not assert that any other woman is able to follow her example.

Margaret always said that the old place was beautiful, and that I ought to be proud of it. I dare say she is right. She has even more imagination than I. But I have a good answer and a plain one, which is this – that all the beauty of the castle comes from her. She has breathed upon it all, as the children blow upon the cold glass window panes in winter; and as their warm breath crystallises into landscapes from fairyland, full of exquisite shapes and traceries upon the blank surface, so her spirit has transformed every grey stone of the old towers, every ancient tree and hedge in the gardens, every thought of my once melancholy self. All that was old is young, and all that was sad is glad, and I am the gladdest of all. Whatever heaven may be, there is no earthly paradise without woman, nor is there anywhere a place so desolate, so dreary, so unutterably miserable that a woman cannot make it seem heaven to the man she loves and who loves her.

I hear certain cynics laugh, and cry that all that has been said before. Do not laugh, my good cynic. You are too small a man to laugh at such a great thing as love. Prayers have been said before now by many, and perhaps you say yours, too. I do not think they lose anything by being repeated, nor you by repeating them. You say that the world is bitter, and full of the waters of bitterness. Love, and so live that you may be loved – the world will turn sweet for you, and you shall rest like me by the waters of paradise.

GUY DE MAUPASSANT

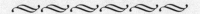

Guy de Maupassant (1850–93), novelist, born probably at the Château de Miromesnil, Dieppe, in north-west France. He studied at Rouen, and spent his life in Normandy. After serving as a soldier and a government clerk, he took to writing, encouraged by Flaubert, a friend of his mother's, and joined the Naturalist group led by Zola. His stories range from the short tale to the full-length novel. His first success 'Boule de Suife' (1880) led to his being in great demand by newspapers. There followed about three hundred stories and several novels, including the supposedly autobiographical *Bel-Ami* (1885). His stories describe madness and fear with a horrifying accuracy which foreshadows the insanity which beset Maupassant in 1892 when he was committed to an asylum in Paris.

The Wreck

It was yesterday, the 31st of December.

I had just finished breakfast with my old friend Georges Garin when the servant handed him a letter covered with seals and foreign stamps.

Georges said: 'Will you excuse me?'

'Certainly.'

And so he began to read the letter, which was written in a large English handwriting, crossed and recrossed in every direction. He read slowly, with serious attention and the interest which we only pay to things which touch our hearts.

Then he put the letter on the mantelpiece and said: 'That was a curious story! I've never told you about it, I think. Yet it was a sentimental adventure, and it really happened to me. That was a strange New Year's Day, indeed! It must have been twenty years ago, for I was then thirty and am now fifty years old.

'I was then an inspector in the Maritime Insurance Company, of which I am now director. I had arranged to pass New Year's Day in Paris – since it is customary to make that day a fête – when I received a letter from the manager, asking me to proceed at once to the Island of Ré, where a three-masted vessel from St-Nazaire, insured by us, had just been driven ashore. It was then eight o'clock in the morning. I arrived at the office at ten to get my advices, and that evening I took the express, which put me down in La Rochelle the next day, the 31st of December.

'I had two hours to wait before going aboard the boat for Ré. So I made a tour of the town. It is certainly a queer city, La Rochelle, with strong characteristics of its own – streets tangled like a labyrinth, sidewalks running under endless arcaded galleries like those of the Rue de Rivoli, but low, mysterious, built as if to form a suitable setting for conspirators and making a striking background for those old-time wars, the savage heroic wars of religion. It is indeed the typical old Huguenot city, conservative, discreet, with no fine art to show, with no wonderful monuments, such as make Rouen; but it is remarkable for its severe, somewhat sullen look; it is a city of obstinate fighters, a city where fanaticism might well blossom, where the faith of the Calvinists became enthusiastic and which gave birth to the plot of the "Four Sergeants".

'After I had wandered for some time about these curious streets, I went aboard the black, rotund little steamboat which was to take me to the Island of Ré. It was called the *Jean Guiton*. It started with angry puffings, passed between the two old towers which guard the harbour, crossed the roadstead and issued from the mole built by Richelieu, the great stones of which can be seen at the water's edge, enclosing the town like a great necklace. Then the steamboat turned to the right.

'It was one of those sad days which give one the blues, tighten the heart and take away all strength and energy and force – a grey, cold day, with a heavy mist which was as wet as rain, as cold as frost, as bad to breathe as the steam of a washtub.

'Under this low sky of dismal fog the shallow, yellow, sandy sea beyond practically level beaches lay without a wrinkle, without a movement, without life, a sea of turbid water, of greasy water, of stagnant water. The *Jean Guiton* passed over it, rolling a little from habit, dividing the smooth surface of the water and leaving behind a few waves, a little splashing, a slight swell, which soon calmed down.

'I began to talk to the captain, a little man with small feet, as round as his boat and rolling in the same manner. I wanted some details of the disaster on which I was to draw up a report. A great square-rigged three-master, the *Marie Joseph*, of St-Nazaire, had gone ashore one night in a hurricane on the sands of the Island of Ré.

'The owner wrote us that the storm had thrown the ship so far ashore that it was impossible to float her and that they had to remove everything which could be detached with the utmost possible haste. Nevertheless I must examine the situation of the wreck, estimate what must have been her condition before the disaster and decide whether all efforts had been used to get her afloat. I came as an agent of the company in order to give contradictory testimony, if necessary, at the trial.

'On receipt of my report, the manager would take what measures he might think necessary to protect our interests.

'The captain of the *Jean Guiton* knew all about the affair, having been summoned with his boat to assist in the attempts at salvage.

'He was from Bordeaux. He told me the story of the disaster. The *Marie Joseph*, driven by a furious gale, lost her bearings completely in the night, and steering haphazardly over a heavy foaming sea – "a milk-soup sea", said the captain – had gone ashore on those immense sandbanks which make the coasts of this country look like limitless Saharas when the tide is low.

'While talking I looked around and ahead. Between the ocean and the lowering sky lay an open space where the eye could see into the distance. We were following a coast. I asked: ' "Is that the Island of Ré?"

' "Yes, sir."

'And suddenly the captain stretched his right hand out before us, pointed to something almost imperceptible in the open sea, and said: "There's your ship!"

' "The *Marie Joseph*!"

' "Yes."

'I was amazed. This black, almost imperceptible speck, which looked to me like a rock, seemed at least three miles from land. "But, captain," I said, "there must be a hundred fathoms of water in that place."

'He began to laugh. "A hundred fathoms, my child! Well, I should say about two! It's now nine-forty, just high tide. Go down along the beach with your hands in your pockets after you've had lunch at the Hôtel du Dauphin, and I'll wager that at ten minutes to three, or three o'clock, you'll reach the wreck without wetting your feet, and have from an hour and three-quarters to two hours aboard of her; but not more, or you'll be caught. The faster the sea goes out the faster it comes back. This coast is as flat as a turtle! But start away at ten minutes to five, as I tell you, and at half-past seven you will be again aboard of the *Jean Guiton*, which will put you down this same evening on the quay at La Rochelle."

'I thanked the captain and I went and sat down in the bow of the steamer to get a good look at the little town of St-Martin, which we were now rapidly approaching.

'It was just like all small seaports which serve as capitals of the barren islands scattered along the coast – a large fishing village, one foot on sea and one on shore, subsisting on fish and wild fowl, vegetables and shellfish, radishes and mussels. The island is very low and little cultivated, yet it seems to be thickly populated. However, I did not penetrate into the interior.

'After lunch I climbed across a little promontory, and then, as the tide was rapidly falling, I started out across the sands towards the black object which I could just perceive above the surface of the water, out a considerable distance.

'I walked quickly over the yellow plain. It was elastic, like flesh, and seemed to sweat beneath my tread. The sea had been there very lately. Now I perceived it at a distance, escaping out of sight, and I no longer could distinguish the line which separated the sands from ocean. I felt as though I were looking at a gigantic supernatural work of enchantment. The Atlantic had just now been before me, then it had disappeared into the sands, just as stage scenery disappears through a trap; and I was now walking in the midst of a desert. Only the feeling, the breath of the salt water, remained with me. I perceived the smell of the wrack, the smell of the sea, the good strong smell of sea coasts. I walked fast; I was no longer cold. I looked at the stranded wreck, which grew in size as I approached, and came now to resemble an enormous shipwrecked whale.

'It seemed fairly to rise out of the ground, and on that great, flat, yellow stretch of sand assumed wonderful proportions. After an hour's walk I at last reached it. It lay upon its side, ruined and shattered, its broken bones showing as though it were an animal, bones of tarred wood pierced with great bolts. The sand had already invaded it, entering it by all the crannies, and held it and refused to let it go. It seemed to have taken root in it. The bow had entered deep into this soft, treacherous beach, while the stern, high in the air, seemed to cast at heaven, like a cry of despairing appeal, the two white words on the black planking, *Marie Joseph*.

'I climbed upon this carcass of a ship by the lowest side; then, having reached the deck, I went below. The daylight, which entered by the stove-in hatches and the cracks in the sides, showed me dimly long dark cavities full of demolished woodwork. They contained nothing but sand, which served as a floor in this cavern of planks.

'I began to take some notes about the condition of the ship. I was seated on a broken empty cask, writing by the light of a great crack, through which I could perceive the boundless stretch of the strand. A strange shivering of cold and loneliness ran over my skin from time to time, and I would often stop writing for a moment to listen to the mysterious noises in the derelict: the noise of crabs scratching the planking with their crooked claws; the noise of a thousand little creatures of the sea already crawling over this dead body or else boring into the wood.

'Suddenly, very near me, I heard human voices. I started as though I had seen a ghost. For a second I really thought I was about to see drowned men rise from the sinister depths of the hold, who would tell me about their death. At any rate, it did not take me long to swing myself on deck. There, standing by the bows, was a tall Englishman with his three young daughters. Certainly they were a good deal more frightened at seeing this sudden apparition on the abandoned three-master than I was at seeing them. The youngest girl turned and ran, the two others threw their arms round their father. As for him, he opened his mouth – that was the only sign of emotion which he showed.

'Then, after several seconds, he spoke: "Monsieur, are you the owner of this ship?"

' "I am."

' "May I go over it?"

' "You may."

'Then he uttered a long sentence in English, in which I only distinguished the word "gracious", repeated several times.

'As he was looking for a place to climb up I showed him the easiest way, and gave him a hand. He climbed up. Then we helped up the three girls, who had now quite recovered their composure. They were charming, especially the oldest, a blonde of eighteen, fresh as a flower, and very dainty and pretty! Ah, yes! the pretty Englishwomen have indeed the look of tender sea plants. One would have said of this one that she had just risen out of the sands and that her hair had kept their tint. They all, with their exquisite freshness, make you think of the delicate colours of pink seashells and of shining pearls hidden in the unknown depths of the ocean.

'She spoke French a little better than her father and acted as interpreter. I had to tell all about the shipwreck, and I romanced as though I had been present at the catastrophe. Then the whole family descended into the interior of the wreck. As soon as they had penetrated into this sombre, dimly lit cavity they uttered cries of astonishment and admiration. Suddenly the father and his three daughters were holding sketchbooks in their hands, which they had doubtless carried hidden somewhere in their heavy weather-proof clothes, and were all beginning at once to make pencil sketches of this melancholy and weird place.

'They had seated themselves side by side on a projecting beam, and the four sketchbooks on the eight knees were being rapidly covered with little black lines which were intended to represent the half-opened hulk of the *Marie Joseph*.

'I continued to inspect the skeleton of the ship, and the oldest girl talked to me while she worked.

'They had none of the usual English arrogance; they were simple honest members of that class of continuous travellers with which England covers the globe. The father was long and thin, with a red face framed in white whiskers, which gave him the look of a living sandwich, a piece of ham carved like a face between two wads of hair. The daughters, who had long legs like young storks, were just as gangling – except the oldest. All three were pretty, especially the tallest.

'She had such a droll way of speaking, of laughing, of understanding and of not understanding, of raising her eyes to ask a question (eyes blue as the deep ocean), of stopping her drawing a moment to make a guess at what you meant, of returning once more to her work, of saying yes or no – that I could have listened and looked indefinitely.

'Suddenly she murmured: ' "I hear a little sound on this boat."

'I listened and I immediately distinguished a low, steady, curious sound. I rose and looked out of the crack and gave a scream. The sea had come up to us; it would soon surround us!

'We were on deck in an instant. It was too late. The water circled us about and was running towards the coast at tremendous speed. No, it did not run, it glided, crept, spread like an immense, limitless blot. The water was barely a few centimetres deep, but the rising flood had gone so far that we no longer saw the vanishing line of the imperceptible tide.

'The Englishman wanted to jump. I held him back. Flight was impossible because of the deep places which we had been obliged to go round on our way out and into which we should fall on our return.

'There was a minute of horrible anguish in our hearts. Then the little English girl began to smile and murmured: "Now it is we who are shipwrecked."

'I tried to laugh, but fear held me, a fear which was cowardly and horrid and base and treacherous like the tide. All the danger which we ran appeared to me at once. I wanted to shriek: "Help!" But to whom?

'The two younger girls were clinging to their father, who looked in consternation at the measureless sea which hedged us round about.

'The night fell as swiftly as the ocean rose – a lowering, wet, icy night.

'I said:"There's nothing to do but to stay on the ship."

'The Englishman answered: "Oh, yes!"'

'And we waited there a quarter of an hour, half an hour, indeed I don't know how long, watching that creeping water growing deeper as it swirled around us, as though it were playing on the beach, which it had regained.

'One of the young girls was cold, and we thought to go below to shelter ourselves from the light but freezing wind that made our skins tingle.

'I leaned over the hatchway. The ship was full of water. So we had to cower against the stern planking, which shielded us a little.

'Darkness was now coming on, and we remained huddled together. I felt the shoulder of the little English girl trembling against mine, her teeth chattering from time to time. But I also felt the gentle warmth of her body through her ulster, and that warmth was as delicious to me as a kiss. We no longer spoke; we sat motionless, mute, cowering down like animals in a ditch when a hurricane is raging. And, nevertheless, despite the night, despite the terrible and increasing danger, I began to feel happy that I was there, glad of the cold and the peril, glad of the long hours of darkness and anguish that I must pass huddled so near this dainty, pretty young girl.

'I asked myself, "Why this strange sensation of well-being and of joy?"

'Why! Who knows? Because she was there? Who was she? A little unknown English girl? I did not love her, I did not even know her. And for all that, I was touched and conquered. I wanted to save her, to sacrifice myself for her, to commit a thousand follies! Strange thing! How does it happen that the presence of a woman overwhelms us so? Is it the power of her grace which enfolds us? Is it the seduction of beauty and youth, which intoxicates one like wine?

'Is it not rather the touch of Love the Mysterious, who seeks constantly to unite two beings, who tries his strength the instant he has put a man and a woman face to face?

'The silence of the darkness became terrible, the stillness of the sky dreadful, because we could hear vaguely about us a slight, continuous sound, the sound of the rising tide and the monotonous plashing of the water against the ship.

'Suddenly I heard the sound of sobs. The youngest of the girls was crying. Her father tried to console her, and they began to talk in their own tongue, which I did not understand. I guessed that he was reassuring her and that she was still afraid.

'I asked my neighbour: "You are not too cold, are you, mademoiselle?"

' "Oh, yes. I am very cold."

'I offered to give her my cloak; she refused it.

'But I had taken it off and I covered her with it against her will. In the short struggle her hand touched mine. It made a delicious thrill run through my body.

'For some minutes the air had been growing brisker, the dashing of the water stronger against the flanks of the ship. I raised myself; a great gust of wind blew in my face. The wind was rising!

'The Englishman perceived this at the same time as I did and said simply: ' "This is bad for us, this – "

'Of course it was bad, it was certain death if any breakers, however feeble, should attack and shake the wreck, which was already so shattered and rickety that the first big sea would carry it off.

'So our anguish increased momentarily as the squalls grew stronger and stronger. Now the sea broke a little, and I saw in the darkness white lines appearing and disappearing, lines of foam, while each wave struck the *Marie Joseph* and shook her with a short quiver which clutched at our hearts.

'The English girl was trembling. I felt her shiver against me. And I had a wild desire to take her in my arms.

'Down there, before and behind us, to the left and right, lighthouses were shining along the shore – lighthouses white, yellow and red, revolving like the enormous eyes of giants who were watching us, waiting eagerly for us to disappear. One of them in particular irritated me. It went out every thirty seconds and it lit up again immediately. It was indeed an eye, that one, with its lid incessantly lowered over its fiery glance.

'From time to time the Englishman struck a match to see the hour; then he put his watch back in his pocket. Suddenly he said to me, over the heads of his daughters, with tremendous gravity: "I wish you a happy New Year, monsieur."

'It was midnight. I held out my hand, which he pressed. Then he said something in English, and suddenly he and his daughters began to sing 'God Save the Queen', which rose through the black and silent air and vanished into space.

'At first I felt a desire to laugh; then I was seized by a powerful, strange emotion.

'It was something sinister and superb, this chant of the shipwrecked, the condemned, something like a prayer and also like something grander, something comparable to the ancient: "Hail, Caesar, those about to die salute thee!"

'When they had finished I asked my neighbour to sing a ballad alone, anything she liked, to make us forget our terrors. She consented, and immediately her clear young voice rang out into the night. She sang something which was doubtless sad, because the notes were long drawn out and hovered, like wounded birds, above the waves.

'The sea was rising now and beating upon our wreck. As for me, I thought only of that voice. And I thought also of the sirens. If a ship had passed near by us what would the sailors have said? My troubled spirit lost itself in the dream! A siren! Was she not really a siren, this daughter of the sea, who had kept me on this worm-eaten ship and who was soon to go down with me deep into the waters?

'But suddenly we were all five rolling on the deck, because the *Marie Joseph* had sunk on her right side. The English girl had fallen upon me, and before I knew what I was doing, thinking that my last moment was come, I had caught her in my arms and kissed her cheek, her temple and her hair.

'The ship did not move again, and we, we also, remained motionless.

'The father said, "Kate!" The one whom I was holding answered, "Yes," and made a movement to free herself. And at that moment I should have wished the ship to split in two and let me fall with her into the sea.

'The Englishman sounded relieved: "A little rocking; it's nothing. I have my three daughters safe." Not having seen the oldest, he had thought she was lost overboard!

'I rose slowly, and suddenly I made out a light on the sea quite close to us. I shouted; they answered. It was a boat sent out in search of us by the hotel keeper, who had guessed at our imprudence.

'We were saved. I was in despair. They picked us up and they brought us back to St-Martin.

'The Englishman began to rub his hands and murmur: "A good supper! A good supper!"

'We did sup. I was not happy. I regretted the *Marie Joseph*.

'We had to separate the next day after much hand-shaking and many promises to write. They departed for Biarritz. I wanted to follow them.

'I was hard hit. I wanted to ask this little girl to marry me. If we had passed eight days together, I should have done so! How weak and incomprehensible a man sometimes is!

'Two years passed without my hearing a word from them. Then I received a letter from New York. She was married and wrote to tell me. And since then we write to each other every year, on New Year's Day. She tells me about her life, talks of her children, her sisters, never of her husband! Why? Ah! why? And as for me, I only talk of the *Marie Joseph*.

She was perhaps the only woman I have ever loved – no – that I ever should have loved. Ah, well! who can tell? Circumstances rule one. And then – and then – all passes. She must be old now; I should not know her. Ah! she of the bygone time, she of the wreck! What a creature! Divine! She writes that her hair is white. That caused me terrible pain. Ah! her yellow hair. No, my English girl exists no longer. How sad it all is!'

The Terror

You say you cannot possibly understand it, and I believe you. You think I am losing my mind? Perhaps I am, but for other reasons than those you imagine, my dear friend.

Yes, I am going to be married, and will tell you what has led me to take that step.

I may add that I know very little of the girl who is going to become my wife tomorrow; I have only seen her four or five times. I know that there is nothing unpleasing about her, and that is enough for my purpose. She is small, fair and stout; so, of course, the day after tomorrow I shall ardently wish for a tall, dark, thin woman.

She is not rich, and belongs to the middle classes. She is a girl such as you may find by the gross, well adapted for matrimony, without any apparent faults, and with no particularly striking qualities. People say of her: 'Mlle Lajolle is a very nice girl,' and tomorrow they will say: 'What a very nice woman Madame Raymon is.'

She belongs, in a word, to that immense number of girls whom one is glad to have for one's wife, till the moment comes when one discovers that one happens to prefer all other women to that particular woman whom one has married.

'Well,' you will say to me, 'what on earth did you get married for?'

I hardly like to tell you the strange and seemingly improbable reason that urged me on to this senseless act; the fact, however, is that I am afraid of being alone.

I don't know how to tell you or to make you understand me, but my state of mind is so wretched that you will pity me and despise me.

I do not want to be alone any longer at night. I want to feel that there is someone close to me, touching me, a being who can speak and say something, no matter what it be.

I wish to be able to awaken somebody by my side, so that I may be able to ask some sudden question, a stupid question even, if I feel inclined, so that I may hear a human voice, and feel that there is some waking soul close to me, someone whose reason is at work; so that when I hastily light the candle I may see some human face by my side – because – because – I am ashamed to confess it – because I am afraid of being alone.

Oh, you don't understand me yet.

I am not afraid of any danger; if a man were to come into the room, I should kill him without trembling. I am not afraid of ghosts, nor do I believe in the supernatural. I am not afraid of dead people, for I believe in the total annihilation of every being that disappears from the face of this earth.

Well – yes, well, it must be told: I am afraid of myself, afraid of that horrible sensation of incomprehensible fear.

You may laugh, if you like. It is terrible, and I cannot get over it. I am afraid of the walls, of the furniture, of the familiar objects; they are animated, as far as I am concerned, by a kind of animal life. Above all, I am afraid of my own dreadful thoughts, of my reason, which seems as if it were about to leave me, driven away by a mysterious and invisible agony.

At first I feel a vague uneasiness in my mind, which causes a cold shiver to run all over me. I look round, and of course nothing is to be seen, and I wish that there were something there, no matter what, as long as it were something tangible. I am frightened merely because I cannot understand my own terror.

If I speak, I am afraid of my own voice. If I walk, I am afraid of I know not what, behind the door, behind the curtains, in the cupboard or under my bed, and yet all the time I know there is nothing anywhere; and I turn round suddenly because I am afraid of what is behind me, although there is nothing there, and I know it.

I become agitated. I feel that my fear increases, and so I shut myself up in my own room, get into bed and hide under the clothes; and there, cowering down, rolled into a ball, I close my eyes in despair, and remain thus for an indefinite time, remembering that my candle is alight on the table by my bedside and that I ought to put it out, and yet – I dare not do it.

It is very terrible, is it not, to be like that?

Formerly I felt nothing of all that. I came home quite calm, and went up and down my apartment without anything disturbing my peace of mind. Had anyone told me that I should be attacked by a malady – for I can call it nothing else – of most improbable fear, such a stupid and terrible malady as it is, I should have laughed outright. I was certainly never afraid of opening the door in the dark. I went to bed slowly, without locking it, and never got up in the middle of the night to make sure that everything was firmly closed.

It began last year in a very strange manner on a damp autumn evening. When my servant had left the room, after I had dined, I asked myself what I was going to do. I walked up and down my room for some time, feeling tired without any reason for it, unable to work, and even without energy to read. A fine rain was falling, and I felt unhappy, a prey to one of those fits of despondency, without any apparent cause, which make us feel inclined to cry, or to talk, no matter to whom, so as to shake off our depressing thoughts.

I felt that I was alone, and my rooms seemed to me to be more empty than they had ever been before. I was in the midst of infinite and overwhelming solitude. What was I to do? I sat down, but a kind of nervous impatience seemed to affect my legs, so I got up and began to walk about again. I was, perhaps, rather feverish, for my hands, which I had clasped behind me, as one often does when walking slowly, almost seemed to burn one another. Then suddenly a cold shiver ran down my back, and I thought the damp air might have penetrated into my rooms, so I lit the fire for the first time that year, and sat down again and looked at the flames. But soon I felt that I could not possibly remain quiet, and so I got up again and determined to go out, to pull myself together and to find a friend to bear me company.

I could not find anyone, so I walked to the boulevard to try and meet some acquaintance or other there.

It was wretched everywhere, and the wet pavement glistened in the gaslight, while the oppressive warmth of the almost impalpable rain lay heavily over the streets and seemed to obscure the light of the lamps.

I went on slowly, saying to myself: 'I shall not find a soul to talk to.'

I glanced into several cafés, from the Madeleine as far as the Faubourg Poissonière, and saw many unhappy-looking individuals sitting at the tables who did not seem even to have enough energy left to finish the refreshments they had ordered.

For a long time I wandered aimlessly up and down, and about midnight I started for home. I was very calm and very tired. My janitor opened the door at once, which was quite unusual for him, and I thought that another lodger had probably just come in.

When I go out I always double-lock the door of my room, and I found it merely closed, which surprised me; but I supposed that some letters had been brought up for me in the course of the evening.

I went in, and found my fire still burning so that it lighted up the room a little, and, while in the act of taking up a candle, I noticed somebody sitting in my armchair by the fire, warming his feet, with his back towards me.

I was not in the slightest degree frightened. I thought, very naturally, that some friend or other had come to see me. No doubt the porter, to whom I had said I was going out, had lent him his own key. In a moment I remembered all the circumstances of my return, how the street door had been opened immediately, and that my own door was only latched and not locked.

I could see nothing of my friend but his head, and he had evidently gone to sleep while waiting for me, so I went up to him to rouse him. I saw him quite distinctly; his right arm was hanging down and his legs were crossed; the position of his head, which was somewhat inclined to the left of the armchair, seemed to indicate that he was asleep. 'Who can it be?' I asked myself. I could not see clearly, as the room was rather dark, so I put out my hand to touch him on the shoulder, and it came in contact with the back of the chair. There was nobody there; the seat was empty.

I fairly jumped with fright. For a moment I drew back as if confronted by some terrible danger; then I turned round again, impelled to do so but panting with fear, so upset that I could not collect my thoughts and ready to faint.

But I am a cool man, and soon recovered myself. I thought: 'It is a mere hallucination, that is all,' and I immediately began to reflect on this phenomenon. Thoughts fly quickly at such moments.

I had been suffering from an hallucination, that was an incontestable fact. My mind had been perfectly lucid and had acted regularly and logically, so there was nothing the matter with the brain. It was only my eyes that had been deceived; they had had a vision, one of those visions which lead simple folk to believe in miracles. It was a nervous seizure of the optical apparatus, nothing more; the eyes were rather congested, perhaps.

I lit my candle, and when I stooped down to the fire in doing so I noticed that I was trembling, and I raised myself up with a jump, as if somebody had touched me from behind.

I was certainly not by any means calm.

I walked up and down a little, and hummed a tune or two. Then I double-locked the door and felt rather reassured; now, at any rate, nobody could come in.

I sat down again and thought over my adventure for a long time; then I went to bed and blew out my light.

For some minutes all went well; I lay quietly on my back, but presently an irresistible desire seized me to look round the room, and I turned over on my side.

My fire was nearly out, and the few glowing embers threw a faint light on the floor by the chair, where I fancied I saw the man sitting again.

I quickly struck a match, but I had been mistaken; there was nothing there. I got up, however, and hid the chair behind my bed, and tried to get to sleep, as the room was now dark; but I had not forgotten myself for more than five minutes, when in my dream I saw all the scene which I had previously witnessed as clearly as if it were reality. I woke up with a start, and having lit the candle, sat up in bed, without venturing even to try to go to sleep again.

Twice, however, sleep overcame me for a few moments in spite of myself, and twice I saw the same thing again, till I fancied I was going mad. When day broke, however, I thought that I was cured, and slept peacefully till noon.

It was all past and over. I had been feverish, had had the nightmare. I know not what. I had been ill, in fact, but yet thought I was a great fool.

I enjoyed myself thoroughly that evening. I dined at a restaurant and afterwards went to the theatre, and then started for home. But as I got near the house I was once more seized by a strange feeling of uneasiness. I was afraid of seeing him again. I was not afraid of him, not afraid of his presence, in which I did not believe; but I was afraid of being deceived again. I was afraid of some fresh hallucination, afraid lest fear should take possession of me.

For more than an hour I wandered up and down the pavement; then, feeling that I was really too foolish, I returned home. I breathed so hard that I could hardly get upstairs, and remained standing outside my door for more than ten minutes; then suddenly I had a courageous impulse and my will asserted itself. I inserted my key into the lock, and went into the apartment with a candle in my hand. I kicked open my bedroom door, which was partly open, and cast a frightened glance towards the fireplace. There was nothing there. A–h! What a relief and what a delight! What a deliverance! I walked up and down briskly and boldly, but I was not altogether reassured, and kept turning round with a jump; the very shadows in the corners disquieted me.

I slept badly, and was constantly disturbed by imaginary noises, but did not see him; no, that was all over.

Since that time I have been afraid of being alone at night. I feel that the spectre is there, close to me, around me; but it has not appeared to me again.

And supposing it did, what would it matter, since I do not believe in it and know that it is nothing?

However, it still worries me, because I am constantly thinking of it. His right arm hanging down and his head inclined to the left like a man who was asleep – I don't want to think about it!

Why, however, am I so persistently possessed with this idea? His feet were close to the fire!

He haunts me; it is very stupid, but who and what is he? I know that he does not exist except in my cowardly imagination, in my fears, and in my agony. There – enough of that!

Yes, it is all very well for me to reason with myself, to stiffen my backbone, so to say; but I cannot remain at home because I know he is there. I know I shall not see him again; he will not show himself again; that is all over. But he is there, all the same, in my thoughts. He remains invisible, but that does not prevent his being there. He is behind the doors, in the closed cupboard, in the wardrobe, under the bed, in every dark corner. If I open the door or the cupboard, if I take the candle to look under the bed and throw a light on the dark places, he is there no longer, but I feel that he is behind me. I turn round, certain that I shall not see him, that I shall never see him again; but for all that, he is behind me.

It is very stupid, it is dreadful; but what am I to do? I cannot help it.

But if there were two of us in the place I feel certain that he would not be there any longer, for he is there just because I am alone, simply and solely because I am alone!

JOHN CHARLES DENT

John Charles Dent (1841–1888) was a Canadian journalist, author and historian. He was born in Kendal in Westmorland but shortly after his birth his family emigrated to Canada. Dent studied law in Brantford, Ontario, and became an attorney in 1865. He practised law for a few years, but found the profession did not suit him, and was drawn to pursue literary endeavours instead. He accordingly relinquished his practice as soon as he felt himself in a position to do so, and went to England. He developed his journalistic skills working for the *Daily Telegraph*. He also contributed a series of articles to the periodical *Once a Week*. After remaining in England for several years, Dent and his family moved to America in 1867, his having obtained a position in Boston. Subsequently, he returned to Canada to work on the editorial staff of the *Toronto Evening Telegram*. For several years Dent devoted himself to journalistic labours on various newspapers, but principally the *Toronto Weekly Globe*. In addition, he wrote a great many sketches, essays and stories. A collection of his stories was published posthumously as *The Gerrard Street Mystery and Other Weird Tales*.

Gagtooth's Image

About three o'clock on the afternoon of Wednesday, the 4th of September 1884, I was riding up Yonge Street, in the city of Toronto, on the top of a crowded omnibus. The omnibus was bound for Thornhill, and my own destination was the intermediate village of Willowdale. Having been in Canada only a short time, and being almost a stranger in Toronto, I dare say I was looking around me with more attention and curiosity than persons who are 'native here and to the manner born' are accustomed to exhibit. We had just passed Isabella Street, and were rapidly nearing Charles Street, when I noticed on my right hand a large, dilapidated frame building, standing in solitary isolation a few feet back from the highway, and presenting the appearance of a veritable Old Curiosity Shop.

A business was carried on here in second-hand furniture of the poorest description, and the object of the proprietor seemed to have been to collect about him all sorts of worn-out commodities and objects which were utterly unmarketable. Everybody who lived in Toronto at the time indicated will remember the establishment, which, as I subsequently learned, was owned and carried on by a man named Robert Southworth, familiarly known to his customers as 'Old Bob'. I had no sooner arrived abreast of the gateway leading into the yard immediately adjoining the building to the southward than my eyes rested upon something which instantly caused them to open themselves to their very widest capacity, and constrained me to signal the driver to stop; which he had no sooner done than I alighted from my seat and requested him to proceed on his journey without me. The driver eyed me suspiciously, and evidently regarded me as an odd customer, but he obeyed my request, and drove on northward, leaving me standing in the middle of the street.

From my elevated seat on the roof of the bus, I had caught a hurried glimpse of a commonplace-looking little marble figure, placed on the top of a pedestal, in the yard already referred to, where several other figures in marble, wood, bronze, stucco and what not were exposed for sale.

The particular figure which had attracted my attention was about fifteen inches in height, and represented a little child in the attitude of prayer. Anyone seeing it for the first time would probably have taken it for a representation of the Infant Samuel. I have called it commonplace, and considered as a work of art, such it undoubtedly was; yet it must have possessed a certain distinctive individuality, for the brief glance which I had caught of it, even at that distance, had been sufficient to convince me that the figure was an old acquaintance of mine. It was in consequence of that conviction that I had dismounted from the omnibus, forgetful, for the moment, of everything but the matter which was uppermost in my mind.

I lost no time in passing through the gateway leading into the yard, and in walking up to the pedestal upon which the little figure was placed. Taking the latter in my hand, I found, as I had expected, that it was not attached to the pedestal, which was of totally different material, and much more elaborate workmanship. Turning the figure upside down, my eyes rested on these words, deeply cut into the little circular throne upon which the figure rested: ' JACKSON: PEORIA, 1854'.

At this juncture the proprietor of the establishment walked up to where I was standing beside the pedestal. 'Like to look at something in that way, sir?' he asked – 'we have more inside.'

'What is the price of this?' I asked, indicating the figure in my hand.

'That, sir; you may have that for fifty cents – of course without the pedestal, which don't belong to it.'

'Have you had it on hand long?'

'I don't know, but if you'll step inside for a moment I can tell you. This way, sir.'

Taking the figure under my arm, I followed him into what he called 'the office' – a small and dirty room, crowded with old furniture in the last stages of dilapidation. From a desk in one corner he took a large tome labelled 'Stock Book', to which he referred, after glancing at a hieroglyphical device pasted on the figure which I held under my arm.

'Yes, sir – had that ever since the 14th of March 1880 – bought it at Morris & Blackwell's sale, sir.'

'Who and what are Messrs Morris & Blackwell?' I enquired.

'They *were* auctioneers, down on Adelaide Street, in the city, sir. Failed sometime last winter. Mr Morris has since died, and I believe Blackwell, the other partner, went to the States.'

After a few more questions, finding that he knew nothing whatever about the matter beyond what he had already told me, I paid over the fifty cents; and, declining with thanks his offer to send my purchase home to me, I marched off with it down the street, and made the best of my way back to the hotel where I had been staying for some days before.

From what has been said, it will be inferred that I – a stranger in Canada – must have had some special reason for encumbering myself in my travels with an intrinsically worthless piece of common Columbia marble.

I *had* a reason. I had often seen that little figure before; and the last time I had seen it, previous to the occasion above mentioned, had been at the town of Peoria, in the State of Illinois, sometime in the month of June 1855.

There is a story connected with that little praying figure; a story, which, to me, is a very touching one; and I believe myself to be the only human being capable of telling it. Indeed, *I* am only able to tell a part of it. How the figure came to be sold by auction, in the city of Toronto, at Messrs Morris & Blackwell's sale on the 14th of March 1880, or how it ever came to be in this part of the world at all, I know no more than the reader does; but I can probably tell all that is worth knowing about the matter.

In the year 1850, and for I know not how long previously, there lived at Peoria, Illinois, a journeyman-blacksmith named Abner Fink. I mention the date, 1850, because it was in that year that I myself settled in Peoria, and first had any knowledge of him; but I believe he had then been living there for some length of time. He was employed at the foundry of Messrs Gowanlock and Van Duzer, and was known for an excellent workman, of steady habits, and good moral character – qualifications which were by no means universal, nor even common, among persons of his calling and degree of life, at the time and place of which I am writing. But he was still more conspicuous (on the *lucus a non lucendo* principle) for another quality – that of reticence. It was very rarely indeed that he spoke to anyone, except when called upon to reply to a question; and even then it was noticeable that he invariably employed the fewest and most concise words in his vocabulary. If brevity were the body, as well as the soul of wit, Fink must have been about the wittiest man that ever lived, the Monosyllabic Traveller not excepted. He never received a letter from anyone during the whole time of his stay at Peoria; nor, so far as was known, did he ever write to anyone. Indeed, there was no evidence that he was able to write. He never went to church, nor even to 'meeting'; never attended any public entertainment; never took any holidays. All his time was spent either at the foundry where he worked, or at the boarding-house where he lodged. In the latter place, the greater part of his hours of relaxation were spent in looking either out of the window or into the fire; thinking, apparently, about nothing in particular. All endeavours on the part of his fellow boarders to draw him into conversation were utterly fruitless. No one in the place knew anything about his past life, and when his fellow-journey-men in the workshop attempted to inveigle him into any confidence on that subject, he had a trick of calling up a harsh and sinister expression of countenance which effectually nipped all such experiments in the bud. Even his employers failed to elicit anything from him on this head, beyond the somewhat vague piece of intelligence that he hailed from 'down east'. The foreman of the establishment, with a desperate attempt at facetiousness, used to say of him that no one knew who he was, where he came from, where he was going to or what he was going to do when he got there.

And yet, this utter lack of sociability could scarcely have arisen from positive surliness or unkindness of disposition. Instances were not wanting in which he had given pretty strong evidence that he carried beneath that rugged and uncouth exterior a kinder and more gentle heart than is possessed by most men. Upon one occasion he had jumped, at the imminent peril of his life, from the bridge which spans the Illinois river just above the entrance to the lake, and had fished up a drowning child from its depths and borne it to the shore in safety. In doing so he had been compelled to swim through a swift and strong current which would have swamped any swimmer with one particle less strength, endurance and pluck. At another time, hearing his landlady say, at dinner, that an execution was in progress in the house of a sick man with a large family, at the other end of the town, he left his dinner untouched, trudged off to the place indicated, and – though the debtor was an utter stranger to him – paid off the debt and costs in full, without taking any assignment of the judgment or other security. Then he went quietly back to his work. From my knowledge of the worthless and impecunious character of the debtor, I am of opinion that Fink never received a cent in the way of reimbursement.

In personal appearance he was short and stout. His age, when I first knew him, must have been somewhere in the neighbourhood of thirty-five. The only peculiarity about his face was an abnormal formation of one of his front teeth, which protruded, and stuck out almost horizontally. This, as may be supposed, did not tend to improve an expression of countenance which in other respects was not very prepossessing. One of the anvil-strikers happening to allude to him one day in his absence by the name of 'Gagtooth', the felicity of the sobriquet at once commended itself to the good taste of the other hands in the shop, who thereafter commonly spoke of him by that name, and eventually it came to be applied to him by everyone in the town.

My acquaintance with him began when I had been in Peoria about a week. I may premise that I am a physician and surgeon – a graduate of Harvard. Peoria was at that time a comparatively new place, but it gave promise of going ahead rapidly; a promise, by the way, which it has since amply redeemed. Messrs Gowanlock and Van Duzer's foundry was a pretty extensive one for a small town in a comparatively new district. They kept about a hundred and fifty hands employed all the year round, and during the busy season this number was more than doubled. It was in consequence of my having received the appointment of medical attendant to that establishment that I buried myself in the west, instead of settling down in my native state of Massachusetts.

Poor Gagtooth was one of my first surgical patients. It came about in this wise. At the foundry, two days in the week, viz., Tuesdays and Fridays, were chiefly devoted to what is called 'casting'. On these days it was necessary to convey large masses of melted iron, in vessels specially manufactured for that purpose, from one end of the moulding shop to the other. It was, of course, very desirable that the metal should not be allowed to cool while in transit, and that as little time as possible should be lost in transferring it from the furnace to the moulds. For this purpose Gagtooth's services were frequently called into requisition, as he was by far the strongest man about the place, and could without assistance carry one end of one of the vessels, which was considered pretty good work for two ordinary men.

Well, one unlucky Friday afternoon he was hard at work at this employment, and as was usual with all the hands in the moulding shop at such times, he was stripped naked from the waist upwards. He was gallantly supporting one end of one of the large receptacles already mentioned, which happened to be rather fuller than usual of the red-hot molten metal. He had nearly reached the moulding-box into which the contents of the vessel were to be poured, when he stumbled against a piece of scantling which was lying in his way. He fell, and as a necessary consequence his end of the vessel fell likewise, spilling the contents all over his body, which was literally deluged by the red, hissing, boiling liquid fire. It must have seemed to the terror-stricken onlookers like a bath of blood.

Further details of the frightful accident, and of my treatment of the case, might be interesting to such of the readers of this book as happen to belong to my own profession; but to general readers such details would be simply shocking. How even his tremendous vitality and vigour of constitution brought him through it all is a mystery to me to this day. I am thirty-six years older than I was at that time. Since then I have acted as surgeon to a fighting regiment all through the great rebellion. I have had patients of all sorts of temperaments and constitutions under my charge, but never have I been brought into contact with a case which seemed more hopeless in my eyes. He must surely have had more than one life in him. I have never had my hands on so magnificent a specimen of the human frame as his was; and better still – and this doubtless contributed materially to his recovery – I have never had a case under my management where the patient bore his sufferings with such uniform fortitude and endurance. Suffice it to say that he recovered, and that his face bore no traces of the frightful ordeal through which he had passed. I don't think he was ever quite the same man as before his accident. I think his nervous system received a shock which eventually tended to shorten his life. But he was still known as incomparably the strongest man in Peoria, and continued to perform the work of two men at the moulding-shop on casting days. In every other respect he was apparently the same; not a whit more disposed to be companionable than before his accident. I used frequently to meet him on the street, as he was going to and fro between his boarding-house and the workshop. He was always alone, and more than once I came to a full stop and enquired after his health, or anything else that seemed to afford a feasible topic for conversation. He was uniformly civil, and even respectful, but confined his remarks to replying to my questions, which, as usual, was done in the fewest words.

During the twelve months succeeding his recovery, so far as I am aware, nothing occurred worthy of being recorded in Gagtooth's annals. About the expiration of that time, however, his landlady, by his authority, at his request, and in his presence, made an announcement to the boarders assembled at the dinner-table which, I should think, must literally have taken away their breaths.

Gagtooth was going to be married!

I don't suppose it would have occasioned greater astonishment if it had been announced as an actual fact that the Illinois river had commenced to flow backwards. It was surprising, incredible, but, like many other surprising and incredible things, it was true. Gagtooth was really and truly about to marry. The object of his choice was his landlady's sister, by name Lucinda Bowlsby. How or when the wooing had been carried on, how the engagement had been led up to, and in what terms the all-important question had been propounded, I am not prepared to say. I need hardly observe that none of the boarders had entertained the faintest suspicion that anything of the kind was impending. The courtship, from first to last, must have been somewhat of a piece with that of the late Mr Barkis. But alas! Gagtooth did not settle his affections so judiciously, nor did he draw such a prize in the matrimonial lottery as Barkis did. Two women more entirely dissimilar, in every respect, than Peggotty and Lucinda Bowlsby can hardly be imagined. Lucinda was nineteen years of age. She was pretty and, for a girl of her class and station in life, tolerably well educated. But she was notwithstanding a light, giddy creature – and, I fear, something worse, at that time. At all events, she had a very questionable sort of reputation among the boarders in the house, and was regarded with suspicion by everyone who knew anything about her, poor Gagtooth alone excepted.

In due time the wedding took place. It was solemnised at the boarding-house; and the bride and bridegroom disdaining to defer to the common usage, spent their honeymoon in their own house. Gagtooth had rented and furnished a little frame dwelling on the outskirts of the town, on the bank of the river; and thither the couple retired as soon as the hymeneal knot was tied. Next morning the bridegroom made his appearance at his forge and went to work as usual, as though nothing had occurred to disturb the serenity of his life.

Time passed by. Rumours now and then reached my ears to the effect that Mrs Fink was not behaving herself very well, and that she was leading her husband rather a hard life of it. She had been seen driving out into the country with a young lawyer from Springfield, who occasionally came over to Peoria to attend the sittings of the District Court. She moreover had the reputation of habitually indulging in the contents of the cup that cheers and likewise inebriates. However, in the regular course of things, I was called upon to assist at the first appearance upon life's stage of a little boy, upon whom his parents bestowed the name of Charlie.

The night of Charlie's birth was the first time I had ever been in the house, and if I remember aright it was the first time I had ever set eyes on Mrs Fink since her marriage. I was not long in making up my mind about her; and I had ample opportunity of forming an opinion as to her character, for she was unable to leave her bed for more than a month, during which time I was in attendance upon her almost daily. I also attended little Charlie through measels, scarlet-rash, whooping-cough and all his childish ailments; and in fact I was a pretty regular visitor at the house from the time of his birth until his father left the neighbourhood, as I shall presently have to relate. I believe Mrs Fink to have been not merely a profligate woman, but a thoroughly bad and heartless one in every respect. She was perfectly indifferent to her husband, whom she shamefully neglected, and almost indifferent to her child. She seemed to care for nothing in the world but dress and strong waters; and to procure these there was no depth of degradation to which she would not stoop.

As a result of my constant professional attendance upon his mother during the first month of little Charlie's life, I became better acquainted with his father than anyone in Peoria had ever done. He seemed to know that I saw into and sympathised with his domestic troubles, and my silent sympathy seemed to afford him some consolation. As the months and years passed by, his wife's conduct became worse and worse, and his affections centred themselves entirely upon his child, whom he loved with a passionate affection to which I have never seen a parallel.

And Charlie was a child made to be loved. When he was two years old he was beyond all comparison the dearest and most beautiful little fellow I have ever seen. His fat, plump, chubby little figure, modelled after Cupid's own; his curly flaxen hair; his matchless complexion, fair and clear as the sky on a sunny summer day; and his bright, round, expressive eyes, which imparted intelligence to his every feature, combined to make him the idol of his father, the envy of all the mothers in town, and the admiration of everyone who saw him. At noon, when the great foundry-bell rang, which was the signal for the workmen to go to dinner, Charlie might regularly be seen, toddling as fast as his stout little legs could spin, along the footpath leading over the common in the direction of the workshops. When about halfway across, he would be certain to meet his father, who, taking the child up in his bare, brawny, smoke-begrimed arms, would carry him home – the contrast between the two strongly suggesting Vulcan and Cupid. At six o'clock in the evening, when the bell announced that work was over for the day, a similar little drama was enacted. It would be difficult to say whether Vulcan or Cupid derived the greater amount of pleasure from these semi-daily incidents. After tea, the two were never separate for a moment. While the mother was perhaps busily engaged in the perusal of some worthless novel, the father would sit with his darling on his knee, listening to his childish prattle, and perhaps so far going out of himself as to tell the child a little story. It seemed to be an understood thing that the mother should take no care or notice of the boy during her husband's presence in the house. Regularly, when the clock on the chimney-piece struck eight, Charlie would jump down from his father's knee and run across the room for his night-dress, returning to his father to have it put on. When this had been done he would kneel down and repeat a simple little prayer, in which One who loved little children like Charlie was invoked to bless father and mother and make him a good boy; after which his father would place him in his little crib, where he soon slept the sleep of happy childhood.

My own house was not far from theirs, and I was so fond of Charlie that it was no uncommon thing for me to drop in upon them for a few minutes, when returning from my office in the evening. Upon one occasion I noticed the child more particularly than usual while he was in the act of saying his prayers. His eyes were closed, his plump little hands were clasped, and his cherubic little face was turned upwards with an expression of infantile trustfulness and adoration which I shall never forget. I have never seen, nor do I ever expect to see, anything else half so beautiful. When he arose from his knees and came up to me to say good-night, I kissed his upturned little face with even greater fervour than usual. After he had been put to bed I mentioned the matter to his father, and said something about my regret that the child's expression had not been caught by a sculptor and fixed in stone.

I had little idea of the effect my remarks were destined to produce. A few evenings afterwards he informed me, much to my surprise, that he had determined to act upon the idea which my words had suggested to his mind, and that he had instructed Heber Jackson, the marble-cutter, to go to work at a 'stone likeness' of little Charlie, and to finish it up as soon as possible. He did not seem to understand that the proper performance of such a task required anything more than mere mechanical skill, and that an ordinary tombstone cutter was scarcely the sort of artist to do justice to it.

However, when the 'stone-likeness' was finished and sent home, I confess I was astonished to see how well Jackson had succeeded. He had not, of course, caught the child's exact expression. It is probable, indeed, that he never saw the expression on Charlie's face which had seemed so beautiful to me, and which had suggested to me the idea of its being 'embodied in marble', as the professionals call it. But the image was at all events, according to order, a 'likeness'. The true lineaments were there and I would have recognised it for a representation of my little friend at the first glance, wherever I might have seen it. In short, it was precisely one of those works of art which have no artistic value whatever for anyone who is unacquainted with, or uninterested in, the subject represented; but knowing and loving little Charlie as I did, I confess that I used to contemplate Jackson's piece of workmanship with an admiration and enthusiasm which the contents of Italian galleries have failed to arouse in me.

Well, the months flew by until some time in the spring of 1855, when the town was electrified by the sudden and totally unexpected failure of Messrs Gowanlock and Van Duzer, who up to that time were currently reported to be one of the wealthiest and most thriving firms in the state. Their failure was not only a great misfortune for the workmen, who were thus thrown out of present employment – for the creditors did not carry on the business – but was regarded as a public calamity to the town and neighbourhood, the prosperity whereof had been enhanced in no inconsiderable degree by the carrying on of so extensive an establishment in their midst, and by the enterprise and energy of the proprietors, both of whom were first-rate businessmen. The failure was in no measure attributed either to dishonesty or want of prudence on the part of Messrs Gowanlock and Van Duzer, but simply to the invention of a new patent which rendered valueless the particular agricultural implement which constituted the speciality of the establishment, and of which there was an enormous stock on hand. There was not the shadow of a hope of the firm being able to get upon its legs again. The partners surrendered everything almost to the last dollar, and shortly afterwards left Illinois for California.

Now, this failure, which more or less affected the entire population of Peoria, was especially disastrous to poor Fink. For past years he had been saving money, and as Messrs Gowanlock and Van Duzer allowed interest at a liberal rate upon all deposits left in their hands by their workmen, all his surplus earnings remained untouched. The consequence was that the accumulations of years were swamped at one fell swoop, and he found himself reduced to poverty. And as though misfortune was not satisfied with visiting him thus heavily, the very day of the failure he was stricken down by typhoid fever: not the typhoid fever known in Canada – which is bad enough – but the terrible putrid typhoid of the west, which is known nowhere else on the face of the globe, and in which the mortality in some years reaches forty per cent.

Of course I was at once called in. I did my best for the patient, which was very little. I tried hard, however, to keep his wife sober, and to compel her to nurse him judiciously. As for little Charlie, I took him home with me to my own house, where he remained until his father was so far convalescent as to prevent all fear of infection. Meanwhile I knew nothing about Gagtooth's money having been deposited in the hands of his employers, and consequently was ignorant of his loss. I did not learn this circumstance for weeks afterwards, and of course had no reason for supposing that his wife was in anywise straitened for money. Once, when her husband had been prostrated for about a fortnight, I saw her with a roll of bank notes in her hand. Little did I suspect how they had been obtained.

Shortly after my patient had begun to sit up in his armchair for a little while every day, he begged so hard for little Charlie's presence that, as soon as I was satisfied that all danger of infection was past, I consented to allow the child to return to his own home. In less than a month afterwards the invalid was able to walk out in the garden for a few minutes every day when the weather was favourable, and in these walks Charlie was his constant companion. The affection of the poor fellow for his flaxen-haired darling was manifested in every glance of his eye, and in every tone of his voice. He would kiss the little chap and pat him on the head a hundred times a day. He would tell him stories until he himself was completely exhausted; and although I knew that this tended to retard his complete recovery, I had not the heart to forbid it. I have often since felt thankful that I never made any attempt to do so.

At last the 15th of September arrived. On the morning of that day Messrs Rockwell and Dunbar's Combined Circus and Menagerie made a triumphal entry into Peoria, and was to exhibit on the green, down by the riverbank. The performance had been ostentatiously advertised and placarded on every dead wall in town for a month back, and all the children in the place, little Charlie included, were wild on the subject. Signor Martigny was to enter a den containing three full-grown lions, and was to go through the terrific and disgusting ordeal usual on such occasions. Gagtooth, of course, was unable to go; but, being unwilling to deny his child any reasonable pleasure, he had consented to Charlie's going with his mother. I happened to be passing the house on my way homewards to dinner just as the pair, about to start, had called in to say goodbye to my patient. Never shall I forget the embrace and the kiss which the father bestowed upon the little fellow. I can see them now, after all these years, almost as distinctly as I saw them on that terrible 15th of September 1855. They perfectly clung to each other, and seemed unwilling to part even for the two or three hours during which the performance was to last. I can see the mother too, impatiently waiting in the doorway, and telling Charlie that if he didn't stop that nonsense they would be too late to see Sampson killing the lion. She – heaven help her! – thought nothing and cared nothing about the pleasure the child was to derive from the entertainment. She was only anxious on her own account; impatient to show her good looks and her cheap finery to the two thousand and odd people assembled under the huge tent.

At last they started. Gagtooth got up and walked to the door, following them with his eye as far as he could see them down the dusty street. Then he returned and sat down in his chair. Poor fellow! he was destined never to see either of them alive again.

Notwithstanding her fear lest she might not arrive in time for the commencement of the performance, Mrs Fink and her charge reached the ground at least half an hour before the ticket office was opened; and I regret to say that that half hour was sufficient to enable her to form an acquaintance with one of the property men of the establishment, to whom she contrived to make herself so agreeable that he passed her and Charlie into the tent free of charge. She was not admitted at the front entrance, but from the tiring-room at the back whence the performers enter. She sat down just at the left of this entrance, immediately adjoining the lion's cage. Ere long the performance commenced. Signor Martigny, when his turn came, entered the cage as per announcement; but he was not long in discovering by various signs not to be mistaken that his charges were in no humour to be played with on that day. Even the ringmaster from his place in the centre of the ring, perceived that old King of the Forest, the largest and most vicious of the lions, was meditating mischief, and called to the signor to come out of the cage. The signor, keeping his eye steadily fixed on the brute, began a retrograde movement from the den. He had the door open, and was swiftly backing through, when, with a roar that seemed to shake the very earth, old King sprang upon him from the opposite side of the cage, dashing him to the ground like a ninepin, and rushed through the aperture into the crowd. Quick as lightning the other two followed, and thus three savage lions were loose and unshackled in the midst of upwards of two thousand men, women and children.

I wish to linger over the details as briefly as possible. I am thankful to say that I was not present, and that I am unable to describe the occurrence from personal observation.

Poor little Charlie and his mother, sitting close to the cage, were the very first victims. The child himself, I think, and hope, never knew what hurt him. His skull was fractured by one stroke of the brute's paw. Signor Martigny escaped with his right arm slit into ribbons. Big Joe Pentland, the clown, with one well-directed stroke of a crowbar, smashed Old King of the Forest's jaw into a hundred pieces, but not before it had closed in the left breast of Charlie's mother. She lived for nearly an hour afterwards, but never uttered a syllable. I wonder if she was conscious. I wonder if it was permitted to her to realise what her sin – for sin it must have been, in contemplation, if not in deed – had brought upon herself and her child. Had she paid her way into the circus, and entered in front, instead of coquetting with the property-man, she would have been sitting under a different part of the tent, and neither she nor Charlie would have sustained any injury, for the two younger lions were shot before they had leapt ten paces from the cage door. Old King was easily despatched after Joe Pentland's tremendous blow. Besides Charlie and his mother, two men and one woman were killed on the spot: another woman died next day from the injuries she received, and several other persons were more or less severely hurt.

Immediately after dinner I had driven out into the country to pay a professional visit, so that I heard nothing about what had occurred until some hours afterwards. I was informed of it, however, before I reached the town, on my way homeward. To say that I was inexpressibly shocked and grieved would merely be to repeat a very stupid platitude, and to say that I was a human being. I had learned to love poor little Charlie almost as dearly as I loved my own children. And his father – what would be the consequence to him?

I drove direct to his house, which was filled with people – neighbours and others who had called to administer such consolation as the circumstances would admit of. I am not ashamed to confess that the moment my eyes rested upon the bereaved father I burst into tears. He sat with his child's body in his lap, and seemed literally transformed into stone. A breeze came in through the open doorway and stirred his thin iron-grey locks, as he sat there in his armchair. He was unconscious of everything – even of the presence of strangers. His eyes were fixed and glazed. Not a sound of any kind, not even a moan, passed his lips; and it was only after feeling his pulse that I was able to pronounce with certainty that he was alive. One single gleam of animation overspread his features for an instant when I gently removed the crushed corpse from his knees, and laid it on the bed, but he quickly relapsed into stolidity. I was informed that he had sat thus ever since he had first received the corpse from the arms of Joe Pentland, who had brought it home without changing his clown's dress. Heaven grant that I may never look upon such a sight again as the poor, half-recovered invalid presented during the whole of that night and for several days afterwards.

For the next three days I spent all the time with him I possibly could, for I dreaded either a relapse of the fever or the loss of his reason. The neighbours were very kind, and took upon themselves the burden of everything connected with the funeral. As for Fink himself, he seemed to take everything for granted, and interfered with nothing. When the time arrived for fastening down the coffin lids, I could not bear to permit that ceremony to be performed without affording him an opportunity of kissing the dead lips of his darling for the last time. I gently led him up to the side of the bed upon which the two coffins were placed. At sight of his little boy's dead face, he fainted, and before he revived I had the lids fastened down. It would have been cruelty to subject him to the ordeal a second time.

The day after the funeral he was sufficiently recovered from the shock to be able to talk. He informed me that he had concluded to leave the neighbourhood, and requested me to draw up a poster, advertising all his furniture and effects for sale by auction. He intended, he said, to sell everything except Charlie's clothes and his own, and these, together with a lock of the child's hair and a few of his toys, were all he intended to take away with him.

'But of course,' I remarked, 'you don't intend to sell the stone likeness?'

He looked at me rather strangely, and made no reply. I glanced around the room, and, to my surprise, the little statue was nowhere to be seen. It then occurred to me that I had not noticed it since Gagtooth had been taken ill.

'By the by, where is it?' I enquired – 'I don't see it.'

After a moment's hesitation he told me the whole story. It was then that I learned for the first time that he had lost all his savings through the failure of Messrs Gowanlock and Van Duzer, and that the morning when he had been taken ill there had been only a dollar in the house. On that morning he had acquainted his wife with his loss, but had strictly enjoined secrecy upon her, as both Gowanlock and Van Duzer had promised him most solemnly that inasmuch as they regarded their indebtedness to him as being upon a different footing from their ordinary liabilities, he should assuredly be paid in full out of the first money at their command. He had implicit reliance upon their word, and requested me to take charge of the money upon its arrival, and to keep it until he instructed me, by post or otherwise, how to dispose of it. To this I, of course, consented. The rest of the story he could only repeat upon the authority of his wife, but I have no reason for disbelieving any portion of it. It seems that a day or two after his illness commenced, and after he had become insensible, his wife had been at her wits' end for money to provide necessaries for the house, and I dare say she spent more on liquor than on necessaries. She declared that she had made up her mind to apply to me for a loan, when a stranger called at the house, attracted, as he said, by the little image, which had been placed in the front window, and was thus visible to passers-by. He announced himself as Mr Silas Pomeroy, merchant, of Myrtle Street, Springfield. He said that the face of the little image strikingly reminded him of the face of a child of his own which had died some time before. He had not supposed that the figure was a likeness of anyone, and had stepped in, upon the impulse of the moment, in the hope that he might be able to purchase it. He was willing to pay a liberal price. The negotiation ended in his taking the image away with him, and leaving a hundred dollars in its stead; on which sum Mrs Fink had kept house ever since. Her husband, of course, knew nothing of this for weeks afterwards. When he began to get better, his wife had acquainted him with the facts. He had found no fault with her, as he had determined to repurchase the image at any cost, so soon as he might be able to earn money enough. As for getting a duplicate, that was out of the question, for Heber Jackson had been carried off by the typhoid epidemic, and Charlie had changed considerably during the fifteen months which had elapsed since the image had been finished. And now poor little Charlie himself was gone, and the great desire of his father's heart was to regain possession of the image. With that in view, as soon as the sale should be over he would start for Springfield, tell his story to Pomeroy, and offer him his money back again. As to any further plans, he did not know, he said, what he would do, or where he would go; but he would certainly never live in Peoria again.

In a few days the sale took place, and Gagtooth started for Springfield with about three hundred dollars in his pocket. Springfield is seventy miles from Peoria. He was to return in about ten days, by which time a tombstone was to be ready for Charlie's grave. He had not ordered one for his wife, who was not buried in the same grave with the child, but in one just beside him.

He returned within the ten days. His journey had been a fruitless one. Pomeroy had become insolvent, and had absconded from Springfield a month before. No one knew whither he had gone, but he must have taken the image with him, as it was not among the effects which he had left behind him. His friends knew that he was greatly attached to the image, in consequence of its real or fancied resemblance to his dead child. Nothing more reasonable then than to suppose that he had taken it away with him.

Gagtooth announced to me his determination of starting on an expedition to find Pomeroy, and never giving up the search while his money held out. He had no idea where to look for the fugitive, but rather thought he would try California first. He could hardly expect to receive any remittance from Gowanlock and Van Duzer for some months to come, but he would acquaint me with his address from time to time, and if anything arrived from them I could forward it to him.

And so, having seen the tombstone set up over little Charlie's grave, he bade me goodbye, and that was the last time I ever saw him, alive.

There is little more to tell. I supposed him to be in the far west, prosecuting his researches, until one night in the early spring of the following year. Charlie and his mother had been interred in a corner of the churchyard adjoining the second Baptist Church, which at that time was on the very outskirts of the town, in a lonely, unfrequented spot, not far from the iron bridge. Late in the evening of the 7th of April 1856, a woman passing along the road in the cold, dim twilight, saw a bulky object stretched out on Charlie's grave. She called at the nearest house, and stated her belief that a man was lying dead in the churchyard. Upon investigation, her surmise proved to be correct.

And that man was Gagtooth.

Dead; partially no doubt, from cold and exposure, but chiefly, I believe, from a broken heart. Where had he spent the six months which had elapsed since I bade him farewell?

To this question I am unable to reply; but this much was evident: he had dragged himself back just in time to die on the grave of the little boy whom he had loved so dearly, and whose brief existence had probably supplied the one bright spot in his father's life.

I had him buried in the same grave with Charlie; and there, on the banks of the Illinois river,

> After life's fitful fever he sleeps well.

I never received any remittance from his former employers, nor did I ever learn anything further of Silas Pomeroy. Indeed, so many years have rolled away since the occurrence of the events above narrated – years pregnant with great events to the American Republic; events, I am proud to say, in which I bore my part – that the wear and tear of life had nearly obliterated all memory of the episode from my mind, until, as detailed in the opening paragraphs of this story, I saw Gagtooth's image from the top of a Thornhill omnibus. That image is now in my possession, and no extremity less urgent than that under which it was sold to Silas Pomeroy, of Myrtle Street, Springfield, will ever induce me to part with it.

THOMAS DE QUINCEY

Thomas de Quincey (1785–1859), writer and critic, born in Manchester, son of a merchant. Educated at Manchester Grammar School, he ran away and wandered in Wales and London. He then spent a short time at Oxford, where he became addicted to opium. On a visit to Bath, he met Coleridge, and through him Southey and Wordsworth, and in 1809 went to live near them in Grasmere. There he set up as an author, largely writing magazine articles. His *Confessions of an English Opium-Eater*, written in sonorous prose, appeared as a serial in 1821, and brought him instant fame. In 1828 he moved to Edinburgh, and for twenty years wrote for various magazines. At the time of his death he was paying rent on six sets of lodgings.

The Avenger

'Why callest thou me murderer, and not rather the wrath of God burning after the steps of the oppressor, and cleansing the earth when it is wet with blood?'

That series of terrific events by which our quiet city and university in the north-eastern quarter of Germany were convulsed during the year 1816 has in itself, and considered merely as a blind movement of human tiger-passion ranging unchained among men, something too memorable to be forgotten or left without its own separate record; but the moral lesson impressed by these events is yet more memorable, and deserves the deep attention of coming generations in their struggle after human improvement, not merely in its own limited field of interest directly awakened, but in all analogous fields of interest; as in fact already, and more than once, in connection with these very events, this lesson has obtained the effectual attention of Christian kings and princes assembled in congress. No tragedy, indeed, among all the sad ones by which the charities of the human heart or of the fireside have ever been outraged, can better merit a separate chapter in the private history of German manners or social life than this unparalleled case. And, on the other hand, no one can put in a better claim to be the historian than myself.

I was at the time, and still am, a professor in that city and university which had the melancholy distinction of being its theatre. I knew familiarly all the parties who were concerned in it, either as sufferers or as agents. I was present from first to last, and watched the whole course of the mysterious storm which fell upon our devoted city in a strength like that of a West Indian hurricane, and which did seriously threaten at one time to depopulate our university, through the dark suspicions which settled upon its members and the natural reaction of generous indignation in repelling them; while the city in its more stationary and native classes would very soon have manifested *their* awful sense of things, of the hideous insecurity for life, and of the unfathomable dangers which had undermined their hearths below their very feet, by sacrificing, whenever circumstances allowed them, their houses and beautiful gardens in exchange for days uncursed by panic and nights unpolluted by blood. Nothing, I can take upon myself to assert, was left undone of all that human foresight could suggest or human ingenuity could accomplish. But observe the melancholy result: the more certain did these arrangements strike people as remedies for the evil, so much the more effectually did they aid the terror, but, above all, the awe, the sense of mystery, when ten cases of total extermination, applied to separate households, had occurred, in every one of which these precautionary aids had failed to yield the slightest assistance. The horror, the perfect frenzy of fear, which seized upon the town after that experience, baffles all attempt at description. Had these various contrivances failed merely in some human and intelligible way, as by bringing the aid too tardily – still, in such cases, though the danger would no less have been evidently deepened, nobody would have felt any further mystery than what, from the very first, rested upon the persons and the motives of the murderers. But, as it was, when, in ten separate cases of exterminating carnage, the astounded police, after an examination the most searching, pursued from day to day, and almost exhausting the patience by the minuteness of the investigation, had finally pronounced that no attempt apparently had been made to benefit by any of the signals preconcerted, that no footstep apparently had moved in that direction – then, and after that result, a blind misery of fear fell upon the population, so much the worse than any anguish of a beleaguered city that is awaiting the storming fury of a victorious enemy, by how much the shadowy, the uncertain, the infinite, is at all times more potent in mastering the mind than a danger that is known, measurable, palpable and human. The very police, instead of offering protection or encouragement, were seized with terror for themselves. And the general feeling, as it was described to me by a grave citizen whom I met in a morning walk (for the overmastering sense of a public calamity broke down every barrier of reserve, and all men talked freely to all men in the streets, as they would have done during the rockings of an earthquake), was, even among the boldest, like that which sometimes takes possession of the mind in dreams – when one feels oneself sleeping alone, utterly divided from all call or hearing of friends, doors open that should be shut, or unlocked that should be triply secured, the very walls gone, barriers swallowed up by unknown abysses, nothing around one but frail curtains, and a world of illimitable night, whisperings at a distance, correspondence going on between darkness and darkness, like one deep calling to another, and the dreamer's own heart the centre from which the whole network of this unimaginable chaos radiates, by means of which the blank privations of silence and darkness become powers the most positive and awful.

Agencies of fear, as of any other passion, and, above all, of passion felt in communion with thousands, and in which the heart beats in conscious sympathy with an entire city, through all its regions of high and low, young and old, strong and weak; such agencies avail to raise and transfigure the natures of men; mean minds become elevated; dull men become eloquent; and when matters came to this crisis, the public feeling, as made known by voice, gesture, manner or words, was such that no stranger could represent it to his fancy. In that respect, therefore, I had an advantage, being upon the spot through the whole course of the affair, for giving a faithful narrative; as I had still more eminently, from the sort of central station which I occupied, with respect to all the movements of the case. I may add that I had another advantage, not possessed, or not in the same degree, by any other inhabitant of the town. I was personally acquainted with every family of the slightest account belonging to the resident population; whether among the old local gentry, or the new settlers whom the late wars had driven to take refuge within our walls.

It was in September 1815 that I received a letter from the chief secretary to the Prince of M—, a nobleman connected with the diplomacy of Russia, from which I quote an extract:

I wish, in short, to recommend to your attentions, and in terms stronger than I know how to devise, a young man on whose behalf the czar himself is privately known to have expressed the very strongest interest. He was at the battle of Waterloo as an aide-de-camp to a Dutch general officer, and is decorated with distinctions won upon that awful day. However, though serving in that instance under English orders, and although an Englishman of rank, he does not belong to the English military service. He has served, young as he is, under various banners, and under ours, in particular, in the cavalry of our imperial guard. He is English by birth, nephew to the Earl of E—, and heir presumptive to his immense estates. There is a wild story current that his mother was a gypsy of transcendent beauty, which may account for his somewhat Moorish complexion, though, after all, that is not of a deeper tinge than I have seen among many an Englishman. He is himself one of the noblest looking of God's creatures. Both father and mother, however, are now dead. Since then he has become the favourite of his uncle, who detained him in England after the emperor had departed – and, as this uncle is now in the last stage of infirmity, Mr Wyndham's succession to the vast family estates is inevitable, and probably near at hand. Meantime, he is anxious for some assistance in his studies. Intellectually he stands in the very first rank of men, as I am sure you will not be slow to discover; but his long military service, and the unparalleled tumult of our European history since 1805, have interfered (as you may suppose) with the cultivation of his mind; for he entered the cavalry service of a German power when a mere boy, and shifted about from service to service as the hurricane of war blew from this point or from that. During the French anabasis to Moscow he entered our service, made himself a prodigious favourite with the whole imperial family, and even now is only in his twenty-second year. As to his accomplishments, they will speak for themselves; they are infinite, and applicable to every situation of life.

Greek is what he wants from you – never ask about terms. He will acknowledge any trouble he may give you, as he acknowledges all trouble, *en prince*. And ten years hence you will look back with pride upon having contributed your part to the formation of one whom all here at St Petersburg, not soldiers only, but we diplomats, look upon as certain to prove a great man, and a leader among the intellects of Christendom.

Two or three other letters followed; and at length it was arranged that Mr Maximilian Wyndham should take up his residence at my monastic abode for one year. He was to keep a table, and an establishment of servants, at his own cost; was to have an apartment of some dozen or so rooms; the unrestricted use of the library; with some other public privileges willingly conceded by the magistracy of the town; in return for all of which he was to pay me a thousand guineas; and already beforehand, by way of acknowledgement for the public civilities of the town, he sent, through my hands, a contribution of three hundred guineas to the various local institutions for the education of the poor, or for charity.

The Russian secretary had latterly corresponded with me from a little German town, not more than ninety miles distant; and, as he had special couriers at his service, the negotiations advanced so rapidly that all was closed before the end of September. And, when once that consummation was attained, I, that previously had breathed no syllable of what was stirring, now gave loose to the interesting tidings, and suffered them to spread through the whole compass of the town. It will be easily imagined that such a story, already romantic enough in its first outline, would lose nothing in the telling. An Englishman to begin with, which name of itself, and at all times, is a passport into German favour, but much more since the late memorable wars that but for Englishmen would have drooped into disconnected efforts – next, an Englishman of rank and of the *haute noblesse* – then a soldier covered with brilliant distinctions, and in the most brilliant arm of the service; young, moreover, and yet a veteran by his experience – fresh from the most awful battle of this planet since the day of Pharsalia – radiant with the favour of courts and of imperial ladies; finally (which alone would have given him an interest in all female hearts), an Antinous of faultless beauty, a Grecian statue, as it were, into which the breath of life had been breathed by some modern Pygmalion; such a pomp of gifts and endowments settling upon one man's head, should not have required for its effect the vulgar consummation (and yet to many it *was* the consummation and crest of the whole) that he was reputed to be rich beyond the dreams of romance or the necessities of a fairy tale. Unparalleled was the impression made upon our stagnant society; every tongue was busy in discussing the marvellous young Englishman from morning to night; every female fancy was busy in depicting the personal appearance of this brave apparition.

On his arrival at my house, I became sensible of a truth which I had observed some years before. The commonplace maxim is that it is dangerous to raise expectations too high. This, which is thus generally expressed, and without limitation, is true only conditionally; it is true then and there only where there is but little merit to sustain and justify the expectation. But in any case where the merit is transcendent of its kind, it is always useful to rack the expectation up to the highest point. In anything which partakes of the infinite, the most unlimited expectations will find ample room for gratification; while it is certain that ordinary observers, possessing little sensibility, unless where they have been warned to expect, will often fail to see what exists in the most conspicuous splendour. In this instance it certainly did no harm to the subject of expectation that I had been warned to look for so much. The warning, at any rate, put me on the lookout for whatever eminence there might be of grandeur in his personal appearance; while, on the other hand, this existed in such excess, so far transcending anything I had ever met with in my experience, that no expectation which it is in words to raise could have been disappointed.

These thoughts travelled with the rapidity of light through my brain, as at one glance my eye took in the supremacy of beauty and power which seemed to have alighted from the clouds before me. Power, and the contemplation of power, in any absolute incarnation of grandeur or excess, necessarily have the instantaneous effect of quelling all perturbation. My composure was restored in a moment. I looked steadily at him. We both bowed. And, at the moment when he raised his head from that inclination, I caught the glance of his eye; an eye such as might have been looked for in a face of such noble lineaments 'Blending the nature of the star With that of summer skies'; and, therefore, meant by nature for the residence and organ of serene and gentle emotions; but it surprised, and at the same time filled me more almost with consternation than with pity, to observe that in those eyes a light of sadness had settled more profound than seemed possible for youth, or almost commensurate to a human sorrow; a sadness that might have become a Jewish prophet, when laden with inspirations of woe.

Two months had now passed away since the arrival of Mr Wyndham. He had been universally introduced to the superior society of the place; and, as I need hardly say, universally received with favour and distinction. In reality, his wealth and importance, his military honours, and the dignity of his character, as expressed in his manners and deportment, were too eminent to allow of his being treated with less than the highest attention in any society whatever. But the effect of these various advantages, enforced and recommended as they were by a personal beauty so rare, was somewhat too potent for the comfort and self-possession of ordinary people; and really exceeded in a painful degree the standard of pretensions under which such people could feel themselves at their ease. He was not naturally of a reserved turn; far from it. His disposition had been open, frank, and confiding, originally; and his roving, adventurous life, of which considerably more than one half had been passed in camps, had communicated to his manners a more than military frankness. But the profound melancholy which possessed him, from whatever cause it arose, necessarily chilled the native freedom of his demeanour, unless when it was revived by strength of friendship or of love. The effect was awkward and embarrassing to all parties. Every voice paused or faltered when he entered a room – dead silence ensued – not an eye but was directed upon him, or else, sunk in timidity, settled upon the floor; and young ladies seriously lost the power, for a time, of doing more than murmuring a few confused, half-inarticulate syllables or half-inarticulate sounds. The solemnity, in fact, of a first present-ation, and the utter impossibility of soon recovering a free, unembarrassed movement of conversation, made such scenes really distressing to all who participated in them, either as actors or spectators. Certainly this result was not a pure effect of manly beauty, however heroic, and in whatever excess; it arose in part from the many and extraordinary endowments which had centred in his person, not less from fortune than from nature; in part also, as I have said, from the profound sadness and freezing gravity of Mr Wyndham's manner; but still more from the perplexing mystery which surrounded that sadness.

Were there, then, no exceptions to this condition of awestruck admiration? Yes; one at least there was in whose bosom the spell of all-conquering passion soon thawed every trace of icy reserve. While the rest of the world retained a dim sentiment of awe toward Mr Wyndham, Margaret Lieben-heim only heard of such a feeling to wonder that it could exist towards *him*. Never was there so victorious a conquest interchanged between two youthful hearts – never before such a rapture of instantaneous sympathy. I did not witness the first meeting of this mysterious Maximilian and this magnificent Margaret, and do not know whether Margaret manifested that trepidation and embarrassment which distressed so many of her youthful co-rivals; but, if she did, it must have fled before the first glance of the young man's eye, which would interpret, past all misunderstanding, the homage of his soul and the surrender of his heart. Their third meeting I *did* see; and there all shadow of embarrassment had vanished, except, indeed, of that delicate embarrassment which clings to impassioned admiration. On the part of Margaret, it seemed as if a new world had dawned upon her that she had not so much as suspected among the capacities of human experience. Like some bird she seemed, with powers unexercised for soaring and flying, not under-stood even as yet, and that never until now had found an element of air capable of sustaining her wings, or tempting her to put forth her buoyant instincts. He, on the other hand, now first found the realisation of his dreams, and for a mere possibility which he had long too deeply contemplated, fearing, however, that in his own case it might prove a chimera, or that he might never meet a woman answering the demands of his heart, he now found a corresponding reality that left nothing to seek.

Here, then, and thus far, nothing but happiness had resulted from the new arrangement. But, if this had been little anticipated by many, far less had I, for my part, anticipated the unhappy revolution which was wrought in the whole nature of Ferdinand von Harrelstein. He was the son of a German baron; a man of good family, but of small estate who had been pretty nearly a soldier of fortune in the Prussian service, and had, late in life, won sufficient favour with the king and other military superiors to have an early prospect of obtaining a commission, under flattering auspices, for this only son – a son endeared to him as the companion of unprosperous years, and as a dutifully affectionate child. Ferdinand had yet another hold upon his father's affections: his features preserved to the baron's unclouded remembrance a most faithful and living memorial of that angelic wife who had died in giving birth to this third child – the only one who had long survived her. Anxious that his son should go through a regular course of mathematical instruction, now becoming annually more important in all the artillery services through-out Europe, and that he should receive a tincture of other liberal studies which he had painfully missed in his own military career, the baron chose to keep his son for the last seven years at our college, until he was now entering upon his twenty-third year. For the four last he had lived with me as the sole pupil whom I had, or meant to have, had not the brilliant proposals of the young Russian guardsman persuaded me to break my resolution. Ferdinand von Harrelstein had good talents, not dazzling but respectable; and so amiable were his temper and manners that I had introduced him every-where, and everywhere he was a favourite; and everywhere, indeed, except exactly there where only in this world he cared for favour. Margaret Lieben-heim, she it was whom he loved, and had loved for years, with the whole ardour of his ardent soul; she it was for whom, or at whose command, he would willingly have died. Early he had felt that in her hands lay his destiny; that she it was who must be his good or his evil genius.

At first, and perhaps to the last, I pitied him exceedingly. But my pity soon ceased to be mingled with respect. Before the arrival of Mr Wyndham he had shown himself generous, indeed magnanimous. But never was there so painful an overthrow of a noble nature as manifested itself in him. I believe that he had not himself suspected the strength of his passion; and the sole resource for him, as I said often, was to quit the city – to engage in active pursuits of enterprise, of ambition, or of science. But he heard me as a somnambulist might have heard me – dreaming with his eyes open. Sometimes he had fits of reverie, starting, fearful, agitated; sometimes he broke out into maniacal movements of wrath, invoking some absent person, praying, beseeching, menacing some air-wove phantom; sometimes he slunk into solitary corners, muttering to himself, and with gestures sorrowfully significant, or with tones and fragments of expostulation that moved the most callous to compassion. Still he turned a deaf ear to the only practical counsel that had a chance for reaching his ears. Like a bird under the fascination of a rattlesnake, he would not summon up the energies of his nature to make an effort at flying away. 'Begone, while it is time!' said others, as well as myself; for more than I saw enough to fear some fearful catastrophe. 'Lead us not into temptation!' said his confessor to him in my hearing (for, though Prussians, the von Harrelsteins were Roman Catholics), 'lead us not into temptation! – that is our daily prayer to God. Then, my son, being led into temptation, do not you persist in courting, nay, almost tempting temptation. Try the effects of absence, though but for a month.' The good father even made an overture toward imposing a penance upon him, that would have involved an absence of some duration. But he was obliged to desist; for he saw that, without effecting any good, he would merely add spiritual disobedience to the other offences of the young man. Ferdinand himself drew his attention to this; for he said: 'Reverend father! do not you, with the purpose of removing me from temptation, be yourself the instrument for tempting me into a rebellion against the church. Do not you weave snares about my steps; snares there are already, and but too many.' The old man sighed, and desisted.

Then came – But enough! From pity, from sympathy, from counsel, and from consolation, and from scorn – from each of these alike the poor stricken deer 'recoiled into the wilderness'; he fled for days together into solitary parts of the forest; fled, as I still hoped and prayed, in good earnest and for a long farewell; but, alas! no: still he returned to the haunts of his ruined happiness and his buried hopes, at each return looking more like the wreck of his former self; and once I heard a penetrating monk observe, whose convent stood near the city gates: 'There goes one ready equally for doing or suffering, and of whom we shall soon hear that he is involved in some great catastrophe – it may be of deep calamity – it may be of memorable guilt.'

So stood matters among us. January was drawing to its close; the weather was growing more and more winterly; high winds, piercingly cold, were raving through our narrow streets; and still the spirit of social festivity bade defiance to the storms which sang through our ancient forests. From the accident of our magistracy being selected from the tradesmen of the city, the hospitalities of the place were far more extensive than would otherwise have happened; for every member of the corporation gave two annual entertainments in his official character. And such was the rivalship which prevailed, that often one quarter of the year's income was spent upon these galas. Nor was any ridicule thus incurred; for the costliness of the entertainment was understood to be an expression of official pride, done in honour of the city, not as an effort of personal display. It followed, from the spirit in which these half-yearly dances originated, that, being given on the part of the city, every stranger of rank was marked out as a privileged guest, and the hospitality of the community would have been equally affronted by failing to offer or by failing to accept the invitation.

Hence it had happened that the Russian guardsman had been introduced into many a family which otherwise could not have hoped for such a distinction. Upon the evening at which I am now arrived, the 22nd of January 1816, the whole city, in its wealthier classes, was assembled beneath the roof of a tradesman who had the heart of a prince. In every point our entertainment was superb; and I remarked that the music was the finest I had heard for years. Our host was in joyous spirits; proud to survey the splendid company he had gathered under his roof; happy to witness their happiness; elated in their elation. Joyous was the dance – joyous were all faces that I saw – up to midnight, very soon after which time supper was announced; and that also, I think, was the most joyous of all the banquets I ever witnessed. The accomplished guardsman outshone himself in brilliancy; even his melancholy relaxed. In fact, how could it be otherwise? near to him sat Margaret Liebenheim – hanging upon his words – more lustrous and bewitching than ever I had beheld her. There she had been placed by the host; and everybody knew why. That is one of the luxuries attached to love; all men cede their places with pleasure; women make way. Even she herself knew, though not obliged to know, why she was seated in that neighbourhood; and took her place, if with a rosy suffusion upon her cheeks, yet with fullness of happiness at her heart.

The guardsman pressed forward to claim Miss Liebenheim's hand for the next dance; a movement which she was quick to favour, by retreating behind one or two parties from a person who seemed coming towards her. The music again began to pour its voluptuous tides through the bounding pulses of the youthful company; again the flying feet of the dancers began to respond to the measures; again the mounting spirit of delight began to fill the sails of the hurrying night with steady inspiration. All went happily. Already had one dance finished; some were pacing up and down, leaning on the arms of their partners; some were reposing from their exertions; when – O heavens! what a shriek! what a gathering tumult!

Every eye was bent towards the doors – every eye strained forward to discover what was passing. But there, every moment, less and less could be seen, for the gathering crowd more and more intercepted the view; so much the more was the ear at leisure for the shrieks redoubled upon shrieks. Miss Liebenheim had moved downward to the crowd. From her superior height she overlooked all the ladies at the point where she stood. In the centre stood a rustic girl, whose features had been familiar to her for some months. She had recently come into the city, and had lived with her uncle, a tradesman, not ten doors from Margaret's own residence, partly on the terms of a kinswoman, partly as a servant on trial. At this moment she was exhausted with excitement, and the nature of the shock she had sustained. Mere panic seemed to have mastered her; and she was leaning, unconscious and weeping, upon the shoulder of some gentleman, who was endeavoring to soothe her. A silence of horror seemed to possess the company, most of whom were still unacquainted with the cause of the alarming interruption. A few, however, who had heard her first agitated words, finding that they waited in vain for a fuller explanation, now rushed tumultuously out of the ballroom to satisfy themselves on the spot. The distance was not great; and within five minutes several persons returned hastily, and cried out to the crowd of ladies that all was true which the young girl had said. 'What was true?' That her uncle Mr Weishaupt's family had been murdered; that not one member of the family had been spared – namely, Mr Weishaupt himself and his wife, neither of them much above sixty, but both infirm beyond their years; two maiden sisters of Mr Weishaupt, from forty to forty-six years of age, and an elderly female domestic.

An incident happened during the recital of these horrors, and of the details which followed, that furnished matter for conversation even in these hours when so thrilling an interest had possession of all minds. Many ladies fainted, among them Miss Liebenheim – and she would have fallen to the ground but for Maximilian, who sprang forward and caught her in his arms. She was long of returning to herself; and, during the agony of his suspense, he stooped and kissed her pallid lips. That sight was more than could be borne by one who stood a little behind the group. He rushed forward, with eyes glaring like a tiger's, and levelled a blow at Maximilian. It was poor, maniacal von Harrelstein, who had been absent in the forest for a week. Many people stepped forward and checked his arm, uplifted for a repetition of this outrage. One or two had some influence with him, and led him away from the spot; while as to Maximilian, so absorbed was he that he had not so much as perceived the affront offered to himself. Margaret, on reviving, was confounded at finding herself so situated amid a great crowd; and yet the prudes complained that there was a look of love exchanged between herself and Maximilian that ought not to have escaped her in such a situation. If they meant by such a situation, one so public, it must be also recollected that it was a situation of excessive agitation; but, if they alluded to the horrors of the moment, no situation more naturally opens the heart to affection and confiding love than the recoil from scenes of exquisite terror.

An examination went on that night before the magistrates, but all was dark; although suspicion attached to a negro named Aaron, who had occasionally been employed in menial services by the family, and had been in the house immediately before the murder. The circumstances were such as to leave every man in utter perplexity as to the presumption for and against him. His mode of defending himself, and his general deportment, were marked by the coolest, nay, the most sneering indifference. The first thing he did, on being acquainted with the suspicions against himself, was to laugh ferociously, and to all appearance most cordially and unaffectedly. He demanded whether a poor man like himself would have left so much wealth as lay scattered abroad in that house – gold repeaters, massy plate, gold snuff boxes – untouched? That argument certainly weighed much in his favour. And yet again it was turned against him; for a magistrate asked him how he happened to know already that nothing had been touched. True it was, and a fact which had puzzled no less than it had awed the magistrates, that, upon their examination of the premises, many rich articles of *bijouterie*, jewellery and personal ornaments had been found lying underanged, and apparently in their usual situations; articles so portable that in the very hastiest flight some might have been carried off. In particular, there was a crucifix of gold, enriched with jewels so large and rare that of itself it would have constituted a prize of great magnitude. Yet this was left untouched, though suspended in a little oratory that had been magnificently adorned by the elder of the maiden sisters. There was an altar, in itself a splendid object, furnished with every article of the most costly material and workmanship, for the private celebration of mass. This crucifix, as well as everything else in the little closet, must have been seen by one at least of the murderous party; for hither had one of the ladies fled; hither had one of the murderers pursued. She had clasped the golden pillars which supported the altar – had turned perhaps her dying looks upon the crucifix; for there, with one arm still wreathed about the altar foot, though in her agony she had turned round upon her face, did the elder sister lie when the magistrates first broke open the street door. And upon the beautiful parquet, or inlaid floor which ran round the room, were still impressed the footsteps of the murderer. These, it was hoped, might furnish a clue to the discovery of one at least among the murderous band. They were rather difficult to trace accurately, those parts of the traces which lay upon the black tessellae being less distinct in outline than the others upon the white or coloured. Most unquestionably, so far as this went, it furnished a negative circumstance in favour of the negro, for the footsteps were very different in outline from his, and smaller, for Aaron was a man of colossal build. And as to his knowledge of the state in which the premises had been found, and his having so familiarly relied upon the fact of no robbery having taken place as an argument on his own behalf, he contended that he had himself been among the crowd that pushed into the house along with the magistrates; that, from his previous acquaintance with the rooms and their ordinary condition, a glance of the eye had been sufficient for him to ascertain the undisturbed condition of all the valuable property most obvious to the grasp of a robber; that, in fact, he had seen enough for his argument before he and the rest of the mob had been ejected by the magistrates; but, finally, that independently of all this, he had heard both the officers, as they conducted him, and all the tumultuous gatherings of people in the street, arguing for the mysteriousness of the bloody transaction upon that very circumstance of so much gold, silver and jewels being left behind untouched.

In six weeks or less from the date of this terrific event, the negro was set at liberty by a majority of voices among the magistrates. In that short interval other events had occurred no less terrific and mysterious. In this first murder, though the motive was dark and unintelligible, yet the agency was not so; ordinary assassins apparently, and with ordinary means, had assailed a helpless and unprepared family; had separated them; attacked them singly in flight (for in this first case all but one of the murdered persons appeared to have been making for the street door); and in all this there was no subject for wonder, except the original one as to the motive. But now came a series of cases destined to fling this earliest murder into the shade. Nobody could now be unprepared; and yet the tragedies, henceforward, which passed before us, one by one or in terrific groups, seemed to argue a lethargy like that of apoplexy in the victims, one and all. The very midnight of mysterious awe fell upon all minds.

Three weeks had passed since the murder at Mr Weishaupt's – three weeks the most agitated that had been known in this sequestered city. We felt ourselves solitary, and thrown upon our own resources; all combination with other towns being unavailing from their great distance. Our situation was no ordinary one. Had there been some mysterious robbers among us, the chances of a visit, divided among so many, would have been too small to distress the most timid; while to young and high-spirited people, with courage to spare for ordinary trials, such a state of expectation would have sent pulses of pleasurable anxiety among the nerves. But murderers! exterminating murderers! – clothed in mystery and utter darkness – these were objects too terrific for any family to contemplate with fortitude. Had these very murderers added to their functions those of robbery, they would have become less terrific; nine out of every ten would have found themselves discharged, as it were, from the roll of those who were liable to a visit; while such as knew themselves liable would have had warning of their danger in the fact of being rich; and would, from the very riches which constituted that danger, have derived the means of repelling it. But, as things were, no man could guess what it was that must make him obnoxious to the murderers. Imagination exhausted itself in vain guesses at the causes which could by possibility have made the poor Weishaupts objects of such hatred to any man. True, they were bigoted in a degree which indicated feebleness of intellect; but *that* wounded no man in particular, while to many it recommended them. True, their charity was narrow and exclusive, but to those of their own religious body it expanded munificently; and, being rich beyond their wants, or any means of employing wealth which their gloomy asceticism allowed, they had the power of doing a great deal of good among the indigent papists of the suburbs. As to the old gentleman and his wife, their infirmities confined them to the house. Nobody remembered to have seen them abroad for years. How, therefore, or when could they have made an enemy? And, with respect to the maiden sisters of Mr Weishaupt, they were simply weak-minded persons, now and then too censorious, but not placed in a situation to incur serious anger from any quarter, and too little heard of in society to occupy much of anybody's attention.

Conceive, then, that three weeks have passed away, that the poor Weis-haupts have been laid in that narrow sanctuary which no murderer's voice will ever violate. Quiet has not returned to us, but the first flutterings of panic have subsided. People are beginning to respire freely again; and such another space of time would have cicatrised our wounds – when, hark! a church bell rings out a loud alarm; the night is starlit and frosty – the iron notes are heard clear, solemn, but agitated. What could this mean? I hurried to a room over the porter's lodge, and, opening the window, I cried out to a man passing hastily below, 'What, in God's name, is the meaning of this?' It was a watchman belonging to our district. I knew his voice, he knew mine, and he replied in great agitation: 'It is another murder, sir, at the old town councillor's, Albernass; and this time they have made a clear house of it.'

'God preserve us! Has a curse been pronounced upon this city? What can be done? What are the magistrates going to do?'

'I don't know, sir. I have orders to run to the Black Friars, where another meeting is gathering. Shall I say you will attend, sir?'

'Yes – no – stop a little. No matter, you may go on; I'll follow immediately.'

I went instantly to Maximilian's room. He was lying asleep on a sofa, at which I was not surprised, for there had been a severe stag chase in the morning. Even at this moment I found myself arrested by two objects, and I paused to survey them. One was Maximilian himself. A person so mysterious took precedence of other interests even at a time like this; and especially by his features, which, composed in profound sleep, as sometimes happens, assumed a new expression, which arrested me chiefly by awaking some confused remembrance of the same features seen under other circumstances and in times long past; but where? This was what I could not recollect, though once before a thought of the same sort had crossed my mind. The other object of my interest was a miniature, which Maximilian was holding in his hand. He had gone to sleep apparently looking at this picture; and the hand which held it had slipped down upon the sofa, so that it was in danger of falling. I released the miniature from his hand, and surveyed it attentively. It represented a lady of sunny, oriental complexion, and features the most noble that it is possible to conceive. One might have imagined such a lady, with her raven locks and imperial eyes, to be the favourite sultana of some Amurath or Mohammed. What was she to Maximilian, or what had she been? For, by the tear which I had once seen him drop upon this miniature when he believed himself unobserved, I conjectured that her dark tresses were already laid low, and her name among the list of vanished things. Probably she was his mother, for the dress was rich with pearls, and evidently that of a person in the highest rank of court beauties. I sighed as I thought of the stern melancholy of her son, if Maximilian were he, as connected, probably, with the fate and fortunes of this majestic beauty; somewhat haughty, perhaps, in the expression of her fine features, but still noble – generous – confiding. Laying the picture on the table, I awoke Maximilian, and told him of the dreadful news. He listened attentively, made no remark, but proposed that we should go together to the meeting of our quarter at the Black Friars. He coloured upon observing the miniature on the table; and, therefore, I frankly told him in what situation I had found it, and that I had taken the liberty of admiring it for a few moments. He pressed it tenderly to his lips, sighed heavily, and we walked away together.

I pass over the frenzied state of feeling in which we found the meeting. Fear, or rather horror, did not promote harmony; many quarrelled with each other in discussing the suggestions brought forward, and Maximilian was the only person attended to. He proposed a nightly mounted patrol for every district. And in particular he offered, as being himself a member of the university, that the students should form themselves into a guard, and go out by rotation to keep watch and ward from sunset to sunrise. Arrangements were made towards that object by the few people who retained possession of their senses, and for the present we separated.

Never, in fact, did any events so keenly try the difference between man and man. Some started up into heroes under the excitement. Some, alas for the dignity of man! drooped into helpless imbecility. Women, in some cases, rose superior to men, but yet not so often as might have happened under a less mysterious danger. A woman is not unwomanly because she confronts danger boldly. But I have remarked, with respect to female courage, that it requires, more than that of men, to be sustained by hope; and that it droops more certainly in the presence of a *mysterious* danger. The fancy of women is more active, if not stronger, and it influences more directly the physical nature. In this case few were the women who made even a show of defying the danger. On the contrary, with them fear took the form of sadness, while with many of the men it took that of wrath.

And how did the Russian guardsman conduct himself amidst this panic? Many were surprised at his behaviour; some complained of it; I did neither. He took a reasonable interest in each separate case, listened to the details with attention, and, in the examination of persons able to furnish evidence, never failed to suggest judicious questions. But still he manifested a coolness almost amounting to carelessness, which to many appeared revolting. But these people I desired to notice that all the other military students, who had been long in the army, felt exactly in the same way. In fact, the military service of Christendom, for the last ten years, had been anything but a parade service; and to those, therefore, who were familiar with every form of horrid butchery, the mere outside horrors of death had lost much of their terror. In the recent murder there had not been much to call forth sympathy. The family consisted of two old bachelors, two sisters, and one grandniece. The niece was absent on a visit, and the two old men were cynical misers, to whom little personal interest attached. Still, in this case as in that of the Weishaupts, the same twofold mystery confounded the public mind – the mystery of the *how*, and the profounder mystery of the *why*. Here, again, no atom of property was taken, though both the misers had hordes of ducats and English guineas in the very room where they died. Their bias, again, though of an unpopular character, had rather availed to make them unknown than to make them hateful. In one point this case differed memorably from the other – that, instead of falling helpless, or flying victims (as the Weishaupts had done), these old men, strong, resolute, and not so much taken by surprise, left proofs that they had made a desperate defence. The furniture was partly smashed to pieces, and the other details furnished evidence still more revolting of the acharnement with which the struggle had been maintained. In fact, with *them* a surprise must have been impracticable, as they admitted nobody into their house on visiting terms. It was thought singular that from each of these domestic tragedies a benefit of the same sort should result to young persons standing in nearly the same relation. The girl who gave the alarm at the ball, with two little sisters and a little orphan nephew, their cousin, divided the very large inheritance of the Weishaupts; and in this latter case the accumulated savings of two long lives all vested in the person of the amiable grandniece.

But now, as if in mockery of all our anxious consultations and elaborate devices, three fresh murders took place on the two consecutive nights succeeding these new arrangements. And in one case, as nearly as time could be noted, the mounted patrol must have been within call at the very moment when the awful work was going on. I shall not dwell much upon them; but a few circumstances are too interesting to be passed over. The earliest case on the first of the two nights was that of a currier. He was fifty years old; not rich, but well off. His first wife was dead, and his daughters by her were married away from their father's house. He had married a second wife, but, having no children by her, and keeping no servants, it is probable that, but for an accident, no third person would have been in the house at the time when the murderers got admittance. About seven o'clock, a way-faring man, a journeyman currier, who, according to our German system, was now in his *wanderjahr*, entered the city from the forest. At the gate he made some enquiries about the curriers and tanners of our town; and, agreeably to the information he received, made his way to this Mr Heinberg. Mr Heinberg refused to admit him, until he mentioned his errand, and pushed below the door a letter of recommendation from a Silesian correspondent, describing him as an excellent and steady workman. Wanting such a man, and satisfied by the answers returned that he was what he represented himself, Mr Heinberg unbolted his door and admitted him. Then, after slipping the bolt into its place, he bade him sit to the fire, brought him a glass of beer, conversed with him for ten minutes, and said: 'You had better stay here tonight; I'll tell you why afterwards; but now I'll step upstairs, and ask my wife whether she can make up a bed for you; and do you mind the door while I'm away.' So saying, he went out of the room. Not one minute had he been gone when there came a gentle knock at the door. It was raining heavily, and, being a stranger to the city, not dreaming that in any crowded town such a state of things could exist as really did in this, the young man, without hesitation, admitted the person knocking. He has declared since – but, perhaps, confounding the feelings gained from better knowledge with the feelings of the moment – that from the moment he drew the bolt he had a misgiving that he had done wrong. A man entered in a horseman's cloak, and so muffled up that the journeyman could dis-cover none of his features. In a low tone the stranger said, 'Where's Heinberg?' – 'Upstairs.' – 'Call him down, then.' The journeyman went to the door by which Mr Heinberg had left him, and called, 'Mr Heinberg, here's one wanting you!' Mr Heinberg heard him, for the man could distinctly catch these words: 'God bless me! has the man opened the door? O, the traitor! I see it.' Upon this he felt more and more consternation, though not knowing why. Just then he heard a sound of feet behind him. On turning round, he beheld three more men in the room; one was fastening the outer door; one was drawing some arms from a cupboard, and two others were whispering together. He himself was disturbed and perplexed, and felt that all was not right. Such was his confusion, that either all the men's faces must have been muffled up, or at least he remembered nothing distinctly but one fierce pair of eyes glaring upon him. Then, before he could look round, came a man from behind and threw a sack over his head, which was drawn tight about his waist, so as to confine his arms, as well as to impede his hearing in part, and his voice altogether. He was then pushed into a room; but previously he had heard a rush upstairs, and words like those of a person exulting, and then a door closed. Once it opened, and he could distinguish the words, in one voice, 'And for *that*!' to which another voice replied, in tones that made his heart quake, 'Aye, for *that*, sir.' And then the same voice went on rapidly to say, 'O dog! could you hope' – at which word the door closed again. Once he thought that he heard a scuffle, and he was sure that he heard the sound of feet, as if rushing from one corner of a room to another. But then all was hushed and still for about six or seven minutes, until a voice close to his ear said, 'Now, wait quietly till some persons come in to release you. This will happen within half an hour.' Accordingly, in less than that time, he again heard the sound of feet within the house, his own bandages were liberated, and he was brought to tell his story at the police office. Mr Heinberg was found in his bedroom. He had died by strangulation, and the cord was still tightened about his neck. During the whole dreadful scene his youthful wife had been locked into a closet, where she heard or saw nothing.

In the second case, the object of vengeance was again an elderly man. Of the ordinary family, all were absent at a country house, except the master and a female servant. She was a woman of courage, and blessed with the firmest nerves; so that she might have been relied on for reporting accurately everything seen or heard. But things took another course. The first warning that she had of the murderers' presence was from their steps and voices already in the hall. She heard her master run hastily into the hall, crying out, 'Lord Jesus! – Mary, Mary, save me!' The servant resolved to give what aid she could, seized a large poker, and was hurrying to his assistance, when she found that they had nailed up the door of communication at the head of the stairs. What passed after this she could not tell; for, when the impulse of intrepid fidelity had been balked, and she found that her own safety was provided for by means which made it impossible to aid a poor fellow creature who had just invoked her name, the generous-hearted creature was overcome by anguish of mind, and sank down on the stair, where she lay, unconscious of all that succeeded, until she found herself raised in the arms of a mob who had entered the house. And how came they to have entered? In a way characteristically dreadful. The night was starlit; the patrols had perambulated the street without noticing anything suspicious, when two foot passengers, who were following in their rear, observed a dark-coloured stream traversing the causeway. One of them, at the same instant tracing the stream backward with his eyes, observed that it flowed from under the door of Mr Munzer, and, dipping his finger in the trickling fluid, he held it up to the lamplight, yelling out at the moment, 'Why, this is blood!' It was so, indeed, and it was yet warm. The other saw, heard, and like an arrow flew after the horse patrol, then in the act of turning the corner. One cry, full of meaning, was sufficient for ears full of expectation. The horsemen pulled up, wheeled, and in another moment reined up at Mr Munzer's door. The crowd, gathering like the drifting of snow, supplied implements which soon forced the chains of the door and all other obstacles. But the murderous party had escaped, and all traces of their persons had vanished, as usual.

Rarely did any case occur without some peculiarity more or less interesting. In that which happened on the following night, making the fifth in the series, an impressive incident varied the monotony of horrors. In this case the parties aimed at were two elderly ladies, who conducted a female boarding school. None of the pupils had as yet returned to school from their vacation; but two sisters, young girls of thirteen and sixteen, coming from a distance, had stayed at school throughout the Christmas holidays. It was the younger of these who gave the only evidence of any value, and one which added a new feature of alarm to the existing panic. Thus it was that her testimony was given: On the day before the murder, she and her sister were sitting with the old ladies in a room fronting to the street; the elder ladies were reading, the younger ones drawing. Louisa, the youngest, never had her ear inattentive to the slightest sound, and once it struck her that she heard the creaking of a foot upon the stairs. She said nothing, but, slipping out of the room, she ascertained that the two female servants were in the kitchen, and could not have been absent; that all the doors and windows, by which ingress was possible, were not only locked, but bolted and barred – a fact which excluded all possibility of invasion by means of false keys. Still she felt persuaded that she had heard the sound of a heavy foot upon the stairs. It was, however, daylight, and this gave her confidence; so that, without communicating her alarm to anybody, she found courage to traverse the house in every direction; and, as nothing was either seen or heard, she concluded that her ears had been too sensitively awake. Yet that night, as she lay in bed, dim terrors assailed her, especially because she considered that, in so large a house, some closet or other might have been overlooked, and, in particular, she did not remember to have examined one or two chests, in which a man could have lain concealed. Through the greater part of the night she lay awake; but as one of the town clocks struck four, she dismissed her anxieties, and fell asleep. The next day, wearied with this unusual watching, she proposed to her sister that they should go to bed earlier than usual. This they did; and, on their way upstairs, Louisa happened to think suddenly of a heavy cloak, which would improve the coverings of her bed against the severity of the night. The cloak was hanging up in a closet within a closet, both leading off from a large room used as the young ladies' dancing school. These closets she had examined on the previous day, and therefore she felt no particular alarm at this moment. The cloak was the first article which met her sight; it was suspended from a hook in the wall, and close to the door. She took it down, but, in doing so, exposed part of the wall and of the floor, which its folds had previously concealed. Turning away hastily, the chances were that she had gone without making any discovery. In the act of turning, however, her light fell brightly on a man's foot and leg. Matchless was her presence of mind; having previously been humming an air, she continued to do so. But now came the trial; her sister was bending her steps to the same closet. If she suffered her to do so, Lottchen would stumble on the same discovery, and expire of fright. On the other hand, if she gave her a hint, Lottchen would either fail to understand her, or, gaining but a glimpse of her meaning, would shriek aloud, or by some equally decisive expression convey the fatal news to the assassin that he had been discovered. In this torturing dilemma fear prompted an expedient, which to Lottchen appeared madness, and to Louisa herself the act of a sibyl instinct with blind inspiration. 'Here,' said she, 'is our dancing room. When shall we all meet and dance again together?' Saying which, she commenced a wild dance, whirling her candle round her head until the motion extinguished it; then, eddying round her sister in narrowing circles, she seized Lottchen's candle also, blew it out, and then interrupted her own singing to attempt a laugh. But the laugh was hysterical. The darkness, however, favoured her; and, seizing her sister's arm, she forced her along, whispering, 'Come, come, come!' Lottchen could not be so dull as entirely to misunderstand her. She suffered herself to be led up the first flight of stairs, at the head of which was a room looking into the street. In this they would have gained an asylum, for the door had a strong bolt. But, as they were on the last steps of the landing, they could hear the hard breathing and long strides of the murderer ascending behind them. He had watched them through a crevice, and had been satisfied by the hysterical laugh of Louisa that she had seen him. In the darkness he could not follow fast, from ignorance of the localities, until he found himself upon the stairs. Louisa, dragging her sister along, felt strong as with the strength of lunacy, but Lottchen hung like a weight of lead upon her. She rushed into the room, but at the very entrance Lottchen fell. At that moment the assassin exchanged his stealthy pace for a loud clattering ascent. Already he was on the topmost stair; already he was throwing himself at a bound against the door, when Louisa, having dragged her sister into the room, closed the door and sent the bolt home in the very instant that the murderer's hand came into contact with the handle. Then, from the violence of her emotions, she fell down in a fit, with her arm around the sister whom she had saved.

How long they lay in this state neither ever knew. The two old ladies had rushed upstairs on hearing the tumult. Other persons had been concealed in other parts of the house. The servants found themselves suddenly locked in, and were not sorry to be saved from a collision which involved so awful a danger. The old ladies had rushed, side by side, into the very centre of those who were seeking them. Retreat was impossible; two persons at least were heard following them upstairs. Something like a shrieking expostulation and counter-expostulation went on between the ladies and the murderers; then came louder voices – then one heart-piercing shriek, and then another – and then a slow moaning and a dead silence. Shortly afterwards was heard the first crashing of the door inwards by the mob; but the murderers had fled upon the first alarm, and, to the astonishment of the servants, had fled upwards. Examination, however, explained this: from a window in the roof they had passed to an adjoining house recently left empty; and here, as in other cases, we had proof how apt people are, in the midst of elaborate provisions against remote dangers, to neglect those which are obvious.

The reign of terror, it may be supposed, had now reached its acme. The two old ladies were both lying dead at different points on the staircase, and, as usual, no conjecture could be made as to the nature of the offence which they had given; but that the murder *was* a vindictive one, the usual evidence remained behind, in the proofs that no robbery had been attempted. Two new features, however, were now brought forward in this system of horrors, one of which riveted the sense of their insecurity in all families occupying extensive houses, and the other raised ill blood between the city and the university, such as required years to allay. The first arose out of the experience, now first obtained, that these assassins pursued the plan of secreting themselves within the house where they meditated a murder. All the care, therefore, previously directed to the securing of doors and windows after nightfall appeared nugatory. The other feature brought to light on this occasion was vouched for by one of the servants, who declared that, the moment before the door of the kitchen was fastened upon herself and fellow servant, she saw two men in the hall, one on the point of ascending the stairs, the other making towards the kitchen; that she could not distinguish the faces of either, but that both were dressed in the academic costume belonging to the students of the university. The consequences of such a declaration need scarcely be mentioned. Suspicion settled upon the students, who were more numerous since the general peace, in a much larger proportion military, and less select or respectable than heretofore. Still, no part of the mystery was cleared up by this discovery. Many of the students were poor enough to feel the temptation that might be offered by any *lucrative* system of outrage. Jealous and painful conclusions were, in the meantime, produced; and, during the latter two months of this winter, it may be said that our city exhibited the very anarchy of evil passions. This condition of things lasted until the dawning of another spring.

It will be supposed that communications were made to the supreme government of the land as soon as the murders in our city were understood to be no casual occurrences but links in a systematic series. Perhaps it might have happened from some other business, of a higher kind, just then engaging the attention of our governors that our representations did not make the impression we had expected. We could not, indeed, complain of absolute neglect from the government. They sent down one or two of their most accomplished police officers, and they suggested some counsels, especially that we should examine more strictly into the quality of the miscellaneous population who occupied our large suburb. But they more than hinted that no necessity was seen either for quartering troops upon us, or for arming our local magistracy with ampler powers.

This correspondence with the central government occupied the month of March, and, before that time, the bloody system had ceased as abruptly as it began. The new police officer flattered himself that the terror of his name had wrought this effect; but judicious people thought otherwise. All, however, was quiet until the depth of summer, when, by way of hinting to us, perhaps, that the dreadful power which clothed itself with darkness had not expired, but was only reposing from its labours, all at once the chief jailer of the city was missing. He had been in the habit of taking long rides in the forest, his present situation being much of a sinecure. It was on the 1st of July that he was missed. In riding through the city gates that morning, he had mentioned the direction which he meant to pursue; and the last time he was seen alive was in one of the forest avenues, about eight miles from the city, leading toward the point he had indicated. This jailer was not a man to be regretted on his own account; his life had been a tissue of cruelty and brutal abuse of his powers, in which he had been too much supported by the magistrates, partly on the plea that it was their duty to back their own officers against all complainers, partly also from the necessities created by the turbulent times for a more summary exercise of their magisterial authority. No man, therefore, on his own separate account, could more willingly have been spared than this brutal jailer; and it was a general remark that, had the murderous band within our walls swept away this man only, they would have merited the public gratitude as purifiers from a public nuisance. But was it certain that the jailer had died by the same hands as had so deeply afflicted the peace of our city during the winter – or, indeed, that he had been murdered at all? The forest was too extensive to be searched; and it was possible that he might have met with some fatal accident. His horse had returned to the city gates in the night, and was found there in the morning. Nobody, however, for months could give information about his rider; and it seemed probable that he would not be discovered until the autumn and the winter should again carry the sportsman into every thicket and dingle of this sylvan tract. One person only seemed to have more knowledge on this subject than others, and that was poor Ferdinand von Harrelstein. He was now a mere ruin of what he had once been, both as to intellect and moral feeling; and I observed him frequently smile when the jailer was mentioned. 'Wait,' he would say, 'till the leaves begin to drop; then you will see what fine fruit our forest bears.' I did not repeat these expressions to anybody except one friend, who agreed with me that the jailer had probably been hanged in some recess of the forest, which summer veiled with its luxuriant umbrage; and that Ferdinand, constantly wandering in the forest, had discovered the body; but we both acquitted him of having been an accomplice in the murder.

Meantime the marriage between Margaret Liebenheim and Maximilian was understood to be drawing near. Yet one thing struck everybody with astonishment. As far as the young people were concerned, nobody could doubt that all was arranged; for never was happiness more perfect than that which seemed to unite them. Margaret was the impersonation of May-time and youthful rapture; even Maximilian in her presence seemed to forget his gloom, and the worm which gnawed at his heart was charmed asleep by the music of her voice, and the paradise of her smiles. But, until the autumn came, Margaret's grandfather had never ceased to frown upon this connection, and to support the pretensions of Ferdinand. The dislike, indeed, seemed reciprocal between him and Maximilian. Each avoided the other's company, and as to the old man, he went so far as to speak sneeringly of Maximilian. Maximilian despised him too heartily to speak of him at all. When he could not avoid meeting him, he treated him with a stern courtesy, which distressed Margaret as often as she witnessed it. She felt that her grandfather had been the aggressor; and she felt also that he did injustice to the merits of her lover. But she had a filial tenderness for the old man, as the father of her sainted mother, and on his own account she found him continually making more claims on her pity, as the decay of his memory, and a childish fretfulness growing upon him from day to day, marked his increasing imbecility.

Equally mysterious it seemed was that about this time Miss Liebenheim began to receive anonymous letters, written in the darkest and most menacing terms. Some of them she showed to me. I could not guess at their drift. Evidently they glanced at Maximilian, and bade her beware of connection with him; and dreadful things were insinuated about him. Could these letters be written by Ferdinand? Written they were not, but could they be dictated by him? Much I feared that they were; and the more so for one reason.

All at once, and most inexplicably, Margaret's grandfather showed a total change of opinion in his views as to her marriage. Instead of favouring Harrelstein's pretensions, as he had hitherto done, he now threw the feeble weight of his encouragement into Maximilian's scale; though, from the situation of all the parties, nobody attached any practical importance to the change in Mr Liebenheim's way of thinking. Nobody? Is that true? No; one person *did* attach the greatest weight to the change – poor, ruined Ferdinand. He, so long as there was one person to take his part, so long as the grandfather of Margaret showed countenance to himself, had still felt his situation not utterly desperate.

Thus were things situated, when in November, all the leaves daily blowing off from the woods, and leaving bare the most secret haunts of the thickets, the body of the jailer was left exposed in the forest; but not, as I and my friend had conjectured, hanged. No; he had died apparently by a more horrid death – by that of crucifixion. The tree, a remarkable one, bore upon a part of its trunk this brief but savage inscription: 'T. H., jailer at — ; Crucified 1 July 1816'.

A great deal of talk went on throughout the city upon this discovery; nobody uttered one word of regret on account of the wretched jailer; on the contrary, the voice of vengeance, rising up in many a cottage, reached my ears from every direction as I walked abroad. The hatred in itself seemed horrid and unchristian, and still more so after the man's death; but, though horrid and fiendish in itself, it was much more impressive, considered as the measure and exponent of the damnable oppression which must have existed to produce it.

At first, when the absence of the jailer was a recent occurrence, and the presence of the murderers among us was, in consequence, revived to our anxious thoughts, it was an event which few alluded to without fear. But matters were changed now; the jailer had been dead for months, and this interval, during which the murderer's hand had slept, encouraged everybody to hope that the storm had passed over our city; that peace had returned to our hearths; and that henceforth weakness might sleep in safety, and innocence without anxiety. Once more we had peace within our walls, and tranquillity by our firesides. Again the child went to bed in cheerfulness, and the old man said his prayers in serenity. Confidence was restored; peace was re-established; and once again the sanctity of human life became the rule and the principle for all human hands among us. Great was the joy; the happiness was universal.

O heavens! by what a thunderbolt were we awakened from our security! On the night of the 27th of December, half an hour, it might be, after twelve o'clock, an alarm was given that all was not right in the house of Mr Liebenheim. Vast was the crowd which soon collected in breathless agitation.

In two minutes a man who had gone round by the back of the house was heard unbarring Mr Liebenheim's door: he was incapable of uttering a word; but his gestures, as he threw the door open and beckoned to the crowd, were quite enough. In the hall, at the farther extremity, and as if arrested in the act of making for the back door, lay the bodies of old Mr Liebenheim and one of his sisters, an aged widow; on the stair lay another sister, younger and unmarried, but upward of sixty. The hall and lower flight of stairs were floating with blood. Where, then, was Miss Liebenheim, the granddaughter? That was the universal cry; for she was beloved as generally as she was admired. Had the infernal murderers been devilish enough to break into that temple of innocent and happy life? Everyone asked the question, and everyone held his breath to listen; but for a few moments no one dared to advance; for the silence of the house was ominous. At length someone cried out that Miss Liebenheim had that day gone upon a visit to a friend, whose house was forty miles distant in the forest. 'Aye,' replied another, 'she had settled to go; but I heard that something had stopped her.' The suspense was now at its height, and the crowd passed from room to room, but found no traces of Miss Liebenheim. At length they ascended the stair, and in the very first room, a small closet, or boudoir, lay Margaret, with her dress soiled hideously with blood. The first impression was that she also had been murdered; but, on a nearer approach, she appeared to be unwounded, and was manifestly alive. Life had not departed, for her breath sent a haze over a mirror, but it was suspended, and she was labouring in some kind of fit. The first act of the crowd was to carry her into the house of a friend on the opposite side of the street, by which time medical assistance had crowded to the spot. Their attentions to Miss Liebenheim had naturally deranged the condition of things in the little room, but not before many people found time to remark that one of the murderers must have carried her with his bloody hands to the sofa on which she lay, for water had been sprinkled profusely over her face and throat, and water was even placed ready to her hand, when she might happen to recover, upon a low footstool by the side of the sofa.

On the following morning, Maximilian, who had been upon a hunting party in the forest, returned to the city, and immediately learned the news. I did not see him for some hours after, but he then appeared to me thoroughly agitated, for the first time I had known him to be so. In the evening another perplexing piece of intelligence transpired with regard to Miss Liebenheim, which at first afflicted every friend of that young lady. It was that she had been seized with the pains of childbirth, and delivered of a son, who, however, being born prematurely, did not live many hours. Scandal, however, was not allowed long to batten upon this imaginary triumph, for within two hours after the circulation of this first rumour followed a second, authenticated, announcing that Maximilian had appeared with the confessor of the Liebenheim family, at the residence of the chief magistrate, and there produced satisfactory proofs of his marriage with Miss Liebenheim, which had been duly celebrated, though with great secrecy, nearly eight months before. In our city, as in all the cities of our country, clandestine marriages, witnessed, perhaps, by two friends only of the parties, besides the officiating priest, are exceedingly common. In the mere fact, therefore, taken separately, there was nothing to surprise us, but, taken in connection with the general position of the parties, it *did* surprise us all; nor could we conjecture the reason for a step apparently so needless. For that Maximilian could have thought it any point of prudence or necessity to secure the hand of Margaret Liebenheim by a private marriage, against the final opposition of her grandfather, nobody who knew the parties, who knew the perfect love which possessed Miss Liebenheim, the growing imbecility of her grandfather or the utter contempt with which Maximilian regarded him, could for a moment believe. Altogether, the matter was one of profound mystery.

Meantime, it rejoiced me that poor Margaret's name had been thus rescued from the fangs of the scandalmongers. These harpies had their prey torn from them at the very moment when they were sitting down to the unhallowed banquet. For this I rejoiced, but else there was little subject for rejoicing in anything which concerned poor Margaret. Long she lay in deep insensibility, taking no notice of anything, rarely opening her eyes, and apparently unconscious of the revolutions, as they succeeded, of morning or evening, light or darkness, yesterday or today. Great was the agitation which convulsed the heart of Maximilian during this period; he walked up and down in the cathedral nearly all day long, and the ravages which anxiety was working in his physical system might be read in his face. People felt it an intrusion upon the sanctity of his grief to look at him too narrowly, and the whole town sympathised with his situation.

At length a change took place in Margaret, but one which the medical men announced to Maximilian as boding ill for her recovery. The wanderings of her mind did not depart, but they altered their character. She became more agitated; she would start up suddenly, and strain her eyesight after some figure which she seemed to see; then she would apostrophise some person in the most piteous terms, beseeching him, with streaming eyes, to spare her old grandfather. 'Look, look,' she would cry out, 'look at his grey hairs! O, sir! he is but a child; he does not know what he says; and he will soon be out of the way and in his grave; and very soon, sir, he will give you no more trouble.' Then, again, she would mutter indistinctly for hours together; sometimes she would cry out frantically, and say things which terrified the bystanders, and which the physicians would solemnly caution them how they repeated; then she would weep, and invoke Maximilian to come and aid her. But seldom, indeed, did that name pass her lips that she did not again begin to strain her eyeballs, and start up in bed to watch some phantom of her poor, fevered heart, as if it seemed vanishing into some mighty distance.

After nearly seven weeks passed in this agitating state, suddenly, on one morning, the earliest and the loveliest of dawning spring, a change was announced to us all as having taken place in Margaret; but it was a change, alas! that ushered in the last great change of all. The conflict, which had for so long a period raged within her, and overthrown her reason, was at an end; the strife was over, and nature was settling into an everlasting rest. In the course of the night she had recovered her senses. When the morning light penetrated through her curtain, she recognised her attendants, made enquiries as to the month and the day of the month, and then, sensible that she could not outlive the day, she requested that her confessor might be summoned.

About an hour and a half the confessor remained alone with her. At the end of that time he came out, and hastily summoned the attendants, for Margaret, he said, was sinking into a fainting fit. The confessor himself might have passed through many a fit, so much was he changed by the results of this interview. I crossed him coming out of the house. I spoke to him – I called to him; but he heard me not – he saw me not. He saw nobody. Onward he strode to the cathedral, where Maximilian was sure to be found, pacing about upon the graves. Him he seized by the arm, whispered something into his ear, and then both retired into one of the many sequestered chapels in which lights are continually burning. There they had some conversation, but not very long, for within five minutes Maximilian strode away to the house in which his young wife was dying. One step seemed to carry him upstairs. The attendants, according to the directions they had received from the physicians, mustered at the head of the stairs to oppose him. But that was idle: before the rights which he held as a lover and a husband – before the still more sacred rights of grief, which he carried in his countenance – all opposition fled like a dream. There was, besides, a fury in his eye. A motion of his hand waved them off like summer flies; he entered the room, and once again, for the last time, he was in company with his beloved.

What passed who could pretend to guess? Something more than two hours had elapsed, during which Margaret had been able to talk occasionally, which was known, because at times the attendants heard the sound of Maximilian's voice evidently in tones of reply to something which she had said. At the end of that time, a little bell, placed near the bedside, was rung hastily. A fainting fit had seized Margaret; but she recovered almost before her women applied the usual remedies. They lingered, however, a little, looking at the youthful couple with an interest which no restraints availed to check. Their hands were locked together, and in Margaret's eyes there gleamed a farewell light of love, which settled upon Maximilian, and seemed to indicate that she was becoming speechless. Just at this moment she made a feeble effort to draw Maximilian towards her; he bent forward and kissed her with an anguish that made the most callous weep, and then he whispered something into her ear, upon which the attendants retired, taking this as a proof that their presence was a hindrance to a free communication. But they heard no more talking, and in less than ten minutes they returned. Maximilian and Margaret still retained their former position. Their hands were fast locked together; the same parting ray of affection, the same farewell light of love, was in the eye of Margaret, and still it settled upon Maximilian. But her eyes were beginning to grow dim; mists were rapidly stealing over them. Maximilian, who sat stupefied and like one not in his right mind, now, at the gentle request of the women, resigned his seat, for the hand which had clasped his had already relaxed its hold; the farewell gleam of love had departed. One of the women closed her eyelids; and there fell asleep for ever the loveliest flower that our city had reared for generations.

The funeral took place on the fourth day after her death. In the morning of that day, from strong affection – having known her from an infant – I begged permission to see the corpse. She was in her coffin; snowdrops and crocuses were laid upon her innocent bosom, and roses, of that sort which the season allowed, over her person. These and other lovely symbols of youth, of springtime, and of resurrection, caught my eye for the first moment; but in the next it fell upon her face. Mighty God! what a change! what a transfiguration! Still, indeed, there was the same innocent sweetness; still there was something of the same loveliness; the expression still remained; but for the features – all trace of flesh seemed to have vanished; mere outline of bony structure remained; mere pencillings and shadowings of what she once had been. This is, indeed, I exclaimed, 'dust to dust – ashes to ashes!'

Maximilian, to the astonishment of everybody, attended the funeral. It was celebrated in the cathedral. All made way for him, and at times he seemed collected; at times he reeled like one who was drunk. He heard as one who hears not; he saw as one in a dream. The whole ceremony went on by torchlight, and toward the close he stood like a pillar, motionless, torpid, frozen. But the great burst of the choir, and the mighty blare ascending from our vast organ at the closing of the grave, recalled him to himself, and he strode rapidly homeward. Half an hour after I returned, I was summoned to his bedroom. He was in bed, calm and collected. What he said to me I remember as if it had been yesterday, and the very tone with which he said it, although more than twenty years have passed since then. He began thus: 'I have not long to live'; and when he saw me start, suddenly awakened into a consciousness that perhaps he had taken poison, and meant to intimate as much, he continued: 'You fancy I have taken poison; – no matter whether I have or not; if I have, the poison is such that no antidote will now avail; or, if it would, you well know that some griefs are of a kind which leave no opening to any hope. What difference, therefore, can it make whether I leave this earth today, tomorrow or the next day? Be assured of this – that whatever I have determined to do is past all power of being affected by a human opposition. Occupy yourself not with any fruitless attempts, but calmly listen to me, else I know what to do.' Seeing a suppressed fury in his eye, notwithstanding I saw also some change stealing over his features as if from some subtle poison beginning to work upon his frame; awestruck I consented to listen, and sat still. 'It is well that you do so, for my time is short. Here is my will, legally drawn up, and you will see that I have committed an immense property to your discretion. Here, again, is a paper still more important in my eyes; it is also testamentary, and binds you to duties which may not be so easy to execute as the disposal of my property. But now listen to something else, which concerns neither of these papers. Promise me, in the first place, solemnly, that whenever I die you will see me buried in the same grave as my wife, from whose funeral we are just returned. Promise.' I promised. 'Swear.' I swore. 'Finally, promise me that when you read this second paper which I have put into your hands, whatsoever you may think of it, you will say nothing – publish nothing to the world until three years shall have passed.' I promised. 'And now farewell for three hours. Come to me again about ten o'clock, and take a glass of wine in memory of old times.' This he said laughingly; but even then a dark spasm crossed his face. Yet, thinking that this might be the mere working of mental anguish within him, I complied with his desire, and retired. Feeling, however, but little at ease, I devised an excuse for looking in upon him about one hour and a half after I had left him. I knocked gently at his door; there was no answer. I knocked louder; still no answer. I went in. The light of day was gone, and I could see nothing. But I was alarmed by the utter stillness of the room. I listened earnestly, but not a breath could be heard. I rushed back hastily into the hall for a lamp; I returned; I looked in upon this marvel of manly beauty, and the first glance informed me that he and all his splendid endowments had departed for ever. He had died, probably, soon after I left him, and had dismissed me from some growing instinct which informed him that his last agonies were at hand.

I took up his two testamentary documents; both were addressed in the shape of letters to myself. The first was a rapid though distinct appropriation of his enormous property. General rules were laid down, upon which the property was to be distributed, but the details were left to my discretion, and to the guidance of circumstances as they should happen to emerge from the various enquiries which it would become necessary to set on foot. This first document I soon laid aside, both because I found that its provisions were dependent for their meaning upon the second, and because to this second document I looked with confidence for a solution of many mysteries; of the profound sadness which had, from the first of my acquaintance with him, possessed a man so gorgeously endowed as the favourite of nature and fortune; of his motives for huddling up, in a clandestine manner, that connection which formed the glory of his life; and possibly (but then I hesitated) of the late unintelligible murders, which still lay under as profound a cloud as ever. Much of this *would* be unveiled – all might be: and there and then, with the corpse lying beside me of the gifted and mysterious writer, I seated myself and read the following statement:

26 March 1817

My trial is finished; my conscience, my duty, my honour, are liberated; my 'warfare is accomplished'. Margaret, my innocent young wife, I have seen for the last time. Her, the crown that might have been of my earthly felicity – her, the one temptation to put aside the bitter cup which awaited me – her, sole seductress (O innocent seductress!) from the stern duties which my fate had imposed upon me – her, even her, I have sacrificed.

Before I go, partly lest the innocent should be brought into question for acts almost exclusively mine, but still more lest the lesson and the warning, which God, by my hand, has written in blood upon your guilty walls, should perish for want of its authentic exposition, hear my last dying avowal, that the murders which have desolated so many families within your walls, and made the household hearth no sanctuary, age no charter of protection, are all due originally to my head, if not always to my hand, as the minister of a dreadful retribution.

That account of my history, and my prospects, which you received from the Russian diplomatist, among some errors of little importance, is essentially correct. My father was not so immediately connected with English blood as is there represented. However, it is true that he claimed descent from an English family of even higher distinction than that which is assigned in the Russian statement. He was proud of this English descent, and the more so as the war with revolutionary France brought out more prominently than ever the moral and civil grandeur of England. This pride was generous, but it was imprudent in his situation. His immediate progenitors had been settled in Italy – at Rome first, but latterly at Milan; and his whole property, large and scattered, came, by the progress of the revolution, to stand under French domination. Many spoliations he suffered; but still he was too rich to be seriously injured. But he foresaw, in the progress of events, still greater perils menacing his most capital resources. Many of the states or princes in Italy were deeply in his debt; and, in the great convulsions which threatened his country, he saw that both the contending parties would find a colourable excuse for absolving themselves from engagements which pressed unpleasantly upon their finances. In this embarrassment he formed an intimacy with a French officer of high rank and high principle. My father's friend saw his danger, and advised him to enter the French service. In his younger days, my father had served extensively under many princes, and had found in every other military service a spirit of honour governing the conduct of the officers. Here only, and for the first time, he found ruffian manners and universal rapacity. He could not draw his sword in company with such men, nor in such a cause. But at length, under the pressure of necessity, he accepted (or rather bought with an immense bribe) the place of a commissary to the French forces in Italy. With this one resource, eventually he succeeded in making good the whole of his public claims upon the Italian states. These vast sums he remitted, through various channels, to England, where he became proprietor in the funds to an immense amount. Incautiously, however, something of this transpired, and the result was doubly unfortunate; for, while his intentions were thus made known as finally pointing to England, which of itself made him an object of hatred and suspicion, it also diminished his means of bribery. These considerations, along with another, made some French officers of high rank and influence the bitter enemies of my father. My mother, whom he had married when holding a brigadier-general's commission in the Austrian service, was, by birth and by religion, a Jewess. She was of exquisite beauty, and had been sought in morganatic marriage by an archduke of the Austrian family; but she had relied upon this plea, that hers was the purest and noblest blood among all Jewish families – that her family traced themselves, by tradition and a vast series of attestations under the hands of the Jewish high priests, to the Maccabees, and to the royal houses of Judea; and that for her it would be a degradation to accept even of a sovereign prince on the terms of such marriage. This was no vain pretension of ostentatious vanity. It was one which had been admitted as valid for time immemorial in Transylvania and adjacent countries, where my mother's family were rich and honoured, and took their seat among the dignitaries of the land. The French officers I have alluded to, without capacity for anything so dignified as a deep passion, but merely in pursuit of a vagrant fancy that would, on the next day, have given place to another equally fleeting, had dared to insult my mother with proposals the most licentious – proposals as much below her rank and birth, as, at any rate, they would have been below her dignity of mind and her purity. These she had communicated to my father, who bitterly resented the chains of subordination which tied up his hands from avenging his injuries.

Still his eye told a tale which his superiors could brook as little as they could the disdainful neglect of his wife. More than one had been concerned in the injuries to my father and mother; more than one were interested in obtaining revenge. Things could be done in German towns, and by favour of old German laws or usages, which even in France could not have been tolerated. This my father's enemies well knew, but this my father also knew; and he endeavoured to lay down his office of commissary. That, however, was a favour which he could not obtain. He was compelled to serve on the German campaign then commencing, and on the subsequent one of Friedland and Eylau. Here he was caught in some one of the snares laid for him; first trepanned into an act which violated some rule of the service; and then provoked into a breach of discipline against the general officer who had thus trepanned him. Now was the long-sought opportunity gained, and in that very quarter of Germany best fitted for improving it. My father was thrown into prison in your city, subjected to the atrocious oppression of your jailer, and the more detestable oppression of your local laws. The charges against him were thought even to affect his life; and he was humbled into suing for permission to send for his wife and children. Already, to his proud spirit, it was punishment enough that he should be reduced to sue for favour to one of his bitterest foes. But it was no part of their plan to refuse *that*. By way of expediting my mother's arrival, a military courier, with every facility for the journey, was forwarded to her without delay. My mother, her two daughters and myself were then residing in Venice. I had, through the aid of my father's connections in Austria, been appointed in the imperial service, and held a high commission for my age. But, on my father's marching northward with the French army, I had been recalled as an indispensable support to my mother. Not that my years could have made me such, for I had barely accomplished my twelfth year; but my premature growth, and my military station, had given me considerable knowledge of the world and presence of mind.

Our journey I pass over; but as I approach your city, that sepulchre of honour and happiness to my poor family, my heart beats with frantic emotions. Never do I see that venerable dome of your minster from the forest, but I curse its form, which reminds me of what we then surveyed for many a mile as we traversed the forest. For leagues before we approached the city, this object lay before us in relief upon the frosty blue sky; and still it seemed never to increase. Such was the complaint of my little sister Mariamne. Most innocent child! would that it never had increased for thy eyes, but remained for ever at a distance! That same hour began the series of monstrous indignities which terminated the career of my ill-fated family. As we drew up to the city gates, the officer

597

who inspected the passports, finding my mother and sisters described as Jewesses, which in my mother's ears (reared in a region where Jews are not dishonoured) always sounded a title of distinction, summoned a subordinate agent, who in coarse terms demanded his toll. We presumed this to be a road tax for the carriage and horses, but we were quickly undeceived; a small sum was demanded for each of my sisters and my mother, as for so many head of cattle. I, fancying some mistake, spoke to the man temperately, and, to do him justice, he did not seem desirous of insulting us; but he produced a printed board, on which, along with the vilest animals, Jews and Jewesses were rated at so much a head. While we were debating the point, the officers of the gate wore a sneering smile upon their faces – the postilions were laughing together; and this, too, in the presence of three creatures whose exquisite beauty, in different styles, agreeably to their different ages, would have caused noblemen to have fallen down and worshipped. My mother, who had never yet met with any flagrant insult on account of her national distinctions, was too much shocked to be capable of speaking. I whispered to her a few words, recalling her to her native dignity of mind, paid the money, and we drove to the prison. But the hour was past at which we could be admitted, and, as Jewesses, my mother and sisters could not be allowed to stay in the city; they were to go into the Jewish quarter, a part of the suburb set apart for Jews, in which it was scarcely possible to obtain a lodging tolerably clean. My father, on the next day, we found, to our horror, at the point of death. To my mother he did not tell the worst of what he had endured. To me he told that, driven to madness by the insults offered to him, he had upbraided the court martial with their corrupt propensities, and had even mentioned that overtures had been made to him for quashing the proceedings in return for a sum of two millions of francs; and that his sole reason for not entertaining the proposal was his distrust of those who made it. 'They would have taken my money,' said he, 'and then found a pretext for putting me to death, that I might tell no secrets.' This was too near the truth to be tolerated; in concert with the local authorities, the military enemies of my father conspired against him – witnesses were suborned; and, finally, under some antiquated law of the place, he was subjected, in secret, to a mode of torture which still lingers in the east of Europe.

He sank under the torture and the degradation. I, too, thoughtlessly, but by a natural movement of filial indignation, suffered the truth to escape me in conversing with my mother. And she – but I will preserve the regular succession of things. My father died; but he had taken such measures, in concert with me, that his enemies should never benefit by his property. Meantime my mother and sisters had closed my father's eyes;

had attended his remains to the grave; and in every act connected with this last sad rite had met with insults and degradations too mighty for human patience. My mother, now become incapable of self-command, in the fury of her righteous grief, publicly and in court denounced the conduct of the magistracy – taxed some of them with the vilest proposals to herself – taxed them as a body with having used instruments of torture upon my father; and, finally, accused them of collusion with the French military oppressors of the district. This last was a charge under which they quailed; for by that time the French had made themselves odious to all who retained a spark of patriotic feeling. My heart sank within me when I looked up at the bench, this tribunal of tyrants, all purple or livid with rage; when I looked at them alternately and at my noble mother with her weeping daughters – these so powerless, those so basely vindictive and locally so omnipotent. Willingly I would have sacrificed all my wealth for a simple permission to quit this infernal city with my poor female relations safe and undishonored. But far other were the intentions of that incensed magistracy. My mother was arrested, charged with some offence equal to petty treason, or *scandalum magnatum*, or the sowing of sedition; and, though what she said was true, where, alas! was she to look for evidence? Here was seen the want of gentlemen. Gentlemen, had they been even equally tyrannical, would have recoiled with shame from taking vengeance on a woman. And what a vengeance! O heavenly powers! that I should live to mention such a thing! Man that is born of woman, to inflict upon woman personal scourging on the bare back, and through the streets at noonday! Even for Christian women the punishment was severe which the laws assigned to the offence in question. But for Jewesses, by one of the ancient laws against that persecuted people, far heavier and more degrading punishments were annexed to almost every offence. What else could be looked for in a city which welcomed its Jewish guests by valuing them at its gates as brute beasts? Sentence was passed, and the punishment was to be inflicted on two separate days, with an interval between each – doubtless to prolong the tortures of mind, but under a vile pretence of alleviating the physical torture. Three days after would come the first day of punishment. My mother spent the time in reading her native scriptures; she spent it in prayer and in musing; while her daughters clung and wept around her day and night – grovelling on the ground at the feet of any people in authority that entered their mother's cell. That same interval – how was it passed by me? Now mark, my friend. Every man in office, or that could be presumed to bear the slightest influence, every wife, mother, sister, daughter of such men, I besieged morning, noon and night. I wearied them with my supplications. I humbled myself to the dust; I, the haughtiest of God's creatures, knelt and prayed to them for the sake of my mother. I besought them that I might undergo the punishment ten times over in her stead. And once or twice I *did* obtain the encouragement of a few natural tears – given more, however, as I was told, to my piety than to my mother's deserts. But rarely was I heard out with patience; and from some houses repelled with personal indignities. The day came: I saw my mother half undressed by the base officials; I heard the prison gates expand; I heard the trumpets of the magistracy sound. She had warned me what to do; I had warned myself. Would I sacrifice a retribution sacred and comprehensive, for the momentary triumph over an individual? If not, let me forbear to look out of doors; for I felt that in the selfsame moment in which I saw the dog of an executioner raise his accursed hand against my mother, swifter than the lightning would my dagger search his heart. When I heard the roar of the cruel mob, I paused – endured – forbore. I stole out by by-lanes of the city from my poor exhausted sisters, whom I left sleeping in each other's innocent arms, into the forest. There I listened to the shouting populace; there even I fancied that I could trace my poor mother's route by the course of the triumphant cries. There, even then, even then, I made – O silent forest! thou heardst me when I made – a vow that I have kept too faithfully. Mother, thou art avenged: sleep, daughter of Jerusalem! for at length the oppressor sleeps with thee. And thy poor son has paid, in discharge of his vow, the forfeit of his own happiness, of a paradise opening upon earth, of a heart as innocent as thine, and a face as fair.

I returned, and found my mother returned. She slept by starts, but she was feverish and agitated; and when she awoke and first saw me, she blushed, as if I could think that real degradation had settled upon her. Then it was that I told her of my vow. Her eyes were lambent with fierce light for a moment; but, when I went on more eagerly to speak of my hopes and projects, she called me to her – kissed me, and whispered: 'Oh, not so, my son! think not of me – think not of vengeance – think only of poor Berenice and Mariamne.' Aye, that thought *was* startling. Yet this magnanimous and forbearing mother, as I knew by the report of Rachael, our one faithful female servant, had, in the morning, during her bitter trial, behaved as might have become a daughter of Judas Maccabaeus: she had looked serenely upon the vile mob, and awed even them by her serenity; she had disdained to utter a shriek when the cruel lash fell upon her fair skin. There is a point that makes the triumph over natural feelings of pain easy or not easy – the degree in which we count upon the sympathy of the bystanders. My mother had it not in the beginning; but, long before the end, her celestial beauty, the divinity of injured innocence, the pleading of common womanhood in the minds of the lowest class, and the reaction of manly feeling in the men, had worked a great change in the mob. Some began now to threaten those who had been active in insulting her. The silence of awe and respect succeeded to noise and uproar; and feelings which they scarcely understood mastered the rude rabble as they witnessed more and more the patient fortitude of the sufferer. Menaces began to rise towards the executioner. Things wore such an aspect that the magistrates put a sudden end to the scene.

That day we received permission to go home to our poor house in the Jewish quarter. I know not whether you are learned enough in Jewish usages to be aware that in every Jewish house, where old traditions are kept up, there is one room consecrated to confusion: a room always locked up and sequestered from vulgar use, except on occasions of memorable affliction, where everything is purposely in disorder – broken – shattered – mutilated; to typify, by symbols appalling to the eye, that desolation which has so long trampled on Jerusalem, and the ravages of the boar within the vineyards of Judaea. My mother, as a Hebrew princess, maintained all traditional customs. Even in this wretched suburb she had her 'chamber of desolation'. There it was that I and my sisters heard her last words. The rest of her sentence was to be carried into effect within a week. She, meantime, had disdained to utter any word of fear; but that energy of self-control had made the suffering but the more bitter. Fever and dreadful agitation had succeeded. Her dreams showed sufficiently to us, who watched her couch, that terror for the future mingled with the sense of degradation for the past. Nature asserted her rights. But the more she shrank from the suffering, the more did she proclaim how severe it had been, and consequently how noble the self-conquest. Yet, as her weakness increased, so did her terror; until I besought her to take comfort, assuring her that, in case any attempt should be made to force her out again to public exposure, I would kill the man who came to execute the order – that we would all die together – and there would be a common end to her injuries and her fears. She was reassured by what I told her of my belief that no future attempt would be made upon her. She slept more tranquilly – but her fever increased; and slowly she slept away into the everlasting sleep which knows of no tomorrow.

Here came a crisis in my fate. Should I stay and attempt to protect my sisters? But, alas! what power had I to do so among our enemies? Rachael and I consulted; and many a scheme we planned. Even while we consulted, and the very night after my mother had been committed to the Jewish burying ground, came an officer, bearing an order for me to repair to Vienna. Some officer in the French army, having watched the transaction respecting my parents, was filled with shame and grief. He wrote a statement of the whole to an Austrian officer of rank, my father's friend, who obtained from the emperor an order, claiming me as a page of his own, and an officer in the household service. O heavens! what a neglect that it did not include my sisters! However, the next best thing was that I should use my influence at the imperial court to get them passed to Vienna. This I did, to the utmost of my power. But seven months elapsed before I saw the emperor. If my applications ever met his eye he might readily suppose that your city, my friend, was as safe a place as another for my sisters. Nor did I myself know all its dangers. At length, with the emperor's leave of absence, I returned. And what did I find? Eight months had passed, and the faithful Rachael had died. The poor sisters, clinging together, but now utterly bereft of friends, knew not which way to turn. In this abandonment they fell into the insidious hands of the ruffian jailer. My elder sister, Berenice, the stateliest and noblest of beauties, had attracted this ruffian's admiration while she was in the prison with her mother. And when I returned to your city, armed with the imperial passports for all, I found that Berenice had died in the villain's custody; nor could I obtain anything beyond a legal certificate of her death. And, finally, the blooming, laughing Mariamne, she also had died – and of affliction for the loss of her sister. You, my friend, had been absent upon your travels during the calamitous history I have recited. You had seen neither my father nor my mother. But you came in time to take under your protection, from the abhorred wretch the jailer, my little broken-hearted Mariamne. And when sometimes you fancied that you had seen me under other circumstances, in her it was, my dear friend, and in her features that you saw mine.

Now was the world a desert to me. I cared little, in the way of love, which way I turned. But in the way of hatred I cared everything. I transferred myself to the Russian service, with the view of gaining some appointment on the Polish frontier, which might put it in my power to execute my vow of destroying all the magistrates of your city. War, however, raged, and carried me into far other regions. It ceased, and there was little prospect that another generation would see it relighted; for the disturber of peace was a prisoner for ever, and all nations were exhausted. Now, then, it became necessary that I should adopt some new mode for executing my vengeance; and the more so, because annually some were dying of those whom it was my mission to punish. A voice ascended to me, day and night, from the graves of my father and mother, calling for vengeance before it should be too late.

I took my measures thus: Many Jews were present at Waterloo. From among these, all irritated against Napoleon for the expectations he had raised, only to disappoint, by his great assembly of Jews at Paris, I selected eight, whom I knew familiarly as men hardened by military experience against the movements of pity. With these as my beagles,

I hunted for some time in your forest before opening my regular campaign; and I am surprised that you did not hear of the death which met the executioner – him I mean who dared to lift his hand against my mother. This man I met by accident in the forest; and I slew him. I talked with the wretch, as a stranger at first, upon the memorable case of the Jewish lady. Had he relented, had he expressed compunction, I might have relented. But far otherwise: the dog, not dreaming to whom he spoke, exulted; he – but why repeat the villain's words? I cut him to pieces. Next I did this: My agents I caused to matriculate separately at the college. They assumed the college dress. And now mark the solution of that mystery which caused such perplexity. Simply as students we all had an unsuspected admission at any house. Just then there was a common practice, as you will remember, among the younger students, of going out a-masking – that is, of entering houses in the academic dress, and with the face masked. This practice subsisted even during the most intense alarm from the murderers; for the dress of the students was supposed to bring protection along with it. But, even after suspicion had connected itself with this dress, it was sufficient that I should appear unmasked at the head of the maskers, to insure them a friendly reception. Hence the facility with which death was inflicted, and that unaccountable absence of any motion towards an alarm. I took hold of my victim, and he looked at me with smiling security. Our weapons were hid under our academic robes; and even when we drew them out, and at the moment of applying them to the threat, they still supposed our gestures to be part of the pantomime we were performing. Did I relish this abuse of personal confidence in myself? No – I loathed it, and I grieved for its necessity; but my mother, a phantom not seen with bodily eyes, but ever present to my mind, continually ascended before me; and still I shouted aloud to my astounded victim, 'This comes from the Jewess! Hound of hounds! Do you remember the Jewess whom you dishonoured, and the oaths which you broke in order that you might dishonour her, and the righteous law which you violated, and the cry of anguish from her son which you scoffed at?' Who I was, what I avenged, and whom, I made every man aware of, and every woman, before I punished them. The details of the cases I need not repeat. One or two I was obliged, at the beginning, to commit to my Jews. The suspicion was thus, from the first, turned aside by the notoriety of my presence elsewhere; but I took care that none suffered who had not either been upon the guilty list of magistrates who condemned the mother or of those who turned away with mockery from the supplication of the son.

It pleased God, however, to place a mighty temptation in my path, which might have persuaded me to forgo all thoughts of vengeance, to forget my vow, to forget the voices which invoked me from the grave. This was Margaret Liebenheim. Ah! how terrific appeared my duty of bloody retribution, after her angel's face and angel's voice had calmed me. With respect to her grandfather, strange it is to mention that never did my innocent wife appear so lovely as precisely in the relation of grand-daughter. So beautiful was her goodness to the old man, and so divine was the childlike innocence on her part, contrasted with the guilty recollections associated with him – for he was among the guiltiest towards my mother – still I delayed *his* punishment to the last; and, for his child's sake, I would have pardoned him – nay, I had resolved to do so, when a fierce Jew, who had a deep malignity toward this man, swore that he would accomplish *his* vengeance at all events, and perhaps might be obliged to include Margaret in the ruin, unless I adhered to the original scheme. Then I yielded; for circumstances armed this man with momentary power. But the night fixed on was one in which I had reason to know that my wife would be absent; for so I had myself arranged with her, and the unhappy counter-arrangement I do not yet understand. Let me add, that the sole purpose of my clandestine marriage was to sting her grandfather's mind with the belief that *his* family had been dishonoured, even as he had dishonoured mine. He learned, as I took care that he should, that his granddaughter carried about with her the promise of a mother, and did not know that she had the sanction of a wife. This discovery made him, in one day, become eager for the marriage he had previously opposed; and this discovery also embittered the misery of his death. At that moment I attempted to think only of my mother's wrongs; but, in spite of all I could do, this old man appeared to me in the light of Margaret's grandfather – and, had I been left to myself, he would have been saved. As it was, never was horror equal to mine when I met her flying to his succour. I had relied upon her absence; and the misery of that moment, when her eye fell upon me in the very act of seizing her grandfather, far transcended all else that I have suffered in these terrific scenes. She fainted in my arms, and I and another carried her upstairs and procured water. Meantime her grand-father had been murdered, even while Margaret fainted. I had, however, under the fear of discovery, though never anticipating a re-encounter with herself, forestalled the explanation requisite in such a case to make my conduct intelligible. I had told her, under feigned names, the story of my mother and my sisters. She knew their wrongs: she had heard me contend for the right of vengeance. Consequently, in our parting interview, one word only was required to place myself in a new position to her thoughts. I needed only to say I was that son; that unhappy mother, so miserably degraded and outraged, was mine.

As to the jailer, he was met by a party of us. Not suspecting that any of us could be connected with the family, he was led to talk of the most hideous details with regard to my poor Berenice. The child had not, as had been insinuated, aided her own degradation, but had nobly sustained the dignity of her sex and her family. Such advantages as the monster pretended to have gained over her – sick, desolate and latterly delirious – were, by his own confession, not obtained without violence. This was too much. Forty thousand lives, had he possessed them, could not have gratified my thirst for revenge. Yet, had he but showed courage, he should have died the death of a soldier. But the wretch showed cowardice the most abject, and – but you know his fate.

Now, then, all is finished, and human nature is avenged. Yet, if you complain of the bloodshed and the terror, think of the wrongs which created my rights; think of the sacrifice by which I gave a tenfold strength to those rights; think of the necessity for a dreadful concussion and shock to society, in order to carry my lesson into the councils of princes.

This will now have been effected. And ye, victims of dishonour, will be glorified in your deaths; ye will not have suffered in vain, nor died without a monument. Sleep, therefore, sister Berenice – sleep, gentle Mariamne, in peace. And thou, noble mother, let the outrages sown in thy dishonour, rise again and blossom in wide harvests of honour for the women of thy afflicted race. Sleep, daughters of Jerusalem, in the sanctity of your sufferings. And thou, if it be possible, even more beloved daughter of a Christian fold, whose company was too soon denied to him in life, open thy grave to receive him, who, in the hour of death, wishes to remember no title which he wore on earth but that of thy chosen and adoring lover,

MAXIMILIAN

ARTHUR CONAN DOYLE

Sir Arthur Conan Doyle (1859–1930), novelist, was born in Edinburgh of an Irish Roman Catholic family. His father was a clerk in the Board of Works, and his uncle, Richard Doyle, was the artist who drew the well-known cover design of *Punch*. Doyle was educated at Stonyhurst and Edinburgh University, where he qualified as a doctor, practising at Southsea from 1882 to 1890. In 1882 he published *A Study in Scarlet*, an adventure story which introduced the famous character Sherlock Holmes. A later Holmes novel was *The Sign of Four* (1890), but he first became really famous with the publication in the *Strand Magazine* of the *Adventures of Sherlock Holmes* (1892), short stories of which the first was 'A Scandal in Bohemia'.

Among novels which Doyle wrote on other themes the best are *Micah Clarke* (1889), *The Refugees* (1893) and *Rodney Stone* (1896), a boxing story. *The White Company* (1890) and *Sir Nigel* (1906) are historical romances with a strong appeal for the young, while *The Exploits of Brigadier Gerard* (1895) recounts with humorous irony the adventures of a young Napoleonic officer. Doyle served as a doctor in the South African War and wrote a history of the conflict, *The Great Boer War* (1900). In 1902 he was knighted. Later he created an amusing new character in the belligerent Professor Challenger, who is the hero of the scientific romances *The Lost World* (1912) and *The Poison Belt* (1913). *Songs of Action* is a book of poems, and *Memories and Adventures* (1924) contains his reminiscences. In his latter years Doyle was deeply interested in psychic phenomena, and wrote a *History of Spiritualism* (1926).

A Foreign Office Romance

There are many folk who knew Alphonse Lacour in his old age. From about the time of the Revolution of 1848 until he died in the second year of the Crimean War he was always to be found in the same corner of the Café de Provence, at the end of the Rue St Honoré, coming down about nine in the evening, and going when he could find no one to talk with. It took some self-restraint to listen to the old diplomatist, for his stories were beyond all belief, and yet he was quick at detecting the shadow of a smile or the slightest little raising of the eyebrows. Then his huge, rounded back would straighten itself, his bulldog chin would project, and his r's would burr like a kettle-drum. When he got as far as, 'Ah, monsieur r–r–r–rit!' or 'Vous ne me cr–r–r–royez pas donc!' it was quite time to remember that you had a ticket for the opera.

There was his story of Talleyrand and the five oyster-shells, and there was his utterly absurd account of Napoleon's second visit to Ajaccio. Then there was that most circumstantial romance (which he never ventured upon until his second bottle had been uncorked) of the Emperor's escape from St Helena – how he lived for a whole year in Philadelphia, while Count Herbert de Bertrand, who was his living image, personated him at Longwood. But of all his stories there was none which was more notorious than that of the Koran and the Foreign Office messenger. And yet when Monsieur Otto's memoirs were written it was found that there really was some foundation for old Lacour's incredible statement.

'You must know, monsieur,' he would say, 'that I left Egypt after Kleber's assassination. I would gladly have stayed on, for I was engaged in a trans-lation of the Koran, and between ourselves I had thoughts at the time of embracing Muhammadanism, for I was deeply struck by the wisdom of their views about marriage. They had made an incredible mistake, however, upon the subject of wine, and this was what the *mufti* who attempted to convert me could never get over. Then when old Kleber died and Menou came to the top, I felt that it was time for me to go. It is not for me to speak of my own capacities, monsieur, but you will readily understand that the man does not care to be ridden by the mule. I carried my Koran and my papers to London, where Monsieur Otto had been sent by the First Consul to arrange a treaty of peace; for both nations were very weary of the war, which had already lasted ten years. Here I was most useful to Monsieur Otto on account of my knowledge of the English tongue, and also, if I may say so, on account of my natural capacity. They were happy days during which I lived in the Square of Bloomsbury. The climate of monsieur's country is, it must be confessed, detestable. But then what would you have? Flowers grow best in the rain. One has but to point to monsieur's fellow country-women to prove it.

'Well, Monsieur Otto, our Ambassador, was kept terribly busy over that treaty, and all of his staff were worked to death. We had not Pitt to deal with, which was, perhaps, as well for us. He was a terrible man that Pitt, and wherever half a dozen enemies of France were plotting together, there was his sharp-pointed nose right in the middle of them. The nation, however, had been thoughtful enough to put him out of office, and we had to do with Monsieur Addington. But Milord Hawkesbury was the Foreign Minister, and it was with him that we were obliged to do our bargaining.

'You can understand that it was no child's play. After ten years of war each nation had got hold of a great deal which had belonged to the other, or to the other's allies. What was to be given back, and what was to be kept? Is this island worth that peninsula? If we do this at Venice, will you do that at Sierra Leone? If we give up Egypt to the Sultan, will you restore the Cape of Good Hope, which you have taken from our allies the Dutch? So we wrangled and wrestled, and I have seen Monsieur Otto come back to the Embassy so exhausted that his secretary and I had to help him from his carriage to his sofa. But at last things adjusted themselves, and the night came round when the treaty was to be finally signed. Now, you must know that the one great card which we held, and which we played, played, played at every point of the game, was that we had Egypt. The English were very nervous about our being there. It gave us a foot at each end of the Mediterranean, you see. And they were not sure that that wonderful little Napoleon of ours might not make it the base of an advance against India. So whenever Lord Hawkesbury proposed to retain anything, we had only to reply, "In *that* case, of course, we cannot consent to evacuate Egypt," and in this way we quickly brought him to reason. It was by the help of Egypt that we gained terms which were remarkably favourable, and especially that we caused the English to consent to give up the Cape of Good Hope. We did not wish your people, monsieur, to have any foothold in South Africa, for history has taught us that the British foothold of one half-century is the British Empire of the next. It is not your army or your navy against which we have to guard, but it is your terrible younger son and your man in search of a career. When we French have a possession across the seas, we like to sit in Paris and to felicitate ourselves upon it. With you it is different. You take your wives and your children, and you run away to see what kind of place this may be, and after that we might as well try to take that old Square of Bloomsbury away from you.

'Well, it was upon the first of October that the treaty was finally to be signed. In the morning I was congratulating Monsieur Otto upon the happy conclusion of his labours. He was a little pale shrimp of a man, very quick and nervous, and he was so delighted now at his own success that he could not sit still, but ran about the room chattering and laughing, while I sat on a cushion in the corner, as I had learned to do in the East. Suddenly, in came a messenger with a letter which had been forwarded from Paris. Monsieur Otto cast his eye upon it, and then, without a word, his knees gave way, and he fell senseless upon the floor. I ran to him, as did the courier, and between us we carried him to the sofa. He might have been dead from his appearance, but I could still feel his heart thrilling beneath my palm. "What is this, then?" I asked.

' "I do not know," answered the messenger. "Monsieur Talleyrand told me to hurry as never man hurried before, and to put this letter into the hands of Monsieur Otto. I was in Paris at midday yesterday."

'I know that I am to blame, but I could not help glancing at the letter, picking it out of the senseless hand of Monsieur Otto. My God! the thunderbolt that it was! I did not faint, but I sat down beside my chief and I burst into tears. It was but a few words, but they told us that Egypt had been evacuated by our troops a month before. All our treaty was undone then, and the one consideration which had induced our enemies to give us good terms had vanished. In twelve hours it would not have mattered. But now the treaty was not yet signed. We should have to give up the Cape. We should have to let England have Malta. Now that Egypt was gone we had nothing left to offer in exchange.

'But we are not so easily beaten, we Frenchmen. You English misjudge us when you think that because we show emotions which you conceal, that we are therefore of a weak and womanly nature. You cannot read your histories and believe that. Monsieur Otto recovered his senses presently, and we took counsel what we should do.

' "It is useless to go on, Alphonse," said he. "This Englishman will laugh at me when I ask him to sign."

' "Courage!" I cried; and then a sudden thought coming into my head – "How do we know that the English will have news of this? Perhaps they may sign the treaty before they know of it."

'Monsieur Otto sprang from the sofa and flung himself into my arms.

' "Alphonse," he cried, "you have saved me! Why should they know about it? Our news has come from Toulon to Paris, and thence straight to London. Theirs will come by sea through the Straits of Gibraltar. At this moment it is unlikely that anyone in Paris knows of it, save only Talleyrand and the First Consul. If we keep our secret, we may still get our treaty signed."

'Ah! monsieur, you can imagine the horrible uncertainty in which we spent the day. Never, never shall I forget those slow hours during which we sat together, starting at every distant shout lest it should be the first sign of the rejoicing which this news would cause in London. Monsieur Otto passed from youth to age in a day. As for me, I find it easier to go out and meet danger than to wait for it. I set forth, therefore, towards evening. I wandered here, and wandered there. I was in the fencing-rooms of Monsieur Angelo, and in the *salon-de-boxe* of Monsieur Jackson, and in the club of Brooks, and in the lobby of the Chamber of Deputies, but nowhere did I hear any news. Still, it was possible that Milord Hawkesbury had received it himself just as we had. He lived in Harley Street, and there it was that the treaty was to be finally signed that night at eight. I entreated Monsieur Otto to drink two glasses of Burgundy before he went, for I feared lest his haggard face and trembling hands should rouse suspicion in the English minister.

'Well, we went round together in one of the Embassy's carriages about half-past seven. Monsieur Otto went in alone; but presently, on excuse of getting his portfolio, he came out again, with his cheeks flushed with joy, to tell me that all was well.

' "He knows nothing," he whispered. "Ah, if the next half-hour were over!"

' "Give me a sign when it is settled," said I.

' "For what reason?"

' "Because until then no messenger shall interrupt you. I give you my promise – I, Alphonse Lacour."

'He clasped my hand in both of his.

' "I shall make an excuse to move one of the candles on to the table in the window," said he, and hurried into the house, whilst I was left waiting beside the carriage.

'Well, if we could but secure ourselves from interruption for a single half-hour the day would be our own. I had hardly begun to form my plans when I saw the lights of a carriage coming swiftly from the direction of Oxford Street. Ah! if it should be the messenger! What could I do? I was prepared to kill him – yes, even to kill him – rather than at this last moment allow our work to be undone. Thousands die to make a glorious war. Why should not one die to make a glorious peace? What though they hurried me to the scaffold? I should have sacrificed myself for my country. I had a little curved Turkish knife strapped to my waist. My hand was on the hilt of it when the carriage which had alarmed me so rattled safely past me.

'But another might come. I must be prepared. Above all, I must not compromise the Embassy. I ordered our carriage to move on, and I engaged what you call a hackney coach. Then I spoke to the driver, and gave him a guinea. He understood that it was a special service.

' "You shall have another guinea if you do what you are told," said I.

' "All right, master," said he, turning his slow eyes upon me without a trace of excitement or curiosity.

' "If I enter your coach with another gentleman, you will drive up and down Harley Street, and take no orders from anyone but me. When I get out, you will carry the other gentleman to Watier's Club, in Bruton Street."

' "All right, master," said he again.

'So I stood outside Milord Hawkesbury's house, and you can think how often my eyes went up to that window in the hope of seeing the candle twinkle in it. Five minutes passed, and another five. Oh, how slowly they crept along! It was a true October night, raw and cold, with a white fog crawling over the wet, shining cobblestones, and blurring the dim oil-lamps. I could not see fifty paces in either direction, but my ears were straining, straining, to catch the rattle of hoofs or the rumble of wheels. It is not a cheering place, monsieur, that Street of Harley, even upon a sunny day. The houses are solid and very respectable over yonder, but there is nothing of the feminine about them. It is a city to be inhabited by males. But on that raw night, amid the damp and the fog, with the anxiety gnawing at my heart, it seemed the saddest, weariest spot in the whole wide world. I paced up and down slapping my hands to keep them warm, and still straining my ears. And then suddenly out of the dull hum of the traffic down in Oxford Street I heard a sound detach itself, and grow louder and louder, and clearer and clearer, with every instant, until two yellow lights came flashing through the fog, and a light cabriolet whirled up to the door of the Foreign Minister. It had not stopped before a young fellow sprang out of it and hurried to the steps, while the driver turned his horse and rattled off into the fog once more.

'Ah, it is in the moment of action that I am best, monsieur. You, who only see me when I am drinking my wine in the Café de Provence, cannot conceive the heights to which I rise. At that moment, when I knew that the fruits of a ten years' war were at stake, I was magnificent. It was the last French campaign and I the general and army in one.

' "Sir," said I, touching him upon the arm, "are you the messenger for Lord Hawkesbury?"

' "Yes," said he.

' "I have been waiting for you half an hour," said I. "You are to follow me at once. He is with the French Ambassador."

'I spoke with such assurance that he never hesitated for an instant. When he entered the hackney coach and I followed him in, my heart gave such a thrill of joy that I could hardly keep from shouting aloud. He was a poor little creature, this Foreign Office messenger, not much bigger than Monsieur Otto, and I – monsieur can see my hands now, and imagine what they were like when I was seven-and-twenty years of age.

'Well, now that I had him in my coach, the question was what I should do with him. I did not wish to hurt him if I could help it.

' "This is a pressing business," said he. "I have a dispatch which I must deliver instantly."

'Our coach had rattled down Harley Street and now, in accordance with my instruction, it turned and began to go up again.

' "Hullo!" he cried. "What's this?"

' "What then?" I asked.

' "We are driving back. Where is Lord Hawkesbury?"

' "We shall see him presently."

' "Let me out!" he shouted. "There's some trickery in this. Coachman, stop the coach! Let me out, I say!"

'I dashed him back into his seat as he tried to turn the handle of the door. He roared for help. I clapped my palm across his mouth. He made his teeth meet through the side of it. I seized his own cravat and bound it over his lips. He still mumbled and gurgled, but the noise was covered by the rattle of our wheels. We were passing the minister's house, and there was no candle in the window.

'The messenger sat quiet for a little, and I could see the glint of his eyes as he stared at me through the gloom. He was partly stunned, I think, by the force with which I had hurled him into his seat. And also he was pondering, perhaps, what he should do next. Presently he got his mouth partly free from the cravat.

' "You shall have my watch and my purse if you will let me go," said he.

' "Sir," said I, "I am as honourable a man as you are yourself."

' "Who are you, then?"

' "My name is of no importance."

' "What do you want with me?"

' "It is a bet."

' "A bet? What d'you mean? Do you understand that I am on government service, and that you will see the inside of a gaol for this?"

' "That is the bet. That is the sport, said I."

' "You may find it poor sport before you finish," he cried. "What is this insane bet of yours then?"

' "I have bet," I answered, "that I will recite a chapter of the Koran to the first gentleman whom I should meet in the street."

'I do not know what made me think of it, save that my translation was always running in my head. He clutched at the door-handle, and again I had to hurl him back into his seat.

' "How long will it take?" he gasped.

' "It depends on the chapter," I answered.

' "A short one, then, and let me go!"

' "But is it fair?" I argued. "When I say a chapter, I do not mean the shortest chapter, but rather one which should be of average length."

' "Help! help! help!" he squealed, and I was compelled again to adjust his cravat.

' "A little patience," said I, "and it will soon be over. I should like to recite the chapter which would be of most interest to yourself. You will confess that I am trying to make things as pleasant as I can for you?"

He slipped his mouth free again.

' "Quick, then, quick!" he groaned.

' "The Chapter of the Camel?" I suggested.

' "Yes, yes."

' "Or that of the Fleet Stallion?"

' "Yes, yes. Only proceed!"

'We had passed the window and there was no candle. I settled down to recite the Chapter of the Stallion to him. Perhaps you do not know your Koran very well, monsieur? Well, I knew it by heart then, as I know it by heart now. The style is a little exasperating for anyone who is in a hurry. But, then, what would you have? The people in the East are never in a hurry, and it was written for them. I repeated it all with the dignity and solemnity which a sacred book demands, and the young Englishman he wriggled and groaned.

' " 'When the horses, standing on three feet and placing the tip of their fourth foot upon the ground, were mustered in front of him in the evening, he said, I have loved the love of earthly good above the remembrance of things on high, and have spent the time in viewing these horses. Bring the horses back to me. And when they were brought back he began to cut off their legs and – ' "

'It was at this moment that the young Englishman sprang at me. My God! how little can I remember of the next few minutes! He was a boxer, this shred of a man. He had been trained to strike. I tried to catch him by the hands. Pac, pac, he came upon my nose and upon my eye. I put down my head and thrust at him with it. Pac, he came from below. But ah! I was too much for him. I hurled myself upon him, and he had no place where he could escape from my weight. He fell flat upon the cushions and I seated myself upon him with such conviction that the wind flew from him as from a burst bellows.

'Then I searched to see what there was with which I could tie him. I drew the strings from my shoes, and with one I secured his wrists, and with another his ankles. Then I tied the cravat round his mouth again, so that he could only lie and glare at me. When I had done all this, and had stopped the bleeding of my own nose, I looked out of the coach and ah, monsieur, the very first thing which caught my eyes was that candle – that dear little candle – glimmering in the window of the minister. Alone, with these two hands, I had retrieved the capitulation of an army and the loss of a province. Yes, monsieur, what Abercrombie and five thousand men had done upon the beach at Aboukir was undone by me, single-handed, in a hackney coach in Harley Street.

'Well, I had no time to lose, for at any moment Monsieur Otto might be down. I shouted to my driver, gave him his second guinea, and allowed him to proceed to Watier's. For myself, I sprang into our Embassy's carriage, and a moment later the door of the minister opened. He had himself escorted Monsieur Otto downstairs, and now so deep was he in talk that he walked out bareheaded as far as the carriage. As he stood there by the open door, there came the rattle of wheels, and a man rushed down the pavement.

' "A despatch of great importance for Milord Hawkesbury!" he cried.

'I could see that it was not my messenger, but a second one. Milord Hawkesbury caught the paper from his hand, and read it by the light of the carriage lamp. His face, monsieur, was as white as this plate, before he had finished.

' "Monsieur Otto," he cried, "we have signed this treaty upon a false understanding. Egypt is in our hands."

' "What!" cried Monsieur Otto. "Impossible!"

' "It is certain. It fell to Abercrombie last month."

' "In that case," said Monsieur Otto, "it is very fortunate that the treaty is signed."

' "Very fortunate for you, sir," cried Milord Hawkesbury, as he turned back to the house.

'Next day, monsieur, what they call the Bow Street Runners were after me, but they could not run across salt water, and Alphonse Lacour was receiving the congratulations of Monsieur Talleyrand and the First Consul before ever his pursuers had got as far as Dover.'

The Striped Chest

'What do you make of her, Allardyce?' I asked.

My second mate was standing beside me upon the poop, with his short, thick legs astretch, for the gale had left a considerable swell behind it, and our two quarter-boats nearly touched the water with every roll. He steadied his glass against the mizzen-shrouds, and he looked long and hard at this disconsolate stranger every time she came reeling up on to the crest of a roller and hung balanced for a few seconds before swooping down upon the other side. She lay so low in the water that I could only catch an occasional glimpse of a pea-green line of bulwark. She was a brig, but her mainmast had been snapped short off some ten feet above the deck, and no effort seemed to have been made to cut away the wreckage, which floated, sails and yards, like the broken wing of a wounded gull upon the water beside her. The foremast was still standing, but the foretopsail was flying loose, and the headsails were streaming out in long, white pennons in front of her. Never have I seen a vessel which appeared to have gone through rougher handling. But we could not be surprised at that, for there had been times during the last three days when it was a question whether our own barque would ever see land again. For thirty-six hours we had kept her nose to it, and if the *Mary Sinclair* had not been as good a seaboat as ever left the Clyde, we could not have come through. And yet here we were at the end of it with the loss only of our gig and of part of the starboard bulwark. It did not astonish us, therefore, when the smother had cleared away, to find that others had been less lucky, and that this mutilated brig staggering about upon a blue sea and under a cloudless sky, had been left, like a blinded man after a lightning flash, to tell of the terror which is past. Allardyce, who was a slow and methodical Scotchman, stared long and hard at the little craft, while our seamen lined the bulwark or clustered upon the fore shrouds to have a view of the stranger. In latitude 20 degrees and longitude 10 degrees, which were about our bearings, one becomes a little curious as to whom one meets, for one has left the main lines of Atlantic commerce to the north. For ten days we had been sailing over a solitary sea.

'She's derelict, I'm thinking,' said the second mate.

I had come to the same conclusion, for I could see no signs of life upon her deck, and there was no answer to the friendly wavings from our seamen. The crew had probably deserted her under the impression that she was about to founder.

'She can't last long,' continued Allardyce, in his measured way. 'She may put her nose down and her tail up any minute. The water's lipping up to the edge of her rail.'

'What's her flag?' I asked.

'I'm trying to make out. It's got all twisted and tangled with the halyards. Yes, I've got it now, clear enough. It's the Brazilian flag, but it's wrong side up.'

She had hoisted a signal of distress, then, before her people had abandoned her. Perhaps they had only just gone. I took the mate's glass and looked round over the tumultuous face of the deep blue Atlantic, still veined and starred with white lines and spoutings of foam. But nowhere could I see anything human beyond ourselves.

'There may be living men aboard,' said I.

'There may be salvage,' muttered the second mate.

'Then we will run down upon her lee side, and lie to.'

We were not more than a hundred yards from her when we swung our foreyard aback, and there we were, the barque and the brig, ducking and bowing like two clowns in a dance.

'Drop one of the quarter-boats,' said I. 'Take four men, Mr Allardyce, and see what you can learn of her.'

But just at that moment my first officer, Mr Armstrong, came on deck, for seven bells had struck, and it was but a few minutes off his watch. It would interest me to go myself to this abandoned vessel and to see what there might be aboard of her. So, with a word to Armstrong, I swung myself over the side, slipped down the falls, and took my place in the sheets of the boat.

It was but a little distance, but it took some time to traverse, and so heavy was the roll that often when we were in the trough of the sea, we could not see either the barque which we had left or the brig which we were approaching. The sinking sun did not penetrate down there, and it was cold and dark in the hollows of the waves, but each passing billow heaved us up into the warmth and the sunshine once more. At each of these moments, as we hung upon a white-capped ridge between the two dark valleys, I caught a glimpse of the long, pea-green line and the nodding foremast of the brig, and I steered so as to come round by her stern, so that we might determine which was the best way of boarding her. As we passed her we saw the name *Nossa Sehnora da Vittoria* painted across her dripping counter.

'The weather side, sir,' said the second mate. 'Stand by with the boat-hook, carpenter!' An instant later we had jumped over the bulwarks, which were hardly higher than our boat, and found ourselves upon the deck of the abandoned vessel. Our first thought was to provide for our own safety in case – as seemed very probable – the vessel should settle down beneath our feet. With this object two of our men held on to the painter of the boat, and fended her off from the vessel's side, so that she might be ready in case we had to make a hurried retreat. The carpenter was sent to find out how much water there was, and whether it was still gaining, while the other seaman, Allardyce and myself, made a rapid inspection of the vessel and her cargo.

The deck was littered with wreckage and with hen-coops, in which the dead birds were washing about. The boats were gone, with the exception of one, the bottom of which had been stove, and it was certain that the crew had abandoned the vessel. The cabin was in a deck-house, one side of which had been beaten in by a heavy sea. Allardyce and I entered it, and found the captain's table as he had left it, his books and papers – all Spanish or Portuguese – scattered over it, with piles of cigarette ash everywhere. I looked about for the log, but could not find it.

'As likely as not he never kept one,' said Allardyce. 'Things are pretty slack aboard a South American trader, and they don't do more than they can help. If there was one it must have been taken away with him in the boat.'

'I should like to take all these books and papers,' said I. 'Ask the carpenter how much time we have.'

His report was reassuring. The vessel was full of water, but some of the cargo was buoyant, and there was no immediate danger of her sinking. Probably she would never sink, but would drift about as one of those terrible unmarked reefs which have sent so many stout vessels to the bottom.

'In that case there is no danger in your going below, Mr Allardyce,' said I. 'See what you can make of her and find out how much of her cargo may be saved. I'll look through these papers while you are gone.'

The bills of lading, and some notes and letters which lay upon the desk, sufficed to inform me that the Brazilian brig *Nossa Sehnora da Vittoria* had cleared from Bahia a month before. The name of the captain was Texeira, but there was no record as to the number of the crew. She was bound for London, and a glance at the bills of lading was sufficient to show me that we were not likely to profit much in the way of salvage. Her cargo consisted of nuts, ginger and wood, the latter in the shape of great logs of valuable tropical growths. It was these, no doubt, which had prevented the ill-fated vessel from going to the bottom, but they were of such a size as to make it impossible for us to extract them. Besides these, there were a few fancy goods, such as a number of ornamental birds for millinery purposes, and a hundred cases of preserved fruits. And then, as I turned over the papers, I came upon a short note in English, which arrested my attention.

It is requested (said the note) that the various old Spanish and Indian curiosities, which came out of the Santarem Collection, and which are consigned to Prontfoot & Neuman of Oxford Street, London, should be put in some place where there may be no danger of these very valuable and unique articles being injured or tampered with. This applies most particularly to the treasure-chest of Don Ramirez di Leyra, which must on no account be placed where anyone can get at it.

The treasure-chest of Don Ramirez! Unique and valuable articles! Here was a chance of salvage after all. I had risen to my feet with the paper in my hand when my Scotch mate appeared in the doorway.

'I'm thinking all isn't quite as it should be aboard of this ship, sir,' said he. He was a hard-faced man, and yet I could see that he had been startled.

'What's the matter?'

'Murder's the matter, sir. There's a man here with his brains beaten out.'

'Killed in the storm?' said I.

'Maybe so, sir, but I'll be surprised if you think so after you have seen him.'

'Where is he, then?'

'This way, sir; here in the maindeck house.'

There appeared to have been no accommodation below in the brig, for there was the after-house for the captain, another by the main hatchway, with the cook's galley attached to it, and a third in the forecastle for the men. It was to this middle one that the mate led me. As you entered, the galley, with its litter of tumbled pots and dishes, was upon the right, and upon the left was a small room with two bunks for the officers. Then beyond there was a place about twelve feet square, which was littered with flags and spare canvas. All round the walls were a number of packets done up in coarse cloth and carefully lashed to the woodwork. At the other end was a great box, striped red and white, though the red was so faded and the white so dirty that it was only where the light fell directly upon it that one could see the colouring. The box was, by subsequent measurement, 4ft 3ins in length, 3ft 2ins in height and 3ft across – considerably larger than a seaman's chest. But it was not to the box that my eyes or my thoughts were turned as I entered the store-room. On the floor, lying across the litter of bunting, there was stretched a small, dark man with a short, curling beard. He lay as far as it was possible from the box, with his feet towards it and his head away. A crimson patch was printed upon the white canvas on which his head was resting, and little red ribbons wreathed themselves round his swarthy neck and trailed away on to the floor, but there was no sign of a wound that I could see, and his face was as placid as that of a sleeping child. It was only when I stooped that I could perceive his injury, and then I turned away with an exclamation of horror. He had been pole-axed; apparently by some person standing behind him. A frightful blow had smashed in the top of his head and penetrated deeply into his brains. His face might well be placid, for death must have been absolutely instantaneous, and the position of the wound showed that he could never have seen the person who had inflicted it.

'Is that foul play or accident, Captain Barclay?' asked my second mate, demurely.

'You are quite right, Mr Allardyce. The man has been murdered – struck down from above by a sharp and heavy weapon. But who was he, and why did they murder him?'

'He was a common seaman, sir,' said the mate. 'You can see that if you look at his fingers.' He turned out his pockets as he spoke and brought to light a pack of cards, some tarred string and a bundle of Brazilian tobacco.

'Hello, look at this!' said he.

It was a large, open knife with a stiff spring blade which he had picked up from the floor. The steel was shining and bright, so that we could not associate it with the crime, and yet the dead man had apparently held it in his hand when he was struck down, for it still lay within his grasp.

'It looks to me, sir, as if he knew he was in danger and kept his knife handy,' said the mate. 'However, we can't help the poor beggar now. I can't make out these things that are lashed to the wall. They seem to be idols and weapons and curios of all sorts done up in old sacking.'

'That's right,' said I. 'They are the only things of value that we are likely to get from the cargo. Hail the barque and tell them to send the other quarter-boat to help us to get the stuff aboard.'

While he was away I examined this curious plunder which had come into our possession. The curiosities were so wrapped up that I could only form a general idea as to their nature, but the striped box stood in a good light where I could thoroughly examine it. On the lid, which was clamped and cornered with metalwork, there was engraved a complex coat of arms, and beneath it was a line of Spanish which I was able to decipher as meaning, 'The treasure-chest of Don Ramirez di Leyra, Knight of the Order of Saint James, Governor and Captain-General of Terra Firma and of the Province of Veraquas.' In one corner was the date, 1606, and on the other a large white label, upon which was written in English, 'You are earnestly requested, upon no account, to open this box.' The same warning was repeated underneath in Spanish. As to the lock, it was a very complex and heavy one of engraved steel, with a Latin motto, which was above a seaman's comprehension. By the time I had finished this examination of the peculiar box, the other quarter-boat with Mr Armstrong, the first officer, had come alongside, and we began to carry out and place in her the various curiosities which appeared to be the only objects worth moving from the derelict ship. When she was full I sent her back to the barque, and then Allardyce and I, with the carpenter and one seaman, shifted the striped box, which was the only thing left, to our boat, and lowered it over, balancing it upon the two middle thwarts, for it was so heavy that it would have given the boat a dangerous tilt had we placed it at either end. As to the dead man, we left him where we had found him. The mate had a theory that, at the moment of the desertion of the ship, this fellow had started plundering, and that the captain, in an attempt to preserve discipline, had struck him down with a hatchet or some other heavy weapon. It seemed more probable than any other explanation, and yet it did not entirely satisfy me either. But the ocean is full of mysteries, and we were content to leave the fate of the dead seaman of the Brazilian brig to be added to that long list which every sailor can recall.

The heavy box was slung up by ropes on to the deck of the *Mary Sinclair*, and was carried by four seamen into the cabin, where, between the table and the after-lockers, there was just space for it to stand. There it remained during supper, and after that meal the mates remained with me, and discussed over a glass of grog the event of the day. Mr Armstrong was a long, thin, vulture-like man, an excellent seaman, but famous for his nearness and cupidity. Our treasure-trove had excited him greatly, and already he had begun with glistening eyes to reckon up how much it might be worth to each of us when the shares of the salvage came to be divided.

'If the paper said that they were unique, Mr Barclay, then they may be worth anything that you like to name. You wouldn't believe the sums that the rich collectors give. A thousand pounds is nothing to them. We'll have something to show for our voyage, or I am mistaken.'

'I don't think that,' said I. 'As far as I can see, they are not very different from any other South American curios.'

'Well, sir, I've traded there for fourteen voyages, and I have never seen anything like that chest before. That's worth a pile of money, just as it stands. But it's so heavy that surely there must be something valuable inside it. Don't you think that we ought to open it and see?'

'If you break it open you will spoil it, as likely as not,' said the second mate.

Armstrong squatted down in front of it, with his head on one side, and his long, thin nose within a few inches of the lock.

'The wood is oak,' said he, 'and it has shrunk a little with age. If I had a chisel or a strong-bladed knife I could force the lock back without doing any damage at all.'

The mention of a strong-bladed knife made me think of the dead seaman upon the brig.

'I wonder if he could have been on the job when someone came to interfere with him,' said I.

'I don't know about that, sir, but I am perfectly certain that I could open the box. There's a screwdriver here in the locker. Just hold the lamp, Allardyce, and I'll have it done in a brace of shakes.'

'Wait a bit,' said I, for already, with eyes which gleamed with curiosity and with avarice, he was stooping over the lid. 'I don't see that there is any hurry over this matter. You've read that card which warns us not to open it.

It may mean anything or it may mean nothing, but somehow I feel inclined to obey it. After all, whatever is in it will keep, and if it is valuable it will be worth as much if it is opened in the owner's offices as in the cabin of the *Mary Sinclair*.'

The first officer seemed bitterly disappointed at my decision.

'Surely, sir, you are not superstitious about it,' said he, with a slight sneer upon his thin lips. 'If it gets out of our own hands, and we don't see for ourselves what is inside it, we may be done out of our rights; besides – '

'That's enough, Mr Armstrong,' said I, abruptly. 'You may have every confidence that you will get your rights, but I will not have that box opened tonight.'

'Why, the label itself shows that the box has been examined by Europeans,' Allardyce added. 'Because a box is a treasure-box is no reason that it has treasures inside it now. A good many folk have had a peep into it since the days of the old Governor of Terra Firma.'

Armstrong threw the screwdriver down upon the table and shrugged his shoulders.

'Just as you like,' said he; but for the rest of the evening, although we spoke upon many subjects, I noticed that his eyes were continually coming round, with the same expression of curiosity and greed, to the old striped box.

And now I come to that portion of my story which fills me even now with a shuddering horror when I think of it. The main cabin had the rooms of the officers round it, but mine was the farthest away from it at the end of the little passage which led to the companion. No regular watch was kept by me, except in cases of emergency, and the three mates divided the watches among them. Armstrong had the middle watch, which ends at four in the morning, and he was relieved by Allardyce. For my part I have always been one of the soundest of sleepers, and it is rare for anything less than a hand upon my shoulder to arouse me.

And yet I was aroused that night, or rather in the early grey of the morning. It was just half-past four by my chronometer when something caused me to sit up in my berth wide awake and with every nerve tingling. It was a sound of some sort, a crash with a human cry at the end of it, which still jarred on my ears. I sat listening, but all was now silent. And yet it could not have been imagination, that hideous cry, for the echo of it still rang in my head, and it seemed to have come from some place quite close to me. I sprang from my bunk, and, pulling on some clothes, I made my way into the cabin. At first I saw nothing unusual there. In the cold, grey light I made out the red-clothed table, the six rotating chairs, the walnut lockers, the swinging barometer, and there, at the end, the big striped chest. I was turning away, with the intention of going upon deck and asking the second mate if he had heard anything, when my eyes fell suddenly upon something which projected from under the table. It was the leg of a man – a leg with a long sea-boot upon it. I stooped, and there was a figure sprawling upon his face, his arms thrown forward and his body twisted. One glance told me that it was Armstrong, the first officer, and a second that he was a dead man. For a few moments I stood gasping. Then I rushed on to the deck, called Allardyce to my assistance, and came back with him into the cabin.

Together we pulled the unfortunate fellow from under the table, and as we looked at his dripping head we exchanged glances, and I do not know which was the paler of the two.

'The same as the Spanish sailor,' said I.

'The very same. God preserve us! It's that infernal chest! Look at Armstrong's hand!'

He held up the mate's right hand, and there was the screwdriver which he had wished to use the night before.

'He's been at the chest, sir. He knew that I was on deck and you were asleep. He knelt down in front of it, and he pushed the lock back with that tool. Then something happened to him, and he cried out so that you heard him.'

'Allardyce,' I whispered, 'what *could* have happened to him?'

The second mate put his hand upon my sleeve and drew me into his cabin. 'We can talk here, sir, for we don't know who may be listening to us in there. What do you suppose is in that box, Captain Barclay?'

'I give you my word, Allardyce, that I have no idea.'

'Well, I can only find one theory which will fit all the facts. Look at the size of the box. Look at all the carving and metalwork which may conceal any number of holes. Look at the weight of it; it took four men to carry it. On top of that, remember that two men have tried to open it, and both have come to their end through it. Now, sir, what can it mean except one thing?'

'You mean there is a man in it?'

'Of course there is a man in it. You know how it is in these South American States, sir. A man may be president one week and hunted like a dog the next – they are forever flying for their lives. My idea is that there is some fellow in hiding there, who is armed and desperate, and who will fight to the death before he is taken.'

'But his food and drink?'

'It's a roomy chest, sir, and he may have some provisions stowed away. As to his drink, he had a friend among the crew upon the brig who saw that he had what he needed.'

'You think, then, that the label asking people not to open the box was simply written in his interest?'

'Yes, sir, that is my idea. Have you any other way of explaining the facts?'

I had to confess that I had not.

'The question is what we are to do?' I asked.

'The man's a dangerous ruffian, who sticks at nothing. I'm thinking it wouldn't be a bad thing to put a rope round the chest and tow it alongside for half an hour; then we could open it at our ease. Or if we just tied the box up and kept him from getting any water maybe that would do as well. Or the carpenter could put a coat of varnish over it and stop all the blow-holes.'

'Come, Allardyce,' said I, angrily. 'You don't seriously mean to say that a whole ship's company are going to be terrorised by a single man in a box. If he's there, I'll engage to fetch him out!' I went to my room and came back with my revolver in my hand. 'Now, Allardyce,' said I, 'do you open the lock, and I'll stand on guard.'

'For God's sake, think what you are doing, sir!' cried the mate. 'Two men have lost their lives over it, and the blood of one not yet dry upon the carpet.'

'The more reason why we should revenge him.'

'Well, sir, at least let me call the carpenter. Three are better than two, and he is a good stout man.'

He went off in search of him, and I was left alone with the striped chest in the cabin. I don't think that I'm a nervous man, but I kept the table between me and this solid old relic of the Spanish Main. In the growing light of morning the red and white striping was beginning to appear, and the curious scrolls and wreaths of metal and carving which showed the loving pains which cunning craftsmen had expended upon it. Presently the carpenter and the mate came back together, the former with a hammer in his hand.

'It's a bad business, this, sir,' said he, shaking his head, as he looked at the body of the mate. 'And you think there's someone hiding in the box?'

'There's no doubt about it,' said Allardyce, picking up the screwdriver and setting his jaw like a man who needs to brace his courage. 'I'll drive the lock back if you will both stand by. If he rises let him have it on the head with your hammer, carpenter. Shoot at once, sir, if he raises his hand. Now!'

He had knelt down in front of the striped chest, and passed the blade of the tool under the lid. With a sharp snick the lock flew back. 'Stand by!' yelled the mate, and with a heave he threw open the massive top of the box. As it swung up we all three sprang back, I with my pistol levelled, and the carpenter with the hammer above his head. Then, as nothing happened, we each took a step forward and peeped in. The box was empty.

Not quite empty either, for in one corner was lying an old yellow candle-stick, elaborately engraved, which appeared to be as old as the box itself. Its rich yellow tone and artistic shape suggested that it was an object of value. For the rest there was nothing more weighty or valuable than dust in the old striped treasure-chest.

'Well, I'm blessed!' cried Allardyce, staring blankly into it. 'Where does the weight come in, then?'

'Look at the thickness of the sides, and look at the lid. Why, it's five inches through. And see that great metal spring across it.'

'That's for holding the lid up,' said the mate. 'You see, it won't lean back. What's that German printing on the inside?'

'It means that it was made by Johann Rothstein of Augsburg, in 1606.'

'And a solid bit of work, too. But it doesn't throw much light on what has passed, does it, Captain Barclay? That candlestick looks like gold. We shall have something for our trouble after all.'

He leant forward to grasp it, and from that moment I have never doubted as to the reality of inspiration, for on the instant I caught him by the collar and pulled him straight again. It may have been some story of the Middle Ages which had come back to my mind, or it may have been that my eye had caught some red which was not that of rust upon the upper part of the lock, but to him and to me it will always seem an inspiration, so prompt and sudden was my action.

'There's devilry here,' said I. 'Give me the crooked stick from the corner.'

It was an ordinary walking-cane with a hooked top. I passed it over the candlestick and gave it a pull. With a flash a row of polished steel fangs shot out from below the upper lip, and the great striped chest snapped at us like a wild animal. Clang came the huge lid into its place, and the glasses on the swinging rack sang and tinkled with the shock. The mate sat down on the edge of the table and shivered like a frightened horse.

'You've saved my life, Captain Barclay!' said he.

So this was the secret of the striped treasure-chest of old Don Ramirez di Leyra, and this was how he preserved his ill-gotten gains from Terra Firma and the Province of Veraquas. Be the thief ever so cunning he could not tell that golden candlestick from the other articles of value, and the instant that he laid hand upon it the terrible spring was unloosed and the murderous steel pikes were driven into his brain, while the shock of the blow sent the victim backwards and enabled the chest automatically to close itself. How many, I wondered, had fallen victims to the ingenuity of the mechanic of Ausgburg? And as I thought of the possible history of that grim striped chest my resolution was very quickly taken.

'Carpenter, bring three men and carry this on deck.'

'Going to throw it overboard, sir?'

'Yes, Mr Allardyce. I'm not superstitious as a rule, but there are some things which are more than a sailor can be called upon to stand.'

'No wonder that brig made heavy weather, Captain Barclay, with such a thing on board. The glass is dropping fast, sir, and we are only just in time.'

So we did not even wait for the three sailors, but we carried it out, the mate, the carpenter, and I, and we pushed it with our own hands over the bulwarks. There was a white spout of water, and it was gone. There it lies, the striped chest, a thousand fathoms deep, and if, as they say, the sea will some day be dry land, I grieve for the man who finds that old box and tries to penetrate into its secret.

The Croxley Master

ONE

Mr Robert Montgomery was seated at his desk, his head upon his hands, in a state of the blackest despondency. Before him was the open ledger with the long columns of Dr Oldacre's prescriptions. At his elbow lay the wooden tray with the labels in various partitions, the cork box, the lumps of twisted sealing-wax, while in front a rank of bottles waited to be filled. But his spirits were too low for work. He sat in silence with his fine shoulders bowed and his head upon his hands.

Outside, through the grimy surgery window over a foreground of blackened brick and slate, a line of enormous chimneys like Cyclopean pillars upheld the lowering, dun-coloured cloud-bank. For six days in the week they spouted smoke, but today the furnace fires were banked, for it was Sunday. Sordid and polluting gloom hung over a district blighted and blasted by the greed of man. There was nothing in the surroundings to cheer a desponding soul, but it was more than his dismal environment which weighed upon the medical assistant. His trouble was deeper and more personal. The winter session was approaching. He should be back again at the university completing the last year which would give him his medical degree; but, alas! he had not the money with which to pay his class fees, nor could he imagine how he could procure it. Sixty pounds were wanted to make his career, and it might have been as many thousand for any chance there seemed to be of his obtaining it. He was roused from his black meditation by the entrance of Dr Oldacre himself, a large, clean-shaven, respectable man, with a prim manner and an austere face. He had prospered exceedingly by the support of the local Church interest, and the rule of his life was never by word or action to run the risk of offending the sentiment which had made him. His standard of respectability and of dignity was exceedingly high, and he expected the same from his assistants. His appearance and words were always vaguely benevolent. A sudden impulse came over the despondent student. He would test the reality of this philanthropy.

'I beg your pardon, Dr Oldacre,' said he, rising from his chair; 'I have a great favour to ask of you.'

The doctor's appearance was not encouraging. His mouth suddenly tightened, and his eyes fell.

'Yes, Mr Montgomery?'

'You are aware, sir, that I need only one more session to complete my course.'

'So you have told me.'

'It is very important to me, sir.'

'Naturally.'

'The fees, Dr Oldacre, would amount to about sixty pounds.'

'I am afraid that my duties call me elsewhere, Mr Montgomery.'

'One moment, sir! I had hoped, sir, that perhaps, if I signed a paper promising you interest upon your money, you would advance this sum to me. I will pay you back, sir, I really will. Or, if you like, I will work it off after I am qualified.'

The doctor's lips had thinned into a narrow line. His eyes were raised again, and sparkled indignantly.

'Your request is unreasonable, Mr Montgomery. I am surprised that you should have made it. Consider, sir, how many thousands of medical students there are in this country. No doubt there are many of them who have a difficulty in finding their fees. Am I to provide for them all? Or why should I make an exception in your favour? I am grieved and disappointed, Mr Montgomery, that you should have put me into the painful position of having to refuse you.' He turned upon his heel, and walked with offended dignity out of the surgery.

The student smiled bitterly, and turned to his work of making up the morning prescriptions. It was poor and unworthy work – work which any weakling might have done as well, and this was a man of exceptional nerve and sinew. But, such as it was, it brought him his board and one pound a week – enough to help him during the summer months and let him save a few pounds towards his winter keep. But those class fees! Where were they to come from? He could not save them out of his scanty wage. Dr Oldacre would not advance them. He saw no way of earning them. His brains were fairly good, but brains of that quality were a drug in the market. He only excelled in his strength, and where was he to find a customer for that? But the ways of fate are strange, and his customer was at hand.

'Look y'ere!' said a voice at the door. Montgomery looked up, for the voice was a loud and rasping one. A young man stood at the entrance – a stocky, bull-necked young miner, in tweed Sunday clothes and an aggressive neck-tie. He was a sinister-looking figure, with dark, insolent eyes, and the jaw and throat of a bulldog.

'Look y'ere!' said he again. 'Why hast thou not sent t' medicine oop as thy master ordered?'

Montgomery had become accustomed to the brutal frankness of the northern worker. At first it had enraged him, but after a time he had grown callous to it, and accepted it as it was meant. But this was something different. It was insolence – brutal, overbearing insolence, with physical menace behind it.

'What name?' he asked coldly.

'Barton. Happen I may give thee cause to mind that name, yoong man. Mak' oop t' wife's medicine this very moment, look ye, or it will be the worse for thee.'

Montgomery smiled. A pleasant sense of relief thrilled softly through him. What blessed safety-valve was this through which his jangled nerves might find some outlet. The provocation was so gross, the insult so unprovoked, that he could have none of those qualms which take the edge off a man's mettle. He finished sealing the bottle upon which he was occupied, and he addressed it and placed it carefully in the rack. 'Look here!' said he, turning round to the miner, 'your medicine will be made up in its turn and sent down to you. I don't allow folk in the surgery. Wait outside in the waiting-room if you wish to wait at all.'

'Yoong man,' said the miner, 'thou's got to mak' t' wife's medicine here, and now, and quick, while I wait and watch thee, or else happen thou might need some medicine thysel' before all is over.'

'I shouldn't advise you to fasten a quarrel upon me.' Montgomery was speaking in the hard, staccato voice of a man who is holding himself in with difficulty. 'You'll save trouble if you'll go quietly. If you don't you'll be hurt. Ah, you would? Take it, then!'

The blows were almost simultaneous – a savage swing which whistled past Montgomery's ear, and a straight drive which took the workman on the chin. Luck was with the assistant. That single whizzing uppercut, and the way in which it was delivered, warned him that he had a formidable man to deal with. But if he had underrated his antagonist, his antagonist had also underrated him, and had laid himself open to a fatal blow.

The miner's head had come with a crash against the corner of the surgery shelves, and he had dropped heavily on to the ground. There he lay with his bandy legs drawn up and his hands thrown abroad, the blood trickling over the surgery tiles.

'Had enough?' asked the assistant, breathing fiercely through his nose.

But no answer came. The man was insensible. And then the danger of his position came upon Montgomery, and he turned as white as his antagonist. A Sunday, the immaculate Dr Oldacre with his pious connection, a savage brawl with a patient; he would irretrievably lose his situation if the facts came out. It was not much of a situation, but he could not get another without a reference, and Oldacre might refuse him one. Without money for his classes, and without a situation – what was to become of him? It was absolute ruin.

But perhaps he could escape exposure after all. He seized his insensible adversary, dragged him out into the centre of he room, loosened his collar, and squeezed the surgery sponge over his face. He sat up at last with a gasp and a scowl. 'Domn thee, thou's spoilt my neck-tie,' said he, mopping up the water from his breast.

'I'm sorry I hit you so hard,' said Montgomery, apologetically.

'Thou hit me hard! I could stan' such fly-flappin' all day. 'Twas this here press that cracked my pate for me, and thou art a looky man to be able to boast as thou hast outed me. And now I'd be obliged to thee if thou wilt give me t' wife's medicine.'

Montgomery gladly made it up and handed it to the miner.

'You are weak still,' said he. 'Won't you stay awhile and rest?'

'T' wife wants her medicine,' said the man, and lurched out at the door.

The assistant, looking after him, saw him rolling, with an uncertain step, down the street, until a friend met him and they walked on arm in arm. The man seemed in his rough Northern fashion to bear no grudge, and so Montgomery's fears left him. There was no reason why the doctor should know anything about it. He wiped the blood from the floor, put the surgery in order, and went on with his interrupted task, hoping that he had come scathless out of a very dangerous business.

Yet all day he was aware of a sense of vague uneasiness, which sharpened into dismay when, late in the afternoon, he was informed that three gentlemen had called and were waiting for him in the surgery. A coroner's inquest, a descent of detectives, an invasion of angry relatives – all sorts of possibilities rose to scare him. With tense nerves and a rigid face he went to meet his visitors.

They were a very singular trio. Each was known to him by sight; but what on earth the three could be doing together, and, above all, what they could expect from *him*, was a most inexplicable problem. The first was Sorley Wilson, the son of the owner of the Nonpareil Coalpit. He was a young blood of twenty, heir to a fortune, a keen sportsman, and down for the Easter vacation from Magdalene College. He sat now upon the edge of the surgery table, looking in thoughtful silence at Montgomery and twisting the ends of his small, black, waxed moustache. The second was Purvis, the publican, owner of the chief beer-shop, and well known as the local bookmaker. He was a coarse, clean-shaven man, whose fiery face made a singular contrast with his ivory-white bald head. He had shrewd, light-blue eyes with foxy lashes, and he also leaned forward in silence from his chair, a fat, red hand upon either knee, and stared critically at the young assistant. So did the third visitor, Fawcett, the horse-breaker, who leaned back, his long, thin legs, with their boxcloth riding-gaiters, thrust out in front of him, tapping his protruding teeth with his riding-whip, with anxious thought in every line of his rugged, bony face. Publican, exquisite and horse-breaker were all three equally silent, equally earnest and equally critical. Montgomery seated in the midst of them, looked from one to the other.

'Well, gentlemen?' he observed, but no answer came.

The position was embarrassing.

'No,' said the horse-breaker, at last. 'No. It's off. It's nowt.'

'Stand oop, lad; let's see thee standin'.' It was the publican who spoke. Montgomery obeyed. He would learn all about it, no doubt, if he were patient. He stood up and turned slowly round, as if in front of his tailor.

'It's off! It's off!' cried the horse-breaker. 'Why, mon, the Master would break him over his knee.'

'Oh, that be hanged for a yarn!' said the young Cantab. 'You can drop out if you like, Fawcett, but I'll see this thing through, if I have to do it alone. I don't hedge a penny. I like the cut of him a great deal better than I liked Ted Barton.'

'Look at Barton's shoulders, Mr Wilson.'

'Lumpiness isn't always strength. Give me nerve and fire and breed. That's what wins.'

'Ay, sir, you have it theer – you have it theer!' said the fat, red-faced publican, in a thick suety voice. 'It's the same wi' poops. Get 'em clean-bred an' fine, an' they'll yark the thick 'uns – yark 'em out o' their skins.'

'He's ten good pund on the light side,' growled the horse-breaker.

'He's a welter weight, anyhow.'

'A hundred and thirty.'

'A hundred and fifty, if he's an ounce.'

'Well, the Master doesn't scale much more than that.'

'A hundred and seventy-five.'

'That was when he was hog-fat and living high. Work the grease out of him and I lay there's no great difference between them. Have you been weighed lately, Mr Montgomery?'

It was the first direct question which had been asked him. He had stood in the midst of them like a horse at a fair, and he was just beginning to wonder whether he was more angry or amused.

'I am just eleven stone,' said he.

'I said that he was a welter weight.'

'But suppose you was trained?' said the publican. 'Wot then?'

'I am always in training.'

'In a manner of speakin', no doubt, he *is* always in trainin',' remarked the horse-breaker. 'But trainin' for everyday work ain't the same as trainin' with a trainer; and I dare bet, with all respec' to your opinion, Mr Wilson, that there's half a stone of tallow on him at this minute.'

The young Cantab put his fingers on the assistant's upper arm, then with his other hand on his wrist, he bent the forearm sharply, and felt the biceps, as round and hard as a cricket-ball, spring up under his fingers.

'Feel that!' said he.

The publican and horse-breaker felt it with an air of reverence. 'Good lad! He'll do yet!' cried Purvis.

'Gentlemen,' said Montgomery, 'I think that you will acknowledge that I have been very patient with you. I have listened to all that you have to say about my personal appearance, and now I must really beg that you will have the goodness to tell me what is the matter.'

They all sat down in their serious, businesslike way.

'That's easy done, Mr Montgomery,' said the fat-voiced publican. 'But before sayin' anything we had to wait and see whether, in a way of speakin', there was any need for us to say anything at all. Mr Wilson thinks there is. Mr Fawcett, who has the same right to his opinion, bein' also a backer and one o' the committee, thinks the other way.'

'I thought him too light built, and I think so now,' said the horse-breaker, still tapping his prominent teeth with the metal head of his riding-whip. 'But happen he may pull through, and he's a fine-made, buirdly young chap, so if you mean to back him, Mr Wilson –

'Which I do.'

'And you, Purvis?'

'I ain't one to go back, Fawcett.'

'Well, I'll stan' to my share of the purse.'

'And well I knew you would,' said Purvis, 'for it would be somethin' new to find Isaac Fawcett as a spoil-sport. Well, then, we will make up the hundred for the stake among us, and the fight stands – always supposin' the young man is willin'.'

'Excuse all this rot, Mr Montgomery,' said the university man, in a genial voice. 'We've begun at the wrong end, I know, but we'll soon straighten it out, and I hope that you will see your way to falling in with our views. In the first place, you remember the man whom you knocked out this morning? He is Barton – the famous Ted Barton.'

'I'm sure, sir, you may well be proud to have outed him in one round,' said the publican. 'Why, it took Morris, the ten-stone-six champion, a deal more trouble than that before he put Barton to sleep. You've done a fine performance, sir, and happen you'll do a finer, if you give yourself the chance.'

'I never heard of Ted Barton, beyond seeing the name on a medicine label,' said the assistant.

'Well, you may take it from me that he's a slaughterer,' said the horse-breaker. 'You've taught him a lesson that he needed, for it was always a word and a blow with him, and the word alone was worth five shillin' in a public court. He won't be so ready now to shake his nief in the face of everyone he meets. However, that's neither here nor there.'

Montgomery looked at them in bewilderment.

'For goodness' sake, gentlemen, tell me what it is you want me to do!' he cried.

'We want you to fight Silas Craggs, better known as the Master of Croxley.'

'But why?'

'Because Ted Barton was to have fought him next Saturday. He was the champion of the Wilson coal-pits, and the other was the Master of the iron-folk down at the Croxley smelters. We'd matched our man for a purse of a hundred against the Master. But you've queered our man, and he can't face such a battle with a two-inch cut at the back of his head. There's only one thing to be done, sir, and that is for you to take his place. If you can lick Ted Barton you may lick the Master of Croxley, but if you don't we're done, for there's no one else who is in the same street with him in this district. It's twenty rounds, two-ounce gloves, Queensberry rules, and a decision on points if you fight to the finish.'

For a moment the absurdity of the thing drove every other thought out of Montgomery's head. But then there came a sudden revulsion. A hundred pounds! – all he wanted to complete his education was lying there ready to his hand, if only that hand were strong enough to pick it up. He had thought bitterly that morning that there was no market for his strength, but here was one where his muscle might earn more in an hour than his brains in a year. But a chill of doubt came over him. 'How can I fight for the coal-pits?' said he. 'I am not connected with them.'

'Eh, lad, but thou art!' cried old Purvis. 'We've got it down in writin', and it's clear enough: "Anyone connected with the coal-pits". Doctor Oldacre is the coal-pit club doctor; thou art his assistant. What more can they want?'

'Yes, that's right enough,' said the Cantab. 'It would be a very sporting thing of you, Mr Montgomery, if you would come to our help when we are in such a hole. Of course, you might not like to take the hundred pounds; but I have no doubt that, in the case of your winning, we could arrange that it should take the form of a watch or piece of plate, or any other shape which might suggest itself to you. You see, you are responsible for our having lost our champion, so we really feel that we have a claim upon you.'

'Give me a moment, gentlemen. It is very unexpected. I am afraid the doctor would never consent to my going – in fact, I am sure that he would not.'

'But he need never know – not before the fight, at any rate. We are not bound to give the name of our man. So long as he is within the weight limits on the day of the fight, that is all that concerns anyone.'

The adventure and the profit would either of them have attracted Montgomery. The two combined were irresistible. 'Gentlemen,' said he, 'I'll do it!'

The three sprang from their seats. The publican had seized his right hand, the horse-dealer his left, and the Cantab slapped him on the back.

'Good lad! good lad!' croaked the publican. 'Eh, mon, but if thou yark him, thou'll rise in one day from being just a common doctor to the best-known mon 'twixt here and Bradford. Thou art a witherin' tyke, thou art, and no mistake; and if thou beat the Master of Croxley, thou'll find all the beer thou want for the rest of thy life waiting for thee at the Four Sacks.

'It is the most sporting thing I ever heard of in my life,' said young Wilson. 'By George, sir, if you pull it off, you've got the constituency in your pocket, if you care to stand. You know the out-house in my garden?'

'Next the road?'

'Exactly. I turned it into a gymnasium for Ted Barton. You'll find all you want there: clubs, punching ball, bars, dumb-bells, everything. Then you'll want a sparring partner. Ogilvy has been acting for Barton, but we don't think that he is class enough. Barton bears you no grudge. He's a good-hearted fellow, though cross-grained with strangers. He looked upon you as a stranger this morning, but he says he knows you now. He is quite ready to spar with you for practice, and he will come any hour you will name.'

'Thank you; I will let you know the hour,' said Montgomery; and so the committee departed jubilant upon their way.

The medical assistant sat for a time in the surgery turning it over a little in his mind. He had been trained originally at the university by the man who had been middleweight champion in his day. It was true that his teacher was long past his prime, slow upon his feet, and stiff in his joints, but even so he was still a tough antagonist; but Montgomery had found at last that he could more than hold his own with him. He had won the university medal, and his teacher, who had trained so many students, was emphatic in his opinion that he had never had one who was in the same class with him. He had been exhorted to go in for the Amateur Championships, but he had no particular ambition in that direction. Once he had put on the gloves with Hammer Tunstall in a booth at a fair and had fought three rattling rounds, in which he had the worst of it, but he had made the prize fighter stretch himself to the uttermost. There was his whole record, and was it enough to encourage him to stand up to the Master of Croxley? He had never heard of the Master before, but then he had lost touch of the ring during the last few years of hard work. After all, what did it matter? If he won, there was the money, which meant so much to him. If he lost, it would only mean a thrashing. He could take punishment without flinching, of that he was certain. If there were only one chance in a hundred of pulling it off, then it was worth his while to attempt it.

Dr Oldacre, new come from church, with an ostentatious prayer-book in his kid-gloved hand, broke in upon his meditation.

'You don't go to service, I observe, Mr Montgomery,' said he, coldly.

'No, sir; I have had some business to detain me.'

'It is very near to my heart that my household should set a good example. There are so few educated people in this district that a great responsibility devolves upon us. If we do not live up to the highest, how can we expect these poor workers to do so? It is a dreadful thing to reflect that the parish takes a great deal more interest in an approaching glove fight than in their religious duties.'

'A glove fight, sir?' said Montgomery, guiltily.

'I believe that to be the correct term. One of my patients tells me that it is the talk of the district. A local ruffian, a patient of ours, by the way, matched against a pugilist over at Croxley. I cannot understand why the law does not step in and stop so degrading an exhibition. It is really a prize fight.'

'A glove fight, you said.'

'I am informed that a two-ounce glove is an evasion by which they dodge the law, and make it difficult for the police to interfere. They contend for a sum of money. It seems dreadful and almost incredible – does it not? – to think that such scenes can be enacted within a few miles of our peaceful home. But you will realise, Mr Montgomery, that while there are such influences for us to counteract, it is very necessary that we should live up to our highest.'

The doctor's sermon would have had more effect if the assistant had not once or twice had occasion to test his highest, and come upon it at unexpectedly humble elevations. It is always so particularly easy to 'compound for sins we're most inclined to by damning those we have no mind to'. In any case, Montgomery felt that of all the men concerned in such a fight – promoters, backers, spectators – it is the actual fighter who holds the strongest and most honourable position. His conscience gave him no concern upon the subject. Endurance and courage are virtues, not vices, and brutality is, at least, better than effeminacy.

There was a little tobacco-shop at the corner of the street, where Montgomery got his bird's-eye and also his local information, for the shopman was a garrulous soul, who knew everything about the affairs of the district. The assistant strolled down there after tea and asked, in a casual way, whether the tobacconist had ever heard of the Master of Croxley.

'Heard of him! Heard of him!' the little man could hardly articulate in his astonishment. 'Why, sir, he's the first mon o' the district, an' his name's as well known in the West Riding as the winner o' t' Derby. But Lor,' sir' – here he stopped and rummaged among a heap of papers – 'they are makin' a fuss about him on account o' his fight wi' Ted Barton, and so the *Croxley Herald* has his life an' record, an' here it is, an' thou canst read it for thysel'.'

The sheet of the paper which he held up was a lake of print around an islet of illustration. The latter was a coarse woodcut of a pugilist's head and neck set in a cross-barred jersey. It was a sinister but powerful face, the face of a debauched hero, clean-shaven, strongly eye-browed, keen-eyed, with huge, aggressive jaw and an animal dewlap beneath it. The long, obstinate cheeks ran flush up to the narrow, sinister eyes. The mighty neck came down square from the ears and curved outwards into shoulders which had lost nothing at the hands of the local artist. Above was written 'Silas Craggs', and beneath, 'The Master of Croxley'.

'Thou'll find all about him there, sir,' said the tobacconist. 'He's a witherin' tyke, he is, and we're proud to have him in the county. If he hadn't broke his leg he'd have been champion of England.'

'Broke his leg, has he?'

'Yes, and it set badly. They ca' him owd K, behind his back, for that is how his two legs look. But his arms – well, if they was both stropped to a bench, as the sayin' is, I wonder where the champion of England would be then.'

'I'll take this with me,' said Montgomery; and putting the paper into his pocket he returned home.

It was not a cheering record which he read there. The whole history of the Croxley Master was given in full, his many victories, his few defeats.

'Born in 1857 [said the provincial biographer], Silas Craggs, better known in sporting circles as the Master of Croxley, is now in his fortieth year.'

'Hang it, I'm only twenty-three!' said Montgomery to himself, and read on more cheerfully.

Having in his youth shown a surprising aptitude for the game, he fought his way up among his comrades, until he became the recognised champion of the district and won the proud title which he still holds. Ambitious of a more than local fame, he secured a patron, and fought his first fight against Jack Barton, of Birmingham, in May 1880, at the old Loiterers' Club. Craggs, who fought at ten stone two at the time, had the better of fifteen rattling rounds, and gained an award on points against the Midlander. Having disposed of James Dunn of Rotherhithe, Cameron of Glasgow and a youth named Fernie, he was thought so highly of by the fancy that he was matched against Ernest Willox, at that time middleweight champion of the North of England, and defeated him in a hard-fought battle, knocking him out in the tenth round after a punishing contest. At this period it looked as if the very highest honours of the ring were within the reach of the young Yorkshireman, but he was laid upon the shelf by a most unfortunate accident. The kick of a horse broke his thigh, and for a year he was compelled to rest himself. When he returned to his work the fracture had set badly, and his activity was much impaired. It was owing to this that he was defeated in seven rounds by Willox, the man whom he had previously beaten, and afterwards by James Shaw, of London, though the latter acknowledged that he had found the toughest customer of his career. Undismayed by his reverses, the Master adapted the style of his fighting to his physical disabilities and resumed his career of victory – defeating Norton (the black), Hobby Wilson and Levi Cohen, the latter a heavy-weight. Conceding two stone, he fought a draw with the famous Billy McQuire, and afterwards, for a purse of fifty pounds, he defeated Sam Hare at the Pelican Club, London. In 1891 a decision was given against him upon a foul when fighting a winning fight against Jim Taylor, the Australian middleweight, and so mortified was he by the decision, that he withdrew from the ring. Since then he has hardly fought at all save to accommodate any local aspirant who may wish to learn the difference between a bar-room scramble and a scientific contest. The latest of these ambitious souls comes from the Wilson coal-pits, which have undertaken to put up a stake of a hundred pounds and back their local champion. There are various rumours afloat as to who their representative is to be, the name of Ted Barton being freely mentioned; but the betting, which is seven to one on the Master against any untried man, is a fair reflection of the feeling of the community.

Montgomery read it over twice, and it left him with a very serious face. No light matter this which he had undertaken; no battle with a rough-and-tumble fighter who presumed upon a local reputation. The man's record showed that he was first-class – or nearly so. There were a few points in his favour, and he must make the most of them. There was age – twenty-three against forty. There was an old ring proverb that 'Youth will be served', but the annals of the ring offer a great number of exceptions. A hard veteran full of cool valour and ring-craft, could give ten or fifteen years and a beating to most striplings. He could not rely too much upon his advantage in age. But then there was the lameness; that must surely count for a great deal. And, lastly, there was the chance that the Master might underrate his opponent, that he might be remiss in his training, and refuse to abandon his usual way of life, if he thought that he had an easy task before him. In a man of his age and habits this seemed very possible. Montgomery prayed that it might be so. Meanwhile, if his opponent were the best man who ever jumped the ropes into a ring, his own duty was clear. He must prepare himself carefully, throw away no chance, and do the very best that he could. But he knew enough to appreciate the difference which exists in boxing, as in every sport, between the amateur and the professional. The coolness, the power of hitting, above all the capability of taking punishment, count for so much.

Those specially developed, gutta-percha-like abdominal muscles of the hardened pugilist will take without flinching a blow which would leave another man writhing on the ground. Such things are not to be acquired in a week, but all that could be done in a week should be done.

The medical assistant had a good basis to start from. He was 5ft 11 ins – tall enough for anything on two legs, as the old ring men used to say – lithe and spare, with the activity of a panther and a strength which had hardly yet ever found its limitations. His muscular development was finely hard, but his power came rather from that higher nerve-energy which counts for nothing upon a measuring tape. He had the well-curved nose and the widely opened eye which never yet were seen upon the face of a craven, and behind everything he had the driving force, which came from the knowledge that his whole career was at stake upon the contest. The three backers rubbed their hands when they saw him at work punching the ball in the gymnasium next morning; and Fawcett, the horse-breaker, who had written to Leeds to hedge his bets, sent a wire to cancel the letter, and to lay another fifty at the market price of seven to one.

Montgomery's chief difficulty was to find time for his training without any interference from the doctor. His work took him a large part of the day, but as the visiting was done on foot, and considerable distances had to be traversed, it was a training in itself. For the rest, he punched the swinging ball and worked with the dumb-bells for an hour every morning and evening, and boxed twice a day with Ted Barton in the gymnasium, gaining as much profit as could be got from a rushing, two-handed slogger. Barton was full of admiration for his cleverness and quickness, but doubtful about his strength. Hard hitting was the feature of his own style, and he exacted it from others.

'Lord, sir, that's a turble poor poonch for an eleven-stone man!' he would cry. 'Thou wilt have to hit harder than that afore t' Master will know that thou art theer. All, thot's better, mon, thot's fine!' he would add, as his opponent lifted him across the room on the end of a right counter. 'Thot's how I likes to feel 'em. Happen thou'lt pull through yet.' He chuckled with joy when Montgomery knocked him into a corner. 'Eh, mon, thou art coming along grand. Thou hast fair yarked me off my legs. Do it again, lad, do it again!'

The only part of Montgomery's training which came within the doctor's observation was his diet, and that puzzled him considerably.

'You will excuse my remarking, Mr Montgomery, that you are becoming rather particular in your tastes. Such fads are not to be encouraged in one's youth. Why do you eat toast with every meal?'

'I find that it suits me better than bread, sir.'

'It entails unnecessary work upon the cook. I observe, also, that you have turned against potatoes.'

'Yes, sir; I think that I am better without them.'

'And you no longer drink your beer?'

'No, sir.'

'These causeless whims and fancies are very much to be deprecated, Mr Montgomery. Consider how many there are to whom these very potatoes and this very beer would be most acceptable.'

'No doubt, sir, but at present I prefer to do without them.'

They were sitting alone at lunch, and the assistant thought that it would be a good opportunity of asking leave for the day of the fight.

'I should be glad if you could let me have leave for Saturday, Dr Oldacre.'

'It is very inconvenient upon so busy a day.'

'I should do a double day's work on Friday so as to leave everything in order. I should hope to be back in the evening.'

'I am afraid I cannot spare you, Mr Montgomery.'

This was a facer. If he could not get leave he would go without it.

'You will remember, Dr Oldacre, that when I came to you it was understood that I should have a clear day every month. I have never claimed one. But now there are reasons why I wish to have a holiday upon Saturday.'

Dr Oldacre gave in with a very bad grace. 'Of course, if you insist upon your formal rights, there is no more to be said, Mr Montgomery, though I feel that it shows a certain indifference to my comfort and the welfare of the practice. Do you still insist?'

'Yes, sir.'

'Very good. Have your way.'

The doctor was boiling over with anger, but Montgomery was a valuable assistant – steady, capable and hardworking – and he could not afford to lose him. Even if he had been prompted to advance those class fees, for which his assistant had appealed, it would have been against his interests to do so, for he did not wish him to qualify, and he desired him to remain in his subordinate position, in which he worked so hard for so small a wage. There was something in the cool insistence of the young man, a quiet resolution in his voice as he claimed his Saturday, which aroused his curiosity.

'I have no desire to interfere unduly with your affairs, Mr Montgomery, but were you thinking of having a day in Leeds upon Saturday?'

'No, sir.

'In the country?'

'Yes, sir.'

'You are very wise. You will find a quiet day among the wild flowers a very valuable restorative. Have you thought of any particular direction?'

'I am going over Croxley way.'

'Well, there is no prettier country when once you are past the ironworks. What could be more delightful than to lie upon the fells, basking in the sunshine, with perhaps some instructive and elevating book as your companion? I should recommend a visit to the ruins of St Bridget's Church, a very interesting relic of the early Norman era. By the way, there is one objection which I see to your going to Croxley on Saturday. It is upon that date, as I am informed, that that ruffianly glove fight takes place. You may find yourself molested by the blackguards whom it will attract.'

'I will take my chance of that, sir,' said the assistant.

On the Friday night, which was the last night before the fight, Montgomery's three backers assembled in the gymnasium and inspected their man as he went through some light exercises to keep his muscles supple. He was certainly in splendid condition, his skin shining with health, and his eyes with energy and confidence. The three walked round him and exulted.

'He's simply ripping!' said the undergraduate.

'By gad, you've come out of it splendidly. You're as hard as a pebble, and fit to fight for your life.'

'Happen he's a trifle on the fine side,' said the publican. 'Runs a bit light at the loins, to my way of thinkin'.'

'What weight today?'

'Ten stone eleven,' the assistant answered.

'That's only three pund off in a week's trainin',' said the horse-breaker. 'He said right when he said that he was in condition. Well, it's fine stuff all there is of it, but I'm none so sure as there is enough.' He kept poking his finger into Montgomery as if he were one of his horses. 'I hear that the Master will scale a hundred and sixty odd at the ringside.'

'But there's some of that which he'd like well to pull off and leave behind wi' his shirt,' said Purvis. 'I hear they've had a rare job to get him to drop his beer, and if it had not been for that great red-headed wench of his they'd never ha' done it. She fair scratted the face off a potman that had brought him a gallon from t' Chequers. They say the hussy is his sparrin' partner, as well as his sweetheart, and that his poor wife is just breakin' her heart over it. Hullo, young 'un, what do you want?'

The door of the gymnasium had opened and a lad, about sixteen, grimy and black with soot and iron, stepped into the yellow glare of the oil lamp. Ted Barton seized him by the collar.

'See here, thou yoong whelp, this is private, and we want noan o' thy spyin'!'

'But I maun speak to Mr Wilson.'

The young Cantab stepped forward.

'Well, my lad, what is it?'

'It's aboot t' fight, Mr Wilson, sir. I wanted to tell your mon somethin' aboot t' Maister.'

'We've no time to listen to gossip, my boy. We know all about the Master.'

'But thou doan't, sir. Nobody knows but me and mother, and we thought as we'd like thy mon to know, sir, for we want him to fair bray him.'

'Oh, you want the Master fair brayed, do you? So do we. Well, what have you to say?'

'Is this your mon, sir?'

'Well, suppose it is?'

'Then it's him I want to tell aboot it. T' Maister is blind o' the left eye.'

'Nonsense!'

'It's true, sir. Not stone blind, but rarely fogged. He keeps it secret, but mother knows, and so do I. If thou slip him on the left side he can't cop thee. Thou'll find it right as I tell thee. And mark him when he sinks his right. 'Tis his best blow, his right upper-cut. T' Maister's finisher, they ca' it at t' works. It's a turble blow when it do come home.'

'Thank you, my boy. This is information worth having about his sight,' said Wilson. 'How came you to know so much? Who are you?'

'I'm his son, sir.'

Wilson whistled. 'And who sent you to us?'

'My mother. I maun get back to her again.'

'Take this half-crown.'

'No, sir, I don't seek money in comin' here. I do it – '

'For love?' suggested the publican.

'For hate!' said the boy, and darted off into the darkness.

'Seems to me t' red-headed wench may do him more harm than good, after all,' remarked the publican. 'And now, Mr Montgomery, sir, you've done enough for this evenin', an' a nine-hours' sleep is the best trainin' before a battle. Happen this time tomorrow night you'll be safe back again with your hundred pound in your pocket.'

TWO

Work was struck at one o'clock at the coal-pits and the ironworks, and the fight was arranged for three. From the Croxley Furnaces, from Wilson's Coal-Pits, from the Heartsease Mine, from the Dodd Mills, from the Leverworth Smelters the workmen came trooping, each with his fox-terrier or his lurcher at his heels. Warped with labour and twisted by toil, bent double by week-long work in the cramped coal galleries or half-blinded with years spent in front of white-hot fluid metal, these men still gilded their harsh and hopeless lives by their devotion to sport. It was their one relief, the only thing which could distract their minds from sordid surroundings, and give them an interest beyond the blackened circle which enclosed them. Literature, art, science, all these things were beyond their horizon; but the race, the football match, the cricket, the fight, these were things which they could understand, which they could speculate upon in advance and comment upon afterwards. Sometimes brutal, sometimes grotesque, the love of sport is still one of the great agencies which make for the happiness of our people. It lies very deeply in the springs of our nature, and when it has been educated out, a higher, more refined nature may be left, but it will not be of that robust British type which has left its mark so deeply on the world. Every one of these raddled workers, slouching with his dog at his heels to see something of the fight, was a true unit of his race.

It was a squally May day, with bright sunbursts and driving showers. Montgomery worked all morning in the surgery getting his medicine made up.

'The weather seems so very unsettled, Mr Montgomery,' remarked the doctor, 'that I am inclined to think that you had better postpone your little country excursion until a later date.'

'I am afraid that I must go today, sir.'

'I have just had an intimation that Mrs Potter, at the other side of Angleton, wishes to see me. It is probable that I shall be there all day. It will be extremely inconvenient to leave the house empty so long.'

'I am very sorry, sir, but I must go,' said the assistant, doggedly.

The doctor saw that it would be useless to argue, and departed in the worst of bad tempers upon his mission. Montgomery felt easier now that he was gone. He went up to his room and packed his running-shoes, his fighting-drawers and his cricket sash into a hand-bag. When he came down, Mr Wilson was waiting for him in the surgery. 'I hear the doctor has gone.'

'Yes; he is likely to be away all day.'

'I don't see that it matters much. It's bound to come to his ears by tonight.'

'Yes; it's serious with me, Mr Wilson. If I win, it's all right. I don't mind telling you that the hundred pounds will make all the difference to me. But if I lose, I shall lose my situation, for, as you say, I can't keep it secret.'

'Never mind. We'll see you through among us. I only wonder the doctor has not heard, for it's all over the country that you are to fight the Croxley Champion. We've had Armitage up about it already. He's the Master's backer, you know. He wasn't sure that you were eligible. The Master said he wanted you whether you were eligible or not. Armitage has money on, and would have made trouble if he could. But I showed him that you came within the conditions of the challenge, and he agreed that it was all right. They think they have a soft thing on.'

'Well, I can only do my best,' said Montgomery.

They lunched together; a silent and rather nervous repast, for Montgomery's mind was full of what was before him, and Wilson had himself more money at stake than he cared to lose.

Wilson's carriage and pair were at the door, the horses with blue-and-white rosettes at their ears, which were the colours of the Wilson Coal-Pits, well known on many a football field. At the avenue gate a crowd of some hundred pit-men and their wives gave a cheer as the carriage passed. To the assistant it all seemed dreamlike and extraordinary – the strangest experience of his life, but with a thrill of human action and interest in it which made it passionately absorbing. He lay back in the open carriage and saw the fluttering hand-kerchiefs from the doors and windows of the miners' cottages. Wilson had pinned a blue-and-white rosette upon his coat, and everybody knew him as their champion. 'Good luck, sir! good luck to thee!' they shouted from the roadside. He felt that he was like some unromantic knight riding down to sordid lists, but there was something of chivalry in it all the same. He fought for others as well as for himself. He might fail from want of skill or strength, but deep in his sombre soul he vowed that it should never be for want of heart.

Mr Fawcett was just mounting into his high-wheeled, spidery dogcart, with his little bit of blood between the shafts. He waved his whip and fell in behind the carriage. They overtook Purvis, the tomato-faced publican, upon the road, with his wife in her Sunday bonnet. They also dropped into the pro-cession, and then, as they traversed the seven miles of the high road to Croxley, their two-horsed, rosetted carriage became gradually the nucleus of a comet with a loosely radiating tail. From every side-road came the miners' carts, the humble, ramshackle traps, black and bulging with their loads of noisy, foul-tongued, open-hearted partisans. They trailed for a long quarter of a mile behind them – cracking, whipping, shouting, galloping, swearing. Horsemen and runners were mixed with the vehicles. And then suddenly a squad of the Sheffield Yeomanry, who were having their annual training in those parts, clattered and jingled out of a field, and rode as an escort to the carriage. Through the dust-clouds round him Montgomery saw the gleaming brass helmets, the bright coats, the tossing heads of the chargers and the delighted brown faces of the troopers. It was more dreamlike than ever.

And then, as they approached the monstrous, uncouth line of bottle-shaped buildings which marked the smelting-works of Croxley, their long, writhing snake of dust was headed off by another but longer one which wound across their path. The main road into which their own opened was filled by the rushing current of traps. The Wilson contingent halted until the others should get past. The iron-men cheered and groaned, according to their humour, as they whirled past their antagonist. Rough chaff flew back and forwards like iron nuts and splinters of coal. 'Brought him up, then!' 'Got t' hearse for to fetch him back?' 'Where's t' owd K-legs?' 'Mon, mon, have thy photograph took – 'twill mind thee of what thou used to look!' 'He fight? – he's nowt but a half-baked doctor!' 'Happen he'll doctor thy Croxley Champion afore he's through wi't.'

So they flashed at each other as the one side waited and the other passed. Then there came a rolling murmur swelling into a shout, and a great brake with four horses came clattering along, all streaming with salmon-pink ribbons. The driver wore a white hat with pink rosette, and beside him, on the high seat, were a man and a woman – she with her arm round his waist. Montgomery had one glimpse of them as they flashed past; he with a furry cap drawn low over his brow, a great frieze coat and a pink comforter round his throat; she brazen, red-headed, bright-coloured, laughing excitedly. The Master, for it was he, turned as he passed, gazed hard at Montgomery, and gave him a menacing, gap-toothed grin. It was a hard, wicked face, blue-jowled and craggy, with long, obstinate cheeks and inexorable eyes. The brake behind was full of patrons of the sport – flushed iron-foremen, heads of departments, managers. One was drinking from a metal flask, and raised it to Montgomery as he passed; and then the crowd thinned, and the Wilson cortège with their dragoons swept in at the rear of the others.

The road led away from Croxley, between curving green hills, gashed and polluted by the searchers for coal and iron. The whole country had been gutted, and vast piles of refuse and mountains of slag suggested the mighty chambers which the labour of man had burrowed beneath. On the left the road curved up to where a huge building, roofless and dismantled, stood crumbling and forlorn, with the light shining through the windowless squares.

'That's the old Arrowsmith's factory. That's where the fight is to be,' said Wilson. 'How are you feeling now?'

'Thank you, I was never better in my life,' Montgomery answered.

'By Gad, I like your nerve!' said Wilson, who was himself flushed and uneasy. 'You'll give us a fight for our money, come what may. That place on the right is the office, and that has been set aside as the dressing and weighing-room.'

The carriage drove up to it amidst the shouts of the folk upon the hillside. Lines of empty carriages and traps curved down upon the winding road, and a black crowd surged round the door of the ruined factory. The seats, as a huge placard announced, were five shillings, three shillings and a shilling, with half-price for dogs. The takings, deducting expenses, were to go to the winner, and it was already evident that a larger stake than a hundred pounds was in question. A babel of voices rose from the door. The workers wished to bring their dogs in free. The men scuffled. The dogs barked. The crowd was a whirling, eddying pool surging with a roar up to the narrow cleft which was its only outlet.

The brake, with its salmon-coloured streamers and four reeking horses, stood empty before the door of the office; Wilson, Purvis, Fawcett and Montgomery passed in.

There was a large, bare room inside with square, clean patches upon the grimy walls, where pictures and almanacs had once hung. Worn linoleum covered the floor, but there was no furniture save some benches and a deal table with a ewer and a basin upon it. Two of the corners were curtained off. In the middle of the room was a weighing-chair. A hugely fat man, with a salmon tie and a blue waistcoat with birds'-eye spots, came bustling up to them. It was Armitage, the butcher and grazier, well known for miles round as a warm man, and the most liberal patron of sport in the Riding. 'Well, well,' he grunted, in a thick, fussy, wheezy voice, 'you have come, then. Got your man? Got your man?'

'Here he is, fit and well. Mr Montgomery, let me present you to Mr Armitage.'

'Glad to meet you, sir. Happy to make your acquaintance. I make bold to say, sir, that we of Croxley admire your courage, Mr Montgomery, and that our only hope is a fair fight and no favour, and the best man win. That's our sentiments at Croxley.'

'And it is my sentiment, also,' said the assistant.

'Well, you can't say fairer than that, Mr Montgomery. You've taken a large contrac' in hand, but a large contrac' may be carried through, sir, as anyone that knows my dealings could testify. The Master is ready to weigh in!'

'So am I.'

'You must weigh in the buff.' Montgomery looked askance at the tall, red-headed woman who was standing gazing out of the window.

'That's all right,' said Wilson. 'Get behind the curtain and put on your fighting kit.'

He did so, and came out the picture of an athlete, in white, loose drawers, canvas shoes, and the sash of a well-known cricket club round his waist. He was trained to a hair, his skin gleaming like silk, and every muscle rippling down his broad shoulders and along his beautiful arms as he moved them. They bunched into ivory knobs, or slid into long, sinuous curves, as he raised or lowered his hands.

'What thinkest thou o' that?' asked Ted Barton, his second, of the woman in the window.

She glanced contemptuously at the young athlete. 'It's but a poor kindness thou dost him to put a thread-paper yoong gentleman like yon against a mon as is a mon. Why, my Jock would throttle him wi' one hond lashed behind him.'

'Happen he may – happen not,' said Barton. 'I have but twa pund in the world, but it's on him, every penny, and no hedgin'. But here's t' Maister, and rarely fine he do look.'

The prize-fighter had come out from his curtain, a squat, formidable figure, monstrous in chest and arms, limping slightly on his distorted leg.

His skin bad none of the freshness and clearness of Montgomery's, but was dusky and mottled, with one huge mole amid the mat of tangled black hair which thatched his mighty breast. His weight bore no relation to his strength, for those huge shoulders and great arms, with brown, sledge-hammer fists, would have fitted the heaviest man that ever threw his cap into a ring. But his loins and legs were slight in proportion. Montgomery, on the other hand, was as symmetrical as a Greek statue. It would be an encounter between a man who was specially fitted for one sport, and one who was equally capable of any. The two looked curiously at each other: a bulldog, and a high-bred clean-limbed terrier, each full of spirit.

'How do you do?'

'How do?' The Master grinned again, and his three jagged front teeth gleamed for an instant. The rest had been beaten out of him in twenty years of battle. He spat upon the floor. 'We have a rare fine day for't.'

'Capital,' said Montgomery.

'That's the good feelin' I like,' wheezed the fat butcher. 'Good lads, both of them! – prime lads! – hard meat an' good bone. There's no ill-feelin'.'

'If he downs me, Gawd bless him!' said the Master,

'An' if we down him, Gawd help him!' interrupted the woman.

'Haud thy tongue, wench!' said the Master, impatiently. 'Who art thou to put in thy word? Happen I might draw my hand across thy face.'

The woman did not take the threat amiss. 'Wilt have enough for thy hand to do, Jock,' said she. 'Get quit o' this gradely man afore thou turn on me.'

The lovers' quarrel was interrupted by the entrance of a newcomer, a gentleman with a fur-collared overcoat and a very shiny top-hat – a top-hat of a degree of glossiness which is seldom seen five miles from Hyde Park. This hat he wore at the extreme back of his head, so that the lower surface of the brim made a kind of frame for his high, bald forehead, his keen eyes, his rugged and yet kindly face. He bustled in with the quiet air of possession with which the ringmaster enters the circus.

'It's Mr Stapleton, the referee from London,' said Wilson. 'How do you do, Mr Stapleton? I was introduced to you at the big fight at the Corinthian Club in Piccadilly.'

'Ah! I dare say,' said the other, shaking hands. 'Fact is, I'm introduced to so many that I can't undertake to carry their names. Wilson, is it? Well, Mr Wilson, glad to see you. Couldn't get a fly at the station, and that's why I'm late.'

'I'm sure, sir,' said Armitage, 'we should be proud that anyone so well known in the boxing world should come down to our little exhibition.'

'Not at all. Not at all. Anything in the interests of boxin'. All ready? Men weighed?'

'Weighing now, sir.'

647

'Ah! Just as well that I should see it done. Seen you before, Craggs. Saw you fight your second battle against Willox. You had beaten him once, but he came back on you. What does the indicator say – a hundred and sixty-three pounds – two off for the kit – a hundred and sixty-one. Now, my lad, you jump. My goodness, what colours are you wearing?'

'The Anonymi Cricket Club.'

'What right have you to wear them? I belong to the club myself.'

'So do I.'

'You an amateur?'

'Yes, sir.'

'And you are fighting for a money prize?'

'Yes.'

'I suppose you know what you are doing? You realise that you're a professional pug from this onwards, and that if ever you fight again – '

'I'll never fight again.'

'Happen you won't,' said the woman, and the Master turned a terrible eye upon her.

'Well, I suppose you know your own business best. Up you jump. One hundred and fifty-one, minus two, a hundred and forty-nine – twelve pounds' difference, but youth and condition on the other scale. Well, the sooner we get to work the better, for I wish to catch the seven o'clock express at Hellifield. Twenty three-minute rounds, with one-minute intervals, and Queensberry rules. Those are the conditions, are they not?'

'Yes, sir.'

'Very good, then – we may go across.'

The two combatants had overcoats thrown over their shoulders, and the whole party, backers, fighters, seconds and the referee filed out of the room. A police inspector was waiting for them in the road. He had a note-book in his hand – that terrible weapon which awes even the London cabman.

'I must take your names, gentlemen, in case it should be necessary to proceed for breach of peace.'

'You don't mean to stop the fight?' cried Armitage, in a passion of indignation. 'I'm Mr Armitage, of Croxley, and this is Mr Wilson, and we'll be responsible that all is fair and as it should be.'

'I'll take the names in case it should be necessary to proceed,' said the inspector, impassively.

'But you know me well.'

'If you was a dook or even a judge it would be all the same,' said the inspector. 'It's the law, and there's an end. I'll not take upon myself to stop the fight, seeing that gloves are to be used, but I'll take the names of all concerned. Silas Craggs, Robert Montgomery, Edward Barton, James Stapleton of London. Who seconds Silas Craggs?'

'I do,' said the woman. 'Yes, you can stare, but it's my job, and no one else's. Anastasia's the name – four a's.'

'Craggs?'

'Johnson – Anastasia Johnson. If you jug him you can jug me.'

'Who talked of juggin', ye fool?' growled the Master. 'Coom on, Mr Armitage, for I'm fair sick o' this loiterin'.'

The inspector fell in with the procession, and proceeded, as they walked up the hill, to bargain in his official capacity for a front seat, where he could safeguard the interests of the law, and in his private capacity to lay out thirty shillings at seven to one with Mr Armitage. Through the door they passed, down a narrow lane walled with a dense bank of humanity, up a wooden ladder to a platform, over a rope which was slung waist-high from four corner-stakes, and then Montgomery realised that he was in that ring in which his immediate destiny was to be worked out. On the stake at one corner there hung a blue-and-white streamer. Barton led him across, the overcoat dangling loosely from his shoulders, and he sat down on a wooden stool. Barton and another man, both wearing white sweaters, stood beside him. The so-called ring was a square, twenty feet each way. At the opposite angle was the sinister figure of the Master, with his red-headed woman and a rough-faced friend to look after him. At each corner were metal basins, pitchers of water, and sponges.

During the hubbub and uproar of the entrance Montgomery was too bewildered to take things in. But now there was a few minutes' delay, for the referee had lingered behind, and so he looked quietly about him. It was a sight to haunt him for a lifetime. Wooden seats had been built in, sloping upwards to the tops of the walls. Above, instead of a ceiling, a great flight of crows passed slowly across a square of grey cloud. Right up to the topmost benches the folk were banked – broadcloth in front, corduroys and fustian behind; faces turned everywhere upon him. The grey reek of the pipes filled the building, and the air was pungent with the acrid smell of cheap, strong tobacco. Everywhere among the human faces were to be seen the heads of the dogs. They growled and yapped from the back benches. In that dense mass of humanity, one could hardly pick out individuals, but Montgomery's eyes caught the brazen gleam of the helmets held upon the knees of the ten yeomen of his escort. At the very edge of the platform sat the reporters, five of them – three locals and two all the way from London. But where was the all-important referee? There was no sign of him, unless he were in the centre of that angry swirl of men near the door.

Mr Stapleton had stopped to examine the gloves which were to be used, and entered the building after the combatants. He had started to come down that narrow lane with the human walls which led to the ring. But already it had gone abroad that the Wilson champion was a gentleman, and that another gentleman had been appointed as referee. A wave of suspicion passed through the Croxley folk. They would have one of their own people for a referee. They would not have a stranger. His path was stopped as he made for the ring. Excited men flung themselves in front of him; they waved their fists in his face and cursed him. A woman howled vile names in his ear. Somebody struck at him with an umbrella. 'Go thou back to Lunnon. We want noan o' thee. Go thou back!' they yelled.

Stapleton, with his shiny hat cocked backwards, and his large, bulging forehead swelling from under it, looked round him from beneath his bushy brows. He was in the centre of a savage and dangerous mob. Then he drew his watch from his pocket and held it dial upwards in his palm.

'In three minutes,' said he, 'I will declare the fight off.'

They raged round him. His cool face and that aggressive top-hat irritated them. Grimy hands were raised. But it was difficult, somehow, to strike a man who was so absolutely indifferent.

'In two minutes I declare the fight off.'

They exploded into blasphemy. The breath of angry men smoked into his placid face. A gnarled, grimy fist vibrated at the end of his nose. 'We tell thee we want noan o' thee. Get thou back where thou com'st from.'

'In one minute I declare the fight off.'

Then the calm persistence of the man conquered the swaying, mutable, passionate crowd.

'Let him through, mon. Happen there'll be no fight after a'.'

'Let him through.'

'Bill, thou loomp, let him pass. Dost want the fight declared off?'

'Make room for the referee! – room for the Lunnon referee!'

And half pushed, half carried, he was swept up to the ring. There were two chairs by the side of it, one for him and one for the timekeeper. He sat down, his hands on his knees, his hat at a more wonderful angle than ever, impassive but solemn, with the aspect of one who appreciates his responsibilities.

Mr Armitage, the portly butcher, made his way into the ring and held up two fat hands, sparkling with rings, as a signal for silence.

'Gentlemen!' he yelled. And then in a crescendo shriek, 'Gentlemen!'

'And ladies!' cried somebody, for, indeed, there was a fair sprinkling of women among the crowd. 'Speak up, owd man!' shouted another. 'What price pork chops?' cried somebody at the back. Everybody laughed, and the dogs began to bark. Armitage waved his hands amidst the uproar as if he were conducting an orchestra. At last the babel thinned into silence.

'Gentlemen,' he yelled, 'the match is between Silas Craggs, whom we call the Master of Croxley, and Robert Montgomery, of the Wilson Coal-Pits. The match was to be under eleven-eight. When they were weighed just now, Craggs weighed eleven-seven and Montgomery ten-nine. The conditions of the contest are the best of twenty three-minute rounds with two-ounce gloves. Should the fight run to its full length, it will, of course, be decided upon points. Mr Stapleton, the well-known London referee, has kindly consented to see fair play. I wish to say that Mr Wilson and I, the chief backers of the two men, have every confidence in Mr Stapleton, and that we beg that you will accept his rulings without dispute.'

He then turned from one combatant to the other, with a wave of his hand.

THREE

'Montgomery – Craggs!' said he.

A great hush fell over the huge assembly. Even the dogs stopped yapping; one might have thought that the monstrous room was empty. The two men had stood up, the small white gloves over their hands They advanced from their corners and shook hands, Montgomery gravely, Craggs with a smile. Then they fell into position. The crowd gave a long sigh – the intake of a thousand excited breaths. The referee tilted his chair on to its back legs, and looked moodily critical from the one to the other.

It was strength against activity – that was evident from the first. The Master stood stolidly upon his K leg. It gave him a tremendous pedestal; one could hardly imagine his being knocked down. And he could pivot round upon it with extraordinary quickness; but his advance or retreat was ungainly. His frame, however, was so much larger and broader than that of the student, and his brown, massive face looked so resolute and menacing that the hearts of the Wilson party sank within them. There was one heart, however, which had not done so. It was that of Robert Montgomery.

Any nervousness which he may have had completely passed away now that he had his work before him. Here was something definite – this hard-faced, deformed Hercules to beat, with a career as the price of beating him. He glowed with the joy of action; it thrilled through his nerves. He faced his man with little in-and-out steps, breaking to the left, breaking to the right, feeling his way, while Craggs, with a dull, malignant eye, pivoted slowly upon his weak leg, his left arm half extended, his right sunk low across the mark. Montgomery led with his left, and then led again, getting lightly home each time. He tried again, but the Master had his counter ready, and Montgomery reeled back from a harder blow than he had given. Anastasia, the woman, gave a shrill cry of encouragement, and her man let fly his right. Montgomery ducked under it, and in an instant the two were in each other's arms.

'Break away! Break away!' said the referee.

The Master struck upwards on the break, and shook Montgomery with the blow. Then it was time. It had been a spirited opening round. The people buzzed into comment and applause. Montgomery was quite fresh, but the hairy chest of the Master was rising and falling. The man passed a sponge over his head while Anastasia flapped the towel before him. 'Good lass! good lass!' cried the crowd, and cheered her.

The men were up again, the Master grimly watchful, Montgomery as alert as a kitten. The Master tried a sudden rush, squattering along with his awkward gait, but coming faster than one would think. The student slipped aside and avoided him. The Master stopped, grinned, and shook his head. Then he motioned with his hand as an invitation to Montgomery to come to him. The student did so and led with his left, but got a swinging right counter in the ribs in exchange. The heavy blow staggered him, and the Master came scrambling in to complete his advantage; but Montgomery, with his greater activity, kept out of danger until the call of time. A tame round, and the advantage with the Master.

'T' Maister's too strong for him,' said a smelter to his neighbour.

'Ay; but t'other's a likely lad. Happen we'll see some sport yet. He can joomp rarely.'

'But t' Maister can stop and hit rarely. Happen he'll mak' him joomp when he gets his nief upon him.'

They were up again, the water glistening upon their faces. Montgomery led instantly, and got his right home with a sounding smack upon the Master's forehead. There was a shout from the colliers, and 'Silence! Order!' from the referee. Montgomery avoided the counter, and scored with his left. Fresh applause, and the referee upon his feet in indignation. 'No comments, gentlemen, if *you* please, during the rounds.'

'Just bide a bit!' growled the Master.

'Don't talk – fight!' said the referee, angrily.

Montgomery rubbed in the point by a flush hit upon the mouth, and the Master shambled back to his corner like an angry bear, having had all the worst of the round.

'Where's thot seven to one?' shouted Purvis, the publican. 'I'll take six to one!'

There were no answers.

'Five to one!'

There were givers at that. Purvis booked them in a tattered notebook.

Montgomery began to feel happy. He lay back with his legs outstretched, his back against the corner-post, and one gloved hand upon each rope. What a delicious minute it was between each round. If he could only keep out of harm's way, he must surely wear this man out before the end of twenty rounds. He was so slow that all his strength went for nothing.

'You're fightin' a winnin' fight – a winnin' fight,' Ted Barton whispered in his ear. 'Go canny; tak' no chances; you have him proper.'

But the Master was crafty. He had fought so many battles with his maimed limb that he knew how to make the best of it. Warily and slowly he manoeuvred round Montgomery, stepping forward and yet again forward until he had imperceptibly backed him into his corner. The student suddenly saw a flash of triumph upon the grim face, and a gleam in the dull, malignant eyes. The Master was upon him. He sprang aside and was on the ropes. The Master smashed in one of his terrible upper-cuts, and Montgomery half broke it with his guard. The student sprang the other way and was against the other converging rope. He was trapped in the angle. The Master sent in another with a hoggish grunt which spoke of the energy behind it. Montgomery ducked, but got a jab from the left upon the mark. He closed with his man.

'Break away! Break away!' cried the referee. Montgomery disengaged, and got a swinging blow on the ear as he did so. It had been a damaging round for him, and the Croxley people were shouting their delight. 'Gentlemen, I will *not* have this noise!' Stapleton roared. 'I have been accustomed to preside at a well-conducted club, and not at a bear-garden.' This little man, with the tilted hat and the bulging forehead, dominated the whole assembly. He was like a headmaster among his boys. He glared round him, and nobody cared to meet his eye.

Anastasia had kissed the Master when he resumed his seat. 'Good lass. Do't again!' cried the laughing crowd, and the angry Master shook his glove at her, as she flapped her towel in front of him. Montgomery was weary and a little sore, but not depressed. He had learned something. He would not again be tempted into danger.

For three rounds the honours were fairly equal. The student's hitting was the quicker, the Master's the harder. Profiting by his lesson, Montgomery kept himself in the open, and refused to be herded into a corner. Sometimes the Master succeeded in rushing him to the side-ropes, but the younger man slipped away, or closed and then disengaged. The monotonous, 'Break away! Break away!' of the referee broke in upon the quick, low patter of rubber-soled shoes, the dull thud of the blows, and the sharp, hissing breath of two tired men.

The ninth round found both of them in fairly good condition. Montgomery's head was still singing from the blow that he had in the corner, and one of his thumbs pained him acutely and seemed to be dislocated. The Master showed no sign of a touch, but his breathing was the more laboured, and a long line of ticks upon the referee's paper showed that the student had a good show of points. But one of this iron-man's blows was worth three of his, and he knew that without the gloves he could not have stood for three rounds against him. All the amateur work that he had done was the merest tapping and flapping when compared to those frightful blows from arms toughened by the shovel and the crowbar.

It was the tenth round, and the fight was half over. The betting now was only three to one, for the Wilson champion had held his own much better than had been expected. But those who knew the ring-craft as well as the staying power of the old prizefighter knew that the odds were still a long way in his favour.

'Have a care of him!' whispered Barton, as he sent his man up to the scratch. 'Have a care! He'll play thee a trick, if he can.'

But Montgomery saw, or imagined he saw, that his antagonist was tiring. He looked jaded and listless, and his hands drooped a little from their position. His own youth and condition were beginning to tell. He sprang in and brought off a fine left-handed lead. The Master's return lacked his usual fire. Again Montgomery led, and again he got home. Then he tried his right upon the mark, and the Master guarded it downwards.

'Too low! Too low! A foul! A foul!' yelled a thousand voices.

The referee rolled his sardonic eyes slowly round. 'Seems to me this buildin' is chock-full of referees,' said he. The people laughed and applauded, but their favour was as immaterial to him as their anger. 'No applause, please! This is not a theatre!' he yelled.

Montgomery was very pleased with himself. His adversary was evidently in a bad way. He was piling on his points and establishing a lead. He might as well make hay while the sun shone. The Master was looking all abroad. Montgomery popped one upon his blue jowl and got away without a return. And then the Master suddenly dropped both his hands and began rubbing his thigh. Ah! that was it, was it? He had muscular cramp.

'Go in! Go in!' cried Teddy Barton.

Montgomery sprang wildly forward, and the next instant was lying half senseless, with his neck nearly broken, in the middle of the ring.

The whole round had been a long conspiracy to tempt him within reach of one of those terrible right-hand upper-cuts for which the Master was famous. For this the listless, weary bearing, for this the cramp in the thigh. When Montgomery had sprung in so hotly he had exposed himself to such a blow as neither flesh nor blood could stand. Whizzing up from below with a rigid arm, which put the Master's eleven stone into its force, it struck him under the jaw; he whirled half round, and fell a helpless and half-paralysed mass. A vague groan and murmur, inarticulate, too excited for words, rose from the great audience. With open mouths and staring eyes they gazed at the twitching and quivering figure.

'Stand back! Stand right back!' shrieked the referee, for the Master was standing over his man ready to give him the *coup-de-grâce* as he rose.

'Stand back, Craggs, this instant!' Stapleton repeated.

The Master sank his hands sulkily and walked backwards to the rope with his ferocious eyes fixed upon his fallen antagonist. The timekeeper called the seconds. If ten of them passed before Montgomery rose to his feet, the fight was ended. Ted Barton wrung his hands and danced about in an agony in his corner.

As if in a dream – a terrible nightmare – the student could hear the voice of the timekeeper – three – four – five – he got up on his hand – six – seven – he was on his knee, sick, swimming, faint, but resolute to rise. Eight – he was up, and the Master was on him like a tiger, lashing savagely at him with both hands. Folk held their breath as they watched those terrible blows, and anticipated the pitiful end – so much more pitiful where a game but helpless man refuses to accept defeat.

Strangely automatic is the human brain. Without volition, without effort, there shot into the memory of this bewildered, staggering, half-stupefied man the one thing which could have saved him – that blind eye of which the Master's son had spoken. It was the same as the other to look at, but Montgomery remembered that he had said that it was the left. He reeled to the left side, half felled by a drive which lit upon his shoulder. The Master pivoted round upon his leg and was at him in an instant.

'Yark him, lad! Yark him!' screamed the woman.

'Hold your tongue!' said the referee.

Montgomery slipped to the left again and yet again, but the Master was too quick and clever for him. He struck round and got him full on the face as he tried once more to break away. Montgomery's knees weakened under him, and he fell with a groan on the floor. This time he knew that he was done. With bitter agony he realised, as he groped blindly with his hands, that he could not possibly raise himself. Far away and muffled he heard, amid the murmurs of the multitude, the fateful voice of the timekeeper counting off the seconds.

'One – two – three – four – five – six – '

'Time!' said the referee.

Then the pent-up passion of the great assembly broke loose. Croxley gave a deep groan of disappointment. The Wilsons were on their feet, yelling with delight. There was still a chance for them. In four more seconds their man would have been solemnly counted out. But now he had a minute in which to recover. The referee looked round with relaxed features and laughing eyes. He loved this rough game, this school for humble heroes, and it was pleasant to him to intervene as a *deus ex machina* at so dramatic a moment. His chair and his hat were both tilted at an extreme angle; he and the timekeeper smiled at each other. Ted Barton and the other second had rushed out and thrust an arm each under Montgomery's knee, the other behind his loins, and so carried him back to his stool. His head lolled upon his shoulder, but a douche of cold water sent a shiver through him, and he started and looked round him.

'He's a' right!' cried the people round. 'He's a rare brave lad. Good lad! Good lad!' Barton poured some brandy into his mouth. The mists cleared a little, and he realised where he was and what he had to do. But he was still very weak, and he hardly dared to hope that he could survive another round.

'Seconds out of the ring!' cried the referee. 'Time!'

The Croxley Master sprang eagerly off his stool.

'Keep clear of him! Go easy for a bit,' said Barton, and Montgomery walked out to meet his man once more.

He had had two lessons – the one when the Master got him into his corner, the other when he had been lured into mixing it up with so powerful an antagonist. Now he would be wary. Another blow would finish him; he could afford to run no risks. The Master was determined to follow up his advantage, and rushed at him, slogging furiously right and left. But Montgomery was too young and active to be caught. He was strong upon his legs once more, and his wits had all come back to him. It was a gallant sight – the line-of-battle ship trying to pour its overwhelming broadside into the frigate, and the frigate manoeuvring always so as to avoid it. The Master tried all his ring-craft. He coaxed the student up by pretended inactivity; he rushed at him with furious rushes towards the ropes. For three rounds he exhausted every wile in trying to get at him. Montgomery during all this time was conscious that his strength was minute by minute coming back to him. The spinal jar from an upper-cut is overwhelming, but evanescent. He was losing all sense of it beyond a great stiffness of the neck. For the first round after his downfall he had been content to be entirely on the defensive, only too happy if he could stall off the furious attacks of the Master. In the second he occasionally ventured upon a light counter. In the third he was smacking back merrily where he saw an opening. His people yelled their approval of him at the end of every round. Even the iron-workers cheered him with that fine unselfishness which true sport engenders. To most of them, unspiritual and unimaginative, the sight of this clean-limbed young Apollo, rising above disaster and holding on while consciousness was in him to his appointed task, was the greatest thing their experience had ever known.

But the Master's naturally morose temper became more and more murderous at this postponement of his hopes. Three rounds ago the battle had been in his hands; now it was all to do over again. Round by round his man was recovering his strength. By the fifteenth he was strong again in wind and limb. But the vigilant Anastasia saw something which encouraged her.

'That bash in t' ribs is telling on him, Jock,' she whispered. 'Why else should he be gulping t' brandy? Go in, lad, and thou hast him yet.'

Montgomery had suddenly taken the flask from Barton's hand, and had a deep pull at the contents. Then, with his face a little flushed, and with a curious look of purpose, which made the referee stare hard at him, in his eyes, he rose for the sixteenth round.

'Game as a pairtridge!' cried the publican, as he looked at the hard-set face.

'Mix it oop, lad! Mix it oop!' cried the iron-men to their Master. And then a hum of exultation ran through their ranks as they realised that their tougher, harder, stronger man held the vantage, after all. Neither of the men showed much sign of punishment. Small gloves crush and numb, but they do not cut. One of the Master's eyes was even more flush with his cheek than Nature had made it. Montgomery had two or three livid marks upon his body, and his face was haggard, save for that pink spot which the brandy had brought into either cheek. He rocked a little as he stood opposite his man, and his hands drooped as if he felt the gloves to be an unutterable weight. It was evident that he was spent and desperately weary. If he received one other blow it must surely be fatal to him. If he brought one home, what power could there be behind it, and what chance was there of its harming the colossus in front of him? It was the crisis of the fight. This round must decide it. 'Mix it oop, lad! Mix it oop!' the iron-men whooped. Even the savage eyes of the referee were unable to restrain the excited crowd.

Now, at last, the chance had come for Montgomery. He had learned a lesson from his more experienced rival. Why should he not play his own game upon him? He was spent, but not nearly so spent as he pretended. That brandy was to call up his reserves, to let him have strength to take full advantage of the opening when it came. It was thrilling and tingling through his veins at the very moment when he was lurching and rocking like a beaten man. He acted his part admirably. The Master felt that there was an easy task before him, and rushed in with ungainly activity to finish it once for all. He slap-banged away left and right, boring Montgomery up against the ropes, swinging in his ferocious blows with those animal grunts which told of the vicious energy behind them.

But Montgomery was too cool to fall a victim to any of those murderous upper-cuts. He kept out of harm's way with a rigid guard, an active foot, and a head which was swift to duck. And yet he contrived to present the same appearance of a man who is hopelessly done. The Master, weary from his own shower of blows, and fearing nothing from so weak a man, dropped his hand for an instant, and at that instant Montgomery's right came home.

It was a magnificent blow, straight, clean, crisp, with the force of the loins and the back behind it. And it landed where he had meant it to – upon the exact point of that blue-grained chin. Flesh and blood could not stand such a blow in such a place. Neither valour nor hardihood can save the man to whom it comes. The Master fell backwards, flat, prostrate, striking the ground with so simultaneous a clap that it was like a shutter falling from a wall. A yell, which no referee could control, broke from the crowded benches as the giant went down. He lay upon his back, his knees a little drawn up, his huge chest panting. He twitched and shook, but could not move. His feet pawed convulsively once or twice. It was no use. He was done. 'Eight – nine – ten!' said the timekeeper, and the roar of a thousand voices, with a deafening clap like the broadside of a ship, told that the Master of Croxley was the Master no more.

Montgomery stood half dazed, looking down at the huge, prostrate figure. He could hardly realise that it was indeed all over. He saw the referee motion towards him with his hand. He heard his name bellowed in triumph from every side. And then he was aware of someone rushing towards him; he caught a glimpse of a flushed face and an aureole of flying red hair, a gloveless fist struck him between the eyes, and he was on his back in the ring beside his antagonist, while a dozen of his supporters were endeavouring to secure the frantic Anastasia. He heard the angry shouting of the referee, the screaming of the furious woman and the cries of the mob. Then something seemed to break like an over-stretched banjo string, and he sank into the deep, deep, mist-girt abyss of unconsciousness.

The dressing was like a thing in a dream, and so was a vision of the Master with the grin of a bulldog upon his face, and his three teeth amiably protruded. He shook Montgomery heartily by the hand.

'I would have been rare pleased to shake thee by the throttle, lad, a short while syne,' said he. 'But I bear no ill-feeling again' thee. It was a rare poonch that brought me down – I have not had a better since my second fight wi' Billy Edwards in '89. Happen thou might think o' goin' further wi' this business. If thou dost, and want a trainer, there's not much inside t' ropes as I don't know. Or happen thou might like to try it wi' me old style and bare knuckles. Thou hast but to write to t' ironworks to find me.'

But Montgomery disclaimed any such ambition. A canvas bag with his share – a hundred and ninety sovereigns – was handed to him, of which he gave ten to the Master, who also received some share of the gate-money. Then, with young Wilson escorting him on one side, Purvis on the other, and Fawcett carrying his bag behind, he went in triumph to his carriage, and drove amid a long roar, which lined the highway like a hedge for the seven miles, back to his starting-point.

'It's the greatest thing I ever saw in my life. By George, it's ripping!' cried Wilson, who had been left in a kind of ecstasy by the events of the day. 'There's a chap over Barnsley way who fancies himself a bit. Let us spring you on him, and let him see what he can make of you. We'll put up a purse – won't we, Purvis? You shall never want a backer.'

'At his weight,' said the publican, 'I'm behind him, I am, for twenty rounds, and no age, country or colour barred.'

'So am I,' cried Fawcett; 'middleweight champion of the world, that's what he is – here, in the same carriage with us.'

But Montgomery was not to be beguiled.

'No; I have my own work to do now.'

'And what may that be?'

'I'll use this money to get my medical degree.'

'Well, we've plenty of doctors, but you're the only man in the Riding that could smack the Croxley Master off his legs. However, I suppose you know your own business best. When you're a doctor, you'd best come down into these parts, and you'll always find a job waiting for you at the Wilson Coal-Pits.'

Montgomery had returned by devious ways to the surgery. The horses were smoking at the door, and the doctor was just back from his long journey. Several patients had called in his absence, and he was in the worst of tempers.

'I suppose I should be glad that you have come back at all, Mr Montgomery!' he snarled. 'When next you elect to take a holiday, I trust it will not be at so busy a time.'

'I am sorry, sir, that you should have been inconvenienced.'

'Yes, sir, I have been exceedingly inconvenienced.' Here, for the first time, he looked hard at the assistant. 'Good Heavens, Mr Montgomery, what have you been doing with your left eye?'

It was where Anastasia had lodged her protest. Montgomery laughed. 'It is nothing, sir,' said he.

'And you have a livid mark under your jaw. It is, indeed, terrible that my representative should be going about in so disreputable a condition. How did you receive these injuries?'

'Well, sir, as you know, there was a little glove-fight today over at Croxley.'

'And you got mixed up with that brutal crowd?'

'I *was* rather mixed up with them.'

'And who assaulted you?'

'One of the fighters.'

'Which of them?'

'The Master of Croxley.'

'Good Heavens! Perhaps you interfered with him?'

'Well, to tell the truth, I did a little.'

'Mr Montgomery, in such a practice as mine, intimately associated as it is with the highest and most progressive elements of our small community, it is impossible – '

But just then the tentative bray of a cornet-player searching for his key-note jarred upon their ears, and an instant later the Wilson Colliery brass band was in full cry with 'See the Conquering Hero Comes' outside the surgery window. There was a banner waving and a shouting crowd of miners.

'What is it? What does it mean?' cried the angry doctor.

'It means, sir, that I have, in the only way which was open to me, earned the money which is necessary for my education. It is my duty, Dr Oldacre, to warn you that I am about to return to the university, and that you should lose no time in appointing my successor.'

The New Catacomb

'Look here, Burger,' said Kennedy, 'I do wish that you would confide in me.'

The two famous students of Roman remains sat together in Kennedy's comfortable room overlooking the Corso. The night was cold, and they had both pulled up their chairs to the unsatisfactory Italian stove which threw out a zone of stuffiness rather than of warmth.

Outside under the bright winter stars lay the modern Rome, the long, double chain of the electric lamps, the brilliantly lighted cafés, the rushing carriages, and the dense throng upon the footpaths. But inside, in the sumptuous chamber of the rich young English archaeologist, there was only old Rome to be seen. Cracked and time-worn friezes hung upon the walls, grey old busts of senators and soldiers with their fighting heads and their hard, cruel faces peered out from the corners. On the centre table, amidst a litter of inscriptions, fragments and ornaments, there stood the famous reconstruction by Kennedy of the Baths of Caracalla, which excited such interest and admiration when it was exhibited in Berlin.

Amphorae hung from the ceiling, and a litter of curiosities strewed the rich red Turkey carpet. And of them all there was not one which was not of the most unimpeachable authenticity, and of the utmost rarity and value; for Kennedy, though little more than thirty, had a European reputation in this particular branch of research, and was, moreover, provided with that long purse which either proves to be a fatal handicap to the student's energies, or, if his mind is still true to its purpose, gives him an enormous advantage in the race for fame. Kennedy had often been seduced by whim and pleasure from his studies, but his mind was an incisive one, capable of long and concentrated efforts which ended in sharp reactions of sensuous languor. His handsome face, with its high, white forehead, its aggressive nose, and its somewhat loose and sensuous mouth, was a fair index of the compromise between strength and weakness in his nature.

Of a very different type was his companion, Julius Burger. He came of a curious blend, a German father and an Italian mother, with the robust qualities of the North mingling strangely with the softer graces of the South. Blue Teutonic eyes lightened his sun-browned face, and above them rose a square, massive forehead, with a fringe of close yellow curls lying round it. His strong, firm jaw was clean-shaven, and his companion had frequently remarked how much it suggested those old Roman busts which peered out from the shadows in the corners of his chamber. Under its bluff German strength there lay always a suggestion of Italian subtlety, but the smile was so honest, and the eyes so frank, that one understood that this was only an indication of his ancestry, with no actual bearing upon his character.

In age and in reputation he was on the same level as his English companion, but his life and his work had both been far more arduous. Twelve years before he had come as a poor student to Rome, and had lived ever since upon some small endowment for research which had been awarded to him by the University of Bonn.

Painfully, slowly and doggedly, with extraordinary tenacity and single-mindedness, he had climbed from rung to rung of the ladder of fame, until now he was a member of the Berlin Academy, and there was every reason to believe that he would shortly be promoted to the chair of the greatest of German universities. But the singleness of purpose which had brought him to the same high level as the rich and brilliant Englishman, had caused him in everything outside their work to stand infinitely below him. He had never found a pause in his studies in which to cultivate the social graces. It was only when he spoke of his own subject that his face was filled with life and soul. At other times he was silent and embarrassed, too conscious of his own limitations in larger subjects, and impatient of that small talk which is the conventional refuge of those who have no thoughts to express.

And yet for some years there had been an acquaintanceship which appeared to be slowly ripening into a friendship between these two very different rivals. The base and origin of this lay in the fact that in their own studies each was the only one of the younger men who had knowledge and enthusiasm enough properly to appreciate the other. Their common interests and pursuits had brought them together, and each had been attracted by the other's knowledge. And then gradually something had been added to this. Kennedy had been amused by the frankness and simplicity of his rival, while Burger in turn had been fascinated by the brilliancy and vivacity which had made Kennedy such a favourite in Roman society. I say 'had', because just at the moment the young Englishman was somewhat under a cloud.

A love affair, the details of which had never quite come out, had indicated a heartlessness and callousness upon his part which shocked many of his friends. But in the bachelor circles of students and artists in which he preferred to move there is no very rigid code of honour in such matters, and though a head might be shaken or a pair of shoulders shrugged over the flight of two and the return of one, the general sentiment was probably one of curiosity and perhaps of envy rather than of reprobation.

'Look here, Burger,' said Kennedy, looking hard at the placid face of his companion, 'I do wish that you would confide in me.'

As he spoke he waved his hand in the direction of a rug which lay upon the floor.

On the rug stood a long, shallow fruit-basket of the light wickerwork which is used in the Campagna, and this was heaped with a litter of objects, inscribed tiles, broken inscriptions, cracked mosaics, torn papyri, rusty metal ornaments, which to the uninitiated might have seemed to have come straight from a dustman's bin, but which a specialist would have speedily recognised as unique of their kind.

The pile of odds and ends in the flat wickerwork basket supplied exactly one of those missing links of social development which are of such interest to the student. It was the German who had brought them in, and the Englishman's eyes were hungry as he looked at them.

'I won't interfere with your treasure-trove, but I should very much like to hear about it,' he continued, while Burger very deliberately lit a cigar. 'It is evidently a discovery of the first importance. These inscriptions will make a sensation throughout Europe.'

'For every one here there are a million there!' said the German. 'There are so many that a dozen savants might spend a lifetime over them, and build up a reputation as solid as the Castle of St Angelo.'

Kennedy was thinking with his fine forehead wrinkled and his fingers playing with his long, fair moustache.

'You have given yourself away, Burger!' said he at last. 'Your words can only apply to one thing. You have discovered a new catacomb.'

'I had no doubt that you had already come to that conclusion from an examination of these objects.'

'Well, they certainly appeared to indicate it, but your last remarks make it certain. There is no place except a catacomb which could contain so vast a store of relics as you describe.'

'Quite so. There is no mystery about that. I *have* discovered a new catacomb.'

'Where?'

'Ah, that is my secret, my dear Kennedy! Suffice it that it is so situated that there is not one chance in a million of anyone else coming upon it. Its date is different from that of any known catacomb, and it has been reserved for the burial of the highest Christians, so that the remains and the relics are quite different from anything which has ever been seen before. If I was not aware of your knowledge and of your energy, my friend, I would not hesitate, under the pledge of secrecy, to tell you everything about it. But as it is I think that I must certainly prepare my own report of the matter before I expose myself to such formidable competition.'

Kennedy loved his subject with a love which was almost a mania – a love which held him true to it, amidst all the distractions which come to a wealthy and dissipated young man. He had ambition, but his ambition was secondary to his mere abstract joy and interest in everything which concerned the old life and history of the city. He yearned to see this new underworld which his companion had discovered.

'Look here, Burger,' said he, earnestly, 'I assure you that you can trust me most implicitly in the matter. Nothing would induce me to put pen to paper about anything which I see until I have your express permission. I quite understand your feeling, and I think it is most natural, but you have really nothing whatever to fear from me. On the other hand, if you don't tell me I shall make a systematic search, and I shall most certainly discover it. In that case, of course, I should make what use I liked of it, since I should be under no obligation to you.'

Burger smiled thoughtfully over his cigar.

'I have noticed, friend Kennedy,' said he, 'that when I want information over any point you are not always so ready to supply it.'

'When did you ever ask me anything that I did not tell you? You remember, for example, my giving you the material for your paper about the temple of the Vestals.'

'Ah, well, that was not a matter of much importance. If I were to question you upon some intimate thing, would you give me an answer, I wonder! This new catacomb is a very intimate thing to me, and I should certainly expect some sign of confidence in return.'

'What you are driving at I cannot imagine,' said the Englishman, 'but if you mean that you will answer my question about the catacomb if I answer any question which you may put to me, I can assure you that I will certainly do so.'

'Well, then,' said Burger, leaning luxuriously back in his settee, and puffing a blue tree of cigar-smoke into the air, 'tell me all about your relations with Miss Mary Saunderson.'

Kennedy sprang up in his chair and glared angrily at his impassive companion.

'What the devil do you mean?' he cried. 'What sort of a question is this? You may mean it as a joke, but you never made a worse one.'

'No, I don't mean it as a joke,' said Burger, simply. 'I am really rather interested in the details of the matter. I don't know much about the world and women and social life and that sort of thing, and such an incident has the fascination of the unknown for me. I know you, and I knew her by sight – I had even spoken to her once or twice. I should very much like to hear from your own lips exactly what it was which occurred between you.'

'I won't tell you a word.'

'That's all right. It was only my whim to see if you would give up a secret as easily as you expected me to give up my secret of the new catacomb. You wouldn't, and I didn't expect you to. But why should you expect otherwise of me? There's St John's clock striking ten. It is quite time that I was going home.'

'No, wait a bit, Burger,' said Kennedy; 'this is really a ridiculous caprice of yours to wish to know about an old love affair which has burned out months ago. You know we look upon a man who kisses and tells as the greatest coward and villain possible.'

'Certainly,' said the German, gathering up his basket of curiosities, 'when he tells anything about a girl which is previously unknown, he must be so. But in this case, as you must be aware, it was a public matter which was the common talk of Rome, so that you are not really doing Miss Mary Saunderson any injury by discussing her case with me. But still, I respect your scruples; and so good-night!'

'Wait a bit, Burger,' said Kennedy, laying his hand upon the other's arm; 'I am very keen upon this catacomb business, and I can't let it drop quite so easily. Would you mind asking me something else in return – something not quite so eccentric this time?'

'No, no; you have refused, and there is an end of it,' said Burger, with his basket on his arm. 'No doubt you are quite right not to answer, and no doubt I am quite right also – and so again, my dear Kennedy, good-night!'

The Englishman watched Burger cross the room, and he had his hand on the handle of the door before his host sprang up with the air of a man who is making the best of that which cannot be helped. 'Hold on, old fellow,' said he. 'I think you are behaving in a most ridiculous fashion, but still, if this is your condition, I suppose that I must submit to it. I hate saying anything about a girl, but, as you say, it is all over Rome, and I don't suppose I can tell you anything which you do not know already. What was it you wanted to know?'

The German came back to the stove, and, laying down his basket, he sank into his chair once more. 'May I have another cigar?' said he. 'Thank you very much! I never smoke when I work, but I enjoy a chat much more when I am under the influence of tobacco. Now, as regards this young lady, with whom you had this little adventure. What in the world has become of her?'

'She is at home with her own people.'

'Oh, really – in England?'

'Yes.'

'What part of England – London?'

'No, Twickenham.'

'You must excuse my curiosity, my dear Kennedy, and you must put it down to my ignorance of the world. No doubt it is quite a simple thing to persuade a young lady to go off with you for three weeks or so, and then to hand her over to her own family at – what did you call the place?'

'Twickenham.'

'Quite so – at Twickenham. But it is something so entirely outside my own experience that I cannot even imagine how you set about it. For example, if you had loved this girl your love could hardly disappear in three weeks, so I presume that you could not have loved her at all. But if you did not love her why should you make this great scandal which has damaged you and ruined her?'

Kennedy looked moodily into the red eye of the stove. 'That's a logical way of looking at it, certainly,' said he. 'Love is a big word, and it represents a good many different shades of feeling. I liked her, and – well, you say you've seen her – you know how charming she can look. But still I am willing to admit, looking back, that I could never have really loved her.'

'Then, my dear Kennedy, why did you do it?'

'The adventure of the thing had a great deal to do with it.'

'What! You are so fond of adventures!'

'Where would the variety of life be without them? It was for an adventure that I first began to pay my attentions to her. I've chased a good deal of game in my time, but there's no chase like that of a pretty woman. There was the piquant difficulty of it also, for, as she was the companion of Lady Emily Rood, it was almost impossible to see her alone. On the top of all the other obstacles which attracted me, I learned from her own lips very early in the proceedings that she was engaged.'

'Mein Gott! To whom?'

'She mentioned no names.'

'I do not think that anyone knows that. So that made the adventure more alluring, did it?'

'Well, it did certainly give a spice to it. Don't you think so?'

'I tell you that I am very ignorant about these things.'

'My dear fellow, you can remember that the apple you stole from your neighbour's tree was always sweeter than that which fell from your own. And then I found that she cared for me.'

'What – at once?'

'Oh, no, it took about three months of sapping and mining. But at last I won her over. She understood that my judicial separation from my wife made it impossible for me to do the right thing by her – but she came all the same, and we had a delightful time, as long as it lasted.'

'But how about the other man?'

Kennedy shrugged his shoulders. 'I suppose it is the survival of the fittest,' said he. 'If he had been the better man she would not have deserted him. Let's drop the subject, for I have had enough of it!'

'Only one other thing. How did you get rid of her in three weeks?'

'Well, we had both cooled down a bit, you understand. She absolutely refused, under any circumstances, to come back to face the people she had known in Rome. Now, of course, Rome is necessary to me, and I was already pining to be back at my work – so there was one obvious cause of separation.

Then, again, her old father turned up at the hotel in London, and there was a scene, and the whole thing became so unpleasant that really – though I missed her dreadfully at first – I was very glad to slip out of it. Now, I rely upon you not to repeat anything of what I have said.'

'My dear Kennedy, I should not dream of repeating it. But all that you say interests me very much, for it gives me an insight into your way of looking at things, which is entirely different from mine, for I have seen so little of life. And now you want to know about my new catacomb. There's no use my trying to describe it, for you would never find it by that. There is only one thing, and that is for me to take you there.'

'That would be splendid.'

'When would you like to come?'

'The sooner the better. I am all impatience to see it.'

'Well, it is a beautiful night – though a trifle cold. Suppose we start in an hour. We must be very careful to keep the matter to ourselves. If anyone saw us hunting in couples they would suspect that there was something going on.'

'We can't be too cautious,' said Kennedy. 'Is it far?'

'Some miles.'

'Not too far to walk?'

'Oh, no, we could walk there easily.'

'We had better do so, then. A cabman's suspicions would be aroused if he dropped us both at some lonely spot in the dead of the night.'

'Quite so. I think it would be best for us to meet at the gate of the Appian Way at midnight. I must go back to my lodgings for the matches and candles and things.'

'All right, Burger! I think it is very kind of you to let me into this secret, and I promise you that I will write nothing about it until you have published your report. Goodbye for the present! You will find me at the gate at twelve.'

The cold, clear air was filled with the musical chimes from that city of clocks as Burger, wrapped in an Italian overcoat, with a lantern hanging from his hand, walked up to the rendezvous. Kennedy stepped out of the shadow to meet him.

'You are ardent in work as well as in love!' said the German, laughing.

'Yes; I have been waiting here for nearly half an hour.'

'I hope you left no clue as to where we were going.'

'Not such a fool! By Jove, I am chilled to the bone! Come on, Burger, let us warm ourselves by a spurt of hard walking.'

Their footsteps sounded loud and crisp upon the rough stone paving of the disappointing road which is all that is left of the most famous highway of the world. A peasant or two going home from the wine-shop, and a few carts of country produce coming up to Rome, were the only things which they met. They swung along, with the huge tombs looming up through the darkness upon each side of them, until they had come as far as the Catacombs of St Calixtus, and saw against a rising moon the great circular bastion of Cecilia Metella in front of them. Then Burger stopped with his hand to his side. 'Your legs are longer than mine, and you are more accustomed to walking,' said he, laughing. 'I think that the place where we turn off is somewhere here. Yes, this is it, round the corner of the trattoria. Now, it is a very narrow path, so perhaps I had better go in front, and you can follow.' He had lit his lantern, and by its light they were enabled to follow a narrow and devious track which wound across the marshes of the Campagna. The great aqueduct of old Rome lay like a monstrous caterpillar across the moonlit landscape, and their road led them under one of its huge arches, and past the circle of crumbling bricks which marks the old arena. At last Burger stopped at a solitary wooden cowhouse, and he drew a key from his pocket.

'Surely your catacomb is not inside a house!' cried Kennedy.

'The entrance to it is. That is just the safeguard which we have against anyone else discovering it.'

'Does the proprietor know of it?'

'Not he. He had found one or two objects which made me almost certain that his house was built on the entrance to such a place. So I rented it from him, and did my excavations for myself. Come in, and shut the door behind you.'

It was a long, empty building, with the mangers of the cows along one wall. Burger put his lantern down on the ground, and shaded its light in all directions save one by draping his overcoat round it. 'It might excite remark if anyone saw a light in this lonely place,' said he. 'Just help me to move this boarding.' The flooring was loose in the corner, and plank by plank the two savants raised it and leaned it against the wall. Below there was a square aperture and a stair of old stone steps which led away down into the bowels of the earth.

'Be careful!' cried Burger, as Kennedy, in his impatience, hurried down them. 'It is a perfect rabbits' warren below, and if you were once to lose your way there, the chances would be a hundred to one against your ever coming out again. Wait until I bring the light.'

'How do you find your own way if it is so complicated?'

'I had some very narrow escapes at first, but I have gradually learned to go about. There is a certain system to it, but it is one which a lost man, if he were in the dark, could not possibly find out. Even now I always spin out a ball of string behind me when I am going far into the catacomb. You can see for yourself that it is difficult, for every one of these passages divides and subdivides a dozen times before you go a hundred yards.' They had descended some twenty feet from the level of the byre, and they were standing now in a square chamber cut out of the soft tufa. The lantern cast a flickering light, bright below and dim above, over the cracked brown walls. In every direction were the black openings of passages which radiated from this common centre.

'I want you to follow me closely, my friend,' said Burger. 'Do not loiter to look at anything upon the way, for the place to which I will take you contains all that you can see, and more. It will save time for us to go there direct.' He led the way down one of the corridors, and the Englishman followed closely at his heels. Every now and then the passage bifurcated, but Burger was evidently following some secret marks of his own, for he neither stopped nor hesitated. Everywhere along the walls, packed like the berths upon an emigrant ship, lay the Christians of old Rome. The yellow light flickered over the shrivelled features of the mummies, and gleamed upon rounded skulls and long white arm-bones crossed over fleshless chests. And everywhere as he passed Kennedy looked with wistful eyes upon inscriptions, funeral vessels, pictures, vestments, utensils, all lying as pious hands had placed them so many centuries ago. It was apparent to him, even in those hurried, passing glances, that this was the earliest and finest of the catacombs, containing such a storehouse of Roman remains as had never before come at one time under the observation of the student. 'What would happen if the light went out?' he asked, as they hurried on.

'I have a spare candle and a box of matches in my pocket. By the way, Kennedy, have you any matches?'

'No; you had better give me some.'

'Oh, that is all right. There is no chance of our separating.'

'How far are we going? It seems to me that we have walked at least a quarter of a mile.'

'More than that, I think. There is really no limit to the tombs – at least, I have never been able to find any. This is a very difficult place, so I think that I will use our ball of string.' He fastened one end of it to a projecting stone and he carried the coil in the breast of his coat, paying it out as he advanced. Kennedy saw that it was no unnecessary precaution, for the passages had become more complex and tortuous than ever, with a perfect network of intersecting corridors. But these all ended in one large circular hall with a square pedestal of tufa topped with a slab of marble at one end of it. 'By Jove!' cried Kennedy in an ecstasy, as Burger swung his lantern over the marble. 'It is a Christian altar – probably the first one in existence. Here is the little consecration cross cut upon the corner of it. No doubt this circular space was used as a church.'

'Precisely,' said Burger. 'If I had more time I should like to show you all the bodies which are buried in these niches upon the walls, for they are the early popes and bishops of the Church, with their mitres, their croziers, and full canonicals. Go over to that one and look at it!' Kennedy went across, and stared at the ghastly head which lay loosely on the shredded and mouldering mitre.

'This is most interesting,' said he, and his voice seemed to boom against the concave vault. 'As far as my experience goes, it is unique. Bring the lantern over, Burger, for I want to see them all.' But the German had strolled away, and was standing in the middle of a yellow circle of light at the other side of the hall.

'Do you know how many wrong turnings there are between this and the stairs?' he asked. 'There are over two thousand. No doubt it was one of the means of protection which the Christians adopted. The odds are two thousand to one against a man getting out, even if he had a light; but if he were in the dark it would, of course, be far more difficult.'

'So I should think.'

'And the darkness is something dreadful. I tried it once for an experiment. Let us try it again!' He stooped to the lantern, and in an instant it was as if an invisible hand was squeezed tightly over each of Kennedy's eyes. Never had he known what darkness was. It seemed to press upon him and to smother him. It was a solid obstacle against which the body shrank from advancing. He put his hands out to push it back from him. 'That will do, Burger,' said he, 'let's have the light again.'

But his companion began to laugh, and in that circular room the sound seemed to come from every side at once. 'You seem uneasy, friend Kennedy,' said he.

'Go on, man, light the candle!' said Kennedy, impatiently.

'It's very strange, Kennedy, but I could not in the least tell by the sound in which direction you stand. Could you tell where I am?'

'No; you seem to be on every side of me.'

'If it were not for this string which I hold in my hand I should not have a notion which way to go.'

'I dare say not. Strike a light, man, and have an end of this nonsense.'

'Well, Kennedy, there are two things which I understand that you are very fond of. The one is adventure, and the other is an obstacle to surmount. The adventure must be the finding of your way out of this catacomb. The obstacle will be the darkness and the two thousand wrong turns which make the way a little difficult to find. But you need not hurry, for you have plenty of time, and when you halt for a rest now and then, I should like you just to think of Miss Mary Saunderson, and whether you treated her quite fairly.'

'You devil, what do you mean?' roared Kennedy. He was running about in little circles and clasping at the solid blackness with both hands.

'Goodbye,' said the mocking voice, and it was already at some distance. 'I really do not think, Kennedy, even by your own showing that you did the right thing by that girl. There was only one little thing which you appeared not to know, and I can supply it. Miss Saunderson was engaged to a poor, ungainly devil of a student, and his name was Julius Burger.' There was a rustle somewhere – the vague sound of a foot striking a stone – and then there fell silence upon that old Christian church – a stagnant heavy silence which closed round Kennedy and shut him in like water round a drowning man.

Some two months afterwards the following paragraph made the round of the European press:

> One of the most interesting discoveries of recent years is that of the new catacomb in Rome, which lies some distance to the east of the well-known vaults of St Calixtus. The finding of this important burial-place, which is exceedingly rich in most interesting early Christian remains, is due to the energy and sagacity of Dr Julius Burger, the young German specialist, who is rapidly taking the first place as an authority upon ancient Rome. Although the first to publish his discovery, it appears that a less fortunate adventurer had anticipated Dr Burger. Some months ago Mr Kennedy, the well-known English student, disappeared suddenly from his rooms in the Corso, and it was conjectured that his association with a recent scandal had driven him to leave Rome. It appears now that he had in reality fallen a victim to that fervid love of archaeology which had raised him to a distinguished place among living scholars. His body was discovered in the heart of the new catacomb, and it was evident from the condition of his feet and boots that he had tramped for days through the tortuous corridors which make these subterranean tombs so dangerous to explorers. The deceased gentleman had, with inexplicable rashness, made his way into this labyrinth without, as far as can be discovered, taking with him either candles or matches, so that his sad fate was the natural result of his own temerity. What makes the matter more painful is that Dr Julius Burger was an intimate friend of the deceased. His joy at the extraordinary find which he has been so fortunate as to make has been greatly marred by the terrible fate of his comrade and fellow-worker.

The King of the Foxes

It was after a hunting dinner, and there were as many scarlet coats as black ones round the table. The conversation over the cigars had turned, therefore, in the direction of horses and horsemen, with reminiscences of phenomenal runs where foxes had led the pack from end to end of a county, and been overtaken at last by two or three limping hounds and a huntsman on foot, while every rider in the field had been pounded. As the port circulated the runs became longer and more apocryphal, until we had the whips enquiring their way and failing to understand the dialect of the people who answered them. The foxes, too, became more eccentric, and we had foxes up pollard willows, foxes which were dragged by the tail out of horses' mangers, and foxes which had raced through an open front door and gone to ground in a lady's bonnet-box. The master had told one or two tall reminiscences, and when he cleared his throat for another we were all curious, for he was a bit of an artist in his way, and produced his effects in a crescendo fashion. His face wore the earnest, practical, severely accurate expression which heralded some of his finest efforts.

'It was before I was master,' said he. 'Sir Charles Adair had the hounds at that time, and then afterwards they passed to old Lathom, and then to me. It may possibly have been just after Lathom took them over, but my strong impression is that it was in Adair's time. That would be early in the eighteen seventies – about 'seventy-two, I should say.

'The man I mean has moved to another part of the country, but I dare say that some of you can remember him. Danbury was the name – Walter Danbury, or Wat Danbury, as the people used to call him. He was the son of old Joe Danbury, of High Ascombe, and when his father died he came into a very good thing, for his only brother was drowned when the *Magna Charta* foundered, so he inherited the whole estate. It was but a few hundred acres, but it was good arable land, and those were the great days of farming. Besides, it was freehold, and a yeoman farmer without a mortgage was a warmish man before the great fall in wheat came. Foreign wheat and barbed wire – those are the two curses of this country, for the one spoils the farmer's work and the other spoils his play.

'This young Wat Danbury was a very fine fellow, a keen rider, and a thorough sportsman, but his head was a little turned at having come, when so young, into a comfortable fortune, and he went the pace for a year or two. The lad had no vice in him, but there was a hard-drinking set in the neighbourhood at that time, and Danbury got drawn in among them; and, being an amiable fellow who liked to do what his friends were doing, he very soon took to drinking a great deal more than was good for him. As a rule, a man who takes his exercise may drink as much as he likes in the evening, and do himself no very great harm, if he will leave it alone during the day. Danbury had too many friends for that, however, and it really looked as if the poor chap was going to the bad, when a very curious thing happened which pulled him up with such a sudden jerk that he never put his hand upon the neck of a whisky bottle again.

'He had a peculiarity which I have noticed in a good many other men, that though he was always playing tricks with his own health, he was none the less very anxious about it, and was extremely fidgety if ever he had any trivial symptom. Being a tough, open-air fellow, who was always as hard as a nail, it was seldom that there was anything amiss with him; but at last the drink began to tell, and he woke one morning with his hands shaking and all his nerves tingling like over-stretched fiddle-strings. He had been dining at some very wet house the night before, and the wine had, perhaps, been more plentiful than choice; at any rate, there he was, with a tongue like a bath towel and a head that ticked like an eight-day clock. He was very alarmed at his own condition, and he sent for Dr Middleton, of Ascombe, the father of the man who practises there now.

'Middleton had been a great friend of old Danbury's, and he was very sorry to see his son going to the devil; so he improved the occasion by taking his case very seriously, and lecturing him upon the danger of his ways. He shook his head and talked about the possibility of *delirium tremens*, or even of mania, if he continued to lead such a life. Wat Danbury was horribly frightened.

' "Do you think I am going to get anything of the sort?" he wailed.

' "Well, really, I don't know," said the doctor gravely. "I cannot undertake to say that you are out of danger. Your system is very much out of order. At any time during the day you might have those grave symptoms of which I warn you."

' "You think I shall be safe by evening?"

' "If you drink nothing during the day, and have no nervous symptoms before evening, I think you may consider yourself safe," the doctor answered. A little fright would, he thought, do his patient good, so he made the most of the matter.

' "What symptoms may I expect?" asked Danebury.

' "It generally takes the form of optical delusions."

' "I see specks floating all about."

' "That is mere biliousness," said the doctor soothingly, for he saw that the lad was highly strung, and he did not wish to overdo it. "I dare say that you will have no symptoms of the kind, but when they do come they usually take the shape of insects, or reptiles, or curious animals."

' "And if I see anything of the kind?"

' "If you do, you will at once send for me;" and so, with a promise of medicine, the doctor departed.

'Young Wat Danbury rose and dressed and moped about the room feeling very miserable and unstrung, with a vision of the County Asylum forever in his mind. He had the doctor's word for it that if he could get through to evening in safety he would be all right; but it is not very exhilarating to be waiting for symptoms, and to keep on glancing at your bootjack to see whether it is still a bootjack or whether it has begun to develop antennae and legs. At last he could stand it no longer, and an overpowering longing for the fresh air and the green grass came over him. Why should he stay indoors when the Ascombe Hunt was meeting within half a mile of him? If he was going to have these delusions which the doctor talked of, he would not have them the sooner nor the worse because he was on horseback in the open. He was sure, too, it would ease his aching head. And so it came about that in ten minutes he was in his hunting-kit, and in ten more he was riding out of his stableyard with his roan mare Matilda between his knees. He was a little unsteady in his saddle just at first, but the farther he went the better he felt, until by the time he reached the meet his head was almost clear, and there was nothing troubling him except those haunting words of the doctor's about the possibility of delusions any time before nightfall.

'But soon he forgot that also, for as he came up the hounds were thrown off, and they drew the Gravel Hanger, and afterwards the Hickory Copse. It was just the morning for a scent – no wind to blow it away, no water to wash it out, and just damp enough to make it cling. There was a field of forty, all keen men and good riders, so when they came to the Black Hanger they knew that there would be some sport, for that's a cover which never draws blank. The woods were thicker in those days than now, and the foxes were thicker also, and that great dark oak grove was swarming with them. The only difficulty was to make them break, for it is, as you know, a very close country, and you must coax them out into the open before you can hope for a run.

'When they came to the Black Hanger the field took their positions along the cover-side wherever they thought that they were most likely to get a good start. Some went in with the hounds, some clustered at the ends of the drives, and some kept outside in the hope of the fox breaking in that direction. Young Wat Danbury knew the country like the palm of his hand, so he made for a place where several drives intersected, and there he waited. He had a feeling that the faster and the farther he galloped the better he should be, and so he was chafing to be off. His mare, too, was in the height of fettle and one of the fastest goers in the county. Wat was a splendid lightweight rider – under ten stone with his saddle – and the mare was a powerful creature, all quarters and shoulders, fit to carry a lifeguardsman; and so it was no wonder that there was hardly a man in the field who could hope to stay with him. There he waited and listened to the shouting of the huntsman and the whips, catching a glimpse now and then in the darkness of the wood of a whisking tail, or the gleam of a white-and-tan side amongst the underwood. It was a well-trained pack, and there was not so much as a whine to tell you that forty hounds were working all round you.

'And then suddenly there came one long-drawn yell from one of them, and it was taken up by another, and another, until within a few seconds the whole pack was giving tongue together and running on a hot scent. Danbury saw them stream across one of the drives and disappear upon the other side, and an instant later the three red coats of the hunt servants flashed after them upon the same line. He might have made a shorter cut down one of the other drives, but he was afraid of heading the fox, so he followed the lead of the huntsman. Right through the wood they went in a bee-line, galloping with their faces brushed by their horses' manes as they stooped under the branches.

'It's ugly going, as you know, with the roots all wriggling about in the darkness, but you can take a risk when you catch an occasional glimpse of the pack running with a breast-high scent; so in and out they dodged until the wood began to thin at the edges, and they found themselves in the long bottom where the river runs. It is clear going there upon grassland, and the hounds were running very strong about two hundred yards ahead, keeping parallel with the stream. The field, who had come round the wood instead of going through, were coming hard over the fields upon the left; but Danbury, with the hunt servants, had a clear lead, and they never lost it.

'Two of the field got on terms with them – Parson Geddes on a big seventeen-hand bay which he used to ride in those days, and Squire Foley, who rode as a featherweight, and made his hunters out of cast thorough-breds from the Newmarket sales; but the others never had a look-in from start to finish, for there was no check and no pulling, and it was clear cross-country racing from start to finish. If you had drawn a line right across the map with a pencil you couldn't go straighter than that fox ran, heading for the South Downs and the sea, and the hounds ran as surely as if they were running to view, and yet from the beginning no one ever saw the fox, and there was never a halloo forrard to tell them that he had been spied. This, however, is not so surprising, for if you've been over that line of country you will know that there are not very many people about.

'There were six of them then in the front row – Parson Geddes, Squire Foley, the huntsman, two whips, and Wat Danbury, who had forgotten all about his head and the doctor by this time, and had not a thought for anything but the run. All six were galloping just as hard as they could lay hoofs to the ground. One of the whips dropped back, however, as some of the hounds were tailing off, and that brought them down to five. Then Foley's thoroughbred strained herself, as these slim-legged, dainty-fetlocked thoroughbreds will do when the going is rough, and he had to take a back seat. But the other four were still going strong, and they did four or five miles down the river flat at a rasping pace. It had been a wet winter, and the waters had been out a little time before, so there was a deal of sliding and splashing; but by the time they came to the bridge the whole field was out of sight, and these four had the hunt to themselves.

'The fox had crossed the bridge – for foxes do not care to swim a chilly river any more than humans do – and from that point he had streaked away southward as hard as he could tear. It is broken country, rolling heaths, down one slope and up another, and it's hard to say whether the up or the down is the more trying for the horses. This sort of switchback work is all right for a cobby, short-backed, short-legged little horse, but it is killing work for a big, long-striding hunter such as one wants in the Midlands. Anyhow, it was too much for Parson Geddes' seventeen-hand bay, and though he tried the Irish trick – for he was a rare keen sportsman – of running up the hills by his horse's head, it was all to no use, and he had to give it up. So then there were only the huntsman, the whip and Wat Danbury – all going strong.

'But the country got worse and worse and the hills were steeper and more thickly covered in heather and bracken. The horses were over their hocks all the time, and the place was pitted with rabbit-holes; but the hounds were still streaming along, and the riders could not afford to pick their steps. As they raced down one slope, the hounds were always flowing up the opposite one, until it looked like that game where the one figure in falling makes the other one rise.

'But never a glimpse did they get of the fox, although they knew very well that he must be only a very short way ahead for the scent to be so strong. And then Wat Danbury heard a crash and a thud at his elbow, and looking round he saw a pair of white cords and top-boots kicking out of a tussock of brambles. The whip's horse had stumbled, and the whip was out of the running. Danbury and the huntsman eased down for an instant; and then, seeing the man staggering to his feet all right, they turned and settled into their saddles once more.

'Joe Clarke, the huntsman, was a famous old rider, known for five counties round; but he reckoned upon his second horse, and the second horses had all been left many miles behind. However, the one he was riding was good enough for anything with such a horseman upon his back, and he was going as well as when he started. As to Wat Danbury, he was going better. With every stride his own feelings improved, and the mind of the rider had its influence upon the mind of the horse. The stout little roan was gathering its muscular limbs under it, and stretching to the gallop as if it were steel and whalebone instead of flesh and blood. Wat had never come to the end of its powers yet, and today he had such a chance of testing them as he had never had before.

'There was a pasture country beyond the heather slopes, and for several miles the two riders were either losing ground as they fumbled with their crop-handles at the bars of gates, or gaining it again as they galloped over the fields. Those were the days before this accursed wire came into the country, and you could generally break a hedge where you could not fly it, so they did not trouble the gates more than they could help. Then they were down in a hard lane, where they had to slacken their pace, and through a farm where a man came shouting excitedly after them; but they had no time to stop and listen to him, for the hounds were on some ploughland, only two fields ahead. It was sloping upwards, that ploughland, and the horses were over their fetlocks in the red, soft soil.

'When they reached the top they were blowing badly, but a grand valley sloped before them, leading up to the open country of the South Downs. Between, there lay a belt of pinewoods, into which the hounds were streaming, running now in a long, straggling line, and shedding one here and one there as they ran. You could see the white-and-tan dots here and there where the limpers were tailing away. But half the pack were still going well, though the pace and distance had both been tremendous – two clear hours now without a check.

'There was a drive through the pinewood – one of those green, slightly rutted drives where a horse can get the last yard out of itself, for the ground is hard enough to give him clean going and yet springy enough to help him. Wat Danbury got alongside of the huntsman and they galloped together with their stirrup-irons touching, and the hounds within a hundred yards of them.

' "We have it all to ourselves," said he.

' "Yes, sir, we've shook on the lot of 'em this time," said old Joe Clarke. "If we get this fox it's worthwhile 'aving 'im skinned an' stuffed, for 'e's a curiosity 'e is."

' "It's the fastest run I ever had in my life!" cried Danbury.

' "And the fastest that ever I 'ad, an' that means more," said the old huntsman. "But what licks me is that we've never 'ad a look at the beast. 'E must leave an amazin' scent be'ind 'im when these 'ounds can follow 'im like this, and yet none of us have seen 'im when we've 'ad a clear 'alf mile view in front of us."

' "I expect we'll have a view of him presently," said Danbury; and in his mind he added, "at least, I shall", for the huntsman's horse was gasping as it ran, and the white foam was pouring down it like the side of a washing-tub.

'They had followed the hounds on to one of the side tracks which led out of the main drive, and that divided into a smaller track still, where the branches switched across their faces as they went, and there was barely room for one horse at a time. Wat Danbury took the lead, and he heard the huntsman's horse clumping along heavily behind him, while his own mare was going with less spring than when she had started. She answered to a touch of his crop or spur, however, and he felt that there was something still left to draw upon. And then he looked up, and there was a heavy wooden stile at the end of the narrow track, with a lane of stiff young saplings leading down to it, which was far too thick to break through. The hounds were running clear upon the grassland on the other side, and you were bound either to get over that stile or lose sight of them, for the pace was too hot to let you go round.

'Well, Wat Danbury was not the lad to flinch, and at it he went full split, like a man who means what he is doing. She rose gallantly to it, rapped it hard with her front hoof, shook him on to her withers, recovered herself, and was over. Wat had hardly got back into his saddle when there was a clatter behind him like the fall of a woodstack, and there was the top bar in splinters, the horse on its belly, and the huntsman on hands and knees half a dozen yards in front of him. Wat pulled up for an instant, for the fall was a smasher; but he saw old Joe spring to his feet and get to his horse's bridle. The horse staggered up, but the moment it put one foot in front of the other, Wat saw that it was hopelessly lame – a slipped shoulder and a six weeks' job. There was nothing he could do, and Joe was shouting to him not to lose the hounds, so off he went again, the one solitary survivor of the whole hunt. When a man finds himself there, he can retire from fox-hunting, for he has tasted the highest which it has to offer. I remember once when I was out with the Royal Surrey – but I'll tell you that story afterwards.

'The pack, or what was left of them, had got a bit ahead during this time; but he had a clear view of them on the downland, and the mare seemed full of pride at being the only one left, for she was stepping out rarely and tossing her head as she went. There were two miles over the green shoulder of a hill, a rattle down a stony, deep-rutted country lane, where the mare stumbled and nearly came down, a jump over a five-foot brook, a cut through a hazel copse, another dose of heavy ploughland, a couple of gates to open, and then the green, unbroken Downs beyond.

'Well,' said Wat Danbury to himself, 'I'll see this fox run into or I shall see it drowned, for it's all clear going now between this and the chalk cliffs which line the sea.' But he was wrong in that, as he speedily discovered. In all the little hollows of the downs at that part there are plantations of fir woods, some of which have grown to a good size. You do not see them until you come upon the edge of the valleys in which they lie. Danbury was galloping hard over the short, springy turf when he came over the lip of one of these depressions, and there was the dark clump of wood lying in front of and beneath him. There were only a dozen hounds still running, and they were just disappearing among the trees. The sunlight was shining straight upon the long olive-green slopes which curved down towards this wood, and Danbury, who had the eyes of a hawk, swept them over this great expanse; but there was nothing moving upon it. A few sheep were grazing far up on the right, but there was no other sight of any living creature. He was certain then that he was very near to the end, for either the fox must have gone to ground in the wood or the hounds' noses must be at his very brush. The mare seemed to know also what that great empty sweep of countryside meant, for she quickened her stride, and a few minutes afterwards Danbury was galloping into the fir wood.

'He had come from bright sunshine, but the wood was very closely planted, and so dim that he could hardly see to right or to left out of the narrow path down which he was riding. You know what a solemn, church-yardy sort of place a fir wood is. I suppose it is the absence of any under-growth, and the fact that the trees never move at all. At any rate a kind of chill suddenly struck Wat Danbury, and it flashed through his mind that there had been some very singular points about this run – its length and its straightness, and the fact that from the first find no one had ever caught a glimpse of the creature. Some silly talk which had been going round the country about the king of the foxes – a sort of demon fox, so fast that it could outrun any pack, and so fierce that they could do nothing with it if they overtook it – suddenly came back into his mind, and it did not seem so laughable now in the dim fir wood as it had done when the story had been told over the wine and cigars. The nervousness which had been on him in the morning, and which he had hoped that he had shaken off, swept over him again in an overpowering wave. He had been so proud of being alone, and yet he would have given ten pounds now to have had Joe Clarke's homely face beside him. And then, just at that moment, there broke out from the thickest part of the wood the most frantic hullabaloo that ever he had heard in his life. The hounds had run into their fox.

'Well, you know, or you ought to know, what your duty is in such a case. You have to be whip, huntsman and everything else if you are the first man up. You get in among the hounds, lash them off, and keep the brush and pads from being destroyed. Of course, Wat Danbury knew all about that, and he tried to force his mare through the trees to the place where all this hideous screaming and howling came from, but the wood was so thick that it was impossible to ride it. He sprang off, therefore, left the mare standing, and broke his way through as best he could with his hunting-lash ready over his shoulder.

'But as he ran forward he felt his flesh go cold and creepy all over. He had heard hounds run into foxes many times before, but he had never heard such sounds as these. They were not the cries of triumph, but of fear. Every now and then came a shrill yelp of mortal agony. Holding his breath, he ran on until he broke through the interlacing branches and found himself in a little clearing, with the hounds all crowding round a patch of tangled bramble at the farther end.

'When he first caught sight of them the hounds were standing in a half-circle round this bramble patch, with their backs bristling and their jaws gaping. In front of the brambles lay one of them with his throat torn out, all crimson and white-and-tan. Wat came running out into the clearing, and at the sight of him the hounds took heart again, and one of them sprang with a growl into the bushes. At the same instant, a creature the size of a donkey jumped on to its feet, a huge grey head, with monstrous glistening fangs and tapering fox jaws, shot out from among the branches, and the hound was thrown several feet into the air, and fell howling among the cover. Then there was a clashing snap, like a rat-trap closing, and the howls sharpened into a scream and then were still.

'Danbury had been on the lookout for symptoms all day, and now he had found them. He looked once more at the thicket, saw a pair of savage red eyes fixed upon him, and fairly took to his heels. It might only be a passing delusion, or it might be the permanent mania of which the doctor had spoken, but anyhow, the thing to do was to get back to bed and to quiet, and to hope for the best.

'He forgot the hounds, the hunt, and everything else in his desperate fears for his own reason. He sprang upon his mare, galloped her madly over the downs, and only stopped when he found himself at a country station. There he left his mare at the inn, and made back for home as quickly as steam would take him. It was evening before he got there, shivering with apprehension, and seeing those red eyes and savage teeth at every turn. He went straight to bed and sent for Dr Middleton.

' "I've got 'em, doctor," said he. "It came about exactly as you said – strange creatures, optical delusions, and everything. All I ask you now is to save my reason." The doctor listened to his story, and was shocked as he heard it.

' "It appears to be a very clear case," said he. "This must be a lesson to you for life."

' "Never a drop again if I only come safely through this," cried Wat Danbury.

' "Well, my dear boy, if you will stick to that it may prove a blessing in disguise. But the difficulty in this case is to know where fact ends and fancy begins. You see, it is not as if there was only one delusion. There have been several. The dead dogs, for example, must have been one as well as the creature in the bush."

' "I saw it all as clearly as I see you."

' "One of the characteristics of this form of delirium is that what you see is even clearer than reality. I was wondering whether the whole run was not a delusion also."

'Wat Danbury pointed to his hunting boots still lying upon the floor, flecked with the splashings of two counties.

' "Hum! that looks very real, certainly. No doubt, in your weak state, you over-exerted yourself and so brought this attack upon yourself. Well, whatever the cause, our treatment is clear. You will take the soothing mixture which I will send to you, and we shall put two leeches upon your temples tonight to relieve any congestion of the brain."

'So Wat Danbury spent the night in tossing about and reflecting what a sensitive thing this machinery of ours is, and how very foolish it is to play tricks with what is so easily put out of gear and so difficult to mend. And so he repeated and repeated his oath that this first lesson should be his last, and that from that time forward he would be a sober, hard-working yeoman as his father had been before him. So he lay, tossing and still repentant, when his door flew open in the morning and in rushed the doctor with a news-paper crumpled up in his hand.

' "My dear boy," he cried, "I owe you a thousand apologies. You're the most ill-used lad and I the greatest numskull in the county. Listen to this!" And he sat down upon the side of the bed, flattened out his paper upon his knee, and began to read.

'The paragraph was headed "Disaster to the Ascombe Hounds" and it went on to say that four of the hounds, shockingly torn and mangled, had been found in Winton Fir Wood upon the South Downs. The run had been so severe that half the pack were lamed; but the four found in the wood were actually dead, although the cause of their extraordinary injuries was still unknown.

' "So, you see," said the doctor, looking up, "that I was wrong when I put the dead hounds among the delusions."

' "But the cause?" cried Wat.

' "Well, I think we may guess the cause from an item which has been inserted just as the paper went to press: 'Late last night, Mr Brown, of Shipton Farm, to the east of Hastings, perceived what he imagined to be an enormous dog worrying one of his sheep. He shot the creature, which proves to be a grey Siberian wolf of the variety known as *Lupus giganticus*. It is supposed to have escaped from some travelling menagerie.' "

'That's the story, gentlemen, and Wat Danbury stuck to his good reso-lutions, for the fright which he had had cured him of all wish to run such a risk again; and he never touches anything stronger than lime-juice – at least, he hadn't before he left this part of the country, five years ago next Lady Day.'

The Green Flag

When Jack Conolly, of the Irish Shotgun Brigade, the Rory of the Hills Inner Circle, and the extreme left wing of the Land League, was incontinently shot by Sergeant Murdoch of the constabulary, in a little moonlight frolic near Kanturk, his twin-brother Dennis joined the British Army. The countryside had become too hot for him; and, as the seventy-five shillings were wanting which might have carried him to America, he took the only way handy of getting himself out of the way. Seldom has Her Majesty had a less promising recruit, for his hot Celtic blood seethed with hatred against Britain and all things British. The sergeant, however, smiling complacently over his six feet of brawn and his forty-four-inch chest, whisked him off with a dozen other of the boys to the depot at Fermoy, whence in a few weeks they were sent on, with the spade-work kinks taken out of their backs, to the first battalion of the Royal Mallows, at the top of the roster for foreign service.

The Royal Mallows, at about that date, were as strange a lot of men as ever were paid by a great empire to fight its battles. It was the darkest hour of the land struggle, when the one side came out with crowbar and battering-ram by day, and the other with mask and with shotgun by night. Men driven from their homes and potato-patches found their way even into the service of the government to which it seemed to them that they owed their troubles, and now and then they did wild things before they came. There were recruits in the Irish regiments who would forget to answer to their own names, so short had been their acquaintance with them. Of these the Royal Mallows had their full share; and, while they still retained their fame as being one of the smartest corps in the army, no one knew better than their officers that they were dry-rotted with treason and with bitter hatred of the flag under which they served.

And the centre of all the disaffection was C Company, in which Dennis Conolly found himself enrolled. They were Celts, Catholics and men of the tenant class to a man; and their whole experience of the British government had been an inexorable landlord and a constabulary who seemed to them to be always on the side of the rent-collector. Dennis was not the only moonlighter in the ranks, nor was he alone in having an intolerable family blood-feud to harden his heart. Savagery had begotten savagery in that veiled civil war. A landlord with an iron mortgage weighing down upon him had small bowels for his tenantry. He did but take what the law allowed, and yet, with men like Jim Holan, or Patrick McQuire, or Peter Flynn, who had seen the roofs torn from their cottages and their folk huddled among their pitiable furniture upon the roadside, it was ill to argue about abstract law. What matter that in that long and bitter struggle there was many another outrage on the part of the tenant, and many another grievance on the side of the landowner! A stricken man can only feel his own wound, and the rank and file of the C Company of the Royal Mallows were sore and savage to the soul. There were low whisperings in barrack-rooms and canteens, stealthy meetings in public-house parlours, bandying of passwords from mouth to mouth, and many other signs which made their officers right glad when the order came which sent them to foreign and, better still, to active service.

For Irish regiments have before now been disaffected, and have at a distance looked upon the foe as though he might, in truth, be the friend; but when they have been put face on to him, and when their officers have dashed to the front with a wave and halloo, those rebel hearts have softened and their gallant Celtic blood has boiled with the mad joy of the fight, until the slower Britons have marvelled that they ever could have doubted the loyalty of their Irish comrades. So it would be again, according to the officers, and so it would not be if Dennis Conolly and a few others could have their way.

It was a March morning upon the eastern fringe of the Nubian desert. The sun had not yet risen, but a tinge of pink flushed up as far as the cloudless zenith, and the long strip of sea lay like a rosy ribbon across the horizon. From the coast inland stretched dreary sand-plains, dotted over with thick clumps of mimosa scrub and mottled patches of thorny bush. No tree broke the monotony of that vast desert. The dull, dusty hue of the thickets, and the yellow glare of the sand, were the only colours, save at one point, where, from a distance, it seemed that a land-slip of snow-white stones had shot itself across a low foot-hill. But as the traveller approached he saw, with a thrill, that these were no stones, but the bleaching bones of a slaughtered army. With its dull tints, its gnarled, viperous bushes, its arid, barren soil, and this death streak trailed across it, it was indeed a nightmare country.

Some eight or ten miles inland the rolling plain curved upwards with a steeper slope until it ran into a line of red basaltic rock which zigzagged from north to south, heaping itself up at one point into a fantastic knoll. On the summit of this there stood upon that March morning three Arab chieftains – the Sheikh Kadra of the Hadendowas, Moussa Wad Aburhegel, who led the Berber dervishes, and Hamid Wad Hussein, who had come northward with his fighting men from the land of the Baggaras. They had all three just risen from their praying-carpets, and were peering out, with fierce, high-nosed faces thrust forward, at the stretch of country revealed by the spreading dawn.

The red rim of the sun was pushing itself now above the distant sea, and the whole coastline stood out brilliantly yellow against the rich deep blue beyond. At one spot lay a huddle of white-walled houses, a mere splotch in the distance; while four tiny cock-boats, which lay beyond, marked the position of three of Her Majesty's 10,000-ton troopers and the admiral's flagship. But it was not upon the distant town, nor upon the great vessels, nor yet upon the sinister white litter which gleamed in the plain beneath them, that the Arab chieftains gazed. Two miles from where they stood, amid the sand-hills and the mimosa scrub, a great parallelogram had been marked by piled-up bushes. From the inside of this dozens of tiny blue smoke-reeks curled up into the still morning air; while there rose from it a confused deep murmur, the voices of men and the gruntings of camels blended into the same insect buzz.

'The unbelievers have cooked their morning food,' said the Baggara chief, shading his eyes with his tawny, sinewy hand. 'Truly their sleep has been scanty; for Hamid and a hundred of his men have fired upon them since the rising of the moon.'

'So it was with these others,' answered the Sheikh Kadra, pointing with his sheathed sword towards the old battlefield. 'They also had a day of little water and a night of little rest, and the heart was gone out of them ere ever the sons of the Prophet had looked them in the eyes. This blade drank deep that day, and will again before the sun has travelled from the sea to the hill.'

'And yet these are other men,' remarked the Berber dervish. 'Well I know that Allah has placed them in the clutch of our fingers, yet it may be that they with the big hats will stand firmer than the cursed men of Egypt.'

'Pray Allah that it may be so,' cried the fierce Baggara, with a flash of his black eyes. 'It was not to chase women that I brought seven hundred men from the river to the coast. See, my brother, already they are forming their array.'

A fanfare of bugle-calls burst from the distant camp. At the same time the bank of bushes at one side had been thrown or trampled down, and the little army within began to move slowly out on to the plain. Once clear of the camp they halted, and the slant rays of the sun struck flashes from bayonet and from gun-barrel as the ranks closed up until the big pith helmets joined into a single long white ribbon. Two streaks of scarlet glowed on either side of the square, but elsewhere the fringe of fighting-men was of the dull yellow khaki tint which hardly shows against the desert sand. Inside their array was a dense mass of camels and mules bearing stores and ambulance needs. Outside a twinkling clump of cavalry was drawn up on each flank, and in front a thin, scattered line of mounted infantry was already slowly advancing over the bush-strewn plain, halting on every eminence, and peering warily round as men might who have to pick their steps among the bones of those who have preceded them.

The three chieftains still lingered upon the knoll, looking down with hungry eyes and compressed lips at the dark steel-tipped patch. 'They are slower to start than the men of Egypt,' the Sheikh of the Hadendowas growled in his beard.

'Slower also to go back, perchance, my brother,' murmured the dervish.

'And yet they are not many – three thousand at the most.'

'And we ten thousand, with the Prophet's grip upon our spear-hafts and his words upon our banner. See their chieftain, how he rides upon the right and looks up at us with the glass that sees from afar! It may be that he sees this also.' The Arab shook his sword at the small clump of horsemen who had spurred out from the square.

'Lo! he beckons,' cried the dervish; 'and see those others at the corner, how they bend and heave. Ha! by the Prophet, I had thought it.' As he spoke, a little woolly puff of smoke spurted up at the corner of the square, and a seven-pound shell burst with a hard metallic smack just over their heads. The splinters knocked chips from the red rocks around them.

'Bismillah!' cried the Hadendowa; 'if the gun can carry thus far, then ours can answer to it. Ride to the left, Moussa, and tell Ben Ali to cut the skin from the Egyptians if they cannot hit yonder mark. And you, Hamid, to the right, and see that three thousand men lie close in the wadi that we have chosen. Let the others beat the drum and show the banner of the Prophet, for by the black stone their spears will have drunk deep ere they look upon the stars again.'

A long, straggling, boulder-strewn plateau lay on the summit of the red hills, sloping very precipitously to the plain, save at one point, where a winding gully curved downwards, its mouth choked with sand-mounds and olive-hued scrub. Along the edge of this position lay the Arab host – a motley crew of shock-headed desert clansmen, fierce predatory slave dealers of the interior and wild dervishes from the Upper Nile, all blent together by their common fearlessness and fanaticism. Two races were there, as wide as the poles apart – the thin-lipped, straight-haired Arab and the thick-lipped, curly negro – yet the faith of Islam had bound them closer than a blood tie. Squatting among the rocks, or lying thickly in the shadow, they peered out at the slow-moving square beneath them, while women with water-skins and bags of *dhoora* fluttered from group to group, calling out to each other those fighting texts from the Koran which in the hour of battle are maddening as wine to the true believer. A score of banners waved over the ragged, valiant crew, and among them, upon desert horses and white Bishareen camels, were the emirs and sheikhs who were to lead them against the infidels.

As the Sheikh Kadra sprang into his saddle and drew his sword there was a wild whoop and a clatter of waving spears, while the one-ended war-drums burst into a dull crash like a wave upon shingle. For a moment ten thousand men were up on the rocks with brandished arms and leaping figures; the next they were under cover again, waiting sternly and silently for their chieftain's orders. The square was less than half a mile from the ridge now, and shell after shell from the seven-pound guns were pitching over it. A deep roar on the right, and then a second one showed that the Egyptian Krupps were in action. Sheikh Kadra's hawk eyes saw that the shells burst far beyond the mark, and he spurred his horse along to where a knot of mounted chiefs were gathered round the two guns, which were served by their captured crews.

'How is this, Ben Ali?' he cried. 'It was not thus that the dogs fired when it was their own brothers in faith at whom they aimed!'

A chieftain reined his horse back, and thrust a blood-smeared sword into its sheath. Beside him two Egyptian artillerymen with their throats cut were sobbing out their lives upon the ground. 'Who lays the gun this time?' asked the fierce chief, glaring at the frightened gunners. 'Here, thou black-browed child of Shaitan, aim, and aim for thy life.'

It may have been chance, or it may have been skill, but the third and fourth shells burst over the square. Sheikh Kadra smiled grimly and galloped back to the left, where his spearmen were streaming down into the gully. As he joined them a deep growling rose from the plain beneath, like the snarling of a sullen wild beast, and a little knot of tribesmen fell into a struggling heap, caught in the blast of lead from a Gardner. Their comrades pressed on over them, and sprang down into the ravine. From all along the crest burst the hard, sharp crackle of Remington fire.

The square had slowly advanced, rippling over the low sand-hills, and halting every few minutes to rearrange its formation. Now, having made sure that there was no force of the enemy in the scrub, it changed its direction, and began to take a line parallel to the Arab position. It was too steep to assail from the front, and if they moved far enough to the right the general hoped that he might turn it. On the top of those ruddy hills lay a baronetcy for him, and a few extra hundreds in his pension, and he meant having them both that day. The Remington fire was annoying, and so were those two Krupp guns; already there were more cacolets full than he cared to see. But on the whole he thought it better to hold his fire until he had more to aim at than a few hundred fuzzy heads peeping over a razor-back ridge. He was a bulky, red-faced man, a fine whist-player and a soldier who knew his work. His men believed in him, and he had good reason to believe in them, for he had excellent stuff under him that day. Being an ardent champion of the short-service system, he took particular care to work with veteran first battalions, and his little force was the compressed essence of an army corps.

The left front of the square was formed by four companies of the Royal Wessex, and the right by four of the Royal Mallows. On either side the other halves of the same regiments marched in quarter column of companies. Behind them, on the right was a battalion of Guards, and on the left one of Marines, while the rear was closed in by a Rifle battalion. Two Royal Artillery seven-pound screw-guns kept pace with the square, and a dozen white-bloused sailors, under their blue-coated, tight-waisted officers, trailed their Gardner in front, turning every now and then to spit up at the draggled banners which waved over the cragged ridge. Hussars and Lancers scouted in the scrub at each side, and within moved the clump of camels, with humorous eyes and supercilious lips, their comic faces a contrast to the blood-stained men who already lay huddled in the cacolets on either side.

The square was now moving slowly on a line parallel with the rocks, stopping every few minutes to pick up wounded, and to allow the screw-guns and Gardner to make themselves felt. The men looked serious, for that spring on to the rocks of the Arab army had given them a vague glimpse of the number and ferocity of their foes; but their faces were set like stone, for they knew to a man that they must win or they must die – and die, too, in a particularly unlovely fashion. But most serious of all was the general, for he had seen that which brought a flush to his cheeks and a frown to his brow.

'I say, Stephen,' said he to his galloper, 'those Mallows seem a trifle jumpy. The right flank company bulged a bit when the blacks showed on the hill.'

'Youngest troops in the square, sir,' murmured the aide, looking at them critically through his eye-glass.

'Tell Colonel Flanagan to see to it, Stephen,' said the general; and the galloper sped upon his way. The colonel, a fine old Celtic warrior, was over at C Company in an instant.

'How are the men, Captain Foley?'

'Never better, sir,' answered the senior captain, in the spirit that makes a Madras officer look murder if you suggest recruiting his regiment from the Punjab.

'Stiffen them up!' cried the colonel. As he rode away a colour-sergeant seemed to trip, and fell forward into a mimosa bush. He made no effort to rise, but lay in a heap among the thorns.

'Sergeant O'Rooke's gone, sorr,' cried a voice.

'Never mind, lads,' said Captain Foley. 'He's died like a soldier, fighting for his Queen.'

'Down with the Queen!' shouted a hoarse voice from the ranks.

But the roar of the Gardner and the typewriter-like clicking of the hopper burst in at the tail of the words. Captain Foley heard them, and Subalterns Grice and Murphy heard them; but there are times when a deaf ear is a gift from the gods.

'Steady, Mallows!' cried the captain, in a pause of the grunting machine-gun. 'We have the honour of Ireland to guard this day.'

'And well we know how to guard it, captin!' cried the same ominous voice; and there was a buzz from the length of the company.

The captain and the two subs. came together behind the marching line.

'They seem a bit out of hand,' murmured the captain.

'Bedad,' said the Galway boy, 'they mean to scoot like redshanks.'

'They nearly broke when the blacks showed on the hill,' said Grice.

'The first man that turns, my sword is through him,' cried Foley, loud enough to be heard by five files on either side of him. Then, in a lower voice, 'It's a bitter drop to swallow, but it's my duty to report what you think to the chief, and have a company of Jollies put behind us.' He turned away with the safety of the square upon his mind, and before he had reached his goal the square had ceased to exist.

In their march in front of what looked like a face of cliff, they had come opposite to the mouth of the gully, in which, screened by scrub and boulders, three thousand chosen dervishes, under Hamid Wad Hussein of the Baggaras, were crouching. Tat, tat, tat, went the rifles of three mounted infantrymen in front of the left shoulder of the square, and an instant later they were spurring it for their lives, crouching over the manes of their horses and pelting over the sand-hills with thirty or forty galloping chieftains at their heels. Rocks and scrub and mimosa swarmed suddenly into life. Rushing black figures came and went in the gaps of the bushes. A howl that drowned the shouts of the officers, a long quavering yell, burst from the ambuscade. Two rolling volleys from the Royal Wessex, one crash from the screw-gun firing shrapnel, and then before a second cartridge could be rammed in, a living, glistening black wave, tipped with steel, had rolled over the gun, the Royal Wessex had been dashed back among the camels, and a thousand fanatics were hewing and hacking in the heart of what had been the square.

The camels and mules in the centre, jammed more and more together as their leaders flinched from the rush of the tribesmen, shut out the view of the other three faces, who could only tell that the Arabs had got in by the yells upon Allah, which rose ever nearer and nearer amid the clouds of sand-dust, the struggling animals and the dense mass of swaying, cursing men. Some of the Wessex fired back at the Arabs who had passed them, as excited Tommies will, and it is whispered among doctors that it was not always a Remington bullet which was cut from a wound that day. Some rallied in little knots, stabbing furiously with their bayonets at the rushing spearmen. Others turned at bay with their backs against the camels, and others round the general and his staff, who, revolver in hand, had flung themselves into the heart of it. But the whole square was sidling slowly away from the gorge, pushed back by the pressure at the shattered corner.

The officers and men at the other faces were glancing nervously to the rear, uncertain what was going on, and unable to take help to their comrades without breaking the formation.

'By Jove, they've got through the Wessex!' cried Grice of the Mallows.

'The divils have hurrooshed us, Ted,' said his brother subaltern, cocking his revolver.

The ranks were breaking, and crowding towards Private Conolly, all talking together as the officers peered back through the veil of dust. The sailors had run their Gardner out, and she was squirting death out of her five barrels into the flank of the rushing stream of savages. 'Oh, this bloody gun!' shouted a voice. 'She's jammed again.' The fierce metallic grunting had ceased, and her crew were straining and hauling at the breech.

'This damned vertical feed!' cried an officer.

'The spanner, Wilson! – the spanner! Stand to your cutlasses, boys, or they're into us.' His voice rose into a shriek as he ended, for a shovel-headed spear had been buried in his chest. A second wave of dervishes lapped over the hillocks, and burst upon the machine-gun and the right front of the line. The sailors were overborne in an instant, but the Mallows, with their fighting blood aflame, met the yell of the Moslem with an even wilder, fiercer cry, and dropped two hundred of them with a single point-blank volley. The howling, leaping crew swerved away to the right, and dashed on into the gap which had already been made for them.

But C Company had drawn no trigger to stop that fiery rush. The men leaned moodily upon their Martinis. Some had even thrown them upon the ground. Conolly was talking fiercely to those about him. Captain Foley, thrusting his way through the press, rushed up to him with a revolver in his hand.

'This is your doing, you villain!' he cried.

'If you raise your pistol, captin, your brains will be over your coat,' said a low voice at his side.

He saw that several rifles were turned on him. The two subalterns had pressed forward, and were by his side. 'What is it, then?' he cried, looking round from one fierce mutinous face to another. 'Are you Irishmen? Are you soldiers? What are you here for but to fight for your country?'

'England is no country of ours,' cried several.

'You are not fighting for England. You are fighting for Ireland, and for the Empire of which it as part.'

'A black curse on the Impire!' shouted Private McQuire, throwing down his rifle. ' 'Twas the Impire that backed the man that druv me on to the roadside. May me hand stiffen before I draw trigger for it.'

'What's the Impire to us, Captain Foley, and what's the Widdy to us ayther?' cried a voice.

'Let the constabulary foight for her.'

'Ay, be God, they'd be better imployed than pullin' a poor man's thatch about his ears.'

'Or shootin' his brother, as they did mine.'

'It was the Impire laid my groanin' mother by the wayside. Her son will rot before he upholds it, and ye can put that in the charge-sheet in the next coort-martial.'

In vain the three officers begged, menaced, persuaded. The square was still moving, ever moving, with the same bloody fight raging in its entrails. Even while they had been speaking they had been shuffling backwards, and the useless Gardner, with her slaughtered crew, was already a good hundred yards from them. And the pace was accelerating. The mass of men, tormented and writhing, was trying, by a common instinct, to reach some clearer ground where they could re-form. Three faces were still intact, but the fourth had been caved in, and badly mauled, without its comrades being able to help it. The Guards had met a fresh rush of the Hadendowas, and had blown back the tribesmen with a volley, and the cavalry had ridden over another stream of them, as they welled out of the gully. A litter of hamstrung horses, and haggled men behind them, showed that a spearman on his face among the bushes can show some sport to the man who charges him. But, in spite of all, the square was still reeling swiftly backwards, trying to shake itself clear of this torment which clung to its heart. Would it break or would it reform? The lives of five regiments and the honour of the flag hung upon the answer.

Some, at least, were breaking. C Company of the Mallows had lost all military order, and was pushing back in spite of the haggard officers, who cursed, and shoved, and prayed in the vain attempt to hold them. The captain and the subalterns were elbowed and jostled, while the men crowded towards Private Conolly for their orders. The confusion had not spread, for the other companies, in the dust and smoke and turmoil, had lost touch with their mutinous comrades. Captain Foley saw that even now there might be time to avert a disaster. 'Think what you are doing, man,' he yelled, rushing towards the ringleader. 'There are a thousand Irish in the square, and they are dead men if we break.'

The words alone might have had little effect on the old moonlighter. It is possible that, in his scheming brain, he had already planned how he was to club his Irish together and lead them to the sea. But at that moment the Arabs broke through the screen of camels which had fended them off. There was a struggle, a screaming, a mule rolled over, a wounded man sprang up in a cacolet with a spear through him, and then through the narrow gap surged a stream of naked savages, mad with battle, drunk with slaughter, spotted and splashed with blood – blood dripping from their spears, their arms, their faces. Their yells, their bounds, their crouching, darting figures, the horrid energy of their spear-thrusts, made them look like a blast of fiends from the pit. And were these the allies of Ireland? Were these the men who were to strike for her against her enemies? Conolly's soul rose up in loathing at the thought.

He was a man of firm purpose, and yet at the first sight of those howling fiends that purpose faltered, and at the second it was blown to the winds. He saw a huge coal-black negro seize a shrieking camel-driver and saw at his throat with a knife. He saw a shock-headed tribesman plunge his great spear through the back of their own little bugler from Mill Street. He saw a dozen deeds of blood – the murder of the wounded, the hacking of the unarmed – and caught, too, in a glance, the good wholesome faces of the faced-about rear rank of the Marines. The Mallows, too, had faced about, and in an instant Conolly had thrown himself into the heart of C Company, striving with the officers to form the men up with their comrades.

But the mischief had gone too far. The rank and file had no heart in their work. They had broken before, and this last rush of murderous savages was a hard thing for broken men to stand against. They flinched from the furious faces and dripping forearms. Why should they throw away their lives for a flag for which they cared nothing? Why should their leader urge them to break, and now shriek to them to re-form? They would not re-form. They wanted to get to the sea and to safety. He flung himself among them with outstretched arms, with words of reason, with shouts, with gaspings. It was useless; the tide was beyond his control. They were shredding out into the desert with their faces set for the coast.

'Bhoys, will ye stand for this?' screamed a voice. It was so ringing, so strenuous, that the breaking Mallows glanced backwards. They were held by what they saw. Private Conolly had planted his rifle-stock downwards in a mimosa bush. From the fixed bayonet there fluttered a little green flag with the crownless harp. God knows for what black mutiny, for what signal of revolt, that flag had been treasured up within the corporal's tunic! Now its green wisp stood amid the rush, while three proud regimental colours were reeling slowly backwards.

'What for the flag?' yelled the private.

'My heart's blood for it! and mine! and mine!' cried a score of voices. 'God bless it! The flag, boys – the flag!'

C Company were rallying upon it. The stragglers clutched at each other, and pointed. 'Here, McQuire, Flynn, O'Hara,' ran the shoutings. 'Close on the flag! Back to the flag!' The three standards reeled backwards, and the seething square strove for a clearer space where they could form their shattered ranks; but C Company, grim and powder-stained, choked with enemies and falling fast, still closed in on the little rebel ensign that flapped from the mimosa bush.

It was a good half-hour before the square, having disentangled itself from its difficulties and dressed its ranks, began to move slowly forward over the ground across which in its labour and anguish it had been driven. The long trail of Wessex men and Arabs showed but too clearly the path they had come.

'How many got into us, Stephen?' asked the general, tapping his snuff-box.

'I should put them down at a thousand or twelve hundred, sir.'

'I did not see any get out again. What the devil were the Wessex thinking about? The Guards stood well, though; so did the Mallows.'

'Colonel Flanagan reports that his front flank company was cut off, sir.'

'Why, that's the company that was out of hand when we advanced!'

'Colonel Flanagan reports, sir, that the company took the whole brunt of the attack, and gave the square time to re-form.'

'Tell the Hussars to ride forward, Stephen,' said the general, 'and try if they can see anything of them. There's no firing, and I fear that the Mallows will want to do some recruiting. Let the square take ground by the right, and then advance!'

But Sheikh Kadra of the Hadendowas saw from his knoll that the men with the big hats had rallied, and that they were coming back in the quiet business fashion of men whose work was before them. He took counsel with Moussa the Berber and Hussein the Baggara, and a woestruck man was he when he learned that the third of his men were safe in the Moslem paradise. So, having still some signs of victory to show, he gave the word, and the desert warriors flitted off unseen and unheard, even as they had come.

A red-rock plateau, a few hundred spears and Remingtons, and a plain which for the second time was strewn with slaughtered men, was all that his day's fighting gave to the English general.

It was a squadron of Hussars which came first to the spot where the rebel flag had waved. A dense litter of Arab dead marked the place. Within, the flag waved no longer, but the rifle stood in the mimosa bush, and round it, with their wounds in front, lay the Fenian private and the silent ranks of the Irishry. Sentiment is not an English failing, but the Hussar captain raised his hilt in a salute as he rode past the blood-soaked ring.

The British general sent home dispatches, and so did the chief of the Hadendowas, though the style and manner differed somewhat. The latter ran thus:

> Sheikh Kadra of the Hadendowa people to Mohammed Ahmed, the chosen of Allah, homage and greeting. Know by this that on the fourth day of this moon we gave battle to the Kaffirs who call themselves Inglees, having with us the Chief Hussein with ten thousand of the faithful. By the blessing of Allah we have broken them, and chased them for a mile, though indeed these infidels are different from the dogs of Egypt, and have slain very many of our men. Yet we hope to smite them again ere the new moon be come, to which end I trust that thou wilt send us a thousand dervishes from Omdurman. In token of our victory I send you by this messenger a flag which we have taken. By the colour it might well seem to have belonged to those of the true faith, but the Kaffirs gave their blood freely to save it, and so we think that, though small, it is very dear to them.

The Lord of Château Noir

It was in the days when the German armies had broken their way across France, and when the shattered forces of the young Republic had been swept away to the north of the Aisne and to the south of the Loire. Three broad streams of armed men had rolled slowly but irresistibly from the Rhine, now meandering to the north, now to the south, dividing, coalescing, but all uniting to form one great lake round Paris. And from this lake there welled out smaller streams – one to the north, one southward, to Orleans, and a third westward to Normandy. Many a German trooper saw the sea for the first time when he rode his horse girth-deep into the waves at Dieppe.

Black and bitter were the thoughts of Frenchmen when they saw this weal of dishonour slashed across the fair face of their country. They had fought and they had been overborne. That swarming cavalry, those countless footmen, the masterful guns – they had tried and tried to make head against them. In battalions their invaders were not to be beaten, but man to man, or ten to ten, they were their equals. A brave Frenchman might still make a single German rue the day that he had left his own bank of the Rhine. Thus, unchronicled amid the battles and the sieges, there broke out another war, a war of individuals, with foul murder upon the one side and brutal reprisal on the other.

Colonel von Gramm, of the 24th Posen Infantry, had suffered severely during this new development. He commanded in the little Norman town of Les Andelys, and his outposts stretched amid the hamlets and farmhouses of the district round. No French force was within fifty miles of him, and yet morning after morning he had to listen to a black report of sentries found dead at their posts, or of foraging parties which had never returned. Then the colonel would go forth in his wrath, and farmsteadings would blaze and villages tremble; but next morning there was still that same dismal tale to be told. Do what he might, he could not shake off his invisible enemies. And yet it should not have been so hard, for, from certain signs in common, in the plan and in the deed, it was certain that all these outrages came from a single source.

Colonel von Gramm had tried violence, and it had failed. Gold might be more successful. He published it abroad over the countryside that five hundred francs would be paid for information. There was no response. Then eight hundred francs. The peasants were incorruptible. Then, goaded on by a murdered corporal, he rose to a thousand, and so bought the soul of

François Rejane, farm labourer, whose Norman avarice was a stronger passion than his French hatred.

'You say that you know who did these crimes?' asked the Prussian colonel, eyeing with loathing the blue-bloused, rat-faced creature before him.

'Yes, colonel.'

'And it was – ?'

'Those thousand francs, colonel – '

'Not a sou until your story has been tested. Come! Who is it who has murdered my men?'

'It is Count Eustace of Château Noir.'

'You lie!' cried the colonel, angrily. 'A gentleman and a nobleman could not have done such crimes.'

The peasant shrugged his shoulders. 'It is evident to me that you do not know the count. It is this way, colonel. What I tell you is the truth, and I am not afraid that you should test it. The Count of Château Noir is a hard man, even at the best time he was a hard man. But of late he has been terrible. It was his son's death, you know. His son was under Douay, and he was taken, and then in escaping from Germany he met his death. It was the count's only child, and indeed we all think that it has driven him mad. With his peasants he follows the German armies. I do not know how many he has killed, but it is he who cut the cross upon the foreheads, for it is the badge of his house.'

It was true. The murdered sentries had each had a saltire cross slashed across their brows, as by a hunting-knife. The colonel bent his stiff back and ran his forefinger over the map which lay upon the table.

'The Château Noir is not more than four leagues,' he said.

'Three and a kilometre, colonel.'

'You know the place?'

'I used to work there.'

Colonel von Gramm rang the bell. 'Give this man food and detain him,' said he to the sergeant.

'Why detain me, colonel? I can tell you no more.'

'We shall need you as guide.'

'As guide? But the count? If I were to fall into his hands? Ah, colonel – '

The Prussian commander waved him away. 'Send Captain Baumgarten to me at once,' said he.

The officer who answered the summons was a man of middle-age, heavy-jawed, blue-eyed, with a curving yellow moustache, and a brick-red face which turned to an ivory white where his helmet had sheltered it. He was bald, with a shining, tightly stretched scalp, at the back of which, as in a mirror, it was a favourite mess-joke of the subalterns to trim their moustaches. As a soldier he was slow, but reliable and brave. The colonel could trust him where a more dashing officer might be in danger.

'You will proceed to Château Noir tonight, captain,' said he. 'A guide has been provided. You will arrest the count and bring him back. If there is an attempt at rescue, shoot him at once.'

'How many men shall I take, colonel?'

'Well, we are surrounded by spies, and our only chance is to pounce upon him before he knows that we are on the way. A large force will attract attention. On the other hand, you must not risk being cut off.'

'I might march north, colonel, as if to join General Goeben. Then I could turn down this road which I see upon your map, and get to Château Noir before they could hear of us. In that case, with twenty men – '

'Very good, captain. I hope to see you with your prisoner tomorrow morning.'

It was a cold December night when Captain Baumgarten marched out of Les Andelys with his twenty Poseners, and took the main road to the north-west. Two miles out he turned suddenly down a narrow, deeply rutted track, and made swiftly for his man. A thin, cold rain was falling, swishing among the tall poplar trees and rustling in the fields on either side. The captain walked first with Moser, a veteran sergeant, beside him. The sergeant's wrist was fastened to that of the French peasant, and it had been whispered in his ear that in case of an ambush the first bullet fired would be through his head. Behind them the twenty infantrymen plodded along through the darkness with their faces sunk to the rain, and their boots squeaking in the soft, wet clay. They knew where they were going, and why, and the thought upheld them, for they were bitter at the loss of their comrades. It was a cavalry job, they knew, but the cavalry were all on with the advance, and, besides, it was more fitting that the regiment should avenge its own dead men.

It was nearly eight when they left Les Andelys. At half-past eleven their guide stopped at a place where two high pillars, crowned with some heraldic stonework, flanked a huge iron gate. The wall in which it had been the opening had crumbled away, but the great gate still towered above the brambles and weeds which had overgrown its base. The Prussians made their way round it and advanced stealthily, under the shadow of a tunnel of oak branches, up the long avenue, which was still cumbered by the leaves of last autumn. At the top they halted and reconnoitred.

The black château lay in front of them. The moon had shone out between two rain-clouds, and threw the old house into silver and shadow. It was shaped like an L, with a low arched door in front and lines of small windows like the open ports of a man-of-war. Above was a dark roof, breaking at the corners into little round overhanging turrets, the whole lying silent in the moonshine, with a drift of ragged clouds blackening the heavens behind it. A single light gleamed in one of the lower windows.

The captain whispered his orders to his men. Some were to creep to the front door, some to the back. Some were to watch the east, and some the west. He and the sergeant stole on tiptoe to the lighted window.

It was a small room into which they looked, very meanly furnished. An elderly man, in the dress of a menial, was reading a tattered paper by the light of a guttering candle. He leaned back in his wooden chair with his feet upon a box, while a bottle of white wine stood with a half-filled tumbler upon a stool beside him. The sergeant thrust his needle-gun through the glass, and the man sprang to his feet with a shriek.

'Silence, for your life! The house is surrounded, and you cannot escape. Come round and open the door, or we will show you no mercy when we come in.'

'For God's sake, don't shoot! I will open it! I will open it!' He rushed from the room with his paper still crumpled up in his hand. An instant later, with a groaning of old locks and a rasping of bars, the low door swung open, and the Prussians poured into the stone-flagged passage.

'Where is Count Eustace de Château Noir?'

'My master! He is out, sir.'

'Out at this time of night? Your life for a lie!'

'It is true, sir. He is out!'

'Where?'

'I do not know.'

'Doing what?'

'I cannot tell. No, it is no use your cocking your pistol, sir. You may kill me, but you cannot make me tell you that which I do not know.'

'Is he often out at this hour?'

'Frequently.'

'And when does he come home?'

'Before daybreak.'

Captain Baumgarten rasped out a German oath. He had had his journey for nothing, then. The man's answers were only too likely to be true. It was what he might have expected. But at least he would search the house and make sure. Leaving a picket at the front door and another at the back, the sergeant and he drove the trembling butler in front of them – his shaking candle sending strange, flickering shadows over the old tapestries and the low, oak-raftered ceilings. They searched the whole house, from the huge stone-flagged kitchen below to the dining-hall on the second floor, with its gallery for musicians, and its panelling black with age, but nowhere was there a living creature. Up above, in an attic, they found Marie, the elderly wife of the butler; but the owner kept no other servants, and of his own presence there was no trace.

It was long, however, before Captain Baumgarten had satisfied himself upon the point. It was a difficult house to search. Thin stairs, which only one man could ascend at a time, connected lines of tortuous corridors. The walls were so thick that each room was cut off from its neighbour. Huge fireplaces yawned in each, while the windows were six feet deep in the wall. Captain Baumgarten stamped with his feet, tore down curtains, and struck with the pommel of his sword. If there were secret hiding-places, he was not fortunate enough to find them.

'I have an idea,' said he, at last, speaking in German to the sergeant. 'You will place a guard over this fellow, and make sure that he communicates with no one.'

'Yes, captain.'

'And you will place four men in ambush at the front and at the back. It is likely enough that about daybreak our bird may return to the nest.'

'And the others, captain?'

'Let them have their suppers in the kitchen. The fellow will serve you with meat and wine. It is a wild night, and we shall be better here than on the country road.'

'And yourself, captain?'

'I will take my supper up here in the dining-hall. The logs are laid and we can light the fire. You will call me if there is any alarm. What can you give me for supper – you?'

'Alas, monsieur, there was a time when I might have answered, 'What you wish!' but now it is all that we can do to find a bottle of new claret and a cold pullet.'

'That will do very well. Let a guard go about with him, sergeant, and let him feel the end of a bayonet if he plays us any tricks.'

Captain Baumgarten was an old campaigner. In the Eastern provinces, and before that in Bohemia, he had learned the art of quartering himself upon the enemy. While the butler brought his supper he occupied himself in making his preparations for a comfortable night. He lit the candelabrum of ten candles upon the centre table. The fire was already burning up, crackling merrily, and sending spurts of blue, pungent smoke into the room. The captain walked to the window and looked out. The moon had gone in again, and it was raining heavily. He could hear the deep sough of the wind, and see the dark loom of the trees, all swaying in the one direction. It was a sight which gave a zest to his comfortable quarters, and to the cold fowl and the bottle of wine which the butler had brought up for him. He was tired and hungry after his long tramp, so he threw his sword, his helmet and his revolver-belt down upon a chair, and fell to eagerly upon his supper. Then, with his glass of wine before him and his cigar between his lips, he tilted his chair back and looked about him.

He sat within a small circle of brilliant light which gleamed upon his silver shoulder-straps and threw out his terracotta face, his heavy eyebrows and his yellow moustache. But outside that circle things were vague and shadowy in the old dining-hall. Two sides were oak-panelled and two were hung with faded tapestry, across which huntsmen and dogs and stags were still dimly streaming. Above the fireplace were rows of heraldic shields with the blazonings of the family and of its alliances, the fatal saltire cross breaking out on each of them.

Four paintings of old seigneurs of Château Noir faced the fireplace, all men with hawk noses and bold, high features, so like each other that only the dress could distinguish the Crusader from the Cavalier of the Fronde. Captain Baumgarten, heavy with his repast, lay back in his chair looking up at them through the clouds of his tobacco smoke, and pondering over the strange chance which had sent him, a man from the Baltic coast, to eat his supper in the ancestral hall of these proud Norman chieftains. But the fire was hot, and the captain's eyes were heavy. His chin sank slowly upon his chest, and the ten candles gleamed upon the broad, white scalp.

Suddenly a slight noise brought him to his feet. For an instant it seemed to his dazed senses that one of the pictures opposite had walked from its frame. There, beside the table, and almost within arm's length of him, was standing a huge man, silent, motionless, with no sign of life save his fierce-glinting eyes. He was black-haired, olive-skinned, with a pointed tuft of black beard, and a great, fierce nose, towards which all his features seemed to run. His cheeks were wrinkled like a last year's apple, but his sweep of shoulder, and bony, corded hands, told of a strength which was unsapped by age. His arms were folded across his arching chest, and his mouth was set in a fixed smile.

'Pray do not trouble yourself to look for your weapons,' he said, as the Prussian cast a swift glance at the empty chair in which they had been laid. 'You have been, if you will allow me to say so, a little indiscreet to make yourself so much at home in a house every wall of which is honeycombed with secret passages. You will be amused to hear that forty men were watching you at your supper. Ah! what then?'

Captain Baumgarten had taken a step forward with clenched fists. The Frenchman held up the revolver which he grasped in his right hand, while with the left he hurled the German back into his chair.

'Pray keep your seat,' said he. 'You have no cause to trouble about your men. They have already been provided for. It is astonishing with these stone floors how little one can hear what goes on beneath. You have been relieved of your command, and have now only to think of yourself. May I ask what your name is?'

'I am Captain Baumgarten of the 24th Posen Regiment.'

'Your French is excellent, though you incline, like most of your country-men, to turn the p into a b. I have been amused to hear them cry, "Avez bitie sur moi!" You know, doubtless, who it is who addresses you.'

'The Count of Château Noir.'

'Precisely. It would have been a misfortune if you had visited my château and I had been unable to have a word with you. I have had to do with many German soldiers, but never with an officer before. I have much to talk to you about.'

Captain Baumgarten sat still in his chair. Brave as he was, there was something in this man's manner which made his skin creep with apprehension. His eyes glanced to right and to left, but his weapons were gone, and in a struggle he saw that he was but a child to this gigantic adversary. The count had picked up the claret bottle and held it to the light.

'Tut! tut!' said he. 'And was this the best that Pierre could do for you? I am ashamed to look you in the face, Captain Baumgarten. We must improve upon this.'

He blew a call upon a whistle which hung from his shooting-jacket. The old manservant was in the room in an instant.

'Chambertin from bin 15!' he cried, and a minute later a grey bottle, streaked with cobwebs, was carried in as a nurse bears an infant. The count filled two glasses to the brim.

'Drink!' said he. 'It is the very best in my cellars, and not to be matched between Rouen and Paris. Drink, sir, and be happy! There are cold joints below. There are two lobsters, fresh from Honfleur. Will you not venture upon a second and more savoury supper?'

The German officer shook his head. He drained the glass, however, and his host filled it once more, pressing him to give an order for this or that dainty.

'There is nothing in my house which is not at your disposal. You have but to say the word. Well, then, you will allow me to tell you a story while you drink your wine. I have so longed to tell it to some German officer. It is about my son, my only child, Eustace, who was taken and died in escaping. It is a curious little story, and I think that I can promise you that you will never forget it.

'You must know, then, that my boy was in the artillery – a fine young fellow, Captain Baumgarten, and the pride of his mother. She died within a week of the news of his death reaching us. It was brought by a brother officer who was at his side throughout, and who escaped while my lad died. I want to tell you all that he told me.

'Eustace was taken at Weissenburg on the 4th of August. The prisoners were broken up into parties, and sent back into Germany by different routes. Eustace was taken upon the 5th to a village called Lauterburg, where he met with kindness from the German officer in command. This good colonel had the hungry lad to supper, offered him the best he had, opened a bottle of good wine, as I have tried to do for you, and gave him a cigar from his own case. Might I entreat you to take one from mine?'

The German again shook his head. His horror of his companion had increased as he sat watching the lips that smiled and the eyes that glared.

'The colonel, as I say, was good to my boy. But, unluckily, the prisoners were moved next day across the Rhine into Ettlingen. They were not equally fortunate there. The officer who guarded them was a ruffian and a villain, Captain Baumgarten. He took a pleasure in humiliating and ill-treating the brave men who had fallen into his power. That night upon my son answering fiercely back to some taunt of his, he struck him in the eye, like this!'

The crash of the blow rang through the hall. The German's face fell forward, his hand up, and blood oozing through his fingers. The count settled down in his chair once more.

'My boy was disfigured by the blow, and this villain made his appearance the object of his jeers. By the way, you look a little comical yourself at the present moment, captain, and your colonel would certainly say that you had been getting into mischief. To continue, however, my boy's youth and his destitution – for his pockets were empty – moved the pity of a kind-hearted major, and he advanced him ten Napoleons from his own pocket without security of any kind. Into your hands, Captain Baumgarten, I return these ten gold pieces, since I cannot learn the name of the lender. I am grateful from my heart for this kindness shown to my boy.

'The vile tyrant who commanded the escort accompanied the prisoners to Durlack, and from there to Carlsruhe. He heaped every outrage upon my lad, because the spirit of the Château Noirs would not stoop to turn away his wrath by a feigned submission. Ay, this cowardly villain, whose heart's blood shall yet clot upon this hand, dared to strike my son with his open hand, to kick him, to tear hairs from his moustache – to use him thus – and thus – and thus!'

The German writhed and struggled. He was helpless in the hands of this huge giant whose blows were raining upon him. When at last, blinded and half-senseless, he staggered to his feet, it was only to be hurled back again into the great oaken chair. He sobbed in his impotent anger and shame.

'My boy was frequently moved to tears by the humiliation of his position,' continued the count. 'You will understand me when I say that it is a bitter thing to be helpless in the hands of an insolent and remorseless enemy. On arriving at Carlsruhe, however, his face, which had been wounded by the brutality of his guard, was bound up by a young Bavarian subaltern who was touched by his appearance. I regret to see that your eye is bleeding so. Will you permit me to bind it with my silk handkerchief?'

He leaned forward, but the German dashed his hand aside.

'I am in your power, you monster!' he cried; 'I can endure your brutalities, but not your hypocrisy.'

The count shrugged his shoulders.

'I am taking things in their order, just as they occurred,' said he. 'I was under vow to tell it to the first German officer with whom I could talk tête-à-tête. Let me see, I had got as far as the young Bavarian at Carlsruhe. I regret extremely that you will not permit me to use such slight skill in surgery as I possess. At Carlsruhe, my lad was shut up in the old *caserne*, where he remained for a fortnight. The worst pang of his captivity was that some unmannerly curs in the garrison would taunt him with his position as he sat by his window in the evening. That reminds me, captain, that you are not quite situated upon a bed of roses yourself, are you now? You came to trap a wolf, my man, and now the beast has you down with his fangs in your throat. A family man, too, I should judge, by that well-filled tunic. Well, a widow the more will make little matter, and they do not usually remain widows long. Get back into the chair, you dog!

'Well, to continue my story – at the end of a fortnight my son and his friend escaped. I need not trouble you with the dangers which they ran, or with the privations which they endured. Suffice it that to disguise themselves they had to take the clothes of two peasants, whom they waylaid in a wood. Hiding by day and travelling by night, they had got as far into France as Remilly, and were within a mile – a single mile, captain – of crossing the German lines when a patrol of Uhlans came right upon them. Ah! it was hard, was it not, when they had come so far and were so near to safety?' The count blew a double call upon his whistle, and three hard-faced peasants entered the room.

'These must represent my Uhlans,' said he. 'Well, then, the captain in command, finding that these men were French soldiers in civilian dress within the German lines, proceeded to hang them without trial or ceremony. I think, Jean, that the centre beam is the strongest.'

The unfortunate soldier was dragged from his chair to where a noosed rope had been flung over one of the huge oaken rafters which spanned the room. The cord was slipped over his head, and he felt its harsh grip round his throat. The three peasants seized the other end, and looked to the count for his orders. The officer, pale, but firm, folded his arms and stared defiantly at the man who tortured him.

'You are now face to face with death, and I perceive from your lips that you are praying. My son was also face to face with death, and he prayed, also. It happened that a general officer came up, and he heard the lad praying for his mother, and it moved him so – he being himself a father – that he ordered his Uhlans away, and he remained with his aide-de-camp only beside the condemned men. And when he heard all the lad had to tell – that he was the only child of an old family, and that his mother was in failing health – he threw off the rope as I throw off this, and he kissed him on either cheek, as I kiss you, and he bade him go, as I bid you go, and may every kind wish of that noble general, though it could not stave off the fever which slew my son, descend now upon your head.'

And so it was that Captain Baumgarten, disfigured, blinded and bleeding, staggered out into the wind and the rain of that wild December dawn.

The Three Correspondents

There was only the one little feathery clump of palms in all that great wilderness of black rocks and orange sand. It stood high on the bank, and below it the brown Nile swirled swiftly towards the Ambigole Cataract, fitting a little frill of foam round each of the boulders which studded its surface. Above, out of a naked blue sky, the sun was beating down upon the sand, and up again from the sand under the brims of the pith-hats of the horsemen with the scorching glare of a blast-furnace. It had risen so high that the shadows of the horses were no larger than themselves.

'Whew!' cried Mortimer, mopping his forehead, 'you'd pay five shillings for this at the hammam.'

'Precisely,' said Scott. 'But you are not asked to ride twenty miles in a Turkish bath with field-glasses and a revolver and a water-bottle and a whole Christmas-treeful of things dangling from you. The hot-house at Kew is excellent as a conservatory, but not adapted for exhibitions upon the horizontal bar. I vote for a camp in the palm-grove and a halt until evening.'

Mortimer rose on his stirrups and looked hard to the southward. Everywhere were the same black burned rocks and deep orange sand. At one spot only an intermittent line appeared to have been cut through the rugged spurs which ran down to the river. It was the bed of the old railway, long destroyed by the Arabs, but now in process of reconstruction by the advancing Egyptians. There was no other sign of man's handiwork in all that desolate scene.

'It's palm trees or nothing,' said Scott.

'Well, I suppose we must; and yet I grudge every hour until we catch the force up. What *would* our editors say if we were late for the action?'

'My dear chap, an old bird like you doesn't need to be told that no sane modern general would ever attack until the press is up.'

'You don't mean that?' said young Anerley. 'I thought we were looked upon as an unmitigated nuisance.'

' "Newspaper correspondents and travelling gentlemen, and all that tribe of useless drones" – being an extract from Lord Wolseley's *Soldier's Pocket-Book*,' cried Scott. 'We know all about *that*, Anerley;' and he winked behind his blue spectacles. 'If there was going to be a battle we should very soon have an escort of cavalry to hurry us up. I've been in fifteen, and I never saw one where they had not arranged for a reporter's table.'

'That's very well; but the enemy may be less considerate,' said Mortimer.

'They are not strong enough to force a battle.'

'A skirmish, then?'

'Much more likely to be a raid upon the rear. In that case we are just where we should be.'

'So we are! What a score over Reuters' man up with the advance! Well, we'll outspan and have our tiffin under the palms.'

There were three of them, and they stood for three great London dailies. Reuters was thirty miles ahead; two evening pennies upon camels were twenty miles behind. And among them they represented the eyes and ears of the public – the great silent millions and millions who had paid for every-thing, and who waited so patiently to know the result of their outlay.

They were remarkable men these body-servants of the press; two of them already veterans in camps, the other setting out upon his first campaign, and full of deference for his famous comrades.

This first one, who had just dismounted from his bay polo-pony, was Mortimer, of the *Intelligence* – tall, straight and hawk-faced, with khaki tunic and riding-breeches, drab putties, a scarlet cummerbund, and a skin tanned to the red of a Scotch fir by sun and wind, and mottled by the mosquito and the sand-fly. The other – small, quick, mercurial, with blue-black, curling beard and hair, a fly-switch for ever flicking in his left hand – was Scott, of the *Courier*, who had come through more dangers and brought off more brilliant *coups* than any man in the profession, save the eminent Chandler, now no longer in a condition to take the field. They were a singular contrast, Mortimer and Scott, and it was in their differences that the secret of their close friendship lay. Each dovetailed into the other. The strength of each was in the other's weakness. Together they formed a perfect unit. Mortimer was Saxon – slow, conscientious and deliberate; Scott was Celtic – quick, happy-go-lucky and brilliant. Mortimer was the more solid, Scott the more attractive. Mortimer was the deeper thinker, Scott the brighter talker. By a curious coincidence, though each had seen much of warfare, their campaigns had never coincided. Together they covered all recent military history. Scott had done Plevna, the Shipka, the Zulus, Egypt, Suakim; Mortimer had seen the Boer War, the Chilian, the Bulgaria and Serbian, the Gordon relief, the Indian frontier, Brazilian rebellion and Madagascar. This intimate personal knowledge gave a peculiar flavour to their talk. There was none of the second-hand surmise and conjecture which form so much of our conversation; it was all concrete and final. The speaker had been there, had seen it, and there was an end of it.

In spite of their friendship there was the keenest professional rivalry between the two men. Either would have sacrificed himself to help his companion, but either would also have sacrificed his companion to help his paper. Never did a jockey yearn for a winning mount as keenly as each of them longed to have a full column in a morning edition whilst every other daily was blank. They were perfectly frank about the matter. Each professed himself ready to steal a march on his neighbour, and each recognised that the other's duty to his employer was far higher than any personal consideration.

The third man was Anerley, of the *Gazette* – young, inexperienced, and rather simple-looking. He had a droop of the lip, which some of his more intimate friends regarded as a libel upon his character, and his eyes were so slow and so sleepy that they suggested an affectation. A leaning towards soldiering had sent him twice to autumn manoeuvres, and a touch of colour in his descriptions had induced the proprietors of the *Gazette* to give him a trial as a war-special. There was a pleasing diffidence about his bearing which recommended him to his experienced companions, and if they had a smile sometimes at his guileless ways, it was soothing to them to have a comrade from whom nothing was to be feared. From the day that they left the telegraph-wire behind them at Sarras, the man who was mounted upon a fifteen-guinea thirteen-four Syrian was delivered over into the hands of the owners of the two fastest polo-ponies that ever shot down the Ghezireh ground. The three had dismounted and led their beasts under the welcome shade. In the brassy, yellow glare every branch above threw so black and solid a shadow that the men involuntarily raised their feet to step over them.

'The palm makes an excellent hat-rack,' said Scott, slinging his revolver and his water-bottle over the little upward-pointing pegs which bristle from the trunk. 'As a shade tree, however, it isn't an unqualified success. Curious that in the universal adaptation of means to ends something a little less flimsy could not have been devised for the tropics.'

'Like the banyan in India.'

'Or the fine hardwood trees in Ashantee, where a whole regiment could picnic under the shade.'

'The teak tree isn't bad in Burmah, either. By Jove, the baccy has all come loose in the saddle-bag! That long-cut mixture smokes rather hot for this climate. How about the baggles, Anerley?'

'They'll be here in five minutes.'

Down the winding path which curved among the rocks the little train of baggage-camels was daintily picking its way. They came mincing and undulating along, turning their heads slowly from side to side with the air of self-conscious women. In front rode the three Berberee body-servants upon donkeys, and behind walked the Arab camel-boys. They had been travelling for nine long hours, ever since the first rising of the moon, at the weary camel-drag of two and a half miles an hour, but now they brightened, both beasts and men, at the sight of the grove and the riderless horses. In a few minutes the loads were unstrapped, the animals tethered, a fire lighted, fresh water carried up from the river, and each camel-boy provided with his own little heap of tiffin laid in the centre of the table-cloth, without which no well-bred Arabian will condescend to feed. The dazzling light without, the subdued half-tones within, the green palm-fronds outlined against the deep blue sky, the flitting, silent-footed Arab servants, the crackling of sticks, the reek of a lighting fire, the placid supercilious heads of the camels, they all come back in their dreams to those who have known them.

Scott was breaking eggs into a pan and rolling out a love-song in his rich, deep voice. Anerley, with his head and arms buried in a deal packing-case, was working his way through strata of tinned soups, bully beef, potted chicken and sardines to reach the jams which lay beneath. The conscientious Mortimer, with his notebook upon his knee, was jotting down what the railway engineer had told him at the line-end the day before. Suddenly he raised his eyes and saw the man himself on his chestnut pony, dipping and rising over the broken ground.

'Hallo! Here's Merryweather!'

'A pretty lather his pony is in! He's had her at that hand-gallop for hours, by the look of her. Hallo, Merryweather, hallo!'

The engineer, a small, compact man with a pointed red beard, had made as though he would ride past their camp without word or halt. Now he swerved, and easing his pony down to a canter, he headed her towards them.

'For God's sake, a drink!' he croaked. 'My tongue is stuck to the roof of my mouth.'

Mortimer ran with the water-bottle, Scott with the whisky-flask and Anerley with the tin pannikin. The engineer drank until his breath failed him.

'Well, I must be off,' said he, striking the drops from his red moustache.

'Any news?'

'A hitch in the railway construction. I must see the general. It's the devil not having a telegraph.'

'Anything we can report?' Out came three notebooks.

'I'll tell you after I've seen the general.'

'Any dervishes?'

'The usual shaves. Hud-up, Jinny! Goodbye!'

With a soft thudding upon the sand and a clatter among the stones the weary pony was off upon her journey once more.

'Nothing serious, I suppose?' said Mortimer, staring after him.

'Deuced serious,' cried Scott. 'The ham and eggs are burned! No – it's all right – saved, and done to a turn! Pull the box up, Anerley. Come on, Mortimer, stow that notebook! The fork is mightier than the pen just at present. What's the matter with you, Anerley?'

'I was wondering whether what we have just seen was worth a telegram.'

'Well, it's for the proprietors to say if it's worth it. Sordid money considerations are not for us. We must wire about something just to justify our khaki coats and our putties.'

'But what is there to say?'

Mortimer's long, austere face broke into a smile over the youngster's innocence. 'It's not quite usual in our profession to give each other tips,' said he. 'However, as my telegram is written, I've no objection to your reading it. You may be sure that I would not show it to you if it were of the slightest importance.'

Anerley took up the slip of paper and read:

Merryweather obstacles stop journey confer general stop nature difficulties later stop rumours dervishes.

'This is very condensed,' said Anerley, with wrinkled brows.

'Condensed!' cried Scott. 'Why, it's sinfully garrulous. If my old man got a wire like that his language would crack the lampshades. I'd cut out half this; for example, I'd have out "journey", and "nature", and "rumours". But my old man would make a ten-line paragraph of it for all that.'

'How?'

'Well, I'll do it myself just to show you. Lend me that stylo.' He scribbled for a minute in his notebook. 'It works out somewhat on these lines:

Mr Charles H. Merryweather, the eminent railway engineer, who is at present engaged in superintending the construction of the line from Sarras to the front, has met with considerable obstacles to the rapid completion of his important task –

Of course the old man knows who Merryweather is, and what he is about, so the word "obstacles" would suggest all that to him.

He has today been compelled to make a journey of forty miles to the front, in order to confer with the general upon the steps which are necessary in order to facilitate the work. Further particulars of the exact nature of the difficulties met with will be made public at a later date. All is quiet upon the line of communications, though the usual persistent rumours of the presence of dervishes in the Eastern desert continue to circulate.   Our own correspondent.

'How's that?' cried Scott, triumphantly, and his white teeth gleamed suddenly through his black beard. 'That's the sort of flapdoodle for the dear old public.'

'Will it interest them?'

'Oh, everything interests them. They want to know all about it; and they like to think that there is a man who is getting a hundred a month simply in order to tell it to them.'

'It's very kind of you to teach me all this.'

'Well, it is a little unconventional, for, after all, we are here to score over each other if we can. There are no more eggs, and you must take it out in jam. Of course, as Mortimer says, such a telegram as this is of no importance one way or another, except to prove to the office that we *are* in the Sudan, and not at Monte Carlo. But when it comes to serious work it must be every man for himself.'

'Is that quite necessary?'

'Why, of course it is.'

'I should have thought if three men were to combine and to share their news, they would do better than if they were each to act for himself, and they would have a much pleasanter time of it.'

The two older men sat with their bread-and-jam in their hands, and an expression of genuine disgust upon their faces.

'We are not here to have a pleasant time,' said Mortimer, with a flash through his glasses. 'We are here to do our best for our papers. How can they score over each other if we do not do the same? If we all combine we might as well amalgamate with Reuters at once.'

'Why, it would take away the whole glory of the profession!' cried Scott. 'At present the smartest man gets his stuff first on the wires. What inducement is there to be smart if we all share and share alike?'

'And at present the man with the best equipment has the best chance,' remarked Mortimer, glancing across at the shot-silk polo ponies and the cheap little Syrian grey. 'That is the fair reward of foresight and enterprise. Every man for himself, and let the best man win.'

'That's the way to find who the best man is. Look at Chandler. He would never have got his chance if he had not played always off his own bat. You've heard how he pretended to break his leg, sent his fellow-correspondent off for the doctor, and so got a fair start for the telegraph-office.'

'Do you mean to say that was legitimate?'

'Everything is legitimate. It's your wits against my wits.'

'I should call it dishonourable.'

'You may call it what you like. Chandler's paper got the battle and the other's didn't. It made Chandler's name.'

'Or take Westlake,' said Mortimer, cramming the tobacco into his pipe. 'Hi, Abdul, you may have the dishes! Westlake brought his stuff down by pretending to be the government courier, and using the relays of government horses. Westlake's paper sold half a million.'

'Is that legitimate also?' asked Anerley, thoughtfully.

'Why not?'

'Well, it looks a little like horse-stealing and lying.'

'Well, *I* think I should do a little horse-stealing and lying if I could have a column to myself in a London daily. What do you say, Scott?'

'Anything short of manslaughter.'

'And I'm not sure that I'd trust you there.'

'Well, I don't think I should be guilty of newspaper-man-slaughter. That I regard as a distinct breach of professional etiquette. But if any outsider comes between a highly charged correspondent and an electric wire, he does it at his peril. My dear Anerley, I tell you frankly that if you are going to handicap yourself with scruple you may just as well be in Fleet Street as in the Sudan. Our life is irregular. Our work has never been systematised. No doubt it will be someday, but the time is not yet. Do what you can and how you can, and be first on the wires; that's my advice to you; and also, that when next you come upon a campaign you bring with you the best horse that money can buy. Mortimer may beat me or I may beat Mortimer, but at least we know that between us we have the fastest ponies in the country. We have neglected no chance.'

'I am not so certain of that,' said Mortimer, slowly. 'You are aware, of course, that though a horse beats a camel on twenty miles, a camel beats a horse on thirty.'

'What, one of those camels?' cried Anerley in astonishment. The two seniors burst out laughing.

'No, no, the real high-bred trotter – the kind of beast the dervishes ride when they make their lightning raids.'

'Faster than a galloping horse?'

'Well, it tires a horse down. It goes the same gait all the way, and it wants neither halt nor drink, and it takes rough ground much better than a horse. They used to have long-distance races at Haifa, and the camel always won at thirty.'

'Still, we need not reproach ourselves, Scott, for we are not very likely to have to carry a thirty-mile message, they will have the field telegraph next week.'

'Quite so. But at the present moment – '

'I know, my dear chap; but there is no motion of urgency before the house. Load baggles at five o'clock; so you have just three hours clear. Any sign of the evening pennies?'

Mortimer swept the northern horizon with his binoculars. 'Not in sight yet.'

'They are quite capable of travelling during the heat of the day. Just the sort of thing evening pennies *would* do. Take care of your match, Anerley. These palm groves go up like a powder magazine if you set them alight. Bye-bye.' The two men crawled under their mosquito-nets and sank instantly into the easy sleep of those whose lives are spent in the open.

Young Anerley stood with his back against a palm tree and his briar between his lips, thinking over the advice which he had received. After all, they were the heads of the profession, these men, and it was not for him, the newcomer, to reform their methods. If they served their papers in this fashion, then he must do the same. They had at least been frank and generous in teaching him the rules of the game. If it was good enough for them it was good enough for him.

It was a broiling afternoon, and those thin frills of foam round the black, glistening necks of the Nile boulders looked delightfully cool and alluring. But it would not be safe to bathe for some hours to come. The air shimmered and vibrated over the baking stretch of sand and rock. There was not a breath of wind, and the droning and piping of the insects inclined one for sleep. Somewhere above a hoopoe was calling. Anerley knocked out his ashes, and was turning towards his couch, when his eye caught something moving in the desert to the south. It was a horseman riding towards them as swiftly as the broken ground would permit. A messenger from the army, thought Anerley; and then, as he watched, the sun suddenly struck the man on the side of the head, and his chin flamed into gold. There could not be two horsemen with beards of such a colour. It was Merryweather, the engineer, and he was returning. What on earth was he returning for? He had been so keen to see the general, and yet he was coming back with his mission unaccomplished. Was it that his pony was hopelessly foundered? It seemed to be moving well. Anerley picked up Mortimer's binoculars, and a foam-bespattered horse and a weary *koorbash*-cracking man came cantering up the centre of the field. But there was nothing in his appearance to explain the mystery of his return. Then as he watched them they dipped into a hollow and disappeared. He could see that it was one of those narrow *khors* which led to the river, and he waited, glass in hand, for their immediate reappearance. But minute passed after minute and there was no sign of them. That narrow gully appeared to have swallowed them up. And then with a curious gulp and start he saw a little grey cloud wreathe itself slowly from among the rocks and drift in a long, hazy shred over the desert. In an instant he had torn Scott and Mortimer from their slumbers.

'Get up, you chaps!' he cried. 'I believe Merryweather has been shot by dervishes.'

'And Reuters not here!' cried the two veterans, exultantly clutching at their notebooks. 'Merryweather shot! Where? When? How?'

In a few words Anerley explained what he had seen.

'You heard nothing?'

'Nothing.'

'Well, a shot loses itself very easily among rocks. By George, look at the buzzards!'

Two large brown birds were soaring in the deep blue heaven. As Scott spoke they circled down and dropped into the little *khor*.

'That's good enough,' said Mortimer, with his nose between the leaves of his book. ' "Merryweather headed dervishes stop return stop shot mutilated stop raid communications." How's that?'

'You think he was headed off?'

'Why else should he return?'

'In that case, if they were out in front of him and others cut him off, there must be several small raiding parties.'

'I should judge so.'

'How about the "mutilated"?'

'I've fought against Arabs before.'

'Where are you off to?'

'Sarras.'

'I think I'll race you in,' said Scott.

Anerley stared in astonishment at the absolutely impersonal way in which these men regarded the situation. In their zeal for news it had apparently never struck them that they, their camp and their servants were all in the lion's mouth. But even as they talked there came the harsh, importunate rat-tat-tat of an irregular volley from among the rocks, and the high, keening whistle of bullets over their heads. A palm spray fluttered down among them. At the same instant the six frightened servants came running wildly in for protection.

It was the cool-headed Mortimer who organised the defence, for Scott's Celtic soul was so aflame at all this 'copy' in hand and more to come that he was too exuberantly boisterous for a commander. The other, with his spectacles and his stern face, soon had the servants in hand. *'Tali henna! Egri!* What the deuce are you frightened about? Put the camels between the palm trunks. That's right. Now get the knee-tethers on them. *Quies!* Did you never hear bullets before? Now put the donkeys here. Not much – you don't get my polo-pony to make a zariba with. Picket the ponies between the grove and the river out of danger's way. These fellows seem to fire even higher than they did in '85.'

'That's got home, anyhow,' said Scott, as they heard a soft, splashing thud like a stone in a mud-bank.

'Who's hit, then?'

'The brown camel that's chewing the cud.' As he spoke the creature, its jaw still working, laid its long neck along the ground and closed its large dark eyes.

'That shot cost me fifteen pounds,' said Mortimer, ruefully. 'How many of them do you make?'

'Four, I think.'

'Only four Bezingers, at any rate; there may be some spearmen.'

'I think not; it is a little raiding-party of riflemen. By the way, Anerley, you've never been under fire before, have you?'

'Never,' said the young pressman, who was conscious of a curious feeling of nervous elation.

'Love and poverty and war, they are all experiences necessary to make a complete life. Pass over those cartridges. This is a very mild baptism that you are undergoing, for behind these camels you are as safe as if you were sitting in the back room of the Authors' Club.'

'As safe, but hardly as comfortable,' said Scott. 'A long glass of hock and seltzer would be exceedingly acceptable. But oh, Mortimer, what a chance! Think of the general's feelings when he hears that the first action of the war has been fought by the press column. Think of Reuters, who has been stewing at the front for a week! Think of the evening pennies just too late for the fun. By George, that slug brushed a mosquito off me!'

'And one of the donkeys is hit.'

'This is sinful. It will end in our having to carry our own kits to Khartoum.'

'Never mind, my boy, it all goes to make copy. I can see the headlines – "Raid on Communications"; "Murder of British Engineer"; "Press Column Attacked". Won't it be ripping?'

'I wonder what the next line will be,' said Anerley.

' "Our Special Wounded"!' cried Scott, rolling over on to his back. 'No harm done,' he added, gathering himself up again; 'only a chip off my knee. This is getting sultry. I confess that the idea of that back room at the Authors' Club begins to grow upon me.'

'I have some diachylon.'

'Afterwards will do. We're having an 'appy day with Fuzzy on the rush. I wish he *would* rush.'

'They're coming nearer.'

'This is an excellent revolver of mine if it didn't throw so devilish high. I always aim at a man's toes if I want to stimulate his digestion. O Lord, there's our kettle gone!' With a boom like a dinner-gong a Remington bullet had passed through the kettle, and a cloud of steam hissed up from the fire. A wild shout came from the rocks above.

'The idiots think that they have blown us up. They'll rush us now, as sure as fate; then it will be our turn to lead. Got your revolver, Anerley?'

'I have this double-barrelled fowling-piece.'

'Sensible man! It's the best weapon in the world at this sort of rough-and-tumble work. What cartridges?'

'Swan-shot.'

'That will do all right. I carry this big-bore double-barrelled pistol loaded with slugs. You might as well try to stop one of these fellows with a pea-shooter as with a service revolver.'

'There are ways and means,' said Scott. 'The Geneva Convention does not hold south of the first cataract. It's easy to make a bullet mushroom by a little manipulation of the tip of it. When I was in the broken square at Tamai – '

'Wait a bit,' cried Mortimer, adjusting his glasses. 'I think they are coming now.'

'The time,' said Scott, snapping up his watch, 'being exactly seventeen minutes past four.'

Anerley had been lying behind a camel staring with an interest which bordered upon fascination at the rocks opposite. Here was a little woolly puff of smoke, and there was another one, but never once had they caught a glimpse of the attackers. To him there was something weird and awesome in these unseen, persistent men who, minute by minute, were drawing closer to them. He had heard them cry out when the kettle was broken, and once, immediately afterwards, an enormously strong voice had roared something which had set Scott shrugging his shoulders.

'They've got to take us first,' said he, and Anerley thought his nerve might be better if he did not ask for a translation.

The firing had begun at a distance of some hundred yards, which put it out of the question for them, with their lighter weapons, to make any reply to it. Had their antagonists continued to keep that range the defenders must either have made a hopeless sally or tried to shelter themselves behind their zariba as best they might on the chance that the sound might bring up help. But, luckily for them, the African has never taken kindly to the rifle, and his primitive instinct to close with his enemy is always too strong for his sense of strategy. They were drawing in, therefore, and now, for the first time, Anerley caught sight of a face looking at them from over a rock. It was a huge, virile, strong-jawed head of a pure negro type, with silver trinkets gleaming in the ears. The man raised a great arm from behind the rock, and shook his Remington at them.

'Shall I fire?' asked Anerley.

'No, no; it is too far. Your shot would scatter all over the place.'

'It's a picturesque ruffian,' said Scott. 'Couldn't you kodak him, Mortimer? There's another!' A fine-featured brown Arab, with a black, pointed beard, was peeping from behind another boulder. He wore the green turban which proclaimed him *hadji*, and his face showed the keen, nervous exultation of the religious fanatic.

'They seem a piebald crowd,' said Scott.

'That last is one of the real fighting Baggara,' remarked Mortimer. 'He's a dangerous man.'

'He looks pretty vicious. There's another negro!'

'Two more! Dingas, by the look of them. Just the same chaps we get our own black battalions from. As long as they get a fight they don't mind who it's for; but if the idiots had only sense enough to understand, they would know that the Arab is their hereditary enemy, and we their hereditary friends. Look at the silly juggins, gnashing his teeth at the very men who put down the slave trade!'

'Couldn't you explain?'

'I'll explain with this pistol when he comes a little nearer. Now sit tight, Anerley. They're off!'

They were indeed. It was the brown man with the green turban who headed the rush. Close at his heels was the negro with the silver earrings – a giant of a man – and the other two were only a little behind. As they sprang over the rocks one after the other, it took Anerley back to the school sports when he held the tape for the hurdle-race. It was magnificent, the wild spirit and abandon of it, the flutter of the chequered jellabas, the gleam of steel, the wave of black arms, the frenzied faces, the quick pitter-patter of the rushing feet. The law-abiding Briton is so imbued with the idea of the sanctity of human life that it was hard for the young pressman to realise that these men had every intention of killing him, and that he was at perfect liberty to do as much for them. He lay staring as if this were a show and he a spectator.

'Now, Anerley, now! Take the Arab!' cried somebody.

He put up the gun and saw the brown fierce face at the other end of the barrel. He tugged at the trigger, but the face grew larger and fiercer with every stride. Again and again he tugged. A revolver-shot rang out at his elbow, then another one, and he saw a red spot spring out on the Arab's brown breast. But he was still coming on.

'Shoot, you ass, shoot!' screamed Scott.

Again he strained unavailingly at the trigger. There were two more pistol-shots, and the big negro had fallen and risen and fallen again.

'Cock it, you fool!' shouted a furious voice; and at the same instant, with a rush and flutter, the Arab bounded over the prostrate camel and came down with his bare feet upon Anerley's chest. In a dream he seemed to be struggling frantically with someone upon the ground, then he was conscious of a tremendous explosion in his very face, and so ended for him the first action of the war.

'Goodbye, old chap. You'll be all right. Give yourself time.' It was Mortimer's voice, and he became dimly conscious of a long, spectacled face, and of a heavy hand upon his shoulder.

'Sorry to leave you. We'll be lucky now if we are in time for the morning editions.' Scott was tightening his girth as he spoke.

'We'll put in our wire that you have been hurt, so your people will know why they don't hear from you. If Reuters or the evening pennies come up, don't give the thing away. Abbas will look after you, and we'll be back tomorrow afternoon. Bye-bye!'

Anerley heard it all, though he did not feel energy enough to answer. Then, as he watched two sleek, brown ponies with their yellow-clad riders dwindling among the rocks, his memory cleared suddenly, and he realised that the first great journalistic chance of his life was slipping away from him. It was a small fight, but it was the first of the war, and the great public at home were all athirst for news. They would have it in the *Courier*, they would have it in the *Intelligence* – but not a word in the *Gazette*. The thought brought him to his feet, though he had to throw his arm round the stem of the palm tree to steady his swimming head. There was a big black man lying where he had fallen, his huge chest pocked with bullet-marks, every wound rosetted with its circle of flies. The Arab was stretched out within a few yards of him, with two hands clasped over the dreadful thing which had been his head. Across him was lying Anerley's fowling-piece, one barrel discharged, the other at half cock.

'Scott effendi shoot him your gun,' said a voice. It was Abbas, his English-speaking body-servant.

Anerley groaned at the disgrace of it. He had lost his head so completely that he had forgotten to cock his gun; and yet he knew that it was not fear but interest which had so absorbed him. He put his hand up to his head and felt that a wet handkerchief was bound round his forehead.

'Where are the two other dervishes?'

'They ran away. One got shot in arm.'

'What's happened to me?'

'Effendi got cut on head. Effendi catch bad man by arms, and Scott effendi shot him. Face burn very bad.'

Anerley became conscious suddenly that there was a pringling about his skin and an overpowering smell of burned hair under his nostrils. He put his hand to his moustache. It was gone. His eyebrows too? He could not find them. His head, no doubt, was very near to the dervish's when they were rolling upon the ground together, and this was the effect of the explosion of his own gun. Well, he would have time to grow some more hair before he saw Fleet Street again. But the cut, perhaps, was a more serious matter. Was it enough to prevent him getting to the telegraph-office at Sarras? The only way was to try and see. But there was only that poor little Syrian grey of his. There it stood in the evening sunshine, with a sunk head and a bent knee, as if its morning's work was still heavy upon it. What hope was there of being able to do thirty-five miles of heavy going upon that? It would be a strain upon the splendid ponies of his companions – and they were the swiftest and most enduring in the country. The most enduring? There was one creature more enduring, and that was a real trotting camel. If he had had one he might have got to the wires first after all, for Mortimer had said that over thirty miles they have the better of any horse. Yes, if he had only had a real trotting camel! And then like a flash came Mortimer's words, 'It is the kind of beast that the dervishes ride when they make their lightning raids.'

The beasts the dervishes ride! What had these dead dervishes ridden? In an instant he was clambering up the rocks, with Abbas protesting at his heels. Had the two fugitives carried away all the camels, or had they been content to save themselves? The brass gleam from a litter of empty Remington cases caught his eye, and showed where the enemy had been crouching. And then he could have shouted for joy, for there, in the hollow, some little distance off, rose the high, graceful white neck and the elegant head of such a camel as he had never set eyes upon before – a swanlike, beautiful creature, as far from the rough, clumsy baggles as the cart-horse is from the racer.

The beast was kneeling under the shelter of the rocks with its waterskin and bag of *doora* slung over its shoulders, and its forelegs tethered Arab fashion with a rope around the knees. Anerley threw his leg over the front pommel while Abbas slipped off the cord. Forward flew Anerley towards the creature's neck, then violently backwards, clawing madly at anything which might save him, and then, with a jerk which nearly snapped his loins, he was thrown forward again. But the camel was on its legs now, and the young pressman was safely seated upon one of the fliers of the desert. It was as gentle as it was swift, and it stood oscillating its long neck and gazing round with its large brown eyes, whilst Anerley coiled his legs round the peg and grasped the curved camel-stick which Abbas had handed up to him. There were two bridle-cords, one from the nostril and one from the neck, but he remembered that Scott had said that it was the servant's and not the house-bell which had to be pulled, so he kept his grasp upon the lower. Then he touched the long, vibrating neck with his stick, and in an instant Abbas's farewell seemed to come from far behind him, and the black rocks and yellow sand were dancing past on either side.

It was his first experience of a trotting camel, and at first the motion, although irregular and abrupt, was not unpleasant. Having no stirrup or fixed point of any kind, he could not rise to it, but he gripped as tightly as he could with his knees, and he tried to sway backwards and forwards as he had seen the Arabs do. It was a large, very concave Makloofa saddle, and he was conscious that he was bouncing about on it with as little power of adhesion as a billiard-ball upon a tea-tray. He gripped the two sides with his hands to hold himself steady. The creature had got into its long, swinging, stealthy trot, its sponge-like feet making no sound upon the hard sand. Anerley leaned back with his two hands gripping hard behind him, and he whooped the creature on. The sun had already sunk behind the line of black volcanic peaks, which look like huge slag-heaps at the mouth of a mine. The western sky had taken that lovely light green and pale pink tint which makes evening beautiful upon the Nile, and the old brown river itself, swirling down amongst the black rocks, caught some shimmer of the colours above. The glare, the heat and the piping of the insects had all ceased together. In spite of his aching head, Anerley could have cried out for pure physical joy as the swift creature beneath him flew along with him through that cool, invigorating air, with the virile north wind soothing his pringling face.

He had looked at his watch, and now he made a swift calculation of times and distances. It was past six when he had left the camp. Over broken ground it was impossible that he could hope to do more than seven miles an hour – less on bad parts, more on the smooth. His recollection of the track was that there were few smooth and many bad. He would be lucky, then, if he reached Sarras anywhere from twelve to one. Then the messages took a good two hours to go through, for they had to be transcribed at Cairo. At the best he could only hope to have told his story in Fleet Street at two or three in the morning. It was possible that he might manage it, but the chances seemed enormously against him. About three the morning edition would be made up, and his chance gone for ever. The one thing clear was that only the first man at the wires would have any chance at all, and Anerley meant to be first if hard riding could do it. So he tapped away at the bird-like neck, and the creature's long, loose limbs went faster and faster at every tap. Where the rocky spurs ran down to the river, horses would have to go round, while camels might get across, so that Anerley felt that he was always gaining upon his companions.

But there was a price to be paid for the feeling. He had heard of men who had burst when on camel journeys, and he knew that the Arabs swathe their bodies tightly in broad cloth bandages when they prepare for a long march. It had seemed unnecessary and ridiculous when he first began to speed over the level track, but now, when he got on the rocky paths, he understood what it meant. Never for an instant was he at the same angle. Backwards, forwards he swung, with a tingling jar at the end of each sway, until he ached from his neck to his knees. It caught him across the shoulders, it caught him down the spine, it gripped him over the loins, it marked the lower line of his ribs with one heavy, dull throb. He clutched here and there with his hands to try and ease the strain upon his muscles. He drew up his knees, altered his seat, and set his teeth with a grim determination to go through with it should it kill him. His head was splitting, his flayed face smarting, and every joint in his body aching as if it were dislocated. But he forgot all that when, with the rising of the moon, he heard the clinking of horses' hoofs down upon the track by the river, and knew that, unseen by them, he had already got well abreast of his companions. But he was hardly halfway, and the time already eleven.

All day the needles had been ticking away without intermission in the little corrugated iron hut which served as a telegraph station at Sarras. With its bare walls and its packing-case seats, it was none the less for the moment one of the vital spots upon the earth's surface, and the crisp, importunate ticking might have come from the world-old clock of destiny. Many august people had been at the other end of those wires, and had communed with the moist-faced military clerk. A French premier had demanded a pledge, and an English marquis had passed on the request to the general in command, with a question as to how it would affect the situation. Cipher telegrams had nearly driven the clerk out of his wits, for of all crazy occupations the taking of a cipher message, when you are without the key to the cipher, is the worst. Much high diplomacy had been going on all day in the innermost chambers of European chancelleries, and the results of it had been whispered into this little corrugated-iron hut. About two in the morning an enormous dispatch had come at last to an end, and the weary operator had opened the door, and was lighting his pipe in the cool, fresh air, when he saw a camel plump down in the dust, and a man, who seemed to be in the last stage of drunkenness, come rolling towards him.

'What's the time?' he cried, in a voice which appeared to be the only sober thing about him.

It was on the clerk's lips to say that it was time that the questioner was in his bed, but it is not safe upon a campaign to be ironical at the expense of khaki-clad men. He contented himself, therefore, with the bald statement that it was after two. But no retort that he could have devised could have had a more crushing effect. The voice turned drunken also, and the man caught at the door-post to uphold him.

'Two o'clock! I'm done after all!' said he. His head was tied up in a bloody handkerchief, his face was crimson, and he stood with his legs crooked as if the pith had all gone out of his back. The clerk began to realise that something out of the ordinary was in the wind.

'How long does it take to get a wire to London?'

'About two hours.'

'And it's two now. I could not get it there before four.'

'Before three.'

'Four.'

'No, three.'

'But you said two hours.'

'Yes, but there's more than an hour's difference in longitude.'

'By heaven, I'll do it yet!' cried Anerley, and staggering to a packing-case, he began the dictation of his famous dispatch.

And so it came about that the *Gazette* had a long column, with headlines like an epitaph, when the sheets of the *Intelligence* and the *Courier* were as blank as the faces of their editors. And so, too, it happened that when two weary men, upon two foundered horses, arrived about four in the morning at the Sarras post-office, they looked at each other in silence and departed noiselessly, with the conviction that there are some situations with which the English language is not capable of dealing.

The Début of Bimbashi Joyce

It was in the days when the tide of Mahdism, which had swept in such a flood from the Great Lakes and Darfur to the confines of Egypt, had at last come to its full, and even begun, as some hoped, to show signs of a turn. At its outset it had been terrible. It had engulfed Hicks's army, swept over Gordon and Khartoum, rolled behind the British forces as they retired down the river, and finally cast up a spray of raiding parties as far north as Aswan. Then it found other channels to east and west, to Central Africa and to Abyssinia, and retired a little on the side of Egypt. For ten years there ensued a lull, during which the frontier garrisons looked out upon those distant blue hills of Dongola. Behind the violet mists which draped them lay a land of blood and horror. From time to time some adventurer went south towards those haze-girt mountains, tempted by stories of gum and ivory, but none ever returned. Once a mutilated Egyptian and once a Greek woman, mad with thirst and fear, made their way to the lines. They were the only exports of that country of darkness. Sometimes the sunset would turn those distant mists into a bank of crimson, and the dark mountains would rise from that sinister reek like islands in a sea of blood. It seemed a grim symbol in the southern heaven when seen from the fort-capped hills by Wadi Halfa. Ten years of lust in Khartoum, ten years of silent work in Cairo, and then all was ready, and it was time for civilisation to take a trip south once more, travelling as her wont is in an armoured train. Everything was ready, down to the last pack-saddle of the last camel, and yet no one suspected it, for an unconstitutional government has its advantage. A great administrator had argued, and managed, and cajoled; a great soldier had organised and planned, and made piastres do the work of pounds. And then one night these two master spirits met and clasped hands, and the soldier vanished away upon some business of his own. And just at that very time, Bimbashi Hilary Joyce, seconded from the Royal Mallow Fusiliers, and temporarily attached to the Ninth Sudanese, made his first appearance in Cairo.

Napoleon had said, and Hilary Joyce had noted, that great reputations are only to be made in the East. Here he was in the East with four tin cases of baggage, a Wilkinson sword, a Bond's slug-throwing pistol and a copy of Green's *Introduction to the Study of Arabic*. With such a start, and the blood of youth running hot in his veins, everything seemed easy. He was a little frightened of the general; he had heard stories of his sternness to young officers, but with tact and suavity he hoped for the best. So, leaving his effects at Shepheard's Hotel, he reported himself at headquarters. It was not the general but the head of the Intelligence Department who received him, the chief being still absent upon that business which had called him. Hilary Joyce found himself in the presence of a short, thick-set officer, with a gentle voice and a placid expression which covered a remarkably acute and energetic spirit. With that quiet smile and guileless manner he had undercut and outwitted the most cunning of Orientals. He stood, a cigarette between his fingers, looking at the newcomer. 'I heard that you had come. Sorry the chief isn't here to see you. Gone up to the frontier, you know.'

'My regiment is at Wadi Halfa. I suppose, sir, that I should report myself there at once?'

'No; I was to give you your orders.' He led the way to a map upon the wall, and pointed with the end of his cigarette. 'You see this place. It's the Oasis of Kurkur – a little quiet, I am afraid, but excellent air. You are to get out there as quickly as possible. You'll find a company of the Ninth, and half a squadron of cavalry. You will be in command.'

Hilary Joyce looked at the name, printed at the intersection of two black lines without another dot upon the map for several inches around it. 'A village, sir?'

'No, a well. Not very good water, I'm afraid, but you soon get accustomed to natron. It's an important post, as being at the junction of two caravan routes. All routes are closed now, of course, but still you never know who *might* come along them.'

'We are there, I presume, to prevent raiding?'

'Well, between you and me, there's really nothing to raid. You are there to intercept messengers. They must call at the wells. Of course you have only just come out, but you probably understand already enough about the conditions of this country to know that there is a great deal of disaffection about, and that the Khalifa is likely to try and keep in touch with his adherents. Then, again, Senoussi lives up that way' – he waved his cigarette to the westward – 'the Khalifa might send a message to him along that route. Anyhow, your duty is to arrest everyone coming along, and get some account of him before you let him go. You don't talk Arabic, I suppose?'

'I am learning, sir.'

'Well, well, you'll have time enough for study there. And you'll have a native officer, Ali something or other, who speaks English, and can interpret for you. Well, goodbye – I'll tell the chief that you reported yourself. Get on to your post now as quickly as you can.'

Railway to Baliani, the post-boat to Aswan, and then two days on a camel in the Libyan Desert, with an Ababdeh guide, and three baggage-camels to tie one down to their own exasperating pace. However, even two and a half miles an hour mount up in time, and at last, on the third evening, from the blackened slag-heap of a hill which is called the Jebel Kurkur, Hilary Joyce looked down upon a distant clump of palms, and thought that this cool patch of green in the midst of the merciless blacks and yellows was the fairest colour effect that he had ever seen. An hour later he had ridden into the little camp, the guard had turned out to salute him, his native subordinate had greeted him in excellent English, and he had fairly entered into his own. It was not an exhilarating place for a lengthy residence. There was one large, bowl-shaped, grassy depression sloping down to the three pits of brown and brackish water. There was the grove of palm trees also, beautiful to look upon, but exasperating in view of the fact that nature has provided her least shady trees on the very spot where shade is needed most. A single wide-spread acacia did something to restore the balance. Here Hilary Joyce slumbered in the heat, and in the cool he inspected his square-shouldered, spindle-shanked Soudanese, with their cheery black faces and their funny little pork-pie forage caps. Joyce was a martinet at drill, and the blacks loved being drilled, so the Bimbashi was soon popular among them. But one day was exactly like another. The weather, the view, the employment, the food – everything was the same. At the end of three weeks he felt that he had been there for interminable years. And then at last there came something to break the monotony.

One evening, as the sun was sinking, Hilary Joyce rode slowly down the old caravan road. It had a fascination for him, this narrow track, winding among the boulders and curving up the nullahs, for he remembered how in the map it had gone on and on, stretching away into the unknown heart of Africa. The countless pads of innumerable camels through many centuries had beaten it smooth, so that now, unused and deserted, it still wound away, the strangest of roads, a foot broad, and perhaps two thousand miles in length. Joyce wondered as he rode how long it was since any traveller had journeyed up it from the south, and then he raised his eyes, and there was a man coming along the path. For an instant Joyce thought that it might be one of his own men, but a second glance assured him that this could not be so. The stranger was dressed in the flowing robes of an Arab, and not in the close-fitting khaki of a soldier. He was very tall, and a high turban made him seem gigantic. He strode swiftly along, with head erect and the bearing of a man who knows no fear.

Who could he be, this formidable giant coming out of the unknown? The precursor possibly of a horde of savage spearmen? And where could he have walked from? The nearest well was a long hundred miles down the track. At any rate the frontier post of Kurkur could not afford to receive casual visitors. Hilary Joyce whisked round his horse, galloped into camp, and gave the alarm. Then, with twenty horsemen at his back, he rode out again to reconnoitre. The man was still coming on in spite of these hostile preparations. For an instant he hesitated when first he saw the cavalry, but escape was out of the question, and he advanced with the air of one who makes the best of a bad job. He made no resistance, and said nothing when the hands of two troopers clutched at his shoulders, but walked quietly between their horses into camp. Shortly afterwards the patrol came in again. There were no signs of any dervishes. The man was alone. A splendid trotting camel had been found lying dead a little way down the track. The mystery of the stranger's arrival was explained. But why, and whence, and whither? – these were questions for which a zealous officer must find an answer.

Hilary Joyce was disappointed that there were no dervishes. It would have been a great start for him in the Egyptian army had he fought a little action on his own account. But even as it was, he had a rare chance of impressing the authorities. He would love to show his capacity to the head of the Intelligence, and even more to that grim chief who never forgot what was smart or forgave what was slack. The prisoner's dress and bearing showed that he was of importance. Mean men do not ride pure-bred trotting camels. Joyce sponged his head with cold water, drank a cup of strong coffee, put on an imposing official tarboosh instead of his sun-helmet, and formed himself into a court of inquiry and judgment under the acacia tree. He would have liked his people to have seen him now, with his two black orderlies in waiting, and his Egyptian native officer at his side. He sat behind a camp-table, and the prisoner, strongly guarded, was led up to him. The man was a handsome fellow, with bold grey eyes and a long black beard.

'Why!' cried Joyce, 'the rascal is making faces at me.' A curious contraction had passed over the man's features, but so swiftly that it might have been a nervous twitch. He was now a model of Oriental gravity. 'Ask him who he is, and what he wants?' The native officer did so, but the stranger made no reply, save that the same sharp spasm passed once more over his face. 'Well, I'm blessed!' cried Hilary Joyce. 'Of all the impudent scoundrels! He keeps on winking at me. Who are you, you rascal? Give an account of yourself! D'ye hear?' But the tall Arab was as impervious to English as to Arabic. The Egyptian tried again and again. The prisoner looked at Joyce with his inscrutable eyes, and occasionally twitched his face at him, but never opened his mouth. The Bimbashi scratched his head in bewilderment.

'Look here, Ali Mahomet, we've got to get some sense out of this fellow. You say there are no papers on him?'

'No, sir; we found no papers.'

'No clue of any kind?'

'He has come far, sir. A trotting camel does not die easily. He has come from Dongola, at least.'

'Well, we must get him to talk.'

'It is possible that he is deaf and dumb.'

'Not he. I never saw a man look more all there in my life.'

'You might send him across to Aswan.'

'And give someone else the credit? No, thank you. This is my bird. But how are we going to get him to find his tongue?'

The Egyptian's dark eyes skirted the encampment and rested on the cook's fire. 'Perhaps,' said he, 'if the Bimbashi thought fit – ' He looked at the prisoner and then at the burning wood.

'No, no; it wouldn't do. No, by Jove, that's going too far.'

'A very little might do it.'

'No, no. It's all very well here, but it would sound just awful if ever it got as far as Fleet Street. But, I say,' he whispered, 'we might frighten him a bit. There's no harm in that.'

'No, sir.'

'Tell them to undo the man's jellaba. Order them to put a horseshoe in the fire and make it red-hot.' The prisoner watched the proceedings with an air which had more of amusement than of uneasiness. He never winced as the black sergeant approached with the glowing shoe held upon two bayonets.

'Will you speak now?' asked the Bimbashi, savagely.

The prisoner smiled gently and stroked his beard.

'Oh, chuck the infernal thing away!' cried Joyce, jumping up in a passion. 'There's no use trying to bluff the fellow. He knows we won't do it. But I *can* and I *will* flog him, and you can tell him from me that if he hasn't found his tongue by tomorrow morning I'll take the skin off his back as sure as my name's Joyce. Have you said all that?'

'Yes, sir.'

'Well, you can sleep upon it, you beauty, and a good night's rest may it give you!' He adjourned the court, and the prisoner, as imperturbable as ever, was led away by the guard to his supper of rice and water. Hilary Joyce was a kind-hearted man, and his own sleep was considerably disturbed by the prospect of the punishment which he must inflict next day. He had hopes that the mere sight of the *koorbash* and the thongs might prevail over his prisoner's obstinacy. And then, again, he thought how shocking it would be if the man proved to be really dumb after all. The possibility shook him so that he had almost determined by daybreak that he would send the stranger on unhurt to Aswan. And yet what a tame conclusion it would be to the incident! He lay upon his *angareeb* still debating it when the question suddenly and effectively settled itself. Ali Mahomet rushed into his tent. 'Sir,' he cried, 'the prisoner is gone!'

'Gone!'

'Yes, sir, and your own best riding camel as well. There is a slit cut in the tent, and he got away unseen in the early morning.'

The Bimbashi acted with all energy. Cavalry rode along every track; scouts examined the soft sand of the wadis for signs of the fugitive, but no trace was discovered. The man had utterly disappeared. With a heavy heart, Hilary Joyce wrote an official report of the matter and forwarded it to Aswan. Five days later there came a curt order from the chief that he should report himself there. He feared the worst from the stern soldier, who spared others as little as he spared himself. And his worst forebodings were realised. Travel-stained and weary, he reported himself one night at the general's quarters. Behind a table piled with papers and strewn with maps the famous soldier and his chief of Intelligence were deep in plans and figures. Their greeting was a cold one.

'I understand, Captain Joyce,' said the general, 'that you have allowed a very important prisoner to slip through your fingers.'

'I am sorry, sir.'

'No doubt. But that will not mend matters. Did you ascertain anything about him before you lost him?'

'No, sir.'

'How was that?'

'I could get nothing out of him, sir.'

'Did you try?'

'Yes, sir; I did what I could.'

'What did you do?'

'Well, sir, I threatened to use physical force.'

'What did he say?'

'He said nothing.'

'What was he like?'

'A tall man, sir. Rather a desperate character, I should think.'

'Any way by which we could identify him?'

'A long black beard, sir. Grey eyes. And a nervous way of twitching his face.'

'Well, Captain Joyce,' said the general, in his stern, inflexible voice, 'I cannot congratulate you upon your first exploit in the Egyptian army. You are aware that every English officer in this force is a picked man. I have the whole British army from which to draw. It is necessary, therefore, that I should insist upon the very highest efficiency. It would be unfair upon the others to pass over any obvious want of zeal or intelligence. You are seconded from the Royal Mallows, I understand?'

'Yes, sir.'

'I have no doubt that your colonel will be glad to see you fulfilling your regimental duties again.' Hilary Joyce's heart was too heavy for words. He was silent. 'I will let you know my final decision tomorrow morning.' Joyce saluted and turned upon his heel.

'You can sleep upon that, you beauty, and a good night's rest may it give you!'

Joyce turned in bewilderment. Where had those words been used before? Who was it who had used them? The general was standing erect. Both he and the chief of the Intelligence were laughing. Joyce stared at the tall figure, the erect bearing, the inscrutable grey eyes.

'Good Lord!' he gasped.

'Well, well, Captain Joyce, we are quits!' said the general, holding out his hand. 'You gave me a bad ten minutes with that infernal red-hot horseshoe of yours. I've done as much for you. I don't think we can spare you for the Royal Mallows just yet awhile.'

'But, sir; but – !'

'The fewer questions the better, perhaps. But of course it must seem rather amazing. I had a little private business with the Kabbabish. It must be done in person. I did it, and came to your post in my return. I kept on winking at you as a sign that I wanted a word with you alone.'

'Yes, yes. I begin to understand.'

'I couldn't give it away before all those blacks, or where should I have been the next time I used my false beard and Arab dress? You put me in a very awkward position. But at last I had a word alone with your Egyptian officer, who managed my escape all right.'

'He! Ali Mahomet!'

'I ordered him to say nothing. I had a score to settle with you. But we dine at eight, Captain Joyce. We live plainly here, but I think I can do you a little better than you did me at Kurkur.'

The Doings of Raffles Haw

A Double Enigma

'I'm afraid that he won't come,' said Laura McIntyre, in a disconsolate voice.
  'Why not?'
  'Oh, look at the weather; it is something too awful.'
  As she spoke a whirl of snow beat with a muffled patter against the cosy red-curtained window, while a long blast of wind shrieked and whistled through the branches of the great white-limbed elms which skirted the garden.

Robert McIntyre rose from the sketch upon which he had been working, and taking one of the lamps in his hand peered out into the darkness. The long skeleton limbs of the bare trees tossed and quivered dimly amid the whirling drift. His sister sat by the fire, her fancy-work in her lap, and looked up at her brother's profile which showed against the brilliant yellow light. It was a handsome face, young and fair and clear cut, with wavy brown hair combed backwards and rippling down into that outward curve at the ends which one associates with the artistic temperament. There was refinement too in his slightly puckered eyes, his dainty gold-rimmed *pince-nez* glasses, and in the black velveteen coat which caught the light so richly upon its shoulder. In his mouth only there was something – a suspicion of coarseness, a possibility of weakness – which in the eyes of some, and of his sister among them, marred the grace and beauty of his features. Yet, as he was wont himself to say, when one thinks that each poor mortal is heir to a legacy of every evil trait or bodily taint of so vast a line of ancestors, lucky indeed is the man who does not find that nature has scored up some long-owing family debt upon his features.

And indeed in this case the remorseless creditor had gone so far as to exact a claim from the lady also, though in her case the extreme beauty of the upper part of the face drew the eye away from any weakness which might be found in the lower. She was darker than her brother – so dark that her heavily coiled hair seemed to be black until the light shone slantwise across it. The delicate, half-petulant features, the finely traced brows and the thoughtful, humorous eyes were all perfect in their way, and yet the combination left something to be desired. There was a vague sense of a flaw somewhere, in feature or in expression, which resolved itself, when analysed, into a slight out-turning and droop of the lower lip; small indeed, and yet pronounced enough to turn what would have been a beautiful face into a merely pretty one. Very despondent and somewhat cross she looked as she leaned back in the armchair, the tangle of bright-coloured silks and of drab holland upon her lap, her hands clasped behind her head, with her snowy forearms and little pink elbows projecting on either side.

'I know he won't come,' she repeated.

'Nonsense, Laura! Of course he'll come. A sailor and afraid of the weather!'

'Ha!' She raised her finger, and a smile of triumph played over her face, only to die away again into a blank look of disappointment. 'It is only papa,' she murmured.

A shuffling step was heard in the hall, and a little peaky man, with his slippers very much down at the heels, came shambling into the room. Mr McIntyre senior was pale and furtive-looking, with a thin straggling red beard shot with grey and a sunken downcast face. Ill-fortune and ill-health had both left their marks upon him. Ten years before he had been one of the largest and richest gunmakers in Birmingham, but a long run of commercial bad luck had sapped his great fortune, and had finally driven him into the Bankruptcy Court. The death of his wife on the very day of his insolvency had filled his cup of sorrow, and he had gone about since with a stunned, half-dazed expression upon his weak pallid face which spoke of a mind unhinged. So complete had been his downfall that the family would have been reduced to absolute poverty were it not for a small legacy of two hundred a year which both the children had received from one of their uncles upon the mother's side who had amassed a fortune in Australia. By combining their incomes, and by taking a house in the quiet country district of Tamfield, some fourteen miles from the great Midland city, they were still able to live with some approach to comfort. The change, however, was a bitter one to all – to Robert, who had to forgo the luxuries dear to his artistic temperament, and to think of turning what had been merely an overruling hobby into a means of earning a living; and even more to Laura, who winced before the pity of her old friends, and found the lanes and fields of Tamfield intolerably dull after the life and bustle of Edgbaston. Their discomfort was aggravated by the conduct of their father, whose life now was one long wail over his misfortunes, and who alternately sought comfort in the prayer-book and in the decanter for the ills which had befallen him.

To Laura, however, Tamfield presented one attraction, which was now about to be taken from her. Their choice of the little country hamlet as their residence had been determined by the fact of their old friend, the Reverend John Spurling, having been nominated as the vicar. Hector

Spurling, the elder son, two months Laura's senior, had been engaged to her for some years, and was, indeed, upon the point of marrying her when the sudden financial crash had disarranged their plans. A sub-lieutenant in the navy, he was home on leave at present, and hardly an evening passed without his making his way from the Vicarage to Elmdene, where the McIntyres resided. Today, however, a note had reached them to the effect that he had been suddenly ordered on duty, and that he must rejoin his ship at Portsmouth by the next evening. He would look in, were it but for half an hour, to bid them adieu.

'Why, where's Hector?' asked Mr McIntyre, blinking round from side to side.

'He's not come, father. How could you expect him to come on such a night as this? Why, there must be two feet of snow in the glebe field.'

'Not come, eh?' croaked the old man, throwing himself down upon the sofa. 'Well, well, it only wants him and his father to throw us over, and the thing will be complete'

'How can you even hint at such a thing, father?' cried Laura indignantly. 'They have been as true as steel. What would they think if they heard you?'

'I think, Robert,' he said, disregarding his daughter's protest, 'that I will have a drop, just the very smallest possible drop, of brandy. A mere thimbleful will do; but I rather think I have caught cold during the snowstorm today.'

Robert went on sketching stolidly in his folding book, but Laura looked up from her work.

'I'm afraid there is nothing in the house, father,' she said.

'Laura! Laura!' He shook his head as one more in sorrow than in anger. 'You are no longer a girl, Laura; you are a woman, the manager of a household, Laura. We trust in you. We look entirely towards you. And yet you leave your poor brother Robert without any brandy, to say nothing of me, your father. Good heavens, Laura! what would your mother have said? Think of accidents, think of sudden illness, think of apoplectic fits, Laura. It is a very grave res – a very grave respons – a very great risk that you run.'

'I hardly touch the stuff,' said Robert curtly; 'Laura need not provide any for me.'

'As a medicine it is invaluable, Robert. To be used, you understand, and not to be abused. That's the whole secret of it. But I'll step down to the Three Pigeons for half an hour.'

'My dear father,' cried the young man, 'you surely are not going out upon such a night. If you must have brandy could I not send Sarah for some? Please let me send Sarah; or I would go myself, or – '

Pip! came a little paper pellet from his sister's chair on to the sketch-book in front of him! He unrolled it and held it to the light.

'For heaven's sake let him go!' was scrawled across it.

'Well, in any case, wrap yourself up warm,' he continued, laying bare his sudden change of front with a masculine clumsiness which horrified his sister. 'Perhaps it is not so cold as it looks. You can't lose your way, that is one blessing. And it is not more than a hundred yards.'

With many mumbles and grumbles at his daughter's want of foresight, old McIntyre struggled into his greatcoat and wrapped his scarf round his long thin throat. A sharp gust of cold wind made the lamps flicker as he threw open the hall-door. His two children listened to the dull fall of his footsteps as he slowly picked out the winding garden path.

'He gets worse – he becomes intolerable,' said Robert at last. 'We should not have let him out; he may make a public exhibition of himself.'

'But it's Hector's last night,' pleaded Laura. 'It would be dreadful if they met and he noticed anything. That was why I wished him to go.'

'Then you were only just in time,' remarked her brother, 'for I hear the gate go, and – yes, you see.'

As he spoke a cheery hail came from outside, with a sharp rat-tat at the window. Robert stepped out and threw open the door to admit a tall young man, whose black frieze jacket was all mottled and glistening with snow crystals. Laughing loudly he shook himself like a Newfoundland dog, and kicked the snow from his boots before entering the little lamplit room.

Hector Spurling's profession was written in every line of his face. The clean-shaven lip and chin, the little fringe of side whisker, the straight decisive mouth, and the hard weather-tanned cheeks all spoke of the Royal Navy. Fifty such faces may be seen any night of the year round the mess-table of the Royal Naval College in Portsmouth Dockyard – faces which bear a closer resemblance to each other than brother does commonly to brother. They are all cast in a common mould, the products of a system which teaches early self-reliance, hardihood and manliness – a fine type upon the whole; less refined and less intellectual, perhaps, than their brothers of the land, but full of truth and energy and heroism. In figure he was straight, tall and well-knit, with keen grey eyes, and the sharp prompt manner of a man who has been accustomed both to command and to obey.

'You had my note?' he said, as he entered the room. 'I have to go again, Laura. Isn't it a bore? Old Smithers is short-handed, and wants me back at once.' He sat down by the girl, and put his brown hand across her white one. 'It won't be a very large order this time,' he continued. 'It's the flying squadron business – Madeira, Gibraltar, Lisbon, and home. I shouldn't wonder if we were back in March.'

'It seems only the other day that you landed,' she answered.

'Poor little girl! But it won't be long. Mind you take good care of her, Robert, when I am gone. And when I come again, Laura, it will be the last time mind! Hang the money! There are plenty who manage on less. We need not have a house. Why should we? You can get very nice rooms in Southsea at two pounds a week. McDougall, our paymaster, has just married, and he only gives thirty shillings. You would not be afraid, Laura?'

'No, indeed.'

'The dear old governor is so awfully cautious. Wait, wait, wait, that's always his cry. I tell him that he ought to have been in the Government Heavy Ordnance Department. But I'll speak to him tonight. I'll talk him round. See if I don't. And you must speak to your own governor. Robert here will back you up. And here are the ports and the dates that we are due at each. Mind that you have a letter waiting for me at every one.'

He took a slip of paper from the side pocket of his coat, but, instead of handing it to the young lady, he remained staring at it with the utmost astonishment upon his face.

'Well, I never!' he exclaimed. 'Look here, Robert; what do you call this?'

'Hold it to the light. Why, it's a fifty-pound Bank of England note. Nothing remarkable about it that I can see.'

'On the contrary. It's the queerest thing that ever happened to me. I can't make head or tail of it.'

'Come, then, Hector,' cried Miss McIntyre with a challenge in her eyes. 'Something very queer happened to me also today. I'll bet a pair of gloves that my adventure was more out of the common than yours, though I have nothing so nice to show at the end of it.'

'Come, I'll take that, and Robert here shall be the judge.'

'State your cases.' The young artist shut up his sketch-book, and rested his head upon his hands with a face of mock solemnity. 'Ladies first! Go along Laura, though I think I know something of your adventure already.'

'It was this morning, Hector,' she said. 'Oh, by the way, the story will make you wild. I had forgotten that. However, you mustn't mind, because, really, the poor fellow was perfectly mad.'

'What on earth was it?' asked the young officer, his eyes travelling from the bank-note to his fiancée.

'Oh, it was harmless enough, and yet you will confess it was very queer. I had gone out for a walk, but as the snow began to fall I took shelter under the shed which the workmen have built at the near end of the great new house. The men have gone, you know, and the owner is supposed to be coming tomorrow, but the shed is still standing. I was sitting there upon a packing-case when a man came down the road and stopped under the same shelter. He was a quiet, pale-faced man, very tall and thin, not much more than thirty, I should think, poorly dressed, but with the look and bearing of a gentleman. He asked me one or two questions about the village and the people, which, of course, I answered, until at last we found ourselves chatting away in the pleasantest and easiest fashion about all sorts of things.

The time passed so quickly that I forgot all about the snow until he drew my attention to its having stopped for the moment. Then, just as I was turning to go, what in the world do you suppose that he did? He took a step towards me, looked in a sad pensive way into my face, and said: 'I wonder whether you could care for me if I were without a penny.' Wasn't it strange? I was so frightened that I whisked out of the shed, and was off down the road before he could add another word. But really, Hector, you need not look so black, for when I look back at it I can quite see from his tone and manner that he meant no harm. He was thinking aloud, without the least intention of being offensive. I am convinced that the poor fellow was mad.'

'Hum! There was some method in his madness, it seems to me,' remarked her brother.

'There would have been some method in my kicking,' said the lieutenant savagely. 'I never heard of a more outrageous thing in my life.'

'Now, I said that you would be wild!' She laid her white hand upon the sleeve of his rough frieze jacket. 'It was nothing. I shall never see the poor fellow again. He was evidently a stranger to this part of the country. But that was my little adventure. Now let us have yours.'

The young man crackled the banknote between his fingers and thumb, while he passed his other hand over his hair with the action of a man who strives to collect himself.

'It is some ridiculous mistake,' he said. 'I must try and set it right. Yet I don't know how to set about it either. I was going down to the village from the Vicarage just after dusk when I found a fellow in a trap who had got himself into broken water. One wheel had sunk into the edge of the ditch which had been hidden by the snow, and the whole thing was high and dry, with a list to starboard enough to slide him out of his seat. I lent a hand, of course, and soon had the wheel in the road again. It was quite dark, and I fancy that the fellow thought that I was a bumpkin, for we did not exchange five words. As he drove off he shoved this into my hand. It is the merest chance that I did not chuck it away, for, feeling that it was a crumpled piece of paper, I imagined that it must be a tradesman's advertisement or something of the kind. However, as luck would have it, I put it in my pocket, and there I found it when I looked for the dates of our cruise. Now you know as much of the matter as I do.'

Brother and sister stared at the black and white crinkled note with astonishment upon their faces.

Why, your unknown traveller must have been Monte Cristo, or Rothschild at the least!' said Robert. 'I am bound to say, Laura, that I think you have lost your bet.'

'Oh, I am quite content to lose it. I never heard of such a piece of luck.

What a perfectly delightful man this must be to know.'

'But I can't take his money,' said Hector Spurling, looking somewhat ruefully at the note. 'A little prize-money is all very well in its way, but a Johnny must draw the line somewhere. Besides it must have been a mistake. And yet he meant to give me something big, for he could not mistake a note for a coin. I suppose I must advertise for the fellow.'

'It seems a pity too,' remarked Robert. 'I must say that I don't quite see it in the same light that you do.'

'Indeed I think that you are very Quixotic, Hector,' said Laura McIntyre. 'Why should you not accept it in the spirit in which it was meant? You did this stranger a service – perhaps a greater service than you know of – and he meant this as a little memento of the occasion. I do not see that there is any possible reason against your keeping it.'

'Oh, come!' said the young sailor, with an embarrassed laugh, 'it is not quite the thing – not the sort of story one would care to tell at mess.'

'In any case you are off tomorrow morning,' observed Robert. 'You have no time to make enquiries about the mysterious Croesus. You must really make the best of it.'

'Well, look here, Laura, you put it in your work-basket,' cried Hector Spurling. 'You shall be my banker, and if the rightful owner turns up then I can refer him to you. If not, I suppose we must look on it as a kind of salvage-money, though I am bound to say I don't feel entirely comfortable about it.' He rose to his feet, and threw the note down into the brown basket of coloured wools which stood beside her. 'Now, Laura, I must up anchor, for I promised the governor to be back by nine. It won't be long this time, dear, and it shall be the last. Goodbye, Robert! Good luck!'

'Goodbye, Hector! *Bon voyage!*'

The young artist remained by the table, while his sister followed her lover to the door. In the dim light of the hall he could see their figures and overhear their words.

'Next time, little girl?'

'Next time be it, Hector.'

'And nothing can part us?'

'Nothing.'

'In the whole world?'

'Nothing.'

Robert discreetly closed the door. A moment later a thud from without, and the quick footsteps crunching on the snow told him that their visitor had departed.

TWO

The Tenant of the New Hall

The snow had ceased to fall, but for a week a hard frost had held the country-side in its iron grip. The roads rang under the horses' hoofs, and every wayside ditch and runlet was a sheet of ice. Over the long undulating landscape the red-brick houses peeped out warmly against the spotless background, and the lines of grey smoke streamed straight up into the windless air. The sky was of the lightest, palest blue, and the morning sun, shining through the distant fog-wreaths of Birmingham, struck a subdued glow from the broad-spread snowfields which might have gladdened the eyes of an artist.

It did gladden the heart of one who viewed it that morning from the summit of the gently-curving Tamfield Hill. Robert McIntyre stood with his elbows upon a gate-rail, his tam-o'-shanter over his eyes and a short briar-root pipe in his mouth, looking slowly about him with the absorbed air of one who breathes his fill of nature. Beneath him to the north lay the village of Tamfield, red walls, grey roofs and a scattered bristle of dark trees, with his own little Elmdene nestling back from the broad, white, winding Birmingham road. At the other side, as he slowly faced round, lay a vast stone building, white and clear-cut, fresh from the builders' hands. A great tower shot up from one corner of it, and a hundred windows twinkled ruddily in the light of the morning sun. A little distance from it stood a square low-lying structure, with a tall chimney rising from the midst of it, rolling out a long plume of smoke into the frosty air. The whole vast mansion stood within its own grounds, enclosed by a stately park wall, and surrounded by what would in time be an extensive plantation of fir trees. By the lodge gates a vast pile of debris, with lines of sheds for workmen and huge heaps of planks from scaffoldings, all proclaimed that the work had only just been brought to an end.

Robert McIntyre looked down with curious eyes at the broad-spread building. It had long been a mystery and a subject of gossip for the whole countryside. Hardly a year had elapsed since the rumour had first gone about that a millionaire had bought a tract of land, and that it was his intention to build a country seat upon it. Since then the work had been pushed on night and day, until now it was finished to the last detail in a shorter time than it takes to build many a six-roomed cottage. Every morning two long special trains had arrived from Birmingham, carrying down a great army of labourers, who were relieved in the evening by a fresh gang, who carried on their task under the rays of twelve enormous electric lights. The number of workmen appeared to be only limited by the space into which they could be fitted. Great lines of wagons conveyed the white Portland stone from the depot by the station. Hundreds of busy toilers handed it over, shaped and squared, to the actual masons, who swung it up with steam cranes on to the growing walls, where it was instantly fitted and mortared by their companions. Day by day the house shot higher, while pillar and cornice and carving seemed to bud out from it as if by magic. Nor was the work confined to the main building. A second structure sprang up at the same time, and there came gangs of pale-faced men from London with much extraordinary machinery, vast cylinders, wheels and wires, which they fitted up in this outlying building. The great chimney which rose from the centre of it, combined with these strange furnishings, seemed to mean that it was reserved as a factory or place of business, for it was rumoured that this rich man's hobby was the same as a poor man's necessity, and that he was fond of working with his own hands amid chemicals and furnaces. Scarce, too, was the second storey begun ere the woodworkers and plumbers and furnishers were busy beneath, carrying out a thousand strange and costly schemes for the greater comfort and convenience of the owner. Singular stories were told all round the country, and even in Birmingham itself, of the extraordinary luxury and the absolute disregard for money which marked all these arrangements. No sum appeared to be too great to spend upon the smallest detail which might do away with or lessen any of the petty inconveniences of life. Wagons and wagons of the richest furniture had passed through the village between lines of staring villagers. Costly skins, glossy carpets, rich rugs, ivory, and ebony, and metal; every glimpse into these storehouses of treasure had given rise to some new legend. And finally, when all had been arranged, there had come a staff of forty servants, who heralded the approach of the owner, Mr Raffles Haw himself.

It was no wonder, then, that it was with considerable curiosity that Robert McIntyre looked down at the great house, and marked the smoking chimneys, the curtained windows, and the other signs which showed that its tenant had arrived. A vast area of greenhouses gleamed like a lake on the farther side, and beyond were the long lines of stables and outhouses. Fifty horses had passed through Tamfield the week before, so that, large as were the preparations, they were not more than would be needed. Who and what could this man be who spent his money with so lavish a hand? His name was unknown. Birmingham was as ignorant as Tamfield as to his origin or the sources of his wealth. Robert McIntyre brooded languidly over the problem as he leaned against the gate, puffing his blue clouds of bird's-eye into the crisp, still air.

Suddenly his eye caught a dark figure emerging from the avenue gates and striding up the winding road. A few minutes brought him near enough to show a familiar face looking over the stiff collar and from under the soft black hat of an English clergyman.

'Good-morning, Mr Spurling.'

'Ah, good-morning, Robert. How are you? Are you coming my way? How slippery the roads are!'

His round, kindly face was beaming with good nature, and he took little jumps as he walked, like a man who can hardly contain himself for pleasure.

'Have you heard from Hector?'

'Oh, yes. He went off all right last Wednesday from Spithead, and he will write from Madeira. But you generally have later news at Elmdene than I have.'

'I don't know whether Laura has heard. Have you been up to see the new-comer?'

'Yes; I have just left him.'

'Is he a married man – this Mr Raffles Haw?'

'No, he is a bachelor. He does not seem to have any relations either, as far as I could learn. He lives alone, amid his huge staff of servants. It is a most remarkable establishment. It made me think of *The Arabian Nights*.'

'And the man? What is he like?'

'He is an angel – a positive angel. I never heard or read of such kindness in my life. He has made me a happy man.'

The clergyman's eyes sparkled with emotion, and he blew his nose loudly in his big red handkerchief.

Robert McIntyre looked at him in surprise.

'I am delighted to hear it,' he said. 'May I ask what he has done?'

'I went up to him by appointment this morning. I had written asking him if I might call. I spoke to him of the parish and its needs, of my long struggle to restore the south side of the church, and of our efforts to help my poor parishioners during this hard weather. While I spoke he said not a word, but sat with a vacant face, as though he were not listening to me. When I had finished he took up his pen. "How much will it take to do the church?" he asked. "A thousand pounds," I answered; "but we have already raised three hundred among ourselves. The squire has very handsomely given fifty pounds." "Well," said he, "how about the poor folk? How many families are there?" "About three hundred," I answered. "And coals, I believe, are at about a pound a ton," said he. "Three tons ought to see them through the rest of the winter. Then you can get a very fair pair of blankets for two pounds. That would make five pounds per family, and seven hundred for the church." He dipped his pen in the ink, and, as I am a living man, Robert, he wrote me a cheque then and there for two thousand two hundred pounds. I don't know what I said; I felt like a fool; I could not stammer out words with which to thank him. All my troubles have been taken from my shoulders in an instant, and indeed, Robert, I can hardly realise it.'

'He must be a most charitable man.'

'Extraordinarily so. And so unpretending. One would think that it was I who was doing the favour and he who was the beggar. I thought of that passage about making the heart of the widow sing for joy. He made my heart sing for joy, I can tell you. Are you coming up to the Vicarage?'

'No, thank you, Mr Spurling. I must go home and get to work on my new picture. It's a five-foot canvas – the landing of the Romans in Kent. I must have another try for the Academy. Good-morning.'

He raised his hat and continued down the road, while the vicar turned off into the path which led to his home.

Robert McIntyre had converted a large bare room in the upper storey of Elmdene into a studio, and thither he retreated after lunch. It was as well that he should have some little den of his own, for his father would talk of little save his ledgers and accounts, while Laura had become peevish and querulous since the one tie which held her to Tamfield had been removed. The chamber was a bare and bleak one, un-papered and un-carpeted, but a good fire sparkled in the grate, and two large windows gave him the needful light. His easel stood in the centre, with the great canvas balanced across it, while against the walls there leaned his two last attempts, 'The Murder of Thomas of Canterbury' and 'The Signing of Magna Charta'. Robert had a weakness for large subjects and broad effects. If his ambition was greater than his skill, he had still all the love of his art and the patience under discouragement which are the stuff out of which successful painters are made. Twice his brace of pictures had journeyed to town, and twice they had come back to him, until the finely gilded frames which had made such a call upon his purse began to show signs of these varied adventures. Yet, in spite of their depressing company, Robert turned to his fresh work with all the enthusiasm which a conviction of ultimate success can inspire.

But he could not work that afternoon.

In vain he dashed in his background and outlined the long curves of the Roman galleys. Do what he would, his mind would still wander from his work to dwell upon his conversation with the vicar in the morning. His imagination was fascinated by the idea of this strange man living alone amid a crowd, and yet wielding such a power that with one dash of his pen he could change sorrow into joy, and transform the condition of a whole parish. The incident of the fifty-pound note came back to his mind. It must surely have been Raffles Haw with whom Hector Spurling had come in contact. There could not be two men in one parish to whom so large a sum was of so small an account as to be thrown to a bystander in return for a trifling piece of assistance. Of course, it must have been Raffles Haw. And his sister had

737

the note, with instructions to return it to the owner, could he be found. He threw aside his palette, and descending into the sitting-room he told Laura and his father of his morning's interview with the vicar, and of his conviction that this was the man of whom Hector was in quest.

'Tut! Tut!' said old McIntyre. 'How is this, Laura? I knew nothing of this. What do women know of money or of business? Hand the note over to me and I shall relieve you of all responsibility. I will take everything upon myself.'

'I cannot possibly, papa,' said Laura, with decision. 'I should not think of parting with it.'

'What is the world coming to?' cried the old man, with his thin hands held up in protest. 'You grow more undutiful every day, Laura. This money would be of use to me – of use, you understand. It may be the cornerstone of the vast business which I shall reconstruct. I will use it, Laura, and I will pay something – four, shall we say, or even four and a half – and you may have it back on any day. And I will give security – the security of my – well, of my word of honour.'

'It is quite impossible, papa,' his daughter answered coldly. 'It is not my money. Hector asked me to be his banker. Those were his very words. It is not in my power to lend it. As to what you say, Robert, you may be right or you may be wrong, but I certainly shall not give Mr Raffles Haw or anyone else the money without Hector's express command.'

'You are very right about not giving it to Mr Raffles Haw,' cried old McIntyre, with many nods of approbation. 'I should certainly not let it go out of the family.'

'Well, I thought that I would tell you.'

Robert picked up his tam-o'-shanter and strolled out to avoid the discussion between his father and sister, which he saw was about to be renewed. His artistic nature revolted at these petty and sordid disputes, and he turned to the crisp air and the broad landscape to soothe his ruffled feelings. Avarice had no place among his failings, and his father's perpetual chatter about money inspired him with a positive loathing and disgust for the subject.

Robert was lounging slowly along his favourite walk which curled over the hill, with his mind turning from the Roman invasion to the mysterious millionaire, when his eyes fell upon a tall, lean man in front of him, who, with a pipe between his lips, was endeavouring to light a match under cover of his cap. The man was clad in a rough pea-jacket, and bore traces of smoke and grime upon his face and hands. Yet there is a Freemasonry among smokers which overrides every social difference, so Robert stopped and held out his case of fusees.

'A light?' said he.

'Thank you.' The man picked out a fusee, struck it, and bent his head to it. He had a pale, thin face, a short straggling beard, and a very sharp and curving nose, with decision and character in the straight thick eyebrows which almost met on either side of it. Clearly a superior kind of workman, and possibly one of those who had been employed in the construction of the new house. Here was a chance of getting some first-hand information on the question which had aroused his curiosity. Robert waited until he had lit his pipe, and then walked on beside him.

'Are you going in the direction of the new Hall?' he asked.

'Yes.' The man's voice was cold, and his manner reserved.

'Perhaps you were engaged in the building of it?'

'Yes, I had a hand in it.'

'They say that it is a wonderful place inside. It has been quite the talk of the district. Is it as rich as they say?'

'I am sure I don't know. I have not heard what they say.'

His attitude was certainly not encouraging, and it seemed to Robert that he gave little sidelong suspicious glances at him out of his keen grey eyes. Yet, if he were so careful and discreet there was the more reason to think that there was information to be extracted, if he could but find a way to it.

'Ah, there it lies!' he remarked, as they topped the brow of the hill, and looked down once more at the great building. 'Well, no doubt it is very gorgeous and splendid, but really for my own part I would rather live in my own little box down yonder in the village.'

The workman puffed gravely at his pipe.

'You are no great admirer of wealth, then?' he said.

'Not I. I should not care to be a penny richer than I am. Of course I should like to sell my pictures. One must make a living. But beyond that I ask nothing. I dare say that I, a poor artist, or you, a man who work for your bread, have more happiness out of life than the owner of that great palace.'

'Indeed, I think that it is more than likely,' the other answered, in a much more conciliatory voice.

'Art,' said Robert, warming to the subject, 'is her own reward. What mere bodily indulgence is there which money could buy which can give that deep thrill of satisfaction which comes on the man who has conceived something new, something beautiful, and the daily delight as he sees it grow under his hand, until it stands before him a completed whole? With my art and without wealth I am happy. Without my art I should have a void which no money could fill. But I really don't know why I should say all this to you.'

The workman had stopped, and was staring at him earnestly with a look of the deepest interest upon his smoke-darkened features.

'I am very glad to hear what you say,' said he. 'It is a pleasure to know that the worship of gold is not quite universal, and that there are at least some who can rise above it. Would you mind my shaking you by the hand?'

It was a somewhat extraordinary request, but Robert rather prided himself upon his bohemianism, and upon his happy facility for making friends with all sorts and conditions of men. He readily exchanged a cordial grip with his chance acquaintance.

'You expressed some curiosity as to this house. I know the grounds pretty well, and might perhaps show you one or two little things which would interest you. Here are the gates. Will you come in with me?'

Here was, indeed, a chance. Robert eagerly assented, and walked up the winding drive amid the growing fir trees. When he found his uncouth guide, however, marching straight across the broad gravel square to the main entrance, he felt that he had placed himself in a false position.

'Surely not through the front door,' he whispered, plucking his companion by the sleeve. 'Perhaps Mr Raffles Haw might not like it.'

'I don't think there will be any difficulty,' said the other, with a quiet smile. 'My name is Raffles Haw.'

THREE

A House of Wonders

Robert McIntyre's face must have expressed the utter astonishment which filled his mind at this most unlooked-for announcement. For a moment he thought that his companion must be joking, but the ease and assurance with which he lounged up the steps, and the deep respect with which a richly-clad functionary in the hall swung open the door to admit him, showed that he spoke in sober earnest. Raffles Haw glanced back, and seeing the look of absolute amazement upon the young artist's features, he chuckled quietly to himself.

'You will forgive me, won't you, for not disclosing my identity?' he said, laying his hand with a friendly gesture upon the other's sleeve. 'Had you known me you would have spoken less freely, and I should not have had the opportunity of learning your true worth. For example, you might hardly have been so frank upon the matter of wealth had you known that you were speaking to the master of the Hall.'

'I don't think that I was ever so astonished in my life,' gasped Robert.

'Naturally you are. How could you take me for anything but a workman? So I am. Chemistry is one of my hobbies, and I spend hours a day in my laboratory yonder. I have only just struck work, and as I had inhaled some not-over-pleasant gases, I thought that a turn down the road and a whiff of tobacco might do me good. That was how I came to meet you, and my toilet, I fear, corresponded only too well with my smoke-grimed face. But I rather fancy I know you by repute. Your name is Robert McIntyre, is it not?'

'Yes, though I cannot imagine how you knew.'

'Well, I naturally took some little trouble to learn something of my neighbours. I had heard that there was an artist of that name, and I presume that artists are not very numerous in Tamfield. But how do you like the design? I hope it does not offend your trained taste.'

'Indeed, it is wonderful – marvellous! You must yourself have an extraordinary eye for effect.'

'Oh, I have no taste at all; not the slightest. I cannot tell good from bad. There never was such a complete Philistine. But I had the best man in London down, and another fellow from Vienna. They fixed it up between them.'

They had been standing just within the folding doors upon a huge mat of bison skins. In front of them lay a great square court, paved with many-coloured marbles laid out in a labyrinth of arabesque design. In the centre a high fountain of carved jade shot five thin feathers of spray into the air, four of which curved towards each corner of the court to descend into broad marble basins, while the fifth mounted straight up to an immense height, and then tinkled back into the central reservoir. On either side of the court a tall, graceful palm tree shot up its slender stem to break into a crown of drooping green leaves some fifty feet above their heads. All round were a series of Moorish arches, in jade and serpentine marble, with heavy curtains of the deepest purple to cover the doors which lay between them. In front, to right and to left, a broad staircase of marble, carpeted with rich thick Smyrna rug work, led upwards to the upper storeys, which were arranged around the central court. The temperature within was warm and yet fresh, like the air of an English May.

'It's taken from the Alhambra,' said Raffles Haw. 'The palm trees are pretty. They strike right through the building into the ground beneath, and their roots are all girt round with hot-water pipes. They seem to thrive very well.'

'What beautifully delicate brasswork!' cried Robert, looking up with admiring eyes at the bright and infinitely fragile metal trellis screens which adorned the spaces between the Moorish arches.

'It is rather neat. But it is not brasswork. Brass is not tough enough to allow them to work it to that degree of fineness. It is gold. But just come this way with me. You won't mind waiting while I remove this smoke?'

He led the way to a door upon the left side of the court, which, to Robert's surprise, swung slowly open as they approached it. 'That is a little improvement which I have adopted,' remarked the master of the house. 'As you go up to a door your weight upon the planks releases a spring which causes the hinges to revolve. Pray step in. This is my own little sanctum, and furnished after my own heart.'

If Robert expected to see some fresh exhibition of wealth and luxury he was woefully disappointed, for he found himself in a large but bare room, with a little iron truckle-bed in one corner, a few scattered wooden chairs, a dingy carpet and a large table heaped with books, bottles, papers and all the other debris which collect around a busy and untidy man. Motioning his visitor into a chair, Raffles Haw pulled off his coat, and, turning up the sleeves of his coarse flannel shirt, he began to plunge and scrub in the warm water which flowed from a tap in the wall.

'You see how simple my own tastes are,' he remarked, as he mopped his dripping face and hair with the towel. 'This is the only room in my great house where I find myself in a congenial atmosphere. It is homely to me. I can read here and smoke my pipe in peace. Anything like luxury is abhorrent to me.'

'Really, I should not have thought it,' observed Robert.

'It is a fact, I assure you. You see, even with your views as to the worth-lessness of wealth, views which, I am sure, are very sensible and much to your credit, you must allow that if a man should happen to be the possessor of vast – well, let us say of considerable – sums of money, it is his duty to get that money into circulation, so that the community may be the better for it. There is the secret of my fine feathers. I have to exert all my ingenuity in order to spend my income, and yet keep the money in legitimate channels. For example, it is very easy to give money away, and no doubt I could dispose of my surplus, or part of my surplus, in that fashion, but I have no wish to pauperise anyone, or to do mischief by indiscriminate charity. I must exact some sort of money's worth for all the money which I lay out. You see my point, don't you?'

'Entirely; though really it is something novel to hear a man complain of the difficulty of spending his income.'

'I assure you that it is a very serious difficulty with me. But I have hit upon some plans – some very pretty plans. Will you wash your hands? Well, then, perhaps you would care to have a look round. Just come into this corner of the room, and sit upon this chair. So. Now I will sit upon this one, and we are ready to start.'

The angle of the chamber in which they sat was painted for about six feet in each direction a dark chocolate-brown, and was furnished with two red plush seats, protruding from the walls and in striking contrast with the simplicity of the rest of the apartment.

'This,' remarked Raffles Haw, 'is a lift, though it is so closely joined to the rest of the room that without the change in colour it might puzzle you to find the division. It is made to run either horizontally or vertically. This line of knobs represents the various rooms. You can see "Dining", "Smoking", "Billiard", "Library" and so on upon them. I will show you the upward action. I press this one with "Kitchen" upon it.'

There was a sense of motion, a very slight jar, and Robert, without moving from his seat, was conscious that the room had vanished, and that a large arched oaken door stood in the place which it had occupied.

'That is the kitchen door,' said Raffles Haw. 'I have my kitchen at the top of the house. I cannot tolerate the smell of cooking. We have come up eighty feet in a very few seconds. Now I press again and here we are in my room once more.'

Robert McIntyre stared about him in astonishment.

'The wonders of science are greater than those of magic,' he remarked.

'Yes, it is a pretty little mechanism. Now we try the horizontal. I press the "Dining" knob and here we are, you see. Step towards the door, and you will find it open in front of you.'

Robert did as he was bid, and found himself with his companion in a large and lofty room, while the lift, the instant that it was freed from their weight, flashed back to its original position. With his feet sinking into the soft rich carpet, as though he were ankle-deep in some mossy bank, he stared about him at the great pictures which lined the walls.

'Surely, surely, I see Raphael's touch there,' he cried, pointing up at the one which faced him.

'Yes, it is a Raphael, and I believe one of his best. I had a very exciting bid for it with the French Government. They wanted it for the Louvre, but of course at an auction the longest purse must win.'

'And this "Arrest of Catiline" must be a Rubens. One cannot mistake his splendid men and his infamous women.'

'Yes, it is a Rubens. The other two are a Velasquez and a Teniers, fair specimens of the Spanish and of the Dutch schools. I have only old masters here. The moderns are in the billiard-room. The furniture here is a little curious. In fact, I fancy that it is unique. It is made of ebony and narwhals' horns. You see that the legs of everything are of spiral ivory, both the table and the chairs. It cost the upholsterer some little pains, for the supply of these things is a strictly limited one. Curiously enough, the Chinese Emperor had given a large order for narwhals' horns to repair some ancient pagoda, which was fenced in with them, but I outbid him in the market, and his celestial highness has had to wait. There is a lift here in the corner, but we do not need it. Pray step through this door. This is the billiard-room,' he continued as they advanced into the adjoining room. 'You see I have a few recent pictures of merit upon the walls. Here is a Corot, two Meissoniers, a Bouguereau, a Millais, an Orchardson and two Alma-Tademas. It seems to me to be a pity to hang pictures over these walls of carved oak. Look at those birds hopping and singing in the branches. They really seem to move and twitter, don't they?'

'They are perfect. I never saw such exquisite work. But why do you call it a billiard-room, Mr Haw? I do not see any board.'

'Oh, a board is such a clumsy uncompromising piece of furniture. It is always in the way unless you actually need to use it. In this case the board is covered by that square of polished maple which you see let into the floor. Now I put my foot upon this motor. You see!' As he spoke, the central portion of the flooring flew up, and a most beautiful tortoiseshell-plated billiard-table rose up to its proper position. He pressed a second spring, and a bagatelle-table appeared in the same fashion. 'You may have card-tables or what you will by setting the levers in motion,' he remarked. 'But all this is very trifling. Perhaps we may find something in the museum which may be of more interest to you.'

He led the way into another chamber, which was furnished in antique style, with hangings of the rarest and richest tapestry. The floor was a mosaic of coloured marbles, scattered over with mats of costly fur. There was little furniture, but a number of Louis-Quatorze cabinets of ebony and silver with delicately-painted plaques were ranged round the apartment.

'It is perhaps hardly fair to dignify it by the name of a museum,' said Raffles Haw. 'It consists merely of a few elegant trifles which I have picked up here and there. Gems are my strongest point. I fancy that there, perhaps, I might challenge comparison with any private collector in the world. I lock them up, for even the best servants may be tempted.'

He took a silver key from his watch chain, and began to unlock and draw out the drawers. A cry of wonder and of admiration burst from Robert McIntyre, as his eyes rested upon case after case filled with the most magnificent stones. The deep still red of the rubies, the clear scintillating green of the emeralds, the hard glitter of the diamonds, the many shifting shades of beryls, of amethysts, of onyxes, of cats'-eyes, of opals, of agates, of cornelians seemed to fill the whole chamber with a vague twinkling, many-coloured light. Long slabs of the beautiful blue lapis lazuli, magnificent bloodstones, specimens of pink and red and white coral, long strings of lustrous pearls, all these were tossed out by their owner as a careless schoolboy might pour marbles from his bag.

'This isn't bad,' he said, holding up a great glowing yellow mass as large as his own head. 'It is really a very fine piece of amber. It was forwarded to me by my agent in the Baltic. Twenty-eight pounds, it weighs. I never heard of so fine a one. I have no very large brilliants – there were no very large ones in the market – but my average is good. Pretty toys, are they not?' He picked up a double handful of emeralds from a drawer, and then let them trickle slowly back into the heap.

'Good heavens!' cried Robert, as he gazed from case to case. 'It is an immense fortune in itself. Surely a hundred thousand pounds would hardly buy so splendid a collection.'

'I don't think that you would do for a valuer of precious stones,' said

Raffles Haw, laughing. 'Why, the contents of that one little drawer of brilliants could not be bought for the sum which you name. I have a memorandum here of what I have expended up to date on my collection, though I have agents at work who will probably make very considerable additions to it within the next few weeks. As matters stand, however, I have spent – let me see – pearls, one forty thousand; emeralds, seven fifty; rubies, eight forty; brilliants, nine twenty; onyxes – I have several very nice onyxes – two thirty. Other gems, carbuncles, agates – hum! Yes, it figures out at just over four million seven hundred and forty thousand. I dare say that we may say five million, for I have not counted the odd money.'

'Good gracious!' cried the young artist, with staring eyes.

'I have a certain feeling of duty in the matter. You see the cutting, polishing, and general sale of stones is one of those industries which is entirely dependent upon wealth. If we do not support it, it must languish, which means misfortune to a considerable number of people. The same applies to the gold filigree work which you noticed in the court. Wealth has its responsibilities, and the encouragement of these handicrafts are among the most obvious of them. Here is a nice ruby. It is Burmese, and the fifth largest in existence. I am inclined to think that if it were uncut it would be the second, but of course cutting takes away a great deal.' He held up the blazing red stone, about the size of a chestnut, between his finger and thumb for a moment, and then threw it carelessly back into its drawer. 'Come into the smoking-room,' he said; 'you will need some little refreshment, for they say that sightseeing is the most exhausting occupation in the world.'

FOUR

From Clime to Clime

The chamber in which the bewildered Robert now found himself was more luxurious, if less rich, than any which he had yet seen. Low settees of claret-coloured plush were scattered in orderly disorder over a mossy Eastern carpet. Deep lounges, reclining sofas, American rocking-chairs, all were to be had for the choosing. One end of the room was walled by glass, and appeared to open upon a luxuriant hot-house. At the farther end a double line of gilt rails supported a profusion of the most recent magazines and periodicals. A rack at each side of the inlaid fireplace sustained a long line of the pipes of all places and nations – English cherrywoods, French briars, German china-bowls, carved meerschaums, scented cedar and myall-wood, with Eastern narghiles, Turkish chibouks and two great golden-topped hookahs. To right and left were a series of small lockers, extending in a treble row for the whole length of the room, with the names of the various brands of tobacco scrolled in ivory work across them. Above were other larger tiers of polished oak, which held cigars and cigarettes.

'Try that Damascus settee,' said the master of the house, as he threw himself into a rocking-chair. 'It is from the Sultan's upholsterer. The Turks have a very good notion of comfort. I am a confirmed smoker myself, Mr McIntyre, so I have been able, perhaps, to check my architect here more than in most of the other departments. Of pictures, for example, I know nothing, as you would very speedily find out. On a tobacco, I might, perhaps, offer an opinion. Now these' – he drew out some long, beautifully-rolled, mellow-coloured cigars – 'these are really something a little out of the common. Do try one.'

Robert lit the weed which was offered to him, and leaned back luxuriously amid his cushions, gazing through the blue balmy fragrant cloud-wreaths at the extraordinary man in the dirty pea-jacket who spoke of millions as another might of sovereigns. With his pale face, his sad, languid air, and his bowed shoulders, it was as though he were crushed down under the weight of his own gold. There was a mute apology, an attitude of deprecation in his manner and speech, which was strangely at variance with the immense power which he wielded. To Robert the whole whimsical incident had been intensely interesting and amusing. His artistic nature blossomed out in this atmosphere of perfect luxury and comfort, and he was conscious of a sense of repose and of absolute sensual contentment such as he had never before experienced.

'Shall it be coffee, or Rhine wine, or Tokay, or perhaps something stronger?' asked Raffles Haw, stretching out his hand to what looked like a piano-board projecting from the wall. 'I can recommend the Tokay. I have it from the man who supplies the Emperor of Austria, though I think I may say that I get the cream of it.'

He struck twice upon one of the piano-notes, and sat expectant. With a sharp click at the end of ten seconds a sliding shutter flew open, and a small tray protruded bearing two long tapering Venetian glasses filled with wine.

'It works very nicely,' said Raffles Haw. 'It is quite a new thing – never before done, as far as I know. You see the names of the various wines and so on printed on the notes. By pressing the note down I complete an electric circuit which causes the tap in the cellars beneath to remain open long enough to fill the glass which always stands beneath it. The glasses, you understand, stand upon a revolving drum, so that there must always be one there. The glasses are then brought up through a pneumatic tube, which is set working by the increased weight of the glass when the wine is added to it. It is a pretty little idea. But I am afraid that I bore you rather with all these petty contrivances. It is a whim of mine to push mechanism as far as it will go.'

'On the contrary, I am filled with interest and wonder,' said Robert warmly. 'It is as if I had been suddenly whipped up out of prosaic old England and transferred in an instant to some enchanted palace, some Eastern home of the genii. I could not have believed that there existed upon this earth such adaptation of means to an end, such complete mastery of every detail which may aid in stripping life of any of its petty worries.'

'I have something yet to show you,' remarked Raffles Haw; 'but we will rest here for a few minutes, for I wished to have a word with you. How is the cigar?'

'Most excellent.'

'It was rolled in Louisiana in the old slavery days. There is nothing made like them now. The man who had them did not know their value. He let them go at merely a few shillings apiece. Now I want you to do me a favour, Mr McIntyre.'

'I shall be so glad.'

'You can see more or less how I am situated. I am a complete stranger here. With the well-to-do classes I have little in common. I am no society man. I don't want to call or be called on. I am a student in a small way, and a man of quiet tastes. I have no social ambitions at all. Do you understand?'

'Entirely.'

'On the other hand, my experience of the world has been that it is the rarest thing to be able to form a friendship with a poorer man – I mean with a man who is at all eager to increase his income. They think much of your wealth, and little of yourself. I have tried, you understand, and I know.' He paused and ran his fingers through his thin beard.

Robert McIntyre nodded to show that he appreciated his position.

'Now, you see,' he continued, 'if I am to be cut off from the rich by my own tastes, and from those who are not rich by my distrust of their motives, my situation is an isolated one. Not that I mind isolation: I am used to it. But it limits my field of usefulness. I have no trustworthy means of informing myself when and where I may do good. I have already, I am glad to say, met a man today, your vicar, who appears to be thoroughly unselfish and trustworthy. He shall be one of my channels of communication with the outer world. Might I ask you whether you would be willing to become another?'

'With the greatest pleasure,' said Robert eagerly.

The proposition filled his heart with joy, for it seemed to give him an almost official connection with this paradise of a house. He could not have asked for anything more to his taste.

'I was fortunate enough to discover by your conversation how high a ground you take in such matters, and how entirely disinterested you are. You may have observed that I was short and almost rude with you at first. I have had reason to fear and suspect all chance friendships. Too often they have proved to be carefully planned beforehand, with some sordid object in view. Good heavens, what stories I could tell you! A lady pursued by a bull – I have risked my life to save her, and have learned afterwards that the scene had been arranged by the mother as an effective introduction, and that the bull had been hired by the hour. But I won't shake your faith in human nature. I have had some rude shocks myself. I look, perhaps, with a jaundiced eye on all who come near me. It is the more needful that I should have one whom I can trust to advise me.'

'If you will only show me where my opinion can be of any use I shall be most happy,' said Robert. 'My people come from Birmingham, but I know most of the folk here and their position.'

'That is just what I want. Money can do so much good, and it may do so much harm. I shall consult you when I am in doubt. By the way, there is one small question which I might ask you now. Can you tell me who a young lady is with very dark hair, grey eyes and a finely chiselled face? She wore a blue dress when I saw her, with astrachan about her neck and cuffs.'

Robert chuckled to himself.

'I know that dress pretty well,' he said. 'It is my sister Laura whom you describe.'

'Your sister! Really! Why, there is a resemblance, now that my attention is called to it. I saw her the other day, and wondered who she might be. She lives with you, of course?'

'Yes; my father, she and I live together at Elmdene.'

'Where I hope to have the pleasure of making their acquaintance. You have finished your cigar? Have another, or try a pipe. To the real smoker all is mere trifling save the pipe. I have most brands of tobacco here. The lockers are filled on Monday, and on Saturday their contents are handed over to the old folk at the alms-houses, so I manage to keep it pretty fresh always. Well, if you won't take anything else, perhaps you would care to see one or two of the other effects which I have devised. On this side is the armoury, and beyond it the library. My collection of books is a limited one; there are just over the fifty thousand volumes. But it is to some extent remarkable for quality. I have a Visigoth Bible of the fifth century, which I rather fancy is unique; there is a *Biblia Pauperum* of 1430; a manuscript of Genesis done upon mulberry leaves, probably of the second century; a *Tristan and Iseult* of the eighth century; and some hundred black-letters, with five very fine specimens of Schoffer and Fust. But those you may turn over any wet afternoon when you have nothing better to do. Meanwhile, I have a little device connected with this smoking-room which may amuse you. Light this other cigar. Now sit with me upon this lounge which stands at the farther end of the room.'

The sofa in question was in a niche which was lined in three sides and above with perfectly clear transparent crystal. As they sat down the master of the house drew a cord which pulled out a crystal shutter behind them, so that they were enclosed on all sides in a great box of glass, so pure and so highly polished that its presence might very easily be forgotten. A number of golden cords with crystal handles hung down into this small chamber, and appeared to be connected with a long shining bar outside.

'Now, where would you like to smoke your cigar?' said Raffles Haw, with a twinkle in his demure eyes. 'Shall we go to India, or to Egypt, or to China, or to – '

'To South America,' said Robert.

There was a whirr and a sense of motion. The young artist gazed about him in absolute amazement. Look where he would all round were tree-ferns and palms with long drooping creepers, and a blaze of brilliant orchids. Smoking-room, house, England, all were gone, and he sat on a settee in the heart of a virgin forest of the Amazon. It was no mere optical delusion or trick. He could see the hot steam rising from the tropical undergrowth, the heavy drops falling from the huge green leaves, the very grain and fibre of the rough bark which clothed the trunks. Even as he gazed a green mottled snake curled noiselessly over a branch above his head, and a bright-coloured paroquet broke suddenly from amid the foliage and flashed off among the tree-trunks. Robert gazed around, speechless with surprise, and finally turned upon his host a face in which curiosity was not unmixed with a suspicion of fear.

'People have been burned for less, have they not?' cried Raffles Haw laughing heartily. 'Have you had enough of the Amazon? What do you say to a spell of Egypt?'

Again the whirr, the swift flash of passing objects, and in an instant a huge desert stretched on every side of them, as far as the eye could reach. In the foreground a clump of five palm trees towered into the air, with a profusion of rough cactus-like plants bristling from their base. On the other side rose a rugged, gnarled, grey monolith, carved at the base into a huge scarabaeus. A group of lizards played about on the surface of the old carved stone. Beyond, the yellow sand stretched away into farthest space, where the dim mirage mist played along the horizon.

'Mr Haw, I cannot understand it!' Robert grasped the velvet edge of the settee, and gazed wildly about him.

'The effect is rather startling, is it not? This Egyptian desert is my favourite when I lay myself out for a contemplative smoke. It seems strange that tobacco should have come from the busy, practical West. It has much more affinity with the dreamy, languid East. But perhaps you would like to run over to China for a change?'

'Not today,' said Robert, passing his hand over his forehead. 'I feel rather confused by all these wonders, and indeed I think that they have affected my nerves a little. Besides, it is time that I returned to my prosaic Elmdene, if I can find my way out of this wilderness to which you have transplanted me. But would you ease my mind, Mr Haw, by showing me how this thing is done?'

'It is the merest toy – a complex plaything, nothing more. Allow me to explain. I have a line of very large greenhouses which extends from one end of my smoking-room. These different houses are kept at varying degrees of heat and humidity so as to reproduce the exact climates of Egypt, China, and the rest. You see, our crystal chamber is a tramway running with a minimum of friction along a steel rod. By pulling this or that handle I regulate how far it shall go, and it travels, as you have seen, with amazing speed. The effect of my hot-houses is heightened by the roofs being invariably concealed by skies, which are really very admirably painted, and by the introduction of birds and other creatures, which seem to flourish quite as well in artificial as in natural heat. This explains the South American effect.'

'But not the Egyptian.'

'No. It is certainly rather clever. I had the best man in France, at least the best at those large effects, to paint in that circular background. You understand, the palms, cacti, obelisk, and so on, are perfectly genuine, and so is the sand for fifty yards or so, and I defy the keenest-eyed man in England to tell where the deception commences. It is the familiar and perhaps rather meretricious effect of a circular panorama, but carried out in the most complete manner. Was there any other point?'

'The crystal box? Why was it?'

'To preserve my guests from the effects of the changes of temperature. It would be a poor kindness to bring them back to my smoking-room drenched through, and with the seeds of a violent cold. The crystal has to be kept warm, too, otherwise vapour would deposit, and you would have your view spoiled. But must you really go? Then here we are back in the smoking-room. I hope that it will not be your last visit by many a one. And if I may come down to Elmdene I should be very glad to do so. This is the way through the museum.'

As Robert McIntyre emerged from the balmy aromatic atmosphere of the great house into the harsh, raw, biting air of an English winter evening he felt as though he had been away for a long visit in some foreign country. Time is measured by impressions, and so vivid and novel had been his feelings, that weeks and weeks might have elapsed since his chat with the smoke-grimed stranger in the road. He walked along with his head in a whirl, his whole mind possessed and intoxicated by the one idea of the boundless wealth and the immense power of this extraordinary stranger.

Small and sordid and mean seemed his own Elmdene as he approached it, and he passed over its threshold full of restless discontent against himself and his surroundings.

FIVE

Laura's Request

That night after supper Robert McIntyre poured forth all that he had seen to his father and to his sister. So full was he of the one subject that it was a relief to him to share his knowledge with others. Rather for his own sake, then, than for theirs he depicted vividly all the marvels which he had seen; the profusion of wealth, the regal treasure-house of gems, the gold, the marble, the extraordinary devices, the absolute lavishness and complete disregard for money which was shown in every detail. For an hour he pictured with glowing words all the wonders which had been shown him, and ended with some pride by describing the request which Mr Raffles Haw had made, and the complete confidence which he had placed in him.

His words had a very different effect upon his two listeners. Old McIntyre leaned back in his chair with a bitter smile upon his lips, his thin face crinkled into a thousand puckers, and his small eyes shining with envy and greed. His lean yellow hand upon the table was clenched until the knuckles gleamed white in the lamplight. Laura, on the other hand, leaned forward, her lips parted, drinking in her brother's words with a glow of colour upon either cheek. It seemed to Robert, as he glanced from one to the other of them, that he had never seen his father look so evil, or his sister so beautiful.

'Who is the fellow, then?' asked the old man after a considerable pause. 'I hope he got all this in an honest fashion. Five millions in jewels, you say. Good gracious me! Ready to give it away, too, but afraid of pauperising anyone. You can tell him, Robert, that you know of one very deserving case which has not the slightest objection to being pauperised.'

'But who can he possibly be, Robert?' cried Laura. 'Haw cannot be his real name. He must be some disguised prince, or perhaps a king in exile. Oh, I should have loved to have seen those diamonds and the emeralds! I always think that emeralds suit dark people best. You must tell me again all about that museum, Robert.'

'I don't think that he is anything more than he pretends to be,' her brother answered. 'He has the plain, quiet manners of an ordinary middle-class Englishman. There was no particular polish that I could see. He knew a little about books and pictures, just enough to appreciate them, but nothing more. No, I fancy that he is a man quite in our own position of life, who has in some way inherited a vast sum. Of course it is difficult for me to form an estimate, but I should judge that what I saw today – house, pictures, jewels, books, and so on – could never have been bought under twenty millions, and I am sure that that figure is entirely an understatement.'

'I never knew but one Haw,' said old McIntyre, drumming his fingers on the table; 'he was a foreman in my pin-fire cartridge-case department. But he was an elderly single man. Well, I hope he got it all honestly. I hope the money is clean.'

'And really, really, he is coming to see us!' cried Laura, clapping her hands. 'Oh, when do you think he will come, Robert? Do give me warning. Do you think it will be tomorrow?'

'I am sure I cannot say.'

'I should so love to see him. I don't know when I have been so interested.'

'Why, you have a letter there,' remarked Robert. 'From Hector, too, by the foreign stamp. How is he?'

'It only came this evening. I have not opened it yet. To tell the truth, I have been so interested in your story that I had forgotten all about it. Poor old Hector! It is from Madeira.' She glanced rapidly over the four pages of straggling writing in the young sailor's bold schoolboyish hand. 'Oh, he is all right,' she said. 'They had a gale on the way out, and that sort of thing, but he is all right now. He thinks he may be back by March. I wonder whether your new friend will come tomorrow – your knight of the enchanted castle.'

'Hardly so soon, I should fancy.'

'If he should be looking about for an investment. Robert,' said the father, 'you won't forget to tell him what a fine opening there is now in the gun trade. With my knowledge, and a few thousands at my back, I could bring him in his thirty per cent. as regular as the bank. After all, he must lay out his money somehow. He cannot sink it all in books and precious stones. I am sure that I could give him the highest references.'

'It may be a long time before he comes, father,' said Robert coldly; 'and when he does I am afraid that I can hardly use his friendship as a means of advancing your interest.'

'We are his equals, father,' cried Laura with spirit. 'Would you put us on the footing of beggars? He would think we cared for him only for his money. I wonder that you should think of such a thing.'

'If I had not thought of such things where would your education have been, miss?' retorted the angry old man; and Robert stole quietly away to his room, whence amid his canvases he could still hear the hoarse voice and the clear in their never-ending family jangle. More and more sordid seemed the surroundings of his life, and more and more to be valued the peace which money can buy.

Breakfast had hardly been cleared in the morning, and Robert had not yet ascended to his work, when there came a timid tapping at the door, and there was Raffles Haw on the mat outside. Robert ran out and welcomed him with all cordiality.

'I am afraid that I am a very early visitor,' he said apologetically; 'but I often take a walk after breakfast.' He had no traces of work upon him now, but was trim and neat with a dark suit, and carefully brushed hair. 'You spoke yesterday of your work. Perhaps, early as it is, you would allow me the privilege of looking over your studio?'

'Pray step in, Mr Haw,' cried Robert, all in a flutter at this advance from so munificent a patron of art; 'I should be only too happy to show you such little work as I have on hand, though, indeed, I am almost afraid when I think how familiar you are with some of the greatest masterpieces. Allow me to introduce you to my father and to my sister Laura.'

Old McIntyre bowed low and rubbed his thin hands together; but the young lady gave a gasp of surprise, and stared with widely-opened eyes at the millionaire.

Haw stepped forward, however, and shook her quietly by the hand. 'I expected to find that it was you,' he said. 'I have already met your sister, Mr McIntyre, on the very first day that I came here. We took shelter in a shed from a snowstorm, and had quite a pleasant little chat.'

'I had no notion that I was speaking to the owner of the Hall,' said Laura in some confusion. 'How funnily things turn out, to be sure!'

'I had often wondered who it was that I spoke to, but it was only yesterday that I discovered. What a sweet little place you have here! It must be charming in summer. Why, if it were not for this hill my windows would look straight across at yours.'

'Yes, and we should see all your beautiful plantations,' said Laura, standing beside him in the window. 'I was wishing only yesterday that the hill was not there.'

'Really! I shall be happy to have it removed for you if you would like it.'

'Good gracious!' cried Laura. 'Why, where would you put it?'

'Oh, they could run it along the line and dump it anywhere. It is not much of a hill. A few thousand men with proper machinery and a line of rails brought right up to them could easily dispose of it in a few months.'

'And the poor vicar's house?' Laura asked, laughing.

'I think that might be got over. We could run him up a facsimile, which would, perhaps, be more convenient to him. Your brother will tell you that I am quite an expert at the designing of houses. But, seriously, if you think it would be an improvement I will see what can be done.'

'Not for the world, Mr Haw. Why, I should be a traitor to the whole village if I were to encourage such a scheme. The hill is the one thing which gives Tamfield the slightest individuality. It would be the height of selfishness to sacrifice it in order to improve the view from Elmdene.'

'It is a little box of a place this, Mr Haw,' said old McIntyre. 'I should think you must feel quite stifled in it after your grand mansion, of which my son tells me such wonders. But we were not always accustomed to this sort of thing, Mr Haw. Humble as I stand here, there was a time, and not so long ago, when I could write as many figures on a cheque as any gunmaker in Birmingham. It was – '

'He is a dear discontented old papa,' cried Laura, throwing her arm round him in a caressing manner. He gave a sharp squeak and a grimace of pain, which he endeavoured to hide by an outbreak of painfully artificial coughing.

'Shall we go upstairs?' said Robert hurriedly, anxious to divert his guest's attention from this little domestic incident. 'My studio is the real atelier, for it is right up under the tiles. I shall lead the way, if you will have the kindness to follow me.'

Leaving Laura and Mr McIntyre, they went up together to the work-room. Mr Haw stood long in front of the 'Signing of Magna Charta', and the 'Murder of Thomas à Becket', screwing up his eyes and twitching nervously at his beard, while Robert stood by in anxious expectancy.

'And how much are these?' asked Raffles Haw at last.

'I priced them at a hundred apiece when I sent them to London.'

'Then the best I can wish you is that the day may come when you would gladly give ten times the sum to have them back again. I am sure that there are great possibilities in you, and I see that in grouping and in boldness of design you have already achieved much. But your drawing, if you will excuse my saying so, is just a little crude, and your colouring perhaps a trifle thin. Now, I will make a bargain with you, Mr McIntyre, if you will consent to it. I know that money has no charms for you, but still, as you said when I first met you, a man must live. I shall buy these two canvases from you at the price which you name, subject to the condition that you may always have them back again by repaying the same sum.'

'You are really very kind.' Robert hardly knew whether to be delighted at having sold his pictures or humiliated at the frank criticism of the buyer.

'May I write a cheque at once?' said Raffles Haw. 'Here is pen and ink. So! I shall send a couple of footmen down for them in the afternoon. Well, I shall keep them in trust for you. I dare say that when you are famous they will be of value as specimens of your early manner.'

'I am sure that I am extremely obliged to you, Mr Haw,' said the young artist, placing the cheque in his notebook. He glanced at it as he folded it up, in the vague hope that perhaps this man of whims had assessed his pictures at a higher rate than he had named. The figures, however, were exact. Robert began dimly to perceive that there were drawbacks as well as advantages to the reputation of a money-scorner, which he had gained by a few chance words, prompted rather by the reaction against his father's than by his own real convictions.

'I hope, Miss McIntyre,' said Raffles Haw, when they had descended to the sitting-room once more, 'that you will do me the honour of coming to see the little curiosities which I have gathered together. Your brother will, I am sure, escort you up; or perhaps Mr McIntyre would care to come?'

'I shall be delighted to come, Mr Haw,' cried Laura, with her sweetest smile. 'A good deal of my time just now is taken up in looking after the poor people, who find the cold weather very trying.' Robert raised his eyebrows, for it was the first he had heard of his sister's missions of mercy, but Mr Raffles Haw nodded approvingly. 'Robert was telling us of your wonderful hot-houses. I am sure I wish I could transport the whole parish into one of them, and give them a good warm.'

'Nothing would be easier, but I am afraid that they might find it a little trying when they came out again. I have one house which is only just finished. Your brother has not seen it yet, but I think it is the best of them all. It represents an Indian jungle, and is hot enough in all conscience.'

'I shall so look forward to seeing it,' cried Laura, clasping her hands. 'It has been one of the dreams of my life to see India. I have read so much of it – the temples, the forests, the great rivers, and the tigers. Why, you would hardly believe it, but I have never seen a tiger except in a picture.'

'That can easily be set right,' said Raffles Haw, with his quiet smile. 'Would you care to see one?'

'Oh, immensely.'

'I will have one sent down. Let me see, it is nearly twelve o'clock. I can get a wire to Liverpool by one. There is a man there who deals in such things. I should think he would be due tomorrow morning. Well, I shall look forward to seeing you all before very long. I have rather outstayed my time, for I am a man of routine, and I always put in a certain number of hours in my laboratory.' He shook hands cordially with them all, and lighting his pipe at the doorstep, strolled off upon his way.

'Well, what do you think of him now?' asked Robert, as they watched his black figure against the white snow.

'I think that he is no more fit to be trusted with all that money than a child,' cried the old man. 'It made me positively sick to hear him talk of moving hills and buying tigers, and suchlike nonsense, when there are honest men without a business, and great businesses starving for a little capital. It's unchristian – that's what I call it.'

'I think he is most delightful, Robert,' said Laura. 'Remember, you have promised to take us up to the Hall. And he evidently wishes us to go soon. Don't you think we might go this afternoon?'

'I hardly think that, Laura. You leave it in my hands, and I will arrange it all. And now I must get to work, for the light is so very short on these winter days.'

That night Robert McIntyre had gone to bed and was dozing off when a hand plucked at his shoulder, and he started up to find his sister in some white drapery, with a shawl thrown over her shoulders, standing beside him in the moonlight.

'Robert, dear,' she whispered, stooping over him, 'there was something I wanted to ask you, but papa was always in the way. You will do something to please me, won't you, Robert?'

'Of course, Laura. What is it?'

'I do so hate having my affairs talked over, dear. If Mr Raffles Haw says anything to you about me, or asks any questions, please don't say anything about Hector. You won't, will you, Robert, for the sake of your little sister?'

'No; not unless you wish it.'

'There is a dear good brother.' She stooped over him and kissed him tenderly.

It was a rare thing for Laura to show any emotion, and her brother marvelled sleepily over it until he relapsed into his interrupted doze.

SIX

A Strange Visitor

The McIntyre family was seated at breakfast on the morning which followed the first visit of Raffles Haw when they were surprised to hear the buzz and hum of a multitude of voices in the village street. Nearer and nearer came the tumult, and then, of a sudden, two maddened horses reared themselves up on the other side of the garden hedge, prancing and pawing, with ears laid back and eyes ever glancing at some horror behind them. Two men hung shouting to their bridles, while a third came rushing up the curved gravel path. Before the McIntyres could realise the situation, their maid, Mary, darted into the sitting-room with terror in her round freckled face:

'If you please, miss,' she screamed, 'your tiger has arrove.'

'Good heavens!' cried Robert, rushing to the door with his half-filled teacup in his hand. 'This is too much. Here is an iron cage on a trolly with a great ramping tiger, and the whole village with their mouths open.'

'Mad as a hatter!' shrieked old Mr McIntyre. 'I could see it in his eye. He spent enough on this beast to start me in business. Whoever heard of such a thing? Tell the driver to take it to the police-station.'

'Nothing of the sort, papa,' said Laura, rising with dignity and wrapping a shawl about her shoulders. Her eyes were shining, her cheeks flushed, and she carried herself like a triumphant queen.

Robert, with his teacup in his hand, allowed his attention to be diverted from their strange visitor while he gazed at his beautiful sister.

'Mr Raffles Haw has done this out of kindness to me,' she said, sweeping towards the door. 'I look upon it as a great attention on his part. I shall certainly go out and look at it.'

'If you please, sir,' said the carman, reappearing at the door, 'it's all as we can do to 'old in the 'osses.'

'Let us all go out together then,' suggested Robert.

They went as far as the garden fence and stared over, while the whole village, from the schoolchildren to the old grey-haired men from the almshouses, gathered round in mute astonishment. The tiger, a long, lithe, venomous-looking creature, with two blazing green eyes, paced stealthily round the little cage, lashing its sides with its tail, and rubbing its muzzle against the bars.

'What were your orders?' asked Robert of the carman.

'It came through by special express from Liverpool, sir, and the train is drawn up at the Tamfield siding all ready to take it back. If it 'ad been royalty the railway folk couldn't ha' shown it more respec'. We are to take it back when you're done with it. It's been a cruel job, sir, for our arms is pulled clean out of the sockets a-'olding in of the 'osses.'

'What a dear, sweet creature it is,' cried Laura. 'How sleek and how graceful! I cannot understand how people could be afraid of anything so beautiful.'

'If you please, marm,' said the carman, touching his skin cap, 'he out with his paw between the bars as we stood in the station yard, and if I 'adn't pulled my mate Bill back it would ha' been a case of kingdom come. It was a proper near squeak, I can tell ye.'

'I never saw anything more lovely,' continued Laura, loftily overlooking the remarks of the driver. 'It has been a very great pleasure to me to see it, and I hope that you will tell Mr Haw so if you see him, Robert.'

'The horses are very restive,' said her brother. 'Perhaps, Laura, if you have seen enough, it would be as well to let them go.'

She bowed in the regal fashion which she had so suddenly adopted. Robert shouted the order, the driver sprang up, his comrades let the horses go, and away rattled the wagon and the trolly with half the Tamfielders streaming vainly behind it.

'Is it not wonderful what money can do?' Laura remarked, as they knocked the snow from their shoes within the porch. 'There seems to be no wish which Mr Haw could not at once gratify.'

'No wish of yours, you mean,' broke in her father. 'It's different when he is dealing with a wrinkled old man who has spent himself in working for his children. A plainer case of love at first sight I never saw.'

'How can you be so coarse, papa?' cried Laura, but her eyes flashed, and her teeth gleamed, as though the remark had not altogether displeased her.

'For heaven's sake, be careful, Laura!' cried Robert. 'It had not struck me before, but really it does look rather like it. You know how you stand. Raffles Haw is not a man to play with.'

'You dear old boy!' said Laura, laying her hand upon his shoulder, 'what do you know of such things? All you have to do is to go on with your painting, and to remember the promise you made last night.'

'What promise was that, then?' cried old McIntyre suspiciously.

'Never you mind, papa. But if you forget it, Robert, I shall never forgive you as long as I live.'

SEVEN

The Workings of Wealth

It can easily be believed that as the weeks passed the name and fame of the mysterious owner of the New Hall resounded over the quiet countryside until the rumour of him had spread to the remotest corners of Warwickshire and Staffordshire. In Birmingham on the one side, and in Coventry and Leamington on the other, there was gossip as to his untold riches, his extraordinary whims, and the remarkable life which he led. His name was bandied from mouth to mouth, and a thousand efforts were made to find out who and what he was. In spite of all their pains, however, the newsmongers were unable to discover the slightest trace of his antecedents, or to form even a guess as to the secret of his riches.

It was no wonder that conjecture was rife upon the subject, for hardly a day passed without furnishing some new instance of the boundlessness of his power and of the goodness of his heart. Through the vicar, Robert and others, he had learned much of the inner life of the parish, and many were the times when the struggling man, harassed and driven to the wall, found thrust into his hand some morning a brief note with an enclosure which rolled all the sorrow back from his life. One day a thick double-breasted pea-jacket and a pair of good sturdy boots were served out to every old man in the almshouse. On another, Miss Swire, the decayed gentlewoman who eked out her small annuity by needlework, had a brand new first-class sewing-machine handed in to her to take the place of the old worn-out treadle which tried her rheumatic joints. The pale-faced schoolmaster, who had spent years with hardly a break in struggling with the juvenile obtuseness of Tamfield, received through the post a circular ticket for a two months' tour through Southern Europe, with hotel coupons and all complete. John Hackett, the farmer, after five long years of bad seasons, borne with a brave heart, had at last been overthrown by the sixth, and had the bailiffs actually in the house when the good vicar had rushed in, waving a note above his head, to tell him not only that his deficit had been made up, but that enough remained over to provide the improved machinery which would enable him to hold his own for the future. An almost superstitious feeling came upon the rustic folk as they looked at the great palace when the sun gleamed upon the huge hot-houses, or even more so, perhaps, when at night the brilliant electric lights shot their white radiance through the countless rows of windows. To them it was as if some minor providence presided in that great place, unseen but seeing all, boundless in its power and its graciousness, ever ready to assist and to befriend. In every good deed, however, Raffles Haw still remained in the background, while the vicar and Robert had the pleasant task of conveying his benefits to the lowly and the suffering.

Once only did he appear in his own person, and that was upon the famous occasion when he saved the well-known bank of Garraweg Brothers in Birmingham. The most charitable and upright of men, the two brothers, Louis and Rupert, had built up a business which extended its ramifications into every townlet of four counties. The failure of their London agents had suddenly brought a heavy loss upon them, and the circumstance leaking out had caused a sudden and most dangerous run upon their establishment. Urgent telegrams for bullion from all their forty branches poured in at the very instant when the head office was crowded with anxious clients all waving their deposit-books, and clamouring for their money. Bravely did the two brothers with their staff stand with smiling faces behind the shining counter, while swift messengers sped and telegrams flashed to draw in all the available resources of the bank. All day the stream poured through the office, and when four o'clock came, and the doors were closed for the day, the street without was still blocked by the expectant crowd, while there remained scarce a thousand pounds of bullion in the cellars.

'It is only postponed, Louis,' said brother Rupert despairingly, when the last clerk had left the office, and when at last they could relax the fixed smile upon their haggard faces.

'Those shutters will never come down again,' cried brother Louis, and the two suddenly burst out sobbing in each other's arms, not for their own griefs, but for the miseries which they might bring upon those who had trusted them.

But who shall ever dare to say that there is no hope, if he will but give his griefs to the world? That very night Mrs Spurling had received a letter from her old schoolfriend, Mrs Louis Garraweg, with all her fears and her hopes poured out in it, and the whole sad story of their troubles. Swift from the Vicarage went the message to the Hall, and early next morning Mr Raffles Haw, with a great black carpet-bag in his hand, found means to draw the cashier of the local branch of the Bank of England from his breakfast, and to persuade him to open his doors at unofficial hours. By half-past nine the crowd had already begun to collect around Garraweg's, when a stranger, pale and thin, with a bloated carpet-bag, was shown at his own very pressing request into the bank parlour.

'It is no use, sir,' said the elder brother humbly, as they stood together encouraging each other to turn a brave face to misfortune, 'we can do no more. We have little left, and it would be unfair to the others to pay you now. We can but hope that when our assets are realised no one will be the loser save ourselves.'

'I did not come to draw out, but to put in,' said Raffles Haw in his demure apologetic fashion. 'I have in my bag five thousand hundred-pound Bank of England notes. If you will have the goodness to place them to my credit account I should be extremely obliged.'

'But, good heavens, sir!' stammered Rupert Garraweg, 'have you not heard? Have you not seen? We cannot allow you to do this thing blindfold; can we Louis?'

'Most certainly not. We cannot recommend our bank, sir, at the present moment, for there is a run upon us, and we do not know to what lengths it may go.'

'Tut! tut!' said Raffles Haw. 'If the run continues you must send me a wire, and I shall make a small addition to my account. You will send me a receipt by post. Good-morning, gentlemen!' He bowed himself out ere the astounded partners could realise what had befallen them, or raise their eyes from the huge black bag and the visiting card which lay upon their table. There was no great failure in Birmingham that day, and the house of Garraweg still survives to enjoy the success which it deserves.

Such were the deeds by which Raffles Haw made himself known throughout the Midlands, and yet, in spite of all his open-handedness, he was not a man to be imposed upon. In vain the sturdy beggar cringed at his gate, and in vain the crafty letter-writer poured out a thousand fabulous woes upon paper. Robert was astonished when he brought some tale of trouble to the Hall to observe how swift was the perception of the recluse, and how unerringly he could detect a flaw in a narrative or lay his finger upon the one point which rang false. Were a man strong enough to help himself, or of such a nature as to profit nothing by help, none would he get from the master of the New Hall. In vain, for example, did old McIntyre throw himself continually across the path of the millionaire, and impress upon him, by a thousand hints and innuendoes, the hard fortune which had been dealt him, and the ease with which his fallen greatness might be restored. Raffles Haw listened politely, bowed, smiled, but never showed the slightest inclination to restore the querulous old gunmaker to his pedestal.

But if the recluse's wealth was a lure which drew the beggars from far and near, as the lamp draws the moths, it had the same power of attraction upon another and much more dangerous class. Strange hard faces were seen in the village street, prowling figures were marked at night stealing about among the fir plantations, and warning messages arrived from city police and county constabulary to say that evil visitors were known to have taken train to Tamfield. But if, as Raffles Haw held, there were few limits to the power of immense wealth, it possessed, among other things, the power of self-preservation, as one or two people were to learn to their cost.

'Would you mind stepping up to the Hall?' he said one morning, putting his head in at the door of the Elmdene sitting-room. 'I have something there that might amuse you.' He was on intimate terms with the McIntyres now, and there were few days on which they did not see something of each other.

They gladly accompanied him, all three, for such invitations were usually the prelude of some agreeable surprise which he had in store for them.

'I have shown you a tiger,' he remarked to Laura, as he led them into the dining-room. 'I will now show you something quite as dangerous, though not nearly so pretty.' There was an arrangement of mirrors at one end of the room, with a large circular glass set at a sharp angle at the top.

'Look in there – in the upper glass,' said Raffles Haw.

'Good gracious! what dreadful-looking men!' cried Laura. 'There are two of them, and I don't know which is the worse.'

'What on earth are they doing?' asked Robert. 'They appear to be sitting on the ground in some sort of a cellar.'

'Most dangerous-looking characters,' said the old man. 'I should strongly recommend you to send for a policeman.'

'I have done so. But it seems a work of supererogation to take them to prison, for they are very snugly in prison already. However, I suppose that the law must have its own.'

'And who are they, and how did they come there? Do tell us, Mr Haw.'

Laura McIntyre had a pretty beseeching way with her, which went rather piquantly with her queenly style of beauty.

'I know no more than you do. They were not there last night, and they are here this morning, so I suppose it is a safe inference that they came in during the night, especially as my servants found the window open when they came down. As to their character and intentions, I should think that is pretty legible upon their faces. They look a pair of beauties, don't they?'

'But I cannot understand in the least where they are,' said Robert, staring into the mirror. 'One of them has taken to butting his head against the wall. No, he is bending so that the other may stand upon his back. He is up there now, and the light is shining upon his face. What a bewildered ruffianly face it is too. I should so like to sketch it. It would be a study for the picture I am planning of the Reign of Terror.'

'I have caught them in my patent burglar trap,' said Haw. 'They are my first birds, but I have no doubt that they will not be the last. I will show you how it works. It is quite a new thing. This flooring is now as strong as possible, but every night I disconnect it. It is done simultaneously by a central machine for every room on the ground-floor. When the floor is disconnected one may advance three or four steps, either from the window or door, and then that whole part turns on a hinge and slides you into a padded strong-room beneath, where you may kick your heels until you are released. There is a central oasis between the hinges, where the furniture is grouped for the night. The flooring flies into position again when the weight of the intruder is removed, and there he must bide, while I can always take a peep at him by this simple little optical arrangement. I thought it might amuse you to have a look at my prisoners before I handed them over to the head-constable, who I see is now coming up the avenue.'

'The poor burglars!' cried Laura. 'It is no wonder that they look bewildered, for I suppose, Mr Haw, that they neither know where they are, nor how they came there. I am so glad to know that you guard yourself in this way, for I have often thought that you ran a danger.'

'Have you so?' said he, smiling round at her. 'I think that my house is fairly burglar-proof. I have one window which may be used as an entrance, the centre one of the three of my laboratory. I keep it so because, to tell the truth, I am somewhat of a night prowler myself, and when I treat myself to a ramble under the stars I like to slip in and out without ceremony. It would, however, be a fortunate rogue who picked the only safe entrance out of a hundred, and even then he might find pitfalls. Here is the constable, but you must not go, for Miss McIntyre has still something to see in my little place. If you will step into the billiard-room I shall be with you in a very few moments.'

EIGHT

A Billionaire's Plans

That morning, and many mornings both before and afterwards, were spent by Laura at the New Hall examining the treasures of the museum, playing with the thousand costly toys which Raffles Haw had collected or sallying out from the smoking-room in the crystal chamber into the long line of luxurious hot-houses. Haw would walk demurely beside her as she flitted from one thing to another like a butterfly among flowers, watching her out of the corner of his eye and taking a quiet pleasure in her delight. The only joy which his costly possessions had ever brought him was that which came from the entertainment of others.

By this time his attentions towards Laura McIntyre had become so marked that they could hardly be mistaken. He visibly brightened in her presence, and was never weary of devising a thousand methods of surprising and pleasing her. Every morning ere the McIntyre family were astir a great bouquet of strange and beautiful flowers was brought down by a footman from the Hall to brighten their breakfast-table. Her slightest wish, however fantastic, was instantly satisfied, if human money or ingenuity could do it. When the frost lasted a stream was dammed and turned from its course that it might flood two meadows, solely in order that she might have a place upon which to skate. With the thaw there came a groom every afternoon with a sleek and beautiful mare in case Miss McIntyre should care to ride. Everything went to show that she had made a conquest of the recluse of the New Hall.

And she on her side played her part admirably. With female adaptiveness she fell in with his humour, and looked at the world through his eyes. Her talk was of almshouses and free libraries, of charities and of improvements. He had never a scheme to which she could not add some detail making it more complete and more effective. To Haw it seemed that at last he had met a mind which was in absolute affinity with his own. Here was a help-mate, who could not only follow, but even lead him in the path which he had chosen.

Neither Robert nor his father could fail to see what was going forward, but to the latter nothing could possibly be more acceptable than a family tie which should connect him, however indirectly, with a man of vast fortune. The glamour of the gold bags had crept over Robert also, and froze the remonstrance upon his lips. It was very pleasant to have the handling of all this wealth, even as a mere agent. Why should he do or say what might disturb their present happy relations? It was his sister's business, not his; and as to Hector Spurling, he must take his chance as other men did. It was obviously best not to move one way or the other in the matter.

But to Robert himself, his work and his surroundings were becoming more and more irksome. His joy in his art had become less keen since he had known Raffles Haw. It seemed so hard to toil and slave to earn such a trifling sum, when money could really be had for the asking. It was true that he had asked for none, but large sums were forever passing through his hands for those who were needy, and if he were needy himself his friend would surely not grudge it to him. So the Roman galleys still remained faintly outlined upon the great canvas, while Robert's days were spent either in the luxurious library at the Hall, or in strolling about the country listening to tales of trouble, and returning like a tweed-suited ministering angel to carry Raffles Haw's help to the unfortunate. It was not an ambitious life, but it was one which was very congenial to his weak and easy-going nature.

Robert had observed that fits of depression had frequently come upon the millionaire, and it had sometimes struck him that the enormous sums which he spent had possibly made a serious inroad into his capital, and that his mind was troubled as to the future. His abstracted manner, his clouded brow, and his bent head all spoke of a soul which was weighed down with care, and it was only in Laura's presence that he could throw off the load of his secret trouble. For five hours a day he buried himself in the laboratory and amused himself with his hobby, but it was one of his whims that no one, neither any of his servants, nor even Laura or Robert, should ever cross the threshold of that outlying building. Day after day he vanished into it, to reappear hours afterwards pale and exhausted, while the whirr of machinery and the smoke which streamed from his high chimney showed how considerable were the operations which he undertook single-handed.

'Could I not assist you in any way?' suggested Robert, as they sat together after luncheon in the smoking-room. 'I am convinced that you over-try your strength. I should be so glad to help you, and I know a little of chemistry.'

'Do you, indeed?' said Raffles Haw, raising his eyebrows. 'I had no idea of that; it is very seldom that the artistic and the scientific faculties go together.'

'I don't know that I have either particularly developed. But I have taken classes, and I worked for two years in the laboratory at Sir Josiah Mason's Institute.'

'I am delighted to hear it,' Haw replied with emphasis. 'That may be of great importance to us. It is very possible – indeed, almost certain – that I shall avail myself of your offer of assistance, and teach you something of my chemical methods, which I may say differ considerably from those of the orthodox school. The time, however, is hardly ripe for that. What is it, Jones?'

'A note, sir.'

The butler handed it in upon a silver salver. Haw broke the seal and ran his eye over it.

'Tut! tut! It is from Lady Morsley, asking me to the Lord-Lieutenant's ball. I cannot possibly accept. It is very kind of them, but I do wish they would leave me alone. Very well, Jones. I shall write. Do you know, Robert, I am often very unhappy.'

He frequently called the young artist by his Christian name, especially in his more confidential moments.

'I have sometimes feared that you were,' said the other sympathetically. 'But how strange it seems, you who are yet young, healthy, with every faculty for enjoyment, and a millionaire.'

'Ah, Robert,' cried Haw, leaning back in his chair, and sending up thick blue wreaths from his pipe. 'You have put your finger upon my trouble. If I were a millionaire I might be happy, but, alas, I am no millionaire!'

'Good heavens!' gasped Robert.

Cold seemed to shoot to his inmost soul as it flashed upon him that this was a prelude to a confession of impending bankruptcy, and that all this glorious life, all the excitement and the colour and change, were about to vanish into thin air.

'No millionaire!' he stammered.

'No, Robert; I am a billionaire – perhaps the only one in the world. That is what is on my mind, and why I am unhappy sometimes. I feel that I should spend this money – that I should put it in circulation – and yet it is so hard to do it without failing to do good – without doing positive harm. I feel my responsibility deeply. It weighs me down. Am I justified in continuing to live this quiet life when there are so many millions whom I might save and comfort if I could but reach them?'

Robert heaved a long sigh of relief. 'Perhaps you take too grave a view of your responsibilities,' he said. 'Everybody knows that the good which you have done is immense. What more could you desire? If you really wished to extend your benevolence further, there are organised charities everywhere which would be very glad of your help.'

'I have the names of two hundred and seventy of them,' Haw answered. 'You must run your eye over them sometime, and see if you can suggest any others. I send my annual mite to each of them. I don't think there is much room for expansion in that direction.'

'Well, really you have done your share, and more than your share. I would settle down to lead a happy life, and think no more of the matter.'

'I could not do that,' Haw answered earnestly. 'I have not been singled out to wield this immense power simply in order that I might lead a happy life. I can never believe that. Now, can you not use your imagination,

Robert, and devise methods by which a man who has command of – well, let us say, for argument's sake, boundless wealth, could benefit mankind by it, without taking away anyone's independence or in any way doing harm?'

'Well, really, now that I come to think of it, it is a very difficult problem,' said Robert.

'Now I will submit a few schemes to you, and you may give me your opinion on them. Supposing that such a man were to buy ten square miles of ground here in Staffordshire, and were to build upon it a neat city, consisting entirely of clean, comfortable little four-roomed houses, furnished in a simple style, with shops and so forth, but no public-houses. Supposing, too, that he were to offer a house free to all the homeless folk, all the tramps, and broken men, and out-of-workers in Great Britain. Then, having collected them together, let him employ them, under fitting superintendence, upon some colossal piece of work which would last for many years, and perhaps be of permanent value to humanity. Give them a good rate of pay, and let their hours of labour be reasonable, and those of recreation be pleasant. Might you not benefit them and benefit humanity at one stroke?'

'But what form of work could you devise which would employ so vast a number for so long a time, and yet not compete with any existing industry? To do the latter would simply mean to shift the misery from one class to another.'

'Precisely so. I should compete with no one. What I thought of doing was of sinking a shaft through the earth's crust, and of establishing rapid communication with the Antipodes. When you had got a certain distance down – how far is an interesting mathematical problem – the centre of gravity would be beneath you, presuming that your boring was not quite directed towards the centre, and you could then lay down rails and tunnel as if you were on the level.'

Then for the first time it flashed into Robert McIntyre's head that his father's chance words were correct, and that he was in the presence of a madman. His great wealth had clearly turned his brain, and made him a monomaniac. He nodded indulgently, as when one humours a child.

'It would be very nice,' he said. 'I have heard, however, that the interior of the earth is molten, and your workmen would need to be salamanders.'

'The latest scientific data do not bear out the idea that the earth is so hot,' answered Raffles Haw. 'It is certain that the increased temperature in coal mines depends upon the barometric pressure. There are gases in the earth which may be ignited, and there are combustible materials as we see in the volcanoes; but if we came across anything of the sort in our borings, we could turn a river or two down the shaft, and get the better of it in that fashion.'

'It would be rather awkward if the other end of your shaft came out under the Pacific Ocean,' said Robert, choking down his inclination to laugh.

'I have had estimates and calculations from the finest living engineers – French, English and American. The point of exit of the tunnel could be calculated to the yard. That portfolio in the corner is full of sections, plans and diagrams. I have agents employed in buying up land, and if all goes well, we may get to work in the autumn. That is one device which may produce results. Another is canal-cutting.'

'Ah, there you would compete with the railways.'

'You don't quite understand. I intend to cut canals through every neck of land where such a convenience would facilitate commerce. Such a scheme, when unaccompanied by any toll upon vessels, would, I think, be a very judicious way of helping the human race.'

'And where, pray, would you cut the canals?' asked Robert.

'I have a map of the world here,' Haw answered, rising and taking one down from the paper-rack. 'You see the blue pencil marks. Those are the points where I propose to establish communication. Of course, I should begin with the obvious duty of finishing the Panama business.'

'Naturally.' The man's lunacy was becoming more and more obvious, and yet there was such precision and coolness in his manner, that Robert found himself against his own reason endorsing and speculating over his plans.

'The Isthmus of Corinth also occurs to one. That, however, is a small matter, from either a financial or an engineering point of view. I propose, however, to make a junction here, through Kiel between the German Ocean and the Baltic. It saves, you will observe, the whole journey round the coast of Denmark, and would facilitate our trade with Germany and Russia. Another very obvious improvement is to join the Forth and the Clyde, so as to connect Leith with the Irish and American routes. You see the blue line?'

'Quite so.'

'And we will have a little cutting here. It will run from Uleaborg to Kem, and will connect the White Sea with the Gulf of Bothnia. We must not allow our sympathies to be insular, must we? Our little charities should be cosmopolitan. We will try and give the good people of Archangel a better outlet for their furs and their tallow.'

'But it will freeze.'

'For six months in the year. Still, it will be something. Then we must do something for the East. It would never do to overlook the East.'

'It would certainly be an oversight,' said Robert, who was keenly alive to the comical side of the question. Raffles Haw, however, in deadly earnest, sat scratching away at his map with his blue pencil.

'Here is a point where we might be of some little use. If we cut through from Batoum to the Kura River we might tap the trade of the Caspian, and open up communication with all the rivers which run into it. You notice that they include a considerable tract of country. Then, again, I think that we might venture upon a little cutting between Beirut, on the Mediterranean, and the upper waters of the Euphrates, which would lead us into the Persian Gulf. Those are one or two of the more obvious canals which might knit the human race into a closer whole.'

'Your plans are certainly stupendous,' said Robert, uncertain whether to laugh or to be awe-struck. 'You will cease to be a man, and become one of the great forces of nature, altering, moulding and improving.'

'That is precisely the view which I take of myself. That is why I feel my responsibility so acutely.'

'But surely if you will do all this you may rest. It is a considerable programme.'

'Not at all. I am a patriotic Briton, and I should like to do something to leave my name in the annals of my country. I should prefer, however, to do it after my own death, as anything in the shape of publicity and honour is very offensive to me. I have, therefore, put by eight hundred million in a place which shall be duly mentioned in my will, which I propose to devote to paying off the National Debt. I cannot see that any harm could arise from its extinction.'

Robert sat staring, struck dumb by the audacity of the strange man's words.

'Then there is the heating of the soil. There is room for improvement there. You have no doubt read of the immense yields which have resulted in Jersey and elsewhere, from the running of hot-water pipes through the soil. The crops are trebled and quadrupled. I would propose to try the experiment upon a larger scale. We might possibly reserve the Isle of Man to serve as a pumping and heating station. The main pipes would run to England, Ireland and Scotland, where they would subdivide rapidly until they formed a network two feet deep under the whole country. A pipe at distances of a yard would suffice for every purpose.'

'I am afraid,' suggested Robert, 'that the water which left the Isle of Man warm might lose a little of its virtue before it reached Caithness, for example.'

'There need not be any difficulty there. Every few miles a furnace might be arranged to keep up the temperature. These are a few of my plans for the future, Robert, and I shall want the co-operation of disinterested men like yourself in all of them. But how brightly the sun shines, and how sweet the countryside looks! The world is very beautiful, and I should like to leave it happier than I found it. Let us walk out together, Robert, and you will tell me of any fresh cases where I may be of assistance.'

NINE

A New Departure

Whatever good Mr Raffles Haw's wealth did to the world, there could be no doubt that there were cases where it did harm. The very contemplation and thought of it had upon many a disturbing and mischievous effect. Especially was this the case with the old gunmaker. From being merely a querulous and grasping man, he had now become bitter, brooding and dangerous. Week by week, as he saw the tide of wealth flow as it were through his very house without being able to divert the smallest rill to nourish his own fortunes, he became more wolfish and more hungry-eyed. He spoke less of his own wrongs, but he brooded more, and would stand for hours on Tamfield Hill looking down at the great palace beneath, as a thirst-stricken man might gaze at the desert mirage.

He had worked, and peeped and pried, too, until there were points upon which he knew more than either his son or his daughter.

'I suppose that you still don't know where your friend gets his money?' he remarked to Robert one morning, as they walked together through the village.

'No, father, I do not. I only know that he spends it very well.'

'Well!' snarled the old man. 'Yes, very well! He has helped every tramp and slut and worthless vagabond over the countryside, but he will not advance a pound, even on the best security, to help a respectable business man to fight against misfortune.'

'My dear father, I really cannot argue with you about it,' said Robert. 'I have already told you more than once what I think. Mr Haw's object is to help those who are destitute. He looks upon us as his equals, and would not presume to patronise us, or to act as if we could not help ourselves. It would be a humiliation to us to take his money.'

'Pshaw! Besides, it is only a question of an advance, and advances are made every day among businessmen. How can you talk such nonsense, Robert?'

Early as it was, his son could see from his excited, quarrelsome manner that the old man had been drinking. The habit had grown upon him of late and it was seldom now that he was entirely sober.

'Mr Raffles Haw is the best judge,' said Robert coldly. 'If he earns the money, he has a right to spend it as he likes.'

'And how does he earn it? You don't know, Robert. You don't know that you aren't aiding and abetting a felony when you help him to fritter it away. Was ever so much money earned in an honest fashion? I tell you there never was. I tell you, also, that lumps of gold are no more to that man than chunks of coal to the miners over yonder. He could build his house of them and think nothing of it.'

'I know that he is very rich, father. I think, however, that he has an extravagant way of talking sometimes, and that his imagination carries him away. I have heard him talk of plans which the richest man upon earth could not possibly hope to carry through.'

'Don't you make any mistake, my son. Your poor old father isn't quite a fool, though he is only an honest broken merchant.' He looked up sideways at his son with a wink and a most unpleasant leer. 'Where there's money I can smell it. There's money there, and heaps of it. It's my belief that he is the richest man in the world, though how he came to be so I should not like to guarantee. I'm not quite blind yet, Robert. Have you seen the weekly wagon?'

'The weekly wagon!'

'Yes, Robert. You see I can find some news for you yet. It is due this morning. Every Saturday morning you will see the wagon come in. Why, here it is now, as I am a living man, coming round the curve.'

Robert glanced back and saw a great heavy wagon drawn by two strong horses lumbering slowly along the road which led to the New Hall. From the efforts of the animals and its slow pace the contents seemed to be of great weight.

'Just you wait here,' old McIntyre cried, plucking at his son's sleeve with his thin bony hand. 'Wait here and see it pass. Then we will watch what becomes of it.'

They stood by the side of the road until it came abreast of them. The wagon was covered with tarpaulin sheetings in front and at the sides, but behind some glimpse could be caught of the contents. They consisted, as far as Robert could see, of a number of packets of the same shape, each about two feet long and six inches high, arranged symmetrically upon the top of each other. Each packet was surrounded by a covering of coarse sacking.

'What do you think of that?' asked old McIntyre triumphantly as the load creaked past.

'Why, father? What do you make of it?'

'I have watched it, Robert – I have watched it every Saturday, and I had my chance of looking a little deeper into it. You remember the day when the elm blew down, and the road was blocked until they could saw it in two. That was on a Saturday, and the wagon came to a stand until they could clear a way for it. I was there, Robert, and I saw my chance. I strolled behind the wagon, and I placed my hands upon one of those packets. They look small, do they not? It would take a strong man to lift one. They are heavy, Robert, heavy, and hard with the hardness of metal. I tell you, boy, that that wagon is loaded with gold.'

'Gold!'

'With solid bars of gold, Robert. But come into the plantation and we shall see what becomes of it.'

They passed through the lodge gates, behind the wagon, and then wandered off among the fir trees until they gained a spot where they could command a view. The load had halted, not in front of the house, but at the door of the out-building with the chimney. A staff of stablemen and footmen were in readiness, who proceeded swiftly to unload and to carry the packages through the door. It was the first time that Robert had ever seen anyone save the master of the house enter the laboratory. No sign was seen of him now, however, and in half an hour the contents had all been safely stored and the wagon had driven briskly away.

'I cannot understand it, father,' said Robert thoughtfully, as they resumed their walk. 'Supposing that your supposition is correct, who would send him such quantities of gold, and where could it come from?'

'Ha, you have to come to the old man after all!' chuckled his companion. 'I can see the little game. It is clear enough to me. There are two of them in it, you understand. The other one gets the gold. Never mind how, but we will hope that there is no harm. Let us suppose, for example, that they have found a marvellous mine, where you can just shovel it out like clay from a pit. Well, then, he sends it on to this one, and he has his furnaces and his chemicals, and he refines and purifies it and makes it fit to sell. That's my explanation of it, Robert. Eh, has the old man put his finger on it?'

'But if that were true, father, the gold must go back again.'

'So it does, Robert, but a little at a time. Ha, ha! I've had my eyes open, you see. Every night it goes down in a small cart, and is sent on to London by the 7.40. Not in bars this time, but done up in iron-bound chests. I've seen them, boy, and I've had this hand upon them.'

'Well,' said the young man thoughtfully, 'maybe you are right. It is possible that you are right.'

While father and son were prying into his secrets, Raffles Haw had found his way to Elmdene, where Laura sat reading the *Queen* by the fire.

'I am so sorry,' she said, throwing down her paper and springing to her feet. 'They are all out except me. But I am sure that they won't be long. I expect Robert every moment.'

'I would rather speak with you alone,' answered Raffles Haw quietly. 'Pray sit down, for I want to have a little chat with you.'

Laura resumed her seat with a flush upon her cheeks and a quickening of the breath. She turned her face away and gazed into the fire; but there was a sparkle in her eyes which was not caught from the leaping flames.

'Do you remember the first time that we met, Miss McIntyre?' he asked, standing on the rug and looking down at her dark hair, and the beautifully feminine curve of her ivory neck.

'As if it were yesterday,' she answered in her sweet mellow tones.

'Then you must also remember the wild words that I said when we parted. It was very foolish of me. I am sure that I am most sorry if I frightened or disturbed you, but I have been a very solitary man for a long time, and I have dropped into a bad habit of thinking aloud. Your voice, your face, your manner, were all so like my ideal of a true woman, loving, faithful and sympathetic, that I could not help wondering whether, if I were a poor man, I might ever hope to win the affection of such a one.'

'Your good opinion, Mr Raffles Haw, is very dear to me,' said Laura. 'I assure you that I was not frightened, and that there is no need to apologise for what was really a compliment.'

'Since then I have found,' he continued, 'that all that I had read upon your face was true. That your mind is indeed that of the true woman, full of the noblest and sweetest qualities which human nature can aspire to. You know that I am a man of fortune, but I wish you to dismiss that consideration from your mind. Do you think from what you know of my character that you could be happy as my wife, Laura?'

She made no answer, but still sat with her head turned away and her sparkling eyes fixed upon the fire. One little foot from under her skirt tapped nervously upon the rug.

'It is only right that you should know a little more about me before you decide. There is, however, little to know. I am an orphan, and, as far as I know, without a relation upon earth. My father was a respectable man, a country surgeon in Wales, and he brought me up to his own profession. Before I had passed my examinations, however, he died and left me a small annuity. I had conceived a great liking for the subjects of chemistry and electricity, and instead of going on with my medical work I devoted myself entirely to these studies, and eventually built myself a laboratory where I could follow out my own researches. At about this time I came into a very large sum of money, so large as to make me feel that a vast responsibility rested upon me in the use which I made of it. After some thought I determined to build a large house in a quiet part of the country, not too far from a great centre. There I could be in touch with the world, and yet would have quiet and leisure to mature the schemes which were in my head. As it chanced, I chose Tamfield as my site. All that remains now is to carry out the plans which I have made, and to endeavour to lighten the earth of some of the misery and injustice which weigh it down. I again ask you, Laura, will you throw in your lot with mine, and help me in the life's work which lies before me?'

Laura looked up at him, at his stringy figure, his pale face, his keen, yet gentle eyes. Somehow as she looked there seemed to form itself beside him some shadow of Hector Spurling, the manly features, the clear, firm mouth, the frank manner. Now, in the very moment of her triumph, it sprang clearly up in her mind how at the hour of their ruin he had stood firmly by them, and had loved the penniless girl as tenderly as the heiress to fortune. That last embrace at the door, too, came back to her, and she felt his lips warm upon her own.

'I am very much honoured, Mr Haw,' she stammered, 'but this is so sudden. I have not had time to think. I do not know what to say.'

'Do not let me hurry you,' he cried earnestly. 'I beg that you will think well over it. I shall come again for my answer. When shall I come? Tonight?'

'Yes, come tonight.'

'Then, adieu. Believe me that I think more highly of you for your hesitation. I shall live in hope.' He raised her hand to his lips, and left her to her own thoughts.

But what those thoughts were did not long remain in doubt. Dimmer and dimmer grew the vision of the distant sailor face, clearer and clearer the image of the vast palace, of the queenly power, of the diamonds, the gold, the ambitious future. It all lay at her feet, waiting to be picked up. How could she have hesitated, even for a moment? She rose, and, walking over to her desk, she took out a sheet of paper and an envelope. The latter she addressed to Lieutenant Spurling, HMS *Active*, Gibraltar. The note cost some little trouble, but at last she got it worded to her mind.

> DEAR HECTOR [she said] – I am convinced that your father has never entirely approved of our engagement, otherwise he would not have thrown obstacles in the way of our marriage. I am sure, too, that since my poor father's misfortune it is only your own sense of honour and feeling of duty which have kept you true to me, and that you would have done infinitely better had you never seen me. I cannot bear, Hector, to allow you to imperil your future for my sake, and I have determined, after thinking well over the matter, to release you from our boy-and-girl engagement, so that you may be entirely free in every way. It is possible that you may think it unkind of me to do this now, but I am quite sure, dear Hector, that when you are an admiral and a very distinguished man, you will look back at this and you will see that I have been a true friend to you and have prevented you from making a false step early in your career. For myself, whether I marry or not, I have determined to devote the remainder of my life to trying to do good, and to leaving the world happier than I found it. Your father is very well, and gave us a capital sermon last Sunday. I enclose the banknote which you asked me to keep for you. Goodbye, for ever, dear Hector, and believe me when I say that, come what may, I am ever your true friend,
>
> LAURA S. McINTYRE

She had hardly sealed her letter before her father and Robert returned.

She closed the door behind them, and made them a little curtsey.

'I await my family's congratulations,' she said, with her head in the air. 'Mr Raffles Haw has been here, and he has asked me to be his wife.'

'The deuce he did!' cried the old man. 'And you said – ?'

'I am to see him again.'

'And you will say – ?'

'I will accept him.'

'You were always a good girl, Laura,' said old McIntyre, standing on his tiptoes to kiss her.

'But Laura, Laura, how about Hector?' asked Robert in mild remonstrance.

'Oh, I have written to him,' his sister answered carelessly. 'I wish you would be good enough to post the letter.'

TEN

The Great Secret

And so Laura McIntyre became duly engaged to Raffles Haw, and old McIntyre grew even more hungry-looking as he felt himself a step nearer to the source of wealth, while Robert thought less of work than ever, and never gave as much as a thought to the great canvas which still stood, dust-covered, upon his easel. Haw gave Laura an engagement ring of old gold, with a great blazing diamond bulging out of it. There was little talk about the matter, however, for it was Haw's wish that all should be done very quietly. Nearly all his evenings were spent at Elmdene, where he and Laura would build up the most colossal schemes of philanthropy for the future. With a map stretched out on the table in front of them, these two young people would, as it were, hover over the world, planning, devising and improving.

'Bless the girl!' said old McIntyre to his son; 'she speaks about it as if she were born to millions. Maybe, when once she is married, she won't be so ready to chuck her money into every mad scheme that her husband can think of.'

'Laura is greatly changed,' Robert answered; 'she has grown much more serious in her ideas.'

'You wait a bit!' sniggered his father. 'She is a good girl, is Laura, and she knows what she is about. She's not a girl to let her old dad go to the wall if she can set him right. It's a pretty state of things,' he added bitterly: 'here's my daughter going to marry a man who thinks no more of gold than I used to of gun-metal; and here's my son going about with all the money he cares to ask for to help every ne'er-do-well in Staffordshire; and here's their father, who loved them and cared for them, and brought them both up, without money enough very often to buy a bottle of brandy. I don't know what your poor dear mother would have thought of it.'

'You have only to ask for what you want.'

'Yes, as if I were a five-year-old child. But I tell you, Robert, I'll have my rights, and if I can't get them one way I will another. I won't be treated as if I were no one. And there's one thing: if I am to be this man's pa-in-law, I'll want to know something about him and his money first. We may be poor, but we are honest. I'll up to the Hall now, and have it out with him.' He seized his hat and stick and made for the door.

'No, no, father,' cried Robert, catching him by the sleeve. 'You had better leave the matter alone. Mr Haw is a very sensitive man. He would not like to be examined upon such a point. It might lead to a serious quarrel. I beg that you will not go.'

'I am not to be put off for ever,' snarled the old man, who had been drinking heavily. 'I'll put my foot down now, once and for ever.' He tugged at his sleeve to free himself from his son's grasp.

'At least you shall not go without Laura knowing. I will call her down, and we shall have her opinion.'

'Oh, I don't want to have any scenes,' said McIntyre sulkily, relaxing his efforts. He lived in dread of his daughter, and at his worst moments the mention of her name would serve to restrain him.

'Besides,' said Robert, 'I have not the slightest doubt that Raffles Haw will see the necessity for giving us some sort of explanation before matters go further. He must understand that we have some claim now to be taken into his confidence.'

He had hardly spoken when there was a tap at the door, and the man of whom they were speaking walked in.

'Good-morning, Mr McIntyre,' said he. 'Robert, would you mind stepping up to the Hall with me? I want to have a little business chat.' He looked serious, like a man who is carrying out something which he has well weighed.

They walked up together with hardly a word on either side. Raffles Haw was absorbed in his own thoughts. Robert felt expectant and nervous, for he knew that something of importance lay before him. The winter had almost passed now, and the first young shoots were beginning to peep out timidly in the face of the wind and the rain of an English March. The snows were gone, but the countryside looked bleaker and drearier, all shrouded in the haze from the damp, sodden meadows.

'By the way, Robert,' said Raffles Haw suddenly, as they walked up the Avenue. 'Has your great Roman picture gone to London?'

'I have not finished it yet.'

'But I know that you are a quick worker. You must be nearly at the end of it.'

'No, I am afraid that it has not advanced much since you saw it. For one thing, the light has not been very good.'

Raffles Haw said nothing, but a pained expression flashed over his face. When they reached the house he led the way through the museum. Two great metal cases were lying on the floor.

'I have a small addition there to the gem collection,' he remarked as he passed. 'They only arrived last night, and I have not opened them yet, but I am given to understand from the letters and invoices that there are some fine specimens. We might arrange them this afternoon, if you care to assist me. Let us go into the smoking-room now.'

He threw himself down into a settee, and motioned Robert into the armchair in front of him.

'Light a cigar,' he said. 'Press the spring if there is any refreshment which you would like. Now, my dear Robert, confess to me in the first place that you have often thought me mad.'

The charge was so direct and so true that the young artist hesitated, hardly knowing how to answer.

'My dear boy, I do not blame you. It was the most natural thing in the world. I should have looked upon anyone as a madman who had talked to me as I have talked to you. But for all that, Robert, you were wrong, and I have never yet in our conversations proposed any scheme which it was not well within my power to carry out. I tell you in all sober earnest that the amount of my income is limited only by my desire, and that all the bankers and financiers combined could not furnish the sums which I can put forward without an effort.'

'I have had ample proof of your immense wealth,' said Robert.

'And you are very naturally curious as to how that wealth was obtained. Well, I can tell you one thing. The money is perfectly clean. I have robbed no one, cheated no one, sweated no one, ground no one down in the gaining of it. I can read your father's eye, Robert. I can see that he has done me an injustice in this matter. Well, perhaps he is not to be blamed. Perhaps I also might think uncharitable things if I were in his place. But that is why I now give an explanation to you, Robert, and not to him. You, at least, have trusted me, and you have a right, before I become one of your family, to know all that I can tell you. Laura also has trusted me, but I know well that she is content still to trust me.'

'I would not intrude upon your secrets, Mr Haw,' said Robert, 'but of course I cannot deny that I should be very proud and pleased if you cared to confide them to me.'

'And I will. Not all. I do not think that I shall ever, while I live, tell all. But

I shall leave directions behind me so that when I die you may be able to carry on my unfinished work. I shall tell you where those directions are to be found. In the meantime, you must be content to learn the effects which I produce without knowing every detail as to the means.'

Robert settled himself down in his chair and concentrated his attention upon his companion's words, while Haw bent forward his eager, earnest face, like a man who knows the value of the words which he is saying.

'You are already aware,' he remarked, 'that I have devoted a great deal of energy and of time to the study of chemistry.'

'So you told me.'

'I commenced my studies under a famous English chemist, I continued them under the best man in France, and I completed them in the most celebrated laboratory of Germany. I was not rich, but my father had left me enough to keep me comfortably, and by living economically I had a sum at my command which enabled me to carry out my studies in a very complete way. When I returned to England I built myself a laboratory in a quiet country place where I could work without distraction or interruption. There I began a series of investigations which soon took me into regions of science to which none of the three famous men who taught me had ever penetrated.

'You say, Robert, that you have some slight knowledge of chemistry, and you will find it easier to follow what I say. Chemistry is to a large extent an empirical science, and the chance experiment may lead to greater results than could, with our present data, be derived from the closest study or the keenest reasoning. The most important chemical discoveries from the first manufacture of glass to the whitening and refining of sugar have all been due to some happy chance which might have befallen a mere dabbler as easily as a deep student.

'Well, it was to such a chance that my own great discovery – perhaps the greatest that the world has seen – was due, though I may claim the credit of having originated the line of thought which led up to it. I had frequently speculated as to the effect which powerful currents of electricity exercise upon any substance through which they are poured for a considerable time. I did not here mean such feeble currents as are passed along a telegraph wire, but I mean the very highest possible developments. Well, I tried a series of experiments upon this point. I found that in liquids, and in compounds, the force had a disintegrating effect. The well-known experiment of the electrolysis of water will, of course, occur to you. But I found that in the case of elemental solids the effect was a remarkable one. The element slowly decreased in weight, without perceptibly altering in composition. I hope that I make myself clear to you?'

'I follow you entirely,' said Robert, deeply interested in his companion's narrative.

'I tried upon several elements, and always with the same result. In every case an hour's current would produce a perceptible loss of weight. My theory at that stage was that there was a loosening of the molecules caused by the electric fluid, and that a certain number of these molecules were shed off like an impalpable dust, all round the lump of earth or of metal, which remained, of course, the lighter by their loss. I had entirely accepted this theory, when a very remarkable chance led me completely to alter my opinions.

'I had one Saturday night fastened a bar of bismuth in a clamp, and had attached it on either side to an electric wire, in order to observe what effect the current would have upon it. I had been testing each metal in turn, exposing them to the influence for from one to two hours. I had just got everything in position, and had completed my connection, when I received a telegram to say that John Stillingfleet, an old chemist in London with whom I had been on terms of intimacy, was dangerously ill, and had expressed a wish to see me. The last train was due to leave in twenty minutes, and I lived a good mile from the station, I thrust a few things into a bag, locked my laboratory, and ran as hard as I could to catch it.

'It was not until I was in London that it suddenly occurred to me that I had neglected to shut off the current, and that it would continue to pass through the bar of bismuth until the batteries were exhausted. The fact, however, seemed to be of small importance, and I dismissed it from my mind. I was detained in London until the Tuesday night, and it was Wednesday morning before I got back to my work. As I unlocked the laboratory door my mind reverted to the uncompleted experiment, and it struck me that in all probability my piece of bismuth would have been entirely disintegrated and reduced to its primitive molecules. I was utterly unprepared for the truth.

'When I approached the table I found, sure enough, that the bar of metal had vanished, and that the clamp was empty. Having noted the fact, I was about to turn away to something else, when my attention was attracted to the fact that the table upon which the clamp stood was starred over with little patches of some liquid silvery matter, which lay in single drops or coalesced into little pools. I had a very distinct recollection of having thoroughly cleared the table before beginning my experiment, so that this substance had been deposited there since I had left for London. Much interested, I very carefully collected it all into one vessel, and examined it minutely. There could be no question as to what it was. It was the purest mercury, and gave no response to any test for bismuth.

'I at once grasped the fact that chance had placed in my hands a chemical discovery of the very first importance. If bismuth were, under certain conditions, to be subjected to the action of electricity, it would begin by losing weight, and would finally be transformed into mercury. I had broken down the partition which separated two elements.

'But the process would be a constant one. It would presumably prove to be a general law, and not an isolated fact. If bismuth turned into mercury, what would mercury turn into? There would be no rest for me until I had solved the question. I renewed the exhausted batteries and passed the current through the bowl of quicksilver. For sixteen hours I sat watching the metal, marking how it slowly seemed to curdle, to grow firmer, to lose its silvery glitter and to take a dull yellow hue. When I at last picked it up in a forceps, and threw it upon the table, it had lost every characteristic of mercury, and had obviously become another metal. A few simple tests were enough to show me that this other metal was platinum.

'Now, to a chemist, there was something very suggestive in the order in which these changes had been effected. Perhaps you can see the relation, Robert, which they bear to each other?'

'No, I cannot say that I do.'

Robert had sat listening to this strange statement with parted lips and staring eyes.

'I will show you. Speaking atomically, bismuth is the heaviest of the metals. Its atomic weight is 210. The next in weight is lead, 207, and then comes mercury at 200. Possibly the long period during which the current had acted in my absence had reduced the bismuth to lead and the lead in turn to mercury. Now platinum stands at 197.5, and it was accordingly the next metal to be produced by the continued current. Do you see now?'

'It is quite clear.'

'And then there came the inference, which sent my heart into my mouth and caused my head to swim round. Gold is the next in the series. Its atomic weight is 197. I remembered now, and for the first time understood why it was always lead and mercury winch were mentioned by the old alchemists as being the two metals which might be used in their calling. With fingers which trembled with excitement I adjusted the wires again, and in little more than an hour – for the length of the process was always in proportion to the difference in the metals – I had before me a knob of ruddy crinkled metal, which answered to every reaction for gold.

'Well, Robert, this is a long story, but I think that you will agree with me that its importance justifies me in going into detail. When I had satisfied myself that I had really manufactured gold I cut the nugget in two. One half I sent to a jeweller and worker in precious metals, with whom I had some slight acquaintance, asking him to report upon the quality of the metal. With the other half I continued my series of experiments, and reduced it in successive stages through all the long series of metals, through silver and zinc and manganese, until I brought it to lithium, which is the lightest of all.'

'And what did it turn to then?' asked Robert.

'Then came what to chemists is likely to be the most interesting portion of my discovery. It turned to a greyish fine powder, which powder gave no further results, however much I might treat it with electricity. And that powder is the base of all things; it is the mother of all the elements; it is, in short, the substance whose existence has been recently surmised by a leading chemist, and which has been christened protyle by him. I am the discoverer of the great law of the electrical transposition of the metals, and I am the first to demonstrate protyle; so, I think, Robert, if all my schemes in other directions come to nothing, my name is at least likely to live in the chemical world.

'There is not very much more for me to tell you. I had my nugget back from my friend the jeweller, confirming my opinion as to its nature and its quality. I soon found several methods by which the process might be simplified, and especially a modification of the ordinary electric current, which was very much more effective. Having made a certain amount of gold, I disposed of it for a sum which enabled me to buy improved materials and stronger batteries. In this way I enlarged my operations until at last I was in a position to build this house and to have a laboratory where I could carry out my work on a much larger scale. As I said before, I can now state with all truth that the amount of my income is only limited by my desires.'

'It is wonderful!' gasped Robert. 'It is like a fairy tale. But with this great discovery in your mind you must have been sorely tempted to confide it to others.'

'I thought well over it. I gave it every consideration. It was obvious to me that if my invention were made public, its immediate result would be to deprive the present precious metals of all their special value. Some other substance – amber, we will say, or ivory – would be chosen as a medium for barter, and gold would be inferior to brass, as being heavier and yet not so hard. No one would be the better for such a consummation as that. Now, if I retained my secret, and used it with wisdom, I might make myself the greatest benefactor to mankind that has ever lived. Those were the chief reasons, and I trust that they are not dishonourable ones, which led me to form the resolution, which I have today for the first time broken.'

'But your secret is safe with me,' cried Robert. 'My lips shall be sealed until I have your permission to speak.'

'If I had not known that I could trust you I should have withheld it from your knowledge. And now, my dear Robert, theory is very weak work, and practice is infinitely more interesting. I have given you more than enough of the first. If you will be good enough to accompany me to the laboratory I shall give you a little of the latter.'

ELEVEN

A Chemical Demonstration

Raffles Haw led the way through the front door, and crossing over the gravelled drive pushed open the outer door of the laboratory – the same through which the McIntyres had seen the packages conveyed from the wagon. On passing through it Robert found that they were not really within the building, but merely in a large bare ante-chamber, around the walls of which were stacked the very objects which had aroused his curiosity and his father's speculations. All mystery had gone from them now, however, for while some were still wrapped in their sackcloth coverings, others had been undone, and revealed themselves as great pigs of lead.

'There is my raw material,' said Raffles Haw carelessly, nodding at the heap. 'Every Saturday I have a wagon-load sent up, which serves me for a week, but we shall need to work double tides when Laura and I are married and we get our great schemes under way. I have to be very careful about the quality of the lead, for, of course, every impurity is reproduced in the gold.'

A heavy iron door led into the inner chamber. Haw unlocked it, but only to disclose a second one about five feet further on.

'This flooring is all disconnected at night,' he remarked. 'I have no doubt that there is a good deal of gossip in the servants'-hall about this sealed chamber, so I have to guard myself against some inquisitive ostler or too adventurous butler.'

The inner door admitted them into the laboratory, a high, bare, white-washed room with a glass roof. At one end was the furnace and boiler, the iron mouth of which was closed, though the fierce red light beat through the cracks, and a dull roar sounded through the building. On either side innumerable huge Leyden jars stood ranged in rows, tier topping tier, while above them were columns of voltaic cells. Robert's eyes, as he glanced around, lit on vast wheels, complicated networks of wire, stands, test-tubes, coloured bottles, graduated glasses, Bunsen burners, porcelain insulators, and all the varied debris of a chemical and electrical workshop.

'Come across here,' said Raffles Haw, picking his way among the heaps of metal, the coke, the packing-cases and the carboys of acid. 'Yours is the first foot except my own which has ever penetrated to this room since the workmen left it. My servants carry the lead into the ante-room, but come no farther. The furnace can be cleaned and stoked from without. I employ a fellow to do nothing else. Now take a look in here.'

He threw open a door on the farther side, and motioned to the young artist to enter. The latter stood silent with one foot over the threshold, staring in amazement around him. The room, which may have been some thirty feet square, was paved and walled with gold. Great brick-shaped ingots, closely packed, covered the whole floor, while on every side they were reared up in compact barriers to the very ceiling. The single electric lamp which lighted the windowless chamber struck a dull, murky, yellow light from the vast piles of precious metal, and gleamed ruddily upon the golden floor.

'This is my treasure house,' remarked the owner. 'You see that I have rather an accumulation just now. My imports have been exceeding my exports. You can understand that I have other and more important duties even than the making of gold, just now. This is where I store my output until I am ready to send it off. Every night almost I am in the habit of sending a case of it to London. I employ seventeen brokers in its sale. Each thinks that he is the only one, and each is dying to know where I can get such large quantities of virgin gold. They say that it is the purest which comes into the market. The popular theory is, I believe, that I am a middleman acting on behalf of some new South African mine, which wishes to keep its where-abouts a secret. What value would you put upon the gold in this chamber? It ought to be worth something, for it represents nearly a week's work.'

'Something fabulous, I have no doubt,' said Robert, glancing round at the yellow barriers. 'Shall I say a hundred and fifty thousand pounds?'

'Oh dear me, it is surely worth very much more than that,' cried Raffles Haw, laughing. 'Let me see. Suppose that we put it at three ten an ounce, which is nearly ten shillings under the mark. That makes, roughly, fifty-six pounds for a pound in weight. Now each of these ingots weighs thirty-six pounds, which brings their value to two thousand and a few odd pounds. There are five hundred ingots on each of these three sides of the room, but on the fourth there are only three hundred, on account of the door, but there cannot be less than two hundred on the floor, which gives us a rough total of two thousand ingots. So you see, my dear boy, that any broker who could get the contents of this chamber for four million pounds would be doing a nice little stroke of business.'

'And a week's work!' gasped Robert. 'It makes my head swim.'

'You will follow me now when I repeat that none of the great schemes which I intend simultaneously to set in motion are at all likely to languish for want of funds. Now come into the laboratory with me and see how it is done.'

In the centre of the workroom was an instrument like a huge vice, with two large brass-coloured plates, and a great steel screw for bringing them together. Numerous wires ran into these metal plates, and were attached at the other end to the rows of dynamic machines. Beneath was a glass stand, which was hollowed out in the centre into a succession of troughs.

'You will soon understand all about it,' said Raffles Haw, throwing off his coat, and pulling on a smoke-stained and dirty linen jacket. 'We must first stoke up a little.' He put his weight on a pair of great bellows, and an answering roar came from the furnace. 'That will do. The more heat the more electric force, and the quicker our task. Now for the lead! Just give me a hand in carrying it.'

They lifted a dozen of the pigs of lead from the floor on to the glass stand, and having adjusted the plates on either side, Haw screwed up the handle so as to hold them in position.

'It used in the early days to be a slow process,' he remarked; 'but now that I have immense facilities for my work it takes a very short time. I have now only to complete the connection in order to begin.'

He took hold of a long glass lever which projected from among the wires, and drew it downwards. A sharp click was heard, followed by a loud, sparkling, crackling noise. Great spurts of flame sprang from the two electrodes, and the mass of lead was surrounded by an aureole of golden sparks, which hissed and snapped like pistol-shots. The air was filled with the peculiar acid smell of ozone.

'The power there is immense,' said Raffles Haw, superintending the process, with his watch upon the palm of his hand. 'It would reduce an organic substance to protyle instantly. It is well to understand the mechanism thoroughly, for any mistake might be a grave matter for the operator. You are dealing with gigantic forces. But you perceive that the lead is already beginning to turn.'

Silvery dew-like drops had indeed begun to form upon the dull-coloured mass, and to drop with a tinkle and splash into the glass troughs. Slowly the lead melted away, like an icicle in the sun, the electrodes ever closing upon it as it contracted, until they came together in the centre, and a row of pools of quicksilver had taken the place of the solid metal. Two smaller electrodes were plunged into the mercury, which gradually curdled and solidified, until it had resumed the solid form, with a yellowish brassy shimmer.

'What lies in the moulds now is platinum,' remarked Raffles Haw. 'We must take it from the troughs and refix it in the large electrodes. So! Now we turn on the current again. You see that it gradually takes a darker and richer tint. Now I think that it is perfect.' He drew up the lever, removed the electrodes, and there lay a dozen bricks of ruddy sparkling gold.

'You see, according to our calculations, our morning's work has been worth twenty-four thousand pounds, and it has not taken us more than twenty minutes,' remarked the alchemist, as he picked up the newly-made ingots, and threw them down among the others.

'We will devote one of them to experiment,' said he, leaving the last standing upon the glass insulator. 'To the world it would seem an expensive demonstration which cost two thousand pounds, but our standard, you see, is a different one. Now you will see me run through the whole gamut of metallic nature.'

First of all men after the discoverer, Robert saw the gold mass, when the electrodes were again applied to it, change swiftly and successively to barium, to tin, to silver, to copper, to iron. He saw the long white electric sparks change to crimson with the strontium, to purple with the potassium, to yellow with the manganese. Then, finally, after a hundred transformations, it disintegrated before his eyes, and lay as a little mound of fluffy grey dust upon the glass table.

'And this is protyle,' said Haw, passing his fingers through it. 'The chemist of the future may resolve it into further constituents, but to me it is the *ultima Thule.*'

'And now, Robert,' he continued, after a pause, 'I have shown you enough to enable you to understand something of my system. This is the great secret. It is the secret which endows the man who knows it with such a universal power as no man has ever enjoyed since the world was made. This secret it is the dearest wish of my heart to use for good, and I swear to you, Robert McIntyre, that if I thought it would tend to anything but good I would have done with it for ever. No, I would neither use it myself nor would any other man learn it from my lips. I swear it by all that is holy and solemn!'

His eyes flashed as he spoke, and his voice quivered with emotion. Standing, pale and lanky, amid his electrodes and his retorts, there was still something majestic about this man, who, amid all his stupendous good fortune, could still keep his moral sense undazzled by the glitter of his gold. Robert's weak nature had never before realised the strength which lay in those thin, firm lips and earnest eyes.

'Surely in your hands, Mr Haw, nothing but good can come of it,' he said.

'I hope not – I pray not – most earnestly do I pray not. I have done for you, Robert, what I might not have done for my own brother had I one, and I have done it because I believe and hope that you are a man who would not use this power, should you inherit it, for selfish ends. But even now I have not told you all. There is one link which I have withheld from you, and which shall be withheld from you while I live. But look at this chest, Robert.'

He led him to a great iron-clamped chest which stood in the corner, and, throwing it open, he took from it a small case of carved ivory.

'Inside this,' he said, 'I have left a paper which makes clear anything which is still hidden from you. Should anything happen to me you will always be able to inherit my powers, and to continue my plans by following the directions which are there expressed. And now,' he continued, throwing his casket back again into the box, 'I shall frequently require your help, but I do not think it will be necessary this morning. I have already taken up too much of your time. If you are going back to Elmdene, I wish that you would tell Laura that I shall be with her in the afternoon.'

TWELVE

A Family Jar

And so the great secret was out, and Robert walked home with his head in a whirl and the blood tingling in his veins. He had shivered as he came up at the damp cold of the wind and the sight of the mist-mottled landscape. That was all gone now. His own thoughts tinged everything with sunshine, and he felt inclined to sing and dance as he walked down the muddy, deeply rutted country lane. Wonderful had been the fate allotted to Raffles Haw, but surely hardly less important was that which had come upon himself. He was the sharer of the alchemist's secret, and the heir to an inheritance which combined a wealth greater than that of monarchs with a freedom such as monarchs cannot enjoy. This was a destiny indeed! A thousand gold-tinted visions of his future life rose up before him, and in fancy he already sat high above the human race, with prostrate thousands imploring his aid or thanking him for his benevolence.

How sordid seemed the untidy garden, with its scrappy bushes and gaunt elm trees! How mean the plain brick front, with the green wooden porch! It had always offended his artistic sense, but now it was obtrusive in its ugliness. The plain room, too, with the American leather chairs, the dull-coloured carpet and the patchwork rug, he felt a loathing for it all. The only pretty thing in it, upon which his eyes could rest with satisfaction, was his sister, as she leaned back in her chair by the fire with her white, clear beautiful face outlined against the dark background.

'Do you know, Robert,' she said, glancing up at him from under her long black lashes, 'papa grows unendurable. I have had to speak very plainly to him, and to make him understand that I am marrying for my own benefit and not for his.'

'Where is he, then?'

'I don't know. At the Three Pigeons, no doubt. He spends most of his time there now. He flew off in a passion, and talked such nonsense about marriage settlements, and forbidding the banns, and so on. His notion of a marriage settlement appears to be a settlement upon the bride's father. He should wait quietly, and see what can be done for him.'

'I think, Laura, that we must make a good deal of allowance for him,' said Robert earnestly. 'I have noticed a great change in him lately. I don't think he is himself at all. I must get some medical advice. But I have been up at the Hall this morning.'

'Have you? Have you seen Raffles? Did he send anything for me?'

'He said that he would come down when he had finished his work.'

'But what is the matter, Robert?' cried Laura, with the swift perception of womanhood. 'You are flushed, and your eyes are shining, and really you look quite handsome. Raffles has been telling you something! What was it? Oh, I know! He has been telling you how he made his money. Hasn't he, now?'

'Well, yes. He took me partly into his confidence. I congratulate you, Laura, with all my heart, for you will be a very wealthy woman.'

'How strange it seems that he should have come to us in our poverty. It is all owing to you, you dear old Robert; for if he had not taken a fancy to you, he would never have come down to Elmdene and taken a fancy to someone else.'

'Not at all,' Robert answered, sitting down by his sister, and patting her hand affectionately. 'It was a clear case of love at first sight. He was in love with you before he ever knew your name. He asked me about you the very first time I saw him.'

'But tell me about his money, Bob,' said his sister. 'He has not told me yet, and I am so curious. How did he make it? It was not from his father; he told me that himself. His father was just a country doctor. How did he do it?'

'I am bound over to secrecy. He will tell you himself.'

'Oh, but only tell me if I guess right. He had it left him by an uncle, eh? Well, by a friend? Or he took out some wonderful patent? Or he discovered a mine? Or oil? Do tell me, Robert!'

'I mustn't, really,' cried her brother laughing. 'And I must not talk to you any more. You are much too sharp. I feel a responsibility about it; and, besides, I must really do some work.'

'It is very unkind of you,' said Laura, pouting. 'But I must put my things on, for I go into Birmingham by the one-twenty.'

'To Birmingham?'

'Yes, I have a hundred things to order. There is everything to be got. You men forget about these details. Raffles wishes to have the wedding in little more than a fortnight. Of course it will be very quiet, but still one needs something.'

'So early as that!' said Robert, thoughtfully. 'Well, perhaps it is better so.'

'Much better, Robert. Would it not be dreadful if Hector came back first and there was a scene? If I were once married I should not mind. Why should I? But of course Raffles knows nothing about him, and it would be terrible if they came together.'

'That must be avoided at any cost.'

'Oh, I cannot bear even to think of it. Poor Hector! And yet what could I do, Robert? You know that it was only a boy-and-girl affair. And how could I refuse such an offer as this? It was a duty to my family, was it not?'

'You were placed in a difficult position – very difficult,' her brother answered. 'But all will be right, and I have no doubt Hector will see it as you do. But does Mr Spurling know of your engagement?'

'Not a word. He was here yesterday, and talked of Hector, but indeed I did not know how to tell him. We are to be married by special licence in Birmingham, so really there is no reason why he should know. But now I must hurry or I shall miss my train.'

When his sister was gone Robert went up to his studio, and having ground some colours upon his palette he stood for some time, brush and maulstick in hand, in front of his big bare canvas. But how profitless all his work seemed to him now! What object had he in doing it? Was it to earn money? Money could be had for the asking, or, for that matter, without the asking. Or was it to produce a thing of beauty? But he had artistic faults. Raffles Haw had said so, and he knew that he was right. After all his pains the thing might not please; and with money he could at all times buy pictures which would please, and which would be things of beauty. What, then, was the object of his working? He could see none. He threw down his brush, and, lighting his pipe, he strolled downstairs once more.

His father was standing in front of the fire, and in no very good humour, as his red face and puckered eyes sufficed to show.

'Well, Robert,' he began, 'I suppose that, as usual, you have spent your morning plotting against your father?'

'What do you mean, father?'

'I mean what I say. What is it but plotting when three folk – you and she and this Raffles Haw – whisper and arrange and have meetings without a word to me about it? What do I know of your plans?'

'I cannot tell you secrets which are not my own, father.'

'But I'll have a voice in the matter, for all that. Secrets or no secrets, you will find that Laura has a father, and that he is not a man to be set aside. I may have had my ups and downs in trade, but I have not quite fallen so low that I am nothing in my own family. What am I to get out of this precious marriage?'

'What should you get? Surely Laura's happiness and welfare are enough for you?'

'If this man were really fond of Laura he would show proper con-sideration for Laura's father. It was only yesterday that I asked him for a loan – condescended actually to ask for it – I, who have been within an ace of being Mayor of Birmingham! And he refused me point blank.'

'Oh, father! How could you expose yourself to such humiliation?'

'Refused me point blank!' cried the old man excitedly. 'It was against his principles, if you please. But I'll be even with him – you see if I am not. I know one or two things about him. What is it they call him at the Three Pigeons? A 'smasher' – that's the word – a coiner of false money. Why else should he have this metal sent him, and that great smoky chimney of his going all day?'

'Why can you not leave him alone, father?' expostulated Robert. 'You seem to think of nothing but his money. If he had not a penny he would still be a very kind-hearted, pleasant gentleman.'

Old McIntyre burst into a hoarse laugh.

'I like to hear you preach,' said he. 'Without a penny, indeed! Do you think that you would dance attendance upon him if he were a poor man? Do you think that Laura would ever have looked twice at him? You know as well as I do that she is marrying him only for his money.'

Robert gave a cry of dismay. There was the alchemist standing in the doorway, pale and silent, looking from one to the other of them with his searching eyes.

'I must apologise,' he said coldly. 'I did not mean to listen to your words. I could not help it. But I have heard them. As to you, Mr McIntyre, I believe that you speak from your own bad heart. I will not let myself be moved by your words. In Robert I have a true friend. Laura also loves me for my own sake. You cannot shake my faith in them. But with you, Mr McIntyre, I have nothing in common; and it is as well, perhaps, that we should both recognise the fact.'

He bowed, and was gone ere either of the McIntyres could say a word.

'You see!' said Robert at last. 'You have done now what you cannot undo!'

'I will be even with him!' cried the old man furiously, shaking his fist through the window at the dark slow-pacing figure. 'You just wait, Robert, and see if your old dad is a man to be played with.'

THIRTEEN

A Midnight Venture

Not a word was said to Laura when she returned as to the scene which had occurred in her absence. She was in the gayest of spirits, and prattled merrily about her purchases and her arrangements, wondering from time to time when Raffles Haw would come. As night fell, however, without any word from him, she became uneasy.

'What can be the matter that he does not come?' she said. 'It is the first day since our engagement that I have not seen him.'

Robert looked out through the window.

'It is a gusty night, and raining hard,' he remarked. 'I do not at all expect him.'

'Poor Hector used to come, rain, snow or fine. But, then, of course, he was a sailor. It was nothing to him. I hope that Raffles is not ill.'

'He was quite well when I saw him this morning,' answered her brother, and they relapsed into silence, while the rain pattered against the windows, and the wind screamed amid the branches of the elms outside.

Old McIntyre had sat in the corner most of the day biting his nails and glowering into the fire, with a brooding, malignant expression upon his wrinkled features. Contrary to his usual habits, he did not go to the village inn, but shuffled off early to bed without a word to his children. Laura and Robert remained chatting for some time by the fire, she talking of the thousand and one wonderful things which were to be done when she was mistress of the New Hall. There was less philanthropy in her talk when her future husband was absent, and Robert could not but remark that her carriages, her dresses, her receptions and her travels in distant countries were the topics into which she threw all the enthusiasm which he had formerly heard her bestow upon refuge homes and labour organisations.

'I think that greys are the nicest horses,' she said. 'Bays are nice too, but greys are more showy. We could manage with a brougham and a landau, and perhaps a high dog-cart for Raffles. He has the coach-house full at present, but he never uses them, and I am sure that those fifty horses would all die for want of exercise, or get livers like Strasburg geese, if they waited for him to ride or drive them.'

'I suppose that you will still live here?' said her brother.

'We must have a house in London as well, and run up for the season. I don't, of course, like to make suggestions now, but it will be different afterwards. I am sure that Raffles will do it if I ask him. It is all very well for him to say that he does not want any thanks or honours, but I should like to know what is the use of being a public benefactor if you are to have no return for it. I am sure that if he does only half what he talks of doing, they will make him a peer – Lord Tamfield, perhaps – and then, of course, I shall be my Lady Tamfield, and what would you think of that, Bob?' She dropped him a stately curtsey, and tossed her head in the air, as one who was born to wear a coronet.

'Father must be pensioned off,' she remarked presently. 'He shall have so much a year on condition that he keeps away. As to you, Bob, I don't know what we shall do for you. We shall make you President of the Royal Academy if money can do it.'

It was late before they ceased building their air-castles and retired to their rooms. But Robert's brain was excited, and he could not sleep. The events of the day had been enough to shake a stronger man. There had been the revelation of the morning, the strange sights which he had witnessed in the laboratory and the immense secret which had been confided to his keeping. Then there had been his conversation with his father in the afternoon, their disagreement and the sudden intrusion of Raffles Haw. Finally the talk with his sister had excited his imagination, and driven sleep from his eyelids. In vain he turned and twisted in his bed, or paced the floor of his chamber. He was not only awake, but abnormally awake, with every nerve highly strung, and every sense at the keenest. What was he to do to gain a little sleep? It flashed across him that there was brandy in the decanter downstairs, and that a glass might act as a sedative.

He had opened the door of his room, when suddenly his ear caught the sound of slow and stealthy footsteps upon the stairs. His own lamp was unlit, but a dim glimmer came from a moving taper, and a long black shadow travelled down the wall. He stood motionless, listening intently. The steps were in the hall now, and he heard a gentle creaking as the key was cautiously turned in the door. The next instant there came a gust of cold air, the taper was extinguished, and a sharp snap announced that the door had been closed from without.

Robert stood astonished. Who could this night wanderer be? It must be his father. But what errand could take him out at three in the morning? And such a morning, too! With every blast of the wind the rain beat up against his chamber-window as though it would drive it in. The glass rattled in the frames, and the tree outside creaked and groaned as its great branches were tossed about by the gale. What could draw any man forth upon such a night?

Hurriedly Robert struck a match and lit his lamp. His father's room was opposite his own, and the door was ajar. He pushed it open and looked about him. It was empty. The bed had not even been lain upon. The single chair stood by the window, and there the old man must have sat since he left them. There was no book, no paper, no means by which he could have amused himself, nothing but a razor-strop lying on the window-sill.

A feeling of impending misfortune struck cold to Robert's heart. There was some ill-meaning in this journey of his father's. He thought of his brooding of yesterday, his scowling face, his bitter threats. Yes, there was some mischief underlying it. But perhaps he might even now be in time to prevent it. There was no use calling Laura. She could be no help in the matter. He hurriedly threw on his clothes, muffled himself in his top-coat, and, seizing his hat and stick, he set off after his father.

As he came out into the village street the wind whirled down it, so that he had to put his ear and shoulder against it, and push his way forward. It was better, however, when he turned into the lane. The high bank and the hedge sheltered him upon one side. The road, however, was deep in mud, and the rain fell in a steady swish. Not a soul was to be seen, but he needed to make no enquiries, for he knew whither his father had gone as certainly as though he had seen him.

The iron side-gate of the avenue was half open, and Robert stumbled his way up the gravelled drive amid the dripping fir trees. What could his father's intention be when he reached the Hall? Was it merely that he wished to spy and prowl, or did he intend to call up the master and enter into some discussion as to his wrongs? Or was it possible that some blacker and more sinister design lay beneath his strange doings? Robert thought suddenly of the razor-strop, and gasped with horror. What had the old man been doing with that? He quickened his pace to a run, and hurried on until he found himself at the door of the Hall.

Thank God! all was quiet there. He stood by the big silent door and listened intently. There was nothing to be heard save the wind and the rain. Where, then, could his father be? If he wished to enter the Hall he would not attempt to do so by one of the windows, for had he not been present when Raffles Haw had shown them the precautions which he had taken? But then a sudden thought struck Robert. There was one window which was left unguarded. Haw had been imprudent enough to tell them so. It was the middle window of the laboratory. If he remembered it so clearly, of course his father would remember it too. There was the point of danger.

The moment he rounded the corner of the building he found that his surmise had been correct. An electric lamp burned in the laboratory, and the silver squares of the three large windows stood out clear and bright in the darkness. The centre one had been thrown open, and, even as he gazed, Robert saw a dark monkey-like figure spring up on to the sill, and vanish into the room beyond. For a moment only it outlined itself against the brilliant light beyond, but in that moment Robert had space to see that it was indeed his father. On tiptoe he crossed the intervening space, and peeped in through the open window. It was a singular spectacle which met his eyes.

There stood upon the glass table some half-dozen large ingots of gold, which had been made the night before, but which had not been removed to the treasure-house. On these the old man had thrown himself, as one who enters into his rightful inheritance. He lay across the table, his arms clasping the bars of gold, his cheek pressed against them, crooning and muttering to himself. Under the clear, still light, amid the giant wheels and strange engines, that one little dark figure clutching and clinging to the ingots had in it something both weird and piteous.

For five minutes or more Robert stood in the darkness amid the rain, looking in at this strange sight, while his father hardly moved save to cuddle closer to the gold, and to pat it with his thin hands. Robert was still uncertain what he should do, when his eyes wandered from the central figure and fell on something else which made him give a little cry of astonishment – a cry which was drowned amid the howling of the gale.

Raffles Haw was standing in the corner of the room. Where he had come from Robert could not say, but he was certain that he had not been there when he first looked in. He stood silent, wrapped in some long, dark dressing-gown, his arms folded, and a bitter smile upon his pale face. Old McIntyre seemed to see him at almost the same moment, for he snarled out an oath, and clutched still closer at his treasure, looking slantwise at the master of the house with furtive, treacherous eyes.

'And it has really come to this!' said Haw at last, taking a step forward. 'You have actually fallen so low, Mr McIntyre, as to steal into my house at night like a common burglar. You knew that this window was unguarded. I remember telling you as much. But I did not tell you what other means I had adopted by which I might be warned if knaves made an entrance. But that you should have come! You!'

The old gunmaker made no attempt to justify himself, but he muttered some few hoarse words, and continued to cling to the treasure.

'I love your daughter,' said Raffles Haw, 'and for her sake I will not expose you. Your hideous and infamous secret shall be safe with me. No ear shall hear what has happened this night. I will not, as I might, arouse my servants and send for the police. But you must leave my house without further words. I have nothing more to say to you. Go as you have come.'

He took a step forward, and held out his hand as if to detach the old man's grasp from the golden bars. The other thrust his hand into the breast of his coat, and with a shrill scream of rage flung himself upon the alchemist. So sudden and so fierce was the movement that Haw had no time for defence. A bony hand gripped him by the throat, and the blade of a razor flashed in the air. Fortunately, as it fell, the weapon struck against one of the many wires which spanned the room, and flying out of the old man's grasp, tinkled upon the stone floor. But, though disarmed, he was still dangerous. With a horrible silent energy he pushed Haw back and back until, coming to a bench, they both fell over it, McIntyre remaining uppermost. His other hand was on the alchemist's throat, and it might have fared ill with him had Robert not climbed through the window and dragged his father off. With the aid of Haw, he pinned the old man down, and passed a long cravat around his arms. It was terrible to look at him, for his face was convulsed, his eyes bulging from his head, and his lips white with foam.

Haw leaned against the glass table panting, with his hand to his side.

'You here, Robert?' he gasped. 'Is it not horrible? How did you come?'

'I followed him. I heard him go out.'

'He would have robbed me. And he would have murdered me. But he is mad – stark, staring mad!'

There could be no doubt of it. Old McIntyre was sitting up now, and burst suddenly into a hoarse peal of laughter, rocking himself backwards and forwards, and looking up at them with little twinkling, cunning eyes. It was clear to both of them that his mind, weakened by long brooding over the one idea, had now at last become that of a monomaniac. His horrid causeless mirth was more terrible even than his fury.

'What shall we do with him?' asked Haw. 'We cannot take him back to Elmdene. It would be a terrible shock to Laura.'

'We could have doctors to certify him in the morning. Could we not keep him here until then? If we take him back, someone will meet us, and there will be a scandal.'

'I know. We will take him to one of the padded rooms, where he can neither hurt himself nor anyone else. I am somewhat shaken myself. But I am better now. Do you take one arm, and I will take the other.'

Half-leading and half-dragging him they managed between them to convey the old gunmaker away from the scene of his disaster, and to lodge him for the night in a place of safety. At five in the morning Robert had started in the gig to make the medical arrangements, while Raffles Haw paced his palatial house with a troubled face and a sad heart.

FOURTEEN

The Spread of the Blight

It may be that Laura did not look upon the removal of her father as an unmixed misfortune. Nothing was said to her as to the manner of the old man's seizure, but Robert informed her at breakfast that he had thought it best, acting under medical advice, to place him for a time under some restraint. She had herself frequently remarked upon the growing eccentricity of his manner, so that the announcement could have been no great surprise to her. It is certain that it did not diminish her appetite for the coffee and the scrambled eggs, nor prevent her from chatting a good deal about her approaching wedding.

But it was very different with Raffles Haw. The incident had shocked him to his inmost soul. He had often feared lest his money should do indirect evil, but here were crime and madness arising before his very eyes from its influence. In vain he tried to choke down his feelings, and to persuade himself that this attack of old McIntyre's was something which came of itself – something which had no connection with himself or his wealth. He remembered the man as he had first met him, garrulous, foolish, but with no obvious vices. He recalled the change which, week by week, had come over him – his greedy eye, his furtive manner, his hints and innuendoes, ending only the day before in a positive demand for money. It was too certain that there was a chain of events there leading direct to the horrible encounter in the laboratory. His money had cast a blight where he had hoped to shed a blessing.

Mr Spurling, the vicar, was up shortly after breakfast, some rumour of evil having come to his ears. It was good for Haw to talk with him, for the fresh breezy manner of the old clergyman was a corrective to his own sombre and introspective mood.

'Prut, tut!' said he. 'This is very bad – very bad indeed! Mind unhinged, you say, and not likely to get over it! Dear, dear! I have noticed a change in him these last few weeks. He looked like a man who had something upon his mind. And how is Mr Robert McIntyre?'

'He is very well. He was with me this morning when his father had this attack.'

'Ha! There is a change in that young man. I observe an alteration in him. You will forgive me, Mr Raffles Haw, if I say a few serious words of advice to you. Apart from my spiritual functions I am old enough to be your father. You are a very wealthy man, and you have used your wealth nobly – yes, sir, nobly. I do not think that there is a man in a thousand who would have done as well. But don't you think sometimes that it has a dangerous influence upon those who are around you?'

'I have sometimes feared so.'

'We may pass over old Mr McIntyre. It would hardly be just, perhaps, to mention him in this connection. But there is Robert. He used to take such an interest in his profession. He was so keen about art. If you met him, the first words he said were usually some reference to his plans, or the progress he was making in his latest picture. He was ambitious, pushing, self-reliant. Now he does nothing. I know for a fact that it is two months since he put brush to canvas. He has turned from a student into an idler, and, what is worse, I fear into a parasite. You will forgive me for speaking so plainly?'

Raffles Haw said nothing, but he threw out his hands with a gesture of pain.

'And then there is something to be said about the country folk,' said the vicar. 'Your kindness has been, perhaps, a little indiscriminate there. They don't seem to be as helpful or as self-reliant as they used. There was old Blaxton, whose cowhouse roof was blown off the other day. He used to be a man who was full of energy and resource. Three months ago he would have got a ladder and had that roof on again in two days' work. But now he must sit down, and wring his hands, and write letters, because he knew that it would come to your ears, and that you would make it good. There's old Ellary, too! Well, of course he was always poor, but at least he did something, and so kept himself out of mischief. Not a stroke will he do now, but smokes and talks scandal from morning to night. And the worst of it is that it not only hurts those who have had your help but it unsettles those who have not. They all have an injured, surly feeling as if other folk were getting what they had an equal right to. It has really come to such a pitch that I thought it was a duty to speak to you about it. Well, it is a new experience to me. I have often had to reprove my parishioners for not being charitable enough, but it is very strange to find one who is too charitable. It is a noble error.'

'I thank you very much for letting me know about it,' answered Raffles Haw, as he shook the good old clergyman's hand. 'I shall certainly reconsider my conduct in that respect.'

He kept a rigid and unmoved face until his visitor had gone, and then retiring to his own little room, he threw himself upon the bed and burst out sobbing with his face buried in the pillow. Of all men in England, this, the richest, was on that day the most miserable. How could he use this great power which he held? Every blessing which he tried to give turned itself into a curse. His intentions were so good, and yet the results were so terrible. It was as if he had some foul leprosy of the mind which all caught who were exposed to his influence. His charity, so well meant, so carefully bestowed, had yet poisoned the whole countryside. And if in small things his results were so evil, how could he tell that they would be better in the larger plans which he had formed? If he could not pay the debts of a simple yokel without disturbing the great laws of cause and effect which lie at the base of all things, what could he hope for when he came to fill the treasury of nations, to interfere with the complex conditions of trade, or to provide for great masses of the population? He drew back with horror as he dimly saw that vast problems faced him in which he might make errors which all his money could not repair. The way of providence was the straight way. Yet he, a half-blind creature, must needs push in and strive to alter and correct it. Would he be a benefactor? Might he not rather prove to be the greatest malefactor that the world had seen?

But soon a calmer mood came upon him, and he rose and bathed his flushed face and fevered brow. After all, was not there a field where all were agreed that money might be well spent? It was not the way of nature, but rather the way of man which he would alter. It was not providence that had ordained that folk should live half-starved and overcrowded in dreary slums. That was the result of artificial conditions, and it might well be healed by artificial means. Why should not his plans be successful after all, and the world better for his discovery? Then again, it was not the truth that he cast a blight on those with whom he was brought in contact. There was Laura; who knew more of him than she did, and yet how good and sweet and true she was! She at least had lost nothing through knowing him. He would go down and see her. It would be soothing to hear her voice, and to turn to her for words of sympathy in this his hour of darkness.

The storm had died away, but a soft wind was blowing, and the smack of the coming spring was in the air. He drew in the aromatic scent of the fir trees as he passed down the curving drive. Before him lay the long sloping countryside, all dotted over with the farmsteadings and little red cottages, with the morning sun striking slantwise upon their grey roofs and glimmering windows. His heart yearned over all these people with their manifold troubles, their little sordid miseries, their strivings and hopings and petty soul-killing cares. How could he get at them? How could he manage to lift the burden from them, and yet not hinder them in their life aim? For more and more could he see that all refinement is through sorrow, and that the life which does not refine is the life without an aim.

Laura was alone in the sitting-room at Elmdene, for Robert had gone out to make some final arrangements about his father. She sprang up as her lover entered, and ran forward with a pretty girlish gesture to greet him.

'Oh, Raffles!' she cried, 'I knew that you would come. Is it not dreadful about papa?'

'You must not fret, dearest,' he answered gently. 'It may not prove to be so very grave after all.'

'But it all happened before I was stirring. I knew nothing about it until breakfast-time. They must have gone up to the Hall very early.'

'Yes, they did come up rather early.'

'What is the matter with you, Raffles?' cried Laura, looking up into his face. 'You look so sad and weary!'

'I have been a little in the blues. The fact is, Laura, that I have had a long talk with Mr Spurling this morning.'

The girl started, and turned white to the lips. A long talk with Mr Spurling! Did that mean that he had learned her secret?

'Well?' she gasped.

'He tells me that my charity has done more harm than good, and in fact, that I have had an evil influence upon everyone whom I have come near. He said it in the most delicate way, but that was really what it amounted to.'

'Oh, is that all?' said Laura, with a long sigh of relief. 'You must not think of minding what Mr Spurling says. Why, it is absurd on the face of it! Everybody knows that there are dozens of men all over the country who would have been ruined and turned out of their houses if you had not stood their friend. How could they be the worse for having known you? I wonder that Mr Spurling can talk such nonsense!'

'How is Robert's picture getting on?'

'Oh, he has a lazy fit on him. He has not touched it for ever so long. But why do you ask that? You have that furrow on your brow again. Put it away, sir!'

She smoothed it away with her little white hand.

'Well, at any rate, I don't think that quite everybody is the worse,' said he, looking down at her. 'There is one, at least, who is beyond taint, one who is good, and pure, and true, and who would love me as well if I were a poor clerk struggling for a livelihood. You would, would you not, Laura?'

'You foolish boy! of course I would.'

'And yet how strange it is that it should be so. That you, who are the only woman whom I have ever loved, should be the only one in whom I also have raised an affection which is free from greed or interest. I wonder whether you may not have been sent by providence simply to restore my confidence in the world. How barren a place would it not be if it were not for woman's love! When all seemed black around me this morning, I tell you, Laura, that I seemed to turn to you and to your love as the one thing on earth upon which I could rely. All else seemed shifting, unstable, influenced by this or that base consideration. In you, and you only, could I trust.'

'And I in you, dear Raffles! I never knew what love was until I met you.'

She took a step towards him, her hands advanced, love shining in her features, when in an instant Raffles saw the colour struck from her face, and a staring horror spring into her eyes. Her blanched and rigid face was turned towards the open door, while he, standing partly behind it, could not see what it was that had so moved her.

'Hector!' she gasped, with dry lips.

A quick step in the hall, and a slim, weather-tanned young man sprang forward into the room, and caught her up in his arms as if she had been a feather.

'You darling!' he said. 'I knew that I would surprise you. I came right up from Plymouth by the night train. And I have long leave, and plenty of time to get married. Isn't it jolly, dear Laura?'

He pirouetted round with her in the exuberance of his delight. As he spun round, however, his eyes fell suddenly upon the pale and silent stranger who stood by the door. Hector blushed furiously, and made an awkward sailor bow, standing with Laura's cold and unresponsive hand still clasped in his.

'Very sorry, sir – didn't see you,' he said. 'You'll excuse my going on in this mad sort of way, but if you had served you would know what it is to get away from quarter-deck manners, and to be a free man. Miss McIntyre will tell you that we have known each other since we were children, and as we are to be married in, I hope, a month at the latest, we understand each other pretty well.'

Raffles Haw still stood cold and motionless. He was stunned, benumbed, by what he saw and heard. Laura drew away from Hector, and tried to free her hand from his grasp.

'Didn't you get my letter at Gibraltar?' she asked.

'Never went to Gibraltar. Were ordered home by wire from Madeira. Those chaps at the Admiralty never know their own minds for two hours together. But what matter about a letter, Laura, so long as I can see you and speak with you? You have not introduced me to your friend here.'

'One word, sir,' cried Raffles Haw in a quivering voice. 'Do I entirely understand you? Let me be sure that there is no mistake. You say that you are engaged to be married to Miss McIntyre?'

'Of course I am. I've just come back from a four months' cruise, and I am going to be married before I drag my anchor again.'

'Four months!' gasped Haw. 'Why, it is just four months since I came here. And one last question, sir. Does Robert McIntyre know of your engagement?'

'Does Bob know? Of course he knows. Why, it was to his care I left Laura when I started. But what is the meaning of all this? What is the matter with you, Laura? Why are you so white and silent? And – hallo! Hold up, sir! The man is fainting!'

'It is all right!' gasped Haw, steadying himself against the edge of the door.

He was as white as paper, and his hand was pressed close to his side as though some sudden pain had shot through him. For a moment he tottered there like a stricken man, and then, with a hoarse cry, he turned and fled out through the open door.

'Poor devil!' said Hector, gazing in amazement after him. 'He seems hard hit anyhow. But what is the meaning of all this, Laura?'

His face had darkened, and his mouth had set.

She had not said a word, but had stood with a face like a mask looking blankly in front of her. Now she tore herself away from him, and, casting herself down with her face buried in the cushion of the sofa, she burst into a passion of sobbing.

'It means that you have ruined me,' she cried. 'That you have ruined – ruined – ruined me! Could you not leave us alone? Why must you come at the last moment? A few more days, and we were safe. And you never had my letter.'

'And what was in your letter, then?' he asked coldly, standing with his arms folded, looking down at her.

'It was to tell you that I released you. I love Raffles Haw, and I was to have been his wife. And now it is all gone. Oh, Hector, I hate you, and I shall always hate you as long as I live, for you have stepped between me and the only good fortune that ever came to me. Leave me alone, and I hope that you will never cross our threshold again.'

'Is that your last word, Laura?'

'The last that I shall ever speak to you.'

'Then, goodbye. I shall see the pater and then go straight back to Plymouth.' He waited an instant, in hopes of an answer, and then walked sadly from the room.

FIFTEEN

The Great Secret

It was late that night that a startled knocking came at the door of Elmdene. Laura had been in her room all day, and Robert was moodily smoking his pipe by the fire, when this harsh and sudden summons broke in upon his thoughts. There in the porch was Jones, the stout head-butler of the Hall, hatless, scared, with the raindrops shining in the lamplight upon his smooth, bald head.

'If you please, Mr McIntyre, sir, would it trouble you to step up to the Hall?' he cried. 'We are all frightened, sir, about master.'

Robert caught up his hat and started at a run, the frightened butler trotting heavily beside him. It had been a day of excitement and disaster. The young artist's heart was heavy within him, and the shadow of some crowning trouble seemed to have fallen upon his soul.

'What is the matter with your master, then?' he asked, as he slowed down into a walk.

'We don't know, sir; but we can't get an answer when we knock at the laboratory door. Yet he's there, for it's locked on the inside. It has given us all a scare, sir, that, and his goin's-on during the day.'

'His goings-on?'

'Yes, sir; for he came back this morning like a man demented, a-talkin' to himself, and with his eyes starin' so that it was dreadful to look at the poor dear gentleman. Then he walked about the passages a long time, and he wouldn't so much as look at his luncheon, but he went into the museum, and gathered all his jewels and things, and carried them into the laboratory. We don't know what he's done since then, sir, but his furnace has been a-roarin', and his big chimney spoutin' smoke like a Birmingham factory. When night came we could see his figure against the light, a-workin' and a-heavin' like a man possessed. No dinner would he have, but work, and work, and work. Now it's all quiet, and the furnace cold, and no smoke from above, but we can't get no answer from him, sir, so we are scared, and Miller has gone for the police, and I came away for you.'

They reached the Hall as the butler finished his explanation, and there outside the laboratory door stood the little knot of footmen and ostlers, while the village policeman, who had just arrived, was holding his bull's-eye to the keyhole, and endeavouring to peep through.

'The key is half-turned,' he said. 'I can't see nothing except just the light.'

'Here's Mr McIntyre,' cried half a dozen voices, as Robert came forward.

'We'll have to beat the door in, sir,' said the policeman. 'We can't get any sort of answer, and there's something wrong.'

Twice and thrice they threw their united weights against it until at last with a sharp snap the lock broke, and they crowded into the narrow passage. The inner door was ajar, and the laboratory lay before them.

In the centre was an enormous heap of fluffy grey ash, reaching up halfway to the ceiling. Beside it was another heap, much smaller, of some brilliant scintillating dust, which shimmered brightly in the rays of the electric light. All round was a bewildering chaos of broken jars, shattered bottles, cracked machinery, and tangled wires, all bent and draggled. And there in the midst of this universal ruin, leaning back in his chair with his hands clasped upon his lap, and the easy pose of one who rests after hard work safely carried through, sat Raffles Haw, the master of the house, and the richest of mankind, with the pallor of death upon his face. So easily he sat and so naturally, with such a serene expression upon his features, that it was not until they raised him, and touched his cold and rigid limbs, that they could realise that he had indeed passed away.

Reverently and slowly they bore him to his room, for he was beloved by all who had served him. Robert alone lingered with the policeman in the laboratory. Like a man in a dream he wandered about, marvelling at the universal destruction. A large broad-headed hammer lay upon the ground, and with this Haw had apparently set himself to destroy all his apparatus, having first used his electrical machines to reduce to protyle all the stock of gold which he had accumulated. The treasure-room which had so dazzled Robert consisted now of merely four bare walls, while the gleaming dust upon the floor proclaimed the fate of that magnificent collection of gems which had alone amounted to a royal fortune. Of all the machinery no single piece remained intact, and even the glass table was shattered into three pieces. Strenuously earnest must have been the work which Raffles Haw had done that day.

And suddenly Robert thought of the secret which had been treasured in the casket within the iron-clamped box. It was to tell him the one last essential link which would make his knowledge of the process complete. Was it still there? Thrilling all over, he opened the great chest, and drew out the ivory box. It was locked, but the key was in it. He turned it and threw open the lid. There was a white slip of paper with his own name written upon it. With trembling fingers he unfolded it. Was he the heir to the riches of El Dorado, or was he destined to be a poor struggling artist? The note was dated that very evening, and ran in this way:

My DEAR ROBERT – My secret shall never be used again. I cannot tell you how I thank heaven that I did not entirely confide it to you, for I should have been handing over an inheritance of misery both to yourself and others. For myself I have hardly had a happy moment since I discovered it. This I could have borne had I been able to feel that I was doing good, but, alas! the only effect of my attempts has been to turn workers into idlers, contented men into greedy parasites, and, worst of all, true, pure women into deceivers and hypocrites. If this is the effect of my interference on a small scale, I cannot hope for anything better were I to carry out the plans which we have so often discussed. The schemes of my life have all turned to nothing. For myself, you shall never see me again. I shall go back to the student life from which I emerged. There, at least, if I can do little good, I can do no harm. It is my wish that such valuables as remain in the Hall should be sold, and the proceeds divided amidst all the charities of Birmingham. I shall leave tonight if I am well enough, but I have been much troubled all day by a stabbing pain in my side. It is as if wealth were as bad for health as it is for peace of mind. Goodbye, Robert, and may you never have as sad a heart as I have tonight.

Yours very truly,

RAFFLES HAW

'Was it suicide, sir? Was it suicide?' broke in the policeman as Robert put the note in his pocket.

'No,' he answered; 'I think it was a broken heart.'

And so the wonders of the New Hall were all dismantled, the carvings and the gold, the books and the pictures, and many a struggling man or woman who had heard nothing of Raffles Haw during his life had cause to bless him after his death. The house has been bought by a company now, who have turned it into a hydropathic establishment, and of all the folk who frequent it in search of health or of pleasure there are few who know the strange story which is connected with it.

The blight which Haw's wealth cast around it seemed to last even after his death. Old McIntyre still raves in the County Lunatic Asylum, and treasures up old scraps of wood and metal under the impression that they are all ingots of gold. Robert McIntyre is a moody and irritable man, forever pursuing a quest which will always evade him. His art is forgotten, and he spends his whole small income upon chemical and electrical appliances, with which he vainly seeks to rediscover that one hidden link. His sister keeps house for him, a silent and brooding woman, still queenly and beautiful, but of a bitter, dissatisfied mind. Of late, however, she has devoted herself to charity, and has been of so much help to Mr Spurling's new curate that it is thought that he may be tempted to secure her assistance for ever. So runs the gossip of the village, and in small places such gossip is seldom wrong. As to Hector Spurling, he is still in Her Majesty's service, and seems inclined to abide by his father's wise advice, that he should not think of marrying until he is a commander. It is possible that of all who were brought within the spell of Raffles Haw he was the only one who had occasion to bless it.

ARTHUR ELCK

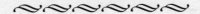

The Tower Room

There were many wonderful things that aroused our childish fantasy, when Balint Orzo and I were boys, but none so much as the old tower that stands a few feet from the castle, shadowy and mysterious. It is an old, curious, square tower, and at the brink of its notched edge there is a shingled helmet which was erected by one of the late Orzos.

There is many and many a legend told about this old tower. A rumour exists that it has a secret chamber into which none is permitted to enter, except the head of the family. Some great secret is concealed in the tower room, and when the first-born son of the Orzo family becomes of age his father takes him there and reveals it. And the effect of the revelation is such that every young man who enters that room comes out with grey hair.

As to what the secret might be, there was much conjecturing. One legend had it that once some Orzo imprisoned his enemies in the tower and starved them until the unfortunates ate each other in their crazed suffering.

According to another story Kelemen Orzo ordered his faithless wife Krisztina Olaszi to be plastered into the wall of the room. Every night since, sobbing is heard from the tower.

Another runs that every hundred years a child with a dog's face is born in the Orzo family and that this little monster has to perish in the tower room, so as to hide the disgrace of the family.

Another conjecture was that once the notorious Menyhart Orzo, who was supreme under King Rudolph in the castle, played a game of draughts with his neighbour, Boldizsar Zomolnoky. They commenced to play on a Monday and continued the game and drank all week until Sunday morning dawned upon them. Then Menyhart Orzo's confessor came and pleaded with the gamblers. He begged them to stop the game on the holy day of Sunday, when all true Christians are in church praising the Lord. But Menyhart, bringing his fist down on the table in such rage that all the wine glasses and bottles danced, cried: 'And if we have to sit here till the world comes to an end, we won't stop till we have finished this game!'

Scarcely had he uttered his vow when, somewhere from the earth, or from the wall, a thundering voice was heard promising to take him at his word – that they would continue playing till the end of the world. And ever since, the draughts are heard rattling, and the two damned souls are still playing the game in the tower room.

When we were boys, the secret did not give us any rest, and we were always discussing and plotting as to how we could discover it. We made at least a hundred various plans, but all failed. It was an impossibility to get into the tower, because of a heavy iron-barred oaken door. The windows were too high to be reached. We had to satisfy ourselves with throwing the odd well-aimed stone, which hit the room through the window. Such an achievement was somewhat of a success, for oftentimes we merely drove out an alarmed flock of birds.

One day I decided that the best way would be to find out the secret of the tower from Balint's father himself. 'He is the head of the family,' I thought, 'and if any light is to be had on the mystery, it is through him.' But Balint didn't like the idea of approaching the old man; he knew his father's temper.

However, once he ventured the question, but he was sorry for it afterwards, for the older Orzo flew into a passion, and scolded and raged, ending by telling him that he must not listen to such nursery-tales; that the tower was mouldering and decaying with age; that the floor timbers and staircase were so infirm that it would fall to pieces should anyone approach it; and that this was why no one could gain admittance.

For a long time afterwards neither of us spoke of it.

But curiosity was incessantly working within us, and one evening Balint solemnly vowed to me that as soon as he became of age and had looked into the room, he would call for me, should I be even at the end of the world, and would let me into the secret. In order to make it more solemn, we called this a 'blood-contract'.

With this vow we parted. My parents sent me to college; Balint had a private tutor and was kept at home in the castle. After that we only met at vacation time.

Eight years passed before I saw the Orzo home again. At Balint's urgent, sudden invitation I had hurriedly journeyed back to my rocky fatherland.

I had scarcely stepped on the wide stone stairway leading from the terrace in the front of the castle, when someone shouted that the honourable master was near! He came galloping in on a foaming horse. I looked at him and started, as if I had seen a ghost, for this thin, tall rider was the perfect resemblance of his father. The same knotty hair and beard, the same densely furrowed face, the same deep, calm, grey eyes. And his hair and beard were almost as white as his father's!

He came galloping through the gate, pulled the bridle with a sudden jerk, and the next moment was on the paving; then with one bound he reached the terrace, and had me in his strong arms. With wild eagerness he showed me into the castle and at the same time kept talking and questioning me without ceasing. Then he thrust me into my room and declared that he gave me fifteen minutes – no more – to dress.

The time had not even expired, when he came, like a whirlwind, embraced me again and carried me into the dining-room. There chandeliers and lamps were already lit; the table was elaborately decorated, and bore plenty of wine.

At the meal he spoke again. Nervously jerking out his words, he was continually questioning me on one subject and then another, without waiting for the answer. He laughed often and harshly. When we came to the drinking, he winked to the servants, and immediately five Czigany musicians entered the room. Balint noticed the astonishment on my face, and half evasively said: 'I have sent to Iglo for them in honour of you. Let the music sound, and the wine flow; who knows when we will see each other again?'

He put his face into his palm. The Cziganys played old Magyar songs. Balint glanced at me now and then, and filled the glasses; we clinked them together, but he always seemed to be worried.

It was dawning. The soft sound of a church bell rose to us. Balint put his hand on my shoulder and bent to my ear.

'Do you know how my father died?' he asked in a husky voice. 'He killed himself.'

I looked at him with amazement; I wanted to speak, but he shook his head, and grasped my hand.

'Do you remember my father?' he asked me. Of course; while I looked at him it seemed as if his father were standing before me. The very same fibrous, skinny figure, the muscles and flesh seeming peeled off. Even through his coat arm I felt the naked, unveiled nerves.

'I always admired and honoured my father, but we were never true intimates; I knew that he loved me, but I felt as if it was not for my own sake; as if he loved something in my soul that was strange to me. I never saw him smile; sometimes he was so harsh that I was afraid of him; at another time he was unmanageable.

'I did not understand him, but the older I became the better did I feel that there was a sad secret germinating in the bottom of his soul, where it grew like a spreading tree, the branches of which crept up to the castle and covered the walls, little by little overshadowed the sunlight, absorbed the air, and darkened everyone's heart. I gritted my teeth in vain; I could not work; I could not start to accomplish anything. I struggled with hundreds and hundreds of determinations; today I prepared for this or that; tomorrow for something else; ambition pressed me within; I could not make up my mind. Behind every resolution I made, I noticed my father's countenance, like a note of interrogation. The old fables that we heard together in our childhood were renewed in my memory. Little by little the thought grew within me, like a fixed delusion, that my father's fatal secret was locked up in the tower room. After that I lived by the calendar and dwelt on the passing of time on the clock. And when the sun that shone on me when I was born arose the twenty-fourth time, I pressed my hand on my heart and entered my father's room – this very room.

' "Father," I said, "I became of age today, everything may be opened before me, and I am at liberty to know everything." Father looked at me and pondered over this.

' "Oh, yes!" he whispered, "this is the day."

' "I may know everything now," continued I; "I am not afraid of any secrets. In the name of our family tradition, I beg of you, please open the tower room."

'Father raised his hand, as if he wanted me to be silent. His face was as white as that of a ghost.

' "Very well," he murmured, "I will open the tower room for you."

'And then he pulled off his coat, tore his shirt open at his breast, and pointed to his heart.

' "Here is the tower room, my boy!" did he whisper in a husky voice. "Here is the tower room, and within our family secret. Do you see it?"

'That is all he said, but when I looked at him I immediately perceived the secret; everything was clear before me and I had a presentiment that something was nearing its end, something about to break.

'Father walked up and down; and then he stopped and pointed to this picture; to this very picture.

' "Did you ever thoroughly look at your ancestors? They are all here, the Orzos. If you scrutinise their faces you will recognise in them your father, yourself and your grandfather; and if you ever read their documents, which were left to us – there they are in the box – then you will know that they are just the same material as we are. Their way of thinking was the same as ours and so were their desires, their wills, their lives and deaths. We had among them soldiers, clergymen, scientists, but not even one great, celebrated man, although their talent, their strength almost tore them asunder.

' "In every one of them the family curse took root: not one of them could be a great man, neither my father nor yours."

'Then I felt as if something horrible was coming from his lips. My breath almost ceased. Father did not finish what he was going to say, but stopped and listened for a minute.

' "I was my father's only hope," he went on after a while; "I too was born talented and prepared for great things, but the Orzos' destiny overtook me, and you see now what became of me. I looked into the tower room. You know what it contains? You know what the name of our secret is? He who saw this secret lost faith in himself. For him it would have been better not to have come into this world at all. But I loved to live and did not want to abandon all my hopes. I married your mother; she consoled me until you were born, and then I regained my delight in life. I knew what I had to keep before my eyes to bring up my son to be such a man as his father could not be.

' "I acquiesced when you left for the foreign countries; then your letters came. I made a special study of every sentence and of every word, for I did not want to trust my reason. I thought the first time that the fault was in me; that I saw unnecessary phantoms. But it wasn't so, for what I read out of your words was our destiny, the curse of the Orzos; from the way of your thinking, I found out that everything is in vain; you too turned your head backwards, you too looked into yourself and noticed there the thing that makes the perceiver sterile for ever. You did not even notice what you had done; you could not grasp it with your reason, but the poison was already within you."

' "It cannot be, father!" I broke out, terrified.

'But he sadly shook his head. "I am old; I cannot believe in anything now. I wish you were right, and would never come to know what I know. God bless you, my son; it is getting late, and I am getting tired."

'It struck me that he was trying to cover his disbelief with sarcasm. Both of us were without sleep that night. At dawn there was silence in his room. I bitterly thought, "When will I go to rest?" When I went into his room in the morning he was lying in his bed. All was over. He had taken poison, and written his farewell on a piece of paper. His last wish was that no one should ever know under what circumstances he died.'

Balint left off speaking and gazed with outstretched eyes towards the window in the darkness. I slowly went to him and put my hand upon his shoulder. He started at my touch.

'I more than once thought of the woman who could be the mother of my son. How many times have I been tempted to fulfil my father's last wish! But at such a time it has always come to my mind that I too might have such a son, who would cast into his father's teeth that he was a coward and a selfish man; that he sacrificed a life for his illusive hopes.

'No! I won't do it. I won't do it. I am the last of the Orzos. With me this damned family will die out. My fathers were cowards and rascals. I do not want anybody to curse my memory.'

I kissed Balint's wet forehead; I knew that this was the last time I would see him. The next day I left the castle, and the day after, his death was made public. He committed suicide, like his father. He was the last Orzo, and I turned about the coat of arms above his head.

A. J. EVANS

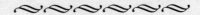

Exploits of the Escaping Club

In the early days of the war, Fort 9, Ingolstadt, had been a quiet, well-behaved sort of place, according to its oldest inmates. But for the six months previous to my arrival before its forbidding gates at the end of 1916, the Germans had collected into it all the naughty boys who had tried to escape from other camps. There were about a hundred and fifty officer prisoners of different nationalities in the place, and at least a hundred and thirty of these had successfully broken out of other camps, and had only been recaught after from three days' to three weeks' temporary freedom. I myself had escaped from Clausthal in the Harz Mountains – but had been recaptured on the Dutch frontier after I'd been at large for a few days.

When I arrived at Fort 9, Ingolstadt, seventy-five per cent of the prisoners were scheming and working continually to escape again. Escaping, and how it should be done, was the most frequent subject of conversation. In fact, the camp was nothing less than an escaping club. We pooled our knowledge and each man was ready to help anyone who wished to escape, quite regardless of his own risk or the punishment he might bring upon himself. No one cared twopence for court martials, and nearly everyone in the fort had done considerable spells of solitary confinement.

It is scarcely necessary to say that the Germans, having herded some hundred and fifty officers with the blackest characters into one camp, took considerable precautions to keep them there. But there were some of the most ingenious people in Fort 9 that I've ever met – particularly among the French – and attempts to escape took place at least once a week.

Fort 9 had been built in 1866 after the Austrian wars. There was a wide moat, about fifteen yards broad and five feet deep, round the whole fort and inside the moat the ramparts rose to a height of forty feet. Our living rooms were actually in the ramparts and the barred windows looked down upon the moat, across a grass path along which a number of sentries were posted. It looked as though there were only two possible ways of getting out: to go out the way we'd come in, past three sentries, three gates and a guardhouse; or to swim the moat. It was impossible to tunnel under the moat. It had been tried, but the water came into the tunnel as soon as it got below the water level. An aeroplane seemed the only other solution. That was the problem we were up against, and however you looked at it, it always boiled down to a nasty cold swim or a colossal piece of bluff. We came to the conclusion that we must have more accurate knowledge of the numbers, positions and movements of the sentries on the ramparts and round the moat at night, so we decided that one of us must spend the night out. It would be a rotten job; fifteen hours' wait on a freezing night, for it was now winter. For the first three and last three hours of this time it would be almost impossible to move a muscle without discovery, and discovery probably meant getting bayoneted. We cast lots for this job – and it fell to a man named Oliphant. I owned I breathed a sigh of relief. There would be two roll-calls to be faked, the roll-call just before sunset and the early morning one. How was this to be done? Our room was separated from the one next door, which was occupied by Frenchmen, by a three-foot-thick wall, and in the wall was an archway. This archway was boarded up and formed a recess which was used as a hanging cupboard for clothes. Under cover of these clothes we cut a hole in the boarding big enough for a man to slip quickly through from one room to the other. The planks which we took out could be put buck easily and we pasted pictures over the cracks to conceal them. It was rather difficult work. We had only a heated table knife to cut the first plank with, but later on we managed to steal a saw from a German carpenter, who was doing some work in one of the rooms, and return it before he missed it. You must remember that there was absolutely no privacy in the fort, and a sentry passed the window and probably stared into the room every minute or two. We then rehearsed the taking of the roll-calls. One of us pretended to be the German NCO taking the roll. First he tapped at the Frenchman's door and counted the men in the room, shut the door and walked about seven paces to our door, tapped and entered. Between the time he shut the first door till he opened ours only six or eight seconds elapsed, but during these seconds one of the Frenchmen had to slip through the hole, put on a British warm, and pretent to be Oliphant; the German NCOs knew every man by sight in every room, but so long as the numbers were correct they often didn't bother to examine our faces. That accounted for the evening roll-call. The early morning one was really easier. For several mornings the fellow in bed nearest the hole in our room made a habit of covering his face with the bedclothes. The German NCO soon got used to seeing him like that, and if he saw him breathing or moving didn't bother to pull the clothes off his face. So the Frenchman next door had simply to jump out of bed as soon as he had been counted, slip through the hole, get into the bed in our room and cover up his face. We practised this until we got it perfect, and the rehearsals were great fun.

The next thing to do was to hide Oliphant below the ramparts. Two of us dug a grave for him there while the others kept watch. Then just before the roll-call went we buried him and covered him with sods of grass. It was freezing at the time. It was about 4.30 p.m. when we buried him, and he wouldn't be able to return to our room till 8.15 the next morning, when the doors were open. The faking of the evening roll-call went of splendidly, but the morning one was a little ticklish, as we couldn't be quite sure which room the NCO would enter first. However, we listened carefully, and fixed it all right, and when he poked our substitute, who groaned and moved in the rehearsed manner, we nearly died with suppressed laughter. About an hour later Oliphant walked in very cold and hungry but otherwise cheerful. He had had quite a successful night. A bright moon had prevented him from crawling about much, but he had seen enough to show that it would be a pretty difficult job to get through the sentries and swim the moat on a dark night. However, providence came to our help.

The winter of 1916 was a hard one, and the moat froze over, and although the Germans went round in a boat every day and tried to keep the ice broken, they eventually had to give it up. It was difficult to know whether the ice would bear or not, but I tested it as well as I could by throwing stones on to it, and decided one morning that I would risk it and make a dash across the moat that evening. A man named Wilkin, and Kicq, a little Belgian officer, who had accompanied me on my previous attempt to escape, agreed to come with me.

Our plan was to start when the *appell* or roll-call bell went at 5 p.m., for it got dark soon afterwards, and I trusted that this would cover our flight. We had to run down a steep bank on to the ice, about fifteen yards across the ice, and then another two hundred yards or so before we could put a cottage between ourselves and the sentries. There was sure to be some shooting, but we reckoned the men's hands would be very cold, for they would already have been two hours at their posts. Moreover they were only armed with old French rifles, which they handled badly. We arranged with some of the other officers to create a diversion when the roll-call bell went by yelling and throwing stones on to the ice to distract the attention of the two nearest sentries. Our main anxiety was: would the ice bear? I felt confident it would. Wilkin said he was awfully frightened, but would go on with it. Kicq said that if I was confident, so was he. It would be extremely unpleasant if the ice broke, for we would be wearing a lot of very heavy clothes. Still, anyone who thinks too much of what may happen will never escape from prison. We filled our rucksacks with rations for a ten days' march and enough solidified alcohol for at least one hot drink a day. We then concealed them and our coats at the jumping-off place.

A few minutes before the bell went we were all three dressed and in our places. It was a bad few minutes. At last it rang and almost immediately I heard laughter and shouting and the sound of stones falling on the ice. We jumped up and bolted over the path and down the slope. I was slightly ahead of the others, and when I got to the moat I gave a little jump on to the ice, thinking that if it was going to break at all it would break at the edge instead of in the middle. It didn't break, and I shuffled across at good speed. When I was about halfway over I heard furious yells of 'Halt!' behind me, followed by a fair amount of shooting; but I was soon up the bank on the far side and through a few scattered trees. Then I looked back.

The others were only just clambering up the bank from the moat, and were a good hundred yards behind me. It turned out that instead of taking a little jump on to the ice as I had done they'd stepped carefully on to the edge, which had broken under their weight, and they had fallen flat on their faces. Wilkin had somehow got upside down, his heavy rucksack falling over his head, so that he couldn't move, but Kicq had freed himself and pulled Wilkin out.

The covering parties had done their job well. They'd managed to divert the attention of the most formidable sentry until I was well on the ice. He had then noticed me, yelled: 'Halt!', loaded his rifle as fast as possible, dropped on one knee, fired and missed. Cold fingers, abuse and some stones hurled at him by the party on the ramparts above had not helped to steady his aim. After one or two shots his rifle jammed. Yells and cheers from the spectators. He tore at the bolt, cursing and swearing, and then put up his rifle at the crowd of jeering prisoners above him, but they could see that the bolt hadn't gone home, and only yelled louder.

Meanwhile, I'd nearly reached the cottage, when I saw a large, four-horse wagon on the main road on my right with a number of civilians by it. They were only about a hundred and fifty yards away, and they started after us, led by a strong, healthy-looking fellow with a cart-whip. The going through the snow was heavy, especially with the weight we were carrying; so the carter quickly overtook me and slashed me across the shoulders with his whip. I turned and rushed at him, but he jumped out of my reach. His companions then arrived, and I saw, too, some armed soldiers coming on bicycles along the road from the fort. The game was up, and the next thing to do was to avoid being shot in the excitement of recapture. So I beckoned the smallest man and said in German: 'Come here, and I'll give myself up to you.' The chap with the whip immediately came forward. 'No, not to you,' I said, 'you hit me with that whip.' The little fellow was very pleased, for there was a hundred marks reward for the capture of an officer, so he hung on to my coat-tails as we started back to the fort. I tore up my map and dropped it into a stream as we went.

The scene in the commandant's office was quite amusing. We were stripped and searched. I had nothing more to hide, but both Kicq and Wilkin had compasses, which they smuggled through with great skill. Kicq's was hidden in the lining of his greatcoat, and Wilkin had his in his hand-kerchief, which he pulled out of his pocket and waved to show that there was nothing in it. All our foodstuffs and clothes were returned to us, except my tin of solidified alcohol. I protested, but in vain. I was given a receipt for it and told I could have it back at the end of the war. As we left the office I saw it standing almost within my reach, and nearly managed to pocket it as I went out. However, I found a friend of mine – a French officer – outside and explained to him the position of the tin and suggested that he should go in with a few pals and steal it back for me under the cover of a row. This was the kind of joke that the Frenchmen loved, and they were past-masters at it. They were always rushing off to the commandant's office with frivolous complaints about one thing or another, just for a rag, which never failed to reduce the commandant and his officers to a state of dithering rage. Within ten minutes I had my solid alcohol back all right, and kept my receipt for it as well.

Compasses and maps were, of course, forbidden, but we managed to get them smuggled in in parcels all the same and watching a German open a parcel in which you knew there was a concealed compass was one of the most exciting things I've ever done.

For the next six weeks life was rather hard. It froze continuously, even in the daytime, and at night the thermometer registered more than 27 degrees of frost. Fuel and light shortage became very serious. We stole wood and coal freely from the Germans, and although the sentries had strict orders to shoot at sight anyone seen taking wood, nearly all the woodwork in the fort was eventually torn down and burnt.

The Germans didn't allow us much oil for our lamps, so we used to steal the oil out of the lamps in the passage, until the Germans realised that they were being robbed and substituted acetylene for oil. However, this didn't deter us, for now, instead of taking the oil out of the lamps, we took the lamps themselves, and lamp-stealing became one of the recognised sports of the camp. How it was done has nothing to do with escaping, but was amusing. Outside our living rooms there was a passage seventy yards long, in which were two acetylene lamps. The sentry in the passage had special orders, a loaded rifle and fixed bayonet, to see that these lamps weren't stolen, and since the *feldwebel*, or sergeant-major, had stuffed up the sentries with horrible stories about our murderous characters, it isn't surprising that each sentry was very keen to prevent us stealing the lamps and leaving him – an isolated German – in total darkness and at our mercy. So whenever a prisoner came out of his room and passed one of the lamps, the sentry would eye him anxiously and get ready to charge at him. The lamps were about thirty yards apart, and this is how we got them. One of us would come out, walk to a lamp and stop beneath it. This would unnerve the sentry, who would advance upon him. The prisoner would then take out his watch and look at it by the light of the lamp, as if that were all he had stopped for. Meanwhile a second officer would come quickly out of a room farther down the passage and take down the other lamp behind the sentry's back. The sentry would immediately turn and charge with loud yells of: 'Halt! Halt!' whereupon the first lamp would also be grabbed, both would be blown out simultaneously, and the prisoners would disappear into their respective rooms leaving the passage in total darkness. The amusing part was that this used to happen every night, and the sentries *knew* it was going to happen, but they were quite powerless against tactics of this kind.

At about this time an officer named Medlicott and I learnt that some Frenchmen were planning to escape across the frozen moat by cutting a window-bar in the latrines which overlooked it. The Germans, however, smelt a rat, but though they inspected the bars carefully they couldn't find the cuts which had been artfully sealed up with a mixture of flour and ashes. Then the *feldwebel* went round and shook each bar violently in turn until the fourth one came off in his hands and he fell down flat on his back. They then wired up the hole, but Medlicott and I saw a chance of cutting the wire and making another bolt for it about a week later, and we took it. We were only at large however for about two hours. The snow on the ground gave our tracks away; we were pursued, surrounded, and eventually had to surrender again. This time we had a somewhat hostile reception when we got back to the fort.

They searched us and took away my tin of solidified alcohol again. They recognised it. 'I know how you stole this back,' said the senior clerk as he gave me another receipt for it, 'but you shan't have it any more.' We both laughed over it. I laughed last, however, as I stole it back again in about a week's time, and kept my two receipts for it as well.

It may seem extraordinary that we weren't punished severely for these attempts to escape, but there were no convenient cells in which to punish us. All the cells at Fort 9 were always full and there was a very long waiting list besides.

After this failure I joined some Frenchmen who were making a tunnel. The shaft was sunk in the corner of one of their rooms close to the window, and the idea was to come out in the steep bank of the moat on a level with the ice and crawl over on a dark night. It was all very unpleasant. Most of the time one lay in a pool of water and in an extremely confined space and worked in pitch darkness, as the air was so bad that no candle would keep alight. Moreover, when we got close to the frozen surface of the ground it was always a question whether the sentry outside wouldn't put his foot through the tunnel, and if he did so whether one would be suffocated or stuck with a bayonet. It was most unpleasant lying there and waiting for him to pass within six inches of your head. All the earth had to be carried in bags along the passage and emptied down the latrines.

Unfortunately, just before the work was finished the thaw set in, and it was generally agreed that we couldn't afford to get our clothes wet swimming the moat. However, the Frenchmen were undaunted and determined to wade through the moat naked, carrying two bundles of kit sewn in waterproof cloths. The rest of us disliked the idea of being chased naked in the middle of winter carrying two twenty-pound bundles, so we decided to make ourselves diving suits out of mackintoshes. We waterproofed the worn patches of these with candle grease, and sewed them up in various places. The Frenchmen would have to fake roll-call, so they made most lifelike dummies, which breathed when you pulled a string, to put in their beds. Whether this attempt to escape would have been successful I can't say, for, thank heaven, we never tried it. When we were all ready and the French colonel, who was going first, had stripped naked and greased himself from head to foot, we learnt that the trap-door which we had made at the exit of the tunnel couldn't be opened under two hours owing to unexpected roots and stones. We had to put off the attempt for that night, and we were unable to make another as the end of the tunnel suddenly fell in, and the cavity was noticed by the sentry.

This was practically the end of my residence in Fort 9, for soon after the Germans decided to send the more unruly of us to other camps. We learnt that we were to be transferred to Zorndorf, in East Prussia, an intolerable spot from all accounts, and a man named Buckley and myself decided to get off the train at the first opportunity and make another bid for freedom. The train would be taking us directly away from the Swiss frontier, so it behoved us to leave it as soon as possible. We equipped ourselves as well as we could with condensed foods before starting, and wore Burberrys to cover our uniforms. Although there were only thirty of us going we had a guard of an officer and fifteen men, which *we* thought a little excessive. We had two hours' wait at the station and amused ourselves by taking as little notice as possible of the officer's orders, which annoyed him and made him shout. Six of us and a sentry were then packed rather tightly into a second-class carriage. We gave him the corner seat next to the corridor, and another sentry marched up and down the corridor outside. Buckley and I took the seats by the window, which we were compelled to keep closed, and there was no door in that side of the carriage. The position didn't look very hopeful, for there wasn't much chance of our sentry going to sleep with the other one outside continually looking in. Just before we started the officer came fussing in: he was obviously very anxious and nervous, and said he hoped that we would have a comfortable, quiet journey and no more trouble. The train started, night fell, and the frontier was left farther and farther behind. We shut our eyes for an hour to try to induce the sentry to go to sleep, but this didn't work.

The carriage was crowded, and both racks were full of small luggage, and, noticing this, I had an idea. I arranged with the others to act in a certain way when the train next went slowly, and I gave the word by saying to the sentry, in German: 'Will you have some food? We are going to eat.' Five or ten minutes of tense excitement followed. Suddenly the train began to slow up. I leant across and said to the sentry, 'Will you have some food? We are going to eat.' Immediately everyone in the carriage stood up with one accord and pulled their stuff off the racks. The sentry also stood up, but was almost completely hidden from the window by a confused mass of men and bags. Under cover of this confusion, Buckley and I stood up on our seats. I slipped the strap of my haversack over my shoulder, pushed down the window, put my leg over and jumped into the night. I fell – not very heavily – on the wires at the side of the track, and lay still in the dark shadow. Three seconds later Buckley came flying out after me, and seemed to take rather a heavy toss. The end of the train wasn't yet past me, and we knew there was a man with a rifle in the last carriage; so when Buckley came running along the track calling out to me, I caught him and pulled him into the ditch at the side. The train went by, and its tail lights vanished round a corner and apparently no one saw or heard us.

I have not space to say much about our walk to the German-Swiss frontier, about two hundred miles away. We only walked by night, and lay up in hiding all through the hours of daylight which was, I think, the worst part of the business and wore out our nerves and physical strength far more than the six or seven hours marching at night, for the day seemed intolerably long from 4.30 a.m. to 9.30 p.m. – seventeen hours – the sun was very hot, and there was little shade, and we were consumed with impatience to get on. Moreover, we could never be free from anxiety at any moment of those seventeen hours. The strain at night of passing through a village, where a few lights still burnt and dogs seemed to wake and bark at us in every house, or of crossing a bridge when one expected to be challenged at any moment, never worried me so much as a cart passing or men talking near our daytime hiding-places.

We went into hiding at dawn or soon after, and when we'd taken off our boots and put on clean socks we would both drop asleep at once. It was a bit of a risk – perhaps one of us ought to have stayed awake, but we took it deliberately since we got great benefit from a sound sleep while we were still warm from walking. But it was only about an hour before we woke again shivering, for the mornings were very cold and we were usually soaked with dew up to our waists. Then we had breakfast – the great moment of the day – and rations were pretty good at first. However, we underestimated the time we would take by about four days, so later on we had to help things out with raw potatoes from the fields, which eventually became our mainstay. All day long we were pestered by stinging insects. Our hands and faces became swollen all over, and the bites on my feet came up in blisters which broke and left raw places when I put on my boots again.

On the fifteenth day our impatience got the better of us, and we started out before it was properly dark, and suddenly came upon a man in soldier's uniform scything grass at the side of the road. We were filthily dirty and unshaven and must have looked the most villainous tramps; it was stupid of us to have risked being seen; but it would have aroused his suspicion if we'd turned back, so we walked on past him. He looked up and said something we didn't catch. We answered: 'Good-evening,' as usual. But he called after us, and then when we took no notice, shouted: 'Halt! Halt!' and ran after us with his scythe.

We were both too weak to run fast or far, and moreover we saw at that moment a man with a gun about fifty yards to our right. There was only one thing to be done, and we did it.

We turned haughtily and waited for our pursuer, and when he was a few yards away Buckley demanded in a voice quivering with indignant German what the devil he meant by shouting at us. He almost dropped his scythe with astonishment then turned round and went slowly back to his work. Buckley had saved the day.

The end of our march on the following night brought us within fifteen kilometres of the Swiss frontier, and we decided to eat the rest of our food and cross the next night. However, I kept back a few small meat lozenges. We learnt the map by heart so as to avoid having to strike matches later on, and left all our spare kit behind us in order to travel light for this last lap. But it wasn't to be our last lap.

We were awfully weak by now and made slow progress through the heavy going, and about two hours after we'd started a full bright moon rose which made us feel frightfully conspicuous. Moreover, we began to doubt our actual position, for a road we'd expected to find wasn't there. However, we tramped on by compass and reached a village which we hoped was a place named Riedheim, within half a mile of the frontier. But here we suddenly came on a single line railway which wasn't on our map. We were aghast – we were lost – and moreover Buckley was fearfully exhausted for want of food, so we decided to lie up for another night in a thick wood on a hill. The meat lozenges I'd saved now came in very handy and we also managed to find water and some more raw potatoes. Then we slept, and when daylight came studied our small-scale map and tried to make head or tail of our situation.

We had a good view of the countryside from our position but could make nothing of it. Perhaps we were already in Switzerland? It was essential to know and it was no good looking for signposts since they'd all been removed within a radius of ten miles of the frontier. I think we were both slightly insane by now from hunger and fatigue; anyhow, I decided to take a great risk. I took off my tunic and walking down into the fields asked a girl who was making hay what the name of the village was. It was Riedheim as I'd originally thought. The railway of course had been made after the map was printed. I don't know what the girl thought of my question and appearance; she gave me a sly look, but went on with her work. I returned to Buckley, and when it was quite dark we left our hiding-place. We had three-quarters of an hour to cross the frontier before the moon rose – and we had to go with the greatest care. For a time we walked bent double, and then we went down on our hands and knees, pushing our way through the thick long grass of water meadows. The night was so still – surely the swishing of the grass as we moved through it must be audible for hundreds of yards. On and on we went – endlessly it seemed – making for a stream which we had seen from our hill and now knew must be the boundary line. Then the edge of the moon peered at us over the hills. We crawled at top speed now, until Buckley's hand on my heel suddenly brought me to a halt. About fifteen yards ahead was a sentry. He was walking along a footpath on the bank of a stream. *The* stream. He had no rifle, and had probably just been relieved. He passed without seeing us. One last spurt and we were in the stream and up the other bank. 'Crawl,' said Buckley. 'Run,' said I, and we ran. It was just after midnight when we crossed into Switzerland and freedom on our eighteenth night out.

J. S. FLETCHER

Joseph Smith Fletcher (1863–1935), novelist, was born in Halifax, son of a minister. Going to London at the age of eighteen, he became a freelance journalist and then a writer, pouring out a stream of poetry, biography and fiction, and producing over a hundred books. He wrote an authoritative history of Yorkshire (1901) and lives of Lord Roberts and Cardinal Newman, as well as some historical novels, but was best known for his detective stories, of which the most notable are *Middle Temple Murder* (1918), popularised by President Wilson's approval, *The Charing Cross Mystery* (1923) and *Murder in the Squire's Pew* (1932). His *Collected Verse* was published in 1931.

The Lighthouse on Shivering Sand

When Mordecai Chiddock came to join the lighthouse staff on Shivering Sand, Jezreel Cornish was taking his allowance of sleep, and Chiddock, being new to the place, did not know who it was he would meet when Cornish woke up. Otherwise, the boat which had brought him and a month's provisions over from the mainland would never have gone back without him.

Until Chiddock came we had never been more than two at the Shivering Sand. That was a bad arrangement, of course, and it was I who got the worst of it. Once Reuben Cleary fell sick, and had to take to his bed. That was just after the monthly boat had been, and until it came again I had to work night and day and nurse him into the bargain. Then there was Pharaoh Nanjulian; he was a melancholy sort from his youth, and the loneliness and monotony affected his brain. His wits gave out at last, and he used to spend the whole day in singing psalms and hymns, and preaching to the sea-birds. We had great storms that autumn, and the monthly boat came a fortnight late, and found me about done for, what with living day and night with a madman, and doing work for two. And it was because of what I said – not mincing matters – that it was decided to send a third man, so that in such cases as those of Cleary and Nanjulian the other man should not be utterly and badly alone.

Chiddock was the man who was sent. Of course, neither Cornish nor myself knew who would be sent; all we knew was that the September boat would bring a third keeper off with it.

It was a fine, bright morning when he came, and I watched him narrowly as he came on to the platform at the foot of the lighthouse, which you could only make at certain times. He was a thickset, swarthy man of middle age; he had curling black hair and beard, and his eyes were shiftier than I cared about. However, he bade me good-morning civilly enough, and when he had got his own things up from the boat, gave me a ready hand with the month's stores. It was not till the boat was off again that he seemed disposed for conversation.

'My name's Chiddock,' he says. 'Mordecai Chiddock.'

'Mine's John Graburn,' I answered him.

He offered me a plug of tobacco, and took a sort of comprehensive glance all around him.

'This,' he says, 'is a lonelier place than most of 'em.'

'You'll make all the more company,' I says. 'There'll be three of us now.'

He gave a glance at the door at the top of the stone stairway, as if he expected to see the third man appear.

'Ah,' he said, 'and what sort of shipmate is the other partner?'

'Oh, he's all right,' said I, offhand. 'He's only been here this last month, but he's a decent man, is Jezreel.'

Chiddock turned round on me like a flash, and I saw a queer look come into his eyes.

'Jezreel!' he said, short and sharp-like. 'That's an uncommon name. I knew a man of that name once. This man's other name, what might it be, now, Graburn?'

'Cornish,' I answered, 'Jezreel Cornish.'

Then I knew that something was amiss, for his cheeks lost all their dark colour and turned a strange pasty white, and I saw sweat burst out on them. He came a step nearer and looked at me with burning eyes, and his lips quivered under his black moustache.

'Jezreel Cornish!' he says, almost in a whisper. 'Jezreel Cornish! A tallish, scraggy-built man with a long, sharp nose and red hair and ferrety eyes; is it a man like that?'

'And what if it is?' I said, watching him.

He drew a long breath, and, turning, looked out across the bay after the boat from the mainland, as if he would call her back. But she was already a speck in the distance, and he turned again to me, breathing hard.

'If it is,' he says, muttering his words, 'if it is, mister – well, then, I wish I was in that craft out there, or on shore, or anywhere, that's all. Jezreel Cornish – ah!'

I saw his face suddenly change from white to red, and from red to white, and, turning, there was Cornish himself coming down the stairs, yawning and stretching after his sleep. And quick as lightning the newcomer's hand went round to his hip-pocket, and I guessed what he had there.

'If that's a pistol you've got,' I says, sharp and quick, 'you can leave it where it is. I'm boss here, and – '

He seemed to give no more heed to me than if I had been a child, and he kept his eyes on Cornish with the watchfulness of a dog that expects a blow. And I turned then to look at Cornish, wondering what it was that was about to happen.

He was not a quick man at noticing things, Cornish, and he had got to the foot of the stairs before he looked fully at Chiddock. But when he looked, I saw all the colour go out of his face, too, and when it came back it was a sort of dark red, and there was that in his eyes which meant murder. He crouched his body up and together, as an animal does when it's going to spring, and he came forward with his sharp teeth showing under his ragged red moustache; and I knew then that I was going to have a troublous time before the boat came again. For these two, Chiddock and Cornish, stood glaring at each other for all the world like wild beasts that are mad to be at grips, and I could see that it needed but a word to let hell loose between them.

Cornish was the first to speak, and I shouldn't have known his voice; it was so changed and so awful. And it was to me that he spoke, and not to Chiddock.

'Is this the new keeper, Graburn?' says he. 'Am I looking at him?'

'You are,' I says, 'and not any pleasanter than he's looking at you, Jezreel Cornish. And I'm not so blind that I can't see that there's black, cruel, bad blood between you two, and I tell you I'll have none of that sort of thing here; so mind your manners, both of you.'

'And he'll be here with us, night and day, shut up with us on Shivering Sand!' says Cornish, watching Chiddock with the eyes of a hungry devil. 'Shut up on Shivering Sand, and with me!'

'And with me, and both of you under my orders!' I rapped out sternly. 'And I'll see that – '

Cornish spat on the ground at his feet.

'Last time I set eyes on your devil's face, Mordecai Chiddock,' he says, in a voice that had suddenly turned as mild as milk, 'I told you I'd murder you when the time came for my chance. It's come! I've got you to myself now, and by God above, I'll kill you!'

What next happened was over in a flash. For Chiddock suddenly whipped the revolver out of his pocket and had Cornish covered. But before he could shoot I knocked it out of his hand, and the next instant had kicked it clean over the edge of the rock into the sea. And with that Chiddock suddenly turned more frightened than before, and it seemed to me that he was going to whimper like a child whose nurse has just checked it.

But Cornish only laughed in a sniggering, sneering fashion, and he turned away from us and went slowly up the stairway into the lighthouse, leaving Chiddock standing there before me with his limbs trembling as if he'd suddenly got the ague, and his damp face whiter than ever. When he spoke his voice was as spiritless as could be, and I saw the man was badly frightened.

'You've left me defenceless, Mr Graburn,' he says, in a queer-sounding voice. 'He'll kill me!'

'There's going to be no killing while I'm about here, my man,' I answered; 'and you'd best tell me what all this is about. There's a blood feud between you?'

But, instead of answering me directly, he began to talk and murmur to himself, and I could make nothing of what I overheard; and all the time he talked his eyes, as restless as a freshly trapped animal's, were searching the sea all round us, as if he hoped to signal some vessel to come and take him off.

'There's no living soul will come to this rock until the boat comes a month hence, Chiddock,' says I. 'You can make up your mind to that. So if you want me to help you you'd best speak, quick.'

He turned then, and glowered at me with a sullen rage burning in his eyes. 'If you hadn't treated me as you have,' he said, nodding towards the spot where the revolver had gone, 'I'd have shot him there and then, and been free of him. As it is, you'll have to stand between us.'

'Jezreel Cornish has no firearms,' I said. 'There's nothing on the rock but an old fowling-piece, and the powder and shot are in my care, and nobody but me can come at them.'

Now, this was not strictly true, because I had a revolver of my own carefully hidden away for emergencies; but I was not going to let anybody know of it. However, Chiddock seemed to think nothing of what I had just said.

'He'll kill me,' he repeated, 'and it'll be murder on your part if you let him! You'll have to get me away, Mr Graburn; and till you do, how will I get meat or sleep? I'm hungry and thirsty now.'

'It strikes me you're a coward!' says I. 'Sit you down while I go up and see what Cornish can tell me about this.'

He sat himself down on a rock as obediently as a child might, and I climbed the stair and made into our living-room, where I found Cornish eating and drinking as unconcernedly as if nothing had happened.

'Now then, Cornish,' I says, sitting down between him and the door, 'what's all this about? I'm headkeeper here, and I'm going to know what you're after.'

'What I'm after,' he says, coolly, 'is killing that man outside, which I shall surely do. There's no hurry. The last time I met him I told him what I should do, and I should have done it then, but he was too cunning, and gave me the slip. That he cannot do this time. He can't swim to the mainland, and he can't fly; he's netted. I can bide my time, but he'll never go off this rock alive!'

'What's he done to you?' I asked him. 'As you're so candid about killing him, you might as well be candid about the crime you've got against him.'

Before he answered he cut himself a great slab of the corned beef and ate heartily of it, just as if he hadn't a trouble in the world.

'That man,' he said at last, nodding towards the open door, through which you could see a patch of dancing sea, 'that man isn't a man at all; he's a devil! A low, mean, black devil, Mr Graburn. Him and me was shipmates once, and we were in Valparaiso together, and there we made a nice bit of money – never mind how. I was struck down with a bad fever; the last thing I remembered was trusting him with my money, and his promising to send most of it home to my wife in England. Then the deliriums came on, and I never knew any more until I came to in a charity hospital. The skunk had taken all I had and left me. What's more, he sailed home to England, found my wife, got her to sell up the home and a bit of a little shop she'd got together on pretence of sending the money to me, and persuaded her to trust him with the sending of it – which, naturally, he never did. And when I did come home, my wife was dead – died in the workhouse, where I found the kids. And, of course, I've got to kill him!'

'If all you say's true, Cornish,' I said, 'he deserves more than that. But I'll have no killing here, understand, now!'

'I don't say that I'll kill him today or tomorrow,' he says, paying no more heed to me than if I hadn't been there. 'Any time'll do me, now that he's trapped. I'll play with him as a cat plays with a mouse. I'll make him as he can't sleep o' nights with fear that death's close upon him. I shall enjoy thinking what way I'll kill him; I'll invent something good!'

'I'm inclined to think trouble and anger have turned your brain, Cornish,' says I.

'You can think what you're pleased to think,' he says, still as cold in his manner as a jellyfish, 'but you'll see Mordecai Chiddock's corpse before the boat comes again.'

'If his living body's turned into a corpse by you, Jezreel Cornish,' says I, 'you'll only swing for it.'

He laughed at that in his sneering fashion.

The sound of it made me frightened, for I could not bring myself to decide whether the man was in his right mind or gone out of his senses like Pharaoh Nanjulian.

'You wouldn't have a chance of escape,' I said.

'Who says I wanted one?' he says. 'Since I found my wife dead in the workhouse I've only lived to kill Mordecai Chiddock. And I say you shall see his corpse, Mr Graburn – and I don't care if you see mine after you've seen his. But I tell you, once for all, I'll kill him!'

I left him sitting there, still eating, and went down to the rocks again, to find Chiddock where I had left him. He turned round on me with fright in his eyes.

'If what I've heard about you is true,' I said, 'you're the lowest-down scoundrel I ever heard of, Chiddock. Death's too good for you, it's too easy. You ought to be skinned alive!'

'I knew that you'd side with him!' he growled. 'But it'll be found out, and it'll be murder against the two of you – mind you that, mister.'

'Leave that to me,' says I, and put down at his side some victuals and drink that I had brought out with me. 'And in the meantime,' I says, 'get that food into you and be more of a man.'

He made no reply to that, but fell upon the victuals like a famished wolf, while I turned back again to the lighthouse. I had a notion in my head, and I was going to put it into shape at once.

There was nothing for it but to keep these two men apart. That Cornish would kill Chiddock I now had no doubt – no more than that Chiddock would have killed Cornish if I had not knocked the revolver out of his hand. Now, that revolver had given me an idea. I, being the only man of the three with a weapon, was certainly master of the situation. And accordingly, as soon as I re-entered the lighthouse, I went to my own chamber, secured and loaded my revolver, and turned into the living-room to speak, with authority, to Jezreel Cornish.

Jezreel had finished his eating, but he still sat at his end of the table, staring moodily at the empty plate. I sat down at the other end; when he at last looked up it was to look straight into the barrel of the revolver.

'What's – what's the meaning of that?' he growled.

'The meaning, Jezreel, my lad, is that,' says I, 'I'm master here in more ways than one, but especially because I'm the only man of the three that's got a weapon. Now, you and the man outside are not going to meet. It's your turn for duty; you'll go up that stair, and I shall lock you in. When it's your hour for coming off I'll let you out; but you'll not see him, because he'll be locked up, too, until you're locked in your own chamber. You and him, Cornish, are going to do all the work this next month; I'm going to do nothing but play gaoler and cook until the boat comes and takes one of you off. Now you can just go up to your duty, and I'll draw the bolt on you. Get under way, Cornish!'

'And what if I don't?' he says, looking ugly.

'There's no ifs in this case,' says I. 'Come!'

He stared hard at me and the revolver for a good minute, then he pushed back his chair and got up.

'I want some tobacco out of the cupboard,' he says. 'I suppose I can get that?'

'You can get what you like out of the cupboard,' I answered him, 'so long as you get upstairs thereafter. And remember I've got the drop on you, Cornish.'

He mumbled something that I couldn't catch, and going over to the cupboard where we kept our general stores, went in. He mumbled and grumbled all the time he was in the cupboard, and his face was angry and scowling when he came out. But he marched straight off to the door of the winding stair which led up to the lantern, and in another second I had turned the key on him.

Now, I ought to tell you what this lighthouse was like. Some fifteen miles from the mainland, it stood on a gaunt, bare rock which rose behind a permanent bank in the sea, that had long been known as the Shivering Sand because of the strange motion of the water over it. The entrance was gained by a stone stairway, which led to a double door some twenty feet above the rock; when you passed that door you found yourself in the living-room, which made a half of the circular space of the lighthouse; the other half was divided into four segments, each forming a separate chamber. A winding stair went out of the living-room into an upper room, which we used for stores, material and suchlike; where it passed from one to the other was a strong door, the one that I had secured against Cornish's descent.

Above that was a stair of eighty-nine steps to the lamp-room and lantern, from which a revolving light shone out to warn all craft away from us.

So long as I was master I saw no difficulty in keeping Chiddock and Cornish separate. Every door in the place was fitted with a good strong lock; on Cornish's I resolved to fit a bolt from a store of hardware which I had by me. Before I released one man from duty I would lock the other in his room; when the released man was safely locked up I would let the other out.

All this being settled, and Cornish safely secured, I went to the door and called to Chiddock, telling him that it would now be safe for him to enter. He came to the foot of the stairway, cringing and fearful; the more I saw of him the more I knew what an arrant coward he was. As things turned out I had to go halfway down the stair and explain what I had done before he would consent to gather his things together and come up.

'Now then, Chiddock,' I said, showing him his chamber, 'this is your room. You know the arrangement. You came here to do one turn of work in three, as things are you'll do one in two. And keep to what I've arranged, or I'll let Jezreel Cornish loose on you.'

'He'll not forgive you for baulking him,' he muttered. 'Look to yourself, mister. You did me a bad turn in knocking that revolver away. I know Cornish when he's roused.'

I made no answer to that, but went about the job of fixing the bolt on the outside of Cornish's door. And with this and other things the afternoon passed quietly, and at the usual time I began to busy myself in making ready for supper.

Mordecai Chiddock sat watching me as if he meant to eat all that I was preparing for the table. For a man in his position and under such fear, he was the hungriest man I ever met, and when we sat down he fell upon the food and the hot coffee as if he had tasted nothing for years.

It gave me no pleasure to sit at meat with a man who had robbed his mate and his mate's wife and children, and I soon got up and left him to finish, after which I served out our usual allowance of rum. I made no answer when he gave me some sort of pledge or toast; instead, I carried my tot into my own chamber and sat down on my bunk to drink it at my leisure. After that I remember lying down for my usual forty winks and feeling more than usually sleepy, and then I remember nothing until I woke to find myself staring at Jezreel Cornish, whose sharp nose and ferrety eyes were very close to my face. It did not take a moment to realise that I was bound about arms and shoulders with a rope that pressed somewhat unpleasantly, and that my revolver was in Cornish's right hand.

'You made a mistake in letting me go to that cupboard, Graburn,' he said, sneering at me. 'I drugged the coffee and the rum.

'And as for locking me up like a gaolbird, you forgot that a man like me thinks nothing of coming down a hundred-foot rope. I told you I should kill Mordecai Chiddock.'

'You've murdered him!' I gasped.

'I'm murdering him,' he says, as cool as ever. 'He's a-staring his death in the face. I'm a merciful man, Graburn, I'm giving him time to repent. Come and see him die. And – quick!'

He suddenly menaced me so meaningly with the revolver that I struggled to my feet and let him half-pull, half-thrust me from the room. He forced me across the living-room, and through the double door, and down the stair upon the plateau of rock into the brightest and silverest moonlight I ever remember – a night so calm and still and beautiful that you'd have wondered any human being could have had anything but good thoughts in his heart between then and sunrise. But Jezreel Cornish was no longer a human being; the devil had taken possession of him.

'Come and see Mordecai Chiddock being a-murdered of, Graburn,' he said, chuckling as if it was all a joke. 'Come and hear him a-begging and a-praying for mercy – Mordecai what never had no mercy on man nor woman! Come, I tell you!' and he dragged me along as if I had been no more than an infant. 'Now look at Mordecai Chiddock, a-facing of his death like the brave sailorman he is!'

From the point to which he dragged me I could see all the devilish ingenuity of what Cornish had done. In the outline of the rock on which Shivering Sand Lighthouse stood there was a crescent-shaped indentation which might have been cut through as you cut into a cheese with a tin scoop. We stood on the edge of one side of this; on the other, dangling from ropes which had been fastened about his waist and under his armpits, the bright moonlight shining full upon him, hung Mordecai Chiddock, a swaying, trembling figure against the silent, pitiless rock behind him.

And he was up to his waist in the advancing tide, and he would soon be submerged and drowned!

I felt myself seized with a sudden fury at the sight of this specimen of Cornish's cruelty, and turned on him with a feeling that would have manifested itself in an attack on him if I had not been bound.

'You devil!' I cried. 'You – '

But he raised the revolver, and for a second I thought my time was come.

'Keep a civil tongue, Mr Graburn,' he said, sullenly. 'It doesn't much matter to me whether you live or die, but I don't want to murder you. After all, I'm not murdering Chiddock; I'm carrying out justice on him. Nice to hear him, isn't it?'

The wretch, swinging in the rising sea not ten yards in front of us, had caught sight of me and burst into frantic entreaties for help. But these entreaties were mingled with the most awful curses and blasphemies I had ever heard, and suddenly Cornish began to add a demoniac laughter and jeering to them.

There was nothing but Chiddock's head left above the waves at last. I knew exactly where the water would rise to, and that in another five minutes he would have gone. And Cornish knew that too, and an idea seemed to strike him. He laughed aloud – a devilish laugh that made my blood turn to ice.

'He's only a few minutes left,' he said. 'I'll go nearer and whisper a few words of parting to him. It'll be a friendly thing to remind him of what a lot of friends he'll meet presently.'

He made off towards the point where Chiddock was hanging, with the evident intention of calling over the edge into the wretched man's very ears.

As he came near, just as if providence had it in mind that he should be cheated of seeing his victim die, he tripped over the rope by which Chiddock was secured. He pitched head foremost over the edge of the rock, and I heard his head strike on the ledge beneath, and saw him cleave the oily-faced water like a plummet. And after that neither I nor any man ever saw Jezreel Cornish alive again.

It was then that I fainted, hearing a long cry of final despair from Chiddock. It may have been unconsciousness rather than fainting, for it was long after daybreak when I came round. I crawled to the edge of the rock, and looked into the cove. Chiddock hung limp against the rock, his head dangling on his shoulder.

I could do nothing to help myself; Cornish had made certain in securing me. During the day I contrived to drag myself into shelter against the fierce sunlight, but I almost went mad with hunger and thirst and horror of my situation. That night no light shone out from the Shivering Sand. But its failure saved me, for the darkened lighthouse roused suspicion, and before midnight a fast government vessel was at the rock to find one dead man hanging over the waves where another was tossing, and a man who was not far from dead, and utterly delirious, babbling incoherently of what he had seen.

MARY E. WILKINS FREEMAN

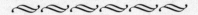

Mary Eleanor Wilkins Freeman was born in Randolph, Massachusetts on 31 October 1852. She passed the greater part of her life in Massachusetts and Vermont and for many years was the private secretary of Oliver Wendell Holmes. Freeman began writing stories and verse for children while still a teenager to help support her family and was quickly successful. Her best known work was written in the 1880s and 1890s while she lived in Randolph. She produced more than two dozen volumes of published short stories and novels. She is best known for two collections of stories, *A Humble Romance and Other Stories* (1887) and *A New England Nun and Other Stories* (1891), which deal mostly with New England life and are among the best of their kind. Freeman is also remembered for her novel *Pembroke* (1894), and she contributed a notable chapter to the collaborative novel *The Whole Family* (1908). In 1902 she married Dr Charles M. Freeman of Metuchen, New Jersey. In April 1926, Freeman became the first recipient of the William Dean Howells Medal for Distinction in Fiction from the American Academy of Arts and Letters. She died on 13 March 1930 and was interred in Hillside Cemetery in Scotch Plains, New Jersey.

The Shadows on the Wall

'Henry had words with Edward here in the study the night before Edward died,' said Caroline Glynn.

She was elderly, tall and harshly thin, with a hard colourlessness of face. She spoke not with acrimony, but with grave severity. Rebecca Ann Glynn, younger, stouter and rosy of face between her crinkling puffs of grey hair, gasped, by way of assent. She sat in a wide flounce of black silk in the corner of the sofa, and rolled terrified eyes from her sister Caroline to her sister Mrs Stephen Brigham, who had been Emma Glynn, the one beauty of the family. She was beautiful still, with a large, splendid, full-blown beauty; she filled a great rocking-chair with her superb bulk of femininity, and swayed gently back and forth, her black silks whispering and her black frills fluttering. Even the shock of death (for her brother Edward lay dead in the house) could not disturb her outward serenity of demeanour. She was grieved over the loss of her brother: he had been the youngest, and she had been fond of him, but never had Emma Brigham lost sight of her own importance amidst the waters of tribulation. She was always awake to the consciousness of her own stability in the midst of vicissitudes and the splendour of her permanent bearing.

But even her expression of masterly placidity changed before her sister Caroline's announcement and her sister Rebecca Ann's gasp of terror and distress in response.

'I think Henry might have controlled his temper, when poor Edward was so near his end,' said she with an asperity which disturbed slightly the roseate curves of her beautiful mouth.

'Of course he did not *know*,' murmured Rebecca Ann in a faint tone strangely out of keeping with her appearance.

One involuntarily looked again to be sure that such a feeble pipe came from that full-swelling chest.

'Of course he did not know it,' said Caroline quickly. She turned on her sister with a strange sharp look of suspicion. 'How could he have known it?' said she. Then she shrank as if from the other's possible answer. 'Of course you and I both know he could not,' said she conclusively, but her pale face was paler than it had been before.

Rebecca gasped again. The married sister was now sitting up straight in her chair; she had ceased rocking, and was eyeing them both intently with a sudden accentuation of family likeness in her face. Given one common intensity of emotion and similar lines showed the three sisters to be of one race.

'What do you mean?' said she impartially to them both. Then she, too, seemed to shrink before a possible answer. She even laughed an evasive sort of laugh. 'I guess you don't mean anything,' said she, but her face wore still the expression of shrinking horror.

'Nobody means anything,' said Caroline firmly. She rose and crossed the room towards the door with grim decisiveness.

'Where are you going?' asked Mrs Brigham.

'I have something to see to,' replied Caroline, and the others at once knew by her tone that she had some solemn and sad duty to perform in the chamber of death.

'Oh,' said Mrs Brigham.

After the door had closed behind Caroline, she turned to Rebecca.

'Did Henry have many words with him?' she asked.

'They were talking very loud,' replied Rebecca evasively, yet with an answering gleam of ready response to the other's curiosity in the quick lift of her soft blue eyes.

Mrs Brigham looked at her. She had not resumed rocking. She still sat up straight with a slight knitting of intensity on her fair forehead, between the pretty rippling curves of her auburn hair.

'Did you – hear anything?' she asked in a low voice with a glance towards the door.

'I was just across the hall in the south parlour, and that door was open and this door ajar,' replied Rebecca with a slight flush.

'Then you must have – '

'I couldn't help it.'

'Everything?'

'Most of it.'

'What was it?'

'The old story.'

'I suppose Henry was mad, as he always was, because Edward was living on here for nothing, when he had wasted all the money father left him.'

Rebecca nodded with a fearful glance at the door.

When Emma spoke again her voice was still more hushed. 'I know how he felt,' said she. 'He had always been so prudent himself, and worked hard at his profession, and there Edward had never done anything but spend, and it must have looked to him as if Edward was living at his expense, but he wasn't.'

'No, he wasn't.'

'It was the way father left the property – that all the children should have a home here – and he left money enough to buy the food and all if we had all come home.'

'Yes.'

'And Edward had a right here according to the terms of father's will, and Henry ought to have remembered it.'

'Yes, he ought.'

'Did he say hard things?'

'Pretty hard from what I heard.'

'What?'

'I heard him tell Edward that he had no business here at all, and he thought he had better go away.'

'What did Edward say?'

'That he would stay here as long as he lived and afterwards, too, if he had a mind to, and he would like to see Henry get him out; and then – '

'What?'

'Then he laughed.'

'What did Henry say.'

'I didn't hear him say anything, but – '

'But what?'

'I saw him when he came out of this room.'

'He looked mad?'

'You've seen him when he looked so.'

Emma nodded; the expression of horror on her face had deepened.

'Do you remember that time he killed the cat because she had scratched him?'

'Yes. Don't!'

Then Caroline re-entered the room. She went up to the stove in which a wood fire was burning – it was a cold, gloomy day of fall – and she warmed her hands, which were reddened from recent washing in cold water.

Mrs Brigham looked at her and hesitated. She glanced at the door, which was still ajar, as it did not easily shut, being still swollen with the damp weather of the summer. She rose and pushed it together with a sharp thud which jarred the house. Rebecca started painfully with a half exclamation. Caroline looked at her disapprovingly.

'It is time you controlled your nerves, Rebecca,' said she.

'I can't help it,' replied Rebecca with almost a wail. 'I am nervous. There's enough to make me so, the Lord knows.'

'What do you mean by that?' asked Caroline with her old air of sharp suspicion, and something between challenge and dread of its being met.

Rebecca shrank.

'Nothing,' said she.

'Then I wouldn't keep speaking in such a fashion.'

Emma, returning from the closed door, said imperiously that it ought to be fixed, it shut so hard.

'It will shrink enough after we have had the fire a few days,' replied Caroline. 'If anything is done to it it will be too small; there will be a crack at the sill.'

'I think Henry ought to be ashamed of himself for talking as he did to Edward,' said Mrs Brigham abruptly, but in an almost inaudible voice.

'Hush!' said Caroline, with a glance of actual fear at the closed door.

'Nobody can hear with the door shut.'

'He must have heard it shut, and – '

'Well, I can say what I want to before he comes down, and *I* am not afraid of him.'

'I don't know who is afraid of him! What reason is there for anybody to be afraid of Henry?' demanded Caroline.

Mrs Brigham trembled before her sister's look. Rebecca gasped again. 'There isn't any reason, of course. Why should there be?'

'I wouldn't speak so, then. Somebody might overhear you and think it was queer. Miranda Joy is in the south parlour sewing, you know.'

'I thought she went upstairs to stitch on the machine.'

'She did, but she has come down again.'

'Well, she can't hear.'

'I say again I think Henry ought to be ashamed of himself. I shouldn't think he'd ever get over it, having words with poor Edward the very night before he died. Edward was enough sight better disposition than Henry, with all his faults. I always thought a great deal of poor Edward, myself.'

Mrs Brigham passed a large fluff of handkerchief across her eyes; Rebecca sobbed outright.

'Rebecca,' said Caroline admonishingly, keeping her mouth stiff and swallowing determinately.

'I never heard him speak a cross word, but perhaps he spoke cross to Henry that last night. I don't know, but he did from what Rebecca overheard,' said Emma.

'Not so much cross as sort of soft, and sweet, and aggravating,' sniffled Rebecca.

'He never raised his voice,' said Caroline; 'but he had his way.'

'He had a right to in this case.'

'Yes, he did.'

'He had as much of a right here as Henry,' sobbed Rebecca, 'and now he's gone, and he will never be in this home that poor father left him and the rest of us again.'

'What do you really think ailed Edward?' asked Emma in hardly more than a whisper. She did not look at her sister.

Caroline sat down in a nearby armchair, and clutched the arms convulsively until her thin knuckles whitened.

'I told you,' said she.

Rebecca held her handkerchief over her mouth, and looked at them above it with terrified, streaming eyes.

'I know you said that he had terrible pains in his stomach, and had spasms, but what do you think made him have them?'

'Henry called it gastric trouble. You know Edward has always had dyspepsia.'

Mrs Brigham hesitated a moment. 'Was there any talk of an – examination?' said she.

Then Caroline turned on her fiercely.

'No,' said she in a terrible voice. 'No.'

The three sisters' souls seemed to meet on one common ground of terrified understanding through their eyes. The old-fashioned latch of the door was heard to rattle, and a push from without made the door shake ineffectually. 'It's Henry,' Rebecca sighed rather than whispered. Mrs Brigham settled herself after a noiseless rush across the floor into her rocking-chair again, and was swaying back and forth with her head comfortably leaning back, when the door at last yielded and Henry Glynn entered. He cast a covertly sharp, comprehensive glance at Mrs Brigham with her elaborate calm; at Rebecca quietly huddled in the corner of the sofa with her handkerchief to her face and only one small reddened ear as attentive as a dog's uncovered and revealing her alertness for his presence; at Caroline sitting with a strained composure in her armchair by the stove. She met his eyes quite firmly with a look of inscrutable fear, and defiance of the fear and of him.

Henry Glynn looked more like this sister than the others. Both had the same hard delicacy of form and feature, both were tall and almost emaciated, both had a sparse growth of grey blond hair far back from high intellectual foreheads, both had an almost noble aquilinity of feature. They confronted each other with the pitiless immovability of two statues in whose marble lineaments emotions were fixed for all eternity.

Then Henry Glynn smiled and the smile transformed his face. He looked suddenly years younger, and an almost boyish recklessness and irresolution appeared in his face. He flung himself into a chair with a gesture which was bewildering from its incongruity with his general appearance. He leaned his head back, flung one leg over the other, and looked laughingly at Mrs Brigham.

'I declare, Emma, you grow younger every year,' he said.

She flushed a little, and her placid mouth widened at the corners. She was susceptible to praise.

'Our thoughts today ought to belong to the one of us who will never grow older,' said Caroline in a hard voice.

Henry looked at her, still smiling. 'Of course, we none of us forget that,' said he, in a deep, gentle voice, 'but we have to speak to the living, Caroline, and I have not seen Emma for a long time, and the living are as dear as the dead.'

'Not to me,' said Caroline.

She rose, and went abruptly out of the room again. Rebecca also rose and hurried after her, sobbing loudly.

Henry looked slowly after them.

'Caroline is completely unstrung,' said he. Mrs Brigham rocked. A confidence in him inspired by his manner was stealing over her. Out of that confidence she spoke quite easily and naturally.

'His death was very sudden,' said she.

Henry's eyelids quivered slightly but his gaze was unswerving.

'Yes,' said he; 'it was very sudden. He was sick only a few hours.'

'What did you call it?'

'Gastric.'

'You did not think of an examination?'

'There was no need. I am perfectly certain as to the cause of his death.'

Suddenly Mrs Brigham felt a creep as of some live horror over her very soul. Her flesh prickled with cold, before an inflection of his voice. She rose, tottering on weak knees.

'Where are you going?' asked Henry in a strange, breathless voice.

Mrs Brigham said something incoherent about some sewing which she had to do, some black for the funeral, and was out of the room. She went up to the front chamber which she occupied. Caroline was there. She went close to her and took her hands, and the two sisters looked at each other.

'Don't speak, don't, I won't have it!' said Caroline finally in an awful whisper.

'I won't,' replied Emma.

That afternoon the three sisters were in the study, the large front room on the ground floor across the hall from the south parlour, when the dusk deepened.

Mrs Brigham was hemming some black material. She sat close to the west window for the waning light. At last she laid her work on her lap.

'It's no use, I cannot see to sew another stitch until we have a light,' said she.

Caroline, who was writing some letters at the table, turned to Rebecca, in her usual place on the sofa.

'Rebecca, you had better get a lamp,' she said.

Rebecca started up; even in the dusk her face showed her agitation.

'It doesn't seem to me that we need a lamp quite yet,' she said in a piteous, pleading voice like a child's.

'Yes, we do,' returned Mrs Brigham peremptorily. 'We must have a light.

I must finish this tonight or I can't go to the funeral, and I can't see to sew another stitch.'

'Caroline can see to write letters, and she is farther from the window than you are,' said Rebecca.

'Are you trying to save kerosene or are you lazy, Rebecca Glynn?' cried Mrs Brigham. 'I can go and get the light myself, but I have this work all in my lap.'

Caroline's pen stopped scratching.

'Rebecca, we must have the light,' said she.

'Had we better have it in here?' asked Rebecca weakly.

'Of course! Why not?' cried Caroline sternly.

'I am sure I don't want to take my sewing into the other room, when it is all cleaned up for tomorrow,' said Mrs Brigham.

'Why, I never heard such a to-do about lighting a lamp.'

Rebecca rose and left the room. Presently she entered with a lamp – a large one with a white porcelain shade. She set it on a table, an old-fashioned card-table which was placed against the opposite wall from the window. That wall was clear of bookcases and books, which were only on three sides of the room. That opposite wall was taken up with three doors, the one small space being occupied by the table. Above the table on the old-fashioned paper, of a white satin gloss, traversed by an indeterminate green scroll, hung quite high a small gilt-and-black-framed ivory miniature taken in her girlhood of the mother of the family. When the lamp was set on the table beneath it, the tiny pretty face painted on the ivory seemed to gleam out with a look of intelligence.

'What have you put that lamp over there for?' asked Mrs Brigham, with more of impatience than her voice usually revealed. 'Why didn't you set it in the hall and have done with it. Neither Caroline nor I can see if it is on that table.'

'I thought perhaps you would move,' replied Rebecca hoarsely.

'If I do move, we can't both sit at that table. Caroline has her paper all spread around. Why don't you set the lamp on the study table in the middle of the room, then we can both see?'

Rebecca hesitated. Her face was very pale. She looked with an appeal that was fairly agonising at her sister Caroline.

'Why don't you put the lamp on this table, as she says?' asked Caroline, almost fiercely. 'Why do you act so, Rebecca?'

'I should think you *would* ask her that,' said Mrs Brigham. 'She doesn't act like herself at all.'

Rebecca took the lamp and set it on the table in the middle of the room without another word. Then she turned her back upon it quickly and seated herself on the sofa, and placed a hand over her eyes as if to shade them, and remained so.

'Does the light hurt your eyes, and is that the reason why you didn't want the lamp?' asked Mrs Brigham kindly.

'I always like to sit in the dark,' replied Rebecca chokingly. Then she snatched her handkerchief hastily from her pocket and began to weep. Caroline continued to write, Mrs Brigham to sew.

Suddenly Mrs Brigham as she sewed glanced at the opposite wall. The glance became a steady stare. She looked intently, her work suspended in her hands. Then she looked away again and took a few more stitches, then she looked again, and again turned to her task. At last she laid her work in her lap and stared concentratedly. She looked from the wall around the room, taking note of the various objects; she looked at the wall long and intently. Then she turned to her sisters.

'What *is* that?' said she.

'What?' asked Caroline harshly; her pen scratched loudly across the paper.

Rebecca gave one of her convulsive gasps.

'That strange shadow on the wall,' replied Mrs Brigham.

Rebecca sat with her face hidden: Caroline dipped her pen in the inkstand.

'Why don't you turn around and look?' asked Mrs Brigham in a wondering and somewhat aggrieved way.

'I am in a hurry to finish this letter, if Mrs Wilson Ebbit is going to get word in time to come to the funeral,' replied Caroline shortly.

Mrs Brigham rose, her work slipping to the floor, and she began walking around the room, moving various articles of furniture, with her eyes on the shadow.

Then suddenly she shrieked out: 'Look at this awful shadow! What is it? Caroline, look, look! Rebecca, look! *What is it?*'

All Mrs Brigham's triumphant placidity was gone. Her handsome face was livid with horror. She stood stiffly pointing at the shadow.

'Look!' said she, pointing her finger at it. 'Look! What is it?'

Then Rebecca burst out in a wild wail after a shuddering glance at the wall: 'Oh, Caroline, there it is again! There it is again!'

'Caroline Glynn, you look!' said Mrs Brigham. 'Look! What is that dreadful shadow?'

Caroline rose, turned, and stood confronting the wall.

'How should I know?' she said.

'It has been there every night since he died,' cried Rebecca.

'Every night?'

'Yes. He died Thursday and this is Saturday; tonight makes three nights,' said Caroline rigidly. She stood as if holding herself calm with a vice of concentrated will.

'It – it looks like – like – ' stammered Mrs Brigham in a tone of intense horror.

'I know what it looks like well enough,' said Caroline. 'I've got eyes in my head.'

'It looks like Edward,' burst out Rebecca in a sort of frenzy of fear. 'Only – '

'Yes, it does,' assented Mrs Brigham, whose horror-stricken tone matched her sister's, 'only – Oh, it is awful! What is it, Caroline?'

'I ask you again, how should I know?' replied Caroline. 'I see it there like you. How should I know any more than you?'

'It *must* be something in the room,' said Mrs Brigham, staring wildly around.

'We moved everything in the room the first night it came,' said Rebecca; 'it is not anything in the room.'

Caroline turned upon her with a sort of fury. 'Of course it is something in the room,' said she. 'How you act! What do you mean by talking so? Of course it is something in the room.'

'Of course, it is,' agreed Mrs Brigham, looking at Caroline suspiciously. 'Of course it must be. It is only a coincidence. It just happens so. Perhaps it is that fold of the window curtain that makes it. It must be something in the room.'

'It is not anything in the room,' repeated Rebecca with obstinate horror.

The door opened suddenly and Henry Glynn entered. He began to speak, then his eyes followed the direction of the others' gaze. He stood stock still staring at the shadow on the wall. It was life size and stretched half across the white parallelogram of a door, half across the wall space on which the picture hung.

'What is that?' he demanded in a strange voice.

'It must be due to something in the room,' Mrs Brigham said faintly.

'It is not due to anything in the room,' said Rebecca again with the shrill insistency of terror.

'How you act, Rebecca Glynn,' said Caroline.

Henry Glynn stood and stared a moment longer. His face showed a gamut of emotions – horror, conviction, then furious incredulity. Suddenly he began hastening hither and thither about the room. He moved the furniture with fierce jerks, turning ever to see the effect upon the shadow on the wall. Not a line of its terrible outline wavered.

'It must be something in the room!' he declared in a voice which seemed to snap like a lash.

His face changed. The inmost secrecy of his nature seemed evident until one almost lost sight of his lineaments. Rebecca stood close to her sofa, regarding him with woeful, fascinated eyes. Mrs Brigham clutched Caroline's hand. They both stood in a corner out of his way. For a few moments he raged about the room like a caged wild animal. He moved every piece of furniture; when the moving of a piece did not affect the shadow, he flung it to the floor, his sisters watching.

Then suddenly he desisted. He laughed and began straightening the furniture which he had flung down.

'What an absurdity,' he said easily. 'Such a to-do about a shadow.'

'That's so,' assented Mrs Brigham, in a scared voice which she tried to make natural. As she spoke she lifted a chair near her.

'I think you have broken the chair that Edward was so fond of,' said Caroline.

Terror and wrath were struggling for expression on her face. Her mouth was set, her eyes shrinking. Henry lifted the chair with a show of anxiety.

'Just as good as ever,' he said pleasantly. He laughed again, looking at his sisters. 'Did I scare you?' he said. 'I should think you might be used to me by this time. You know my way of wanting to leap to the bottom of a mystery, and that shadow does look – queer – and I thought if there was any way of accounting for it I would like to without any delay.'

'You don't seem to have succeeded,' remarked Caroline dryly, with a slight glance at the wall.

Henry's eyes followed hers and he quivered perceptibly.

'Oh, there is no accounting for shadows,' he said, and he laughed again. 'A man is a fool to try to account for shadows.'

Then the supper bell rang, and they all left the room, but Henry kept his back to the wall, as did, indeed, the others.

Mrs Brigham pressed close to Caroline as she crossed the hall. 'He looked like a demon!' she breathed in her ear.

Henry led the way with an alert motion like a boy; Rebecca brought up the rear; she could scarcely walk, her knees trembled so.

'I can't sit in that room again this evening,' she whispered to Caroline after supper.

'Very well, we will sit in the south room,' replied Caroline. 'I think we will sit in the south parlour,' she said aloud; 'it isn't as damp as the study, and I have a cold.'

So they all sat in the south room with their sewing. Henry read the newspaper, his chair drawn close to the lamp on the table. About nine o'clock he rose abruptly and crossed the hall to the study. The three sisters looked at one another. Mrs Brigham rose, folded her rustling skirts compactly around her, and began tiptoeing towards the door.

'What are you going to do?' enquired Rebecca agitatedly.

'I am going to see what he is about,' replied Mrs Brigham cautiously.

She pointed as she spoke to the study door across the hall; it was ajar. Henry had striven to pull it together behind him, but it had somehow swollen beyond the limit with curious speed. It was still ajar and a streak of light showed from top to bottom. The hall lamp was not lit.

'You had better stay where you are,' said Caroline with guarded sharpness.

'I am going to see,' repeated Mrs Brigham firmly.

Then she folded her skirts so tightly that her bulk with its swelling curves was revealed in a black silk sheath, and she went with a slow toddle across the hall to the study door. She stood there, her eye at the crack.

In the south room Rebecca stopped sewing and sat watching with dilated eyes. Caroline sewed steadily. What Mrs Brigham, standing at the crack in the study door, saw was this:

Henry Glynn, evidently reasoning that the source of the strange shadow must be between the table on which the lamp stood and the wall, was making systematic passes and thrusts all over and through the intervening space with an old sword which had belonged to his father. Not an inch was left unpierced. He seemed to have divided the space into mathematical sections. He brandished the sword with a sort of cold fury and calculation; the blade gave out flashes of light, the shadow remained unmoved. Mrs Brigham, watching, felt herself cold with horror.

Finally Henry ceased and stood with the sword in hand and raised as if to strike, surveying the shadow on the wall threateningly. Mrs Brigham toddled back across the hall and shut the south-room door behind her before she related what she had seen.

'He looked like a demon!' she said again. 'Have you got any of that old wine in the house, Caroline? I don't feel as if I could stand much more.'

Indeed, she looked overcome. Her handsome placid face was worn and strained and pale.

'Yes, plenty,' said Caroline; 'you can have some when you go to bed.'

'I think we had all better take some,' said Mrs Brigham. 'Oh, my God, Caroline, what – '

'Don't ask and don't speak,' said Caroline.

'No, I am not going to,' replied Mrs Brigham; 'but – '

Rebecca moaned aloud.

'What are you doing that for?' asked Caroline harshly.

'Poor Edward,' returned Rebecca.

'That is all you have to groan for,' said Caroline. 'There is nothing else.'

'I am going to bed,' said Mrs Brigham. 'I shan't be able to be at the funeral if I don't.'

Soon the three sisters went to their chambers and the south parlour was deserted. Caroline called to Henry in the study to put out the light before he came upstairs. They had been gone about an hour when he came into the room bringing the lamp which had stood in the study. He set it on the table and waited a few minutes, pacing up and down. His face was terrible, his fair complexion showed livid; his blue eyes seemed dark blanks of awful reflections.

Then he took the lamp up and returned to the library. He set the lamp on the centre table, and the shadow sprang out on the wall. Again he studied the furniture and moved it about, but deliberately, with none of his former frenzy. Nothing affected the shadow. Then he returned to the south room with the lamp and again waited. Again he returned to the study and placed the lamp on the table, and the shadow sprang out upon the wall. It was midnight before he went upstairs. Mrs Brigham and the other sisters, who could not sleep, heard him.

The next day was the funeral. That evening the family sat in the south room. Some relatives were with them. Nobody entered the study until Henry carried a lamp in there after the others had retired for the night. He saw again the shadow on the wall leap to an awful life before the light.

The next morning at breakfast Henry Glynn announced that he had to go to the city for three days. The sisters looked at him with surprise. He very seldom left home, and just now his practice had been neglected on account of Edward's death. He was a physician.

'How can you leave your patients now?' asked Mrs Brigham wonderingly.

'I don't know how to, but there is no other way,' replied Henry easily. 'I have had a telegram from Dr Mitford.'

'Consultation?' enquired Mrs Brigham.

'I have business,' replied Henry.

Dr Mitford was an old classmate of his who lived in a neighbouring city and who occasionally called upon him in the case of a consultation.

After he had gone Mrs Brigham said to Caroline that after all Henry had not said that he was going to consult with Dr Mitford, and she thought it very strange.

'Everything is very strange,' said Rebecca with a shudder.

'What do you mean?' enquired Caroline sharply.

'Nothing,' replied Rebecca.

Nobody entered the library that day, nor the next, nor the next. The third day Henry was expected home, but he did not arrive and the last train from the city had come.

'I call it pretty queer work,' said Mrs Brigham. 'The idea of a doctor leaving his patients for three days anyhow, at such a time as this, and I know he has some very sick ones; he said so. And the idea of a consultation lasting three days! There is no sense in it, and *now* he is not returned. I don't understand it, for my part.'

'I don't either,' said Rebecca.

They were all in the south parlour. There was no light in the study opposite, and the door was ajar.

Presently Mrs Brigham rose – she could not have told why; something seemed to impel her, some will outside her own. She went out of the room, again wrapping her rustling skirts around that she might pass noiselessly, and began pushing at the swollen door of the study.

'She has not got any lamp,' said Rebecca in a shaking voice.

Caroline, who was writing letters, rose again, took a lamp (there were two in the room) and followed her sister. Rebecca had risen, but she stood trembling, not venturing to follow.

The doorbell rang, but the others did not hear it; it was on the south door on the other side of the house from the study. Rebecca, after hesitating until the bell rang the second time, went to the door; she remembered that the servant was out.

Caroline and her sister Emma entered the study. Caroline set the lamp on the table. They looked at the wall. 'Oh, my God,' gasped Mrs Brigham, 'there are – there are *two*– shadows.' The sisters stood clutching each other, staring at the awful things on the wall. Then Rebecca came in, staggering, with a telegram in her hand. 'Here is – a telegram,' she gasped. 'Henry is – dead.'

E. W. HORNUNG

Ernest William Hornung (1866–1921), novelist, was born at
Middlesbrough, Yorkshire, and educated at Uppingham. From
1884 to 1886 he lived in Australia for his health and afterwards
he wrote two novels with an Australian background, *A Bride from
the Bush* (1890) and *The Boss of Taroomba* (1894). Returning to
England, he married Constance Doyle, sister of Conan Doyle,
in 1893. In 1899 his well-known book *The Amateur Cracksman*
appeared, with its hero Raffles the gentleman-burglar making a
sort of foil to his brother-in-law's detective Sherlock Holmes.
Three further collections of these adventures appeared, *Raffles*
(1901), *A Thief in the Night* (1905) and *Mr Justice Raffles* (1909).
During the First World War Hornung travelled in France with
a mobile library for the use of the troops. *Notes of a Camp
Follower on the Western Front* (1919) tells of his experiences and
The Young Guard is a book of war poems.

The Wrong House

My old school friend Ralph, who now lived with me on the edge of Ham
Common, had come home from Australia with a curious affection of the
eyes, due to long exposure to the glare out there, which necessitated the use
of clouded spectacles in the open air. He had not the rich complexion of the
typical colonist, being indeed peculiarly pale, but it appeared that he had
been confined to his berth for the greater part of the voyage home, while his
prematurely grey hair was further proof that the rigours of bush life had at
last undermined an originally tough constitution. Our landlady, who spoilt
him from the first, was much concerned on his behalf, and wished to call in
the local doctor; but Ralph said dreadful things about the profession, and
quite frightened the good woman by arbitrarily forbidding her ever to let a
doctor inside her door. I had to apologise to her for the painful prejudices
and violent language of 'these colonists', but the old soul was easily mollified.
She had fallen in love with Raffles at first sight, and she never could do too
much for him. It was owing to our landlady that I took to calling him Ralph,
for the first time in our lives, on her beginning to speak of and to him as 'Mr
Raffles'.

'This won't do,' said he to me. 'It's a name that sticks.'

'It must be my fault! She must have heard it from me,' said I self-
reproachfully.

'You must tell her it's the short for Ralph.'

'But it's longer.'

'It's the short,' said he; 'and you've got to tell her so.'

Henceforth I heard so much of 'Mr Ralph', his likes and dislikes, what he
would fancy and what he would not, and oh, what a dear gentleman he was,
that I often remembered to say, 'Ralph, old chap,' myself.

It was an ideal cottage, as I said when I found it, and in it our delicate man
became rapidly robust. Not that the air was also ideal, for, when it was not
raining, we had the same faithful mist from November to March. But it was
something to Ralph to get any air at all, other than night-air, and the bicycle
did the rest. We taught ourselves, and may I never forget our earlier rides,
through and through Richmond Park when the afternoons were shortest,
upon the incomparable Ripley Road when we gave a day to it. Raffles rode a
Beeston Humber, a Royal Sunbeam was good enough for me, but he
insisted on our both having Dunlop tires.

'They seem the most popular brand. I had my eye on the road all the way from Ripley to Cobham, and there were more Dunlop marks than any other kind. Bless you, yes, they all leave their special tracks, and we don't want ours to be extra special; the Dunlop's like a rattlesnake, and the Palmer leaves telegraph-wires, but surely the serpent is more in our line.'

That was the winter when there were so many burglaries in the Thames Valley from Richmond upward. It was said that the thieves used bicycles in every case, but what is not said? They were sometimes on foot to my knowledge, and we took a great interest in the series, or rather sequence of successful crimes. Raffles would often get his devoted old lady to read him the latest local accounts, while I was busy with my writing (much I wrote) in my own room. We even rode out by night ourselves, to see if we could not get on the tracks of the thieves, and never did we fail to find hot coffee on the hob for our return. We had indeed fallen upon our feet. Also, the misty nights might have been made for the thieves. But their success was not so consistent, and never so enormous as people said, especially the sufferers, who lost more valuables than they had ever been known to possess. Failure was often the caitiff's portion, and disaster once; owing, ironically enough, to that very mist which should have served them. But as I am going to tell the story with some particularity, and perhaps some gusto, you will see why who read.

The right house stood on high ground near the river, with quite a drive (in at one gate and out at the other) sweeping past the steps. Between the two gates was a half-moon of shrubs, to the left of the steps a conservatory, and to their right the walk leading to the tradesmen's entrance and the back premises; here also was the pantry window, of which more anon. The right house was the residence of an opulent stockbroker who wore a heavy watch-chain and seemed fair game. There would have been two objections to it had I been the stockbroker. The house was one of a row, though a goodly row, and an army-crammer had established himself next door. There is a type of such institutions in the suburbs; the youths go about in knickerbockers, smoking pipes, except on Saturday nights, when they lead each other home from the last train. It was none of our business to spy upon these boys, but their manners and customs fell within the field of observation. And we did not choose the night upon which the whole row was likely to be kept awake.

The night that we did choose was as misty as even the Thames Valley is capable of making them. Raffles smeared vaseline upon the plated parts of his Beeston Humber before starting, and our dear landlady cosseted us both, and prayed we might see nothing of the nasty burglars, not denying as the reward would be very handy to them that got it, to say nothing of the honour and glory. We had promised her a liberal perquisite in the event of our success, but she must not give other cyclists our idea by mentioning it to a soul. It was about midnight when we cycled through Kingston to Surbiton, having trundled our machines across Ham Fields, mournful in the mist as those by Acheron, and so over Teddington Bridge.

I often wonder why the pantry window is the vulnerable point of nine houses out of ten. This house of ours was almost the tenth, for the window in question had bars of sorts, but not the right sort. The only bars that Raffles allowed to beat him were the kind that are let into the stone outside; those fixed within are merely screwed to the woodwork, and you can unscrew as many as necessary if you take the trouble and have the time. Barred windows are usually devoid of other fasteners worthy the name; this one was no exception to that foolish rule, and a push with the penknife did its business. I am giving householders some valuable hints, and perhaps deserving a good mark from the critics. These, in any case, are the points that I would see to, were I a rich stockbroker in a riverside suburb. In giving good advice, however, I should not have omitted to say that we had left our machines in the semicircular shrubbery in front, or that Raffles had most ingeniously fitted our lamps with dark slides, which enabled us to leave them burning.

It proved sufficient to unscrew the bars at the bottom only, and then to wrench them to either side. Neither of us had grown stout with advancing years, and in a few minutes we both had wormed through into the sink, and thence to the floor. It was not an absolutely noiseless process, but once in the pantry we were mice, and no longer blind mice. There was a gas-bracket, but we did not meddle with that. Raffles went armed these nights with a better light than gas; if it were not immoral, I might recommend a dark-lantern which was more or less his patent. It was that handy invention, the electric torch, fitted by Raffles with a dark hood to fulfil the functions of a slide. I had held it through the bars while he undid the screws, and now he held it to the keyhole, in which a key had been turned upon the other side.

There was a pause for consideration, and in the pause we put on our masks. It was never known that these Thames Valley robberies were all committed by miscreants decked in the livery of crime, but that was because until this night we had never even shown our masks. It was a point upon which Raffles had insisted on all feasible occasions since his furtive return to the world. Tonight it twice nearly lost us everything – but you shall hear.

There is a forceps for turning keys from the wrong side of the door, but the implement is not so easy of manipulation as it might be. Raffles for one preferred a sharp knife and the corner of the panel. You go through the panel because that is thinnest, of course in the corner nearest the key, and you use a knife when you can, because it makes least noise. But it does take minutes, and even I can remember shifting the electric torch from one hand to the other before the aperture was large enough to receive the hand and wrist of Raffles.

He had at such times a motto of which I might have made earlier use, but the fact is that I have only once before described a downright burglary in which I assisted, and that without knowing it at the time. The most solemn student of these annals cannot affirm that he has cut through many doors in our company, since (what was to me) the maiden effort to which I allude. I, however, have cracked only too many a crib in conjunction with A. J. Raffles, and at the crucial moment he would whisper 'Victory or Wormwood Scrubbs, Bunny!' or instead of Wormwood Scrubbs it might be Portland Bill. This time it was neither one nor the other, for with that very word 'victory' upon his lips, they whitened and parted with the first taste of defeat.

'My hand's held!' gasped Raffles, and the white of his eyes showed all round the iris, a rarer thing than you may think.

At the same moment I heard the shuffling feet and the low, excited young voices on the other side of the door, and a faint light shone round Raffles's wrist.

'Well done, Beefy!'

'Hang on to him!'

'Good old Beefy!'

'Beefy's got him!'

'So have I – so have I!'

And Raffles caught my arm with his one free hand. 'They've got me tight,' he whispered. 'I'm done.'

'Blaze through the door,' I urged, and might have done it had I been armed. But I never was. It was Raffles who monopolised that risk.

'I can't – it's the boys – the wrong house!' he whispered. 'Curse the fog – it's done me. But you get out, Bunn, while you can; never mind me; it's my turn, old chap.'

His one hand tightened in affectionate farewell. I put the electric torch in it before I went, trembling in every inch, but without a word.

Get out! His turn! Yes, I would get out, but only to come in again, for it was my turn – mine – not his. Would Raffles leave me held by a hand through a hole in a door? What he would have done in my place was the thing for me to do now. I began by diving headfirst through the pantry window and coming to earth upon all fours. But even as I stood up, and brushed the gravel from the palms of my hands and the knees of my knickerbockers, I had no notion what to do next. And yet I was halfway to the front door before I remembered the vile crape mask upon my face, and tore it off as the door flew open and my feet were on the steps.

'He's into the next garden,' I cried to a bevy of pyjamas with bare feet and young faces at either end of them.

'Who? Who?' said they, giving way before me.

'Some fellow who came through one of your windows headfirst.'

'The other Johnny, the other Johnny,' the cherubs chorused.

'Biking past – saw the light – why, what have you there?'

Of course it was Raffles's hand that they had, but now I was in the hall among them. A red-faced barrel of a boy did all the holding, one hand round the wrist, the other palm to palm, and his knees braced up against the panel. Another was rendering ostentatious but ineffectual aid, and three or four others danced about in their pyjamas. After all, they were not more than four to one. I had raised my voice, so that Raffles might hear me and take heart, and now I raised it again. Yet to this day I cannot account for my inspiration – it proved nothing less.

'Don't talk so loud,' they were crying below their breath; 'don't wake 'em upstairs, this is our show.'

'Then I see you've got one of them,' said I, as desired. 'Well, if you want the other you can have him, too. I believe he's hurt himself.'

'After him, after him!' they exclaimed as one.

'But I think he got over the wall – '

'Come on, you chaps, come on!'

And there was a soft stampede to the hall door.

'Don't all desert me, I say!' gasped the red-faced hero who held Raffles prisoner.

'We must have them both, Beefy!'

'That's all very well – '

'Look here,' I interposed, 'I'll stay by you. I've a friend outside, I'll get him too.'

'Thanks awfully,' said the valiant Beefy.

The hall was empty now. My heart beat high.

'How did you hear them?' I enquired, my eye running over him.

'We were down having drinks – game o' nap – in there.'

Beefy jerked his great head towards an open door, and the tail of my eye caught the glint of glasses in the firelight, but the rest of it was otherwise engaged.

'Let me relieve you,' I said, trembling.

'No, I'm all right.'

'Then I must insist.'

And before he could answer I had him round the neck with such a will that not a gurgle passed my fingers, for they were almost buried in his hot, smooth flesh. Oh, I am not proud of it; the act was as vile as act could be; but I was not going to see Raffles taken, my one desire was to be the saving of him, and I tremble even now to think to what lengths I might have gone for its fulfilment. As it was, I squeezed and tugged until one strong hand gave way after the other and came feeling round for me, but feebly because they had held on so long. And what do you suppose was happening at the same moment? The pinched white hand of Raffles, reddening with returning blood, and with a clot of blood upon the wrist, was craning upward and turning the key in the lock without a moment's loss.

'Steady on, Bunny!'

And I saw that Beefy's ears were blue; but Raffles was feeling in his pockets as he spoke. 'Now let him breathe,' said he, clapping his handkerchief over the poor youth's mouth. An empty vial was in his other hand, and the first few stertorous breaths that the poor boy took were the end of him for the time being. Oh, but it was villainous, my part especially, for he must have been far gone to go the rest of the way so readily. I began by saying I was not proud of this deed, but its dastardly character has come home to me more than ever with the penance of writing it out. I see in myself, at least my then self, things that I never saw quite so clearly before. Yet let me be quite sure that I would not do the same again. I had not the smallest desire to throttle this innocent lad (nor did I), but only to extricate Raffles from the most hopeless position he was ever in; and after all it was better than a blow from behind. On the whole, I will not alter a word, nor whine about the thing any more.

We lifted the plucky fellow into Raffles's place in the pantry, locked the door on him, and put the key through the panel. Now was the moment for thinking of ourselves, and again that infernal mask which Raffles swore by came near the undoing of us both. We had reached the steps when we were hailed by a voice, not from without but from within, and I had just time to tear the accursed thing from Raffles's face before he turned.

A stout man with a blond moustache was on the stairs, in his pyjamas like the boys.

'What are you doing here?' said he.

'There has been an attempt upon your house,' said I, still spokesman for the night, and still on the wings of inspiration. 'Your sons – '

'My pupils.'

'Indeed. Well, they heard it, drove off the thieves, and have given chase.'

'And where do you come in?' enquired the stout man, descending.

'We were bicycling past, and I actually saw one fellow come headfirst through your pantry window. I think he got over the wall.'

Here a breathless boy returned.

'Can't see anything of him,' he gasped.

'It's true, then,' remarked the crammer.

'Look at that door,' said I.

But unfortunately the breathless boy looked also, and now he was being joined by others equally short of wind.

'Where's Beefy?' he screamed. 'What on earth's happened to Beefy?'

'My good boys,' exclaimed the crammer, 'will one of you be kind enough to tell me what you've been doing, and what these gentlemen have been doing for you? Come in all, before you get your death. I see lights in the classroom, and more than lights. Can these be signs of a carouse?'

'A very innocent one, sir,' said a well-set-up youth with more moustache than I have yet.

'Well, Olphert, boys will be boys. Suppose you tell me what happened, before we come to recriminations.'

The bad old proverb was my first warning. I caught two of the youths exchanging glances under raised eyebrows. Yet their stout, easy-going mentor had given me such a reassuring glance of sidelong humour, as between man of the world and man of the world, that it was difficult to suspect him of suspicion. I was nevertheless itching to be gone.

Young Olphert told his story with engaging candour. It was true that they had come down for an hour's nap and cigarettes; well, and there was no denying that there was whisky in the glasses. The boys were now all back in their classroom, I think entirely for the sake of warmth; but Raffles and I were in knickerbockers and Norfolk jackets, and very naturally remained without, while the army-crammer (who wore bedroom slippers) stood on the threshold, with an eye each way. The more I saw of the man the better I liked and the more I feared him. His chief annoyance thus far was that they had not called him when they heard the noise, that they had dreamt of leaving him out of the fun. But he seemed more hurt than angry about that.

'Well, sir,' concluded Olphert, 'we left old Beefy Smith hanging on to his hand, and this gentleman with him, so perhaps he can tell us what happened next?'

'I wish I could,' I cried with all their eyes upon me, for I had had time to think. 'Some of you must have heard me say I'd fetch my friend in from the road?'

'Yes, I did,' piped an innocent from within.

'Well, and when I came back with him things were exactly as you see them now. Evidently the man's strength was too much for the boy's; but whether he ran upstairs or outside I know no more than you do.'

'It wasn't like that boy to run either way,' said the crammer, cocking a clear blue eye on me.

'But if he gave chase!'

'It wasn't like him even to let go.'

'I don't believe Beefy ever would,' put in Olphert. 'That's why we gave him the billet.'

'He may have followed him through the pantry window,' I suggested wildly.

'But the door's shut,' put in a boy.

'I'll have a look at it,' said the crammer.

And the key no longer in the lock, and the insensible youth within! The key would be missed, the door kicked in; nay, with the man's eye still upon me, I thought I could smell the chloroform,

I thought I could hear a moan, and prepared for either any moment. And how he did stare! I have detested blue eyes ever since, and blond moustaches, and the whole stout easy-going type that is not such a fool as it looks. I had brazened it out with the boys, but the first grown man was too many for me, and the blood ran out of my heart as though there was no Raffles at my back. Indeed, I had forgotten him. I had so longed to put this thing through by myself! Even in my extremity it was almost a disappointment to me when his dear, cool voice fell like a delicious draught upon my ears. But its effect upon the others is more interesting to recall. Until now the crammer had the centre of the stage, but at this point Raffles usurped a place which was always his at will. People would wait for what he had to say, as these people waited now for the simplest and most natural thing in the world.

'One moment!' he had begun.

'Well?' said the crammer, relieving me of his eyes at last.

'I don't want to lose any of the fun –'

'Nor must you,' said the crammer, with emphasis.

'But we've left our bikes outside, and mine's a Beeston Humber,' continued Raffles. 'If you don't mind, we'll bring 'em in before these fellows get away on them.'

And out he went without a look to see the effect of his words, I after him with a determined imitation of his self-control. But I would have given something to turn round. I believe that for one moment the shrewd instructor was taken in, but as I reached the steps I heard him asking his pupils whether any of them had seen any bicycles outside.

That moment, however, made the difference. We were in the shrubbery, Raffles with his electric torch drawn and blazing, when we heard the kicking at the pantry door, and in the drive with our bicycles before man and boys poured pell-mell down the steps.

We rushed our machines to the nearer gate, for both were shut, and we got through and swung it home behind us in the nick of time. Even I could mount before they could reopen the gate, which Raffles held against them for half an instant with unnecessary gallantry. But he would see me in front of him, and so it fell to me to lead the way.

Now, I have said that it was a very misty night (hence the whole thing), and also that these houses were on a hill. But they were not nearly on the top of the hill, and I did what I firmly believe that almost everybody would have done in my place. Raffles, indeed, said he would have done it himself, but that was his generosity, and he was the one man who would not. What I did was to turn in the opposite direction to the other gate, where we might so easily have been cut off, and to pedal for my life – uphill!

'My God!' I shouted when I found it out.

'Can you turn in your own length?' asked Raffles, following loyally.

'Not certain.'

'Then stick to it. You couldn't help it. But it's the devil of a hill!'

'And here they come!'

'Let them,' said Raffles, and brandished his electric torch, our only light as yet.

A hill seems endless in the dark, for you cannot see the end, and with the patter of bare feet gaining on us, I thought this one could have no end at all. Of course the boys could charge up it quicker than we could pedal, but I even heard the voice of their stout instructor growing louder through the mist.

'Oh, to think I've let you in for this!' I groaned, my head over the handlebars, every ounce of my weight first on one foot and then on the other. I glanced at Raffles, and in the white light of his torch he was doing it all with his ankles, exactly as though he had been riding in a gymkhana.

'It's the most sporting chase I was ever in,' said he.

'All my fault!'

'My dear Bunny, I wouldn't have missed it for the world!'

Nor would he forge ahead of me, though he could have done so in a moment, he who from his boyhood had done everything of the kind so much better than anybody else. No, he must ride a wheel's length behind me, and now we could not only hear the boys running, but breathing also. And then of a sudden I saw Raffles on my right striking with his torch; a face flew out of the darkness to meet the thick glass bulb with the glowing wire enclosed; it was the face of the boy Olphert, with his enviable moustache, but it vanished with the crash of glass, and the naked wire thickened to the eye like a tuning-fork struck red-hot.

I saw no more of that. One of them had crept up on my side also; as I looked, hearing him pant, he was grabbing at my left handle, and I nearly sent Raffles into the hedge by the sharp turn I took to the right. His wheel's length saved him. But my boy could run, was overhauling me again, seemed certain of me this time, when all at once the Sunbeam ran easily; every ounce of my weight with either foot once more, and I was over the crest of the hill, the grey road reeling out from under me as I felt for my brake. I looked back at Raffles. He had put up his feet. I screwed my head round still farther, and there were the boys in their pyjamas, their hands upon their knees, like so many wicketkeepers, and a big man shaking his fist. There was a lamp-post on the hilltop, and that was the last I saw.

We sailed down to the river, then on through Thames Ditton as far as

Esher Station, when we turned sharp to the right, and from the dark stretch by Imber Court came to light in Molesey, and were soon pedalling like gentlemen of leisure through Bushey Park, our lights turned up, the broken torch put out and away. The big gates had long been shut, but you can manoeuvre a bicycle through the others. We had no further adventures on the way home, and our coffee was still warm upon the hob.

'But I think it's an occasion for Sullivans,' said Raffles, who now kept them for such. 'By all my gods, Bunny, it's been the most sporting night we ever had in our lives! And do you know which was the most sporting part of it?'

'That uphill ride?'

'I wasn't thinking of it.'

'Turning your torch into a truncheon?'

'My dear Bunny! A gallant lad – I hated hitting him.'

'I know,' I said. 'The way you got us out of the house!'

'No, Bunny,' said Raffles, blowing rings. 'It came before that, you sinner, and you know it!'

'You don't mean anything I did?' said I, self-consciously, for I began to see that this was what he did mean. And now at latest it will also be seen why this story has been told with undue and inexcusable gusto; there is none other like it for me to tell; it is my one ewe-lamb in all these annals.

But Raffles had a ruder name for it. 'It was the Apotheosis of the Bunny,' said he, but in a tone I never shall forget.

'I hardly knew what I was doing or saying,' I said. 'The whole thing was a fluke.'

'Then,' said Raffles, 'it was the kind of fluke I always trusted you to make when runs were wanted.'

And he held out his dear old hand.

The Rest Cure

I had not seen Raffles for a month or more, and I was sadly in need of his advice. My life was being made a burden to me by a wretch who had obtained a bill of sale over the furniture in Mount Street, and it was only by living elsewhere that I could keep the vulpine villain from my door. This cost ready money, and my balance at the bank was sorely in need of another lift from Raffles. Yet, had he been in my shoes, he could not have vanished more effectually than he had done, both from the face of the town and from the ken of all who knew him.

It was late in August; he never played first-class cricket after July, when a scholastic understudy took his place in the Middlesex eleven. And in vain did I scour my *Field* and my *Sportsman* for the country-house matches with which he wilfully preferred to wind up the season; the matches were there, but never the magic name of A. J. Raffles. Nothing was known of him at the Albany; he had left no instructions about his letters, either there or at the club. I began to fear that some evil had overtaken him. I scanned the features of captured criminals in the illustrated Sunday papers; on each occasion I breathed again; nor was anything worthy of Raffles going on. I will not deny that I was less anxious on his account than on my own. But it was a double relief to me when he gave a first characteristic sign of life.

I had called at the Albany for the fiftieth time, and returned to Piccadilly in my usual despair, when a street sloucher sidled up to me in furtive fashion and enquired if my name was what it is.

' 'Cause this 'ere's for you,' he rejoined to my affirmative, and with that I felt a crumpled note in my palm.

It was from Raffles. I smoothed out the twisted scrap of paper, and on it were just a couple of lines in pencil:

Meet me in Holland Walk at dark tonight. Walk up and down till I come.

A. J. R.

That was all! Not another syllable after all these weeks, and the few words scribbled in a wild caricature of his scholarly and dainty hand! I was no longer to be alarmed by this sort of thing; it was all so like the Raffles I loved least; and to add to my indignation, when at length I looked up from the mysterious missive, the equally mysterious messenger had disappeared in a manner worthy of the whole affair. He was, however, the first creature I espied under the tattered trees of Holland Walk that evening.

'Seen 'im yet?' he enquired confidentially, blowing a vile cloud from his horrid pipe.

'No, I haven't; and I want to know where you've seen him,' I replied sternly. 'Why did you run away like that the moment you had given me his note?'

'Orders, orders,' was the reply. 'I ain't such a juggins as to go agen a toff as makes it worf me while to do as I'm bid an' 'old me tongue.'

'And who may you be?' I asked jealously. 'And what are you to Mr Raffles?'

'You silly ass, Bunny, don't tell all Kensington that I'm in town!' replied my tatterdemalion, shooting up and smoothing out into a merely shabby Raffles. 'Here, take my arm – I'm not so beastly as I look. But neither am I in town, nor in England, nor yet on the face of the earth, for all that's known of me to a single soul but you.'

'Then where are you,' I asked, 'between ourselves?'

'I've taken a house near here for the holidays, where I'm going in for a Rest Cure of my own description. Why? Oh, for lots of reasons, my dear Bunny; among others, I have long had a wish to grow my own beard; under the next lamp-post you will agree that it's training on very nicely. Then, you mayn't know it, but there's a canny man at Scotland Yard who has had a quiet eye on me longer than I like. I thought it about time to have an eye on him, and I stared him in the face outside the Albany this very morning. That was when I saw you go in, and scribbled a line to give you when you came out. If he had caught us talking he would have spotted me at once.'

'So you are lying low out here!'

'I prefer to call it my Rest Cure,' returned Raffles, 'and it's really nothing else. I've got a furnished house at a time when no one else would have dreamed of taking one in town; and my very neighbours don't know I'm there, though I'm bound to say there are hardly any of them at home. I don't keep a servant, and do everything for myself. It's the next best fun to a desert island. Not that I make much work, for I'm really resting, but I haven't done so much solid reading for years. Rather a joke, Bunny: the man whose house I've taken is one of Her Majesty's inspectors of prisons, and his study's a storehouse of criminology. It has been quite amusing to lie on one's back and have a good look at oneself as others fondly imagine they see one.'

'But surely you get some exercise?' I asked; for he was leading me at a good rate through the leafy byways of Campden Hill; and his step was as springy and as light as ever.

'The best exercise I ever had in my life,' said Raffles; 'and you would never live to guess what it is. It's one of the reasons why I went in for this seedy kit. I follow cabs. Yes, Bunny, I turn out about dusk and meet the expresses at Euston or King's Cross; that is, of course, I loaf outside and pick my cab, and often run my three or four miles for a bob or less. And it not only keeps you in the very pink: if you're good they let you carry the trunks upstairs; and I've taken notes from the inside of more than one commodious residence which will come in useful in the autumn. In fact, Bunny, what with these new Rowton Houses, my beard, and my otherwise well-spent holiday, I hope to have quite a good autumn season before the erratic Raffles turns up in town.'

I felt it high time to wedge in a word about my own far less satisfactory affairs. But it was not necessary for me to recount half my troubles. Raffles could be as full of himself as many a worse man, and I did not like his society the less for these human outpourings. They had rather the effect of putting me on better terms with myself, through bringing him down to my level for the time being. But his egoism was not even skin-deep; it was rather a cloak, which Raffles could cast off quicker than any man I ever knew, as he did not fail to show me now.

'Why, Bunny, this is the very thing!' he cried. 'You must come and stay with me, and we'll lie low side by side. Only remember it really is a Rest Cure. I want to keep literally as quiet as I was without you. What do you say to forming ourselves at once into a practically Silent Order? You agree? Very well, then, here's the street and that's the house.'

It was ever such a quiet little street, turning out of one of those which climb right over the pleasant hill. One side was monopolised by the garden wall of an ugly but enviable mansion standing in its own ground; opposite were a solid file of smaller but taller houses; on neither side were there many windows alight, nor a solitary soul on the pavement or in the road. Raffles led the way to one of the small tall houses. It stood immediately behind a lamp-post, and I could not but notice that a love-lock of Virginia creeper was trailing almost to the step, and that the bow-window on the ground floor was closely shuttered. Raffles admitted himself with his latchkey, and I squeezed past him into a very narrow hall. I did not hear him shut the door, but we were no longer in the lamplight, and he pushed softly past me in his turn.

'I'll get a light,' he muttered as he went; but to let him pass I had leaned against some electric switches, and while his back was turned I tried one of these without thinking. In an instant hall and staircase were flooded with light; in another Raffles was upon me in a fury, and all was dark once more. He had not said a word, but I heard him breathing through his teeth.

Nor was there anything to tell me now. The mere flash of electric light upon a hail of chaos and uncarpeted stairs, and on the face of Raffles as he sprang to switch it off, had been enough even for me.

'So this is how you have taken the house,' said I in his own undertone. ' "Taken" is good; "taken" is beautiful!'

'Did you think I'd done it through an agent?' he snarled. 'Upon my word, Bunny, I did you the credit of supposing you saw the joke all the time!'

'Why shouldn't you take a house,' I asked, 'and pay for it?'

'Why should I,' he retorted, 'within three miles of the Albany? Besides, I should have had no peace; and I meant every word I said about my Rest Cure.'

'You are actually staying in a house where you've broken in to steal?'

'Not to steal, Bunny! I haven't stolen a thing. But staying here I certainly am, and having the most complete rest a busy man could wish.'

'There'll be no rest for me!'

Raffles laughed as he struck a match. I had followed him into what would have been the back drawing-room in the ordinary little London house; the inspector of prisons had converted it into a separate study by filling the folding doors with bookshelves, which I scanned at once for the congenial works of which Raffles had spoken. I was not able to carry my examination very far. Raffles had lighted a candle, stuck (by its own grease) in the crown of an opera hat, which he opened the moment the wick caught. The light thus struck the ceiling in an oval shaft, which left the rest of the room almost as dark as it had been before.

'Sorry, Bunny!' said Raffles, sitting on one pedestal of a desk from which the top had been removed, and setting his makeshift lantern on the other. 'In broad daylight, when it can't be spotted from the outside, you shall have as much artificial light as you like. If you want to do some writing, that's the top of the desk on end against the mantelpiece. You'll never have a better chance so far as interruption goes. But no midnight oil or electricity! You observe that their last care was to fix up these shutters; they appear to have taken the top off the desk to get at 'em without standing on it; but the beastly things wouldn't go all the way up, and the strip they leave would give us away to the backs of the other houses if we lit up after dark. Mind that telephone! If you touch the receiver they will know at the exchange that the house is not empty, and I wouldn't put it past the colonel to have told them exactly how long he was going to be away. He's pretty particular: look at the strips of paper to keep the dust off his precious books!'

'Is he a colonel?' I asked, perceiving that Raffles referred to the absentee householder.

'Of sappers,' he replied, 'and a vc into the bargain, confound him! Got it at Rorke's Drift; prison governor or inspector ever since; favourite recreation, what do you think? Revolver shooting! You can read all about him in his own *Who's Who*. A devil of a chap to tackle, Bunny, when he's at home!'

'And where is he now?' I asked uneasily. And do you know he isn't on his way home?'

'Switzerland,' replied Raffles, chuckling; 'he wrote one too many labels, and was considerate enough to leave it behind for our guidance. Well, no one ever comes back from Switzerland at the beginning of September, you know; and nobody ever thinks of coming back before the servants. When they turn up they won't get in. I keep the latch jammed, but the servants will think it's jammed itself, and while they're gone for the locksmith we shall walk out like gentlemen – if we haven't done so already.'

'As you walked in, I suppose?'

Raffles shook his head in the dim light to which my sight was growing inured.

'No, Bunny, I regret to say I came in through the dormer window. They were painting next door but one. I never did like ladder work, but it takes less time than picking a lock in the broad light of a street lamp.'

'So they left you a latchkey as well as everything else!'

'No, Bunny. I was just able to make that for myself. I am playing at *Robinson Crusoe*, not *The Swiss Family Robinson*. And now, my dear Friday, if you will kindly take off those boots, we can explore the island before we turn in for the night.'

The stairs were very steep and narrow, and they creaked alarmingly as Raffles led the way up, with the single candle in the crown of the colonel's hat. He blew it out before we reached the half-landing, where a naked window stared upon the backs of the houses in the next road, but lit it again at the drawing-room door. I just peeped in upon a semi-grand swathed in white and a row of watercolours mounted in gold. An excellent bathroom broke our journey to the second floor.

'I'll have one tonight,' said I, taking heart of a luxury unknown in my last sordid sanctuary.

'You'll do no such thing,' snapped Raffles. 'Have the goodness to remember that our island is one of a group inhabited by hostile tribes. You can fill the bath quietly if you try, but it empties under the study window, and makes the very devil of a noise about it. No, Bunny, I bale out every drop and pour it away through the scullery sink, so you will kindly consult me before you turn a tap. Here's your room; hold the light outside while I draw the curtains; it's the old chap's dressing-room. Now you can bring the glim. How's that for a jolly wardrobe? And look at his coats on their cross trees inside: dapper old dog, shouldn't you say? Mark the boots on the shelf above, and the little brass rail for his ties! Didn't I tell you he was particular? And wouldn't he simply love to catch us at his kit?'

'Let's only hope it would give him an apoplexy,' said I shuddering.

'I shouldn't build on it,' replied Raffles. 'That's a big man's trouble, and neither you nor I could get into the old chap's clothes. But come into the best bedroom, Bunny. You won't think me selfish if I don't give it up to you? Look at this, my boy, look at this! It's the only one I use in all the house.'

I had followed him into a good room, with ample windows closely curtained, and he had switched on the light in a hanging lamp at the bedside. The rays fell from a thick green funnel in a plateful of strong light upon a table deep in books. I noticed several volumes of the *Invasion of the Crimea*.

'That's where I rest the body and exercise the brain,' said Raffles. 'I have long wanted to read my Kinglake from A to Z, and I manage about a volume a night. There's a style for you, Bunny! I love the punctilious thoroughness of the whole thing; one can understand its appeal to our careful colonel. His name, did you say? Crutchley, Bunny – Colonel Crutchley, RE, VC.'

'We'd put his valour to the test!' said I, feeling more valiant myself after our tour of inspection.

'Not so loud on the stairs,' whispered Raffles. 'There's only one door between us and – '

Raffles stood still at my feet, and well he might! A deafening double knock had resounded through the empty house; and to add to the utter horror of the moment, Raffles instantly blew out the light. I heard my heart pounding. Neither of us breathed. We were on our way down to the first landing, and for a moment we stood like mice; then Raffles heaved a deep sigh, and in the depths I heard the gate swing home.

'Only the postman, Bunny! He will come now and again, though they have obviously left instructions at the post-office. I hope the old colonel will let them have it when he gets back. I confess it gave me a turn.'

'Turn!' I gasped. 'I must have a drink, if I die for it.'

'My dear Bunny, that's no part of my Rest Cure.'

'Then goodbye! I can't stand it; feel my forehead; listen to my heart! Crusoe found a footprint, but he never heard a double-knock at the street door!'

' "Better live in the midst of alarms",' quoted Raffles, ' "than dwell in this horrible place." I must confess we get it both ways, Bunny. Yet I've nothing but tea in the house.'

'And where do you make that? Aren't you afraid of smoke?'

'There's a gas-stove in the dining-room.'

'But surely to goodness,' I cried, 'there's a cellar lower down!'

'My dear, good Bunny,' said Raffles, 'I've told you already that I didn't come in here on business. I came in for the Cure. Not a penny will these people be the worse, except for their washing and their electric light, and I mean to leave enough to cover both items.'

'Then,' said I, 'since Brutus is such a very honourable man, we will borrow a bottle from the cellar, and replace it before we go.'

Raffles slapped me softly on the back, and I knew that I had gained my point. It was often the case when I had the presence of heart and mind to stand up to him. But never was little victory of mine quite so grateful as this.

Certainly it was a very small cellar, indeed a mere cupboard under the kitchen stairs, with a most ridiculous lock. Nor was this cupboard overstocked with wine. But I made out a jar of whisky, a shelf of Zeltinger, another of claret, and a short one at the top which presented a little battery of golden-leafed necks and corks. Raffles set his hand no lower. He examined the labels while I held folded hat and naked light.

'Mumm 1884!' he whispered. 'G. H. Mumm, and AD 1884! I am no wine-bibber, Bunny, as you know, but I hope you appreciate the specifications as I do. It looks to me like the only bottle, the last of its case, and it does seem a bit of a shame; but more shame for the miser who hoards in his cellar what was meant for mankind! Come, Bunny, lead the way. This baby is worth nursing. It would break my heart if anything happened to it now!'

So we celebrated my first night in the furnished house; and I slept beyond belief, slept as I never was to sleep there again. But it was strange to hear the milkman in the early morning, and the postman knocking his way along the street an hour later, and to be passed over by one destroying angel after another. I had come down early enough, and watched through the drawing-room blind the cleansing of all the steps in the street but ours. Yet Raffles had evidently been up some time; the house seemed far purer than overnight as though he had managed to air it room by room; and from the one with the gas-stove there came a frizzling sound that fattened the heart.

I only wish I had the pen to do justice to the week I spent indoors on Campden Hill! It might make amusing reading; the reality for me was far removed from the realm of amusement. Not that I was denied many a laugh of suppressed heartiness when Raffles and I were together. But half our time we very literally saw nothing of each other. I need not say whose fault that was. He would be quiet; he was in ridiculous and offensive earnest about his egregious Cure. Kinglake he would read by the hour together, day and night, by the hanging lamp, lying upstairs on the best bed. There was daylight enough for me in the drawing-room below; and there I would sit immersed in criminous tomes, weakly fascinated until I shivered and shook in my stocking soles. Often I longed to do something hysterically desperate, to rouse Raffles and bring the street about our ears; once I did bring him about mine by striking a single note on the piano, with the soft pedal down. His neglect of me seemed wanton at the time. I have long realised that he was only wise to maintain silence at the expense of perilous amenities, and as fully justified in those secret and solitary sorties which made bad blood in my veins. He was far cleverer than I at getting in and out; but even had I been his match for stealth and wariness, my company would have doubled every risk. I admit now that he treated me with quite as much sympathy as common caution would permit. But at the time I took it so badly as to plan a small revenge.

What with his flourishing beard and the increasing shabbiness of the only suit he had brought with him to the house, there was no denying that Raffles had now the advantage of a permanent disguise. That was another of his excuses for leaving me as he did, and it was the one I was determined to remove. On a morning, therefore, when I awoke to find him flown again, I proceeded to execute a plan which I had already matured in my mind. Colonel Crutchley was a married man; there were no signs of children in the house; on the other hand, there was much evidence that the wife was a woman of fashion. Her dresses overflowed the wardrobe and her room; large, flat, cardboard boxes were to be found in every corner of the upper floors. She was a tall woman; I was not too tall a man. Like Raffles, I had not shaved on Campden Hill. That morning, however, I did my best with a very fair razor which the colonel had left behind in my room; then I turned out the lady's wardrobe and the cardboard boxes, and took my choice.

I have fair hair, and at the time it was rather long. With a pair of Mrs Crutchley's tongs and a discarded hairnet, I was able to produce an almost immodest fringe. A big black hat with a wintry feather completed a head-dress as unseasonable as my skating skirt and feather boa; of course, the good lady had all her summer frocks away with her in Switzerland. This was all the more annoying from the fact that we were having a very warm September; so I was not sorry to hear Raffles return as I was busy adding a layer of powder to my heated countenance. I listened a moment on the landing, but as he went into the study I determined to complete my toilet in every detail. My idea was first to give him the fright he deserved, and secondly to show him that I was quite as fit to move abroad as he. It was, however, I confess, a pair of the colonel's gloves that I was buttoning as I slipped down to the study even more quietly than usual. The electric light was on, as it generally was by day, and under it stood as formidable a figure as ever I encountered in my life of crime.

Imagine a thin but extremely wiry man, past middle age, brown and bloodless as any crab apple, but as coolly truculent and as casually alert as Raffles at his worst. It was, it could only be, the fire-eating and prison-inspecting colonel himself! He was ready for me, a revolver in his hand, taken, as I could see, from one of those locked drawers in the pedestal desk with which Raffles had refused to tamper; the drawer was open, and a bunch of keys depended from the lock. A grim smile crumpled up the parchment face, so that one eye was puckered out of sight; the other was propped open by an eyeglass, which, however, dangled on its string when I appeared.

'A woman, begad!' the warrior exclaimed. 'And where's the man, you scarlet hussy?'

Not a word could I utter. But, in my horror and my amazement, I have no sort of doubt that I acted the part I had assumed in a manner I never should have approached in happier circumstances.

'Come, come, my lass,' cried the old oak veteran, 'I'm not going to put a bullet through you, you know! You tell me all about it, and it'll do you more good than harm. There, I'll put the nasty thing away and – God bless me, if the brazen wench hasn't squeezed into the wife's kit!'

A squeeze it happened to have been, and in my emotion it felt more of one than ever; but his sudden discovery had not heightened the veteran's animosity against me. On the contrary, I caught a glint of humour through his gleaming glass, and he proceeded to pocket his revolver like the gentleman he was.

'Well, well, it's lucky I looked in,' he continued. 'I only came round on the off-chance of letters, but if I hadn't you'd have had another week in clover. Begad, though, I saw your handwriting the moment I'd got my nose inside! Now just be sensible and tell me where your good man is.'

I had no man. I was alone, had broken in alone. There was not a soul in the affair (much less the house) except myself. So much I stuttered out in tones too hoarse to betray me on the spot. But the old man of the world shook a hard old head.

'Quite right not to give away your pal,' said he. 'But I'm not one of the marines, my dear, and you mustn't expect me to swallow all that. Well, if you won't say, you won't, and we must just send for those who will.'

In a flash I saw his fell design. The telephone directory lay open on one of the pedestals. He must have been consulting it when he heard me on the stairs; he had another look at it now; and that gave me my opportunity. With a presence of mind rare enough in me to excuse the boast, I flung myself upon the instrument in the corner and hurled it to the ground with all my might. I was myself sent spinning into the opposite corner at the same instant. But the instrument happened to be a standard of the more elaborate pattern, and I flattered myself that I had put the delicate engine out of action for the day.

Not that my adversary took the trouble to ascertain. He was looking at me strangely in the electric light, standing intently on his guard, his right hand in the pocket where he had dropped his revolver. And I – I hardly knew it – but I caught up the first thing handy for self-defence, and was brandishing the bottle which Raffles and I had emptied in honour of my arrival on this fatal scene.

'Be shot if I don't believe you're the man himself!' cried the colonel, shaking an armed fist in my face. 'You young wolf in sheep's clothing. Been at my wine, of course! Put down that bottle; down with it this instant, or I'll drill a tunnel through your middle. I thought so! Begad, sir, you shall pay for this! Don't you give me an excuse for potting you now or I'll jump at the chance! My last bottle of '84 – you miserable blackguard – you unutterable beast!'

He had browbeaten me into his own chair in his own corner; he was standing over me, empty bottle in one hand, revolver in the other, and murder itself in the purple puckers of his raging face. His language I will not even pretend to indicate: his skinny throat swelled and trembled with the monstrous volleys. He could smile at my appearance in his wife's clothes; he would have had my blood for the last bottle of his best champagne. His eyes were not hidden now; they needed no eyeglass to prop them open; large with fury, they started from the livid mask. I watched nothing else. I could not understand why they should start out as they did. I did not try. I say I watched nothing else – until I saw the face of Raffles over the unfortunate officer's shoulder.

Raffles had crept in unheard while our altercation was at its height, had watched his opportunity and stolen on his man unobserved by either of us. While my own attention was completely engrossed, he had seized the colonel's pistol-hand and twisted it behind the colonel's back until his eyes bulged out as I have endeavoured to describe. But the fighting man had some fight in him still; and scarcely had I grasped the situation when he hit out venomously behind with the bottle, which was smashed to bits on Raffles's shin. Then I threw my strength into the scale; and before many minutes we had our officer gagged and bound in his chair. But it was not one of our bloodless victories. Raffles had been cut to the bone by the broken glass; his leg bled wherever he limped and the fierce eyes of the bound man followed the wet trail with gleams of sinister satisfaction.

I thought I had never seen a man better bound or better gagged. But the humanity seemed to have run out of Raffles with his blood. He tore up tablecloths, he cut down blind-cords, he brought the dust-sheets from the drawing-room and multiplied every bond. The unfortunate man's legs were lashed to the legs of his chair, his arms to its arms, his thighs and back fairly welded to the leather. Either end of his own ruler protruded from his bulging cheeks – the middle was hidden by his moustache – and the gag kept in place by remorseless lashings at the back of his head. It was a spectacle I could not bear to contemplate at length, while from the first I found myself physically unable to face the ferocious gaze of those implacable eyes. But Raffles only laughed at my squeamishness, and flung a dust-sheet over man and chair; and the stark outline drove me from the room.

It was Raffles at his worst, Raffles as I never knew him before or after – a Raffles mad with pain and rage, and desperate as any other criminal in the land. Yet he had struck no brutal blow, he had uttered no disgraceful taunt, and probably not inflicted a tithe of the pain he had himself to bear. It is true that he was flagrantly in the wrong, his victim as laudably in the right.

Nevertheless, granting the original sin of the situation, and given this unforeseen development, even I failed to see how Raffles could have combined greater humanity with any regard for our joint safety; and had his barbarities ended here, I for one should not have considered them an extraordinary aggravation of an otherwise minor offence. But in the broad daylight of the bathroom, which had a ground-glass window but no blind, I saw at once the serious nature of his wound and of its effect upon the man.

'It will maim me for a month,' said he; 'and if the vc comes out alive, the wound he gave may be identified with the wound I've got.'

The vc! There, indeed, was an aggravation to one illogical mind. But to cast a moment's doubt upon the certainty of his coming out alive!

'Of course he'll come out,' said I. 'We must make up our minds to that.'

'Did he tell you he was expecting the servants or his wife? If so, of course we must hurry up.'

'No, Raffles, I'm afraid he's not expecting anybody. He told me, if he hadn't looked in for letters, we should have had the place to ourselves another week. That's the worst of it.'

Raffles smiled as he secured a regular puttee of dust-sheeting. No blood was coming through.

'I don't agree, Bunny,' said he. 'It's quite the best of it, if you ask me.'

'What, that he should die the death?'

'Why not?'

And Raffles stared me out with a hard and merciless light in his clear blue eyes – a light that chilled the blood.

'If it's a choice between his life and our liberty, you're entitled to your decision and I'm entitled to mine, and I took it before I bound him as I did,' said Raffles. 'I'm only sorry I took so much trouble if you're going to stay behind and put him in the way of releasing himself before he gives up the ghost. Perhaps you will go and think it over while I wash my bags and dry 'em at the gas stove. It will take me at least an hour, which will just give me time to finish the last volume of Kinglake.'

Long before he was ready to go, however, I was waiting in the hall, clothed indeed, but not in a mind which I care to recall. Once or twice I peered into the dining-room where Raffles sat before the stove, without letting him hear me. He, too, was ready for the street at a moment's notice; but a steam ascended from his left leg, as he sat immersed in his red volume. Into the study I never went again; but Raffles did, to restore to its proper shelf this and every other book he had taken out and so destroy that clue to the manner of man who had made himself at home in the house. On his last visit I heard him whisk off the dust-sheet; then he waited a minute; and when he came out it was to lead the way into the open air as though the accursed house belonged to him.

'We shall be seen,' I whispered at his heels. 'Raffles, Raffles, there's a policeman at the corner!'

'I know him intimately,' replied Raffles, turning, however, the other way. 'He accosted me on Monday, when I explained that I was an old soldier of the colonel's regiment, who came in every few days to air the place and send on any odd letters. You see, I have always carried one or two about me, redirected to that address in Switzerland, and when I showed them to him it was all right. But after that it was no use listening at the letter-box for a clear coast, was it?'

I did not answer; there was too much to exasperate in these prodigies of cunning which he could never trouble to tell me at the time. And I knew why he had kept his latest feats to himself: unwilling to trust me outside the house, he had systematically exaggerated the dangers of his own walks abroad; and when to these injuries he added the insult of a patronising compliment on my late disguise, I again made no reply.

'What's the good of your coming with me?' he asked, when I had followed him across the main stream of Notting Hill.

'We may as well sink or swim together,' I answered sullenly.

'Yes? Well, I'm going to swim into the provinces, have a shave on the way, buy a new kit piecemeal, including a cricket-bag (which I really want), and come limping back to the Albany with the same old strain in my bowling leg. I needn't add that I have been playing country-house cricket for the last month under an alias; it's the only decent way to do it when one's county has need of one. That's my itinerary, Bunny, but I really can't see why you should come with me.'

'We may as well swing together!' I growled.

'As you will, my dear fellow,' replied Raffles. 'But I begin to dread your company on the drop!'

I shall hold my pen on that provincial tour. Not that I joined Raffles in any of the little enterprises with which he beguiled the breaks in our journey; our last deed in London was far too great a weight upon my soul. I could see that gallant officer in his chair, see him at every hour of the day and night, now with his indomitable eyes meeting mine ferociously, now a stark outline underneath a sheet. The vision darkened my day and gave me sleepless nights. I was with our victim in all his agony; my mind would only leave him for that gallows of which Raffles had said true things in jest. No, I could not face so vile a death lightly, but I could meet it, somehow, better than I could endure a guilty suspense. In the watches of the second night I made up my mind to meet it halfway, that very morning, while still there might be time to save the life that we had left in jeopardy. And I got up early to tell Raffles of my resolve.

His room in the hotel where we were staying was littered with clothes and luggage new enough for any bridegroom; I lifted the locked cricket-bag, and found it heavier than a cricket-bag has any right to be. But in the bed Raffles was sleeping like an infant, his shaven self once more. And when I shook him he awoke with a smile.

'Going to confess, eh, Bunny? Well, wait a bit; the local police won't thank you for knocking them up at this hour. And I bought a late edition which you ought to see; that must be it on the floor. You have a look in the stop-press column, Bunny.'

I found the place with a sunken heart, and this is what I read:

WEST END OUTRAGE – Colonel Crutchley, RE, VC, has been the victim of a dastardly outrage at his residence, Peter Street, Campden Hill. Returning unexpectedly to the house, which had been left untenanted during the absence of the family abroad, he found it occupied by two ruffians, who overcame and secured the distinguished officer by the exercise of considerable violence. When discovered through the intelligence of the Kensington police, the gallant victim was gagged and bound, hand and foot, and in an advanced stage of exhaustion.

'Thanks to the Kensington police,' observed Raffles, as I read the last words aloud in my horror. 'They can't have gone when they got my letter.'

'Your letter?'

'I printed them a line while we were waiting for our train at Euston. They must have got it that night, but they can't have paid any attention to it until yesterday morning. And when they do, they take all the credit and give me no more than you did, Bunny!'

I looked at the curly head upon the pillow, at the smiling, handsome face under the curls. And at last I understood.

'So all the time you never meant it!'

'Slow murder? You should have known me better. A few hours' enforced rest cure was the worst I wished him.'

'You might have told me, Raffles!'

'That may be, Bunny, but you ought certainly to have trusted me!'

A Bad Night

There was to be a certain little wedding in which Raffles and I took a surreptitious interest. The bride-elect was living in some retirement, with a recently widowed mother and an asthmatical brother, in a mellow hermitage on the banks of the Mole. The bridegroom was a prosperous son of the same suburban soil which had nourished both families for generations. The wedding presents were so numerous as to fill several rooms at the pretty retreat upon the Mole, and of an intrinsic value calling for a special transaction with the Burglary Insurance Company in Cheapside. I cannot say how Raffles obtained all this information. I only know that it proved correct in each particular. I was not indeed deeply interested before the event, since Raffles assured me that it was 'a one-man job', and naturally intended to be the one man himself. It was only at the eleventh hour that our positions were inverted by the wholly unexpected selection of Raffles for the English team in the Second Test Match.

In a flash I saw the chance of my criminal career. It was some years since Raffles had served his country in these encounters; he had never thought to be called upon again, and his gratification was only less than his embarrassment. The match was at Old Trafford, on the third Thursday, Friday and Saturday in July; the other affair had been all arranged for the Thursday night, the night of the wedding at East Molesey. It was for Raffles to choose between the two excitements, and for once I helped him to make up his mind. I duly pointed out to him that in Surrey, at all events, I was quite capable of taking his place. Nay, more, I insisted at once on my prescriptive right and on his patriotic obligation in the matter. In the country's name and in my own, I implored him to give it and me a chance; and for once, as I say, my arguments prevailed. Raffles sent his telegram – it was the day before the match. We then rushed down to Esher, and over every inch of the ground, by that characteristically circuitous route which he enjoined on me for the next night. And at six in the evening I was receiving the last of my many instructions through a window of the restaurant car.

'Only promise me not to take a revolver,' said Raffles in a whisper. 'Here are my keys; there's an old life-preserver somewhere in the bureau; take that, if you like – though what you take I rather fear you are the chap to use!'

'Then the rope be round my own neck!' I whispered back. 'Whatever else I may do, Raffles, I shan't give you away; and you'll find I do better than you think, and am worth trusting with a little more to do, or I'll know the reason why!'

And I meant to know it, as he was borne out of Euston with raised eyebrows and I turned grimly on my heel. I saw his fears for me; and nothing could have made me more fearless for myself. Raffles had been wrong about me all these years; now was my chance to set him right. It was galling to feel that he had no confidence in my coolness or my nerve, when neither had ever failed him at a pinch. I had been loyal to him through rough and smooth. In many an ugly corner I had stood as firm as Raffles himself. I was his right hand, and yet he never hesitated to make me his cat's-paw. This time, at all events, I should be neither one nor the other; this time I was the understudy playing lead at last; and I wish I could think that Raffles ever realised with what gusto I threw myself into his part.

Thus I was first out of a crowded theatre train at Esher next night, and first down the stairs into the open air. The night was close and cloudy; and the road to Hampton Court, even now that the suburban builder has marked much of it for his own, is one of the darkest I know. The first mile is still a narrow avenue, a mere tunnel of leaves at midsummer; but at that time there was not a lighted pane or cranny by the way. Naturally, it was in this blind reach that I fancied I was being followed. I stopped in my stride; so did the steps I made sure I had heard not far behind; and when I went on, they followed suit. I dried my forehead as I walked, but soon brought myself to repeat the experiment, when an exact repetition of the result went to convince me that it had been my own echo all the time. And since I lost it on getting quit of the avenue, and coming out upon the straight and open road, I was not long in recovering from my scare. But now I could see my way, and found the rest of it without mishap, though not without another semblance of adventure. Over the bridge across the Mole, when about to turn to the left, I marched straight upon a policeman in rubber soles. I had to call him 'officer' as I passed, and to pass my turning by a couple of hundred yards, before venturing back another way.

At last I had crept through a garden gate, and round by black windows to a black lawn drenched with dew. It had been a heating walk, and I was glad to blunder on a garden seat, most considerately placed under a cedar which added its own darkness to that of the night. Here I rested a few minutes, putting up my feet to keep them dry, untying my shoes to save time, and generally facing the task before me with a coolness which I strove to make worthy of my absent chief. But mine was a self-conscious quality, as far removed from the original as any other deliberate imitation of genius. I actually struck a match on my trousers, and lit one of the shorter Sullivans. Raffles himself would not have done such a thing at such a moment. But I wished to tell him that I had done it; and in truth I was not more than pleasurably afraid; I had rather that impersonal curiosity as to the issue which has been the saving of me in still more precarious situations. I even grew impatient for the fray, and could not after all sit still as long as I had intended. So it happened that I was finishing my cigarette on the edge of the wet lawn, and about to slip off my shoes before stepping across the gravel to the conservatory door, when a most singular sound arrested me in the act. It was a muffled gasping somewhere overhead. I stood like stone; and my listening attitude must have been visible against the milky sheen of the lawn, for a laboured voice hailed me sternly from a window.

'Who on earth are you?' it wheezed.

'A detective officer,' I replied, 'sent down by the Burglary Insurance Company.'

Not a moment had I paused for my precious fable. It had all been prepared for me by Raffles, in case of need. I was merely repeating a lesson in which I had been closely schooled. But at the window there was pause enough, filled only by the uncanny wheezing of the man I could not see.

'I don't see why they should have sent you down,' he said at length. 'We are being quite well looked after by the local police; they're giving us a special call every hour.'

'I know that, Mr Medlicott,' I rejoined on my own account. 'I met one of them at the corner just now, and we passed the time of night.'

My heart was knocking me to bits. I had started for myself at last.

'Did you get my name from him?' pursued my questioner, in a suspicious wheeze.

'No; they gave me that before I started,' I replied. 'But I'm sorry you saw me, sir; it's a mere matter of routine, and not intended to annoy anybody. I propose to keep a watch on the place all night, but I own it wasn't necessary to trespass as I've done. I'll take myself off the actual premises, if you prefer it.'

This again was all my own; and it met with a success that might have given me confidence.

'Not a bit of it,' replied young Medlicott, with a grim geniality. 'I've just woke up with the devil of an attack of asthma, and may have to sit up in my chair till morning. You'd better come up and see me through, and kill two birds while you're about it. Stay where you are, and I'll come down and let you in.'

Here was a dilemma which Raffles himself had not foreseen! Outside, in the dark, my audacious part was not hard to play; but to carry the improvisation indoors was to double at once the difficulty and the risk. It was true that I had purposely come down in a true detective's overcoat and bowler; but my personal appearance was hardly of the detective type. On the other hand as the soi-disant guardian of the gifts one might only excite suspicion by refusing to enter the house where they were. Nor could I forget that it was my purpose to effect such entry first or last. That was the casting consideration. I decided to take my dilemma by the horns.

There had been a scraping of matches in the room over the conservatory; the open window had shown for a moment, like an empty picture-frame, a gigantic shadow wavering on the ceiling; and in the next half-minute I remembered to tie my shoes. But the light was slow to reappear through the leaded glasses of an outer door farther along the path. And when the door opened, it was a figure of woe that stood within and held an unsteady candle between our faces.

I have seen old men look half their age, and young men look double theirs; but never before or since have I seen a beardless boy bent into a man of eighty, gasping for every breath, shaken by every gasp, swaying, tottering and choking, as if about to die upon his feet. Yet with it all, young Medlicott overhauled me shrewdly, and it was several moments before he would let me take the candle from him.

'I shouldn't have come down – made me worse,' he began whispering in spurts. 'Worse still going up again. You must give me an arm. You will come up? That's right! Not as bad as I look, you know. Got some good whisky, too. Presents are all right; but if they aren't you'll hear of it indoors sooner than out. Now I'm ready – thanks! Mustn't make more noise than we can help – wake my mother.'

It must have taken us minutes to climb that single flight of stairs. There was just room for me to keep his arm in mine; with the other he hauled on the banisters; and so we mounted, step by step, a panting pause on each, and a pitched battle for breath on the half-landing. In the end we gained a cosy library, with an open door leading to a bedroom beyond. But the effort had deprived my poor companion of all power of speech; his labouring lungs shrieked like the wind; he could just point to the door by which we had entered, and which I shut in obedience to his gestures, and then to the decanter and its accessories on the table where he had left them overnight. I gave him nearly half a glassful, and his paroxysm subsided a little as he sat hunched up in a chair.

'I was a fool . . . to turn in,' he blurted in more whispers between longer pauses. 'Lying down is the devil . . . when you're in for a real bad night. You might get me the brown cigarettes . . . on the table in there. That's right . . . thanks awfully . . . and now a match!'

The asthmatic had bitten off either end of the stramonium cigarette, and was soon choking himself with the crude fumes, which he inhaled in desperate gulps, to exhale in furious fits of coughing. Never was more heroic remedy; it seemed a form of lingering suicide; but by degrees some slight improvement became apparent, and at length the sufferer was able to sit upright, and to drain his glass with a sigh of rare relief. I sighed also, for I had witnessed a struggle for dear life by a man in the flower of his youth, whose looks I liked, whose smile came like the sun through the first break in his torments, and whose first words were to thank me for the little I had done in bare humanity.

That made me feel the thing I was. But the feeling put me on my guard. And I was not unready for the remark which followed a more exhaustive scrutiny than I had hitherto sustained.

'Do you know,' said young Medlicott, 'that you aren't a bit like the detective of my dreams?'

'Only too proud to hear it,' I replied. 'There would be no point in my being in plain clothes if I looked exactly what I was.'

My companion reassured me with a wheezy laugh.

'There's something in that,' said he, 'although I do congratulate the insurance people on getting a man of your class to do their dirty work. And I congratulate myself,' he was quick enough to add, 'on having you to see me through as bad a night as I've had for a long time. You're like flowers in the depths of winter. Got a drink? That's right! I suppose you didn't happen to bring down an evening paper?'

I said I had brought one, but had unfortunately left it in the train.

'What about the Test Match?' cried my asthmatic, shooting forward in his chair.

'I can tell you that,' said I. 'We went in first – '

'Oh, I know all about that,' he interrupted. 'I've seen the miserable score up to lunch. How many did we scrape altogether?'

'We're scraping them still.'

'No! How many?'

'Over two hundred for seven wickets.'

'Who made the stand?'

'Raffles, for one. He was sixty-two not out at close of play!'

And the note of admiration rang in my voice, though I tried in my self-consciousness to keep it out. But young Medlicott's enthusiasm proved an ample cloak for mine; it was he who might have been the personal friend of Raffles; and in his delight he chuckled till he puffed and blew again.

'Good old Raffles!' he panted in every pause. 'After being chosen last, and as a bowler-man! That's the cricketer for me, sir; by Jove, we must have another drink in his honour! Funny thing, asthma; your liquor affects your head no more than it does a man with a snakebite; but it eases everything else, and sees you through. Doctors will tell you so, but you've got to ask 'em first; they're no good for asthma! I've only known one who could stop an attack, and he knocked me sideways with nitrite of amyl. Funny complaint in other ways; raises your spirits, if anything. You can't look beyond the next breath. Nothing else worries you. Well, well, here's luck to A. J. Raffles, and may he get his century in the morning!'

And he struggled to his feet for the toast; but I drank it sitting down. I felt unreasonably wroth with Raffles, for coming into the conversation as he had done – for taking centuries in test matches as he was doing, without bothering his head about me. A failure would have been in better taste; it would have shown at least some imagination, some anxiety on one's account. I did not reflect that even Raffles could scarcely be expected to picture me in my cups with the son of the house that I had come to rob; chatting with him, ministering to him; admiring his cheery courage, and honestly attempting to lighten his load! Truly it was an infernal position: how could I rob him or his after this? And yet I had thrust myself into it; and Raffles would never, never understand!

Even that was not the worst. I was not quite sure that young Medlicott was sure of me. I had feared this from the beginning, and now (over the second glass that could not possibly affect a man in his condition) he practically admitted as much to me. Asthma was such a funny thing (he insisted) that it would not worry him a bit to discover that I had come to take the presents instead of to take care of them! I showed a sufficiently faint appreciation of the jest. And it was presently punished as it deserved, by the most violent paroxysm that had seized the sufferer yet: the fight for breath became faster and more furious, and the former weapons of no more avail. I prepared a cigarette, but the poor brute was too breathless to inhale. I poured out yet more whisky, but he put it from him with a gesture.

'Amyl – get me amyl!' he gasped. 'The tin on the table by my bed.'

I rushed into his room, and returned with a little tin of tiny cylinders done up like miniature crackers in scraps of calico; the spent youth broke one in his handkerchief, in which he immediately buried his face. I watched him closely as a subtle odour reached my nostrils; and it was like the miracle of oil upon the billows. His shoulders rested from long travail; the stertorous gasping died away to a quick but natural respiration; and in the sudden cessation of the cruel contest, an uncanny stillness fell upon the scene. Meanwhile the hidden face had flushed to the ears, and, when at length it was raised to mine, its crimson calm was as incongruous as an optical illusion.

'It takes the blood from the heart,' he murmured, 'and clears the whole show for the moment. If it only lasted! But you can't take two without a doctor; one's quite enough to make you smell the brimstone . . . I say, what's up? You're listening to something! If it's the policeman we'll have a word with him.'

It was not the policeman; it was no outdoor sound that I had caught in the sudden cessation of the bout for breath. It was a noise, a footstep, in the room below us. I went to the window and leaned out: right underneath, in the conservatory, was the faintest glimmer of a light in the adjoining room.

'One of the rooms where the presents are!' whispered Medlicott at my elbow. And as we withdrew together, I looked him in the face as I had not done all night.

I looked him in the face like an honest man, for a miracle was to make me one once more. My knot was cut – my course inevitable. Mine, after all, to prevent the very thing that I had come to do! My gorge had long since risen at the deed; the unforeseen circumstances had rendered it impossible from the first; but now I could afford to recognise the impossibility, and to think of Raffles and the asthmatic alike without a qualm. I could play the game by them both, for it was one and the same game. I could preserve thieves' honour, and yet regain some shred of that which I had forfeited as a man!

So I thought as we stood face to face, our ears straining for the least movement below, our eyes locked in a common anxiety. Another muffled footfall – felt rather than heard – and we exchanged grim nods of simultaneous excitement. But by this time Medlicott was as helpless as he had been before; the flush had faded from his face, and his breathing alone would have spoiled everything. In dumb show I had to order him to stay where he was, to leave my man to me. And then it was that in a gusty whisper, with the same shrewd look that had disconcerted me more than once during our vigil, young Medlicott froze and fired my blood by turns.

'I've been unjust to you,' he said, with his right hand in his dressing-gown pocket. 'I thought for a bit – never mind what I thought – I soon saw I was wrong. But – I've had this thing in my pocket all the time!'

And he would have thrust his revolver upon me as a peace-offering, but I would not even take his hand, as I tapped the life-preserver in my pocket, and crept out to earn his honest grip or to fall in the attempt. On the landing I drew Raffles's little weapon, slipped my right wrist through the leathern loop, and held it in readiness over my right shoulder. Then, downstairs I stole, as Raffles himself had taught me, close to the wall, where the planks are nailed. Nor had I made a sound, to my knowledge; for a door was open, and a light was burning, and the light did not flicker as I approached the door. I clenched my teeth and pushed it open; and here was the veriest villain waiting for me, his little lantern held aloft.

'You blackguard!' I cried, and with a single thwack I felled the ruffian to the floor.

There was no question of a foul blow. He had been just as ready to pounce on me; it was simply my luck to have got the first blow home. Yet a fellow-feeling touched me with remorse, as I stood over the senseless body, sprawling prone, and perceived that I had struck an unarmed man. The lantern only had fallen from his hands; it lay on one side, smoking horribly;

and a something in the reek caused me to set it up in haste and turn the body over with both hands.

Shall I ever forget the incredulous horror of that moment?

It was Raffles himself!

How it was possible, I did not pause to ask myself; if one man on earth could annihilate space and time, it was the man lying senseless at my feet; and that was Raffles, without an instant's doubt. He was in villainous guise, which I knew of old, now that I knew the unhappy wearer. His face was grimy, and dexterously plastered with a growth of reddish hair; his clothes were those in which he had followed cabs from the London termini; his boots were muffled in thick socks; and I had laid him low with a bloody scalp that filled my cup of horror. I groaned aloud as I knelt over him and felt his heart. And I was answered by a bronchial whistle from the door.

'Jolly well done!' cheered my asthmatical friend. 'I heard the whole thing – only hope my mother didn't. We must keep it from her if we can.'

I could have cursed the creature's mother from my full heart; yet even with my hand on that of Raffles, as I felt his feeble pulse, I told myself that this served him right. Even had I brained him, the fault had been his, not mine. And it was a characteristic, an inveterate fault, that galled me for all my anguish: to trust and yet distrust me to the end, to race through England in the night, to spy upon me at his work – to do it himself after all!

'Is he dead?' wheezed the asthmatic coolly.

'Not he,' I answered, with an indignation that I dared not show.

'You must have hit him pretty hard,' pursued young Medlicott, 'but I suppose it was a case of getting first knock. And a good job you got it, if this was his,' he added, picking up the murderous little life-preserver which poor Raffles had provided for his own destruction.

'Look here,' I answered, sitting back on my heels. 'He isn't dead, Mr Medlicott, and I don't know how long he'll be as much as stunned. He's a powerful brute, and you're not fit to lend a hand. But that policeman of yours can't be far away. Do you think you could struggle out and look for him?'

'I suppose I am a bit better than I was,' he replied doubtfully. 'The excitement seems to have done me good. If you like to leave me on guard with my revolver, I'll undertake that he doesn't escape me.'

I shook my head with an impatient smile.

'I should never hear the last of it,' said I. 'No, in that case all I can do is to handcuff the fellow and wait till morning if he won't go quietly; and he'll be a fool if he does, while there's a fighting chance.'

Young Medlicott glanced upstairs from his post on the threshold. I refrained from watching him too keenly, but I knew what was in his mind.

'I'll go,' he said hurriedly. 'I'll go as I am, before my mother is disturbed and frightened out of her life. I owe you something, too, not only for what you've done for me, but for what I was fool enough to think about you at the first blush. It's entirely through you that I feel as fit as I do for the moment. So I'll take your tip, and go just as I am, before my poor old pipes strike up another tune.'

I scarcely looked up until the good fellow had turned his back upon the final tableau of watchful officer and prostrate prisoner and gone out wheezing into the night. But I was at the door to hear the last of him down the path and round the corner of the house. And when I rushed back into the room, there was Raffles sitting cross-legged on the floor, and slowly shaking his broken head as he stanched the blood.

'Et tu, Bunny!' he groaned. 'Mine own familiar friend!'

'Then you weren't even stunned!' I exclaimed. 'Thank God for that!'

'Of course I was stunned,' he murmured, 'and no thanks to you that I wasn't brained. Not to know me in the kit you've seen scores of times! You never looked at me, Bunny; you didn't give me time to open my mouth. I was going to let you run me in so prettily! We'd have walked off arm-in-arm; now it's as tight a place as ever we were in, though you did get rid of old blow-pipes rather nicely. But we shall have the devil's own run for our money!'

Raffles had picked himself up between his mutterings, and I had followed him to the door into the garden, where he stood busy with the key in the dark, having blown out his lantern and handed it to me. But though I followed Raffles, as my nature must, I was far too embittered to answer him again. And so it was for some minutes that might furnish forth a thrilling page, but not a novel one to those who know their Raffles and put up with me. Suffice it that we left a locked door behind us, and the key on the garden wall, which was the first of half a dozen that we scaled before dropping into a lane that led to a footbridge higher up the backwater. And when we paused upon the footbridge, the houses along the bank were still in peace and darkness.

Knowing my Raffles as I did, I was not surprised when he dived under one end of this bridge, and came up with his Inverness cape and opera hat, which he had hidden there on his way to the house. The thick socks were peeled from his patent-leathers, the ragged trousers stripped from an evening pair, bloodstains and Newgate fringe removed at the water's edge, and the whole sepulchre whited in less time than the thing takes to tell. Nor was that enough for Raffles, but he must alter me as well, by wearing my overcoat under his cape, and putting his Zingari scarf about my neck.

'And now,' said he, 'you may be glad to hear there's a 3:12 from Surbiton, which we could catch on all fours. If you like we'll go separately, but I don't think there's the slightest danger now, and I begin to wonder what's happening to old blow-pipes.'

So, indeed, did I, and with no small concern, until I read of his adventures (and our own) in the newspapers. It seemed that he had made a gallant spurt into the road, and there paid the penalty of his rashness by a sudden incapacity to move another inch. It had eventually taken him twenty minutes to creep back to locked doors, and another ten to ring up the inmates. His description of my personal appearance, as reported in the papers, is the only thing that reconciles me to the thought of his sufferings during that half-hour.

But at the time I had other thoughts, and they lay too deep for idle words, for to me also it was a bitter hour. I had not only failed in my self-sought task; I had nearly killed my comrade into the bargain. I had meant well by friend and foe in turn, and I had ended in doing execrably by both. It was not all my fault, but I knew how much my weakness had contributed to the sum. And I must walk with the man whose fault it was, who had travelled two hundred miles to obtain this last proof of my weakness, to bring it home to me, and to make our intimacy intolerable from that hour. I must walk with him to Surbiton, but I need not talk; all through Thames Ditton I had ignored his sallies; nor yet when he ran his arm through mine, on the river front, when we were nearly there, would I break the seal my pride had set upon my lips.

'Come, Bunny,' he said at last, 'I have been the one to suffer most, when all's said and done, and I'll be the first to say that I deserved it. You've broken my head; my hair's all glued up in my gore; and what yarn I'm to put up at Manchester, or how I shall take the field at all, I really don't know. Yet I don't blame you, Bunny, and I do blame myself. Isn't it rather hard luck if I am to go unforgiven into the bargain? I admit that I made a mistake; but, my dear fellow, I made it entirely for your sake.'

'For my sake!' I echoed bitterly.

Raffles was more generous; he ignored my tone.

'I was miserable about you – frankly – miserable!' he went on. 'I couldn't get it out of my head that somehow you would be laid by the heels. It was not your pluck that I distrusted, my dear fellow, but it was your very pluck that made me tremble for you. I couldn't get you out of my head. I went in when runs were wanted, but I give you my word that I was more anxious about you; and no doubt that's why I helped to put on some runs. Didn't you see it in the paper, Bunny? It's the innings of my life, so far.'

'Yes,' I said, 'I saw that you were in at close of play. But I don't believe it was you – I believe you have a double who plays your cricket for you!'

And at the moment that seemed less incredible than the fact.

'I'm afraid you didn't read your paper very carefully,' said Raffles, with the first trace of pique in his tone. 'It was rain that closed play before five o'clock. I hear it was a sultry day in town, but at Manchester we got the storm, and the ground was under water in ten minutes. I never saw such a thing in my life. There was absolutely not the ghost of a chance of another ball being bowled. But I had changed before I thought of doing what I did. It was only when I was on my way back to the hotel, by myself, because I couldn't talk to a soul for thinking of you, that on the spur of the moment I made the man take me to the station instead, and was under way in the restaurant car before I had time to think twice about it. I am not sure that of all the mad deeds I have ever done, this was not the maddest of the lot!'

'It was the finest,' I said in a low voice; for now I marvelled more at the impulse which had prompted his feat, and at the circumstances surrounding it, than even at the feat itself.

'Heaven knows,' he went on, 'what they are saying and doing in Manchester! But what can they say? What business is it of theirs? I was there when play stopped, and I shall be there when it starts again. We shall be at Waterloo just after half-past three, and that's going to give me an hour at the Albany on my way to Euston, and another hour at Old Trafford before play begins. What's the matter with that? I don't suppose I shall notch any more, but all the better if I don't; if we have a hot sun after the storm, the sooner they get in the better; and may I have a bowl at them while the ground bites!'

'I'll come up with you,' I said, 'and see you at it.'

'My dear fellow,' replied Raffles, 'that was my whole feeling about you. I wanted to "see you at it" – that was absolutely all. I wanted to be near enough to lend a hand if you got tied up, as the best of us will at times. I knew the ground better than you, and I simply couldn't keep away from it. But I didn't mean you to know that I was there; if everything had gone as I hoped it might, I should have sneaked back to town without ever letting you know I had been up. You should never have dreamt that I had been at your elbow; you would have believed in yourself, and in my belief in you, and the rest would have been silence till the grave. So I dodged you at Waterloo, and I tried not to let you know that I was following you from Esher station. But you suspected somebody was; you stopped to listen more than once; after the second time I dropped behind, but gained on you by taking the short cut by Imber Court and over the footbridge where I left my coat and hat. I was actually in the garden before you were. I saw you smoke your Sullivan, and I was rather proud of you for it, though you must never do that sort of thing again. I heard almost every word between you and the poor devil upstairs. And up to a certain point, Bunny, I really thought you played the scene to perfection.'

The station lights were twinkling ahead of us in the fading velvet of the summer's night. I let them increase and multiply before I spoke.

'And where,' I asked, 'did you think I first went wrong?'

'In going indoors at all,' said Raffles. 'If I had done that, I should have done exactly what you did from that point on. You couldn't help yourself, with that poor brute in that state. And I admired you immensely, Bunny, if that's any comfort to you now.'

Comfort! It was wine in every vein, for I knew that Raffles meant what he said, and with his eyes I soon saw myself in braver colours. I ceased to blush for the vacillations of the night, since he condoned them. I could even see that I had behaved with a measure of decency, in a truly trying situation, now that Raffles seemed to think so. He had changed my whole view of his proceedings and my own, in every incident of the night but one. There was one thing, however, which he might forgive me, but which I felt that I could forgive neither Raffles nor myself. And that was the contused scalp wound over which I shuddered in the train.

'And to think that I did that,' I groaned, 'and that you laid yourself open to it, and that we have neither of us got another thing to show for our night's work! That poor chap said it was as bad a night as he had ever had in his life; but I call it the very worst that you and I ever had in ours.'

Raffles was smiling under the double lamps of the first-class compartment that we had to ourselves.

'I wouldn't say that, Bunny. We have done worse.'

'Do you mean to tell me that you did anything at all?'

'My dear Bunny,' replied Raffles, 'you should remember how long I had been maturing the felonious little plan, what a blow it was to me to have to turn it over to you, and how far I had travelled to see that you did it by yourself as well as might be. You know what I did see, and how well I understood. I tell you again that I should have done the same thing myself, in your place. But I was not in your place, Bunny. My hands were not tied like yours. Unfortunately, most of the jewels have gone on the honeymoon with the happy pair; but these emerald links are all right, and I don't know what the bride was doing to leave this diamond comb behind. Here, too, is the old silver skewer I've been wanting for years – they make the most charming paperknives in the world – and this gold cigarette-case will just do for your smaller Sullivans.'

Nor were these the only pretty things that Raffles set out in twinkling array upon the opposite cushions. But I do not pretend that this was one of our heavy hauls, or deny that its chief interest still resides in the score of the Second Test Match of that Australian tour.

The Spoils of Sacrilege

There was one deed of those days which deserved a place in our original annals. It is the deed of which I am personally most ashamed. I have traced the course of a score of felonies, from their source in the brain of Raffles to their issue in his hands. I have omitted all mention of the one which emanated from my own miserable mind. But in these supplementary memoirs, wherein I pledged myself to extenuate nothing more that I might have to tell of Raffles, it is only fair that I should make as clean a breast of my own baseness. It was I, then, and I alone, who outraged natural sentiment and trampled the expiring embers of elementary decency by proposing and planning the raid upon my own old home.

I would not accuse myself the more vehemently by making excuses at this point. Yet I feel bound to state that it was already many years since the place had passed from our possession into that of an utter alien, against whom I harboured a prejudice which was some excuse in itself. He had enlarged and altered the dear old place out of all knowledge; nothing had been good enough for him as it stood in our day. The man was a hunting maniac, and where my dear father used to grow prize peaches under glass, this vandal was soon stabling his hot-house thoroughbreds, which took prizes in their turn at all the country shows. It was a southern county, and I never went down there without missing another greenhouse and noting a corresponding extension to the stables. Not that I ever set foot in the grounds from the day we left; but for some years I used to visit old friends in the neighbourhood, and could never resist the temptation to reconnoitre the scenes of my childhood. And so far as could be seen from the road – which it stood too near – the house itself appeared to be the one thing that the horsey purchaser had left much as he found it.

My only other excuse may be none at all in any eyes but mine. It was my passionate desire at this period to 'keep up my end' with Raffles in every department of the game felonious. He would insist upon an equal division of all proceeds; it was for me to earn my share. So far I had been useful only at a pinch; the whole credit of any real success belonged invariably to Raffles. It had always been his idea. That was the tradition which I sought to end, and no means could compare with that of my unscrupulous choice. There was the one house in England of which I knew every inch, and Raffles only what I told him. For once I must lead, and Raffles follow, whether he liked it or not. He saw that himself; and I think he liked it better than he liked me for the desecration in view; but I had hardened my heart, and his feelings were too fine for actual remonstrance on such a point.

I, in my obduracy, went to foul extremes. I drew plans of all the floors from memory. I actually descended upon my friends in the neighbourhood, with the sole object of obtaining snapshots over our own old garden wall. Even Raffles could not keep his eyebrows down when I showed him the prints one morning in the Albany. But he confined his open criticisms to the house.

'Built in the late 'sixties, I see,' said Raffles, 'or else very early in the 'seventies.'

'Exactly when it was built,' I replied. 'But that's worthy of a sixpenny detective, Raffles! How on earth did you know?'

'That slate tower bang over the porch, with the dormer windows and the iron railing and flagstaff atop makes us a present of the period. You see them on almost every house of a certain size built about thirty years ago. They are quite the most useless excrescences I know.'

'Ours wasn't,' I answered, with some warmth. 'It was my *sanctum sanctorum* in the holidays. I smoked my first pipe up there, and wrote my first verses.'

Raffles laid a kindly hand upon my shoulder – 'Bunny, Bunny, you can rob the old place, and yet you can't hear a word against it?'

'That's different,' said I relentlessly. 'The tower was there in my time, but the man I mean to rob was not.'

'You really do mean to do it, Bunny?'

'By myself, if necessary!' I averred.

'Not again, Bunny, not again,' rejoined Raffles, laughing as he shook his head. 'But do you think the man has enough to make it worth our while to go so far afield?'

'Far afield! It's not forty miles on the London and Brighton.'

'Well, that's as bad as a hundred on most lines. And when did you say it was to be?'

'Friday week.'

'I don't much like a Friday, Bunny. Why make it one?'

'It's the night of their hunt point-to-point. They wind up the season with it every year; and the bloated Guillemard usually sweeps the board with his fancy flyers.'

'You mean the man in your old house?'

'Yes; and he tops up with no end of a dinner there,' I went on, 'for his hunting pals and the bloods who ride for him. If the festive board doesn't groan under a new regiment of challenge cups, it will be no fault of theirs, and old Guillemard will have to do them top-hole all the same.'

'So it's a case of common pot-hunting,' remarked Raffles, eyeing me shrewdly through the cigarette smoke.

'Not for us, my dear fellow,' I made answer in his own tone. 'I wouldn't ask you to break into the next set of chambers here in the Albany for a few pieces of modern silver, Raffles. Not that we need scorn the cups if we get a chance of lifting them, and if Guillemard does so in the first instance. It's by no means certain that he will. But it is pretty certain to be a lively night for him and his pals – and a vulnerable one for the best bedroom!'

'Capital!' said Raffles, throwing coils of smoke between his smiles. 'Still, if it's a dinner-party, the hostess won't leave her jewels upstairs. She'll wear them, my boy.'

'Not all of them, Raffles; she has far too many for that. Besides, it isn't an ordinary dinner-party; they say Mrs Guillemard is generally the only lady there, and that she's quite charming in herself. Now, no charming woman would clap on all sail in jewels for a roomful of fox-hunters.'

'It depends what jewels she has.'

'Well, she might wear her rope of pearls.'

'I should have said so.'

'And, of course, her rings.'

'Exactly, Bunny.'

'But not necessarily her diamond tiara – '

'Has she got one?'

' – and certainly not her emerald and diamond necklace on top of all!' Raffles snatched the Sullivan from his lips, and his eyes burned like its end.

'Bunny, do you mean to tell me there are all these things?'

'Of course I do,' said I. 'They are rich people, and he's not such a brute as to spend everything on his stable. Her jewels are as much the talk as his hunters. My friends told me all about both the other day when I was down making enquiries. They thought my curiosity as natural as my wish for a few snapshots of the old place. In their opinion the emerald necklace alone must be worth thousands of pounds.'

Raffles rubbed his hands in playful pantomime.

'I only hope you didn't ask too many questions, Bunny! But if your friends are such old friends, you will never enter their heads when they hear what has happened, unless you are seen down there on the night, which might be fatal. Your approach will require some thought: if you like I can work out the shot for you. I shall go down independently, and the best thing may be to meet outside the house itself on the night of nights. But from that moment I am in your hands.'

And on these refreshing lines our plan of campaign was gradually developed and elaborated into that finished study on which Raffles would rely like any artist of the footlights. None were more capable than he of coping with the occasion as it rose, of rising himself with the emergency of the moment, of snatching a victory from the very dust of defeat. Yet, for choice, every detail was premeditated, and an alternative expedient at each finger's end for as many bare and awful possibilities. In this case, however, the finished study stopped short at the garden gate or wall; there I was to assume command; and though Raffles carried the actual tools of the trade of which he alone was master, it was on the understanding that for once I should control and direct their use.

I had gone down in evening-clothes by an evening train, but had carefully overshot old landmarks, and alighted at a small station some miles south of the one where I was still remembered. This committed me to a solitary and somewhat lengthy tramp; but the night was mild and starry, and I marched into it with a high stomach; for this was to be no costume crime, and yet I should have Raffles at my elbow all the night. Long before I reached my destination, indeed, he stood in wait for me on the white highway, and we finished with linked arms.

'I came down early,' said Raffles, 'and had a look at the races. I always prefer to measure my man, Bunny; and you needn't sit in the front row of the stalls to take stock of your friend Guillemard. No wonder he doesn't ride his own horses! The steeplechaser isn't foaled that would carry him round that course. But he's a fine monument of a man, and he takes his troubles in a way that makes me blush to add to them.'

'Did he lose a horse?' I enquired cheerfully.

'No, Bunny, but he didn't win a race! His horses were by chalks the best there, and his pals rode them like the foul fiend, but with the worst of luck every time. Not that you'd think it, from the row they're making. I've been listening to them from the road – you always did say the house stood too near it.'

'Then you didn't go in?'

'When it's your show? You should know me better. Not a foot would I set on the premises behind your back. But here they are, so perhaps you'll lead the way.'

And I led it without a moment's hesitation, through the unpretentious six-barred gate into the long but shallow crescent of the drive. There were two such gates, one at each end of the drive, but no lodge at either, and not a light nearer than those of the house. The shape and altitude of the lighted windows, the whisper of the laurels on either hand, the very feel of the gravel underfoot, were at once familiar to my senses as the sweet, relaxing, immemorial air that one drank deeper at every breath. Our stealthy advance was to me like stealing back into my childhood; and yet I could conduct it without compunction. I was too excited to feel immediate remorse, albeit not too lost in excitement to know that remorse for every step that I was taking would be my portion soon enough. I mean every word that I have written of my peculiar shame for this night's work. And it was all to come over me before the night was out. But in the garden I never felt it once.

The dining-room windows blazed in the side of the house facing the road. That was an objection to peeping through the venetian blinds, as we nevertheless did, at our peril of observation from the road. Raffles would never have led me into danger so gratuitous and unnecessary, but he followed me into it without a word. I can only plead that we both had our reward. There was a sufficient chink in the obsolete venetians, and through it we saw every inch of the picturesque board. Mrs Guillemard was still in her place, but she really was the only lady, and dressed as quietly as I had prophesied; round her neck was her rope of pearls, but not the glimmer of an emerald nor the glint of a diamond, nor yet the flashing constellation of a tiara in her hair. I gripped Raffles in token of my triumph, and he nodded as he scanned the overwhelming majority of flushed fox-hunters. With the exception of one stripling, evidently the son of the house, they were in evening pink to a man; and as I say, their faces matched their coats. An enormous fellow, with a great red face and cropped moustache, occupied my poor father's place; he it was who had replaced our fruitful vineries with his stinking stables; but I am bound to own he looked a genial clod, as he sat in his fat and listened to the young bloods boasting of their prowess, or elaborately explaining their mishaps. And for a minute we listened also, before I remembered my responsibilities and led Raffles round to the back of the house.

There never was an easier house to enter. I used to feel that keenly as a boy, when, by a prophetic irony, burglars were my bugbear, and I looked under my bed every night in life. The bow-windows on the ground floor finished in inane balconies to the first-floor windows. These balconies had ornamental iron railings, to which a less ingenious rope-ladder than ours could have been hitched with equal ease. Raffles had brought it with him, round his waist, and he carried the telescopic stick for fixing it in place. The one was unwound and the other put together in a secluded corner of the red-brick walls, where of old I had played my own game of squash-rackets in the holidays. I made further investigations in the starlight, and even found a trace of my original white line along the red wall.

But it was not until we had effected our entry through the room which had been my very own, and made our parlous way across the lighted landing, to the best bedroom of those days and these, that I really felt myself a worm. Twin brass bedsteads occupied the site of the old four-poster from which I had first beheld the light. The doors were the same; my childish hands had grasped these very handles. And there was Raffles securing the landing door with wedge and gimlet, the very second after softly closing it behind us.

'The other leads into the dressing-room, of course? Then you might be fixing the outer dressing-room door,' he whispered at his work, 'but not the middle one Bunny, unless you want to. The stuff will be in there, you see, if it isn't in here.'

My door was done in a moment, being fitted with a powerful bolt; but now an aching conscience made me busier than I need have been. I had raised the rope-ladder after us into my own old room, and while Raffles wedged his door I lowered the ladder from one of the best bedroom windows, in order to prepare that way of escape which was a fundamental feature of his own strategy. I meant to show Raffles that I had not followed in his train for nothing. But I left it to him to unearth the jewels. I had begun by turning up the gas; there appeared to be no possible risk in that; and Raffles went to work with a will in the excellent light. There were some good pieces in the room, including an ancient tallboy in fruity mahogany, every drawer of which was turned out on the bed without avail. A few of the drawers had locks to pick, yet not one trifle to our taste lay within. The situation became serious as the minutes flew. We had left the party at its sweets; the solitary lady might be free to roam her house at any minute. In the end we turned our attention to the dressing-room. And no sooner did Raffles behold the bolted door than up went his hands.

'A bathroom bolt,' he cried below his breath, 'and no bath in the room! Why didn't you tell me, Bunny? A bolt like that speaks volumes; there's none on the bedroom door, remember, and this one's worthy of a strong room! What if it is their strong room, Bunny! Oh, Bunny, what if this is their safe?' Raffles had dropped upon his knees before a carved oak chest of indisputable antiquity. Its panels were delightfully irregular, its angles faultlessly faulty, its one modern defilement a strong lock to the lid. Raffles was smiling as he produced his jimmy. R–r–r–rip went lock or lid in another ten seconds – I was not there to see which. I had wandered back into the bedroom in a paroxysm of excitement and suspense. I must keep busy as well as Raffles, and it was not too soon to see whether the rope-ladder was all right. In another minute . . .

I stood frozen to the floor. I had hooked the ladder beautifully to the inner sill of wood, and had also let down the extended rod for the more expeditious removal of both on our return to terra firma. Conceive my cold horror on arriving at the open window just in time to see the last of hooks and bending rod as they floated out of sight and reach into the outer darkness of the night, removed by some silent and invisible hand below!

'Raffles! Raffles – they've spotted us and moved the ladder this very instant!'

So I panted as I rushed on tiptoe to the dressing-room. Raffles had the working end of his jimmy under the lid of a leathern jewel case. It flew open at the vicious twist of his wrist that preceded his reply.

'Did you let them see that you'd spotted that?'

'No.'

'Good! Pocket some of these cases – no time to open them. Which door's nearest the backstairs?'

'The other.'

'Come on then?'

'No, no, I'll lead the way. I know every inch of it.'

And, as I leaned against the bedroom door, handle in hand, while Raffles stooped to unscrew the gimlet and withdraw the wedge, I hit upon the ideal port in the storm that was evidently about to burst on our devoted heads. It was the last place in which they would look for a couple of expert cracksmen with no previous knowledge of the house. If only we could gain my haven unobserved, there we might lie in unsuspected hiding, and by the hour, if not for days and nights.

Alas for that sanguine dream! The wedge was out, and Raffles on his feet behind me. I opened the door, and for a second the pair of us stood upon the threshold.

Creeping up the stairs before us, each on the tip of his silken toes, was a serried file of pink barbarians, redder in the face than anywhere else, and armed with crops carried by the wrong end. The monumental person with the short moustache led the advance. The fool stood still upon the top step to let out the loudest and cheeriest view-holloo that ever smote my ears.

It cost him more than he may know until I tell him. There was the wide part of the landing between us; we had just that much start along the narrow part, with the walls and doors upon our left, the banisters on our right, and the baize door at the end. But if the great Guillemard had not stopped to live up to his sporting reputation, he would assuredly have laid one or other of us by the heels, and either would have been tantamount to both.

As I gave Raffles a headlong lead to the baize door, I glanced down the great well of stairs, and up came the daft yells of these sporting oafs: 'Gone away – gone away!'

'Yoick – yoick – yoick!'

'Yonder they go!'

And gone I had, through the baize door to the back landing, with Raffles at my heels. I held the swing door for him, and heard him bang it in the face of the spluttering and blustering master of the house. Other feet were already in the lower flight of the backstairs; but the upper flight was the one for me, and in an instant we were racing along the upper corridor with the chuckle-headed pack at our heels. Here it was all but dark – they were the servants' bedrooms that we were passing now – but I knew what I was doing. Round the last corner to the right, through the first door to the left and we were in the room underneath the tower. In our time a long stepladder had led to the tower itself. I rushed in the dark to the old corner. Thank God, the ladder was there still! It leaped under us as we rushed aloft like one quadruped. The breakneck trapdoor was still protected by a curved brass stanchion; this I grasped with one hand and then Raffles with the other as I felt my feet firm upon the tower floor. In he sprawled after me, and down went the trapdoor with a bang upon the leading hound.

I hoped to feel his dead-weight shake the house, as he crashed upon the floor below; but the fellow must have ducked, and no crash came. Meanwhile not a word passed between Raffles and me; he had followed me, as I had led him, without waste of breath upon a single syllable. But the merry lot below were still yelling and bellowing in full cry.

'Gone to ground?' screamed one.

'Where's the terrier?' screeched another.

But their host of the mighty girth – a man like a soda-water bottle, from my one glimpse of him on his feet – seemed sobered rather than stunned by the crack on that head of his. We heard his fine voice no more, but we could feel him straining every thew against the trapdoor upon which Raffles and I stood side by side. At least I thought Raffles was standing, until he asked me to strike a light and I found him on his knees instead of on his feet, busy screwing down the trapdoor with his gimlet. He carried three or four gimlets for wedging doors, and he drove them all in to the handle, while I pulled at the stanchion and pushed with my feet.

But the upward pressure ceased before our efforts. We heard the ladder creak again under a ponderous and slow descent; and we stood upright in the dim flicker of a candle-end that I had lit and left burning on the floor. Raffles glanced at the four small windows in turn and then at me. 'Is there any way out at all?' he whispered, as no other being would or could have whispered to the man who had led him into such a trap. 'We've no rope-ladder, you know.'

'Thanks to me,' I groaned. 'The whole thing's my fault!'

'Nonsense, Bunny; there was no other way to run. But what about these windows?'

His magnanimity took me by the throat; without a word I led him to the one window looking inward upon sloping slates and level leads. Often as a boy I had clambered over them, for the fearful fun of risking life and limb, or the fascination of peering through the great square skylight, down the well of the house into the hall below. There were, however, several smaller skylights, for the benefit of the top floor, through any one of which I thought we might have made a dash. But at a glance I saw we were too late: one of these skylights became a brilliant square before our eyes; it opened and admitted a flushed face on flaming shoulders.

'I'll give them a fright!' said Raffles through his teeth. In an instant he had plucked out his revolver and smashed the window with its butt and the slates with a bullet not a yard from the protruding head. And that, I believe, was the only shot that Raffles ever fired in his whole career as a midnight marauder.

'You didn't hit him?' I gasped, as the head disappeared, and we heard a crash in the corridor.

'Of course I didn't, Bunny,' he replied, backing into the tower; 'but no one will believe I didn't mean to, and it'll stick on ten years if we're caught. That's nothing, if it gives us an extra five minutes now, while they hold a council of war. Is that a working flagstaff overhead?'

'It used to be.'

'Then there'll be halliards.'

'They were as thin as clotheslines.'

'And they're sure to be rotten, and we should be seen cutting them down. No, Bunny, that won't do. Wait a bit. Is there a lightning conductor?'

'There was.'

I opened one of the side windows and reached out as far as I could. 'You'll be seen from that skylight!' cried Raffles in a warning undertone.

'No, I won't. I can't see it myself. But here's the lightning-conductor, where it always was.'

'How thick,' asked Raffles, as I drew in and rejoined him.

'Rather thicker than a lead-pencil.'

'They sometimes bear you,' said Raffles, slipping on a pair of white kid gloves, and stuffing his handkerchief into the palm of one. 'The difficulty is to keep a grip; but I've been up and down them before tonight. And it's our only chance. I'll go first, Bunny: you watch me, and do exactly as I do if I get down all right.'

'But if you don't?'

'If I don't,' whispered Raffles, as he wormed through the window feet foremost, 'I'm afraid you'll have to face the music where you are, and I shall have the best of it down in Acheron!'

And he slid out of reach without another word, leaving me to shudder alike at his levity and his peril; nor could I follow him very far by the wan light of the April stars; but I saw his forearms resting a moment in the spout that ran around the tower, between bricks and slates, on the level of the floor; and I had another dim glimpse of him lower still, on the eaves over the very room that we had ransacked. Thence the conductor ran straight to earth in an angle of the façade. And since it had borne him thus far without mishap, I felt that Raffles was as good as down. But I had neither his muscles nor his nerves, and my head swam as I mounted to the window and prepared to creep out backwards in my turn.

So it was that at the last moment I had my first unobstructed view of the little old tower of other days. Raffles was out of the way; the bit of candle was still burning on the floor, and in its dim light the familiar haunt was cruelly like itself of innocent memory. A lesser ladder still ascended to a tinier trapdoor in the apex of the tower; the fixed seats looked to me to be wearing their old, old coat of grained varnish; nay the varnish had its ancient smell, and the very vanes outside creaked their message to my ears.

I remembered whole days that I had spent, whole books that I had read, here in this favourite fastness of my boyhood. The dirty little place, with the dormer window in each of its four sloping sides, became a gallery hung with poignant pictures of the past. And here was I leaving it with my life in my hands and my pockets full of stolen jewels! A superstition seized me. Suppose the conductor came down with me . . . suppose I slipped . . . and was picked up dead, with the proceeds of my shameful crime upon me, under the very windows . . . where the sun came peeping in at dawn . . .

I hardly remember what I did or left undone. I only know that nothing broke, that somehow I kept my hold, and that in the end the wire ran red-hot through my palms so that both were torn and bleeding when I stood panting beside Raffles in the flowerbeds. There was no time for thinking then. Already there was a fresh commotion indoors; the tidal wave of excitement which had swept all before it to the upper regions was subsiding in as swift a rush downstairs; and I raced after Raffles along the edge of the drive without daring to look behind.

We came out by the opposite gate to that by which we had stolen in. Sharp to the right ran the private lane behind the stables and sharp to the right dashed Raffles, instead of straight along the open road. It was not the course I should have chosen, but I followed Raffles without a murmur, only too thankful that he had assumed the lead at last. Already the stables were lit up like a chandelier; there was a staccato rattle of horseshoes in the stable yard, and the great gates were opening as we skimmed past in the nick of time. In another minute we were skulking in the shadow of the kitchen-garden wall while the high road rang with the dying tattoo of galloping hoofs.

'That's for the police,' said Raffles, waiting for me. 'But the fun's only beginning in the stables. Hear the uproar, and see the lights! In another minute they'll be turning out the hunters for the last run of the season.'

'We mustn't give them one, Raffles!'

'Of course we mustn't; but that means stopping where we are.'

'We can't do that!'

'If they're wise they'll send a man to every railway station within ten miles and draw every cover inside the radius. I can only think of one that's not likely to occur to them.'

'What's that?'

'The other side of this wall. How big is the garden, Bunny?'

'Six or seven acres.'

'Well, you must take me to another of your old haunts, where we can lie low till morning.'

'And then?'

'Sufficient for the night, Bunny! The first thing is to find a burrow. What are those trees at the end of this lane?'

'St Leonard's Forest.'

'Magnificent! They'll scour every inch of that before they come back to their own garden. Come, Bunny, give me a leg up, and I'll pull you after me in two ticks!'

There was indeed nothing better to be done; and, much as I loathed and dreaded entering the place again, I had already thought of a second sanctuary of old days, which might as well be put to the base uses of this disgraceful night. In a far corner of the garden, over a hundred yards from the house, a little ornamental lake had been dug within my own memory; its shores were shelving lawn and steep banks of rhododendrons; and among the rhododendrons nestled a tiny boathouse which had been my childish joy. It was half a dock for the dingy in which one ploughed these miniature waters and half a bathing-box for those who preferred their morning tub among the goldfish. I could not think of a safer asylum than this, if we must spend the night upon the premises; and Raffles agreed with me when I had led him by sheltering shrubbery and perilous lawn to the diminutive chalet between the rhododendrons and the water.

But what a night it was! The little bathing-box had two doors, one to the water, the other to the path. To hear all that could be heard, it was necessary to keep both doors open, and quite imperative not to talk. The damp night air of April filled the place, and crept through our evening clothes and light overcoats into the very marrow; the mental torture of the situation was renewed and multiplied in my brain; and all the time one's ears were pricked for footsteps on the path between the rhododendrons. The only sounds we could at first identify came one and all from the stables. Yet there the excitement subsided sooner than we had expected, and it was Raffles himself who breathed a doubt as to whether they were turning out the hunters after all. On the other hand, we heard wheels in the drive not long after midnight; and Raffles, who was beginning to scout among the shrubberies, stole back to tell me that the guests were departing, and being sped, with an unimpaired conviviality which he failed to understand. I said I could not understand it either, but suggested the general influence of liquor, and expressed my envy of their state. I had drawn my knees up to my chin on the bench where one used to dry oneself after bathing, and there I sat in a seeming stolidity at utter variance with my inward temper. I heard Raffles creep forth again and I let him go without a word. I never doubted that he would be back again in a minute, and so let many minutes elapse before I realised his continued absence, and finally crept out myself to look for him.

Even then I only supposed that he had posted himself outside in some more commanding position. I took a catlike stride and breathed his name. There was no answer. I ventured further, till I could overlook the lawns: they lay like clean slates in the starlight: there was no sign of living thing nearer than the house, which was still lit up, but quiet enough now. Was it a cunning and deliberate quiet assumed as a snare? Had they caught Raffles, and were they waiting for me? I returned to the boat-house in an agony of fear and indignation. It was fear for the long hours that I sat there waiting for him; it was indignation when at last I heard his stealthy step upon the gravel. I would not go out to meet him. I sat where I was while the stealthy step came nearer, nearer; and there I was sitting when the door opened, and a huge man in riding-clothes stood before me in the steely dawn.

I leaped to my feet, and the huge man clapped me playfully on the shoulder.

'Sorry I've been so long, Bunny, but we should never have got away as we were; this riding-suit makes a new man of me, on top of my own, and here's a youth's kit that should do you down to the ground.'

'So you broke into the house again?'

'I was obliged to, Bunny; but I had to watch the lights out one by one, and give them a good hour after that. I went through that dressing room at my leisure this time; the only difficulty was to spot the son's quarters at the back of the house; but I overcame it, as you see, in the end. I only hope they'll fit, Bunny. Give me your patent leathers, and I'll fill them with stones and sink them in the pond. I'm doing the same with mine. Here's a brown pair apiece, and we mustn't let the grass grow under them if we're to get to the station in time for the early train while the coast's still clear.'

The early train leaves the station in question at 6.20 a.m.; and that fine spring morning there was a police officer in a peaked cap to see it off; but he was too busy peering into the compartments for a pair of very swell mobsmen that he took no notice of the huge man in riding-clothes, who was obviously intoxicated, or the more insignificant but not less horsy character who had him in hand. The early train is due at Victoria at 8.28, but these worthies left it at Clapham Junction, and changed cabs more than once between Battersea and Piccadilly, and left a few of their garments in each four-wheeler. It was barely nine o'clock when they sat together in the Albany, and might have been recognised once more as Raffles and myself.

'And now,' said Raffles, 'before we do anything else, let us turn out those little cases that we hadn't time to open when we took them. I mean the ones I handed to you, Bunny. I had a look into mine in the garden, and I'm sorry to say there was nothing in them. The lady must have been wearing their proper contents.'

Raffles held out his hand for the substantial leather cases which I had produced at his request. But that was the extent of my compliance; instead of handing them over, I looked boldly into the eyes that seemed to have discerned my wretched secret at one glance.

'It is no use my giving them to you,' I said. 'They are empty also.'

'When did you look into them?'

'In the tower.'

'Well, let me see for myself.'

'As you like.'

'My dear Bunny, this one must have contained the necklace you boasted about.'

'Very likely.'

'And this one the tiara.'

'I dare say.'

'Yet she was wearing neither, as you prophesied, and as we both saw for ourselves!'

I had not taken my eyes from his. 'Raffles,' I said, 'I'll be frank with you after all. I meant you never to know, but it's easier than telling you a lie. I left both things behind me in the tower. I won't attempt to explain or defend myself; it was probably the influence of the tower, and nothing else; but the whole thing came over me at the last moment, when you had gone and I was going. I felt that I should very probably break my neck, that I cared very little whether I did or not, but that it would be frightful to break it at that house with those things in my pocket. You may say I ought to have thought of all that before! you may say what you like, and you won't say more than I deserve. It was hysterical, and it was mean, for I kept the cases to impose on you.'

'You were always a bad liar, Bunny,' said Raffles, smiling. 'Will you think me one when I tell you that I can understand what you felt, and even what you did? As a matter of fact, I have understood for several hours now.'

'You mean what I felt, Raffles?'

'And what you did. I guessed it in the boat-house. I knew that something must have happened or been discovered to disperse that truculent party of sportsmen so soon and on such good terms with themselves. They had not got us; they might have got something better worth having; and your phlegmatic attitude suggested what. As luck would have it, the cases that I personally had collared were the empty ones; the two prizes had fallen to you. Well, to allay my horrid suspicion, I went and had another peep through the lighted venetians. And what do you think I saw?'

I shook my head. I had no idea, nor was I very eager for enlightenment.

'The two poor people whom it was your own idea to despoil,' quoth Raffles, 'prematurely gloating over these two pretty things!' He withdrew a hand from either pocket of his crumpled dinner-jacket, and opened the pair under my nose. In one was a diamond tiara, and in the other a necklace of fine emeralds set in clusters of brilliants.

'You must try to forgive me, Bunny,' continued Raffles before I could speak. 'I don't say a word against what you did, or undid; in fact, now it's all over, I am rather glad to think that you did try to undo it. But, my dear fellow, we had both risked life, limb and liberty; and I had not your sentimental scruples. Why should I go empty away? If you want to know the inner history of my second visit to that good fellow's dressing-room, drive home for a fresh kit and meet me at the Turkish bath in twenty minutes. I feel more than a little grubby, and we can have our breakfast in the cooling gallery. Besides, after a whole night in your old haunts, Bunny, it's only in order to wind up in Northumberland Avenue.'

BERNHARD SEVERIN INGEMANN

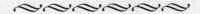

B. S. Ingemann (1789–1862), the father of the Danish novel. For the Danes, Ingemann is a celebrated literary figure, and his works are well known to every child, youth and adult in Denmark. His themes are all taken from the historical events of the Middle Ages, their chief characters being national heroes and heroines.

The Sealed Room

For many years there stood in a side street in Kiel an unpretentious old frame house which had a forbidding, almost sinister appearance, with its old-fashioned balcony and its overhanging upper stories. For the last twenty years the house had been occupied by a greatly respected widow, Madame Wolff, to whom the dwelling had come by inheritance. She lived there quietly with her one daughter, in somewhat straitened circumstances.

What gave the house a mysterious notoriety, augmenting the sinister quality in its appearance, was the fact that one of its rooms, a corner room on the main floor, had not been opened for generations. The door was firmly fastened and sealed with plaster, as well as the window looking out upon the street. Above the door was an old inscription, dated 1603, which threatened sudden death and eternal damnation to any human being who dared to open the door or efface the inscription. Neither door nor window had been opened in the two hundred years that had passed since the inscription was put up. But for a generation back or more, the partition wall and the sealed door had been covered with wallpaper, and the inscription had been almost forgotten.

The room adjoining the sealed chamber was a large hall, utilised only for rare important events. Such an occasion arose with the wedding of the only daughter of the house. For that evening the great hall, as it was called, was brilliantly decorated and illuminated for a ball. The building had deep cellars and the old floors were elastic. Madame Wolff had in vain endeavoured to avoid using the great hall at all, for the foolish old legend of the sealed chamber aroused a certain superstitious dread in her heart, and she rarely if ever entered the hall herself. But merry Miss Elizabeth, her pretty young daughter, was passionately fond of dancing, and her mother had promised that she should have a ball on her wedding day. Her betrothed, Secretary Winther, was also a good dancer, and the two young people combated the mother's prejudice against the hall and laughed at her fear of the sealed room. They thought it would be wiser to appear to ignore the stupid legend altogether, and thus to force the world to forget it. In spite of secret misgivings Madame Wolff yielded to their arguments. And for the first time in many years the merry strains of dance music were heard in the great hall that lay next to the mysterious sealed chamber.

The bridal couple, as well as the wedding guests, were in the gayest mood, and the ball was an undoubted success. The dancing was interrupted for an hour while supper was served in an adjoining room. After the repast the guests returned to the hall, and it was several hours more before the last dance was called. The season was early autumn and the weather still balmy. The windows had been opened to freshen the air. But the walls retained their dampness and suddenly the dancers noticed that the old wallpaper which covered the partition wall between the hall and the sealed chamber had been loosened through the jarring of the building, and had fallen away from the sealed door with its mysterious inscription.

The story of the sealed chamber had been almost forgotten by most of those present, forgotten with many other old legends heard in childhood. The inscription thus suddenly revealed naturally aroused great interest, and there was a general curiosity to know what the mysterious closed room might hide. Conjectures flew from mouth to mouth. Some insisted that the closed door must hide the traces of a hideous murder, or some other equally terrible crime. Others suggested that perhaps the room had been used as a hiding place for garments and other articles belonging to some person who had died of a pestilence, and that the room had been sealed for fear of spreading the disease. Still others thought that in the sealed chamber there might be found a secret entrance from the cellars, which had made the room available as a hiding place for robbers or smugglers. The guests had quite forgotten their dancing in the interest awakened by the sight of the mysterious door.

'For mercy's sake, don't let's go too near it!' exclaimed some of the young ladies. But the majority thought it would be great fun to see what was hidden there. Most of the men said that they considered it foolish not to have opened the door long ago, and examined the room. The young bridegroom did not join in this opinion, however. He upheld the decision of his mother-in-law not to allow any attempt to effect an entrance into the room. He knew that there was a clause in the title deeds to the house which made the express stipulation that no owner should ever permit the corner room to be opened. There was discussion among the guests as to whether such a clause in a title deed could be binding for several hundred years, and many doubted its validity at any time. But most of them understood why Madame Wolff did not wish any investigation, even should any of those present have sufficient courage to dare the curse and break open the door.

'Nonsense! What great courage is necessary for that?' exclaimed Lieutenant Flemming Wolff, a cousin of the bride of the evening. This gentleman had a reputation that was not of the best. He was known to live mostly on debt and pawn tickets, and was of a most quarrelsome disposition. As a duelist he was feared because of his speciality. This was the ability, and the inclination, through a trick in the use of the foils, to disfigure his opponent's face badly, without at all endangering his life. In this manner he had already sadly mutilated several brave officers and students, who had had the bad luck to stand up against him. He himself was anything but pleasant to look upon, his natural plainness having been rendered repellent by a life of low debauchery. He cherished a secret grudge against the bridegroom and bitter feelings toward the bride, because the latter had so plainly shown her aversion for him when he had ventured to pay suit to her.

The family had not desired any open break with this disagreeable relative, and had therefore sent him an invitation to the wedding. They had taken it for granted that, under the circumstances, he would prefer to stay away. But he had appeared at the ball, and, perhaps to conceal his resentment, he had been the most indefatigable dancer of the evening. At supper he had partaken freely of the strongest wines and was plainly showing the effect of them by this time. His eyes rolled wildly, and those who knew him took care not to contradict him, or to have anything to say to him at all.

With a boastful laugh he repeated his assertion that it didn't take much courage to open a sealed door, especially when there might be a fortune concealed behind it. In his opinion it was cowardly to let oneself be frightened by a centuries-old legend. *He* wouldn't let that bother him if *he* had influence enough in the family to win the daughter and induce the mother to give a ball in the haunted hall. With this last hit he hoped to arouse the young husband's ire. But the latter merely shrugged his shoulders and turned away with a smile of contempt.

Lieutenant Wolff fired up at this, and demanded to know whether the other intended to call his, the lieutenant's, courage into question by his behaviour.

'Not in the slightest, when it is a matter of obtaining a loan, or of mutilating an adversary with a trick at fencing,' answered the bridegroom angrily, taking care, however, that neither the bride nor any of the other ladies should hear his words. Then he continued in a whisper: 'But I don't believe you'd have the courage to remain here alone and in darkness before this closed door for a single hour. If you wish to challenge me for this doubt, I am at your disposal as soon as you have proven me in the wrong. But I choose the weapons.'

'They must be chosen by lot, sir cousin,' replied the lieutenant, his cheek pale and his jaws set. 'I will expect you to breakfast tomorrow morning at eight o'clock.'

The bridegroom nodded, and took the other's cold dry hand for an instant. The men who had overheard the short conversation looked upon it as a meaningless incident, the memory of which would disappear from the lieutenant's brain with the vanishing wine fumes.

The ball was now over. The bride left the hall with her husband and several of the guests who were to accompany the young couple to their new home. The lights went out in the old house. The door of the dancing hall had been locked from the outside. Lieutenant Flemming Wolff remained alone in the room, having hidden himself in a dark corner where he had not been seen by the servants who had extinguished the lights and locked the door. The night-watchman had just called out two o'clock when the solitary guest found himself, still giddy from the heavy wine, alone in the great dark hall in front of the mysterious door.

The windows were at only a slight elevation from the street, and a spring would take him to safety should his desire to remain there, or to solve the mystery of the sealed room, vanish. But next morning all the windows in the great hall were found closed, just as the servants had left them the night before. The night-watchman reported that he had heard a hollow-sounding crash in that unoccupied part of the house during the night. But that was nothing unusual, as there was a general belief in the neighbourhood that the house was haunted.

For hollow noises were often heard there, and sounds as of money falling on the floor, and rattling and clinking as of a factory machine. Enlightened people, it is true, explained these sounds as echoes of the stamping and other natural noises from a large stable just behind the old house. But in spite of these explanations and their eminent feasibility, the dread of the unoccupied portion of the house was so great that not even the most reckless man-servant could be persuaded to enter it alone after nightfall.

Next morning at eight o'clock Winther appeared at his mother-in-law's door, saying that he had forgotten something of importance in the great hall the night before. Madame Wolff had not yet arisen, but the maid who let in the early visitor noticed with surprise that he had a large pistol sticking out of one of his pockets.

Winther had been to his cousin's apartment and found it locked. He now entered the great hall, and at first glance thought it empty. To his alarm and astonishment, however, he saw that the sealed door had been broken open. He approached it with anxiety, and found his wife's cousin, the doughty duelist, lying pale and lifeless on the threshold. Beside him lay a large stone which had struck his head in falling and must have killed him at once. Over the door was a hole in the wall, just the size of the stone. The latter had evidently rested on the upper edge of the door, and must certainly have fallen on its opening. The unfortunate man lay half in the mysterious chamber and half in the hall, just as he must have fallen when the stone struck him.

The formal investigation of the closed room was made in the presence of the police authorities. It contained nothing but a small safe which was built into the wall. When the safe had been opened by force, an inner chamber, which had to be broken open by itself, was found to contain a number of rolls of gold pieces, many jewels and numerous notes and IOUs. The treasure was covered by an old document. From this latter it was learned that the owner of the house two hundred years ago had been a silk weaver by the name of Flemming Ambrosius Wolff. He was said to have lent money on security for many years, but had died apparently a poor man, because he had so carefully hidden his wealth that little of it was found after his death.

With a niggardliness that bordered on madness, he had believed that he could hide his treasure for ever by shutting it up in the sealed room. The curse over the door was to frighten away any venturesome mortal, and further security was given by the clause in the title deed.

The universally disliked Lieutenant Flemming Wolff must have had many characteristics in common with this disagreeable old ancestor, to whose treasure he would have fallen heir had he not lost his life in the discovering of it. The old miser had not hidden his wealth for all eternity, as he had hoped, but had only brought about the inheriting of it by Madame Wolff, the owner of the house, and the next of kin. The first use to which this lady put the money was the tearing down of the uncanny old building and the erection in its stead of a beautiful new home for her daughter and son-in-law.

MAURUS JOKAI

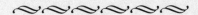

Maurus Jokai (1825–1904), the best known Hungarian novelist, did not lose faith after the disastrous outcome of the Hungarian War of Independence of 1848–9. In many novels, he revived the former glory of his native land. He is still the most widely read author in Hungary and twenty-two of his hundred novels have appeared in English. In his immense output, many weaknesses are apparent. His novels lack depth; many aim solely at entertaining. But his optimism, his humour, his imagination captivate the reader; he has an unsurpassed talent as a *raconteur*. No other author has so masterfully described the beauties of the Hungarian landscape and the typical characters of Hungary. His novels are essentially modern fairy tales told in colourful, expressive language.

Thirteen at Table

We are far amidst the snow-clad mountains of Transylvania.

The scenery is magnificent. In clear weather, the plains of Hungary as far as the Rez promontory may be seen from the summit of the mountains. Groups of hills rise one above the other, covered with thick forest, which, at the period when our tale commences, had just begun to assume the first light green of spring.

Towards sunset, a slight purple mist overspread the farther pinnacles, leaving their ridges still tinged with gold. On the side of one of these hills the white turrets of an ancient family mansion gleamed from amid the trees.

Its situation was peculiarly romantic. A steep rock descended on one side, on whose pinnacle rose a simple cross. In the depth of the valley beneath lay a scattered village, whose evening bells melodiously broke the stillness of nature.

Farther off, some broken roofs arose among the trees, from whence the sound of the mill, and the yellow-tinted stream, betrayed the miners' dwellings.

Through the meadows in the valley beneath a serpentine rivulet wound its silvery way, interrupted by numerous falls and huge blocks of stone, which had been carried down in bygone ages from the mountains during the melting of the snows.

A little path, cut in the side of the rock, ascended to the castle; while higher up, a broad road, somewhat broken by the mountain streams, conducted across the hills to more distant regions.

The castle itself was an old family mansion, which had received many additions at different periods, as the wealth or necessities of the family suggested. It was surrounded by groups of ancient chestnut trees, and the terrace before the court was laid out in gardens, which were now filled with anemones, hyacinths and other early flowers. Now and then the head of a joyous child appeared at the windows, which were opened to admit the evening breeze; while various members of the household retinue were seen hastening through the corridors, or standing at the doors in their embroidered liveries.

The castle was completely surrounded by a strong rail-work of iron, the stone pillars were overgrown by the evergreen leaves of the gobea and epomoea.

It was the early spring of 1848.

A party, consisting of thirteen persons, had assembled in the dining-room. They were all members of one family, and all bore the name of Bardy.

At the head of the board sat the grandmother, an old lady of eighty years of age, whose snow-white hair was dressed according to the fashion of her times beneath her high white cap. Her face was pale and much wrinkled, and the eyes turned constantly upwards, as is the case with persons who have lost their sight. Her hand and voice trembled with age, and there was something peculiarly striking in the thick snow-white eyebrows.

On her right hand sat her eldest son, Tamas Bardy, a man of between fifty and sixty. With a haughty and commanding countenance, penetrating glance, lofty figure and noble mien, he was a true type of that ancient aristocracy which is now beginning to die out.

Opposite to him, at the old lady's left hand, sat the darling of the family – a lovely girl of about fifteen. Her golden hair fell in luxuriant tresses round a countenance of singular beauty and sweetness. The large and lustrous deep-blue eyes were shaded by long dark lashes, and her complexion was pale as the lily, excepting when she smiled or spoke, and a slight flush like the dawn of morning overspread her cheeks. Jolanka was the orphan child of a distant relative, whom the Bardys had adopted. They could not allow one who bore their name to suffer want; and it seemed as if each member of the family had united to heap affection and endearment on the orphan girl, and thus prevented her from feeling herself a stranger among them.

There were still two other female members of the family: Katalin, the old lady's daughter, who had been for many years a widow; and the wife of one of her sons, a pretty young woman, who was trying to teach a little prattler at her side to use the golden spoon which she had placed in his small, fat hand, while he laughed and crowed, and the family did their best to guess what he said, or what he most preferred.

Opposite to them there sat two gentlemen. One of them was the husband of the young mother, Jozsef Bardy – a handsome man of about thirty-five, with regular features, and black hair and beard; a constant smile beamed on his gay countenance, while he playfully addressed his little son and gentle wife across the table. The other was his brother, Barnabas – a man of herculean form and strength. His face was marked by smallpox; he wore neither beard nor moustache, and his hair was combed smoothly back, like a peasant's. His disposition was melancholy and taciturn; but he seemed constantly striving to atone, by the amiability of his manners, for an unprepossessing exterior.

Next to him sat a little cripple, whose pale countenance bore that expression of suffering sweetness so peculiar to the deformed, while his lank hair, bony hands and misshapen shoulders awakened the beholder's pity. He, too, was an orphan – a grandchild of the old lady's – his parents having died some years before.

Two little boys of about five years old sat opposite to him. They were dressed alike, and the resemblance between them was so striking that they were constantly mistaken. They were twin-children of the young couple.

At the lower end of the table sat Imre Bardy, a young man of twenty, whose handsome countenance was full of life and intelligence, his figure manly and graceful, and his manner courteous and agreeable. A slight moustache was beginning to shade his upper lip, and his dark hair fell in natural ringlets around his head. He was the only son of Tamas Bardy, and resembled him much in form and feature.

Beside him sat an old gentleman, with white hair and ruddy complexion. This was Simon Bardy, an ancient relative, who had grown old with the grandmother of the family.

The same peculiarity characterised every countenance in the Bardy family – namely the lofty forehead and marked brows, and the large deep-blue eyes, shaded by their heavy dark lashes. (There is a race of the Hungarians in the Carpath who, unlike the Hungarians of the plain, have blue eyes and often fair hair.)

'How singular!' exclaimed one of the party; 'we are thirteen at table today.'

'One of us will surely die,' said the old lady; and there was a mournful conviction in the faint, trembling tones.

'Oh, no, grandmother, we are only twelve and a half!' exclaimed the young mother, taking the little one on her knee.

'This little fellow only counts half on the railroad.'

All the party laughed at this remark, even the little cripple's countenance relaxed into a sickly smile.

'Ay, ay,' continued the old lady, 'the trees are now putting forth their verdure, but at the fall of the leaf who knows if all of us, or any of us, may still be sitting here?'

*　　*　　*

Several months had passed since this slight incident.

In one of the apartments of the castle, the eldest Bardy and his son were engaged in earnest conversation.

The father paced hastily up and down the apartment, now and then stopping short to address his son, who stood in the embrasure of one of the windows. The latter wore the dress of the Magyar Hussars – a grey dolman, with crimson cord; he held a crimson shako, with a tricoloured cockade, in his hand.

'Go,' said the father, speaking in broken accents; 'the sooner the better; let me not see you! Do not think I speak in anger, but I cannot bear to look at you, and think where you are going. You are my only son, and you know how I have loved you – how all my hopes have been concentrated in you. But do not think that these tears, which you see me shed for the first time, are on your account; for if I knew I should lose you – if your blood were to flow at the next battle – I should only bow my head in dust and say, "The Lord gave, and the Lord taketh away, blessed be His holy name!" Yes, if I heard that you and your infatuated companions were cut to pieces, I could stifle the burning tears; but to know that your blood, when it flows, will be a curse upon the earth, and your death will be the death of two kingdoms – '

'They may die now; but they will regenerate – '

'This is not true; you only deceive yourselves with the idea that you can build up a new edifice when you have overthrown the old one. Great God, what sacrilege! Who has entrusted you with the fate of our country, to tempt the Almighty? Who authorises you to lose all there is for the hope of what may be? For centuries past have so many honourable men fought in vain to uphold the old tottering constitution, as you call it? Or were they not true patriots and heroes? Your companions have hissed their persecuted countrymen in the Diet; but do they love their country better than we do, who have shed our blood and sacrificed our interests for her from generation to generation, and even suffered disgrace, if necessary, to keep her in life? – for though that life has been gradually weakened, still it is life. You promise her glory; but the name of glory is death!'

'It may be so, father; we may lose our country as regards ourselves, but we give one instead of ten millions, who were hitherto our own people, and yet strangers in their native land.'

'Chimera! The people will not understand you. They never even dreamt of what you wish to give them. The true way to seek the people's welfare is to give them what they need.

'Ask my dependants! Is there one among them whom I have allowed to suffer want or ruin, whom I have not assisted in times of need? – or have I ever treated them unjustly? You will not hear a murmur. Tell them that I am unjust notwithstanding, because I do not call the peasant from his plough to give his opinions on forming the laws and constitution – and what will be the consequence? They will stare at you in astonishment; and yet, in their mistaken wrath, they will come down some night and burn this house over my head.'

'That is the unnatural state of the times. It is all the fault of past bad management, if the people have no better idea. But let the peasant once be free, let him be a man, and he will understand all that is now strange to him.'

'But that freedom will cost the lives of thousands!'

'I do not deny it. Indeed, I believe that neither I nor any of the present generation will reap the fruits of this movement. I think it probable that in a few years not one of those whose names we now hear spoken of may still be living; and what is more, disgrace and curses may be heaped upon their dust. But a time will come when the great institutions of which they have laid the foundation will arise and render justice to the memory of those who sacrificed themselves for the happiness of future generations. To die for our country is a glorious death, but to carry with us the curses of thousands, to die despised and hated for the salvation of future millions, oh! that is sublime – it is Messiah-like!'

'My son – my only son!' cried his father, throwing himself passionately on the young man's neck and sobbing bitterly. 'Do you see these tears?'

'For the first time in my life I see them, father – I see you weep; my heart can scarcely bear the weight of these tears – and yet I go! You have reason to weep, for I bring neither joy nor glory on your head – and yet I go! A feeling stronger than the desire of glory, stronger than the love of my country, inspires my soul; and it is a proof of the strength of my faith that I see your tears, my father – and yet I go!'

'Go!' murmured his father, in a voice of despair. 'You may never return again, or, when you do, you may find neither your father's house nor the grave in which he is laid! But know, even then, in the hour of your death, or in the hour of mine, I do not curse you – and now, leave me.' With these words he turned away and motioned to his son to depart.

Imre silently left the apartment, and as soon as he had closed the door the tears streamed from his eyes; but before his sword had struck the last step his countenance had regained its former determination, and the fire of enthusiasm had kindled in his eye.

He then went to take leave of his Uncle Jozsef, whom he found surrounded by his family. The twins were sitting at his feet, while his wife was playing bo-peep with the little one, who laughed and shouted, while his mother hid herself behind his father's armchair.

Imre's entrance interrupted the general mirth. The little boy ran over to examine the sword and golden tassels, while the little one began to cry in alarm at the sight of the strange dress.

'Csitt, baba!' said his mother, taking him from his father's arms; 'your cousin is going to wars, and will bring you a golden horse.'

Jozsef wrung his nephew's hand. 'God be with you!' he exclaimed, and added in a lower voice, 'You are the noblest of us all – you have done well!'

They then all embraced him in turns, and Imre left them, amidst clamours of the little ones, and proceeded to his grandmother's apartments.

On the way, he met his Uncle Barnabas, who embraced him again and again in silence, and then tore himself away without saying a word.

The old lady sat in her great armchair, which she seldom quitted, and as she heard the clash of Imre's sword, she looked up and asked who was coming.

'It is Imre!' said the fair-haired maiden, blushing, and her heart beat quickly as she pronounced his name.

Jolanka felt that Imre was more than a brother to her, and the feeling with which she had learnt to return his affection was warmer than even a sister's love.

The widow lady and the cripple were also in the grandmother's apartment; the child sat on a stool at the old lady's feet, and smiled sadly as the young man entered.

'Why that sword at your side, Imre?' asked the old lady in a feeble voice. 'Ah, this is no good world – no good world! But if God is against us, who can resist His hand? I have spoken with the dead again in dreams. I thought they all came around me and beckoned me to follow them; but I am ready to go, and place my life with gratitude and confidence in the hands of the Lord. Last night I saw the year 1848 written in the skies in letters of fire. Who knows what may come over us yet? This is no good world – no good world!'

Imre bent silently over the old lady's hand and kissed it.

'And so you are going? Well, God bless and speed you, if you go beneath the cross, and never forget in life or in death to raise your heart to the Lord;' and the old lady placed her withered hand upon her grandson's head, and murmured, 'God Almighty bless you!'

'My husband was just such a handsome youth when I lost him,' sighed the widowed aunt as she embraced her nephew. 'God bless you!'

The little cripple threw his arms around his cousin's knees and, sobbing, entreated him not to stay long away.

The last who bade farewell was Jolanka. She approached with downcast eyes, holding in her small white hands an embroidered cockade, which she placed on his breast. It was composed of five colours – blue and gold, red, white and green.

'I understand,' said the young man, in a tone of joyful surprise, as he pressed the sweet girl to his heart, 'Transylvania and Hungary united! I shall win glory for your colours!'

The maiden yielded to his warm embrace, murmuring, as he released her, 'Remember me!'

'When I cease to remember you, I shall be no more,' replied the youth fervently.

And then he kissed the young girl's brow, and once more bidding farewell, he hurried from the apartment.

Old Simon Bardy lived on the first floor: Imre did not forget him.

'Well, nephew,' said the old man cheerfully, 'God speed you, and give you strength to cut down many Turks!'

'It is not with the Turks that we shall have to do,' replied the young man, smiling.

'Well, with the French,' said the old soldier of the past century, correcting himself.

A page waited at the gate with two horses saddled and bridled.

'I shall not require you – you may remain at home,' said Imre, as, taking the bridle of one of the horses and vaulting lightly into the saddle, he pressed his shako over his brow and galloped from the castle.

As he rode under the cross, he checked his horse and looked back. Was it of his grandmother's words or of the golden-haired Jolanka that he thought?

A white handkerchief waved from the window. 'Farewell, light of my soul!' murmured the youth; and kissing his hand, he once more dashed his spurs into his horse's flank, and turned down the steep hill.

Those were strange times. All at once the villages began to be depopulated; the inhabitants disappeared, none knew whither. The doors of the houses were closed.

The bells were no longer heard in the evening, nor the maiden's song as she returned from her work. The barking of dogs which had lost their masters alone interrupted the silence of the streets, where the grass began to grow.

Imre Bardy rode through the streets of the village without meeting a soul; few of the chimneys had smoke, and no fires gleamed through the kitchen windows.

Evening was drawing on, and a slight transparent mist had overspread the valley. Imre was desirous of reaching Kolozsvar early on the next morning, and continued his route all night.

About midnight the moon rose behind the trees, shedding her silvery light over the forest. All was still, excepting the echo of the miner's hammer, and the monotonous sound of his horse's step along the rocky path. He rode on, lost in thought; when suddenly the horse stopped short and pricked his ears.

'Come, come,' said Imre, stroking his neck, 'you have not heard the cannon yet.'

The animal at last proceeded, turning his head impatiently from side to side, and snorting and neighing with fear.

The road now led through a narrow pass between two rocks, whose summits almost met, and a slight bridge, formed of one or two rotten planks, was thrown across the dry channel of a mountain stream which cut up the path.

As Imre reached the bridge, the horse backed, and no spurring could induce him to cross. Imre at last pressed his knee angrily against the trembling animal, striking him at the same time across the neck with the bridle, on which the horse suddenly cleared the chasm at one bound and then again turned and began to back.

At that instant a fearful cry arose from beneath, which was echoed from the rocks around, and ten or fifteen savage-looking beings climbed from under the bridge, with lances formed of upright scythes.

Even then there would have been time for the horseman to turn back, and dash through the handful of men behind him, but either he was ashamed of turning from the first conflict, or he was desirous, at any risk, to reach Kolozsvar at the appointed time, and instead of retreating by the bridge, he galloped towards the other end of the pass, where the enemy rushed upon him from every side, yelling hideously.

'Back, Wallachian dogs!' cried Imre, cutting two of them down, while several others sprang forward with the scythes.

Two shots whistled by, and Imre, letting go the bridle, cut right and left, his sword gleaming rapidly among the awkward weapons; and taking advantage of a moment in which the enemy's charge began to slacken, he suddenly dashed through the crowd towards the outlet of the rock, without perceiving that another party awaited him above the rocks with great stones, with which they prepared to crush him as he passed.

He was only a few paces from the spot, when a gigantic figure, armed with a short broad-axe, and with a Roman helmet on his head, descended from the rock in front of him, and seizing the reins of the horse, forced him to halt. The young man aimed a blow at his enemy's head, and the helmet fell back, cut through the middle, but the force of the blow had broken his sword in two; and the horse, lifted by his giant foe, reared, so that the rider, losing his balance, was thrown against the side of the rock and fell senseless to the ground.

At the same instant a shot was fired towards them from the top of the rock.

'Who fired there?' cried the giant, in a voice of thunder. The bloodthirsty Wallachians would have rushed madly on their defenceless prey, had not the giant stood between him and them.

'Who fired on me?' he sternly exclaimed. The Wallachians stood back in terror.

'It was not on you, Decurio, that I fired, but on the hussar,' stammered out one of the men, on whom the giant had fixed his eye.

'You lie, traitor! Your ball struck my armour, and had I not worn a shirt of mail, it would have pierced my heart.'

The man turned deadly pale, trembling from head to foot.

'My enemies have paid you to murder me!'

The savage tried to speak, but words died upon his lips.

'Hang him instantly – he is a traitor!'

The rest of the gang immediately seized the culprit and carried him to the nearest tree, from whence his shrieks soon testified that his sentence was being put in execution.

The Decurio remained alone with the young man and hastily lifting him, still senseless, from the ground, he mounted his horse; placing him before him, ere the savage horde had returned he had galloped some distance along the road from whence the youth had come, covering him with his mantle as he passed the bridge, to conceal him from several of the gang who stood there, and exclaiming, 'Follow me to the Tapanfalva.'

As soon as they were out of sight, he suddenly turned to the left, down a steep, hilly path, and struck into the depth of the forest.

The morning sun had just shot its first beams across the hills, tinting with golden hue the reddening autumn leaves, when the young hussar began to move in his fevered dreams, and murmured the name, 'Jolanka.'

In a few moments he opened his eyes. He was lying in a small chamber, through the only window of which the sunbeams shone upon his face.

The bed on which he lay was made of lime-boughs, simply woven together, and covered with wolves' skins. A gigantic form was leaning against the foot of the bed with his arms folded, and as the young man awoke, he turned round. It was the Decurio.

'Where am I?' asked the young man, vaguely endeavouring to recall the events of the past night.

'In my house,' replied the Decurio.

'And who are you?'

'I am Numa, Decurio of the Roumin Legion, your foe in battle, but now your host and protector.'

'And why did you save me from your men?' asked the young man, after a short silence.

'Because the strife was unequal – a hundred against one.'

'But had it not been for you, I could have freed myself from them.'

'Without me you had been lost. Ten paces from where I stopped your horse, you would inevitably have been dashed to pieces by huge stones which they were preparing to throw down upon you from the rock.'

'And you did not desire my death?'

'No, because it would have reflected dishonour on the Roumin name.'

'You are a chivalrous man, Decurio!'

'I am what you are; I know your character, and the same feeling inspires us both. You love your nation, as I do mine. Your nation is great and cultivated; mine is despised and neglected, and my love is more bitterly devoted. Your love for your country makes you happy; mine deprives me of peace. You have taken up arms to defend your country without knowing your own strength, or the number of the foe; I have done the same. Either of us may lose, or we may both be blotted out; but though the arms may be buried in the earth, rust will not eat them.'

'I do not understand your grievances.'

'You do not understand? Know, then, that although fourteen centuries have passed since the Roman eagle overthrew Diurbanus, there are still those among us – the now barbarous people – who can trace their descent from generation to generation, up to the times of its past glory. We have still our traditions, if we have nothing more; and can point out what forest stands in the place of the ancient Sarmisaegethusa, and what town is built where one Decebalus overthrew the far-famed troops of the Consulate. And alas for that town! if the graves over which its houses are built should once more open, and turn the populous streets into a field of battle! What is become of the nation, the heir of so much glory? – the proud Dacians, the descendants of the far-famed legions? I do not reproach any nation for having brought us to what we now are; but let none reproach me if I desire to restore my people to what they once were.'

'And do you believe that this is the time?'

'We have no prophets to point out the hour, but it seems yours do not see more clearly. We shall attempt it now, and if we fail our grandchildren will attempt it again. We have nothing to lose but a few lives; you risk much that is worth losing, and yet you assemble beneath the banner of war. Then what would you do if you were like us? – a people who possess nothing in this world, among whom there is not one able or one instructed head; for although every third man bears the name of Papa, it is not every hundredth who can read! A people excluded from every employment; who live a miserable life in the severest manual labour; who have not one noble city in their country, the home of three-fourths of their people. Why should we seek to know the signs of the times in which we are to die, or be regenerated! We have nothing but our wretchedness, and if we are conquered we lose nothing. Oh! you did wrong for your own peace to leave a nation to such utter neglect!'

'We do not take up arms for our nation alone, but for freedom in general.'

'You do wrong. It is all the same to us who our sovereign may be; only let him be just towards us, and raise up our fallen people; but you will destroy your nation – its power, its influence and privileges – merely that you may live in a country without a head.'

A loud uproar interrupted the conversation. A disorderly troop of Wallachians approached the Decurio's house, triumphantly bearing the hussar's shako on a pole before them.

'Had I left you there last night, they would now have exhibited your head instead of your shako.'

The crowd halted before the Decurio's window, greeting him with loud vociferations.

The Decurio spoke a few words in the Wallachian language, on which they replied more vehemently than before, at the same time thrusting forward the trophy on the pole.

The Decurio turned hastily round. 'Was your name written on your shako?' he asked the young man, in evident embarrassment.

'It was.'

'Unhappy youth! The people, furious at not having found you, are determined to attack your father's house.'

'And you will permit them?' asked the youth, starting from bed.

'I dare not contradict them, unless I would lose their confidence. I can prevent nothing.'

'Give me up – let them wreak their bloody vengeance on my head!'

'I should only betray myself for having concealed you; and it would not save your father's house.'

'And if they murder the innocent and unprotected, on whom will the ignominy of their blood fall?'

'On me; but I will give you the means of preventing this disgrace. Do you accept it?'

'Speak!'

'I will give you a disguise; hasten to Kolozsvar and assemble your comrades – then return and protect your house. I will wait you there, and man to man, in open honourable combat, the strife will no longer be ignominious.'

'Thanks, thanks!' murmured the youth, pressing the Decurio's hand.

'There is not a moment to lose; here is a peasant's mantle – if you should be interrogated, you have only to show this *paszura* [everything on which a double-headed eagle – the emblem of the Austrian government – was painted, engraved or sculptured, the Wallachians called *paszura*] and mention my name. Your not knowing the language is of no consequence; my men are accustomed to see Hungarian gentlemen visit me in disguise, and having only seen you by night, they will not recognise you.'

Imre hastily took the dress, while Decurio spoke to the people, made arrangements for the execution of their plans, and pointed out the way to the castle, promising to follow them immediately.

'Accept my horse as a remembrance,' said the young man, turning to the Decurio.

'I accept it, as it would only raise suspicion were you to mount it; but you may recover it again in the field. Haste, and lose no time! If you delay you will bring mourning on your own head and disgrace on mine!'

In a few minutes the young man, disguised as a Wallachian peasant, was hastening on foot across the hills to Kolozsvar.

*   *   *

It was past midnight.

The inhabitants of the Bardy castle had all retired to rest.

The iron gate was locked and the windows barred, when suddenly the sound of demoniac cries roused the slumberers from their dreams.

'What is that noise?' cried Jozsef Bardy, springing from his bed, and rushing to the window.

'The Olahok!' cried a hussar, who had rushed to his master's apartments on hearing the sounds.

'The Olah! the Olah!' was echoed through the corridors by the terrified servants.

By the light of a few torches, a hideous crowd was seen before the windows, armed with scythes and axes, which they were brandishing with fearful menaces.

'Lock all the doors!' cried Jozsef Bardy, with calm presence of mind. 'Barricade the great entrance, and take the ladies and children to the back rooms. You must not lose your heads, but all assemble together in the turret-chamber, from whence the whole building may be protected. And taking down two good rifles from over his bed, he hastened to his elder brother Tamas's apartments, which overlooked the court.

Have you heard the noise?' asked his brother as he entered.

'I knew it would come,' Tamas replied, and coolly continued to pace the room.

'And are you not preparing for defence?'

'To what purpose? – they will kill us all. I am quite prepared for what must inevitably happen.'

'But it will not happen if we defend ourselves courageously. We are eight men – the walls of the castle are strong – the besiegers have no guns, and no place to protect them; we may hold out for days until assistance comes from Kolozsvar.'

'We shall lose,' replied Tamas coldly, and without the slightest change of countenance.

'Then I shall defend the castle myself. I have a wife and children, our old mother and our sisters are here, and I shall protect them, if necessary alone.'

At that instant Barnabas and old Simon entered with the widowed sister.

Barnabas had a huge twenty-pound iron club in his hand; grinding his teeth, and with eyes darting fire, he seemed capable of meeting single-handed the whole troop.

He was followed by the widow, with two loaded pistols in her hands, and old Simon, who entreated them not to use violence or exasperate the enemy.

'Conduct yourselves bravely!' replied the widow dryly; 'let us not die in vain.'

'Come with me – we shall send them all to hell!' cried Barnabas, swinging his club with his herculean arm as if it had been a reed.

'Let us not be too hasty,' interrupted Jozsef; we will stand here in the tower, from whence we can shoot everyone that approaches, and if they break in, we can meet them on the stairs.'

'For heaven's sake!' cried Simon, 'what are you going to do? If you kill one of them they will massacre us all. Speak to them peaceably – promise them wine – take them to the cellar – give them money – try to pacify them! Nephew Tamas, you will speak to them?' continued the old man, turning to Tamas, who still paced up and down, without the slightest visible emotion.

'Pacification and resistance are equally vain,' he replied coldly; 'we are inevitably lost!'

'We have no time for delay,' said Jozsef impatiently; 'take the arms from the wall, Barnabas, give one to each servant – let them stand at the back windows of the house, we two are enough here. Sister, stand between the windows, that the stones may not hit you; and when you load, do not strike the balls too far in, that our aim may be the more secure!'

'No! no! – I cannot let you fire,' exclaimed the old man, endeavouring to drag Jozsef from the window. 'You must not fire yet – only remain quiet.'

'Go to the hurricane, old man! would you have us use holy water against a shower of stones?'

At that instant several large stones were dashed through the windows, breaking the furniture against which they fell.

'Only wait,' said Simon, 'until I speak with them. I am sure I shall pacify them. I can speak their language and I know them all – just let me go to them.'

'A vain idea! If you sue for mercy they will certainly kill you, but if you show courage, you may bring them to their senses. You had better stay and take a gun.'

But the old man was already out of hearing, and hurrying downstairs, he went out of a back door into the court, which the Wallachians had not yet taken possession of.

They were endeavouring to break down one of the stone pillars of the iron gate with their axes and hammers, and had already succeeded in making an aperture, through which one of the gang now climbed.

Old Simon recognised him. 'Lupey, my son, what do you want here?' said the old man. 'Have we ever offended you? Do you forget all that I have done for you? – how I cured your wife when she was so ill, and got you off from the military; and how, when your ox died, I gave you two fine bullocks to replace it? Do you not know me, my son Lupey?'

'I am not your son Lupey now; I am a "malcontent!" ' cried the Wallachian, aiming a blow with a heavy hammer at the old man's head.

Uttering a deep groan, Simon fell lifeless to the ground.

The rest of the party saw the scene from the tower.

Barnabas rushed from the room like a maddened tiger, while Jozsef, retiring cautiously behind the embrasure of the window, aimed his gun as they were placing his uncle's head upon a spike, and shot the first who raised it. Another seized it, and the next instant he, too, fell to the earth; another and another, as many as attempted to raise the head, till, finally, none dared approach.

The widow loaded the guns while Tamas sat quietly in an armchair.

Meanwhile Barnabas had hurried to the attic, where several large fragments of iron had been stowed away, and dragging them to a window which overlooked the entrance, he waited until the gang had assembled round the door, and were trying to break in; then, lifting an enormous piece with gigantic strength, he dropped it on the heads of the besiegers.

Fearful cries arose and the gang, who were at the door, fled right and left, leaving four or five of their number crushed beneath the ponderous mass.

The next moment they returned with redoubled fury, dashing stones against the windows and the roof, while the door resounded with the blows of their clubs.

Notwithstanding the stones which were flying round him, Barnabas stood at the window dashing down heavy iron masses, and killing two or three men every time.

His brother meanwhile continued firing from the tower, and not a ball was aimed in vain. The besiegers had lost a great number, and began to fall back, after fruitless efforts to break in the door, when a footman entered breathless to inform Barnabas that the Wallachians were beginning to scale the opposite side of the castle with ladders, and that the servants were unable to resist them.

Barnabas rushed to the spot.

Two servants lay mortally wounded in one of the back rooms, through the window of which the Wallachians were already beginning to enter, while another ladder had been placed against the opposite window, which they were beginning to scale as Barnabas entered.

'Here, wretches!' he roared furiously, and, seizing the ladder with both hands, shook it so violently that the men were precipitated from it, and then lifting it with supernatural strength, he dashed it against the opposite one, which broke with the force of the weight thrown against it, the upper part falling backwards with the men upon it, while one of the party remained hanging from the window-sill, and, after immense exertions to gain a footing, he too fell to the earth.

Barnabas rushed into the next room grinding his teeth, his lips foaming, and his face of a livid hue; so appalling was his appearance, that one of the gang, who had been the first to enter by the window, turned pale with terror and dropped his axe.

Taking advantage of this, Barnabas darted on his enemy, and dragging him with irresistible force to the window, he dashed him from it.

'On here! as many as you are!' he shouted furiously, the blood gushing from his mouth from the blow of a stone. 'On! all who wish a fearful death!'

At that instant, a shriek of terror rose within the house.

The Wallachians had discovered the little back door which Simon had left open, and, stealing through it, were already inside the house, when the shrieks of a servant girl gave the besieged notice of their danger.

Barnabas, seizing his club, hurried in the direction of the sounds; he met his brother on the stairs, who had likewise heard the cry, and hastened thither with his gun in his hand, accompanied by the widow.

'Go, sister!' said Jozsef, 'take my wife and children to the attics; we will try to guard the staircase step by step. Kiss them all for me. If we die, the villains will put us all in one grave – we shall meet again!'

The widow retired.

The two brothers silently pressed hands, and then, standing on the steps, awaited their enemies. They did not wait long.

The bloodhounds with shouts of vengeance rushed on the narrow stone stairs.

'Hah! thus near I love to have you, dogs of hell!' cried Barnabas, raising his iron club with both hands, and dealing such blows right and left, that none whom it reached rose again. The stairs were covered with the dead and wounded, while their death cries, and the sound of the heavy club, echoed fearfully through the vaulted building.

The foremost of the gang retreated as precipitately as they had advanced, but were continually pressed forward again by the members from behind, while Barnabas drove them back unweariedly, cutting an opening through them with the blows of his club.

He had already beaten them back nearly to the bottom of the stairs, when one of the gang, who had concealed himself in a niche, pierced him through the back with a spike.

Dashing his club amongst the retreating crowd, he turned with a cry of rage, and seizing his murderer by the shoulders, dragged him down with him to the ground.

The first four who rushed to help the murderer were shot dead by Jozsef Bardy, who, when he had fired off both his muskets, still defended his prostrated brother with the butt-end of one, until he was overpowered and disarmed; after which a party of them carried him out to the iron cross, and crucified him on it amidst the most shocking tortures.

On trying to separate the other brother from his murderer, they found them both dead. With his last strength Barnabas had choked his enemy, whom he still held firmly in his deadly grip, and they were obliged to cut off his hand in order to disengage the Wallachian's body.

Tamas, the eldest brother, now alone survived. Seated in his armchair he calmly awaited his enemies, with a large silver chandelier burning on the table before him.

As the noise approached his chamber, he drew from its jewelled sheath his broad curved sword, and, placing it on the table before him, proceeded coolly to examine the ancient blade, which was inscribed with unknown characters.

At last the steps were at the door; the handle was turned – it had not even been locked.

The magnate rose, and, taking his sword from the table, he stood silently and calmly before his enemies, who rushed upon him with fearful oaths, brandishing their weapons still reeking with the blood of his brothers.

The nobleman stood motionless as a statue until they came within two paces of him, when suddenly the bright black steel gleamed above his head, and the foremost man fell at his feet with his skull split to the chin. The next received a deep gash in the shoulder of his outstretched arm, but not a word escaped the magnate's lips, his countenance retained its cold and stern expression as he looked at his enemies in calm disdain, as if to say, 'Even in combat a nobleman is worth ten boors.'

Warding off with the skill of a consummate swordsman every blow aimed at him, he coolly measured his own thrusts, inflicting severe wounds on his enemies' faces and heads; but the more he evaded them the more furious they became. At last he received a severe wound in the leg from a scythe, and fell on one knee; but without evincing the slightest pain, he still continued fighting with the savage mob, until, after a long and obstinate struggle, he fell without a murmur or even a death-groan.

The enraged gang cut his body to pieces, and in a few minutes they had hoisted his head on his own sword. Even then the features retained their haughty, contemptuous expression.

He was the last man of the family with whom they had to contend, but more than a hundred of their own band lay stretched in the court and before the windows, covering the stairs and rooms with heaps of bodies, and when the shouts of triumph ceased for an instant, the groans of the wounded and the dying were heard from every side.

None now remained but women and children. When the Wallachians broke into the castle, the widow had taken them all to the attics, leaving the door open, that her brothers might find refuge in case they were forced to retreat; and here the weaker members of the family awaited the issue of the combat which was to bring them life or death, listening breathlessly to the uproar, and endeavouring, from its confused sounds, to determine good or evil.

At last the voices died away, and the hideous cries of the besiegers ceased. The trembling women believed that the Wallachians had been driven out, and, breathing more freely, each awaited with impatience the approach of brothers – husband – sons.

At last a heavy step was heard on the stairs leading to the garret.

'This is Barnabas's step!' cried the widow, joyfully, and still holding the pistols in her hands, she ran to the door of the garret.

Instead of her expected brother, a savage form, drunken with blood, strode towards her, his countenance burning with rage and triumph.

The widow started back, uttering a shriek of terror, and then with that unaccountable courage of desperation, she aimed one of the pistols at the Wallachian's breast, and he instantly fell backwards on one of his comrades, who followed close behind. The other pistol she discharged into her own bosom.

And now we must draw a veil over the scene that followed. What happened there must not be witnessed by human eyes.

Suffice it to say, they murdered every one, women and children, with the most refined and brutal cruelty, and then threw their dead bodies out of the window from which Barnabas had dashed down the iron fragments on the besiegers' heads.

They left the old grandmother to the last, that she might witness the extermination of her whole family. Happily for her, her eyes had ceased to distinguish the light of the sun, and ere long the light of an eternal glory had risen upon them.

The Wallachians then dug a common grave for the bodies, and threw them all in together. The little one, whom his parents loved so well, they cast in alive, his nurse having escaped from the attics and carried him downstairs, before being overtaken by the savages.

'There are only eleven here!' cried one of the gang, who had counted the bodies, 'one of them must be still alive somewhere – there ought to be twelve!' And then they once more rushed through the empty rooms, overturning all the furniture, and cutting up and breaking everything they met with. They searched the garrets and every corner of the cellars, but without success.

At last a yell of triumph was heard. One of them had discovered a door which, being painted of the same colour as the walls, had hitherto escaped their observation. It concealed a small apartment in the turret. With a few blows of their axes it was broken open, and they rushed in.

'Ah! a rare booty!' cried the foremost of the ruffians, while, with blood-thirsty curiosity, the others pressed round to see the new victim.

There lay the little orphan with the golden hair; her eyes were closed and a deathlike hue had overspread her beautiful features.

Her aunt, with an instinctive foreboding, had concealed her here when she took the others to the attic.

The orphan grasped a sharp knife in her hand, with which she had attempted to kill herself; and when her fainting hands refused the fearful service, she had swooned in despair.

'Ah!' cried the Wallachians, in savage admiration, their bloodthirsty countenances assuming a still more hellish expression.

'This is a common booty!' cried several voices together.

'A beautiful girl! A noble lady! ha, ha! She will just suit the tattered Wallachians!' And with their foul and bloody hands, they seized the young girl by her fair slight arms.

'Ha! what is going on here?' thundered a voice from behind.

The Wallachians looked round.

A figure stood among them fully a head taller than all the rest. He wore a brass helmet, in which a deep cleft was visible, and held in his left hand a Roman sword. His features bore the ancient Roman character.

'The Decurio!' they murmured, making way for him.

'What is going on here?' he repeated; and seeing the fainting girl in the arms of a Wallachian, he ordered him to lay her down.

'She is one of our enemies,' replied the savage insolently.

'Silence, knave! Does one of the Roumin nation seek enemies in women? Lay her down instantly.'

'Not so, leader,' interrupted Lupey; 'our laws entitle us to a division of the spoil. This girl is our booty; she belongs to us after the victory.'

'I know our laws better than you do, churl! Due division of spoil is just and fair; but we cast lots for what cannot be divided.'

'True, leader: a horse or an ox cannot be divided, and for them we cast lots, but in this case – '

'I have said it cannot, and I should like to know who dares to say it can!'

Lupey knew the Decurio too well to proffer another syllable, and the rest turned silently from the girl; one voice alone was heard to exclaim, 'It can!'

'Who dares to say that?' cried the Decurio; 'let him come forward!'

A Wallachian, with long plaited hair, confronted the Decurio. He was evidently intoxicated, and replied, striking his breast with his fist: 'I said so.'

Scarcely had the words escaped his lips than the Decurio, raising his left hand, severed the contradictor's head at one stroke from his body; and as it fell back, the lifeless trunk dropped on its knees before the Decurio, with its arms around him, as if in supplication.

'Dare anyone still say it can?' asked Numa, with merciless rigour.

The Wallachians turned silently away.

'Put the horses immediately to the carriage; the girl must be placed in it, and brought to Topanfalvo. Whoever has the good fortune of winning her, has a right to receive her as I confide her to you; but if anyone of you should dare to offend her in the slightest degree, even by a look or a smile, remember this and take example from it,' continued the Decurio, pointing with his sword to the headless body of the young man. 'And now you may go – destroy and pillage.'

At these words the band scattered right and left, the Decurio with the fainting girl, whom he lifted into the carriage and confided to some faithful retainers of the family, pointing out the road across the hills.

In half an hour the castle was in flames and the Wallachians, descending into the cellars, had knocked out the bottoms of the casks, and bathed in the sea of flowing wine and brandy, singing wild songs, while the fire burst from every window enveloping the blackened walls; after which the revellers departed, leaving their dead, and those who were too helplessly intoxicated to follow them.

Meanwhile they brought the young girl to the Decurio's house, and as each man considered that he had an equal right to the prize, they kept a vigilant eye upon her, and none dared offend her so much as by a look.

When the Decurio arrived, they all crowded into the house with him, filling the rooms, as well as the entrance and porch.

Having laid out the spoil before them on the ground, the leader proceeded to divide it into equal shares, retaining for himself a portion of ten men, after which most of the band dispersed to their homes; but a good many remained, greedily eyeing their still unappropriated victim, who lay pale and motionless on the couch of lime-boughs where they had laid her.

'You are waiting, I suppose, to cast lots for the girl?' said Numa dryly.

'Certainly,' replied Lupey, with an insolent leer; 'and his she will be who casts highest. If two, or ten, or twenty of us should cast the same, we have an equal right to her.'

'I tell you only one can have her,' interrupted Numa sternly.

'Then those who win must cast again among themselves.'

'Casting the die will not do; we may throw all day long, and two may remain at the end.'

'Well, let us play cards for her.'

'I cannot allow that, the more cunning will deceive the simpler.'

'Well, write our names upon bricks, and throw them all into a barrel; and whichever name you draw will take away the girl.'

'I can say what name I please, for none of you can read.'

The Wallachian shook his head impatiently. 'Well, propose something yourself, Decurio.'

'I will. Let us try which of us can give the best proof of courage and daring; and whoever can do that, shall have the girl, for he best deserves her.'

'Well said!' cried the men unanimously. 'Let us each relate what we have done, and then you can judge which among us is the boldest.'

'I killed the first Bardy in the court in sight of his family.'

'I broke in the door, when that terrible man was dashing down the iron on our heads.'

'I mounted the stairs first.'

'I fought nearly half an hour with the noble in the cloth of gold.'

And thus they continued. Each man, according to his own account, was the first and the bravest – each had performed miracles of valour.

'You have all behaved with great daring, but it is impossible now to prove what has happened. The proof must be given here, by all of us together, before my eyes, indisputably.'

'Well, tell us how,' said Lupey impatiently, always fearing that the Decurio was going to deceive them.

'Look here,' said Numa, drawing a small cask from beneath the bed – and in doing so he observed that the young girl half opened her eyes, glanced at him, and then closed them. She was awake, and had heard all.

As he stooped down, Numa whispered gently in her ear: 'Fear nothing,' and then drew the cask into the middle of the room.

The Wallachians stared with impatient curiosity as he knocked out the bottom of the cask with a hatchet.

'This cask contains gunpowder,' continued Decurio. 'We will light a match and place it in the middle of the cask, and whoever remains longest in the room is undoubtedly the most courageous; for there is enough here to blow up not only this house, but the whole of the neighbouring village.'

At this proposition several of the men began to murmur.

'If any are afraid they are not obliged to remain,' said the Decurio dryly.

'I agree,' said Lupey doggedly. 'I will remain here; and perhaps, after all, it is poppy-seeds you have got there – it looks very much like them.'

The Decurio stooped down, and taking a small quantity between his fingers, threw it into the Wallachian's pipe, which immediately exploded, causing him to stagger back; in the next instant he stood with a blackened visage, *sans* beard and moustache, amidst the jeers and laughter of his comrades.

This only exasperated him the more.

'I will stay for all that!' he exclaimed; and lifting up the pipe which he had dropped, he walked over and lit it at the burning match which the Decurio was placing in the cask.

Upon this, two-thirds of the men left the room.

The rest assembled around the cask with much noise and bravado, swearing by heaven and earth that they would stay until the match burned out; but the more they swore, the more they looked at the burning match, the flame of which was slowly approaching the gunpowder.

For some minutes their courage remained unshaken, but after that they ceased to boast, and began to look at each other in silent consternation, while their faces grew paler every instant. At last one or two rose and stood aloof; the others followed their example; then, some grinding their teeth with rage, others chattering with terror, they all began to leave the room.

Only two remained beside the cask; Numa, who stood with his arms folded leaning against the foot of the bed; and Lupey, who was sitting on the iron of the cask with his back turned to the danger, and smoking furiously.

As soon as they were alone, the latter glanced behind him and saw the flame was within an inch of the powder.

'I'll tell you what, Decurio,' he said, springing up, 'we are only two left, don't let us make fools of each other; let us come to an understanding on this matter.'

'If you are tired of waiting, I can press the match lower.'

'This is no jest, Numa; you are risking your own life. How can you wish to send us both to hell for the sake of a pale girl? But I'll tell you what – I'll give her up to you if you will only promise that she shall be mine when you are tired of her.'

'Remain here and win her – if you dare.'

'To what purpose?' said the Wallachian, in a whining voice, and in his impatience he began to tear his clothes and stamp with his feet, like a petted child.

'What I have said stands good,' said the Decurio; 'whoever remains longest has the sole right to the lady.'

'Well, I will stay, of course; but what do I gain by it? I know you will stay, too, and then the devil will have us both; and I speak not only for myself when I say I do not wish that.'

'If you do not wish it, you had better be gone.'

'Decurio, this is madness! The flame will reach the powder immediately.'

'I see it.'

'May a thunderbolt strike you on St Michael's Day!' roared the Wallachian fiercely, as he rushed to the door; but after he had gone out, he once more thrust his head in and cried: 'Will you give in? I am not gone yet.'

'Nor have I removed the match; you may come back.' The Wallachian slammed the door, and ran for his life, till exhausted and breathless he sank under a tree, where he lay with his tunic over his head, and his ears covered with his hands, only now and then raising his head nervously, to listen for the awful explosion which was to blow up the world.

Meanwhile Numa coolly removed the match, which was entirely burnt down; and throwing it into the grate, he stepped over to the bed and whispered into the young girl's ear: 'You are free!'

Trembling, she raised herself in the bed and taking the Decurio's large, sinewy hands within her own, she murmured: 'Be merciful! Oh hear my prayer, and kill me!'

The Decurio stroked the fair hair of the lovely suppliant. 'Poor child!' he replied gently; 'you have nothing to fear; nobody will hurt you now.'

'You have saved me from these fearful people – now save me from yourself!'

'You have nothing to fear from me,' replied the Dacian, proudly; 'I fight for liberty alone, and you may rest as securely within my threshold as on the steps of the altar. When I am absent you need have no anxiety, for these walls are impregnable, and if anyone should dare offend you by the slightest look, that moment shall be the last of his mortal career. And when I am at home you have nothing to fear, for woman's image never dwelt within my heart. Accept my poor couch, and may your rest be sweet! – Imre Bardy slept on it last night.'

'Imre!' exclaimed the starting girl. 'You have seen him, then? – oh! where is he!'

The Decurio hesitated. 'He should not have delayed so long,' he murmured, pressing his hand against his brow; 'all would have been otherwise.'

'Oh! let me go to him; if you know where he is.'

'I do not know, but I am certain he will come here if he is alive – indeed he must come.'

'Why do you think that?'

'Because he will seek you.'

'Did he then speak – before you?'

'As he lay wounded on that couch, he pronounced your name in his dreams. Are you not that Jolanka Bardy whom they call "The Angel"? I knew you by your golden locks.'

The young girl cast down her eyes. 'Then you think he will come?' she said in a low voice. And my relations?'

'He will come as soon as possible; and now you must take some food and rest. Do not think about your relations now; they are all in a safe place – nobody can hurt them more.

The Decurio brought some refreshment, laid a small prayer-book on the pillow, and left the orphan by herself.

The poor girl opened the prayer-book, and her tears fell like raindrops on the blessed page; but, overcome by the fatigue and terror she had undergone, her head ere long sank gently back, and she slept calmly and sweetly the sleep of exhausted innocence.

As evening closed, the Decurio returned, and softly approaching the bed, looked long and earnestly at the fair sleeper's face, until two large tears stood unconsciously in his eyes.

The Roumin hastily brushed away the unwonted moisture, and as if afraid of the feeling which had stolen into his breast, he hastened from the room, and laid himself upon his woollen rug before the open door.

The deserted castle still burned on, shedding a ghastly light on the surrounding landscape, while the deepest silence reigned around, only broken now and then by an expiring groan, or the hoarse song of a drunken reveller.

Day was beginning to dawn as a troop of horsemen galloped furiously towards the castle from the direction of Kolozsvar.

They were Imre and his comrades.

Silently and anxiously they pursued their course, their eyes fixed upon one point as they seemed to fly rather than gallop along the road. 'We are too late!' exclaimed one of the party at last, pointing to a dim red smoke along the horizon. 'Your castle is burning!'

Without returning an answer, Imre spurred his panting horse to a swifter pace. A turn in the road suddenly brought the castle to their view, its blackened walls still burning, while red smoke rose high against the side of the hill.

The young man uttered a fierce cry of despair, and galloped madly down the declivity. In less than a quarter of an hour he stood before the ruined walls.

'Where is my father? where are my family? where is my bride?' he shrieked in frantic despair, brandishing his sword over the head of a half-drunken Wallachian, who was leaning against the ruined portico.

The latter fell to his knees, imploring mercy, and declaring that it was not he who killed them.

'Then they are dead!' exclaimed the unhappy youth, as, half-choked by his sobs, he fell forward on his horse's neck.

Meanwhile his companions had ridden up, and immediately sounded the Wallachian, whom, but for Imre's interference, they would have cut down.

'Lead us to where you have buried them. Are they all dead?' he entreated; 'have you not left one alive? Accursed be the sun that rises after such a night!'

The Wallachian pointed to a large heap of fresh-raised mould. 'They are all there!' he said.

Imre fell from his horse without another word, as if struck down.

His companions removed him to a little distance, where the grass was least red.

They then began to dig twelve graves with their swords. Imre watched them in silence. He seemed unconscious what they were about.

When they had finished the graves they proceeded to open the large pit, but the sight was too horrible, and they carried Imre away by force. He could not have looked on what was there and still retain his senses.

In a short time, one of his comrades approached and told him that there were only eleven bodies in the grave.

'Then one of them must be alive!' cried Imre, a slight gleam of hope passing over his pale features; 'which is it? – speak! Is there not a young girl with golden locks among them?'

'I know not,' stammered his comrade, in great embarrassment.

'You do not know? – go and look again.'

His friend hesitated.

'Let me go – I must know,' said Imre impatiently, as the young man endeavoured to detain him.

'Oh stay, Imre, you cannot look on them; they are all headless!'

'My God!' exclaimed the young man, covering his face with both hands, and bursting into tears he threw himself down with his face upon the earth.

His comrades questioned the Wallachian closely as to what he knew about the young girl. First he returned no answer, pretending to be drunk and not to understand; but on their promising to spare his life, on the sole condition that he would speak the truth, he confessed that she had been carried away to the mountains, where the band were to cast lots for her.

'I must go!' said Imre, starting as if in a trance.

'Whither?' enquired his comrades.

'To seek her! Take off your dress,' he continued, turning to the Wallachian, 'you may have mine in exchange,' and, hastily putting on the tunic, he concealed his pistols in the girdle beneath it.

'We will follow you,' said his comrades, taking up their arms; 'we will seek her from village to village.'

'No, no, I must go alone! I shall find her more easily alone. If I do not return, avenge this for me,' he said, pointing to the moat; then, turning to the Wallachian, he added sternly: 'I have found beneath your girdle a gold medallion, which my grandmother wore suspended from her neck, and by which I know you to be one of her murderers, and had I not promised to spare your life, you should now receive the punishment that you deserve. Keep him here,' he said to his comrades, 'until I have crossed the hills, and then let him go.'

And taking leave of his friends, he cast one glance at the eleven heaps, and at the burning castle of his ancestors, and hastened towards the mountains.

The hoary autumn nights had dyed the leaves of the forest. The whole country looked as if it had been washed in blood.

Deep amidst the wildest forest the path suddenly descends into a narrow valley, surrounded by steep rocks, at the foot of which lies a little village half concealed among the trees.

It seemed as if the settlers there had only cleared sufficient ground to build their dwellings, leaving all around them a dense forest. Apart from the rest, on the top of a rock, stood a cottage, which, unlike the others, was constructed entirely of large blocks of stone, and only approachable by a small path cut in the rock.

A young man ascended this path. He was attired in a peasant's garb and although he evidently had travelled far, his step was light and fleet. When he had ascended about halfway, he was suddenly stopped by an armed Wallachian, who had been kneeling before a shrine in the rock, and seeing the stranger, rose and stood in his path.

The latter pronounced the Decurio's name, and produced his *paszura*.

The Wallachian examined it on every side, and then stepped back to let the stranger pass, after which he once more laid down his scythe and cap, and knelt before the shrine.

The stranger knocked at the Decurio's door, which was locked, and an armed Wallachian appeared from behind the rocks and informed him that the Decurio was not at home, only his wife.

'His wife?' exclaimed the stranger in surprise.

'Yes, that pale girl who fell to him by lot.'

'And she is his wife.'

'He told us so himself, and swore that if any of us dared so much as lift his eye upon her, he would send him to St Nicholas in paradise.'

'Can I not see her?'

'I would not advise you; for if the Decurio hears of it, he will make halves of you; but you may go around to the window if you like – only let me get out of the way first, that the Decurio may not find me here.'

The stranger hastened to the window, and looking in, he saw the young girl seated on an armchair made of rough birch boughs, with a little prayer-book on her knee; her fair arm supporting her head, while a mass of golden ringlets half veiled her face, which was as pale as an alabaster statue; the extreme sadness of its expression rendering her beauty still more touching.

'Jolanka!' exclaimed the stranger passionately.

She started at the well-known voice, and, uttering a cry of joy, rushed to the window.

'Oh, Imre!' she murmured, 'are you come at last!'

'Can I not enter? can I not speak with you?'

The young girl hastened to unbar the door, which was locked on the inside, and as Imre entered she threw herself into his arms, while he pressed her fondly to his heart.

The Wallachian, who had stolen to the window, stood aghast with terror and, as soon as the Decurio arrived, he ran to meet him, and related, with vehement gesticulations, how the girl had thrown herself into the peasant's arms.

'And how did you know that?' asked Numa coldly.

'I saw them through the window.'

'And dared you look through my window? Did I not forbid you? Down on your knees, and pray!'

The Wallachian fell on his knees, and clasped his hands.

'Rebel! you deserve your punishment of death for having disobeyed my commands; and if you ever dare to open your lips on the subject, depend upon it, you shall not escape!' And with these words he strode away, leaving the astonished informer on his knees, in which posture he remained for some time afterwards, not daring to raise his head until the Decurio's steps had died away.

As Numa entered the house, the lovers hastened to meet him. For an instant or two he stood at the threshold, regarding the young man with a look of silent reproach. 'Why did you come so late?' he asked.

Imre held out his hand, but the Decurio did not accept it. 'The blood of your family is on my hand,' he whispered. 'You have let dishonour come on me, and mourning on yourself.'

The young man's head sank on his breast in silent anguish.

'Take his hand,' said Jolanka, in her low, sweet accents; and then turning to Imre: 'He saved your life – he saved us both, and he will rescue our family, too.'

Imre looked at her in astonishment.

The Decurio seized his arms and drew him aside. 'She does not know that they are dead,' he whispered; 'she was not with them, and knows nothing of their fate; and I have consoled her with the idea that they are all prisoners, she must never know the horrors of that fearful night.'

'But sooner or later she will hear it.'

'Never! you must leave the place and the kingdom. You must go to Turkey.'

'My way lies towards Hungary.'

'You must not think of it. Evil days await that country; your prophets do not see them, but I know, and see them clearly. Go to Turkey; I will give you letters by which you may pass in security through Wallachia and Moldavia; and here is a purse of gold – do not scruple to accept it, for it is your own, it belonged to *them*. Promise me, for her sake,' he continued earnestly, pointing to Jolanka, 'that you will not go to Hungary.'

Imre hesitated. 'I cannot promise what I am not sure I shall fulfil; but I shall remember your advice.'

Numa took the hands of the two lovers, and, gazing long and earnestly on their faces, he said, in a voice of deep feeling, 'You love one another?'

They pressed his hand in silence.

'You will be happy – you will forget your misfortunes. God bless and guide you on your way! Take these letters, and keep the direct road to Brasso, by the Saxon-land. You will find free passage everywhere, and never look behind until the last pinnacles of the snowy mountains are beyond your sight. Go! we will not take leave, not a word, let us forget each other!'

* * *

The Decurio watched the lovers until they were out of sight; and called to them, even when they could hear him no longer: 'Do not go towards Hungary.'

He then entered his house. The prayer-book lay open as the young girl had left it; the page was still damp with her tears. Numa's hand trembled, as he kissed the volume fervently and placed it in his bosom.

When night came on, the Roumin lay down on his wolf-skin couch, where the golden-haired maiden, and her lover before her, had slept, but it seemed as if they had stolen his rest – he could not close his eyes there; so he rose and went out on the porch, where he spread his rug before the open door; but it was long ere he could sleep – there was an unwonted feeling at his heart, something like happiness, yet inexpressibly sad; and, buried in deep reverie, he lay with his eyes fixed on the dark blue starry vault above him till past midnight. Suddenly he thought he heard the report of some firearms at a great distance, and at the same moment two stars sank beneath the horizon. Numa thought of the travellers, and a voice seemed to whisper, 'They are now happy!'

The moon had risen high in the heavens when the Decurio was roused from his sleep by heavy footsteps, and five or six Wallachians, among whom was Lupey, stood before him.

'We have brought two enemies' heads,' said the latter, with a dark look at the Decurio; 'pay us their worth!' and taking two heads from his pouch he laid them on Numa's mat.

The Wallachians watched their leader's countenance with sharp, suspicious glances.

Numa recognised the two heads by the light of the moon. They were those of Imre and Jolanka, but his features did not betray the slightest emotion.

'You will know them probably,' continued Lupey. 'The young magnate, who escaped us at the pass, came for the girl in your absence, and at the same time stole your money, and, what is more, we found your *paszura* upon him also.'

'Who killed them?' asked the Decurio, in his usual calm voice.

'None of us,' replied the Wallachian; 'as we rushed upon them, the young magnate drew two pistols from his girdle, and shot the girl through the head first, and himself afterwards.'

'Were you all there?'

'And more of us besides.'

'Go back and bring the rest. I will divide the money you have found on them among you. Make haste; and should one of you remain behind, his share will be divided among the rest.'

The Wallachians hastened to seek their comrades with cries of joy.

The Decurio then locked the door, and, throwing himself upon the ground beside the two heads, he kissed them a hundred times, and sobbed like a child.

'I warned you not to go towards Hungary!' he said bitterly. 'Why did you not hear me, unhappy children? why did you not take my word?' and he wept over his enemies' heads as if he had been their father.

He then rose, his eyes darting fire, and, shaking his terrible fist, he cried, in a voice hoarse with rage: 'Czine mintye!' – a Wallachian term signifying revenge.

In a few hours, the Wallachians had assembled before the Decurio's house. They were about fifty or sixty, all wild, fearful-looking men.

Numa covered the two heads with a cloth, and laid them on the bed, after which he opened the door.

Lupey entered last.

'Lock the door,' said Numa, when they were all in; we must not be interrupted;' and, making them stand in a circle, he looked around at them all, one by one.

'Are you all here?' he asked at last.

'Not one is absent.'

'Do you consider yourselves all equally deserving of a share of *the booty*?'

'All of us.'

'It was you,' he continued to Lupey, 'who struck down the old man?'

'It was.'

'And you who struck the magnate with a scythe?'

'You are right, leader.'

'And you really killed all the women in the castle?' turning to a third.

'With my own hand.'

'And one and all of you can boast of having massacred, and plundered, and set on fire?'

'All! all!' they cried, striking their breasts.

'Do not lie before heaven. See! your wives are listening at the window to what you say, and will betray you if you do not speak the truth.'

'We speak the truth!'

'It is well!' said the leader, as he calmly approached the bed; and, seating himself on it, uncovered the two heads and placed them on his knee. 'Where did you put their bodies?' he asked.

'We cut them in pieces and strewed them on the highroad.'

There was a short silence. Numa's breathing became more and more oppressed, and his large chest heaved convulsively. 'Have you prayed yet?' he asked in an altered voice.

'Not yet, leader. What should we pray for?' said Lupey.

'Fall down on your knees and pray, for this is the last morning which will dawn on any of you.'

'Are you in your senses, leader? What are you going to do?'

'I am going to purge the Roumin nation of a set of ruthless murderers and brigands. Miserable wretches; instead of glory, you have brought dishonour and disgrace upon our arms wherever you have appeared. While the brave fought on the field of battle, you slaughtered their wives and children; while they risked their lives before the cannon's mouth you attacked the house of the sleepers and robbed and massacred the helpless and the innocent. Fall down on your knees and pray for your souls, for the angel of death stands over you, to blot out your memory from among the Roumin people!'

The last words were pronounced in a fearful tone. Numa was no longer the cold unmoved statue he had hitherto appeared, he was like a fiery genius of wrath, whose very breath was destruction.

The Wallachians fell upon their knees in silent awe, while the women who had been standing outside, rushed shrieking down the rocks.

The Decurio drew a pistol from his breast, and approached the cask of gunpowder.

With a fearful howl, they rushed upon him; the shriek of despair was heard for an instant, then came a terrible explosion, which caused the rocks to tremble, while the flames rose with a momentary flash amidst clouds of dust and smoke, scaring the beasts of the forest and scattering stones and beams, and hundreds of dismembered limbs, far through the valley and over the houses of the terrified inhabitants!

When the smoke had dissipated, a smoking ruin stood in the place of Numa's dwelling.

The sun rose and smiled upon the earth, which was strewn with the last leaves of autumn, but where were those who had assembled at the spring-time of the year?

The evening breezes whispered mournfully through the ruined walls, and stirred the faded leaves upon eleven grassy mounds.

The pen trembles in my hand – my heart sickens at the recital of such misery.

Would that I could believe it an imagination – the ghostly horror of a fevered brain!

Would that I could bid my gentle readers check the falling tear or tell them: 'Start not with horror; it is but romance – the creation of some fearful dream – let us awake, and see it no more!'

RUDYARD KIPLING

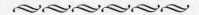

Rudyard Kipling (1865–1936) was named after the Staffordshire reservoir near Leek beside which his parents became engaged. He was born in India, and spent the first six years of his life there, acquiring Hindustani as a second language and living in a bungalow like that in *The Jungle Book*. In 1871 he was taken with his sister Alice to England to board at Lorne Lodge in Southsea and there had a miserable time before being sent to the United Services College at Westward Ho! in Devon, the model for *Stalky & Co*. He left school at sixteen to return to India and work on the *Civil and Military Gazette* in Lahore, and his familiarity with all classes of society provided him with material for *Barrack Room Ballads* and *Plain Tales from the Hills*. In 1889 he returned to England and in 1891 published his novel *The Light That Failed*. He married Caroline (Carrie) Balestier the following year and they returned to her home at Brattleboro, Vermont, where Kipling wrote *The Jungle Book*, *The Second Jungle Book* and *Captains Courageous*. In 1896 the family returned to England, where Kipling continued to write prolifically. In 1907 he was the first Englishman to receive the Nobel Prize for Literature. His later years were darkened by the death of his son John at the Battle of Loos in 1915.

My Own True Ghost Story

There are, in India, ghosts who take the form of fat, cold, pobby corpses, and hide in trees near the roadside till a traveller passes. Then they drop upon his neck and remain. There are also terrible ghosts of women who have died in child-bed. These wander along the pathways at dusk, or hide in the crops near a village, and call seductively. But to answer their call is death in this world and the next. Their feet are turned backwards that all sober men may recognise them. There are ghosts of little children who have been thrown into wells. These haunt well curbs and the fringes of jungles, and wail under the stars, or catch women by the wrist and beg to be taken up and carried. These and the corpse ghosts, however, are only vernacular articles and do not attack sahibs. No native ghost has yet been authentically reported to have frightened an Englishman; but many English ghosts have scared the life out of both white and black.

Nearly every other station owns a ghost. There are said to be two at Simla, not counting the woman who blows the bellows at Syree dak-bungalow on the Old Road; Mussoorie has a house haunted of a very lively Thing; a White Lady is supposed to do night-watchman round a house in Lahore; Dalhousie says that one of her houses 'repeats' on autumn evenings all the incidents of a horrible horse-and-precipice accident; Murree has a merry ghost, and, now that she has been swept by cholera, will have room for a sorrowful one; there are Officers' Quarters in Mian Mir whose doors open without reason, and whose furniture is guaranteed to creak, not with the heat of June but with the weight of Invisibles who come to lounge in the chairs; Peshawar possesses houses that none will willingly rent; and there is something – not fever – wrong with a big bungalow in Allahabad. The older provinces simply bristle with haunted houses, and march phantom armies along their main thoroughfares.

Some of the dak-bungalows on the Grand Trunk Road have handy little cemeteries in their compound – witnesses to the 'changes and chances of this mortal life' in the days when men drove from Calcutta to the Northwest. These bungalows are objectionable places to put up in. They are generally very old, always dirty, while the *khansamah* is as ancient as the bungalow. He either chatters senilely, or falls into the long trances of age. In both moods he is useless. If you get angry with him, he refers to some sahib dead and buried these thirty years, and says that when he was in that sahib's service not a *khansamah* in the province could touch him. Then he jabbers and mows and trembles and fidgets among the dishes, and you repent of your irritation.

In these dak-bungalows, ghosts are most likely to be found, and when found, they should be made a note of. Not long ago it was my business to live in dak-bungalows. I never inhabited the same house for three nights running, and grew to be learned in the breed. I lived in government-built ones with red brick walls and rail ceilings, an inventory of the furniture posted in every room, and an excited snake at the threshold to give welcome. I lived in 'converted' ones – old houses officiating as dak-bungalows – where nothing was in its proper place and there wasn't even a fowl for dinner. I lived in second-hand palaces where the wind blew through open-work marble tracery just as uncomfortably as through a broken pane. I lived in dak-bungalows where the last entry in the visitors' book was fifteen months old, and where they slashed off the curry-kid's head with a sword. It was my good luck to meet all sorts of men, from sober travelling missionaries and deserters flying from British regiments, to drunken loafers who threw whisky bottles at all who passed; and my still greater good fortune just to escape a maternity case. Seeing that a fair proportion of the tragedy of our lives out here acted itself in dak-bungalows, I wondered that I had met no ghosts. A ghost that would voluntarily hang about a dak-bungalow would be mad of course; but so many men have died mad in dak-bungalows that there must be a fair percentage of lunatic ghosts.

In due time I found my ghost, or ghosts rather, for there were two of them. We will call the bungalow Katmal dak-bungalow. But *that* was the smallest part of the horror. A man with a sensitive hide has no right to sleep in dak-bungalows. He should marry. Katmal dak-bungalow was old and rotten and unrepaired. The floor was of worn brick, the walls were filthy and the windows were nearly black with grime. It stood on a bypath largely used by native sub-deputy assistants of all kinds, from finance to forests; but real sahibs were rare. The *khansamah*, who was nearly bent double with old age, said so.

When I arrived, there was a fitful, undecided rain on the face of the land, accompanied by a restless wind, and every gust made a noise like the rattling of dry bones in the stiff toddy palms outside. The *khansamah* completely lost his head on my arrival. He had served a sahib once. Did I know that sahib? He gave me the name of a well-known man who has been buried for more than a quarter of a century, and showed me an ancient daguerreotype of that man in his prehistoric youth. I had seen a steel engraving of him at the head of a double volume of *Memoirs* a month before, and I felt ancient beyond telling.

The day shut in and the *khansamah* went to get me food. He did not go through the pretence of calling it '*khana*' – man's victuals. He said '*ratub*', and that means, among other things, 'grub' – dog's rations. There was no insult in his choice of the term. He had forgotten the other word, I suppose.

While he was cutting up the dead bodies of animals, I settled myself down, after exploring the dak-bungalow. There were three rooms, beside my own, which was a corner kennel, each giving into the other through dingy white doors fastened with long iron bars. The bungalow was a very solid one, but the partition walls of the rooms were almost jerry-built in their flimsiness. Every step or bang of a trunk echoed from my room down the other three, and every footfall came back tremulously from the far walls. For this reason I shut the door. There were no lamps – only candles in long glass shades. An oil wick was set in the bathroom.

For bleak, unadulterated misery that dak-bungalow was the worst of the many that I had ever set foot in. There was no fireplace, and the windows would not open; so a brazier of charcoal would have been useless. The rain and the wind splashed and gurgled and moaned round the house, and the toddy palms rattled and roared. Half a dozen jackals went through the compound singing, and a hyena stood afar off and mocked them. A hyena would convince a Sadducee of the Resurrection of the Dead – the worst sort of Dead. Then came the *ratub* – a curious meal, half native and half English in composition – with the old *khansamah* babbling behind my chair about dead and gone English people, and the wind-blown candles playing shadow-bo-peep with the bed and the mosquito-curtains. It was just the sort of dinner and evening to make a man think of every single one of his past sins, and of all the others that he intended to commit if he lived.

Sleep, for several hundred reasons, was not easy. The lamp in the bathroom threw the most absurd shadows into the room, and the wind was beginning to talk nonsense.

Just when the reasons were drowsy with blood-sucking I heard the regular 'Let-us-take-and-heave-him-over' grunt of doolie-bearers in the compound. First one doolie came in, then a second, and then a third. I heard the doolies dumped on the ground, and the shutter in front of my door shook. 'That's someone trying to come in,' I said. But no one spoke, and I persuaded myself that it was the gusty wind. The shutter of the room next to mine was attacked, flung back, and the inner door opened. 'That's some sub-deputy assistant,' I said, 'and he has brought his friends with him. Now they'll talk and spit and smoke for an hour.'

But there were no voices and no footsteps. No one was putting his luggage into the next room. The door shut, and I thanked providence that I was to be left in peace. But I was curious to know where the doolies had gone. I got out of bed and looked into the darkness. There was never a sign of a doolie. Just as I was getting into bed again, I heard, in the next room, the sound that no man in his senses can possibly mistake – the whir of a billiard ball down the length of the slates when the striker is stringing for break. No

947

other sound is like it. A minute afterwards there was another whir, and I got into bed. I was not frightened – indeed I was not. I was very curious to know what had become of the doolies. I jumped into bed for that reason.

Next minute I heard the double click of a cannon and my hair sat up. It is a mistake to say that hair stands up. The skin of the head tightens and you can feel a faint, prickly, bristling all over the scalp. That is the hair sitting up.

There was a whir and a click, and both sounds could only have been made by one thing – a billiard ball. I argued the matter out at great length with myself; and the more I argued the less probable it seemed that one bed, one table and two chairs – all the furniture of the room next to mine – could so exactly duplicate the sounds of a game of billiards. After another cannon, a three-cushion one to judge by the whir, I argued no more. I had found my ghost and would have given worlds to have escaped from that dak-bungalow. I listened, and with each listen the game grew clearer. There was whir on whir and click on click. Sometimes there was a double click and a whir and another click. Beyond any sort of doubt, people were playing billiards in the next room. And the next room was not big enough to hold a billiard table!

Between the pauses of the wind I heard the game go forward – stroke after stroke. I tried to believe that I could not hear voices; but that attempt was a failure.

Do you know what fear is? Not ordinary fear of insult, injury or death, but abject, quivering dread of something that you cannot see – fear that dries the inside of the mouth and half of the throat – fear that makes you sweat on the palms of the hands and gulp in order to keep the uvula at work? This is a fine fear – a great cowardice, and must be felt to be appreciated. The very improbability of billiards in a dak-bungalow proved the reality of the thing. No man – drunk or sober – could imagine a game at billiards, or invent the spitting crack of a 'screw-cannon'.

A severe course of dak-bungalows has this disadvantage – it breeds infinite credulity. If a man said to a confirmed dak-bungalow-haunter: 'There is a corpse in the next room, and there's a mad girl in the next but one, and the woman and man on that camel have just eloped from a place sixty miles away,' the hearer would not disbelieve because he would know that nothing is too wild, grotesque or horrible to happen in a dak-bungalow. This credulity, unfortunately, extends to ghosts. A rational person fresh from his own house would have turned on his side and slept. I did not. So surely as I was given up as a bad carcass by the scores of things in the bed because the bulk of my blood was in my heart, so surely did I hear every stroke of a long game at billiards played in the echoing room behind the iron-barred door. My dominant fear was that the players might want a marker. It was an absurd fear; because creatures who could play in the dark would be above such superfluities. I only know that that was my terror; and it was real.

After a long, long while the game stopped, and the door banged. I slept because I was dead tired. Otherwise I should have preferred to have kept awake. Not for everything in Asia would I have dropped the door-bar and peered into the dark of the next room.

When the morning came, I considered that I had done well and wisely, and enquired for the means of departure.

'By the way, *khansamah*,' I said, 'what were those three doolies doing in my compound in the night?'

'There were no doolies,' said the *khansamah*.

I went into the next room and the daylight streamed through the open door. I was immensely brave. I would, at that hour, have played Black Pool with the owner of the big Black Pool down below.

'Has this place always been a dak-bungalow?' I asked.

'No,' said the *khansamah*. 'Ten or twenty years ago, I have forgotten how long, it was a billiard room.'

'A how much?'

'A billiard room for the sahibs who built the railway. I was *khansamah* then in the big house where all the railway-sahibs lived, and I used to come across with brandy-*shrab*. These three rooms were all one, and they held a big table on which the sahibs played every evening. But the sahibs are all dead now, and the railway runs, you say, nearly to Kabul.'

'Do you remember anything about the sahibs?'

'It is long ago, but I remember that one sahib, a fat man and always angry, was playing here one night, and he said to me: 'Mangal Khan, brandy-*pani do*,' and I filled the glass, and he bent over the table to strike, and his head fell lower and lower till it hit the table, and his spectacles came off, and when we – the sahibs and I myself – ran to lift him he was dead. I helped to carry him out. Aha, he was a strong sahib! But he is dead and I, old Mangal Khan, am still living, by your favour.'

That was more than enough! I had my ghost – a first-hand, authenticated article. I would write to the Society for Psychical Research – I would paralyse the Empire with the news! But I would, first of all, put eighty miles of assessed cropland between myself and that dak-bungalow before nightfall. The Society might send their regular agent to investigate later on.

I went into my own room and prepared to pack after noting down the facts of the case. As I smoked I heard the game begin again – with a miss in balk this time, for the whir was a short one.

The door was open and I could see into the room. *Click – click!* That was a cannon. I entered the room without fear, for there was sunlight within and a fresh breeze without. The unseen game was going on at a tremendous rate. And well it might, when a restless little rat was running to and fro inside the dingy ceiling-cloth, and a piece of loose window-sash was making fifty breaks off the window-bolt as it shook in the breeze!

Impossible to mistake the sound of billiard balls! Impossible to mistake the whir of a ball over the slate! But I was to be excused. Even when I shut my enlightened eyes the sound was marvellously like that of a fast game.

Entered angrily the faithful partner of my sorrows, Kadir Baksh.

'This bungalow is very bad and low-caste! No wonder the sahib was disturbed and is speckled. Three sets of doolie-bearers came to the bungalow late last night when I was sleeping outside, and said that it was their custom to rest in the rooms set apart for the English people! What honour has the *khansamah*? They tried to enter, but I told them to go. No wonder, if these *oorias* have been here, that the sahib is sorely spotted. It is shame, and the work of a dirty man!' Kadir Baksh did not say that he had taken from each gang two annas for rent in advance, and then, beyond my earshot, had beaten them with the big green umbrella whose use I could never before divine. But Kadir Baksh has no notions of morality.

There was an interview with the *khansamah*, but as he promptly lost his head, wrath gave place to pity, and pity led to a long conversation, in the course of which he put the fat engineer-sahib's tragic death in three separate stations – two of them fifty miles away. The third shift was to Calcutta, and there the sahib died while driving a dog-cart.

If I had encouraged him the *khansamah* would have wandered all through Bengal with his corpse.

I did not go away as soon as I intended. I stayed for the night, while the wind and the rat and the sash and the window-bolt played a ding-dong 'hundred and fifty up'. Then the wind ran out and the billiards stopped, and I felt that I had ruined my one genuine, hall-marked ghost story.

Had I only stopped at the proper time, I could have made *anything* out of it. That was the bitterest thought of all!

Bubbling-Well Road

Look out on a large-scale map the place where the Chenab River falls into the Indus fifteen miles or so above the hamlet of Chachuran. Five miles west of Chachuran lies Bubbling-Well Road, and the house of the *gosain* or priest of Arti-goth. It was the priest who showed me the road, but it is no thanks to him that I am able to tell this story.

Five miles west of Chachuran is a patch of the plumed jungle-grass, that turns over in silver when the wind blows, from ten to twenty feet high and from three to four miles square. In the heart of the patch hides the *gosain* of Bubbling-Well Road. The villagers stone him when he peers into the daylight, although he is a priest, and he runs back again as a strayed wolf turns into tall crops. He is a one-eyed man and carries, burnt between his brows, the impress of two copper coins. Some say that he was tortured by a native prince in the old days; for he is so old that he must have been capable of mischief in the days of Runjit Singh. His most pressing need at present is a halter, and the care of the British government.

These things happened when the jungle-grass was tall; and the villagers of Chachuran told me that a herd of wild pigs had gone into the Arti-goth patch. To enter jungle-grass is always an unwise proceeding, but I went, partly because I knew nothing of pig-hunting, and partly because the villagers said that the big boar of the herd owned foot-long tusks. Therefore I wished to shoot him, in order to produce the tusks in after years, and say that I had ridden him down in fair chase. I took a gun and went into the hot, close patch, believing that it would be an easy thing to unearth one pig in ten square miles of jungle. Mr Wardle, the terrier, went with me because he believed that I was incapable of existing for an hour without his advice and countenance. He managed to slip in and out between the grass clumps, but I had to force my way, and in twenty minutes was as completely lost as though I had been in the heart of Central Africa. I did not notice this at first till I had grown weary of stumbling and pushing through the grass, and Mr Wardle was beginning to sit down very often and hang out his tongue very far. There was nothing but grass everywhere, and it was impossible to see two yards in any direction. The grass-stems held the heat exactly as boiler-tubes do.

In half an hour, when I was devoutly wishing that I had left the big boar alone, I came to a narrow path which seemed to be a compromise between a native footpath and a pig-run. It was barely six inches wide, but I could sidle along it in comfort. The grass was extremely thick here, and where the path was ill defined it was necessary to crush into the tussocks with both hands before the face, or to back into it leaving both hands free to manage the rifle. None the less it was a path, and valuable because it might lead to a place.

At the end of nearly fifty yards of fair way, just when I was preparing to back into an unusually stiff tussock, I missed Mr Wardle, who for his girth is an unusually frivolous dog and never keeps to heel. I called him three times and said aloud, 'Where has the little beast gone to?' Then I stepped backwards several paces, for almost under my feet a deep voice repeated, 'Where has the little beast gone?' To appreciate an unseen voice thoroughly you should hear it when you are lost in stifling jungle-grass. I called Mr Wardle again and the underground echo assisted me. At that I ceased calling and listened very attentively, because I thought I heard a man laughing in a peculiarly offensive manner. The heat made me sweat, but the laughter made me shake. There is no earthly need for laughter in high grass. It is indecent, as well as impolite. The chuckling stopped, and I took courage and continued to call till I thought that I had located the echo somewhere behind and below the tussock into which I was preparing to back just before I lost Mr Wardle. I drove my rifle up to the triggers between the grass-stems in a downward and forward direction. Then I waggled it to and fro, but it did not seem to touch ground on the far side of the tussock as it should have done. Every time that I grunted with the exertion of driving a heavy rifle through thick grass, the grunt was faithfully repeated from below, and when I stopped to wipe my face the sound of low laughter was distinct beyond doubting.

I went on all fours into the tussock, face first, an inch at a time, my mouth open and my eyes fine, full and prominent. When I had overcome the resistance of the grass I found that I was looking straight across a black gap in the ground – that I was actually lying on my chest leaning over the mouth of a well so deep I could scarcely see the water in it.

There were things in the water – black things – and the water was as black as pitch with blue scum atop. The laughing sound came from the noise of a little spring, spouting out halfway down one side of the well. Sometimes as the black things circled round, the trickle from the spring fell upon their tightly stretched skins, and then the laughter changed into a sputter of mirth. One thing turned over on its back, as I watched, and drifted round and round the circle of the mossy brickwork with a hand and half an arm held clear of the water in a stiff and horrible flourish, as though it were a very wearied guide paid to exhibit the beauties of the place.

I did not spend more than half an hour in creeping round that well and finding the path on the other side. The remainder of the journey I accomplished by feeling every foot of ground in front of me, and crawling like a snail through every tussock. I carried Mr Wardle in my arms and he licked my nose. He was not frightened in the least, nor was I, but we wished to reach open ground in order to enjoy the view. My knees were loose, and the apple in my throat refused to slide up and down. The path on the far side of the well was a very good one, though boxed in on all sides by grass, and it led me in time to the priest's hut in the centre of a little clearing. When that priest saw my very white face coming through the grass he howled with terror and embraced my boots; but when I reached the bedstead set outside his door I sat down quickly and Mr Wardle mounted guard over me. I was not in a condition to take care of myself.

When I awoke I told the priest to lead me into the open, out of the Arti-goth patch, and to walk slowly in front of me. Mr Wardle hates natives, and the priest was more afraid of Mr Wardle than of me, though we were both angry. He walked very slowly down a narrow little path from his hut. That path crossed three paths, such as the one I had come by in the first instance, and every one of the three headed towards the Bubbling Well. Once when we stopped to draw breath, I heard the well laughing to itself alone in the thick grass, and only my need for his services prevented my firing both barrels into the priest's back.

When we came to the open the priest crashed back into cover, and I went to the village of Arti-goth for a drink. It was pleasant to be able to see the horizon all round, as well as the ground underfoot.

The villagers told me that the patch of grass was full of devils and ghosts, all in the service of the priest, and that men and women and children had entered it and had never returned. They said the priest used their livers for purposes of witchcraft. When I asked why they had not told me of this at the outset, they said that they were afraid they would lose their reward for bringing news of the pig.

Before I left I did my best to set the patch alight, but the grass was too green. Some fine summer day, however, if the wind is favourable, a file of old newspapers and a box of matches will make clear the mystery of Bubbling-Well Road.

At the End of the Passage

Four men, each entitled to 'life, liberty, and the pursuit of happiness', sat at a table playing whist. The thermometer marked – for them – one hundred and one degrees of heat. The room was darkened till it was only just possible to distinguish the pips of the cards and the very white faces of the players. A tattered, rotten punkah of whitewashed calico was puddling the hot air and whining dolefully at each stroke. Outside lay gloom worthy of a November day in London. There was neither sky, sun nor horizon – nothing but a brown purple haze of heat. It was as though the earth were dying of apoplexy.

From time to time clouds of tawny dust rose from the ground without wind or warning, flung themselves tablecloth-wise among the tops of the parched trees, and came down again. Then a whirling dust-devil would scutter across the plain for a couple of miles, break, and fall outward, though there was nothing to check its flight save a long low line of piled railway-sleepers white with the dust, a cluster of huts made of mud, condemned rails, and canvas, and the one squat four-roomed bungalow that belonged to the assistant engineer in charge of a section of the Gaudhari state line then under construction.

The four, stripped to the thinnest of sleeping-suits, played whist crossly, with wranglings as to leads and returns. It was not the best kind of whist, but they had taken some trouble to arrive at it. Mottram of the Indian Survey had ridden thirty and railed one hundred miles from his lonely post in the desert since the night before; Lowndes of the Civil Service, on special duty in the political department, had come as far to escape for an instant the miserable intrigues of an impoverished native state whose king alternately fawned and blustered for more money from the pitiful revenues contributed by hard-wrung peasants and despairing camel-breeders; Spurstow, the doctor of the line, had left a cholera-stricken camp of coolies to look after itself for forty-eight hours while he associated with white men once more. Hummil, the assistant engineer, was the host. He stood fast and received his friends thus every Sunday if they could come in. When one of them failed to appear, he would send a telegram to his last address, in order that he might know whether the defaulter were dead or alive. There are very many places in the East where it is not good or kind to let your acquaintances drop out of sight even for one short week.

The players were not conscious of any special regard for each other. They squabbled whenever they met; but they ardently desired to meet, as men without water desire to drink. They were lonely folk who understood the dread meaning of loneliness. They were all under thirty years of age – which is too soon for any man to possess that knowledge.

'Pilsener?' said Spurstow, after the second rubber, mopping his forehead.

'Beer's out, I'm sorry to say, and there's hardly enough soda-water for tonight,' said Hummil.

'What filthy bad management!' Spurstow snarled.

'Can't help it. I've written and wired; but the trains don't come through regularly yet. Last week the ice ran out – as Lowndes knows.'

'Glad I didn't come. I could ha' sent you some if I had known, though. Phew! it's too hot to go on playing bumblepuppy.' This with a savage scowl at Lowndes, who only laughed. He was a hardened offender.

Mottram rose from the table and looked out of a chink in the shutters.

'What a sweet day!' said he.

The company yawned all together and betook themselves to an aimless investigation of all Hummil's possessions – guns, tattered novels, saddlery, spurs and the like. They had fingered them a score of times before, but there was really nothing else to do.

'Got anything fresh?' said Lowndes.

'Last week's *Gazette of India*, and a cutting from a home paper. My father sent it out. It's rather amusing.'

'One of those vestrymen that call 'emselves MPs again, is it?' said Spurstow, who read his newspapers when he could get them.

'Yes. Listen to this. It's to your address, Lowndes. The man was making a speech to his constituents, and he piled it on. Here's a sample: "And I assert unhesitatingly that the Civil Service in India is the preserve – the pet preserve – of the aristocracy of England. What does the democracy – what do the masses – get from that country, which we have step by step fraudulently annexed? I answer, nothing whatever. It is farmed with a single eye to their own interests by the scions of the aristocracy. They take good care to maintain their lavish scale of incomes, to avoid or stifle any enquiries into the nature and conduct of their administration, while they themselves force the unhappy peasant to pay with the sweat of his brow for all the luxuries in which they are lapped." ' Hummil waved the cutting above his head. ' 'Ear! 'ear!' said his audience.

Then Lowndes, meditatively: 'I'd give – I'd give three months' pay to have that gentleman spend one month with me and see how the free and independent native prince works things. Old Timbersides' – this was his flippant title for an honoured and decorated feudatory prince – 'has been wearing my life out this week past for money. By Jove, his latest performance was to send me one of his women as a bribe!'

'Good for you! Did you accept it?' said Mottram.

'No. I rather wish I had, now. She was a pretty little person, and she yarned away to me about the horrible destitution among the king's women-folk. The darlings haven't had any new clothes for nearly a month, and the old man wants to buy a new drag from Calcutta – solid silver railings and silver lamps, and trifles of that kind. I've tried to make him understand that he has played the deuce with the revenues for the last twenty years and must go slow. He can't see it.'

'But he has the ancestral treasure-vaults to draw on. There must be three millions at least in jewels and coin under his palace,' said Hummil.

'Catch a native king disturbing the family treasure! The priests forbid it except as the last resort. Old Timbersides has added something like a quarter of a million to the deposit in his reign.'

'Where the mischief does it all come from?' said Mottram.

'The country. The state of the people is enough to make you sick. I've known the tax-men wait by a milch-camel till the foal was born and then hurry off the mother for arrears. And what can I do? I can't get the court clerks to give me any accounts; I can't raise anything more than a fat smile from the commander-in-chief when I find out the troops are three months in arrears; and old Timbersides begins to weep when I speak to him. He has taken to the King's Peg heavily – liqueur brandy for whisky, and Heidsieck for soda-water.'

'That's what the Rao of Jubela took to. Even a native can't last long at that,' said Spurstow. 'He'll go out.'

'And a good thing, too. Then I suppose we'll have a council of regency, and a tutor for the young prince, and hand him back his kingdom with ten years' accumulations.'

'Whereupon that young prince, having been taught all the vices of the English, will play ducks and drakes with the money and undo ten years' work in eighteen months. I've seen that business before,' said Spurstow. 'I should tackle the king with a light hand, if I were you, Lowndes. They'll hate you quite enough under any circumstances.'

'That's all very well. The man who looks on can talk about the light hand; but you can't clean a pig-stye with a pen dipped in rose-water. I know my risks; but nothing has happened yet. My servant's an old Pathan, and he cooks for me. They are hardly likely to bribe him, and I don't accept food from my true friends, as they call themselves. Oh, but it's weary work! I'd sooner be with you, Spurstow. There's shooting near your camp.'

'Would you? I don't think it. About fifteen deaths a day don't incite a man to shoot anything but himself. And the worst of it is that the poor devils look at you as though you ought to save them. Lord knows, I've tried everything. My last attempt was empirical, but it pulled an old man through. He was brought to me apparently past hope, and I gave him gin and Worcester sauce with cayenne. It cured him; but I don't recommend it.'

'How do the cases run generally?' said Hummil.

'Very simply indeed. Chlorodyne, opium pill, chlorodyne, collapse, nitre, bricks to the feet, and then – the burning-ghat. The last seems to be the only thing that stops the trouble. It's black cholera, you know. Poor devils! But, I will say, little Bunsee Lal, my apothecary, works like a demon. I've recommended him for promotion if he comes through it all alive.'

'And what are your chances, old man?' said Mottram.

'Don't know; don't care much; but I've sent the letter in. What are you doing with yourself generally?'

'Sitting under a table in the tent and spitting on the sextant to keep it cool,' said the man of the survey. 'Washing my eyes to avoid ophthalmia, which I shall certainly get, and trying to make a sub-surveyor understand that an error of five degrees in an angle isn't quite so small as it looks. I'm altogether alone, y' know, and shall be till the end of the hot weather.'

'Hummil's the lucky man,' said Lowndes, flinging himself into a long chair. 'He has an actual roof – torn as to the ceiling-cloth, but still a roof – over his head. He sees one train daily. He can get beer and soda-water and ice 'em when God is good. He has books, pictures' – they were torn from the *Graphic* – 'and the society of the excellent sub-contractor Jevins, besides the pleasure of receiving us weekly.'

Hummil smiled grimly. 'Yes, I'm the lucky man, I suppose. Jevins is luckier.'

'How? Not – '

'Yes. Went out. Last Monday.'

'By his own hand?' said Spurstow quickly, hinting the suspicion that was in everybody's mind. There was no cholera near Hummil's section. Even fever gives a man at least a week's grace, and sudden death generally implied self-slaughter.

'I judge no man this weather,' said Hummil. 'He had a touch of the sun, I fancy; for last week, after you fellows had left, he came into the verandah and told me that he was going home to see his wife, in Market Street, Liverpool, that evening.

'I got the apothecary in to look at him, and we tried to make him lie down. After an hour or two he rubbed his eyes and said he believed he had had a fit – hoped he hadn't said anything rude. Jevins had a great idea of bettering himself socially. He was very like Chucks in his language.'

'Well?'

'Then he went to his own bungalow and began cleaning a rifle. He told the servant that he was going to shoot buck in the morning. Naturally he fumbled with the trigger, and shot himself through the head – accidentally.

The apothecary sent in a report to my chief, and Jevins is buried somewhere out there. I'd have wired to you, Spurstow, if you could have done anything.'

'You're a queer chap,' said Mottram. 'If you'd killed the man yourself you couldn't have been more quiet about the business.'

'Good Lord! what does it matter?' said Hummil calmly. 'I've got to do a lot of his overseeing work in addition to my own. I'm the only person that suffers. Jevins is out of it – by pure accident, of course, but out of it. The apothecary was going to write a long screed on suicide. Trust a babu to drivel when he gets the chance.'

'Why didn't you let it go in as suicide?' said Lowndes.

'No direct proof. A man hasn't many privileges in this country, but he might at least be allowed to mishandle his own rifle. Besides, someday I may need a man to smother up an accident to myself. Live and let live. Die and let die.'

'You take a pill,' said Spurstow, who had been watching Hummil's white face narrowly. 'Take a pill, and don't be an ass. That sort of talk is skittles. Anyhow, suicide is shirking your work. If I were Job ten times over, I should be so interested in what was going to happen next that I'd stay on and watch.'

'Ah! I've lost that curiosity,' said Hummil.

'Liver out of order?' said Lowndes feelingly.

'No. Can't sleep. That's worse.'

'By Jove, it is!' said Mottram. 'I'm that way every now and then, and the fit has to wear itself out. What do you take for it?'

'Nothing. What's the use? I haven't had ten minutes' sleep since Friday morning.'

'Poor chap! Spurstow, you ought to attend to this,' said Mottram. 'Now you mention it, your eyes are rather gummy and swollen.'

Spurstow, still watching Hummil, laughed lightly. 'I'll patch him up, later on. Is it too hot, do you think, to go for a ride?'

'Where to?' said Lowndes wearily. 'We shall have to go away at eight, and there'll be riding enough for us then. I hate a horse, when I have to use him as a necessity. Oh, heavens! what is there to do?'

'Begin whist again, at chick points and a gold mohur on the rub,' said Spurstow promptly.

'Poker. A month's pay all round for the pool – no limit – and fifty-rupee raises. Somebody would be broken before we got up,' said Lowndes.

'Can't say that it would give me any pleasure to break any man in this company,' said Mottram. 'There isn't enough excitement in it, and it's foolish.' He crossed over to the worn and battered little camp-piano – wreckage of a married household that had once held the bungalow – and opened the case.

'It's used up long ago,' said Hummil. 'The servants have picked it to pieces.'

The piano was indeed hopelessly out of order, but Mottram managed to bring the rebellious notes into a sort of agreement, and there rose from the ragged keyboard something that might once have been the ghost of a popular music-hall song. The men in the long chairs turned with evident interest as Mottram banged the more lustily.

'That's good!' said Lowndes. 'By Jove! the last time I heard that song was in '79, or thereabouts, just before I came out.'

'Ah!' said Spurstow with pride, 'I was home in '80.' And he mentioned a song of the streets popular at that date.

Mottram executed it roughly. Lowndes criticised and volunteered emendations. Mottram dashed into another ditty, not of the music-hall character, and made as if to rise.

'Sit down,' said Hummil. 'I didn't know that you had any music in your composition. Go on playing until you can't think of anything more. I'll have that piano tuned up before you come again. Play something festive.'

Very simple indeed were the tunes to which Mottram's art and the limitations of the piano could give effect, but the men listened with pleasure, and in the pauses talked all together of what they had seen or heard when they were last at home. A dense dust-storm sprang up outside, and swept roaring over the house, enveloping it in the choking darkness of midnight, but Mottram continued unheeding, and the crazy tinkle reached the ears of the listeners above the flapping of the tattered ceiling-cloth.

In the silence after the storm he glided from the more directly personal songs of Scotland, half humming them as he played, into the Evening Hymn.

'Sunday,' said he, nodding his head.

'Go on. Don't apologise for it,' said Spurstow.

Hummil laughed long and riotously. 'Play it, by all means. You're full of surprises today. I didn't know you had such a gift of finished sarcasm. How does that thing go?'

Mottram took up the tune.

'Too slow by half. You miss the note of gratitude,' said Hummil. 'It ought to go to the "Grasshopper's Polka" – this way.' And he chanted, *prestissimo* –

> 'Glory to thee, my God, this night,
> For all the blessings of the light.

That shows we really feel our blessings. How does it go on? –

> If in the night I sleepless lie,
> My soul with sacred thoughts supply;

> May no ill dreams disturb my rest –
>
> Quicker, Mottram! –
>
> Or powers of darkness me molest!

Bah! what an old hypocrite you are!'

'Don't be an ass,' said Lowndes. 'You are at full liberty to make fun of anything else you like, but leave that hymn alone. It's associated in my mind with the most sacred recollections – '

'Summer evenings in the country – stained-glass window – light going out, and you and she jamming your heads together over one hymn-book,' said Mottram.

'Yes, and a fat old cockchafer hitting you in the eye when you walked home. Smell of hay, and a moon as big as a bandbox sitting on the top of a haycock; bats – roses – milk and midges,' said Lowndes.

'Also mothers. I can just recollect my mother singing me to sleep with that when I was a little chap,' said Spurstow.

The darkness had fallen on the room. They could hear Hummil squirming in his chair.

'Consequently,' said he testily, 'you sing it when you are seven fathoms deep in hell! It's an insult to the intelligence of the Deity to pretend we're anything but tortured rebels.'

'Take *two* pills,' said Spurstow; 'that's tortured liver.'

'The usually placid Hummil is in a vile bad temper. I'm sorry for his coolies tomorrow,' said Lowndes, as the servants brought in the lights and prepared the table for dinner.

As they were settling into their places about the miserable goat-chops, and the smoked tapioca pudding, Spurstow took occasion to whisper to Mottram, 'Well done, David!'

'Look after Saul, then,' was the reply.

'What are you two whispering about?' said Hummil suspiciously.

'Only saying that you are a damned poor host. This fowl can't be cut,' returned Spurstow with a sweet smile. 'Call this a dinner?'

'I can't help it. You don't expect a banquet, do you?'

Throughout that meal Hummil contrived laboriously to insult directly and pointedly all his guests in succession, and at each insult Spurstow kicked the aggrieved persons under the table; but he dared not exchange a glance of intelligence with either of them. Hummil's face was white and pinched, while his eyes were unnaturally large. No man dreamed for a moment of resenting his savage jibes, but as soon as the meal was over they made haste to get away. 'Don't go. You're just getting amusing, you fellows. I hope I haven't said anything that annoyed you. You're such touchy devils.' Then, changing the note into one of almost abject entreaty, Hummil added, 'I say, you surely aren't going?'

'In the language of the blessed Jorrocks, where I dines I sleeps,' said Spurstow. 'I want to have a look at your coolies tomorrow, if you don't mind. You can give me a place to lie down in, I suppose?'

The others pleaded the urgency of their several duties next day, and, saddling up, departed together, Hummil begging them to come next Sunday.

As they jogged off, Lowndes unbosomed himself to Mottram – ' . . . And I never felt so like kicking a man at his own table in my life. He said I cheated at whist, and reminded me I was in debt! Told you you were as good as a liar to your face! You aren't half indignant enough over it.'

'Not I,' said Mottram. 'Poor devil! Did you ever know old Hummy behave like that before or within a hundred miles of it?'

'That's no excuse. Spurstow was hacking my shin all the time, so I kept a hand on myself. Else I should have – '

'No, you wouldn't. You'd have done as Hummy did about Jevins; judge no man this weather. By Jove! the buckle of my bridle is hot in my hand! Trot out a bit, and 'ware rat-holes.'

Ten minutes' trotting jerked out of Lowndes one very sage remark when he pulled up, sweating from every pore – 'Good thing Spurstow's with him tonight.'

'Ye–es. Good man, Spurstow. Our roads turn here. See you again next Sunday, if the sun doesn't bowl me over.'

'S'pose so, unless old Timbersides' finance minister manages to dress some of my food. Good-night, and – God bless you!'

'What's wrong now?'

'Oh, nothing.' Lowndes gathered up his whip, and, as he flicked Mottram's mare on the flank, added, 'You're not a bad little chap – that's all.' And the mare bolted half a mile across the sand, on the word.

In the assistant engineer's bungalow Spurstow and Hummil smoked the pipe of silence together, each narrowly watching the other. The capacity of a bachelor's establishment is as elastic as its arrangements are simple. A servant cleared away the dining-room table, brought in a couple of rude native bedsteads made of tape strung on light wood frames, flung a square of cool Calcutta matting over each, set them side by side, pinned two towels to the punkah so that their fringes should just sweep clear of the sleepers' nose and mouth, and announced that the couches were ready.

The men flung themselves down, ordering the punkah-coolies by all the powers of hell to pull. Every door and window was shut, for the outside air was that of an oven. The atmosphere within was only 104 degrees, as the thermometer bore witness, and heavy with the foul smell of badly-trimmed kerosene lamps; and this stench, combined with that of native tobacco, baked brick and dried earth, sends the heart of many a strong man down to his boots, for it is the smell of the Great Indian Empire when she turns herself for six months into a house of torment. Spurstow packed his pillows craftily so that he reclined rather than lay, his head at a safe elevation above his feet. It is not good to sleep on a low pillow in the hot weather if you happen to be of thick-necked build, for you may pass with lively snores and gugglings from natural sleep into the deep slumber of heat-apoplexy.

'Pack your pillows,' said the doctor sharply, as he saw Hummil preparing to lie down at full length.

The night-light was trimmed; the shadow of the punkah wavered across the room, and the *flick* of the punkah-towel and the soft whine of the rope through the wall-hole followed it. Then the punkah flagged, almost ceased. The sweat poured from Spurstow's brow. Should he go out and harangue the coolie? It started forward again with a savage jerk, and a pin came out of the towels. When this was replaced, a tom-tom in the coolie-lines began to beat with the steady throb of a swollen artery inside some brain-fevered skull. Spurstow turned on his side and swore gently. There was no movement on Hummil's part. The man had composed himself as rigidly as a corpse, his hands clenched at his sides. The respiration was too hurried for any suspicion of sleep. Spurstow looked at the set face. The jaws were clenched, and there was a pucker round the quivering eyelids.

'He's holding himself as tightly as ever he can,' thought Spurstow. 'What in the world is the matter with him? – Hummil!'

'Yes,' in a thick constrained voice.

'Can't you get to sleep?'

'No.'

'Head hot? Throat feeling bulgy? or how?'

'Neither, thanks. I don't sleep much, you know.'

'Feel pretty bad?'

'Pretty bad, thanks. There is a tom-tom outside, isn't there? I thought it was my head at first . . . Oh, Spurstow, for pity's sake give me something that will put me asleep – sound asleep – if it's only for six hours!' He sprang up, trembling from head to foot. 'I haven't been able to sleep naturally for days, and I can't stand it! – I can't stand it!'

'Poor old chap!'

'That's no use. Give me something to make me sleep. I tell you I'm nearly mad. I don't know what I say half my time. For three weeks I've had to think and spell out every word that has come through my lips before I dared say it. Isn't that enough to drive a man mad? I can't see things correctly now, and I've lost my sense of touch. My skin aches – my skin aches! Make me sleep. Oh, Spurstow, for the love of God make me sleep sound. It isn't enough merely to let me dream. Let me sleep!'

'All right, old man, all right. Go slow; you aren't half as bad as you think.' The floodgates of reserve once broken, Hummil was clinging to him like a frightened child. 'You're pinching my arm to pieces.'

'I'll break your neck if you don't do something for me. No, I didn't mean that. Don't be angry, old fellow.' He wiped the sweat off himself as he fought to regain composure. 'I'm a bit restless and off my oats, and perhaps you could recommend some sort of sleeping mixture – bromide of potassium.'

'Bromide of skittles! Why didn't you tell me this before? Let go of my arm, and I'll see if there's anything in my cigarette-case to suit your complaint.' Spurstow hunted among his day-clothes, turned up the lamp, opened a little silver cigarette-case, and advanced on the expectant Hummil with the daintiest of fairy squirts.

'The last appeal of civilisation,' said he, 'and a thing I hate to use. Hold out your arm. Well, your sleeplessness hasn't ruined your muscle; and what a thick hide it is! Might as well inject a buffalo subcutaneously. Now in a few minutes the morphia will begin working. Lie down and wait.'

A smile of unalloyed and idiotic delight began to creep over Hummil's face. 'I think,' he whispered – 'I think I'm going off now. Gad! it's positively heavenly! Spurstow, you must give me that case to keep; you – ' The voice ceased as the head fell back.

'Not for a good deal,' said Spurstow to the unconscious form. 'And now, my friend, sleeplessness of your kind being very apt to relax the moral fibre in little matters of life and death, I'll just take the liberty of spiking your guns.'

He paddled into Hummil's saddle-room in his bare feet and uncased a twelve-bore rifle, an Express and a revolver. Of the first he unscrewed the nipples and hid them in the bottom of a saddlery-case; of the second he abstracted the lever, kicking it behind a big wardrobe. The third he merely opened, and knocked the doll-head bolt of the grip up with the heel of a riding-boot.

'That's settled,' he said, as he shook the sweat off his hands. 'These little precautions will at least give you time to turn. You have too much sympathy with gun-room accidents.'

And as he rose from his knees, the thick muffled voice of Hummil cried in the doorway, 'You fool!'

Such tones they use who speak in the lucid intervals of delirium to their friends a little before they die.

Spurstow started, dropping the pistol. Hummil stood in the doorway, rocking with helpless laughter.

'That was awf'ly good of you, I'm sure,' he said, very slowly, feeling for his words. 'I don't intend to go out by my own hand at present. I say,

Spurstow, that stuff won't work. What shall I do? What shall I do?' And panic terror stood in his eyes.

'Lie down and give it a chance. Lie down at once.'

'I daren't. It will only take me halfway again, and I shan't be able to get away this time. Do you know it was all I could do to come out just now? Generally I am as quick as lightning; but you had clogged my feet. I was nearly caught.'

'Oh yes, I understand. Go and lie down.'

'No, it isn't delirium; but it was an awfully mean trick to play on me. Do you know I might have died?'

As a sponge rubs a slate clean, so some power unknown to Spurstow had wiped out of Hummil's face all that stamped it for the face of a man, and he stood at the doorway in the expression of his lost innocence. He had slept back into terrified childhood.

'Is he going to die on the spot?' thought Spurstow. Then, aloud, 'All right, my son. Come back to bed, and tell all about it. You couldn't sleep; but what was all the rest of the nonsense?'

'A place – a place down there,' said Hummil, with simple sincerity. The drug was acting on him by waves, and he was flung from the fear of a strong man to the fright of a child as his nerves gathered sense or were dulled.

'Good God! I've been afraid of it for months past, Spurstow. It has made every night hell to me; and yet I'm not conscious of having done anything wrong.'

'Be still, and I'll give you another dose. We'll stop your nightmares, you unutterable idiot!'

'Yes, but you must give me so much that I can't get away. You must make me quite sleepy – not just a little sleepy. It's so hard to run then.'

'I know it; I know it. I've felt it myself. The symptoms are exactly as you describe.'

'Oh, don't laugh at me, confound you! Before this awful sleeplessness came to me I've tried to rest on my elbow and put a spur in the bed to sting me when I fell back. Look!'

'By Jove! the man has been rowelled like a horse! Ridden by the nightmare with a vengeance! And we all thought him sensible enough. Heaven send us understanding!' Aloud, Spurstow said, 'You like to talk, don't you?'

'Yes, sometimes. Not when I'm frightened. *Then* I want to run. Don't you?'

'Always. Before I give you your second dose try to tell me exactly what your trouble is.'

Hummil spoke in broken whispers for nearly ten minutes, whilst Spurstow looked into the pupils of his eyes and passed his hand before them once or twice.

At the end of the narrative the silver cigarette-case was produced, and the last words that Hummil said as he fell back for the second time were, 'Put me quite to sleep; for if I'm caught I die – I die!'

'Yes, yes; we all do that sooner or later – thank heaven, which has set a term to our miseries,' said Spurstow, settling the cushions under the head. 'It occurs to me that unless I drink something I shall go out before my time. I've stopped sweating, and – I wear a seventeen-inch collar.' He brewed himself scalding hot tea, which is an excellent remedy against heat-apoplexy if you take three or four cups of it in time. Then he watched the sleeper.

'A blind face that cries and can't wipe its eyes, a blind face that chases him down corridors! H'm! Decidedly, Hummil ought to go on leave as soon as possible; and, sane or otherwise, he undoubtedly did rowel himself most cruelly. Well heaven send us understanding!'

At midday Hummil rose, with an evil taste in his mouth, but an unclouded eye and a joyful heart.

'I was pretty bad last night, wasn't I?' said he.

'I have seen healthier men. You must have had a touch of the sun. Look here: if I write you a swingeing medical certificate, will you apply for leave on the spot?'

'No.'

'Why not? You want it.'

'Yes, but I can hold on till the weather's a little cooler.'

'Why should you, if you can get relieved on the spot?'

'Burkett is the only man who could be sent; and he's a born fool.'

'Oh, never mind about the line. You aren't so important as all that. Wire for leave, if necessary.'

Hummil looked very uncomfortable.

'I can hold on till the rains,' he said evasively.

'You can't. Wire to headquarters for Burkett.'

'I won't. If you want to know why, particularly, Burkett is married, and his wife's just had a kid, and she's up at Simla, in the cool, and Burkett has a very nice billet that takes him into Simla from Saturday to Monday. That little woman isn't at all well. If Burkett was transferred she'd try to follow him. If she left the baby behind she'd fret herself to death. If she came – and Burkett's one of those selfish little beasts who are always talking about a wife's place being with her husband – she'd die. It's murder to bring a woman here just now. Burkett hasn't the physique of a rat. If he came here he'd go out; and I know she hasn't any money, and I'm pretty sure she'd go out too. I'm salted in a sort of way, and I'm not married. Wait till the Rains, and then Burkett can get thin down here. It'll do him heaps of good.'

'Do you mean to say that you intend to face – what you have faced, till the Rains break?'

'Oh, it won't be so bad, now you've shown me a way out of it. I can always wire to you. Besides, now I've once got into the way of sleeping, it'll be all right. Anyhow, I shan't put in for leave. That's the long and the short of it.'

'My great Scott! I thought all that sort of thing was dead and done with.'

'Bosh! You'd do the same yourself. I feel a new man, thanks to that cigarette-case. You're going over to camp now, aren't you?'

'Yes; but I'll try to look you up every other day, if I can.'

'I'm not bad enough for that. I don't want you to bother. Give the coolies gin and ketchup.'

'Then you feel all right?'

'Fit to fight for my life, but not to stand out in the sun talking to you. Go along, old man, and bless you!'

Hummil turned on his heel to face the echoing desolation of his bungalow, and the first thing he saw standing in the verandah was the figure of himself. He had met a similar apparition once before, when he was suffering from overwork and the strain of the hot weather.

'This is bad – already,' he said, rubbing his eyes. 'If the thing slides away from me all in one piece, like a ghost, I shall know it is only my eyes and stomach that are out of order. If it walks – my head is going.'

He approached the figure, which naturally kept at an unvarying distance from him, as is the way of all spectres that are born of overwork. It slid through the house and dissolved into swimming specks within the eyeball as soon as it reached the burning light of the garden. Hummil went about his business till even. When he came in to dinner he found himself sitting at the table. The vision rose and walked out hastily. Except that it cast no shadow it was in all respects real.

No living man knows what that week held for Hummil. An increase of the epidemic kept Spurstow in camp among the coolies, and all he could do was to telegraph to Mottram, bidding him go to the bungalow and sleep there. But Mottram was forty miles away from the nearest telegraph, and knew nothing of anything save the needs of the survey till he met, early on Sunday morning, Lowndes and Spurstow heading towards Hummil's for the weekly gathering.

'Hope the poor chap's in a better temper,' said the former, swinging himself off his horse at the door. 'I suppose he isn't up yet.'

'I'll just have a look at him,' said the doctor. 'If he's asleep there's no need to wake him.'

And an instant later, by the tone of Spurstow's voice calling upon them to enter, the men knew what had happened. There was no need to wake him.

The punkah was still being pulled over the bed, but Hummil had departed this life some hours before.

The body lay on its back, hands clenched by its sides, as Spurstow had seen it lying seven nights previously. In the staring eyes was written terror beyond the expression of any pen.

Mottram, who had entered behind Lowndes, bent over the dead and touched the forehead lightly with his lips. 'Oh, you lucky, lucky devil!' he whispered.

But Lowndes had seen the eyes, and withdrew shuddering to the other side of the room.

'Poor chap! poor old chap! And the last time I met him I was angry. Spurstow, we should have watched him. Has he – ?'

Deftly Spurstow continued his investigations, ending by a search round the room.

'No, he hasn't,' he snapped. 'There's no trace of anything. Call the servants.'

They came, eight or ten of them, whispering and peering over each other's shoulders.

'When did your sahib go to bed?' said Spurstow.

'At eleven or ten, we think,' said Hummil's personal servant.

'He was well then? But how should you know?'

'He was not ill, as far as our comprehension extended. But he had slept very little for three nights. This I know, because I saw him walking much, and specially in the heart of the night.'

As Spurstow was arranging the sheet, a big straight-necked hunting-spur tumbled on the ground. The doctor groaned. The personal servant peeped at the body.

'What do you think, Chuma?' said Spurstow, catching the look on the dark face.

'Heaven-born, in my poor opinion my master has descended into the Dark Places, and there has been caught because he was not able to escape with sufficient speed. We have the spur for evidence that he fought with Fear. Thus have I seen men of my race do with thorns when a spell was laid upon them to overtake them in their sleeping hours and they dared not sleep.'

'Chuma, you're a mud-head. Go out and prepare seals to be set on the sahib's property.'

'God has made the Heaven-born. God has made me. Who are we to enquire into the dispensations of God? I will bid the other servants hold aloof while you are reckoning the tally of the sahib's property. They are all thieves, and would steal.'

'As far as I can make out, he died from – oh, anything: stoppage of the heart's action, heat-apoplexy or some other visitation,' said Spurstow to his companions. 'We must make an inventory of his effects, and so on.'

'He was scared to death,' insisted Lowndes. 'Look at those eyes! For pity's sake don't let him be buried with them open!'

'Whatever it was, he's clear of all the trouble now,' said Mottram softly.

Spurstow was peering into the open eyes. 'Come here,' said he. 'Can you see anything there?'

'I can't face it!' whimpered Lowndes. 'Cover up the face! Is there any fear on earth that can turn a man into that likeness? It's ghastly. Oh, Spurstow, cover it up!'

'No fear – on earth,' said Spurstow.

Mottram leaned over his shoulder and looked intently. 'I see nothing except some grey blurs in the pupil. There can be nothing there, you know.'

'Even so. Well, let's think. It'll take half a day to knock up any sort of coffin; and he must have died at midnight. Lowndes, old man, go out and tell the coolies to break ground next to Jevins's grave. Mottram, go round the house with Chuma and see that the seals are put on things. Send a couple of men to me here, and I'll arrange.'

The strong-armed servants when they returned to their own kind told a strange story of the doctor sahib vainly trying to call their master back to life by magic arts – to wit, the holding of a little green box that clicked to each of the dead man's eyes, and of a bewildered muttering on the part of the doctor sahib, who took the little green box away with him.

The resonant hammering of a coffin-lid is no pleasant thing to hear, but those who have experience maintain that much more terrible is the soft swish of the bed-linen, the reeving and unreeving of the bed-tapes, when he who has fallen by the roadside is apparelled for burial, sinking gradually as the tapes are tied over, till the swaddled shape touches the floor and there is no protest against the indignity of hasty disposal.

At the last moment Lowndes was seized with scruples of conscience. 'Ought you to read the service – from beginning to end?' said he to Spurstow.

'I intend to. You're my senior as a civilian. You can take it if you like.'

'I didn't mean that for a moment. I only thought if we could get a chaplain from somewhere – I'm willing to ride anywhere – and give poor Hummil a better chance. That's all.'

'Bosh!' said Spurstow, as he framed his lips to the tremendous words that stand at the head of the burial service.

After breakfast they smoked a pipe in silence to the memory of the dead. Then Spurstow said absently – ' 'Tisn't in medical science.'

'What?'

'Things in a dead man's eye.'

'For goodness' sake leave that horror alone!' said Lowndes. 'I've seen a native die of pure fright when a tiger chivied him. I know what killed Hummil.'

'The deuce you do! I'm going to try to see.' And the doctor retreated into the bathroom with a Kodak camera. After a few minutes there was the sound of something being hammered to pieces, and he emerged, very white indeed.

'Have you got a picture?' said Mottram. 'What does the thing look like?'

'It was impossible, of course. You needn't look, Mottram. I've torn up the films. There was nothing there. It was impossible.'

'That,' said Lowndes, very distinctly, watching the shaking hand striving to relight the pipe, 'is a damned lie.'

Mottram laughed uneasily. 'Spurstow's right,' he said. 'We're all in such a state now that we'd believe anything. For pity's sake let's try to be rational.'

There was no further speech for a long time. The hot wind whistled without, and the dry trees sobbed. Presently the daily train, winking brass and burnished steel and spouting steam, pulled up panting in the intense glare.

'We'd better go on on that,' said Spurstow. 'Go back to work. I've written my certificate. We can't do any more good here, and work'll keep our wits together. Come on.'

No one moved. It is not pleasant to face railway journeys at midday in June.

Spurstow gathered up his hat and whip, and, turning in the doorway, said –

> 'There may be Heaven – there must be Hell.
> Meantime, there is our life here. We–ell?'

Neither Mottram nor Lowndes had any answer to the question.

The Return of Imray

Imray achieved the impossible. Without warning, for no conceivable motive, in his youth, at the threshold of his career, he chose to disappear from the world – which is to say, the little Indian station where he lived.

Upon a day he was alive, well, happy, and in great evidence among the billiard-tables at his club. Upon a morning, he was not, and no manner of search could make sure where he might be. He had stepped out of his place; he had not appeared at his office at the proper time, and his dogcart was not upon the public roads. For these reasons, and because he was hampering, in a microscopical degree, the administration of the Indian Empire, that Empire paused for one microscopical moment to make inquiry into the fate of Imray. Ponds were dragged, wells were plumbed, telegrams were dispatched down the lines of railways and to the nearest seaport town – twelve hundred miles away; but Imray was not at the end of the drag-ropes nor the telegraph wires. He was gone, and his place knew him no more.

Then the work of the great Indian Empire swept forward, because it could not be delayed, and Imray from being a man became a mystery – such a thing as men talk over at their tables in the club for a month, and then forget utterly. His guns, horses, and carts were sold to the highest bidder. His superior officer wrote an altogether absurd letter to his mother, saying that Imray had unaccountably disappeared, and his bungalow stood empty.

After three or four months of the scorching hot weather had gone by, my friend Strickland, of the police, saw fit to rent the bungalow from the native landlord. This was before he was engaged to Miss Youghal – an affair which has been described in another place – and while he was pursuing his investigations into native life. His own life was sufficiently peculiar, and men complained of his manners and customs. There was always food in his house, but there were no regular times for meals. He ate, standing up and walking about, whatever he might find at the sideboard, and this is not good for human beings. His domestic equipment was limited to six rifles, three shotguns, five saddles, and a collection of stiff-jointed mahseer-rods, bigger and stronger than the largest salmon-rods. These occupied one-half of his bungalow, and the other half was given up to Strickland and his dog Tietjens – an enormous Rampur slut who devoured daily the rations of two men. She spoke to Strickland in a language of her own; and whenever, walking abroad, she saw things calculated to destroy the peace of Her Majesty the Queen-Empress, she returned to her master and laid information. Strickland would take steps at once, and the end of his labours was trouble and fine and imprisonment for other people. The natives believed that Tietjens was a familiar spirit, and treated her with the great reverence that is born of hate and fear. One room in the bungalow was set apart for her special use. She owned a bedstead, a blanket and a drinking-trough, and if anyone came into Strickland's room at night her custom was to knock down the invader and give tongue till someone came with a light. Strickland owed his life to her, when he was on the Frontier, in search of a local murderer, who came in the grey dawn to send Strickland much farther than the Andaman Islands. Tietjens caught the man as he was crawling into Strickland's tent with a dagger between his teeth; and after his record of iniquity was established in the eyes of the law he was hanged. From that date Tietjens wore a collar of rough silver, and employed a monogram on her night-blanket; and the blanket was of double woven Kashmir cloth, for she was a delicate dog.

Under no circumstances would she be separated from Strickland; and once, when he was ill with fever, made great trouble for the doctors, because she did not know how to help her master and would not allow another creature to attempt aid. Macarnaght, of the Indian Medical Service, beat her over her head with a gun-butt before she could understand that she must give room for those who could give quinine.

A short time after Strickland had taken Imray's bungalow, my business took me through that station, and naturally, the club quarters being full, I quartered myself upon Strickland. It was a desirable bungalow, eight-roomed and heavily thatched against any chance of leakage from rain. Under the pitch of the roof ran a ceiling-cloth which looked just as neat as a whitewashed ceiling. The landlord had repainted it when Strickland took the bungalow. Unless you knew how Indian bungalows were built you would never have suspected that above the cloth lay the dark three-cornered cavern of the roof, where the beams and the underside of the thatch harboured all manner of rats, bats, ants, and foul things.

Tietjens met me in the verandah with a bay like the boom of the bell of St Paul's, putting her paws on my shoulder to show she was glad to see me. Strickland had contrived to claw together a sort of meal which he called lunch, and immediately after it was finished went out about his business. I was left alone with Tietjens and my own affairs. The heat of the summer had broken up and turned to the warm damp of the rains. There was no motion in the heated air, but the rain fell like ramrods on the earth, and flung up a blue mist when it splashed back. The bamboos and the custard-apples, the poinsettias and the mango trees in the garden stood still while the warm water lashed through them, and the frogs began to sing among the aloe hedges. A little before the light failed, and when the rain was at its worst, I sat in the back verandah and heard the water roar from the eaves, and scratched myself because I was covered with the thing called prickly-heat. Tietjens came out with me and put her head in my lap and was very sorrowful; so I gave her biscuits when tea was ready, and I took tea in the back verandah on account of the little coolness found there. The rooms of the house were dark behind me. I could smell Strickland's saddlery and the oil on his guns, and I had no desire to sit among these things. My own servant came to me in the twilight, the muslin of his clothes clinging tightly to his drenched body, and told me that a gentleman had called and wished to see someone. Very much against my will, but only because of the darkness of the rooms, I went into the naked drawing-room, telling my man to bring the lights. There might or might not have been a caller waiting – it seemed to me that I saw a figure by one of the windows – but when the lights came there was nothing save the spikes of the rain without, and the smell of the drinking earth in my nostrils. I explained to my servant that he was no wiser than he ought to be, and went back to the verandah to talk to Tietjens. She had gone out into the wet, and I could hardly coax her back to me; even with biscuits with sugar tops.

Strickland came home, dripping wet, just before dinner, and the first thing he said was, 'Has anyone called?'

I explained, with apologies, that my servant had summoned me into the drawing-room on a false alarm; that perhaps some loafer had tried to call on Strickland, and thinking better of it had fled without giving his name. Strickland ordered dinner, without comment, and since it was a real dinner with a white tablecloth attached, we sat down.

At nine o'clock Strickland wanted to go to bed, and I was tired too. Tietjens, who had been lying underneath the table, rose up, and swung into the least exposed verandah as soon as her master moved to his own room, which was next to the stately chamber set apart for Tietjens. If a mere wife had wished to sleep out of doors in that pelting rain it would not have mattered; but Tietjens was a dog, and therefore the better animal. I looked at Strickland, expecting to see him flay her with a whip. He smiled queerly, as a man would smile after telling some unpleasant domestic tragedy. 'She has done this ever since I moved in here,' said he. 'Let her go.'

The dog was Strickland's dog, so I said nothing, but I felt all that Strickland felt in being thus made light of. Tietjens encamped outside my bedroom window, and storm after storm came up, thundered on the thatch, and died away. The lightning spattered the sky as a thrown egg spatters a barn-door, but the light was pale blue, not yellow; and, looking through my split bamboo blinds, I could see the great dog standing, not sleeping, in the verandah, the hackles alift on her back and her feet anchored as tensely as the drawn wire-rope of a suspension bridge. In the very short pauses of the thunder I tried to sleep, but it seemed that someone wanted me very urgently. He, whoever he was, was trying to call me by name, but his voice was no more than a husky whisper. The thunder ceased, and Tietjens went into the garden and howled at the low moon. Somebody tried to open my door, walked about and about through the house and stood breathing heavily in the verandahs, and just when I was falling asleep I fancied that I heard a wild hammering and clamouring above my head or on the door.

I ran into Strickland's room and asked him whether he was ill and had been calling for me. He was lying on his bed half dressed, a pipe in his mouth. 'I thought you'd come,' he said. 'Have I been walking round the house recently?'

I explained that he had been tramping in the dining-room and the smoking-room and two or three other places, and he laughed and told me to go back to bed. I went back to bed and slept till the morning, but through all my mixed dreams I was sure I was doing someone an injustice in not attending to his wants. What those wants were I could not tell; but a fluttering, whispering, bolt-fumbling, lurking, loitering Someone was reproaching me for my slackness, and, half awake, I heard the howling of Tietjens in the garden and the threshing of the rain.

I lived in that house for two days. Strickland went to his office daily, leaving me alone for eight or ten hours with Tietjens for my only companion. As long as the full light lasted I was comfortable, and so was Tietjens; but in the twilight she and I moved into the back verandah and cuddled each other for company. We were alone in the house, but none the less it was much too fully occupied by a tenant with whom I did not wish to interfere. I never saw him, but I could see the curtains between the rooms quivering where he had just passed through; I could hear the chairs creaking as the bamboos sprang under a weight that had just quitted them; and I could feel when I went to get a book from the dining-room that somebody was waiting in the shadows of the front verandah till I should have gone away. Tietjens made the twilight more interesting by glaring into the darkened rooms with every hair erect, and following the motions of something that I could not see. She never entered the rooms, but her eyes moved interestedly: that was quite sufficient. Only when my servant came to trim the lamps and make all light and habitable she would come in with me and spend her time sitting on her haunches, watching an invisible extra man as he moved about behind my shoulder. Dogs are cheerful companions.

I explained to Strickland, gently as might be, that I would go over to the club and find for myself quarters there. I admired his hospitality, was pleased with his guns and rods, but I did not much care for his house and its atmosphere. He heard me out to the end, and then smiled very wearily, but without contempt, for he is a man who understands things. 'Stay on,' he said, 'and see what this thing means. All you have talked about I have known since I took the bungalow. Stay on and wait. Tietjens has left me. Are you going too?'

I had seen him through one little affair, connected with a heathen idol, that had brought me to the doors of a lunatic asylum, and I had no desire to help him through further experiences. He was a man to whom unpleasant-nesses arrived as do dinners to ordinary people.

Therefore I explained more clearly than ever that I liked him immensely, and would be happy to see him in the daytime; but that I did not care to sleep under his roof. This was after dinner, when Tietjens had gone out to lie in the verandah.

' 'Pon my soul, I don't wonder,' said Strickland, with his eyes on the ceiling-cloth. 'Look at that!'

The tails of two brown snakes were hanging between the cloth and the cornice of the wall. They threw long shadows in the lamplight.

'If you are afraid of snakes of course – ' said Strickland.

I hate and fear snakes, because if you look into the eyes of any snake you will see that it knows all and more of the mystery of man's fall, and that it feels all the contempt that the Devil felt when Adam was evicted from Eden. Besides which its bite is generally fatal, and it twists up trouser legs.

'You ought to get your thatch overhauled,' I said. 'Give me a mahseer-rod, and we'll poke 'em down.'

'They'll hide among the roof-beams,' said Strickland. 'I can't stand snakes overhead. I'm going up into the roof. If I shake 'em down, stand by with a cleaning-rod and break their backs.'

I was not anxious to assist Strickland in his work, but I took the cleaning-rod and waited in the dining-room, while Strickland brought a gardener's ladder from the verandah, and set it against the side of the room.

The snake-tails drew themselves up and disappeared. We could hear the dry rushing scuttle of long bodies running over the baggy ceiling-cloth. Strickland took a lamp with him, while I tried to make clear to him the danger of hunting roof-snakes between a ceiling-cloth and a thatch, apart from the deterioration of property caused by ripping out ceiling-cloths.

'Nonsense!' said Strickland. 'They're sure to hide near the walls by the cloth. The bricks are too cold for 'em, and the heat of the room is just what they like.' He put his hand to the corner of the stuff and ripped it from the cornice. It gave with a great sound of tearing, and Strickland put his head through the opening into the dark of the angle of the roof-beams. I set my teeth and lifted the rod, for I had not the least knowledge of what might descend.

'H'm!' said Strickland, and his voice rolled and rumbled in the roof. 'There's room for another set of rooms up here, and, by Jove, someone is occupying 'em!'

'Snakes?' I said from below.

'No. It's a buffalo. Hand me up the two last joints of a mahseer-rod, and I'll prod it. It's lying on the main roof-beam.'

I handed up the rod.

'What a nest for owls and serpents! No wonder the snakes live here,' said Strickland, climbing farther into the roof. I could see his elbow thrusting with the rod. 'Come out of that, whoever you are! Heads below there! It's falling.'

I saw the ceiling-cloth nearly in the centre of the room bag with a shape that was pressing it downwards and downwards towards the lighted lamp on the table. I snatched the lamp out of danger and stood back. Then the cloth ripped out from the walls, tore, split, swayed, and shot down upon the table something that I dared not look at till Strickland had slid down the ladder and was standing by my side.

He did not say much, being a man of few words; but he picked up the loose end of the tablecloth and threw it over the remnants on the table.

'It strikes me,' said he, putting down the lamp, 'our friend Imray has come back. Oh! you would, would you?'

There was a movement under the cloth, and a little snake wriggled out, to be back-broken by the butt of the mahseer-rod. I was sufficiently sick to make no remarks worth recording.

Strickland meditated, and helped himself to drinks. The arrangement under the cloth made no more signs of life.

'Is it Imray?' I said.

Strickland turned back the cloth for a moment, and looked. 'It is Imray,' he said; 'and his throat is cut from ear to ear.'

Then we spoke, both together and to ourselves: 'That's why he whispered about the house.'

Tietjens, in the garden, began to bay furiously. A little later her great nose heaved open the dining-room door.

She sniffed and was still. The tattered ceiling-cloth hung down almost to the level of the table, and there was hardly room to move away from the discovery.

Tietjens came in and sat down, her teeth bared under her lip and her forepaws planted. She looked at Strickland.

'It's a bad business, old lady,' said he. 'Men don't climb up into the roofs of their bungalows to die, and they don't fasten up the ceiling cloth behind 'em. Let's think it out.'

'Let's think it out somewhere else,' I said.

'Excellent idea! Turn the lamps out. We'll get into my room.'

I did not turn the lamps out. I went into Strickland's room first, and allowed him to make the darkness. Then he followed me, and we lit tobacco and thought. Strickland thought. I smoked furiously, because I was afraid.

'Imray is back,' said Strickland. 'The question is – who killed Imray? Don't talk, I've a notion of my own. When I took this bungalow I took over most of Imray's servants. Imray was guileless and inoffensive, wasn't he?'

I agreed; though the heap under the cloth had looked neither one thing nor the other.

'If I call in all the servants they will stand fast in a crowd and lie like Aryans. What do you suggest?'

'Call 'em in one by one,' I said.

'They'll run away and give the news to all their fellows,' said Strickland. 'We must segregate 'em. Do you suppose your servant knows anything about it?'

'He may, for aught I know; but I don't think it's likely. He has only been here two or three days,' I answered. 'What's your notion?'

'I can't quite tell. How the dickens did the man get the wrong side of the ceiling-cloth?'

There was a heavy coughing outside Strickland's bedroom door. This showed that Bahadur Khan, his body-servant, had waked from sleep and wished to put Strickland to bed.

'Come in,' said Strickland. 'It's a very warm night, isn't it?'

Bahadur Khan, a great, green-turbaned, six-foot Muhammadan, said that it was a very warm night; but that there was more rain pending, which, by his honour's favour, would bring relief to the country.

'It will be so, if God pleases,' said Strickland, tugging off his boots. 'It is in my mind, Bahadur Khan, that I have worked thee remorselessly for many days – ever since that time when thou first camest into my service. What time was that?'

'Has the Heaven-born forgotten? It was when Imray Sahib went secretly to Europe without warning given; and I – even I – came into the honoured service of the protector of the poor.'

'And Imray Sahib went to Europe?'

'It is so said among those who were his servants.'

'And thou wilt take service with him when he returns?'

'Assuredly, sahib. He was a good master, and cherished his dependants.'

'That is true. I am very tired, but I go buck-shooting tomorrow. Give me the little sharp rifle that I use for black-buck; it is in the case yonder.'

The man stooped over the case; handed barrels, stock and fore-end to Strickland, who fitted all together, yawning dolefully. Then he reached down to the gun-case, took a solid-drawn cartridge and slipped it into the breech of the .360 Express.

'And Imray Sahib has gone to Europe secretly! That is very strange, Bahadur Khan, is it not?'

'What do I know of the ways of the white man, Heaven-born?'

'Very little, truly. But thou shalt know more anon. It has reached me that Imray Sahib has returned from his so long journeyings, and that even now he lies in the next room, waiting his servant.'

'Sahib!'

The lamplight slid along the barrels of the rifle as they levelled themselves at Bahadur Khan's broad breast.

'Go and look!' said Strickland. 'Take a lamp. Thy master is tired, and he waits thee. Go!'

The man picked up a lamp, and went into the dining-room, Strickland following, and almost pushing him with the muzzle of the rifle. He looked for a moment at the black depths behind the ceiling-cloth; at the writhing snake under foot; and last, a grey glaze settling on his face, at the thing under the tablecloth.

'Hast thou seen?' said Strickland after a pause.

'I have seen. I am clay in the white man's hands. What does the Presence do?'

'Hang thee within the month. What else?'

'For killing him? Nay, sahib, consider. Walking among us, his servants, he cast his eyes upon my child, who was four years old. Him he bewitched, and in ten days he died of the fever – my child!'

'What said Imray Sahib?'

'He said he was a handsome child, and patted him on the head; wherefore my child died. Wherefore I killed Imray Sahib in the twilight, when he had come back from office, and was sleeping. Wherefore I dragged him up into the roof-beams and made all fast behind him. The Heaven-born knows all things. I am the servant of the Heaven-born.'

Strickland looked at me above the rifle, and said, in the vernacular, 'Thou art witness to this saying? He has killed.'

Bahadur Khan stood ashen grey in the light of the one lamp. The need for justification came upon him very swiftly. 'I am trapped,' he said, 'but the offence was that man's. He cast an evil eye upon my child, and I killed and hid him. Only such as are served by devils,' he glared at Tietjens, couched stolidly before him, 'only such could know what I did.'

'It was clever. But thou shouldst have lashed him to the beam with a rope. Now, thou thyself wilt hang by a rope. Orderly!'

A drowsy policeman answered Strickland's call. He was followed by another, and Tietjens sat wondrous still.

'Take him to the police-station,' said Strickland. 'There is a case toward.'

'Do I hang, then?' said Bahadur Khan, making no attempt to escape, and keeping his eyes on the ground.

'If the sun shines or the water runs – yes!' said Strickland.

Bahadur Khan stepped back one long pace, quivered, and stood still. The two policemen waited further orders.

'Go!' said Strickland.

'Nay; but I go very swiftly,' said Bahadur Khan. 'Look! I am even now a dead man.'

He lifted his foot, and to the little toe there clung the head of the half-killed snake, firm fixed in the agony of death.

'I come of land-holding stock,' said Bahadur Khan, rocking where he stood. 'It were a disgrace to me to go to the public scaffold: therefore I take this way. Be it remembered that the sahib's shirts are correctly enumerated, and that there is an extra piece of soap in his washbasin. My child was bewitched, and I slew the wizard. Why should you seek to slay me with the rope? My honour is saved, and – and – I die.'

At the end of an hour he died, as they die who are bitten by the little brown *karait*, and the policemen bore him and the thing under the tablecloth to their appointed places. All were needed to make clear the disappearance of Imray.

'This,' said Strickland, very calmly, as he climbed into bed, 'is called the nineteenth century. Did you hear what that man said?'

'I heard,' I answered. 'Imray made a mistake.'

'Simply and solely through not knowing the nature of the Oriental, and the coincidence of a little seasonal fever. Bahadur Khan had been with him for four years.'

I shuddered. My own servant had been with me for exactly that length of time. When I went over to my own room I found my man waiting, impassive as the copper head on a penny, to pull off my boots.

'What has befallen Bahadur Khan?' said I.

'He was bitten by a snake and died. The rest the sahib knows,' was the answer.

'And how much of this matter hast thou known?'

'As much as might be gathered from one coming in in the twilight to seek satisfaction. Gently, sahib. Let me pull off those boots.'

I had just settled to the sleep of exhaustion when I heard Strickland shouting from his side of the house – 'Tietjens has come back to her place!'

And so she had. The great deerhound was couched statelily on her own bedstead on her own blanket, while, in the next room, the idle, empty ceiling-cloth waggled as it trailed on the table.

The City of Dreadful Night

The dense wet heat that hung over the face of land, like a blanket, prevented all hope of sleep in the first instance. The cicalas helped the heat; and the yelling jackals the cicalas. It was impossible to sit still in the dark, empty, echoing house and watch the punkah beat the dead air. So, at ten o'clock of the night, I set my walking-stick on end in the middle of the garden, and waited to see how it would fall. It pointed directly down the moonlit road that leads to the City of Dreadful Night. The sound of its fall disturbed a hare. She limped from her form and ran across to a disused Muhammadan burial-ground, where the jawless skulls and rough-butted shank-bones, heartlessly exposed by the July rains, glimmered like mother-of-pearl on the rain-channelled soil. The heated air and the heavy earth had driven the very dead upward for coolness's sake. The hare limped on; snuffed curiously at a fragment of a smoke-stained lamp-shard, and died out, in the shadow of a clump of tamarisk trees.

The mat-weaver's hut under the lee of the Hindu temple was full of sleeping men who lay like sheeted corpses. Overhead blazed the unwinking eye of the moon. Darkness gives at least a false impression of coolness. It was hard not to believe that the flood of light from above was warm. Not so hot as the sun, but still sickly warm, and heating the heavy air beyond what was our due. Straight as a bar of polished steel ran the road to the City of Dreadful Night; and on either side of the road lay corpses disposed on beds in fantastic attitudes – one hundred and seventy bodies of men. Some shrouded all in white with bound-up mouths; some naked and black as ebony in the strong light; and one – that lay face upwards with dropped jaw, far away from the others – silvery white and ashen grey.

A leper asleep; and the remainder wearied coolies, servants, small shop-keepers, and drivers from the hackstand hard by. The scene – a main approach to Lahore city, and the night a warm one in August. This was all that there was to be seen; but by no means all that one could see. The witchery of the moonlight was everywhere; and the world was horribly changed. The long line of the naked dead, flanked by the rigid silver statue, was not pleasant to look upon. It was made up of men alone. Were the womenkind, then, forced to sleep in the shelter of the stifling mud-huts as best they might? The fretful wail of a child from a low mud-roof answered the question. Where the children are the mothers must be also to look after them. They need care on these sweltering nights. A black little bullet-head peeped over the coping, and a thin – a painfully thin – brown leg was slid over on to the gutter pipe. There was a sharp clink of glass bracelets; a woman's arm showed for an instant above the parapet, twined itself round the lean little neck, and the child was dragged back, protesting, to the shelter of the bedstead. His thin, high-pitched shriek died out in the thick air almost as soon as it was raised; for even the children of the soil found it too hot to weep.

More corpses; more stretches of moonlit, white road, a string of sleeping camels at rest by the wayside; a vision of scudding jackals; ekka-ponies asleep – the harness still on their backs, and the brass-studded country carts, winking in the moonlight – and again more corpses. Wherever a grain cart a-tilt, a tree trunk, a sawn log, a couple of bamboos and a few handfuls of thatch cast a shadow, the ground is covered with them. They lie – some face downwards, arms folded, in the dust; some with clasped hands flung up above their heads; some curled up dog-wise; some thrown like limp gunny-bags over the side of the grain carts; and some bowed with their brows on their knees in the full glare of the moon. It would be a comfort if they were only given to snoring; but they are not, and the likeness to corpses is unbroken in all respects save one. The lean dogs snuff at them and turn away. Here and there a tiny child lies on his father's bedstead, and a protecting arm is thrown round it in every instance. But, for the most part, the children sleep with their mothers on the house-tops. Yellow-skinned white-toothed pariahs are not to be trusted within reach of brown bodies.

A stifling hot blast from the mouth of the Delhi Gate nearly ends my resolution of entering the City of Dreadful Night at this hour. It is a compound of all evil savours, animal and vegetable, that a walled city can brew in a day and a night. The temperature within the motionless groves of plantain and orange trees outside the city walls seems chilly by comparison. Heaven help all sick persons and young children within the city tonight! The high house-walls are still radiating heat savagely, and from obscure side gullies fetid breezes eddy that ought to poison a buffalo. But the buffaloes do not heed. A drove of them are parading the vacant main street; stopping now and then to lay their ponderous muzzles against the closed shutters of a grain-dealer's shop and to blow thereon like grampuses.

Then silence follows – the silence that is full of the night noises of a great city. A stringed instrument of some kind is just, and only just, audible. High overhead someone throws open a window, and the rattle of the woodwork echoes down the empty street. On one of the roofs, a hookah is in full blast; and the men are talking softly as the pipe gutters. A little farther on, the noise of conversation is more distinct. A slit of light shows itself between the sliding shutters of a shop. Inside, a stubble-bearded, weary-eyed trader is balancing his account-books among the bales of cotton prints that surround him. Three sheeted figures bear him company, and throw in a remark from time to time. First he makes an entry, then a remark; then passes the back of his hand across his streaming forehead. The heat in the built-in street is fearful. Inside the shops it must be almost unendurable. But the work goes on steadily; entry, guttural growl and uplifted hand-stroke succeeding each other with the precision of clockwork.

A policeman – turbanless and fast asleep – lies across the road on the way to the Mosque of Wazir Khan. A bar of moonlight falls across the forehead and eyes of the sleeper, but he never stirs. It is close upon midnight, and the heat seems to be increasing. The open square in front of the mosque is crowded with corpses; and a man must pick his way carefully for fear of treading on them. The moonlight stripes the mosque's high front of coloured enamel work in broad diagonal bands; and each separate dreaming pigeon in the niches and corners of the masonry throws a squab little shadow. Sheeted ghosts rise up wearily from their pallets, and flit into the dark depths of the building. Is it possible to climb to the top of the great minaret, and thence to look down on the city? At all events the attempt is worth making, and the chances are that the door of the staircase will be unlocked. Unlocked it is; but a deeply sleeping janitor lies across the threshold, face turned to the moon. A rat dashes out of his turban at the sound of approaching footsteps. The man grunts, opens his eyes for a minute, turns round, and goes to sleep again. All the heat of a decade of fierce Indian summers is stored in the pitch-black, polished walls of the corkscrew staircase. Halfway up, there is something alive, warm and feathery; and it snores. Driven from step to step as it catches the sound of my advance, it flutters to the top and reveals itself as a yellow-eyed, angry kite. Dozens of kites are asleep on this and the other minarets, and on the domes below. There is the shadow of a cool, or at least a less sultry breeze at this height; and, refreshed thereby, I turn to look on the City of Dreadful Night.

Doré might have drawn it! Zola could describe it – this spectacle of sleeping thousands in the moonlight and in the shadow of the moon. The rooftops are crammed with men, women and children; and the air is full of undistinguishable noises. They are restless in the City of Dreadful Night; and small wonder. The marvel is that they can even breathe. If you gaze intently at the multitude, you can see that they are almost as uneasy as a daylight crowd; but the tumult is subdued. Everywhere, in the strong light, you can watch the sleepers turning to and fro; shifting their beds and again resettling them. In the pit-like courtyards of the houses there is the same movement.

The pitiless moon shows it all. Shows, too, the plains outside the city, and here and there a hand's-breadth of the Ravi river without the walls. Shows, lastly, a splash of glittering silver on a house-top almost directly below the mosque minaret. Some poor soul has risen to throw a jar of water over his fevered body; the tinkle of the falling water strikes faintly on the ear. Two or three other men, in far-off corners of the City of Dreadful Night, follow his example, and the water flashes like heliographic signals. A small cloud passes over the face of the moon, and the city and its inhabitants – clear drawn in black and white before – fade into masses of black and deeper black. Still the unrestful noise continues, the sigh of a great city overwhelmed with the heat, and of a people seeking in vain for rest. It is only the lower-class women who sleep on the house-tops. What must the torment be in the latticed zenanas, where a few lamps are still twinkling? There are footfalls in the court below. It is the muezzin – faithful minister; but he ought to have been here an hour ago to tell the Faithful that prayer is better than sleep – the sleep that will not come to the city.

The muezzin fumbles for a moment with the door of one of the minarets, disappears awhile, and a bull-like roar – a magnificent bass thunder – tells that he has reached the top of the stairway. They must hear the cry to the banks of the shrunken Ravi itself! Even across the courtyard it is almost overpowering. The cloud drifts by and shows him outlined in black against the sky, hands laid upon his ears, and broad chest heaving with the play of his lungs – 'Allah ho Akbar'; then a pause while another muezzin somewhere in the direction of the Golden Temple takes up the call – 'Allah ho Akbar.' Again and again; four times in all; and from the bedsteads a dozen men have risen up already. 'I bear witness that there is no God but God.' What a splendid cry it is, the proclamation of the creed that brings men out of their beds by scores at midnight! Once again he thunders through the same phrase, shaking with the vehemence of his own voice; and then, far and near, the night air rings with, 'Muhammad is the Prophet of God.' It is as though he were flinging his defiance to the far-off horizon, where the summer lightning plays and leaps like a bared sword. Every muezzin in the city is in full cry, and some men on the roof-tops are beginning to kneel. A long pause precedes the last cry, 'La ilaha Illallah,' and the silence closes upon it, as the ram on the head of a cotton-bale.

The muezzin stumbles down the dark stairway grumbling in his beard. He passes the arch of the entrance and disappears. Then the stifling silence settles down over the City of Dreadful Night. The kites on the minaret sleep again, snoring more loudly, the hot breeze comes up in puffs and lazy eddies and the moon slides down towards the horizon. Seated with both elbows on the parapet of the tower, one can watch and wonder over that heat-tortured hive till the dawn. 'How do they live down there? What do they think of? When will they awake?' More tinkling of sluiced water-pots; faint jarring of wooden bedsteads moved into or out of the shadows; uncouth music of stringed instruments softened by distance into a plaintive wail, and one low grumble of far-off thunder. In the courtyard of the mosque the janitor, who lay across the threshold of the minaret when I came up, starts wildly in his sleep, throws his hands above his head, mutters something, and falls back again. Lulled by the snoring of the kites – they snore like over-gorged humans – I drop off into an uneasy doze, conscious that three o'clock has struck, and that there is a slight – a very slight – coolness in the atmosphere. The city is absolutely quiet now, but for some vagrant dog's love-song. Nothing save dead heavy sleep.

Several weeks of darkness pass after this. For the moon has gone out. The very dogs are still, and I watch for the first light of the dawn before making my way homeward. Again the noise of shuffling feet. The morning call is about to begin, and my night watch is over. 'Allah ho Akbar! Allah ho Akbar!' The east grows grey, and presently saffron; the dawn wind comes up as though the muezzin had summoned it; and, as one man, the City of Dreadful Night rises from its bed and turns its face towards the dawning day. With return of life comes return of sound. First a low whisper, then a deep bass hum; for it must be remembered that the entire city is on the house-tops. My eyelids weighed down with the arrears of long deferred sleep, I escape from the minaret through the courtyard and out into the square beyond, where the sleepers have risen, stowed away the bedsteads, and are discussing the morning hookah. The minute's freshness of the air has gone, and it is as hot as at first.

'Will the sahib, out of his kindness, make room?' What is it? Something borne on men's shoulders comes by in the half-light, and I stand back. A woman's corpse going down to the burning-ghat, and a bystander says, 'She died at midnight from the heat.' So the city was of death as well as night after all.

LEOPOLD LEWIS

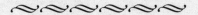

A Dreadful Bell

It was one of those large and important hotels that seem to swoop down and take possession of little villages. The first object that caught the eye of the traveller as he approached the hamlet over the neighbouring hill was the new grand hotel, with its white staring walls and numberless windows, and the letters of its name in black paint running across it. It had scattered the little houses to the right and left of it. It had fixed itself in the best possible situation in front of the sea, and had swallowed up in its erection all the most time-honoured and distinguished characteristics of the locality. In short, instead of the hotel being considered as belonging to the village, the village was now looked upon as an accessory to the hotel. The cause of this change was that the little fishing hamlet being prettily situated on the seacoast in North Wales, the travelling élite had passed its opinion in favour of the place, and the hotel had in consequence sprung up like magic – the Montmorency Hotel, with plate-glass windows and a grand portico, hundreds of bedrooms and sitting-rooms, bathing-machines, hot and vapour baths, invalid chairs and various other conveniences.

How I came to be stopping at the Montmorency was in this way: my old college chum, Tom Marlowe, had just got married to his Julia, and having spent their honeymoon abroad, they took it into their heads that a little repose and a little peaceful enjoyment of each other's society would not be an inappropriate change. Accordingly they had taken apartments in one of the houses in Montmorency Terrace. Tom had heard that I was going to Ireland for my vacation, and had written to ask me to stop and see him on my way.

I accepted the invitation, and put up at the hotel, as there was no vacant room in Tom's house, and I intended to make only a flying visit.

On an evening when the village was undergoing one of its very heartiest squalls, and the wind and the rain and the sea were all roaring together, I had enjoyed a pleasant dinner with Tom and his Julia. The storm without had made the windows rattle rather noisily in their frames; and the street door would persist in flying open suddenly, and when once open, banging itself; the chimneys, too, were altogether uncomfortable, and grumbled incessantly, and the whole establishment had exhibited decided symptoms of a general shakiness of constitution peculiar to mansions that are rapidly 'run up' in rising localities. But we were so merry, and had so much to talk about – Tom was in such good spirits, and his Julia was emphatically what he had so often described her to me to be, 'a born angel' – that I believe if the house itself had been carried away bodily out to sea, it would have been a matter of indifference to them, provided they had gone with it, in each other's society. The time had passed so pleasantly and quickly that I was quite startled when a clock struck eleven; and, as I knew they were early people at the Montmorency, I rose to take my leave.

'By Jove! What a night!' said Tom, as he opened the street door to let me out. 'Will you have a rug to put round you, or my topcoat?'

'No, thank you.'

'Well, get home as fast as you can. How it does come down, and as dark as pitch. Come round in the morning, there's a good fellow.'

'All right. Good-night, old boy.'

The Montmorency was only about five hundred yards distant. I ran as fast as I could, and soon reached the portico, but the whole of the hotel was in darkness. Everybody had evidently gone to bed.

'They are early people with a vengeance,' I muttered, as I seized the bell and rang vigorously. 'They will think that rather a strong pull, but one can't wait out long on such a night as this.'

And it was a night! The portico afforded no protection. The wind howled round its columns, and the rain dashed through it. There was not a soul about. The sky and the sea were both as black as ink.

'Confound it,' I said, after I had waited some considerable time. 'I wonder when they're going to open the door. I'll wait two minutes more and then I'll ring again.'

The two minutes seemed to be twenty, and no one came.

Surely it was not intentional to keep me out in the rain, to give me the street for shelter, because I was not in before the door was shut. It certainly was a hotel where such an arrangement might have been adopted as a rule, but the mere thought of such an absurdity gave me new vigour, and I rang the bell violently for several minutes, and only desisted from sheer exhaustion. I had just commenced to consider whether in the circumstances I should not be justified in throwing a few stones and smashing one or two of the upstairs windows, when, through the pane of glass at the side of the door, I saw to my great relief a faint glimmer of light thrown into the hall. This gradually became brighter and brighter, as if someone were slowly coming down the principal staircase, which was at right angles to the door, bearing a light. It proved to be so, for the next moment I saw, standing on the last step of the stairs, an old gentleman of about sixty, with perfectly white hair, habited in a dressing-gown, and carrying high above his head a lighted bedroom candle.

'Someone I have awakened at last by my ringing,' thought I. 'One of the visitors, no doubt. I shall apologise to him when he has opened the door, and the early hour at which I commenced to ring and the state of the night will surely be a sufficient excuse.'

I steadily fixed my eyes on the old gentleman, and got nearer to the door ready for the chain to be dropped and the bolts to be drawn, for I was becoming more bitterly cold every minute. The old gentleman advanced cautiously into the hall and crossed it, without however once looking towards the door. When he had reached the side of the hall farthest from the stairs he looked up, as if contemplating something fearfully high upon the wall, and as he did so I saw that the arm which held the candle trembled violently.

'You shall hear me at any rate,' thought I, and I rang again.

To my utter astonishment, immediately I had done this, the old gentleman, still without looking towards the door, gave a start, and appeared to shake from head to foot. By his profile, which was towards me, I could see that the expression of his face was one of intense alarm. I heard him utter a shout of horror, and then with a bound he turned on his heel, dashed up the stairs he had so lately descended, and the hall was once more plunged in darkness.

I had scarcely time to question myself as to what could possibly be the meaning of these strange proceedings, before my attention was attracted by a great noise in the upper part of the hotel. It sounded to me as if a number of people were running about. Then doors banged violently. Then there was a succession of crashes. Then shouts of men and screams of women. Nobody, however, appeared in the hall. I rushed into the road and looked up at the hotel. Gracious heavens! What was the matter? Nearly all the windows, before so black, were now illuminated with a bright light. Dark outlines of the human form passed hurriedly backwards and forwards upon the blinds looking like struggling and excited phantoms. Still not a window opened. The noise continued with unabated fury; then, as gradually as it had commenced, the shouting ceased and became murmurs, the doors banged off one by one, until there seemed no more to bang, the lights went out like specks of fire upon a burnt paper, and then all was again in darkness and silence.

What could it mean? In vain I asked myself the question, and no one came to the door to enlighten me upon the subject, or to give me admittance. 'I'll try once more,' I exclaimed, 'and this shall be the last time.' I rang feebly and despairingly. Instantly bells seemed to ring all over the house and passages. Big bells and little bells, near bells and distant bells, upstairs bells and downstairs bells, burst out together in one long continuous angry jangle. The last little bell was still tinkling away somewhere up in the garrets, when a light once again appeared, and this time as if it were coming up a trap in the floor of the hall. I saw it was borne by the head-waiter. He was only partly dressed, and he wore a nightcap made out of a red handkerchief. He looked for an instant towards where I stood, and then shambled in his slippers to the door, let down the chain, half opened the door, put his nose through the opening, and breathed out a ghostly, inflamed, husky whisper, 'Who is it?'

'It's me,' I said somewhat petulantly, 'open the door.'

He rubbed his eyes, held up the light, looked intensely hard at the wick of the candle, said 'Oh!' and opened the door.

'Well, you have kept me a pretty time outside,' I said as I entered. 'I have been ringing the bell since eleven, and by George, there goes one o'clock. I'm wet to the skin and nearly dead with cold.'

The head-waiter was putting the chain up in a fumbling uncertain sort of gaoler fashion. He didn't seem to be altogether quite awake yet, and from the fumes of rum and the smell of tobacco smoke that pervaded him, and the very fishy and winking condition of his eyes, I concluded that Bacchus had assisted Morpheus in the task of lulling him to sleep. In reply to my observation he simply breathed out another rum-and-water 'Oh!' and hoisted his apparel about his waist in a dreamy way.

'Has anything been the matter?' I continued, as I lighted a bedroom candle. 'What a terrible row there was in the house at about half-past twelve.'

'Was there, though?' he said, with a yawn, a hiccup and a lurch. 'Now was there, though? Well, you knows best, I've no doubt.'

And without another word he shuffled away, with his two long braces dragging behind him and bumping their buckles on the floor, looking like a drunken old bashaw, while I went off to bed. I never slept so sound in my life as I did that night. It was nearly eleven o'clock before I came downstairs and entered the coffee-room to order breakfast. There was only one gentleman in the room, and he was seated at a table at the extreme end having breakfast, with a newspaper balancing against the coffee biggin, and simultaneously devouring the news and the buttered toast in the heartiest manner possible. He was a small, middle-aged gentleman, and was evidently suffering from severe nervousness, for he made a great clatter with the cups and spoons, knocking them together loudly; and I noticed that his hands and head shook so continuously that he had the greatest difficulty in carrying anything in a direct line to his mouth. His hair:, which was short and black, stood up very straight and stiff, and he wore a large pair of gold eye-glasses. As I entered and took my seat at a table near the window, he fixed his glasses with greater steadiness upon his nose, and directed at me a long and anxious gaze. Apparently, however, finding that I was a stranger, he turned the newspaper with much gesticulation, and went on with his breakfast.

It was not a rude look. It was only the stare of a short-sighted man; but still it made me think of three trifling incidents that had occurred to me on my passage downstairs from my bedroom to the coffee-room. On the first landing I had met the chambermaid. Immediately she had seen me she had backed into a corner, and had stared at me with mingled curiosity and terror until I had passed. On a lower floor I had encountered the boots. On seeing me, he had instantly dropped a bootjack, two chamber-candlesticks, three pairs of slippers and a warming-pan, with a terrible clatter, and then wagged his head reprovingly at me as if I had done it. Finally, in crossing the hall, the second waiter – a limp wretch in a perpetual perspiration – on meeting me, turned on his heel, and, with a half-smothered cry, fled up a passage. The head-waiter here entered the room. He had resumed his usual dignified appearance; his white cravat was stiff and spotless, and his black wig was curled and oiled into quite a lustrous condition. He made a complete circuit of the room, walking in a solemn manner, and looking at me gravely the while; and, having done this, he approached my table, leant over it on the knuckles of his hands, and contemplated me sternly and enquiringly.

'Breakfast, waiter, if you please.'

'Oh! breakfast?' he repeated, without altering his position. 'Well now, sir, did you order breakfast?'

'Yes,' I answered; 'and I should like it as quickly as possible.'

'Ah!' said the waiter, heaving a deep sigh, and still in a contemplative condition. 'Should you? Mind, I don't say you shouldn't. Only it may be difficult – and then, again, it's rather unnatural – that's all.' And then, before I could express my surprise at this extraordinary conduct on his part, he bent his head near to mine, and whispered in my ear: 'You've done it.'

'Done it! Done what? What do you mean?' I said, instinctively adopting a whispered tone.

'Horful!' gasped the waiter in the same horrid whisper, and throwing his head and eyes up. 'No one could have believed it. I am not a bad sort, sir; but I am a family man, sir; I have a wife and three small children, one of 'em, sir, now in arms and cutting its teeth, sir; and when a family man has been examined in the way I have been; when it's been extricated out of me by threats – threats of the most horrid nature – when a hinder waiter has been threatened to be put over my head – a hinder waiter so ignorant of arithmetic that he don't know plated spoons from silver ones – how could I help it?'

'Help what?' I said. 'What are you talking about? I don't understand a word of what you are saying. Am I to have any breakfast or not?'

At this last question the head-waiter drew himself up to his full height, and in a perfectly serious – indeed, solemn – manner, said: 'Well, sir, if you ask me as a matter of opinion, I should say that you are *not* to have any breakfast. Mind, it is a matter of opinion on my part. However, no one have ever accused me of possessing the feelings of a wolf, and so I will go and make the enquiry,'

Either the waiter was mad, or he had not entirely recovered from his last night's drinking. I ordered him again to bring the breakfast, and threatened to speak to the proprietor of the hotel if he any longer delayed doing so.

'Well!' he said, looking at me curiously. 'Well, I always said philosophy were a wonderful invention, but if ever I see such a go as this – skewer me! You knows what I mean, and what you've done – you knows you did!' And then, with a look full of meaning and reproach, he whispered, 'F.D!' and slid gravely out of the room.

I was still lost in astonishment at the waiter's conduct, when, happening to look round, I perceived that the little gentleman at the other end of the room, having by this time clattered through his breakfast and finished with the newspaper, was now steadily observing me. He had certainly not been able to overhear my whispered conversation with the waiter, but he had evidently noticed that what had taken place had been the cause of exciting my anger, for he now said: 'Stupid fellow, that!'

I experienced quite a feeling of gratitude towards the stranger for his sympathy. 'I cannot think what is the matter with him,' I said, as I passed down the room to a table nearer to the little gentleman. 'He don't seem in a condition to take an order for breakfast.'

'Oh!' said the stranger, fidgeting in his chair, and nervously endeavouring to fix the cruets in their stand. 'Ah, it's very extraordinary! I can't make him out either. He has been bringing me wrong things all the morning. I ordered fish, and he brought me cutlets. I don't like cutlets. Then he brought me a fish-slice to cut the butter with. Ridiculous! And, look at these cruets, not one of them will go into the stand. As an excuse, he says he has been greatly agitated. So have I been agitated! So has everyone been agitated after the disgraceful proceedings of last night.'

'Indeed?' said I. 'I heard something, but I was unable to distinguish what it was.'

The little gentleman stared hard at me. 'You must be a sound sleeper, young man – a very sound sleeper; but perhaps it did not happen to you. Did it?'

Not having the remotest idea to what the question referred, I answered in the negative.

'Perhaps,' said the little gentleman, 'you do not even know what did happen – eh?'

'No.'

'Very extraordinary,' said the little gentleman, and then he went on nervously: 'I never went through such a night – never. A man of my weak nerves, too. My doctor sent me down here for quiet and repose. "Go down,

Bamby," he said, "no railway station within three miles, no organs, no yelling black men, no Punches and Judies, in fact, a paradise of peace and comfort." So I came. I arrived yesterday in the midst of the most terrible storm I ever saw. I went to bed about half-past ten, and, contrary to my usual custom, soon dropped off to sleep.

'I am a bad sleeper, young man. About half-past twelve o'clock I was woken by someone knocking violently at my door. I had bolted it before getting into bed. Judge of my alarm at such a proceeding at such an hour. The knocking continued in violence, then a heavy body seemed to be thrown against the door, which, after repeated shocks, burst open, and a man fell head foremost into my room – a tall, powerful man, in a coloured gown and wellington boots, with a pair of trousers tied round his throat. Before I had time to utter a word, he had started to his feet and assumed a threatening attitude. "Help! Murder! Fire! Thieves!" I shouted out at the top of my voice. "I'll help you," he cried, dancing wildly round me, "come out of this!" And in a moment he had seized the bedclothes and had dragged off the counterpane and blankets. "Come out of this!" he again cried, and again pounced upon me, this time clutching me by the ankle of my left leg and commencing to drag me – a man of my weak nerves – bodily off the bed.

'Maddened with terror, I clung to the head of the bedstead, and shouted still louder for assistance. The more I shouted the more the villain tugged at my leg. The struggle was fearful. Chairs, table, drawers, looking-glasses and fire-irons all seemed to be tumbling and crashing about the room indiscriminately. The very bedstead, with myself still madly clinging to it, seemed to be whirled round and round in the fury of the conflict. At length my assailant appeared to weaken in his efforts, and summoning all my remaining strength with my disengaged leg, I gave him one terrible kick full in the chest that sent him staggering back on to the washstand, in his fall knocking it down, smashing the jugs and basins into atoms, and deluging the room with water. Just fancy the situation to a man of my weak nerves!'

'Did you capture him?'

'No. Before I could recover myself he was on his legs again – had rushed out of the room and was gone. Winding the remains of the bedclothes round me, I dashed out after him, shouting, "Stop thief!" To my astonishment I found the whole house in an uproar. Ladies and gentlemen, in the most extraordinary state of *déshabillé* I ever saw, were running about with lights, asking each other what it was, and where it was, and who had done it, and what it meant? Everybody seemed to have been served in the way I had been. The mistress of the hotel appeased us by saying that the matter should have full inquiry in the morning, and eventually we retired to rest again. You must admit, young man, you were a very sound sleeper not to have been awakened by these proceedings.'

I was considerably astonished at this recital. This, then, accounted for the excitement in the hotel while I was ringing at the door.

'And what was the explanation of this extraordinary affair?' I enquired.

'The explanation,' continued Mr Bamby, 'as far as I have heard it, is more mysterious to me than the affair itself. The landlady, in answer to my enquiries this morning, informed me it was the F.D., and everybody I have asked has answered me in the same way; but who the F.D. is, or what the F.D. is, or why the deuce the F.D. pulled everybody out of bed last night, by the leg, is a problem I mean to have unravelled before I leave this place.'

I gave quite a start of astonishment. The head-waiter had whispered these mysterious letters into my ear. For a moment a thought flashed through my mind that I might be suspected of being the perpetrator of the outrages described by Mr Bamby; but then I was not in the hotel at the time they occurred, and no one knew this better than the head-waiter, who had opened the door to me. 'Do you think you would know your aggressor again,' I said, 'if you saw him?'

'I don't know,' said Mr Bamby. 'It was so dark at the time, and I was so bewildered; but dear me, how very late it is. What a thing it is to have one's rest disturbed. It loses one's whole day. I should like to catch my friend the F.D., or the Funny Devil, or whatever he is, I'd show him some fun, although I am a man of weak nerves. Good-morning.'

And Mr Bamby took up his hat and umbrella, and trotted out of the room. As he went out the head-waiter came in. I looked hungrily towards him, but he only carried an empty plate in one hand, and advanced with great solemnity, bearing it before him like a churchwarden going round after a charity sermon. He presented it to me. I looked at him and then at the plate.

'What's this? Where is the breakfast, fellow? What in the name of heaven is the meaning of all this? What's that plate for?'

Without a movement of his face he still advanced the plate before me. I really think I was about to take it out of his hand and hurl it through the window, when I caught sight of a paper lying upon it. I took it up and looked at it. It was my bill!

'What's this?' I demanded fiercely.

'What is that, sir?' said the head-waiter. 'That is the bill, sir. We have *not* charged for breakfast. We have *not*, I believe, charged for a bed tonight; but the attendance is included.'

'I will see the proprietor at once,' I cried, 'and have this affair explained. A pretty hotel this seems to be. I am kept waiting half the night ringing at the bell. Breakfast is refused me, and my bill is thrust upon me without my asking for it. What do you take me for? Eh?'

I advanced upon the head-waiter; he retreated in terror.

'Don't, sir, don't. I am a family man, and not a bad sort: but hotels is hotels, sir, and can't afford to be ruined. Whole families turning out – families from the Philippine Islands – two nabobs, and one a general – ain't they nothing? Then, to see the deluges – the breakages – the spoiled linen – oh! to see it – '

It was clear I was taken for the author of the last night's proceedings – the mysterious F. D. referred to by Mr Bamby. I heard no more. I rushed out of the room, intending at once to have an interview with the proprietor of the hotel and explain matters. In the hall there were groups of servants, all talking anxiously. As I made my appearance there was a general movement of excitement among them; all eyes were directed towards me, and I again heard the mention of the mysterious letters in an undertone, clearly, in reference to myself.

'Can I see the proprietor?' I addressed a young woman in the bar of the hotel.

'Walk this way,' she answered, in a sharp, snappish tone.

I passed through the bar and into a back room. Here was seated the landlady, with a large book before her. As I entered, and she saw who it was, she started up, took off her spectacles, and confronted me with a glare of terrible indignation.

'So, Number twenty-four,' she said, before I could open my mouth, 'I hope you are satisfied with the mischief of which you have been the cause. The affair of last night may be my ruin, and I have to thank you for it.' She pointed to the book. 'I am now making out the bill of Number four, a gentleman suffering from the gout. How can he be expected to remain in a hotel where he is pulled out of bed in the middle of the night, and dragged about his room by the leg? Here is the family in Number eighteen, who have been in hysterics ever since, and who threaten me with an action for the loss of wigs and teeth and all sorts of valuable property. And here is the Indian general in Number eighty-two, who declares he will have your life, and then there will be murder on the premises in the height of the season. It's shameful, disgraceful.'

'Madam,' I interrupted, 'I assure you I am perfectly innocent of the outrages which I have heard were committed last night in this hotel.'

'How dare you, Number twenty-four,' cried the landlady, 'utter such wilful falsehoods? Is it not enough, what you have done? I have perfect confidence in the statement made to me by Mr Loverock, our head-waiter.'

'If Mr Loverock,' I urged, 'has made a charge against me of being the author of this affair, he is a villain, since he knows that such a charge is false.'

'He is no villain,' said the landlady, now in a towering passion. 'He is no villain; and he is not false. He was not at first willing to divulge you; and it was only when I threatened to remove him from his situation that he made the statement he did. He is no villain, Number twenty-four. It is you, and you alone, who are the villain. You, who have been the cause of all this misery and ruin.'

The matter was becoming to me momentarily more inexplicable. I was about to make further reply to the landlady, when I was startled by a loud noise outside the bar, and I heard a man's voice demanding: 'Where is he? Where is he? Where is the ruffian? Let me reach him. Let me grasp his throat. Let me revenge my wife. Let me revenge my three daughters. Out of the way!'

'It is the general!' shrieked the landlady; and at the same moment a gentleman in a furious rage bounded into the room. He carried a bootjack in one hand, which he waved wildly over his head, and he was advancing to seize me, when another gentleman jumped into the room after him, threw his arms round his waist, and held him as if he were in a vice.

'Let me go,' shouted the first gentleman, struggling to get free.

'I shan't,' shouted the second gentleman. 'What do you want to do?'

I knew the voice. It was Tom Marlowe.

'Tom,' I cried, 'what is all this about? I am charged with the most extraordinary conduct. Speak for me, old fellow.'

'Why – what – ' exclaimed Tom, putting his head round the general's body without relaxing his hold. 'Good gracious! Is it you? If this gentleman would only have the kindness to leave off struggling, and abandon his bloodthirsty intentions, I could discuss the matter with him. There is some mistake.'

'There's not!' roared the general.

'There is!' I shouted.

'You had better retire, sir,' interposed the landlady, addressing me. 'Your presence only serves to excite the general's frenzy. I am willing to explain matters to Mr Marlowe.'

'Go into the next room, will you,' said Tom, again putting his head round the general's body, 'and lock the door on him, ma'am. I won't let go of this gentleman unless you do.'

'Go, sir!' exclaimed the landlady to me, and pointing to an inner room in a Lady Macbeth attitude.

I entered. The door was immediately closed and locked upon me. It was quite an hour before Tom made his appearance. Directly he came in he fell into a chair, and burst into a fit of laughter. When he had partially recovered himself, he said: 'Excuse me, my dear fellow, laughing in this wild manner; but for the last hour I have been dying with suppressed emotion. I have been wanting to laugh, and have not dared.'

'What is it all about?'

'Well, my dear boy,' said Tom, 'it seems it was you who did it after all.'

'Impossible! I wasn't in the hotel.'

'Just listen for one moment. I have been making enquiries all over the house, and have had interviews with the parties concerned. I think I have found it all out, and if I know anything of the laws of cause and effect, it was you who did it. However, don't make yourself uneasy. I have cleared up the matter now, and appeased the landlady, and they have determined to forgive you.'

'Forgive me – but what for? What have I done?'

'It seems,' said Tom, 'that there is an elderly gentleman from America stopping in the house with his family. He is of very nervous temperament, and from having some short time ago severely suffered from the effects of a fire on his premises, exists in a perpetual state of alarm as to one breaking out wherever he may be. In fact, he is almost a monomaniac upon the subject. Now, it appears that it was you who rang the bell last night. Loverock, the waiter, who sleeps downstairs, says he opened the street door to you at one o'clock. You left me at eleven, so that you were at it about two hours.'

'That's true,' I said. 'They wouldn't open the door. What was I to do?'

'Precisely,' continued Tom. 'At about half-past twelve o'clock it further appears that the fire-fearing gentleman, having listened to a violent and almost continuous ringing of a bell for an hour and a half, at length took it into his head to travel out of his bedroom to discover the cause. On reaching the hall – '

'Yes, I saw him through the door-window.'

'On reaching the hall, he examined all the bells upon the wall, and seeing a particularly large one madly ringing came to the conclusion it was the fire-bell. The alarm of fire always drives him out of his senses, and the instinct of preserving his fellow-creatures at such a time is so strong upon him that it becomes a madness. It was this feeling that drove him through the house shouting for help, bursting open doors, pulling the furniture out of the rooms and the people out of their beds – in fact, acting as if a fire were actually raging in the hotel.'

'But why should he have thought it was the fire-bell?'

'Come and see,' said Tom.

We passed into the hall. In the midst of a cluster of bells hanging upon the wall, each of which had its number, was one bell of an unusually large size, and underneath this, painted in red, were the mysterious letters 'F.D.'.

'That's the bell you rang,' said Tom. 'The American gentleman, in his excitement, not unnaturally concluded it gave the alarm of fire. You see, in the United States, where this gentleman comes from, the letters 'F.D.' represent the Fire Department.'

'And what, in the name of heaven, do those initials really stand for?'

'Front door!'

JACK LONDON

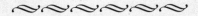

John Griffith London (1876–1916), novelist who wrote under the name Jack London, was born in San Francisco, the illegitimate son of an Irish vagabond and an American girl who afterwards married John London, a grocer. Brought up in poverty, he worked at all sorts of odd jobs, but read omnivorously. About the age of nineteen he attended Oakland High School for a short time and then had a year at the University of California. But an ordered existence was impossible for him. The open sea and the open road were his passions, and at one time he was arrested as a vagrant. In 1897 he took part in the Klondike gold rush; he got no gold, but from his experiences he afterwards wrote *The Call of the Wild* (1903), which sold nearly a million and a half copies. In 1904 he was a special correspondent in the Russo-Japanese War, and in 1907 he set off with his wife on a world cruise; after visiting Honolulu they abandoned the voyage in Australia, and he wrote of it in *The Cruise of the Snark* (1911). In 1912 he sailed round the Horn. At this time he was reckoned the best paid and most popular writer in America, but drink and extravagance caused his work to deteriorate, and he finally committed suicide. He is best remembered for his primitive and sensational stories, such as *The God of his Fathers* (1901), *The Sea Wolf* (1904), *White Fang* (1905), *Before Adam* (1906), *Smoke Bellew* (1912), *John Barleycorn* (1913), *The Star Rover* (1914) and *Jerry of the Islands* (1917).

Siwash

'If I was a man – ' Her words were in themselves indecisive, but the withering contempt which flashed from her black eyes was not lost upon the menfolk in the tent.

Tommy, the English sailor, squirmed, but chivalrous old Dick Humphries, Cornish fisherman and erstwhile American salmon capitalist, beamed upon her benevolently as ever. He bore women too large a portion of his rough heart to mind them, as he said, when they were in the doldrums, or when their limited vision would not permit them to see all around a thing. So they said nothing, these two men who had taken the half-frozen woman into their tent three days back, and who had warmed her, and fed her, and rescued her goods from the Indian packers. This latter had necessitated the payment of numerous dollars, to say nothing of a demonstration in force – Dick Humphries squinting along the sights of a Winchester while Tommy apportioned their wages among them at his own appraisement. It had been a little thing in itself, but it meant much to a woman playing a desperate single-hand in the equally desperate Klondike rush of '97. Men were occupied with their own pressing needs, nor did they approve of women playing, single-handed, the odds of the arctic winter. 'If I was a man, I know what I would do.' Thus reiterated Molly, she of the flashing eyes, and therein spoke the cumulative grit of five American-born generations.

In the succeeding silence, Tommy thrust a pan of biscuits into the Yukon stove and piled on fresh fuel. A reddish flood pounded along under his suntanned skin, and as he stooped, the skin of his neck was scarlet. Dick palmed a three-cornered sail needle through a set of broken pack straps, his good nature in nowise disturbed by the feminine cataclysm which was threatening to burst in the storm-beaten tent.

'And if you was a man?' he asked, his voice vibrant with kindness. The three-cornered needle jammed in the damp leather, and he suspended work for the moment.

'I'd be a man. I'd put the straps on my back and light out. I wouldn't lay in camp here, with the Yukon like to freeze most any day, and the goods not half over the portage. And you – you are men, and you sit here, holding your hands, afraid of a little wind and wet. I tell you straight, Yankee-men are made of different stuff. They'd be hitting the trail for Dawson if they had to wade through hellfire. And you, you – I wish I was a man.'

'I'm very glad, my dear, that you're not.' Dick Humphries threw the bight of the sail twine over the point of the needle and drew it clear with a couple of deft turns and a jerk.

A snort of the gale dealt the tent a broad-handed slap as it hurtled past, and the sleet rat-tat-tatted with snappy spite against the thin canvas. The smoke, smothered in its exit, drove back through the firebox door, carrying with it the pungent odour of green spruce.

'Good Gawd! Why can't a woman listen to reason?' Tommy lifted his head from the denser depths and turned upon her a pair of smoke-outraged eyes.

'And why can't a man show his manhood?'

Tommy sprang to his feet with an oath which would have shocked a woman of lesser heart, ripped loose the sturdy reef-knots and flung back the flaps of the tent.

The trio peered out. It was not a heartening spectacle. A few water-soaked tents formed the miserable foreground, from which the streaming ground sloped to a foaming gorge. Down this ramped a mountain torrent. Here and there, dwarf spruce, rooting and grovelling in the shallow alluvium, marked the proximity of the timber line. Beyond, on the opposing slope, the vague outlines of a glacier loomed dead-white through the driving rain. Even as they looked, its massive front crumbled into the valley, on the breast of some subterranean vomit, and it lifted its hoarse thunder above the screeching voice of the storm. Involuntarily, Molly shrank back.

'Look, woman! Look with all your eyes! Three miles in the teeth of the gale to Crater Lake, across two glaciers, along the slippery rim-rock, knee-deep in a howling river! Look, I say, you Yankee woman! Look! There's your Yankee-men!' Tommy pointed a passionate hand in the direction of the straggling tents. 'Yankees, the last mother's son of them. Are they on trail? Is there one of them with the straps to his back? And you would teach us men our work? Look, I say!'

Another tremendous section of the glacier rumbled earthward. The wind whipped in at the open doorway, bulging out the sides of the tent till it swayed like a huge bladder at its guy ropes. The smoke swirled about them, and the sleet drove sharply into their flesh. Tommy pulled the flaps together hastily, and returned to his tearful task at the firebox. Dick Humphries threw the mended pack straps into a corner and lighted his pipe. Even Molly was for the moment persuaded.

'There's my clothes,' she half-whimpered, the feminine for the moment prevailing. 'They're right at the top of the cache, and they'll be ruined! I tell you, ruined!'

'There, there,' Dick interposed, when the last quavering syllable had wailed itself out. 'Don't let that worry you, little woman. I'm old enough to be your father's brother, and I've a daughter older than you, and I'll tog you out in fripperies when we get to Dawson if it takes my last dollar.'

'When we get to Dawson!' The scorn had come back to her throat with a sudden surge. 'You'll rot on the way, first. You'll drown in a mudhole. You – you – Britishers!'

The last word, explosive, intensive, had strained the limits of her vituperation. If that would not stir these men, what could? Tommy's neck ran red again, but he kept his tongue between his teeth. Dick's eyes mellowed. He had the advantage over Tommy, for he had once had a white woman for a wife.

The blood of five American-born generations is, under certain circumstances, an uncomfortable heritage; and among these circumstances might be enumerated that of being quartered with next of kin. These men were Britons. On sea and land her ancestry and the generations thereof had thrashed them and theirs. On sea and land they would continue to do so. The traditions of her race clamoured for vindication. She was but a woman of the present, but in her bubbled the whole mighty past. It was not alone Molly Travis who pulled on gum boots, mackintosh and straps; for the phantom hands of ten thousand forbears drew tight the buckles, just so as they squared her jaw and set her eyes with determination. She, Molly Travis, intended to shame these Britishers; they, the innumerable shades, were asserting the dominance of the common race.

The menfolk did not interfere. Once Dick suggested that she take his oilskins, as her mackintosh was worth no more than paper in such a storm. But she sniffed her independence so sharply that he communed with his pipe till she tied the flaps on the outside and slushed away on the flooded trail.

'Think she'll make it?' Dick's face belied the indifference of his voice.

'Make it? If she stands the pressure till she gets to the cache, what of the cold and misery, she'll be stark, raving mad. Stand it? She'll be dumb-crazed. You know it yourself, Dick. You've wind-jammed round the Horn. You know what it is to lay out on a topsail yard in the thick of it, bucking sleet and snow and frozen canvas till you're ready to just let go and cry like a baby. Clothes? She won't be able to tell a bundle of skirts from a gold pan or a tea-kettle.'

'Kind of think we were wrong in letting her go, then?'

'Not a bit of it. So help me, Dick, she'd 'a' made this tent a hell for the rest of the trip if we hadn't. Trouble with her she's got too much spirit. This'll tone it down a bit.'

'Yes,' Dick admitted, 'she's too ambitious. But then Molly's all right. A cussed little fool to tackle a trip like this, but a plucky sight better than those pick-me-up-and-carry-me kind of women. She's the stock that carried you and me, Tommy, and you've got to make allowance for the spirit. Takes a woman to breed a man. You can't suck manhood from the dugs of a creature whose only claim to womanhood is her petticoats. Takes a she-cat, not a cow, to mother a tiger.'

'And when they're unreasonable we've got to put up with it, eh?'

'The proposition. A sharp sheath-knife cuts deeper on a slip than a dull one; but that's no reason for to hack the edge off over a capstan bar.'

'All right, if you say so, but when it comes to woman, I guess I'll take mine with a little less edge.'

'What do you know about it?' Dick demanded.

'Some.' Tommy reached over for a pair of Molly's wet stockings and stretched them across his knees to dry.

Dick, eying him querulously, went fishing in her hand satchel, then hitched up to the front of the stove with divers articles of damp clothing spread likewise to the heat.

'Thought you said you never were married?' he asked.

'Did I? No more was I – that is – yes, by Gawd! I was. And as good a woman as ever cooked grub for a man.'

'Slipped her moorings?' Dick symbolised infinity with a wave of his hand.

'Ay . . . Childbirth,' he added, after a moment's pause.

The beans bubbled rowdily on the front lid, and he pushed the pot back to a cooler surface. After that he investigated the biscuits, tested them with a splinter of wood, and placed them aside under cover of a damp cloth. Dick, after the manner of his kind, stifled his interest and waited silently. 'A different woman to Molly. Siwash.'

Dick nodded his understanding.

'Not so proud and wilful, but stick by a fellow through thick and thin. Sling a paddle with the next and starve as contentedly as Job. Go for'ard when the sloop's nose was more often under than not, and take in sail like a man. Went prospecting once, up Teslin way, past Surprise Lake and the Little Yellow-Head. Grub gave out, and we ate the dogs. Dogs gave out, and we ate harnesses, moccasins and furs. Never a whimper; never a pick-me-up-and-carry-me. Before we went she said look out for grub, but when it happened, never a I-told-you-so. "Never mind, Tommy," she'd say, day after day, that weak she could bare lift a snowshoe and her feet raw with the work. "Never mind. I'd sooner be flat-bellied of hunger and be your woman, Tommy, than have a *potlach* every day and be Chief George's *klooch*." George was chief of the Chilcats, you know, and wanted her bad.

'Great days, those. Was a likely chap myself when I struck the coast. Jumped a whaler, the *Pole Star*, at Unalaska, and worked my way down to Sitka on an otter hunter. Picked up with Happy Jack there – know him?'

'Had charge of my traps for me,' Dick answered, 'down on the Columbia. Pretty wild, wasn't he, with a warm place in his heart for whiskey and women?'

'The very chap. Went trading with him for a couple of seasons – hooch, and blankets and such stuff. Then got a sloop of my own, and not to cut him out, came down Juneau way. That's where I met Killisnoo; I called her Tilly for short. Met her at a squaw dance down on the beach. Chief George had finished the year's trade with the Sticks over the passes, and was down from Dyea with half his tribe. No end of Siwashes at the dance, and I the only white. No one knew me, barring a few of the bucks I'd met over Sitka way, but I'd got most of their histories from Happy Jack.

'Everybody talking Chinook, not guessing that I could spit it better than most; and principally two girls who'd run away from Haine's Mission up the Lynn Canal. They were trim creatures, good to the eye, and I kind of thought of casting that way; but they were fresh as fresh-caught cod. Too much edge, you see. Being a newcomer, they started to twist me, not knowing I gathered in every word of Chinook they uttered.

'I never let on, but set to dancing with Tilly, and the more we danced the more our hearts warmed to each other. "Looking for a woman," one of the girls says, and the other tosses her head and answers, "Small chance he'll get one when the women are looking for men." And the bucks and squaws standing around began to grin and giggle and repeat what had been said. "Quite a pretty boy," says the first one. I'll not deny I was rather smooth-faced and youngish, but I'd been a man amongst men many's the day, and it rankled me. "Dancing with Chief George's girl," pipes the second. "First thing George'll give him the flat of a paddle and send him about his business." Chief George had been looking pretty black up to now, but at this he laughed and slapped his knees. He was a husky beggar and would have used the paddle too.

' "Who's the girls?" I asked Tilly, as we went ripping down the centre in a reel. And as soon as she told me their names I remembered all about them from Happy Jack. Had their pedigree down fine – several things he'd told me that not even their own tribe knew. But I held my hush, and went on courting Tilly, they a-casting sharp remarks and everybody roaring. 'Bide a wee, Tommy, I says to myself; 'bide a wee.'

'And bide I did, till the dance was ripe to break up, and Chief George had brought a paddle all ready for me. Everybody was on the lookout for mischief when we stopped; but I marched, easy as you please, slap into the thick of them. The Mission girls cut me up something clever, and for all I was angry I had to set my teeth to keep from laughing. I turned upon them suddenly.

' "Are you done?" I asked.

'You should have seen them when they heard me spitting Chinook. Then I broke loose. I told them all about themselves, and their people before them; their fathers, mothers, sisters, brothers – everybody, everything. Each mean trick they'd played; every scrape they'd got into; every shame that'd fallen them. And I burned them without fear or favour. All hands crowded round.

Never had they heard a white man sling their lingo as I did. Everybody was laughing save the Mission girls. Even Chief George forgot the paddle, or at least he was swallowing too much respect to dare to use it.

'But the girls. "Oh, don't, Tommy," they cried, the tears running down their cheeks. "Please don't. We'll be good. Sure, Tommy, sure." But I knew them well, and I scorched them on every tender spot. Nor did I slack away till they came down on their knees, begging and pleading with me to keep quiet. Then I shot a glance at Chief George; but he did not know whether to have at me or not, and passed it off by laughing hollowly.

'So be. When I passed the parting with Tilly that night I gave her the word that I was going to be around for a week or so, and that I wanted to see more of her. Not thick-skinned, her kind, when it came to showing like and dislike, and she looked her pleasure for the honest girl she was. Ay, a striking lass, and I didn't wonder that Chief George was taken with her.

'Everything my way. Took the wind from his sails on the first leg. I was for getting her aboard and sailing down Wrangle way till it blew over, leaving him to whistle; but I wasn't to get her that easy. Seems she was living with an uncle of hers – guardian, the way such things go – and seems he was nigh to shuffling off with consumption or some sort of lung trouble. He was good and bad by turns, and she wouldn't leave him till it was over with. Went up to the tepee just before I left, to speculate on how long it'd be; but the old beggar had promised her to Chief George, and when he clapped eyes on me his anger brought on a haemorrhage.

' "Come and take me, Tommy," she says when we bid goodbye on the beach. "Ay," I answers; "when you give the word." And I kissed her, white-man-fashion and lover-fashion, till she was all of a tremble like a quaking aspen, and I was so beside myself I'd half a mind to go up and give the uncle a lift over the divide.

'So I went down Wrangle way, past St Mary's and even to the Queen Charlottes, trading, running whiskey, turning the sloop to most anything. Winter was on, stiff and crisp, and I was back to Juneau, when the word came. "Come," the beggar says who brought the news. "Killisnoo say, 'Come now.' " "What's the row?" I asks. "Chief George," says he. "*Potlach*. Killisnoo, makum *klooch*."

'Ay, it was bitter – the Taku howling down out of the north, the salt water freezing quick as it struck the deck, and the old sloop and I hammering into the teeth of it for a hundred miles to Dyea. Had a Douglass Islander for crew when I started, but midway up he was washed over from the bows. Jibed all over and crossed the course three times, but never a sign of him.'

'Doubled up with the cold most likely,' Dick suggested, putting a pause into the narrative while he hung one of Molly's skirts up to dry, 'and went down like a pot of lead.'

'My idea. So I finished the course alone, half-dead when I made Dyea in the dark of the evening. The tide favoured, and I ran the sloop plump to the bank, in the shelter of the river. Couldn't go an inch farther, for the fresh water was frozen solid. Halyards and blocks were that iced up I didn't dare lower mainsail or jib. First I broached a pint of the cargo raw, and then, leaving all standing, ready for the start, and with a blanket around me, headed across the flat to the camp. No mistaking, it was a grand layout. The Chilcats had come in a body – dogs, babies and canoes – to say nothing of the Dog-Ears, the Little Salmons and the Missions. Full half a thousand of them to celebrate Tilly's wedding, and never a white man in a score of miles.

'Nobody took note of me, the blanket over my head and hiding my face, and I waded knee deep through the dogs and youngsters till I was well up to the front. The show was being pulled off in a big open place among the trees, with great fires burning and the snow moccasin-packed as hard as Portland cement. Next me was Tilly, beaded and scarlet-clothed galore, and against her Chief George and his head men. The shaman was being helped out by the big medicines from the other tribes, and it shivered my spine up and down, the deviltries they cut. I caught myself wondering if the folks in Liverpool could only see me now; and I thought of yellow-haired Gussie, whose brother I licked after my first voyage, just because he was not for having a sailorman courting his sister. And with Gussie in my eyes I looked at Tilly. A rum old world, thinks I, with a man a-stepping in trails the mother little dreamed of when he lay at suck.

'So be. When the noise was loudest, walrus hides booming and priests a-singing, I says, "Are you ready?" Gawd! Not a start, not a shot of the eyes my way, not the twitch of a muscle. "I knew," she answers, slow and steady as a calm spring tide. "Where?" "The high bank at the edge of the ice," I whispers back. "Jump out when I give the word."

'Did I say there was no end of huskies? Well, there was no end. Here, there, everywhere, they were scattered about – tame wolves and nothing less. When the strain runs thin they breed them in the bush with the wild, and they're bitter fighters. Right at the toe of my moccasin lay a big brute, and by the heel another. I doubled the first one's tail, quick, till it snapped in my grip. As his jaws clipped together where my hand should have been, I threw the second one by the scruff straight into his mouth. "Go!" I cried to Tilly.

'You know how they fight. In the wink of an eye there was a raging hundred of them, top and bottom, ripping and tearing each other, kids and squaws tumbling which way and the camp gone wild. Tilly'd slipped away, so I followed. But when I looked over my shoulder at the skirt of the crowd, the devil laid me by the heart, and I dropped the blanket and went back.

'By then the dogs'd been knocked apart and the crowd was untangling itself. Nobody was in proper place, so they didn't note that Tilly'd gone. "Hallo," I says, gripping Chief George by the hand. "May your *potlach*-smoke rise often, and the Sticks bring many furs with the spring."

'Lord love me, Dick, but he was joyed to see me – him with the upper hand and wedding Tilly. Chance to puff big over me. The tale that I was hot after her had spread through the camps, and my presence did him proud. All hands knew me, without my blanket, and set to grinning and giggling. It was rich, but I made it richer by playing unbeknowing.

' "What's the row?" I asks. "Who's getting married now?"

' "Chief George," the shaman says, ducking his reverence to him.

' "Thought he had two *klooches*."

' "Him takum more – three," with another duck.

' "Oh!" And I turned away as though it didn't interest me.

'But this wouldn't do, and everybody begins singing out, "Killisnoo! Killisnoo!"

' "Killisnoo what?" I asked.

' "Killisnoo, *klooch*, Chief George," they blathered. "Killisnoo, *klooch*."

'I jumped and looked at Chief George. He nodded his head and threw out his chest.

' "She'll be no *klooch* of yours," I says solemnly. "No *klooch* of yours," I repeats, while his face went black and his hand began dropping to his hunting-knife.

' "Look!" I cries, striking an attitude. "Big Medicine. You watch my smoke."

'I pulled off my mittens, rolled back my sleeves, and made half a dozen passes in the air.

' "Killisnoo!" I shouts. "Killisnoo! Killisnoo!"

'I was making medicine, and they began to scare. Every eye was on me; no time to find out that Tilly wasn't there. Then I called Killisnoo three times again, and waited; and three times more. All for mystery and to make them nervous. Chief George couldn't guess what I was up to, and wanted to put a stop to the foolery; but the shamans said to wait, and that they'd see me and go me one better, or words to that effect. Besides, he was a superstitious cuss, and I fancy a bit afraid of the white man's magic.

'Then I called Killisnoo, long and soft like the howl of a wolf, till the women were all a-tremble and the bucks looking serious.

' "Look!" I sprang for'ard, pointing my finger into a bunch of squaws – easier to deceive women than men, you know. "Look!" And I raised it aloft as though following the flight of a bird. Up, up, straight overhead, making to follow it with my eyes till it disappeared in the sky.

' "Killisnoo," I said, looking at Chief George and pointing upward again. "Killisnoo."

'So help me, Dick, the gammon worked. Half of them, at least, saw Tilly disappear in the air. They'd drunk my whiskey at Juneau and seen stranger sights, I'll warrant. Why should I not do this thing, I, who sold bad spirits corked in bottles? Some of the women shrieked. Everybody fell to whispering in bunches. I folded my arms and held my head high, and they drew farther away from me. The time was ripe to go. "Grab him," Chief George cries. Three or four of them came at me, but I whirled, quick, made a couple of passes like to send them after Tilly, and pointed up. Touch me? Not for the kingdoms of the earth. Chief George harangued them, but he couldn't get them to lift a leg. Then he made to take me himself; but I repeated the mummery and his grit went out through his fingers.

' "Let your shamans work wonders the like of which I have done this night," I says. "Let them call Killisnoo down out of the sky whither I have sent her." But the priests knew their limits. "May your *klooches* bear you sons as the spawn of the salmon," I says, turning to go; "and may your totem pole stand long in the land, and the smoke of your camp rise always."

'But if the beggars could have seen me hitting the high places for the sloop as soon as I was clear of them, they'd have thought my own medicine had got after me. Tilly'd kept warm by chopping the ice away, and was all ready to cast off. Gawd! how we ran before it, the Taku howling after us and the freezing seas sweeping over at every clip. With everything battened down, me a-steering and Tilly chopping ice, we held on half the night, till I plumped the sloop ashore on Porcupine Island, and we shivered it out on the beach; blankets wet, and Tilly drying the matches on her breast.

'So I think I know something about it. Seven years, Dick, man and wife, in rough sailing and smooth. And then she died, in the heart of the winter, died in childbirth, up there on the Chilcat Station. She held my hand to the last, the ice creeping up inside the door and spreading thick on the gut of the window. Outside, the lone howl of the wolf and the Silence; inside, death and the Silence. You've never heard the Silence yet, Dick, and Gawd grant you don't ever have to hear it when you sit by the side of death. Hear it? Ay, till the breath whistles like a siren, and the heart booms, booms, booms, like the surf on the shore.

'Siwash, Dick, but a woman. White, Dick, white, clear through. Towards the last she says, "Keep my feather bed, Tommy, keep it always." And I agreed. Then she opened her eyes, full with the pain. "I've been a good woman to you, Tommy, and because of that I want you to promise – to promise" – the words seemed to stick in her throat – "that when you marry, the woman be white. No more Siwash, Tommy. I know. Plenty white women down to Juneau now. I know. Your people call you 'squaw-man', your women turn their heads to the one side on the street, and you do not go to their cabins like other men. Why? Your wife Siwash. Is it not so? And this is not good. Wherefore I die. Promise me. Kiss me in token of your promise."

'I kissed her, and she dozed off, whispering, "It is good." At the end, that near gone my ear was at her lips, she roused for the last time. "Remember, Tommy; remember my feather bed." Then she died, in childbirth, up there on the Chilcat Station.'

The tent heeled over and half flattened before the gale. Dick refilled his pipe, while Tommy drew the tea and set it aside against Molly's return.

And she of the flashing eyes and Yankee blood? Blinded, falling, crawling on hand and knee, the wind thrust back in her throat by the wind, she was heading for the tent. On her shoulders a bulky pack caught the full fury of the storm. She plucked feebly at the knotted flaps, but it was Tommy and Dick who cast them loose. Then she set her soul for the last effort, staggered in, and fell exhausted on the floor.

Tommy unbuckled the straps and took the pack from her. As he lifted it there was a clanging of pots and pans. Dick, pouring out a mug of whiskey, paused long enough to pass the wink across her body. Tommy winked back. His lips pursed the monosyllable, 'Clothes,' but Dick shook his head reprovingly.

'Here, little woman,' he said, after she had drunk the whiskey and straightened up a bit. 'Here's some dry togs. Climb into them. We're going out to extra-peg the tent. After that, give us the call, and we'll come in and have dinner. Sing out when you're ready.'

'So help me, Dick, that's knocked the edge off her for the rest of this trip,' Tommy spluttered as they crouched to the lee of the tent.

'But it's the edge is her saving grace,' Dick replied, ducking his head to a volley of sleet that drove around a corner of the canvas. 'The edge that you and I've got, Tommy, and the edge of our mothers before us.'

The Man with the Gash

Jacob Kent had suffered from cupidity all the days of his life. This, in turn, had engendered a chronic distrustfulness, and his mind and character had become so warped that he was a very disagreeable man to deal with. He was also a victim to somnambulic propensities, and very set in his ideas. He had been a weaver of cloth from the cradle, until the fever of Klondike had entered his blood and torn him away from his loom. His cabin stood midway between Sixty Mile Post and the Stuart River; and men who made it a custom to travel the trail to Dawson, likened him to a robber baron, perched in his fortress and exacting toll from the caravans that used his ill-kept roads. Since a certain amount of history was required in the construction of this figure, the less cultured wayfarers from Stuart River were prone to describe him after a still more primordial fashion, in which a command of strong adjectives was to be chiefly noted.

This cabin was not his, by the way, having been built several years previously by a couple of miners who had got out a raft of logs at that point for a grub-stake. They had been most hospitable lads, and, after they abandoned it, travellers who knew the route made it an object to arrive there at nightfall. It was very handy, saving them all the time and toil of pitching camp; and it was an unwritten rule that the last man left a neat pile of firewood for the next comer. Rarely a night passed but from half a dozen to a score of men crowded into its shelter. Jacob Kent noted these things, exercised squatter sovereignty, and moved in. Thenceforth, the weary travellers were mulcted a dollar per head for the privilege of sleeping on the floor, Jacob Kent weighing the dust and never failing to steal the down-weight. Besides, he so contrived that his transient guests chopped his wood for him and carried his water. This was rank piracy, but his victims were an easy-going breed, and while they detested him, they yet permitted him to flourish in his sins.

One afternoon in April he sat by his door – for all the world like a predatory spider – marvelling at the heat of the returning sun, and keeping an eye on the trail for prospective flies. The Yukon lay at his feet, a sea of ice, disappearing around two great bends to the north and south, and stretching an honest two miles from bank to bank. Over its rough breast ran the sled-trail, a slender sunken line, eighteen inches wide and two thousand miles in length, with more curses distributed to the linear foot than any other road in or out of all Christendom.

Jacob Kent was feeling particularly good that afternoon. The record had been broken the previous night, and he had sold his hospitality to no fewer than twenty-eight visitors. True, it had been quite uncomfortable, and four had snored beneath his bunk all night; but then it had added appreciable weight to the sack in which he kept his gold dust. That sack, with its glittering yellow treasure, was at once the chief delight and the chief bane of his existence. Heaven and hell lay within its slender mouth. In the nature of things, there being no privacy to his one-roomed dwelling, he was tortured by a constant fear of theft. It would be very easy for these bearded, desperate-looking strangers to make away with it. Often he dreamed that such was the case, and awoke in the grip of nightmare. A select number of these robbers haunted him through his dreams, and he came to know them quite well, especially the bronzed leader with the gash on his right cheek. This fellow was the most persistent of the lot, and, because of him, he had, in his waking moments, constructed several score of hiding-places in and about the cabin. After a concealment he would breathe freely again, perhaps for several nights, only to collar the Man with the Gash in the very act of unearthing the sack. Then, on awakening in the midst of the usual struggle, he would at once get up and transfer the bag to a new and more ingenious crypt. It was not that he was the direct victim of these phantasms; but he believed in omens and thought-transference, and he deemed these dream-robbers to be the astral projection of real personages who happened at those particular moments, no matter where they were in the flesh, to be harbouring designs, in the spirit, upon his wealth. So he continued to bleed the unfortunates who crossed his threshold, and at the same time to add to his trouble with every ounce that went into the sack.

As he sat sunning himself, a thought came to Jacob Kent that brought him to his feet with a jerk. The pleasures of life had culminated in the continual weighing and reweighing of his dust; but a shadow had been thrown upon this pleasant avocation, which he had hitherto failed to brush aside. His gold-scales were quite small; in fact, their maximum was a pound and a half – eighteen ounces – while his hoard mounted up to something like three and a third times that. He had never been able to weigh it all at one operation, and hence considered himself to have been shut out from a new and most edifying coign of contemplation. Being denied this, half the pleasure of possession had been lost; nay, he felt that this miserable obstacle actually minimised the fact, as it did the strength, of possession. It was the solution of this problem flashing across his mind that had just brought him to his feet. He searched the trail carefully in either direction. There was nothing in sight, so he went inside.

In a few seconds he had the table cleared away and the scales set up. On one side he placed the stamped disks to the equivalent of fifteen ounces, and balanced it with dust on the other. Replacing the weights with dust, he then had thirty ounces precisely balanced. These, in turn, he placed together on one side and again balanced with more dust. By this time the gold was exhausted, and he was sweating liberally. He trembled with ecstasy, ravished beyond measure. Nevertheless he dusted the sack thoroughly, to the last least grain, till the balance was overcome and one side of the scales sank to the table. Equilibrium, however, was restored by the addition of a pennyweight and five grains to the opposite side. He stood, head thrown back, transfixed. The sack was empty, but the potentiality of the scales had become immeasurable. Upon them he could weigh any amount, from the tiniest grain to pounds upon pounds. Mammon laid hot fingers on his heart. The sun swung on its westering way till it flashed through the open doorway, full upon the yellow-burdened scales. The precious heaps, like the golden breasts of a bronze Cleopatra, flung back the light in a mellow glow. Time and space were not.

'Gawd blime me! but you 'ave the makin' of several quid there, 'aven't you?'

Jacob Kent wheeled about, at the same time reaching for his double-barrelled shotgun, which stood handy. But when his eyes lit on the intruder's face, he staggered back dizzily. *It was the face of the Man with the Gash!*

The man looked at him curiously.

'Oh, that's all right,' he said, waving his hand deprecatingly. 'You needn't think as I'll 'arm you or your blasted dust. You're a rum 'un, you are,' he added reflectively, as he watched the sweat pouring from off Kent's face and the quavering of his knees.

'W'y don't you pipe up an' say somethin'?' he went on, as the other struggled for breath. 'Wot's gone wrong o' your gaff? Anythink the matter?'

'W–w–where'd you get it?' Kent at last managed to articulate, raising a shaking forefinger to the ghastly scar which seamed the other's cheek.

'Shipmate stove me down with a marlin-spike from the main-royal. An' now as you 'ave your figger'ead in trim, wot I want to know is, wot's it to you? That's wot I want to know – wot's it to you? Gawd blime me! do it 'urt you? Ain't it smug enough for the likes o' you? That's wot I want to know!'

'No, no,' Kent answered, sinking upon a stool with a sickly grin. 'I was just wondering.'

'Did you ever see the like?' the other went on truculently.

'No.'

'Ain't it a beute?'

'Yes.' Kent nodded his head approvingly, intent on humouring this strange visitor, but wholly unprepared for the outburst which was to follow his effort to be agreeable.

'You blasted, bloomin', burgoo-eatin' son-of-a-sea-swab! Wot do you mean, a-sayin' the most onsightly thing Gawd Almighty ever put on the face o' man is a beute? Wot do you mean, you –'

And thereat this fiery son of the sea broke off into a string of Oriental profanity, mingling gods and devils, lineages and men, metaphors and monsters, with so savage a virility that Jacob Kent was paralysed. He shrank back, his arms lifted as though to ward off physical violence. So utterly unnerved was he that the other paused in the mid-swing of a gorgeous peroration and burst into thunderous laughter.

'The sun's knocked the bottom out o' the trail,' said the Man with the Gash, between departing paroxysms of mirth. 'An' I only 'ope as you'll appreciate the hoppertunity of consortin' with a man o' my mug. Get steam up in that firebox o' your'n. I'm goin' to unrig the dogs an' grub 'em. An' don't be shy o' the wood, my lad; there's plenty more where that come from, and it's you've got the time to sling an axe. An' tote up a bucket o' water while you're about it. Lively! or I'll run you down, so 'elp me!'

Such a thing was unheard of. Jacob Kent was making the fire, chopping wood, packing water – doing menial tasks for a guest! When Jim Cardegee left Dawson, it was with his head filled with the iniquities of this roadside Shylock; and all along the trail his numerous victims had added to the sum of his crimes. Now, Jim Cardegee, with the sailor's love for a sailor's joke, had determined, when he pulled into the cabin, to bring its inmate down a peg or so. That he had succeeded beyond expectation he could not help but remark, though he was in the dark as to the part the gash on his cheek had played in it. But while he could not understand, he saw the terror it created, and resolved to exploit it as remorselessly as would any modern trader a choice bit of merchandise.

'Strike me blind, but you're a 'ustler,' he said admiringly, his head cocked to one side, as his host bustled about. 'You never 'ort to 'ave gone Klondiking. It's the keeper of a pub you was laid out for. An' it's often as I 'ave 'eard the lads up an' down the river speak o' you, but I 'adn't no idea you was so jolly nice.'

Jacob Kent experienced a tremendous yearning to try his shotgun on him, but the fascination of the gash was too potent. This was the real Man with the Gash, the man who had so often robbed him in the spirit. This, then, was the embodied entity of the being whose astral form had been projected into his dreams, the man who had so frequently harboured designs against his hoard; hence – there could be no other conclusion – this Man with the Gash had now come in the flesh to dispossess him. And that gash! He could no more keep his eyes from it than stop the beating of his heart. Try as he would, they wandered back to that one point as inevitably as the needle to the pole.

'Do it 'urt you?' Jim Cardegee thundered suddenly, looking up from the spreading of his blankets and encountering the rapt gaze of the other. 'It strikes me as 'ow it 'ud be the proper thing for you to draw your jib, douse the glim, an' turn in, seein' as 'ow it worrits you. Jes' lay to that, you swab, or so 'elp me I'll take a pull on your peak-purchases!'

Kent was so nervous that it took three puffs to blow out the slush-lamp, and he crawled into his blankets without even removing his moccasins. The sailor was soon snoring lustily from his hard bed on the floor, but Kent lay staring up into the blackness, one hand on the shotgun, resolved not to close his eyes the whole night. He had not had an opportunity to secrete his five pounds of gold, and it lay in the ammunition box at the head of his bunk. But, try as he would, he at last dozed off with the weight of his dust heavy on his soul. Had he not inadvertently fallen asleep with his mind in such condition, the somnambulic demon would not have been invoked, nor would Jim Cardegee have gone mining next day with a dish-pan.

The fire fought a losing battle, and at last died away, while the frost penetrated the mossy chinks between the logs and chilled the inner atmosphere. The dogs outside ceased their howling, and, curled up in the snow, dreamed of salmon-stocked heavens where dog-drivers and kindred task-masters were not. Within, the sailor lay like a log, while his host tossed restlessly about, the victim of strange fantasies. As midnight drew near he suddenly threw off the blankets and got up. It was remarkable that he could do what he then did without ever striking a light. Perhaps it was because of the darkness that he kept his eyes shut, and perhaps it was for fear he would see the terrible gash on the cheek of his visitor; but, be this as it may, it is a fact that, unseeing, he opened his ammunition box, put a heavy charge into the muzzle of the shotgun without spilling a particle, rammed it down with double wads, and then put everything away and got back into bed.

Just as daylight laid its steel-grey fingers on the parchment window, Jacob Kent awoke. Turning on his elbow, he raised the lid and peered into the ammunition box. Whatever he saw, or whatever he did not see, exercised a very peculiar effect upon him, considering his neurotic temperament. He glanced at the sleeping man on the floor, let the lid down gently, and rolled over on his back. It was an unwonted calm that rested on his face. Not a muscle quivered. There was not the least sign of excitement or perturbation. He lay there a long while, thinking, and when he got up and began to move about, it was in a cool, collected manner, without noise and without hurry.

It happened that a heavy wooden peg had been driven into the ridgepole just above Jim Cardegee's head. Jacob Kent, working softly, ran a piece of half-inch manila over it, bringing both ends to the ground. One end he tied about his waist, and in the other he rove a running noose. Then he cocked his shotgun and laid it within reach, by the side of numerous moose-hide thongs. By an effort of will he bore the sight of the scar, slipped the noose over the sleeper's head, and drew it taut by throwing back on his weight, at the same time seizing the gun and bringing it to bear.

Jim Cardegee awoke, choking, bewildered, staring down the twin wells of steel.

'Where is it?' Kent asked, at the same time slacking on the rope.

'You blasted – ugh – '

Kent merely threw back his weight, shutting off the other's wind.

'Bloomin' – Bur – ugh – '

'Where is it?' Kent repeated.

'Wot?' Cardegee asked, as soon as he had caught his breath.

'The gold-dust.'

'Wot gold-dust?' the perplexed sailor demanded.

'You know well enough – mine.'

'Ain't seen nothink of it. Wot do ye take me for? A safe-deposit? Wot 'ave I got to do with it, any'ow?'

'Mebbe you know, and mebbe you don't know, but anyway, I'm going to stop your breath till you do know. And if you lift a hand, I'll blow your head off!'

'Vast heavin'!' Cardegee roared, as the rope tightened.

Kent eased away a moment, and the sailor, wriggling his neck as though from the pressure, managed to loosen the noose a bit and work it up so the point of contact was just under the chin.

'Well?' Kent questioned, expecting the disclosure.

But Cardegee grinned. 'Go ahead with your 'angin', you bloomin' old pot-wolloper!'

Then, as the sailor had anticipated, the tragedy became a farce. Cardegee being the heavier of the two, Kent, throwing his body backward and down, could not lift him clear of the ground. Strain and strive to the uttermost, the sailor's feet still stuck to the floor and sustained a part of his weight. The remaining portion was supported by the point of contact just under his chin. Failing to swing him clear, Kent clung on, resolved slowly to throttle him or force him to tell what he had done with the hoard. But the Man with the Gash would not throttle. Five, ten, fifteen minutes passed, and at the end of that time, in despair, Kent let his prisoner down.

'Well,' he remarked, wiping away the sweat, 'if you won't hang you'll shoot. Some men wasn't born to be hanged, anyway.'

'An' it's a pretty mess as you'll make o' this 'ere cabin floor.' Cardegee was fighting for time. 'Now, look 'ere, I'll tell you wot we'll do; we'll lay our 'eads 'longside an' reason together. You've lost some dust. You say as 'ow I know, an' I say as 'ow I don't. Let's get a hobservation an' shape a course – '

'Vast heavin'!' Kent dashed in, maliciously imitating the other's enunciation. 'I'm going to shape all the courses of this shebang, and you observe; and if you do anything more, I'll bore you as sure as Moses!'

'For the sake of my mother – '

'Whom God have mercy upon if she loves you. Ah! Would you?' He frustrated a hostile move on the part of the other by pressing the cold muzzle against his forehead. 'Lay quiet, now! If you lift as much as a hair, you'll get it.'

It was rather an awkward task, with the trigger of the gun always within pulling distance of the finger, but Kent was a weaver, and in a few minutes had the sailor tied hand and foot. Then he dragged him without and laid him by the side of the cabin, where he could overlook the river and watch the sun climb to the meridian.

'Now I'll give you till noon, and then – '

'Wot?'

'You'll be hitting the brimstone trail. But if you speak up, I'll keep you till the next bunch of mounted police come by.'

'Well, Gawd blime me, if this ain't a go! 'Ere I be, innercent as a lamb, an' 'ere you be, lost all o' your top 'amper an' out o' your reckonin', run me foul an' goin' to rake me into 'ell-fire. You bloomin' old pirut! You – ' Jim Cardegee loosed the strings of his profanity and fairly outdid himself.

Jacob Kent brought out a stool that he might enjoy it in comfort. Having exhausted all the possible combinations of his vocabulary, the sailor quieted down to hard thinking, his eyes constantly gauging the progress of the sun, which tore up the eastern slope of the heavens with unseemly haste. His dogs, surprised that they had not long since been put to harness, crowded around him. His helplessness appealed to the brutes. They felt that something was wrong, though they knew not what, and they crowded about, howling their mournful sympathy.

'Chook! Mush-on! you Siwashes!' he cried, attempting, in a vermicular way, to kick at them, and discovering himself to be tottering on the edge of a declivity. As soon as the animals had scattered, he devoted himself to the significance of that declivity, which he felt to be there but could not see. Nor was he long in arriving at a correct conclusion. In the nature of things, he figured, man is lazy. He does no more than he has to. When he builds a cabin he must put dirt on the roof. From these premises it was logical that he should carry that dirt no farther than was absolutely necessary. Therefore, he lay upon the edge of the hole from which the dirt had been taken to roof Jacob Kent's cabin. This knowledge, properly utilised, might prolong things, he thought; and he then turned his attention to the moose-hide thongs which bound him. His hands were tied behind him, and pressing against the snow, they were wet with the contact. This moistening of the rawhide he knew would tend to make it stretch, and, without apparent effort, he endeavoured to stretch it more and more.

He watched the trail hungrily, and when in the direction of Sixty Mile a dark speck appeared for a moment against the white background of an ice-jam, he cast an anxious eye at the sun. It had climbed nearly to the zenith.

Now and again he caught the black speck clearing the hills of ice and sinking into the intervening hollows; but he dared not permit himself more than the most cursory glances for fear of rousing his enemy's suspicion. Once, when Jacob Kent rose to his feet and searched the trail with care, Cardegee was frightened, but the dog-sled had struck a piece of trail running parallel with a jam, and remained out of sight till the danger was past.

'I'll see you 'ung for this,' Cardegee threatened, attempting to draw the other's attention. 'An' you'll rot in 'ell, jes' you see if you don't.

'I say,' he cried, after another pause; 'd'ye b'lieve in ghosts?' Kent's sudden start made him sure of his ground, and he went on: 'Now a ghost 'as the right to 'aunt a man wot don't do wot he says; and you can't shuffle me off till eight bells – wot I mean is twelve o'clock – can you? 'Cos if you do, it'll 'appen as 'ow I'll 'aunt you. D'ye 'ear? A minute, a second too quick, an' I'll 'aunt you, so 'elp me, I will!'

Jacob Kent looked dubious, but declined to talk.

' 'Ow's your chronometer? Wot's your longitude? 'Ow do you know as your time's correct?' Cardegee persisted, vainly hoping to beat his executioner out of a few minutes. 'Is it Barrack's time you 'ave, or is it the Company time? 'Cos if you do it before the stroke o' the bell, I'll not rest. I give you fair warnin'. I'll come back. An' if you 'aven't the time, 'ow will you know? That's wot I want – 'ow will you tell?'

'I'll send you off all right,' Kent replied. 'Got a sundial here.'

'No good. Thirty-two degrees variation o' the needle.'

'Stakes are all set.'

' 'Ow did you set 'em? Compass?'

'No; lined them up with the North Star.'

'Sure?'

'Sure.'

Cardegee groaned, then stole a glance at the trail. The sled was just clearing a rise, barely a mile away, and the dogs were in full lope, running lightly.

' 'Ow close is the shadows to the line?'

Kent walked to the primitive timepiece and studied it. 'Three inches,' he announced, after a careful survey.

'Say, jes' sing out "eight bells" afore you pull the gun, will you?'

Kent agreed, and they lapsed into silence. The thongs about Cardegee's wrists were slowly stretching, and he had begun to work them over his hands.

'Say, 'ow close is the shadows?'

'One inch.'

The sailor wriggled slightly to assure himself that he would topple over at the right moment, and slipped the first turn over his hands.

' 'Ow close?'

'Half an inch.' Just then Kent heard the jarring churn of the runners and turned his eyes to the trail. The driver was lying flat on the sled and the dogs swinging down the straight stretch to the cabin. Kent whirled back, bringing his rifle to shoulder.

'It ain't eight bells yet!' Cardegee expostulated. 'I'll 'aunt you, sure!'

Jacob Kent faltered. He was standing by the sundial, perhaps ten paces from his victim. The man on the sled must have seen that something unusual was taking place, for he had risen to his knees, his whip singing viciously among the dogs.

The shadows swept into line. Kent looked along the sights.

'Make ready!' he commanded solemnly. 'Eight b – '

But just a fraction of a second too soon, Cardegee rolled backward into the hole. Kent held his fire and ran to the edge. Bang! The gun exploded full in the sailor's face as he rose to his feet. But no smoke came from the muzzle; instead, a sheet of flame burst from the side of the barrel near its butt, and Jacob Kent went down. The dogs dashed up the bank, dragging the sled over his body, and the driver sprang off as Jim Cardegee freed his hands and drew himself from the hole.

'Jim!' The newcomer recognised him. 'What's the matter?'

'Wot's the matter? Oh, nothink at all. It jest 'appens as I do little things like this for my 'ealth. Wot's the matter, you bloomin' idjit? Wot's the matter, eh? Cast me loose or I'll show you wot! 'Urry up, or I'll 'olystone the decks with you! Huh!' he added, as the other went to work with his sheath-knife. 'Wot's the matter? I want to know. Jes' tell me that, will you, wot's the matter? Hey?'

Kent was quite dead when they rolled him over. The gun, an old-fashioned, heavy-weighted muzzle-loader, lay near him. Steel and wood had parted company. Near the butt of the right-hand barrel, with lips pressed outward, gaped a fissure several inches in length. The sailor picked it up, curiously. A glittering stream of yellow dust ran out through the crack. The facts of the case dawned upon Jim Cardegee.

'Strike me standin'!' he roared; ' 'ere's a go! 'Ere's 'is bloomin' dust! Gawd blime me, an' you, too, Charley, if you don't run an' get the dish-pan!'

Where the Trail Forks

'Must I, then, must I, then, now leave this town –
And you, my love, stay here?'

The singer, clean-faced and cheery-eyed, bent over and added water to a pot of simmering beans, and then, rising, a stick of firewood in hand, drove back the circling dogs from the grub-box and cooking-gear. He was blue of eye, and his long hair was golden, and it was a pleasure to look upon his lusty freshness. A new moon was thrusting a dim horn above the white line of close-packed snowcapped pines which ringed the camp and segregated it from all the world. Overhead, so clear it was and cold, the stars danced with quick, pulsating movements. To the south-east an evanescent greenish glow heralded the opening revels of the aurora borealis. Two men, in the immediate foreground, lay upon the bearskin which was their bed. Between the skin and naked snow was a six-inch layer of pine boughs. The blankets were rolled back. For shelter, there was a fly at their backs – a sheet of canvas stretched between two trees and angling at forty-five degrees. This caught the radiating heat from the fire and flung it down upon the skin. Another man sat on a sled, drawn close to the blaze, mending moccasins. To the right, a heap of frozen gravel and a rude windlass denoted where they toiled each day in dismal groping for the pay-streak. To the left, four pairs of snowshoes stood erect, showing the mode of travel which obtained when the stamped snow of the camp was left behind.

That Schwabian folk-song sounded strangely pathetic under the cold northern stars, and did not do the men good who lounged about the fire after the toil of the day. It put a dull ache into their hearts, and a yearning which was akin to belly-hunger, and sent their souls questing southward across the divides to the sun-lands.

'For the love of God, Sigmund, shut up!' expostulated one of the men. His hands were clenched painfully, but he hid them from sight in the folds of the bearskin upon which he lay.

'And what for, Dave Wertz?' Sigmund demanded. 'Why shall I not sing when the heart is glad?'

'Because you've got no call to, that's why. Look about you, man, and think of the grub we've been defiling our bodies with for the last twelve-month, and the way we've lived and worked like beasts!'

Thus abjured, Sigmund, the golden-haired, surveyed it all, and the frost-rimmed wolf-dogs and the vapour breaths of the men. 'And why shall not the heart be glad?' he laughed. 'It is good; it is all good. As for the grub – ' He doubled up his arm and caressed the swelling biceps. 'And if we have lived and worked like beasts, have we not been paid like kings? Twenty dollars to the pan the streak is running, and we know it to be eight feet thick. It is another Klondike – and we know it – Jim Hawes there, by your elbow, knows it and complains not. And there's Hitchcock! He sews moccasins like an old woman, and waits against the time. Only you can't wait and work until the wash-up in the spring. Then we shall all be rich, rich as kings, only you cannot wait. You want to go back to the States. So do I, and I was born there, but I can wait, when each day the gold in the pan shows up yellow as butter in the churning. But you want your good time, and, like a child, you cry for it now. Bah! Why shall I not sing:

> In a year, in a year, when the grapes are ripe,
> I shall stay no more away.
> Then if you still are true, my love,
> It will be our wedding day.
> In a year, in a year, when my time is past,
> Then I'll live in your love for aye.
> Then if you still are true, my love,
> It will be our wedding day.'

The dogs, bristling and growling, drew in closer to the firelight. There was a monotonous crunch-crunch of webbed shoes, and between each crunch the dragging forward of the heel of the shoe like the sound of sifting sugar. Sigmund broke off from his song to hurl oaths and firewood at the animals. Then the light was parted by a fur-clad figure, and an Indian girl slipped out of the webs, threw back the hood of her squirrel-skin *parka*, and stood in their midst. Sigmund and the men on the bearskin greeted her as 'Sipsu', with the customary, 'Hallo,' but Hitchcock made room on the sled that she might sit beside him.

'And how goes it, Sipsu?' he asked, talking, after her fashion, in broken English and bastard Chinook. 'Is the hunger still mighty in the camp? and has the witch doctor yet found the cause wherefore game is scarce and no moose in the land?'

'Yes; even so. There is little game, and we prepare to eat the dogs. Also has the witch doctor found the cause of all this evil, and tomorrow will he make sacrifice and cleanse the camp.'

'And what does the sacrifice chance to be? – a new-born babe or some poor devil of a squaw, old and shaky, who is a care to the tribe and better out of the way?'

'It chanced not that wise; for the need was great, and he chose none other than the chief's daughter; none other than I, Sipsu.'

'Hell!' The word rose slowly to Hitchcock's lips, and brimmed over full and deep, in a way which bespoke wonder and consideration.

'Wherefore we stand by a forking of the trail, you and I,' she went on calmly, 'and I have come that we may look once more upon each other, and once more only.'

She was born of primitive stock, and primitive had been her traditions and her days; so she regarded life stoically, and human sacrifice as part of the natural order. The powers which ruled the daylight and the dark, the flood and the frost, the bursting of the bud and the withering of the leaf, were angry and in need of propitiation. This they exacted in many ways – death in the bad water, through the treacherous ice-crust, by the grip of the grizzly or a wasting sickness which fell upon a man in his own lodge till he coughed, and the life of his lungs went out through his mouth and nostrils. Likewise did the powers receive sacrifice. It was all one. And the witch doctor was versed in the thoughts of the powers and chose unerringly. It was very natural. Death came by many ways, yet was it all one after all – a manifestation of the all-powerful and inscrutable.

But Hitchcock came of a later world-breed. His traditions were less concrete and without reverence, and he said, 'Not so, Sipsu. You are young, and yet in the full joy of life. The witch doctor is a fool, and his choice is evil. This thing shall not be.'

She smiled and answered, 'Life is not kind, and for many reasons. First, it made of us twain the one white and the other red, which is bad. Then it crossed our trails, and now it parts them again; and we can do nothing. Once before, when the gods were angry, did your brothers come to the camp. They were three, big men and white, and they said the thing shall not be. But they died quickly, and the thing was.'

Hitchcock nodded that he heard, half-turned, and lifted his voice. 'Look here, you fellows! There's a lot of foolery going on over to the camp, and they're getting ready to murder Sipsu. What d'ye say?'

Wertz looked at Hawes, and Hawes looked back, but neither spoke. Sigmund dropped his head and petted the shepherd dog between his knees. He had brought Shep in with him from the outside, and thought a great deal of the animal. In fact, a certain girl, who was much in his thoughts, and whose picture in the little locket on his breast often inspired him to sing, had given him the dog and her blessing when they kissed goodbye and he started on his Northland quest.

'What d'ye say?' Hitchcock repeated.

'Mebbe it's not so serious,' Hawes answered with deliberation. 'Most likely it's only a girl's story.'

'That isn't the point!' Hitchcock felt a hot flush of anger sweep over him at their evident reluctance. 'The question is, if it is so, are we going to stand it? What are we going to do?'

'I don't see any call to interfere,' spoke up Wertz. 'If it is so, it is so, and that's all there is about it. It's a way these people have of doing. It's their religion, and it's no concern of ours. Our concern is to get the dust and then get out of this Godforsaken land. 'T isn't fit for naught else but beasts! And what are these black devils but beasts? Besides, it'd be damn poor policy.'

'That's what I say,' chimed in Hawes. 'Here we are, four of us, three hundred miles from the Yukon or a white face. And what can we do against half a hundred Indians? If we quarrel with them, we have to vamoose; if we fight, we are wiped out. Further, we've struck pay, and, by God! I, for one, am going to stick by it!'

'Ditto here,' supplemented Wertz.

Hitchcock turned impatiently to Sigmund, who was softly singing,

> 'In a year, in a year, when the grapes are ripe,
> I shall stay no more away.

'Well, it's this way, Hitchcock,' he finally said, 'I'm in the same boat with the rest. If three score bucks have made up their mind to kill the girl, why, we can't help it. One rush, and we'd be wiped off the landscape. And what good'd that be? They'd still have the girl. There's no use in going against the customs of a people except you're in force.'

'But we are in force!' Hitchcock broke in. 'Four whites are a match for a hundred times as many reds. And think of the girl!'

Sigmund stroked the dog meditatively. 'But I do think of the girl. And her eyes are blue like summer skies, and laughing like summer seas, and her hair is yellow, like mine, and braided in ropes the size of a big man's arms. She's waiting for me, out there, in a better land. And she's waited long, and now my pile's in sight I'm not going to throw it away.'

'And shamed I would be to look into the girl's blue eyes and remember the black ones of the girl whose blood was on my hands,' Hitchcock sneered; for he was born to honour and championship, and to do the thing for the thing's sake, nor stop to weigh or measure.

Sigmund shook his head. 'You can't make me mad, Hitchcock, nor do mad things because of your madness. It's a cold business proposition and a question of facts. I didn't come to this country for my health, and, further, it's impossible for us to raise a hand. If it is so, it is too bad for the girl, that's all. It's a way of her people, and it just happens we're on the spot this one time. They've done the same for a thousand thousand years, and they're going to do it now, and they'll go on doing it for all time to come. Besides, they're not our kind. Nor's the girl. No, I take my stand with Wertz and Hawes, and – '

But the dogs snarled and drew in, and he broke off, listening to the crunch-crunch of many snowshoes. Indian after Indian stalked into the firelight, tall and grim, fur-clad and silent, their shadows dancing grotesquely on the snow. One, the witch doctor, spoke gutturally to Sipsu. His face was daubed with savage paint blotches, and over his shoulders was drawn a wolfskin, the gleaming teeth and cruel snout surmounting his head. No other word was spoken. The prospectors held the peace. Sipsu arose and slipped into her snowshoes.

'Goodbye, O my man,' she said to Hitchcock. But the man who had sat beside her on the sled gave no sign nor lifted his head as they filed away into the white forest.

Unlike many men, his faculty of adaptation, while large, had never suggested the expediency of an alliance with the women of the Northland. His broad cosmopolitanism had never impelled toward covenanting in marriage with the daughters of the soil. If it had, his philosophy of life would not have stood between. But it simply had not. Sipsu? He had pleasured in campfire chats with her, not as a man who knew himself to be man and she woman, but as a man might with a child, and as a man of his make certainly would if for no other reason than to vary the tedium of a bleak existence. That was all. But there was a certain chivalric thrill of warm blood in him, despite his Yankee ancestry and New England upbringing, and he was so made that the commercial aspect of life often seemed meaningless and bore contradiction to his deeper impulses.

So he sat silent, with head bowed forward, an organic force, greater than himself, as great as his race, at work within him. Wertz and Hawes looked askance at him from time to time, a faint but perceptible trepidation in their manner. Sigmund also felt this. Hitchcock was strong, and his strength had been impressed upon them in the course of many an event in their precarious life. So they stood in a certain definite awe and curiosity as to what his conduct would be when he moved to action.

But his silence was long, and the fire was nigh out when Wertz stretched his arms and yawned and thought he'd go to bed. Then Hitchcock stood up his full height.

'May God damn your souls to the deepest hells, you chicken-hearted cowards! I'm done with you!' He said it calmly enough, but his strength spoke in every syllable, and every intonation was advertisement of intention. 'Come on,' he continued, 'whack up, and in whatever way suits you best. I own a quarter interest in the claims; our contracts show that. There're twenty-five or thirty ounces in the sack from the test pans. Fetch out the scales. We'll divide that now. And you, Sigmund, measure me my quarter-share of the grub and set it apart. Four of the dogs are mine, and I want four more. I'll trade you my share in the camp outfit and mining-gear for the dogs. And I'll throw in my six or seven ounces and the spare colt with the ammunition. What d'ye say?'

The three men drew apart and conferred. When they returned, Sigmund acted as spokesman. 'We'll whack up fair with you, Hitchcock. In everything you'll get your quarter-share, neither more nor less; and you can take it or leave it. But we want the dogs as bad as you do, so you get four, and that's all. If you don't want to take your share of the outfit and gear, why, that's your lookout. If you want it, you can have it; if you don't, leave it.'

'The letter of the law,' Hitchcock sneered. 'But go ahead. I'm willing. And hurry up. I can't get out of this camp and away from its vermin any too quick.'

The division was effected without further comment. He lashed his meagre belongings upon one of the sleds, rounded in his four dogs and harnessed up. His portion of outfit and gear he did not touch, though he threw on to the sled half a dozen dog harnesses, and challenged them with his eyes to interfere. But they shrugged their shoulders and watched him disappear into the forest.

*   *   *

A man crawled upon his belly through the snow. On every hand loomed the moose-hide lodges of the camp. Here and there a miserable dog howled or snarled abuse upon his neighbour. Once, one of them approached the creeping man, but the man became motionless. The dog came closer and sniffed, and came yet closer, till its nose touched the strange object which had not been there when darkness fell. Then Hitchcock, for it was Hitchcock, upreared suddenly, shooting an unmittened hand out to the brute's shaggy throat. And the dog knew its death in that clutch and when the man moved on was left broken-necked under the stars. In this manner Hitchcock made the chief's lodge. For long he lay in the snow without, listening to the voices of the occupants and striving to locate Sipsu. Evidently there were many in the tent, and from the sounds they were in high excitement. At last he heard the girl's voice, and crawled around so that only the moose-hide divided them. Then burrowing in the snow, he slowly wormed his head and shoulders underneath. When the warm inner air smote his face, he stopped and waited, his legs and the greater part of his body still on the outside. He could see nothing, nor did he dare lift his head. On one side of him was a skin bale. He could smell it, though he carefully felt to be certain. On the other side his face barely touched a furry garment which he knew clothed a body. This must be Sipsu. Though he wished she would speak again, he resolved to risk it.

He could hear the chief and the witch doctor talking high, and in a far corner some hungry child whimpering to sleep. Squirming over on his side, he carefully raised his head, still just touching the furry garment. He listened to the breathing. It was a woman's breathing; he would chance it.

He pressed against her side softly but firmly, and felt her start at the contact. Again he waited, till a questioning hand slipped down upon his head and paused among the curls. The next instant the hand turned his face gently upward, and he was gazing into Sipsu's eyes.

She was quite collected. Changing her position casually, she threw an elbow well over on the skin bale, rested her body upon it, and arranged her *parka*. In this way he was completely concealed. Then, and still most casually, she reclined across him, so that he could breathe between her arm and breast, and when she lowered her head her ear pressed lightly against his lips.

'When the time suits, go thou,' he whispered, 'out of the lodge and across the snow, down the wind to the bunch of jackpine in the curve of the creek. There wilt thou find my dogs and my sled, packed for the trail. This night we go down to the Yukon; and since we go fast, lay thou hands upon what dogs come nigh thee, by the scruff of the neck, and drag them to the sled in the curve of the creek.'

Sipsu shook her head in dissent; but her eyes glistened with gladness, and she was proud that this man had shown towards her such favour. But she, like the women of all her race, was born to obey the masculine will, and when Hitchcock repeated, 'Go!' he did it with authority, and though she made no answer he knew that his will was law.

'And never mind harness for the dogs,' he added, preparing to go. 'I shall wait. But waste no time. The day chaseth the night alway, nor does it linger for man's pleasure.'

Half an hour later, stamping his feet and swinging his arms by the sled, he saw her coming, a surly dog in either hand. At the approach of these his own animals waxed truculent, and he favoured them with the butt of his whip till they quieted. He had approached the camp up the wind, and sound was the thing to be most feared in making his presence known.

'Put them into the sled,' he ordered when she had got the harness on the two dogs. 'I want my leaders to the fore.'

But when she had done this, the displaced animals pitched upon the aliens. Though Hitchcock plunged among them with clubbed rifle, a riot of sound went up and across the sleeping camp.

'Now we shall have dogs, and in plenty,' he remarked grimly, slipping an axe from the sled lashings. 'Do thou harness whichever I fling thee, and betweenwhiles protect the team.'

He stepped a space in advance and waited between two pines. The dogs of the camp were disturbing the night with their jangle, and he watched for their coming. A dark spot, growing rapidly, took form upon the dim white expanse of snow. It was a forerunner of the pack, leaping cleanly, and, after the wolf fashion, singing direction to its brothers. Hitchcock stood in the shadow. As it sprang past, he reached out, gripped its forelegs in mid-career, and sent it whirling earthward. Then he struck it a well-judged blow beneath the ear and flung it to Sipsu. And while she clapped on the harness, he, with his axe, held the passage between the trees, till a shaggy flood of white teeth and glistening eyes surged and crested just beyond reach. Sipsu worked rapidly. When she had finished, he leaped forward, seized and stunned a second, and flung it to her. This he repeated thrice again, and when the sled team stood snarling in a string of ten, he called, 'Enough!'

But at this instant a young buck, the forerunner of the tribe, and swift of limb, wading through the dogs and, cuffing right and left, attempted the passage. The butt of Hitchcock's rifle drove him to his knees, whence he toppled over sideways. The witch doctor, running lustily, saw the blow fall.

Hitchcock called to Sipsu to pull out. At her shrill, 'Chook!' the maddened brutes shot straight ahead, and the sled, bounding mightily, just missed unseating her. The powers were evidently angry with the witch doctor, for at this moment they plunged him upon the trail. The lead-dog fouled his snowshoes and tripped him up, and the nine succeeding dogs trod him under foot and the sled bumped over him. But he was quick to his feet, and the night might have turned out differently had not Sipsu struck backwards with the long dog-whip and smitten him a blinding blow across the eyes. Hitchcock, hurrying to overtake her, collided against him as he swayed with pain in the middle of the trail. Thus it was, when this primitive theologian got back to the chief's lodge, that his wisdom had been increased in so far as concerns the efficacy of the white man's fist. So, when he orated then and there in the council, he was wroth against all white men.

*   *   *

'Tumble out, you loafers! Tumble out! Grub'll be ready before you get into your footgear!'

Dave Wertz threw off the bearskin, sat up, and yawned.

Hawes stretched, discovered a lame muscle in his arm, and rubbed it sleepily. 'Wonder where Hitchcock bunked last night?' he queried, reaching for his moccasins. They were stiff, and he walked gingerly in his socks to the fire to thaw them out. 'It's a blessing he's gone,' he added, 'though he was a mighty good worker.'

'Yep. Too masterful. That was his trouble. Too bad for Sipsu. Think he cared for her much?'

'Don't think so. Just principle. That's all. He thought it wasn't right –

and, of course, it wasn't – but that was no reason for us to interfere and get hustled over the divide before our time.'

'Principle is principle, and it's good in its place, but it's best left at home when you go to Alaska. Eh?' Wertz had joined his mate, and both were working pliability into their frozen moccasins. 'Think we ought to have taken a hand?'

Sigmund shook his head. He was very busy. A scud of chocolate-coloured foam was rising in the coffeepot, and the bacon needed turning. Also, he was thinking about the girl with laughing eyes like summer seas, and he was humming softly.

His mates chuckled to each other and ceased talking. Though it was past seven, daybreak was still three hours distant. The aurora borealis had passed out of the sky, and the camp was an oasis of light in the midst of deep darkness. And in this light the forms of the three men were sharply defined. Emboldened by the silence, Sigmund raised his voice and opened the last stanza of the old song:

'In a year, in a year, when the grapes are ripe – '

Then the night was split with a rattling volley of rifle-shots. Hawes sighed, made an effort to straighten himself, and collapsed. Wertz went over on an elbow with drooping head. He choked a little, and a dark stream flowed from his mouth. And Sigmund, the Golden-Haired, his throat a-gurgle with the song, threw up his arms and pitched across the fire.

*   *   *

The witch doctor's eyes were well blackened, and his temper none of the best; for he quarrelled with the chief over the possession of Wertz's rifle, and took more than his share of the part-sack of beans. Also he appropriated the bearskin, and caused grumbling among the tribesmen. And finally, he tried to kill Sigmund's dog, which the girl had given him, but the dog ran away, while he fell into the shaft and dislocated his shoulder on the bucket. When the camp was well looted they went back to their own lodges, and there was a great rejoicing among the women. Further, a band of moose strayed over the south divide and fell before the hunters, so the witch doctor attained yet greater honour, and the people whispered among themselves that he spoke in council with the gods.

But later, when all were gone, the shepherd dog crept back to the deserted camp, and all the night long and a day it wailed the dead. After that it disappeared, though the years were not many before the Indian hunters noted a change in the breed of timber wolves, and there were dashes of bright colour and variegated markings such as no wolf bore before.

ANSELME MARCHAL

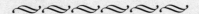

Hoodwinking the Germans

After my release from the civilian prison of Magdeburg, I was sent back to Scharnhörst, the most rigorous prison camp in Germany. A little later, towards the end of December 1917, a new companion in captivity was given, or rather returned, to me. It was Roland Garros.

He and I had been imprisoned together before, but separated because we had refused to answer the incessant roll-calls with which we were plagued and had incited the rest of the prisoners to do the same. Garros had been confined in the camp of Burg, but now all French officers were being evacuated from Burg in order to make room for the Russian officers who were being concentrated there. Germany and Russia were making the peace of Brest-Litovsk, so it had been decided to prevent any contact between our wavering allies and ourselves.

After Burg, Garros was at first transferred to the Wagenhaus with the French officers who were not undergoing reprisals. He was kept there for about two weeks. At the end of that time a search proved him to be the possessor of the important sum of two marks in German money and a pair of pincers. It needed no more to earn him a few days' confinement in the cells. Afterwards, as penance for his two crimes, he was sent to Scharnhörst.

I found in Garros the good friend of peacetime, who had always had my affection, and the great pilot of wartime, who had as yet been prevented by circumstances from giving his full measure.

The close intimacy in which we lived at Scharnhörst and the trials we were soon to undergo together could not do otherwise than transform our former good-comradeship into the deepest of affections. Nobody could be admitted to the intimacy of Garros's mind without feeling respect and admiration for his very superior intelligence, nor into the intimacy of his heart without loving him.

As soon as we found ourselves together again at Scharnhörst, we 'pooled' all the different projects for escape that he and I had imagined. Garros had only one idea – to escape and take his revenge. Before six weeks were out we had found a possible way of getting out of the camp.

When I first came to Scharnhöst I talked freely of my intention to escape. One day a Russian officer came to me with a most engaging air, saying how much he deplored the lack of success of my previous attempt, and offering to help me in a new effort, all this being seasoned with so many compliments on my coolness and courage as to put me well on my guard. Finally, he bluntly offered to take me to a room of which he had the key, and from which he assured me I could escape into the moat without being seen.

While I had few illusions as to the sincerity of this most devoted of Russians, I took him at his word and let him show me the little room he had described. Once there I had only to put an eye to the window to assure myself that it would be impossible to find a less promising place. At ten metres' distance was silhouetted the grey form of a sentinel, and as he would undoubtedly be given very good reasons for being on his guard, it is easy to imagine what would have been the fate of Lieutenant Marchal, the runaway rather than the sitting duck.

My Russian was, as you choose, either a most extraordinary imbecile or something of a dirty dog; for myself, I lean towards the second hypothesis.

After that I was more discreet, in case some other amateur Judas should try to betray me; but my constant preoccupation was how to part company with my guardians, and I did not stop examining every possible plan of escape.

Escape in the twilight, by boldly walking through one of the gates, past the sentries, still seemed to me to be the method requiring the greatest amount of assurance, but at the same time offering the greatest chance of success, as being the least expected.

Since my previous attempt I had been particularly recommended to the vigilance of the non-commissioned officers of the guard, and confronted with each one in turn, so that in future they would have no difficulty in recognising me, whatever my disguise. I had to get over this difficulty. Ever since the beginning of the winter I had never shown myself in the courtyard except wrapped up in my overcoat, the collar turned up so as to hide almost the whole of my face. As the months passed I hoped that the guard would have forgotten my face, and anyway my face would have become blurred in the memories of the non-coms. Garros agreed with me that this was the best plan, and we prepared accordingly.

We would both dress up as German officers and walk boldly out of the prison.

The *first* thing was to fake the kits. We begged some permanganate of potash from a doctor and made a strong solution. In this we washed our two French officers' coats, until they ceased to be horizon blue and became campaign grey. The buttons we carved out of wood with penknives, and painted them greenish bronze. Out of our pilots' overalls we got enough fur to make collars for the coats.

One of our friends made us caps. They were a great success. He made the frames out of pieces of cardboard from a box. The tops he covered with blue cloth cut out of a pair of trousers, and then made bands out of a red-flannel belt. This he stole from an old colonel who wore it at night. We hoped the poor old man would not catch a chill. With some nickel he made cockades such as the Germans carried on their caps; and no one at a distance, or in a bad light, could have told them from the real thing. They were 'creations'.

We cut down some slats of wood into the shape of sabres and blacked them over with shoe-blacking.

Garros produced two suits of civilian clothes. Goodness knows how he had kept them concealed in his trips from prison to prison. He had, however, brought them to Scharnhörst and secreted them between a wall and a wood fence where there was a loose plank. The Germans never knew where those civilian suits came from, and I cannot tell. I don't know.

The hardest task was to forge false passes with false names. I knew German and Germany well, for I had lived there and travelled in the country before the war, and I managed these pretty successfully after several tries.

As the date we had chosen arrived we got the assistance of our comrades. There were none of the 'amateur Judases' among them. They worked for us like blacks, and they gave us all their assistance loyally. Two other officers – Captain Meyer and Lieutenant Gille – also determined to escape, but were prepared to let us get away first.

It was important to keep our escape concealed as long as possible, so as to give us a good start. We intended to go as dusk came, so the evening roll-call was the first problem. We devised a complicated plan.

Garros and I were in Room 7 in the right wing of the Scharnhörst on the first floor. A wooden partition that divided the casement in two separated us from Room 8. A trap-door had been made in this partition, by means of which two of our comrades from No. 8 proposed to pass at the opportune moment and replace us in No. 7. But on reflection our friends decided that the proximity of the two rooms would not allow the substitution, however rapidly carried out, to be made in the too-short time that it would take the inspecting officer of the week to reach the second room after having assured himself that the first had its full number of occupants. So it was decided to ask two French officers of Room 11, also situated on the first floor, but in the left wing of the bastion, to come and occupy Garros's and my beds when the non-commissioned officer of the week had visited their room and had been able to announce to his lieutenant, '*Alles da!*' ('All present and correct!')

This time, in order that no absences should be remarked from Room 11, it was essential that our two substitutes should be found in it when the officer came, condemned though they were to spend the whole night in No. 7. They were found there, if not in person, at least in the shape of two friends from Room 15 on the second floor, which was situated immediately over theirs. Lieutenant Chalon, our renowned engineer in the Scharnhörst, cut a hole through the solid masonry of Room 15 down into Room 11 and concealed it. As soon as we were gone our two friends from No. 11 would come to No. 7 and get into our beds. The two from No. 15 on the second floor would drop through the hole in the floors and take the place of the two who should have been in No. 11. As soon as the German officer had inspected No. 11 and started up the staircase to the second floor, they were to be hoisted up again into their own room by main force, so that by the time the Prussian officer and his NCOs had got to their room they would be back in their own places and the Prussians could report, 'All present and correct!'

The falsification of the morning roll-call, however, would not be so easy, for it was held in the open courtyard. The inmates of each room were fallen in as a group and counted, while the rooms were guarded by sentries, so that no one could go in or out.

The day arrived – the 14th of February 1918. Two of our friends kept watch in the passage, to see that we were not disturbed. Several others came to help us with our kit. We rigged ourselves out in our civilian suits and put our faked German overcoats over them. To cover our trousers legs we had some gaiters. Then we strapped on our 'swords', adjusted our caps to a good angle with a touch of swagger, and as complete German officers were ready.

As it began to get to twilight we marched out and up to the gate known as the Wagenhaus Gate.

We were a little behind our schedule and the twilight had already turned to darkness. Garros's watch – I no longer had one – marked ten minutes to six, and the train we wanted to catch left Magdeburg at half-past six. There was no time to be lost, and we lost none.

Approaching the first sentry I put on my most impressive voice and roared at Garros that it was insufferable that a German colonel should be whistled after and hooted at by the prisoners, and that it was our duty to go immediately to the general and ask him to take energetic measures to bring those insolent Frenchmen back into the paths of virtue.

The first sentry heard my words very plainly. His attitude was proof enough of that. Without uttering a syllable he drew aside, and stood at attention.

We arrived before the second. He asked us, in a timid voice, some question that I did not catch. Was it a password he wanted? If such a word existed, it would be the only one that we were quite incapable of uttering. I made good anything that may have been lacking in our reply by the crescendo in which I continued my fierce invectives against the disgraceful *Franzosen* who were making the life of the camp commandant a misery to him. It was time that a stop was put to such a monstrous state of affairs. Garros agreed energetically by a sort of hoarse growling. Out tactics were successful. The sentry opened the great gates and let us through.

A little farther along another sentry guarded the barbed-wire barrier that had been laid across the slope leading up to the gates. But this third guard considered himself to be covered by the second, and he said nothing to us. He stood to attention, and then saluted and opened the barrier for us.

We had now reached the footbridge over the moat. Before it was a sentry, who demanded to see our passes. Although we had them in our pockets we preferred not to show them unless it was absolutely necessary. In my most terrible voice I roared an emphatic, 'Mind your own affairs!' at him, and added, 'That makes the third time we've been asked for those damned papers!' and we brushed past, and he made no further attempt to stop us.

We walked in step slowly across that bridge, and even more slowly into the darkness beyond it, our hearts in our mouths, expecting at any minute to hear some pursuit, some of the sentries or the guard after us.

As soon as we judged we were clear and out of sight we hurried to the edge of a railway track, and in a broad ditch we crouched while we tore off our overcoats, our leggings, the officers' caps and our wooden swords, and, hiding them in a drain, we turned into peaceful German citizens. Garros had a soft felt hat and I a most disreputable cloth cap. Sticking these on our heads, we made back to the road and walked with the utmost nonchalance to Magdeburg and into the railway station.

We hoped that we had a good start. Later we heard that everything had worked well. The German officer inspecting at the evening roll-call had not noticed our absence, though our two friends from No. 15 had only been hauled back up from No. 11 just in time. Though out of breath and covered with dust they bamboozled the guards successfully.

The morning roll-call had also been successful. Garros's absence was missed. A friend from our room put on his pilot's leather coat, turned the fur collar up to his eyes as was Garros's habit, and took his place in the ranks. The 'dancing master ' on duty that day was superbly oblivious to this masquerade; but not seeing me in the group, and hearing that I had reported sick, he sent up to No. 7 the non-com. especially detailed to watch me.

The man – who was known to us as Bismarck – came into the room, where he found only one officer, whose head and shoulders he was unable to see, their owner being busily occupied in searching for some unknown object under my bed. Without changing his position the officer in question addressed a few words of German to Bismarck, which sufficed to reassure him, as I was the only occupant of No. 7 able to speak to him in his own language.

The officer who pretended to be myself was Lieutenant Buel, who knew a little German. How he found a substitute for himself and bluffed Bismarck and the sentries I don't know. It is a mystery I have never been able to fathom, for if any prisoner for any reason did not fall in on morning roll-call his room was specially guarded by a sentry, with strict orders to see that no one went in or out.

None the less, the result was that we got a good twenty-four hours' start, and it was not until the following evening roll-call that the Germans spotted that we were gone.

When they did find out there was a real blow-up. The German papers demanded that the Chancellor make new arrangements so that no other prisoners should get away. The commandant of the camp was dismissed in disgrace. We, none of us, had any sympathy with him in that. Then a whole army of Berlin secret police descended on the prison and investigated everything and everybody, but could not for the life of them find out how we had got away.

Those in themselves were good enough results, but they were not the best. The Berlin secret-police officers, the *ersatz* Sherlock Holmeses, not only had their trouble for nothing in so far as finding the smallest clue as to how our own escape had been managed, but they facilitated – oh, most certainly against their will! – the successful accomplishment of another. Absorbed as they were in ransacking the rooms and searching our fellow-prisoners they neglected to keep watch over their own pockets. And the result was that Captain Meyer, who had given up to us his turn of escape, rendered to one of the detectives the sincere flattery of imitation – though he carried out his investigations more discretely than did the German, for he relieved him of all his identity papers.

Two days later, with Lieutenant Gille, Meyer marched out of the prison. At the gates he presented the papers of the secret-service officer. The doors and barred gates opened before him and he was gone.

Staggering at this escape right under their noses, while they were in charge and investigating, the Berlin sleuth-hounds had to set out on a new inquiry, and even then found nothing, for I expect the 'tec' didn't let on that he'd had his pocket picked.

Meanwhile, while the officers of four different rooms were managing, with such ingenuity, to hide our absence from Scharnhörst for a night and a morning, we were going full-steam ahead towards the north-west.

Several times we were treated as if suspicious characters. Once several peasants who were travelling in the same direction kept asking us questions of all sorts. It may just have been their native curiosity. In order to appease this curiosity, I told them that we were going to Brunswick to install some motors for the Swiss Company, Oerlikon. They swallowed the story and left us in peace, and we accomplished the first day's journey without further incident.

The train deposited us in the evening at Brunswick, and that which was to carry us towards Cologne would not pass for another six hours. What to do in the meantime? We decided to kill time by walking. The night was very dark, cold and dry. We followed a sleeping street bordered by a high fence, on the other side of which was a cemetery. If only we could get into that we would be certain of finding the safest of resting-places. The opportunity was presented to us before very long; we found a loose paling, and managed to squeeze through the narrow opening.

Our only impression, in the midst of tombs surrounded by trees black and sombre in the night, was one of security – security such as only a cemetery could possibly procure for individuals in our position. A little alley led us away from the street, and, sitting down on a tomb, we began to talk in whispers.

Hours passed. It was midnight. Suddenly I felt Garros's hand grip my arm.

'Listen,' he whispered, and we both strained our ears. It was an eerie sound that we heard, indefinable, a sort of rustling, coming from where we did not know, caused by what we did not know. It seemed to draw closer – but no, it receded, stopped, and then we heard it again, approaching. It may have been only the dragging steps of some guardian making his rounds, but even that earthly explanation was not too reassuring, and the sound was not at all like that of footsteps. Whatever it was, we did not like it, and with one accord we took to our heels. I do not doubt that in our undignified flight we trampled more than one flower-border, stumbled over more than one grave, tore down more than one wreath; but at last we reached the gap in the palisade and in an instant found ourselves out in the street, where no strange thing moved about.

Train time was approaching, and we went back to the station. In the second-class carriage where chance more than our own desire led us we found two officers occupying the corners on the corridor. Never was there so undesirable a meeting; yet to turn about and leave them would have been of the utmost imprudence. We were in the soup, and the best thing we could do for the moment was to stay in it. Passing before our uncomfortable travelling companions we gave them the politest of *Guten Abends*. They replied with a nod of the head.

Squeezed into the two other corners, we sat and waited for the train to pull out. The four or five minutes we had to wait seemed an eternity. Anybody in our position is invariably afflicted by the constant and painful impression that a policeman is following on his trail, scenting the escaped prisoner from afar. At Brunswick we suffered again that agonising sensation. Whoever was the individual who walked steadily up and down the platform, keeping close to our compartment and apparently never for a minute quitting it with his eye, he can flatter himself on having made us pass a most unpleasant interlude.

At last the train drew quietly out. The night passed without incident, and in the morning we found ourselves at Cologne.

Feeling somewhat ashamed of my cap, I bought a hat, and then we wandered idly about the town. But in spite of the crowded streets that made it highly improbable that anybody would pay any attention to us, we were still harassed by the fear of spies. The most reassuring manner of passing the morning that we could think of was to spend it in the cathedral; we would hardly be looked for there. We went, and heard three masses, one after the other in rapid succession.

At a certain moment my companion nudged me with his elbow. He drew my attention to two other civilians whom we had already noticed at the preceding mass, and who now seemed to have every intention of hearing the next, like ourselves. After examining them carefully out of the corner of our eyes, we felt reassured. They were probably only very pious folk, unless like ourselves, they had raken refuge in the cathedral in order to avoid undesirable encounters.

Prudence bade us not to venture into a restaurant, so for lunch we ate some chocolate without bread, and washed it down with beer in a bar. Afterwards we bought an electric torch that we would need for our future nocturnal peregrinations. Then we sought in the darkness of a cinema the relative security that we had found in the morning under the lofty and cold roof of the cathedral.

At the fall of evening we took a workmen's train for Aix-la-Chapelle. It was crowded. The intermediary stations being as numerous as in the out-skirts of Paris, the halts were very frequent. As we drew into one of them someone in our compartment cried out: 'Ah, there are the police again, watching all the exits of the station . . . I wonder what it means?'

Naturally, the meaning to us was that we had been tracked and it was for our benefit that the police had been mobilised. By a coincidence that we judged to be most fortunate the train slowed down at that moment. The stop-signal was down. I whispered to Garros, 'Let's take the chance!' I opened the carriage door, and a German soldier who was standing by it said, 'What are you up to?'

'Don't you worry about that,' I said; 'we are already an hour late, and we don't want to miss the last tram.'

While I was talking Garros had jumped from the train. I followed him, and the soldier closed the carriage door behind me.

We found ourselves in the open country, close to the railway embankment. As we were not certain of the direction of Aix, we decided to steer north-west. We walked on until we reached a spot where the houses, that had been widely scattered, began to group themselves in successive and well-populated agglomerations. Obviously, the outskirts of a big town.

We knew that one of the characteristics of Aix-la-Chapelle was a wide exterior boulevard, lined with trees, and at about eight o'clock we came out on a boulevard that answered that description.

We had an annotated map, which we had had smuggled through to us in the prison. This told us that we should turn to the right, down a street that because of the unevenness of the ground presented the peculiarity of having one pavement raised up by four steps. The boulevard led us to that street, which we entered and followed. On a signpost we were able to read 'Direction de Tivoli'. We were on the right track, so, quite sure of ourselves now, we continued along the street, which rapidly became suburban in character. We had penetrated on to the territory of Aix, but not for more than ten minutes.

Once more in the open country, we directed our course by map and compass. The compass, too, had been smuggled into the prison in a parcel of food. The weather was chilly, but dry and seasonable – far from the fifteen and twenty degrees of frost from which I had suffered so cruelly during my first terrible journey in trying to escape.

Keeping off the roads as much as possible, jumping the little rivers in order to avoid having to show our passports at the bridges, throwing ourselves flat on the ground at the least alarm, we had yet managed to make some thirteen or fourteen kilometres by two o'clock in the morning. We calculated that only two more kilometres, at the most, still separated us from the frontier.

We entered a wood. The dried leaves with which the ground was covered made a continual crackling noise under our feet which, it seemed to us, must be audible at a great distance. Fearing that it might betray us, and looking for a path on which our footsteps would make less noise, we flashed our lamp along the ground. Immediately a shrill whistle rang out. It seemed to emanate from a little cabin that we could see on a height above the woods.

Undoubtedly our light had been seen. If that cabin should prove to be a guardhouse filled with soldiers set there to watch the passages over the frontier we would be pursued and perhaps caught – and taken back to Magdeburg. No! We had no intention of accepting that. Turning to the right, and without quitting the copse, we took to our heels.

After a few minutes we came out on a transversal road, which, we realised, would lead us back in the direction of Aix. But we had no choice. Above all, we must get out of that patrol- and sentry-infested zone. A prey to nervous apprehensions that the high stakes for which we were playing may render excusable, we felt that an enemy lurked in every shadow, ready to leap out on us. At one time we heard footsteps both behind and before us. Turning again to the left, we fled across the open fields. Ditches and unseen obstacles made traps for us in the dark. Garros tore his face and I my hands in climbing over artificial thorn hedges of barbed wire.

The alarming noises continued. Suspicious lights, quickly flashed on and off, showed here and there in the distance. All those noises and lights were not necessarily a menace to us – we knew that quite well, but were incapable of distinguishing the innocuous from the dangerous. This perhaps needs some explanation, and it is this.

In that frontier region between Germany and Holland smuggling was never at a standstill. The smugglers made signals to each other by whistling, modulating their voices to imitate the cries of all kinds of birds – somewhat after the fashion of the *Pirates of Savannah*, an old melodrama of my childhood's days.

Optical signals were also used. Thus, in the fields, we often saw certain individuals who followed along the railroad track, bent double under heavy loads, and who from time to time, in order to warn the others, gave short flashes of light with their electric torches. We said to ourselves that perhaps back there in the woods it was only with *maltouziers* of this kind that we had had dealings, and whose whistling was no more than an answer to what they mistook for the signal of one of their acolytes. But hardly had we conceived that comforting thought than other shadows appeared, going in the same direction along the railway track; and this time there was no doubt about it. The silhouettes were those of soldiers on patrol . . . The business was comic enough to watch, had it not proved to us that we ran the double risk of being pursued on sight, either as escaped prisoners or as smugglers; and once captured, there would be little choice between the two; the result for us would be the same.

In any case we were doomed to postpone our attempt to cross the frontier until the next night; and the only thing to do in the meantime was to return to Aix-la-Chapelle. We must in any case be fairly close to it, as we had been walking for three hours and must easily have covered on the return road the thirteen or fourteen kilometres that we had previously made in the opposite direction.

Going straight in front of us, we came to a high railway embankment under which passed the road we were following. The spot was guarded by a sentry. Like all his kind, he was provided with an electric torch, the light of which he turned full on our faces.

'Have you got your papers?'

Without any previous collaboration the same idea came simultaneously to both of us. We put on the voices and the gestures of extreme intoxication. I replied to the soldier.

'Ole man, now you jus' lissen to me . . . You can't 'rrest us jus' because we live at Aix . . . Got paid today, we did . . . Had a rousing ole beano with some of the chaps . . . '

'Where?'

I gave the name of a village on the outskirts of Aix, and launched out into a complicated but circumstantial description of our bacchic prowess. The sentry showed himself indulgent. He clapped us on the back in friendly fashion, and, 'Get along with you,' he said. 'Pass, but don't let me catch you around here again.' To which I answered with the profoundest conviction, 'You can count on that, ole man.'

When we reached Aix-la-Chapelle it was nearly five o'clock in the morning. In the street we came across a night-watchman whose business it was to see that all doors were properly closed. I went up to him and said: 'We are strangers in town. Could you tell us of an hotel?' Doing better than merely tell us of one, he led us to it.

We had to register – using of necessity false names – and indicate the identity papers that we would be able to produce, and the information we gave on that second point was of exactly the same value as on the first, and we had to pay in advance, having no baggage of any kind.

The red marks that Garros had on his face from his fall in the barbed wire earned for him more than one suspicious glance, from which I also suffered by ricochet, thanks to my lacerated hands. Nevertheless, we were allowed to have our two beds, of which we stood in considerable need, after our nocturnal stroll of twenty-five or thirty kilometres. However, we did not linger over-long in them, fear of being denounced to the police effectually driving away all desire for a sluggish morning. By ten o'clock we were already downstairs, and making for the front door.

The hall porter called after us in a voice that seemed to us full of curiosity: 'What! Going already?'

'Yes, yes, we are in a hurry;' and without more ado we briskly left his company.

Condemned as we were to wait for evening before again venturing out into the country, we drifted aimlessly about the streets of Aix. But our stomachs clamoured for a remittance somewhat more substantial than that with which we had so far gratified them. Since our last meal at Scharnhörst, that is to say twice twenty-four hours ago, we had in all, and for all, eaten eight small tablets of chocolate – somewhat meagre fare. And now that the eighth and last tablet had disappeared we could discover no means of replenishing our larder. Unprovided with cards or food-tickets of any kind, to present ourselves anywhere either as a diner on the premises or a purchaser of comestibles would have been to denounce ourselves infallibly; if not for what we were, at least as persons whose irregular position recommended them highly to the curiosity of the police.

Good luck led us to a mechanical bar. There, at least, we thought, there could be no danger, the machine being endowed neither with eyes nor ears. We soon found out our mistake. If the machines were deaf and blind the same could not be said of the urchins detailed to watch over them. One of these, about twelve years old and as sharp as a razor, came and planted himself next to us, obviously all ears. I broke into a voluble flood of speech, and succeeded in allaying the suspicions of the young spy to such an extent that he at last left us, and went to carry on his small affairs elsewhere.

We at once prepared for a good feed, but disappointment awaited us. The only dish that was left was jellied mussels. We could do no other than resign ourselves to the inevitable – and it had to be better than nothing. In return for forty pfennigs the distributor produced for our benefit seven mussels on a plate. Both of us returned twice to the charge. Then we departed, having failed to lose any great proportion of our hunger, but having gained an undeniable feeling of nausea.

In default of more solid nourishment we fell back on glasses of beer, absorbed at frequent intervals during our aimless wanderings. Unfortunately, it was Einheilsbier, which only had the vaguest of resemblances to the good, solid beer of peacetime.

One of these pauses we made at the Theatrellatz Tavern, where Munich Spartenbrau used to be served. Momentarily discouraged by our failure of the night before, we were afraid of having to spend an indefinite period between Aix-la-Chapelle and the spot we had marked out for crossing the frontier. It occurred to us that help from outside would be invaluable . . . I had a good friend, almost a brother, on whose affection and intelligence I had always been able to count throughout the fifteen years of our acquaintance – Raoul Humbert. I knew him to be at Leysin in Switzerland, at the sanatorium Les Fougères. I wrote to him. I sent my letter in an envelope of the tavern, where he was to reply to me, using the name of Munder. Disguising my handwriting, I told him that with a fellow-machinist from the firm of Oerlikon, I was held up at Aix-la-Chapelle by an accident to my arm, sustained during a first and unsuccessful attempt to install the motor; that I hoped to have better luck with my second attempt, but that nevertheless I should be glad of his helpful intervention in whatever form he could give it. The terms of my letter were of necessity ambiguous, but my friend Humbert would certainly decipher its meaning without difficulty. I may as well say now that the letter reached him – he has since shown it to me, with the tavern's stamp on it – but on that same day the newspapers announced that Garros and I had reached Holland in safety, and so he did nothing.

Towards evening we went into a sort of café. We were served with *ersatz* coffee, accompanied by a sort of tart, the crust of which was artificial – as indeed were the cream and the strawberries with which it was filled. Our stomachs did not receive it with any better grace than the morning's mussels.

Night came. Our previous failure would at least have served to teach us the lie of the land, so it was with greater confidence that we started off again towards the frontier. Alas! we went farther astray than ever, only extricating ourselves with the greatest difficulty from the barbed wire and with only the satisfaction of not having attracted the attention of a patrol. Aix had the privilege of seeing our second return between three and four o'clock.

With no food save that which I have already described, this new march of thirty kilometres would leave us thoroughly exhausted, and we began to fear that we would never succeed in getting out of the damned country. First we had to find a place to sleep. I led Garros to an inn near the station, where I knocked while my companion waited at a distance. A sleepy woman opened to me. I said that I was called Schmidt, and asked her if a friend of mine, a commercial traveller, had not enquired for me that night. She replied in the negative. 'Then he hasn't yet arrived. He will very likely come by a later train, but he will certainly join me before long. In any case, I will take a room for myself and reserve another for him.' My friend, strangely enough, arrived almost immediately. And now for a good sleep. We had earned it.

At midday Garros said: 'Listen, old man. Today is the end. Either we pass the frontier or we are done for. But after two days and three nights of almost total abstinence we are not in the best form for the last pull at the traces. At whatever risk we must have a good feed.'

I agreed with him only too well. In order not to remain for ever at the inn we moved to another hotel in the same quarter. I booked two rooms for the sake of appearances. Then I called the restaurant attendant aside. 'Look here,' I said, 'we have come a long way and are very hungry – only I warn you we have lost our food cards.' He gave me to understand that, if I did not look too closely at the price, the matter might be arranged.

It was arranged. We were served with a dinner, washed down with wine, that would have been perfection save for a total lack of bread. It seemed that everywhere, even in this land of regulations, the severest of restrictive organisations could be circumvented. And that night again, beside the official menu endorsed by the police, we had an enormous steak with potatoes, an omelette and some jam. Nothing was lacking save the bread.

Well ballasted, thoroughly revived, we felt full of courage and spirits. Nevertheless, we redoubled our precautions. Once on our way, we took frequent bearings, in order to make no error in our itinerary, and at the slightest alarm we took refuge behind a bush or in a ditch.

At seven or eight kilometres from the frontier the immediate proximity of the principal guardhouse was made clearly visible to us by its external illuminations – a huge electric light. In that vicinity the slightest imprudence would be the end of us. We advanced only on hands and knees, ears and eyes well opened. At last we came on a little stream that was noted on our map as marking the last line of sentries. But here we were condemned to a lengthy wait. We were in the first night of the first quarter of the moon; and it shed a considerable amount of light. Until it had set we could not walk, nor even crawl, in the open. We found that it took its time about it. Never had I realised how slowly the moon travels. We cursed it for its sloth. We even accused it of being an hour late according to the meteorological schedule announced for it in the *Magdeburg Journal* that we had consulted. However, neither the moon nor the newspaper was at fault; the error was due to an idiosyncrasy of Garros's watch.

At last the night was dark. We set off again, on all-fours, until we came to a perfectly naked plain. Not a tree, not a house to be seen. No further doubt was possible – we were approaching the goal.

Nevertheless, we were worried by the fact that we could not find the landmark that had been indicated to us – a mountain peak that dominated the otherwise flat country. We could see no slightest trace of the smallest peak, yet we still felt that we were on the right track. This idea was confirmed by the sight, in the distance, of a brilliantly illuminated building, which we had been told to use as a lighthouse. But we had been told that it was the guardhouse from which the frontier was watched, whereas in reality it was a coke factory situated in Holland itself. Yet, save for that error of identification, it was the same luminous landmark of which we had been told.

As for the famous mountain peak, which we saw later, it was no more than one of those huge slag-heaps that are so often found in industrial areas.

We advanced now flat on our stomachs, and crossed in that fashion a ploughed field which we saw to be traversed on our right by numerous footprints. 'That must be the route for the relief of the sentries,' we said to ourselves. No matter – we must get on. Crawling thus we made barely five hundred metres an hour – and in what state of mind may be imagined – a curious mixture of terror and hope.

Now, twenty metres in front of us, there rose a little thorn hedge. In the breath of a whisper we said to each other that it must border the road along which, if our information was reliable, the sentries patrolled.

At that moment we heard someone cough to our right. Garros seized my arm and pressed it, indicating that we must neither speak nor move.

Holding our breath, we did our best to disappear into the ground.

All at once the sentry who had coughed began to walk towards us. Suddenly he stopped. We had the agonising sensation that he could see us perfectly well in the dark. But no, he went on, paused a few metres in front of us, and continued on his way to our left.

He came back, walked to the right, and halted.

Then we heard a voice, to which another replied. It was the conversation of people speaking face to face – nose to nose, judging by the tone of their voices.

Now, we knew that the sentries on that line were posted at intervals of a hundred and fifty metres; so if one of them had moved to go and talk to his right-hand neighbour it was highly probable that he had thus opened in front of us a gap double the usual width. We must take advantage of it.

Crawling obliquely towards the left, we reached the thorn hedge. Fortunately there were gaps in it, between the little trunks where they emerged from the soil. By groping, Garros found his and I mine. We slid through.

Beyond it the ground sloped slightly, and a metre and a half farther on a strand of barbed wire was stretched low across the grass.

The wire was arranged in such a manner as to trip up anybody who passed, so that the noise made by his stumbling might warn the sentries. As we were crawling we felt the wire, and did not trip.

We found ourselves now in a little field, about a hundred metres wide. Still flat on our stomachs we crossed it. A perfect hedge of barbed wire bounded it. It was the last obstacle. In one bound, taking no heed of torn skin or clothing or rifles or sentries, we leaped on to and over it, and in another we cleared a stream whose sinuous course marked the frontier. Then, with beating hearts, soaring spirits and smarting eyes, we literally fell into each other's arms.

We were in Holland! We were out of reach of the Germans.

Here end my souvenirs of captivity. It only remains to me to relate briefly the circumstances of our repatriation.

From the point where we had crossed the last line of German barbed wire we took train for The Hague, where we reported ourselves to the French ambassador. Garros never forgot, as I shall never forget, the charming manner in which General Boucabeille, the military attaché, the general's wife and the members of the French colony received us.

Then we took ship for England. The crossing was effected in the usual manner, that is to say, under the protection of British destroyers. During the voyage if a mine or two were signalled no fuss was made – our ship and her escort knew well enough how to avoid them. I may note, too, that a German hydroplane attacked us, but its bombs made no victims in our flotilla: the inoffensive fish of the North Sea were the only sufferers.

At last we reached London, and from there we left for Boulogne and the front.

The nightmare was over. We were soldiers once more.

FERENC MOLNÁR

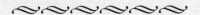

Ferenc Molnár (1876–1952), novelist and playwright, born in Budapest, Hungary. He trained as a lawyer, but became a journalist and war correspondent. He had considerable success with his short stories, but is best known for his novel *The Paul Street Boys* (1907), and his plays *The Devil* (1907), *Liliom* (1909) and *The Good Fairy* (1930), all of which have achieved success in English translation.

The Living Death

Here is a very serious reason, my dear sisters, why at last, after an absence of twenty years in America, I am confiding to you this strange secret in the life of our beloved and lamented father, and of the old house where we were children together. The truth is, if I read rightly the countenances of my physicians as they whisper to each other by the window of the chamber in which I am lying, that only a few days of this life remain to me.

It is not right that this secret should die with me, my dear sisters. Though it will seem terrible to you, as it has to me, it will enable you to better understand our blessed father, help you to account for what must have seemed to you to be strange inconsistencies in his character. That this secret was revealed to me was due to my indolence and childish curiosity.

For the first, and the last, time in my life I listened at a keyhole. With shame and a hotly chiding conscience I yielded to that insatiable curiosity – and when you have read these lines you will understand why I do not regret that inexcusable, furtive act.

I was only a lad when we went to live in that odd little house. You remember it stood in the outskirts of Rakos, near the new cemetery. It stood on a deep lot, and was roughly boarded on the side which looked on the highway. You remember that on the first floor, next the street, were the room of our father, the dining-room and the children's room. In the rear of the house was the sculpture studio. There we had the large white hall with big windows, where white-clothed labourers worked. They mixed the plaster, made forms, chiselled, scratched and sawed. Here in this large hall had our father worked for thirty years.

When I arrived, in the holidays, I noted a change in our father's countenance. His beard was white, even when he did not work with the plaster. Through his strong spectacles his eyes glittered peculiarly. He was less calm than formerly. And he did not speak much, but all the more did he read.

Why, we all knew that after the passing away of our mother he became a bookworm, reading very often by candlelight until morning.

Then did it happen, about the fourth day after my arrival. I spent my leisure hours in the studio; I carved little figures, formed little pillar heads from the white plaster. In the corner a big barrel stood filled with water. It was noon; the labourers went to lunch.

I sat down close to the barrel and carved a Corinthian pillar. Father came into the studio and did not notice me. He carried in his hands two plates of soup. When he came into the studio he closed the door behind him and looked around in the shop, as though to make sure he was not observed. As I have said, he did not notice me. I was astonished. Holding my breath, I listened. Father went through the large hall, and then opened a small door, of which I knew only so much that it led into a chamber three steps lower than the studio.

I was full of expectation: I listened. I did not hear a word of conversation. Presently father came back with the empty plates in his hand. Somebody bolted the chamber's door behind him.

Father went out of the studio, and I, much embarrassed, crept from behind the barrel.

I knew that the chamber had a window, which looked back towards the ploughed fields. I ran out of the studio and around the house. Much to my astonishment, the chamber's window was curtained inside. A large yellow plaid curtain hid everything from view. But I had to go, anyway, for I heard Irma's voice calling from the yard: 'Antal, to lunch!'

I sat down to the table with you, my sisters, and looked at father. He was sitting at the head of the table, and ate without saying a word.

Day after day I troubled my head about this mystery in the chamber, but said not a word to anybody. I went into the studio, as usual, but I did not notice anything peculiar. Not a sound came from the chamber, and when our father worked in the shop with his ten labourers he passed by the small door as if beyond it there was nothing out of the ordinary.

On Thursday I had to go back to Germany. On Tuesday night curiosity seized me again. Suddenly I felt that perhaps never would I know what was going on in my father's house. That night, when the working people were gone, I went into the studio. For a long time I was lost in my thoughts. All kinds of romantic ideas passed through my head, while my gaze rested on that small mysterious chamber door.

In the studio it was dark already, and from under the small door in a thin border a yellow radiance poured out. Suddenly I regained my courage. I went to the door and listened. Somebody was speaking. It was a man's voice, but I did not understand what he was saying. I was putting my ear close to the door, when I heard steps at the front of the studio. Father came.

I quickly withdrew myself behind the barrel. Father walked through the hall and knocked on the door softly. The bolt clicked and the door opened. Father went into the chamber and closed the door immediately and locked it.

Now all discretion and sense of honour in me came to an end. Curiosity mastered me. I knew that last year one part of this small room had been partitioned off and was used as a woodhouse. And I knew that there was a possibility of going into the woodhouse through the yard.

I went out, therefore, but found the woodhouse was closed. Driven by trembling curiosity, I ran into the house, took the key of the woodhouse from its nail, and in a minute, through the crevice between two planks, I was looking into that mysterious little room.

There was a table in the middle of the room, and beside the wall were two straw mattresses. On the table a lighted candle stood. A bottle of wine was beside it, and around the table were sitting father and two strangers. Both the strangers were all in black. Something in their appearance froze me with terror.

I fled in a panic of unreasoning fear, but returned soon, devoured by curiosity.

You, my sister Irma, must remember how I found you there, gazing with starting eyeballs on the same mysteriously terrifying scene – and how I drew you away with a laugh and a trifling explanation, so that I might return and resume my ghastly vigil alone.

One of the strangers wore a frock coat and had a sunburned, brown face. He was not old yet, not more than forty-five or forty-eight. He seemed to be a tradesman in his Sunday clothes. That did not interest me much.

I looked at the other old man, and then a shiver of cold went through me. He was a famous physician, a professor, Mr H—. I desire to lay stress upon it that he it was, for I had read two weeks before in the papers that he had died and was buried!

And now he was sitting, in evening dress, in the chamber of a poor plaster sculptor, in the chamber of my father, behind a bolted door!

I was aware of the fact that the physician knew father. Why, you can recall that when father had asthma he consulted Mr H—. Moreover, the professor visited us very frequently. The papers said he was dead, yet here he was!

With beating heart and in terror, I looked and listened.

The professor put some shining little thing on the table.

'Here is my diamond shirt stud,' he said to my father. 'It is yours.'

Father pushed the jewel aside, refusing the gift.

'Why, you are spending money on me,' said the professor.

'It makes no difference,' replied father; 'I shan't take the diamond.'

Then they were silent for a long while. At length the professor smiled and said: 'The pair of cuff buttons which I had from Prince Eugene I presented to the watchman in the cemetery. They are worth a thousand guldens.'

And he showed his cuffs, from which the buttons were missing. Then he turned to the sunburned man: 'What did you give him, General Gardener?'

The tall, strong man unbuttoned his frock coat.

'Everything I had – my gold chain, my scarf pin, and my ring.'

I did not understand all this. What did it mean? Where did they come from? A horrible presentiment arose in me. They came from the cemetery! They wore the very clothes in which they were buried!

What had happened to them? Were they only apparently dead? Did they awake? Did they rise from the dead? What were they seeking here?

They had a very low-voiced conversation with father. I listened in vain. Only later on, when they warmed to their subject and spoke more audibly, did I understand them.

'There is no other way,' said the professor. 'Put it in your will that the coroner shall pierce your heart through with a knife.'

Do you remember, my sisters, the last will of our father, which was thus executed?

Father did not say a word. Then the professor went on, saying: 'That would be a splendid invention. Had I been living till now I would have published a book about it. Nobody takes the Indian fakir seriously here in Europe. But despite this, the buried fakirs, who are two months under ground and then come back into life, are very serious men. Perhaps they are more serious than ourselves, with all our scientific knowledge. There are strange, new, dreadful things for which we are not yet matured enough.

'I died upon their methods; I can state that now. The mental state which they reach systematically I reached accidentally. The solitude, the absorbedness, the lying in a bed month by month, the gazing upon a fixed point hour by hour – these are all self-evident facts with me, a deserted misanthrope.

'I died as the Indian fakirs do, and were I not a descendant of an old noble family, who have a tomb in this country, I would have died really.

'God knows how it happened. I don't think there is any use of worrying ourselves about it. I have still four days. Then we go for good and all. But not back, no, no, not back to life!'

He pointed with his hand towards the city. His face was burning from fever, and he knitted his brows. His countenance was horrible at this moment. Then he looked at the man with the sunburned face. 'The case of Mr Gardener is quite different. This is an ordinary physician's error. But he has less than four days. He will be gone tomorrow or positively the day after tomorrow.'

He grasped the pulse of the sunburned man.

'At this minute his pulse beats a hundred and twelve. You have a day left, Mr Gardener. But not back. We don't go back. Never!'

Father said nothing. He looked at the professor with seriousness, and fondly. The professor drank a glass of wine, and then turned towards father.

'Go to bed. You have to get up early; you still live; you have children. We shall sleep if we can do so. It is very likely that General Gardener won't see another morning. You must not witness that.'

Now father began to speak, slowly, reverently.

'If you, professor, have to send word – or perhaps Mr Gardener – somebody we must take care of – a command, if you have – '

The professor looked at him sternly, saying but one word: 'Nothing.'

Father was still waiting.

'Absolutely nothing,' repeated the professor. 'I have died, but I have four days yet. I live those here, my dear old friend, with you. But I don't go back any more. I don't even turn my face backward. I don't want to know where the others live. I don't want life, old man. It is not honourable to go back. Go, my friend – go to bed.'

Father shook hands with them and disappeared. General Gardener sat stiffly on his chair. The professor gazed into the air.

I began to be aware of all that had happened here. These two apparently dead men had come back from the cemetery, but how, in what manner, by what means? I don't understand it perfectly even now. There, in the small room, near to the cemetery, they were living their few remaining days. They did not want to go back again into life.

I shuddered. During these few minutes I seemed to have learned the meaning of life and of death. Now I myself felt that the life of the city was at a vast distance. I had a feeling that the professor was right. It was not worth while. I, too, felt tired, tired of life, like the professor, the feverish, clever, serious old man who came from the coffin and was sitting there in his grave clothes waiting for the final death.

They did not speak a word to each other. They were simply waiting. I did not have power to move from the crack in the wall through which I saw them.

And now there happened the awful thing that drove me away from our home, never to return.

It was about half-past one when someone tapped on the window. The professor took alarm and looked at Mr Gardener a warning to take no notice. But the tapping grew louder. The professor got up and went to the window. He lifted the yellow curtain and looked out into the night. Quickly he returned and spoke to General Gardener, and then both went to the window and spoke with the person who had knocked. After a long conversation they lifted the man through the window.

On this terrible day nothing could happen that would surprise me. I was benumbed. The man who was lifted through the window was clad in white linen to his feet. He was a Hebrew, a poor, thin, weak, pale Hebrew. He wore his white funeral dress. He shivered from cold, trembled, seemed almost unconscious. The professor gave him some wine. The Hebrew stammered: 'Terrible! Oh, horrible!'

I learned from his broken language that he had not been buried yet, like the professor. He had not yet known the smell of the earth. He had come from his bier.

'I was laid out a corpse,' he whimpered. 'My God, they would have buried me by tomorrow!'

The professor gave him wine again.

'I saw a light here,' he went on. 'I beg you will give me some clothes – some soup, if you please – and I am going back again.' Then he said in German: 'Meine gute, theure Frau! Meine Kinder!' (My good wife, my children.)

He began to weep. The professor's countenance changed to a devilish expression when he heard this lament. He despised the lamenting Hebrew.

'You are going back?' he thundered. 'But you won't go back! Don't shame yourself!'

The Hebrew gazed at him stupidly.

'I live in Rottenbiller Street,' he stammered. 'My name is Joseph Braun.'

He bit his nails in his nervous agitation. Tears filled his eyes.

'Ich muss zu meine Kinder,' he said in German again. (I must go to my children.)

'No!' exclaimed the professor. 'You'll never go back!'

'But why?'

'I will not permit it!'

The Hebrew looked around. He felt that something was wrong here. His startled manner seemed to ask: 'Am I in a lunatic asylum?' He dropped his head and said to the professor simply: 'I am tired.'

The professor pointed to the straw mattress.

'Go to sleep. We will speak further in the morning.'

Fever blazed in the professor's face. On the other straw mattress General Gardener now slept with his face to the wall.

The Hebrew staggered to the straw mattress, threw himself down, and wept. The weeping shook him terribly. The professor sat at the table and smiled.

Finally the Hebrew fell asleep. Hours passed in silence. I stood motionless looking at the professor, who gazed into the candlelight. There was not much left of it. Presently he sighed and blew it out. For a little while there was dark, and then I saw the dawn penetrating the yellow curtain at the window. The professor leaned back in his chair, stretched out his feet, and closed his eyes.

All at once the Hebrew got up silently and went to the window. He believed the professor was asleep. He opened the window carefully and started to creep out. The professor leaped from his chair, shouting: 'No!'

He caught the Hebrew by his shroud and held him back. There was a long knife in his hand. Without another word, the professor pierced the Hebrew through the heart.

He put the limp body on the straw mattress, then went out of the chamber into the studio. In a few minutes he came back with father. Father was pale and did not speak. They covered the dead Hebrew with a rug, and then, one after the other, crept out through the window, lifted the corpse out, and carried it away. In a quarter of an hour they came back. They exchanged a few words, from which I learned that they had succeeded in putting the dead Hebrew back on his bier without having been observed.

They shut the window. The professor drank a glass of wine and again stretched out his legs on the chair.

'It is impossible to go back,' he said. 'It is not allowed.'

Father went away. I did not see him any more. I staggered up to my room, went to bed and slept immediately. The next day I got up at ten o'clock. I left the city at noon.

Since that time, my dear sisters, you have not seen me. I don't know anything more. At this minute I say to myself that what I know, what I have set down here, is not true. Maybe it never happened, maybe I have dreamed it all. I am not clear in my mind. I have a fever.

But I am not afraid of death. Here, on my hospital bed, I see the professor's feverish but calm and wise face. When he grasped the Hebrew by the throat he looked like a lover of Death, like one who has a secret relation with the passing of life, who advocates the claims of Death, and who punishes him who would cheat Death.

Now Death urges his claim upon me. I have no desire to cheat him – I am so tired, so very tired.

God be with you, my dear sisters.

FRANK NORRIS

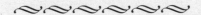

Frank Norris (1870–1902), novelist, was born in Chicago, son of a jeweller, and christened Benjamin Franklin Norris; later the family moved to San Francisco. In 1887 he studied art in London and Paris, then spent some time studying at the University of California and at Harvard. In 1895 he went to South Africa as a newspaper correspondent, and after that was a journalist in San Francisco and New York. In 1899 he published *McTeague*, a grim Zolaesque novel about the more sordid parts of San Francisco. He then planned a trilogy on the subject of wheat: *The Octopus* (1901) deals with its production; *The Pit* (1903) with the speculation that accompanies its marketing, and *The Wolf* was to have described the consumption of bread in a famine-stricken village. But before he could complete this or another trilogy he had planned on Gettysburg, Norris succumbed to an attack of appendicitis at the age thirty-two. Others of his novels are *Moran of the Lady Letty* (1898), *Blix* (1899), *A Man's Woman* (1900) and *Vandover and the Brute* (1914). *A Deal in Wheat* (1903) and *The Third Circle* (1909) are collections of short stories, and *Responsibilities of the Novelist* (1903) is a book of essays.

A Memorandum of Sudden Death

The manuscript of the account that follows belongs to a harness-maker in Albuquerque, Juan Tejada by name, and he is welcome to whatever of advertisement this notice may bring him. He is a good fellow, and his patented martingale for stage horses may be recommended. I understand he got the manuscript from a man named Bass, or possibly Bass left it with him for safe-keeping. I know that Tejada has some things of Bass's now – things that Bass left with him last November: a mess-kit, a lantern and a broken theodolite – a whole saddle-box full of contraptions. I forgot to ask Tejada how Bass got the manuscript, and I wish I had done so now, for the finding of it might be a story itself. The probabilities are that Bass simply picked it up page by page off the desert, blown about the spot where the fight occurred and at some little distance from the bodies. Bass, I am told, is a bone-gatherer by profession, and one can easily understand how he would come across the scene of the encounter in one of his tours into western Arizona. My interest in the affair is impersonal, but none the less keen. Though I did not know young Karslake, I knew his stuff – as everybody still does, when you come to that. For the matter of that, the mere mention of his pen-name, 'Anson Qualtraugh', recalls at once to thousands of the readers of a certain world-famous monthly magazine of New York articles and stories he wrote for it while he was alive; as, for instance, his admirable descriptive work called 'Traces of the Aztecs on the Mogolon Mesa', in the October number of 1890. Also, in the January issue of 1892 there are two specimens of his work, one signed Anson Qualtraugh and the other Justin Blisset. Why he should have used the Blisset signature I do not know. It occurs only this once in all his writings. In this case it is signed to a very indifferent New Year's story. The Qualtraugh 'stuff' of the same number is, so the editor writes to me, a much shortened transcript of a monograph on 'Primitive Methods of Moki Irrigation', which are now in the archives of the Smithsonian. The admirable novel, 'The Peculiar Treasure of Kings', is of course well known. Karslake wrote it in 1888–9, and the controversy that arose about the incident of the third chapter is still – sporadically and intermittently – continued.

The manuscript that follows now appears, of course, for the first time in print, and I acknowledge herewith my obligations to Karslake's father, Mr Patterson Karslake, for permission to publish.

I have set the account down word for word, with all the hiatuses and breaks that by nature of the extraordinary circumstances under which it was written were bound to appear in it. I have allowed it to end precisely as Karslake was forced to end it, in the middle of a sentence. God knows the real end is plain enough and was not far off when the poor fellow began the last phrase that never was to be finished.

The value of the thing is self-apparent. Besides the narrative of incidents it is a simple setting forth of a young man's emotions in the very face of violent death. You will remember the distinguished victim of the guillotine, a lady who on the scaffold begged that she might be permitted to write out the great thoughts that began to throng her mind. She was not allowed to do so, and the record is lost. Here is a case where the record is preserved. But Karslake, being a young man not very much given to introspection, his work is more a picture of things seen than a transcription of things thought. However, one may read between the lines; the very breaks are eloquent, while the break at the end speaks with a significance that no words could attain.

The manuscript in itself is interesting. It is written partly in pencil, partly in ink (no doubt from a fountain pen), on sheets of manila paper torn from some sort of long and narrow account-book. In two or three places there are smudges where the powder-blackened finger and thumb held the sheets momentarily. I would give much to own it, but Tejada will not give it up without Bass's permission, and Bass has gone to the Klondike.

As to Karslake himself. He was born in Raleigh, in North Carolina, in 1868, studied law at the State University, and went to the Bahamas in 1885 with the members of a government coast-survey commission. Gave up the practice of law and 'went in' for fiction and the study of the ethnology of North America about 1887. He was unmarried.

The reasons for his enlisting have long been misunderstood. It was known that at the time of his death he was a member of B Troop of the Sixth Regiment of United States Cavalry, and it was assumed that because of this fact Karslake was in financial difficulties and not upon good terms with his family. All this, of course, is untrue, and I have every reason to believe that Karslake at this time was planning a novel of military life in the Southwest, and, wishing to get in closer touch with the *milieu* of the story, actually enlisted in order to be able to write authoritatively. He saw no active service until the time when his narrative begins. The year of his death is uncertain. It was in the spring probably of 1896, in the twenty-eighth year of his age.

There is no doubt he would have become in time a great writer. A young man of twenty-eight who had so lively a sense of the value of accurate observation, and so eager a desire to produce that in the very face of death he could faithfully set down a description of his surroundings, actually laying down the rifle to pick up the pen, certainly was possessed of extraordinary faculties.

They came in sight early this morning just after we had had breakfast and had broken camp. The four of us – 'Bunt', 'Idaho', Estorijo and myself – were jogging on to the southward and had just come up out of the dry bed of some water-hole – the alkali was white as snow in the crevices – when Idaho pointed them out to us, three to the rear, two on one side, one on the other and – very far away – two ahead. Five minutes before, the desert was as empty as the flat of my hand. They seemed literally to have *grown* out of the sage-brush. We took them in through my field-glasses and Bunt made sure they were an outlying band of Hunt-in-the-Morning's bucks. I had thought, and so had all of us, that the rest of the boys had rounded up the whole of the old man's hostiles long since. We are at a loss to account for these fellows here. They seem to be well mounted.

We held a council of war from the saddle without halting, but there seemed very little to be done – but to go right along and wait for developments. At about eleven we found water – just a pocket in the bed of a dried stream – and stopped to water the ponies. I am writing this during the halt.

We have one hundred and sixteen rifle cartridges. Yesterday was Friday, and all day, as the newspapers say, 'the situation remained unchanged'. We expected surely that the night would see some rather radical change, but nothing happened, though we stood watch and watch till morning. Of yesterday's eight only six are in sight and the other two may have gone to bring up reserves. We now have two to the front, one on each side, and two to the rear, all far out of rifle-range.

The following paragraph is in an unsteady script and would appear to have been written in the saddle. The same peculiarity occurs from time to time in the narrative, and occasionally the writing is so broken as to be illegible.

On again after breakfast. It is about eight-fifteen. The other two have come back – without 'reserves', thank God. Very possibly they did not go away at all, but were hidden by a dip in the ground. I cannot see that any of them are nearer. I have watched one to the left of us steadily for more than half an hour and I am sure that he has not shortened the distance between himself and us. What their plans are hell only knows, but this silent, persistent escorting tells on the nerves. I do not think I am afraid – as yet. It does not seem possible but that we will ride into La Paz at the end of the fortnight exactly as we had planned, meet Greenock according to arrangements and take the stage on to the railroad. Then next month I shall be in San Antonio and report at headquarters. Of course, all this is to be, of course; and this business of today will make a good story to tell. It's an experience – good 'material'. Very naturally I cannot now see how I am going to get out of this [the word 'alive' has here been erased], but of course I *will*. Why 'of course'? I don't know. Maybe I am trying to deceive myself. Frankly, it looks like a situation insoluble; but the solution will surely come right enough in good time.

Eleven o'clock – No change.

Two-thirty p.m. – We are halted to tighten girths and to take a single swallow of the canteens. One of them rode in a wide circle from the rear to the flank, about ten minutes ago, conferred a moment with his fellow, then fell back to his old position. He wears some sort of red cloth or blanket. We reach no more water till day after tomorrow. But we have sufficient. Estorijo has been telling funny stories *en route*.

Four o'clock p.m. – They have closed up perceptibly, and we have been debating about trying one of them with Idaho's Winchester. No use; better save the ammunition. It looks . . .'

The next words are undecipherable, but from the context they would appear to be 'as if they would attack tonight'.

. . . we have come to know certain of them now by nicknames. We speak of the Red One, or the Little One, or the One with the Feather, and Idaho has named a short thickset fellow on our right 'Little Willie'. By God, I wish something would turn up – relief or fight. I don't care which. How Estorijo can cackle on, reeling off his senseless, pointless funny stories, is beyond me. Bunt is almost as bad. They understand the fix we are in, I *know*, but how they can take it so easily is the staggering surprise. I feel that I am as courageous as either of them, but levity seems horribly inappropriate. I could kill Estorijo joyfully.

Sunday morning – Still no developments. We were so sure of something turning up last night that none of us pretended to sleep. But nothing stirred. There is no sneaking out of the circle at night. The moon is full. A jack-rabbit could not have slipped by them unseen last night.

Nine o'clock (in the saddle) – We had coffee and bacon as usual at sunrise; then on again to the southeast just as before. For half an hour after starting the Red One and two others were well within rifle-shot, nearer than ever before. They had worked in from the flank. But before Idaho could get a chance at them they dipped into a shallow arroyo, and when they came out on the other side were too far away to think of shooting.

Ten o'clock – All at once we find there are nine instead of eight; where and when this last one joined the band we cannot tell. He wears a sombrero and army trousers, but the upper part of his body is bare. Idaho calls him 'Half and half'. He is riding a – They're coming.

Later – For a moment we thought it was the long-expected rush. The

Red One – he had been in the front – wheeled quick as a flash and came straight for us, and the others followed suit. Great Heavens, how they rode! We could hear them yelling on every side of us. We jumped off our ponies and stood behind them, the rifles across the saddles. But at four hundred yards they all pivoted about and cantered off again leisurely. Now they followed us as before – three in the front, two in the rear and two on either side. I do not think I am going to be frightened when the rush does come. I watched myself just now. I was excited, and I remember Bunt saying to me, 'Keep your shirt on, m'son'; but I was not afraid of being killed. Thank God for that! It is something I've long wished to find out, and now that I know it I am proud of it. Neither side fired a shot. I was not afraid. It's glorious. Estorijo is all right.

Sunday afternoon, one-thirty – No change. It is unspeakably hot.

Three-fifteen – The One with the Feather is walking, leading his pony. It seems to be lame.

With this entry Karslake ended page five, and the next page of the manuscript is numbered seven. It is very probable, however, that he made a mistake in the numerical sequence of his pages, for the narrative is continuous, and, at this point at least, unbroken. There does not seem to be any sixth page.

Four o'clock – Is it possible that we are to pass another night of suspense? They certainly show no signs of bringing on the crisis, and they surely would not attempt anything so late in the afternoon as this. It is a relief to feel that we have nothing to fear till morning, but the tension of watching all night long is fearful.

Later – Idaho has just killed the Little One.

Later – Still firing.

Later – Still at it.

Later, about five – A bullet struck within three feet of me.

Five-ten – Still firing.

Seven-thirty p.m., in camp – It happened so quickly that it was all over before I realised. We had our first interchange of shots with them late this afternoon. The Little One was riding from the front to the flank. Evidently he did not think he was in range – nor did any of us. All at once Idaho tossed up his rifle and let go without aiming – or so it seemed to me. The stock was not at his shoulder before the report came. About six seconds after the smoke had cleared away we could see the Little One begin to lean backwards in the saddle, and Idaho said grimly, 'I guess I got *you*.' The Little One leaned farther and farther till suddenly his head dropped back between his shoulder-blades. He held to his pony's mane with both hands for a long time and then all at once went off feet first.

His legs bent under him like putty as his feet touched the ground. The pony bolted.

Just as soon as Idaho fired the others closed right up and began riding around us at top speed, firing as they went. Their aim was bad as a rule, but one bullet came very close to me. At about half-past five they drew off out of range again and we made camp right where we stood. Estorijo and I are both sure that Idaho hit the Red One, but Idaho himself is doubtful, and Bunt did not see the shot. I could swear that the Red One all but went off his pony. However, he seems active enough now.

Monday morning – Still another night without attack. I have not slept since Friday evening. The strain is terrific. At daybreak this morning, when one of our ponies snorted suddenly, I cried out at the top of my voice. I could no more have repressed it than I could have stopped my blood flowing; and for half an hour afterwards I could feel my flesh crisping and pringling, and there was a sickening weakness at the pit of my stomach. At breakfast I had to force down my coffee. They are still in place, but now there are two on each side, two in the front, two in the rear. The killing of the Little One seems to have heartened us all wonderfully. I am sure we will get out – somehow. But oh! the suspense of it.

Monday morning, nine-thirty – Under way for over two hours. There is no new development. But Idaho has just said that they seem to be edging in. We hope to reach water today. Our supply is low, and the ponies are beginning to hang their heads. It promises to be a blazing hot day. There is alkali all to the west of us, and we just commence to see the rise of ground miles to the southward that Idaho says is the San Jacinto Mountains. Plenty of water there. The desert hereabout is vast and lonesome beyond words; leagues of sparse sage-brush, leagues of leper-white alkali, leagues of baking grey sand, empty, heat-ridden, the abomination of desolation; and always – in whichever direction I turn my eyes – always, in the midst of this pale-yellow blur, a single figure in the distance, blanketed, watchful, solitary, standing out sharp and distinct against the background of sage and sand.

Monday, about eleven o'clock – No change. The heat is appalling. There is just a –

Later – I was on the point of saying that there was just a mouthful of water left for each of us in our canteens when Estorijo and Idaho both at the same time cried out that they were moving in. It is true. They are within rifle range, but do not fire. We, as well, have decided to reserve our fire until something more positive happens.

Noon – The first shot – for today – from the Red One. We are halted. The shot struck low and to the left. We could see the sand spout up in a cloud just as though a bubble had burst on the surface of the ground.

They have separated from each other, and the whole eight of them are now in a circle around us. Idaho believes the Red One fired as a signal. Estorijo is getting ready to take a shot at the One with the Feather. We have the ponies in a circle around us. It looks as if now at last this is the beginning of the real business.

Later, twelve-thirty-five – Estorijo missed. Idaho will try with the Winchester as soon as the One with the Feather halts. He is galloping towards the Red One.

All at once, about two o'clock, the fighting began. This is the first let-up. It is now – God knows what time. They closed up suddenly and began galloping about us in a circle, firing all the time. They rode like madmen. I would not have believed that Indian ponies could run so quickly. What with their yelling and the incessant crack of their rifles and the thud of their ponies' feet our horses at first became very restless, and at last Idaho's mustang bolted clean away. We all stood to it as hard as we could. For about the first fifteen minutes it was hot work. The Spotted One is hit. We are certain of that much, though we do not know whose gun did the work. My poor old horse is bleeding dreadfully from the mouth. He has two bullets in the stomach, and I do not believe he can stand much longer. They have let up for the last few moments, but are still riding around us, their guns at 'ready'. Every now and then one of us fires, but the heat shimmer has come up over the ground since noon and the range is extraordinarily deceiving.

Three-ten – Estorijo's horse is down, shot clean through the head. Mine has gone long since. We have made a rampart of the bodies.

Three-twenty – They are at it again, tearing around us incredibly fast, every now and then narrowing the circle. The bullets are striking every-where now. I have no rifle, do what I can with my revolver, and try to watch what is going on in front of me and warn the others when they press in too close on my side.

Karslake nowhere accounts for the absence of his carbine. That a US trooper should be without his gun while traversing a hostile country is a fact difficult to account for.

Three-thirty – They have winged me – through the shoulder. Not bad, but it is bothersome. I sit up to fire, and Bunt gives me his knee on which to rest my right arm. When it hangs it is painful.

Quarter to four – It is horrible. Bunt is dying. He cannot speak, the ball having gone through the lower part of his face, but back, near the neck. It happened through his trying to catch his horse. The animal was struck in the breast and tried to bolt. He reared up, backing away, and as we had to keep him close to us to serve as a bulwark Bunt followed him out from the little circle that we formed, his gun in one hand, his other gripping the bridle. I suppose every one of the eight fired at him simultaneously, and down he went. The pony dragged him a little ways still clutching the bridle, then fell itself, its whole weight rolling on Bunt's chest. We have managed to get him in and secure his rifle, but he will not live. None of us knows him very well. He only joined us about a week ago, but we all liked him from the start. He never spoke of himself, so we cannot tell much about him. Idaho says he has a wife in Torreon, but that he has not lived with her for two years; they did not get along well together, it seems. This is the first violent death I have ever seen, and it astonishes me to note how *unimportant* it seems. How little anybody cares – after all. If I had been told of his death – the details of it, in a story or in the form of fiction – it is easily conceivable that it would have impressed me more with its importance than the actual scene has done. Possibly my mental vision is scaled to a larger field since Friday, and as the greater issues loom up one man more or less seems to be but a unit – more or less – in an eternal series. When he was hit he swung back against the horse, still holding by the rein. His feet slid from under him, and he cried out, 'My *God*!' just once. We divided his cartridges between us and Idaho passed me his carbine. The barrel was scorching hot.

They have drawn off a little and for fifteen minutes, though they still circle us slowly, there has been no firing. Forty cartridges left. Bunt's body (I think he is dead now) lies just back of me, and already the gnats – I can't speak of it.

Karslake evidently made the next few entries at successive intervals of time, but neglected in his excitement to note the exact hour as above. We may gather that 'They' made another attack and then repeated the assault so quickly that he had no chance to record it properly. I transcribe the entries in exactly the disjointed manner in which they occur in the original. The reference to the 'fire' is unexplainable.

I shall do my best to set down exactly what happened and what I do and think, and what I see.

The heat-shimmer spoiled my aim, but I am quite sure that either

This last rush was the nearest. I had started to say that though the heat-shimmer was bad, either Estorijo or myself wounded one of their ponies. We saw him stumble.

Another rush –

Our ammunition

Only a few cartridges left.

The Red One like a whirlwind only fifty yards away.

We fire separately now as they sneak up under cover of our smoke.

We put the fire out. Estorijo –

It is possible that Karslake had begun here to chronicle the death of the Mexican.

I have killed the Spotted One. Just as he wheeled his horse I saw him in a line with the rifle-sights and let him have it squarely. It took him straight in the breast. I could *feel* that shot strike. He went down like a sack of lead weights. By God, it was superb!

Later – They have drawn off out of range again, and we are allowed a breathing-spell. Our ponies are either dead or dying, and we have dragged them around us to form a barricade. We lie on the ground behind the bodies and fire over them. There are twenty-seven cartridges left.

It is now mid-afternoon. Our plan is to stand them off if we can till night and then to try an escape between them. But to what purpose? They would trail us so soon as it was light.

We think now that they followed us without attacking for so long because they were waiting till the lie of the land suited them. They wanted – no doubt – an absolutely flat piece of country, with no depressions, no hills or stream-beds in which we could hide, but which should be high upon the edges, like an amphitheatre. They would get us in the centre and occupy the rim themselves. Roughly, this is the bit of desert which witnesses our 'last stand'. On three sides the ground swells a very little – the rise is not four feet. On the third side it is open, and so flat that even lying on the ground as we do we can see (leagues away) the San Jacinto hills – 'from whence cometh no help'. It is all sand and sage, for ever and for ever. Even the sage is sparse – a bad place even for a coyote. The whole is flagellated with an intolerable heat and – now that the shooting is relaxed – oppressed with a benumbing, sodden silence – the silence of a primordial world. Such a silence as must have brooded over the Face of the Waters on the Eve of Creation – desolate, desolate, as though a colossal, invisible pillar – a pillar of the Infinitely Still, the pillar of Nirvana – rose for ever into the empty blue, human life an atom of microscopic dust crushed under its basis, and at the summit God Himself. And I find time to ask myself why, at this of all moments of my tiny lifespan, I am able to write as I do, registering impressions, keeping a finger upon the pulse of the spirit. But oh! if I had time now – time to write down the great thoughts that do throng the brain. They are there, I feel them, know them. No doubt the supreme exaltation of approaching death is the stimulus that one never experiences in the humdrum business of day-to-day existence. Such mighty thoughts! Unintelligible, but if I had time I could spell them out, *and how I could write then*! I feel that the whole secret of Life is within my reach; I can almost grasp it; I seem to feel that in just another instant I can see it all plainly, as the archangels see it all the time, as the great minds of the world, the great philosophers, have seen it once or twice, vaguely – a glimpse here and there, after years of patient study. Seeing thus I should be the equal of the gods. But it is not meant to be. There is a sacrilege in it. I almost seem to understand why it is kept from us. But the very reason of this withholding is in itself a part of the secret. If I could only, only set it down! – for whose eyes? Those of a wandering hawk? God knows. But never mind. I should have spoken – once; should have said the great Word for which the World since the evening and the morning of the First Day has listened. God knows. God knows. What a whirl is this? Monstrous incongruity. Philosophy and fighting troopers. The Infinite and dead horses. There's humour for you. The Sublime takes off its hat to the Ridiculous. Slip a cartridge into the breech and speculate about the Absolute. Keep one eye on your sights and the other on the Cosmos. Blow the reek of burned powder from before you so you may look over the edge of the abyss of the Great Primal Cause. Duck to the whistle of a bullet and commune with Schopenhauer. Perhaps I am a little mad. Perhaps I am supremely intelligent. But in either case I am not understandable to myself. How, then, be understandable to others? If these sheets of paper, this incoherence, is ever read, the others will understand it about as much as the investigating hawk. But none the less be it of record that I, Karslake, *saw*. It reads like Revelation: 'I, John, saw.' It is just that. There is something apocalyptic in it all. I have seen a vision, but cannot – there is the pitch of anguish in the impotence – bear record. If time were allowed to order and arrange the words of description, this exaltation of spirit, in that very space of time, would relax, and the describer lapse back to the level of the average again before he could set down the things he saw, the things he thought. The machinery of the mind that could coin the great Word is automatic, and the very force that brings the die near the blank metal supplies the motor power of the reaction before the impression is made . . . I stopped for an instant, looking up from the page, and at once the great vague panorama faded. I lost it all. The Cosmos has dwindled again to an amphitheatre of sage and sand, a vista of distant purple hills, the shimmer of scorching alkali, and in the middle distance there, those figures, blanketed, beaded, feathered, rifle in hand.

But for a moment I stood on Patmos.

The Ridiculous jostles the elbow of the Sublime and shoulders it from place as Idaho announces that he has found two more cartridges in Estorijo's pockets.

They rushed again. Eight more cartridges gone. Twenty-one left. They rush in this manner – at first the circle, rapid beyond expression, one figure succeeding the other so swiftly that the dizzied vision loses count and instead of seven of them there appear to be seventy. Then suddenly, on some indistinguishable signal, they contract this circle, and through the jets of powder-smoke Idaho and I see them whirling past our rifle-sights not one hundred yards away. Then their fire suddenly slackens, the smoke drifts by, and we see them in the distance again, moving about us at a slow canter. Then the blessed breathing-spell, while we peer out to know if we have killed or not, and count our cartridges. We have laid the twenty-one loaded shells that remain in a row between us, and after our first glance outward to see if any of them are down, our next is inward at that ever-shrinking line of brass and lead. We do not talk much. This is the end. We know it now. All of a sudden the conviction that I am to die here has hardened within me. It is, all at once, absurd that I should ever have supposed that I was to reach La Paz, take the east-bound train and report at San Antonio. It seems to me that I *knew*, weeks ago, that our trip was to end thus. I knew it – somehow – in Sonora, while we were waiting orders, and I tell myself that if I had only stopped to really think of it I could have foreseen today's bloody business.

Later – The Red One got off his horse and bound up the creature's leg. One of us hit him, evidently. A little higher, it would have reached the heart. Our aim is ridiculously bad – the heat-shimmer –

Later – Idaho is wounded. This last time, for a moment, I was sure the end had come. They were within revolver range and we could feel the vibration of the ground under their ponies' hoofs. But suddenly they drew off. I have looked at my watch; it is four o'clock.

Four o'clock – Idaho's wound is bad – a long, raking furrow in the right forearm. I bind it up for him, but he is losing a great deal of blood and is very weak.

They seem to know that we are only two by now, for with each rush they grow bolder. The slackening of our fire must tell them how scant is our ammunition.

Later – This last was magnificent. The Red One and one other with lines of blue paint across his cheek galloped right at us. Idaho had been lying with his head and shoulders propped against the neck of his dead pony. His eyes were shut, and I thought he had fainted. But as he heard them coming he struggled up, first to his knees and then to his feet – to his full height – dragging his revolver from his hip with his left hand. The whole right arm swung useless. He was so weak that he could only lift the revolver halfway – could not get the muzzle up. But though it sagged and dropped in his grip, he *would* die fighting. When he fired, the bullet threw up the sand not a yard from his feet, and then he fell on his face across the body of the horse. During the charge I fired as fast as I could, but evidently to no purpose. They must have thought that Idaho was dead, for as soon as they saw him getting to his feet they sheered their horses off and went by on either side of us. I have made Idaho comfortable. He is unconscious; have used the last of the water to give him a drink. He does not seem –

They continue to circle us. Their fire is incessant, but very wild. So long as I keep my head down I am comparatively safe.

Later – I think Idaho is dying. It seems he was hit a second time when he stood up to fire. Estorijo is still breathing; I thought him dead long since.

Four-ten – Idaho gone. Twelve cartridges left. Am all alone now.

Four-twenty-five – I am very weak.

Karslake was evidently wounded sometime between ten and twenty-five minutes after four. His notes make no mention of the fact.

Eight cartridges remain. I leave my library to my brother, Walter Patterson Karslake; all my personal effects to my parents, except the picture of myself taken in Baltimore in 1897, which I direct to be . . .

The next lines are undecipherable.

. . . at Washington, DC, as soon as possible. I appoint as my literary –

Four forty-five – Seven cartridges. Very weak and unable to move lower part of my body. Am in no pain. They rode in very close. The Red One is – An intolerable thirst –

I appoint as my literary executor my brother, Patterson Karslake. The notes on 'Coronado in New Mexico' should be revised.

My death occurred in western Arizona, April 15th, at the hands of a roving band of Hunt-in-the-Morning's bucks. They have –

Five o'clock – The last cartridge gone.

Estorijo still breathing. I cover his face with my hat. Their fire is incessant. Am much weaker. Convey news of death to Patterson Karslake, care of Corn Exchange Bank, New York City.

Five-fifteen – about – They have ceased firing, and draw together in a bunch. I have four cartridges left . . .

See conflicting note dated five o'clock.

. . . but am extremely weak. Idaho was the best friend I had in all the Southwest. I wish it to be known that he was a generous, open-hearted fellow, a kindly man, clean of speech and absolutely unselfish. He may be known as follows: Sandy beard, long sandy hair, scar on forehead, about six feet one inch in height. His real name is James Monroe Herndon; his profession that of government scout. Notify Mrs Herndon, Trinidad, New Mexico.

The writer is Arthur Staples Karslake, dark hair, height five feet eleven, body will be found near that of Herndon.

Luis Estorijo, Mexican –

Later – Two more cartridges.

Five-thirty – Estorijo dead.

It is half-past five in the afternoon of April fifteenth. They followed us from the eleventh – Friday – till today. It will . . .

The manuscript ends here.

The Ghost in the Crosstrees

ONE

Cyrus Ryder, the President of the South Pacific Exploitation Company, had at last got hold of a 'proposition' – all Ryder's schemes were, in his vernacular, 'propositions' – that was not only profitable beyond precedent or belief, but that also was, wonderful to say, more or less legitimate. He had got an 'island'. He had not discovered it. Ryder had not felt a deck under his shoes for twenty years other than the promenade deck of the ferry-boat *San Rafael* that takes him home to Berkeley every evening after 'business hours'. He had not discovered it, but 'Old Rosemary', captain of the barkentine *Scottish Chief* of Blyth, had done that very thing, and, dying before he was able to perfect the title, had made over his interest in it to his best friend and old comrade, Cyrus Ryder.

'Old Rosemary', I am told, first landed on the island – it is called Paa – in the later 1860s.

He established its location and took its latitude and longitude, but as minutes and degrees mean nothing to the lay reader, let it be said that the Island of Paa lies just below the equator, some 200 miles west of the Gilberts and 1,600 miles due east from Brisbane, in Australia. It is six miles long, three wide, and because of the prevailing winds and precipitous character of the coast can only be approached from the west during December and January.

'Old Rosemary' landed on the island, raised the American flag, had the crew witness the document by virtue of which he made himself the possessor, and then, returning to San Francisco, forwarded to the Secretary of State at Washington application for title. This was withheld till it could be shown that no other nation had a prior claim. While 'Old Rosemary' was working out the proof, he died, and the whole matter was left in abeyance till Cyrus Ryder took it up. By then there was a new Secretary in Washington and times were changed, so that the government of Ryder's native land was not so averse towards acquiring eastern possessions. The Secretary of State wrote to Ryder to say that the application would be granted upon his furnishing a bond for $50,000; and you may believe that the bond was forthcoming.

For in the first report upon Paa, 'Old Rosemary' had used the magic word 'guano'.

He averred, and his crew attested over their sworn statements, that Paa was covered to an average depth of six feet with the stuff, so that this last and biggest of 'Cy' Ryder's propositions was a vast slab of an extremely marketable product six feet thick, three miles wide and six miles long.

But no sooner had the title been granted when there came a dislocation in the proceedings that until then had been going forward so smoothly. Ryder called the Three Black Crows to him at this juncture, one certain afternoon in the month of April. They were his best agents. The plums that the 'Company' had at its disposal generally went to the trio, and if any man could 'put through' a dangerous and desperate piece of work, Strokher, Hardenberg and Ally Bazan were those men.

Of late they had been unlucky, and the affair of the contraband arms, which had ended in failure of cataclysmic proportions, yet rankled in Ryder's memory, but he had no one else to whom he could entrust the present proposition and he still believed Hardenberg to be the best boss on his list.

If Paa was to be fought for, Hardenberg, backed by Strokher and Ally Bazan, was the man of all men for the job, for it looked as though Ryder would not get the Island of Paa without a fight after all, and nitrate beds were worth fighting for.

'You see, boys, it's this way,' Ryder explained to the three as they sat around the spavined table in the grimy back room of Ryder's 'office'. 'It's this way. There's a scoovy after Paa, I'm told; he says he was there before "Rosemary", which is a lie, and that his gov'ment has given him title. He's got a kind of dough-dish up Portland way and starts for Paa as soon as ever he kin fit out. He's got no title, in course, but if he gits there afore we do and takes possession it'll take fifty years o' lawing an' injunctioning to git him off. So hustle is the word for you from the word go. We got a good start o' the scoovy. He can't put to sea within a week, while over yonder in Oakland Basin there's the *Idaho Lass*, as good a schooner, boys, as ever wore paint, all ready but to fit her new sails on her. Ye kin do it in less than no time. The stores will be goin' into her while ye're workin', and within the week I expect to see the *Idaho Lass* showing her heels to the Presidio. You see the point now, boys. If ye beat the scoovy – his name is Petersen, and his boat is called the *Elftruda* – we're to the wind'ard of a pretty pot o' money. If he gets away before you do – well, there's no telling; we prob'ly lose the island.'

TWO

About ten days before the morning set for their departure I went over to the Oakland Basin to see how the Three Black Crows were getting on.

Hardenberg welcomed me as my boat bumped alongside, and extending a great tarry paw, hauled me over the rail. The schooner was a wilderness of confusion, with the sails covering, apparently, nine-tenths of the decks, the remaining tenth encumbered by spars, cordage, tangled rigging, chains, cables and the like, all helter-skeltered together in such a haze of entanglements that my heart misgave me as I looked on it. Surely order would not issue from this chaos in four days' time with only three men to speed the work.

But Hardenberg was reassuring, and little Ally Bazan, the colonial, told me they would 'snatch her shipshape in the shorter end o' two days, if so be they must'.

I stayed with the Three Crows all that day and shared their dinner with them on the quarterdeck when, wearied to death with the strain of wrestling with the slatting canvas and ponderous boom, they at last threw themselves upon the hamper of 'cold snack' I had brought off with me and pledged the success of the venture in tin dippers full of Pilsener.

'And I'm thinking,' said Ally Bazan, 'as 'ow ye might as well turn in along o' us on board 'ere, instead o' hykin' back to town tonight. There's a fairish set o' currents up and daown 'ere about this time o' dye, and ye'd find it a stiff bit o' rowing.'

'We'll sling a hammick for you on the quarterdeck, m'son,' urged Hardenberg.

And so it happened that I passed my first night aboard the *Idaho Lass*.

We turned in early. The Three Crows were very tired, and only Ally Bazan and I were left awake at the time when we saw the eight-thirty ferryboat negotiating for her slip on the Oakland side. Then we also went to bed.

And now it becomes necessary, for a better understanding of what is to follow, to mention with some degree of particularisation the places and manners in which my three friends elected to take their sleep, as well as the condition and berth of the schooner *Idaho Lass*.

Hardenberg slept upon the quarterdeck, rolled up in an army blanket and a tarpaulin. Strokher turned in below in the cabin upon the fixed lounge by the dining-table, while Ally Bazan stretched himself in one of the bunks in the fo'c'sle.

As for the location of the schooner, she lay out in the stream, some three or four cables' length off the yards and docks of a ship-building concern. No other ship or boat of any description was anchored nearer than at least three hundred yards. She was a fine, roomy vessel, three-masted, about a hundred and fifty feet in length overall. She lay head upstream, and from where I slung my hammock by Hardenberg on the quarterdeck I could see her tops sharply outlined against the sky above the Golden Gate before I went to sleep.

I suppose it was very early in the morning – nearer two than three – when I awoke. Some movement on the part of Hardenberg – as I afterwards found out – had aroused me. But I lay inert for a long minute trying to find out why I was not in my own bed, in my own home, and to account for the rushing, rippling sound of the tide eddies sucking and chuckling around the *Lass*'s rudder-post.

Then I became aware that Hardenberg was awake. I lay in my hammock, facing the stern of the schooner, and as Hardenberg had made up his bed between me and the wheel he was directly in my line of vision when I opened my eyes, and I could see him without any other movement than that of raising the eyelids. Just now, as I drifted more and more into wakefulness, I grew proportionately puzzled and perplexed to account for a singularly strange demeanour and conduct on the part of my friend.

He was sitting up in his place, his knees drawn up under the blanket, one arm thrown around both, the hand of the other arm resting on the neck and supporting the weight of his body. He was broad awake. I could see the green shine of our riding lantern in his wide-open eyes, and from time to time I could hear him muttering to himself, 'What is it? What is it? What the devil is it, anyhow?' But it was not his attitude, nor the fact of his being so broad awake at the unseasonable hour, nor yet his unaccountable words that puzzled me the most. It was the man's eyes and the direction in which they looked that startled me.

His gaze was directed not upon anything on the deck of the boat, nor upon the surface of the water near it, but upon something behind me and at a great height in the air. I was not long in getting myself broad awake.

THREE

I rolled out on the deck and crossed over to where Hardenberg sat huddled in his blankets.

'What the devil – ' I began.

He jumped suddenly at the sound of my voice, then raised an arm and pointed towards the top of the foremast.

'D'ye see it?' he muttered. 'Say, huh? D'ye see it? I thought I saw it last night, but I wasn't sure. But there's no mistake now. D'ye see it, Mr Dixon?'

I looked where he pointed. The schooner was riding easily at anchor, the surface of the bay was calm, but overhead the high white sea-fog was rolling in. Against it the foremast stood out like the hand of an illuminated town clock, and there was not a detail of its rigging that was not as distinct as if etched against the sky.

And yet I saw nothing.

'Where?' I demanded, and again and again, 'where?'

'In the crosstrees,' whispered Hardenberg. 'Ah, look there.'

He was right. Something was stirring there, something that I had mistaken for the furled tops'l. At first it was but a formless bundle, but as Hardenberg spoke it stretched itself, it grew upright, it assumed an erect attitude, it took the outlines of a human being. From head to heel a casing housed it in, a casing that might have been anything at that hour of the night and in that strange place – a shroud, if you like, a winding-sheet – anything; and it is without shame that I confess to a creep of the most disagreeable sensation I have ever known as I stood at Hardenberg's side on that still, foggy night and watched the stirring of that nameless, formless shape standing gaunt and tall and grisly and wrapped in its winding-sheet upon the crosstrees of the foremast of the *Idaho Lass*.

We watched and waited breathless for an instant. Then the creature on the foremast laid a hand upon the lashings of the tops'l and undid them. Then it turned, slid to the deck by I know not what strange process, and, still hooded, still shrouded, still lapped about by its mummy-wrappings, seized a rope's end. In an instant the jib was set and stood on hard and billowing against the night wind. The tops'l followed. Then the figure moved forward and passed behind the companionway of the fo'c'sle.

We looked for it to appear upon the other side, but looked in vain. We saw it no more that night.

What Hardenberg and I told each other between the time of the disappearing and the hour of breakfast I am now ashamed to recall. But at last we agreed to say nothing to the others – for the time being. Just after breakfast, however, we two had a few words by the wheel on the quarterdeck. Ally Bazan and Strokher were forward.

'The proper thing to do,' said I – it was a glorious, exhilarating morning, and the sunlight was flooding every angle and corner of the schooner – 'the proper thing to do is to sleep on deck by the foremast tonight with our pistols handy and interview the – party if it walks again.'

'Oh, yes,' cried Hardenberg heartily. 'Oh, yes; that's the proper thing. Of course it is. No manner o' doubt about that, Mr Dixon. Watch for the party – yes, with pistols. Of course it's the proper thing. But I know one man that ain't going to do no such thing.'

'Well,' I remember to have said reflectively, 'well – I guess I know another.'

But for all our resolutions to say nothing to the others about the night's occurrences, we forgot that the tops'l and jib were both set and both drawing.

'An' w'at might be the bloomin' notion o' setting the bloomin' kite and jib?' demanded Ally Bazan not half an hour after breakfast. Shamelessly Hardenberg, at a loss for an answer, feigned an interest in the grummets of the life-boat cover and left me to lie as best I might.

But it is not easy to explain why one should raise the sails of an anchored ship during the night, and Ally Bazan grew very suspicious. Strokher, too, had something to say, and in the end the whole matter came out.

Trust a sailor to give full value to anything savouring of the supernatural. Strokher promptly voted the ship a 'queer old hooker anyhow, and about as seaworthy as a hen-coop'. He held forth at great length upon the subject.

'You mark my words, now,' he said. 'There's been some fishy doin's in this 'ere vessel, and it's like somebody's bin done to death crool hard, an' 'e wants to git away from the smell o' land, just like them as is killed on blue water. That's w'y 'e takes an' sets the sails between dark an' dawn.'

But Ally Bazan was thoroughly and wholly upset, so much so that at first he could not speak. He went pale and paler while we stood talking it over, and crossed himself – he was a Catholic – furtively behind the water-butt.

'I ain't never 'a' been keen on ha'nts anyhow, Mr Dixon,' he told me aggrievedly at dinner that evening. 'I got no use for 'em. I ain't never known any good to come o' anything with a ha'nt tagged to it, an' we're makin' a ill beginnin' o' this island business, Mr Dixon – a blyme ill beginnin'. I mean to stye awyke tonight.'

But if he was awake the little colonial was keeping close to his bunk at the time when Strokher and Hardenberg woke me at about three in the morning.

I rolled out and joined them on the quarterdeck and stood beside them watching. The same figure again towered, as before, grey and ominous in the crosstrees. As before, it set the tops'l; as before, it came down to the deck and raised the jib; as before, it passed out of sight amid the confusion of the forward deck.

But this time we all ran towards where we last had seen it, stumbling over the encumbered decks, jostling and tripping, but keeping wonderfully close together. It was not twenty seconds from the time the creature had disappeared before we stood panting upon the exact spot we had last seen it. We searched every corner of the forward deck in vain. We looked over the side. The moon was up. This night there was no fog. We could see for miles each side of us, but never a trace of a boat was visible, and it was impossible that any swimmer could have escaped the merciless scrutiny to which we subjected the waters of the bay in every direction.

Hardenberg and I dived down into the fo'c'sle. Ally Bazan was sound asleep in his bunk and woke stammering, blinking and bewildered by the lantern we carried.

'I sye,' he cried, all at once scrambling up and clawing at our arms, 'D'd the bally ha'nt show up agyne?' And as we nodded he went on more aggrievedly than ever – 'Oh, I sye, y' know, I daon't like this. I eyen't shipping in no bloomin' 'ooker wot carries a ha'nt for supercargo. They waon't no good come o' this cruise – no, they waon't. It's a sign, that's wot it is. I eyen't goin' to buck ag'in' no signs – it eyen't human nature, no it eyen't. You mark my words, Bud Hardenberg, we clear this port with a ship wot has a ha'nt an' we waon't never come back agyne, my hearty.'

That night he berthed aft with us on the quarterdeck, but though we stood watch and watch till well into the dawn, nothing stirred about the foremast. So it was the next night, and so the night after that. When three successive days had passed without any manifestation the keen edge of the business became a little blunted and we declared that an end had been made.

Ally Bazan returned to his bunk in the fo'c'sle on the fourth night, and the rest of us slept the hours through unconcernedly.

But in the morning there were the jib and tops'l set and drawing as before.

FOUR

After this we began experimenting – on Ally Bazan. We bunked him forward and we bunked him aft, for someone had pointed out that the 'ha'nt' walked only at the times when the colonial slept in the fo'c'sle. We found this to be true. Let the little fellow watch on the quarterdeck with us and the night passed without disturbance. As soon as he took up his quarters forward the haunting recommenced. Furthermore, it began to appear that the 'ha'nt' carefully refrained from appearing to him. He of us all had never seen the thing. He of us all was spared the chills and the harrowings that laid hold upon the rest of us during these still grey hours after midnight when we huddled on the deck of the *Idaho Lass* and watched the sheeted apparition in the rigging; for by now there was no more charging forward in attempts to run the ghost down. We had passed that stage long since.

But so far from rejoicing in this immunity or drawing courage therefrom, Ally Bazan filled the air with his fears and expostulations. Just the fact that he was in some way differentiated from the others – that he was singled out, if only for exemption – worked upon him. And that he was unable to scale his terrors by actual sight of their object excited them all the more.

And there issued from this a curious consequence. He, the very one who had never seen the haunting, was also the very one to unsettle what little common sense yet remained to Hardenberg and Strokher. He never allowed the subject to be ignored – never lost an opportunity of referring to the doom that o'erhung the vessel. By the hour he poured into the ears of his friends lugubrious tales of ships, warned as this one was, that had cleared from port never to be seen again. He recalled to their minds parallel incidents that they themselves had heard; he foretold the fate of the *Idaho Lass* when the land should lie behind and she should be alone in mid-ocean with this horrid supercargo that took liberties with the rigging, and at last one particular morning, two days before that which was to witness the schooner's departure, he came out flatfooted to the effect that 'Gaw-blyme him, he couldn't stand the gaff no longer, no he couldn't, so help him, that if the owners were wishful for to put to sea' (doomed to some unnamable destruction) 'he for one wa'n't fit to die, an' was going to quit that blessed day'. For the sake of appearances, Hardenberg and Strokher blustered and fumed, but I could hear the crack in Strokher's voice as plain as in a broken ship's bell. I was not surprised at what happened later in the day, when he told the others that he was a very sick man. A congenital stomach trouble, it seemed – or was it a liver complaint – had found him out again. He had contracted it when a lad at Trincomalee, diving for pearls; it was acutely painful, it appeared. Why, gentlemen, even at that very moment, as he stood there talking – Hi, yi! O Lord ! – talking, it was a-griping of him something uncommon, so it was. And no, it was no manner of use for him to think of going on this voyage; sorry he was, too, for he'd made up his mind, so he had, to find out just what was wrong with the foremast, etc.

And thereupon Hardenberg swore a great oath and threw down the capstan bar he held in his hand.

'Well, then,' he cried wrathfully, 'we might as well chuck up the whole business. No use going to sea with a sick man and a scared man.'

'An' there's the first word o' sense,' cried Ally Bazan, 'I've heard this long day. "Scared", he says; aye, right ye are, me bully.'

'It's Cy Rider's fault,' the three declared after a two-hours' talk. 'No business giving us a schooner with a ghost aboard. Scoovy or no scoovy, island or no island, guano or no guano, we don't go to sea in the haunted hooker called the *Idaho Lass*.'

No more they did. On board the schooner they had faced the supernatural with some kind of courage born of the occasion. Once on shore, and no money could hire, no power force them to go aboard a second time.

The affair ended in a grand wrangle in Cy Rider's back office, and just twenty-four hours later the bark *Elftruda*, under the command of Captain Jens Petersen, cleared from Portland, bound for 'a cruise to South Pacific ports – in ballast'.

*   *   *

Two years after this I took Ally Bazan with me on a duck-shooting excursion in the 'Toolies' back of Sacramento, for he is a handy man about a camp and can row a boat as softly as a drifting cloud.

We went about in a cabin cat of some thirty feet over all, the rowboat towing astern. Sometimes we did not go ashore to camp, but slept aboard. On the second night of this expedient I woke in my blankets on the floor of the cabin to see the square of grey light that stood for the cabin door darkened by – it gave me the same old start – a sheeted figure. It was going up the two steps to the deck. Beyond question it had been in the cabin. I started up and followed it. I was too frightened not to – if you can see what

I mean. By the time I had got the blankets off and had thrust my head above the level of the cabin hatch the figure was already in the bows, and, as a matter of course, hoisting the jib.

I thought of calling Ally Bazan, who slept by me on the cabin floor, but it seemed to me at the time that if I did not keep that figure in sight it would elude me again, and, besides, if I went back in the cabin I was afraid that I would bolt the door and remain under the bedclothes till morning. I was afraid to go on with the adventure, but I was much more afraid to go back.

So I crept forward over the deck of the sloop. The 'ha'nt' had its back towards me, fumbling with the ends of the jib halyards. I could hear the creak of new ropes as it undid the knot, and the sound was certainly substantial and commonplace. I was so close by now that I could see every outline of the shape. It was precisely as it had appeared on the crosstrees of the *Idaho*, only, seen without perspective, and brought down to the level of the eye, it lost its exaggerated height.

It had been kneeling upon the deck. Now, at last, it rose and turned about, the end of the halyards in its hand. The light of the earliest dawn fell squarely on the face and form, and I saw, if you please, Ally Bazan himself. His eyes were half shut, and through his open lips came the sound of his deep and regular breathing.

At breakfast the next morning I asked, 'Ally Bazan, did you ever walk in your sleep.'

'Aye,' he answered, 'years ago, when I was by wye o' being a lad, I used allus to wrap the bloomin' sheets around me. An' crysy things I'd do the times. But the 'abit left me when I grew old enough to tyke me whisky strite and have hair on me fyce.'

I did not 'explain away' the ghost in the crosstrees either to Ally Bazan or to the other two Black Crows. Furthermore, I do not now refer to the Island of Paa in the hearing of the trio. The claims and title of Norway to the island have long since been made good and conceded – even by the State Department at Washington – and I understand that Captain Petersen has made a very pretty fortune out of the affair.

FITZ JAMES O'BRIEN

Fitz James O'Brien (1828–1862) is often considered one of the forerunners of modern science fiction. He was born Michael O'Brien in County Cork, and educated at the University of Dublin. He is believed to have been at one time a soldier in the British service. On leaving college he went to London, where he edited a periodical in aid of the World's Fair of 1851. About 1852, having spent his inheritance of eight thousand pounds, he went to the United States, changed his name to Fitz James and devoted his attention to literature. His first important literary connection was with *Harper's Magazine*, and beginning in February 1853 with 'The Two Skulls', he contributed more than sixty pieces in prose and verse to that periodical. Among the short stories he wrote for the popular magazines of the day, 'The Diamond Lens' (1858) and 'The Wonder Smith' (1859) are unsurpassed as creations of the imagination, and 'Horrors Unknown' (1858) has been referred to as 'the single most striking example of surrealistic fiction to pre-date *Alice in Wonderland*'. Two of his poems were published in *The Ballads of Ireland* (1856). In New York he was ranked as the most able among the brilliant set of Bohemians in Manhattan. In 1861, at the outbreak of the Civil War, he joined the New York National Guard and was severely wounded in a skirmish on 26 February 1862; he lingered until April, when he died at Cumberland, Maryland.

My Wife's Tempter

ONE

A Predestined Marriage

Elsie and I were to be married in less than a week. It was rather a strange match, and I knew that some of our neighbours shook their heads over it and said that no good would come. The way it came to pass was thus.

I loved Elsie Burns for two years, during which time she refused me three times. I could no more help asking her to have me, when the chance offered, than I could help breathing or living. To love her seemed natural to me as existence. I felt no shame, only sorrow, when she rejected me; I felt no shame either when I renewed my suit. The neighbours called me mean-spirited to take up with any girl that had refused me as often as Elsie Burns had done; but what cared I about the neighbours? If it is black weather, and the sun is under a cloud every day for a month, is that any reason why the poor farmer should not hope for the blue sky and the plentiful burst of warm light when the dark month is over? I never entirely lost heart. Do not, however, mistake me. I did not mope, and moan, and grow pale, after the manner of poetical lovers. No such thing. I went bravely about my business, ate and drank as usual, laughed when the laugh went round, and slept soundly and woke refreshed. Yet all this time I loved – desperately loved – Elsie Burns. I went wherever I hoped to meet her, but did not haunt her with my attentions. I behaved to her as any friendly young man would have behaved: I met her and parted from her cheerfully. She was a good girl, too, and behaved well. She had me in her power – how a woman in Elsie's situation could have mortified a man in mine! – but she never took the slightest advantage of it. She danced with me when I asked her, and had no foolish fears of allowing me to see her home of nights, after a ball was over, or of wandering with me through the pleasant New England fields when the wild flowers made the paths like roads in fairyland.

On the several disastrous occasions when I presented my suit I did it simply and manfully, telling her that I loved her very much, and would do everything to make her happy if she would be my wife. I made no fulsome protestations, and did not once allude to suicide. She, on the other hand, calmly and gravely thanked me for my good opinion, but with the same calm gravity rejected me. I used to tell her that I was grieved; that I would not press her; that I would wait and hope for some change in her feelings. She had an esteem for me, she would say, but could not marry me. I never asked her for any reasons. I hold it to be an insult to a woman of sense to demand her reasons on such an occasion. Enough for me that she did not then wish to be my wife; so that the old intercourse went on – she cordial and polite as ever, I never for one moment doubting that the day would come when my roof tree would shelter her, and we should smile together over our fireside at my long and indefatigable wooing.

I will confess that at times I felt a little jealous – jealous of a man named Hammond Brake, who lived in our village. He was a weird, saturnine fellow, who made no friends among the young men of the neighbourhood, but who loved to go alone, with his books and his own thoughts for company. He was a studious and, I believe, a learned young man, and there was no avoiding the fact that he possessed considerable influence over Elsie. She liked to talk with him in corners, or in secluded nooks of the forest, when we all went out blackberry gathering or picnicking. She read books that he gave her, and whenever a discussion arose relative to any topic higher than those ordinary ones we usually canvassed, Elsie appealed to Brake for his opinion, as a disciple consulting a beloved master. I confess that for a time I feared this man as a rival. A little closer observation, however, convinced me that my suspicions were unfounded. The relations between Elsie and Hammond Brake were purely intellectual. She reverenced his talents and acquirements, but she did not love him. His influence over her, nevertheless, was none the less decided.

In time – as I thought all along – Elsie yielded. I was what was considered a most eligible match, being tolerably rich, and Elsie's parents were most anxious to have me for a son-in-law. I was good-looking and well educated enough, and the old people, I believe, pertinaciously dinned all my advantages into my little girl's ears. She battled against the marriage for a long time with a strange persistence – all the more strange because she never alleged the slightest personal dislike of me; but after a vigorous cannonading from her own garrison (in which, I am proud to say, I did not in any way join), she hoisted the white flag and surrendered.

I was very happy. I had no fear about being able to gain Elsie's heart. I think – indeed I know – that she had liked me all along, and that her refusals were dictated by other feelings than those of a personal nature. I only guessed as much then. It was some time before I knew all.

As the day approached for our wedding Elsie did not appear at all stricken with woe. The village gossips had not the smallest opportunity for establishing a romance with a compulsory bride for the heroine. Yet to me it seemed as if there was something strange about her. A vague terror appeared to beset her. Even in her most loving moments, when resting in my arms, she would shrink away from me, and shudder as if some cold wind had suddenly struck upon her. That it was caused by no aversion to me was evident, for she would the moment after, as if to make amends, give me one of those voluntary kisses that are sweeter than all others.

Once only did she show any emotion. When the solemn question was put to her, the answer to which was to decide her destiny, I felt her hand – which was in mine – tremble. As she gasped out a convulsive, 'Yes,' she gave one brief, imploring glance at the gallery on the right. I placed the ring upon her finger, and looked in the direction in which she gazed. Hammond Brake's dark countenance was visible looking over the railings, and his eyes were bent sternly on Elsie. I turned quickly round to my bride, but her brief emotion, of whatever nature, had vanished. She was looking at me anxiously, and smiling – somewhat sadly – through her maiden's tears.

The months went by quickly, and we were very happy. I learned that Elsie really loved me, and of my love for her she had proof long ago. I will not say that there was no cloud upon our little horizon. There was one, but it was so small, and appeared so seldom, that I scarcely feared it. The old vague terror seemed still to attack my wife. If I did not know her to be pure as heaven's snow, I would have said it was a *remorse*. At times she scarcely appeared to hear what I said, so deep would be her reverie. Nor did those moods seem pleasant ones. When rapt in such, her sweet features would contract, as if in a hopeless effort to solve some mysterious problem. A sad pain, as it were, quivered in her white, drooped eyelids. One thing I particularly remarked: *She spent hours at a time gazing at the west.* There was a small room in our house whose windows, every evening, flamed with the red light of the setting sun. Here Elsie would sit and gaze westward, so motionless and entranced that it seemed as if her soul was going down with the day. Her conduct to me was curiously varied. She apparently loved me very much, yet there were times when she absolutely avoided me. I have seen her strolling through the fields, and left the house with the intention of joining her, but the moment she caught sight of me approaching she has fled into the neighbouring copse, with so evident a wish to avoid me that it would have been absolutely cruel to follow.

Once or twice the old jealousy of Hammond Brake crossed my mind, but I was obliged to dismiss it as a frivolous suspicion. Nothing in my wife's conduct justified any such theory. Brake visited us once or twice a week – in fact, when I returned from my business in the village, I used to find him seated in the parlour with Elsie, reading some favourite author, or conversing on some novel literary topic; but there was no disposition to avoid my scrutiny. Brake seemed to come as a matter of right; and the perfect unconsciousness of furnishing any grounds for suspicion with which he acted was a sufficient answer to my mind for any wild doubts that my heart may have suggested.

Still I could not but remark that Brake's visits were in some manner connected with Elsie's melancholy. On the days when he had appeared and departed, the gloom seemed to hang more thickly than ever over her head. She sat, on such occasions, all the evening at the western window, silently gazing at the cleft in the hills through which the sun passed to his repose.

At last I made up my mind to speak to her. It seemed to me to be my duty, if she had a sorrow, to partake of it. I approached her on the matter with the most perfect confidence that I had nothing to learn beyond the existence of some girlish grief, which a confession and a few loving kisses would exorcise for ever.

'Elsie,' I said to her one night, as she sat, according to her custom, gazing westward, like those maidens of the old ballads of chivalry watching for the knights that never came – 'Elsie, what is the matter with you, darling? I have noticed a strange melancholy in you for some time past. Tell me all about it.'

She turned quickly round and gazed at me with eyes wide open and face filled with a sudden fear. 'Why do you ask me that, Mark?' she answered. 'I have nothing to tell.'

From the strange, startled manner in which this reply was given, I felt convinced that she had something to tell, and instantly formed a determination to discover what it was. A pang shot through my heart as I thought that the woman whom I held dearer than anything on earth hesitated to trust me with a petty secret.

I believed I understood. I was tolerably rich. I knew it could not be any secret over milliners' bills or women's usual money troubles. God help me! I felt sad enough at the moment, though I kissed her back and ceased to question her. I felt sad, because my instinct told me that she deceived me; and it is very hard to be deceived, even in trifles, by those we love. I left her sitting at her favourite window, and walked out into the fields. I wanted to think.

I remained out until I saw lights in the parlour shining through the dusky evening; then I returned slowly. As I passed the windows – which were near the ground, our house being cottage-built – I looked in. Hammond Brake was sitting with my wife. She was sitting in a rocking chair opposite to him, holding a small volume open on her lap. Brake was talking to her very earnestly, and she was listening to him with an expression I had never before seen on her countenance. Awe, fear and admiration were all blent together in those dilating eyes. She seemed absorbed, body and soul, in what this man said. I shuddered at the sight. A vague terror seized upon me; I hastened into the house. As I entered the room rather suddenly, my wife started and hastily concealed the little volume that lay on her lap in one of her wide pockets. As she did so, a loose leaf escaped from the volume and slowly fluttered to the floor, unobserved by either her or her companion. But I had my eye upon it. I felt that it was a clue.

'What new novel or philosophical wonder have you both been poring over?' I asked quite jovially, stealthily watching at the same time the telltale embarrassment under which Elsie was labouring.

Brake, who was not in the least discomposed, replied. 'That,' said he, 'is a secret which must be kept from you. It is an advance copy, and is not to be shown to anyone except your wife.'

'Ha!' cried I, 'I know what it is. It is your volume of poems that Ticknor is publishing. Well, I can wait until it is regularly for sale.'

I knew that Brake had a volume in the hands of the publishing house I mentioned, with a vague promise of publication some time in the present century. Hammond smiled significantly, but did not reply. He evidently wished to cultivate this supposed impression of mine. Elsie looked relieved, and heaved a deep sigh. I felt more than ever convinced that a secret was beneath all this. So I drew my chair over the fallen leaf that lay unnoticed on the carpet, and talked and laughed with Hammond Brake genially, as if nothing was on my mind, while all the time a great load of suspicion lay heavily at my heart.

At length Hammond Brake rose to go. I wished him good-night, but did not offer to accompany him to the door. My wife supplied this omitted courtesy, as I had expected. The moment I was alone I picked up the book leaf from the floor. It was *not* the leaf of a volume of poems. Beyond that, however, I learned nothing. It contained a string of paragraphs printed in the biblical fashion, and the language was biblical in style. It seemed to be a portion of some religious book. Was it possible that my wife was being converted to the Romish faith? Yes, that was it. Brake was a Jesuit in disguise – I had heard of such things – and had stolen into the bosom of my family to plant there his destructive errors. There could be no longer any doubt of it. This was some portion of a Romish book – some infamous Popish publication. Fool that I was not to see it all before! But there was yet time. I would forbid him the house.

I had just formed this resolution when my wife entered. I put the strange leaf in my pocket and took my hat.

'Why, you are not going out, surely?' cried Elsie, surprised.

'I have a headache,' I answered. 'I will take a short walk.'

Elsie looked at me with a peculiar air of distrust. Her woman's instinct told her that there was something wrong. Before she could question me, however, I had left the room and was walking rapidly on Hammond Brake's track.

He heard the footsteps, and I saw his figure, black against the sky, stop and peer back through the dusk to see who was following him.

'It is I, Brake,' I called out. 'Stop; I wish to speak with you.'

He stopped, and in a minute or so we were walking side by side along the road. My fingers itched at that moment to be on his throat. I commenced the conversation.

'Brake,' I said, 'I'm a very plain sort of man, and I never say anything without good reason. What I came after you to tell you is that I don't wish you to come to my house any more, or to speak with Elsie any further than the ordinary salutations go. It's no joke. I'm quite in earnest.'

Brake started, and, stopping short, faced me suddenly in the road. 'What have I done?' he asked. 'You surely are too sensible a man to be jealous, Dayton.'

'Oh,' I answered scornfully, 'not jealous in the ordinary sense of the word, a bit. But I don't think your company good company for my wife, Brake. If you *will* have it out of me, I suspect you of being a Roman Catholic, and of trying to convert my wife.'

A smile shot across his face, and I saw his sharp white teeth gleam for an instant in the dusk.

'Well, what if I am a Papist?' he said, with a strange tone of triumph in his voice. 'The faith is not criminal. Besides, what proof have you that I was attempting to proselyte your wife?'

'This,' said I, pulling the leaf from my pocket – 'this leaf from one of those devilish Papist books you and she were reading this evening. I picked it up from the floor. Proof enough, I think!'

In an instant Brake had snatched the leaf from my hand and torn it into atoms.

'You shall be obeyed,' he said. 'I will not speak with Elsie as long as she is your wife. Good-night. You think I'm a Papist, then, Dayton? You're a clever fellow!'

And with rather a sneering chuckle he marched on along the road and vanished into the darkness.

TWO

The Secret Discovered

Brake came no more. I said nothing to Elsie about his prohibition, and his name was never mentioned. It seemed strange to me that she should not speak of his absence, and I was very much puzzled by her silence. Her moodiness seemed to have increased, and, what was most remarkable, in proportion as she grew more and more reserved, the intenser were the bursts of affection which she exhibited for me. She would strain me to her bosom and kiss me, as if she and I were about to be parted for ever. Then for hours she would remain sitting at her window, silently gazing, with that terrible, wistful gaze of hers, at the west.

I will confess to having watched my wife at this time. I could not help it. That some mystery hung about her I felt convinced. I must fathom it or die. Her honour I never for a moment doubted; yet there seemed to weigh continually upon me the prophecy of some awful domestic calamity. This time the prophecy was not in vain.

About three weeks after I had forbidden Brake my house, I was strolling over my farm in the evening, apparently inspecting my agriculture but in reality speculating on that topic which latterly was ever present to me.

There was a little knoll covered with evergreen oaks at the end of the lawn. It was a picturesque spot, for on one side the bank went off into a sheer precipice of about eighty feet in depth, at the bottom of which a pretty pool lay, that in the summer time was fringed with white water-lilies. I had thought of building a summerhouse at this spot, and now my steps mechanically directed themselves towards the place. As I approached I heard voices. I stopped and listened eagerly. A few seconds enabled me to ascertain that Hammond Brake and my wife were in the copse talking together. She still followed him, then; and he, scoundrel that he was, had broken his promise. A fury seemed to fill my veins as I made this discovery. I felt the impulse strong upon me to rush into the grove, and then and there strangle the villain who was poisoning my peace. But with a powerful effort I restrained myself. It was necessary that I should overhear what was said. I threw myself flat on the grass, and so glided silently into the copse until I was completely within earshot. This was what I heard.

My wife was sobbing. 'So soon – so soon? I – Hammond, give me a little time!'

'I cannot, Elsie. My chief orders me to join him. You must prepare to accompany me.'

'No, no!' murmured Elsie. 'He loves me so! And I love him. Our child, too – how can I rob him of our unborn babe?'

'Another sheep for our flock,' answered Brake solemnly. 'Elsie, do you forget your oath? Are you one of us, or are you a common hypocrite, who will be of us until the hour of self-sacrifice, and then fly like a coward? Elsie, you must leave tonight.'

'Ah! my husband, my husband!' sobbed the unhappy woman.

'You have no husband, woman,' cried Brake harshly. 'I promised Dayton not to speak to you as long as you were his wife, but the vow was annulled before it was made. Your husband in God yet awaits you. You will yet be blessed with the true spouse.'

'I feel as if I were going to die,' cried Elsie. 'How can I ever forsake him – he who was so good to me?'

'Nonsense! no weakness. He is not worthy of you. Go home and prepare for your journey. You know where to meet me. I will have everything ready, and by daybreak there shall be no trace of us left. Beware of permitting your husband to suspect anything. He is not very shrewd at such things – he thought I was a Jesuit in disguise – but we had better be careful. Now go. You have been too long here already. Bless you, sister.'

A few faint sobs, a rustling of leaves, and I knew that Brake was alone. I rose, and stepped silently into the open space in which he stood. His back was towards me. His arms were lifted high over his head with an exultant gesture, and I could see his profile, as it slightly turned towards me, illuminated with a smile of scornful triumph. I put my hand suddenly on his throat from behind, and flung him on the ground before he could utter a cry.

'Not a word,' I said, unclasping a short-bladed knife which I carried; 'answer my questions, or, by heaven, I will cut your throat from ear to ear!'

He looked up into my face with an unflinching eye, and set his lips as if resolved to suffer all.

'What are you? Who are you? What object have you in the seduction of my wife?'

He smiled, but was silent.

'Ah! you won't answer. We'll see.'

I pressed the knife slowly against his throat. His face contracted spasmodically, but although a thin red thread of blood sprang out along the edge of the blade, Brake remained mute. An idea suddenly seized me. This sort of death had no terrors for him. I would try another. There was the precipice. I was twice as powerful as he was, so I seized him in my arms, and in a moment transported him to the margin of the steep, smooth cliff, the edge of which was garnished with the tough stems of the wild vine. He seemed to feel it was useless to struggle with me, so passively allowed me to roll him over the edge. When he was suspended in the air, I gave him a vine stem to cling to and let him go. He swung at a height of eighty feet, with face upturned and pale. He dared not look down. I seated myself on the edge of the cliff, and with my knife began to cut into the thick vine a foot or two above the place of his grasp. I was correct in my calculation. This terror was too much for him. As he saw the notch in the vine getting deeper and deeper, his determination gave way.

'I'll answer you,' he gasped out, gazing at me with starting eyeballs; 'what do you ask?'

'What are you?' was my question, as I ceased cutting at the stem.

'A Mormon,' was the answer, uttered with a groan. 'Take me up. My hands are slipping. Quick!'

'And you wanted my wife to follow you to that infernal Salt Lake City, I suppose?'

'For God's sake, release me! I'll quit the place, never to come back. Do help me up, Dayton – I'm falling!'

I felt mightily inclined to let the villain drop; but it did not suit my purpose to be hung for murder, so I swung him back again on the sward, where he fell panting and exhausted.

'Will you quit the place tonight?' I said. 'You'd better. By heaven, if you don't, I'll tell all the men in the village, and we'll lynch you, as sure as your name is Brake.'

'I'll go – I'll go,' he groaned. 'I swear never to trouble you again.'

'You ought to be hanged, you villain. Be off!'

He slunk away through the trees like a beaten dog; and I went home in a state bordering on despair. I found Elsie crying. She was sitting by the window as of old. I knew now why she gazed so constantly at the west. It was her Mecca. Something in my face, I suppose, told her that I was labouring under great excitement. She rose startled as soon as I entered the room.

'Elsie,' said I, 'I am come to take you home.'

'Home? Why, *I am* at home, am I not? What do you mean?'

'No. This is no longer your home. You have deceived me. You are a Mormon. I know all. You have become a convert to that apostle of hell, Brigham Young, and you cannot live with me. I love you still, Elsie, dearly; but – you must go and live with your father.'

DAVID PHILLIPS

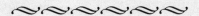

At a Sap-Head

A fellow named Kendall and I palled up the day after he joined our company. We were in a sugar factory at the time, where we were to spend the night before going into the line. I had found two planks and trestles, and thought, in my ignorance, to make a bed where the rats would not disturb me, and while I surveyed the available floor space the slinking form of a large rat, just discernible in the dimming light, made me turn sharply round. My planks struck Kendall's and, in trying to save them, he received the full weight of one on his foot.

'Clumsy swine!' he shouted, and hopped in a threatening attitude towards me. As I put up my fists, I appraised his ability. He was lean and lanky. I decided to punch him in the stomach and upper-cut him as he crumpled. But the platoon-sergeant intervened and warned us both for guard from two to four o'clock the following morning.

Kendall spat copiously after the retiring sergeant.

'Stop that!' I said in mock seriousness, 'or I'll have you up for dumb insolence.'

Kendall laughed outright.

'Well, if we've got to go on guard together we may as well kip together.' He had two planks but no trestles, so we jammed the four planks together on my trestles, and next morning on guard we got to know each other better.

Looking back, I am vaguely conscious that the human associations of those war years live more vividly in my memory than the horror and unspeakable realities of war, much as they tormented me.

Kendal and I did many duties together after that and we grew in each other's regard. Of course we never voiced it – at twenty years of age one does not, nor, I suppose, at sixty. I don't know. But how else can I explain why he cursed me more abusively than my fellows? Or that my references to his mode of travel along the trenches as being due to chronic 'wind-up' caused him to smile and make dumb signs with his fingers, yet when others said so he would rise in a flash to silence them with his clenched fists.

One night when Kendall and I, together with two others, were over the parados busily digging, the enemy's machine-guns traversed in our direction. It was soon after nine o'clock when Jerry started to strafe us pretty generally along the line with 'minnies', 'coal-boxes', 'flying pigs', 'toffee apples', aerial torpedoes, 'flying fishes,' 'pipsqueaks' – a very mixed assortment from his stock, to be recognised by whichever of their names you knew them.

Soon we heard the cry: 'Stretcher bearers!' Again and again it was repeated as we crouched lower in our now deepening pit.

'Down Sap 26 – shouldn't wonder,' Kendall said, rising and plying his spade once more. D Company's getting it good and heavy. Damned if I don't think we are better off out here over the – ' A pipsqueak exploded near by and the sprayed earth tinkled on our steel helmets.

The next minute our captain dropped into the pit. We stopped working and wondered what he wanted. He spoke to me: 'A minnie has dropped plump into the middle of the support bay of Sap 26 and wiped all four of them out, poor chaps, and the two men at the sap-head have been sent down with shell-shock. I want you and someone else to man the sap-head and hang out as long as you possibly can, because the company is short of men and I can't spare any to remain in support. If you get into trouble you must send up a couple of Verey lights and make your way back to the front line. Now, who'll you take with you?'

'Me, sir!' Kendall answered quickly.

'Right! You others must come to the front line. This job must wait.'

We gathered our tools together and prepared to make our way back to the front line.

'Sergeant Popple and I will come with you as far as the support bay. Wait for us at the entrance to the sap.'

Arrived at the entrance, we waited for the captain and Sergeant Popple. They soon came up, bringing the Verey light pistol with them.

'All OK?' the captain asked.

We nodded.

'Then lead the way – you'll find it's knee deep in mud. Halt at the support bay, or where the bay was before the minnie dropped. We're sure to straggle out going through the mud.'

For the first few yards of the sap – a roughly hewn trench leading forwards from our front line – the going was good and the desultory shelling ceased. Then the mud became thicker, almost knee high, and footholds none too easy. And the squelching as each foot was lifted out of the mud seemed deafening in contrast with the piercing quiet that had descended on our sector.

I floundered into a hole, loin high in the mud. ' 'Ware hole,' I whispered over my shoulder to Kendall and heard him pass the warning on to the captain, who in turn passed it on to Sergeant Popple. And in a few moments more I heard the captain's muffled curses as he floundered as I had done.

At last we arrived at the minnie hole, where the support bay had been.

'Jerry could hear us a mile off,' Kendall whispered.

'How much farther to the sap-head?' the captain asked.

'Another sixty feet or so,' I replied.

'All right. We'll give you ten minutes by my watch, and unless you signal us before that we'll return to the front line. I'll have you relieved as soon as I can, but it won't be before morning. Don't make yourselves objectionable, because I can't spare any men to support you. Good luck!'

The mud was not so deep at the sap-head. Kendall made himself comfortable on the small fire-step close to the supply of Mills bombs, having first put a couple handy beside him. He looked at his watch: 'Five minutes to ten,' he whispered. 'They'll be back in the front line by now. Say, Jerry's only a few yards away, isn't he?'

'Yes,' I answered. 'No need to whisper, but don't shout. Jerry's sap-head is about twenty-five yards from here. Sometimes, when it's quiet, you can hear him knock a tin over. I believe they've got a little dug-out at their sap-head.'

'Seems damn silly, doesn't it.' Kendall remarked. 'Couple of Jerries, or so, twenty-five yards over there, and us over here, sitting on our backsides doing nothing.'

'Shift farther up, then I can sit down and help you. When Jerry sends a couple of bombs over after he's had his supper we'll send one over just to let him know we're still awake.'

'We shan't have had any supper though. Have you anything to eat?' Kendall asked.

'No. Have you?'

'Not a thing, only these hard biscuits.'

Apart from two small explosions near by and our reply, the night was comparatively quiet. But a continuous booming as of distant thunder came from the direction of the Somme. Kendall noted it: 'Worse places than this, I suppose,' he said.

'Yes. Still you might have had a soft lookout job in the front line. What did you want to come down here for, anyway? Always thought you were windy,' I bantered.

'So I am,' he confessed; 'windy as hell.'

'So am I.'

'Then why did the captain call on –'

'Shut up! I haven't told him yet.'

Kendall became reminiscent as a rat scuttled up the bank to the side of us. 'Funny, that night in the sugar factory. Lord, how I cursed that sergeant sticking us on guard together! And here we are – snug as a couple of bugs in a rug.'

'Not so strange after all. Perhaps, if we knew Jerry better, there'd be none of this,' I ventured.

'Perhaps so. Yes. And here we sit, and over there Jerry sits, lousy as hell – platoons of 'em in column, route-marching all over you; drink that's one part water and four parts chloride of lime and brought up from the well at

Ecurie in two-gallon petrol tins; a bath every eighteen days and a shave when you're lucky enough to find a puddle that hasn't been stirred for an hour or so. What the devil made you join up?'

'The papers talked me into it – and vanity, I suppose,' I answered.

And so we talked through the night, gathering our greatcoats around us in the chill of the morning before dawn. A night crammed full of self-revelation – interesting as nothing else – of intimacies conveyed half-banteringly, yet with a veneer of cynicism!

And at dawn we eyed each other, a little shamefacedly perhaps, with a new interest and greater understanding.

'Gets colder between stand-to and stand-down,' Kendall remarked. He jumped down from the fire-step, where he had been looking towards the German lines. 'The sun'll get stronger presently. Keep an eye on that poppy' – it grew on the edge of the trench – 'watch it open. That'll help the time to pass. Blimey!' he continued. 'We've done eight hours already. Must report to the union when we get back.'

Sergeant Popple crawled warily up to the sap-head, carrying two hunks of bread, two small pieces of bacon and a dixie of cold tea. We welcomed him as uproariously as the proximity of the two sap-heads allowed.

'Well, Pop,' Kendall said, 'how are things?'

'Lost a lot of men in the bombardment last night – Jerry's got our range to an inch. Davies gone, poor fellow, and Wellshead; Ashton blown to pieces; and Wheeler, poor kid. Only seventeen too! Got out here by bluffing his age and now a shell's taken his head clean off while he was standing on the fire-step. Goodness knows how many have had Blighty ones.'

Sergeant Popple looked grave as he stood with bent back, biting the ends of his grey moustache, the mud dripping from his puttees.

We ate the breakfast he had brought, filled our water bottles with the cold tea that was over, and asked him when he thought we would be relieved.

'Can't say,' he replied. 'Won't be before this afternoon, anyway. And cookie's got a touch of nerves, so I'll bring you along some grub when I get the chance. Captain wants you to keep a sharp lookout from this sap-head, and you're not to leave it on any account.'

'Right-o, Pop! Kiss the captain for me,' Kendall answered, and we watched Sergeant Popple down the sap, crouching low and carrying the empty dixie.

'Some say, "Good old Pop!" ' I ventured.

'Some don't so say,' Kendall replied with gusto.

The afternoon turned in an hour from sunshine to rain. A wind sprang up, a regular gale, and from over the German lines heavy clouds rolled disgorging torrential rains. Dinner-time had long since passed and Sergeant

Popple had not brought us any. We were hungry as we stood in the lee of the firing-plate, which, sand-bagged on the other side except for the peep-hole, formed the sap-head. So we munched the few scraps of hard biscuits that were left and took draughts from our cold tea.

At six o'clock we tossed for sleeping. Kendall won, and tucking himself well into the corner of the fire-step, with his waterproof sheet pegged to the sand-bags so that his head and body were completely covered, he tried to sleep. I heard him muttering to himself every now and then; he cursed the conditions, the rain, the lice and, above all, the relieving party that had not arrived. But it was evident he would not be able to sleep. He was already wet through from the thighs downwards as I was.

'Thank your lucky stars you're not out here,' I said, as I heard the scratching of his lighter and knew, although I could not see, that he was going to light a cigarette. He did not reply, but started cursing again.

The rain came down still heavier and the wind swept it across the open, washing the trunk of the tree on our right – such a tree: dead, shell-torn, barkless!

Night came. We continued to take turns at resting on the fire-step; one resting, the other standing at the far corner and looking out over the lines into the darkness, which was relieved now and again by a fizzing Verey light. At midnight our artillery made a show and the Germans replied vigorously. In no man's land, as we were, it was comparatively safe, though the shells screeching overhead in both directions were particularly nerve-racking in our exhausted state.

Kendall cursed the relieving party again and again for not coming. All that night he cursed them venomously; for no one had been to see us, to bring food, and our biscuits and cold tea were long since finished. We no longer attempted to rest. Drenched to the skin and painfully in need of sleep, we propped ourselves up on the fire-step or in the trench, now a quagmire. And Kendall's obsession, the relieving party, soon made it impossible for him to stay on the lookout. And as for me, every stake in no man's land turned into a stalking German after a momentary stare, and I would have to look away and blink before the Germans would revert to stakes once more.

After stand-to on the following morning we were relieved. Dog-tired and hungry, we returned to the front line, where only the minimum of sentries were on duty owing to the shortage of men. We were given hot tea, bread and bacon, and we went down a dug-out to sleep.

Soon – it seemed about five minutes afterwards – we were roused again and placed on sentry duty in the front line. Perhaps our periscope was a little too high, for Jerry paid us some invidious attention, so with the dirt showering all about us we lowered it for a while.

After two hours Corporal Simpson brought two men to relieve us. I was looking through the periscope at the time and Kendall, who sat cleaning his rifle, was the first to see them.

'What do you want?' Kendall asked the corporal.

'Brought the relief, of course,' the corporal replied.

'Relief! We don't want a bloody relief. We've held this position for thirty-four hours twenty-seven minutes. Clear out or I'll plug you!'

Tired as I was, it was some seconds before I realised that this was no ordinary banter, that Kendall still imagined we were holding the sap-head. I turned round towards him.

'Clear out, you blighter!' Kendall shouted, and with a quick movement slid the bolt of his rifle back and forced a bullet into the breach.

I fell on him, pinning his shoulders to the ground, and, with Corporal Simpson and the assistance of the two men, barely managed to restrain him. And as I sprawled across his chest I looked into his staring, glassy eyes and realised he was mad – stark, staring mad!

WILLIAM PITTENGER

William Pittenger (1840–1904) enlisted with the 2nd Ohio Infantry Regiment shortly after the first Battle of Bull Run, anxious to fight in the Civil War. He served in campaigns in Kentucky and Tennessee, but his singular moment of glory came on the night of 12 April 1862, when he and twenty-one other volunteers embarked on a secret raid deep into Confederate territory to cut the rail link between Marietta and Chattanooga. At Kenesaw Mountain, the raiders pirated the engine *General* and headed off for Chattanooga, only to run out of fuel near Graysville. The Confederate engine in pursuit, the *Texas*, soon caught up with the men and all were captured in short order. J. J. Andrews and seven of his men were executed at Atlanta, and the others were imprisoned in Atlanta, where Pittenger says they were treated very well. At Atlanta, eight of the raiders managed to make their escape late at night and walk their way to the North in pairs. But Pittenger and the rest remained imprisoned, eventually being transferred to Castle Thunder in Richmond, until a parole was arranged in May 1863. Weakened and ill from his imprisonment, Pittenger was discharged from the service in August 1863. For their part in the raid, Pittenger and his comrades were awarded the Congressional Medal of Honor. Pittenger died in California.

The Locomotive Chase in Georgia

The railroad raid to Georgia, in the spring of 1862, has always been considered to rank high among the striking and novel incidents of the Civil War. At that time General O. M. Mitchel, under whose authority it was organised, commanded Union forces in middle Tennessee, consisting of a division of Buell's army. The Confederates were concentrating at Corinth, Mississippi, and Grant and Buell were advancing by different routes towards that point. Mitchel's orders required him to protect Nashville and the country around, but allowed him great latitude in the disposition of his division, which, with detachments and garrisons, numbered nearly seventeen thousand men. His attention had long been strongly turned towards the liberation of east Tennessee, which he knew that President Lincoln also earnestly desired, and which would, if achieved, strike a most damaging blow at the resources of the rebellion. A Union army once in possession of east Tennessee would have the inestimable advantage, found nowhere else in the South, of operating in the midst of a friendly population, and having at hand abundant supplies of all kinds. Mitchel had no reason to believe that Corinth would detain the Union armies much longer than Fort Donelson had done, and was satisfied that as soon as that position had been captured the next movement would be eastward toward Chattanooga, thus throwing his own division in advance. He determined, therefore, to press into the heart of the enemy's country as far as possible, occupying strategical points before they were adequately defended and assured of speedy and powerful reinforcement. To this end his measures were vigorous and well chosen.

On 8 April 1862 – the day after the battle of Pittsburg Landing, of which, however, Mitchel had received no intelligence – he marched swiftly southward from Shelbyville, and seized Huntsville in Alabama on 11 April, and then sent a detachment westward over the Memphis and Charleston Railroad to open railway communication with the Union army at Pittsburg Landing. Another detachment, commanded by Mitchel in person, advanced on the same day seventy miles by rail directly into the enemy's territory, arriving unchecked with two thousand men within thirty miles of Chattanooga – in two hours' time he could now reach that point – the most important position in the West. Why did he not go on? The story of the railroad raid is the answer. The night before breaking camp at Shelbyville, Mitchel sent an expedition secretly into the heart of Georgia to cut the railroad communications of Chattanooga to the south and east. The fortune of this attempt had a most important bearing upon his movements, and will now be narrated.

In the employ of General Buell was a spy named James J. Andrews, who had rendered valuable services in the first year of the war, and had secured the full confidence of the Union commanders. In March 1862, Buell had sent him secretly with eight men to burn the bridges west of Chattanooga; but the failure of expected cooperation defeated the plan, and Andrews, after visiting Atlanta, and inspecting the whole of the enemy's lines in that vicinity and northward, had returned, ambitious to make another attempt. His plans for the second raid were submitted to Mitchel, and on the eve of the movement from Shelbyville to Huntsville Mitchel authorised him to take twenty-four men, secretly enter the enemy's territory, and, by means of capturing a train, burn the bridges on the northern part of the Georgia State Railroad, and also one on the East Tennessee Railroad where it approaches the Georgia State line, thus completely isolating Chattanooga, which was virtually ungarrisoned.

The soldiers for this expedition, of whom the writer was one, were selected from the three Ohio regiments belonging to General J. W. Sill's brigade, being simply told that they were wanted for secret and very dangerous service. So far as is known, not a man chosen declined the perilous honour. Our uniforms were exchanged for ordinary Southern dress, and all arms except revolvers were left in camp. On 7 April, by the roadside about a mile east of Shelbyville, in the late evening twilight, we met our leader. Taking us a little way from the road, he quietly placed before us the outlines of the romantic and adventurous plan, which was: to break into small detachments of three or four, journey eastward into the Cumberland Mountains, then work southward, travelling by rail after we were well within the Confederate lines, and finally, the evening of the third day after the start, meet Andrews at Marietta, Georgia, more than two hundred miles away. When questioned, we were to profess ourselves Kentuckians going to join the Southern army.

On the journey we were a good deal annoyed by the swollen streams and the muddy roads consequent on three days of almost ceaseless rain. Andrews was led to believe that Mitchel's column would inevitably be delayed; and as we were expected to destroy the bridges the very day that Huntsville was entered, he took the responsibility of sending word to our different groups that our attempt would be postponed one day – from Friday to Saturday, April 12. This was a natural but a most lamentable error of judgement.

One of the men detailed was belated, and did not join us at all. Two others were very soon captured by the enemy; and though their true character was not detected, they were forced into the Southern army, and two reached Marietta, but failed to report at the rendezvous. Thus, when we assembled very early in the morning in Andrews's room at the Marietta Hotel for final consultation before the blow was struck we were but twenty, including our leader. All preliminary difficulties had been easily overcome, and we were in good spirits. But some serious obstacles had been revealed on our ride from Chattanooga to Marietta the previous evening. The railroad was found to be crowded with trains, and many soldiers were among the passengers. Then the station – Big Shanty – at which the capture was to be effected had recently been made a Confederate camp. To succeed in our enterprise it would be necessary first to capture the engine in a guarded camp with soldiers standing around as spectators, and then to run it from one to two hundred miles through the enemy's country, and to deceive or overpower all trains that should be met – a large contract for twenty men. Some of our party thought the chances of success so slight, under existing circumstances, that they urged the abandonment of the whole enterprise. But Andrews declared his purpose to succeed or die, offering to each man, however, the privilege of withdrawing from the attempt – an offer no one was in the least disposed to accept. Final instructions were then given, and we hurried to the ticket-office in time for the northward-bound mail-train, and purchased tickets for different stations along the line in the direction of Chattanooga.

Our ride, as passengers, was but eight miles. We swept swiftly around the base of Kenesaw Mountain, and soon saw the tents of the Confederate forces camped at Big Shanty gleam white in the morning mist. Here we were to stop for breakfast, and attempt the seizure of the train. The morning was raw and gloomy, and a rain, which fell all day, had already begun. It was a painfully thrilling moment. We were but twenty, with an army about us, and a long and difficult road before us, crowded with enemies. In an instant we were to throw off the disguise which had been our only protection, and trust to our leader's genius and our own efforts for safety and success. Fortunately we had no time for giving way to reflections and conjectures which could only unfit us for the stern task ahead.

When we stopped, the conductor, the engineer, and many of the passengers hurried to breakfast, leaving the train unguarded. Now was the moment of action. Ascertaining that there was nothing to prevent a rapid start, Andrews, our two engineers, Brown and Knight, and the firemen hurried forward, uncoupling a section of the train consisting of three empty baggage or box-cars, the locomotive and the tender. The engineers and the firemen sprang into the cab of the engine, while Andrews, with hand on the rail and foot on the step, waited to see that the remainder of the party had gained entrance into the rear box-car. This seemed difficult and slow, though it really consumed but a few seconds, for the car stood on a considerable bank, and the first who came were pitched in by their comrades, while these in turn dragged in the others, and the door was instantly closed.

A sentinel, with musket in hand, stood not a dozen feet from the engine, watching the whole proceeding; but before he or any of the soldiers or guards around could make up their minds to interfere all was done, and Andrews, with a nod to his engineer, stepped on board. The valve was pulled wide open, and for a moment the wheels slipped round in rapid, ineffective revolutions; then, with a bound that jerked the soldiers in the box-car from their feet, the little train darted away, leaving the camp and the station in the wildest uproar and confusion. The first step of the enterprise was triumphantly accomplished.

According to the timetable, of which Andrews had secured a copy, there were two trains to be met. These presented no serious hindrance to our attaining high speed, for we could tell just where to expect them. There was also a local freight not down on the timetable, but which could not be far distant. Any danger of collision with it could be avoided by running according to the schedule of the captured train until it was passed; then at the highest possible speed we could run to the Oostenaula and Chickamauga bridges, lay them in ashes, and pass on through Chattanooga to Mitchel at Huntsville, or wherever eastward of that point he might be found, arriving long before the close of the day. It was a brilliant prospect, and so far as human estimates can determine it would have been realised had the day been Friday instead of Saturday. Friday every train had been on time, the day dry, the road in perfect order. Now the road was in disorder, every train far behind time, and two 'extras' were approaching us. But of these unfavourable conditions we knew nothing, and pressed confidently forward.

We stopped frequently, and at one point tore up the track, cut telegraph wires, and loaded on cross-ties to be used in bridge-burning. Wood and water were taken without difficulty, Andrews very coolly telling the story to which he adhered throughout the run – namely, that he was one of General Beauregard's officers, running an impressed powder-train through to that commander at Corinth. We had no good instruments for track-raising, as we had intended rather to depend upon fire; but the amount of time spent in taking up a rail was not material at this stage of our journey, as we easily kept on the time of our captured train. There was a wonderful exhilaration in passing swiftly by towns and stations through the heart of an enemy's country in this manner. It possessed just enough of the spice of danger, in this part of the run, to render it thoroughly enjoyable. The slightest accident to our engine, however, or a miscarriage in any part of our programme, would have completely changed the conditions.

At Etowah we found the *Yonah*, an old locomotive owned by an iron company, standing with steam up; but not wishing to alarm the enemy till the local freight had been safely met, we left it unharmed. Kingston, thirty miles from the starting-point, was safely reached. A train from Rome,

Georgia, on a branch road, had just arrived and was waiting for the morning mail – our train. We learned that the local freight would soon come also, and, taking the side-track, waited for it. When it arrived, however, Andrews saw, to his surprise and chagrin, that it bore a red flag, indicating another train not far behind. Stepping over to the conductor, he boldly asked: 'What does it mean that the road is blocked in this manner when I have orders to take this powder to Beauregard without a minute's delay?' The answer was interesting, but not reassuring: 'Mitchel has captured Huntsville, and is said to be coming to Chattanooga, and we are getting everything out of there.' He was asked by Andrews to pull his train a long way down the track out of the way, and promptly obeyed.

It seemed an exceedingly long time before the expected 'extra' arrived, and when it did come it bore another red flag. The reason given was that the 'local', being too great for one engine, had been made up in two sections, and the second section would doubtless be along in a short time. This was terribly vexatious; yet there seemed nothing to do but to wait. To start out between the sections of an extra train would be to court destruction. There were already three trains around us, and their many passengers and others were all growing very curious about the mysterious train, manned by strangers, which had arrived on the time of the morning mail. For an hour and five minutes from the time of arrival at Kingston we remained in this most critical position. The sixteen of us who were shut up tightly in a box-car – personating Beauregard's ammunition – hearing sounds outside, but unable to distinguish words, had perhaps the most trying position. Andrews sent us, by one of the engineers, a cautious warning to be ready to fight in case the uneasiness of the crowd around led them to make any investigation, while he himself kept near the station to prevent the sending off of any alarming telegram. So intolerable was our suspense, that the order for a deadly conflict would have been felt as a relief. But the assurance of Andrews quieted the crowd until the whistle of the expected train from the north was heard; then as it glided up to the depot, past the end of our side-track, we were off without more words.

But unexpected danger had arisen behind us. Out of the panic at Big Shanty two men emerged, determined, if possible, to foil the unknown captors of their train. There was no telegraph station, and no locomotive at hand with which to follow; but the conductor of the train, W. A. Fuller, and Anthony Murphy, foreman of the Atlanta railway machine-shops, who happened to be on board of Fuller's train, started on foot after us as hard as they could run. Finding a hand-car they mounted it and pushed forward till they neared Etowah, where they ran on the break we had made in the road, and were precipitated down the embankment into the ditch. Continuing with more caution, they reached Etowah and found the *Yonah*, which was at once pressed into service, loaded with soldiers who were at hand, and hurried with flying wheels towards Kingston. Fuller prepared to fight at that point, for he knew of the tangle of extra trains, and of the lateness of the regular trains, and did not think we should be able to pass. We had been gone only four minutes when he arrived and found himself stopped by three long, heavy trains of cars, headed in the wrong direction. To move them out of the way so as to pass would cause a delay he was little inclined to afford – would, indeed, have almost certainly given us the victory. So, abandoning his engine, he with Murphy ran across to the Rome train, and, uncoupling the engine and one car, pushed forward with about forty armed men. As the Rome branch connected with the main road above the depot, he encountered no hindrance, and it was now a fair race. We were not many minutes ahead.

Four miles from Kingston we again stopped and cut the telegraph. While trying to take up a rail at this point we were greatly startled. One end of the rail was loosened, and eight of us were pulling at it, when in the distance we distinctly heard the whistle of a pursuing engine. With a frantic effort we broke the rail, and all tumbled over the embankment with the effort. We moved on, and at Adairsville we found a mixed train (freight and passenger) waiting, but there was an express on the road that had not yet arrived. We could afford no more delay, and set out for the next station, Calhoun, at terrible speed, hoping to reach that point before the express, which was behind time, should arrive. The nine miles which we had to travel were left behind in less than the same number of minutes. The express was just pulling out, but, hearing our whistle, backed before us until we were able to take the side-track. It stopped, however, in such a manner as completely to close up the other end of the switch. The two trains, side by side, almost touched each other, and our precipitate arrival caused natural suspicion. Many searching questions were asked, which had to be answered before we could get the opportunity of proceeding. We in the box-car could hear the altercation, and were almost sure that a fight would be necessary before the conductor would consent to 'pull up' in order to let us out. Here again our position was most critical, for the pursuers were rapidly approaching.

Fuller and Murphy saw the obstruction of the broken rail in time and reversed their engine, to prevent wreck, but the hindrance was for the present insuperable. Leaving all their men behind, they started for a second foot-race. Before they had gone far they met the train we had passed at Adairsville and turned it back after us. At Adairsville they dropped the cars, and with locomotive and tender loaded with armed men, they drove forward at the highest speed possible. They knew that we were not many minutes ahead, and trusted to overhaul us before the express train could be safely passed.

But Andrews had told the powder story again with all his skill, and added a direct request in peremptory form to have the way opened before him, which the Confederate conductor did not see fit to resist; and just before the pursuers arrived at Calhoun we were again under way. Stopping once more to cut wires and tear up the track, we felt a thrill of exhilaration to which we had long been strangers. The track was now clear before us to Chattanooga; and even west of that city we had good reason to believe that we should find no other train in the way till we had reached Mitchel's lines. If one rail could now be lifted we would be in a few minutes at the Oostenaula bridge; and that burned, the rest of the task would be little more than simple manual labour, with the enemy absolutely powerless. We worked with a will.

But in a moment the tables were turned. Not far behind we heard the scream of a locomotive bearing down upon us at lightning speed. The men on board were in plain sight and well armed. Two minutes – perhaps one – would have removed the rail at which we were toiling; then the game would have been in our own hands, for there was no other locomotive beyond that could be turned back after us. But the most desperate efforts were in vain. The rail was simply bent, and we hurried to our engine and darted away, while remorselessly after us thundered the enemy.

Now the contestants were in clear view, and a race followed unparalleled in the annals of war. Wishing to gain a little time for the burning of the Oostenaula bridge, we dropped one car, and, shortly after, another; but they were 'picked up' and pushed ahead to Resaca. We were obliged to run over the high trestles and covered bridge at that point without a pause. This was the first failure in the work assigned us.

The Confederates could not overtake and stop us on the road; but their aim was to keep close behind, so that we might not be able to damage the road or take in wood or water. In the former they succeeded, but not in the latter. Both engines were put at the highest rate of speed. We were obliged to cut the wire after every station passed, in order that an alarm might not be sent ahead; and we constantly strove to throw our pursuers off the track, or to obstruct the road permanently in some way, so that we might be able to burn the Chickamauga bridges, still ahead. The chances seemed good that Fuller and Murphy would be wrecked. We broke out the end of our last box-car and dropped cross-ties on the track as we ran, thus checking their progress and getting far enough ahead to take in wood and water at two separate stations. Several times we almost lifted a rail, but each time the coming of the Confederates within rifle-range compelled us to desist and speed on. Our worst hindrance was the rain. The previous day (Friday) had been clear, with a high wind, and on such a day fire would have been easily and tremendously effective. But today a bridge could be burned only with abundance of fuel and careful nursing.

Thus we sped on, mile after mile, in this fearful chase, round curves and past stations in seemingly endless perspective. Whenever we lost sight of the enemy beyond a curve, we hoped that some of our obstructions had been effective in throwing him from the track, and that we should see him no more; but at each long reach backward the smoke was again seen, and the shrill whistle was like the scream of a bird of prey. The time could not have been so very long, for the terrible speed was rapidly devouring the distance; but with our nerves strained to the highest tension each minute seemed an hour. On several occasions the escape of the enemy from wreck was little less than miraculous. At one point a rail was placed across the track on a curve so skilfully that it was not seen till the train ran upon it at full speed. Fuller says that they were terribly jolted, and seemed to bounce altogether from the track, but lighted on the rails in safety. Some of the Confederates wished to leave a train which was driven at such a reckless rate, but their wishes were not gratified.

Before reaching Dalton we urged Andrews to turn and attack the enemy, laying an ambush so as to get into close quarters, that our revolvers might be on equal terms with their guns. I have little doubt that if this had been carried out it would have succeeded. But either because he thought the chance of wrecking or obstructing the enemy still good, or feared that the country ahead had been alarmed by a telegram around the Confederacy by the way of Richmond, Andrews merely gave the plan his sanction without making any attempt to carry it into execution.

Dalton was passed without difficulty, and beyond we stopped again to cut wires and to obstruct the track. It happened that a regiment was encamped not a hundred yards away, but they did not molest us. Fuller had written a despatch to Chattanooga, and dropped a man with orders to have it forwarded instantly, while he pushed on to save the bridges. Part of the message got through and created a wild panic in Chattanooga, although it did not materially influence our fortunes. Our supply of fuel was now very short, and without getting rid of our pursuers long enough to take in more, it was evident that we could not run as far as Chattanooga.

While cutting the wire we made an attempt to get up another rail; but the enemy, as usual, were too quick for us. We had no tool for this purpose except a wedge-pointed iron bar. Two or three bent iron claws for pulling out spikes would have given us such incontestable superiority that, down to almost the last of our run, we should have been able to escape and even to burn all the Chickamauga bridges. But it had not been our intention to rely on this mode of obstruction – an emergency only rendered necessary by our unexpected delay and the pouring rain.

We made no attempt to damage the long tunnel north of Dalton, as our enemies had greatly dreaded. The last hope of the raid was now staked upon an effort of a kind different from any that we had yet made, but which, if successful, would still enable us to destroy the bridges nearest Chattanooga. But, on the other hand, its failure would terminate the chase. Life and success were put upon one throw.

A few more obstructions were dropped on the track, and our own speed increased so that we soon forged a considerable distance ahead. The side and end boards of the last car were torn into shreds, all available fuel was piled upon it, and blazing brands were brought back from the engine. By the time we approached a long, covered bridge a fire in the car was fairly started. We uncoupled it in the middle of the bridge, and with painful suspense waited the issue. Oh for a few minutes till the work of conflagration was fairly begun! There was still steam pressure enough in our boiler to carry us to the next wood-yard, where we could have replenished our fuel by force, if necessary, so as to run as near to Chattanooga as was deemed prudent. We did not know of the telegraph message which the pursuers had sent ahead. But, alas! the minutes were not given. Before the bridge was extensively fired the enemy was upon us, and we moved slowly onward, looking back to see what they would do next. We had not long to conjecture. The Confederates pushed right into the smoke, and drove the burning car before them to the next side-track.

With no car left, and no fuel, the last scrap having been thrown into the engine or upon the burning car, and with no obstruction to drop on the track, our situation was indeed desperate. A few minutes only remained until our steed of iron which had so well served us would be powerless.

But it might still be possible to save ourselves. If we left the train in a body, and, taking a direct course towards the Union lines, hurried over the mountains at right angles with their course, we could not, from the nature of the country, be followed by cavalry, and could easily travel – athletic young men as we were, and fleeing for life – as rapidly as any pursuers. There was no telegraph in the mountainous districts west and northwest of us, and the prospect of reaching the Union lines seemed to me then, and has always since seemed, very fair. Confederate pursuers with whom I have since conversed freely have agreed on two points – that we could have escaped in the manner here pointed out, and that an attack on the pursuing train would likely have been successful. But Andrews thought otherwise, at least in relation to the former plan, and ordered us to jump from the locomotive one by one, and, dispersing in the woods, each endeavour to save himself. Thus ended the Andrews railroad raid.

It is easy now to understand why Mitchel paused thirty miles west of Chattanooga. The Andrews raiders had been forced to stop eighteen miles south of the same town, and no flying train met him with the expected tidings that all railroad communications of Chattanooga were destroyed, and that the town was in a panic and undefended. He dared advance no farther without heavy reinforcements from Pittsburg Landing or the North; and he probably believed to the day of his death, six months later, that the whole Andrews party had perished without accomplishing anything.

A few words will give the sequel to this remarkable enterprise. There was great excitement in Chattanooga and in the whole of the surrounding Confederate territory for scores of miles. The hunt for the fugitive raiders was prompt, energetic and completely successful. Ignorant of the country, disorganised, and far from the Union lines, they strove in vain to escape. Several were captured the same day on which they left the cars, and all but two within a week. Even these two were overtaken and brought back when they supposed that they were virtually out of danger. Two of those who had failed to be on the train were identified and added to the band of prisoners.

Now follows the saddest part of the story. Being in citizens' dress within an enemy's lines, the whole party were held as spies, and closely and vigorously guarded. A court martial was convened, and the leader and seven others out of the twenty-two were condemned and executed. The remainder were never brought to trial, probably because of the advance of Union forces, and the consequent confusion into which the affairs of the departments of east Tennessee and Georgia were thrown. Of the remaining fourteen, eight succeeded by a bold effort – attacking their guard in broad daylight – in making their escape from Atlanta, Georgia, and ultimately in reaching the North. The other six who shared in this effort, but were recaptured, remained prisoners until the latter part of March 1863, when they were exchanged through a special arrangement made with Secretary Stanton. All the survivors of this expedition received medals and promotion. The pursuers also received expressions of gratitude from their fellow-Confederates, notably from the governor and the legislature of Georgia.

*　　*　　*

Below is a list of the participants in the raid: James J. Andrews, leader – *Executed*; William Campbell, a civilian who volunteered to accompany the raiders – *Executed*; George D. Wilson, Company B, 2nd Ohio Volunteers – *Executed*; Marion A. Ross, Company A, 2nd Ohio Volunteers – *Executed*; Perry G. Shadrack, Company K, 2nd Ohio Volunteers – *Executed*; Samuel Slavens, 33rd Ohio Volunteers – *Executed*; Samuel Robinson, Company G, 33rd Ohio Volunteers – *Executed*; John Scott, Company K, 21st Ohio Volunteers – *Executed*; Wilson W. Brown, Company F, 21st Ohio Volunteers – *Escaped*; William Knight, Company E, 21st Ohio Volunteers – *Escaped*; Mark Wood, Company C, 21st Ohio Volunteers – *Escaped*; James A. Wilson, Company C, 21st Ohio Volunteers – *Escaped*; John Wollam, Company C, 33rd Ohio Volunteers – *Escaped*; D. A. Dorsey, Company H, 33rd Ohio Volunteers – *Escaped*; Jacob Parrott, Company K, 33rd Ohio Volunteers – *Exchanged*;

Robert Buffum, Company H, 21st Ohio Volunteers – *Exchanged*; William Benzinger, Company G, 21st Ohio Volunteers – *Exchanged*; William Reddick, Company B, 33rd Ohio Volunteers – *Exchanged*; E. H. Mason, Company K, 21st Ohio Volunteers – *Exchanged*; William Pittenger, Company G, 2nd Ohio Volunteers – *Exchanged*.

J. R. Porter, Company C, 21st Ohio, and Martin J. Hawkins, Company A, 33rd Ohio, reached Marietta, but did not get on board the train. They were captured and imprisoned with their comrades.

A. O. POLLARD

Second Lieutenant A. O. Pollard, MC, DCM, 1st Battalion Honourable Artillery Company, was awarded the Victoria Cross for actions at Gavrelle on the 29th April 1917. The citation read:

> For conspicuous bravery and determination. The troops of various units on the left of this officer's battalion had become disorganised owing to the heavy casualties from shellfire; and a subsequent determined enemy attack with very strong forces caused further confusion and retirement. Closely pressed by hostile forces, 2nd Lt Pollard at once realised the seriousness of the situation, and dashed up to stop the retirement. With only four men he started a counter-attack with bombs and pressed it home till he had broken the enemy offensive; he regained all that had been lost and gained much ground in addition. The enemy had retired in disorder, sustaining many casualties. By his force of will, dash and splendid example, coupled with an utter contempt for danger, this officer, who has already won the DCM and MC, infused courage into every man who saw him.

I Charge!

The 15th of June 1915 was a broiling hot summer's day. There was scarcely a breath of wind as we set off on the eight-mile march which would take us to our 'jumping-off' position. The Poperinghe-Ypres road was, as usual, crowded with traffic; troops in large and small parties, some in full equipment, some in light fatigue dress; limbers drawn by horses, limbers drawn by mules; endless ammunition columns; siege guns and howitzers; strings of lorries; motorcycle dispatch riders; every conceivable branch of the service was represented going about its business in orderly confusion. Even the cavalry who, since the inception of trench warfare, were rather out of fashion, had their part in the pageant. They sat their horses with the same erectness as in peacetime, but their drab equipment was in sad contrast to the shining breast-plates, scarlet cloaks and nodding plumes with which they entrance the nursemaids in the Mall.

On this occasion they rode with something of an air. When we succeeded in boring a hole through the enemy's defences on the following morning they would come once more into their own. Thundering hoofs and steaming nostrils would race in pursuit of a flying enemy. Sharp steel and quivering lance would clear the way for us to consolidate our victory.

We did not go right into Ypres. We turned off short of Hell Fire Corner across the fields. In one of these a stray shell knocked the Adjutant off his horse, though luckily without killing him. It was only a minor incident, but it warned us that we were under fire; our big adventure had commenced.

A student of psychology would notice a subtle difference between troops marching away from the line for a rest, and the same troops going up the line into action. Leaving the line, when every step means a further distance from bullets, and shells, there is an atmosphere of gaiety; songs are heard, jokes are exchanged, laughter is frequent. Going up, on the other hand, is a very different business. There is an air of seriousness, remarks are answered in monosyllables, men are mostly silent, occupied with their own thoughts. Some laugh and chatter from a sense of bravado, or to prevent their imaginations from becoming too active; others to bolster up the shrinking spirits of their weaker comrades. Only a few are natural.

On this occasion there was a tenseness in the bearing of the battalion quite different from our normal visits to the trenches. We started off with a swing as if we were going for a route march. Every one walked jauntily, and one could sense the excitement in the air. Gradually this spirit faded, helped no doubt by the heat of the day, and the sweat of marching. The wounding of the Adjutant was like the period at the end of a paragraph. After that first shell scarcely a word was spoken. We were going into something of which we had no experience. No man felt sure he would live through the coming ordeal.

We were halted in a field to await the coming of dusk. Tea was provided from the cookers, which were afterwards taken back to the transport field. I wonder how many watched them go off with envious eyes for the company cooks and the drivers. I wonder whether any of those returning envied us?

We moved forward in the twilight in single file. Our way lay along a railway line, and we stumbled forward and cursed the sleepers. They were either too far apart or too near; I have never been able to determine which. What I am sure of is that they are damnably awkward things to walk on, especially in full battle order.

At last we reached our position. It consisted of row after row of narrow, shallow trenches, each row being intended to accommodate successive waves of attacking troops. We were herded into ours literally like sardines. There was no room to lie down; the trench was too narrow to sit down in except sideways; if one stood up, one was head and shoulders over the top. Such were the quarters in which we were to pass the night.

Ernest and I and Percy got to work with our entrenching tools and hollowed out a space so that we could crouch in some sort of comfort. It was not worth while to put in too much work, as we should only be there for a few hours. As it was, it took us over an hour to get ourselves settled.

Smoking was strictly forbidden in case Fritz spotted the glow of the cigarettes, but of course we smoked. We managed to get a light from an apparatus which I had had sent out from home. It consisted of some sort of cord which was ignited by sparking a flint with a small wheel. Its merit lay in the fact that it glowed without making a flame. We were able to light up in perfect safety.

Sleep was out of the question. Not only was I too uncomfortable but I was far too excited. In a few hours I was to go over the top for the first time. I felt no trace of fear or even nervousness; only an anxiety to get started. The hours seemed interminable. Would the dawn never come?

Fritz started spasmodic shelling in the small hours. Whether he suspected anything or not I cannot say. I do not think he can have done, for a concentrated bombardment of these congested assembly trenches would have meant a massacre. The stuff he was sending over was shrapnel, and he caused some casualties, though not in our trench.

About an hour before zero hour a message came down the line that I was to report to Captain Boyle. Thankfully, I climbed out of my cramped lodgement and made my way to company headquarters. Captain Boyle had great news for me. Two men were required to accompany the first wave as a connecting link. I was one of the two chosen; the other was a fellow called Springfield, whose father was editor of *London Opinion*.

Springy and I were delighted; I especially so. My ambition was to be realised. I was to take part in a real charge. With luck I might bayonet a Hun.

We reported to Captain Spooner of the 1st Lincolns. The Lincolns were in the British front-line trench, and were consequently very much more comfortable than we were in the assembly trenches. We had scarcely arrived when the barrage commenced.

Bang! Bang! Bang! Bang! Bang! Swish, swish, swish. Crump! Crump! Crump! Crump! Crump! Deafening pandemonium! One had to shout in one's neighbour's ear to make oneself heard at all. I knew the Hun was replying because an occasional shower of dust and earth descended on my head, but the continuous noise of guns and shells rendered my sense of hearing completely inoperative. Guns firing and shells bursting were so intermingled, friend and foe, that there was one endless succession of shattering detonations.

Springy and I stood and waited; Captain Spooner from time to time looked at his watch; the men of the Lincolns fidgeted with their equipment. My pulse raced; the blood pounded through my veins. I looked at Springy and grinned; Springy grinned back. Only a few more minutes.

At last Captain Spooner turned and smiled. His lips formed the words, 'Only a minute to go!' Instantly all was bustle and confusion. Short three-rung ladders were placed against the parapet. A man stood by each one, his foot on the first step, his rifle and bayonet swung over his shoulder.

Captain Spooner raised his hand; then swarmed up the ladder in front of him. I followed close at his heels. Springy was only a second behind me. Right and left along the line men were clambering over the top.

With the memory of the Moulin Rouge fresh in my mind, I fully expected that we should be met with a withering fire as we emerged into the open. I anticipated the crackle of machine-guns, the rattle of musketry, the sweeping away of our gallant charge. Except that I never once dreamed or considered that I myself should be hit. Even in this first attack I had the extraordinary feeling of being myself exempt, though not to the same degree as later on when I was an officer. I shall therefore leave the analysis of this peculiar sense until I record the period when it became more pronounced.

Instead of a hail of machine-gun and rifle bullets, there was – nothing! Not a sign of life was to be seen anywhere around the enemy positron. Overhead the shells still whined and screeched; behind us and in front great spouts of earth went up in bursts. The noise was deafening, but from the menacing line of earthworks opposite, not so much as a puff of smoke.

Just ahead of me Captain Spooner ran in a steady jog-trot across no man's land. Right and left stretched long lines of troops. All were running forward, their rifles gripped in their hands.

Four hundred yards to go! We ran steadily on. Springy and I had lengthened our stride until we were right at Captain Spooner's heels. Still not a movement in the trench we were rapidly approaching.

What should we meet when we got there, I wondered? Perhaps they were reserving their fire until the last moment. Perhaps a hidden machine-gun nest would suddenly sweep us away like chaff before the wind. Or it might be that the infantry would rise to meet us with a yell in a counter bayonet charge. I clenched my teeth and gripped my rifle tighter.

Ten yards from the trench Springy and I both sprinted. Two minds with but a single thought. We both wanted to be first to engage the enemy. There was no wire to bother us. It had been utterly destroyed by our fierce barrage. We passed Captain Spooner in a flash.

What a shock met my eyes as I mounted the German parapet. The trench was full of men; men with sightless eyes and waxen faces. Each gripped his rifle and leaned against the side of the trench in an attitude of defence, but all were dead. We were attacking a position held by corpses!

For a single moment I could not believe my eyes. I thought it must be some trick of the Hun to fill the trench with dummies the better to lure us into a trap. Then, when at length I realised what I was looking at, I felt suddenly sick with horror. This was unvarnished war; war with the gloves off. There was something ludicrous about that trench of dead men. One wanted to laugh at their comical appearance. There was also something fine: every man in his place with his face towards the enemy. But mostly they aroused a feeling of pity. Death must have come to them so suddenly, without giving them a chance in their own defence. They certainly gave me a very different reception from anything I had anticipated.

The Lincolns swept past and on to the second line. Springy and I turned and ran back to the 'jumping off' trench. Our job was to report that the first German line was clear. Captain Boyle was standing on the parapet talking to Major Ward. I informed them that the Lincolns had gone on, and then, without waiting for the battalion to advance, ran back again to the German position. I suppose, strictly speaking, I should have rejoined my section. But I had received no definite orders to do so, and I wanted to get back to the Lincolns and see some of the fighting. I was still sure there would be a hand-to-hand contest.

There was now considerably more activity from the Huns. Machine-guns were intermingling their clatter with the roar of the shells. They were firing from some reserve positions, and I could hear the whine and whistle of the bullets as they passed me or ricocheted overhead.

The German trench I had first entered was situated on the edge of a small wood. This I now passed through to the second trench at the back; then on up to the German communication trench. Here I saw my first live Hun. He was lying half in and half out of a dug-out, pinned down by a beam of wood which prevented him from moving the lower part of his body. All the same he was full of fight. He had a thin face with an aquiline nose on which were perched steel-rimmed glasses. He reminded me forcibly of a German master we had at my preparatory school. In his hand he held an automatic with which he was taking pot-shots at whoever passed him. He had killed one man and wounded one, and I arrived just in time to see a Tommy stick him with his bayonet.

I passed right up the communication trench until I found the Lincolns. They were holding what had been the fourth German line, which they were putting in a condition of defence. I made the mistake of reporting to Captain Spooner, who at once ordered me to rejoin my unit. There was no sign of any hand-to-hand fighting anywhere up there. All was peace and quiet. The Hun had cleared out without waiting for the British advance. I concluded the whole thing was over and returned to the wood.

SAKI

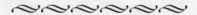

Hector Hugh Munro (1870–1916), novelist who wrote under the name Saki, was born at Akyab, Burma, son of a police official of Scottish extraction, and was brought up by aunts at Pilton in Devon. Educated at Exmouth and Bedford Grammar School, he travelled with his father in France, Germany and Switzerland, then was for a time in the police service in Burma but found the climate too unhealthy. Returning to England, he wrote for the *Westminster Gazette*, and from 1902 to 1908 was a foreign correspondent for the *Morning Post*. In the First World War he served as a private with the Royal Fusiliers and was killed at Beaumont-Hamel. His books of humorous short stories include *Reginald* (1904), *Reginald in Russia* (1910), *The Chronicles of Clovis* (1912), *Beasts and Super-Beasts* (1914) and *The Square Egg* (1924); *The Unbearable Bassington* (1912) and *When William Came* (1914) are novels. His pseudonym Saki is the name of the cup-bearer in *The Rubáiyát* of Omar Khayyám.

Sredni Vashtar

Conradin was ten years old, and the doctor had pronounced his professional opinion that the boy would not live another five years. The doctor was silky and effete, and counted for little, but his opinion was endorsed by Mrs De Ropp, who counted for nearly everything. Mrs De Ropp was Conradin's cousin and guardian, and in his eyes she represented those three-fifths of the world that are necessary and disagreeable and real; the other two-fifths, in perpetual antagonism to the foregoing, were summed up in himself and his imagination. One of these days Conradin supposed he would succumb to the mastering pressure of wearisome necessary things – such as illnesses and coddling restrictions and drawn-out dullness. Without his imagination, which was rampant under the spur of loneliness, he would have succumbed long ago.

Mrs De Ropp would never, in her honestest moments, have confessed to herself that she disliked Conradin, though she might have been dimly aware that thwarting him 'for his good' was a duty which she did not find particularly irksome. Conradin hated her with a desperate sincerity which he was perfectly able to mask. Such few pleasures as he could contrive for himself gained an added relish from the likelihood that they would be displeasing to his guardian, and from the realm of his imagination she was locked out – an unclean thing, which should find no entrance.

In the dull, cheerless garden, overlooked by so many windows that were ready to open with a message not to do this or that, or a reminder that medicines were due, he found little attraction. The few fruit trees that it contained were set jealously apart from his plucking, as though they were rare specimens of their kind blooming in an arid waste; it would probably have been difficult to find a market-gardener who would have offered ten shillings for their entire yearly produce. In a forgotten corner, however, almost hidden behind a dismal shrubbery, was a disused tool-shed of respectable proportions, and within its walls Conradin found a haven, something that took on the varying aspects of a playroom and a cathedral. He had peopled it with a legion of familiar phantoms, evoked partly from fragments of history and partly from his own brain, but it also boasted two inmates of flesh and blood. In one corner lived a ragged-plumaged Houdan hen, on which the boy lavished an affection that had scarcely another outlet. Farther back in the gloom stood a large hutch, divided into two compartments, one of which was fronted with close iron bars. This was the abode of a large polecat-ferret, which a friendly butcher-boy had once smuggled, cage and all, into its present quarters, in exchange for a long-secreted hoard of small silver. Conradin was dreadfully afraid of the lithe, sharp-fanged beast, but it was his most treasured possession. Its very presence in the tool-shed was a secret and fearful joy, to be kept scrupulously from the knowledge of the Woman, as he privately dubbed his cousin. And one day, out of heaven knows what material, he spun the beast a wonderful name, and from that moment it grew into a god and a religion. The Woman indulged in religion once a week at a church near by, and took Conradin with her, but to him the church service was an alien rite in the House of Rimmon. Every Thursday, in the dim and musty silence of the tool-shed he worshipped with mystic and elaborate ceremonial before the wooden hutch where dwelt Sredni Vashtar, the great ferret. Red flowers in their season and scarlet berries in the wintertime were offered at his shrine, for he was a god who laid some special stress on the fierce impatient side of things, as opposed to the Woman's religion, which, as far as Conradin could observe, went to great lengths in the contrary direction. And on great festivals powdered nutmeg was strewn in front of his hutch, an important feature of the offering being that the nutmeg had to be stolen. These festivals were of irregular occurrence, and were chiefly appointed to celebrate some passing event. On one occasion, when Mrs De Ropp suffered from acute toothache for three days, Conradin kept up the festival during the entire three days, and almost succeeded in persuading himself that Sredni Vashtar was personally responsible for the toothache. If the malady had lasted for another day the supply of nutmeg would have given out.

The Houdan hen was never drawn into the cult of Sredni Vashtar. Conradin had long ago settled that she was an Anabaptist. He did not pretend to have the remotest knowledge as to what an Anabaptist was, but he privately hoped that it was dashing and not very respectable. Mrs De Ropp was the ground plan on which he based and detested all respectability.

After a while Conradin's absorption in the tool-shed began to attract the notice of his guardian. 'It is not good for him to be pottering down there in all weathers,' she promptly decided, and at breakfast one morning she announced that the Houdan hen had been sold and taken away overnight. With her short-sighted eyes she peered at Conradin, waiting for an outbreak of rage and sorrow, which she was ready to rebuke with a flow of excellent precepts and reasoning. But Conradin said nothing: there was nothing to be said. Something perhaps in his white set face gave her a momentary qualm, for at tea that afternoon there was toast on the table, a delicacy which she usually banned on the ground that it was bad for him; also because the making of it 'gave trouble', a deadly offence in the middle-class feminine eye.

'I thought you liked toast,' she exclaimed, with an injured air, observing that he did not touch it.

'Sometimes,' said Conradin.

In the shed that evening there was an innovation in the worship of the hutch-god. Conradin had been wont to chant his praises, tonight he asked a boon.

'Do one thing for me, Sredni Vashtar.'

The thing was not specified. As Sredni Vashtar was a god he must be supposed to know. And choking back a sob as he looked at that other empty corner, Conradin went back to the world he so hated.

And every night, in the welcome darkness of his bedroom, and every evening in the dusk of the tool-shed, Conradin's bitter litany went up: 'Do one thing for me, Sredni Vashtar.'

Mrs De Ropp noticed that the visits to the shed did not cease, and one day she made a further journey of inspection.

'What are you keeping in that locked hutch?' she asked. 'I believe it's guinea-pigs. I'll have them all cleared away.'

Conradin shut his lips tight, but the Woman ransacked his bedroom till she found the carefully hidden key, and forthwith marched down to the shed to complete her discovery. It was a cold afternoon, and Conradin had been bidden to keep to the house. From the farthest window of the dining-room the door of the shed could just be seen beyond the corner of the shrubbery, and there Conradin stationed himself. He saw the Woman enter, and then he imagined her opening the door of the sacred hutch and peering down with her short-sighted eyes into the thick straw bed where his god lay hidden. Perhaps she would prod at the straw in her clumsy impatience. And Conradin fervently breathed his prayer for the last time. But he knew as he prayed that he did not believe. He knew that the Woman would come out presently with that pursed smile he loathed so well on her face, and that in an hour or two the gardener would carry away his wonderful god, a god no longer, but a simple brown ferret in a hutch. And he knew that the Woman would triumph always as she triumphed now and that he would grow ever more sickly under her pestering and domineering and superior wisdom, till one day nothing would matter much more with him, and the doctor would be proved right. And in the sting and misery of his defeat, he began to chant loudly and defiantly the hymn of his threatened idol:

> Sredni Vashtar went forth,
> His thoughts were red thoughts and his teeth were white.
> His enemies called for peace, but he brought them death.
> Sredni Vashtar the Beautiful.

And then of a sudden he stopped his chanting and drew closer to the window-pane. The door of the shed still stood ajar as it had been left, and the minutes were slipping by. They were long minutes, but they slipped by nevertheless. He watched the starlings running and flying in little parties across the lawn; he counted them over and over again, with one eye always on that swinging door. A sour-faced maid came in to lay the table for tea, and still Conradin stood and waited and watched. Hope had crept by inches into his heart, and now a look of triumph began to blaze in his eyes that had only known the wistful patience of defeat. Under his breath, with a furtive exultation, he began once again the paean of victory and devastation. And presently his eyes were rewarded: out through that doorway came a long, low, yellow-and brown beast, with eyes a-blink at the waning daylight, and dark wet stains around the fur of jaws and throat. Conradin dropped on his knees. The great polecat-ferret made its way down to a small brook at the foot of the garden, drank for a moment, then crossed a little plank bridge and was lost to sight in the bushes. Such was the passing of Sredni Vashtar.

'Tea is ready,' said the sour-faced maid; 'where is the mistress?'

'She went down to the shed some time ago,' said Conradin.

And while the maid went to summon her mistress to tea, Conradin fished a toasting-fork out of the sideboard drawer and proceeded to toast himself a piece of bread. And during the toasting of it and the buttering of it with much butter and the slow enjoyment of eating it, Conradin listened to the noises and silences which fell in quick spasms beyond the dining-room door. The loud foolish screaming of the maid, the answering chorus of wondering ejaculations from the kitchen region, the scuttering footsteps and hurried embassies for outside help, and then, after a lull, the scared sobbings and the shuffling tread of those who bore a heavy burden into the house.

'Whoever will break it to the poor child? I couldn't for the life of me!' exclaimed a shrill voice. And while they debated the matter among themselves, Conradin made himself another piece of toast.

The Hounds of Fate

In the fading light of a close dull autumn afternoon Martin Stoner plodded his way along muddy lanes and rut-seamed cart tracks that led he knew not exactly whither. Somewhere in front of him, he fancied, lay the sea, and towards the sea his footsteps seemed persistently turning; why he was struggling wearily forward to that goal he could scarcely have explained, unless he was possessed by the same instinct that turns a hard-pressed stag cliffward in its last extremity. In his case the hounds of fate were certainly pressing him with unrelenting insistence; hunger, fatigue and despairing hopelessness had numbed his brain, and he could scarcely summon sufficient energy to wonder what underlying impulse was driving him onward. Stoner was one of those unfortunate individuals who seem to have tried everything; a natural slothfulness and improvidence had always intervened to blight any chance of even moderate success, and now he was at the end of his tether, and there was nothing more to try. Desperation had not awakened in him any dormant reserve of energy; on the contrary, a mental torpor grew up round the crisis of his fortunes. With the clothes he stood up in, a halfpenny in his pocket, and no single friend or acquaintance to turn to, with no prospect either of a bed for the night or a meal for the morrow, Martin Stoner trudged stolidly forward, between moist hedgerows and beneath dripping trees, his mind almost a blank, except that he was subconsciously aware that somewhere in front of him lay the sea. Another consciousness obtruded itself now and then – the knowledge that he was miserably hungry. Presently he came to a halt by an open gateway that led into a spacious and rather neglected farm-garden; there was little sign of life about, and the farmhouse at the farther end of the garden looked chill and inhospitable. A drizzling rain, however, was setting in, and Stoner thought that here perhaps he might obtain a few minutes' shelter and buy a glass of milk with his last remaining coin. He turned slowly and wearily into the garden and followed a narrow, flagged path up to a side door. Before he had time to knock the door opened and a bent, withered-looking old man stood aside in the doorway as though to let him pass in.

'Could I come in out of the rain?' Stoner began, but the old man interrupted him.

'Come in, Master Tom. I knew you would come back one of these days.'

Stoner lurched across the threshold and stood staring uncomprehendingly at the other.

'Sit down while I put you out a bit of supper,' said the old man with quavering eagerness. Stoner's legs gave way from very weariness, and he sank inertly into the armchair that had been pushed up to him. In another minute he was devouring the cold meat, cheese and bread that had been placed on the table at his side.

'You'm little changed these four years,' went on the old man, in a voice that sounded to Stoner as something in a dream, far way and inconsequent; 'but you'll find us a deal changed, you will. There's no one about the place same as when you left; nought but me and your old aunt. I'll go and tell her that you'm come; she won't be seeing you, but she'll let you stay right enough. She always did say if you was to come back you should stay, but she'd never set eyes on you or speak to you again.'

The old man placed a mug of beer on the table in front of Stoner and then hobbled away down a long passage. The drizzle of rain had changed to a furious lashing downpour, which beat violently against door and windows. The wanderer thought with a shudder of what the seashore must look like under this drenching rainfall, with night beating down on all sides. He finished the food and beer and sat numbly waiting for the return of his strange host. As the minutes ticked by on the grandfather clock in the corner a new hope began to flicker and grow in the young man's mind; it was merely the expansion of his former craving for food and a few minutes' rest into a longing to find a night's shelter under this seemingly hospitable roof. A clattering of footsteps down the passage heralded the old farm servant's return.

'The old missus won't see you, Master Tom, but she says you are to stay. 'Tis right enough, seeing the farm will be yours when she be put under earth. I've had a fire lit in your room, Master Tom, and the maids has put fresh sheets on to the bed. You'll find nought changed up there. Maybe you'm tired and would like to go there now.'

Without a word Martin Stoner rose heavily to his feet and followed his ministering angel along a passage, up a short creaking stair, along another passage, and into a large room lit with a cheerfully blazing fire. There was but little furniture – plain, old-fashioned and good of its kind; a stuffed squirrel in a case and a wall-calendar of four years ago were about the only symptoms of decoration. But Stoner had eyes for little else than the bed, and could scarce wait to tear his clothes off him before rolling in a luxury of weariness into its comfortable depths. The hounds of fate seemed to have checked for a brief moment.

In the cold light of morning Stoner laughed mirthlessly as he slowly realised the position in which he found himself. Perhaps he might snatch a bit of breakfast on the strength of his likeness to this other missing ne'er-do-well, and get safely away before anyone discovered the fraud that had been thrust on him. In the room downstairs he found the bent old man ready with a dish of bacon and fried eggs for 'Master Tom's' breakfast, while a hard-faced elderly maid brought in a teapot and poured him out a cup of tea. As he sat at the table a small spaniel came up and made friendly advances.

' 'Tis old Bowker's pup,' explained the old man, whom the hard-faced maid had addressed as George. 'She was main fond of you; never seemed the same after you went away to Australee. She died 'bout a year agone. 'Tis her pup.'

Stoner found it difficult to regret her decease; as a witness for identification she would have left nothing to be desired.

'You'll go for a ride, Master Tom?' was the next startling proposition that came from the old man. 'We've a nice little roan cob that goes well in saddle. Old Biddy is getting a bit up in years, though 'er goes well still, but I'll have the little roan saddled and brought round to the door.'

'I've got no riding things,' stammered the castaway, almost laughing as he looked down at his one suit of well-worn clothes.

'Master Tom,' said the old man earnestly, almost with an offended air, 'all your things is just as you left them. A bit of airing before the fire and they'll be all right. 'Twill be a bit of a distraction like, a little riding and wild-fowling now and agen. You'll find the folk around here has hard and bitter minds towards you. They hasn't forgotten nor forgiven. No one'll come nigh you, so you'd best get what distraction you can with horse and dog. They'm good company, too.'

Old George hobbled away to give his orders, and Stoner, feeling more than ever like one in a dream, went upstairs to inspect 'Master Tom's' wardrobe. A ride was one of the pleasures dearest to his heart, and there was some protection against immediate discovery of his imposture in the thought that none of Tom's aforetime companions were likely to favour him with a close inspection. As the interloper thrust himself into some tolerably well-fitting riding cords he wondered vaguely what manner of misdeed the genuine Tom had committed to set the whole countryside against him. The thud of quick, eager hoofs on damp earth cut short his speculations. The roan cob had been brought up to the side door.

'Talk of beggars on horseback,' thought Stoner to himself, as he trotted rapidly along the muddy lanes where he had tramped yesterday as a down-at-heel outcast; and then he flung reflection indolently aside and gave himself up to the pleasure of a smart canter along the turf-grown side of a level stretch of road. At an open gateway he checked his pace to allow two carts to turn into a field. The lads driving the carts found time to give him a prolonged stare, and as he passed on he heard an excited voice call out, ''Tis Tom Prikel, I knowed him at once; showing hisself here agen, is he?'

Evidently the likeness which had imposed at close quarters on a doddering old man was good enough to mislead younger eyes at a short distance.

In the course of his ride he met with ample evidence to confirm the statement that local folk had neither forgotten nor forgiven the bygone crime which had come to him as a legacy from the absent Tom. Scowling looks, mutterings and nudgings greeted him whenever he chanced upon human beings; 'Bowker's pup', trotting placidly by his side, seemed the one element of friendliness in a hostile world.

As he dismounted at the side door he caught a fleeting glimpse of a gaunt, elderly woman peering at him from behind the curtain of an upper window. Evidently this was his aunt by adoption.

Over the ample midday meal that stood in readiness for him, Stoner was able to review the possibilities of his extraordinary situation. The real Tom, after four years of absence, might suddenly turn up at the farm, or a letter might come from him at any moment. Again, in the character of heir to the farm, the false Tom might be called on to sign documents, which would be an embarrassing predicament. Or a relative might arrive who would not imitate the aunt's attitude of aloofness. All these things would mean ignominious exposure. On the other hand, the alternative was the open sky and the muddy lanes that led down to the sea. The farm offered him, at any rate, a temporary refuge from destitution; farming was one of the many things he had 'tried', and he would be able to do a certain amount of work in return for the hospitality to which he was so little entitled.

'Will you have cold pork for your supper,' asked the hard-faced maid, as she cleared the table, 'or will you have it hotted up?'

'Hot, with onions,' said Stoner. It was the only time in his life that he had made a rapid decision. And as he gave the order he knew that he meant to stay.

Stoner kept rigidly to those portions of the house which seemed to have been allotted to him by a tacit treaty of delimitation. When he took part in the farm-work it was as one who worked under orders and never initiated them. Old George, the roan cob and Bowker's pup were his sole companions in a world that was otherwise frostily silent and hostile. Of the mistress of the farm he saw nothing. Once, when he knew she had gone forth to church, he made a furtive visit to the farm parlour in an endeavour to glean some fragmentary knowledge of the young man whose place he had usurped, and whose ill-repute he had fastened on himself. There were many photographs hung on the walls, or stuck in prim frames, but the likeness he sought for was not among them. At last, in an album thrust out of sight, he came across what he wanted. There was a whole series, labelled 'Tom': a podgy child of three, in a fantastic frock; an awkward boy of about twelve, holding a cricket bat as though he loathed it; a rather good-looking youth of eighteen with very smooth, evenly parted hair; and, finally, a young man with a somewhat surly dare-devil expression. At this last portrait Stoner looked with particular interest; the likeness to himself was unmistakable.

From the lips of old George, who was garrulous enough on most subjects, he tried again and again to learn something of the nature of the offence which shut him off as a creature to be shunned and hated by his fellowmen.

'What do the folk around here say about me?' he asked one day as they were walking home from an outlying field.

The old man shook his head.

'They be bitter agen you, mortal bitter. Ay, 'tis a sad business, a sad business.'

And never could he be got to say anything more enlightening.

On a clear frosty evening, a few days before the festival of Christmas, Stoner stood in a corner of the orchard which commanded a wide view of the countryside. Here and there he could see the twinkling dots of lamp or candle glow which told of human homes where the goodwill and jollity of the season held their sway. Behind him lay the grim, silent farmhouse, where no one ever laughed, where even a quarrel would have seemed cheerful. As he turned to look at the long grey front of the gloom-shadowed building, a door opened and old George came hurriedly forth. Stoner heard his adopted name called in a tone of strained anxiety. Instantly he knew that something untoward had happened, and with a quick revulsion of outlook his sanctuary became in his eyes a place of peace and contentment, from which he dreaded to be driven.

'Master Tom,' said the old man in a hoarse whisper, 'you must slip away quiet from here for a few days. Michael Ley is back in the village, and he swears to shoot you if he can come across you. He'll do it, too, there's murder in the look of him. Get away under cover of night; 'tis only for a week or so, he won't be here longer.'

'But where am I to go?' stammered Stoner, who had caught the infection of the old man's obvious terror.

'Go right away along the coast to Punchford and keep hid there. When Michael's safe gone I'll ride the roan over to the Green Dragon at Punchford; when you see the cob stabled at the Green Dragon 'tis a sign you may come back agen.'

'But – ' began Stoner hesitatingly.

' 'Tis all right for money,' said the other; 'the old Missus agrees you'd best do as I say, and she's given me this.'

The old man produced three sovereigns and some odd silver.

Stoner felt more of a cheat than ever as he stole away that night from the back gate of the farm with the old woman's money in his pocket. Old George and Bowker's pup stood watching him a silent farewell from the yard. He could scarcely fancy that he would ever come back, and he felt a throb of compunction for those two humble friends who would wait wistfully for his return. Some day perhaps the real Tom would come back, and there would be wild wonderment among those simple farm folks as to the identity of the shadowy guest they had harboured under their roof. For his own fate he felt no immediate anxiety; three pounds goes but little way in the world when there is nothing behind it, but to a man who has counted his exchequer in pennies it seems a good starting-point. Fortune had done him a whimsically kind turn when last he trod these lanes as a hopeless adventurer, and there might yet be a chance of his finding some work and making a fresh start; as he got farther from the farm his spirits rose higher. There was a sense of relief in regaining once more his lost identity and ceasing to be the uneasy ghost of another. He scarcely bothered to speculate about the implacable enemy who had dropped from nowhere into his life; since that life was now behind him, one unreal item the more made little difference. For the first time for many months he began to hum a careless light-hearted refrain.

Then there stepped out from the shadow of an overhanging oak tree a man with a gun. There was no need to wonder who he might be; the moonlight falling on his white set face revealed a glare of human hate such as Stoner in the ups and downs of his wanderings had never seen before. He sprang aside in a wild effort to break through the hedge that bordered the lane, but the tough branches held him fast. The hounds of fate had waited for him in those narrow lanes, and this time they were not to be denied.

MARY SHELLEY

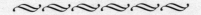

Mary Wollstonecraft Shelley (1797–1851), novelist, born in London, was the only child of William Godwin and Mary Wollstonecraft, his first wife. In 1814 she went to the Continent with Percy Bysshe Shelley and married him, on the death of his wife, two years later. When abroad she saw much of Byron, and it was at his villa on the Lake of Geneva that she conceived the idea of her famous novel *Frankenstein, or the Modern Prometheus* (1818), a ghastly but powerful work. None of her other novels, including *The Last Man* (1826) and *Lodore* (1835), had the same success. She contributed biographies of foreign artists and authors to Lardner's *Cabinet Cyclopaedia* and edited her husband's poems after his death.

The Mortal Immortal

16 July 1833 – This is a memorable anniversary for me; on it I complete my three hundred and twenty-third year!

The Wandering Jew? – certainly not. More than eighteen centuries have passed over his head. In comparison with him, I am a very young Immortal.

Am I, then, immortal? This is a question which I have asked myself, by day and night, for now three hundred and three years, and yet cannot answer it. I detected a grey hair amidst my brown locks this very day – that surely signifies decay. Yet it may have remained concealed there for three hundred years – for some persons have become entirely white-headed before twenty years of age.

I will tell my story, and my reader shall judge for me. I will tell my story, and so contrive to pass some few hours of a long eternity, become so wearisome to me. For ever! Can it be? To live for ever! I have heard of enchantments, in which the victims were plunged into a deep sleep, to wake, after a hundred years, as fresh as ever; I have heard of the Seven Sleepers – thus to be immortal would not be so burthensome; but, oh! the weight of never-ending time – the tedious passage of the still-succeeding hours! How happy was the fabled Nourjahad! But to my task.

All the world has heard of Cornelius Agrippa. His memory is as immortal as his arts have made me. All the world has also heard of his scholar, who, unawares, raised the foul fiend during his master's absence, and was destroyed by him. The report, true or false, of this accident, was attended with many inconveniences to the renowned philosopher. All his scholars at once deserted him – his servants disappeared. He had no one near him to put coals on his ever-burning fires while he slept, or to attend to the changeful colours of his medicines while he studied. Experiment after experiment failed, because one pair of hands was insufficient to complete them: the dark spirits laughed at him for not being able to retain a single mortal in his service.

I was then very young – very poor – and very much in love. I had been for about a year the pupil of Cornelius, though I was absent when this accident took place. On my return, my friends implored me not to return to the alchymist's abode. I trembled as I listened to the dire tale they told; I required no second warning; and when Cornelius came and offered me a purse of gold if I would remain under his roof, I felt as if Satan himself tempted me. My teeth chattered – my hair stood on end – I ran off as fast as my trembling knees would permit.

My failing steps were directed whither for two years they had every evening been attracted – a gently bubbling spring of pure living water, beside which lingered a dark-haired girl, whose beaming eyes were fixed on the path I was accustomed each night to tread. I cannot remember the hour when I did not love Bertha; we had been neighbours and playmates from infancy – her parents, like mine, were of humble life, yet respectable, and our attachment had been a source of pleasure to them. In an evil hour, a malignant fever carried off both her father and mother, and Bertha became an orphan. She would have found a home beneath my paternal roof, but, unfortunately, the old lady of the near castle, rich, childless and solitary, declared her intention to adopt her. Henceforth Bertha was clad in silk, inhabited a marble palace and was looked on as being highly favoured by fortune. But in her new situation among her new associates, Bertha remained true to the friend of her humbler days; she often visited the cottage of my father, and when forbidden to go thither, she would stray towards the neighbouring wood, and meet me beside its shady fountain.

She often declared that she owed no duty to her new protectress equal in sanctity to that which bound us. Yet still I was too poor to marry, and she grew weary of being tormented on my account. She had a haughty but an impatient spirit, and grew angry at the obstacle that prevented our union. We met now after an absence, and she had been sorely beset while I was away; she complained bitterly, and almost reproached me for being poor. I replied hastily: 'I am honest, if I am poor! – were I not, I might soon become rich!'

This exclamation produced a thousand questions. I feared to shock her by owning the truth, but she drew it from me; and then, casting a look of disdain on me, she said: 'You pretend to love me, and you fear to face the Devil for my sake!'

I protested that I had only dreaded to offend her – while she dwelt on the magnitude of the reward that I should receive. Thus encouraged – shamed by her – led on by love and hope, laughing at my later fears, with quick steps and a light heart, I returned to accept the offers of the alchemist, and was instantly installed in my office.

A year passed away. I became possessed of no insignificant sum of money. Custom had banished my fears. In spite of the most painful vigilance, I had never detected the trace of a cloven foot; nor was the studious silence of our abode ever disturbed by demoniac howls. I still continued my stolen interviews with Bertha, and hope dawned on me – hope – but not perfect joy: for Bertha fancied that love and security were enemies, and her pleasure was to divide them in my bosom. Though true of heart, she was something of a coquette in manner; I was jealous as a Turk. She slighted me in a thousand ways, yet would never acknowledge herself to be in the wrong. She would drive me mad with anger, and then force me to beg her pardon. Sometimes she fancied that I was not sufficiently submissive, and then she had some story of a rival, favoured by her protectress. She was surrounded by silk-clad youths – the rich and handsome. What chance had the sad-robed scholar of Cornelius compared with these?

On one occasion, the philosopher made such large demands upon my time that I was unable to meet her as I was wont. He was engaged in some mighty work, and I was forced to remain, day and night, feeding his furnaces and watching his chemical preparations. Bertha waited for me in vain at the fountain. Her haughty spirit fired at this neglect; and when at last I stole out during a few short minutes allotted to me for slumber, and hoped to be consoled by her, she received me with disdain, dismissed me in scorn, and vowed that any man should possess her hand rather than he who could not be in two places at once for her sake. She would be revenged! And truly she was. In my dingy retreat I heard that she had been hunting, attended by Albert Hoffer. Albert Hoffer was favoured by her protectress, and the three passed in cavalcade before my smoky window. Methought that they mentioned my name; it was followed by a laugh of derision, as her dark eyes glanced contemptuously towards my abode.

Jealousy, with all its venom and all its misery, entered my breast. Now I shed a torrent of tears to think that I should never call her mine; and, anon, I imprecated a thousand curses on her inconstancy. Yet, still I must stir the fires of the alchemist, still attend on the changes of his unintelligible medicines.

Cornelius had watched for three days and nights, nor closed his eyes. The progress of his alembics was slower than he expected; in spite of his anxiety, sleep weighted upon his eyelids. Again and again he threw off drowsiness with more than human energy; again and again it stole away his senses. He eyed his crucibles wistfully. 'Not ready yet,' he murmured; 'will another night pass before the work is accomplished? Winzy, you are vigilant – you are faithful – you have slept, my boy – you slept last night. Look at that glass vessel. The liquid it contains is of a soft rose-colour; the moment it begins to change hue, awaken me – till then I may close my eyes. First, it will turn white, and then emit golden flashes; but wait not till then; when the rose-colour fades, rouse me.' I scarcely heard the last words, muttered, as they were, in sleep. Even then he did not quite yield to nature. 'Winzy, my boy,' he again said, 'do not touch the vessel – do not put it to your lips; it is a philtre – a philtre to cure love; you would not cease to love your Bertha – beware to drink!'

And he slept. His venerable head sunk on his breast, and I scarce heard his regular breathing. For a few minutes I watched the vessel – the rosy hue of the liquid remained unchanged. Then my thoughts wandered – they visited the fountain, and dwelt on a thousand charming scenes never to be renewed – never! Serpents and adders were in my heart as the word 'Never!' half formed itself on my lips. False girl! – false and cruel! Never more would she smile on me as that evening she smiled on Albert. Worthless, detested woman! I would not remain unrevenged – she should see Albert expire at her feet – she should die beneath my vengeance. She had smiled in disdain and triumph – she knew my wretchedness and her power. Yet what power had she? – the power of exciting my hate – my utter scorn – my – oh, all but indifference! Could I attain that – could I regard her with careless eyes, transferring my rejected love to one fairer and more true, that were indeed a victory!

A bright flash darted before my eyes. I had forgotten the medicine of the adept; I gazed on it with wonder: flashes of admirable beauty, more bright than those which the diamond emits when the sun's rays are on it, glanced from the surface of the liquid; and odour the most fragrant and grateful stole over my sense; the vessel seemed one globe of living radiance, lovely to the eye, and most inviting to the taste. The first thought, instinctively inspired by the grosser sense, was, I will – I must drink. I raised the vessel to my lips. 'It will cure me of love – of torture!' Already I had quaffed half of the most delicious liquor ever tasted by the palate of man, when the philosopher stirred. I started – I dropped the glass – the fluid flamed and glanced along the floor, while I felt Cornelius's grip at my throat, as he shrieked aloud, 'Wretch! you have destroyed the labour of my life!'

The philosopher was totally unaware that I had drunk any portion of his drug. His idea was, and I gave a tacit assent to it, that I had raised the vessel from curiosity, and that, frightened at its brightness, and the flashes of intense light it gave forth, I had let it fall. I never undeceived him. The fire of the medicine was quenched – the fragrance died away – he grew calm, as a philosopher should under the heaviest trials, and dismissed me to rest.

I will not attempt to describe the sleep of glory and bliss which bathed my soul in paradise during the remaining hours of that memorable night. Words would be faint and shallow types of my enjoyment, or of the gladness that possessed my bosom when I woke. I trod air – my thoughts were in heaven. Earth appeared heaven, and my inheritance upon it was to be one trance of delight. 'This it is to be cured of love,' I thought; 'I will see Bertha this day, and she will find her lover cold and regardless; too happy to be disdainful, yet how utterly indifferent to her!'

The hours danced away. The philosopher, secure that he had once succeeded, and believing that he might again, began to concoct the same medicine once more. He was shut up with his books and drugs, and I had a holiday. I dressed myself with care; I looked in an old but polished shield which served me for a mirror: methoughts my good looks had wonderfully improved. I hurried beyond the precincts of the town, joy in my soul, the beauty of heaven and earth around me. I turned my steps toward the castle – I could look on its lofty turrets with lightness of heart, for I was cured of love. My Bertha saw me afar off, as I came up the avenue. I know not what sudden impulse animated her bosom, but at the sight, she sprang with a light fawnlike bound down the marble steps, and was hastening towards me. But I had been perceived by another person. The old high-born hag, who called herself her protectress, and was her tyrant, had seen me also; she hobbled, panting, up the terrace; a page, as ugly as herself, held up her train, and fanned her as she hurried along, and stopped my fair girl with a, 'How, now, my bold mistress? whither so fast? Back to your cage – hawks are abroad!'

Bertha clasped her hands – her eyes were still bent on my approaching figure. I saw the contest. How I abhorred the old crone who checked the kind impulses of my Bertha's softening heart. Hitherto, respect for her rank had caused me to avoid the lady of the castle; now I disdained such trivial considerations. I was cured of love, and lifted above all human fears; I hastened forwards and soon reached the terrace. How lovely Bertha looked! her eyes flashing fire, her cheeks glowing with impatience and anger, she was a thousand times more graceful and charming than ever. I no longer loved – oh no! I adored – worshipped – idolised her!

She had that morning been persecuted, with more than usual vehemence, to consent to an immediate marriage with my rival. She was reproached with the encouragement that she had shown him – she was threatened with being turned out of doors with disgrace and shame. Her proud spirit rose in arms at the threat; but when she remembered the scorn that she had heaped upon me, and how, perhaps, she had thus lost one whom she now regarded as her only friend, she wept with remorse and rage. At that moment I appeared. 'Oh, Winzy!' she exclaimed, 'take me to your mother's cot; swiftly let me leave the detested luxuries and wretchedness of this noble dwelling – take me to poverty and happiness.'

I clasped her in my arms with transport. The old dame was speechless with fury, and broke forth into invective only when we were far on the road to my natal cottage. My mother received the fair fugitive, escaped from a gilt cage to nature and liberty, with tenderness and joy; my father, who loved her, welcomed her heartily; it was a day of rejoicing, which did not need the addition of the celestial potion of the alchemist to steep me in delight.

Soon after this eventful day, I became the husband of Bertha. I ceased to be the scholar of Cornelius, but I continued his friend. I always felt grateful to him for having, unaware, procured me that delicious draught of a divine elixir, which, instead of curing me of love (sad cure! solitary and joyless remedy for evils which seem blessings to the memory), had inspired me with courage and resolution, thus winning for me an inestimable treasure in my Bertha.

I often called to mind that period of trancelike inebriation with wonder. The drink of Cornelius had not fulfilled the task for which he affirmed that it had been prepared, but its effects were more potent and blissful than words can express. They had faded by degrees, yet they lingered long – and painted life in hues of splendour. Bertha often wondered at my lightness of heart and unaccustomed gaiety; for, before, I had been rather serious, or even sad, in my disposition. She loved me the better for my cheerful temper, and our days were winged by joy.

Five years afterwards I was suddenly summoned to the bedside of the dying Cornelius. He had sent for me in haste, conjuring my instant presence. I found him stretched on his pallet, enfeebled even to death; all of life that yet remained animated his piercing eyes, and they were fixed on a glass vessel, full of roseate liquid.

'Behold,' he said, in a broken and inward voice, 'the vanity of human wishes! a second time my hopes are about to be crowned, a second time they are destroyed. Look at that liquor – you may remember five years ago I had prepared the same, with the same success; then, as now, my thirsting lips expected to taste the immortal elixir – you dashed it from me! and at present it is too late.'

He spoke with difficulty, and fell back on his pillow. I could not help saying: 'How, revered master, can a cure for love restore you to life?'

A faint smile gleamed across his face as I listened earnestly to his scarcely intelligible answer.

'A cure for love and for all things – the Elixir of Immortality. Ah! if now I might drink, I should live for ever!'

As he spoke, a golden flash gleamed from the fluid; a well-remembered fragrance stole over the air; he raised himself, all weak as he was – strength seemed miraculously to re-enter his frame – he stretched forth his hand – a loud explosion startled me – a ray of fire shot up from the elixir, and the glass vessel which contained it was shivered to atoms! I turned my eyes towards the philosopher; he had fallen back – his eyes were glassy – his features rigid – he was dead!

But I lived, and was to live for ever! So said the unfortunate alchemist, and for a few days I believed his words. I remembered the glorious intoxication that had followed my stolen draught. I reflected on the change I had felt in my frame – in my soul. The bounding elasticity of the one – the buoyant lightness of the other. I surveyed myself in a mirror, and could perceive no change in my features during the space of the five years which had elapsed. I remembered the radiant hues and grateful scent of that delicious beverage – worthy the gift it was capable of bestowing – I was, then, *immortal*!

A few days after I laughed at my credulity. The old proverb, that 'a prophet is least regarded in his own country', was true with respect to me and my defunct master. I loved him as a man – I respected him as a sage – but I derided the notion that he could command the powers of darkness, and laughed at the superstitious fears with which he was regarded by the vulgar. He was a wise philosopher, but had no acquaintance with any spirits but those clad in flesh and blood. His science was simply human; and human science, I soon persuaded myself, could never conquer nature's laws so far as to imprison the soul for ever within its carnal habitation. Cornelius had brewed a soul-refreshing drink – more inebriating than wine – sweeter and more fragrant than any fruit: it possessed probably strong medicinal powers, imparting gladness to the heart and vigour to the limbs; but its effects would wear out; already they were diminished in my frame. I was a lucky fellow to have quaffed health and joyous spirits, and perhaps a long life, at my master's hands; but my good fortune ended there; longevity was far different from immortality.

I continued to entertain this belief for many years. Sometimes a thought stole across me – Was the alchemist indeed deceived? But my habitual credence was that I should meet the fate of all the children of Adam at my appointed time – a little late, but still at a natural age. Yet it was certain that I retained a wonderfully youthful look. I was laughed at for my vanity in consulting the mirror so often, but I consulted it in vain – my brow was untrenched – my cheeks – my eyes – my whole person continued as untarnished as in my twentieth year.

I was troubled. I looked at the faded beauty of Bertha – I seemed more like her son. By degrees our neighbours began to make similar observations, and I found at last that I went by the name of the scholar bewitched. Bertha herself grew uneasy. She became jealous and peevish, and at length she began to question me. We had no children; we were all in all to each other; and though, as she grew older, her vivacious spirit became a little allied to ill-temper, and her beauty sadly diminished, I cherished her in my heart as the mistress I idolised, the wife I had sought and won with such perfect love.

At last our situation became intolerable: Bertha was fifty – I twenty years of age. I had, in very shame, in some measure adopted the habits of advanced age; I no longer mingled in the dance among the young and high-spirited, but my heart bounded along with them while I restrained my feet; and a sorry figure I cut among the Nestors of our village. But before the time I mention, things were altered – we were universally shunned; we were – at least, I was – reported to have kept up an iniquitous acquaintance with some of my former master's supposed friends. Poor Bertha was pitied, but deserted. I was regarded with horror and detestation.

What was to be done? we sat by our winter fire – poverty had made itself felt, for none would buy the produce of my farm; and often I had been forced to journey twenty miles to some place where I was not known, to dispose of our property. It is true, we had saved something for an evil day – that day was come.

We sat by our lone fireside – the old-hearted youth and his antiquated wife. Again Bertha insisted on knowing the truth; she recapitulated all she had ever heard said about me, and added her own observations. She conjured me to cast off the spell; she described how much more comely grey hairs were than my chestnut locks; she descanted on the reverence and respect due to age – how preferable to the slight regard paid to mere children: could I imagine that the despicable gifts of youth and good looks outweighed disgrace, hatred and scorn? Nay, in the end I should be burnt as a dealer in the black art, while she, to whom I had not deigned to communicate any portion of my good fortune, might be stoned as my accomplice. At length she insinuated that I must share my secret with her, and bestow on her like benefits to those I myself enjoyed, or she would denounce me – and then she burst into tears.

Thus beset, methought it was the best way to tell the truth. I revealed it as tenderly as I could, and spoke only of a very long life, not of immortality – which representation, indeed, coincided best with my own ideas. When I ended I rose and said: 'And now, my Bertha, will you denounce the lover of your youth? – You will not, I know. But it is too hard, my poor wife, that you should suffer for my ill-luck and the accursed arts of Cornelius. I will leave you – you have wealth enough, and friends will return in my absence. I will go; young as I seem and strong as I am, I can work and gain my bread among strangers, unsuspected and unknown. I loved you in youth; God is my witness that I would not desert you in age, but that your safety and happiness require it.'

I took my cap and moved towards the door; in a moment Bertha's arms were round my neck, and her lips were pressed to mine. 'No, my husband, my Winzy,' she said, 'you shall not go alone – take me with you; we will remove from this place, and, as you say, among strangers we shall be unsuspected and safe. I am not so old as quite to shame you, my Winzy; and I dare say the charm will soon wear off, and, with the blessing of God, you will become more elderly-looking, as is fitting; you shall not leave me.'

I returned the good soul's embrace heartily. 'I will not, my Bertha; but for your sake I had not thought of such a thing. I will be your true, faithful husband while you are spared to me, and do my duty by you to the last.'

The next day we prepared secretly for our emigration. We were obliged to make great pecuniary sacrifices – it could not be helped. We realised a sum sufficient, at least, to maintain us while Bertha lived; and, without saying adieu to anyone, quitted our native country to take refuge in a remote part of western France.

It was a cruel thing to transport poor Bertha from her native village, and the friends of her youth, to a new country, new language, new customs. The strange secret of my destiny rendered this removal immaterial to me; but I compassionated her deeply, and was glad to perceive that she found compensation for her misfortunes in a variety of little ridiculous circumstances. Away from all telltale chroniclers, she sought to decrease the apparent disparity of our ages by a thousand feminine arts – rouge, youthful dress and assumed juvenility of manner. I could not be angry. Did I not myself wear a mask? Why quarrel with hers, because it was less successful? I grieved deeply when I remembered that this was my Bertha, whom I had loved so fondly and won with such transport – the dark-eyed, dark-haired girl, with smiles of enchanting archness and a step like a fawn – this mincing, simpering, jealous old woman. I should have revered her grey locks and withered cheeks; but thus! – It was my work, I knew; but I did not the less deplore this type of human weakness.

Her jealously never slept. Her chief occupation was to discover that, in spite of outward appearances, I was myself growing old. I verily believe that the poor soul loved me truly in her heart, but never had woman so tormenting a mode of displaying fondness. She would discern wrinkles in my face and decrepitude in my walk, while I bounded along in youthful vigour, the youngest-looking of twenty youths. I never dared address another woman. On one occasion, fancying that the belle of the village regarded me with favouring eyes, she brought me a grey wig. Her constant discourse among her acquaintances was that though I looked so young, there was ruin at work within my frame; and she affirmed that the worst symptom about me was my apparent health. My youth was a disease, she said, and I ought at all times to prepare, if not for a sudden and awful death, at least to awake some morning white-headed and bowed down with all the marks of advanced years. I let her talk – I often joined in her conjectures. Her warnings chimed in with my never-ceasing speculations concerning my state, and I took an earnest, though painful, interest in listening to all that her quick wit and excited imagination could say on the subject.

Why dwell on these minute circumstances? We lived on for many long years. Bertha became bedridden and paralytic; I nursed her as a mother might a child. She grew peevish, and still harped upon one string – of how long I should survive her. It has ever been a source of consolation to me that I performed my duty scrupulously towards her. She had been mine in youth, she was mine in age; and at last, when I heaped the sod over her corpse, I wept to feel that I had lost all that really bound me to humanity.

Since then how many have been my cares and woes, how few and empty my enjoyments! I pause here in my history – I will pursue it no further. A sailor without rudder or compass, tossed on a stormy sea – a traveller lost on a widespread heath, without landmark or stone to guide him – such I have been: more lost, more hopeless than either. A nearing ship, a gleam from some far cot, may save them; but I have no beacon except the hope of death.

Death! mysterious, ill-visaged friend of weak humanity! Why alone of all mortals have you cast me from your sheltering fold? Oh, for the peace of the grave! the deep silence of the iron-bound tomb! that thought would cease to work in my brain, and my heart beat no more with emotions varied only by new forms of sadness!

Am I immortal? I return to my first question. In the first place, is it not more probably that the beverage of the alchemist was fraught rather with longevity than eternal life? Such is my hope. And then be it remembered that I only drank half of the potion prepared by him. Was not the whole necessary to complete the charm? To have drained half the Elixir of Immortality is but to be half-immortal – my For Ever is thus truncated and null.

But again, who shall number the years of the half of eternity? I often try to imagine by what rule the infinite may be divided. Sometimes I fancy age advancing upon me. One grey hair I have found. Fool! do I lament? Yes, the fear of age and death often creeps coldly into my heart; and the more I live, the more I dread death, even while I abhor life. Such an enigma is man – born to perish – when he wars, as I do, against the established laws of his nature.

But for this anomaly of feeling surely I might die: the medicine of the alchemist would not be proof against fire – sword – and the strangling waters. I have gazed upon the blue depths of many a placid lake, and the tumultuous rushing of many a mighty river, and have said, peace inhabits those waters; yet I have turned my steps away, to live yet another day. I have asked myself whether suicide would be a crime in one to whom thus only the portals of the other world could be opened. I have done all, except presenting myself as a soldier or duelist, an objection of destruction to my – no, not my fellow mortals, and therefore I have shrunk away. They are not my fellows. The inextinguishable power of life in my frame, and their ephemeral existence, places us wide as the poles asunder. I could not raise a hand against the meanest or the most powerful among them.

Thus have I lived on for many a year – alone, and weary of myself – desirous of death, yet never dying – a mortal immortal. Neither ambition nor avarice can enter my mind, and the ardent love that gnaws at my heart, never to be returned – never to find an equal on which to expend itself – lives there only to torment me.

This very day I conceived a design by which I may end all – without self-slaughter, without making another man a Cain – an expedition, which mortal frame can never survive, even endued with the youth and strength that inhabits mine. Thus I shall put my immortality to the test, and rest for ever – or return, the wonder and benefactor of the human species.

Before I go, a miserable vanity has caused me to pen these pages. I would not die, and leave no name behind. Three centuries have passed since I quaffed the fatal beverage; another year shall not elapse before, encountering gigantic dangers – warring with the powers of frost in their home – beset by famine, toil, and tempest – I yield this body, too tenacious a cage for a soul which thirsts for freedom, to the destructive elements of air and water; or, if I survive, my name shall be recorded as one of the most famous among the sons of men; and, my task achieved, I shall adopt more resolute means, and, by scattering and annihilating the atoms that compose my frame, set at liberty the life imprisoned within and so cruelly prevented from soaring from this dim earth to a sphere more congenial to its immortal essence.

ROBERT LOUIS STEVENSON

Robert Louis Stevenson (1850–94), writer, born in Edinburgh, son of Thomas Stevenson the lighthouse engineer. He studied at Edinburgh, became a lawyer (1875), then turned to writing travel sketches, essays and short stories for magazines. The romantic adventure story *Treasure Island* (1883) brought him fame, and entered him on a course of romantic fiction which included *Kidnapped* (1886), *The Strange Case of Dr Jekyll and Mr Hyde* (1886), *The Master of Ballantrae* (1889), *Catriona* (1893) and the unfinished *Weir of Hermiston* (1896), considered his masterpiece. He suffered from a chronic bronchial condition and in 1888 he settled for health reasons at Vailima, Samoa, where he died of a cerebral haemorrhage six years later.

The Pavilion on the Links

ONE

Tells how I camped in Graden Sea-Wood and beheld a light in the pavilion

I was a great solitary when I was young. I made it my pride to keep aloof and suffice for my own entertainment; and I may say that I had neither friends nor acquaintances until I met that friend who became my wife and the mother of my children. With one man only was I on private terms; this was R. Northmour Esquire, of Graden Easter in Scotland. We had met at college; and though there was not much liking between us, nor even much intimacy, we were so nearly of a humour that we could associate with ease to both. Misanthropes, we believed ourselves to be; but I have thought since that we were only sulky fellows. It was scarcely a companionship, but a coexistence in unsociability. Northmour's exceptional violence of temper made it no easy affair for him to keep the peace with anyone but me; and as he respected my silent ways, and let me come and go as I pleased, I could tolerate his presence without concern. I think we called each other friends.

When Northmour took his degree and I decided to leave the university without one, he invited me on a long visit to Graden Easter; and it was thus that I first became acquainted with the scene of my adventures. The mansion-house of Graden stood in a bleak stretch of country some three miles from the shore of the German Ocean. It was as large as a barrack; and as it had been built of a soft stone, liable to consume the eager air of the seaside, it was damp and draughty within and half-ruinous without. It was impossible for two young men to lodge with comfort in such a dwelling. But there stood in the northern part of the estate, in a wilderness of links and blowing sand-hills and between a plantation and the sea, a small pavilion or belvedere, of modern design, which was exactly suited to our wants; and in this hermitage, speaking little, reading much, and rarely associating except at meals, Northmour and I spent four tempestuous winter months. I might have stayed longer; but one March night there sprang up between us a dispute, which rendered my departure necessary. Northmour spoke hotly, I remember, and I suppose I must have made some tart rejoinder. He leaped from his chair and grappled me; I had to fight, without exaggeration, for my life; and it was only with a great effort that I mastered him, for he was near as strong in body as myself, and seemed filled with the devil. The next morning, we met on our usual terms; but I judged it more delicate to withdraw; nor did he attempt to dissuade me.

It was nine years before I revisited the neighbourhood. I travelled at that time with a tilt cart, a tent and a cooking-stove, tramping all day beside the wagon, and at night, whenever it was possible, gypsying in a cove of the hills or by the side of a wood. I believe I visited in this manner most of the wild and desolate regions both in England and Scotland; and, as I had neither friends nor relations, I was troubled with no correspondence, and had nothing in the nature of headquarters, unless it was the office of my solicitors, from whom I drew my income twice a year. It was a life in which I delighted; and I fully thought to have grown old upon the march and at last died in a ditch.

It was my whole business to find desolate corners, where I could camp without the fear of interruption; and hence, being in another part of the same shire, I bethought me suddenly of the pavilion on the links. No thoroughfare passed within three miles of it. The nearest town, and that was but a fisher village, was at a distance of six or seven. For ten miles of length, and from a depth varying from three miles to half a mile, this belt of barren country lay along the sea. The beach, which was the natural approach, was full of quicksands. Indeed I may say there is hardly a better place of concealment in the United Kingdom. I determined to pass a week in the Sea-Wood of Graden Easter, and making a long stage, reached it about sundown on a wild September day.

The country, I have said, was mixed sand-hill and links; *links* being a Scottish name for sand which has ceased drifting and become more or less solidly covered with turf. The pavilion stood on an even space; a little behind it, the wood began in a hedge of elders huddled together by the wind; in front, a few tumbled sand-hills stood between it and the sea. An outcropping of rock had formed a bastion for the sand, so that there was here a promontory in the coast-line between two shallow bays; and just beyond the tides, the rock again cropped out and formed an islet of small dimensions but strikingly designed. The quicksands were of great extent at low water, and had an infamous reputation in the country. Close in shore, between the islet and the promontory, it was said they would swallow a man in four minutes and a half; but there may have been little ground for this precision. The district was alive with rabbits, and haunted by gulls which made a continual piping about the pavilion. On summer days the outlook was bright and even gladsome; but at sundown in September, with a high wind, and a heavy surf rolling in close along the links, the place told of nothing but dead mariners and sea disaster. A ship beating to windward on the horizon, and a huge truncheon of wreck half-buried in the sands at my feet, completed the innuendo of the scene.

The pavilion – it had been built by the last proprietor, Northmour's uncle, a silly and prodigal virtuoso – presented little signs of age. It was two storeys in height, Italian in design, surrounded by a patch of garden in which nothing had prospered but a few coarse flowers; and looked, with its shuttered windows, not like a house that had been deserted, but like one that had never been tenanted by man. Northmour was plainly from home; whether, as usual, sulking in the cabin of his yacht, or in one of his fitful and extravagant appearances in the world of society, I had, of course, no means of guessing. The place had an air of solitude that daunted even a solitary like myself; the wind cried in the chimneys with a strange and wailing note; and it was with a sense of escape, as if I were going indoors, that I turned away and, driving my cart before me, entered the skirts of the wood.

The Sea-Wood of Graden had been planted to shelter the cultivated fields behind, and check the encroachments of the blowing sand. As you advanced into it from coastward, elders were succeeded by other hardy shrubs; but the timber was all stunted and bushy; it led a life of conflict; the trees were accustomed to swing there all night long in fierce winter tempests; and even in early spring, the leaves were already flying, and autumn was beginning, in this exposed plantation. Inland the ground rose into a little hill, which, along with the islet, served as a sailing mark for seamen. When the hill was open of the islet to the north, vessels must bear well to the eastward to clear Graden Ness and the Graden Bullers. In the lower ground, a streamlet ran among the trees, and, being dammed with dead leaves and clay of its own carrying, spread out every here and there, and lay in stagnant pools. One or two ruined cottages were dotted about the wood; and, according to Northmour, these were ecclesiastical foundations, and in their time had sheltered pious hermits.

I found a den, or small hollow, where there was a spring of pure water; and there, clearing away the brambles, I pitched the tent and made a fire to cook my supper. My horse I picketed farther in the wood where there was a patch of sward. The banks of the den not only concealed the light of my fire, but sheltered me from the wind, which was cold as well as high.

The life I was leading made me both hardy and frugal. I never drank but water, and rarely ate anything more costly than oatmeal; and I required so little sleep, that, although I rose with the peep of day, I would often lie long awake in the dark or starry watches of the night. Thus in Graden Sea-Wood, although I fell thankfully asleep by eight in the evening I was awake again before eleven with a full possession of my faculties, and no sense of drowsiness or fatigue. I rose and sat by the fire, watching the trees and clouds tumultuously tossing and fleeing overhead, and hearkening to the wind and the rollers along the shore; till at length, growing weary of inaction, I quitted the den, and strolled towards the borders of the wood. A young moon, buried in mist, gave a faint illumination to my steps; and the light grew brighter as I walked forth into the links. At the same moment, the wind, smelling of salt from the open ocean and carrying particles of sand, struck me with its full force, so that I had to bow my head.

When I raised it again to look about me, I was aware of a light in the pavilion. It was not stationary; but passed from one window to another, as though someone were reviewing the different apartments with a lamp or candle.

I watched it for some seconds in great surprise. When I had arrived in the afternoon the house had been plainly deserted; now it was as plainly occupied. It was my first idea that a gang of thieves might have broken in and be now ransacking Northmour's cupboards, which were many and not ill supplied. But what should bring thieves to Graden Easter? And, again, all the shutters had been thrown open, and it would have been more in the character of such gentry to close them. I dismissed the notion, and fell back upon another. Northmour himself must have arrived, and was now airing and inspecting the pavilion.

I have said that there was no real affection between this man and me; but, had I loved him like a brother, I was then so much more in love with solitude that I should none the less have shunned his company. As it was, I turned and ran for it; and it was with genuine satisfaction that I found myself safely back beside the fire. I had escaped an acquaintance; I should have one more night in comfort. In the morning, I might either slip away before Northmour was abroad, or pay him as short a visit as I chose.

But when morning came, I thought the situation so diverting that I forgot my shyness. Northmour was at my mercy; I arranged a good practical jest, though I knew well that my neighbour was not the man to jest with in security; and, chuckling beforehand over its success, took my place among the elders at the edge of the wood, whence I could command the door of the pavilion. The shutters were all once more closed, which I remember thinking odd, and the house, with its white walls and green venetians, looked spruce and habitable in the morning light. Hour after hour passed, and still no sign of Northmour. I knew him for a sluggard in the morning; but, as it drew on towards noon, I lost my patience. To say the truth, I had promised myself to break my fast in the pavilion, and hunger began to prick me sharply. It was a pity to let the opportunity go by without some cause for mirth; but the grosser appetite prevailed, and I relinquished my jest with regret, and sallied from the wood.

The appearance of the house affected me, as I drew near, with disquietude. It seemed unchanged since last evening; and I had expected it, I scarce knew why, to wear some external signs of habitation. But no: the windows were all closely shuttered, the chimneys breathed no smoke, and the front door itself was closely padlocked. Northmour, therefore, had entered by the back; this was the natural and, indeed, the necessary conclusion; and you may judge of my surprise when, on turning around the house, I found the back door similarly secured.

My mind at once reverted to the original theory of thieves; and I blamed myself sharply for my last night's inaction. I examined all the windows on the lower storey, but none of them had been tampered with; I tried the padlocks, but they were both secure. It thus became a problem how the thieves, if thieves they were, had managed to enter the house. They must have got, I reasoned, upon the roof of the outhouse where Northmour used to keep his photographic battery; and from thence, either by the window of the study or that of my old bedroom, completed their burglarious entry.

I followed what I supposed was their example; and, getting on the roof, tried the shutters of each room. Both were secure; but I was not to be beaten; and, with a little force, one of them flew open, grazing, as it did so, the back of my hand. I remember, I put the wound to my mouth, and stood for perhaps half a minute licking it like a dog, and mechanically gazing behind me over the waste links and the sea; and, in that space of time, my eye made note of a large schooner yacht some miles to the north-east. Then I threw up the window and climbed in.

I went over the house, and nothing can express my mystification. There was no sign of disorder, but, on the contrary, the rooms were unusually clean and pleasant. I found fires laid, ready for lighting; three bedrooms prepared with a luxury quite foreign to Northmour's habits, and with water in the ewers and the beds turned down; a table set for three in the dining-room; and an ample supply of cold meats, game and vegetables on the pantry shelves. There were guests expected, that was plain; but why guests, when Northmour hated society? And, above all, why was the house thus stealthily prepared at dead of night? and why were the shutters closed and the doors padlocked?

I effaced all traces of my visit, and came forth from the window feeling sobered and concerned.

The schooner yacht was still in the same place; and it flashed for a moment through my mind that this might be the *Red Earl* bringing the owner of the pavilion and his guests. But the vessel's head was set the other way.

TWO

Tells of the nocturnal landing from the yacht

I returned to the den to cook myself a meal, of which I stood in great need, as well as to care for my horse, whom I had somewhat neglected in the morning. From time to time I went down to the edge of the wood; but there was no change in the pavilion, and not a human creature was seen all day upon the links. The schooner in the offing was the one touch of life within my range of vision. She, apparently with no set object, stood off and on or lay to, hour after hour; but as the evening deepened, she drew steadily nearer. I became more convinced that she carried Northmour and his friends, and that they would probably come ashore after dark; not only because that was of a piece with the secrecy of the preparations, but because the tide would not have flowed sufficiently before eleven to cover Graden Floe and the other sea quags that fortified the shore against invaders.

All day the wind had been going down, and the sea along with it; but there was a return towards sunset of the heavy weather of the day before. The night set in pitch dark. The wind came off the sea in squalls, like the firing of a battery of cannon; now and then there was a flaw of rain, and the surf rolled heavier with the rising tide. I was down at my observatory among the elders, when a light was run up to the masthead of the schooner, and showed she was closer in than when I had last seen her by the dying daylight. I concluded that this must be a signal to Northmour's associates on shore; and, stepping forth into the links, looked around me for something in response.

A small footpath ran along the margin of the wood, and formed the most direct communication between the pavilion and the mansion-house; and, as I cast my eyes to that side, I saw a spark of light, not a quarter of a mile away, and rapidly approaching. From its uneven course it appeared to be the light of a lantern carried by a person who followed the windings of the path, and was often staggered and taken aback by the more violent squalls. I concealed myself once more among the elders, and waited eagerly for the newcomer's advance. It proved to be a woman; and, as she passed within half a rod of my ambush, I was able to recognise the features. The deaf and silent old dame, who had nursed Northmour in his childhood, was his associate in this underhand affair.

I followed her at a little distance, taking advantage of the innumerable heights and hollows, concealed by the darkness and favoured not only by the nurse's deafness but by the uproar of the wind and surf. She entered the pavilion, and, going at once to the upper storey, opened and set a light in one of the windows that looked towards the sea. Immediately afterwards the light at the schooner's masthead was run down and extinguished. Its purpose had been attained, and those on board were sure that they were expected. The old woman resumed her preparations; although the other shutters remained closed, I could see a glimmer going to and fro about the house; and a gush of sparks from one chimney after another soon told me that the fires were being kindled.

Northmour and his guests, I was now persuaded, would come ashore as soon as there was water on the floe. It was a wild night for a boat service; and I felt some alarm mingle with my curiosity as I reflected on the danger of the landing. My old acquaintance, it was true, was the most eccentric of men; but the present eccentricity was both disquieting and lugubrious to consider. A variety of feelings thus led me towards the beach, where I lay flat on my face in a hollow within six feet of the track that led to the pavilion. Thence, I should have the satisfaction of recognising the arrivals, and, if they should prove to be acquaintances, greeting them as soon as they had landed.

Some time before eleven, while the tide was still dangerously low, a boat's lantern appeared close in shore; and, my attention being thus awakened, I could perceive another still far to seaward, violently tossed, and sometimes hidden by the billows. The weather, which was getting dirtier as the night went on, and the perilous situation of the yacht upon a lee shore, had probably driven them to attempt a landing at the earliest possible moment.

A little afterwards, four yachtsmen carrying a very heavy chest, and guided by a fifth with a lantern, passed close in front of me as I lay, and were admitted to the pavilion by the nurse. They returned to the beach, and passed me a second time with another chest, larger but apparently not so heavy as the first. A third time they made the transit, and on this occasion one of the yachtsmen carried a leather portmanteau and the others a lady's trunk and carriage bag. My curiosity was sharply excited. If a woman were among the guests of Northmour, it would show a change in his habits and an apostasy from his pet theories of life, well calculated to fill me with surprise. When he and I dwelt there together, the pavilion had been a temple of misogyny. And now, one of the detested sex was to be installed under its roof. I remembered one or two particulars, a few notes of daintiness and almost of coquetry which had struck me the day before as I surveyed the preparations in the house; their purpose was now clear, and I thought myself dull not to have perceived it from the first.

While I was thus reflecting, a second lantern drew near me from the beach. It was carried by a yachtsman whom I had not yet seen, and who was conducting two other persons to the pavilion. These two persons were unquestionably the guests for whom the house was made ready; and, straining eye and ear, I set myself to watch them as they passed. One was an unusually tall man, in a travelling hat slouched over his eyes, and a highland cape closely buttoned and turned up so as to conceal his face. You could make out no more of him than that he was, as I have said, unusually tall, and walked feebly with a heavy stoop. By his side, and either clinging to him or giving him support – I could not make out which – was a young, tall and slender figure of a woman. She was extremely pale; but in the light of the lantern her face was so marred by strong and changing shadows, that she might equally well have been as ugly as sin or as beautiful as I afterwards found her to be.

When they were just abreast of me, the girl made some remark which was drowned by the noise of the wind.

'Hush!' said her companion; and there was something in the tone with which the word was uttered that thrilled and rather shook my spirits. It seemed to breathe from a bosom labouring under the deadliest terror; I have never heard another syllable so expressive; and I still hear it again when I am feverish at night, and my mind runs upon old times. The man turned towards the girl as he spoke; I had a glimpse of much red beard and a nose which seemed to have been broken in youth; and his light eyes seemed shining in his face with some strong and unpleasant emotion.

But these two passed on and were admitted in their turn to the pavilion.

One by one, or in groups, the seamen returned to the beach. The wind brought me the sound of a rough voice crying, 'Shove off!' Then, after a pause, another lantern drew near. It was Northmour alone.

My wife and I, a man and a woman, have often agreed to wonder how a person could be, at the same time, so handsome and so repulsive as Northmour. He had the appearance of a finished gentleman; his face bore every mark of intelligence and courage; but you had only to look at him, even in his most amiable moment, to see that he had the temper of a slaver captain. I never knew a character that was both explosive and revengeful to the same degree; he combined the vivacity of the south with the sustained and deadly hatreds of the north; and both traits were plainly written on his face, which was a sort of danger signal. In person he was tall, strong and active; his hair and complexion very dark; his features handsomely designed, but spoiled by a menacing expression.

At that moment he was somewhat paler than by nature; he wore a heavy frown, and his lips worked and he looked sharply round him as he walked, like a man besieged with apprehensions. And yet I thought he had a look of triumph underlying all, as though he had already done much, and was near the end of an achievement.

Partly from a scruple of delicacy – which I dare say came too late – partly from the pleasure of startling an acquaintance, I desired to make my presence known to him without delay.

I got suddenly to my feet, and stepped forward. 'Northmour!' said I.

I have never had so shocking a surprise in all my days. He leaped on me without a word; something shone in his hand and he struck for my heart with a dagger. At the same moment I knocked him head over heels. Whether it was my quickness, or his own uncertainty, I know not; but the blade only grazed my shoulder, while the hilt and his fist struck me violently on the mouth.

I fled, but not far. I had often and often observed the capabilities of the sand-hills for protracted ambush or stealthy advances and retreats, and not ten yards from the scene of the scuffle, plumped down again upon the grass. The lantern had fallen and gone out. But what was my astonishment to see Northmour slip at a bound into the pavilion, and hear him bar the door behind him with a clang of iron!

He had not pursued me. He had run away. Northmour, whom I knew for the most implacable and daring of men, had run away! I could scarce believe my reason; and yet in this strange business, where all was incredible, there was nothing to make a work about in an incredibility more or less. For why was the pavilion secretly prepared? Why had Northmour landed with his guests at dead of night, in half a gale of wind, and with the floe scarce covered? Why had he sought to kill me? Had he not recognised my voice? I wondered. And, above all, how had he come to have a dagger ready in his hand? A dagger, or even a sharp knife, seemed out of keeping with the age in which we lived; and a gentleman landing from his yacht on the shore of his own estate, even although it was at night and in some mysterious circumstances, does not usually, as a matter of fact, walk thus prepared for deadly onslaught. The more I reflected, the further I felt at sea. I recapitulated the elements of mystery, counting them on my fingers: the pavilion secretly prepared for guests; the guests landed at the risk of their lives and to the imminent peril of the yacht; the guests, or at least one of them, in undisguised and seemingly causeless terror; Northmour with a naked weapon; Northmour stabbing his most intimate acquaintance at a word; last, and not least strange, Northmour fleeing from the man whom he had sought to murder, and barricading himself, like a hunted creature, behind the door of the pavilion. Here were at least six separate causes for extreme surprise; each part and parcel with the others, and forming all together one consistent story. I felt almost ashamed to believe my own senses.

As I thus stood, transfixed with wonder, I began to grow painfully conscious of the injuries I had received in the scuffle; I skulked round among the sand-hills and, by a devious path, regained the shelter of the wood. On the way, the old nurse passed again within several yards of me, still carrying her lantern, on the return journey to the mansion-house of Graden. This made a seventh suspicious feature in the case – Northmour and his guests, it appeared, were to cook and do the cleaning for themselves, while the old woman continued to inhabit the big empty barrack among the policies. There must surely be great cause for secrecy, when so many inconveniences were confronted to preserve it.

So thinking, I made my way to the den. For greater security, I trod out the embers of the fire, and lit my lantern to examine the wound upon my shoulder. It was a trifling hurt, although it bled somewhat freely, and I dressed it as well as I could (for its position made it difficult to reach) with some rag and cold water from the spring. While I was thus busied, I mentally declared war against Northmour and his mystery. I am not an angry man by nature, and I believe there was more curiosity than resentment in my heart. But war I certainly declared; and, by way of preparation, I got out my revolver, and, having drawn the charges, cleaned and reloaded it with scrupulous care. Next I became preoccupied about my horse. It might break loose, or fall to neighing, and so betray my camp in the Sea-Wood. I determined to rid myself of its neighbourhood, and long before dawn I was leading it over the links in the direction of the fisher village.

THREE

Tells how I became acquainted with my wife

For two days I skulked round the pavilion, profiting from the uneven surface of the links. I became an adept in the necessary tactics. These low hillocks and shallow dells, running one into another, became a kind of cloak of darkness for my enthralling, but perhaps dishonourable, pursuit. Yet, in spite of this advantage, I could learn but little of Northmour or his guests.

Fresh provisions were brought under cover of darkness by the old woman from the mansion-house. Northmour, and the young lady, sometimes together, but more often singly, would walk for an hour or two at a time on the beach beside the quicksand. I could not but conclude that this promenade was chosen with an eye to secrecy; for the spot was open only to the seaward. But it suited me not less excellently; the highest and most accidented of the sand-hills immediately adjoined; and from these, lying flat in a hollow, I could overlook Northmour or the young lady as they walked.

The tall man seemed to have disappeared. Not only did he never cross the threshold, but he never so much as showed face at a window; or, at least, not so far as I could see; for I dared not creep forward beyond a certain distance in the day, since the upper floor commanded the bottoms of the links; and at night, when I could venture farther, the lower windows were barricaded as if to stand a siege. Sometimes I thought the tall man must be confined to bed, for I remembered the feebleness of his gait; and sometimes I thought he must have gone clear away, and that Northmour and the young lady remained alone together in the pavilion. The idea, even then, displeased me.

Whether or not this pair were man and wife, I had seen abundant reason to doubt the friendliness of their relation. Although I could hear nothing of what they said, and rarely so much as glean a decided expression on the face of either, there was a distance, almost a stiffness, in their bearing which showed them to be either unfamiliar or at enmity. The girl walked faster when she was with Northmour than when she was alone; and I conceived that any inclination between a man and a woman would rather delay than accelerate the step. Moreover, she kept a good yard free of him, and trailed her umbrella, as if it were a barrier, on the side between them. Northmour kept sidling closer; and, as the girl retired from his advance, their course lay at a sort of diagonal across the beach, and would have landed them in the surf had it been long enough continued. But, when this was imminent, the girl would unostentatiously change sides and put Northmour between her and the sea. I watched these manoeuvres, for my part, with high enjoyment and approval, and chuckled to myself at every move.

On the morning of the third day, she walked alone for some time, and I perceived, to my great concern, that she was more than once in tears. You will see that my heart was already interested more than I supposed. She had a firm yet airy motion of the body, and carried her head with unimaginable grace; every step was a thing to look at, and she seemed in my eyes to breathe sweetness and distinction.

The day was so agreeable, being calm and sunshiny, with a tranquil sea, and yet with a healthful piquancy and vigour in the air, that, contrary to custom, she was tempted forth a second time to walk. On this occasion she was accompanied by Northmour, and they had been but a short while on the beach, when I saw him take forcible possession of her hand. She struggled, and uttered a cry that was almost a scream. I sprang to my feet, unmindful of my strange position; but, ere I had taken a step, I saw Northmour bareheaded and bowing very low, as if to apologise; and dropped again at once into my ambush. A few words were interchanged; and then, with another bow, he left the beach to return to the pavilion. He passed not far from me, and I could see him, flushed and lowering, and cutting savagely with his cane among the grass. It was not without satisfaction that I recognised my own handiwork in a great cut under his right eye, and a considerable discolouration round the socket.

For some time the girl remained where he had left her, looking out past the islet and over the bright sea. Then with a start, as one who throws off preoccupation and puts energy again upon its mettle, she broke into a rapid and decisive walk. She also was much incensed by what had passed. She had forgotten where she was. And I beheld her walk straight into the borders of the quicksand where it is most abrupt and dangerous. Two or three steps farther and her life would have been in serious jeopardy, when I slid down the face of the sand-hill, which is there precipitous, and, running halfway forward, called to her to stop.

She did so, and turned round. There was not a tremor of fear in her behaviour, and she marched directly up to me like a queen. I was barefoot, and clad like a common sailor, save for an Egyptian scarf round my waist; and she probably took me at first for someone from the fisher village, straying after bait. As for her, when I thus saw her face to face, her eyes set steadily and imperiously upon mine, I was filled with admiration and astonishment, and thought her even more beautiful than I had looked to find her. Nor could I think enough of one who, acting with so much boldness, yet preserved a maidenly air that was both quaint and engaging; for my wife kept an old-fashioned precision of manner through all her admirable life – an excellent thing in woman, since it sets another value on her sweet familiarities.

'What does this mean?' she asked.

'You were walking,' I told her, 'directly into Graden Floe.'

'You do not belong to these parts,' she said again. 'You speak like an educated man.'

'I believe I have a right to that name,' said I, 'although in this disguise.'

But her woman's eye had already detected the sash. 'Oh!' she said; 'your sash betrays you.'

'You have said the word *betray*,' I resumed. 'May I ask you not to betray me? I was obliged to disclose myself in your interest; but if Northmour learned my presence it might be worse than disagreeable for me.'

'Do you know,' she asked, 'to whom you are speaking?'

'Not to Mr Northmour's wife?' I asked, by way of answer.

She shook her head. All this while she was studying my face with an embarrassing intentness. Then she broke out –

'You have an honest face. Be honest like your face, sir, and tell me what you want and what you are afraid of. Do you think I could hurt you? I believe you have far more power to injure me! And yet you do not look unkind. What do you mean – you, a gentleman – by skulking like a spy about this desolate place? Tell me,' she said, 'who is it you hate?'

'I hate no one,' I answered; 'and I fear no one face to face. My name is Cassilis – Frank Cassilis. I lead the life of a vagabond for my own good pleasure. I am one of Northmour's oldest friends; and three nights ago, when I addressed him on these links, he stabbed me in the shoulder with a knife.'

'It was you!' she said.

'Why he did so,' I continued, disregarding the interruption, 'is more than I can guess, and more than I care to know. I have not many friends, nor am I very susceptible to friendship; but no man shall drive me from a place by terror. I had camped in Graden Sea-Wood ere he came; I camp in it still. If you think I mean harm to you or yours, madam, the remedy is in your hand. Tell him that my camp is in the Hemlock Den, and tonight he can stab me in safety while I sleep.'

With this I doffed my cap to her, and scrambled up once more among the sand-hills. I do not know why, but I felt a prodigious sense of injustice, and felt like a hero and a martyr; while, as a matter of fact, I had not a word to say in my defence, nor so much as one plausible reason to offer for my conduct. I had stayed at Graden out of a curiosity natural enough, but undignified; and though there was another motive growing in along with the first, it was not one which, at that period, I could have properly explained to the lady of my heart.

Certainly, that night, I thought of no one else; and, though her whole conduct and position seemed suspicious, I could not find it in my heart to entertain a doubt of her integrity. I could have staked my life that she was clear of blame, and, though all was dark at the present, that the explanation of the mystery would show her part in these events to be both right and needful. It was true, let me cudgel my imagination as I pleased, that I could invent no theory of her relations to Northmour; but I felt none the less sure of my conclusion because it was founded on instinct in place of reason, and, as I may say, went to sleep that night with the thought of her under my pillow.

Next day she came out about the same hour alone, and, as soon as the sand-hills concealed her from the pavilion, drew nearer to the edge, and called me by name in guarded tones. I was astonished to observe that she was deadly pale, and seemingly under the influence of strong emotion.

'Mr Cassilis!' she cried; 'Mr Cassilis!'

I appeared at once, and leaped down upon the beach. A remarkable air of relief overspread her countenance as soon as she saw me.

'Oh!' she cried, with a hoarse sound, like one whose bosom has been lightened of a weight. And then, 'Thank God you are still safe!' she added; 'I knew, if you were, you would be here.' (Was not this strange? So swiftly and wisely does Nature prepare our hearts for these great lifelong intimacies, that both my wife and I had been given a presentiment on this the second day of our acquaintance. I had even then hoped that she would seek me; she had felt sure that she would find me.) 'Do not,' she went, on swiftly, 'do not stay in this place. Promise me that you will sleep no longer in that wood. You do not know how I suffer; all last night I could not sleep for thinking of your peril.'

'Peril?' I repeated. 'Peril from whom? From Northmour?'

'Not so,' she said. 'Did you think I would tell him after what you said?'

'Not from Northmour?' I repeated. 'Then how? From whom? I see none to be afraid of.'

'You must not ask me,' was her reply, 'for I am not free to tell you. Only believe me, and go hence – believe me, and go away quickly, quickly, for your life!'

An appeal to his alarm is never a good plan to rid oneself of a spirited young man. My obstinacy was but increased by what she said, and I made it a point of honour to remain. And her solicitude for my safety still more confirmed me in the resolve.

'You must not think me inquisitive, madam,' I replied; 'but, if Graden is so dangerous a place, you yourself perhaps remain here at some risk.'

She only looked at me reproachfully.

'You and your father – ' I resumed; but she interrupted me almost with a gasp.

'My father! How do you know that?' she cried.

'I saw you together when you landed,' was my answer; and I do not know why, but it seemed satisfactory to both of us, as indeed it was the truth. 'But,' I continued, 'you need have no fear from me. I see you have some reason to be secret, and, you may believe me, your secret is as safe with me as if I were in Graden Floe. I have scarce spoken to anyone for years; my horse is my only companion, and even he, poor beast, is not beside me. You see, then, you may count on me for silence. So tell me the truth, my dear young lady, are you not in danger?'

'Mr Northmour says you are an honourable man,' she returned, 'and I believe it when I see you. I will tell you so much; you are right; we are in dreadful, dreadful danger, and you share it by remaining where you are.'

'Ah!' said I; 'you have heard of me from Northmour? And he gives me a good character?'

'I asked him about you last night,' was her reply. 'I pretended,' she hesitated, 'I pretended to have met you long ago, and spoken to you of him. It was not true; but I could not help myself without betraying you, and you had put me in a difficulty. He praised you highly.'

'And – you may permit me one question – does this danger come from Northmour?' I asked.

'From Mr Northmour?' she cried. 'Oh no; he stays with us to share it.'

'While you propose that I should run away?' I said. 'You do not rate me very high.'

'Why should you stay?' she asked. 'You are no friend of ours.'

I know not what came over me, for I had not been conscious of a similar weakness since I was a child, but I was so mortified by this retort that my eyes pricked and filled with tears, as I continued to gaze upon her face.

'No, no,' she said, in a changed voice; 'I did not mean the words unkindly.'

'It was I who offended,' I said; and I held out my hand with a look of appeal that somehow touched her, for she gave me hers at once, and even eagerly. I held it for awhile in mine, and gazed into her eyes. It was she who first tore her hand away, and, forgetting all about her request and the promise she had sought to extort, ran at the top of her speed, and without turning, till she was out of sight.

And then I knew that I loved her, and thought in my glad heart that she – she herself – was not indifferent to my suit. Many a time she has denied it in after days, but it was with a smiling and not a serious denial. For my part, I am sure our hands would not have lain so closely in each other if she had not begun to melt to me already. And, when all is said, it is no great contention, since, by her own avowal, she began to love me on the morrow.

And yet on the morrow very little took place. She came and called me down as on the day before, upbraided me for lingering at Graden, and, when she found I was still obdurate, began to ask me more particularly as to my arrival. I told her by what series of accidents I had come to witness their disembarkation, and how I had determined to remain, partly from the interest which had been wakened in me by Northmour's guests, and partly because of his own murderous attack. As to the former, I fear I was disingenuous, and led her to regard herself as having been an attraction to me from the first moment that I saw her on the links. It relieves my heart to make this confession even now, when my wife is with God, and already knows all things, and the honesty of my purpose even in this; for while she lived, although it often pricked my conscience, I had never the hardihood to undeceive her. Even a little secret, in such a married life as ours, is like the rose-leaf which kept the princess from her sleep.

From this the talk branched into other subjects, and I told her much about my lonely and wandering existence; she, for her part, giving ear, and saying little. Although we spoke very naturally, and latterly on topics that might seem indifferent, we were both sweetly agitated. Too soon it was time for her to go; and we separated, as if by mutual consent, without shaking hands, for both knew that, between us, it was no idle ceremony.

The next, and that was the fourth day of our acquaintance, we met in the same spot, but early in the morning, with much familiarity and yet much timidity on either side. When she had once more spoken about my danger – and that, I understood, was her excuse for coming – I, who had prepared a great deal of talk during the night, began to tell her how highly I valued her kind interest, and how no one had ever cared to hear about my life, nor had I ever cared to relate it, before yesterday.

Suddenly she interrupted me, saying with vehemence, 'And yet, if you knew who I was, you would not so much as speak to me!'

I told her such a thought was madness, and, little as we had met, I counted her already a dear friend; but my protestations seemed only to make her more desperate.

'My father is in hiding!' she cried.

'My dear,' I said, forgetting for the first time to add 'young lady', 'what do I care? If he were in hiding twenty times over, would it make one thought of change in you?'

'Ah, but the cause!' she cried, 'the cause! It is – ' she faltered for a second – 'it is disgraceful to us!'

FOUR

Tells in what a startling manner I learned that I was not alone in Graden Sea-Wood

This was my wife's story, as I drew it from her among tears and sobs. Her name was Clara Huddlestone: it sounded very beautiful in my ears; but not so beautiful as that other name of Clara Cassilis, which she wore during the longer and, I thank God, the happier portion of her life. Her father, Bernard Huddlestone, had been a private banker in a very large way of business. Many years before, his affairs becoming disordered, he had been led to try dangerous, and at last criminal, expedients to retrieve himself from ruin. All was in vain; he became more and more cruelly involved, and found his honour lost at the same moment with his fortune. About this period, Northmour had been courting his daughter with great assiduity, though with small encouragement; and to him, knowing him thus disposed in his favour, Bernard Huddlestone turned for help in his extremity. It was not merely ruin and dishonour, nor merely a legal condemnation, that the unhappy man had brought upon his head. It seems he could have gone to prison with a light heart. What he feared, what kept him awake at night or recalled him from slumber into frenzy, was some secret, sudden and unlawful attempt upon his life. Hence, he desired to bury his existence and escape to one of the islands in the South Pacific, and it was in Northmour's yacht, the *Red Earl*, that he designed to go. The yacht had picked them up clandestinely upon the coast of Wales, and had deposited them at Graden, till she could be refitted and provisioned for the longer voyage. Nor could Clara doubt that her hand had been stipulated as the price of passage. For, although Northmour was neither unkind nor even discourteous, he had shown himself in several instances somewhat overbold in speech and manner.

I listened, I need not say, with fixed attention, and put many questions as to the more mysterious part. It was in vain. She had no clear idea of what the blow was, nor of how it was expected to fall. Her father's alarm was unfeigned and physically prostrating, and he had thought more than once of making an unconditional surrender to the police. But the scheme was finally abandoned, for he was convinced that not even the strength of our English prisons could shelter him from his pursuers. He had had many affairs with Italy, and with Italians resident in London, in the later years of his business; and these last, as Clara fancied, were somehow connected with the doom that threatened him. He had shown great terror at the presence of an Italian seaman on board the *Red Earl*, and had bitterly and repeatedly accused Northmour in consequence. The latter had protested that Beppo (that was the seaman's name) was a capital fellow, and could be trusted to the death; but Mr Huddlestone had continued ever since to declare that all was lost, that it was only a question of days, and that Beppo would be the ruin of him yet.

I regarded the whole story as the hallucination of a mind shaken by calamity. He had suffered heavy loss by his Italian transactions; and hence the sight of an Italian was hateful to him, and the principal part in his nightmare would naturally enough be played by one of that nation.

'What your father wants,' I said, 'is a good doctor and some calming medicine.'

'But Mr Northmour?' objected Clara. 'He is untroubled by losses, and yet he shares in this terror.'

I could not help laughing at what I considered her simplicity.

'My dear,' said I, 'you have told me yourself what reward he has to look for. All is fair in love, you must remember; and if Northmour foments your father's terrors, it is not at all because he is afraid of any Italian man, but simply because he is infatuated with a charming English woman.'

She reminded me of his attack upon myself on the night of the disembarkation, and this I was unable to explain. In short, and from one thing to another, it was agreed between us that I should set out at once for the fisher village, Graden Wester, as it was called, look up all the newspapers I could find, and see for myself if there seemed any basis of fact for these continued alarms. The next morning, at the same hour and place, I was to make my report to Clara. She said no more on that occasion about my departure; nor, indeed, did she make it a secret that she clung to the thought of my proximity as something helpful and pleasant; and, for my part, I could not have left her if she had gone upon her knees to ask it.

I reached Graden Wester before ten in the forenoon; for in those days I was an excellent pedestrian, and the distance, as I think I have said, was little over seven miles; fine walking all the way upon the springy turf. The village is one of the bleakest on that coast, which is saying much: there is a church in a hollow; a miserable haven in the rocks, where many boats have been lost as they returned from fishing; two or three score of stone houses arranged along the beach and in two streets, one leading from the harbour and another striking out from it at right angles; and, at the corner of these two, a very dark and cheerless tavern, by way of principal hotel.

I had dressed myself somewhat more suitably to my station in life, and at once called upon the minister in his little manse beside the graveyard. He knew me, although it was more than nine years since we had met; and when I told him that I had been long upon a walking tour, and was behind with the news, readily lent me an armful of newspapers, dating from a month back to the day before. With these I sought the tavern, and, ordering some break-fast, sat down to study the 'Huddlestone Failure'.

It had been, it appeared, a very flagrant case. Thousands of persons were reduced to poverty, and one in particular had blown out his brains as soon as payment was suspended. It was strange to myself that, while I read these details, I continued rather to sympathise with Mr Huddlestone than with his victims, so complete already was the empire of my love for my wife. A price was naturally set upon the banker's head; and, as the case was inexcusable and the public indignation thoroughly aroused, the unusual figure of seven hundred and fifty pounds was offered for his capture. He was reported to have large sums of money in his possession. One day, he had been heard of in Spain; the next, there was sure intelligence that he was still lurking between Manchester and Liverpool, or along the border of Wales; and the day after, a telegram would announce his arrival in Cuba or Yucatan. But in all this there was no word of an Italian, nor any sign of mystery.

In the very last paper, however, there was one item not so clear. The accountants who were charged to verify the failure had, it seemed, come upon the traces of a very large number of thousands, which figured for some time in the transactions of the house of Huddlestone; but which came from nowhere, and disappeared in the same mysterious fashion. It was only once referred to by name, and then under the initials 'X. X.', but it had plainly been floated for the first time into the business at a period of great depression some six years ago. The name of a distinguished royal personage had been mentioned by rumour in connection with this sum. 'The cowardly desperado' – such, I remember, was the editorial expression – was supposed to have escaped with a large part of this mysterious fund still in his possession.

I was still brooding over the fact, and trying to torture it into some connection with Mr Huddlestone's danger, when a man entered the tavern and asked for some bread and cheese with a decided foreign accent.

'Siete Italiano?' said I.

'Si, signor,' was his reply.

I said it was unusually far north to find one of his compatriots; at which he shrugged his shoulders, and replied that a man would go anywhere to find work. What work he could hope to find at Graden Wester, I was totally unable to conceive; and the incident struck so unpleasantly upon my mind, that I asked the landlord, while he was counting me some change, whether he had ever before seen an Italian in the village. He said he had once seen some Norwegians, who had been shipwrecked on the other side of Graden Ness and rescued by the lifeboat from Cauldhaven.

'No!' said I; 'but an Italian, like the man who has just had bread and cheese?'

'What?' cried he, 'yon black-avised fellow wi' the teeth? Was he an I-talian? Weel, yon's the first that ever I saw, an' I dare say he's like to be the last.'

Even as he was speaking, I raised my eyes, and, casting a glance into the street, beheld three men in earnest conversation together, and not thirty yards away. One of them was my recent companion in the tavern parlour; the other two, by their handsome, sallow features and soft hats, evidently belonged to the same race. A crowd of village children stood around them, gesticulating and talking gibberish in imitation. The trio looked singularly foreign to the bleak dirty street in which they were standing, and the dark grey heaven that overspread them; and I confess my incredulity received at that moment a shock from which it never recovered. I might reason with myself as I pleased, but I could not argue down the effect of what I had seen, and I began to share in the Italian terror.

It was already drawing towards the close of the day before I had returned the newspapers at the manse and got well forward on to the links on my way home. I shall never forget that walk. It grew very cold and boisterous; the wind sang in the short grass about my feet; thin rain showers came running on the gusts; and an immense mountain range of clouds began to arise out of the bosom of the sea. It would be hard to imagine a more dismal evening; and whether it was from these external influences, or because my nerves were already affected by what I had heard and seen, my thoughts were as gloomy as the weather.

The upper windows of the pavilion commanded a considerable spread of links in the direction of Graden Wester. To avoid observation, it was necessary to hug the beach until I had gained cover from the higher sand-hills on the little headland, when I might strike across, through the hollows, for the margin of the wood. The sun was about setting; the tide was low, and all the quicksands uncovered; and I was moving along, lost in unpleasant thought, when I was suddenly thunderstruck to perceive the prints of human feet. They ran parallel to my own course, but low down upon the beach instead of along the border of the turf; and, when I examined them, I saw at once, by the size and coarseness of the impression, that it was a stranger to me and to those in the pavilion who had recently passed that way. Not only so; but from the recklessness of the course which he had followed, steering near to the most formidable portions of the sand, he was as evidently a stranger to the country and to the ill-repute of Graden beach.

Step by step I followed the prints; until, a quarter of a mile farther, I beheld them die away into the south-eastern boundary of Graden Floe. There, whoever he was, the miserable man had perished. One or two gulls, who had, perhaps, seen him disappear, wheeled over his sepulchre with their usual melancholy piping. The sun had broken through the clouds by a last effort, and coloured the wide level of quicksands with a dusky purple. I stood for some time gazing at the spot, chilled and disheartened by my own reflections, and with a strong and commanding consciousness of death. I remember wondering how long the tragedy had taken, and whether his screams had been audible at the pavilion. And then, making a strong resolution, I was about to tear myself away, when a gust fiercer than usual fell upon this quarter of the beach, and I saw, now whirling high in the air, now skimming lightly across the surface of the sands, a soft, black felt hat, somewhat conical in shape, such as I had remarked already on the heads of the Italians.

I believe, but I am not sure, that I uttered a cry. The wind was driving the hat shoreward, and I ran round the border of the floe to be ready against its arrival. The gust fell, dropping the hat for a while upon the quicksand, and then, once more freshening, landed it a few yards from where I stood. I seized it with the interest you may imagine. It had seen some service; indeed, it was rustier than either of those I had seen that day upon the street. The lining was red, stamped with the name of the maker, which I have forgotten, and that of the place of manufacture, Venedig. This (it is not yet forgotten) was the name given by the Austrians to the beautiful city of Venice, then, and for long after, a part of their dominions.

The shock was complete. I saw imaginary Italians upon every side; and for the first, and, I may say, for the last time in my experience, became over-powered by what is called a panic terror. I knew nothing, that is, to be afraid of, and yet I admit that I was heartily afraid; and it was with a sensible reluctance that I returned to my exposed and solitary camp in the Sea-Wood.

There I ate some cold porridge which had been left over from the night before, for I was disinclined to make a fire; and, feeling strengthened and reassured, dismissed all these fanciful terrors from my mind and lay down to sleep with composure.

How long I may have slept it is impossible for me to guess, but I was awakened at last by a sudden, blinding flash of light into my face. It woke me like a blow. In an instant I was upon my knees. But the light had gone as suddenly as it came. The darkness was intense. And, as it was blowing great guns from the sea and pouring with rain, the noises of the storm effectually concealed all others.

It was, I dare say, half a minute before I regained my self-possession. But for two circumstances, I should have thought I had been awakened by some new and vivid form of nightmare. First, the flap of my tent, which I had shut carefully when I retired, was now unfastened; and, second, I could still perceive, with a sharpness that excluded any theory of hallucination, the smell of hot metal and of burning oil. The conclusion was obvious. I had been wakened by someone flashing a bull's-eye lantern in my face. It had been but a flash, and away. He had seen my face, and then gone. I asked myself the object of so strange a proceeding, and the answer came pat. The man, whoever he was, had thought to recognise me, and he had not. There was yet another question unresolved, and to this, I may say, I feared to give an answer; if he had recognised me, what would he have done?

My fears were immediately diverted from myself, for I saw that I had been visited in a mistake; and I became persuaded that some dreadful danger threatened the pavilion. It required some nerve to issue forth into the black and intricate thicket which surrounded and overhung the den; but I groped my way to the links, drenched with rain, beaten upon and deafened by the gusts, and fearing at every step to lay my hand upon some lurking adversary. The darkness was so complete that I might have been surrounded by an army and yet none the wiser, and the uproar of the gale so loud that my hearing was as useless as my sight.

For the rest of that night, which seemed interminably long, I patrolled the vicinity of the pavilion, without seeing a living creature or hearing any noise but the concert of the wind, the sea and the rain. A light in the upper storey filtered through a cranny of the shutter, and kept me company till the approach of dawn.

FIVE

Tells of an interview between Northmour, Clara and myself

With the first peep of day, I retired from the open to my old lair among the sand-hills, there to await the coming of my wife. The morning was grey, wild and melancholy; the wind moderated before sunrise, and then went about and blew in puffs from the shore; the sea began to go down, but the rain still fell without mercy. Over all the wilderness of links there was not a creature to be seen. Yet I felt sure the neighbourhood was alive with skulking foes. The light that had been so suddenly and surprisingly flashed upon my face as I lay sleeping, and the hat that had been blown ashore by the wind from over Graden Floe, were two speaking signals of the peril that environed Clara and the party in the pavilion.

It was, perhaps, half-past seven, or nearer eight, before I saw the door open, and that dear figure come towards me in the rain. I was waiting for her on the beach before she had crossed the sand-hills.

'I have had such trouble to come!' she cried. 'They did not wish me to go walking in the rain.'

'Clara,' I said, 'you are not frightened!'

'No,' said she, with a simplicity that filled my heart with confidence. For my wife was the bravest as well as the best of women; in my experience, I have not found the two go always together, but with her they did; and she combined the extreme of fortitude with the most endearing and beautiful virtues.

I told her what had happened; and, though her cheek grew visibly paler, she retained perfect control over her senses.

'You see now that I am safe,' said I, in conclusion. 'They do not mean to harm me; for, had they chosen, I was a dead man last night.'

She laid her hand upon my arm.

'And I had no presentiment!' she cried.

Her accent thrilled me with delight. I put my arm about her, and strained her to my side; and, before either of us was aware, her hands were on my shoulders and my lips upon her mouth. Yet up to that moment no word of love had passed between us. To this day I remember the touch of her cheek, which was wet and cold with the rain; and many a time since, when she has been washing her face, I have kissed it again for the sake of that morning on the beach. Now that she is taken from me, and I finish my pilgrimage alone, I recall our old loving kindnesses and the deep honesty and affection which united us, and my present loss seems but a trifle in comparison.

We may have thus stood for some seconds – for time passes quickly with lovers – before we were startled by a peal of laughter close at hand. It was not natural mirth, but seemed to be affected in order to conceal an angrier feeling. We both turned, though I still kept my left arm about Clara's waist; nor did she seek to withdraw herself; and there, a few paces off upon the beach, stood Northmour, his head lowered, his hands behind his back, his nostrils white with passion.

'Ah! Cassilis!' he said, as I disclosed my face.

'That same,' said I; for I was not at all put about.

'And so, Miss Huddlestone,' he continued slowly but savagely, 'this is how you keep your faith to your father and to me? This is the value you set upon your father's life? And you are so infatuated with this young gentleman that you must brave ruin, and decency, and common human caution – '

'Miss Huddlestone – ' I was beginning to interrupt him, when he, in his turn, cut in brutally. 'You hold your tongue,' said he; 'I am speaking to that girl.'

'That girl, as you call her, is my wife,' said I; and my wife only leaned a little nearer, so that I knew she had affirmed my words.

'Your what?' he cried. 'You lie!'

'Northmour,' I said, 'we all know you have a bad temper, and I am the last man to be irritated by words. For all that, I propose that you speak lower, for I am convinced that we are not alone.'

He looked round him, and it was plain my remark had in some degree sobered his passion. 'What do you mean?' he asked.

I only said one word: 'Italians.'

He swore a round oath, and looked at us, from one to the other.

'Mr Cassilis knows all that I know,' said my wife.

'What *I* want to know,' he broke out, 'is where the devil Mr Cassilis comes from, and what the devil Mr Cassilis is doing here. You say you are married; that I do not believe. If you were, Graden Floe would soon divorce you; four minutes and a half, Cassilis. I keep my private cemetery for my friends.'

'It took somewhat longer,' said I, 'for that Italian.'

He looked at me for a moment half daunted, and then, almost civilly, asked me to tell my story. 'You have too much the advantage of me, Cassilis,' he added. I complied of course; and he listened, with several ejaculations, while I told him how I had come to Graden; that it was I whom he had tried to murder on the night of landing; and what I had subsequently seen and heard of the Italians.

'Well,' said he, when I had done, 'it is here at last; there is no mistake about that. And what, may I ask, do you propose to do?'

'I propose to stay with you and lend a hand,' said I.

'You are a brave man,' he returned, with a peculiar intonation.

'I am not afraid,' said I.

'And so,' he continued, 'I am to understand that you two are married? And you stand up to it before my face, Miss Huddlestone?'

'We are not yet married,' said Clara; 'but we shall be as soon as we can.'

'Bravo!' cried Northmour. 'And the bargain? Damn it, you're not a fool, young woman; I may call a spade a spade with you. How about the bargain? You know as well as I do what your father's life depends upon. I have only to put my hands under my coat-tails and walk away, and his throat would be cut before the evening.'

'Yes, Mr Northmour,' returned Clara, with great spirit; 'but that is what you will never do. You made a bargain that was unworthy of a gentleman; but you are a gentleman for all that, and you will never desert a man whom you have begun to help.'

'Aha!' said he. 'You think I will give my yacht for nothing? You think I will risk my life and liberty for love of the old gentleman; and then, I suppose, be best man at the wedding, to wind up? Well,' he added, with an odd smile, 'perhaps you are not altogether wrong. But ask Cassilis here. *He* knows me. Am I a man to trust? Am I safe and scrupulous? Am I kind?'

'I know you talk a great deal, and sometimes, I think, very foolishly,' replied Clara, 'but I know you are a gentleman, and I am not the least afraid.'

He looked at her with a peculiar approval and admiration; then, turning to me, 'Do you think I would give her up without a struggle, Frank?' said he. 'I tell you plainly, you look out. The next time we come to blows –'

'Will make the third,' I interrupted, smiling.

'Aye, true; so it will,' he said. 'I had forgotten. Well, the third time's lucky.'

'The third time, you mean, you will have the crew of the *Red Earl* to help,' I said.

'Do you hear him?' he asked, turning to my wife.

'I hear two men speaking like cowards,' said she. 'I should despise myself either to think or speak like that. And neither of you believe one word that you are saying, which makes it the more wicked and silly.'

'She's a trump!' cried Northmour. 'But she's not yet Mrs Cassilis. I say no more. The present is not for me.'

Then my wife surprised me. 'I leave you here,' she said suddenly. 'My father has been too long alone. But remember this: you are to be friends, for you are both good friends to me.'

She has since told me her reason for this step. As long as she remained, she declared that we two would have continued to quarrel; and I suppose that she was right, for when she was gone we fell at once into a sort of confidentiality.

Northmour stared after her as she went away over the sand-hill

'She is the only woman in the world!' he exclaimed with an oath. 'Look at her action.'

I, for my part, leaped at this opportunity for a little further light.

'See here, Northmour,' said I; 'we are all in a tight place, are we not?'

'I believe you, my boy,' he answered, looking me in the eyes, and with great emphasis. 'We have all hell upon us, that's the truth. You may believe me or not, but I'm afraid for my life.'

'Tell me one thing,' said I. 'What are they after, these Italians? What do they want with Mr Huddlestone?'

'Don't you know?' he cried. 'The black old scamp had Carbonarist funds on a deposit – two hundred and eighty thousand; and of course he gambled it away on stocks. There was to have been a revolution in the Tridentino, or Parma; but the revolution is off, and the whole wasps' nest is after Huddlestone. We shall all be lucky if we can save our skins.'

'The Carbonari!' I exclaimed. 'God help him indeed!'

'Amen!' said Northmour. 'And now, look here: I have said that we are in a fix; and, frankly, I shall be glad of your help. If I can't save Huddlestone, I want at least to save the girl. Come and stay in the pavilion; and, there's my hand on it, I shall act as your friend until the old man is either clear or dead. But,' he added, 'once that is settled, you become my rival once again, and I warn you – mind yourself.'

'Done!' said I; and we shook hands.

'And now let us go directly to the fort,' said Northmour; and he began to lead the way through the rain.

SIX

Tells of an introduction to the tall man

We were admitted to the pavilion by Clara, and I was surprised by the completeness and security of the defences. A barricade of great strength, and yet easy to displace, supported the door against any violence from without; and the shutters of the dining-room, into which I was led directly, and which was feebly illuminated by a lamp, were even more elaborately fortified. The panels were strengthened by bars and cross-bars; and these, in their turn, were kept in position by a system of braces and struts, some abutting on the floor, some on the roof, and others, in fine, against the opposite wall of the apartment. It was at once a solid and well-designed piece of carpentry, and I did not seek to conceal my admiration.

'I am the engineer,' said Northmour. 'You remember the planks in the garden? Behold them!'

'I did not know you had so many talents,' said I.

'Are you armed?' he continued, pointing to an array of guns and pistols, all in admirable order, which stood in line against the wall or were displayed upon the sideboard.

'Thank you,' I returned; 'I have gone armed since our last encounter. But, to tell you the truth, I have had nothing to eat since early yesterday evening.'

Northmour produced some cold meat, to which I eagerly set myself, and a bottle of good Burgundy, by which, wet as I was, I did not scruple to profit. I have always been an extreme temperance man on principle; but it is useless to push principle to excess, and on this occasion I believe that I finished three-quarters of the bottle. As I ate, I still continued to admire the preparations for defence.

'We could stand a siege,' I said at length.

'Ye–es,' drawled Northmour; 'a very little one, per–haps. It is not so much the strength of the pavilion I misdoubt; it is the doubled anger that kills me. If we get to shooting, wild as the country is someone is sure to hear it, and then – why then it's the same thing, only different, as they say: caged by law, or killed by the Carbonari. There's the choice. It is a devilish bad thing to have the law against you in this world, and so I tell the old gentleman upstairs. He is quite of my way of thinking.'

'Speaking of that,' said I, 'what kind of person is he?'

'Oh, he!' cried the other; 'he's a rancid fellow, as far as he goes. I should like to have his neck wrung tomorrow by all the devils in Italy. I am not in this affair for him. You take me? I made a bargain for Missy's hand, and I mean to have it too.'

'That by the way,' said I. 'I understand. But how will Mr Huddlestone take my intrusion?'

'Leave that to Clara,' returned Northmour.

I could have struck him in the face for this coarse familiarity; but I respected the truce, as, I am bound to say, did Northmour, and so long as the danger continued not a cloud arose in our relation. I bear him this testimony with the most unfeigned satisfaction; nor am I without pride when I look back upon my own behaviour. For surely no two men were ever left in a position so invidious and irritating.

As soon as I had done eating, we proceeded to inspect the lower floor. Window by window we tried the different supports, now and then making an inconsiderable change – and the strokes of the hammer sounded with startling loudness through the house. I proposed, I remember, to make loop-holes; but he told me they were already made in the windows of the upper storey. It was an anxious business this inspection, and left me down-hearted. There were two doors and five windows to protect, and, counting Clara, only four of us to defend them against an unknown number of foes. I communicated my doubts to Northmour, who assured me, with unmoved composure, that he entirely shared them.

'Before morning,' said he, 'we shall all be butchered and buried in Graden Floe. For me, that is written.'

I could not help shuddering at the mention of the quicksand, but reminded Northmour that our enemies had spared me in the wood.

'Do not flatter yourself,' said he. 'Then you were not in the same boat with the old gentleman; now you are. It's the floe for all of us, mark my words.'

I trembled for Clara; and just then her dear voice was heard calling us to come upstairs. Northmour showed me the way, and, when he had reached the landing, knocked at the door of what used to be called 'My Uncle's Bedroom', as the founder of the pavilion had designed it especially for himself.

'Come in, Northmour; come in, dear Mr Cassilis,' said a voice from within.

Pushing open the door, Northmour admitted me before him into the apartment. As I came in I could see the daughter slipping out by the side door into the study, which had been prepared as her bedroom. In the bed, which was drawn back against the wall, instead of standing, as I had last seen it, boldly across the window, sat Bernard Huddlestone, the defaulting banker. Little as I had seen of him by the shifting light of the lantern on the links, I had no difficulty in recognising him for the same. He had a long and sallow countenance, surrounded by a long red beard and side whiskers. His broken nose and high cheekbones gave him somewhat the air of a Kalmuck, and his light eyes shone with the excitement of a high fever. He wore a skull-cap of black silk; a huge Bible lay open before him on the bed, with a pair of gold spectacles in the place, and a pile of other books lay on the stand by his side. The green curtains lent a cadaverous shade to his cheek; and, as he sat propped on pillows, his great stature was painfully hunched, and his head protruded till it overhung his knees. I believe if he had not died otherwise, he must have fallen a victim to consumption in the course of but a very few weeks.

He held out to me a hand, long, thin and disagreeably hairy.

'Come in, come in, Mr Cassilis,' said he. 'Another protector – ahem! – another protector. Always welcome as a friend of my daughter's, Mr Cassilis. How they have rallied about me, my daughter's friends! May God in heaven bless and reward them for it!'

I gave him my hand, of course, because I could not help it; but the sympathy I had been prepared to feel for Clara's father was immediately soured by his appearance, and the wheedling, unreal tones in which he spoke.

'Cassilis is a good man,' said Northmour; 'worth ten.'

'So I hear,' cried Mr Huddlestone eagerly, 'so my girl tells me. Ah, Mr Cassilis, my sin has found me out, you see! I am very low, very low; but I hope equally penitent. We must all come to the throne of grace at last, Mr Cassilis. For my part, I come late indeed; but with unfeigned humility, I trust.'

'Fiddle-de-dee!' said Northmour roughly.

'No, no, dear Northmour!' cried the banker. 'You must not say that; you must not try to shake me. You forget, my dear, good boy, you forget I may be called this very night before my Maker.'

His excitement was pitiful to behold; and I felt myself grow indignant with Northmour, whose infidel opinions I well knew and heartily derided, as he continued to taunt the poor sinner out of his humour of repentance.

'Pooh, my dear Huddlestone!' said he. 'You do yourself injustice. You are a man of the world inside and out, and were up to all kinds of mischief before

I was born. Your conscience is tanned like South American leather – only you forgot to tan your liver, and that, if you will believe me, is the seat of the annoyance.'

'Rogue, rogue! bad boy!' said Mr Huddlestone, shaking his finger. 'I am no precisian, if you come to that; I always hated a precisian; but I never lost hold of something better through it all. I have been a bad boy, Mr Cassilis; I do not seek to deny that; but it was after my wife's death, and you know, with a widower, it's a different thing: sinful – I won't say no; but there is a gradation, we shall hope. And talking of that – Hark!' he broke out suddenly, his hand raised, his fingers spread, his face racked with interest and terror. 'Only the rain, bless God!' he added, after a pause, and with indescribable relief.

For some seconds he lay back among the pillows like a man near to fainting; then he gathered himself together, and, in somewhat tremulous tones, began once more to thank me for the share I was prepared to take in his defence.

'One question, sir,' said I, when he had paused. 'Is it true that you have money with you?'

He seemed annoyed by the question, but admitted with reluctance that he had a little.

'Well,' I continued, 'it is their money they are after, is it not? Why not give it up to them?'

'Ah!' replied he, shaking his head, 'I have tried that already, Mr Cassilis; and alas that it should be so! but it is blood they want.'

'Huddlestone, that's a little less than fair,' said Northmour. 'You should mention that what you offered them was upwards of two hundred thousand short. The deficit is worth a reference; it is for what they call a cool sum, Frank. Then, you see, the fellows reason in their clear Italian way; and it seems to them, as indeed it seems to me, that they may just as well have both while they're about it – money and blood together, by George, and no more trouble for the extra pleasure.'

'Is it in the pavilion?' I asked.

'It is; and I wish it were in the bottom of the sea instead,' said Northmour; and then suddenly – 'What are you making faces at me for?' he cried to Mr Huddlestone, on whom I had unconsciously turned my back. 'Do you think Cassilis would sell you?'

Mr Huddlestone protested that nothing had been further from his mind.

'It is a good thing,' retorted Northmour in his ugliest manner. 'You might end by wearying us. What were you going to say?' he added, turning to me.

'I was going to propose an occupation for the afternoon,' said I. 'Let us carry that money out, piece by piece, and lay it down before the pavilion door. If the Carbonari come, why, it's theirs at any rate.'

'No, no,' cried Mr Huddlestone, 'it does not, it cannot belong to them! It should be distributed pro rata among all my creditors.'

'Come now, Huddlestone,' said Northmour, 'none of that.'

'Well, but my daughter,' moaned the wretched man.

'Your daughter will do well enough. Here are two suitors, Cassilis and I, neither of us beggars, between whom she has to choose. And as for yourself, to make an end of arguments, you have no right to a farthing, and, unless I'm much mistaken, you are going to die.'

It was certainly very cruelly said; but Mr Huddlestone was a man who attracted little sympathy; and, although I saw him wince and shudder, I mentally endorsed the rebuke; nay, I added a contribution of my own.

'Northmour and I,' I said, 'are willing enough to help you to save your life, but not to escape with stolen property.'

He struggled for a while with himself, as though he were on the point of giving way to anger, but prudence had the best of the controversy.

'My dear boys,' he said, 'do with me or my money what you will. I leave all in your hands. Let me compose myself.'

And so we left him, gladly enough I am sure. The last that I saw, he had once more taken up his great Bible, and with tremulous hands was adjusting his spectacles to read.

SEVEN

Tells how a word was cried through the pavilion window

The recollection of that afternoon will always be graven on my mind. Northmour and I were persuaded that an attack was imminent; and if it had been in our power to alter in any way the order of events, that power would have been used to precipitate rather than delay the critical moment. The worst was to be anticipated; yet we could conceive no extremity so miserable as the suspense we were now suffering. I have never been an eager, though always a great, reader; but I never knew books so insipid as those which I took up and cast aside that afternoon in the pavilion. Even talk became impossible, as the hours went on. One or other was always listening for some sound, or peering from an upstairs window over the links. And yet not a sign indicated the presence of our foes.

We debated over and over again my proposal with regard to the money; and had we been in complete possession of our faculties, I am sure we should have condemned it as unwise; but we were flustered with alarm, grasped at a straw, and determined, although it was as much as advertising Mr Huddlestone's presence in the pavilion, to carry my proposal into effect.

The sum was part in specie, part in bank paper, and part in circular notes payable to the name of James Gregory. We took it out, counted it, enclosed it once more in a despatch-box belonging to Northmour, and prepared a letter in Italian which he tied to the handle. It was signed by both of us under oath, and declared that this was all the money which had escaped the failure of the house of Huddlestone. This was, perhaps, the maddest action ever perpetrated by two persons professing to be sane. Had the despatch-box fallen into other hands than those for which it was intended, we stood criminally convicted on our own written testimony; but, as I have said, we were neither of us in a condition to judge soberly, and had a thirst for action that drove us to do something, right or wrong, rather than endure the agony of waiting. Moreover, as we were both convinced that the hollows of the links were alive with hidden spies upon our movements, we hoped that our appearance with the box might lead to a parley, and, perhaps, a compromise.

It was nearly three when we issued from the pavilion. The rain had taken off; the sun shone quite cheerfully.

I have never seen the gulls fly so close about the house or approach so fearlessly to human beings. On the very doorstep one flapped heavily past our heads, and uttered its wild cry in my very ear.

'There is an omen for you,' said Northmour, who like all freethinkers was much under the influence of superstition. 'They think we are already dead.'

I made some light rejoinder, but it was with half my heart; for the circumstance had impressed me.

A yard or two before the gate, on a patch of smooth turf, we set down the despatch-box; and Northmour waved a white handkerchief over his head. Nothing replied. We raised our voices, and cried aloud in Italian that we were there as ambassadors to resolve the quarrel; but the stillness remained unbroken save by the seagulls and the surf. I had a weight at my heart when we desisted; and I saw that even Northmour was unusually pale. He looked over his shoulder nervously, as though he feared that someone had crept between him and the pavilion door.

'By God,' he said in a whisper, 'this is too much for me!'

I replied in the same key: 'Suppose there should be none, after all!'

'Look there,' he returned, nodding with his head, as though he had been afraid to point.

I glanced in the direction indicated and there, from the northern quarter of the Sea-Wood, beheld a thin column of smoke rising steadily against the now cloudless sky.

'Northmour,' I said (we still continued to talk in whispers), 'it is not possible to endure this suspense. I prefer death fifty times over. Stay you here to watch the pavilion; I will go forward and make sure, if I have to walk right into their camp.'

He looked once again all round him with puckered eyes, and then nodded assentingly to my proposal.

My heart beat like a sledge-hammer as I set out walking rapidly in the direction of the smoke; and, though up to that moment I had felt chill and shivering, I was suddenly conscious of a glow of heat over all my body. The ground in this direction was very uneven: a hundred men might have lain hidden in as many square yards about my path. But I had not practised the business in vain: I chose such routes as cut at the very root of concealment, and, by keeping along the most convenient ridges, commanded several hollows at a time. It was not long before I was rewarded for my caution. Coming suddenly on to a mound somewhat more elevated than the surrounding hummocks, I saw, not thirty yards away, a man bent almost double, and running as fast as his attitude permitted along the bottom of a gully. I had dislodged one of the spies from his ambush. As soon as I sighted him, I called loudly both in English and Italian; and he, seeing concealment was no longer possible, straightened himself up, leaped from the gully and made off as straight as an arrow for the borders of the wood.

It was none of my business to pursue; I had learned what I wanted – that we were beleaguered and watched in the pavilion; and I returned at once, and walking as nearly as possible in my old footsteps, to where Northmour awaited me beside the despatch-box. He was even paler than when I had left him, and his voice shook a little.

'Could you see what he was like?' he asked.

'He kept his back turned,' I replied.

'Let us get into the house, Frank. I don't think I'm a coward, but I can stand no more of this,' he whispered.

All was still and sunshiny about the pavilion as we turned to re-enter it; even the gulls had flown in a wider circuit and were seen flickering along the beach and sand-hills; and this loneliness terrified me more than a regiment under arms. It was not until the door was barricaded that I could draw a full inspiration and relieve the weight that lay upon my bosom. Northmour and I exchanged a steady glance; and I suppose each made his own reflections on the white and startled aspect of the other.

'You were right,' I said. 'All is over. Shake hands, old man, for the last time.'

'Yes,' replied he, 'I will shake hands; for, as sure as I am here, I bear no malice. But remember, if, by some impossible accident, we should give the slip to these blackguards, I'll take the upper hand of you by fair or foul.'

'Oh,' said I, 'you weary me!'

He seemed hurt, and walked away in silence to the foot of the stairs, where he paused.

'You do not understand,' said he. 'I am not a swindler, and I guard myself;

that is all. It may weary you or not, Mr Cassilis, I do not care a rush; I speak for my own satisfaction, and not for your amusement. You had better go upstairs and court the girl; for my part, I stay here.'

'And I stay with you,' I returned. 'Do you think I would steal a march, even with your permission?'

'Frank,' he said, smiling, 'it's a pity you are an ass, for you have the makings of a man. I think I must be fey today; you cannot irritate me even when you try. Do you know,' he continued softly, 'I think we are the two most miserable men in England, you and I? we have got on to thirty without wife or child, or so much as a shop to look after – poor, pitiful, lost devils, both! And now we clash about a girl! As if there were not several millions in the United Kingdom! Ah, Frank, Frank, the one who loses this throw, be it you or me, he has my pity! It were better for him – how does the Bible say? – that a millstone were hanged about his neck and he were cast into the depth of the sea. Let us take a drink,' he concluded suddenly, but without any levity of tone.

I was touched by his words, and consented. He sat down on the table in the dining-room, and held up the glass of sherry to his eye.

'If you beat me, Frank,' he said, 'I shall take to drink. What will you do, if it goes the other way?'

'God knows,' I returned.

'Well,' said he, 'here is a toast in the meantime: "Italia Irredenta!"'

The remainder of the day was passed in the same dreadful tedium and suspense. I laid the table for dinner, while Northmour and Clara prepared the meal together in the kitchen. I could hear their talk as I went to and fro, and was surprised to find it ran all the time upon myself. Northmour again bracketed us together, and rallied Clara on a choice of husbands; but he continued to speak of me with some feeling, and uttered nothing to my prejudice unless he included himself in the condemnation. This awakened a sense of gratitude in my heart, which combined with the immediateness of our peril to fill my eyes with tears. After all, I thought – and perhaps the thought was laughably vain – we were here three very noble human beings to perish in defence of a thieving banker.

Before we sat down to table, I looked forth from an upstairs window. The day was beginning to decline; the links were utterly deserted; the despatch-box still lay untouched where we had left it hours before.

Mr Huddlestone, in a long yellow dressing-gown, took one end of the table, Clara the other, while Northmour and I faced each other from the sides. The lamp was brightly trimmed; the wine was good; the viands, although mostly cold, excellent of their sort. We seemed to have agreed tacitly; all reference to the impending catastrophe was carefully avoided; and, considering our tragic circumstances, we made a merrier party than could have been expected. From time to time, it is true, Northmour or I would rise from table and make a round of the defences; and, on each of these occasions, Mr Huddlestone was recalled to a sense of his tragic predicament, glanced up with ghastly eyes and bore for an instant on his countenance the stamp of terror. But he hastened to empty his glass, wiped his forehead with his handkerchief and joined again in the conversation.

I was astonished at the wit and information he displayed. Mr Huddlestone's was certainly no ordinary character; he had read and observed for himself; his gifts were sound; and, though I could never have learned to love the man, I began to understand his success in business, and the great respect in which he had been held before his failure. He had, above all, the talent of society; and though I never heard him speak but on this one and most unfavourable occasion, I set him down among the most brilliant conversationalists I ever met.

He was relating with great gusto, and seemingly no feeling of shame, the manoeuvres of a scoundrelly commission merchant whom he had known and studied in his youth, and we were all listening with an odd mixture of mirth and embarrassment, when our little party was brought abruptly to an end in the most startling manner.

A noise like that of a wet finger on the window-pane interrupted Mr Huddlestone's tale; and in an instant we were all four as white as paper, and sat tongue-tied and motionless round the table.

'A snail,' I said at last; for I had heard that these animals make a noise somewhat similar in character.

'Snail be damned!' said Northmour. 'Hush!'

The same sound was repeated twice at regular intervals; and then a formidable voice shouted through the shutters the Italian word, 'Traditore!'

Mr Huddlestone threw his head in the air; his eyelids quivered; next moment he fell insensible below the table. Northmour and I had each run to the armoury and seized a gun. Clara was on her feet with her hand at her throat.

So we stood waiting, for we thought the hour of attack was certainly come; but second passed after second, and all but the surf remained silent in the neighbourhood of the pavilion.

'Quick,' said Northmour; 'upstairs with him before they come.'

EIGHT

Tells the story of the tall man

Somehow or other, by hook and crook, and between the three of us, we got Bernard Huddlestone bundled upstairs and laid upon the bed in 'My Uncle's Room'. During the whole process, which was rough enough, he gave no sign of consciousness, and he remained, as we had thrown him, without changing the position of a finger. His daughter opened his shirt and began to wet his head and bosom; while Northmour and I ran to the window. The weather continued clear; the moon, which was now about full, had risen and shed a very clear light upon the links; yet, strain our eyes as we might, we could distinguish nothing moving. A few dark spots, more or less, on the uneven expanse were not to be identified; they might be crouching men, they might be shadows; it was impossible to be sure.

'Thank God,' said Northmour, 'Aggie is not coming tonight.'

Aggie was the name of the old nurse; he had not thought of her till now; but that he should think of her at all was a trait that surprised me in the man.

We were again reduced to waiting. Northmour went to the fireplace and spread his hands before the red embers, as if he were cold. I followed him mechanically with my eyes, and in so doing turned my back upon the window. At that moment a very faint report was audible from without, and a ball shivered a pane of glass and buried itself in the shutter two inches from my head. I heard Clara scream; and though I whipped instantly out of range and into a corner, she was there, so to speak, before me, beseeching to know if I were hurt. I felt that I could stand to be shot at every day and all day long, with such marks of solicitude for a reward; and I continued to reassure her, with the tenderest caresses and in complete forgetfulness of our situation, till the voice of Northmour recalled me to myself.

'An air-gun,' he said. 'They wish to make no noise.'

I put Clara aside, and looked at him. He was standing with his back to the fire and his hands clasped behind him; and I knew by the black look on his face, that passion was boiling within. I had seen just such a look before he attacked me, that March night, in the adjoining chamber; and, though I could make every allowance for his anger, I confess I trembled for the consequences. He gazed straight before him; but he could see us with the tail of his eye, and his temper kept rising like a gale of wind. With regular battle awaiting us outside, this prospect of an internecine strife within the walls began to daunt me.

Suddenly, as I was thus closely watching his expression and prepared against the worst, I saw a change, a flash, a look of relief, upon his face. He took up the lamp which stood beside him on the table, and turned to us with an air of some excitement.

'There is one point that we must know,' said he. 'Are they going to butcher the lot of us, or only Huddlestone? Did they take you for him, or fire at you for your own *beaux yeux*?'

'They took me for him, for certain,' I replied. 'I am near as tall, and my head is fair.'

'I am going to make sure,' returned Northmour; and he stepped up to the window, holding the lamp above his head, and stood there, quietly affronting death, for half a minute.

Clara sought to rush forward and pull him from the place of danger; but I had the pardonable selfishness to hold her back by force.

'Yes,' said Northmour, turning coolly from the window; 'it's only Huddlestone they want.'

'Oh, Mr Northmour!' cried Clara; but found no more to add; the temerity she had just witnessed seeming beyond the reach of words.

He, on his part, looked at me, cocking his head, with a fire of triumph in his eyes; and I understood at once that he had thus hazarded his life merely to attract Clara's notice and depose me from my position as the hero of the hour. He snapped his fingers.

'The fire is only beginning,' said he. 'When they warm up to their work, they won't be so particular.'

A voice was now heard hailing us from the entrance. From the window we could see the figure of a man in the moonlight; he stood motionless, his face uplifted to ours, and a rag of something white on his extended arm; and as we looked right down upon him, though he was a good many yards distant on the links, we could see the moonlight glitter on his eyes.

He opened his lips again, and spoke for some minutes on end, in a key so loud that he might have been heard in every corner of the pavilion and as far away as the borders of the wood. It was the same voice that had already shouted 'Traditore!' through the shutters of the dining-room; this time it made a complete and clear statement. If the traitor 'Oddlestone' were given up, all others should be spared; if not, no one should escape to tell the tale.

'Well, Huddlestone, what do you say to that?' asked Northmour, turning to the bed.

Up to that moment the banker had given no sign of life, and I, at least, had supposed him to be still lying in a faint; but he replied at once, and in such tones as I have never heard elsewhere, save from a delirious patient, adjured and besought us not to desert him. It was the most hideous and abject performance that my imagination could conceive.

'Enough,' cried Northmour; and then he threw open the window, leaned out into the night, and in a tone of exultation, and with a total forgetfulness of what was due to the presence of a lady, poured out upon the ambassador a string of the most abominable raillery both in English and Italian, and bade him be gone where he had come from. I believe that nothing so delighted Northmour at that moment as the thought that we must all infallibly perish before the night was out.

Meantime the Italian put his flag of truce into his pocket and disappeared, at a leisurely pace, among the sand-hills.

'They make honourable war,' said Northmour. 'They are all gentlemen and soldiers. For the credit of the thing, I wish we could change sides – you and I, Frank, and you too, Missy, my darling – and leave that being on the bed to someone else. Tut! Don't look shocked! We are all going post to what they call eternity, and may as well be above-board while there's time. As far as I'm concerned, if I could first strangle Huddlestone and then get Clara in my arms, I could die with some pride and satisfaction. And as it is, by God, I'll have a kiss!'

Before I could do anything to interfere, he had rudely embraced and repeatedly kissed the resisting girl. Next moment I had pulled him away with fury, and flung him heavily against the wall. He laughed loud and long, and I feared his wits had given way under the strain; for even in the best of days he had been a sparing and a quiet laugher.

'Now, Frank,' said he, when his mirth was somewhat appeased, 'it's your turn. Here's my hand. Goodbye; farewell!' Then, seeing me stand rigid and indignant, and holding Clara to my side – 'Man!' he broke out, 'are you angry? Did you think we were going to die with all the airs and graces of society? I took a kiss; I'm glad I had it; and now you can take another if you like, and square accounts.'

I turned from him with a feeling of contempt which I did not seek to dissemble.

'As you please,' said he. 'You've been a prig in life; a prig you'll die.'

And with that he sat down in a chair, a rifle over his knee, and amused himself with snapping the lock; but I could see that his ebullition of light spirits (the only one I ever knew him to display) had already come to an end, and was succeeded by a sullen, scowling humour.

All this time our assailants might have been entering the house, and we been none the wiser; we had in truth almost forgotten the danger that so imminently overhung our days. But just then Mr Huddlestone uttered a cry, and leaped from the bed.

I asked him what was wrong.

'Fire!' he cried. 'They have set the house on fire!'

Northmour was on his feet in an instant, and he and I ran through the door of communication with the study. The room was illuminated by a red and angry light. Almost at the moment of our entrance, a tower of flame arose in front of the window, and, with a tingling report, a pane fell inwards on the carpet. They had set fire to the lean-to outhouse, where Northmour used to nurse his negatives.

'Hot work,' said Northmour. 'Let us try in your old room.'

We ran thither in a breath, threw up the casement, and looked forth. Along the whole back wall of the pavilion piles of fuel had been arranged and kindled; and it is probable they had been drenched with mineral oil, for, in spite of the morning's rain, they all burned bravely. The fire had taken a firm hold already on the outhouse, which blazed higher and higher every moment; the back door was in the centre of a red-hot bonfire; the eaves we could see, as we looked upward, were already smouldering, for the roof overhung, and was supported by considerable beams of wood. At the same time, hot, pungent and choking volumes of smoke began to fill the house. There was not a human being to be seen to right or left.

'Ah, well!' said Northmour, 'here's the end, thank God.'

And we returned to My Uncle's Room. Mr Huddlestone was putting on his boots, still violently trembling, but with an air of determination such as I had not hitherto observed. Clara stood close by him, with her cloak in both hands ready to throw about her shoulders, and a strange look in her eyes, as if she were half hopeful, half doubtful of her father.

'Well, boys and girls,' said Northmour, 'how about a sally? The oven is heating; it is not good to stay here and be baked; and, for my part, I want to come to my hands with them and be done.'

'There is nothing else left,' I replied.

And both Clara and Mr Huddlestone, though with a very different intonation, added, 'Nothing.'

As we went downstairs the heat was excessive, and the roaring of the fire filled our ears; and we had scarce reached the passage before the stairs window fell in, a branch of flame shot brandishing through the aperture, and the interior of the pavilion became lit up with that dreadful and fluctuating glare. At the same moment we heard the fall of something heavy and inelastic in the upper storey. The whole pavilion, it was plain, had gone alight like a box of matches, and now not only flamed sky-high to land and sea, but threatened with every moment to crumble and fall in about our ears.

Northmour and I cocked our revolvers. Mr Huddlestone, who had already refused a firearm, put us behind him with a manner of command.

'Let Clara open the door,' said he. 'So, if they fire a volley, she will be protected. And in the meantime stand behind me. I am the scapegoat; my sins have found me out.'

I heard him, as I stood breathless by his shoulder, with my pistol ready, pattering off prayers in a tremulous, rapid whisper; and I confess, horrid as the thought may seem, I despised him for thinking of supplications in a moment so critical and thrilling. In the meantime, Clara, who was dead white but still possessed her faculties, had displaced the barricade from the front door. Another moment, and she had pulled it open. Firelight and moonlight illuminated the links with confused and changeful lustre, and far away against the sky we could see a long trail of glowing smoke.

Mr Huddlestone, filled for the moment with a strength greater than his own, struck Northmour and myself a back-hander in the chest; and while we were thus for the moment incapacitated from action, lifting his arms above his head like one about to dive, he ran straight forward out of the pavilion.

'Here am!' he cried – 'Huddlestone! Kill me, and spare the others!'

His sudden appearance daunted, I suppose, our hidden enemies; for Northmour and I had time to recover, to seize Clara between us, one by each arm, and to rush forth to his assistance, ere anything further had taken place. But scarce had we passed the threshold when there came near a dozen reports and flashes from every direction among the hollows of the links. Mr Huddlestone staggered, uttered a weird and freezing cry, threw up his arms over his head, and fell backward on the turf.

'Traditore! Traditore!' cried the invisible avengers.

And just then, a part of the roof of the pavilion fell in, so rapid was the progress of the fire. A loud, vague and horrible noise accompanied the collapse, and a vast volume of flame went soaring up to heaven. It must have been visible at that moment from twenty miles out at sea, from the shore at Graden Wester and far inland from the peak of Graystiel, the most eastern summit of the Caulder Hills. Bernard Huddlestone, although God knows what were his obsequies, had a fine pyre at the moment of his death.

NINE

Tells how Northmour carried out his threat

I should have the greatest difficulty to tell you what followed next after this tragic circumstance. It is all to me, as I look back upon it, mixed, strenuous and ineffectual, like the struggles of a sleeper in a nightmare. Clara, I remember, uttered a broken sigh and would have fallen forward to earth, had not Northmour and I supported her insensible body. I do not think we were attacked; I do not remember even to have seen an assailant; and I believe we deserted Mr Huddlestone without a glance. I only remember running like a man in a panic, now carrying Clara altogether in my own arms, now sharing her weight with Northmour, now scuffling confusedly for the possession of that dear burden. Why we should have made for my camp in the Hemlock Den, or how we reached it, are points lost for ever to my recollection. The first moment at which I became definitely sure, Clara had been suffered to fall against the outside of my little tent, Northmour and I were tumbling together on the ground, and he, with contained ferocity, was striking for my head with the butt of his revolver. He had already twice wounded me on the scalp and it is to the consequent loss of blood that I am tempted to attribute the sudden clearness of my mind.

I caught him by the wrist.

'Northmour,' I remember saying, 'you can kill me afterwards. Let us first attend to Clara.'

He was at that moment uppermost. Scarcely had the words passed my lips, when he had leaped to his feet and ran towards the tent; and the next moment, he was straining Clara to his heart and covering her unconscious hands and face with his caresses.

'Shame!' I cried. 'Shame on you, Northmour!'

And, giddy though I still was, I struck him repeatedly upon the head and shoulders.

He relinquished his grasp, and faced me in the broken moonlight.

'I had you under, and I let you go,' said he; 'and now you strike me! Coward!'

'You are the coward,' I retorted. 'Did she wish your kisses while she was still sensible of what she wanted? Not she! And now she may be dying; and you waste this precious time and abuse her helplessness. Stand aside and let me help her.'

He confronted me for a moment, white and menacing; then suddenly he stepped aside.

'Help her then,' said he.

I threw myself on my knees beside her, and loosened, as well as I was able, her dress and corset; but while I was thus engaged, a grasp descended on my shoulder.

'Keep your hands of her,' said Northmour fiercely. 'Do you think I have no blood in my veins?'

'Northmour,' I cried, 'if you will neither help her yourself, nor let me do so, do you know that I shall have to kill you?'

'That is better!' he cried. 'Let her die also, where's the harm? Step aside from that girl and stand up to fight!'

'You will observe,' said I, half rising, 'that I have not kissed her yet.'

'I dare you to,' he cried.

I do not know what possessed me; it was one of the things I am most ashamed of in my life, though, as my wife used to say, I knew that my kisses would be always welcome were she dead or living; down I fell again upon my knees, parted the hair from her forehead, and, with the dearest respect, laid my lips for a moment on that cold brow. It was such a caress as a father might have given; it was such a one as was not unbecoming from a man soon to die to a woman already dead.

'And now,' said I, 'I am at your service, Mr Northmour.'

But I saw, to my surprise, that he had turned his back upon me.

'Do you hear?' I asked.

'Yes,' said he, 'I do. If you wish to fight, I am ready. If not, go on and save Clara. All is one to me.'

I did not wait to be twice bidden; but, stooping again over Clara, continued my efforts to revive her. She still lay white and lifeless; I began to fear that her sweet spirit had indeed fled beyond recall, and horror and a sense of utter desolation seized upon my heart. I called her by name with the most endearing inflections; I chafed and beat her hands; now I laid her head low, now supported it against my knee; but all seemed to be in vain, and the lids still lay heavy on her eyes.

'Northmour,' I said, 'there is my hat. For God's sake bring some water from the spring.'

Almost in a moment he was by my side with the water. 'I have brought it in my own,' he said. 'You do not grudge me the privilege?'

'Northmour – ' I was beginning to say, as I laved her head and breast; but he interrupted me savagely.

'Oh, you hush up!' he said. 'The best thing you can do is to say nothing.'

I had certainly no desire to talk, my mind being swallowed up in concern for my dear love and her condition; so I continued in silence to do my best towards her recovery, and, when the hat was empty, returned it to him, with one word – 'More.' He had, perhaps, gone several times upon this errand, when Clara reopened her eyes.

'Now,' said he, 'since she is better, you can spare me, can you not? I wish you a good-night, Mr Cassilis.'

And with that he was gone among the thicket. I made a fire, for I had now no fear of the Italians, who had even spared all the little possessions left in my encampment; and, broken as she was by the excitement and the hideous catastrophe of the evening, I managed, in one way or another – by persuasion, encouragement, warmth, and such simple remedies as I could lay my hand on – to bring her back to some composure of mind and strength of body.

Day had already come, when a sharp 'Hist!' sounded from the thicket. I started from the ground; but the voice of Northmour was heard adding, in the most tranquil tones: 'Come here, Cassilis, and alone; I want to show you something.'

I consulted Clara with my eyes, and, receiving her tacit permission, left her alone, and clambered out of the den. At some distance off I saw Northmour leaning against an elder; and, as soon as he perceived me, he began walking seaward. I had almost overtaken him as he reached the outskirts of the wood.

'Look,' said he, pausing.

A couple of steps more brought me out of the foliage. The light of the morning lay cold and clear over that well-known scene. The pavilion was but a blackened wreck; the roof had fallen in, one of the gables had fallen out; and, far and near, the face of the links was cicatrised with little patches of burnt furze. Thick smoke still went straight upwards in the windless air of the morning, and a great pile of ardent cinders filled the bare walls of the house, like coals in an open grate. Close by the islet a schooner yacht lay to, and a well-manned boat was pulling vigorously for the shore.

'The *Red Earl*!' I cried. 'The *Red Earl* twelve hours too late!'

'Feel in your pocket, Frank. Are you armed?' asked Northmour.

I obeyed him, and I think I must have become deadly pale. My revolver had been taken from me.

'You see I have you in my power,' he continued. 'I disarmed you last night while you were nursing Clara; but this morning – here – take your pistol. No thanks!' he cried, holding up his hand. 'I do not like them; that is the only way you can annoy me now.'

He began to walk forward across the links to meet the boat, and I followed a step or two behind. In front of the pavilion I paused to see where Mr Huddlestone had fallen; but there was no sign of him, nor so much as a trace of blood.

'Graden Floe,' said Northmour.

He continued to advance till we had come to the head of the beach.

'No farther, please,' said he. 'Would you like to take her to Graden House?'

'Thank you,' replied I; 'I shall try to get her to the minister's at Graden Wester.'

The prow of the boat here grated on the beach, and a sailor jumped ashore with a line in his hand.

'Wait a minute, lads!' cried Northmour; and then lower and to my private ear: 'You had better say nothing of all this to her,' he added.

'On the contrary!' I broke out, 'she shall know everything that I can tell.'

'You do not understand,' he returned, with an air of great dignity. 'It will be nothing to her; she expects it of me. Goodbye!' he added, with a nod.

I offered him my hand.

'Excuse me,' said he. 'It's small, I know; but I can't push things quite so far as that. I don't wish any sentimental business, to sit by your hearth a white-haired wanderer, and all that. Quite the contrary: I hope to God I shall never again clap eyes on either one of you.'

'Well, God bless you, Northmour!' I said heartily.

'Oh, yes,' he returned.

He walked down the beach; and the man who was ashore gave him an arm on board, and then shoved off and leaped into the bows himself. Northmour took the tiller; the boat rose to the waves, and the oars between the thole-pins sounded crisp and measured in the morning air.

They were not yet halfway to the *Red Earl*, and I was still watching their progress, when the sun rose out of the sea.

One word more, and my story is done. Years after, Northmour was killed fighting under the colours of Garibaldi for the liberation of the Tyrol.

The Sire de Maletroit's Door

Denis de Beaulieu was not yet two-and-twenty, but he counted himself a grown man, and a very accomplished cavalier into the bargain. Lads were early formed in that rough, warfaring epoch; and when one has been in a pitched battle and a dozen raids, has killed one's man in an honourable fashion and knows a thing or two of strategy and mankind, a certain swagger in the gait is surely to be pardoned. He had put up his horse with due care, and supped with due deliberation; and then, in a very agreeable frame of mind, went out to pay a visit in the grey of the evening. It was not a very wise proceeding on the young man's part. He would have done better to remain beside the fire or go decently to bed. For the town was full of the troops of Burgundy and England under a mixed command; and though Denis was there on safe-conduct, his safe-conduct was like to serve him little on a chance encounter.

It was September 1429; the weather had fallen sharp; a flighty piping wind, laden with showers, beat about the township; and the dead leaves ran riot along the streets. Here and there a window was already lighted up; and the noise of men-at-arms making merry over supper within, came forth in fits and was swallowed up and carried away by the wind. The night fell swiftly; the flag of England, fluttering on the spire-top, grew ever fainter and fainter against the flying clouds – a black speck like a swallow in the tumultuous, leaden chaos of the sky. As the night fell the wind rose, and began to hoot under archways and roar amid the tree-tops in the valley below the town.

Denis de Beaulieu walked fast and was soon knocking at his friend's door; but though he promised himself to stay only a little while and make an early return, his welcome was so pleasant, and he found so much to delay him, that it was already long past midnight before he said goodbye upon the threshold. The wind had fallen again in the meanwhile; the night was as black as the grave; not a star, nor a glimmer of moonshine, slipped through the canopy of cloud. Denis was ill-acquainted with the intricate lanes of Château Landon; even by daylight he had found some trouble in picking his way and in this absolute darkness he soon lost it altogether. He was certain of one thing only – to keep mounting the hill; for his friend's house lay at the lower end, or tail, of Château Landon, while the inn was up at the head, under the great church spire. With this clue to go upon he stumbled and groped forward, now breathing more freely in open places where there was a good slice of sky overhead, now feeling along the wall in stifling closes. It is an eerie and mysterious position to be thus submerged in opaque blackness in an almost unknown town. The silence is terrifying in its possibilities. The touch of cold window bars to the exploring hand startles the man like the touch of a toad; the inequalities of the pavement shake his heart into his mouth; a piece of denser darkness threatens an ambuscade or a chasm in the pathway; and where the air is brighter, the houses put on strange and bewildering appearances, as if to lead him farther from his way. For Denis, who had to regain his inn without attracting notice, there was real danger as well as mere discomfort in the walk; and he went warily and boldly at once, and at every corner paused to make an observation.

He had been for some time threading a lane so narrow that he could touch a wall with either hand, when it began to open out and go sharply downward. Plainly this lay no longer in the direction of his inn, but the hope of a little more light tempted him forward to reconnoitre. The lane ended in a terrace with a bartizan wall, which gave an outlook between high houses, as out of an embrasure, into the valley lying dark and formless several hundred feet below. Denis looked down, and could discern a few tree-tops waving and a single speck of brightness where the river ran across a weir. The weather was clearing up, and the sky had lightened, so as to show the outline of the heavier clouds and the dark margin of the hills. By the uncertain glimmer, the house on his left hand should be a place of some pretensions; it was surmounted by several pinnacles and turret-tops; the round stern of a chapel, with a fringe of flying buttresses, projected boldly from the main block; and the door was sheltered under a deep porch carved with figures and overhung by two long gargoyles. The windows of the chapel gleamed through their intricate tracery with a light as of many tapers, and threw out the buttresses and the peaked roof in a more intense blackness against the sky. It was plainly the *hôtel* of some great family of the neighbourhood; and as it reminded Denis of a town house of his own at Bourges, he stood for some time gazing up at it and mentally gauging the skill of the architects and the consideration of the two families.

There seemed to be no issue to the terrace but the lane by which he had reached it; he could only retrace his steps, but he had gained some notion of his whereabouts, and hoped by this means to hit the main thoroughfare and speedily regain the inn. He was reckoning without that chapter of accidents which was to make this night memorable above all others in his career; for he had not gone back above a hundred yards before he saw a light coming to meet him, and heard loud voices speaking together in the echoing narrows of the lane. It was a party of men-at-arms going the night round with torches. Denis assured himself that they had all been making free with the wine-bowl, and were in no mood to be particular about safe-conducts or the niceties of chivalrous war. It was as like as not that they would kill him like a dog and leave him where he fell. The situation was inspiriting but nervous. Their own torches would conceal him from sight, he reflected; and he hoped that they would drown the noise of his footsteps with their own empty voices. If he were but fleet and silent, he might evade their notice altogether.

Unfortunately, as he turned to beat a retreat, his foot rolled upon a pebble; he fell against the wall with an ejaculation, and his sword rang loudly on the stones. Two or three voices demanded who went there – some in French, some in English; but Denis made no reply, and ran the faster down the lane. Once upon the terrace, he paused to look back. They still kept calling after him, and just then began to double the pace in pursuit, with a considerable clank of armour, and great tossing of the torchlight to and fro in the narrow jaws of the passage.

Denis cast a look around and darted into the porch. There he might escape observation, or – if that were too much to expect – was in a capital posture whether for parley or defence. So thinking, he drew his sword and tried to set his back against the door. To his surprise, it yielded behind his weight and, though he turned in a moment, continued to swing back on oiled and noiseless hinges, until it stood wide open on a black interior. When things fall out opportunely for the person concerned, he is not apt to be critical about the how or why, his own immediate personal convenience seeming a sufficient reason for the strangest oddities and resolutions in our sublunary things; and so Denis, without a moment's hesitation, stepped within and partly closed the door behind him to conceal his place of refuge. Nothing was further from his thoughts than to close it altogether; but for some inexplicable reason – perhaps by a spring or a weight – the ponderous mass of oak whipped itself out of his fingers and clanked to, with a formidable rumble and a noise like the falling of an automatic bar.

The round, at that very moment, debauched upon the terrace and proceeded to summon him with shouts and curses. He heard them ferreting in the dark corners; the stock of a lance even rattled along the outer surface of the door behind which he stood; but these gentlemen were in too high a humour to be long delayed, and soon made off down a corkscrew pathway which had escaped Denis's observation, and passed out of sight and hearing along the battlements of the town.

Denis breathed again. He gave them a few minutes' grace for fear of accidents, and then groped about for some means of opening the door and slipping forth again. The inner surface was quite smooth, not a handle, not a moulding, not a projection of any sort. He got his fingernails round the edges and pulled, but the mass was immovable. He shook it, it was as firm as a rock. Denis de Beaulieu frowned and gave vent to a little noiseless whistle.

What ailed the door? he wondered. Why was it open? How came it to shut so easily and so effectually after him? There was something obscure and underhand about all this that was little to the young man's fancy. It looked like a snare; and yet who could suppose a snare in such a quiet by-street and in a house of so prosperous and even noble an exterior? And yet – snare or no snare, intentionally or unintentionally – here he was, prettily trapped; and for the life of him he could see no way out of it again. The darkness began to weigh upon him. He gave ear; all was silent without, but within and close by he seemed to catch a faint sighing, a faint sobbing rustle, a little stealthy creak – as though many persons were at his side, holding themselves quite still, and governing even their respiration with the extreme of slyness. The idea went to his vitals with a shock, and he faced about suddenly as if to defend his life. Then, for the first time, he became aware of a light about the level of his eyes and at some distance in the interior of the house – a vertical thread of light, widening towards the bottom, such as might escape between two wings of arras over a doorway. To see anything was a relief to Denis; it was like a piece of solid ground to a man labouring in a morass; his mind seized upon it with avidity; and he stood staring at it and trying to piece together some logical conception of his surroundings. Plainly there was a flight of steps ascending from his own level to that of this illuminated doorway; and indeed he thought he could make out another thread of light, as fine as a needle and as faint as phosphorescence, which might very well be reflected along the polished wood of a handrail. Since he had begun to suspect that he was not alone, his heart had continued to beat with smothering violence, and an intolerable desire for action of any sort had possessed itself of his spirit. He was in deadly peril, he believed. What could be more natural than to mount the staircase, lift the curtain, and confront his difficulty at once? At least he would be dealing with something tangible; at least he would be no longer in the dark. He stepped slowly forward with out-stretched hands, until his foot struck the bottom step; then he rapidly scaled the stairs, stood for a moment to compose his expression, lifted the arras and went in.

He found himself in a large apartment of polished stone. There were three doors; one on each of three sides; all similarly curtained with tapestry. The fourth side was occupied by two large windows and a great stone chimney-piece, carved with the arms of the Maletroits. Denis recognised the bearings, and was gratified to find himself in such good hands. The room was strongly illuminated but it contained little furniture except a heavy table and a chair or two; the hearth was innocent of fire, and the pavement was but sparsely strewn with rushes clearly many days old.

On a high chair beside the chimney, and directly facing Denis as he entered, sat a little old gentleman in a fur tippet. He sat with his legs crossed and his hands folded, and a cup of spiced wine stood by his elbow on a bracket on the wall. His countenance had a strongly masculine cast; not properly human, but such as we see in the bull, the goat or the domestic boar; something equivocal and wheedling, something greedy, brutal and dangerous. The upper lip was inordinately full, as though swollen by a blow or a toothache; and the smile, the peaked eyebrows, and the small, strong eyes were quaintly and almost comically evil in expression. Beautiful white hair hung straight all round his head, like a saint's, and fell in a single curl upon the tippet. His beard and moustache were the pink of venerable sweetness. Age, probably in consequence of inordinate precautions, had left no mark upon his hands; and the Maletroit hand was famous. It would be difficult to imagine anything at once so fleshy and so delicate in design; the taper, sensual fingers were like those of one of Leonardo's women; the fork of the thumb made a dimpled protuberance when closed; the nails were perfectly shaped, and of a dead, surprising whiteness. It rendered his aspect tenfold more redoubtable that a man with hands like these should keep them devoutly folded in his lap like a virgin martyr – that a man with so intense and startling an expression of face should sit patiently on his seat and contemplate people with an unwinking stare, like a god, or a god's statue. His quiescence seemed ironical and treacherous, it fitted so poorly with his looks.

Such was Alain, Sire de Maletroit.

Denis and he looked silently at each other for a second or two.

'Pray step in,' said the Sire de Maletroit. 'I have been expecting you all the evening.'

He had not risen, but he accompanied his words with a smile and a slight but courteous inclination of the head. Partly from the smile, partly from the strange musical murmur with which the Sire prefaced his observation, Denis felt a strong shudder of disgust go through his marrow. And what with disgust and honest confusion of mind, he could scarcely get words together in reply.

'I fear,' he said, 'that this is a double accident. I am not the person you suppose me. It seems you were looking for a visit; but for my part, nothing was further from my thoughts – nothing could be more contrary to my wishes – than this intrusion.'

'Well, well,' replied the old gentleman indulgently, 'here you are, which is the main point. Seat yourself, my friend, and put yourself entirely at your ease. We shall arrange our little affairs presently.'

Denis perceived that the matter was still complicated with some misconception, and he hastened to continue his explanations.

'Your door . . . ' he began.

'About my door?' asked the other, raising his peaked eyebrows. 'A little piece of ingenuity.' And he shrugged his shoulders. 'A hospitable fancy! By your own account, you were not desirous of making my acquaintance. We old people look for such reluctance now and then; and when it touches our honour, we cast about until we find some way of overcoming it. You arrive uninvited, but believe me, very welcome.'

'You persist in error, sir,' said Denis. 'There can be no question between you and me. I am a stranger in this countryside. My name is Denis, damoiseau de Beaulieu. If you see me in your house, it is only – '

'My young friend,' interrupted the other, 'you will permit me to have my own ideas on that subject. They probably differ from yours at the present moment,' he added with a leer, 'but time will show which of us is in the right.'

Denis was convinced he had to do with a lunatic. He seated himself with a shrug, content to wait the upshot; and a pause ensued, during which he thought he could distinguish a hurried gabbling as of prayer from behind the arras immediately opposite him. Sometimes there seemed to be but one person engaged, sometimes two; and the vehemence of the voice, low as it was, seemed to indicate either great haste or an agony of spirit. It occurred to him that this piece of tapestry covered the entrance to the chapel he had noticed from without.

The old gentleman meanwhile surveyed Denis from head to foot with a smile, and from time to time emitted little noises like a bird or a mouse, which seemed to indicate a high degree of satisfaction. This state of matters became rapidly insupportable; and Denis, to put an end to it, remarked politely that the wind had gone down.

The old gentleman fell into a fit of silent laughter, so prolonged and violent that he became quite red in the face. Denis got upon his feet at once, and put on his hat with a flourish.

'Sir,' he said, 'if you are in your wits, you have affronted me grossly. If you are out of them, I flatter myself I can find better employment for my brains than to talk with lunatics. My conscience is clear; you have made a fool of me from the first moment; you have refused to hear my explanations; and now there is no power under God will make me stay here any longer; and if I cannot make my way out in a more decent fashion, I will hack your door in pieces with my sword.'

The Sire de Maletroit raised his right hand and wagged it at Denis with the fore and little fingers extended.

'My dear nephew,' he said, 'sit down.'

'Nephew!' retorted Denis, 'you lie in your throat;' and he snapped his fingers in his face.

'Sit down, you rogue!' cried the old gentleman, in a sudden, harsh voice, like the barking of a dog. 'Do you fancy,' he went on, 'that when I had made my little contrivance for the door I had stopped short with that? If you prefer to be bound hand and foot till your bones ache, rise and try to go away. If you choose to remain a free young buck, agreeably conversing with an old gentleman – why, sit where you are in peace, and God be with you.'

'Do you mean I am a prisoner?' demanded Denis.

'I state the facts,' replied the other. 'I would rather leave the conclusion to yourself.'

Denis sat down again. Externally he managed to keep pretty calm; but within, he was now boiling with anger, now chilled with apprehension. He no longer felt convinced that he was dealing with a madman. And if the old gentleman was sane, what, in God's name, had he to look for? What absurd or tragical adventure had befallen him? What countenance was he to assume?

While he was thus unpleasantly reflecting, the arras that overhung the chapel door was raised, and a tall priest in his robes came forth and, giving a long, keen stare at Denis, said something in an undertone to Sire de Maletroit.

'She is in a better frame of spirit?' asked the latter.

'She is more resigned, messire,' replied the priest.

'Now the Lord help her, she is hard to please!' sneered the old gentleman. 'A likely stripling – not ill-born – and of her own choosing, too? Why, what more would the jade have?'

'The situation is not usual for a young damsel,' said the other, 'and somewhat trying to her blushes.'

'She should have thought of that before she began the dance. It was none of my choosing, God knows that: but since she is in it, by our Lady, she shall carry it to the end.' And then addressing Denis, 'Monsieur de Beaulieu,' he asked, 'may I present you to my niece? She has been waiting your arrival, I may say, with even greater impatience than myself.'

Denis had resigned himself with a good grace – all he desired was to know the worst of it as speedily as possible; so he rose at once, and bowed in acquiescence. The Sire de Maletroit followed his example and limped, with the assistance of the chaplain's arm, towards the chapel door. The priest pulled aside the arras, and all three entered. The building had considerable architectural pretensions. A light groining sprang from six stout columns, and hung down in two rich pendants from the centre of the vault. The place terminated behind the altar in a round end, embossed and honeycombed with a superfluity of ornament in relief, and pierced by many little windows shaped like stars, trefoils or wheels. These windows were imperfectly glazed, so that the night air circulated freely in the chapel. The tapers, of which there must have been half a hundred burning on the altar, were unmercifully blown about; and the light went through many different phases of brilliancy and semi-eclipse. On the steps in front of the altar knelt a young girl richly attired as a bride. A chill settled over Denis as he observed her costume; he fought with desperate energy against the conclusion that was being thrust upon his mind; it could not – it should not – be as he feared.

'Blanche,' said the Sire, in his most flute-like tones, 'I have brought a friend to see you, my little girl; turn round and give him your pretty hand. It is good to be devout, but it is necessary to be polite, my niece.'

The girl rose to her feet and turned towards the newcomers. She moved all of a piece; and shame and exhaustion were expressed in every line of her fresh young body; and she held her head down and kept her eyes upon the pavement, as she came slowly forward. In the course of her advance, her eyes fell upon Denis de Beaulieu's feet – feet of which he was justly vain, be it remarked, and wore in the most elegant accoutrement even while travelling. She paused – started, as if his yellow boots had conveyed some shocking meaning – and glanced suddenly up into the wearer's countenance. Their eyes met; shame gave place to horror and terror in her looks; the blood left her lips; with a piercing scream she covered her face with her hands and sank upon the chapel floor.

'That is not the man!' she cried. 'My uncle, that in not the man!'

The Sire de Maletroit chirped agreeably. 'Of course not,' he said; 'I expected as much. It was so unfortunate you could not remember his name.'

'Indeed,' she cried, 'indeed, I have never seen this person till this moment – I have never so much as set eyes upon him – I never wish to see him again. Sir,' she said, turning to Denis, 'if you are a gentleman, you will bear me out. Have I ever seen you – have you ever seen me – before this accursed hour?'

'To speak for myself, I have never had that pleasure,' answered the young man. 'This is the first time, messire, that I have met with your engaging niece.'

The old gentleman shrugged his shoulders.

'I am distressed to hear it,' he said. 'But it is never too late to begin. I had little more acquaintance with my own late lady ere I married her; which proves,' he added with a grimace, 'that these impromptu marriages may often produce an excellent understanding in the long-run. As the bride-groom is to have a voice in the matter, I will give him two hours to make up for lost time before we proceed with the ceremony.' And he turned towards the door, followed by the clergyman.

The girl was on her feet in a moment. 'My uncle, you cannot be in earnest,' she said. 'I declare before God I will stab myself rather than be forced on that young man. The heart rises at it; God forbids such marriages; you dishonour your white hair. Oh, my uncle, pity me! There is not a woman in all the world but would prefer death to such a nuptial. Is it possible,' she added, faltering – 'is it possible that you do not believe me – that you still think this' – and she pointed at Denis with a tremor of anger and contempt – 'that you still think *this* to be the man?'

'Frankly,' said the old gentleman, pausing on the threshold, 'I do. But let me explain to you once for all, Blanche de Maletroit, my way of thinking about this affair. When you took it into your head to dishonour my family and the name that I have borne, in peace and war, for more than three-score years, you forfeited not only the right to question my designs but that of looking me in the face. If your father had been alive, he would have spat on you and turned you out of doors. His was the hand of iron. You may bless your God you have only to deal with the hand of velvet, mademoiselle. It was my duty to get you married without delay. Out of pure goodwill, I have tried to find your own gallant for you. And I believe I have succeeded. But before God and all the holy angels, Blanche de Maletroit, if I have not, I care not one jack-straw. So let me recommend you to be polite to our young friend; for upon my word, your next groom may be less appetising.'

And with that he went out, with the chaplain at his heels; and the arras fell behind the pair.

The girl turned upon Denis with flashing eyes.

'And what, sir,' she demanded, 'may be the meaning of all this?'

'God knows,' returned Denis gloomily. 'I am a prisoner in this house, which seems full of mad people. More I know not; and nothing do I understand.'

'And pray how came you here?' she asked.

He told her as briefly as he could. 'For the rest,' he added, 'perhaps you will follow my example, and tell me the answer to all these riddles, and what, in God's name, is like to be the end of it.'

She stood silent for a little, and he could see her lips tremble and her tearless eyes burn with a feverish lustre. Then she pressed her forehead in both hands.

'Alas, how my head aches!' she said wearily – 'to say nothing of my poor heart! But it is due to you to know my story, unmaidenly as it must seem. I am called Blanche de Maletroit; I have been without father or mother for – oh! for as long as I can recollect, and indeed I have been most unhappy all my life. Three months ago a young captain began to stand near me every day in church. I could see that I pleased him; I am much to blame, but I was so glad that anyone should love me; and when he passed me a letter, I took it home with me and read it with great pleasure. Since that time he has written many. He was so anxious to speak with me, poor fellow! and kept asking me to leave the door open some evening that we might have two words upon the stair. For he knew how much my uncle trusted me.' She gave something like a sob at that, and it was a moment before she could go on. 'My uncle is a hard man, but he is very shrewd,' she said at last. 'He has performed many feats in war, and was a great person at court, and much trusted by Queen Isabeau in old days. How he came to suspect me I cannot tell; but it is hard to keep anything from his knowledge; and this morning, as we came from mass, he took my hand in his, forced it open, and read my little billet, walking by my side all the while. When he had finished, he gave it back to me with great politeness. It contained another request to have the door left open; and this has been the ruin of us all. My uncle kept me strictly in my room until evening, and then ordered me to dress myself as you see me – a hard mockery for a young girl, do you not think so? I suppose, when he could not prevail with me to tell him the young captain's name, he must have laid a trap for him: into which, alas! you have fallen in the anger of God. I looked for much confusion; for how could I tell whether he was willing to take me for his wife on these sharp terms? He might have been trifling with me from the first; or I might have made myself too cheap in his eyes. But truly I had not looked for such a shameful punishment as this! I could not think that God would let a girl be so disgraced before a young man. And now I have told you all and I can scarcely hope that you will not despise me.'

Denis made her a respectful inclination.

'Madam,' he said, 'you have honoured me by your confidence. It remains for me to prove that I am not unworthy of the honour. Is Messire de Maletroit at hand?'

'I believe he is writing in the *salle* without,' she answered.

'May I lead you thither, madam?' asked Denis, offering his hand with his most courtly bearing.

She accepted it and the pair passed out of the chapel, Blanche in a very drooping and shamefast condition, but Denis strutting and ruffling in the consciousness of a mission, and the boyish certainty of accomplishing it with honour.

The Sire de Maletroit rose to meet them with an ironical obeisance.

'Sir,' said Denis, with the grandest possible air, 'I believe I am to have some say in the matter of this marriage; and let me tell you at once, I will be no party to forcing the inclination of this young lady. Had it been freely offered to me, I should have been proud to accept her hand, for I perceive she is as good as she is beautiful; but as things are, I have now the honour, messire, of refusing.'

Blanche looked at him with gratitude in her eyes; but the old gentleman only smiled and smiled, until his smile grew positively sickening to Denis.

'I am afraid,' he said, 'Monsieur de Beaulieu, that you do not perfectly understand the choice I have to offer you. Follow me, I beseech you, to this window.' And he led the way to one of the large windows which stood open on the night. 'You observe,' he went on, 'there is an iron ring in the upper masonry, and reeved through that, a very efficacious rope. Now, mark my words; if you should find your disinclination to my niece's person insurmountable, I shall have you hanged out of this window before sunrise. I shall only proceed to such an extremity with the greatest regret, you may believe me. For it is not at all your death that I desire, but my niece's establishment in life. At the same time, it must come to that if you prove obstinate. Your family, Monsieur de Beaulieu, is very well in its way; but if you sprang from Charlemagne, you should not refuse the hand of a Maletroit with impunity – not if she had been as common as the Paris road – not if she were as hideous as the gargoyle over my door. Neither my niece nor you, nor my own private feelings, move me at all in this matter. The honour of my house has been compromised; I believe you to be the guilty person; at least you are now in the secret; and you can hardly wonder if I request you to wipe out the stain. If you will not, your blood be on your own head! It will be no great satisfaction to me to have your interesting relics kicking their heels in the breeze below my windows; but half a loaf is better than no bread, and if I cannot cure the dishonour, I shall at least stop the scandal.'

There was a pause.

'I believe there are other ways of settling such imbroglios among gentlemen,' said Denis. 'You wear a sword, and I hear you have used it with distinction.'

The Sire de Maletroit made a signal to the chaplain, who crossed the room with long silent strides and raised the arras over the third of the three doors. It was only a moment before he let it fall again, but Denis had time to see a dusky passage full of armed men.

'When I was a little younger, I should have been delighted to honour you, Monsieur de Beaulieu,' said Sire Alain; 'but I am now too old. Faithful retainers are the sinews of age, and I must employ the strength I have. This is one of the hardest things to swallow as a man grows up in years; but with a little patience, even this becomes habitual. You and the lady seem to prefer the salle for what remains of your two hours; and as I have no desire to cross your preference, I shall resign it to your use with all the pleasure in the world. No haste!' he added, holding up his hand, as he saw a dangerous look come into Denis de Beaulieu's face. 'If your mind revolts against hanging, it will be time enough two hours hence to throw yourself out of the window or upon the pikes of my retainers. Two hours of life are always two hours. A great many things may turn up in even as little a while as that. And, besides, if I understand her appearance, my niece has still something to say to you. You will not disfigure your last hours by a want of politeness to a lady?'

Denis looked at Blanche, and she made him an imploring gesture.

It is likely that the old gentleman was hugely pleased at this symptom of an understanding; for he smiled on both, and added sweetly: 'If you will give

me your word of honour, Monsieur de Beaulieu, to await my return at the
end of the two hours before attempting anything desperate, I shall withdraw
my retainers, and let you speak in greater privacy with mademoiselle.'

Denis again glanced at the girl, who seemed to beseech him to agree.

'I give you my word of honour,' he said.

Messire de Maletroit bowed, and proceeded to limp about the apartment,
clearing his throat the while with that odd musical chirp which had already
grown so irritating in the ears of Denis de Beaulieu. He first possessed
himself of some papers which lay upon the table; then he went to the mouth
of the passage and appeared to give an order to the men behind the arras;
and lastly he hobbled out through the door by which Denis had come in,
turning upon the threshold to address a last smiling bow to the young
couple, and followed by the chaplain with a hand-lamp.

No sooner were they alone than Blanche advanced towards Denis with
her hands extended. Her face was flushed and excited, and her eyes shone
with tears.

'You shall not die!' she cried, 'you shall marry me after all.'

'You seem to think, madam,' replied Denis, 'that I stand much in fear of
death.'

'Oh no, no,' she said, 'I see you are no poltroon. It is for my own sake – I
could not bear to have you slain for such a scruple.'

'I am afraid,' returned Denis, 'that you underrate the difficulty, madam.
What you may be too generous to refuse, I may be too proud to accept. In a
moment of noble feeling towards me, you forgot what you perhaps owe to
others.'

He had the decency to keep his eyes upon the floor as he said this, and after
he had finished, so as not to spy upon her confusion. She stood silent for a
moment, then walked suddenly away, and falling on her uncle's chair, fairly
burst out sobbing. Denis was in the acme of embarrassment. He looked
round, as if to seek for inspiration, and seeing a stool, plumped down upon it
for something to do. There he sat, playing with the guard of his rapier and
wishing himself dead a thousand times over and buried in the nastiest
kitchen-heap in France. His eyes wandered round the apartment, but found
nothing to arrest them. There were such wide spaces between the furniture,
the light fell so baldly and cheerlessly over all, the dark outside air looked in so
coldly through the windows, that he thought he had never seen a church so
vast, nor a tomb so melancholy. The regular sobs of Blanche de Maletroit
measured out the time like the ticking of a clock. He read the device upon the
shield over and over again, until his eyes became obscured; he stared into
shadowy corners until he imagined they were swarming with horrible animals;
and every now and again he awoke with a start, to remember that his last two
hours were running, and death was on the march.

Oftener and oftener, as the time went on, did his glance settle on the girl herself. Her face was bowed forward and covered with her hands, and she was shaken at intervals by the convulsive hiccup of grief. Even thus she was not an unpleasant object to dwell upon, so plump and yet so fine, with a warm brown skin, and the most beautiful hair, Denis thought, in the whole world of womankind. Her hands were like her uncle's; but they were more in place at the end of her young arms, and looked infinitely soft and caressing. He remembered how her blue eyes had shone upon him, full of anger, pity and innocence. And the more he dwelt on her perfections, the uglier death looked, and the more deeply was he smitten with penitence at her continued tears. Now he felt that no man could have the courage to leave a world which contained so beautiful a creature; and now he would have given forty minutes of his last hour to have unsaid his cruel speech.

Suddenly a hoarse and ragged peal of cockcrow rose to their ears from the dark valley below the windows. And this shattering noise in the silence of all around was like a light in a dark place, and shook them both out of their reflections.

'Alas, can I do nothing to help you?' she said, looking up.

'Madam,' replied Denis, with a fine irrelevancy, 'if I have said anything to wound you, believe me, it was for your own sake and not for mine.'

She thanked him with a tearful look.

'I feel your position cruelly,' he went on. 'The world has been bitter hard on you. Your uncle is a disgrace to mankind. Believe me, madam, there is no young gentleman in all France but would be glad of my opportunity, to die in doing you a momentary service.'

'I know already that you can be very brave and generous,' she answered. 'What I want to know is whether I can serve you – now or afterwards,' she added, with a quaver.

'Most certainly,' he answered with a smile. 'Let me sit beside you as if I were a friend, instead of a foolish intruder; try to forget how awkwardly we are placed to one another; make my last moments go pleasantly; and you will do me the chief service possible.'

'You are very gallant,' she added, with a yet deeper sadness . . . 'very gallant . . . and it somehow pains me. But draw nearer, if you please; and if you find anything to say to me, you will at least make certain of a very friendly listener. Ah! Monsieur de Beaulieu,' she broke forth – 'ah! Monsieur de Beaulieu, how can I look you in the face?' And she fell to weeping again with a renewed effusion.

'Madam,' said Denis, taking her hand in both of his, 'reflect on the little time I have before me, and the great bitterness into which I am cast by the sight of your distress. Spare me, in my last moments, the spectacle of what I cannot cure even with the sacrifice of my life.'

'I am very selfish,' answered Blanche. 'I will be braver, Monsieur de Beaulieu, for your sake. But think if I can do you no kindness in the future – if you have no friends to whom I could carry your adieux. Charge me as heavily as you can; every burden will lighten, by so little, the invaluable gratitude I owe you. Put it in my power to do something more for you than weep.'

'My mother is married again, and has a young family to care for. My brother Guichard will inherit my fiefs; and if I am not in error, that will content him amply for my death. Life is a little vapour that passeth away, as we are told by those in holy orders. When a man is in a fair way and sees all life open in front of him, he seems to himself to make a very important figure in the world. His horse whinnies to him; the trumpets blow and the girls look out of window as he rides into town before his company; he receives many assurances of trust and regard – sometimes by express in a letter – sometimes face to face, with persons of great consequence falling on his neck. It is not wonderful if his head is turned for a time. But once he is dead, were he as brave as Hercules or as wise as Solomon, he is soon forgotten. It is not ten years since my father fell, with many other knights around him, in a very fierce encounter, and I do not think that any one of them, nor so much as the name of the fight, is now remembered. No, no, madam, the nearer you come to it, you see that death is a dark and dusty corner, where a man gets into his tomb and has the door shut after him till the judgement day. I have few friends just now, and once I am dead I shall have none.'

'Ah, Monsieur de Beaulieu!' she exclaimed, 'you forget Blanche de Maletroit.'

'You have a sweet nature, madam, and you are pleased to estimate a little service far beyond its worth.'

'It is not that,' she answered. 'You mistake me if you think I am so easily touched by my own concerns. I say so, because you are the noblest man I have ever met; because I recognise in you a spirit that would have made even a common person famous in the land.'

'And yet here I die in a mouse-trap – with no more noise about it than my own squeaking,' answered he.

A look of pain crossed her face, and she was silent for a little while. Then a fight came into her eyes, and with a smile she spoke again.

'I cannot have my champion think meanly of himself. Anyone who gives his life for another will be met in paradise by all the heralds and angels of the Lord God. And you have no such cause to hang your head. For . . . Pray, do you think me beautiful?' she asked, with a deep flush.

'Indeed, madam, I do,' he said.

'I am glad of that,' she answered heartily. 'Do you think there are many men in France who have been asked in marriage by a beautiful maiden – with her own lips – and who have refused her to her face? I know you men would half despise such a triumph; but believe me, we women know more of what is precious in love. There is nothing that should set a person higher in his own esteem; and we women would prize nothing more dearly.'

'You are very good,' he said; 'but you cannot make me forget that I was asked in pity and not for love.'

'I am not so sure of that,' she replied, holding down her head. 'Hear me to an end, Monsieur de Beaulieu. I know how you must despise me; I feel you are right to do so; I am too poor a creature to occupy one thought of your mind, although, alas! you must die for me this morning. But when I asked you to marry me, indeed, and indeed, it was because I respected and admired you, and loved you with my whole soul, from the very moment that you took my part against my uncle. If you had seen yourself, and how noble you looked, you would pity rather than despise me. And now,' she went on, hurriedly checking him with her hand, 'although I have laid aside all reserve and told you so much, remember that I know your sentiments towards me already. I would not, believe me, being nobly born, weary you with importunities into consent. I too have a pride of my own: and I declare before the holy mother of God, if you should now go back from your word already given, I would no more marry you than I would marry my uncle's groom.'

Denis smiled a little bitterly.

'It is a small love,' he said, 'that shies at a little pride.'

She made no answer, although she probably had her own thoughts.

'Come hither to the window,' he said, with a sigh. 'Here is the dawn.'

And indeed the dawn was already beginning. The hollow of the sky was full of essential daylight, colourless and clean; and the valley underneath was flooded with a grey reflection. A few thin vapours clung in the coves of the forest or lay along the winding course of the river. The scene disengaged a surprising effect of stillness, which was hardly interrupted when the cocks began once more to crow among the steadings. Perhaps the same fellow who had made so horrid a clangour in the darkness not half an hour before, now sent up the merriest cheer to greet the coming day. A little wind went bustling and eddying among the tree-tops underneath the windows. And still the daylight kept flooding insensibly out of the east, which was soon to grow incandescent and cast up that red-hot cannon-ball, the rising sun.

Denis looked out over all this with a bit of a shiver. He had taken her hand, and retained it in his almost unconsciously.

'Has the day begun already?' she said; and then, illogically enough: 'the night has been so long! Alas, what shall we say to my uncle when he returns?'

'What you will,' said Denis, and he pressed her fingers in his.

She was silent.

'Blanche,' he said, with a swift, uncertain, passionate utterance, 'you have seen whether I fear death. You must know well enough that I would as gladly leap out of that window into the empty air as lay a finger on you without your free and full consent. But if you care for me at all do not let me lose my life in a misapprehension; for I love you better than the whole world; and though I will die for you blithely, it would be like all the joys of paradise to live on and spend my life in your service.'

As he stopped speaking, a bell began to ring loudly in the interior of the house; and a clatter of armour in the corridor showed that the retainers were returning to their post and the two hours were at an end.

'After all that you have heard?' she whispered, leaning towards him with her lips and eyes.

'I have heard nothing,' he replied.

'The captain's name was Florimond de Champdivers,' she said in his ear.

'I did not hear it,' he answered, taking her supple body in his arms and covering her wet face with kisses.

A melodious chirping was audible behind, followed by a beautiful chuckle, and the voice of Messire de Maletroit wished his new nephew a good-morning.

ANTHONY TROLLOPE

Anthony Trollope, the quintessential Victorian novelist whose
dozens of books illuminate virtually every aspect of late nineteenth century England, was born in London on 24 April 1815.
His father failed as a barrister and his mother, Frances Trollope,
successfully turned to writing in order to improve their finances.
At the age of nineteen Trollope embarked on a career as a civil
servant in London's General Post Office. In 1841 he was transferred to Ireland, where he lived for the next eighteen years. In
1844 he married Rose Heseltine, who became a trusted literary
assistant once he began to write. Trollope's first book was
published in 1847, but it was not until 1855 that he achieved
commercial success with *The Warden*, the initial volume in a six-
book series about clerical life in and around the fictional cathedral
town of Barchester. In October 1859 he returned to England and
quickly became part of London's literary life. With *Can You
Forgive Her?* in 1865 he launched the Palliser novels, a new series
about politics. Trollope resigned from the postal service late in
1867 to become editor of *Saint Paul's Magazine*. The next year he
made an unsuccessful bid for a seat in Parliament. In the final
years of his life he travelled extensively. Anthony Trollope died
on 6 December 1882, a month after suffering a paralysing stroke.

The Man who Kept his Money in a Box

I first saw the man who kept his money in a box in the midst of the ravine of the Via Mala. I interchanged a few words with him or with his wife at the hospice, at the top of the Splugen; and I became acquainted with him in the courtyard of Conradi's hotel at Chiavenna. It was, however, afterwards at Bellaggio, on the lake of Como, that that acquaintance ripened into intimacy. A good many years have rolled by since then, and I believe this little episode in his life may be told without pain to the feelings of anyone.

His name was —; let us for the present say that his name was Greene. How he learned that my name was Robinson I do not know, but I remember well that he addressed me by my name at Chiavenna. To go back, however, for a moment to the Via Mala; I had been staying for a few days at the Golden Eagle at Tusis – which, by the by, I hold to be the best small inn in all Switzerland, and its hostess to be, or to have been, certainly the prettiest landlady – and on the day of my departure southwards, I had walked on, into the Via Mala, so that the diligence might pick me up in the gorge. This pass I regard as one of the grandest spots to which my wandering steps have ever carried me, and though I had already lingered about it for many hours, I now walked thither again to take my last farewell of its dark towering rocks, its narrow causeway and roaring river, trusting to my friend the landlady to see that my luggage was duly packed upon the diligence. I need hardly say that my friend did not betray her trust.

As one goes out from Switzerland towards Italy, the road through the Via Mala ascends somewhat steeply, and passengers by the diligence may walk from the inn at Tusis into the gorge, and make their way through the greater part of the ravine before the vehicle will overtake them. This, however, Mr Greene with his wife and daughter had omitted to do. When the diligence passed me in the defile, the horses trotting for a few yards over some level portion of the road, I saw a man's nose pressed close against the glass of the coupe window. I saw more of his nose than of any other part of his face, but yet I could perceive that his neck was twisted and his eye upturned, and that he was making a painful effort to look upwards to the summit of the rocks from his position inside the carriage.

There was such a roar of wind and waters at the spot that it was not practicable to speak to him, but I beckoned with my finger and then pointed to the road, indicating that he should have walked. He understood me, though I did not at the moment understand his answering gesture. It was subsequently, when I knew somewhat of his habits, that he explained to me that on pointing to his open mouth, he had intended to signify that he would be afraid of a sore throat in exposing himself to the air of that damp and narrow passage.

I got up into the conductor's covered seat at the back of the diligence, and in this position encountered the drifting snow of the Splugen. I think it is coldest of all the passes. Near the top of the pass the diligence stops for a while, and it is here, if I remember, that the Austrian officials demand the travellers' passports. At least in those days they did so. These officials have now retreated behind the Quadrilatere – soon, as we hope, to make a further retreat – and the district belongs to the kingdom of United Italy. There is a place of refreshment or hospice here, into which we all went for a few moments, and I then saw that my friend with the weak throat was accompanied by two ladies.

'You should not have missed the Via Mala,' I said to him, as he stood warming his toes at the huge covered stove.

'We miss everything,' said the elder of the two ladies, who, however, was very much younger than the gentleman, and not very much older than her companion.

'I saw it beautifully, mamma,' said the younger one; whereupon mamma gave her head a toss, and made up her mind, as I thought, to take some little vengeance before long upon her stepdaughter. I observed that Miss Greene always called her stepmother mamma on the first approach of any stranger, so that the nature of the connection between them might be understood. And I observed also that the elder lady always gave her head a toss when she was so addressed.

'We don't mean to enjoy ourselves till we get down to the lake of Como,' said Mr Greene. As I looked at him cowering over the stove, and saw how oppressed he was with great coats and warm wrappings for his throat, I quite agreed with him that he had not begun to enjoy himself as yet. Then we all got into our places again, and I saw no more of the Greenes till we were standing huddled together in the large courtyard of Conradi's hotel at Chiavenna.

Chiavenna is the first Italian town which the tourist reaches by this route, and I know no town in the north of Italy which is so closely surrounded by beautiful scenery. The traveller as he falls down to it from the Splugen road is bewildered by the loveliness of the valleys – that is to say, if he so arranges that he can see them without pressing his nose against the glass of a coach window. And then from the town itself there are walks of two, three and four hours, which I think are unsurpassed for wild and sometimes startling beauties. One gets into little valleys, green as emeralds, and surrounded on all sides by grey broken rocks, in which Italian Rasselases might have lived in perfect bliss; and then again one comes upon distant views up the river courses, bounded far away by the spurs of the Alps, which are perfect – to which the fancy can add no additional charm. Conradi's hotel also is by no means bad; or was not in those days. For my part I am inclined to think that Italian hotels have received a worse name than they deserve; and I must profess that, looking merely to creature comforts, I would much sooner stay a week at the Golden Key at Chiavenna than with mine host of the King's Head in the thriving commercial town of Muddleboro, on the borders of Yorkshire and Lancashire.

I am always rather keen about my room in travelling, and having secured a chamber looking out upon the mountains had returned to the courtyard to collect my baggage before Mr Greene had succeeded in realising his position, or understanding that he had to take upon himself the duties of settling his family for the night in the hotel by which he was surrounded. When I descended he was stripping off the outermost of three greatcoats, and four waiters around him were beseeching him to tell them what accommodation he would require. Mr Greene was giving sundry very urgent instructions to the conductor respecting his boxes; but as these were given in English, I was not surprised to find that they were not accurately followed. The man, however, was much too courteous to say in any language that he did not understand every word that was said to him. Miss Greene was standing apart, doing nothing. As she was only eighteen years of age, it was of course her business to do nothing; and a very pretty little girl she was, by no means ignorant of her own beauty, and possessed of quite sufficient wit to enable her to make the most of it.

Mr Greene was very leisurely in his proceedings, and the four waiters were almost reduced to despair.

'I want two bedrooms, a dressing-room, and some dinner,' he said at last, speaking very slowly, and in his own vernacular. I could not in the least assist him by translating it into Italian, for I did not speak a word of the language myself; but I suggested that the man would understand French. The waiter, however, had understood English. Waiters do understand all languages with a facility that is marvellous; and this one now suggested that Mrs Greene should follow him upstairs. Mrs Greene, however, would not move till she had seen that her boxes were all right; and as Mrs Greene was also a pretty woman, I found myself bound to apply myself to her assistance.

'Oh, thank you,' said she. 'The people are so stupid that one can really do nothing with them. And as for Mr Greene, he is of no use at all. You see that box, the smaller one. I have four hundred pounds' worth of jewellery in that, and therefore I am obliged to look after it.'

'Indeed,' said I, rather startled at this amount of confidence on rather a short acquaintance. 'In that case I do not wonder at your being careful. But is it not rather rash, perhaps – '

'I know what you are going to say. Well, perhaps it is rash. But when you are going to foreign courts, what are you to do? If you have got those sort of things you must wear them.'

As I was not myself possessed of anything of that sort, and had no intention of going to any foreign court, I could not argue the matter with her. But I assisted her in getting together an enormous pile of luggage, among which there were seven large boxes covered with canvas, such as ladies not uncommonly carry with them when travelling. That one which she represented as being smaller than the others, and as holding jewellery, might be about a yard long by a foot and a half deep. Being ignorant in those matters, I should have thought it sufficient to carry all a lady's wardrobe for twelve months. When the boxes were collected together, she sat down upon the jewel-case and looked up into my face. She was a pretty woman, perhaps thirty years of age, with long light yellow hair, which she allowed to escape from her bonnet, knowing, perhaps, that it was not unbecoming to her when thus dishevelled. Her skin was very delicate, and her complexion good. Indeed her face would have been altogether prepossessing had there not been a want of gentleness in her eyes. Her hands, too, were soft and small, and on the whole she may be said to have been possessed of a strong battery of feminine attractions. She also well knew how to use them.

'Whisper,' she said to me, with a peculiar but very proper aspiration on the h – 'Wh–hisper,' and both by the aspiration and the use of the word I knew at once from what island she had come. 'Mr Greene keeps all his money in this box also; so I never let it go out of my sight for a moment. But whatever you do, don't tell him that I told you so.'

I laid my hand on my heart, and made a solemn asseveration that I would not divulge her secret. I need not, however, have troubled myself much on that head, for as I walked upstairs, keeping my eye upon the precious trunk, Mr Greene addressed me.

'You are an Englishman, Mr Robinson,' said he. I acknowledged that I was.

'I am another. My wife, however, is Irish. My daughter – by a former marriage – is English also. You see that box there.'

'Oh, yes,' said I, 'I see it.' I began to be so fascinated by the box that I could not keep my eyes off it.

'I don't know whether or no it is prudent, but I keep all my money there; my money for travelling, I mean.'

'If I were you, then,' I answered, 'I would not say anything about it to anyone.'

'Oh, no, of course not,' said he; 'I should not think of mentioning it. But those brigands in Italy always take away what you have about your person, but they don't meddle with the heavy luggage.'

'Bills of exchange, or circular notes,' I suggested.

'Ah, yes; and if you can't identify yourself, or happen to have a headache, you can't get them changed. I asked an old friend of mine, who has been connected with the Bank of England for the last fifty years, and he assured me that there was nothing like sovereigns.'

'But you never get the value for them.'

'Well, not quite. One loses a franc, or a franc and a half. But still, there's the certainty, and that's the great matter. An English sovereign will go anywhere,' and he spoke these words with considerable triumph.

'Undoubtedly, if you consent to lose a shilling on each sovereign.'

'At any rate, I have got three hundred and fifty in that box,' he said. 'I have them done up in rolls of twenty-five pounds each.'

I again recommended him to keep this arrangement of his as private as possible – a piece of counsel which I confess seemed to me to be much needed – and then I went away to my own room, having first accepted an invitation from Mrs Greene to join their party at dinner. 'Do,' said she; 'we have been so dull, and it will be so pleasant.'

I did not require to be much pressed to join myself to a party in which there was so pretty a girl as Miss Greene, and so attractive a woman as Mrs Greene. I therefore accepted the invitation readily, and went away to make my toilet. As I did so I passed the door of Mr Greene's room, and saw the long file of boxes being borne into the centre of it.

I spent a pleasant evening, with, however, one or two slight drawbacks. As to old Greene himself, he was all that was amiable; but then he was nervous, full of cares, and somewhat apt to be a bore. He wanted information on a thousand points, and did not seem to understand that a young man might prefer the conversation of his daughter to his own. Not that he showed any solicitude to prevent conversation on the part of his daughter. I should have been perfectly at liberty to talk to either of the ladies had he not wished to engross all my attention to himself. He also had found it dull to be alone with his wife and daughter for the last six weeks.

He was a small spare man, probably over fifty years of age, who gave me to understand that he had lived in London all his life, and had made his own fortune in the city. What he had done in the city to make his fortune he did not say. Had I come across him there I should no doubt have found him to be a sharp man of business, quite competent to teach me many a useful lesson of which I was as ignorant as an infant. Had he caught me on the Exchange, or at Lloyd's, or in the big room of the Bank of England, I should have been compelled to ask him everything. Now, in this little town under the Alps, he was as much lost as I should have been in Lombard Street, and was ready enough to look to me for information. I was by no means chary in giving him my counsel and imparting to him my ideas on things in general in that part of the world – only I should have preferred to be allowed to make myself civil to his daughter.

In the course of conversation it was mentioned by him that they intended to stay a few days at Bellaggio, which, as all the world knows, is a central spot on the lake of Como, and a favourite resting-place for travellers. There are three lakes which all meet here, and to all of them we give the name of Como. They are properly called the lakes of Como, Colico and Lecco; and Bellaggio is the spot at which their waters join each other. I had half made up my mind to sleep there one night on my road into Italy, and now, on hearing their purpose, I declared that such was my intention.

'How very pleasant,' said Mrs Greene. 'It will be quite delightful to have someone to show us how to settle ourselves, for really – '

'My dear, I'm sure you can't say that you ever have much trouble.'

'And what if I do, Mr Greene? I am sure Sophonisba does not do much to help me.'

'You won't let me,' said Sophonisba, whose name I had not before heard. Her papa had called her Sophy in the yard of the inn. Sophonisba Greene! Sophonisba Robinson did not sound so badly in my ears, and I confess that I had tried the names together. Her papa had mentioned to me that he had no other child, and had mentioned also that he had made his fortune.

And then there was a little family contest as to the amount of travelling labour which fell to the lot of each of the party, during which I retired to one of the windows of the big front room in which we were sitting. And how much of this labour there is incidental to a tourist's pursuits! And how often these little contests do arise upon a journey! Who has ever travelled and not known them? I had taken up such a position at the window as might, I thought, have removed me out of hearing; but nevertheless from time to time a word would catch my ear about that precious box. 'I have never taken *my* eyes off it since I left England,' said Mrs Greene, speaking quick, and with a considerable brogue superinduced by her energy. 'Where would it have been at Basle if I had not been looking after it?' 'Quite safe,' said Sophonisba; 'those large things always are safe.' 'Are they, miss? That's all you know about it. I suppose your bonnet-box was quite safe when I found it on the platform at – at – I forget the name of the place?'

'Freidrichshafen,' said Sophonisba, with almost an unnecessary amount of Teutonic skill in her pronunciation. 'Well, mamma, you have told me of that at least twenty times.' Soon after that, the ladies took them to their own rooms, weary with the travelling of two days and a night, and Mr Greene went fast asleep in the very comfortless chair in which he was seated.

At four o'clock on the next morning we started on our journey.

> Early to bed, and early to rise,
> Is the way to be healthy, and wealthy, and wise.

We all know that lesson, and many of us believe in it; but if the lesson be true, the Italians ought to be the healthiest and wealthiest and wisest of all men and women. Three or four o'clock seems to them quite a natural hour for commencing the day's work. Why we should have started from Chiavenna at four o'clock in order that we might be kept waiting for the boat an hour and a half on the little quay at Colico, I don't know; but such was our destiny. There we remained an hour and a half; Mrs Greene sitting pertinaciously on the one important box. She had designated it as being smaller than the others, and, as all the seven were now ranged in a row, I had an opportunity of comparing them. It was something smaller – perhaps an inch less high, and an inch and a half shorter. She was a sharp woman, and observed my scrutiny. 'I always know it,' she said in a loud whisper, 'by this little hole in the canvas,' and she put her finger on a slight rent on one of the ends. 'As for Greene, if one of those Italian brigands were to walk off with it on his shoulders, before his eyes, he wouldn't be the wiser. How helpless you men are, Mr Robinson!'

'It is well for us that we have women to look after us.'

'But you have got no one to look after you – or perhaps you have left her behind?'

'No, indeed. I'm all alone in the world as yet. But it's not my own fault. I have asked half a dozen.'

'Now, Mr Robinson!' And in this way the time passed on the quay at Colico, till the boat came and took us away. I should have preferred to pass my time in making myself agreeable to the younger lady; but the younger lady stood aloof, turning up her nose, as I thought, at her mamma.

I will not attempt to describe the scenery about Colico. The little town itself is one of the vilest places under the sun, having no accommodation for travellers, and being excessively unhealthy; but there is very little either north or south of the Alps – and, perhaps, I may add, very little elsewhere – to beat the beauty of the mountains which cluster round the head of the lake. When we had sat upon those boxes that hour and a half, we were taken on board the steamer, which had been lying off a little way from the shore, and then we commenced our journey. Of course there was a good deal of exertion and care necessary in getting the packages off from the shore on to the boat, and I observed that anyone with half an eye in his head might have seen that the mental anxiety expended on that one box which was marked by the small hole in the canvas far exceeded that which was extended to all the other six boxes. 'They deserve that it should be stolen,' I said to myself, 'for being such fools.' And then we went down to breakfast in the cabin.

'I suppose it must be safe,' said Mrs Greene to me, ignoring the fact that the cabin waiter understood English, although she had just ordered some veal cutlets in that language.

'As safe as a church,' I replied, not wishing to give much apparent importance to the subject.

'They can't carry it off here,' said Mr Greene. But he was innocent of any attempt at a joke, and was looking at me with all his eyes.

'They might throw it overboard,' said Sophonisba. I at once made up my mind that she could not be a good-natured girl. The moment that breakfast was over, Mrs Greene returned again upstairs, and I found her seated on one of the benches near the funnel, from which she could keep her eyes fixed upon the box. 'When one is obliged to carry about one's jewels with one, one must be careful, Mr Robinson,' she said to me apologetically. But I was becoming tired of the box, and the funnel was hot and unpleasant, therefore I left her.

I had made up my mind that Sophonisba was ill-natured; but, nevertheless, she was pretty, and I now went through some little manoeuvres with the object of getting into conversation with her. This I soon did, and was surprised by her frankness. 'How tired you must be of mamma and her box,' she said to me. To this I made some answer, declaring that I was rather interested than otherwise in the safety of the precious trunk. 'It makes me sick,' said Sophonisba, 'to hear her go on in that way to a perfect stranger. I heard what she said about her jewellery.'

'It is natural she should be anxious,' I said, 'seeing that it contains so much that is valuable.'

'Why did she bring them?' said Sophonisba. 'She managed to live very well without jewels till papa married her, about a year since; and now she can't travel about for a month without lugging them with her everywhere. I should be so glad if someone would steal them.'

'But all Mr Greene's money is there also.'

'I don't want papa to be bothered, but I declare I wish the box might be lost for a day or so. She is such a fool; don't you think so, Mr Robinson?'

At this time it was just fourteen hours since I first had made their acquaintance in the yard of Conradi's hotel, and of those fourteen hours more than half had been passed in bed. I must confess that I looked upon Sophonisba as being almost more indiscreet than her stepmother. Nevertheless, she was not stupid, and I continued my conversation with her the greatest part of the way down the lake towards Bellaggio.

These steamers which run up and down the lake of Como and the Lago Maggiore, put out their passengers at the towns on the banks of the water by means of small rowing-boats, and the persons who are about to disembark generally have their own articles ready to their hands when their turn comes for leaving the steamer. As we came near to Bellaggio, I looked up my own portmanteau, and, pointing to the beautiful wood-covered hill that stands at the fork of the waters, told my friend Greene that he was near his destination. 'I am very glad to hear it,' said he, complacently, but he did not at the moment busy himself about the boxes. Then the small boat ran up alongside the steamer, and the passengers for Como and Milan crowded up the side.

'We have to go in that boat,' I said to Greene.

'Nonsense!' he exclaimed.

'Oh, but we have.'

'What! put our boxes into that boat,' said Mrs Greene. 'Oh dear! Here, boatman! there are seven of these boxes, all in white like this,' and she pointed to the one that had the hole in the canvas. 'Make haste. And there are two bags, and my dressing case, and Mr Greene's portmanteau. Mr Greene, where is your portmanteau?'

The boatman whom she addressed, no doubt did not understand a word of English, but nevertheless he knew what she meant, and, being well accustomed to the work, got all the luggage together in an incredibly small number of moments.

'If you will get down into the boat,' I said, 'I will see that the luggage follows you before I leave the deck.'

'I won't stir,' she said, 'till I see that box lifted down. Take care; you'll let it fall into the lake. I know you will.'

'I wish they would,' Sophonisba whispered into my ear.

Mr Greene said nothing, but I could see that his eyes were as anxiously fixed on what was going on as were those of his wife. At last, however, the three Greens were in the boat, as also were all the packages. Then I followed them, my portmanteau having gone down before me, and we pushed off for Bellaggio. Up to this period most of the attendants around us had understood a word or two of English, but now it would be well if we could find someone to whose ears French would not be unfamiliar. As regarded Mr Greene and his wife, they, I found, must give up all conversation, as they knew nothing of any language but their own. Sophonisba could make herself understood in French, and was quite at home, as she assured me, in German. And then the boat was beached on the shore at Bellaggio, and we all had to go again to work with the object of getting ourselves lodged at the hotel which overlooks the water.

I had learned before that the Greenes were quite free from any trouble in this respect, for their rooms had been taken for them before they left England. Trusting to this, Mrs Greene gave herself no inconsiderable airs the moment her foot was on the shore, and ordered the people about as though she were the Lady Paramount of Bellaggio. Italians, however, are used to this from travellers of a certain description. They never resent such conduct, but simply put it down in the bill with the other articles. Mrs Greene's words on this occasion were innocent enough, seeing that they were English; but had I been that head waiter who came down to the beach with his nice black shiny hair, and his napkin under his arm, I should have thought her manner very insolent.

Indeed, as it was, I did think so, and was inclined to be angry with her. She was to remain for some time at Bellaggio, and therefore it behoved her, as she thought, to assume the character of the grand lady at once. Hitherto she had been willing enough to do the work, but now she began to order about Mr Greene and Sophonisba; and, as it appeared to me, to order me about also. I did not quite enjoy this; so leaving her still among her luggage and satellites, I walked up to the hotel to see about my own bedroom. I had some seltzer water, stood at the window for three or four minutes, and then walked up and down the room. But still the Greenes were not there. As I had put in at Bellaggio solely with the object of seeing something more of Sophonisba, it would not do for me to quarrel with them, or to allow them so to settle themselves in their private sitting-room that I should be excluded. Therefore I returned again to the road by which they must come up, and met the procession near the house.

Mrs Greene was leading it with great majesty, the waiter with the shiny hair walking by her side to point out to her the way. Then came all the luggage – each porter carrying a white canvas-covered box. That which was so valuable no doubt was carried next to Mrs Greene, so that she might at a moment's notice put her eye upon the well-known valuable rent. I confess that I did not observe the hole as the train passed by me, nor did I count the number of the boxes. Seven boxes, all alike, are very many; and then they were followed by three other men with the inferior articles – Mr Greene's portmanteau, the carpet-bag, &c., &c. At the tail of the line, I found Mr Greene, and behind him Sophonisba. 'All your fatigues will be over now,' I said to the gentleman, thinking it well not to be too particular in my attentions to his daughter. He was panting beneath a terrible greatcoat, having forgotten that the shores of an Italian lake are not so cold as the summits of the Alps, and did not answer me. 'I'm sure I hope so,' said Sophonisba. 'And I shall advise papa not to go any farther unless he can persuade Mrs Greene to send her jewels home.' 'Sophy, my dear,' he said, 'for heaven's sake let us have a little peace since we are here.' From all which I gathered that Mr Green had not been fortunate in his second matrimonial adventure. We then made our way slowly up to the hotel, having been altogether distanced by the porters, and when we reached the house we found that the different packages were already being carried away through the house, some this way and some that. Mrs Green, the meanwhile, was talking loudly at the door of her own sitting-room.

'Mr Greene,' she said, as soon as she saw her heavily oppressed spouse – for the noonday sun was up – 'Mr Greene, where are you?'

'Here, my dear,' and Mr Greene threw himself panting into the corner of a sofa.

'A little seltzer water and brandy,' I suggested. Mr Greene's inmost heart leaped at the hint, and nothing that his remonstrant wife could say would induce him to move until he had enjoyed the delicious draught. In the meantime the box with the hole in the canvas had been lost.

Yes; when we came to look into matters, to count the packages, and to find out where we were, the box with the hole in the canvas was not there. Or, at any rate, Mrs Greene said it was not there. I worked hard to look it up, and even went into Sophonisba's bedroom in my search. In Sophonisba's bedroom there was but one canvas-covered box. 'That is my own,' said she, 'and it is all that I have, except this bag.'

'Where on earth can it be?' said I, sitting down on the trunk in question. At the moment I almost thought that she had been instrumental in hiding it.

'How am I to know?' she answered; and I fancied that even she was dismayed. 'What a fool that woman is!'

'The box must be in the house,' I said.

'Do find it, for papa's sake; there's a good fellow. He will be so wretched without his money. I heard him say that he had only two pounds in his purse.'

'Oh, I can let him have money to go on with,' I answered grandly. And then I went off to prove that I was a good fellow, and searched throughout the house. Two white boxes had by order been left downstairs, as they would not be needed; and these two were in a large cupboard of the hall, which was used expressly for stowing away luggage. And then there were three in Mrs Greene's bedroom, which had been taken there as containing the wardrobe which she would require while remaining at Bellaggio. I searched every one of these myself to see if I could find the hole in the canvas. But the hole in the canvas was not there. And let me count as I would, I could make out only six. Now there certainly had been seven on board the steamer, though I could not swear that I had seen the seven put into the small boat.

'Mr Greene,' said the lady standing in the middle of her remaining treasures, all of which were now open, 'you are worth nothing when travelling. Were you not behind?' But Mr Greene's mind was full, and he did not answer.

'It has been stolen before your very eyes,' she continued.

'Nonsense, mamma,' said Sophonisba. 'If ever it came out of the steamer it certainly came into the house.'

'I saw it out of the steamer,' said Mrs Greene, 'and it certainly is not in the house. Mr Robinson, may I trouble you to send for the police? – at once, if you please, sir.'

I had been at Bellaggio twice before, but nevertheless I was ignorant of their system of police. And then, again, I did not know what was the Italian for the word.

'I will speak to the landlord,' I said.

'If you will have the goodness to send for the police at once, I will be obliged to you.' And as she thus reiterated her command, she stamped with her foot upon the floor.

'There are no police at Bellaggio,' said Sophonisba.

'What on earth shall I do for money to go on with?' said Mr Greene, looking piteously up to the ceiling, and shaking both his hands.

And now the whole house was in an uproar, including not only the landlord, his wife and daughters, and all the servants, but also every other visitor at the hotel. Mrs Greene was not a lady who hid either her glories or her griefs under a bushel, and, though she spoke only in English, she soon made her protestations sufficiently audible. She protested loudly that she had been robbed, and that she had been robbed since she left the steamer. The box had come on shore; of that she was quite certain. If the landlord had any regard either for his own character or for that of his house, he would ascertain before an hour was over where it was, and who had been the thief. She would give him an hour. And then she sat herself down; but in two minutes she was up again, vociferating her wrongs as loudly as ever. All this was filtered through me and Sophonisba to the waiter in French, and from the waiter to the landlord; but the lady's gestures required no translation to make them intelligible, and the state of her mind on the matter was, I believe, perfectly well understood.

Mr Greene I really did pity. His feelings of dismay seemed to be quite as deep, but his sorrow and solicitude were repressed into more decorum. 'What am I to do for money?' he said. 'I have not a shilling to go on with!' And he still looked up at the ceiling.

'You must send to England,' said Sophonisba.

'It will take a month,' he replied.

'Mr Robinson will let you have what you want at present,' added Sophonisba. Now I certainly had said so, and had meant it at the time. But my whole travelling store did not exceed forty or fifty pounds, with which I was going on to Venice, and then back to England through the Tyrol. Waiting a month for Mr Greene's money from England might be even more inconvenient to me than to him. Then it occurred to me that the wants of the Greene family would be numerous and expensive, and that my small stock would go but a little way among so many. And what also if there had been no money and no jewels in that accursed box! I confess that at the moment such an idea did strike my mind. One hears of sharpers on every side committing depredations by means of most singular intrigues and contrivances. Might it not be possible that the whole batch of Greenes belonged to this order of society. It was a base idea, I own; but I confess that I entertained it for a moment.

I retired to my own room for a while that I might think over all the circumstances. There certainly had been seven boxes, and one had had a hole in the canvas. All the seven had certainly been on board the steamer. To so much I felt that I might safely swear. I had not counted the seven into the small boat, but on leaving the larger vessel I had looked about the deck to see that none of the Greene trappings were forgotten. If left on the steamer, it had been so left through an intent on the part of someone there employed. It was quite possible that the contents of the box had been ascertained through the imprudence of Mrs Greene, and that it had been conveyed away so that it might be rifled at Como. As to Mrs Greene's assertion that all the boxes had been put into the small boat, I thought nothing of it. The people at Bellaggio could not have known which box to steal, nor had there been time to concoct the plan in carrying the boxes up to the hotel. I came at last to this conclusion, that the missing trunk had either been purloined and carried on to Como – in which case it would be necessary to lose no time in going after it; or that it had been put out of sight in some uncommonly clever way, by the Greenes themselves, as an excuse for borrowing as much money as they could raise and living without payment of their bills. With reference to the latter hypothesis, I declared to myself that Greene did not look like a swindler; but as to Mrs Greene – ! I confess that I did not feel so confident in regard to her.

Charity begins at home, so I proceeded to make myself comfortable in my room, feeling almost certain that I should not be able to leave Bellaggio on the following morning. I had opened my portmanteau when I first arrived, leaving it open on the floor as is my wont. Some people are always being robbed, and are always locking up everything; while others wander safe over the world and never lock up anything. For myself, I never turn a key any-where, and no one ever purloins from me even a handkerchief. *Cantabit vacuus* – and I am always sufficiently *vacuus*. Perhaps it is that I have not a handkerchief worth the stealing. It is your heavy-laden, suspicious, maladroit Greenes that the thieves attack. I now found out that the accommodating boots, who already knew my ways, had taken my travelling gear into a dark recess which was intended to do for a dressing-room, and had there spread my portmanteau open upon some table or stool in the corner. It was a convenient arrangement, and there I left it during the whole period of my sojourn.

Mrs Greene had given the landlord an hour to find the box, and during that time the landlord, the landlady, their three daughters, and all the servants in the house certainly did exert themselves to the utmost. Half a dozen times they came to my door, but I was luxuriating in a washing-tub, making up for that four-o'clock start from Chiavenna. I assured them, how-ever, that the box was not there, and so the search passed by. At the end of the hour I went back to the Greenes according to promise, having resolved that someone must be sent on to Como to look after the missing article.

There was no necessity to knock at their sitting-room door, for it was wide open. I walked in, and found Mrs Greene still engaged in attacking the landlord, while all the porters who had carried the luggage up to the house were standing round. Her voice was loud above the others, but, luckily for them all, she was speaking English. The landlord, I saw, was becoming sulky. He spoke in Italian, and we none of us understood him, but I gathered that he was declining to do anything further. The box, he was certain, had never come out of the steamer. The boots stood by interpreting into French, and, acting as second interpreter, I put it into English.

Mr Greene, who was seated on the sofa, groaned audibly, but said nothing. Sophonisba, who was sitting by him, beat upon the floor with both her feet.

'Do you hear, Mr Greene?' said she, turning to him. 'Do you mean to allow that vast amount of property to be lost without an effort? Are you prepared to replace my jewels?'

'Her jewels!' said Sophonisba, looking up into my face. 'Papa had to pay the bill for every stitch she had when he married her.' These last words were so spoken as to be audible only by me, but her first exclamation was loud enough. Were they people for whom it would be worth my while to delay my journey, and put myself to serious inconvenience with reference to money?

A few minutes afterwards I found myself with Greene on the terrace before the house. 'What ought I to do?' said he.

'Go to Como,' said I, 'and look after your box. I will remain here and go on board the return steamer. It may perhaps be there.'

'But I can't speak a word of Italian,' said he.

'Take the boots,' said I.

'But I can't speak a word of French.' And then it ended in my undertaking to go to Como. I swear that the thought struck me that I might as well take my portmanteau with me, and cut and run when I got there. The Greenes were nothing to me.

I did not, however, do this. I made the poor man a promise, and I kept it. I took merely a dressing-bag, for I knew that I must sleep at Como; and, thus resolving to disarrange all my plans, I started. I was in the midst of beautiful scenery, but I found it quite impossible to draw any enjoyment from it – from that or from anything around me. My whole mind was given up to anathemas against this odious box, as to which I had undoubtedly heavy cause of complaint. What was the box to me? I went to Como by the afternoon steamer, and spent a long dreary evening down on the steamboat quays searching everywhere, and searching in vain. The boat by which we had left Colico had gone back to Colico, but the people swore that nothing had been left on board it. It was just possible that such a box might have gone on to Milan with the luggage of other passengers.

I slept at Como, and on the following morning I went on to Milan. There was no trace of the box to be found in that city. I went round to every hotel and travelling office, but could hear nothing of it. Parties had gone to Venice, and Florence, and Bologna, and any of them might have taken the box. No one, however, remembered it; and I returned back to Como, and thence to Bellaggio, reaching the latter place at nine in the evening, disappointed, weary and cross.

'Has monsieur found the accursed trunk?' said the Bellaggio boots, meeting me on the quay.

'In the name of the — no. Has it not turned up here?'

'Monsieur,' said the boots, 'we shall all be mad soon. The poor master, he is mad already.'

And then I went up to the house.

'My jewels!' shouted Mrs Greene, rushing to me with her arms stretched out as soon as she heard my step in the corridor. I am sure she would have embraced me had I found the box. I had not, however, earned any such reward.

'I can hear nothing of the box either at Como or Milan,' I said.

'Then what on earth am I to do for my money?' said Mr Greene.

I had had neither dinner nor supper, but the elder Greenes did not care for that. Mr Greene sat silent in despair, and Mrs Greene stormed about the room in her anger.

'I am afraid you are very tired,' said Sophonisba.

'I am tired, and hungry, and thirsty,' said I. I was beginning to get angry, and to think myself ill used. And that idea as to a family of swindlers became strong again. Greene had borrowed ten napoleons from me before I started for Como, and I had spent above four in my fruitless journey to that place and Milan. I was beginning to fear that my whole purpose as to Venice and the Tyrol would be destroyed; and I had promised to meet friends at Innsbruck, who – who were very much preferable to the Greenes. As events turned out, I did meet them. Had I failed in this, the present Mrs Robinson would not have been sitting opposite to me.

I went to my room and dressed myself, and then Sophonisba presided over the tea-table for me. 'What are we to do?' she asked me in a confidential whisper.

'Wait for money from England.'

'But they will think we are all sharpers,' she said; 'and upon my word I do not wonder at it from the way in which that woman goes on.' She then leaned forward, resting her elbow on the table and her face on her hand, and told me a long history of all their family discomforts. Her papa was a very good sort of man, only he had been made a fool of by that intriguing woman, who had been left without a sixpence with which to bless herself. And now they had nothing but quarrels and misery. Papa did not always get the worst of it; papa could rouse himself sometimes; only now he was beaten down and cowed by the loss of his money. This whispering confidence was very nice in its way, seeing that Sophonisba was a pretty girl; but the whole matter seemed to be full of suspicion.

'If they did not want to take you in in one way, they did in another,' said the present Mrs Robinson, when I told the story to her at Innsbruck. I beg that it may be understood that at the time of my meeting the Greenes I was not engaged to the present Mrs Robinson, and was open to make any matrimonial engagement that might have been pleasing to me.

On the next morning, after breakfast, we held a council of war. I had been informed that Mr Greene had made a fortune, and was justified in presuming him to be a rich man. It seemed to me, therefore, that his course was easy. Let him wait at Bellaggio for more money, and when he returned home, let him buy Mrs Greene more jewels. A poor man always presumes that a rich man is indifferent about his money. But in truth a rich man never is indifferent about his money, and poor Greene looked very blank at my proposition.

'Do you mean to say that it's gone for ever?' he asked.

'I'll not leave the country without knowing more about it,' said Mrs Greene.

'It certainly is very odd,' said Sophonisba. Even Sophonisba seemed to think that I was too offhand.

'It will be a month before I can get money, and my bill here will be something tremendous,' said Greene.

'I wouldn't pay them a farthing till I got my box,' said Mrs Greene.

'That's nonsense,' said Sophonisba. And so it was.

'Hold your tongue, miss!' said the stepmother.

'Indeed, I shall not hold my tongue,' said the stepdaughter. Poor Greene! He had lost more than his box within the last twelve months; for, as I had learned in that whispered conversation over the tea-table with Sophonisba, this was in reality her papa's marriage trip.

Another day was now gone, and we all went to bed. Had I not been very foolish I should have had myself called at five in the morning, and have gone away by the early boat, leaving my ten napoleons behind me. But, unfortunately, Sophonisba had exacted a promise from me that I would not do this, and thus all chance of spending a day or two in Venice was lost to me. Moreover, I was thoroughly fatigued, and almost glad of any excuse which would allow me to lie in bed on the following morning. I did lie in bed till nine o'clock, and then found the Greenes at breakfast.

'Let us go and look at the Serbelloni Gardens,' said I, as soon as the silent meal was over; 'or take a boat over to the Sommariva Villa.'

'I should like it so much,' said Sophonisba.

'We will do nothing of the kind till I have found my property,' said Mrs Greene. 'Mr Robinson, what arrangement did you make yesterday with the police at Como?'

'The police at Como?' I said. 'I did not go to the police.'

'Not go to the police? And do you mean to say that I am to be robbed of my jewels and no efforts made for redress? Is there no such thing as a constable in this wretched country? Mr Greene, I do insist upon it that you at once go to the nearest British consul.'

'I suppose I had better write home for money,' said he.

'And do you mean to say that you haven't written yet?' said I, probably with some acrimony in my voice.

'You needn't scold papa,' said Sophonisba.

'I don't know what I am to do,' said Mr Greene, and he began walking up and down the room; but still he did not call for pen and ink, and I began again to feel that he was a swindler. Was it possible that a man of business, who had made his fortune in London, should allow his wife to keep all her jewels in a box, and carry about his own money in the same?

'I don't see why you need be so very unhappy, papa,' said Sophonisba. 'Mr Robinson, I'm sure, will let you have whatever money you may want at present.' This was pleasant!

'And will Mr Robinson return me my jewels which were lost, I must say, in a great measure, through his carelessness,' said Mrs Greene. This was pleasanter!

'Upon my word, Mrs Greene, I must deny that,' said I, jumping up. 'What on earth could I have done more than I did do? I have been to Milan and nearly fagged myself to death.'

'Why didn't you bring a policeman back with you?'

'You would tell everybody on board the boat what there was in it,' said I.

'I told nobody but you,' she answered.

'I suppose you mean to imply that I've taken the box,' I rejoined. So that on this, the third or fourth day of our acquaintance, we did not go on together quite pleasantly.

But what annoyed me, perhaps the most, was the confidence with which it seemed to be Mr Greene's intention to lean upon my resources. He certainly had not written home yet, and had taken my ten napoleons, as one friend may take a few shillings from another when he finds that he has left his own silver on his dressing-table. What could he have wanted of ten napoleons? He had alleged the necessity of paying the porters, but the few francs he had had in his pocket would have been enough for that. And now Sophonisba was ever and again prompt in her assurances that he need not annoy himself about money, because I was at his right hand. I went upstairs into my own room, and counting all my treasures, found that thirty-six pounds and some odd silver was the extent of my wealth. With that I had to go at any rate as far as Innsbruck, and from thence back to London. It was quite impossible that I should make myself responsible for the Greenes' bill at Bellaggio.

We dined early, and after dinner, according to a promise made in the morning, Sophonisba ascended with me into the Serbelloni Gardens, and walked round the terraces on that beautiful hill which commands the view of the three lakes. When we started I confess that I would sooner have gone alone, for I was sick of the Greenes in my very soul. We had had a terrible day. The landlord had been sent for so often that he refused to show himself again. The landlady – though Italians of that class are always courteous – had been so driven that she snapped her fingers in Mrs Greene's face. The three girls would not show themselves. The waiters kept out of the way as much as possible; and the boots, in confidence, abused them to me behind their back. 'Monsieur,' said the boots, 'do you think there ever was such a box?'

'Perhaps not,' said I; and yet I knew that I had seen it.

I would, therefore, have preferred to walk without Sophonisba; but that now was impossible. So I determined that I would utilise the occasion by telling her of my present purpose. I had resolved to start on the following day, and it was now necessary to make my friends understand that it was not in my power to extend to them any further pecuniary assistance.

Sophonisba, when we were on the hill, seemed to have forgotten the box, and to be willing that I should forget it also. But this was impossible. When, therefore, she told me how sweet it was to escape from that terrible woman, and leaned on my arm with all the freedom of old acquaintance, I was obliged to cut short the pleasure of the moment.

'I hope your father has written that letter,' said I.

'He means to write it from Milan. We know you want to get on, so we purpose to leave here the day after tomorrow.'

'Oh!' said I thinking of the bill immediately, and remembering that Mrs Greene had insisted on having champagne for dinner.

'And if anything more is to be done about the nasty box, it may be done there,' continued Sophonisba.

'But I must go tomorrow,' said I, 'at five in the morning.'

'Nonsense,' said Sophonisba. 'Go tomorrow, when I – I mean we – are going on the next day!'

'And I might as well explain,' said I, gently dropping the hand that was on my arm, 'that I find – I find it will be impossible for me – to – to – '

'To what?'

'To advance Mr Greene any more money just at present.'

Then Sophonisba's arm dropped all at once, and she exclaimed, 'Oh, Mr Robinson!'

After all, there was a certain hard good sense about Miss Greene which would have protected her from my evil thoughts had I known all the truth. I found out afterwards that she was a considerable heiress, and, in spite of the opinion expressed by the present Mrs Robinson when Miss Walker, I do not for a moment think she would have accepted me had I offered to her.

'You are quite right not to embarrass yourself,' she said, when I explained to her my immediate circumstances; 'but why did you make papa an offer which you cannot perform? He must remain here now till he hears from England. Had you explained it all at first, the ten napoleons would have carried us to Milan.' This was all true, and yet I thought it hard upon me.

It was evident to me now that Sophonisba was prepared to join her stepmother in thinking that I had ill-treated them, and I had not much doubt that I should find Mr Greene to be of the same opinion. There was very little more said between us during the walk, and when we reached the hotel at seven or half-past seven o'clock, I merely remarked that I would go in and wish her father and mother goodbye. 'I suppose you will drink tea with us,' said Sophonisba, and to this I assented.

I went into my own room, and put all my things into my portmanteau, for according to the custom, which is invariable in Italy when an early start is premeditated, the boots was imperative in his demand that the luggage should be ready overnight. I then went to the Greene's sitting-room, and found that the whole party was now aware of my intentions.

'So you are going to desert us,' said Mrs Greene.

'I must go on upon my journey,' I pleaded in a weak apologetic voice.

'Go on upon your journey, sir!' said Mrs Greene. 'I would not for a moment have you put yourself to inconvenience on our account.' And yet I had already lost fourteen napoleons, and given up all prospect of going to Venice!

'Mr Robinson is certainly right not to break his engagement with Miss Walker,' said Sophonisba. Now I had said not a word about an engagement with Miss Walker, having only mentioned incidentally that she would be one of the party at Innsbruck. 'But,' continued she, 'I think he should not have misled us.' And in this way we enjoyed our evening meal.

I was just about to shake hands with them all, previous to my final departure from their presence, when the boots came into the room.

'I'll leave the portmanteau till tomorrow morning,' said he.

'All right,' said I.

'Because,' said he, 'there will be such a crowd of things in the hall. The big trunk I will take away now.'

'Big trunk – what big trunk?'

'The trunk with your rug over it, on which your portmanteau stood.'

I looked round at Mr, Mrs and Miss Greene, and saw that they were all looking at me. I looked round at them, and as their eyes met mine I felt that I turned as red as fire. I immediately jumped up and rushed away to my own room, hearing as I went that all their steps were following me. I rushed to the inner recess, pulled down the portmanteau, which still remained in its old place, tore away my own carpet rug which covered the support beneath it, and there saw – a white canvas-covered box, with a hole in the canvas on the side next to me!

'It is my box,' said Mrs Greene, pushing me away, as she hurried up and put her finger within the rent.

'It certainly does look like it,' said Mr Greene, peering over his wife's shoulder.

'There's no doubt about the box,' said Sophonisba.

'Not the least in life,' said I, trying to assume an indifferent look.

'Mon Dieu!' said the boots.

'Corpo di Baccho!' exclaimed the landlord, who had now joined the party.

'Oh–h–h–h–!' screamed Mrs Greene, and then she threw herself on to my bed, and shrieked hysterically.

There was no doubt whatsoever about the fact. There was the lost box, and there it had been during all those tedious hours of unavailing search. While I was suffering all that fatigue in Milan, spending my precious zwanzigers in driving about from one hotel to another, the box had been safe, standing in my own room at Bellaggio, hidden by my own rug. And now that it was found everybody looked at me as though it were all my fault.

Mrs Greene's eyes, when she had done being hysterical, were terrible, and Sophonisba looked at me as though I were a convicted thief.

'Who put the box here?' I said, turning fiercely upon the boots.

'I did,' said the boots, 'by monsieur's express order.'

'By my order?' I exclaimed.

'Certainly,' said the boots.

'Corpo di Baccho!' said the landlord, and he also looked at me as though I were a thief. In the meantime the landlady and the three daughters had clustered round Mrs Greene, administering to her all manner of Italian consolation. The box and the money and the jewels were after all a reality; and much incivility can be forgiven to a lady who has really lost her jewels, and has really found them again.

There and then there arose a hurly-burly among us as to the manner in which the odious trunk found its way into my room. Had anybody been just enough to consider the matter coolly, it must have been quite clear that I could not have ordered it there. When I entered the hotel, the boxes were already being lugged about, and I had spoken a word to no one concerning them. That traitorous boots had done it – no doubt without malice prepense; but he had done it; and now that the Greenes were once more known as moneyed people, he turned upon me, and told me to my face that I had desired that box to be taken to my own room as part of my own luggage!

'My dear,' said Mr Greene, turning to his wife, 'you should never mention the contents of your luggage to anyone.'

'I never will again,' said Mrs Greene, with a mock repentant air, 'but I really thought – '

'One never can be sure of sharpers,' said Mr Greene.

'That's true,' said Mrs Greene.

'After all, it may have been accidental,' said Sophonisba, on hearing which good-natured surmise both papa and mamma Greene shook their suspicious heads.

I was resolved to say nothing then. It was all but impossible that they should really think that I had intended to steal their box; nor, if they did think so, would it have become me to vindicate myself before the landlord and all his servants. I stood by therefore in silence, while two of the men raised the trunk, and joined the procession which followed it as it was carried out of my room into that of the legitimate owner. Everybody in the house was there by that time, and Mrs Greene, enjoying the triumph, by no means grudged them the entrance into her sitting-room. She had felt that she was suspected, and now she was determined that the world of Bellaggio should know how much she was above suspicion. The box was put down upon two chairs, the supporters who had borne it retiring a pace each. Mrs Greene then advanced proudly with the selected key, and Mr Greene stood by at her right shoulder, ready to receive his portion of the hidden treasure. Sophonisba was now indifferent, and threw herself on the sofa, while I walked up and down the room thoughtfully – meditating what words I should say when I took my last farewell of the Greenes. But as I walked I could see what occurred. Mrs Greene opened the box, and displayed to view the ample folds of a huge yellow woollen dressing-down. I could fancy that she would not willingly have exhibited this article of her toilet, had she not felt that its existence would speedily be merged in the presence of the glories which were to follow. This had merely been the padding at the top of the box. Under that lay a long papier-mâché case, and in that were all her treasures. 'Ah, they are safe,' she said, opening the lid and looking upon her tawdry pearls and carbuncles.

Mr Greene, in the meantime, well knowing the passage for his hand, had dived down to the very bottom of the box, and seized hold of a small canvas bag. 'It is here,' said he, dragging it up, 'and as far as I can tell, as yet, the knot has not been untied.' Whereupon he sat himself down by Sophonisba, and employing her to assist him in holding them, began to count his rolls. 'They are all right,' said he; and he wiped the perspiration from his brow.

I had not yet made up my mind in what manner I might best utter my last words among them so as to maintain the dignity of my character, and now I was standing over against Mr Greene with my arms folded on my breast. I had on my face a frown of displeasure, which I am able to assume upon occasions, but I had not yet determined what words I would use. After all, perhaps it might be as well that I should leave them without any last words.

'Greene, my dear,' said the lady, 'pay the gentleman his ten napoleons.'

'Oh yes, certainly;' whereupon Mr Greene undid one of the rolls and extracted eight sovereigns. 'I believe that will make it right, sir,' said he, handing them to me.

I took the gold, slipped it with an indifferent air into my waistcoat pocket, and then refolded my arms across my breast.

'Papa,' said Sophonisba, in a very audible whisper, 'Mr Robinson went for you to Como. Indeed, I believe he says he went to Milan.'

'Do not let that be mentioned,' said I.

'By all means pay him his expenses,' said Mrs Greene; 'I would not owe him anything for worlds.'

'He should be paid,' said Sophonisba.

'Oh, certainly,' said Mr Greene. And he at once extracted another sovereign, and tendered it to me in the face of the assembled multitude.

This was too much! 'Mr Greene,' said I, 'I intended to be of service to you when I went to Milan, and you are very welcome to the benefit of my intentions. The expense of that journey, whatever may be its amount, is my own affair.' And I remained standing with my closed arms.

'We will be under no obligation to him,' said Mrs Greene; 'and I shall insist on his taking the money.'

'The servant will put it on his dressing-table,' said Sophonisba. And she handed the sovereign to the boots, giving him instructions.

'Keep it yourself, Antonio,' I said. Whereupon the man chucked it to the ceiling with his thumb, caught it as it fell, and with a well-satisfied air, dropped it into the recesses of his pocket. The air of the Greenes was also well satisfied, for they felt that they had paid me in full for all my services.

And now, with many obsequious bows and assurances of deep respect, the landlord and his family withdrew from the room. 'Was there anything else they could do for Mrs Greene?' Mrs Greene was all affability. She had shown her jewels to the girls, and allowed them to express their admiration in pretty Italian superlatives. There was nothing else she wanted tonight. She was very happy and liked Bellaggio. She would stay yet a week, and would make herself quite happy. And, though none of them understood a word that the other said, each understood that things were now rose-coloured, and so with scrapings, bows and grinning smiles, the landlord and all his myrmidons withdrew. Mr Greene was still counting his money, sovereign by sovereign, and I was still standing with my folded arms upon my bosom.

'I believe I may now go,' said I.

'Good-night,' said Mrs Greene.

'Adieu,' said Sophonisba.

'I have the pleasure of wishing you goodbye,' said Mr Greene.

And then I walked out of the room. After all, what was the use of saying anything? And what could I say that would have done me any service? If they were capable of thinking me a thief – which they certainly did – nothing that I could say would remove the impression. Nor, as I thought, was it suitable that I should defend myself from such an imputation. What were the Greenes to me? So I walked slowly out of the room, and never again saw one of the family from that day to this.

As I stood upon the beach the next morning, while my portmanteau was being handed into the boat, I gave the boots five zwanzigers. I was determined to show him that I did not condescend to feel anger against him.

He took the money, looked into my face, and then whispered to me, 'Why did you not give me a word of notice beforehand?' and winked his eye. He was evidently a thief, and took me to be another – but what did it matter?

I went thence to Milan, in which city I had no heart to look at anything; thence to Verona, and so over the pass of the Brenner to Innsbruck. When I once found myself near to my dear friends the Walkers I was again a happy man; and I may safely declare that, though a portion of my journey was so troublesome and unfortunate, I look back upon that tour as the happiest and the luckiest epoch of my life.

EDGAR WALLACE

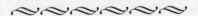

Edgar Wallace (1875–1932), journalist and novelist, born in Greenwich, the illegitimate son of an actor, was baptised Richard Horatio Edgar Wallace. Brought up by a Billingsgate fish-porter and his wife, he attended an elementary school at Peckham and left at twelve to become successively newsboy, errand boy, milk roundsman and labourer. At eighteen he enlisted in the Royal West Kent Regiment and served in South Africa. Discharged in 1899, he became a foreign correspondent for the *Daily Mail*, but was sacked for involving them in a libel suit. His first great success was *The Four Just Men* (1905), with its sequels *The Council of Justice* (1908) and *The Three Just Men* (1926). His early novels include a West African series – *Sanders of the River* (1911), *Bones* (1915) and others – but it was by his thrillers and detective stories that he became really famous. Well meriting his nickname of 'fiction factory', working with a dictaphone and a typist who held the record for speed-typing, he produced some one hundred and seventy books. Wallace also wrote a number of excellent plays in which excitement and horror are skilfully relieved by touches of humour. *People* (1926) is an autobiography. He died in Hollywood of pneumonia, and left an estate cumbered with £150,000 in debts, which his royalties paid off in two years. He was twice married.

The Lone House Mystery

ONE

I am taking no credit out of what the newspapers called the Lone House Mystery. I've been long enough in the police force to know that the man who blows his own trumpet never gets into a good orchestra. So if anybody tells you that Superintendent Minter of Scotland Yard is trying to glorify himself, give them a dirty look for me.

'Superintendent' is a mouthful, and anyway, it is not matey. Not that I encourage young constables to call me 'Sooper' to my face. They never do. I want ' sir ' from them and every other rank, but I like to overhear 'em talking about the old Sooper, always providing they don't use a certain adjective.

Mr John C. Field always called me Superintendent. I never knew until he pronounced the word that there were so many syllables in it.

No man likes to admit he was in error, but I'm owning up that I broke all my rules when I liked him at first sight. It's all very well to go mad about a girl the first time you meet her, but it's wrong to file a man on your first impressions. Because a man who makes a hit the first time you meet him is going out of his way to make you think well of him. And normal men don't do that. Commercial travellers do and actors do, but they're not normal.

John C. Field was the type that anybody could admire. He was tall, broad-shouldered and good-looking, for all his fifty-odd years and his grey hair. He had the manners of a gentleman, could tell a good story and was a perfect host. He never stopped handing out the cigars.

I met him in a curious way. He lived in a smallish house on the banks of the Linder. I don't suppose you know the Linder – it's a stream that pretends to be a river until it runs into the Thames between Reading and Henley, and then it is put into its proper place and called the 'Bourne'. There is a house on the other side of the stream called Hainthorpe, and it was owned by a Mr Max Voss. He built it and had an electric power line carried from Reading. It was over this line that I went down to make enquiries. I was in the special branch of Scotland Yard at the time and did a lot of work that the county police knew nothing about. It is not an offence to use electric power, but just about this time the Flack brothers and Johnny McGarth and two or three of the big forgery gangs were terribly busy with private printing presses, and when we heard of a householder using up a lot of juice we were a bit suspicious.

So I went down to Hainthorpe and saw Mr Voss. He was a stout, red-faced man with a little white moustache, who had lost the use of his legs through frostbite in Russia. And that is how his new house came to be filled with electric contraptions. He had electric chairs that ran him from one room to another, electric elevators, and even in his bathroom a sort of electric hoist that could lift him from his chair into his bath and out again.

'Now,' he said, with a twinkle in his eye, 'you'll want to see the printing presses where I make phoney money!' He chuckled with laughter when he saw he'd hit the right nail on the head.

I went there for an hour and stayed three days.

'Stay tonight, anyway,' he said. 'My man Veddle will give you any sleeping kit you require.'

Voss was an interesting man who had been an engineer in Russia. He wasn't altogether helpless, because he could hobble around on crutches, though it wasn't nice to see him doing it.

It was pretty late when I arrived, so I did not need any persuasion to stay to dinner, especially when I heard that young Garry Thurston was coming. I knew Garry – I'd met him half a dozen times at Marlborough Street and Bow Street and other police courts. He had more endorsements on his driving licence than any other rich young man I knew. His hobbies were speeding through police traps and parking in unauthorised places. A bright boy – one of the new type of criminals that the motoring regulations have created.

He had a big house in the neighbourhood and had struck up a friendship with Mr Voss. I suppose I'm all wrong, but I like these harum-scarum young men that the public schools and universities turn out by the thousand.

He stopped dead at the sight of me in the smoking-room.

'Moses!' he said. 'What have I done?'

When I told him that I was after mere forgers he seemed quite disappointed.

He was a nice boy, and if I ever have the misfortune to be married and have a son, he would be the kind that would annoy me less than any other. I don't know what novelists mean when they write about 'clean-limbed men', unless they're talking about people who have regular baths, but I have an idea that he was the kind of fellow they have in mind.

We were halfway through dinner when I first heard the name of Mr Field. It arose over a question of poaching. Voss remarked that he wished Field's policemen would keep to their own side of the river, and that was the first time I knew that Field was under police protection, and asked why. It was then that young Thurston broke in.

'He'll need a regiment of soldiers to look after him if something happens which I think is happening,' he said, and there was something in his tone which made me look at him. If ever I saw hate in a man's eyes I saw it in Garry Thurston's.

I noticed that Mr Voss changed the subject, and after the young man had gone home he told me why.

'Thurston is not normal about this man Field,' he said, 'and I needn't tell you it's about a girl – Field's secretary. She's a lovely creature, and so far as I can tell Field treats her with every respect and deference. But Garry's got it into his thick head that there's something sinister going on over at Lone House. I think it's the psychological result of poor Field living in a place called Lone House at all!'

That explained a lot to me. Young men in love are naturally murderous young animals. Whether it's normal or abnormal to want to murder the man who squeezes the hand of the young lady you've taken a fancy to, I don't know. I guess it's normal. Personally speaking, I've never been delirious except from natural causes.

'Field's policemen' rather puzzled me till Mr Voss explained. For some reason or other Field went in fear of his life, and paid a handsome sum per annum for individual police attention. There were usually two men on duty near the house all the time.

I couldn't have come to a better man than Max Voss to hear all the news of the neighbourhood. I think that red-faced old gentleman was the biggest gossip I have ever met. He knew the history of everybody for twenty miles round, could tell you all their private business, why engagements were broken off, what made Mrs So-and-So go to the Riviera in such a hurry last March, and why Lord What's-his-name was selling his pictures.

And he told me quite a lot about Field. He lived alone except for a few servants, and had no visitors, with the exception of a negro who came about once a month, a well-dressed young fellow, and a rather pretty half-caste woman who arrived at rare intervals.

'Very few people know about this. She comes up river in a launch, sometimes with the negro and sometimes without him. They usually come in the evening, stay an hour or two and disappear. Before they come, Field sends all his servants out.'

I had to chuckle at this. 'Sounds to me like a mystery.'

Voss smiled. 'It is nothing to the mystery of Lady Kingfether's trip to North Africa,' he said, and began to tell me a long story.

It was a pretty interesting story. Every time I woke up something was happening.

I went to bed late and tired, and getting up at six o'clock in the morning, dressed and went out into the garden. Mr Voss had told me his man Veddle would look after me, but devil a sign of Veddle had I seen, either on the previous night or that morning, and I understood why when I came upon him suddenly on his way from the little cottage in the grounds where he lived. He tried to avoid me, but I've got pretty good eyesight for a man of sixty. No man who had ever seen Veddle could forget him. A heavy-looking man with a roundish face and eyes that never met you. I could have picked him out a mile away. When Voss had said 'Veddle', I never dreamed he was the same Veddle who had passed through my hands three times. Naturally, when criminals take on respectable employment they become Smith.

He knew me, of course.

'Why, Mr Minter,' he said in his oily way, 'this is a surprise!'

'Didn't know I was here, eh?' I said.

He coughed.

'Well, to tell you the truth, I did,' he said, 'but I thought it would be better if I kept out of your way. Mr Voss knows,' he went on quickly.

'About your previous convictions?'

He nodded.

'Does he know that two of them were for blackmail?' I asked.

He smiled lopsidedly at this.

'It's a long lane that has no turning, Mr Minter. I've given up all that sort of thing. Yes, Mr Voss knows. What a splendid gentleman! What a pity the Lord has so afflicted him!'

I didn't waste much time on the man. Blackmail is one of the crimes that makes me sick, and I'd sooner handle a bushel of snakes than deal with this kind of criminal. Naturally I did not mention the conversation to Voss, because the police never give away their clients. Voss brought up the subject himself at lunch.

'That man Veddle of mine is an old lag,' he said. 'I wondered if you'd recognise him. He's a good fellow, and I think I pay him enough to keep him straight.'

I didn't tell him that you couldn't pay any criminal enough to keep him straight, because there isn't so much money in the world, because I did not want to discourage him.

I saw Veddle again that afternoon in peculiar circumstances. He was always a bit of a dandy, and had considerable success with women of all classes. No man can understand the fascination which a certain kind of man exercises over a certain kind of woman. It isn't a question of looks or age, it's a kind of hypnotism.

I was taking a long walk by myself along the river bank. The river separated Mr Voss's property from the Lone House estate. Lone House itself was a square, white building that stood on the crest of a rising lawn that sloped up from the river, which is almost a lake here, for the stream broadens into what is known locally as the Flash.

A small wood on Mr Voss's side of the river hides the house from view. I was coming out of Tadpole Copse, as it was called, when I saw Veddle waiting by the edge of the stream. A girl was rowing across the Flash. Her back was turned to the servant, and she did not see him till she had landed and tied up the boat. It was then that he approached her. I was naturally interested, and walked a little slower. If the girl did not see Veddle, Veddle did not see me, and I was within a dozen yards of the two when he went up to her, raising his hat.

I don't think I've ever seen anybody so lovely as this girl, Marjorie Venn, and I could quite understand why Garry Thurston had fallen for her. Except for police purposes, I can't describe women. I can write down the colour of their eyes and hair, their complexion and height, but I've never been able to say why they're beautiful. I just know they are or they're not; and she was.

She turned quickly and walked away from the man. He followed her, talking all the time, and presently I saw him grip her by the arm and swing her round. She saw me and said something, and Veddle turned and dropped his hand. She did not attempt to meet me, but walked off quickly, leaving the man looking a little foolish. But it's very difficult to embarrass a fellow who's done three stretches for felony. He met me with his sly smile.

'A nice little piece that,' he said – 'A friend of mine.'

'So it appears,' said I. 'Never seen anybody look more friendly than she did.'

He smiled crookedly.

'Women get that way if they like you,' he said.

'Who was the last woman you blackmailed?' I asked; but, bless you, you couldn't make him feel uncomfortable. He just smiled and went on his way.

I watched him, wondering whether he was trying to overtake the girl. He hadn't gone a dozen paces when, round the corner of a clump of trees, came swinging a man who I guessed was Field himself. You can tell from a man's walk just what is in his mind, and I wondered if Veddle was gifted with second sight. If he had been he would have run, but he kept right on.

I saw Field stand squarely in his path. He asked a question, and in another second his fist shot out and Veddle went down. To my surprise he made a fight of it, came up again and took a left swing to the jaw that would have knocked out any ordinary man.

It wasn't any business of mine, but I am an officer of the law and I thought it was the right moment to interfere. By the time I reached Mr Field, Veddle was running for his life. I was a little taken aback when Field held out his hand.

'You're Superintendent Minter? I heard you were staying in the neighbourhood,' he said. 'I hope you're not going to prosecute me for trespass – this is a short cut to Hainthorpe Station and I often use it. I don't know whether Mr Voss objects.'

Before I could tell him I didn't know what was in Mr Voss's mind about trespassing he went on: 'Did you see that little fracas? I'm afraid I lost my temper with that fellow, but this is not the first time he has annoyed the young lady.'

He asked me to come over to his house for a drink and, going back to where the skiff was moored, he rowed me across. We landed at a little stage and walked together up the lawn to the open French windows of his study. I noticed then that in front of these the grass was worn and that there was a patch of bare earth – it's funny how a police officer can register these things automatically.

The little study was beautifully furnished, and evidently Mr Field was a man who had done a lot of travelling, for all the walls were covered with curios: African spears and assegais, and on the shelves was a collection of native pottery. He saw me looking round and, walking to the wall, picked down a broad-bladed sword.

'This will interest you if you know anything about Africa,' he said. 'It is the Sword of Tuna. It belonged to the Chief of Ituri – a man who gave me a lot of trouble and who predicted that it would never be sheathed till it was sheathed in my unworthy person.'

He smiled.

'I took it from his dead body after a fight in the forest, so his prediction is not likely to be fulfilled.'

The blade was extraordinarily bright, and I told him that it must take a lot of work to keep it polished, but to my surprise he said that it was made from an alloy which always kept the blade shining – a native variety of stainless steel.

He replaced the sword, and for about a quarter of an hour we talked about Africa, where, he told me, he had made his money, and of the country, and only towards the end of our conversation did he mention the fact that he had a couple of detectives watching the house.

'I've made many enemies in my life,' he said, but did not explain any further how he had made them.

He rowed me back to the other side of the Flash and asked me to dinner. I was going the following night. He was the kind of man I liked: he smoked good cigars, and not only smoked them but gave them to the right kind of people.

On my way back to Hainthorpe I met Mr Voss, or, rather, he nearly met me. The paths of his estate were as level as a billiard table and as broad as an ordinary drive, and they had need to be, for he drove his little electric chair at thirty miles an hour. It was bigger than a Bath chair and packed with batteries, and if I had not jumped into the bushes I should have known just how heavy it was.

I did not think it was necessary to hide anything about Veddle, and I told him what I had seen. He was blue with rage.

'What a beast!' he said. 'I have given that man his chance and I would have forgiven a little light larceny, but this is an offence beyond forgiveness.'

Every afternoon he was in the habit of driving to the top of Jollyboy Hill, which gave him a wonderful view of the surrounding country, and, as he offered to put his chair into low gear, I walked up by his side, though it was a bit of a climb. From the top of the hill you saw the river stretching for miles, and Lone House looked a pretty insignificant place to be the homestead of a thousand acres.

In the opposite direction I could see Dobey Manor, an old Elizabethan house where Garry Thurston's ancestors had lived for hundreds of years.

'A nice boy, Garry,' said Mr Voss thoughtfully. 'Don't tell him about Veddle – I don't want a murder on my hands.'

I dined with him that night, though I ought to have gone back to London, and he arranged that his car should pick me up at Lone House after my dinner there the following night and take me down.

'You are very much favoured,' he said. 'From what I hear, Field does not invite many people to his house. He is rather a recluse, and all the time I have been here he has not been to see me or asked me to pay him a visit.'

I saw Veddle that evening. He had the most beautiful black eye I had ever seen on a man, but, as he did not speak about the little scrap, I thought I'd be tactful and say nothing.

I was just a little bit uneasy because Veddle was marked on the police books as a dangerous man. He had twice fought off detectives who had been sent to arrest him and had once pulled a gun on them. I happen to know this because I was one of the detectives.

In the morning I was strolling in the garden when I saw him coming from his little cottage, and thought it wise to offer a few words of advice.

'You got what you asked for,' I said, 'and if you are a wise man you'll forget what happened yesterday afternoon.'

He looked at me a bit queerly. I'll swear it was one of the few times he ever looked any man in the eyes. 'He will get what is coming to him,' he said, and turned immediately away.

That afternoon I sat on the terrace at Hainthorpe. It was a warm, drowsy day after a heavy shower of rain, and I was half asleep when I saw Mr Voss move along the path in front of the terrace in his electric chair. He was going very fast. I watched him till he disappeared in the little copse near the river's edge and saw the chair emerge on the other side and come up the winding path towards Jollyboy Hill.

Mr Voss always wore a white bowler hat and grey check suit, and it was easy to pick these up even at a distance of a mile and a half, for, as I say, my eyesight was very good.

He was there longer than usual this day – he told me he never stayed more than ten minutes because he caught cold so easily. While he was there my eyes wandered to the copse, and I saw a little curl of smoke rising and wondered whether somebody had lit a fire. It was pretty hot – the sort of day when wood fires break out very easily. The smoke drifted away and presently I saw Mr Voss's chair coming down the hill and pass through the wood. A few minutes later he was waving his hand to me as he turned the chair on to the gentle incline which led to the front of the house. He guided the machine up to where I sat – the terrace was broad and stone-flagged.

'Did you see some smoke come over that wood? I thought the under-growth was on fire.'

I told him I had seen it.

He shook his head. 'There was nothing there, but I was a little alarmed. Last year I lost a good plantation through gypsies lighting a fire and for-getting to put it out before they left.'

We talked for a little while and he told me he had made arrangements for his Rolls to pick me up at Lone House at ten.

'I hope you won't tell Garry about Veddle,' he said. 'I am getting rid of him – Veddle, I mean. I heard so many stories about this fellow in the village, and I can't afford to have that kind of man round me.' He questioned me about Veddle's past, but naturally I was cautious, for, no matter how bad a man is, the police never give him away. He knew, however, that Veddle had been charged with blackmail, and I thought it necessary that I should tell him also that this ex-convict was marked dangerous at headquarters.

He asked me to come into the house with him as Veddle had gone out for the afternoon, and I helped him into the lift and into the little runabout that he kept on the first floor. I was thoroughly awake by the time I got back to the terrace and sat down to read through a case which was fully reported in that morning's newspaper and in which I had an interest. I had hardly opened the paper before one of the maids came out and said I was wanted on the telephone. I didn't know the man who called me, but he said he was one of the detectives engaged to look after Mr Field. I didn't recognise the voice.

'Is that Superintendent Minter . . . Will you come over to Lone House? Mr Field has been murdered . . .'

I was so surprised that I could not speak for a moment.

'Murdered!' I said. 'Murdered?'

Then, hanging up the receiver, I dashed out of the house and ran along the path through the wood to the place immediately opposite Lone House. The detective was waiting in a boat. He was so agitated and upset that I could not make head or tail of what he was saying. He ran across the lawn and I followed him.

The French windows were wide open, and even before I entered the room I saw, on the damp, brown earth before the door, a distinct imprint of a naked foot. The man had not seen it, and I pushed him aside just as he was going to step on it.

I was first in the room and there I saw Field. He was lying in the centre of the floor, very still, and from his back protruded the hilt of the Sword of Tuna.

TWO

I didn't have to be a doctor to know that Field was dead. There was very little blood on the floor, considering the size of the sword blade, and the only disorder I could detect at the moment was a smashed coffee cup in the fireplace and a little table which had held the coffee service overturned on the floor. The second cup was not broken; the coffee pot had spilt on the carpet – when Field fell he might have overturned the table, as I remarked to the detective, whose name was Wills.

Now in a case like this a detective's work is usually hampered by a lot of squalling servants who run all over the house and destroy every clue that is likely to be useful to a police officer; and the first thing that struck me was the complete silence of the house and the absence of all servants. I asked Wills about this.

'The servants are out; they've been out since lunchtime,' he said. 'Mr Field sent them up to town to a charity matinee that he'd bought tickets for.'

He went out into the hall and I heard him call Miss Venn by name. When he came back: 'She must have gone out too,' he said, 'though I could have sworn I saw her an hour ago on the lawn.'

I sent him to telephone to his chief. I'm the sort of man who never asks for trouble, and there's no better way of getting trouble than interfering with the county constabulary. I don't say they are jealous of us at Scotland Yard, but they can do things so much better. They've often told me this.

While he was phoning, I had a look at Field. On his cheek was a wound about two inches long, little more than a scratch, but this must have happened before his death, because in his pocket I found a handkerchief covered with blood. There was nothing I could see likely to cause this wound except a small paperknife which lay on a table against the wall. I examined the blade: it was perfectly clean, but I put it aside for microscopic examination in case one of these clever Berkshire detectives thought it was necessary. I believe in giving the county police all the help you can, and anyway it was certain they'd call in somebody from the Yard after they'd given the murderer time enough to get out of the country.

Leading from the study were two doors, one into the passage and the other into a room at the back of the house. On the other side of the passage was a sort of drawing-room and the dining-room. I say 'sort of drawing-room' because it was almost too comfortable to be a real drawing-room.

I tried the door of the back room: it was locked. Obviously there was another door into the same room from the passage, but I found this was locked too.

When Wills came back from phoning – he'd already had the intelligence to phone a doctor – he told me the story of the discovery. He was on duty single-handed that afternoon; the second detective attached to the establishment had gone to town in Mr Field's car to the charity matinee. Wills said that he had been told to hang around but keep well away from the house, and not to take any notice of anything he saw or heard. It was not an unusual instruction apparently.

'Sometimes,' said Wills, 'he used to have a coloured woman and a negro lad come down to see him. We always had the same instructions. As a matter of fact, I was watching the river, expecting them to turn up. They usually arrived on a motor-boat from downstream, and moored off the lawn.'

'You didn't see them today?' I asked.

He shook his head.

'No; only the instructions I had today were exactly the same as I had when they were expected, and usually all the servants were sent out – and Miss Venn.'

I made a quick search of the house. I admit that curiosity is my vice, and I wanted to know as much about this case as was possible before the Surrey police came in with their hobnailed boots, laying their big hands over all the fingerprints. At least, that's what I felt at the time.

I was searching Field's bedroom when Wills called me downstairs.

'It's the deputy chief constable,' he said.

I didn't tell him what I thought of the deputy chief constable, because I am strong for discipline, and it's not my job to put young officers against their superiors. Not that I'd ever met the deputy chief constable, but I'd met others.

'Is that you, Minter? Deputy chief constable speaking.'

'Yes, sir,' I said, expecting some fool instructions.

'We've had particulars of this murder phoned to us by Wills, and I've been through to Scotland Yard. Will you take complete charge of the case? I have your own chief constable's permission.'

Naturally, I was very pleased, and told him so. He promised to come over later in the afternoon and see me. I must say this about the Berkshire constabulary, that there isn't a brighter or smarter lot in the whole of England. It's one of the best administered constabularies, and the men are as keen a lot of crime-hounds as you could wish to meet. Don't let anybody say anything against the Berkshire constabulary – I'm all for them.

My first search was of the desk in the study. I found a bundle of letters, a steel box, locked, and to which I could find no key, a loaded revolver, and, in an envelope, a lot of maps and plans of the Kwange Diamond Syndicate. I knew, as a matter of fact, that Field was heavily interested in diamonds, and that he had very valuable properties in Africa.

In another drawer I found his passbook and his bank deposit book and with these a small ledger which showed his investments. As near as I could gather, he was a half-a-million man. I was looking at this when Wills came in to tell me that Mr Voss was on the other bank and wanted to know if I could see him. I went down to the boat and rowed across. He was in his chair, and he held something in his hand which looked like a big gun cartridge.

'I've heard about the murder,' he said. 'I'm wondering whether this has got anything to do with it.'

I took the cartridge from him; it smelt of sulphur. And then, from under the rug which covered his knees, he took an awkward-looking pistol.

'I found them together in the copse,' he said, 'or at least, my servants found them under my directions. Do you remember the smoke, Minter – the smoke we saw coming from the trees?'

I'd forgotten all about that for the moment, but now I understood.

'This is a little smoke bomb. They used them in the war for signals,' said Voss.

His thin face was almost blue with excitement.

'The moment I heard of what had happened at Lone House, I remembered the smoke – it was a signal! I got my chair out and came straight away down with a couple of grooms, and we searched the copse thoroughly. We found these two things behind a bush – and something else.'

He dived again under the rug and produced a second cartridge, which, I could see, had not been discharged.

'Somebody was waiting there to give a signal. There must have been two people in it at least,' he said. And then: 'He is dead, I suppose?'

I nodded. He shook his head and frowned.

'It's queer. I always thought he would come to an end like that. I don't know why. But there was a mystery about the man.'

'Where is Veddle?' I asked, and he stared at me.

'Veddle? At the house, I suppose.'

He turned and shouted to the two grooms who were some distance away. They had not seen Veddle. He sent one of them in search of the man.

Veddle had been in my mind ever since I had seen the body of Field with the sword of Tuna sticking through his back. I hadn't forgotten his threat nor his police record, and if there was one man in the world who had to account for every minute of his time that man was Mr Veddle.

'I hadn't thought of him,' said Voss slowly.

He knitted his white eyebrows again and laughed.

'It couldn't have been Veddle: I saw him – now, when did I see him?' He thought for a little time. 'Now I come to think of it, I haven't seen him all the morning, but he's sure to be able to account for himself. He spends most of his time in the servants' hall trying to get off with my housemaid.'

A few yards beyond the copse was a small pleasure-house which had a view of the river, and this was equipped with a telephone, which the groom must have used, for he came back while I was talking and reported that Veddle was not in the house and had not been seen. Mr Voss brought his electric chair round, and I walked by its side back to the copse.

Locally it was called Tadpole Copse, and for a good reason, for it was that shape; large clumps that thinned off into a long tail, running parallel with the river and following its course downstream. It terminated on the edge of the property, where there was a narrow lane leading to the main road. It struck me at the time that it was quite possible for any man who had been hidden in the copse to have made a getaway without attracting attention even though the other bank of the river had been alive with policemen.

Voss went back to the house to make enquiries about his servant. He promised to telephone to me as soon as they were completed, and I returned to the boat and was ferried across to the house.

Two doctors were there when I arrived, and they said just the things you expect doctors to say . . . that Field had died instantly . . . that only a very powerful man could have killed him, and that it was a terrible business. They had brought an ambulance with them, and I sent the body away under Wills's charge and went on with my search of the desk.

I was really looking for keys. There were two locked rooms in the house, and at the moment I did not feel justified in breaking open any door until the servants returned.

I went round to the back of the house. The window of the locked room was set rather high and a blue blind was drawn down so that I could not see into it. Moreover, the windows were fastened on the inside. In all the circumstances I decided to wait till I found the key, or until the Berkshire police, who were on their way, brought me a pick-lock.

Why had he sent his servants out that afternoon, and what could Marjorie Venn tell me when she came back? Somehow I banked upon the secretary more than upon the servants, because she would know a great deal more of his intimate life.

I went back to the desk and resumed my search amongst the papers. I was turning over the pages of an engineering report dealing with the Kwange Mine when I heard a sound. Somebody was knocking, slowly and deliberately. I confess I am not a nervous man. Superintendents of police seldom are. If you're nervous you die before you reach the rank of sergeant. But this time I could feel my hair lift a little bit, for the knocking came from the door of the locked room.

THREE

There was no doubt about it: the sound of the knocking came from behind that locked door. I went over and tried the handle. I am a believer in miracles, and thought perhaps the knocker might have opened the door from the inside, but it was fast.

Then I heard a voice – the voice of a girl – cry, 'Help!' and the solution of that mystery came at once. I didn't wait for the keys to come; outside the kitchen door I had seen a big axe – in fact, I had thought that it might be useful in case of necessity. Going out, I brought in the axe and, calling the girl to stand aside, I had that door open in two minutes.

She was standing by a large, oriental-looking sofa, holding on to the head for support.

'You're Miss Marjorie Venn, aren't you?'

She couldn't answer, but nodded. Her face was like death; even her lips were almost white.

I set her down and got a glass of water for her. Naturally, as soon as she felt better she began to cry. That's the trouble with women: when they can be useful they become useless. I had to humour her, but it was about ten minutes before she could speak and answer my questions.

'How long have you been there?'

'Where is he?' she asked. 'Has he gone?'

I guessed she was referring to Field. I thought at the moment it was not advisable to tell her that the late Mr Field was just then on his way to a mortuary.

'He's a beast!' she said. 'He gave me something in the coffee. You're a detective, aren't you?'

I had to tell her I was a superintendent. I mean, I'm not a snob, but I like to have credit for my rank.

It took a long time to get the truth out of her. She had lunched alone with Mr Field, and he had become a little too attentive. Apparently it was not the first time that this had happened: it was the first time she had ever spoken about it. And it was only then she discovered that all the servants had been sent out.

As a matter of fact, she had nothing to tell me except what I could already guess. He had not behaved himself, and then he had changed his tactics, apologised, and she thought that the incident was over.

'I'm leaving tonight,' she said. 'I can't stand it any more. It's been terrible! But he pays me a very good salary and I couldn't afford to throw up the work. I never dreamt he would be so base. Even when the coffee tasted bitter, I suspected nothing.' And then she shuddered.

'Do you live here, Miss Venn?' I thought she was a resident secretary, and was surprised when she shook her head. She lodged with a widow woman in a cottage about half a mile away. She had lived at the house, but certain things had happened and she had left. It was not necessary for her to explain what the certain things were. I began to get a new view of Mr Field.

She had heard nothing, could not remember being carried into the room. I think someone must have interrupted him and that he must have come out and locked her in.

Wills admitted to me afterwards that he had come down to the house and that Field had come out in a rage and ordered him to go to his post.

I thought, in the circumstances, as she was calmer, I might tell her what had happened. She was horrified; could hardly believe me. And then she broke into a fit of shuddering which I diagnosed as hysteria. This time it took her some time to get calm again, and the first person she mentioned was Wills, the detective.

'Where was he – when the murder was committed?' she asked.

I was staggered at the question, but she repeated it. I told her that so far as I knew Wills was on the road keeping watch.

'He was here, then!' she said, so emphatically that I opened my eyes.

'Of course he was here.'

She shook her head helplessly.

'I don't understand it.'

'Now look here, young lady,' said I – and although I am not a family man, I have got a fatherly manner which has been highly spoken of – 'what is all this stuff about Wills?'

She was silent for a long time, and then, womanlike, went off at an angle.

'It's dreadful . . . I can't believe it's true.'

'What about Wills?' I asked again.

She brought her mind back to the detective.

'Mr Field was sending him away today. He only found out this morning that he is the brother of that dreadful man – the convict.'

'Veddle?' I said quickly, and she nodded.

'Did you know that it was Mr Field who prosecuted Veddle the last time he went to prison? Or perhaps you didn't know he'd been to prison?'

I knew that all right, as I explained to her.

'But how did he find out that Wills was Veddle's brother?'

Field had found out by accident. He was rowing down the river, as he sometimes did, and had seen the two men talking together on the bank. They were on such good terms that he got suspicious, and when he returned he called Wills into his study and asked him what he meant by associating with a man of Veddle's character, and Wills had blurted out the truth. He hadn't attempted to hide the fact that his brother was an ex-convict. In fact, it was not until that moment really that Field remembered the man.

'Mr Field told me,' she went on, 'that his attitude was very unsatisfactory, and that he was sending him away.'

Just at that moment the deputy chief constable arrived by car and brought a crowd of bright young men, who had got all their detective science out of books. It was pitiful to see them looking for fingerprints and taking plaster casts of the naked foot, just like detectives in fiction, and measuring distances and setting up their cameras when there was nothing to photograph except me.

I told the chief all I knew of the case and got him to send the young lady back to her lodging in his car, and to get a doctor for her. One of his bright assistants suggested that we ought to hold her on suspicion, but there are some suggestions that I don't even answer, and that was one of them.

I went over with the deputy to see Mr Voss, who had sent a message to say that he had heard from Veddle. The man had telephoned him from Guildford. Halfway across the field he came flying down to meet us. I must say that that electric Bath chair of his exceeded all the speed limits, and the wonder to me was that he hadn't been killed years before.

There are some gentlemen who should never be admitted into police cases, because they get enthusiastic. I think they get their ideas of crime out of books written by this fellow whose name I see everywhere. He wanted to know if we'd got any fingerprints, and his red face got purple when I told him about the young lady locked in the room.

'Scandalous! Disgraceful! By gad, that fellow ought to be horsewhipped!'

'He's been killed.' I said, 'which is almost as bad.'

Then I asked him about Veddle.

'How he got to Guildford in the time I haven't the slightest idea. He must have had a car waiting for him. It's the most astounding thing that ever happened.'

'What did he say?' I asked him.

'Nothing very much. He said he would be away for two or three days, that he'd got a call from a sick brother. Before I could say anything about the murder he hung up.'

I decided to search the cottage where Veddle lived. It was on the edge of a plantation, and consisted of two rooms, one of which was a sort of kitchen-cum-dining-room, the other a bedroom. It was plainly but well furnished. Mr Voss, who couldn't get his machine through the door and shouted all his explanations through the windows, said he'd furnished it himself.

There was one cupboard, which contained an old suit and a new suit of clothes and a couple of pairs of boots. But what I particularly noticed was that Veddle hadn't taken his pipe away. It was lying on the table and looked as if it had been put down in a hurry. Another curious thing was a long mackintosh hanging behind the door. It was the longest mackintosh I have ever seen. On top of it hung a black felt hat. I took down the mackintosh and, laying it on the bed, felt in the pockets – it is the sort of thing one does mechanically – and the first thing my fingers closed round was a small cylinder. I took it out. It was a smoke cartridge. I put that on the table and went on with the search.

One of the drawers of the bureau was locked. I took the liberty of opening it. It had a tin cash-box, which was unfastened, and in this I made a discovery. There must have been three hundred pounds in one-pound notes, a passport made out in the name of Wills – Sidney Wills, which was Veddle's real name – and a book of tickets which took him to Constantinople. There was a sleeper ticket also made out in the name of Wills, and the whole was enclosed in a Cook's folder, and, as I discovered from the stamp, had been purchased at Cook's West-End office the day before the murder.

There was a third thing in the drawer which I didn't take very much notice of at the time, but which turned out to be one of the big clues in the case. This was a scrap of paper on which was written: 'Bushes second stone's throw turn to Amberley Church third down.'

I sent this to the deputy chief constable.

'Very mysterious,' he said. 'I know Amberley Church well; it's about eight miles from here. It's got a very famous steeple.'

As I say, I didn't attach a great deal of importance to it. It was too mysterious for me. I put it in my pocket, and a few minutes afterwards I had forgotten it, when I heard that Wills, the detective, was missing.

FOUR

The disappearance of Wills rattled me. And I'm not a man easily rattled. Now and again you meet a crook detective, but mostly in books. I knew just what they'd say at Scotland Yard – they'd blame me for it. If a chimney catches fire, or a gas main blows up, the chief constable says to the deputy: 'Why isn't the Sooper more careful?'

Wills hadn't done anything dramatic: he'd just walked to the station, taken a ticket to London and had gone. I got on to the Yard by phone, but of course he hadn't turned up then, and I placed the chief constable in full possession of all the facts; and from the way he said: 'How did that come to happen, Minter?' I knew that I was halfway to a kick. If I wasn't one of the most efficient officers in the service, and didn't catch every man I was sent after, I should be blamed for their crimes.

I got one bit of evidence. After I'd finished telephoning and come out of the house, I found an assistant gardener waiting to see me. He had seen Veddle walking towards his cottage about the time of the murder. He had particularly noticed him because he wore a long mackintosh that reached to his heels and a black hat; the mackintosh had the collar up and the tab drawn across as though it were raining. This was remarkable because it was a fairly warm day. The gardener thought he was a stranger who was trying to find his way to the house, and had gone across towards him, when he recognised Veddle.

'From which way was he coming?'

'From Tadpole Wood,' said the man. 'I told Mr Voss and he sent me on to tell you.'

I liked Mr Voss: he was a nice man. But the one thing that rattles me is the amateur detective. I suppose the old gentleman found time hanging on his hands, and welcomed this murder as a farmer welcomes rain after a drought. He was what I would describe as a seething mass of excitement. His electric chair was dashing here and there; he was down in Tadpole Wood with half a dozen gamekeepers and gardeners, finding clues that would have baffled the well-known Sherlock Holmes. He meant well, and that's the hardest thing you can say about any man.

He gave me one idea – more than one, if the truth be told. It was after I rowed across to Lone House and had come upon him and his searchers in the wood.

'Why do you trouble to row?' he said. 'Why don't you get Garry Thurston to lend you his submarine?'

I thought he was joking, but he went on: 'It's a motor-boat. I call it the submarine because of its queer build.'

He told me that Garry had had the boat built for him to his own design. The river, though not an important one, is very deep, and leads, of course, to the Thames, where the Conservancy Board have a regulation against speeding. You're not allowed to use speedboats on the Thames, because the wash from them damages the banks and has been known to wreck barges.

As Garry was keen on speed, and had taken a natural science degree at Cambridge, he had designed a boat which offered him a maximum of speed with a minimum of wash.

'It honestly does look a submarine. There's only about four feet of it above water, and the driver's seat is more like a conning tower than a cockpit.'

'Where does he keep it?' I asked.

Apparently he had a boathouse about two hundred yards from the Flash. We afterwards measured and found that it was exactly two hundred and thirty yards in a straight line from Lone House.

Mr Voss was full of enthusiasm, and we went round the edge of the estate, touched a secondary road and in a very short time came to a big, green boathouse, but there was no boat there.

'He must be out in it,' said Mr Voss, a little annoyed, 'but when he comes in – there he is!'

He pointed to the river, and I'll swear to you that although my sight is as good as any man's I couldn't see it.

The boat was moving against a green background, and as it was painted green it was almost invisible. If I hadn't seen Garry Thurston's head and his big face I would never have seen it at all. The top was shaped like a sort of whaleback. The whole boat seemed to be awash and sinking.

It came towards us, moving very quickly, and Garry waved his hand to us, brought the boat alongside and stepped out.

'I've been down to the river,' he said, 'and nearly had an accident – Field's black friends were rowing up and they fouled my bow.'

I had heard about these strange negroes who came to see Field occasionally, and I was very much interested.

'When was this?' I asked.

He told me. It must have been half an hour before the murder was committed.

'They were lying under the bank, and the boy evidently decided to row across into one of the backwaters, and chose the moment I was hitting up a tolerable speed for this little river. I only avoided them by accident. Why doesn't Field bring his native pals here by road?'

I thought it was a bright moment to tell him that John Field had met his death that afternoon. He wasn't shocked, did not even seem surprised, and when he said, 'Poor devil!' I did not think he sounded terribly sincere. Then he asked quickly: 'Where was Miss Venn?'

'She was in the house,' I said, and I saw his face go pale.

'Good God!' he gasped. 'In the house when the murder was committed –' I stopped him.

'She knew nothing about it – that's all I'm prepared to tell you. At least, she said she knew nothing about it.'

'Where is she now?' asked Garry. He looked absolutely ill with worry. I told him that I had sent her to her lodgings, and I think he'd have started right away if I hadn't pointed out that it wasn't quite the thing to go worrying the girl unless she had given him some right.

'And anyway,' I said, 'she's a police witness, and I don't want her interfered with.'

I told him what I'd come for, and told him at the same time that his boat was quite useless for the purpose: it was too long and too full of odd contraptions for me to bother my head about. But he had what I had thought was a row-boat, under a canvas cover, but which proved to be a small motor dinghy, and with this he ran me down to the Flash, showing me in the meantime how to work it.

I hadn't by any means got through Field's papers. In his pocket had been a bunch of keys. There was one odd-looking key for which I could find no lock. I discovered it that evening, when I was trying the walls of his study. Behind a picture, which swung out on hinges, I found the steel door of a safe. It was packed with papers, mostly of a business nature, and I was going through these carefully when Miss Marjorie Venn arrived. About tea-time I had sent her a note, telling her that when she was well enough I would like her assistance to sort out Field's papers. I didn't expect that she'd be well enough to come until the next day, but they telephoned, just before I began my search, to ask me if I would send the car for her.

She was quite calm; some of the colour had come back to her face; and I had a closer view of her than I had had that day on the bank, when Veddle had behaved like a blackguard. She was my ideal of what a woman should be: no hysterics, no swooning, just calm and sensible, which women so seldom are.

The servants had come back from the matinée, and I wanted to know exactly how I was to deal with them. She went out and saw them, and arranged that they were to stay on until further orders. A couple of the women, however, insisted on going home that night. She paid their wages out of money which she kept for that purpose.

There was no doubt about her being a help. She knew almost every document by sight, and saved me the trouble of reading through long legal agreements and contracts.

I sent for coffee when we were well into the work. It was while we were drinking this that she told me something about Field. He paid her a good salary, but she was in fear of him, and once or twice had been on the point of leaving him.

'I hate to say it of him, but he was absolutely unscrupulous,' she said. 'If he had not been a friend of my father's, and I was not obeying my father's wishes, I should never have stayed.'

This was a new one to me, but apparently Field and Miss Venn's father had been great friends in South Africa. Lewis Venn had died there – died apparently within a year of Field finding his gold-mine.

'When Mr Field came back I was about fifteen and at school. He paid for my education and helped my mother in many ways, and after dear mother's death he sent me to Oxford. I had never met him until then. He persuaded me to give up my studies and come and act as his private secretary. I was under that deep obligation to him – ' She paused. 'I think he has cancelled that,' she said quietly.

Her father and Field had been poor men, who had wandered about Africa looking for mythical gold-mines. One day they came to a native village and discovered, under a heap of earth, an immense store of raw gold, the accumulation of centuries, which the natives had won from a river, and which had been handed on from chief to chief.

'The Chief of Tuna,' she said. 'This sword – ' She stopped and shuddered. It was this that had put them on the track of the gold-mine. 'Mr Field often spoke about it.'

She stopped rather abruptly.

'Now I think we ought to get on with our work,' she said.

It was five minutes after this that we made a discovery. There was a false bottom to the safe, and in this was a long envelope, and, written on the outside: 'The Last Will and Testament of John Carlos Field.' The envelope was sealed; I broke the seal and opened it.

It was written on a double sheet of foolscap evidently in Field's own hand, and after the usual flim-flam with which legal documents began, it said: 'I leave all of which I die possessed to Marjorie Anna Venn, of Clive Cottage, in this parish – '

'To me?' Marjorie Venn looked as if she had seen a ghost. She evidently couldn't believe what I was reading.

'If you're Marjorie Anna Venn – '

She nodded. 'That is my full name.' She spoke like somebody who had been running and was out of breath. 'He asked me my full name one day, and I told him. But why – '

There was a big space under the place where he and the witnesses had signed, and here he had written a codicil, which was also witnessed.

'I direct that the sum of five hundred pounds shall be paid to my wife, Lita Field, and the sum of a thousand pounds to my son, Joseph John Field.'

We looked at one another.

'Then he was married!' she said.

At this minute one of my men came in to see me. 'There's a young man called. He says his name is Joseph John Field.'

I pushed back my chair, as much astonished as the girl.

'Show him in,' I said.

We didn't speak a word. And then the door opened, and there walked into the room a tall, young, good-looking negro.

'My name is Joseph John Field,' he said.

FIVE

Did I say I was not easily rattled? Well, I'm not. But I'd been rattled twice in one day.

I looked at the negro, I looked at Marjorie.

The boy – he was about nineteen – stood there motionless; there was no expression on his face or in his brown eyes.

'Joseph John Field?' I said. 'You're not the son of John Field, who was the owner of this house?'

He nodded.

'Yes, I am his son,' he said quietly. 'My mother was the daughter of the Chief of Tuna.'

I could only look at him. I thought these kinds of cases only existed in the minds of people who wrote cinema stories. But there was this negro, making a claim that was so preposterous that I simply couldn't believe him.

'Then your grandfather was the Chief of Tuna – I suppose you know that the Sword of Tuna – '

He interrupted me.

'Yes, I know that.'

'Who told you?' I asked sharply.

He hesitated.

'A detective. He telephoned to my mother tonight.'

'Wills?' I asked.

Again he hesitated.

'Yes, Mr Wills. He has been a good friend of ours. He once saved my mother from – from being beaten by Mr Field.'

'Is your mother black?' I asked. There was no time to consider his feelings, but apparently he was one of these sensible negroes who didn't mind being described as black.

He shook his head.

'She is negroid, but she is almost as pale as a European.'

He had the cultured voice of an English gentleman. I found afterwards that he had been educated at a public school, and was at that time at a university.

'Mr Wills thought that I should come and see you, because, as mother and I were in the neighbourhood today, and we were known to have visited the house recently, suspicion might attach to us.'

'It certainly does, young man,' said I, and it was only then that I asked him if he'd sit down.

I could see Marjorie was listening, fascinated. The young man drew up a chair on the other side of the desk. He wore dark gloves and carried an ebony cane. His clothes were made by a good West-End tailor. He was in fact more like a real swell than any negro I've ever met. There was nothing ostentatious about his clothes, and, as I say, his voice was the voice of a gentleman.

He put his hand in his pocket, took out a leather case, opened it and handed me a folded paper. It was headed: 'March, 17th, being St Patrick's Day, 1907, at the Jesuit Mission, Kobulu.' Written in faded ink were the words:

> I have this day, and in accordance with the rites of Holy Church, performed the ceremony of marriage between John Carlos Field, English, and Lita, daughter of Kosulu, Chief of Tuna, and issue this certificate in proof thereof.
>
> MICHAEL ALOYSIUS VALETTI, SJ

Underneath was written: 'Confirmed – Morou, District Commissioner'.

I handed the document mechanically to Miss Venn.

She read it. 'This is your mother's marriage certificate,' she said.

He nodded. 'You are Miss Marjorie Venn? I've never seen you before, but I know you very well. My mother knew your father. They came to our village more than twenty years ago, my father and yours.'

I thought it was a pretty good moment to ask him about Field's life in Africa, but the boy would tell me nothing, except that Field behaved very badly to his mother and had brought a number of tribes with him to attack the village and had killed the chief – his father-in-law.

I was a little knocked out to find a young negro claiming to be the son of a white man, but if I'd had any sense, I'd have realised that this is one of the jokes that nature plays in marriages of mixed colour. It was understandable now why Field invariably sent his servants away when his wife and son called upon him.

My first inclination was to admire the man for having done the right thing by this coloured son of his, but then I realised that he could not very well do anything else. I didn't suppose his wife blackmailed him, but the possibility of the fact leaking out that this country gentleman was married to a negress would be quite sufficient to make him pay well to keep her quiet. He could not even divorce her or allow her to divorce him without creating a scandal. I mentioned this fact to the boy, who agreed and said that Field had offered his mother a large sum of money to apply in the District Courts – I think they were Belgian – for a divorce, but his mother, having been mission-trained a Catholic, would not hear of divorce.

I wanted to get his reaction to the will, so I told him that he had been practically cut off, except for a thousand pounds. He wasn't a bit surprised, except that he had been left anything at all.

'Where did my father die?' the girl asked suddenly, but Joseph Field would say very little about what happened in Africa twenty-two years before. Possibly he did not know very much, though I am inclined to believe that he knew more than he was prepared to tell.

He did throw some sort of light on the cause of the quarrel between Field and the Chief of Tuna.

'My father had difficulty in locating the mine and came back again and again. He tried to persuade Kosulu – my grandfather – to let him have a share of the gold store which we kept in the village. Kosulu was paramount chief and the gold had been accumulating for centuries. It was to gain possession of this that he attacked the village – '

'Was my father in the attack?' asked the girl quickly.

Joseph Field shook his head.

'No, Miss Venn. The partnership had already been broken. Your father at the time was prospecting elsewhere. He did go back to the village after Kosulu was wounded and nursed him. John Field was bitterly disappointed because he had not been given the gold. He thought when he married my mother he would be able to take possession of the store. Mr Venn at that time was a very sick man. My mother tells me he was planning to go to the coast to make his way back to what you call civilisation' – I saw him smile; I guess he had his own idea of civilisation. 'It was on his way to the coast your father died.'

I cross-examined him as to the number of times he and his mother had visited Lone House, but I could get nothing that helped me very much. They had only come once without invitation and that was the time that Wills had to intervene to save the woman from John Field's hunting crop.

There was nothing for me to do but to take his name and address. He and his mother lived in a flat in Bayswater and I told him that I would call to see them at the first available opportunity.

'What do you make of that?' I asked the girl when he had gone.

She shook her head.

I thought she looked rather sad and wondered why; not that I spend much time in analysing the emotions of females.

We did not do much more searching, but spent the next hour discussing Joseph John Field, and the part he may have played. I told her I knew that they had been in the neighbourhood that day and where I had my information from. When I mentioned Garry Thurston she went very pink and started very quickly to talk about his boat.

'It's curious,' she said. 'Mr Field used to detest that motor-boat. I think it was because he hated being spied upon, as he called it, and he had an idea that Garry used to come down on to the Flash in it to – well, to see me.'

'And did you see him very often?' I asked.

'He is a great friend of mine,' she answered.

It's funny that you can never get a woman to give a straight answer to a straight question. However, it was not a subject that I wanted to pursue at the moment, so I let it drop.

The truth about John Field's marrriage must come out at the inquest: I told Joseph that when I saw him off the premises, but he didn't seem much upset. It was clear to me that there was no love lost between him and his father. Generally when he referred to him he called him 'John Field'. I could see that the horsewhip incident was on his mind, and probably there were other incidents which nobody knew anything about.

It was easy to understand now why Wills was not popular with Field: he knew too much and probably presumed upon his knowledge. I guess that the woman must have told the detective that she was Field's wife.

An idea occurred to me suddenly.

'Do you mind if I ask you a delicate question. Miss Marjorie?' I said, and when she said no, I asked her if Field had proposed marriage to her.

'Three or four times,' she said quietly, and I did not pursue the subject, because it might have been a very painful one for the young lady.

From what she told me it seemed that Field had lived almost the life of a hermit: he knew nobody in the neighbourhood and made no friends.

'Mr Voss asked him to dinner once, but he refused. He tried to buy Hainthorpe – '

'Mr Voss's house?'

She nodded.

'He hated people living so close to him and he had an idea of building a house on top of Jollyboy Hill; in fact, he offered Mr Voss a very considerable sum of money through his agent for the hill alone, but the offer was not accepted.'

There wasn't much more to be done that night. Mr Voss had asked me to stay with him and, after seeing the young lady home, I got one of our men who understands engines to take me across the Flash. Here I found the little two-seater which Mr Voss had put at my disposal: I don't understand motor-boats, but I can drive a car.

As I think I have explained, the house stands in a little stretch of meadow which is wholly encircled by trees. The path to the house is just wide enough to take a small car. The roads runs a little way through Tadpole Wood, through the thickest part of it. I was within a few yards of what I would call the exit, when I saw, in the light of my headlamps, somebody standing by the birch tree. Thinking it was one of the searchers, I slowed my car almost to a walk, and shouted: 'Do you want a lift?'

I had hardly spoken the words before the figure straightened itself and fired twice at me.

SIX

The bullets stung past me so close to my face that I thought I had been hit. For a moment I sat paralysed with astonishment. It was the sight of the figure running that sort of brought me to life. I was out of the car in a second, but by this time he was out of sight. If I'd had the sense to bring my car round on a full lock, the lamps would have made it possible for me to see. As it was I was stumbling about in the dark with no chance of following my gentleman friend.

I think I ought to explain that Mr Voss had made dozens of 'walks' in Tadpole Wood and there were paths running in all directions; it was a real laby – what's the word? Maze. I went back to the car and got my hand lamp, which I should have taken before. I ought to have known that any kind of search was a waste of time, but a man who's been so fired at doesn't think as calmly as the chief constable sitting in his office (as I told him later). I hadn't any difficulty in finding where this bird had stood. I found the two shells of an automatic pistol lying on the grass. They were both hot when I found them. Naturally I kept them, because nowadays there is a new-fangled process by which you can identify from the cartridge the pistol that fired it, and I didn't think it was a satisfactory night's work. To go running through the wood was a waste of time – I realised that. The only hope was that the shots would have aroused one of Mr Voss's gamekeepers and that the man might be seen. Apparently it had aroused them, but in the wrong direction. Their cottages were on the other side of the house and I met them running over the ground on my way to Hainthorpe. By the time I told them what had happened, I remembered that I had two or three detectives at Lone House who would want to know all about the shooting, and I turned back to see them. I was giving instructions about notifying the police stations around, with the idea of putting a barrage on the roads, when I heard two more shots fired in quick succession. They came from the direction of Hainthorpe. I got into the car again and flew up the road, not so fast as I might have done because I had police officers and gamekeepers piled into the machine or hanging on to the footboards.

The entrance of Hainthorpe is a great portico, and the first thing I saw in the light of the motor lamps was a ladder lying across the drive. The house was in commotion. A servant, who looked scared sick, met me and asked me to come up to Mr Voss's room. He took me in the elevator. Mr Voss was sitting in bed. He was very red in the face, all his white hair was standing up and he was in his pyjamas.

'Look at that!' he roared and pointed to the curved bedhead.

It had been made of gilt wood, but now, for a space of about a foot, it was smashed to smithereens.

'They shot at me,' he said. (Did I say 'he said'? He yelled it.) 'Look at that!'

Over the bed was a square hole in the wall that had shivered the plaster and sent it flying in all directions. The damage was so great that it didn't look like an automatic bullet that had done the work.

When he pointed to the French windows leading to the portico I understood why.

One window was smashed to smithereens, one was neatly punctured with a hole – both bullets must have started somersaulting the moment they touched the obstruction of the glass. I went out on to the top of the portico. It was surrounded by a low balustrade and had upon it a canvas awning – Mr Voss used to be pushed out here to enjoy the sunlight and sometimes, he told me, he had slept there.

One of the cartridge cases I discovered on the balustrade, the other on the drive below the next morning.

When I got Mr Voss quiet, he told me what happened. He had not apparently heard the first two shots that were fired at me, but he was awakened by the sound of a ladder being put against the portico. He sat up in bed and switched on the light.

'It was the most stupid thing I could have done, for the devil could see his target. The light was hardly on before – bang! I actually saw the glass smash . . . '

Though he was always regarded as a man of iron nerve, he was trembling from head to foot. One of the splinters from the wood had cut his right hand, which was wrapped up in a handkerchief. I wanted him to see a doctor about it, but he pooh-poohed the idea. I went downstairs while he dressed himself with the assistance of a servant, and after a few minutes he came down in the lift and wheeled himself into the library. He was much calmer and had enough theories to last him for the rest of the night.

I had all the servants in the house brought into the library one by one and questioned them. Nobody had seen the man who had done the shooting. The ladder was one belonging to the gardeners and was used in the orchard, but kept hanging near the house. I questioned everybody closely as to whether they had seen a pistol in the possession of Veddle. They were all very vague, except a gardener who had actually seen an automatic in Veddle's cottage. Mr Voss was very emphatic on the point.

'There was no doubt at all,' he said, 'he had a pistol: I saw him practising with it once and told him to throw it into the river.'

He told me then what he had never told me before: that in the course of the past year he had received two threatening letters written by anonymous correspondents.

'I didn't think it was worth while keeping them,' he said. 'They were written by some illiterate person, and I always suspected some gypsies I had turned off a corner of my land about this time last year.'

'They were not in Veddle's handwriting?'

'No,' he said slowly. 'I don't think I have ever seen Veddle's handwriting now that you mention it.'

I had the little scrap of paper in my pocket which I had taken from Veddle's cottage and I showed it to him. He examined the mysterious message it contained, reading out the words: 'Bushes second stone stop turn to Amberley Church third down.'

I took the paper from him. I could have sworn that the third and fourth words were 'stone's throw', but I saw I had made a mistake. Even with the change of the words it was as plain to me as it had been at first.

'I think that is Veddle's writing,' I said.

'What does it mean?'

'I haven't the slightest idea,' I said. 'The point is: is the writing anything like the anonymous letters you received?'

He shook his head. 'So far as I can remember, it isn't.' He pulled out a handful of letters from his pocket, trying to find some note which Veddle had written to him. He was one of those careless men who keep money, letters and odd memoranda in one pocket. As he went through them he threw half of them away.

'I get my pockets full of this stuff,' he said. 'It is what I call a bachelor's wastepaper basket.'

I stooped and fished into the real wastepaper basket, and handed him something he had thrown away. They might have been old bills, they were so sprinkled with ink, but I've got an instinct for money.

'You may be a rich man,' I said, 'but there is no reason why you should chuck your money into the wastepaper basket.'

They were bank notes, three for ten pounds and one for twenty pounds.

He chuckled at his carelessness.

'Perhaps that is why Veddle always took personal charge of my wastepaper basket. I wonder how much the rascal has made out of my carelessness.'

It was nearly four o'clock when I went up to my room, after a long talk with the chief constable on the wire.

I am one of those old-fashioned police officers who never have got out of their notebook habit. Give me a bit of a pencil and a paper and I can collect all my thoughts on one page. Here were the facts:

1. A very rich man, occupying a lonely house by the river, is killed. The only immediate clue is the impression on the earth outside of a naked footprint.
2. In the house at the time of the murder and locked up in a room is his

private secretary, a girl to whom he had been making love although he was a married man. It was impossible that she could have locked the door herself, for the key of the room was found in the dead man's inside pocket when he was searched.

3. One of the detectives engaged to look after Field disappears, and we discover that he is the brother of Veddle – Mr Voss's servant, a man who had a quarrel and a fight with Field and who threatened to get even with him.

4. Veddle and Wills disappear, but on the night following the murder, some person unknown appears in the grounds and fires at me and attempts to assassinate Mr Voss.

5. Mr Garry Thurston, who is in love with the secretary, possesses a boat which could approach the house unseen. He states, and this is confirmed, he was cruising along the little river at or near the time of the murder, and discovers a negress, who is Field's wife, and a young negro, who is Field's son, within striking distance of the house.

I wrote all this down, and the sun was shining through the windows by the time I had finished. I didn't feel like sleep. It's a queer thing – there is a point beyond which tiredness cannot go: you either drop into a heavy sleep where you sit, or you suddenly become as lively as a cricket. I had got to the cricket stage. I had a bath, shaved and, dressing myself, I went downstairs, unlocked the front door and stepped out. It was going to be a gorgeous day: the sun was up, the air was fresh and sweet. I decided to walk across the park towards Lone House. I knew the detectives would be there and some of them would be awake and could make me some coffee.

I stepped out very cheerfully, never dreaming that I was on the point of making a discovery which would change the whole complexion of the case.

As I think I told you, to reach the place where the river spreads out into a little lake one has to pass through Tadpole Wood. The birds were singing and it was the sort of morning that somehow you could not associate with police work, murders and midnight shootings.

I reached the spot where I had been fired at and, although I didn't expect to find anything, I had a sudden impulse to go off the path and make a search of the undergrowth. There was more than a possibility that I should find something which we had overlooked. I poked about with my stick in the undergrowth and in the grass and was turning to go when suddenly I saw two feet behind a bush; they were wide apart, the toes turned up. The man, whoever he was, must have been lying on his back.

I am not easily agitated, but there was something about these feet and their absolute stillness that sent a shiver down my spine. I walked quickly past the bush. Lying on his back was a man, his arms outstretched, his white face turned up to the sky. It was not necessary to see the blood on his throat to know that he was dead.

I stood looking at him, speechless. He was the one man I didn't expect to find murdered on that summer morning.

SEVEN

The dead man was Veddle. He had been shot at close quarters, and the doctor who saw him afterwards said he must have been killed instantaneously.

What struck me at the time was that he had not been killed in the place he was found. His attitude, the fact that there was little or no blood on the ground, and the fact that I found afterwards traces of a heavy body being dragged to behind the bushes, all gave the OK to my first impression.

I didn't do any searching just then, but, running through the wood, I came to the water's edge, intending to call assistance from Lone House. The first thing I saw was Garry Thurston's queer-looking boat. It was moored to the bank, the painter tied to a tree, and its stern had drifted out so that it lay bow on to the bank. One of our men was on the lawn, and I shouted to him to come over. He travelled across in the little motor dinghy.

'How long has that boat been there?' I asked.

'I don't know. I saw it a quarter of an hour ago when I came out on to the lawn, and wondered what it was doing there. It belongs to Mr Thurston, doesn't it?'

I wasn't worrying about the ownership of the boat at the moment, but took him up to the place where the body lay, and together we began our search.

He had heard nothing in the night, except that, just before daylight, he thought he heard the sound of a motor-car backfiring. It seemed a long way off, and nothing like the sound of the shots he had heard earlier in the evening.

Some rough attempt had been made to search Veddle's body, for the pockets of the jacket and the trouser pockets were turned inside out. It was in his hip pocket, on which he was lying, that we found the money – about two hundred pounds. The money was a bit of a shock to me, and upset all my previous calculations. It only shows how dangerous it is for an experienced police officer to make up his mind too soon.

'A hundred and eighty pounds,' said the sergeant, counting it.

I put it in my pocket without a word.

We began to comb the wood, and in ten minutes we had found the place where the murder was committed. We should have known this by certain signs, but there was an already packed suitcase and an overcoat.

The place was about thirty yards from the drive which runs through Tadpole Copse, very near the spot where I had been shot at on the previous night.

There wasn't time to make more than a rough search of the suitcase, and that told us nothing.

I went down to the Flash and examined Garry Thurston's boat. The floor of the cockpit was covered with a rubber mat, of white and blue check, and on this were the marks of muddy footprints. They weren't so much muddy as wet; it looked as if somebody had been wading in the water before they got into the boat.

Taking the motor dinghy, I went up to the boathouse. The gates facing the river were wide open; the little door on the land side was locked. I knew, because Garry Thurston had told me, that the gates opened automatically at the pull of a lever on the inside of the boathouse, and they could only be opened from the inside. The boathouse itself was supported on piles, and I saw at once that it was possible for anybody who would take the risk to dive under its edge and climb up inside. I told the detective to take the suitcase across to Lone House, and, taking the police car, I drove up to Dobey Manor, where Mr Garry Thurston lived.

It was an old Elizabethan manor house, one of the show places of the county. I am not very well acquainted with the habits of the non-working classes, and I expected it would take me an hour to make anybody hear at that time of the morning. But the first person I saw when I got out of the car was Mr Thurston himself. He was up and dressed, and by the look of him I guessed he had not been to bed all night. He was unshaven, and his eyes had one of those tired, poker-party looks.

'You're up early, Mr Thurston,' I said, and he smiled.

'I haven't been to bed all night. In fact I've only just come in.' And then, abruptly: 'Have they found Veddle?'

That was the one question I didn't expect him to put to me, and I was a little taken aback. The one person I didn't think he would be interested in was Veddle.

'Yes, we've found him,' I replied.

I looked at his face pretty straightly, but it was like a mask and told me nothing. He didn't speak for a moment, and then: 'You found him, eh?' He spoke very slowly, as though he was thinking out every word carefully.

I expected him to ask me where Veddle had been found. I had an instinct that that was the question that was on his lips and which, for some reason, he dared not ask. I had come up to make enquiries about his motor-boat. It was merely a precautionary enquiry to clear up any possibility that he might have an arrangement with somebody in the neighbourhood to use the boat. But his attitude and his appearance changed my angle.

'Yes,' I went on, not taking my eyes off him, 'I found Veddle shot dead in Tadpole Copse.'

He was a good-looking young fellow, but as I spoke his face went grey and old.

'You don't mean that!' It was almost in a whisper that he spoke. 'Shot dead! Good God! How – how awful!'

It wasn't a moment to try to carry on a polite conversation – I put my question to him without trimmings.

'Where have you been all night, Mr Thurston?'

The colour returned to his face in large quantities. He made no attempt to deny the fact that he hadn't been in bed.

'I was just wandering around,' he stammered. 'I couldn't sleep – Veddle dead! How perfectly ghastly!'

Why was he so interested in Veddle, dead or alive? That puzzled me; but so many things had puzzled me in the past twenty-four hours.

He stopped further enquiries by saying: 'Come inside and have some coffee,' and, turning abruptly, he walked ahead of me through the garden and up a broad flight of steps on to the terrace before the house.

The first thing I saw on the terrace was something under a canvas cover that looked like a machine gun. He saw my eyes go in that direction, and I noticed him frown. He would have passed on, but I was curious.

'Oh, that!' he said, and was a little embarrassed. 'That is a telescope. This house, as you see, is built on a rise, and on a clear day I can see objects forty miles away. If it wasn't for Jollyboy Hill one could see St Paul's well enough to tell the time by the clock.'

It was a fairly clear morning. I pointed to a church spire about five miles away.

'What church is that?' I asked.

'That's Amberley,' he said.

Amberley Church! I remembered the note that I had found in Veddle's room: 'Bushes second stone stop turn to Amberley Church third down.'

He seemed anxious to get me indoors, walked ahead of me, turning to see if I was following.

Generally speaking, I am not easily baffled, but the behaviour of this young man, his interest in Veddle, and the fact that he'd been out all night – the night that Veddle was murdered – upset quite a number of interesting theories that were beginning to sort themselves out in my mind.

It was when we were sitting in the big hall of his house, a room that looked like a small chapel, that I told him the reason I had come. He stared when I told him about the boat. 'I can't understand that,' he said. 'No, I haven't used the boat since – well, I haven't used it since you saw me on the river. Will you tell me where you found it?'

I described the position where the boat had been moored, and then, to my surprise, he asked: 'Were any of Veddle's belongings on the bank or in the boat?'

When I told him about the suitcase I thought he turned a little pale. He certainly got up from the table quickly, leaving his coffee untouched, and paced up and down the room. I didn't know what to make of him. His agitation wasn't natural in a man who had nothing more than a casual interest in the death of Veddle.

I put the question again to him. 'What were you doing last night?'

'I went to town,' he said.

There was a 'you be damned' tone in his voice which was a little unexpected.

'Really, inspector, I don't see why my movements should be questioned.'

'What time did you go to town?'

'At seven o'clock last night – it may have been eight. I didn't dine here.'

I looked at his grey suit. He must have gone to town on pretty important business for it to have kept him up all night. I guessed then that he hadn't been back very long when I arrived at the house, but this guess was wrong, because I afterwards discovered he had returned at three o'clock.

There was no sense in alarming him. I put on my best jolly-good-fellow smile.

'Your coffee's getting cold, Mr Thurston,' I said, helping myself to another cup. 'If I've asked you any questions that I oughtn't to have asked I'm very sorry.'

I drank up the coffee.

'I think I'll toddle back to Lone House and see what they've found in Veddle's suitcase. Have you seen Miss Venn lately – '

I had hardly asked the question when I heard a woman's voice behind me.

'Can I come in, please?'

I turned my head. Standing in the doorway was a woman. I guessed she was about forty. She was slim and tall, and dressed in a neat costume; and though she hadn't either the colour or the peculiar features of her race, I knew she was a negress and guessed she was John Field's wife.

EIGHT

The last person in the world I expected to see was the negress whom John Field had married in the wilds of Africa, and I was so taken by surprise that I hadn't a word to say. You can't imagine anything more – what is the word? incongruous, is it? – than the sight of that young woman in this big, vaulted manor hall. She just didn't belong to the country and didn't belong to the house.

The queer thing was that I had made up my mind during the night that I would see her that day.

I turned to Garry Thurston. I expected him to look embarrassed, but he didn't.

'You don't know Mrs Field?' he said as calmly as you please. 'I brought her down from town early this morning – her and her son.'

It was one of those situations where a man can't exactly find the right word to break into a conversation. At least, I couldn't for a long time.

'Why did you bring her here?' I asked at last.

'Because I want to know something more about John Field – a great deal more than I know.'

Now it is a fact that until that moment I had never considered this young man very seriously. I know his boat was seen in the vicinity of the house about the time the murder was committed, and one of my subordinate officers had suggested he should be questioned. But also I know quite a lot about criminals, and when you get an educated man committing a murder he doesn't as a rule fall into any of the errors that upset the applecart of the half-wits.

I looked from him to the woman. She had just realised who I was, and she was looking at me in a curious and understanding way. Mr Thurston beckoned her in and pulled out a chair for her. 'Now, Mr Thurston,' I said, 'perhaps you'll tell me what is it you want to know about Field? I may be able to put you right.'

He shook his head.

'Nothing that I wanted to know about Field immediately concerns this murder,' he said. 'I was anxious to get particulars of his early life, and Mrs Field very kindly agreed to come down.'

'Did you have to bring her down here, Mr Thurston? Couldn't you have questioned her in London?'

He shook his head.

'The questions I wanted to put had to be asked here,' he said shortly, and I knew that nothing I could say would make him give me any further information, and I guessed from the look of the woman that she wasn't going to be helpful.

I put aside all the friend-of-the-family stuff, and began to ask him to account for his movements that night. And he had an alibi as fast as a rock. He'd been in town, and, what is more, his chauffeur had driven him and driven him back again. He couldn't have been anywhere near Tadpole Copse when the murder was committed. I don't think we were such good friends as we had been when I left, but he was the sort of young man who would know I was only doing my duty and would bear no malice.

I didn't go back straight to the house. It took my fancy to go up to the top of Jollyboy Hill. I've been too long in the police service to expect anything that looks or feels like inspiration, but I had an idea that once I got on top of that hill a lot of things would become clear that were at the moment a bit obscure.

Well, they didn't.

I walked down the other side of the hill, through Tadpole Copse, and stood there watching the local police while they were conducting a search which brought nothing to light except a towel. It was a curious thing to find in the bottom of a hollow tree. It hadn't been used very much, and looked to me as though it had not been long from the laundry, though it was crumpled and still damp: On the edge I found stitched one of those names that drapers sell to attach to laundry, and the name was ' Veddle'.

But the most important discovery of the morning was made by a detective officer of the Berkshire police, who took the dinghy down the river on the off-chance of finding some sort of clue. It's funny how amateurs expect to find clues strewn all over the face of the earth. But this fellow was lucky, for he found something that had a big bearing on the case. It was a sheet of paper floating on the water, and anybody who wasn't quite as enthusiastic as he was might have passed it by.

He sent the dinghy up to it and fished it out. It was a large date sheet, evidently torn from a calendar, and the date on it was the 4th of August in the current year. He would have thrown it back again but he saw on the back some writing in pencil, and, having read it, he brought the paper to me.

The first thing that struck me when I saw it was that I had seen a calendar that size before, but for the minute I couldn't place it. The writing on the back was in copying pencil and the water had made it very messy, but it was as easy to read as print. On the top was the number '23', and evidently this was the number of a page, for the writing started in the middle of a sentence:

. . . have always kept my eyes open. And I kept my ears open too. I saw Field once in Tadpole Copse, but he saw me too and went back across the Flash. I went over two nights in succession and had a good look at the girl as she was leaving for her lodgings. I saw what I could do. If I married her my fortune was made, and I did my best to make up to her. After all, she was only a secretary and she didn't know . . .

'She didn't know' were the last words on the paper. What didn't she know? To me it was fairly obvious. She didn't know that she was Field's heiress; but Veddle did.

What interested me about the sheet was that it was evidently part of a long story. Where were the other sheets? I sent the officer back in the dinghy to search the river as far as the Thames, and then I made my way up to the cottage where Veddle had lived.

Some busybody had been up to the house and wakened Mr Voss. I saw his mechanical chair whizzing down the path towards me, and from the fact that he still wore his pyjamas and a dressing-gown I guessed he'd only just got out of bed.

'Is it true about Veddle? When did it happen? Why didn't somebody wake me up?'

I couldn't answer all the questions he put to me, but I told him that I was going to search the cottage and asked him if he would lend me the key. He blew a whistle, and one of his gardeners came running forward and was sent back to the house to get the key, while we went on to the hut. I call it a hut although it was brick-made and was thatched. We had to wait a little time until the gardener returned, and I told Mr Voss as much as I thought he ought to know. He was very thoughtful.

'He must have been in the grounds last night. Do you think it was he who fired at us?'

I couldn't answer that question till the door of the cottage was opened. When I walked in, however, there was the answer on the table – a Browning pistol, the barrel still foul from the shot that had been fired, and seven unused cartridges in the magazine.

The room was just as I had left it, except (I remembered now) that the big calendar I had seen on one of the walls was lying on the table. The sheets had been torn off as far as September 7th. The back of the sheets were blank and could be used for writing paper. I had no doubt that Veddle had used it for that purpose.

The pen and ink were still on the table. How had he obtained admission? I went to the door – Mr Voss could not come in because of the narrowness of the passage – and asked him if there was another key. He shook his head.

'He could easily have had one made, but I know of no other,' he said.

I was returning to the room when he called me back.

'It has just occurred to me that he may have been there all the time.'

'While I was searching before, you mean?'

He nodded.

'Yes. There's a large cellar underneath the house. I think it was used for storing wine in my predecessor's days. It's queer I never thought of that before. You'll find a trapdoor in the bedroom.'

I made a search of the bedroom, turned up the carpet, and sure enough there was the trap! A wooden ladder led to the bottom, and it only needed a casual examination to show that the cellar had been lived in and slept in, for there was a camp bed, half a dozen blankets and a small electric handlamp, the sort you can buy for five shillings at any store.

So that was where Veddle had hidden. The place was well ventilated, and he could have stayed there, without anybody being the wiser, for a week. I found a tin of biscuits, half a dozen bottles of mineral water, and the half of a Dutch cheese in a small cupboard behind the bed.

There was no other clue. I came up the steps, and, closing the trap, whistled for an officer to stay on duty in the cottage until he was relieved. Mr Voss and I went back to the house together. I had to telephone to the chief constable and arrange for a couple more of my men to come down.

Mr Voss had to take his chair by another route. He ran up a long incline to the terrace, but he was waiting for me by the time I got up the steps. And then he made a suggestion which staggered me. When I say it staggered me, I am probably giving you a wrong impression. Nothing staggers me, but it was certainly unexpected.

'Is it possible to keep the story of the Veddle murder out of the newspapers?' he asked.

'Why on earth, Mr Voss?'

He looked at me very thoughtfully.

'You'll probably think that I'm not quite right in my head, but I have a theory that if this news is suppressed today, the murderer will be in your bands tomorrow morning.'

He would give me no reason. I hate people who are mysterious, because in nine cases out of ten they've nothing to be mysterious about. And then I told him about the piece of paper that was found on the river. I have been told by the chief constable that I am a talkative old man. Maybe I am; but I have found that the worst way to get through a case like this is keeping your mouth shut, and I thought this was the moment to talk.

He took the paper which I had in my pocket and examined it. 'Yes, that looks like Veddle's writing,' he said at last; 'obviously part of a long confession. I wonder what happened to the rest of it?'

That was the one thing I intended finding out.

NINE

I took the letter into his study and examined it carefully, and then, with Mr Voss's permission, I sent for his steward, or butler, or whatever he was called. I had seen a telephone in the cottage, and I had meant to ask before whether that phone was fixed up to the house exchange. When the steward told me it was not, a lot of light was thrown on the mystery of Veddle's death.

I got through to the local telephone supervisor and asked a few questions. Naturally he couldn't answer, because he'd only just come on duty; but an hour later, when I was having breakfast, I was informed the supervisor had got all the data I wanted. A call had come through at about ten o'clock on the previous night from the cottage phone, obviously from Veddle, who had asked for a London number and talked for six minutes, but the operator had no idea to whom he was speaking. There was a record of the call, and I got straight through to the number and found it was a small hotel near Paddington Station. Nobody named Wills was staying there, but the night porter had left a record that a 'Mr Staines' had been rung up at something after ten, and that it was a toll call. 'Mr Staines' himself was not in the hotel at the moment I phoned. I took no risks, but got through to the Yard immediately and sent a couple of officers to pick up 'Mr Staines' and see how much like Mr Wills he looked. When I came back I found Mr Voss had hatched out a brand-new theory, and it was so very much like my own that I wondered if I'd been talking aloud to myself.

'I'm sure this man Wills is in it,' he said. 'I shouldn't be surprised if he was the fellow who stole Garry Thurston's boat – my butler was telling me it was found moored on the Flash.'

'In that case,' said I, 'Mr Wills has got the last dying speech and confession of his brother. But why he went away without Veddle is a mystery to me.'

Voss returned to the subject of publicity, and he was very earnest.

'You have to realise, Sooper,' he said, 'that I have a scientific mind. I may not be a good detective, but I have the faculty of deduction. Since I lost the use of my legs I've spent my time working out problems more intricate than this, and I am more satisfied than ever that if you keep the shooting of Veddle out of the newspapers you'll have your man tomorrow morning.'

'Are you suggesting that Wills killed him?' I asked.

He shook his head.

'Of course not! Wills is obviously a confederate. He came up the river, probably by boat, last night, to get his brother away. You've been making enquiries at the exchange, haven't you? Without having stirred from this room or being told by any person who overheard your conversation, I can tell you you have been asking what were the messages that passed between the cottage and some unknown destination last night.'

I grinned at this.

'Oh, no, I'm not guessing, I'm telling you,' said Mr Voss, his face getting pinker and pinker, his white hair almost standing up on his head in his excitement. 'And I'll bet you found that it was his brother he called – or, if you haven't, I can tell you it was! He asked his brother to come down and get him away. His brother arrived by boat.'

'Why not by road?' said I.

'The roads are under observation, aren't they? What chance has a car of getting within a mile of this place? No, he came by river, probably by row-boat – he must have had a row-boat to have got out into the stream and stolen Garry Thurston's odd little launch. He brought that launch down to where you found it, and met his brother, who probably went back to the cottage for his suitcase or something of the sort. Did you find any suitcase, by the way? I see you did. He may have handed over the story of the crime to Wills, who rowed downstream ahead of the motor-boat and got away, quite confident that his brother would escape.'

'I don't see the object of holding this story from the newspapers,' I said.

'Don't you?' Max Voss's voice was very quiet. 'I do! Two people have been killed, both by the same hand.' He tapped on the table-cloth, emphasising every point. 'The one person who knows the murderer is Wills. Publish the news that Veddle has been found killed and Wills will come into the open – and will go the same way as Field and his brother!'

That was a brand-new angle to me. It. never occurred to me that Wills was hiding from anybody but Superintendent Minter. Personally, I don't like my theories upset by other people. Nothing annoys me more than to work out a case so that every little bit of the puzzle fits, and then for somebody to show me I've got one piece upside down. But Mr Voss was a man for whom I had a great respect, and the more I saw him the more I respected him. I don't believe in amateur detectives, the kind you read about in books, but if I had to work with one of those well-known sleuths I'd like him to be as near to Mr Voss as possible, because undoubtedly he had brains.

I thought Marjorie Venn was late when she turned up at Lone House that morning, but the truth was I had been up so early that ten o'clock seemed the middle of the day. I had taken a copy of the writing on the paper, and I showed it to her. She was puzzled, though she remembered several occasions when Veddle had tried to get acquainted with her. She had once paid a visit to a cinema house in Reading (it was on a Saturday afternoon and she had gone into Reading by the bus) and found Veddle sitting by her side.

I didn't tell her for some time about the man being dead. In fact, she got it from one of the servants in the house and came to me very distressed. I could see the business was getting on to her nerves, and I was wondering whether I couldn't get her away from the place to London. Mr Field's lawyer was coming that day, and as she inherited Field's money she could afford to stay at the best hotel in town, and I knew that the lawyer would advance the cash. When I made the suggestion, however, she wouldn't hear of it.

It was a casual reference I made to Garry Thurston which explained why she didn't want to leave the neighbourhood. I saw a flush come to her face, and I guessed that she and Garry were better friends than either of them had admitted.

I think she may have surmised my suspicion, for she very quickly got away from the subject of this young man.

'I'm not at all nervous, and I'd rather stay in the country till this ghastly murder is settled,' she said. 'And I wouldn't dream of leaving until I have all Mr Field's affairs in order.'

That afternoon I had a blow. Our chief constable is as kind a man as you'd meet in a day's march, but he is not what I would call a very sensitive man. Because, if he had been, he wouldn't have sent Superintendent Gurly to exercise, as he called it, a general supervision. Gurly is my senior. I've nothing to say against him; I dare say he's a good father and a moderately good husband. He's fat and I don't like fat men, but I've known fat men I could get on with. I never could get on with Gurly, ever since we were constables together. He was the sort of man who knew everything, except how little he knew; and naturally, the first thing he did when he came on the spot was to take charge of everything, give orders to my men and generally make himself conspicuously useless.

I have been on many cases with Superintendent Gurly, but never found a way of getting over him. If you threw up the case and went back to the Yard, it meant you had to go back to undo all his well-meaning work a few days later. If you complained to the chief constable, the chief would say: 'Well, you know what he is – just humour him.' He fussed about the house till late in the afternoon, and then he came into the study and said, 'I think I'll take a dinghy and row down the river, Minter.'

'Can you swim?' I asked, but even when he said no, I knew it was no good hoping, because fat men float.

I arranged to sleep at Lone House that night, and by the time dinner was over Gurly was back, as full of ideas as a bad egg is full of bouquet. Marjorie Venn had gone back to her lodgings, so that I could use all the bad language I wanted to use without hurting anybody's feelings. Anyway, you couldn't hurt Gurly with a hatchet. If ever I wanted to murder the man, it was when he said: 'I've got all the threads in my hand now, Minter – in fact, I think I could execute a warrant in the morning.'

'Fine,' I said. 'You naturally would know everything in half an hour. Who killed John Field?'

He looked at me and waggled his head, and I know that when Gurly waggles his head he's going to be so silly that you have to laugh or be sick.

'A girl,' he said.

I just gaped at him.

'Who? Miss Venn?'

He nodded.

'Is anything more obvious?' he asked. 'I wonder it hasn't occurred to you before, Minter.'

He leaned over the table, and he's so fat that the table creaked. I was creaking a bit myself.

'She was in the house when the murder was committed – you don't deny that. She was locked in the room, I grant you, but what was to prevent her from locking the door and throwing the key out of the window?'

'The only thing that was likely to prevent her was that the key was in the dead man's pocket,' I said, but that didn't choke him off.

'There may have been two keys, or three,' he said. 'Who benefited by his death? She did! It's pretty well established that she disliked him, Minter. She was having an affair with somebody in the neighbourhood – I haven't found out who it was –'

'You should have taken another five minutes,' I said; but, bless your soul, that kind of kick never reached him.

'He was killed by the Sword of Tuna –' he began again, when I stopped him.

'The man who killed John Field left his naked footprint outside the door. It wasn't a woman, it was a man. Get that silly idea out of your head, Gurly.'

'There are one or two questions I'm going to ask her,' he said, and took out of his pocket a big notebook, which he must have spent hours filling up. 'Will you bring her in?'

'She's gone,' I said very coldly.

'Then she's got to be brought back.'

Now when Gurly is in that kind of mood there's no coping with him. He was perfectly within his rights in wanting to question Marjorie Venn, and I had no authority to stop him. For one thing, it would have looked pretty bad in his report if I had put any obstacle in his way; so, after trying to persuade him to leave the matter over till the morning, I agreed to go down with him to the cottage where she lived and see her.

'She may be gone in the morning,' said Gurly.

It was a waste of time answering.

A police car took us to the little village where Marjorie Venn lived with a widow woman who kept a small shop. Marjorie had the two best rooms in the house, and had furnished them herself, she told me.

The shop was shut, but we knocked up the landlady and told her what we had come about. She looked at us in surprise.

'Miss Venn has gone to London – she went half an hour ago, and took all her things with her – she's not coming back.'

I couldn't believe the news that Marjorie Venn had gone without saying a word to me, especially after all she had told me that afternoon. I had done my best to persuade her to go to London, but she had said she was staying until John Field's affairs were cleared up; and here, without the slightest warning, she had disappeared.

'What did I tell you?' said Gurly. 'I knew it, my boy. You oughtn't to have let her out of your sight –'

I didn't take any notice of him.

'How did she leave? When did she make up her mind?' I asked the widow.

According to her story, a note had been delivered to her and she had gone out immediately, not even putting on her hat. She was gone a quarter of an hour, and when she came back she seemed agitated and went straight up to her room and began packing. The landlady knew this because she had gone up with a glass of milk which the girl usually took before she went to bed. She found her putting her things into a suitcase, and Marjorie told her she had been called to London on very urgent business, and that a car was coming for her. It arrived a few minutes later.

Exactly what kind of car it was the landlady could not say, because it had driven through the village and had pulled up by the side of the road, and all that she saw was its tail light. Marjorie had carried her own suitcase to the car, and paid the woman her lodging money, and that was all the landlady knew.

I went to the village inn, but could find nobody who had seen the car.

Even the village policeman could give me no information. Although the place was not on the highway to anywhere, cars frequently passed through the street. The news knocked me out, but old Gurly was chortling with joy.

'What did I tell you?' he shouted. ' She's bolted! She knew I was here, of course – '

'That's enough to make any woman bolt,' I snarled at him, 'but not a girl like Miss Venn.'

We took the car on to the first police control post, but they could tell us nothing. Any number of cars had passed, none of them so suspicious looking that the sergeant in charge felt called upon to pull it up.

'The car might have taken a circuitous route,' suggested Gurly, and for once in a way his was an intelligent suggestion.

There were half a dozen byways, but unless the car was moving in a circle it must pass one of the 'barrages'.

Driving back to the house, Gurly let himself go – he was more Gurlyish than ever I remembered him.

'It's the obvious things that always escape the ordinary police officer's attention,' he said. 'The moment I came into the house, my suspicions were on that girl. I worked it out a dozen ways, and I came to the conclusion that the only person who could have killed Field – '

'And shot Veddle?' I suggested.

'Why not?' said Gurly.

He was the sort of man who, when he gets into an argument and finds himself cornered, raises his voice to a shout. I kept him shouting all the way back to Lone House.

So far as I knew, the girl had no friends in London and the only thing to do was what Gurly did – circulate a description to the hotels and ask for notification of her arrival. Gurly would have sent out an 'arrest and detain' order, but I stopped that. After all, he's a member of the police force, and I didn't want Scotland Yard to look foolish.

From all our searchings and examinations that day, one or two important facts had come to light. The first of these was that Veddle was the man who had shot at me and at Max Voss. He had used an automatic; the back fire from the cartridge had burnt and blackened his hand. He had made some attempt to get the stain off, but it was very visible; and to prove my theory I found, on a re-search of the cottage, a spare box of ammunition.

We went over together, Gurly and I, and at Mr Voss's invitation went up to the house to supper. Before we went in I told the superintendent of Mr Voss's request, and naturally he took the opposite view to me.

'I quite agree – there's too much publicity about police affairs, Minter. The reporters would only have come down and got a sensational story, and taken away all the credit that's coming to me.'

Now, the curious thing about the Lone House murder was that we'd only had two local reporters on the job. As a rule, in cases like these the whole countryside is overrun with newspaper fellows; but you've got to remember that it wasn't called 'The Lone House Mystery' in the first two or three days. Only four people outside police circles knew how the murder had been committed – even the servants knew no more than that Mr Field had been found dead, for they were all out at the time of the murder, and we tied them all up to secrecy by promising them that they wouldn't lose their jobs (Miss Venn did that for me) if they kept quiet.

So I didn't think the story had reached the press, though I found later that one of the local reporters had phoned a column to an evening newspaper.

There was another reason why I thought the press would miss the Veddle killing. Big police cases usually go in threes, and just then the Tinnings case was holding down a lot of space in the newspapers – it was a poison murder, and a fashionable actress was in it, and, as I happened to know, most of the star men of the London press were quartered in a little town to the north of London, where the suspect lived. But, as I say, I was wrong.

One of the first questions Mr Voss asked me when I went in was whether there was anything about Veddle's murder in the evening newspapers. He had had them all sent down from London, and they contained no reference to the crime, but he was worried as to whether they were in the later editions. I wasn't in a position to tell him, because I never read newspapers except when they contain the account of a trial where I have been specially commended by the judge.

It was the next day that I found that the murder had been splashed on the front page of an evening newspaper.

Naturally, Gurly and Mr Voss became best friends. Gurly has got a weakness for monied people. I had asked him not to discuss the case with Voss, because, as I told him, I didn't want him worried; but we hadn't been seated at the table for five minutes when Gurly started throwing off his theories and deductions.

'You know the girl, Mr Voss?'

Voss looked at him quickly.

'Miss Venn? Yes – why?'

Gurly smiled and spread out his fat hands. 'Who else could it be?'

I thought that Voss was going to have a fit. 'You don't mean to tell me that you suspect Marjorie Venn – '

I think he was going to say something rude, but he checked himself.

'Yes, I do,' said Gurly; 'and the fact that she's disappeared tonight – '

Voss pushed himself back from the table, staring at my thick-headed colleague.

'Disappeared? What do you mean – ?'

I thought it was time to step in.

'She's gone away, Mr Voss – left at a few minutes' notice.'

'When was this?'

He reached out his hands, gripped the edge of the table and pulled the wheelchair back to where it had been, and he seemed to have got the better of his annoyance.

Gurly told him, because Gurly is the sort of man who must speak or perish.

'Just tell me what happened to this young lady,' Voss interrupted him. 'I am very much interested in her; in fact, I had thought of asking you to introduce me. She may want work – '

'Work!' said Gurly. 'My dear fellow, that's the whole point – she's his heiress.'

'Field's?'

I never saw such a blank look of unbelief in a man's face.

'He left her all his money,' Gurly went on, rushing down the road marked 'Angels only'. 'That's my point! She had everything to gain by his death . . . '

He ambled on, but Voss wasn't listening to him. He was staring at me.

'You never told me this, Mr Minter,' he said. 'It is amazing news. Why did he leave her the money? Was there anything – wrong?'

Each question came like the snap of a whip, and as I didn't want Gurly to explain, I told him just as much as I thought an outsider ought to know. I saw the relief in his face before I had finished.

'Conscience, eh? The girl's father was his partner, you say? This rather complicates matters.'

'Upsets your pet solution?' I asked him, and he nodded.

Then without warning he switched on to another subject.

'Have you seen Garry Thurston? He hasn't been up today. I think he ought to know about Miss Venn's disappearance – have you told him?'

He snapped his finger at the butler, who came back with a telephone; it had a long cord attached, and at the end a plug which he pushed into a socket in the wall.

I didn't say anything; I was anxious to know just what Mr Garry Thurston would say, and would have given anything to listen in and discover his reaction – that's the word, isn't it?

Voss jiggled the hook impatiently and presently he got through. He asked one or two questions, and I could tell he was talking to the servant.

'Garry's gone to bed.' He covered the receiver with his hand. 'Do you think I ought to get him up?'

Before I could reply he was speaking again.

'Yes. Tell him I want him. It's very urgent.'

He waited some time, and then: 'Hallo! Is that you, Garry? It's Voss speaking.'

He was silent for a while, evidently listening to what Thurston was saying at the other end.

'Yes,' he said at last, and then again: 'Yes.'

Once he started to interrupt Thurston, but he did not ask the question which I knew was on his lips. I saw his face go paler, and his bushy eyebrows meet, but he said nothing which would tell me what the conversation was all about. Then, to my surprise, he said, 'All right,' and hung up the receiver. He handed the instrument to the butler and met my eye.

'Well,' said I, 'you didn't seem to let him know very much about Miss Venn?'

He had no answer at once, but sat looking at me for quite a long time.

'No, I didn't ask him any questions: he told me all I wanted to know,' he said. 'Miss Venn went to London on Garry Thurston's advice. She went because he thought there was danger to her and – '

Bang!

The glass in the big oriel window smashed and splintered. Something hit the decanter in front of him and cut the neck off as though it had been sliced by a knife. For the second time in twenty-four hours somebody had shot at him.

ELEVEN

How quickly can a man think? Not a second had passed between the shot being fired and the moment I jumped to my feet, but I had travelled nearly twelve thousand miles, I had lived over the life of Field and had gone over every aspect of his killing – and I knew the murderer. I knew him as I stood by that table, half twisted round towards the smashed window. I knew just why that smoke signal had been used in Tadpole Copse, and why I had found the print of the man's foot on the soft earth outside Field's study.

A second? It could not have been a tenth of a second. I'll do Gurly justice: he was out of that room before I could say 'knife', and I was not far behind him. We flew into the hall, over the terrace – there was nobody in sight. The grounds were as black as pitch; we could see nothing. Our only hope was that the couple of men we had left on duty patrolling the river bank near the copse would have heard the shot and might have seen the man who did the shooting, but although they hurried up to the house, they had met nobody.

It was nearly one o'clock before I left Voss. I intended putting my men inside the house, but Gurly wouldn't hear of it.

'I'll stay with Mr Voss,' he said, 'and if I am not as good as any two flat-footed policemen, then it's about time I resigned.'

I had my own views on that subject, but did not give them. What I did do was to take him aside and tell him that for the next twelve hours he must not let Voss out of his sight.

'You had better carry a gun,' I said.

He roared with laughter.

'If I see the gentleman who did the shooting, he will be sorry even if he carries two guns.'

Which was all very fine and large, but didn't impress me.

He went into Voss's bedroom and closed the shutters. He had a camp bed brought, and as soon as Max Voss was inside the room he had the camp bed put right across the door.

A lot of people think I am brave, but I'm not. I was in a bit of a funk when I walked down to the Flash, even though I had two police officers with me, for I knew that somewhere lurking in the darkness was the man who had tried to kill Voss.

I was absolutely dead for want of sleep, but before I lay down I had several little jobs to do, and one of them was to go through the money I had found in Veddle's pocket, count it and seal it up ready to be sent to the Yard in the morning.

Counting that money took me longer than I had expected – it was two o'clock – because that money spoke and confirmed all that had come to me when the shot was fired.

At half-past two I lay down on the bed, but I could not sleep. Being over tired is almost as bad as not being tired at all. I lay there thinking about Veddle and John Field and the girl, Marjorie Venn, and she came into my thoughts more frequently than either of the other two.

Once I thought of getting up and making myself some tea, or pouring out something stronger, but I turned over again on the other side and tried to drop off.

As a matter of precaution I had planted my two men halfway between the house and Tadpole Copse. I don't know whether I am sorry or glad I did that.

I couldn't sleep. I was absolutely like a wet rag, and, getting up, I walked to the window. The dawn was beginning to break. There was just enough light to make shadows. I thought it was a tree in the middle of the lawn – a little tree I had overlooked – until I saw it move towards the water's edge.

'Who is that?' I shouted. 'Stop, or I'll fire.'

I didn't have a gun, but I thought the threat would be enough. Then I saw that it was a woman who was running towards the river, and my heart jumped, for I recognised the figure in the dawn light – it was Marjorie Venn!

I rushed out of the room, switching on the light as I went, and ran down the stairs. The front door leading to the lawn was wide open, so was the door of the study. When I got to the lawn I could see nothing. On the river's edge there was no sign of a boat.

I blew my whistle for the two men. Before they could come down I went back to the house and into the study. The safe door was wide open. The safe had contained a number of documents, and I could not see for the moment if any had been taken. Then, turning my head, I saw on the hearth a little bundle of ashes that was still smoking.

You know how paper burns: it leaves the letters all shiny and visible against the black background. I didn't need my glasses to know that the heap of ashes that was smouldering was the last will and testament of John Field, the will that had left all his money to Marjorie Venn.

I remembered it being in the safe. I remembered too that Marjorie had a key to the safe and a key to the front door.

By the time I finished my examination I heard my name called from the other side of the Flash. The two men had come down to the water's edge, and I ordered them to cross, as the motor-boat was on their side of the lake. They had seen nobody, heard nothing but my shout.

It was getting lighter and things were becoming visible. I was so certain that it was impossible to pick up the traces of Marjorie Venn that, having given the men some instructions, I went back to the study, lay down on the sofa and was asleep in a few minutes.

I suppose an old man does not require the amount of sleep that a youngster needs. The study clock was striking seven when I woke. I had taken a big glass cover which was over a piece of native carved ivory and had put it over the ashes in the grate before I lay down. The nature of the document was as plain as the daylight that showed it. There was the will, and I wondered if a burnt will could be proved. But would Marjorie Venn want to prove it? I wondered for a few minutes whether it was she or the negress who had burned away a fortune. No – I couldn't have mistaken Marjorie.

While the servants were getting breakfast I sat down at the table, took out some paper and wrote out the case as I saw it. That is a weakness of mine. I like to put A to B and B to C. In half an hour I had the whole of the case laid out as I understood it. Exactly what was the beginning of the trouble, and – to me – what was the end. It was not a very long document; it took me nine minutes to read to the chief constable (I got him out of his bed) and to receive my instructions from him.

Our chief constable is a very sensible man who trusts his subordinates, and apparently he did not send Gurly down, but Gurly had sent himself down on the promise that he would not interfere with me. Maybe the chief constable was lying when he said that, but it sounded true.

I finished the telephone talk, went up and had a bath and shaved. When I came down the two night watchers were on the lawn, waiting to be dismissed. If they expected me to put them to bed they were entitled to a grievance. I crossed the Flash with them and we went up to Mr Voss's house together.

He was an early riser, and his staff were usually up and about when most servants were thinking of turning over for their last little snooze. Even the butler was on his job.

'Mr Gurly is still asleep,' he said.

'What time does Mr Voss wake up as a rule?' I asked.

He told me that he usually took in the early-morning tea about eight o'clock when Mr Voss had a late night, and seven when he had an early one.

'I was bringing it up now,' he said.

Gurly was snoring like a pig. I didn't kick him, because he was my superior. I merely made a few faces at him – that didn't harm anybody.

He took a long time to wake up.

'Hullo, Minter!' he growled. He was never at his brightest in the morning. 'What's doing?'

I told him I had come to see Voss, and, getting up, he cleared away his bed.

'I haven't heard from him all night long,' he said as I knocked at the door.

'He doesn't seem to hear us now,' I said, and knocked again.

There was no reply.

I hammered on the panel, but still there was no answer. Peeping down through the keyhole, I saw that the key was still in the lock, and sent the butler to find a crowbar. I knew there was one hanging in a glass case with a fire hatchet farther along the corridor.

With the crowbar I forced the door open and walked in. The room was empty; the lights still burnt, and the closed curtains kept out whatever daylight there was. But the room was empty, and the bed had not been slept in. Max Voss had vanished as completely and as mysteriously as Marjorie Venn!

TWELVE

Pulling aside the curtains, I saw that the shutter was unfastened and that one of the windows was ajar. There was no ladder against the portico; I knew that, because I should have seen it when we came to the house.

Gurly was absolutely shaking with excitement.

'How did they get him away? He's a pretty heavy man to carry, and I heard no sound. Have a look at the balustrade – there'll probably be blood on it . . . '

He was firing off directions to the butler when I left him.

I had Voss's car brought round and went straight to Garry Thurston's house. I expected he would be up, and I wasn't disappointed. He was strolling on the lawn before the house, and he must have been out and about for some little time, for he was wearing tennis flannels, and told me as calmly as you please that he was cooling off after a set.

'Does Mrs Field play tennis?' I asked sharply, and he smiled.

'Mrs Field went to London last night,' he said very deliberately, 'and her son. She told me all I wanted to know. It wasn't very pleasant hearing for me, but then, I knew much worse before she came.'

I sort of scowled at him.

'That sounds like chapter one of a thrilling detective story,' I said.

'The last chapter,' he answered. 'I hope I haven't given you a lot of trouble, Mr Minter – I certainly didn't intend to. The fact is, I've had a perfectly dreadful few days, and I have been so engrossed in my own business that I haven't troubled very much about other people's feelings. How is Mr Voss?' I didn't answer him. 'Is there anything you want to see me about?'

'Yes, there is,' I said. 'Young man, I warn you that I'm out for blood. I've no respect for you nor your manor house nor your money nor – '

'Anything that is thy neighbour's,' he smiled. 'I realise that, super-intendent. I can help you up to a point, and tell you the truth up to a point. Beyond that I am afraid I cannot promise either to be helpful or veracious.'

He pulled up two wicker chairs and, putting them facing each other, sat down in one of them. I didn't feel like sitting; besides, a man standing up has got an advantage when he's cross-examining a man who's sitting down. One of the best lawyers at the Bar told me that.

'Last night,' I said, 'Miss Marjorie Venn left her lodgings very hurriedly – '

'In a motor-car,' said Garry Thurston coolly. 'Somebody sent a note for her, and that somebody was me. I wanted to see her very, very particularly, and I had something to tell her which induced her to go away with me.'

His frankness took my breath away.

'It was you who brought the car for her?'

He nodded.

'And took her to London?'

'No.'

'Where did you take her?' I asked.

He looked towards the house.

'She's there – in fact, she has been there since last night.'

'And she hasn't left the house all night?' I said sarcastically.

'As to that, I am not prepared to say,' said Garry Thurston. 'If she strolled with me in the night you may be sure she had a very good reason. She is not the sort of young lady who does things without a very good cause.'

His cheek was breathtaking.

'She's in the house – can I see her?'

He nodded. 'She's changing. We've been playing tennis all the morning.'

'Have you been near Voss's house?' I asked.

He shook his head. 'No.'

'Do you know where Voss is at this moment, and who took him away?'

He looked at me steadily.

'I've told you all that I'm going to tell you,' he said. 'Fortunately, you cannot put me in a torture chamber; more fortunately still, I am a very rich and influential young man. Not,' he added, 'that that makes a great deal of difference to you, Sooper. When I say that I am paying you a compliment. But your immediate superiors are not going to make the mistake of prosecuting me unless they have a very excellent basis for their prosecution. I did not murder John Field or Veddle; I did not fire at you – I have an idea Veddle did that. In fact, I have done nothing for which the law can touch me.'

I waited till he had finished, and then: 'Are you quite sure about that, Mr Thurston?' I asked quietly. 'Are you absolutely certain that in the past eight hours you have done nothing for which I can put you in the dock?'

He smiled again.

'Come along and have breakfast,' he said, but I wasn't going to allow him to blarney me.

I wanted to see the young lady, and he made no objection. She came down into the big library a few minutes after I had seated myself.

Marjorie Venn was very pale, but I never saw a girl who was more composed or surer of herself. There was a look in her face that I had never seen before, a sort of – what's the word? Serenity, that's it – that made her like somebody new.

She gave me a little smile as she came in, and held out her hand. As I wasn't Gurly I took it.

'Now, young woman,' I said, 'will you explain why you came to my house in the middle of the night?'

'It was to be my house,' she said, her lips twitching. 'Yes, I'm not denying it, superintendent: I did come into the study, I did open the safe, and I did burn Mr Field's will.'

'Why on earth?' I asked her.

'Because I didn't want the money. It belongs to his wife. It was her devotion which helped Field to find the mine. Every penny of it belongs to her and her child. It would have been easy to have accepted the will and to have handed the money and property to her,' she went on, 'but I didn't want my name associated with Mr Field in any way.'

I didn't take my eyes off her.

'And so you prefer to be a poor woman?'

'Miss Venn will not be a poor woman,' Garry broke in. 'There are two reasons why she will not be, and one of them is that she and I are to be married next week.'

I played my trump card. 'With your father's consent?' I asked her, and her colour changed.

'Yes,' she said in a low voice, 'with my father's consent.'

Garry Thurston was looking at me. I felt his eyes searching my face, and I got a little kick out of the knowledge that I'd given him a bit of a shock.

And then I dropped all the friendly stuff and began to ask her questions. Any other girl would have been rattled, but she fenced with me so cleverly that at the end of half an hour I knew no more than I had at the beginning, and, what was worse, she hadn't given me a handle that would help me to force her to speak.

When I got back to Hainthorpe I found Gurly had collected half the Berkshire constabulary and had organised a grand search of the grounds.

'I'm looking for a well. There must be one in the park somewhere . . . A gardener told me that he'd heard there was such a thing.'

'What do you want with a well?' I asked. 'Have the taps gone dry?'

But he was the sort of man who must have a well and a dead body to round off any case in which he was engaged. I often think that Gurly got most of his ideas of police work out of these sensational stories that are so popular nowadays.

I didn't trouble to look for the well, but put through a call supplementing the one I had sent from Garry Thurston's place. But I knew just how small my chance was, and I wasn't disappointed when by noon the County Police reported blank. But I knew London was working, that the ports were being watched, and that every train that drew out of town, or pulled into a seaport, was being combed for my man.

It was early in the afternoon that I got the message from the Bixton Cottage Hospital. Bixton lies on the river; it would be one of the healthiest places in England if it wasn't for the weir, which provides eighty per cent of the casualties that go into the red brick cottage which is called a hospital. That weir is a pretty dangerous spot even in daylight, and doubly dangerous to a man who's rowing for his life in the dark and tries to land in order to avoid observation from the lock.

When they took him out of the water he was so near dead that the policeman who had heard him shout and went in after him didn't think he was worth artificial resuscitation; but being an amateur, and having just passed through his first-aid course, he had a cut at it, and nobody was more surprised than he when he heard the drowned man breathing.

He didn't recover consciousness till round about lunchtime, and the first name he mentioned was that of Superintendent Minter.

They phoned me and I drove at top speed to the hospital. I had to wait for an hour, because the doctor wouldn't have him wakened, and I was taking tea with the matron when the nurse came for me, and I walked into the little ward and straight up to the bedside.

'Hullo, Wills!' I said. Veddle's brother lay on the bed, looking more dead than alive. I could see he was frightened, and I knew why.

'You were a bit excited last night, weren't you?' I asked him. 'That shot you fired at Voss wasn't any too good. You shouldn't have missed him.'

He looked away.

'I didn't shoot at anybody,' he said sullenly. 'You can't prove that I shot at anybody.'

And this was true. If I was going to get a story out of Wills I'd have to hold off on that shooting charge until he did a little confessional work, and I rather fancied he was too wide awake to tell me much.

He didn't seem inclined to say anything, and for a long time he just lay, avoiding my eyes and ignoring my questions. Then, suddenly: 'You've got nothing on me, Sooper, except the disciplinary charge – did they give you my brother's statement? It was in my pocket – I don't think it's been thrown away. I've been carrying it ever since he handed it to me the other night. He knew something was going to happen, and he said he was taking no chances – he had the whole story written in case somebody got him, or they framed up a charge against him. It's written on the back of a calendar and one sheet's missing. But there's nothing against me in it, Sooper. You can talk about shooting as much as you like, and you can be as suspicious as you like, but you can prove nothing. I helped my brother because he's the only pal I ever had. I took the job down at Lone House not to protect Field but to find out something my brother wanted to know.'

It was perfectly true, what Wills said: there was no evidence against him. We never found the gun he used when he shot at Voss; but in those loosely written pages that I read carefully that night I discovered the reason for the shooting.

THIRTEEN

I'm not giving you this document word for word. It was long, and a lot of Veddle's statements were wholly inaccurate.

Field and his partner Venn (he afterwards called himself Voss) located a mine in Africa. Venn, who was married to a charming colonial girl, sent her to England, where her child might be born, and the two partners continued their search. The mine was located through the instrumentality of a native chief, whose daughter Field married.

He tried also to secure from the chief, his father-in-law, a supply of raw gold that was in the village, and, when this was denied him, attacked the village, himself leading a hostile tribe. At the time Venn was living in the chief's hut, a very sick man. He cared very little what became of him. News had reached him that his wife had died in childbirth. He did not know then, or until many years afterwards, that the letter which came to him was written by Field, designed to drive a sick man to suicide.

Field went back to England, an immensely wealthy man, quite confident that his sometime partner had died in the forest. He did not take his black wife with him – she followed, with her child, and located him. She was missionary-trained, spoke good English. Even she did not know that Voss was alive.

He had wandered from one tribe to another, careless of his fate, and quite ignorant of the fact that his partner had found and was working the mine they had sought, or that the attack upon the village had been instigated by Field. He only discovered this when, as a comparatively wealthy trader, he returned to the old village and received from the dying chief a legacy which made him a very rich man – the major portion of that store of crude gold which Field had taken such risks to procure. For the risks were very real. He was working his mine under charter from the Congo government, a charter which would have been instantly revoked if his share in the rebellion had been traced.

Without any very hard feeling against the man who had treated him shabbily, Venn came back to England, and again an accident revealed the truth. The letter he had received in the forest, telling him of his child's death, had been written by Field. Venn's wife had died in poverty a year before he arrived in England, and the child, he learned to his horror, was in Field's employment.

A property which was adjacent to Lone House was on the market, and Voss obviously sat down cold-bloodedly to plan the murder of the man who had allowed his wife to starve, and who now, for all he knew, was victimising

Marjorie Venn. He must prepare his alibi in advance, and he appeared in the county as a man who had lost the use of his legs, could not move except in a mechanically propelled chair. He had the house altered, lifts installed, all the paraphernalia of infirmity were gathered, and the legend of the cripple who could not walk became very well known throughout the county.

He must have been something of an artist in his way. I have met men like that before, but Voss, or Venn, could give points to all of them. He reconnoitred the ground, decided exactly the dramatic manner in which his crime should be committed, and waited patiently for the right assistant to turn up.

Veddle was the man: an ex-convict, utterly dishonest, a man who read his employer's letters, and who, to Venn's consternation, surprised his secret. From that moment Veddle was doomed – from his statement it looked as though he was under the impression that his fortune was made.

Voss seized the opportunity to reveal his whole plan to his subordinate. It promised untold riches to this blackmailer – for Veddle had made another discovery, namely, that Marjorie Venn was his employer's daughter and would one day be a very rich woman. He kept his secret to himself, not even hinting to Voss that he knew as much, and in his clownish way he tried to make good with the young lady.

He had a grievance himself against Field, who had beaten him up, and he became the more willing to help his employer towards his revenge.

You will remember that Mr Voss always wore a grey check jacket and a white hat? On the day of the murder Veddle was waiting in the copse dressed exactly like his master. As the electric chair went into the wood it stopped, and the two men changed places. Veddle had received careful instructions – that was in the first clue I found. He was to go up the hill, stop at a certain bush, turn at a certain stone, so that he faced Amberley Church. In this position he would be visible for miles around. He would also have a commanding view of Tadpole Copse.

The moment he received the signal, he was to come down the hill in third speed. Voss had chosen his man well. Wills, the watching detective, had been got rid of through his brother. The moment the chair moved on, with Veddle in the seat, Voss threw off his check coat and slipped into the water, swimming across the Flash, and made his way over the lawn to the study.

He may have carried a knife; it is unlikely that he went without arms; but the Sword of Tuna was easy to grasp. Field must have had his back to him when he struck.

You must remember that Voss wore nothing but a bathing suit. He was in the water and across the Flash in a few minutes; he was a powerful swimmer. Arriving back in Tadpole Copse, he found the smoke pistol that Veddle had ready in his overcoat pocket and fired his signal. The moment

Veddle saw this, he brought his car down the hill and through the wood. Here Voss was waiting – I don't know whether to call him Voss or Venn. He had dried his head and face roughly with a towel, which he had pushed into a hollow tree, and with his check coat and dummy collar, and a rug over his knees, nobody would have dreamed that the man in the chair that came out of one end of the wood was not the man who went in at the other.

Almost immediately Veddle got into his long coat and hid his clothes and made for his cottage. The moment a hue and cry was raised it was necessary to get Veddle out of the way. Full arrangements had been made, but Veddle was not taking any risks. He refused to leave the same night, and hid himself in his cellar.

I don't know how he discovered that his employer was double-crossing him. I think it may have been the fact that I was at the house.

The moment the hue and cry was raised Veddle lost his nerve and bolted. I found his money – the money that Voss had supplied him with and which was to get him out of England. I've reason to believe that he was actually hiding at Hainthorpe, in the house itself. It was afterwards that he went back to the cottage and hid himself in the cellar.

Voss was in a difficulty: he had to find a new supply of money. I knew exactly what had happened when I counted the money we had found on the dead body of Veddle, for one of the notes was splattered with ink; it was the same note I had seen in the possession of Max Voss.

The mystery of the shooting in the night was never thoroughly cleared up. I am satisfied in my own mind that Veddle was the would-be assassin, and that, believing his employer was trying to double-cross him, he had shot at him through his bedroom window. I don't like to think that Max Voss fired at me in the copse, and worked out a fake attack upon himself, but even this is possible.

There was somebody who knew his secret. The one man in the world he did not wish to know – that was Garry Thurston. Garry had a telescope on his terrace, and on the afternoon that Veddle, disguised as his master, went to the top of Jollyboy Hill, Mr Garry Thurston took a look at him through his telescope and immediately recognised the servant.

He was distracted because he was fond of Voss. He could not betray him. He was, I believe, bewildered, and then he heard that Field had a negro wife and wheedled the address where she was staying out of one of my men and went in search of her. It was she who told him the story of the two partners and in a second he guessed that Marjorie Venn was Voss's daughter. He wanted to get her out of the way. He wanted still more to save the life of the girl's father. Whether he assisted him to escape I cannot prove – escape he did and was never seen again in England.

That he killed Veddle in cold blood I am sure. Veddle had got on to his brother by telephone and arranged that they should meet in Tadpole Copse. He packed his suitcase, went down into the wood, handed over the statement to his brother, who was all along suspected. Wills rowed back to the Thames, never doubting that his brother would follow.

Naturally Voss didn't want the Veddle case to get into the papers: he knew that Wills would be on his track.

A queer case, an unsatisfactory case. I always look upon a murder case as unsatisfactory when nobody is hanged. At the same time I should not have liked Max Voss to have taken the nine o'clock walk: he was a decent fellow as murderers go.

The Dark Horse

When people get short on topics of conversation they say to me; 'Sooper, you ought to write a book.' And I always say: 'I got no time.' Anyway, superintendents of police don't write books. They know too much. And besides, I can't spell. Never could. There was a woman down at Wembley who used to throw my uneducation in my face every time I pinched her husband. He was educated. Wrote five hands, all different. And there was a lady down in Kent who used to report me regular to the Chief Commissioner because I didn't say 'my lady' to her – wife of a city sheriff or something. Anyway, she never asked me why I didn't write a book. She knew I was low.

In my young days police constables didn't have to do much more than read and write. The only etiquette they were supposed to know was never to give backchat to their superiors or argue with a man who threatened to punch 'em on the nose. But nowadays, when everybody's gone scientific and lots of policemen speak French, a chap like me would have no chance of promotion.

I got where I got on merit, as I was explaining to Mr Frank Dewsbury one night. I often tell people this, otherwise they wouldn't know, but would be thinking I got my promotion because the chief was sorry for me.

Mr Dewsbury is a man I respect very highly. Once upon a time I didn't respect him because he was a stockbroker and wasn't rich. I used to think he drank or abused other good habits, but apparently there was nothing wrong with him. He had a house in Elsmere Gardens, and some nights when I had nothing better to do I used to go in and have a chat with him. That's how I discovered he didn't drink – I'd take four whiskies to his two. So you might say he was almost a teetotaller. He was a tall young man, nearly as tall as me, a good looker, a bit of a boxer, and he was an officer in the Territorials. He had a high respect for me – in fact, he was as intelligent a young man as you could wish to meet.

But he wasn't rich. So far as I could discover, there are quite a lot of people on the Stock Exchange who haven't got a million. He was one of them. His uncle was Mr Elijah Larmer. I was sorry to hear this, because Larmer and I have never been best friends. He is a man as old as me, but he hasn't worn as well.

Larmer owns most of West Kensington – land and estates to him are what back gardens are to me and you. He lives on the outskirts of my division in a big, dirty-looking house that is so surrounded by shrubs and trees that you can hardly see it from the roadway. Rich? That man could buy the Bank of England and still have enough money left to buy lunch.

The first time I met him professionally was twelve years ago. He was the kind of man who liked to have a lot of ready money at his hand. I don't say that he distrusted banks, but in the estate agent's business, especially in his early days, most of the deals were done with ready money. He had a big strong-room built in his basement, and he often had as much as a hundred thousand pounds in that safe room of his. And naturally, being a mean old fellow, when he had that strong-room made he got the cheapest builder and the cheapest safemaker and used cut-price material.

Mean? He was so mean he used to count the pips in an orange. When they put the new heating into St Asaph's Church, he went twice a day to save his own gas.

As I say, I came into touch with him over this new strong-room of his. It was only a strong-room to a child with a wooden spade. When Harry Pinford went after it with a kit of tools it was the weakest strong-room you could imagine. They cut a hole through the strongest part of it one night and got away with eight thousand pounds.

'What are the police for?' he says to me (I was acting inspector at the time) when I went to see the job. 'Are they ornaments? I pay rates and taxes to be protected. Look at that strong-room! Burgled under the nose of the police!'

I pointed out that it was under his own nose too. I showed him the rotten lock on the kitchen door and the cheap fastenings on the pantry window and the burglar alarm that didn't go off because he'd been too mean to keep the batteries in order. He reported me for impertinence and threatened to have me broken. He got so that he used to think I was responsible. I took Harry about three weeks afterwards, but he'd planted the money. Larmer was like a lunatic when he didn't get his eight thousand back. He had a new steel door fitted and new burglar alarms.

'My uncle,' said Mr Dewsbury, 'is difficult.'

He was being very difficult with young Dewsbury, who was his uncle's broker. Larmer did quite a lot of speculating on the Stock Exchange and made money. And he had quite a number of friends who also did their business through Frank Dewsbury.

Frank was doing well when he met a girl, Miss Elizabeth Pinder, the daughter of a man who had once caught old Larmer over a law deal. Larmer didn't know anything about the engagement for a long time. When he did he sent for Frank.

'What's this dam' nonsense about the Pinder girl?' he said. 'I'd sooner see you dead than married to the daughter of that old crook Joe Pinder.'

'I'm very fond of her,' said Frank. 'In fact, I'd sooner be dead than not marry her. Be reasonable, Uncle Elijah – Betty is not responsible for her father's actions. Besides, he's dead.'

'Naturally he's dead,' snarled old Larmer, who had a working arrangement with the Almighty, 'but his daughter's alive! Didn't Joe Pinder play the dirtiest trick on me? Wasn't he a crooked-minded twister . . .' And so forth and so on.

I happened to drop in to dinner the night after. There was Frank pretending not to care, and there was Betty, a very pretty, straight-backed girl, who wasn't crying over the business but was looking rather serious. There was a sort of aunt there too. She spoke at intervals, saying the things she'd like to do to Mr Larmer. Most of 'em were strictly illegal.

'He's taking his business away from me, and I suppose his friends will do the same,' said Frank. 'He's also cutting me out of his will –'

'That doesn't mean a lot,' said Betty. 'He told you he was only leaving you a thousand pounds – all his money is going to mental hospitals.'

'If I had my way with him,' said the aunt, who was a Godfearing woman who wore a gold cross round her neck and a copper cross on her waist, 'I'd boil him in oil. A man like that doesn't deserve to live.'

She was Betty's aunt.

I've naturally got a very soft place for young people. They want all the sympathy that we old chaps can give 'em. They're so darned foolish. I never see a young man that I don't think of him as an oyster who's mislaid his shell. At the same time, I never thought I should lower myself to be sorry for a stockbroker. He was a good soldier – he was in the war at sixteen – and a good amateur theatrical player, and they tell me the way he handled a tennis racket would make Lenglen look like Cousin Jane from the country. But I doubt if he was a good stockbroker. I don't know what kind of brain you've got to have to be a good stockbroker, but he hadn't got it. I knew that the minute he told me he wasn't a millionaire.

I didn't see him again for nearly a month, but I heard through my sergeant, who wastes time picking up items about honest people that he ought to be using in the pursuit of his duty, that young Mr Dewsbury was having a bad time.

My sergeant – it was Martin at the time – got very friendly with Mr Dewsbury and used to call in every other night – not that that meant anything: he'd go almost anywhere for a free drink.

'He knows quite a lot about police work,' Martin told me. 'I've never seen a man so interested – I think he's going to write a book.'

About a week after this I saw Mr Dewsbury and Martin up West. It was the sergeant's night off, and he could do pretty well as he liked, but I was kind of curious. I am one of those old-fashioned detectives that can't deduce anything. If I see a man opening a window with a jemmy in the middle of the night, I deduce that he's a burglar, and if he shows fight on the way to the station I get a sort of deduction that he wants clubbing. I used to carry a small rubber truncheon in my right hip pocket, and it's been a good friend of mine. But working out the colour of a man's eyes from the cigar ash he's left on the library carpet has never been a hobby of mine. That's scientific and educated, and I'm neither.

So I didn't start deducing about him and Dewsbury being college chums, but I just started asking, which I've always found is the best way of getting information. It appeared that Dewsbury was very anxious to see some of the underworld. There's a special brand of underworld round the Tottenham Court Road that's just there to be seen. It doesn't mean anything, and whenever I show visitors round and take 'em to this exhibition, I always feel as though I'm deceiving innocent children. It's like being asked to take a man to see the dangerous snakes at the zoo and showing him the lizard house.

'But he knows as much about the game as I do,' said Martin.

'Which isn't much,' said I; for a senior officer should never lose an opportunity of keeping a young detective in his place. Vanity is the curse of the service.

'Soho didn't mean anything to him, so I took him along to the Grands and let him take a look at one or two of the boys. And, Sooper, Jim Mosker is in town – he slipped out as I went into the bar, but I saw him.'

Now, where Jim Mosker is, 'Dowsy' Lightfoot is, and naturally all my interest in Mr Dewsbury's first course in criminal jurisprudence got off the car and made way for Jim and his snaky friend.

Jim Mosker was one of the cleverest safe-blowers in Europe: a nice, quiet-spoken man, who could prove an alibi in three languages. He hadn't been in town for I don't know how long. Jim wasn't one of these vulgar, haphazard burglars that only go after the stuff when they're short of money and generally get caught with the goods because they haven't taken the trouble to reconnoitre the ground. Jim went after the big money in a big way. He'd take a year to prepare, and preparation with Jim meant the last button on the last gaiter, as Napoleon said. If it wasn't Napoleon it was Bismarck.

Before Jim Mosker did the actual work he knew the Christian names and family history of every clerk, cashier, messenger and office boy at the bank – he generally worked banks. He knew just what the manager's private trouble was, her name and what worried her. His partner was another kind. 'Dowsy' Lightfoot supplied any violence that the combination required. He had no conscience, no pity and no eyelashes. He was a pale, hairless man without feeling.

At the earliest opportunity I looked up Jim and found him at the Grands, which is a sort of high-class club for low-class people. It was run by Wilkie

Meed, an old-time boxer, and it was very well conducted, for Wilkie still packed a punch that hurt. In a way it was rather a healthy sort of place: you never saw funny people there, and a fellow who strolled in one night and asked for a shot of dope was taken to the hospital under the impression he'd had it. Just honest-to-God thieves, confidence men, screw-men, but always the élite of the profession.

I found Jim sitting at a corner table in the big bar, and of course that clever sergeant of mine was all wrong when he said that Jim thought he had missed being seen.

'How are you, Sooper?' said Jim, getting up and shaking me by the hand. 'Sit down and have a drink.' And when the waiter had come over, he said: 'Vermouth, with just two drops of absinthe and a little water.'

And mind you, he hadn't seen me for six years. What a memory!

'I saw a fellow here the other night: they tell me he's your sergeant, Martin. I didn't like to talk to him because he had a friend of mine with him.'

'How's Dowsy?' I asked, for there was no sign of the snake man.

Jim smiled. He was a chubby little man who wore rimless glasses.

'Dowsy? He's coming over tomorrow night. I'm getting rather tired of Paris, Sooper. This is the good little town, only you people won't leave me alone. All the time you think I am doing something unlawful.'

He went on in this way for a long time, and I let him have his spiel. I knew he'd been in France and Berlin, but he was not on the books and it was no business of mine to connect him with that big jewel robbery in Friedrich-strasse or an unpleasant little affair in Lyons.

'What's this joke about the gentleman who was with Martin being a friend of yours?' I asked.

Jim smiled quickly.

'He's a man named Dewsbury. I met him three months ago in Paris. A very nice fellow.' He shrugged his shoulders. ' I don't care two hoots whether he knows my sad story or not,' he said, 'but it might hurt his feelings if he had a heart-to-heart talk with you and heard I was a naughty boy. Not that I am,' said Jim. 'I'm spending what you would describe as my declining years regretting my foolish past. Thanks to a legacy which my aunt left me – '

'Let's keep to facts, Jim,' I said. 'Where did you meet this Mr Dewsbury?'

He'd met him at a big restaurant just off the Bois. Somebody introduced him, and they had driven out in Jim's car to Enghien and had a little gamble at the tables.

'It was a very mild affair,' said Jim, 'and there was no private seance afterwards. No, I liked the lad; there's something very straightforward and English about him.'

Which was Jim's way of saying that he thought Frank Dewsbury was a fool.

Now I knew Jim's method as well as I know the road to Clapham Common. That wasn't an accidental meeting in Paris. Jim was after big money – he'd never come to England unless.

After we'd had a couple of drinks Jim began to get truthful and surprising.

'I don't know why I lie to you, Sooper,' he said, in his frank, boyish way, 'but here's the whole strength of Dewsbury and how we met him. It was in a restaurant, but nobody introduced us. Dowsy had had four drinks and was full of danger. When we got to the restaurant we found Dewsbury sitting at our table. We were so late that the head waiter had handed over our park and told him he could sit there. And then Dowsy got a bit unpleasant and whipped in a quick one. It wasn't quick enough for this Dewsbury man, who ducked and landed Dowsy a short-arm jab under the heart that laid him out. Naturally enough, when the tumult and the shouting died, we got together like brothers, and that's how we came to meet him. And that's a fact. Of course, the head waiter said he didn't put Dewsbury at our table at all, but he'd just sat down and wouldn't be moved. The whole proceedings were very queer.'

I knew Mr Dewsbury often went to Paris. He had a great friend there, an estate agent who did a lot of business with old Larmer, his uncle. Just about then, trade was brisk, for some of the Russian nobility who had saved a bit of money were buying estates in England. Dewsbury told me this when I saw him the next night.

He was very cheerful except that he spoke about his uncle and Betty Pinder. He had already bought a house at Purley when old man Larmer came.

'The moral is, Sooper,' he said, with a little laugh, 'never count your wedding presents till after the wedding!'

He told me his business had dropped to nothing, and that every time he met Elijah, as he frequently did, the old man got him by the buttonhole and told him a new one against Joe Pinder.

'I should hate to hang for Uncle Elijah,' he said.

I asked him where he got his interest in crime, and he took me by the arm and led me back to his house. I'd never examined his library before, and I was surprised to find the number of books he had on the subject – almost as many as that bird I got hung over the Big Foot murder.

He told me that when he was in the trenches during the war he read nothing else, and he proved that he wasn't talking stuff when he told me the full history of Jim Mosker.

'Oh, yes, I knew them the moment I spotted them in Paris. I liked Jim, but the skinned one – ugh!'

I was interested. I was terribly interested.

'You didn't by any chance sit down at that table knowing they were coming and that Dowsy would start something?' I asked.

'Maybe I did,' said Mr Frank Dewsbury very carelessly. 'I thought it was a good way of getting acquainted. I tried the Sullivans first, but they're half-wits. Jim Mosker's got brains.'

I didn't ask him why he tried to get acquainted with the Sullivans, who are just second-class thieves in the take-it-as-you-find-it class.

I'd already reported Mosker's presence in my district. He came twice to see Dewsbury. Miss Pinder evidently heard about it, because she called at my lodgings one night.

'You're a great friend of Frank's, aren't you? And I'm a little worried, Superintendent. Frank is the dearest fellow in the world, but he's awfully generous and broad-minded, and I've got a feeling that it isn't good for him to be seen about with Mr Mosker.'

'You've met Mosker?' I asked.

She nodded.

'Yes; I don't like him. I don't know why: he's very nice and polite, but there's something about him . . . '

I didn't give her any biographical details. I thought it best to let Mr Frank Dewsbury do his own excusing.

'You see, Superintendent, what worries me so much is that just now Frank is awfully pinched for money. And knowing how desperate things are with him, I don't like to feel he's keeping bad company. He missed two engagements with me last week to dine with Mr Mosker.'

I soothed her down, but I was a bit puzzled. Frank Dewsbury was not the kind of fellow that'd get so desperate that he'd take a corner with a man like Mosker. On the morning of the 18th of June – that was a few days after I'd spoken with the young lady – Frank Dewsbury asked me if I could see him. I told him to come down to the station, because I was pretty busy, and he arrived in a car packed full of baggage.

He had a little country bungalow within a couple of miles of the sea, and he was going there to write the opening chapters of a book on crime, and he wanted a few facts about the organisation of Scotland Yard. It was the first time I'd heard there was any. It's not for me to knock my superiors, so I did my best to give him a good impression. I saw him off, and at about five o'clock that afternoon we got a trunk call through from his cottage, asking me how London was cut up for police purposes. When I say 'he asked me', I was out, but Martin, who is a rare talker, supplied him with all the information he wanted and more.

I didn't know, because old man Larmer didn't notify us, that at half-past three that afternoon a M. Lacoste arrived from Paris with twenty-four million francs. They were in twelve packages, each containing two thousand *mille* notes, and M. Lacoste was accompanied by a couple of armed guards.

He drove from Victoria to the old man's house, where Elijah and his lawyer were waiting to complete a big land deal. They had a glass of grocery wine together, the old man put the money in his new strong-room, and the Frenchman and the lawyer drove away together.

Nobody had seen Jim Mosker or his pal, but nothing is more certain than that they were on the spot and that the party had been watched all the way from Paris to Mr Larmer's place.

This house stood on an island site; most of the grounds were in front, and behind was a mews containing about eight garages called Steverny Mews. Above each garage was a little flat intended for the chauffeurs, but the old man had turned out all his tenants months before and was converting these garages into flats for artistic people. As everybody knows, artistic people would rather live in a converted stable provided the roofs are low and the stairs are ladders, than they'd stay at the Ritz-Carlton. That's why they're artistic.

He had a garage of his own but he had dismissed his chauffeur and sent his car to a local garage proprietor. At half-past nine that night a big limousine came to the mews, the driver got down and, unlocking the door of Elijah's garage, drove the car in, and the gates were closed behind them. This was seen by a policeman who was standing at the end of the mews. It was a dark night and raining a little, and the policeman thought no more than that it was the old man's car.

A quarter of an hour later a tall policeman called at the front door.

'I've come from the Superintendent. He says he hears you've got a lot of money in the house: would you like me inside, sir, or outside?'

Larmer didn't like me, but I guess he was pretty well relieved to see this tall policeman – did I tell you that Dowsy Lightfoot stood six feet two inches in his socks?

'I'm not going to pay any police charges,' he said, that being the first thought that occurred to him, but the policeman said there was nothing to pay and that it was a part of police duty, so Larmer let him stay in the kitchen.

Soon after there came a phone call from M. Lacoste. It was very important: could Larmer come at once as the deal might have to be cancelled? This touched him on his tender spot. Having the policeman in the house made all the difference, and he went out, first placing the policeman in the little passage that led to the strong-room. Naturally enough, when he got to the Ritz-Carlton he was met by a very nice young man who said that Lacoste had gone out to see the Governor of the Bank of England, and he sat the old boy down in the lounge and told him the story of his life.

*　　　*　　　*

I heard about the robbery at midnight. At three o'clock in the morning we found Mosker; he was lying on the side of the Chiselhurst Road amongst the grass, and Dowsy was lying on the other. They were both handcuffed, and Dowsy was fit for hospital because, as he told me later, he'd had a beating up that he'd remember all the days of his life.

'No, I haven't got the stuff,' said Mosker, when I interviewed him at the local police station. 'I've been doubled, Sooper.'

He then told me what had happened. The car they used for the job was a fast old limousine, one of the kind that has a luggage space on top and a sheet of mackintosh to keep the baggage dry. They had faked the car so as to look as though it were going on a week-end trip, with cardboard boxes under the waterproof. Jim Mosker was the driver; he went straight into the garage, locked the door, and waited till Dowsy was planted in the house. Once they got rid of old man Larmer, the rest was easy. They cut into the strong-room with the kit that Mosker had brought in the car, got the money, threw it into the limousine, and were out of the house long before the young man who was entertaining Mr Larmer had got to the place where he was vaccinated.

'We went straight for the coast. I'd arranged for a tug to take us across to Dunkirk,' said Jim, 'and it looked easy once we shook London astern. We'd got to a lonely sort of common; I don't know the place – Chiselhurst, was it? – when I saw a leg come over the side of the car, and I realised that we'd been carrying a passenger on top under the tarpaulin. How he got there I don't know. He must have got into the garage whilst we were operating, but that doesn't matter.

'Before I could open my mouth he was standing on the running-board, and he pushed a gun under my armpit.

'"Stop", he said. I couldn't see his face, but I could feel the pistol, and thought it best to stop, so I did. The light from the front lamps reflected back from the bushes, and the only thing I could see was that he had a half mask over the top of his face and a black moustache. Until then I thought he was just ordinary police. "Step down and step lively," he said, so I did. But Dowsy, who has never yet realised the inevitable, took a running kick at him. I don't know what he did to Dowsy – my poor pal just disappeared, and I didn't see him again till this feller hauled him out of the ditch and put the irons on him. By this time he'd got 'em on me, and Dowsy and I had to sit and watch our good earnings being dumped into a bag. Not that Dowsy saw much – he just lay there and groaned. I don't know what this feller hit him with but I think it had iron in it. That's all I can tell you, Sooper. I wouldn't have told you so much, if you hadn't found our tools in the car.'

'You don't know who the man was who robbed you?' I asked.

Mosker shook his head.

'No. It's a bit hard, Sooper. And after the trouble we took to find out all that young Dewsbury knew!'

It struck me at the time that young Dewsbury might have been doing a little enquiry work himself.

I made a trip to where the car was found, and, examining the road about a hundred yards farther along, I saw wheel marks: the diamond-pattern tyre of a light car. But there was no trace of the third man, and that afternoon I drove on to see young Dewsbury. I thought, being an expert on crime, he might give me a theory. Besides which, I wanted to have a look at the tyres of his car.

I found him working away very cheerfully, though he didn't seem to have written much. I think he'd been changing his tyres all morning . . .

I make no accusations against any man. I harbour no unkind thoughts. All I know is that when Mr Frank Dewsbury was married he went away in his own Rolls. And he's gone back to stockbroking. I think he's found out how to deal with money. And how to get it.

Clues

I've got a smart Aleck of a detective-sergeant in my division who is strong for clues. The harder they are the better he likes 'em. He reckons fingerprints are too childishly easy for a full-grown officer of the CID.

'I believe there is a lot in that tobacco-ash theory, Sooper,' he said. 'It's fiction, I know – but there's a lot of truth in stories.'

So I put up to him the well-known case of the State against Uriah – or, better still, Uriah against David with Bathsheba intervening.

The chief was saying the other day that there has been nothing new in murder crime since the celebrated Cain and Abel affair.

'In fact, Sooper,' he said, 'you can dig down into the Old Book and find parallels for most every case that comes up at the Old Bailey.'

Which, in a way, is true. All the same, crime was a mighty simple affair round about 3000 BC. If a feller didn't like another feller he just dropped him down a well or snicked off his head, and what happened to the snicker depended on the kind of a pull he had with the chief priest or the king or whoever was the man on top.

There wasn't any come-back with Uriah, for instance, and no complications. They just handed him up to the front-line trenches and sent him out single-handed to see what the Amalekites were thinking up for tomorrow's battle.

But if Uriah had had a tough brother Bill or a sister named Lou, there would surely have been trouble for David, and worse still if Uriah, instead of getting himself carved up by the enemy, had sneaked back to headquarters by a roundabout way.

The David I'm thinking of was a mean man named Mr Penderbury Jonnes, who owned three stores on Oxford Street and had a country mansion near Hertford, to say nothing of a flat in Hanover Square. I happened to know Pen Jonnes. He was a Welshman on the soft-goods side of the race. A tall, red-faced fellow with eyes like a puppy dog's and a moustache like a cavalry officer. We used to think that he was a bachelor in the sense that he hadn't any regular matrimonial arrangement. But this wasn't so.

He had a wife, though nobody seemed to have met her. She had been a shop-girl in one of his stores and he didn't find out until it was too late that her brother was Yorkshire Harry, the only cruiser-weight that ever went ten rounds with that Yankee fellow who held the title till some girl told him he looked grand in a dress suit.

Yorkshire Harry used to do a little blackmailing on the side, and he ran with the Stineys, who were cracksmen on the top scale. Anyway, Penderbury took the shortest way out of trouble and was married at the Henrietta Street Registry Office. I expect he was sorry, because Yorkshire Harry was caught the very next year and died in Gloucester Gaol from some fool thing.

I used to get a whole lot of anonymous letters about Penderbury – written in a woman's hand. Every second word was spelt wrong. Generally the letters had a Hertford postmark, and if half the things they accused Jonnes of doing were true, he's have lived permanently in jail.

It was then I found out about Mrs Jonnes and got a specimen of her handwriting. After that we didn't take too much notice of the anonymous letters, whether they were signed 'A Frend' or 'A lover of Justise'. Interfering between man and wife is the very last instruction in the police code. I gathered that Mrs Jonnes did not like her husband and let it go at that.

One letter I remember very well – I'll spell it according to my ideas of how it ought to be spelt: 'If he wasn't afraid that the police would come after him, why does he keep all that money in his safe ready in case he has to jump out of the country?'

As a matter of fact, I did know that Penderbury kept a lot of money in his safe near Hertford, and so did somebody else. Two burglars tried to 'bust' the house once and it came out at the trial. As the judge says, 'This is not a court of morality,' and people can do pretty well anything they like so long as they don't obstruct the police in the execution of their duty or drive a car without a licence.

Jonnes had a cashier named Banford – Horace Angel Banford. I never quite got the hang of that 'Angel' and I never asked him, though I knew him pretty well. He was one of those Adam's apple tenors who sang so well that nothing could improve him. People used to say what a pity it was that he didn't go to a master for a few lessons. He was that kind of vocalist. But he went fine at our police orphanage concerts, and that is where I came to meet him. He was a tall, thin, sandy man with hollow cheeks, short sight and a schoolgirl complexion, and the last idea that he'd start was that he'd ever qualify for that 9 a.m. walk from cell to gallows.

Crime and music were his hobbies. I was surprised, when he invited me down to his little flat in Bloomsbury, to find the number of books he had about criminals. But he was sensible with it – never thought he could spot a homicide by the colour of his eyes and the curious way he wagged his ears. One thing he was certain about.

'Nine out of every ten murderers wouldn't be caught if they weren't boneheads,' he said to me one night. 'A crime is like any other job. You've got to be efficient to hold it down.'

We were all alone because his wife was out. She went out a lot – she was a great dancer.

'She goes with a lady friend,' said Mr Banford. 'Personally, dancing bores me, but she loves it,'

That made it all right. Anything Dora Banford loved – dresses, dancing, pretty little jewels – was all right. Banford's salary was ten pounds a week – that's about fifty dollars American, isn't it? And he did everything on that – Bloomsbury flat, a well-dressed wife, jewels and dances.

And it can't be done.

I went again, because he had a book on the Leamington murder which he'd lent and was getting back, and naturally, as I was the man who pinched Pike Gurney, I wanted to see if the feller that wrote the book had given me all the credit I deserved.

I met Mrs Banford in the hall: she was pulling on her gloves when I went in, and I can tell you she was a peach. One of those fluffy little things with wild golden hair that never stays put. She sort of gave me a look under her long lashes and said (not out loud, but my receptivity is pretty good), 'Who is the old bird with the big feet?' or something equally interesting.

Horace Angel fussed around her like a nanny before a baby's first party. He sort of leant over her and fanned her with his wings. Down to the street door he went with her, got her a cab and put her inside, and then he came back with his silly, thin face all red and smirky.

'The best wife in the world!' he said.

I was with him for two hours and picked out all the bits in the book about me. I must say that the fellow who wrote it was an honest man and only made one mistake. He said I took Pike as he was going into the Branscombe House Hotel, when in fact I took him as he was coming out.

At one o'clock the next morning I had a pressing engagement with the reserves. We raided the Highlow Club in Fitzroy Square. We had information that Fogini, the manager, was selling booze out of hours and that everybody who went to the Highlow didn't go to dance. There was a baccarat game on the top floor, and there were all sorts of nice little private dining-rooms where people stayed who didn't play cards and weren't keen on dancing.

The raid went according to plan, and in Room 7 I found Mrs Banford and Mr Jonnes. They were sitting at a little table with a very large bottle of champagne, and as far as I could see when I opened the door, he was holding her two hands across the table. She snatched them away when I barged in, and I saw a puzzled sort of look walking alongside her fear – she was trying to place me.

Jonnes went redder than usual.

'What the devil is the idea of this?' he snapped.

'You're under arrest,' said I, 'for consuming spirituous liquor after the hours by law prescribed.'

Which is the classy way of saying that he was boozing out of hours.

That made his colour run.

'Can't this be squared?' he said. 'I'm Mr Jonnes, of Jonnes Mantle Corporation.'

He yanked out his pocket-book.

'Don't insult me with five,' I said, when he slipped me a note. 'My price is ten million. Who is the lady?'

Of course I knew, but I didn't let on. He seemed to have forgotten all about her.

'Oh –' he said, like a man who had to bring his mind down to trifles, 'she's Mrs Smith – an Australian lady.'

I ordered him down to the dance room, where my boys were doing a little asking, and he went. This Mrs Banford's face was the colour of chalk and she was going after him when I called her back.

'I'm playing favourites for the first time in years,' I said. 'There's a pretty good fire-escape at the back – I'll show you the way.'

I did more than that, I took her down and tipped off the man on duty to let her pass out; said she was a highness and we didn't want any highnesses in this kind of scandal.

Jonnes came up next morning before the Marylebone magistrates and got his fine, and so far as I was concerned there was the end of the lady who went dancing with a girl friend.

Only things don't work out that way in life, which is a story that's continued an' continued. About six months after this I stepped into the charge room at Limber Street Station, and what did I see? Horace Angel in the steel pen. He had the colour of a man who wasn't expected to live. Poor old Horace, caught with the goods. Two thousand pounds' worth of embezzlement on his soul. And there, resting his arm on the sergeant's desk, was Jonnes.

Horace Angel had nothing to say, or if he had he was short on speech. The jailer put him below and I strolled up to Penderbury Jonnes.

'He has been swindling me for years. I hate doing this, because I know his wife, poor little woman . . . But I trusted him. Why, I've even sent him down to Hertford with the key of my safe, where there are thousands of pounds . . .'

That was his end of it. When I interviewed Horace Angel in his dugout he gave me another slant to the story. It wasn't easy to get it, I can tell you, because when he wasn't weeping he was cursing Dora Banford and Penderbury Jonnes, and when he wasn't cursing Dora he was forgiving her, though I didn't notice that he forgave Penderbury much.

'We're going to start fresh when I come out,' he said. 'I never gave the little girl a chance, Sooper. All I wanted to do was read an' sing, and that's pretty dull for a woman. I've been a scoundrel and dragged her name in the mud. How that hound caught me I don't know – somebody on the inside must have seen the duplicate set of books – '

'Where did you make them up?' I asked.

'At home,' he gulped. 'God, what a fool I was! And they came straight to my flat and found them, Sooper. The hired girl must have been in their pay.'

I let him go on.

'What's all this about Jonnes and your wife?' I asked.

'Nothing!' he said, very loud, but by and by I got it out of him.

Horace Angel had a friend who took a part in a West End revue. This friend was a genuine tenor and had a couple of Come-my-love-the-moon-is-shining numbers. The queer thing about a stage tenor is that his throat is always going wonky. Just before the curtain goes up he strolls into the manager's office and says: 'Sorry, old boy, but you'll have to put on the understudy,' and naturally that leads to his having a lot of fuss made over him both before and after. But sometimes his throat does really go wrong, and Horace Angel, being a sort of floating understudy, was sometimes sent for to take his place.

One night a hurry-up call came to him – it was just after his wife had gone out to meet her girl friend – and Horace Angel went down to the theatre and made up. He was rather glad she was out because she knew nothing about his understudying – Horace Angel was a little sensitive on the point of his voice.

His entry was towards the end of the first act. He was halfway through that love and moon stuff when he happened to look into the stage box. And there was Dora and Mr Jonnes. They were right at the back of the box and he gathered that they weren't interested in the play.

He got through the numbers and went home. There was a row, I suppose – he didn't tell me anything about that. And a few weeks later Jonnes pinched him.

Now whether Jonnes knew all the time that poor old Horace Angel was robbing him, and kept quiet because of the pull it gave him, or whether the auditors made the discovery, I've never found out.

At the Old Bailey the judge took a serious view of the crime and sent Banford down for three years. Two days after he was sentenced, Mrs Banford paid the rent in advance, locked up the flat, and went to Paris. Mr Jonnes followed the next day.

I had a talk with Uriah at Wormwood Scrubbs.

'There is only one way to hurt Jonnes,' he said, 'and when I come out I'm going to do it.'

You don't take much notice of what newly convicted people say, and I passed it. I said nothing about Mrs Bathsheba except to lie up a message from her to say that she was bearing her affliction patiently. But he got to know when he was in Dartmoor. Every man has a friend who thinks that bad news is the only news worth knowing, and Horace Angel had several friends like that.

He said nothing; gave no trouble, went out of his cell at eight in the morning and had the key turned on him at four in the afternoon; sewed mail-bags, helped with the laundry and sang solos in the prison choir; and nobody guessed how Horace Angel's mind was slipping back to Lombroso and Mantazinni and his little crime library.

I never saw Jonnes and Dora together – not that I had many opportunities, but I never did. One of our inspectors who went over to bring back a bank clerk who had left London hurriedly with a block of the bank's assets, told me that she had a flat in the Avenue Bois de Boulogne (which is going some) but personally I knew nothing about that till later. But just about then I met Mrs Jonnes. The anonymous letters were piling up at the office and the chief was getting a little tired of reading 'em.

'Go down and see this Mrs Jonnes, Sooper, and tell her from me that until we get short on regular crime, we haven't time to investigate the chicken-chasing propensities of the modern husband.'

I went down to Hertford midweek, because Mr Jonnes would be in town, and after a lot of difficulty I saw his wife. She had been a good looker, but years of Penderbury had sort of put an A in her face; if you've seen the nose lines and the drooping mouth of dissatisfied ladies you'll know what I mean. She had a Cockney accent with a sort of whistle in it, and what she didn't say about Mr Jonnes was that he was a perfect gentleman and a model husband.

'I live the life of a dog,' she said. 'One of these days I'll poison him – I will! If my poor darling brother was alive . . . !'

I got in a word or two about anonymous letters and she gave me her views on the police and the way they allowed wives to be beaten and locked up in rooms without food and treated like dirt by the servants.

'One of these days . . . !'

Those were her last words to me, and somehow I didn't feel that they were quite idle, for in Mrs Jonnes's veins ran the blood of three tough generations on both sides of the family.

When Horace was released I made it my business to call on him. He was sitting in the dining-room of the flat going through a lot of letters that had come during his absence. I remember that one of them had a cheque for his performance the night he peeked into the stage box.

'I'm starting all over again, Sooper,' he said, and he was very cheerful. 'A friend of mine has offered me a job in Peckham – not a big salary but enough to carry on with.'

He did not mention his wife but he did speak of Jonnes.

'There is a man who ought to be out of the world,' he said, as calmly as though he was talking about rice pie. 'The more one thinks about Jonnes the more useless a creature he seems. He has never done a stroke of work for the money he has. His father left him the stores and he uses his wealth to corrupt the pure and the foolish.'

'Quite a lot of people ought to be out of the world, Horace Angel,' I said, 'and sooner or later they will be. Give nature a chance and she'll put everybody where they belong.' He smiled at this: a sour, crooked smile. This was a Thursday afternoon. On Saturday afternoon at four o'clock, Penderbury Jonnes went out of his big house at Hertford with a gun under his arm. He said that he was going to shoot rabbits. Field Towers – which was the name of his house – stands in about eighty acres of good rough shooting. The estate is surrounded by a wall except for about three hundred yards, where a bean-shaped covert of beech and pine trees separates his land from Lord Forlmby's estate. At about 5.35 one of Lord Forlmby's game-keepers, stalking a stoat, came through the covert and saw a man lying huddled up on the ground. He ran across the rough and saw that it was Penderbury Jonnes and that he was dead. He had been shot at close range through the right shoulder, and his gun was lying by his side.

The gamekeeper sent for the police, and just about that time I had taken over the duties of chief detective inspector in the absence on leave of Joe Frawlett. There are four chief inspectors attached to Scotland Yard, and these men have the four districts of London, so that when the Hertford police asked for assistance it was my job to go down.

I got to the Towers about nine o'clock that night. It was dark and raining, but on the advice of the local police the body hadn't been moved, and a ring of space had been kept clear around the hurdles which had been put up over the body.

'The man must have been killed by a discharge of the gun,' the doctor told me, 'though the wound is a very slight one. Probably a stray pellet reached his heart. One barrel of the gun has been fired, and the servants at the Towers say that they heard only one explosion.'

The gun had been carefully wrapped in oiled silk and taken to the house to be photographed for fingerprints. I had a talk with the Chief Constable of Hertford, who was on the spot.

'The shot was fired at about 4.15,' he said; 'the only person seen near the spot was a motor-cyclist who was sheltering from the rain under a hedge on Lord Forlmby's side of the plantation. And the only discovery we have made is this glove.'

He took it out of his pocket – a cheap cotton glove, right hand, slightly stained with mud and very damp.

'We found this at the end of the plantation,' said the chief constable. 'It was too dark to look for footprints and there is no other clue.'

I told off three of the Hertford police to make a search of the copse by hand-lamp, and then went up to the house to see Mrs Jonnes, and here I had my first shock.

She had left the Towers at some time in the afternoon.

'They'd been quarrelling all morning,' said the butler; 'the worst shindy I've ever heard!'

'Where did you see her last?' I asked.

'Going into the gun-room,' he said.

I made a search of the gun-room. Jonnes was a methodical sort of a man, who had little ivory labels on every stand showing the maker and date of purchase of every piece. And there were two blank spaces. One was the home of the gun that had been found by Jonnes's side, the other a new gun bought a week before.

I went up into Mrs Jonnes's room. The wardrobe door was open, but there had been no attempt to pack anything. I made further enquiries. Jonnes's two-seated car was gone – had been taken out of the garage some time between four and six.

I inspected the other rooms, and in one on the ground floor, which Jonnes used as a study, I saw the safe. The butler, who was beginning to get more at home with the police, and had lost the feeling that any word he uttered might hang him, became a little more chatty.

'The row was about a woman named Banford. He was throwing her in Mrs Jonnes's face, saying how wonderful she was. Mrs Jonnes went almost mad . . . she was a very jealous woman.'

About now the policemen I had sent to search the wood came back. They had made two finds. A rain-sodden sheet of newspaper in which something had been wrapped, and a small wooden box that somebody had hidden under a holly bush. The newspaper was a week-old copy of the *Echo de Paris*. The box was locked, but there wasn't much trouble in opening it. As a burglar kit it wasn't of much account. A couple of chisels, a jemmy, an electric torch, a key wrapped in tissue paper, a glazier's diamond and a folded square of fly-paper to hold a window pane when it was cut.

'That explains the glove,' I said. 'He carried them in his pocket to avoid fingerprinting – but who goes travelling around with the *Echo de Paris*?'

The key interested me. I tried it on the safe and it opened the door.

There was one man to see, and that was Horace Angel. By twelve o'clock I was ringing the bell of his flat. I was a little surprised when he opened the door to me. He was dressed in an old suit and a pair of slippers, but before the fire was a pair of wet boots, and over the back of a chair was hung a pair of trousers that were wet to the knees.

'Been out?' I asked.

He had been to Wembley Exhibition, he said.

Now Wembley ran a guessing competition. When you entered you received a card on which you wrote down your guess of the number of people who would pay for admission the next day. It was a green card, and was almost the first thing I saw lying on the table.

'There's a chance of a hundred pounds, Sooper,' he said, and smiled as he took up the ticket and handed it to me.

'What time were you there?' I asked.

'About four,' he said.

'You're a bit of a motor-cyclist, aren't you?'

He shook his head.

'I've never ridden one,' he answered. 'Why do you ask?'

Before I could say a word there was a knock on the hall door, and immediately afterwards another knock. I was nearest. I went into the hall and opened the door. A woman was standing there, so drenched, so miserably dressed, that I did not recognise her. There was a light on the landing, and she must have recognised me, for she cowered back as if I was going to strike her.

'Come in, Mrs Banford,' I said, and slowly she shrank past me into the dining-room where Horace Angel was standing by the table. He said nothing; his wide-opened eyes were staring at her as though she were a ghost.

'Hullo . . . Dora!' he whispered. 'My God . . . how awful!'

She looked as if she had found her dress on a junk heap. It was old and ill-fitting . . . I remember that there had been a sort of pattern worked in little beads. Some of the pattern was missing. Two or three threads were hanging loose, losing beads with every movement she made. Her hat was like a man's, shapeless and big and dripping from the brim.

'Hullo . . . Horry!'

The words seemed to strangle her, and though she spoke to him her eyes were on me – big, round, blue eyes, set far back in dark hollows.

'Where have you come from, Mrs Banford?' I asked.

She wore old boots that were soggy with rain and grey with mud; her skirt looked as if it had been soaked in water.

'From Dover . . . I walked,' she said breathlessly. 'I've been waiting outside to see you, Horry – I knew you were in London. I went to the Bloomsbury Garage and saw your old motor-bicycle: they said that you had been in two hours.'

I looked at Horace Angel – who couldn't ride a motor-bicycle – but he had no eyes for me. He was tugging his handkerchief from his pocket to wipe his streaming face, the handkerchief came out and something else – a white cotton glove that fell on the table. It was the left glove, an exact fellow to the other that had been found in the covert.

I said nothing, waiting . . . Dora went on: 'I've been in England four days . . . Jonnes had me put in prison . . . a French prison.'

'Why?'

She shook her head.

'I was mad . . . I don't know . . . the knife was on the table and I was mad.'

'You attacked him and you were put into a French prison: when?'

She put her hand before her eyes as if she was trying to think.

'A year ago. There was no trial, and when he did not appear to sign some papers they released me. They do that sort of thing in France. They paid my fare, third-class to Dover, and I walked.'

'I'm sorry.' Horace Angel was so hoarse that he barked the words.

And then she looked at him, I think for the first time. 'Are you? I'm past that, Horry . . . My God! if that man hadn't come into the wood – !'

'What's that?' I asked sharply. 'Which wood?'

She turned her head.

'There's somebody at the door . . . police . . . but you're a policeman, aren't you?'

Her numbed fingers snapped back the catch of the shabby bag she carried.

'I don't want this – '

She laid a tiny automatic on the table.

And then the door opened slowly and a woman came in. I must have forgotten to fasten the outer door. It was Mrs Jonnes – she wore an oilskin cloak. I noticed this because she kept her hands hidden under it. Her face was white and her eyes were like red lamps.

'You're Dora Banford,' she said.

Dora nodded.

And then the hands came into view and the shot gun. I snatched it from her before her fingers could curl round the trigger, and she dropped into a chair and burst into tears.

I don't exactly remember how I got them all three to the station, but when I got them there it looked as if my troubles were just beginning, for which of them to charge I did not know.

Jonnes's doctor saved me a lot of time next morning.

'The man died of heart failure, as I warned him he would,' he telephoned me. 'The wound was accidental – he probably pulled the trigger as he fell, and anyway it would not have killed a rat.'

And so nobody hanged. Not Horace Angel, who went to burgle the safe with a key that he'd pinched or copied years before; not Mrs Jonnes, who came after Dora with murder in her heart; nor Dora, who tramped to Hertford to settle accounts with the man who had broken her.

But the clues – gosh! I'll never get clues like those again!

Romance in It

Spending money (said the Superintendent) is an art. Have you ever noticed that when people come into money suddenly the first thing they do is to create criminals? It's a fact. They begin right, but they weaken on it. The feller who buys the winning ticket in the Calcutta Sweep always starts by saying that he's just going to jog along at his old job in the grocery department, and the girl who inherits a million dollars from her uncle in Australia tells the reporter that she wants nothing more than a little cottage in the country with roses up the garden path, but one of 'em ends by playing a system at Monte Carlo and the other finishes up as queen of the night clubs.

Neither could understand why swells who hadn't a quarter of their money lived twice as well. You've got to be educated from birth in money-spending: it must be kicked into you at school and at home – it's one of the hardest things a feller can learn.

I knew a bird who never quite learnt it. On the other hand, I know one who did. How many millions he had I've never discovered. Probably none. The moment a man lives in a big house and acts mean, people think he's a millionaire; but certainly Mr Johnson Goott was rich.

He had one child, a girl, and from information received I understand he intended marrying her to a peer of the realm. Instead of which she married a gentleman. I'm not trying to be funny – I know both the fellers. Lord What's-his-name's been married twice since then, and his second divorce is coming up to the courts in the New Year.

Elsie Goott met a young officer at a dance – his name was Fairlight, and so was hers a month after that.

Old Goott said some very unpleasant things about her and her mother, and what happened before she was born when her mother was staying in Scotland, and I hope for the girl's sake he was right, because it was no catch to have a lot of mean Goott blood running through your heart and important blood vessels.

Anyway, he cut her off with nothing and sent her young husband all the bills she'd run up before her marriage.

Captain Fairlight left the army and became a hopeless gambler: in other words, he started a poultry farm. Lot of army gentlemen do this: they like ordering chickens about.

That is how I came to know them. They were on my manor (to use a thieves' expression) when I was in charge of one of the outlying districts of London.

The only man I ever met who understood chickens was a fellow called Linsy, who was the cleverest confidence man in the business. Naturally he would. No chicken could even pretend she could lay eggs with Linsy unless she really could deliver the goods. And when, after knowing the Fairlights for about six months and seeing their stock going down three points a day, I felt it was time to give them a helping hand, I thought of Linsy and went and looked him up.

He was living in a handsome flat in Bayswater, and had a manservant and a maidservant, and maybe an ox and an ass in his back yard. And naturally he was going straight.

'The other game isn't worth the candle, Sooper,' he said. 'There aren't enough clever people in the world. They have to be clever to be caught – no real fool ever bought a gold brick or trusted you with a wad of notes to show you his confidence in you.'

I'm something of a kid myself and fairy stories go a long way with me, but I never believe that any habitual criminal is going straight to anywhere but the assizes. But I'm a polite man, naturally, and I can look as if I believed anything.

He was interested about the chickens.

'Funny how these amateurs always walk into that graft,' he said. 'I remember years ago – '

'Don't let's have any reminiscences, Mike,' I said. 'Can you do anything for these young people? I don't mind introducing you, because there's nothing to be made out of them.'

I'd seen his eyes light up at the mention of chickens. It was the one subject he really got enthusiastic about – he was the fellow that started the chicken farm at Parkhurst, or was it Dartmoor?

'Sure, I'll help you,' he said. 'And you can trust me to give 'em a square deal, unless they've got a breed I specially want, and then I'll try and buy it.'

I heard from Mrs Fairlight a few days after that he'd been down, but it was a month before I saw Linsy.

'That captain fellow knows more than most hen-feeders,' he said, 'but he hasn't enough capital. He wants a place about ten times as big, and I've told him to buy the farm next door – it's for sale. And he ought to put up some new runs and buy a few of Lord Dewin's prize birds. And he should run a motor-van to carry his stock to market. There's a fortune in that farm, with a fellow like Fairlight. What a woman she is, Sooper! You wouldn't think a so-and-so like Goott would have a daughter . . . '

I let him rave on, for I knew there was no harm in Linsy. He was naturally romantic; otherwise he wouldn't have been a confidence man, or at any rate a successful confidence man.

She wrote to the old man and asked him to lend her some money. He wrote back telling her he wouldn't, and didn't even put a stamp on the letter.

'Goott,' said Linsy thoughtfully, and I could see a look in his eye that wasn't quite lawful.

'Unless you want to find yourself sewing mailbags in Wormwood Scrubbs, keep away from Goott,' I warned him. 'He's so wide that you can't get past him.'

'Those are the kind I like,' said Linsy.

Now the funny thing about rich men is that things are always turning up to make them richer. A poor man can dig in his garden all day and never turn up a threepenny bit; but every time a rich man opens his door there's the postman waiting with a registered letter.

Goott had all sorts of successes. He was the only man that ever put money into a treasure-hunting expedition and got a profit on it. If he bought a property in the middle of the Sahara Desert, he'd find gold on it, and a brand-new spring would come up to wash it.

I don't know how he got his start, but I'll bet it was dishonest. He was so wide that even his cook never got a rake-off from the tradesmen. So that when a friend of Linsy's called at Goott's house in Brook Street – Linsy only did the very big jobs himself – with one of Linsy's cleverest little stories about an uncle dying in California and wanting him to distribute the money, Mr Goott didn't wait for the story to finish, but sent for the police.

Linsy's friend didn't even wait for the police.

I heard this from Superintendent Bryne, who was in control of that area. From certain peculiarities of the story I knew that Linsy was behind it, because the yarn wasn't as crude as I have made it. I was a little surprised, because Linsy isn't quite a sap, and must have known that that old con yarn could never get over in Brook Street – not at No. 274, anyway.

As a matter of fact, I heard the yarn at first-hand, because I happened to be up west, and I called on Mr Goott. He was a short man with a bald head and a black moustache, and what he didn't say about confidence men he said about the police.

'These fellows don't understand that I can smell money.' He spoke with a slightly Dutch accent. 'It's an instinct with me.'

He seemed unusually excited – I didn't know why. I couldn't guess that the sailor was waiting in the study for him to come back and continue the conversation.

The sailor had arrived that afternoon with a letter of introduction from a man in Leningrad. It was written on a thin piece of tissue paper and hidden in a cigarette, and it was in Dutch. 'Dear friend Goott, I want you to see this man. He will tell you everything.' It was signed 'Jan van Roos'.

The sailor had had a difficulty in meeting Mr Goott, who kept three people in his house to prevent anybody seeing him. There was the footman at the door, there was the butler, and there was Mr Goott's secretary. But the sailor, who didn't look like a sailor because he was dressed in an old suit of clothes and a Derby hat, got to him at last by sending in the cigarette and asking him to open it.

The sailor's name was Brown. He had been a member of the crew of a ship which had gone to Leningrad, and he had been persuaded by Soviet agents to join their organisation. One night he had been arrested, and in prison he met van Roos, who used to be a prosperous diamond merchant but had been for two years in the prison of St Peter and St Paul. The sailor and van Roos had long conversations. He had nursed the Dutchman through a sickness, and when, for no reason at all, they were both released, they were the best of friends.

'What's all this to do with me?' asked Goott, very impatiently.

The man glanced at him angrily. (This is Goott's own description.)

'I don't know how much it's got to do with you,' he said gruffly. 'If you don't want to hear it, I won't waste my time any more. But I've seen the boxes with my own eyes.'

Goott had an appointment in the city which he couldn't give up. He asked the man to call again that night, and he was there in the study when Bryne and I made our visit – though of course we didn't know this.

Goott hurried back to the sailor the moment we had gone.

'Listen, my friend,' he said. (I am relying entirely on his account of the conversation: it is probably more or less accurate.) ' You tell me that after the Revolution the reserves of the Imperial Bank were packed into six boxes containing English and American banknotes, and that they were taken to the shores of the Baltic and buried there. I'm not a fool. Only this night I've seen two police officers who came to speak to me about another attempting swindler.'

Brown got up and took his hat.

'Then I won't say any more to you,' he said. 'I've told you before what van Roos told me. I've told you I've seen the boxes buried under the floor of an old house, and if you like to come to the place I'm lodging I can show you the plan. I'm not asking for anything, I'm not offering you anything. There's only three people know about this and one of 'em's dead – that's van Roos. He died the week before I smuggled myself on to a Soviet vessel that was coming to Hull.'

'Who's the other man?'

'The Grand Duke Boris,' said the sailor. 'He's in London, and he's been trying to find me. But van Roos said he was only entitled to a very small share. He wouldn't have any of it if I had my way.'

Goott was impressed and agreed to go with the man to his lodgings. He was staying at a small hotel off the Blackfriars Road. But Goott was a careful man.

'I'll go in daylight,' he said, and the man offered no objection.

The next afternoon he arrived at the little temperance hotel and was shown up to the sailor's room. It was a poorish kind of apartment: it had nothing in it beyond the furniture except one sea trunk.

He found Brown sitting on the bed in his shirt-sleeves, smoking a pipe. Goott was taking no risks: he had two private detectives outside watching the house, with instructions to come in after him if he wasn't out in a quarter of an hour. To be on the safe side he told Brown this.

'Don't you worry: nobody's going to hurt you. Besides, I'm not wanting your help any more,' said the sailor, getting up and stretching himself. 'I like dealing with gentlemen who are gentlemen, and when a man doubts my word it makes me mad. I'm very sorry to have troubled you, Mr Goott.'

Goott was standing by the window with an eye on the street. He was also visible to the two detectives who had followed him; and at that moment he saw a big Rolls draw up before the hotel, a footman got down and opened the door, and a very elegant-looking swell got out and looked up at the house with an expression on his face as if he smelt something that he didn't like.

'You promised to show me the plan.'

'It's not necessary,' said Brown. 'I'm not doing any more business with you. And besides, I see it's useless trying to get you to help. I'll tell you plainly that it would cost you ten thousand pounds to charter a boat, and anybody with half an eye could see that you wouldn't put up ten thousand pence.'

'You're right there,' said Goott.

'Well,' said the sailor, knocking out the ashes of his pipe in the fire-grate, 'we won't talk any more about it. I've offered you a lot of money – I don't know how much it is. Van Roos said it was two millions, but he was probably lying –'

There was a knock at the door, and the sailor looked round, rather startled. He glanced at Goott suspiciously.

'Who's that?' he asked. 'One of your pals?'

'No friend of mine,' said Goott, getting nearer to the window so that the detectives could see what was happening to him – if anything did happen.

The knock came again.

'Come in,' said Brown.

The door opened and there entered the swell whom Goott had seen getting out of the car. He saw the Dutchman and frowned.

'Who is this?' he asked sharply.

The sailor grinned.

'It doesn't matter who it is, your highness,' he said roughly. 'A friend of mine if you like.'

He looked at Goott and jerked his head towards the swell.

'This is the Grand Duke I've been talking to you about.'

'Does this man know?' asked the Grand Duke, breathing hard.

'He knows as much as you know,' said Brown. 'He knows that there is stuff, but he doesn't know where it is, and nobody else knows until I get a signed agreement with you that I have my share. You tried to beat me down – '

'Then he does know?' interrupted the Grand Duke between his teeth.

Turning, he locked the door and faced the sailor. He was a head taller than Brown and a strong-looking fellow.

'I'll repeat my offer,' he said. 'I will pay the cost of the expedition, I will guarantee you a hundred thousand pounds – '

'Nothing doing,' said the sailor loudly. 'I don't know how much stuff is there, but I want half.'

The eyes of the Grand Duke half closed, and Goott said he never so much as saw his arm move; but suddenly there appeared in his hand a Browning, with which he covered the sailor.

'More than a half of that money,' he said quietly, 'is the property of my family. You have the plan – you brought this man to see it. I want it.'

Before Goott knew what had happened, the sailor leaped at him like a cat. The pistol dropped from the Grand Duke's hand and he was flung backward across the bed. Goott looked helplessly through the window and saw his detectives, but for a second did not know what to do. But he was a quick thinker. Reaching forward, he jerked the sailor backwards. The Grand Duke came to his feet, breathless and pale.

'Let's talk this thing over,' said Goott. 'We are businessmen . . .'

It was a long time before the Grand Duke could speak. Brown was all for making a rough house, but in the end they made an appointment to meet in Brook Street, and about midnight the sailor and the Grand Duke left, the best of friends, with a bearer cheque for ten thousand pounds and one of the three signed agreements that the money should be split three ways.

I ran across Linsy a year after this: he was in the lounge of the Grand Hotel in Paris. I had gone over to bring back a fellow who had swindled the Midland Bank. It was only just before I left that I heard all this from Mr Goott, because naturally he was sore and didn't want everybody to know that he had backed a loser.

'If you say it was me, it was me,' said Linsy, 'but you've got to prove it. If you say that the Grand Duke was young Allison – why, you'd better ask him. It you tell me you've been down to the Fairlights and that I lent them the money to buy the farm, that doesn't prove anything either. I can only tell you this, Sooper, that the cleverer a man is the easier he is to catch, if you can put a little bit of romance into the catching.'

A few months later I was introduced to an American gentleman who wanted to know all about Linsy. He pointed to Linsy as he crossed the hall.

'You see that man?' he said. 'I will tell you in confidence that he's working for the King of Siam, and he's found a big emerald mine . . .'

A Certain Game

Sanders had been away on a holiday.

The commissioner, whose work lay for the main part in wandering through a malarial country in some discomfort and danger, spent his holiday in travelling through another malarial country in as great discomfort and at no less risk. The only perceptible difference, so far as could be seen, between his work and his holiday was that instead of considering his own worries he had to listen to the troubles of somebody else.

Mr Commissioner Sanders derived no small amount of satisfaction from such a vacation, which is a sure sign that he was most human.

His holiday was a long one, for he went by way of St Paul de Loanda overland to the Congo, shot an elephant or two in the French Congo, went by mission steamer to the Sangar River and made his way back to Stanley Pool.

At Matadi he found letters from his relief, a mild youth who had come from headquarters to take his place as a temporary measure, and was quite satisfied in his inside mind that he was eminently qualified to occupy the seat of the commissioner.

The letter was a little discursive, but Sanders read it as eagerly as a girl reads her first love letter. For he was reading about a land which was very dear to him.

'Umfebi, the headman of Kulanga, has given me a little trouble. He wants sitting on badly, and if I had control . . . ' Sanders grinned unpleasantly and said something about 'impertinent swine', but did he not refer to the erring Umfebi? 'I find M'laka, the chief of the Little River, a very pleasant man to deal with: he was most attentive to me when I visited his village and trotted out all his dancing girls for my amusement.' Sanders made a little grimace. He knew M'laka for a rascal and wondered. 'A chief who has been most civil and courteous is Bosambo of the Ochori. I know this will interest you because Bosambo tells me that he is a special protégé of yours. He tells me how you had paid for his education as a child and had gone to a lot of trouble to teach him the English language. I did not know of this.'

Sanders did not know of it either, and swore an oath to the brazen sky to take this same Bosambo, thief by nature, convict by the wise provision of the Liberian Government, and chief of the Ochori by sheer effrontery, and kick him from one end of the city to the other.

'He is certainly the most civilised of your men,' the letter went on. 'He has been most attentive to the astronomical mission which came out in your absence to observe the eclipse of the moon. They speak very highly of his attention and he has been most active in his attempt to recover some of their property which was either lost or stolen on their way down the river.'

Sanders smiled, for he himself had lost property in Bosambo's territory.

'I think I will go home,' said Sanders.

Home he went by the nearest and the quickest way and came to headquarters early one morning, to the annoyance of his relief, who had planned a great and fairly useless palaver to which all the chiefs of all the land had been invited.

'For,' he explained to Sanders in a grieved tone, 'it seems to me that the only way to ensure peace is to get at the minds of these people, and the only method by which one can get at their minds is to bring them all together.'

Sanders stretched his legs contemptuously and sniffed. They sat at chop on the broad stoep before the commissioner's house, and Mr Franks – so the deputy commissioner was named – was in every sense a guest. Sanders checked the vitriolic appreciation of the native mind which came readily to his lips, and enquired: 'When is this prec – when is this palaver?'

'This evening,' said Franks.

Sanders shrugged his shoulders.

'Since you have gathered all these chiefs together,' he said, 'and they are present in my Houssa lines, with their wives and servants, eating my "special expense" vote out of existence, you had better go through with it.'

That evening the chiefs assembled before the residency, squatting in a semi-circle about the chair on which sat Mr Franks – an enthusiastic young man with a very pink face and gold-mounted spectacles.

Sanders sat a little behind and said nothing, scrutinising the assembly with an unfriendly eye. He observed without emotion that Bosambo of the Ochori occupied the place of honour in the centre, wearing a leopard skin and loop after loop of glittering glass beads. He had ostrich feathers in his hair and bangles of polished brass about his arms and ankles and, chiefest abomination, suspended by a scarlet ribbon from that portion of the skin which covered his left shoulder, hung a large and elaborate decoration.

Beside him the kings and chiefs of other lands were mean, commonplace men. B'fari of the Larger Isisi, Kulala of the N'Gombi, Kandara of the Akasava, Etobi of the River-beyond-the-River, and a score of little kings and overlords might have been so many carriers.

It was M'laka of the Lesser Isisi who opened the palaver.

'Lord Franki,' he began, 'we are great chiefs who are as dogs before the brightness of your face, which is like the sun that sets through a cloud.'

Mr Franks, to whom this was interpreted, coughed and went pinker than ever.

'Now that you are our father,' continued M'laka, 'and that Sandi has gone from us, though you have summoned him to this palaver to testify to your greatness, the land has grown fruitful, sickness has departed, and there is peace among us.'

He avoided Sanders' cold eye whilst the speech was being translated.

'Now that Sandi has gone,' M'laka went on with relish, 'we are sorry, for he was a good man according to some, though he had not the great heart and the gentle spirit of our lord Franki.'

This he said, and much more, especially with regard to the advisability of calling together the chiefs and headmen that they might know of the injustice of taxation, the hardship of life under certain heartless lords – here he looked at Sanders – and the need for restoring the old powers of the chiefs.

Other orations followed. It gave them great sorrow, they said, because Sandi, their lord, was going to leave them. Sandi observed that the blushing Mr Franks was puzzled, and acquitted him of spreading the report of his retirement.

Then Bosambo, sometime of Monrovia, and now chief of the Ochori, from-the-border-of-the-river-to-the-mountains-by-the-forest.

'Lord Franki,' he said, 'I feel shame that I must say what I have to say, for you have been to me as a brother.'

He said this much, and paused as one overcome by his feelings. Franks was doubly affected, but Sanders watched the man suspiciously.

'But Sandi was our father and our mother,' said Bosambo; 'in his arms he carried us across swift rivers, and with his beautiful body he shielded us from our enemies; his eyes were bright for our goodness and dim to our faults, and now that we must lose him my stomach is full of misery, and I wish I were dead.'

He hung his head, shaking it slowly from side to side, and there were tears in his eyes when he lifted them. David lamenting Jonathan was no more woeful than Bosambo of Monrovia taking a mistaken farewell of his master.

'Franki is good,' he went on, mastering himself with visible effort; 'his face is very bright and pretty, and he is as innocent as a child; his heart is pure, and he has no cunning.'

Franks shifted uneasily in his seat as the compliment was translated.

'And when M'laka speaks to him with a tongue of oil,' said Bosambo, 'lo! Franki believes him, though Sandi knows that M'laka is a liar and a breaker of laws, who poisoned his brother in Sandi's absence and is unpunished.'

M'laka half rose from his seat and reached for his elephant sword.

'Down!' snarled Sanders; his hand went swiftly to his jacket pocket, and M'laka cowered.

'And when Kulala of the N'Gombi raids into Alamandy territory stealing girls, our lord is so gentle of spirit – '

'Liar and dog and eater of fish!'

The outraged Kulala was on his feet, his fat figure shaking with wrath.

But Sanders was up now, stiffly standing by his relief, and a gesture sent insulter and insulted squatting to earth.

All that followed was Greek to Mr Franks, because nobody troubled to translate what was said.

'It seems to me,' said Sanders, 'that I may divide my chiefs into three parts, saying this part is made of rogues, this part of fools, and this, and the greater part, of people who are rogues in a foolish way. Now I know only one of you who is a pure rogue, and that is Bosambo of the Ochori, and for the rest you are like children.

'For when Bosambo spread the lie that I was leaving you, and when the master Franki called you together, you, being simpletons, who throw your faces to the shadows, thought, "Now this is the time to speak evilly of Sandi and well of the new master." But Bosambo, who is a rogue and a liar, has more wisdom than all of you, for the cunning one has said, "I will speak well of Sandi, knowing that he will stay with us; and Sandi, hearing me, will love me for my kindness."'

For one of the few times in his life Bosambo was embarrassed, and looked it.

'Tomorrow,' said Sanders, 'when I come from my house, I wish to see no chief or headman, for the sight of you already makes me violently ill. Rather I would prefer to hear from my men that you are hurrying back with all speed to your various homes. Later, I will come and there will be palavers – especially in the matter of poisoning. The palaver is finished.'

He walked into the house with Franks, who was not quite sure whether to be annoyed or apologetic.

'I am afraid my ideas do not exactly tally with yours,' he said, a little ruefully.

Sanders smiled kindly. 'My dear chap,' he said, 'nobody's ideas really tally with anybody's! Native folk are weird folk – that is why I know them. I am a bit of a weird bird myself.'

When he had settled his belongings in their various places the commissioner sent for Bosambo, and that worthy came, stripped of his gaudy furnishings, and sat humbly on the stoep before Sanders.

'Bosambo,' he said briefly, 'you have the tongue of a monkey that chatters all the time.'

'Master, it is good that monkeys chatter,' said the crestfallen chief, 'otherwise the hunter would never catch them.'

'That may be,' said Sanders; 'but if their chattering attracts bigger game to stalk the hunter, then they are dangerous beasts. You shall tell me later about the poisoning of M'laka's brother; but first you shall say why you desire to stand well with me. You need not lie, for we are men talking together.'

Bosambo met his master's eye fearlessly.

'Lord,' he said, 'I am a little chief of a little people. They are not of my race, yet I govern them wisely. I have made them a nation of fighters where they were a nation of women.'

Sanders nodded. 'All this is true; if it were not so, I should have removed you long since. This you know. Also that I have reason to be grateful to you for certain happenings.'

'Lord,' said Bosambo, earnestly, 'I am no beggar for favours, for I am, as you know, a Christian, being acquainted with the blessed Peter and the blessed Paul and other holy saints which I have forgotten. But I am a better man than all these chiefs and I desire to be a king.'

'A what?' asked the astonished Sanders.

'A king, lord,' said Bosambo, unashamed; 'for I am fitted for kingship, and a witch doctor in the K-roo country, to whom I dashed a bottle of gin, predicted I should rule vast lands.'

'Not this side of heaven,' said Sanders decisively. He did not say 'heaven', but let that pass.

Bosambo hesitated.

'Ochori is a little place and a little people,' he said, half to himself; 'and by my borders sits M'laka, who rules a large country three times as large and very rich – '

Sanders clicked his lips impatiently, then the humour of the thing took possession of him.

'Go you to M'laka,' he said, with a little inward grin, 'say to him all that you have said to me. If M'laka will deliver his kingdom into your hands I shall be content.'

'Lord,' said Bosambo, 'this I will do, for I am a man of great attainments and have a winning way.'

With the dignity of an emperor's son he stalked through the garden and disappeared.

The next morning Sanders said goodbye to Mr Franks – a coasting steamer gave the commissioner an excuse for hurrying him off. The chiefs had departed at sunrise, and by the evening life had resumed its normal course for Sanders.

It ran smoothly for two months, at the end of which time M'laka paid a visit to his brother-in-law, Kulala, a chief of N'Gombi, and a man of some importance, since he was lord of five hundred spears and many famous hunters.

They held a palaver which lasted the greater part of a week, and at the end there was a big dance.

It was more than a coincidence that on the last day of the palaver two shivering men of the Ochori were led into the village by their captors and promptly sacrificed.

The dance followed.

The next morning M'laka and his relative went out against the Ochori, capturing on their way a man whom M'laka denounced as a spy of Sandi's. Him they did to death in a conventional fashion, and he died uncomplainingly. Then they rested three days.

M'laka and his men came to the Ochori city at daybreak, and held a brief palaver in the forest.

'Now news of this will come to Sandi,' he said; 'and Sandi, who is a white devil, will come with his soldiers, and we will say that we were driven to do this because Bosambo invited us to a dance, and then endeavoured to destroy us.'

'Bosambo would have destroyed us,' chanted the assembly faithfully.

'Further, if we kill all the Ochori, we will say that it was not our people who did the killing, but the Akasava.'

'Lord, the killing was done by the Akasava,' they chanted again.

Having thus arranged both an excuse and an alibi, M'laka led his men to their quarry.

In the grey light of dawn the Ochori village lay defenceless. No fires spluttered in the long village street, no curl of smoke uprose to indicate activity.

M'laka's army in one long, irregular line went swiftly across the clearing which separated the city from the forest.

'Kill!' breathed M'laka; and along the ranks the order was taken up and repeated.

Nearer and nearer crept the attackers; then from a hut on the outskirts of the town stepped Bosambo, alone. He walked slowly to the centre of the street, and M'laka saw, in a thin-legged tripod, something straight and shining and ominous. Something that caught the first rays of the sun as they topped the trees of the forest, and sent them flashing and gleaming back again.

Six hundred fighting men of the N'Gombi checked and halted dead at the sight of it. Bosambo touched the big brass cylinder with his hand and turned it carelessly on its swivel until it pointed in the direction of M'laka, who was ahead of the others, and no more than thirty paces distant.

As if to make assurance doubly sure, he stooped and glanced along the polished surface, and M'laka dropped his short spear at his feet and raised his hands.

'Lord Bosambo,' he said mildly, 'we come in peace.'

'In peace you shall go,' said Bosambo, and whistled.

The city was suddenly alive with armed men. From every hut they came into the open.

'I love you as a man loves his goats,' said M'laka fervently; 'I saw you in a dream, and my heart led me to you.'

'I, too, saw you in a dream,' said Bosambo; 'therefore I arose to meet you, for M'laka, the king of the Lesser Isisi, is like a brother to me.'

M'laka, who never took his eyes from the brass-coated cylinder, had an inspiration.

'This much I beg of you, master and lord,' he said; 'this I ask, my brother, that my men may be allowed to come into your city and make joyful sacrifices, for that is the custom.'

Bosambo scratched his chin reflectively.

'This I grant,' he said; 'yet every man shall leave his spear, stuck head downwards into earth – which is our custom before sacrifice.'

M'laka shifted his feet awkwardly. He made the two little double-shuffle steps which native men make when they are embarrassed.

Bosambo's hand went slowly to the tripod.

'It shall be as you command,' said M'laka hastily; and gave the order.

Six hundred dejected men, unarmed, filed through the village street, and on either side of them marched a line of Ochori warriors – who were not without weapons. Before Bosambo's hut M'laka, his brother-in-law Kulala, his headmen, and the headmen of the Ochori, sat to conference which was half meal and half palaver.

'Tell me, Lord Bosambo,' asked M'laka, 'how does it come about that Sandi gives you the gun that says, 'Ha-ha-ha'? For it is forbidden that the chiefs and people of this land should be armed with guns.'

Bosambo nodded.

'Sandi loves me,' he said simply, 'for reasons which I should be a dog to speak of, for does not the same blood run in his veins that runs in mine?'

'That is foolish talk,' said Kulala, the brother-in-law; 'for he is white and you are black.'

'None the less it is true,' said the calm Bosambo; 'for he is my cousin, his brother having married my mother, who was a chief's daughter. Sandi wished to marry her,' he went on reminiscently; 'but there are matters which it is shame to talk about. Also he gave me these.'

From beneath the blanket which enveloped his shoulders he produced a leather wallet. From this he took a little package. It looked like a short, stumpy baton. Slowly he removed its wrapping of fine native cloth, till there were revealed three small cups of wood. In shape they favoured the tumbler of commerce, in size they were like very large thimbles.

Each had been cut from a solid piece of wood, and was of extreme thinness. They were fitted one inside the other when he removed them from the cloth, and now he separated them slowly and impressively.

At a word, a man brought a stool from the tent and placed it before him.

Over this he spread the wisp of cloth and placed the cups thereon upside down.

From the interior of one he took a small red ball of copal and camwood kneaded together.

Fascinated, the marauding chiefs watched him.

'These Sandi gave me,' said Bosambo, 'that I might pass the days of the rains pleasantly; with these I play with my headman.'

'Lord Bosambo,' said M'laka, 'how do you play?'

Bosambo looked up to the warm sky and shook his head sadly.

'This is no game for you, M'laka,' he said, addressing the heavens; 'but for one whose eyes are very quick to see; moreover, it is a game played by Christians.'

Now the Isisi folk pride themselves on their keenness of vision. Is it not a proverb of the River, 'The N'Gombi to hear, the Bushman to smell, the Isisi to see, and the Ochori to run'?

'Let me see what I cannot see,' said M'laka; and, with a reluctant air, Bosambo put the little red ball on the improvised table behind the cup.

'Watch then, M'laka! I put this ball under this cup: I move the cup –'

Very leisurely he shifted the cups.

'I have seen no game like this,' said M'laka; and contempt was in his voice.

'Yet it is a game which pleased me and my men of bright eyes,' said Bosambo; 'for we wager so much rods against so much salt that no man can follow the red ball.'

The chief of the Lesser Isisi knew where the red ball was, because there was a slight scratch on the cup which covered it.

'Lord Bosambo,' he said, quoting a saying, 'only the rat comes to dinner and stays to ravage – yet if I did not sit in the shadow of your hut, I would take every rod from you.'

'The nukusa is a small animal, but he has a big voice,' said Bosambo, giving saying for saying; 'and I would wager you could not uncover the red ball.'

M'laka leant forward. 'I will stake the spears of my warriors against the spears of the Ochori,' he said.

Bosambo nodded.

'By my head,' he said.

M'laka stretched forward his hand and lifted the cup, but the red ball was not there. Rather it was under the next cup, as Bosambo demonstrated.

M'laka stared.

'I am no blind man,' he said roughly; 'and your tongue is like the burning of dry sticks – clack, clack, clack!'

Bosambo accepted the insult without resentment.

'It is the eye,' he said meditatively; 'we Ochori folk see quickly.'

M'laka swallowed an offensive saying.

'I have ten bags of salt in my house,' he said shortly, 'and it shall be my salt against the spears you have won.'

'By my heart and life,' said Bosambo, and put the ball under the cup.

Very lazily he moved the cups to and fro, changing their positions.

'My salt against your spears,' said M'laka exultantly, for he saw now which was the cup. It had a little stain near the rim.

Bosambo nodded, and M'laka leant forward and lifted the cup. But the ball was not there.

M'laka drew a deep breath, and swore by Iwa – which is death – and by devils of kinds unknown; by sickness and by his father – who had been hanged, and was in consequence canonised.

'It is the eye,' said Bosambo sadly; 'as they say by the River, 'The Ochori to see – '

'That is a lie!' hissed M'laka; 'the Ochori see nothing but the way they run. Make this game again – '

And again Bosambo covered the red ball; but this time he bungled, for he placed the cup which covered the ball on an uneven place on the stool. And between the rim of the cup and the cloth there was a little space where a small ball showed redly – and M'laka was not blind.

'Bosambo,' he said, holding himself, 'I wager big things, for I am a chief of great possessions, and you are a little chief, yet this time I will wager my all.'

'M'laka of the Isisi,' responded Bosambo slowly, 'I also am a great chief and a relative by marriage to Sandi. Also I am a God-man speaking white men's talk and knowing of Santa Antonio, Marki, Luki, the blessed Timothi, and similar magics. Now this shall be the wager; if you find a red ball you shall find a slave whose name is Bosambo of the Ochori, but if you lose the red one you shall lose your country.'

'May the sickness mango come to me if I do not speak the truth,' swore M'laka, 'but to all this I agree.'

He stretched out his hand and touched the cup.

'It is here!' he shouted and lifted the cover.

There was no red ball.

M'laka was on his feet breathing quickly through his nose.

He opened his mouth to speak, but there was no need, for an Ochori runner came panting through the street with news; before he could reach the hut where his overlord sat and tell it, the head of Sanders' column emerged from the forest path.

It is said that 'the smell of blood carries farther than a man can see'. It had been a tactical error to kill one of Sanders' spies.

The commissioner was stained and soiled and he was unshaven, for the call of war had brought him by forced marches through the worst forest path in the world.

Into the open strode the column, line after line of blue-coated Houssas, bare-legged, sandal-footed, scarlet-headed, spreading out as smoke spreads when it comes from a narrow barrel. Forming in two straggling lines, it felt its way cautiously forward, for the Ochori city might hold an enemy.

Bosambo guessed the meaning of the demonstration and hurried forward to meet the commissioner. At a word from Sanders the lines halted, and midway between the city and the wood they met – Bosambo and his master.

'Lord,' said Bosambo conventionally, 'all that I have is yours.'

'It seems that you have your life, which is more than I expected,' said Sanders. 'I know that M'laka, chief of the Lesser Isisi, is sheltering in your village. You shall deliver this man to me for judgement.'

'M'laka, I know,' said Bosambo, carefully, 'and he shall be delivered; but when you speak of the chief of the Lesser Isisi you speak of me, for I won all his lands by a certain game.'

'We will talk of that later,' said Sanders.

He led his men to the city, posting them on its four sides, then he followed Bosambo to where M'laka and his headman awaited his coming – for the guest of a chief does not come out to welcome other guests.

'M'laka,' said Sanders, 'there are two ways with chiefs who kill the servants of government. One is a high and short way, as you know.'

M'laka's eyes sought a possible tree, and he shivered.

'The other way,' said Sanders, 'is long and tiresome, and that is the way for you. You shall sit down in the Village of Irons for my king's pleasure.'

'Master, how long?' asked M'laka in a shaky voice.

'Whilst you live,' said Sanders.

M'laka accepted what was tantamount to penal servitude for life philosophically – for there are worse things.

'Lord,' he said, 'you have always hated me. Also you have favoured other chiefs and oppressed me. Me, you deny all privilege; yet to Bosambo, your uncle – '

Sanders drew a long breath.

' – you give many favours, such as guns.'

'If my word had not been given,' said Sanders coldly, 'I should hang you, M'laka, for you are the father of liars and the son of liars. What guns have I given Bosambo?'

'Lord, that is for you to see,' said M'laka and jerked his head to the terrifying tripod.

Sanders walked towards the instrument.

'Bosambo,' he said, with a catch in his voice, 'I have in mind three white men who came to see the moon.'

'Lord, that is so,' said Bosambo cheerfully; 'they were mad, and they looked at the moon through this thing; also at stars.'

He pointed to the innocent telescope. 'And this they lost?' said Sanders. Bosambo nodded.

'It was lost by them and found by an Ochori man who brought it to me,' said Bosambo. 'Lord, I have not hidden it, but placed it here where all men can see it.'

Sanders scanned the horizon. To the right of the forest was a broad strip of marshland, beyond, blurred blue in the morning sunlight, rose the little hill that marks the city of the Lesser Isisi.

He stooped down to the telescope and focused it upon the hill. At its foot was a cluster of dark huts.

'Look,' he said, and Bosambo took his place. 'What do you see?' asked Sanders.

'The city of the Lesser Isisi,' said Bosambo.

'Look well,' said Sanders, 'for that is the city you have won by a certain game.'

Bosambo shifted uncomfortably.

'When I come to my new city – ' he began.

'I also will come,' said Sanders significantly. On the stool before the huts the three little wooden cups still stood, and Sanders had seen them, also the red ball. 'Tomorrow I shall appoint a new chief to the Lesser Isisi. When the moon is at full I shall come to see the new chief,' he said, 'and if he has lost his land by "a certain game" I shall appoint two more chiefs, one for the Isisi and one for the Ochori, and there will be sorrow amongst the Ochori, for Bosambo of Monrovia will be gone from them.'

'Lord,' said Bosambo, making one final effort for empire, 'you said that if M'laka gave, Bosambo should keep.'

Sanders picked up the red ball and slipped it under one cup. He changed their positions slightly.

'If your game is a fair game,' he said, 'show me the cup with the ball.'

'Lord, it is the centre one,' said Bosambo without hesitation.

Sanders raised the cup.

There was no ball.

'I see,' said Bosambo slowly, 'I see that my lord Sandi is also a Christian.'

'It was a jest,' explained Bosambo to his headmen when Sanders had departed; 'thus my lord Sandi always jested even when I nursed him as a child. Menchimis, let the *lokali* sound and the people be brought together for a greater palaver and I will tell them the story of Sandi, who is my half-brother by another mother.'

The Swift Walker

They have a legend in the Akasava country of a green devil. He is taller than the trees, swifter than the leopard, more terrible than all other ghosts, for he is green – the fresh, young green of the trees in spring – and has a voice that is a strangled bark, like the hateful, rasping gr–r–r of a wounded crocodile.

This is M'shimba-M'shamba, the Swift Walker.

You sometimes find his erratic track showing clearly through the forest. For the space of twelve yards' width the trees are twisted, broken and uprooted, the thick undergrowth swept together in tangled heaps, as though by two huge clumsy hands.

This way and that goes the path of M'shimba-M'shamba, zigzag through the forest – and woe to the hut or the village that stands in his way!

For he will leave this hut intact; from this hut he will cut the propped verandah of leaves; this he will catch up in his ruthless fingers and tear it away swiftly from piece to piece, strewing the wreckage along the village street.

He has lifted whole families and flung them broken and dying into the forest; he has wiped whole communities from the face of the earth.

Once, by the Big River, was a village called N'kema-N'kema, which means literally 'monkey-monkey'. It was a poor village, and the people lived by catching fish and smoking the same. This they sold to inland villages, profiting on occasions to the equivalent of twelve shillings a week. Generally it was less; but, more or less, some fifty souls lived in comfort on the proceeds.

Some there were in that village who believed in M'shimba-M'shamba, and some who scoffed at him.

And when the votaries of the green devil went out to make sacrifices to him the others laughed. So acute did the division between the worshippers and the non-worshippers become, that the village divided itself into two, some building their dwellings on the farther side of the creek which ran near by, and the disbelievers remaining on the other bank.

For many months the sceptics gathered to revile the famous devil. Then one night M'shimba-M'shamba came. He came furiously, walking along the water of the creek – for he could do such miraculous things – stretching out his hairy arms to grab tree and bush and hut.

In the morning the worshippers were alone alive, and of the village of the faithless there was no sign save one tumbled roof, which heaved now and then very slightly, for under it was the chief of the village, who was still alive.

The worshippers held a palaver, and decided that it would be a sin to rescue him since their lord, M'shimba-M'shamba, had so evidently decreed his death. More than this, they decided that it would be a very holy thing and intensely gratifying to their green devil if they put fire to the hut – the fallen roof of wood and plaited grass heaved pathetically at the suggestion – and completed the destruction.

At this moment there arrived a great chief of an alien tribe, Bosambo of the Ochori, who came up against the tide in his state canoe, with its fifty paddlers and his state drummer.

He was returning from a visit of ceremony and had been travelling since before daylight when he came upon the village and stopped to rest his paddlers and eat.

'Most wonderful chief,' said the leader of the believers, 'you have come at a moment of great holiness.' And he explained the passing of M'shimba-M'shamba, and pointed to the fallen roof, which showed at long intervals a slight movement. 'Him we will burn,' said the headman simply; 'for he has been a sinful reviler of our lord the devil, calling him by horrible names, such as 'snake eater' and 'sand drinker'.

'Little man,' said Bosambo magnificently, 'I will sit down with my men and watch you lift that roof and bring the chief before me; and if he dies, then, by Damnyou – which is our Lord Sandi's own fetish – I will hang you up by your legs over a fire.'

Bosambo did not sit down, but superintended the rescue of the unfortunate chief, accelerating the work – for the people of the village had no heart in it – by timely blows with the butt of his spear.

They lifted the roof and brought an old man to safety. There had been three others in the hut, but they were beyond help.

The old chief was uninjured, and had he been younger he would have required no assistance to free himself. They gave him water and a little corn to eat and he recovered sufficiently to express his contrition. For he had seen M'shimba-M'shamba, the green one.

'Higher than trees, he stood, lord,' he said to the interested Bosambo; 'and round about his head were little tearing clouds, that flew backwards and forwards to him and from him like birds.'

He gave further anatomical particulars. He thought that one leg of the devil was longer than the other, and that he had five arms, one of which proceeded from his chest.

Bosambo left the village, having confirmed the chief in his chieftainship and admonished his would-be murderers.

Now it need not be explained that Bosambo had no more right to re-establish chiefs or to admonish people of the Akasava than you and I have to vote in the Paris municipal elections. For Bosambo was a chief of the

Ochori, which is a small, unimportant tribe, and himself was of no great consequence.

It was not to offer an apology that he directed his paddlers to make for the Akasava city. It lay nearly ten miles out of his way, and Bosambo would not carry politeness to such lengths.

When he beached his canoe before the wondering people of the city and marched his fifty paddlers (who became fifty spearmen by the simple expedient of leaving their paddles behind and taking their spears with them) through the main streets of the city, he walked importantly.

'Chief,' he said to that worthy, hastily coming forth to meet him, 'I come in peace, desiring a palaver on the high matter of M'shimba-M'shamba.'

When the chief, whose name was Sekedimi, recognised him he was sorry that he had troubled to go out to greet him, for the Ochori were by all native reckoning very small fish indeed.

'I will summon the children,' said Sekedimi sourly; 'for they know best of ghosts and such stories.'

'This is a palaver for men,' said Bosambo, his wrath rising; 'and though the Akasava, by my way of thinking, are no men, yet I am willing to descend from my highness, where Sandi's favour has put me, to talk with your people.'

'Go to your canoe, little chief,' snarled Sekedimi, 'before I beat you with rods. For we Akasava folk are very jealous, and three chiefs of this city have been hanged for their pride. And if you meet M'shimba-M'shamba, behold you may take him with you.'

Thus it came about that Bosambo, paramount chief of the Ochori, went stalking back to his canoe with as much dignity as he could summon, followed by the evil jests of the Akasava and the rude words of little boys.

Exactly what capital Bosambo could have made from his chance acquaintance with M'shimba-M'shamba need not be considered.

It is sufficient for the moment, at any rate, to record the fact that he returned to his capital, having lost something of prestige, for his paddlers, who took a most solemn oath not to tell one word of what had happened in the Akasava village, told none – save their several wives.

Bosambo was in many ways a model chief.

He dispensed a justice which was, on the whole, founded on the purest principles of equity. Somewhere, hundreds of miles away, sat Sanders of the River, and upon his method Bosambo, imitative as only a coast man can be, based his own. He punished quickly and obeyed the law himself as far as it lay within him to obey anything.

There was no chief as well disciplined as he, else it would have been a bad day's work for Sekedimi of the Akasava, for Bosambo was a man of high spirit and quick to resent affront to his dignity. And Sekedimi had wounded him deeply.

But Bosambo was a patient man; he had the gift which every native possesses of pigeon-holing his grievances. Therefore he waited, putting aside the matter and living down his people's disapproval.

He carried a pliant stick of hippo hide that helped him considerably in preserving their respect.

All things moved orderly till the rains had come and gone.

Then one day at sunset he came again to the Akasava city, this time with only ten paddlers. He walked through the street unattended, carrying only three light spears in his left hand and a wicker shield on the same arm. In his right hand he had nothing but his thin, pliant stick of hippo skin, curiously carved.

The chief of the Akasava had word of his coming and was puzzled, for Bosambo had arrived in an unaccustomed way – without ostentation.

'The dawn has come early,' he said politely.

'I am the water that reflects the light of your face,' replied Bosambo with conventional courtesy.

'You will find me in a kind mood,' said Sekedimi; 'and ready to listen to you.'

He was fencing cautiously; for who knew what devilish lies Bosambo had told Sandi?

Bosambo seated himself before the chief.

'Sekedimi,' said he, 'though my skin is black, I am of white and paramount people, having been instructed in their magic and knowing their gods intimately.'

'So I have heard; though, for my part, I take no account of their gods, being, as they tell me, for women and gentle things.'

'That is true,' said Bosambo, 'save one god, whose name was Petero, who was a great cutter-off of ears.'

Sekedimi was impressed. 'Him I have not heard about,' he admitted.

'Knowing these,' Bosambo went on, 'I came before the rains to speak of M'shimba-M'shamba, the green one, who walks crookedly.'

'This is the talk of children,' said Sekedimi; 'for M'shimba-M'shamba is the name our fathers gave to the whirlwind that comes through the forest – and it is no devil.'

Sekedimi was the most enlightened chief that ever ruled the Akasava and his explanation of M'shimba-M'shamba was a perfectly true one.

'Lord chief,' said Bosambo earnestly, 'no man may speak with better authority on such high and holy matters as devils as I, Bosambo, for I have seen wonderful sights and know the world from one side to the other. For I have wandered far, even to the edge of the world which looks down into hell; and I have seen wild leopards so great that they have drunk up whole rivers and eaten trees of surprising height and thickness.'

'Ko, ko,' said the awe-stricken counsellors of the chief who stood about his person; and even Sekedimi was impressed.

'Now I come to you,' said Bosambo, 'with joyful news, for my young men have captured M'shimba-M'shamba, the green one, and have carried him to the land of the Ochori.'

This he said with fine dramatic effect, and was pleased to observe the impression he had created.

'We bound the green one,' he went on, 'with N'Gombi chains, and laid the trunk of a tree in his mouth to silence his fearful roaring. We captured him, digging an elephant pit so deep that only men of strongest eyesight could see the bottom, so wide that no man could shout across it and be heard. And we took him to the land of the Ochori on a hundred canoes.'

Sekedimi sat with open mouth.

'The green one?' he asked incredulously.

'The green one,' said Bosambo, nodding his head; 'and we fastened together four shields, like that which I carry, and these we put over each of his eyes, that he might not see the way we took him or find his way back to the Akasava.'

There was a long silence.

'It seems,' said Sekedimi, after a while, 'that you have done a wonderful thing; for you have removed a devil from our midst. Yet the Ochori people will be sorry, for the curse which you have taken from us you have given to your people, and surely they will rise against you.'

'E–wa!' murmured his counsellors, nodding their heads wisely. 'The Ochori will rise against their chief, for he has loosened an evil one in their midst.'

Bosambo rose, for night was falling and he desired to begin the return stage of his journey.

'The Ochori are a very proud people,' he said. 'Never have they had a great devil before; the Isisi, the Akasava, the N'Gombi, the Bush folk, the Lesser Isisi, the Bomongo, the Boungendi – all these tribes have devils in great variety, but the Ochori have had none and they were very sad. Now their stomachs are full of pride for M'shimba-M'shamba, the green one, is with them, roving the forest in which we have loosed him, in a most terrifying way.'

He left the Akasava in a thoughtful mood, and set his state canoe for the juncture of the river.

That night the Akasava chief called together all his headmen, his elders, his chief fighting men and all men of consequence.

The staccato notes of the *lokali* called the little chiefs of outlying villages, and with them their elder men. From the fourth hour of night till the hour before dawn the palaver lasted.

'O chiefs and people,' said Sekedimi, 'I have called you together to tell you of a great happening. For M'shimba-M'shamba, who since the beginning of the world has been the own devil of the Akasava people, is now no longer ours. Bosambo, of the Ochori, has bound him and carried him away.'

'This is certainly a shame,' said one old man; 'for M'shimba-M'shamba is our very own devil, and Bosambo is an evil man to steal that which is not his.'

'That is as I think,' said Sekedimi. 'Let us go to Sandi, who holds court by the border of the N'Gombi country, and he shall give us a book.'

Sanders was at that time settling a marriage dispute, the principal article of contention being: if a man pays six thousand *matakos* (brass rods) for a wife, and in the first twelve months of her married life she develop sleeping-sickness, was her husband entitled to recover his purchase price from her father? It was a long, long palaver, requiring the attendance of many witnesses; and Sanders was deciding it on the very common-sense line that any person selling a damaged article, well knowing the same to be damaged, was guilty of fraud. The evidence, however, exonerated the father from blame, and there only remained a question of equity. He was in the midst of the second half of the trial when the chief of the Akasava, with his headman, his chief slave, and a deputation of the little chiefs waited upon him.

'Lord,' said Sekedimi, without preliminary, 'we have covered many miles of country and traversed rivers of surprising swiftness; also we encountered terrible perils by the way.'

'I will excuse you an account of your adventures,' said the commissioner, 'for I am in no mood for long palavers. Say what is to be said and have done.'

Thereupon Sekedimi told the story of the filched devil from the beginning, when he had, with a fine sarcasm, presented the Swift Walker to the Ochori.

Now Sanders knew all about M'shimba-M'shamba. Moreover, he knew that until very recently the chief himself was in no doubt as to what the 'green one' really was.

It was characteristic of him that he made no attempt to turn the chief to a sense of his folly.

'If Bosambo has taken M'shimba-M'shamba,' he said gravely, 'then he has done no more than you told him to do.'

'Now I spoke in jest,' said Sekedimi, 'for this devil is very dear to us, and since we can no more hear his loud voice in our forests we are sad for one who is gone.'

'Wait!' said Sanders, 'for is this the season when M'shimba-M'shamba walks? Is it not rather midway between the rains that he comes so swiftly? Wait and he will return to you.'

But Sekedimi was in no mood for waiting.

'Master, if I go to Bosambo,' he said, 'and speak kindly to him, will he not return the green one?'

'Who knows?' said Sanders wearily. 'I am no prophet.'

'If my lord gave me a book –' suggested Sekedimi.

'This is no book palaver,' said Sanders briefly; 'but justice between man and man. For if I give you a book to Bosambo, what shall I say when Bosambo asks me also for a book to you?'

'Lord, that is just,' said Sekedimi, and he went his way. With twelve of his principal chiefs he made the journey to the Ochori city, carrying with him gifts of goats and fat dogs, salt and heavy rings of brass.

Bosambo received him ceremoniously, accepted his gifts but declined to favour him.

'Sekedimi,' he said, 'I am wax in the hands of my people. I fear to anger them; for they love M'shimba-M'shamba better than they love their goats or their salt or their wives.'

'But no one sees him till the middle time between the rains,' said Sekedimi.

'Last night we heard him,' persisted Bosambo steadily; 'very terrible he was, and my people trembled and were proud.'

For many hours the chief of the Akasava pleaded and argued, but without avail.

'I see that you have a heart of brass,' said Sekedimi at length; 'therefore, Bosambo, return me the presents I brought, and I will depart.'

'As to the presents,' said Bosambo, 'they are dispersed, for swift messengers have carried them to the place where M'shimba-M'shamba sits and have put them where he may find them, that he may know the Akasava remember him with kindness.'

Empty-handed the chief returned.

He sent courier after courier in the course of the next month, without effect. And as time wore on his people began to speak against him. The crops of two villages failed, and the people cursed him, saying that he had sold the ghost and the spirit of fortune.

At last, in desperation, he paid another visit to Bosambo.

'Chief,' he said, when all ceremonies had been observed, 'I tell you this: I will give you fifty bags of salt and as much corn as ten canoes can hold if you will return to me our green one. And if your pride resists me, then I will call my spears, though Sandi hang me for it.'

Bosambo was a wise man. He knew the limit of human endurance. Also he knew who would suffer if war came, for Sanders had given him private warning.

'My heart is heavy,' he said. 'Yet since you are set upon this matter I will return you M'shimba-M'shamba, though I shall be shamed before my people. Send me the salt and the corn, and when the tide of the river is so high and the moon is nearly full I will find the green one and bring him back to your land.'

Sekedimi went back to his city a happy man. In a week the salt and the corn were delivered and the canoes that brought them carried a message back. On such a day, at such an hour, the green one would be cut loose in the forest of the Akasava. Afterwards, Bosambo would come in state to announce the transfer.

At the appointed time the chief of the Akasava waited by the river beach, two great fires burning behind him to guide Bosambo's canoe through the night. And behind the fires the population of the city and the villages about stood awed and expectant, biting its knuckles.

Tom-tom! Tom-tom! Tom-tom! Over the water came the faint sound of Bosambo's drum and the deep-chested chant of his paddlers. In half an hour his canoe grounded and he waded ashore.

'Lord Sekedimi,' he greeted the chief, 'this night I have loosened M'shimba-M'shamba, the green one, the monster. And he howled fearfully because I left him. My heart is sore, and there is nothing in my poor land which gives me pleasure.'

'Fifty sacks of my salt I sent you,' said Sekedimi unpleasantly; 'also corn.'

'None the less, I am as an orphan who has lost his father and his mother,' moaned Bosambo.

'Let the palaver finish, chief,' said Sekedimi, 'for my heart is also sore, having lost salt and corn.'

'I see that you have no stomach for pity,' said Bosambo, and re-embarked.

Clear of the Akasava city, Bosambo regained his spirits, though the night was stormy and great spots of rain fell at intervals.

The further he drew from the Akasava chief the more jovial he became, and he sang a song.

'There are fools in the forest,' he bawled musically, 'such as the Ingonona who walks with his eyes shut; but he is not so great a fool as Sekedimi.

> He is like a white man who is newly come to this land.
> He is like a child that burns his fingers.
> He is simple and like a great worm.'

He sang all this, and added libellous and picturesque particulars.

'Lord chief,' said the headman suddenly, arresting his song, 'I think we will make for the shore.'

Over the trees on the right bank of the river lightning flickered with increasing brightness, and there was a long continuous rumble of thunder in the air.

'To the middle island,' ordered Bosambo.

The headman shivered.

'Lord, the middle island is filled with spirits,' he said.

'You are a fool,' said Bosambo; but he ordered the canoe to the left bank.

Brighter and more vivid grew the lightning, louder and louder the crackle and crash of thunder. The big raindrops fell fitfully.

Then above the noise of thunder came a new sound – a weird howling that set the paddlers working with quicker strokes.

'Whow–w–w!'

A terrifying shriek deafened them.

The man nearest him dropped his paddle with a frightened whimper, and Bosambo caught it.

'Paddle, dogs!' he thundered.

They were within a dozen yards of the shore when, by the quick flashing lightning, he saw a jagged path suddenly appear in the forest on the bank before him.

It was as though giant hands were plucking at trees. They twisted and reeled like drunken men – cracked, and fell over.

'Paddle!'

Then something caught Bosambo and lifted him from the canoe. Up, up he went; then as swiftly down to the water; up again, and down. He struck out for the shore, choked and half-conscious.

His fingers caught the branches of a stricken tree, and he drew himself to land. He stumbled forward on his hands and knees, panting heavily.

Overhead the storm raged, but Bosambo did not heed it. His forty paddlers, miraculously cast ashore by the whirlwind, lay around him laughing and moaning, according to their temperaments.

But these he forgot.

For he was engaged in the composition of a hurried and apologetic prayer to M'shimba-M'shamba, the green one, the Swift Walker.

Nine Terrible Men

There were nine terrible men in the Forest of O'Tombi, so native report had it.

Nine terrible men who lived on an island set in a swamp. And the swamp was hard to come by, being in the midst of a vast forest. Only a monkey or a leopard could find a way to the inhabitants of this island – they themselves being privy to the secret ways.

No man of the Isisi, of the N'Gombi, of the Akasava, or of the river tribes, attempted to track down the nine, for, as it was generally known, most powerful ju-jus guarded all paths that led to the secret place.

Nine outlawed men, with murder and worse upon their souls, they came together, God knows how, and preyed upon their world.

They raided with impunity, being impartial as to whether Isisi or N'Gombi paid toll.

By night they would steal forth in single file, silent as death, no twig cracking in their path, no word spoken. As relentless as the soldier ant in his march of destruction, they made their way without hindrance to the village they had chosen for the scene of their operations, took what they wanted and returned.

Sometimes they wanted food, sometimes spears – for these lords of the woods were superior to craftsmanship – sometimes a woman or two went and never came back.

Such lawless communities were not uncommon. Occasionally very ordinary circumstances put an end to them; some there were that flourished, like the People-Who-Were-Not-All-Alike.

The Nine Terrible Men of the O'Tombi existed because nothing short of an army corps could have surrounded them, and because, as Sanders thought, they were not a permanent body, but dispersed at times to their several homes.

Sanders once sent two companies of Houssas to dislodge the nine, but they did nothing, for the simple reason that never once did they get within shooting distance. Then Sanders came himself, and caught little else than a vicious attack of malarial fever.

He sent messages to all the chiefs of the people within a radius of a hundred miles to kill at sight any of the nine, offering certain rewards. After three palpably inoffensive men of the Ochori tribe had been killed, and the reward duly claimed, Sanders countermanded the order.

For two years the nine ravaged at will, then a man of the Isisi, one Fembeni, found grace.

Fembeni became a Christian, though there is no harm in that. This is not satire, but a statement with a reservation. There are certain native men who embrace the faith and lose quality thereby, but Fembeni was a Christian and a better man – except –

Here is another reservation.

Up at Musunkusu a certain Ruth Glandynne laboured for the cause, she being a medical missionary, and pretty to boot.

White folk would call her pretty because she had regular features, a faultless complexion, and a tall, well-modelled figure.

Black folk thought she was plain, because her lips were not as they should be by convention; nor was she developed according to their standards.

Also, from the N'Gombi point of view, her long brown hair was ridiculous, and her features made her look 'like a bird'.

Mr Commissioner Sanders thought she was very pretty indeed – when he allowed himself to think about her.

He did not think about her more often than he could help, for two reasons – the only one that is any business of yours and mine being that she was an enormous responsibility. He had little patches of white hair on either side of his temple – when he allowed his hair to grow long enough for these to become visible – which he called grimly his 'missionary patches'. The safety of the solitary stations set in the wilds was a source of great worry.

You must understand that missionaries are very good people. Those ignoramuses who sneer at them place themselves in the same absurd position as those who sneer at Nelson or speak slightingly of other heroes.

Missionaries take terrible risks – they cut themselves adrift from the material life which is worth the living; they endure hardships incomprehensible to the uninitiated; they suffer from tempestuous illnesses which find them hale and hearty in the morning and leave their feeble bodies at the edge of death at sunset.

'And all this they do,' said Bosambo of Monrovia, philosophically and thoughtfully, 'because of certain mysteries which happened when the world was young to do with a famous man called Hesu [the second person of the Trinity is so called in some dialects]. Now I think that is the greatest mystery of all.'

Sanders appreciated the disinterestedness of the work, was immensely impressed by the courage of the people who came to labour in the unhealthy field, but all the time he fretfully wished they wouldn't.

His feelings were those of a professional lion-tamer who sees a light-hearted amateur stepping into the cage of the most savage of his beasts; they were feelings of the skilled matador who watches the novice's awkward handling of an Andalusian bull – a troubled matador with a purple cloak held ready and one neatly-shod foot on the barrier, ready to spring into the ring at the novice's need.

The 'missionary patches' grew larger and whiter in the first few months of Ruth Glandynne's presence at Musunkusu, for this village was too near to the wild N'Gombi, too near the erratic Isisi, for Sanders' liking.

Sanders might easily have made a mistake in his anxiety. He might have sent messengers to the two peoples, or gone in person – threatening them with death and worse than death if they harmed the girl.

But that would have aroused a sense of importance in their childlike bosoms, and when the time came, as it assuredly would come, when their stomachs were angry against him, some chief would say: 'Behold, here is a woman who is the core of Sandi's eye. If we do her harm we shall be revenged on Sandi.'

And, since children do not know any other tomorrow than the tomorrow of good promise, it would have gone badly with the lady missionary.

Instead, Sanders laid upon Bosambo, chief of the Ochori, charge of this woman, and Bosambo he trusted in all big things, though in the matter of goods movable and goods convertible he had no such confidence.

When Fembeni of the Isisi was converted from paganism to Christianity, Sanders was fussing about the little creeks which abound on the big river, looking for a man named Oko, who after a long and mysterious absence had returned to his village, killed his wife and fled to the bush.

The particular bush happened to be in the neighbourhood of the mission station, otherwise Sanders might have been content to allow his policemen to carry out the good work, but no sooner did news come that Oko had broken for that section of the N'Gombi country which impinges on Musunkusu, than Sanders went flying upriver in his steamer, the *Zaire*, because something told him he had identified one of the nine men.

Wrote Sergeant Ahmed, the Houssa, who prided himself on his English, to his wife at headquarters: 'At daylight, when search for murderer was officially resumed, came our Lord Sundah very actively angry. By orders I took left bank of Kulula River with three men, being ordered to shoot aforesaid Oko if resistance offered. Abiboo (sergeant) took right or other bank, and our lord searched bush. Truly Oko must be a very important man that Sundah comes officially searching for same, saying bitter reproach words to his humble servants.'

Ahmed's picture of his chief's agitation may be a little exaggerated, but I do not doubt that there was a substratum of fact therein.

On the second day of the hunt, Sanders' steamer was tied up at the mission station, and he found himself walking in the cool of the evening with Ruth Glandynne. So he learnt about Fembeni, the Isisi man who had found the light and was hot and eager for salvation.

'H'm!' said Sanders, displaying no great enthusiasm.

But she was too elated over her first convert to notice the lack of warmth in his tone.

'It is just splendid,' she said, her grey eyes alight and her pretty face kindling with the thought, 'especially when you remember, Mr Sanders, that I have only an imperfect knowledge of the language.'

'Are you sure,' asked the incredulous Sanders, 'that Fembeni understands what it is all about?'

'Oh, yes!' She smiled at the commissioner's simplicity. 'Why, he met me halfway, as it were; he came out to meet the truth; he – '

'Fembeni?' said Sanders thoughtfully. 'I think I know the man; if I remember him aright he is not the sort of person who would get religion if he did not see a strong business end to it.'

She frowned a little. Her eyebrows made a level line over resentful eyes.

'I think that is unworthy of you,' she said coldly.

He looked at her, the knuckle of his front finger at his lips.

She was very pretty, he thought, or else he had been so long removed from the society of white women that she seemed beautiful only because she stood before a background of brutal ugliness.

Slim, straight, grave-eyed, complexion faultless, though tanned by the African sun, features regular and delicate, hair (a quantity) russet-brown.

Sanders shook his head.

'I wish to heaven you weren't monkeying about in this infernal country,' he said.

'That is beside the question,' she replied with a little smile. 'We are talking of Fembeni, and I think you are being rather horrid.'

They reached the big square hut that Sanders had built for her, and climbed the wooden steps that led to the stoep.

Sanders made no reply, but when she had disappeared into the interior of the hut to make him some tea, he beckoned to Abiboo, who had followed him at a respectful distance.

'Go you,' he said, 'and bring me Fembeni of the Isisi.'

He was stirring his tea while the girl was giving him a rosy account of her work, when Fembeni came, a tall man of middle age, wearing the trousers and waistcoat which were the outward and visible signs of his inward and spiritual grace.

'Come near, Fembeni,' said Sanders gently.

The man walked with confidence up the steps of the stoep, and without invitation drew a chair towards him and seated himself.

Sanders said nothing. He looked at the man for a very long time, then: 'Who asked you to sit in my presence?' he said softly.

'Lord,' said Fembeni pompously, 'since I have found the blessed truth – '

Something in Sanders' eyes caused him to rise hurriedly.

'You may sit – on the ground,' said Sanders quietly, 'after the manner of your people, and I will sit on this chair after the manner of mine. For behold, Fembeni, even the blessed truth shall not make black white or white black; nor shall it make you equal with Sandi, who is your master.'

'Lord, that is so,' said the sullen Fembeni, 'yet we are all equal in the eyes of the great One.'

'Then there are a million people in the Isisi, in the N'Gombi, the Akasava and the Ochori, who are your equals,' said Sanders, 'and it is no shame for you to do as they do.'

Which was unanswerable, according to Fembeni's sense of logic.

The girl had listened to the talk between her novitiate and the commissioner with rising wrath, for she had not Sanders' knowledge of native people.

'I think that is rather small of you, Mr Sanders,' she said hotly. 'It is a much more important matter that a heathen should be brought to the truth than that your dignity should be preserved.'

Sanders frowned horribly – he had no society manners and was not used to disputation.

'I do not agree with you, Miss Glandynne,' he said a little gruffly; 'for, whilst the Isisi cannot see the ecstatic condition of his soul which leads him to be disrespectful to me, they can and do see the gross materialism of his sottish body.'

A thought struck him and he turned to the man. That thought made all the difference between life and death to Fembeni.

'Fembeni,' he said, relapsing into the language of the Isisi, 'you are a rich man by all accounts.'

'Lord, it is so.'

'And wives – how many have you?'

'Four, lord.'

Sanders nodded and turned to the girl.

'He has four wives,' he said.

'Well?'

There was a hint of defiance in the questioning 'Well?'

'He has four wives,' repeated Sanders. 'What is your view on this matter?'

'He shall marry one in the Christian style,' she said, flushing. 'Oh, you know, Mr Sanders, it is impossible for a man to be a Christian and have more wives than one!'

Sanders turned to the man again.

'In this matter of wives, Fembeni,' he said gently; 'how shall you deal with the women of your house?'

Fembeni wriggled his bare shoulders uncomfortably.

'Lord, I shall put them all away, save one,' he said sulkily, 'for that is the blessed way.'

'H'm!' said Sanders for the second time that morning.

He was silent for a long time, then: 'It is rather a problem,' he said.

'It presents no difficulty to my mind,' said the girl stiffly.

She was growing very angry, though Sanders did not realise the fact, being unused to the ways of white women.

'I think it is rather horrid of you, Mr Sanders, to discourage this man, to put obstacles to his faith – '

'I put no obstacle,' interrupted the commissioner. He was short of speech, being rather so intent upon his subject that he took no account of the fine feelings of a zealous lady missionary. 'But I cannot allow this to happen in my district; this man has four wives, each of them has borne him children. What justice or what Christianity is there in turning loose three women who have served this man?'

Here was a problem for the girl, and in her desperation she used an argument which was unanswerable.

'The law allows this,' she said. 'These things happen all over the world where missionary work is in progress. Perhaps I could bring the women to understand; perhaps I could explain – '

'You couldn't explain the babies out of existence,' said Sanders brutally.

That ended the discussion, for with a look of scorn and disgust she passed into the hut, leaving Sanders a prey to some emotion.

He turned a cold eye to the offending Fembeni.

'It seems,' he said, 'that a man by becoming a Christian has less mouths to fill. Now I must investigate this matter.'

Fembeni regarded him apprehensively, for if a woman is questioned, who knows what she will say? And it was fairly unimportant to the man if he had one wife or forty.

There was no possibility of searching any farther that night for the erring Oko, and Sanders was rowed across the river in his canoe to interview the wives of the new convert.

He found one woman who viewed the coming change with considerable philosophy, and three who were very shrill and very voluble.

'Lord,' said one of these three in that insolent tone which only native women assume, 'this white witch has taken our man – '

'I do not hear well,' said Sanders quickly, 'yet I thought I heard a word I do not like.'

He whiffled a pliant stick till it hummed a tune.

'Lord,' said the woman, dropping her voice and speaking more mildly, 'this God-lady has taken our man.'

'God-ladies do not take men,' said Sanders; 'rather they influence their spirits that they may be better men.'

'Fembeni will be no better and no worse,' said the woman bitterly, 'for he goes to the forest by night; often he has risen from my side, and when he has gone, behold the Nine Terrible Men have come from near by and taken that which they wanted.'

She stopped abruptly. There was horror in the eyes which met the commissioner's; in her anger she had said too much.

'That is foolish talk,' said Sanders easily.

He knew there would be no more information here and he played to quieten her fears.

He strolled through the village, talked awhile with the headman, and returned to his canoe.

Once on the *Zaire* he summoned Abiboo.

'Take three men and bring Fembeni to me,' he said, 'and be very ready to shoot him, for I have heard certain things.'

He waited for ten minutes, then Abiboo returned – alone.

'Fembeni has gone into the forest,' he said; 'also the God-lady.'

Sanders looked at him.

'How?'

'Lord, this Fembeni is a Christian, and desired to speak with the God-woman of the new magic. So they walked together, the God-woman reading from a book. Also he had a gift for her, which he bought from a Frenchi trader.'

'I see,' said Sanders.

He poured himself out a stiff whisky, and his hand shook a little.

Then he lifted down a sporting rifle that hung on the wall of his cabin, broke open two packets of cartridges, and dropped them into his coat pocket.

'Let the men come on quickly,' he said, 'you commanding.'

'Lord, there are other sergeants,' said Abiboo. 'I will go with you, for I am at your right hand, though death waits me.'

'As you will,' said Sanders roughly.

He went through the missionary compound, stopping only that a boy should point out the direction the two had taken, then he moved swiftly towards the forest, Abiboo at his heels.

He followed the beaten track for a hundred yards. Then he stopped and sniffed like a dog.

He went on a little farther and came back on his tracks.

He stooped and picked up some pieces of broken glass and turned aside from the path, following his nose.

Ruth Glandynne had supreme faith in the power of the Word which makes martyrs.

'You must have no doubt, Fembeni,' she said in her halting Isisi, 'for with Light, such things as the Word brings, all things will be made plain to you.'

They were beyond the confines of the little mission station, walking slowly towards the forest.

She read little extracts from the book she carried, and so full of her subject was she that she did not observe that they had passed the straggling trees, the outposts of the big forest.

When she did notice this she turned.

'More I will tell you, Fembeni,' she said.

'Lady, tell me now,' he begged, 'for Sandi has made me doubt.'

She frowned. What mischief can a materialist work! She had liked Sanders. Now for one resentful moment she almost hated him.

'There are white men who doubt,' she said, 'and who place pitfalls in the way – '

'Also this have I bought for you,' said Fembeni, 'paying one bag of salt.'

From the leather pouch at his side he produced a long flat flask.

She smiled as she recognised the floral label of the abominable scent beloved of the natives.

'This I bought for you, teacher,' he said, and removed the stopper so that the unoffending evening reeked of a sudden with the odour of musk, 'that you might protect me against Sandi, who is no God-man but a devil.'

She took the bottle and hastily replaced the stopper.

'Sandi is no devil,' she said gently, 'and will do you no harm.'

'He has crossed the river,' said Fembeni sulkily, and there was a curious glitter in his eyes, 'and he will speak with my wives, and they will tell him evil things of me.'

She looked at him gravely.

'What evil things can they say?' she asked.

'They can lie,' he said shortly, 'and Sandi will bring his rope and I shall die.'

She smiled. 'I do not think you need fear,' she said, and began to walk back; but he stood in front of her, and at that instant she realised her danger, and the colour faded from her face.

'If Sandi comes after me to kill me,' he said slowly, 'I shall say to him: 'Behold, I have a woman of your kind, and if you do not pardon me you will be sorry.'

She thought quickly, then of a sudden leapt past him and fled in the direction of the station.

He was after her in a flash. She heard the fast patter of his feet, and suddenly felt his arm about her waist.

She screamed, but there was no one to hear her, and his big hand covered her mouth.

He shook her violently.

'You live or you die,' he said; 'but if you cry out I will beat you till you die.'

He half carried, half dragged her in the direction of the forest.

She was nearly dead with fear; she was dimly conscious of the fact that he did not take the beaten path, that he turned at right angles and moved unerringly through the wood, following a path of his own knowing.

As he turned she made another attempt to secure her liberty. She still held the scent flask in her hand, and struck at him with all her might. He caught her arm and nearly broke it.

The stopper fell out and her dress was drenched with the vile perfume.

He wrenched the flask from her hand and threw it

Grasping her by the arm he led her on. She was nearly exhausted when he stopped, and she sank an inert heap to the ground.

She dare not faint, though she was on the verge of such a breakdown. How long they had been travelling she had no idea. The sun was setting; this she guessed rather than knew, for no sunlight penetrated the aisles.

Fembeni watched her; he sat with his back to a tree and regarded her thoughtfully.

After a while he rose. 'Come,' he said.

They moved on in silence. She made no appeal to him. She knew now the futility of speech. Her mind was still bewildered. 'Why, why, why?' it asked incoherently.

Why had this man professed Christianity?

'Fembeni,' she faltered, 'I have been kind to you.'

'Woman,' he said grimly, 'you may be kinder.' She said no more.

The horror of the thing began to take shape. She half stopped, and he grasped her arm roughly.

'By my head you shall live,' he said, 'if Sandi gives his word that none of us shall hang – for we are the Terrible Men, and Sandi has smelt me out.'

There was a gleam of hope in this speech. If it was only as a hostage that they held her –

Night had fallen when they came to water.

Here Fembeni halted. He searched about in the undergrowth and dragged to view a section of hollow tree-trunk.

Inside were two sticks of iron wood, and squatting down before the *lokali* he rattled a metallic tattoo.

For ten minutes he played his tuneless rhythm. When he stopped there came a faint reply from somewhere across the lake.

They waited, the girl and her captor, for nearly half an hour. She strained her ears for the sound of oars, not knowing that the water did not extend for more than a hundred yards, and that beyond and around lay the great swamp wherein stood the island headquarters of the Nine.

The first intimation of the presence of others was a stealthy rustle, then through the gloom she saw the men coming towards her.

Fembeni grasped her arm and led her forward. He exchanged a few words with the newcomers in a dialect she could not understand. There was a brief exchange of questions, and then the party moved on.

The ground beneath her feet grew soft and sodden. Sometimes the water was up to her ankles. The leader of the men picked his way unerringly, now following a semi-circular route, now turning off at right angles, now winding in and out, till she lost all sense of direction.

Her legs were like lead, her head was swimming and she felt she was on the point of collapse when suddenly the party reached dry land.

A few minutes later they came to the tumbledown village which the outlaws had built themselves.

A fire was burning, screened from view by the arrangement of the huts which had been built in a crescent.

The girl was shown a hut and thrust inside.

Soon afterwards a woman brought her a bowl of boiled fish and a gourd of water.

In her broken Isisi she begged the woman to stay with her, but she was evidently of the N'Gombi people and did not understand.

A few minutes later she was alone.

Outside the hut about the fire sat eight of the Nine Terrible Men. One of these was Oko of the Isisi, a man of some power.

'This woman I do not like,' he said, 'and by my way of thinking Fembeni is a fool and a son of a fool to bring her unless she comes as other women have come – to serve us.'

'Lord Oko,' said Fembeni, 'I am more skilled in the ways of white folk than you, and I tell you that if we keep this woman here it shall be well with us. For if Sandi shall catch you or me, or any of us, we shall say to him: 'There is a woman with us whom you greatly prize, and if you hang me, behold you kill her also.'

Still Oko was not satisfied.

'I also know white people and their ways,' he said. 'Sandi would have left us, now he will not rest till we are scattered and dead, for Sandi has a memory like the river, which never ceases to flow.'

A man of the Akasava suggested an evil thing.

'That we shall consider,' said Oko.

He had already decided. He had none of the subtlety of mind which distinguished Fembeni. He saw an end, and was for crowding in the space of life left to him as much of life as his hand could grasp.

They sat in palaver till early in the morning, the firelight reflected on the polished skin of their bodies.

Then Oko left the circle and crept to the girl's hut. They saw him stoop and enter, and heard a little scream.

'Oko has killed her,' said Fembeni.

'It is best,' said the other men.

Fembeni rose and went to the hut.

'Oko,' he called softly, then stooped and went in.

Facing him was a ragged square of dim light, where a great hole had been cut in the farther side of the hut.

'Oko,' he called sharply, then two hands of steel caught him by the throat and two others pulled his legs from under him.

He went to the ground, too terrified to resist.

'Fembeni,' said a soft voice in his ear, 'I have been waiting for you.'

He was rolled on to his face and he made no resistance. His hands were pulled behind, and he felt the cold steel bands encircle his wrist and heard a 'snick' as they fastened.

He was as expeditiously gagged.

'As for Oko,' said Sanders' voice, 'he is dead, and if you had heard him cry you also would have been dead.'

That ended the one-sided conversation, Sanders and his sergeant sitting patiently in their little lair waiting for the rest of the men to come.

With the morning arrived a detachment of Houssas under Sergeant Ahmed, following the trail Sanders had followed. There were four dead men to be buried – including him who had stood on guard at the edge of the swamp.

There was a white-faced girl to be guarded back across the swamp to the seclusion of the forest, and with her went the women of the outlaws' village.

Fembeni and his four companions stood up for judgement.

'One only thing I would ask you, Fembeni,' said Sanders, 'and that is this: you are by some account a Christian. Do you practise this magic, or are you for the ju-jus and gods of your fathers?'

'Lord,' said Fembeni eagerly, 'I am a Christian in all ways. Remember this, master, I am of your faith.'

Sanders, with his lips parted and his eyes narrowed, looked at the man. 'Then it is proper that I should give you time to say your prayers,' he said. 'Abiboo, we hang this man last.'

'I see that you are a devil,' said Fembeni, 'otherwise you would not follow us in the night with none to show you the way. Now I tell you, Sandi, that I am no Christian, for all God-folk are foolish save you, and I know that you are no God-man. Therefore, if I am to hang, let me hang with the rest.'

Sanders nodded.

The Sickness-Mongo

Sanders taught his people by example, by word of mouth, and by such punishment as occasion required. Of all methods, punishment was the least productive of result, for memory lasts only so long as pain, and men who had watched with quaking hearts a strapped body as it swayed from a tree branch, straightway forgot the crime for which the criminal died just as soon as the malefactor was decently interred.

Sanders taught the men of the *Zaire* to stack wood. He showed them that if it was stacked in the bow, the vessel would sink forward, or if it was stacked all on one side, the vessel would list. He stood over them, day after day, directing and encouraging them, and the same men were invariably his pupils because Sanders did not like new faces.

He was going upriver in some haste when he tied to a wooding to replenish his stock.

At the end of six years' tuition he left them to pile wood while he slept, and they did all the things which they should not have done.

This he discovered when he returned to the boat.

'Master,' said the headman of the wooders, and he spoke with justifiable pride, 'we have cut and stored the wood for the puc-a-puc in one morning, whereas other and slower folk would have worked till sundown, but because we love your lordship we have worked till the sweat fell from our bodies.'

Sanders looked at the wood piled all wrong, and looked at the headman.

'It is not wise,' he said, 'to store the wood in the bow, for thus the ship will sink, as I have often told you.'

'Lord, we did it because it was easiest,' said the man simply.

'That I can well believe,' said Sanders, and ordered the re-stacking, without temper.

You must remember that he was in a desperate hurry: that every hour counted. He had been steaming all night – a dangerous business, for the river was low and there were new sandbanks which did not appear on his home-made chart. Men fret their hearts out dealing with such little problems as ill-stacked wood, but Sanders neither fretted nor worried. If he had, he would have died, for things like this were part of his working day. Yet the headman's remissness worried him a little, for he knew the man was no fool.

In an hour the wood was more evenly distributed and Sanders rang the engines ahead. He put the nose of the boat to the centre of the stream and held on his course till at sunset he came to a place where the river widened abruptly, and where little islands were each a great green tangle of vegetation.

Here he slowed the steamer, carefully circumnavigating each island, till darkness fell, then he picked a cautious way to shore, through much shoal water. The *Zaire* bumped and shivered as she struck or grazed the hidden sandbanks.

Once she stopped dead, and her crew of forty slipped over the side of the boat, and wading, breast high, pushed her along with a deep-chested song.

At last he came to a shelving beach, and here, fastened by her steel hawsers to two trees, the boat waited for dawn.

Sanders had a bath, dressed, and came into his little deck-house to find his dinner waiting.

He ate the tiny chicken, took a stiff peg of whiskey, and lit his cigar. Then he sent for Abiboo.

'Abiboo,' he said, 'once you were a man in these parts.'

'Lord, it is so,' said Abiboo. 'I was a spy here for six months.'

'What do you know of these islands?'

'Lord, I only know that in one of them the Isisi bury their dead, and of another it is said that magic herbs grow; also that witch-doctors come thither to practise certain rites.'

Sanders nodded.

'Tomorrow we seek for the Island of Herbs,' he said, 'for I have information that evil things will be done at the full of the moon.'

'I am your man,' said Abiboo.

It happened two nights following this that a chief of the N'Gombi, a simple old man who had elementary ideas about justice and a considerable faith in devils, stole down the river with twelve men and with labour they fastened two pieces of wood shaped like a St Andrew's Cross between two trees.

They bent a young sapling, trimming the branches from the top, till it reached the head of the cross, and this they made fast with a fishing line. Whatever other preparations they may have contemplated making were indefinitely postponed because Sanders, who had been watching them from behind a convenient copal tree, stepped from his place of concealment, and the further proceedings failed to yield any satisfaction to the chief.

He eyed Sanders with a mild reproach.

'Lord, we set a trap for a leopard,' he explained, 'who is very terrible.'

'In other days,' mused Sanders aloud, 'a man seeing this cross would think of torture, O chief – and, moreover, leopards do not come to the middle island – tell me the truth.'

'Master,' said the old chief in agitation, 'this leopard swims, therefore he fills our hearts with fear.'

Sanders sighed wearily.

'Now you will tell me the truth, or I shall be more than any leopard.'

The chief folded his arms so that the flat of his hands touched his back, he being a lean man, and his hands fidgeted nervously.

'I cannot tell you a lie,' he said, 'because you are as a very bat, seeing into dark places readily and moving at night. Also you are like a sudden storm that comes up from trees without warning, and you are most terrible in your anger.'

'Get along,' said Sanders, passively irritable.

'Now this is the truth,' said the chief huskily. 'There is a man who comes to my village at sunset, and he is an evil one, for he has the protection of the Christ-man and yet he does abominable things – so we are for chopping him.'

Sanders peered at the chief keenly.

'If you chop him, chief, you will surely die,' he said softly, 'even if he be as evil as the devil – whichever type of devil you mostly fear. This is evidently a bad palaver indeed, and I will sit down with you for some days.'

He carried the chief and his party back to the village and held a palaver.

Now Sanders of the River in moments such as these was a man of inexhaustible patience; and of that patience he had considerable need when two hours after his arrival there came stalking grandly into the village a man whose name was Ofalikari, a man of the N'Gombi by a Congolaise father.

His other name was Joseph, and he was an evangelist.

This much Sanders discovered quickly enough.

'Fetch this man to me,' he said to Sergeant Abiboo, for the preacher made his palaver at the other end of the village.

Soon Abiboo returned.

'Master,' he said, 'this man will not come, being only agreeable to the demands of certain gods with which your honour is acquainted.'

Sanders showed his teeth.

'Go to him,' he said softly, 'and bring him; if he will come for no other cause, hit him with the flat of your bayonet.'

Abiboo saluted stiffly – after the style of native non-commissioned officers – and departed, to return with Ofalikari, whom he drew with him somewhat unceremoniously by the ear.

'Now,' said Sanders to the man, 'we will have a little talk, you and I.'

The sun went down, the moon came up, flooding the black river with mellow light, but still the talk went on – for this was a very serious palaver indeed.

A big fire was built in the very middle of the village street and here all the people gathered, whilst Sanders and the man sat face to face.

Occasionally a man or a woman would be sent for from the throng; once Sanders dispatched a messenger to a village five miles away to bring evidence. They came and went, those who testified against Ofalikari.

'Lord, one night we gathered by his command and he sacrificed a white goat,' said one witness.

'We swore by the dried heart of a white goat that we would do certain abominable things,' said another.

'By his order we danced a death dance at one end of the village, and the maidens danced the wedding dance at the other, then a certain slave was killed by him, and . . .'

Sanders nodded gravely.

'And he said that the sons of the White Goat should not die,' said another.

In the end Sanders rose and stretched himself.

'I have heard enough,' he said, and nodded to the sergeant of Houssas, who came forward with a pair of bright steel handcuffs.

One of these he snapped on the man's wrist, the other he held and led him to the boat.

The *Zaire* swung out to midstream, making a difficult way through the night to the mission station.

Ill news travels faster than an eight-knot steamboat can move upstream.

Sanders found the missionary waiting for him at daybreak on the strip of white beach, and the missionary, whose name was Haggin, was in one of those cold passions that saintly men permit themselves, for righteousness' sake.

'All England shall ring with this outrage,' he said, and his voice trembled. 'Woe the day when a British official joins the hosts of Satan . . .'

He said many other disagreeable things.

'Forget it,' said Sanders tersely; 'this man of yours has been playing the fool.'

And in his brief way he described the folly.

'It's a lie!' said the missionary. He was tall and thin, yellow with fever, and his hands shook as he threw them out protestingly. 'He has made converts for the faith, he has striven for souls . . .'

'Now listen to me,' said Sanders and he wagged a solemn forefinger at the other. 'I know this country. I know these people – you don't. I take your man to headquarters, not because he preaches the gospel, but because he holds meetings by night and practises strange rites which are not the rites of any known Church. Because he is a son of the White Goat, and I will have no secret societies in my land.'

If the truth be told, Sanders was in no frame of mind to consider the feelings of missionaries.

There was unrest in his territories – unrest of an elusive kind. There had been a man murdered on the Little River and none knew whose hand it was that struck him down.

His body, curiously carved, came floating downstream one sunny morning, and agents brought the news to Sanders. Then another had been killed and another. A life more or less is nothing in a land where people die by whole villages, but these men with their fantastic slashings worried Sanders terribly.

He had sent for his chief spies.

'Go north to the territory of the killing, which is on the edge of the N'Gombi country, and bring me news,' he said.

One such had sent him a tale of a killing palaver – so he had rushed north to find by the veriest accident that the threatened life was that of a man he desired most of all to place behind bars.

Now he was carrying his prisoner to headquarters. He was anxious to put an end to the growth of a movement which might well get beyond control, for secret societies spread like fire.

At noon he reached a wooding and tied up.

He summoned his headman.

'Lobolo,' he said, 'you shall stack the wood while I sleep, remembering all the wise counsel I gave you.'

'Lord, I am wise in your wisdom,' said the headman, and Abiboo having strung a hammock between two trees, Sanders tumbled in and fell asleep instantly.

Whilst he slept, one of the wooders detached himself from the working party, and came stealthily towards him.

Sanders' sleeping place was removed some distance from the shore, that the noise of chopping and sawing and the rattle of heavy billets on the steel deck should not disturb him.

Noiselessly the man moved until he came to within striking distance of the unconscious commissioner.

He took a firmer grip of the keen steel machette he carried and stepped forward.

Then a long sinewy hand caught him by the throat and pulled him down. He twisted his head and met the passionless gaze of Abiboo.

'We will go from here,' whispered the Houssa, 'lest our talk awake my lord.'

He wrenched the machette from the other's hand and followed him into the woods.

'You came to kill Sandi,' said Abiboo.

'That is true,' said the man, 'for I have a secret ju-ju which told me to do this, Sandi having offended. And if you harm me, the White Goat shall surely slay you, brown man.'

'I have eaten Sandi's salt,' said Abiboo, 'and whether I live or die is ordained. As for you, your fate is about your neck . . .'

Sanders woke from his sleep to find Abiboo squatting on the ground by the side of the hammock.

'What is it?' he asked.

'Nothing, lord,' said the man. 'I watched your sleep, for it is written, "He is a good servant who sees when his master's eyes are shut."'

Sanders heard the serious undertone to the proverb and was on the point of asking a question, then wisely checked himself.

He walked to the shore. The men had finished their work, and the wood was piled in one big, irregular heap in the well of the fore deck. It was piled so that it was impossible (1) for the steersman on the bridge above to see the river; (2) for the stoker to get anywhere near his furnace; (3) for the *Zaire* to float in anything less than three fathoms of water.

Already the little ship was down by the head, and the floats of her stern wheel merely skimming the surface of the river.

Sanders stood on the bank with folded arms looking at the work of the headman's hands. Then his eyes wandered along the length of the vessel. Amidships was a solid iron cage, protected from the heat of the sun by a double roof and broad canvas eaves. His eyes rested here for a long time, for the cage was empty and the emissary of the White Goat gone.

Sanders stood for a few moments in contemplation; then he stepped slowly down the bank and crossed the gangway.

'Be ears and eyes to me, Abiboo,' he said in Arabic, 'find what has become of Ofalikari, also the men who guarded him. Place these under arrest and bring them before me.'

He walked to his cabin, his head sunk in thought. This was serious, though he reserved his judgement till Abiboo returned with his prisoners.

They arrived under escort, a little alarmed, a little indignant.

'Lord, these men have reason,' said Abiboo.

'Why did you allow the prisoner to go?' asked Sanders.

'Thus it was, master,' said the senior of the two; 'whilst you slept the God-man came – him we saw at daybreak this morning. And he told us to let the prisoner come with him, and because he was a white man we obeyed him.'

'Only white men who are of the government may give such orders,' said Sanders; 'therefore I adjudge you guilty of folly, and I hold you for trial.'

There was nothing to be gained by lecturing them. He sent for his headman.

'Lobolo,' he said, 'ten years you have been my headman, and I have been kind to you.'

'Lord, you have been as a father,' said the old man, and his hand was shaking.

'Yonder,' said Sanders, pointing with his finger, 'lies your land and the village you came from is near enough. Let the storeman pay you your wages and never see me again.'

'Lord,' stammered the headman, 'if the stacking of wood was a fault –'

'Well, you know it is a fault,' said Sanders; 'you have eaten my bread and now you have sold me to the White Goats.'

The old man fell sobbing at his feet.

'Lord master,' he moaned, 'I did this because I was afraid, for a certain man told me that if I did not delay your lordship I should die, and, lord, death is very terrible to the old, because they live with it in their hearts.'

'Which man was this?' asked Sanders.

'One called Kema, lord.'

Sanders turned to his orderly.

'Find me Kema,' he said, and Abiboo shifted his feet.

'Lord, he has died the death,' he said simply, 'for while you slept he came to slay you. And I had some palaver with him.'

'And?'

'Lord, I saw him for an evil man and I smote his head from his body with a machette.'

Sanders was silent. He stood looking at the deck, then he turned to his cabin.

'Master,' said the waiting headman, 'what of me?'

The commissioner stretched his finger towards the shore, and with bowed shoulders Lobolo left the ship that had been his home for many years.

It took the greater part of an hour to trim the vessel.

'We will make for the mission station,' said Sanders, though he had no doubt in his mind as to what he would find . . .

The mission house was still burning when the *Zaire* rounded the river's head.

He found the missionary's charred body among the smouldering wreckage.

Of Ofalikari he found no trace.

There had been a secret society suppressed in Niger, and it had been broken by three regiments of native infantry, a battery of mountain guns and some loss of life. The 'British victory' and the 'splendid success of our arms' had given the people of the islands a great deal of satisfaction, but the commissioner who let the matter get to the stage of war was a ruined man, for governments do not like spending the millions they have put aside for the creation of a national pension scheme, which will bring them votes and kudos at the next election, on dirty little wars which bring nothing but vacancies in the junior ranks of the native army.

Sanders had a pigeon post from headquarters containing a straight-away telegram from the administrator.

Your message received and forwarded. Ministers wire settle your palaver by any means. For God's sake keep clear necessity employing army. Sending you one battalion Houssas and field gun. Do the best you can.

There was not much margin for wastage. The whole country was now rotten with rebellion. It had all happened in the twinkling of an eye. From being law-abiding and inoffensive, every village had become of a sudden the headquarters of the White Goats. Terrible rites were being performed on the Isisi; the N'Gombi had danced by whole communities the dance of the Goat; the Akasava killed two of Sanders' spies and had sent their heads to Sanders as proof of their 'earnest spirits' – to quote the message literally.

There was a missionary lady at Kosumkusu. Sanders' first thought was for her. He steamed direct from the smouldering ruins of Haggin's hut to find her.

She was amused at the growth of the secret societies, and thought it all very interesting.

Sanders did not tell her the aspect of the situation which was not amusing.

'Really, Mr Sanders,' she smiled, 'I'm quite safe here – this is the second time in three months you have tried to bring me into your fold.'

'This time you are coming,' said Sanders quietly. 'Abiboo has turned my cabin into a most luxurious boudoir.'

But she fenced with him to the limits of his patience.

'But what of Mr Haggin and Father Wells?' she asked. 'You aren't bothering about them.'

'I'm not bothering about Haggin,' said Sanders, 'because he's dead – I've just come from burying him.'

'Dead!'

'Murdered,' said Sanders briefly, 'and his mission burnt. I've sent an escort for the Jesuits. They may or they may not get down. We pick them up tomorrow, with luck.'

The girl's face had gone white.

'I'll come,' she said. 'I'm not afraid – yes, I am. And I'm giving you a lot of worry – forgive me.'

Sanders said something more or less incoherent, for he was not used to penitent womankind.

He took her straight away, and the *Zaire* was hardly out of sight before her chief convert set fire to the mission buildings.

Sanders picked up the Jesuits. His rescue party had arrived just in time. He landed his guests at headquarters and went back to the Upper River to await developments.

The *Zaire* had a complement of fifty men. They were technically deck hands and their duty lay in collecting wood, in taking aboard and discharging such stores as he brought with him and in assisting in the navigation of the boat.

He went to a wooding on the Calali River to replenish his stock of fuel and very wisely he 'wooded' by daylight.

The same night the whole of his men deserted, and he was left with twenty Houssas, Yoka the engineer and a Congo boy who acted as his cook.

This was his position when he dropped downstream to an Isisi river where he hoped news would await him.

For all the volcano which trembled beneath his feet, he gave no outward sign of perturbation. The movement could be checked, might indeed be destroyed, if Ofalikari were laid by the heels, but the 'missioner' had vanished and there was no reliable word as to his whereabouts.

Somewhere in the country he directed the operations of the society.

There was a lull; a sudden interval of inactivity. That was bad, as bad as it could be.

Sanders reviewed the position and saw no good in it; he remembered the commissioner who brought war to Niger and shivered, for he loved the country and he loved his work.

There were two days of heavy rains, and these were followed by two days of sweltering heat – and then Bosambo, a native chief, with all a native's malignity and indifference to suffering grafted to his knowledge of white men, sent a message to Sanders.

Two fast paddlers brought the messenger, and he stood up in his canoe to deliver his words.

'Thus said our lord Bosambo,' he shouted, keeping a respectful distance from the little boat. 'Go you to Sandi, but go not on board his ship on your life. Say to Sandi: The White Goat dies, and the people of these lands come back to wisdom before the moon is full.'

'Come to the ship and tell me more,' called Sanders. The man shook his head.

'Lord, it is forbidden,' he said, 'for our lord was very sure on that matter; and there is nothing to tell you, for we are ignorant men, only Bosambo being wiser than all men save your lordship.'

Sanders was puzzled. He knew the chief well enough to believe that he did not prophesy lightly, and yet –

'Go back to your chief,' he said, 'tell him that I have faith in him.'

Then he sat down at the junction of the Isisi and Calali Rivers for Bosambo to work miracles.

Bosambo, chief of the Ochori, had had in his time many gods. Some of these he retained for emergencies or because their possession added to his prestige. He neither loved nor feared them. Bosambo loved or feared no man, save Sanders.

The White Goats might have the chief of the Ochori in a cleft stick; they might seduce from their allegiance half and more than half of his people, as they had done, but Bosambo, who knew that weak men who acquire strength of a sudden, invariably signalise their independence by acquiring new masters, accepted the little troubles which accompany the chieftainship of such a tribe as his with pleasing philosophy.

It was a trying time for him, and it was a period not without some excitement for those who tried him.

A dish of fish came to him from his chief cook one morning. Bosambo ate a little, and sent for the same cook, who was one of his titular wives.

'Woman,' said Bosambo, 'if you try to poison me, I will burn you alive, by Ewa!'

She was speechless with terror and fell on her knees before him.

'As matters are,' said Bosambo, 'I shall not speak of your sin to Sandi, who is my sister's own child by a white father, for if Sandi knew of this, he would place you in boiling water till your eyes bulged like a fish. Go now, woman, and cook me clean food.'

Other attempts were made on his life. Once a spear whizzed past his head as he walked alone in the forest. Bosambo uttered a shriek and fell to the ground and the thrower, somewhat incautiously, came to see what mischief he had wrought, and if need be to finish the good work . . . Bosambo returned from his walk alone. He stopped by the river to wash his hands and scour his spears with wet sand, and that was the end of the adventure so far as his assailant was concerned.

But the power of the society was growing. His chief councillor was slain at meat, another was drowned, and his people began to display a marked insolence.

The air became electric. The Akasava had thrown off all disguise, the influence of the White Goat predominated. Chiefs and headmen obeyed the least of their hunters, or themselves joined in the lewd ritual celebrated nightly in the forest. The chief who had brought about the arrest of Ofalikari was pulled down and murdered in the open street by the very men who had lodged complaints, and the first to strike was his own son.

All these things were happening whilst Sanders waited at the junction of the Isisi and Calali Rivers, his Houssas sleeping by the guns.

Bosambo saw the end clearly. He had no illusions as to his ultimate fate. 'Tomorrow, light of my eyes,' he said to his first wife, 'I send you in a canoe to find Sandi, for men of the White Goat come openly – one man from every tribe, calling upon me to dance and make sacrifice.'

His wife was a Kano woman; tall and straight and comely. 'Lord,' she said simply, 'at the end you will take your spear and kill me, for here I sit till the end. When you die, life is death to me.'

Bosambo put his strong arm about her and patted her head.

The following day he sat at palaver, but few were the applicants for justice. There was a stronger force abroad in the land; a higher dispenser of favour.

At the moment he raised his hand to signify the palaver was finished a man came running from the forest. He ran unsteadily, like one who was drunken, throwing out his arms before him as though he was feeling his way.

He gained the village street, and came stumbling along, his sobbing breath being audible above the hum of the Ochoris' wondering talk.

Then suddenly a shrill voice cried a word in fear, and the people went bolting to their huts – and there was excuse, for this wanderer with the glazed eyes was sick to death, and his disease was that dreaded bush plague which decimates territories. It is an epidemic disease which makes its appearance once in twenty years; it has no known origin and no remedy.

Other diseases: sleeping sickness, beri-beri, malaria, are called by courtesy the sickness-mongo – 'The Sickness Itself' – but this mysterious malady alone is entitled to the description.

The man fell flat on the ground at the foot of the little hill where Bosambo sat in solitude – his headmen and councillors having fled in panic at the sick man's approach.

Bosambo looked at him thoughtfully.

'What may I do for you, my brother?' he asked.

'Save me,' moaned the man.

Bosambo was silent. He was a native, and a native mind is difficult to follow. I cannot explain its psychology. The coils were tightening on him, death faced him as assuredly as it stared hollow-eyed on the thing that writhed at his feet.

'I can cure you,' he said softly, 'by certain magic. Go you to the far end of the village, there you will find four new huts and in each hut three beds. Now you shall lie down on each bed and after you shall go into the forest as fast as you can walk and wait for my magic to work.'

Thus spake Bosambo, and the man at his feet, with death's hand already upon his shoulder, listened eagerly.

'Lord, is there any other thing I must do?' he asked in the thin whistling tone which is characteristic of the disease.

'This you must also do,' said Bosambo: 'you must go to these huts secretly so that none see you; and on each bed you shall lie so long as it will take a fish to die.'

Watched from a hundred doorways, the sick man made his way back to the forest; and the men of the village spat on the ground as he passed.

Bosambo sent his messengers to Sanders then and there, and patiently awaited the coming of the emissaries of the Goat.

At ten o'clock that night, before the moon was up, they arrived dramatically. Simultaneously twelve lights appeared, at twelve points about the village, then each light advanced at slow pace and revealed a man bearing a torch.

They advanced at solemn pace until they arrived together at a meeting place, and that place the open roadway before Bosambo's hut. In a blazing semicircle they stood before the chief – and the chief was not impressed.

For these delegates were a curious mixture. They included a petty chief of the Ochori – Bosambo marked him down for an ignominious end – a fisherman of the Isisi, a witch-doctor of the N'Gombi, a hunter of the Calali and, chiefest of all, a tall, broad-shouldered negro in the garb of white men.

This was Ofalikari, sometime preacher of the Word, and supreme head of the terrible order which was devastating the territories.

As they stood the voice of a man broke the silence with a song. He led it in a nasal falsetto, and the others acted as chorus.

'The White Goat is very strong and his horns are of gold.'

'Oai!' chorused the others.

'His blood is red and he teaches mysteries.'

'Oai!'

'When his life goes out his spirit becomes a god.'

'Oai!'

'Woe to those who stand between the White Goat and his freedom.'

'Oai!'

'For his sharp feet will cut them to the bone and his horns will bleed them.'

'Oai!'

They sang, one drum tapping rhythmically, the bangled feet of the chorus jingling as they pranced with deliberation at each 'Oai!'

When they had finished, Ofalikari spoke.

'Bosambo, we know you to be a wise man, and acquainted with white people and their gods, even as I am, for I was a teacher of the blessed Word. Now the White Goat loves you, Bosambo, and will do you no injury. Therefore have we come to summon you to a big palaver tomorrow, and to that palaver we will summon Sandi to answer for his wickedness. Him we will burn slowly, for he is an evil man.'

'Lord Goat,' said Bosambo, 'this is a big matter, and I will ask you to stay with me this night, that I may be guided and strengthened by your lordships' wisdom. I have built you four new huts,' he went on, 'knowing that your honours were coming; here you shall be lodged, and by my heart and my life no living man shall injure you.'

'No dead man can, Bosambo,' said Ofalikari, and there was a rocking shout of laughter. Bosambo laughed too; he laughed louder and longer than all the rest, he laughed so that Ofalikari was pleased with him.

'Go in peace,' said Bosambo, and the delegates went to their huts.

In the early hours of the morning Bosambo sent for Tomba, an enemy and a secret agent of the society.

'Go to the great lords,' he said, 'tell them I come to them tonight by the place where the Isisi River and the big river meet. And say to them that they must go quickly, for I do not wish to see them again, lest our adventure does not carry well, and Sandi punish me.'

At daybreak with his cloak of monkey tails about him – for the dawn was chilly – he watched the delegation leave the village and each member go his separate way.

He noted that Tomba accompanied them out of sight. He wasted half an hour, then went to his hut and emerged naked save for his loin cloth, his great shield on his left arm, and in the hand behind the shield a bundle of throwing spears.

To him moved fifty fighting men, the trusted and the faithful, and each carried his wicker war shield obliquely before him.

And the Ochori people, coward at heart, watched the little company in awe. They stood waiting, these fierce, silent warriors, till at a word they marched till they came to the four huts where Bosambo's guests had lain. Here they waited again. Tomba returned presently and stared uneasily at the armed rank.

'Tomba,' said Bosambo gently, 'did you say farewell to the Goat lords?'

'This I did, chief,' said Tomba.

'Embracing them as is the Goat custom?' asked Bosambo more softly still.

'Lord, I did this.'

Bosambo nodded.

'Go to that hut, O Tomba, great Goat and embracer of Goats.'

Tomba hesitated, then walked slowly to the nearest hut. He reached the door, and half turned.

'Slay!' whispered Bosambo, and threw the first spear.

With a yell of terror the man turned to flee, but four spears struck him within a space which the palm of a hand might cover and he rolled into the hut, dead.

Bosambo selected another spear, one peculiarly prepared, for beneath the spear head a great wad of dried grass had been bound and this had been soaked in copal gum.

A man brought him fire in a little iron cup and he set it to the spear, and with a jerk of his palm sent the blazing javelin to the hut's thatched roof.

In an instant it burst into flame – in ten minutes the four new houses were burning fiercely.

And on the flaming fire, the villagers, summoned to service, added fresh fuel and more and more, till the sweat rolled down their unprotected bodies. In the afternoon Bosambo allowed the fire to die down. He sent two armed men to each of the four roads that led into the village, and his orders were explicit.

'You shall kill any man or woman who leaves this place,' he said; 'also you shall kill any man or woman who, coming in, will not turn aside. And if you do not kill them, I myself will kill you. For I will not have the sickness-mongo in my city, lest our lord Sandi is angry.'

Sanders, waiting for he knew not what, heard the news, and went steaming to headquarters, sending pigeons in front asking for doctors. A week later he came back with sufficient medical stores to put the decks of the *Zaire* awash, but he came too late. The bush plague had run its course. It had swept through cities and lands and villages like a tempest, and strange it was that those cities which sent delegates to Bosambo suffered most, and in the N'Gombi city to which Ofalikari stumbled to die, one eighth of the population were wiped out.

'And how has it fared with you, Bosambo?' asked Sanders when the medical expedition came to Ochori.

'Lord,' said Bosambo, 'it has passed me by.'

There was a doctor in the party of an enquiring mind. 'Ask him how he accounts for his immunity,' he said to Sanders, for he had no knowledge of the vernacular, and Sanders repeated the question.

'Lord,' said Bosambo with simple earnestness, 'I prayed very earnestly, being, as your lordship knows, a *bueno Catolico*.'

And the doctor, who was also a 'good Catholic', was so pleased that he gave Bosambo a sovereign and a little writing pad – at least he did not give Bosambo the latter, but it is an indisputable fact that it was in the chief's hut when the party had gone.

EDITH WHARTON

Edith Wharton was born in 1862 into a prominent and wealthy New York family. In 1885 she married a Boston socialite; the couple travelled frequently and settled in France in 1907, but the marriage was unhappy and they divorced in 1913. On her trips to Europe, Wharton became a close friend of the novelist Henry James. Her first major novel was *The House of Mirth* (1905); many short stories, travel books, memoirs and novels followed, including *Ethan Frome* (1911), *The Reef* (1912) and *The Age of Innocence* (1920). Wharton was decorated for her humanitarian work during the First World War. She died in France in 1937.

A Bottle of Perrier

ONE

A two days' struggle over the treacherous trails in a well-intentioned but short-winded 'flivver', and a ride of two more on a hired mount of unamiable temper, had disposed young Medford, of the American School of Archaeology at Athens, to wonder why his queer English friend, Henry Almodham, had chosen to live in the desert.

Now he understood.

He was leaning against the roof parapet of the old building, half Christian fortress, half Arab palace, which had been Almodham's pretext; or one of them. Below, in an inner court, a little wind, rising as the sun sank, sent through a knot of palms the rain-like rattle so cooling to the pilgrims of the desert. An ancient fig tree, enormous, exuberant, writhed over a white-washed well-head, sucking life from what appeared to be the only source of moisture within the walls. Beyond these, on every side, stretched away the mystery of the sands, all golden with promise, all livid with menace, as the sun alternately touched or abandoned them.

Young Medford, somewhat weary after his journey from the coast, and awed by his first intimate sense of the omnipresence of the desert, shivered and drew back. Undoubtedly, for a scholar and a misogynist, it was a wonderful refuge; but one would have to be, incurably, both.

'Let's take a look at the house,' Medford said to himself, as if speedy contact with man's handiwork were necessary to his reassurance.

The house, he already knew, was empty save for the quick cosmopolitan manservant, who spoke a sort of palimpsest Cockney lined with Mediterranean tongues and desert dialects – English, Italian or Greek, which was he? – and two or three burnoused underlings who, having carried Medford's bags to his room, had relieved the palace of their gliding presences. Mr Almodham, the servant told him, was away; suddenly summoned by a friendly chief to visit some unexplored ruins to the south, he had ridden off at dawn, too hurriedly to write, but leaving messages of excuse and regret. That evening late he might be back, or next morning. Meanwhile Mr Medford was to make himself at home.

Almodham, as young Medford knew, was always making these archaeological explorations; they had been his ostensible reason for settling in that remote place, and his desultory search had already resulted in the discovery of several early Christian ruins of great interest.

Medford was glad that his host had not stood on ceremony, and rather relieved, on the whole, to have the next few hours to himself. He had had a malarial fever the previous summer, and in spite of his cork helmet he had probably caught a touch of the sun; he felt curiously, helplessly tired, yet deeply content.

And what a place it was to rest in! The silence, the remoteness, the illimitable air! And in the heart of the wilderness green leafage, water, comfort – he had already caught a glimpse of wide wicker chairs under the palms – a humane and welcoming habitation. Yes, he began to understand Almodham. To anyone sick of the Western fret and fever the very walls of this desert fortress exuded peace.

As his foot was on the ladder-like stair leading down from the roof, Medford saw the manservant's head rising towards him. It rose slowly and Medford had time to remark that it was sallow, bald on the top, diagonally dented with a long white scar, and ringed with thick ash-blond hair. Hitherto Medford had noticed only the man's face – youngish, but sallow also – and been chiefly struck by its wearing an odd expression which could best be defined as surprise.

The servant, moving aside, looked up, and Medford perceived that his air of surprise was produced by the fact that his intensely blue eyes were rather wider open than most eyes, and fringed with thick ash-blond lashes; otherwise there was nothing noticeable about him.

'Just to ask – what wine for dinner, sir? Champagne, or – '

'No wine, thanks.'

The man's disciplined lips were played over by a faint flicker of deprecation or irony, or both.

'Not any at all, sir?'

Medford smiled back. 'It's not out of respect for Prohibition.' He was sure that the man, of whatever nationality, would understand that; and he did.

'Oh, I didn't suppose, sir – '

'Well, no; but I've been rather seedy, and wine's forbidden.'

The servant remained incredulous. 'Just a little light Moselle, though, to colour the water, sir?'

'No wine at all,' said Medford, growing bored. He was still in the stage of convalescence when it is irritating to be argued with about one's dietary. 'Oh – what's your name, by the way?' he added, to soften the curtness of his refusal.

'Gosling,' said the other unexpectedly, though Medford didn't in the least know what he had expected him to be called.

'You're English, then?'

'Oh, yes, sir.'

'You've been in these parts a good many years, though?'

Yes, he had, Gosling said; rather too long for his own liking; and added that he had been born at Malta. 'But I know England well too.' His deprecating look returned. 'I will confess, sir, I'd like to have 'ad a look at Wembley.* Mr Almodham 'ad promised me – but there –' As if to minimise the abandon of this confidence, he followed it up by a ceremonious request for Medford's keys, and an enquiry as to when he would like to dine. Having received a reply, he still lingered, looking more surprised than ever.

'Just a mineral water, then, sir?'

'Oh, yes – anything.'

'Shall we say a bottle of Perrier?'

Perrier in the desert! Medford smiled assentingly, surrendered his keys and strolled away.

The house turned out to be smaller than he had imagined, or at least the habitable part of it; for above this towered mighty dilapidated walls of yellow stone, and in their crevices clung plaster chambers, one above the other, cedar-beamed, crimson-shuttered but crumbling. Out of this jumble of masonry and stucco, Christian and Moslem, the latest tenant of the fortress had chosen a cluster of rooms tucked into an angle of the ancient keep. These apartments opened on the uppermost court, where the palms chattered and the fig tree coiled above the well. On the broken marble pavement, chairs and a low table were grouped, and a few geraniums and blue morning-glories had been coaxed to grow between the slabs.

A white-skirted boy with watchful eyes was watering the plants; but at Medford's approach he vanished like a wisp of vapour.

There was something vaporous and insubstantial about the whole scene; even the long arcaded room opening on the court, furnished with saddlebag cushions, divans with gazelle skins and rough indigenous rugs; even the table piled with old copies of *The Times* and ultra-modern French and English reviews – all seemed, in that clear mocking air, born of the delusion of some desert wayfarer.

A seat under the fig tree invited Medford to doze, and when he woke the hard blue dome above him was gemmed with stars and the night breeze gossiped with the palms.

Rest – beauty – peace. Wise Almodham!

---

* A famous exhibition at Wembley, near London, took place in 1924.

TWO

Wise Almodham! Having carried out – with somewhat disappointing results – the excavation with which an archaeological society had charged him twenty-five years ago, he had lingered on, taken possession of the Crusaders' stronghold, and turned his attention from ancient to medieval remains. But even these investigations, Medford suspected, he prosecuted only at intervals, when the enchantment of his leisure did not lie on him too heavily.

The young American had met Henry Almodham at Luxor the previous winter; had dined with him at old Colonel Swordsley's, on that perfumed starlit terrace above the Nile; and, having somehow awakened the archaeologist's interest, had been invited to look him up in the desert the following year.

They had spent only that one evening together, with old Swordsley blinking at them under memory-laden lids, and two or three charming women from the Winter Palace chattering and exclaiming; but the two men had ridden back to Luxor together in the moonlight, and during that ride Medford fancied he had puzzled out the essential lines of Henry Almodham's character. A nature saturnine yet sentimental; chronic indolence alternating with spurts of highly intelligent activity; gnawing self-distrust soothed by intimate self-appreciation; a craving for complete solitude coupled with the inability to tolerate it for long.

There was more, too, Medford suspected: a dash of Victorian romance, gratified by the setting, the remoteness, the inaccessibility of his retreat, and by being known as *the* Henry Almodham – 'the one who lives in a Crusaders' castle, you know' – the gradual imprisonment in a pose assumed in youth, and into which middle age had slowly stiffened; and something deeper, darker, too, perhaps, though the young man doubted that; probably just the fact that living in that particular way had brought healing to an old wound, an old mortification, something which years ago had touched a vital part and left him writhing. Above all, in Almodham's hesitating movements and the dreaming look of his long well-featured brown face with its shock of grey hair, Medford detected an inertia, mental and moral, which life in this castle of romance must have fostered and excused.

'Once here, how easy not to leave!' he mused, sinking deeper into his deep chair.

'Dinner, sir,' Gosling announced.

The table stood in an open arch of the living-room; shaded candles made a rosy pool in the dusk. Each time he emerged into their light the servant, white-jacketed, velvet-footed, looked more competent and more surprised than ever. Such dishes, too – the cook also a Maltese? Ah, they were geniuses, these Maltese! Gosling bridled, smiled his acknowledgment, and started to fill the guest's glass with Chablis.

'No wine,' said Medford patiently.

'Sorry, sir. But the fact is – '

'You said there was Perrier?'

'Yes, sir; but I find there's none left. It's been awfully hot, and Mr Almodham has been and drank it all up. The new supply isn't due till next week. We 'ave to depend on the caravans going south.'

'No matter. Water, then. I really prefer it.'

Gosling's surprise widened to amazement. 'Not water, sir? Water – in these parts?'

Medford's irritability stirred again. 'Something wrong with your water? Boil it then, can't you? I won't – ' He pushed away the half-filled wineglass.

'Oh – boiled? Certainly, sir.' The man's voice dropped almost to a whisper. He placed on the table a succulent mess of rice and mutton, and vanished.

Medford leaned back, surrendering himself to the night, the coolness, the ripple of wind in the palms.

One agreeable dish succeeded another. As the last appeared, the diner began to feel the pangs of thirst, and at the same moment a beaker of water was placed at his elbow. 'Boiled, sir, and I squeezed a lemon into it.'

'Right. I suppose at the end of the summer your water gets a bit muddy?'

'That's it, sir. But you'll find this all right, sir.'

Medford tasted. 'Better than Perrier.' He emptied the glass, leaned back and groped in his pocket. A tray was instantly at his hand with cigars and cigarettes.

'You don't – smoke sir?'

Medford, for answer, held up his cigar to the man's light. 'What do you call this?'

'Oh, just so. I meant the other style.' Gosling glanced discreetly at the opium pipes of jade and amber laid out on a low table.

Medford shrugged away the invitation – and wondered. Was that perhaps Almodham's other secret – or one of them? For he began to think there might be many; and all, he was sure, safely stored away behind Gosling's vigilant brow.

'No news yet of Mr Almodham?'

Gosling was gathering up the dishes with dexterous gestures. For a moment he seemed not to hear. Then – from beyond the candle gleam – 'News, sir? There couldn't 'ardly be, could there? There's no wireless in the desert, sir; not like London.' His respectful tone tempered the slight irony. 'But tomorrow evening ought to see him riding in.' Gosling paused, drew nearer, swept one of his swift hands across the table in pursuit of the last crumbs, and added tentatively: 'You'll surely be able, sir, to stay till then?'

Medford laughed. The night was too rich in healing; it sank on his spirit like wings. Time vanished, fret and trouble were no more. 'Stay, I'll stay a year if I have to!'

'Oh – a year?' Gosling echoed it playfully, gathered up the dessert dishes and was gone.

THREE

Medford had said that he would wait for Almodham a year; but the next morning he found that such arbitrary terms had lost their meaning. There were no time measures in a place like this. The silly face of his watch told its daily tale to emptiness. The wheeling of the constellations over those ruined walls marked only the revolutions of the earth; the spasmodic motions of man meant nothing.

The very fact of being hungry, that stroke of the inward clock, was minimised by the slightness of the sensation – just the ghost of a pang, that might have been quieted by dried fruit and honey. Life had the light monotonous smoothness of eternity.

Toward sunset Medford shook off this queer sense of otherwhereness and climbed to the roof. Across the desert he spied for Almodham. Southward the Mountains of Alabaster hung like a blue veil lined with light. In the west a great column of fire shot up, spraying into plumy cloudlets which turned the sky to a fountain of rose-leaves, the sands beneath to gold.

No riders specked them. Medford watched in vain for his absent host till night fell, and the punctual Gosling invited him once more to table.

In the evening Medford absently fingered the ultra-modern reviews – three months old, and already so stale to the touch – then tossed them aside, flung himself on a divan and dreamed. Almodham must spend a lot of time dreaming; that was it. Then, just as he felt himself sinking down into torpor, he would be off on one of these dashes across the desert in quest of unknown ruins. Not such a bad life.

Gosling appeared with Turkish coffee in a cup cased in filigree.

'Are there any horses in the stable?' Medford suddenly asked.

'Horses? Only what you might call pack-horses, sir. Mr Almodham has the two best saddle-horses with him.'

'I was thinking I might ride out to meet him.'

Gosling considered. 'So you might, sir.'

'Do you know which way he went?'

'Not rightly, sir. The caid's man was to guide them.'

'Them? Who went with him?'

'Just one of our men, sir. They've got the two thoroughbreds. There's a third, but he's lame.'

Gosling paused. 'Do you know the trails, sir? Excuse me, but I don't think I ever saw you here before.'

'No,' Medford acquiesced, 'I've never been here before.'

'Oh, then' – Gosling's gesture added: 'In that case, even the best thoroughbred wouldn't help you.'

'I suppose he may still turn up tonight?'

'Oh, easily, sir. I expect to see you both breakfasting here tomorrow morning,' said Gosling cheerfully.

Medford sipped his coffee. 'You said you'd never seen me here before. How long have you been here yourself?'

Gosling answered instantly, as though the figures were never long out of his memory: 'Eleven years and seven months altogether, sir,'

'Nearly twelve years! That's a longish time.'

'Yes, it is.'

'And I don't suppose you often get away?'

Gosling was moving off with the tray. He halted, turned back, and said with sudden emphasis: 'I've never once been away. Not since Mr Almodham first brought me here.'

'Good Lord! Not a single holiday?'

'Not one, sir.'

'But Mr Almodham goes off occasionally. I met him at Luxor last year.'

'Just so, sir. But when he's here he needs me for himself; and when he's away he needs me to watch over the others. So you see –'

'Yes, I see. But it must seem to you devilish long.'

'It seems long, sir.'

'But the others? You mean they're not – wholly trustworthy?'

'Well, sir, they're just Arabs,' said Gosling with careless contempt.

'I see. And not a single old reliable among them?'

'The term isn't in their language, sir.'

Medford was busy lighting his cigar. When he looked up he found that Gosling still stood a few feet off.

'It wasn't as if it 'adn't been a promise, you know, sir,' he said, almost passionately.

'A promise?'

'To let me 'ave my holiday, sir. A promise – agine and agine.'

'And the time never came?'

'No, sir, the days just drifted by –'

'Ah. They would, here. Don't sit up for me,' Medford added. 'I think I shall wait up – wait for Mr Almodham.'

Gosling's stare widened. 'Here, sir? Here in the court?'

The young man nodded, and the servant stood still regarding him, turned by the moonlight to a white spectral figure, the unquiet ghost of a patient butler who might have died without his holiday.

'Down here in the court all night, sir? It's a lonely spot. I couldn't 'ear you if you was to call. You're best in bed, sir. The air's bad. You might bring your fever on again.'

Medford laughed and stretched himself in his long chair. 'Decidedly,' he thought, 'the fellow needs a change.' Aloud he remarked: 'Oh, I'm all right. It's you who are nervous, Gosling. When Mr Almodham comes back I mean to put in a word for you. You shall have your holiday.'

Gosling still stood motionless. For a minute he did not speak. 'You would, sir, you would?' He gasped it out on a high cracked note, and the last word ran into a laugh – a brief shrill cackle, the laugh of one long unused to such indulgences.

'Thank you, sir. Good-night, sir.' He was gone.

FOUR

'You do boil my drinking-water, always?' Medford questioned, his hand clasping the glass without lifting it.

The tone was amicable, almost confidential; Medford felt that since his rash promise to secure a holiday for Gosling he and Gosling were on terms of real friendship.

'Boil it? Always, sir. Naturally.' Gosling spoke with a slight note of reproach, as though Medford's question implied a slur – unconscious, he hoped – on their newly established relation. He scrutinised Medford with his astonished eyes, in which a genuine concern showed itself through the glaze of professional indifference.

'Because, you know, my bath this morning – '

Gosling was in the act of receiving from the hands of a gliding Arab a fragrant dish of couscous. Under his breath he hissed to the native: 'You damned aboriginy, you, can't even 'old a dish steady? Ugh!' The Arab vanished before the imprecation, and Gosling, with a calm deliberate hand, set the dish before Medford. 'All alike, they are.' Fastidiously he wiped a trail of grease from his linen sleeve.

'Because, you know, my bath this morning simply stank,' said Medford, plunging fork and spoon into the dish.

'Your bath, sir?' Gosling stressed the word. Astonishment, to the exclusion of all other emotion, again filled his eyes as he rested them on Medford. 'Now, I wouldn't 'ave 'ad that 'appen for the world,' he said self-reproachfully.

'There's only the one well here, eh? The one in the court?'

Gosling aroused himself from absorbed consideration of the visitor's complaint. 'Yes, sir; only the one.'

'What sort of a well is it? Where does the water come from?'

'Oh, it's just a cistern, sir. Rainwater. There's never been any other here. Not that I ever knew it to fail; but at this season sometimes it does turn queer. Ask any o' them Arabs, sir; they'll tell you. Liars as they are, they won't trouble to lie about that.'

Medford was cautiously tasting the water in his glass. 'This seems all right,' he pronounced.

Sincere satisfaction was depicted on Gosling's countenance. 'I seen to its being boiled myself, sir. I always do. I 'ope that Perrier'll turn up tomorrow, sir.'

'Oh, tomorrow – ' Medford shrugged, taking a second helping. 'Tomorrow I may not be here to drink it.'

'What – going away, sir?' cried Gosling.

Medford, wheeling round abruptly, caught a new and incomprehensible look in Gosling's eyes. The man had seemed to feel a sort of dog-like affection for him; had wanted, Medford could have sworn, to keep him on, persuade him to patience and delay; yet now, Medford could equally have sworn, there was relief in his look, satisfaction, almost, in his voice.

'So soon, sir?'

'Well, this is the fifth day since my arrival. And as there's no news yet of Mr Almodham, and you say he may very well have forgotten all about my coming – '

'Oh, I don't say that, sir; not forgotten! Only, when one of those old piles of stones takes 'old of him, he does forget about the time, sir. That's what I meant. The days drift by – 'e's in a dream. Very likely he thinks you're just due now, sir.' A small thin smile sharpened the lustreless gravity of Gosling's features. It was the first time that Medford had seen him smile.

'Oh, I understand. But still – ' Medford paused. Through the spell of inertia laid on him by the drowsy place and its easeful comforts his instinct of alertness was struggling back. 'It's odd – '

'What's odd?' Gosling echoed unexpectedly, setting the dried dates and figs on the table.

'Everything,' said Medford.

He leaned back in his chair and glanced up through the arch at the lofty sky from which noon was pouring down in cataracts of blue and gold. Almodham was out there somewhere under that canopy of fire, perhaps, as the servant said, absorbed in his dream. The land was full of spells.

'Coffee, sir?' Gosling reminded him. Medford took it.

'It's odd that you say you don't trust any of these fellows – these Arabs –

and yet that you don't seem to feel worried at Mr Almodham's being off God knows where, all alone with them.'

Gosling received this attentively, impartially; he saw the point. 'Well, sir, no – you wouldn't understand. It's the very thing that can't be taught, when to trust 'em and when not. It's 'ow their interests lie, of course, sir; and their religion, as they call it.' His contempt was unlimited. 'But even to begin to understand why I'm not worried about Mr Almodham, you'd 'ave to 'ave lived among them, sir, and you'd 'ave to speak their language.'

'But I – ' Medford began. He pulled himself up short and bent above his coffee.

'Yes, sir.'

'But I've travelled among them more or less.'

'Oh, travelled!' Even Gosling's intonation could hardly conciliate respect with derision in his reception of this boast.

'This makes the fifth day, though,' Medford continued argumentatively. The midday heat lay heavy even on the shaded side of the court, and the sinews of his will were weakening.

'I can understand, sir, a gentleman like you 'aving other engagements – being pressed for time, as it were,' Gosling reasonably conceded.

He cleared the table, committed its freight to a pair of Arab arms that just showed and vanished, and finally took himself off while Medford sank into the divan. A land of dreams . . .

The afternoon hung over the place like a great velarium of cloth-of-gold stretched across the battlements and drooping down in ever slacker folds upon the heavy-headed palms. When at length the gold turned to violet, and the west to a bow of crystal clasping the desert sands, Medford shook off his sleep and wandered out. But this time, instead of mounting to the roof, he took another direction.

He was surprised to find how little he knew of the place after five days of loitering and waiting. Perhaps this was to be his last evening alone in it. He passed out of the court by a vaulted stone passage which led to another walled enclosure. At his approach two or three Arabs who had been squatting there rose and melted out of sight. It was as if the solid masonry had received them.

Beyond, Medford heard a stamping of hoofs, the stir of a stable at night-fall. He went under another archway and found himself among horses and mules. In the fading light an Arab was rubbing down one of the horses, a powerful young chestnut. He too seemed about to vanish; but Medford caught him by the sleeve.

'Go on with your work,' he said in Arabic.

The man, who was young and muscular, with a lean Bedouin face, stopped and looked at him.

'I didn't know your excellency spoke our language.'

'Oh, yes,' said Medford.

The man was silent, one hand on the horse's restless neck, the other thrust into his woollen girdle. He and Medford examined each other in the faint light.

'Is that the horse that's lame?' Medford asked.

'Lame?' The Arab's eyes ran down the animal's legs. 'Oh, yes; lame,' he answered vaguely.

Medford stooped and felt the horses knees and fetlocks. 'He seems pretty fit. Couldn't he carry me for a canter this evening if I felt like it?'

The Arab considered; he was evidently perplexed by the weight of responsibility which the question placed on him.

'Your excellency would like to go for a ride this evening?'

'Oh, just a fancy. I might or I might not.' Medford lit a cigarette and offered one to the groom, whose white teeth flashed his gratification. Over the shared match they drew nearer and the Arab's diffidence seemed to lessen.

'Is this one of Mr Almodham's own mounts?' Medford asked.

'Yes, sir; it's his favourite,' said the groom, his hand passing proudly down the horse's bright shoulder.

'His favourite? Yet he didn't take him on this long expedition?'

The Arab fell silent and stared at the ground.

'Weren't you surprised at that?' Medford queried.

The man's gesture declared that it was not his business to be surprised.

The two remained without speaking while the quick blue night descended.

At length Medford said carelessly: 'Where do you suppose your master is at this moment?'

The moon, unperceived in the radiant fall of day, had now suddenly possessed the world, and a broad white beam lay full on the Arab's white smock, his brown face and the turban of camel's hair knotted above it. His agitated eyeballs glistened like jewels.

'If Allah would vouchsafe to let us know!'

'But you suppose he's safe enough, don't you? You don't think it's necessary yet for a party to go out in search of him?'

The Arab appeared to ponder this deeply. The question must have taken him by surprise. He flung a brown arm about the horse's neck and continued to scrutinise the stones of the court.

'When the master is away Mr Gosling is our master.'

'And he doesn't think it necessary?'

The Arab sighed: 'Not yet.'

'But if Mr Almodham were away much longer – '

The man was again silent, and Medford continued: 'You're the head groom, I suppose?'

'Yes, excellency.'

There was another pause. Medford half turned away; then over his shoulder: 'I suppose you know the direction Mr Almodham took? The place he's gone to?'

'Oh, assuredly, excellency.'

'Then you and I are going to ride after him. Be ready an hour before daylight. Say nothing to anyone – Mr Gosling or anybody else. We two ought to be able to find him without other help.'

The Arab's face was all a responsive flash of eyes and teeth. 'Oh, sir, I undertake that you and my master shall meet before tomorrow night. And none shall know of it.'

'He's as anxious about Almodham as I am,' Medford thought; and a faint shiver ran down his back. 'All right. Be ready,' he repeated.

He strolled back and found the court empty of life, but fantastically peopled by palms of beaten silver and a white marble fig tree.

'After all,' he thought irrelevantly, 'I'm glad I didn't tell Gosling that I speak Arabic.'

He sat down and waited till Gosling, approaching from the living-room, ceremoniously announced for the fifth time that dinner was served.

FIVE

Medford sat up in bed with the jerk which resembles no other. Someone was in his room. The fact reached him not by sight or sound – for the moon had set, and the silence of the night was complete – but by a peculiar faint disturbance of the invisible currents that enclose us.

He was awake in an instant, caught up his electric hand-lamp and flashed it into two astonished eyes. Gosling stood above the bed.

'Mr Almodham – he's back?' Medford exclaimed.

'No, sir; he's not back.' Gosling spoke in low controlled tones. His extreme self-possession gave Medford a sense of danger – he couldn't say why, or of what nature. He sat upright, looking hard at the man.

'Then what's the matter?'

'Well, sir, you might have told me you talk Arabic' – Gosling's tone was now wistfully reproachful – 'before you got 'obnobbing with that Selim. Making randyvoos with 'im by night in the desert.'

Medford reached for his matches and lit the candle by the bed. He did not know whether to kick Gosling out of the room or to listen to what the man had to say; but a quick movement of curiosity made him determine on the latter course.

'Such folly! First I thought I'd lock you in. I might 'ave.' Gosling drew a key from his pocket and held it up. 'Or again I might 'ave let you go. Easier than not. But there was Wembley.'

'Wembley?' Medford echoed. He began to think that the man was going mad. One might, so conceivably, in that place of postponements and enchantments! He wondered whether Almodham himself were not a little mad – if, indeed, Almodham were still in a world where such a fate is possible.

'Wembley. You promised to get Mr Almodham to give me an 'oliday – to let me go back to England in time for a look at Wembley. Every man 'as 'is fancies, 'asn't he, sir? And that's mine. I've told Mr Almodham so, agine and agine. He'd never listen, or only make believe to; say: "We'll see, now, Gosling, we'll see" – and no more 'eard of it. But you was different, sir. You said it, and I knew you meant it – about my 'oliday. So I'm going to lock you in.' Gosling spoke composedly, but with an under-thrill of emotion in his queer Mediterranean-Cockney voice.

'Lock me in?'

'Prevent you somehow from going off with that murderer. You don't suppose you'd ever 'ave come back alive from that ride, do you?'

A shiver ran over Medford, as it had the evening before when he had said to himself that the Arab was as anxious as he was about Almodham. He gave a slight laugh.

'I don't know what you're talking about. But you're not going to lock me in.'

The effect of this was unexpected. Gosling's face was drawn up into a convulsive grimace and two tears rose to his pale eyelashes and ran down his cheeks.

'You don't trust me, after all,' he said plaintively.

Medford leaned on his pillow and considered. Nothing as queer had ever before happened to him. The fellow looked almost ridiculous enough to laugh at; yet his tears were certainly not simulated. Was he weeping for Almodham, already dead, or for Medford, about to be committed to the same grave?

'I should trust you at once,' said Medford, 'if you'd tell me where your master is.'

Gosling's face resumed its usual guarded expression, though the trace of the tears still glittered on it.

'I can't do that, sir.'

'Ah, I thought so!'

'Because – 'ow do I know?'

Medford thrust a leg out of bed. One hand, under the blanket, lay on his revolver.

'Well, you may go now. Put that key down on the table first. And don't try to do anything to interfere with my plans. If you do I'll shoot you,' he added concisely.

'Oh, no, you wouldn't shoot a British subject; it makes such a fuss. Not that I'd care – I've often thought of doing it myself. Sometimes in the sirocco season. That don't scare me. And you shan't go.'

Medford was on his feet now, the revolver visible. Gosling eyed it with indifference.

'Then you do know where Mr Almodham is? And you're determined that I shan't find out?' Medford challenged him.

'Selim's determined,' said Gosling, 'and all the others are. They all want you out of the way. That's why I've kept 'em to their quarters – done all the waiting on you myself. Now will you stay here? For God's sake, sir! The return caravan is going through to the coast the day after tomorrow. Join it, sir – it's the only safe way! I darsn't let you go with one of our men, not even if you was to swear you'd ride straight for the coast and let this business be.'

'This business? What business?'

'This worrying about where Mr Almodham is, sir. Not that there's anything to worry about. The men all know that. But the plain fact is they've stolen some money from his box, since he's been gone, and if I hadn't winked at it they'd 'ave killed me; and all they want is to get you to ride out after 'im, and put you safe away under a 'eap of sand somewhere off the caravan trails. Easy job. There; that's all, sir. My word it is.'

There was a long silence. In the weak candlelight the two men stood considering each other.

Medford's wits began to clear as the sense of peril closed in on him. His mind reached out on all sides into the enfolding mystery, but it was everywhere impenetrable. The odd thing was that, though he did not believe half of what Gosling had told him, the man yet inspired him with a queer sense of confidence as far as their mutual relation was concerned. 'He may be lying about Almodham, to hide God knows what; but I don't believe he's lying about Selim.'

Medford laid his revolver on the table. 'Very well,' he said. 'I won't ride out to look for Mr Almodham, since you advise me not to. But I won't leave by the caravan; I'll wait here till he comes back.'

He saw Gosling whiten under his sallowness. 'Oh, don't do that, sir; I couldn't answer for them if you was to wait. The caravan'll take you to the coast the day after tomorrow as easy as if you was riding in Rotten Row.'

'Ah, then you know that Mr Almodham won't be back by the day after tomorrow?' Medford caught him up.

'I don't know anything, sir.'

'Not even where he is now?'

Gosling reflected. 'He's been gone too long, sir, for me to know that,' he said from the threshold.

The door closed on him.

Medford found sleep unrecoverable. He leaned in his window and watched the stars fade and the dawn break in all its holiness. As the stir of life rose among the ancient walls he marvelled at the contrast between that fountain of purity welling up into the heavens and the evil secrets clinging bat-like to the nest of masonry below.

He no longer knew what to believe or whom. Had some enemy of Almodham's lured him into the desert and bought the connivance of his people? Or had the servants had some reason of their own for spiriting him away, and was Gosling possibly telling the truth when he said that the same fate would befall Medford if he refused to leave?

Medford, as the light brightened, felt his energy return. The very impenetrableness of the mystery stimulated him. He would stay, and he would find out the truth.

SIX

It was always Gosling himself who brought up the water for Medford's bath; but this morning he failed to appear with it, and when he came it was to bring the breakfast tray. Medford noticed that his face was of a pasty pallor, and that his lids were reddened as if with weeping. The contrast was unpleasant, and a dislike for Gosling began to shape itself in the young man's breast.

'My bath?' he queried.

'Well, sir, you complained yesterday of the water – '

'Can't you boil it?'

'I 'ave, sir.'

'Well, then – '

Gosling went out sullenly and presently returned with a brass jug. 'It's the time of year – we're dying for rain,' he grumbled, pouring a scant measure of water into the tub.

Yes, the well must be pretty low, Medford thought. Even boiled, the water had the disagreeable smell that he had noticed the day before, though of course, in a slighter degree. But a bath was a necessity in that climate. He splashed the few cupfuls over himself as best as he could.

He spent the day in rather fruitlessly considering his situation. He had hoped the morning would bring counsel, but it brought only courage and resolution, and these were of small use without enlightenment. Suddenly he remembered that the caravan going south from the coast would pass near the castle that afternoon. Gosling had dwelt on the date often enough, for it was the caravan which was to bring the box of Perrier water.

'Well, I'm not sorry for that,' Medford reflected, with a slight shrinking of the flesh. Something sick and viscous, half smell, half substance, seemed to have clung to his skin since his morning bath, and the idea of having to drink that water again was nauseating.

But his chief reason for welcoming the caravan was the hope of finding in it some European, or at any rate some native official from the coast, to whom he might confide his anxiety. He hung about, listening and waiting, and then mounted to the roof to gaze northward along the trail. But in the afternoon glow he saw only three Bedouins guiding laden pack mules towards the castle.

As they mounted the steep path he recognised some of Almodham's men, and guessed at once that the southward caravan trail did not actually pass under the walls and that the men had been out to meet it, probably at a small oasis behind some fold of the sand-hills. Vexed at his own thoughtlessness in not foreseeing such a possibility, Medford dashed down to the court, hoping the men might have brought back some news of Almodham, though, as the latter had ridden south, he could at best only have crossed the trail by which the caravan had come. Still, even so, someone might know something, some report might have been heard – since everything was always known in the desert.

As Medford reached the court, angry vociferations, and retorts as vehement, rose from the stable-yard. He leaned over the wall and listened. Hitherto nothing had surprised him more than the silence of the place. Gosling must have had a strong arm to subdue the shrill voices of his underlings. Now they had all broken loose, and it was Gosling's own voice – usually so discreet and measured – which dominated them.

Gosling, master of all the desert dialects, was cursing his subordinates in a half-dozen.

'And you didn't bring it – and you tell me it wasn't there, and I tell you it was, and that you know it, and that you either left it on a sand-heap while you were jawing with some of those slimy fellows from the coast, or else fastened it on to the horse so carelessly that it fell off on the way – and all of you too sleepy to notice. Oh, you sons of females I wouldn't soil my lips by naming! Well, back you go to hunt it up, that's all.'

'By Allah and the tomb of his Prophet, you wrong us unpardonably. There was nothing left at the oasis, nor yet dropped off on the way back. It was not there, and that is the truth in its purity.'

'Truth! Purity! You miserable lot of shirks and liars, you – and the gentleman here not touching a drop of anything but water – as you profess to do, you liquor-swilling humbugs!'

Medford drew back from the parapet with a smile of relief. It was nothing but a case of Perrier – the missing case – which had raised the passions of these grown men to the pitch of frenzy! The anti-climax lifted a load from his breast. If Gosling, the calm and self-controlled, could waste his wrath on so slight a hitch in the working of the commissariat, he at least must have a free mind. How absurd this homely incident made Medford's speculations seem!

He was at once touched by Gosling's solicitude, and annoyed that he should have been so duped by the hallucinating fancies of the East.

Almodham was off on his own business; very likely the men knew where and what the business was; and even if they had robbed him in his absence, and quarrelled over the spoils, Medford did not see what he could do. It might even be that his eccentric host – with whom, after all, he had had but one evening's acquaintance – repenting an invitation too rashly given, had ridden away to escape the boredom of entertaining him. As this alternative occurred to Medford it seemed so plausible that he began to wonder if Almodham had not simply withdrawn to some secret suite of that intricate dwelling, and were waiting there for his guest's departure.

So well would this explain Gosling's solicitude to see the visitor off – so completely account for the man's nervous and contradictory behaviour – that Medford, smiling at his own obtuseness, hastily resolved to leave on the morrow. Tranquillised by this decision, he lingered about the court till dusk fell, and then, as usual, went up to the roof. But today his eyes, instead of raking the horizon, fastened on the clustering edifice of which, after six days' residence, he knew so little. Aerial chambers, jutting out at capricious angles, baffled him with closely shuttered windows, or here and there with the enigma of painted panes. Behind which window was his host concealed, spying, it might be, at this very moment on the movements of his lingering guest?

The idea that that strange moody man, with his long brown face and shock of white hair, his half-guessed selfishness and tyranny, and his morbid self-absorption, might be actually within a stone's throw, gave Medford, for the first time, a sharp sense of isolation. He felt himself shut out, unwanted – the place, now that he imagined someone might be living in it unknown to him, became lonely, inhospitable, dangerous.

'Fool that I am – he probably expected me to pack up and go as soon as I found he was away!' the young man reflected. Yes; decidedly he would leave the next morning.

Gosling had not shown himself all the afternoon. When at length, belatedly, he came to set the table, he wore a look of sullen, almost surly, reserve which Medford had not yet seen on his face. He hardly returned the young man's friendly, 'Hallo – dinner?' and when Medford was seated handed him the first dish in silence. Medford's glass remained unfilled till he touched its brim.

'Oh, there's nothing to drink, sir. The men lost the case of Perrier – or dropped it and smashed the bottles. They say it never came. 'Ow do I know, when they never open their 'eathen lips but to lie?' Gosling burst out with sudden violence.

He set down the dish he was handing, and Medford saw that he had been obliged to do so because his whole body was shaking as if with fever.

'My dear man, what does it matter? You're going to be ill,' Medford exclaimed, laying his hand on the servant's arm. But the latter, muttering: 'Oh, God, if I'd only 'a' gone for it myself,' jerked away and vanished from the room.

Medford sat pondering; it certainly looked as if poor Gosling were on the edge of a breakdown. No wonder, when Medford himself was so oppressed by the uncanniness of the place. Gosling reappeared after an interval, correct, close-lipped, with the dessert and a bottle of white wine. 'Sorry, sir.'

To pacify him, Medford sipped the wine and then pushed his chair away and returned to the court. He was making for the fig tree by the well when Gosling, slipping ahead, transferred his chair and wicker table to the other end of the court.

'You'll be better here – there'll be a breeze presently,' he said. 'I'll fetch your coffee.'

He disappeared again, and Medford sat gazing up at the pile of masonry and plaster, and wondering whether he had not been moved away from his favourite corner to get him out of – or into? – the angle of vision of the invisible watcher. Gosling, having brought the coffee, went away and Medford sat on.

At length he rose and began to pace up and down as he smoked. The moon was not up yet, and darkness fell solemnly on the ancient walls. Presently the breeze arose and began its secret commerce with the palms.

Medford went back to his seat; but as soon as he had resumed it he fancied that the gaze of his hidden watcher was jealously fixed on the red spark of his cigar. The sensation became increasingly distasteful; he could almost feel Almodham reaching out long ghostly arms from somewhere above him in the darkness. He moved back into the living-room, where a shaded light hung from the ceiling; but the room was airless, and finally he went out again and dragged his seat to its old place under the fig tree. From there the windows which he suspected could not command him, and he felt easier, though the corner was out of the breeze and the heavy air seemed tainted with the exhalation of the adjoining well.

'The water must be very low,' Medford mused. The smell, though faint, was unpleasant; it smirched the purity of the night. But he felt safer there, somehow, farther from those unseen eyes which seemed mysteriously to have become his enemies.

'If one of the men had knifed me in the desert, I shouldn't wonder if it would have been at Almodham's orders,' Medford thought. He drowsed.

When he woke the moon was pushing up its ponderous orange disk above the walls, and the darkness in the court was less dense. He must have slept for an hour or more. The night was delicious, or would have been anywhere but there. Medford felt a shiver of his old fever and remembered that Gosling had warned him that the court was unhealthy at night.

'On account of the well, I suppose. I've been sitting too close to it,' he reflected. His head ached, and he fancied that the sweetish foulish smell clung to his face as it had after his bath. He stood up and approached the well to see how much water was left in it. But the moon was not yet high enough to light those depths, and he peered down into blackness.

Suddenly he felt both shoulders gripped from behind and forcibly pressed forward, as if by someone seeking to push him over the edge. An instant later, almost coinciding with his own swift resistance, the push became a strong tug backwards, and he swung round to confront Gosling, whose hands immediately dropped from his shoulders.

'I thought you had the fever, sir – I seemed to see you pitching over,' the man stammered.

Medford's wits returned. 'We must both have it, for I fancied you were pitching me,' he said with a laugh.

'Me, sir?' Gosling gasped. 'I pulled you back as 'ard as ever – '

'Of course. I know.'

'Whatever are you doing here, anyhow, sir? I warned you it was un'ealthy at night,' Gosling continued irritably.

Medford leaned against the well-head and contemplated him. 'I believe the whole place is unhealthy.'

Gosling was silent. At length he asked: 'Aren't you going up to bed, sir?'

'No,' said Medford, 'I prefer to stay here.'

Gosling's face took on an expression of dogged anger. 'Well, then, I prefer that you shouldn't.'

Medford laughed again. 'Why? Because it's the hour when Mr Almodham comes out to take the air?'

The effect of this question was unexpected. Gosling dropped back a step or two and flung up his hands, pressing them to his lips as if to stifle a low outcry.

'What's the matter?' Medford queried. The man's antics were beginning to get on his nerves.

'Matter?' Gosling still stood away from him, out of the rising slant of moonlight.

'Come! Own up that he's here and have done with it!' cried Medford impatiently.

'Here? What do you mean by "here"? You 'aven't seen 'im, 'ave you?' Before the words were out of the man's lips he flung up his arms again, stumbled forward and fell in a heap at Medford's feet.

Medford, still leaning against the well-head, smiled down contemptuously at the stricken wretch. His conjecture had been the right one, then; he had not been Gosling's dupe after all.

'Get up, man. Don't be a fool! It's not your fault if I guessed that Mr Almodham walks here at night – '

'Walks here!' wailed the other, still cowering.

'Well, doesn't he? He won't kill you for owning up will he?'

'Kill me? Kill me? I wish I'd killed *you*!' Gosling half got to his feet, his head thrown back in ashen terror. 'And I might 'ave, too, so easy! You felt me pushing of you over, didn't you? Coming 'ere spying and sniffing – ' His anguish seemed to choke him.

Medford had not changed his position. The very abjectness of the creature at his feet gave him an easy sense of power. But Gosling's last cry had suddenly deflected the course of his speculations. Almodham was here, then; that was certain; but just where was he, and in what shape? A new fear scuttled down Medford's spine.

'So you did want to push me over?' he said. 'Why? As the quickest way of joining your master?'

The effect was more immediate than he had foreseen.

Gosling, getting to his feet, stood there bowed and shrunken in the accusing moonlight.

'Oh, God – and I 'ad you 'arf over! You know I did! And then – it was what you said about Wembley. So help me, sir, I felt you meant it, and it 'eld me back.' The man's face was again wet with tears, but this time Medford recoiled from them as if they had been drops splashed up by a falling body from the foul waters below.

Medford was silent. He did not know if Gosling were armed or not, but he was no longer afraid; only aghast, and yet shudderingly lucid.

Gosling continued to ramble on half deliriously: 'And if only that Perrier 'ad of come. I don't believe it'd ever 'ave crossed your mind, if only you'd 'ave had your Perrier regular, now would it? But you say 'e walks – and I knew he would! Only – what was I to do with him, with you turning up like that the very day?'

Still Medford did not move.

'And 'im driving me to madness, sir, sheer madness, that same morning. Will you believe it? The very week before you come, I was to sail for England and 'ave my 'oliday, a 'ole month, sir – and I was entitled to six, if there was any justice – a 'ole month in 'Ammersmith, sir, in a cousin's 'ouse, and the chance to see Wembley thoroughly; and then 'e 'eard you was coming, sir, and 'e was bored and lonely 'ere, you understand – 'e 'ad to have new excitements provided for 'im or 'e'd go off 'is bat – and when 'e 'eard you was coming, 'e come out of his black mood in a flash and was 'arf crazy with pleasure, and said, "I'll keep 'im 'ere all winter – a remarkable young man, Gosling – just my kind." And when I says to him: "And 'ow about my 'oliday?" he stares at me with those stony eyes of 'is and says: "Oliday? Oh, to be sure; why next year – we'll see what can be done about it next year." Next year, sir, as if 'e was doing me a favour! And that's the way it 'ad been for nigh on twelve years.

'But this time, if you 'adn't 'ave come I do believe I'd 'ave got away, for he was getting used to 'aving Selim about 'im and his 'ealth was never better – and, well, I told 'im as much, and 'ow a man 'ad his rights after all, and my youth was going, and me that 'ad served him so well chained up 'ere like 'is watchdog, and always next year and next year – and, well, sir, 'e just laughed, sneering-like, and lit 'is cigarette. "Oh, Gosling, cut it out," 'e says.

'He was standing on the very spot where you are now, sir; and he turned to walk into the 'ouse. And it was then I 'it 'im. He was a heavy man, and he fell against the well kerb. And just when you were expected any minute – oh, my God!'

Gosling's voice died out in a strangled murmur.

Medford, at his last words, had unvoluntarily shrunk back a few feet. The two men stood in the middle of the court and stared at each other without speaking. The moon, swinging high above the battlements, sent a searching spear of light down into the guilty darkness of the well.

The Lady's Maid's Bell

ONE

It was the autumn after I had the typhoid. I'd been three months in hospital, and when I came out I looked so weak and tottery that the two or three ladies I applied to were afraid to engage me. Most of my money was gone, and after I'd boarded for two months, hanging about the employment-agencies, and answering any advertisement that looked any way respectable, I pretty nearly lost heart, for fretting hadn't made me fatter, and I didn't see why my luck should ever turn. It did though – or I thought so at the time. A Mrs Railton, a friend of the lady that first brought me out to the States, met me one day and stopped to speak to me: she was one that had always a friendly way with her. She asked me what ailed me to look so white, and when I told her, 'Why, Hartley,' says she, 'I believe I've got the very place for you. Come in tomorrow and we'll talk about it.'

The next day, when I called, she told me the lady she'd in mind was a niece of hers, a Mrs Brympton, a youngish lady, but something of an invalid, who lived all the year round at her country-place on the Hudson, owing to not being able to stand the fatigue of town life.

'Now, Hartley,' Mrs Railton said, in that cheery way that always made me feel things must be going to take a turn for the better – 'now understand me; it's not a cheerful place I'm sending you to. The house is big and gloomy; my niece is nervous, vaporish; her husband – well, he's generally away; and the two children are dead. A year ago, I would as soon have thought of shutting a rosy active girl like you into a vault; but you're not particularly brisk yourself just now, are you? and a quiet place, with country air and wholesome food and early hours, ought to be the very thing for you. Don't mistake me,' she added, for I suppose I looked a trifle downcast; 'you may find it dull, but you won't be unhappy. My niece is an angel. Her former maid, who died last spring, had been with her twenty years and worshipped the ground she walked on. She's a kind mistress to all, and where the mistress is kind, as you know, the servants are generally good-humoured, so you'll probably get on well enough with the rest of the household. And you're the very woman I want for my niece: quiet, well-mannered, and educated above your station. You read aloud well, I think? That's a good thing; my niece likes to be read to. She wants a maid that can be something of a companion: her last was, and

I can't say how she misses her. It's a lonely life . . . Well, have you decided?'

'Why, ma'am,' I said, 'I'm not afraid of solitude.'

'Well, then, go; my niece will take you on my recommendation. I'll telegraph her at once and you can take the afternoon train. She has no one to wait on her at present, and I don't want you to lose any time.'

I was ready enough to start, yet something in me hung back; and to gain time I asked, 'And the gentleman, ma'am?'

'The gentleman's almost always away, I tell you,' said Mrs Railton, quick-like – 'and when he's there,' says she suddenly, 'you've only to keep out of his way.'

I took the afternoon train and got out at D— station at about four o'clock. A groom in a dog-cart was waiting, and we drove off at a smart pace. It was a dull October day, with rain hanging close overhead, and by the time we turned into Brympton Place woods the daylight was almost gone. The drive wound through the woods for a mile or two, and came out on a gravel court shut in with thickets of tall black-looking shrubs. There were no lights in the windows, and the house *did* look a bit gloomy.

I had asked no questions of the groom, for I never was one to get my notion of new masters from their other servants: I prefer to wait and see for myself. But I could tell by the look of everything that I had got into the right kind of house, and that things were done handsomely. A pleasant-faced cook met me at the back door and called the housemaid to show me up to my room. 'You'll see madam later,' she said. 'Mrs Brympton has a visitor.'

I hadn't fancied Mrs Brympton was a lady to have many visitors, and somehow the words cheered me. I followed the housemaid upstairs, and saw, through a door on the upper landing, that the main part of the house seemed well-furnished, with dark panelling and a number of old portraits. Another flight of stairs led us up to the servants' wing. It was almost dark now, and the housemaid excused herself for not having brought a light. 'But there's matches in your room,' she said, 'and if you go careful you'll be all right. Mind the step at the end of the passage. Your room is just beyond.'

I looked ahead as she spoke, and halfway down the passage, I saw a woman standing. She drew back into a doorway as we passed, and the house-maid didn't appear to notice her. She was a thin woman with a white face, and a darkish stuff gown and apron. I took her for the housekeeper and thought it odd that she didn't speak, but just gave me a long look as we went by. My room opened into a square hall at the end of the passage. Facing my door was another which stood open: the housemaid exclaimed when she saw it.

'There – Mrs Blinder's left that door open again!' said she, closing it.

'Is Mrs Blinder the housekeeper?'

'There's no housekeeper: Mrs Blinder's the cook.'

'And is that her room?'

'Laws, no,' said the housemaid, cross-like. 'That's nobody's room. It's empty, I mean, and the door hadn't ought to be open. Mrs Brympton wants it kept locked.'

She opened my door and led me into a neat room, nicely furnished, with a picture or two on the walls; and having lit a candle she took leave, telling me that the servants'-hall tea was at six, and that Mrs Brympton would see me afterwards.

I found them a pleasant-spoken set in the servants' hall, and by what they let fall I gathered that, as Mrs Railton had said, Mrs Brympton was the kindest of ladies; but I didn't take much notice of their talk, for I was watching to see the pale woman in the dark gown come in. She didn't show herself, however, and I wondered if she ate apart; but if she wasn't the housekeeper, why should she? Suddenly it struck me that she might be a trained nurse, and in that case her meals would of course be served in her room. If Mrs Brympton was an invalid it was likely enough she had a nurse. The idea annoyed me, I own, for they're not always the easiest to get on with, and if I'd known, I shouldn't have taken the place. But there I was, and there was no use pulling a long face over it; and not being one to ask questions, I waited to see what would turn up.

When tea was over, the housemaid said to the footman: 'Has Mr Ranford gone?' and when he said yes, she told me to come up with her to Mrs Brympton.

Mrs Brympton was lying down in her bedroom. Her lounge stood near the fire and beside it was a shaded lamp. She was a delicate-looking lady, but when she smiled I felt there was nothing I wouldn't do for her. She spoke very pleasantly, in a low voice, asking me my name and age and so on, and if I had everything I wanted, and if I wasn't afraid of feeling lonely in the country.

'Not with you I wouldn't be, madam,' I said, and the words surprised me when I'd spoken them, for I'm not an impulsive person; but it was just as if I'd thought aloud.

She seemed pleased at that, and said she hoped I'd continue in the same mind; then she gave me a few directions about her toilet, and said Agnes the housemaid would show me next morning where things were kept.

'I am tired tonight, and shall dine upstairs,' she said. 'Agnes will bring me my tray, that you may have time to unpack and settle yourself; and later you may come and undress me.'

'Very well, ma'am,' I said. 'You'll ring, I suppose?'

I thought she looked odd.

'No – Agnes will fetch you,' says she quickly, and took up her book again.

Well – that was certainly strange: a lady's maid having to be fetched by the housemaid whenever her lady wanted her! I wondered if there were no bells in the house; but the next day I satisfied myself that there was one in every room, and a special one ringing from my mistress's room to mine; and after that it did strike me as queer that, whenever Mrs Brympton wanted anything, she rang for Agnes, who had to walk the whole length of the servants' wing to call me.

But that wasn't the only queer thing in the house. The very next day I found out that Mrs Brympton had no nurse; and then I asked Agnes about the woman I had seen in the passage the afternoon before. Agnes said she had seen no one, and I saw that she thought I was dreaming. To be sure, it was dusk when we went down the passage, and she had excused herself for not bringing a light; but I had seen the woman plain enough to know her again if we should meet. I decided that she must have been a friend of the cook's, or of one of the other women-servants: perhaps she had come down from town for a night's visit, and the servants wanted it kept secret. Some ladies are very stiff about having their servants' friends in the house overnight. At any rate, I made up my mind to ask no more questions.

In a day or two, another odd thing happened. I was chatting one afternoon with Mrs Blinder, who was a friendly disposed woman, and had been longer in the house than the other servants, and she asked me if I was quite comfortable and had everything I needed. I said I had no fault to find with my place or with my mistress, but I thought it odd that in so large a house there was no sewing-room for the lady's maid.

'Why,' says she, 'there *is* one; the room you're in is the old sewing-room.'

'Oh,' said I; 'and where did the other lady's maid sleep?'

At that she grew confused, and said hurriedly that the servants' rooms had all been changed about last year, and she didn't rightly remember.

That struck me as peculiar, but I went on as if I hadn't noticed: 'Well, there's a vacant room opposite mine, and I mean to ask Mrs Brympton if I mayn't use that as a sewing-room.'

To my astonishment, Mrs Blinder went white, and gave my hand a kind of squeeze. 'Don't do that, my dear,' said she, trembling-like. 'To tell you the truth, that was Emma Saxon's room, and my mistress has kept it closed ever since her death.'

'And who was Emma Saxon?'

'Mrs Brympton's former maid.'

'The one that was with her so many years?' said I, remembering what Mrs Railton had told me.

Mrs Blinder nodded.

'What sort of woman was she?'

'No better walked the earth,' said Mrs Blinder. 'My mistress loved her like a sister.'

'But I mean – what did she look like?'

Mrs Blinder got up and gave me a kind of angry stare. 'I'm no great hand at describing,' she said; 'and I believe my pastry's rising.' And she walked off into the kitchen and shut the door after her.

TWO

I had been near a week at Brympton before I saw my master. Word came that he was arriving one afternoon, and a change passed over the whole household. It was plain that nobody loved him below stairs. Mrs Blinder took uncommon care with the dinner that night, but she snapped at the kitchen-maid in a way quite unusual with her; and Mr Wace, the butler, a serious, slow-spoken man, went about his duties as if he'd been getting ready for a funeral. He was a great Bible-reader, Mr Wace was, and had a beautiful assortment of texts at his command; but that day he used such dreadful language that I was about to leave the table, when he assured me it was all out of Isaiah; and I noticed that whenever the master came Mr Wace took to the prophets.

About seven, Agnes called me to my mistress's room; and there I found Mr Brympton. He was standing on the hearth; a big fair bull-necked man, with a red face and little bad-tempered blue eyes: the kind of man a young simpleton might have thought handsome, and would have been like to pay dear for thinking it.

He swung about when I came in, and looked me over in a trice. I knew what the look meant, from having experienced it once or twice in my former places. Then he turned his back on me, and went on talking to his wife; and I knew what *that* meant, too. I was not the kind of morsel he was after. The typhoid had served me well enough in one way: it kept that kind of gentleman at arm's-length.

'This is my new maid, Hartley,' says Mrs Brympton in her kind voice; and he nodded and went on with what he was saying.

In a minute or two he went off, and left my mistress to dress for dinner, and I noticed as I waited on her that she was white, and chill to the touch.

Mr Brympton took himself off the next morning, and the whole house drew a long breath when he drove away. As for my mistress, she put on her hat and furs (for it was a fine winter morning) and went out for a walk in the gardens, coming back quite fresh and rosy, so that for a minute, before her colour faded, I could guess what a pretty young lady she must have been, and not so long ago, either.

She had met Mr Ranford in the grounds, and the two came back together, I remember, smiling and talking as they walked along the terrace under my window. That was the first time I saw Mr Ranford, though I had often heard his name mentioned in the hall. He was a neighbour, it appeared, living a mile or two beyond Brympton, at the end of the village; and as he was in the habit of spending his winters in the country he was almost the only company my mistress had at that season. He was a slight tall gentleman of about thirty, and I thought him rather melancholy-looking till I saw his smile, which had a kind of surprise in it, like the first warm day in spring. He was a great reader, I heard, like my mistress, and the two were forever borrowing books off one another, and sometimes (Mr Wace told me) he would read aloud to Mrs Brympton by the hour, in the big dark library where she sat in the winter afternoons. The servants all liked him, and perhaps that's more of a compliment than the masters suspect. He had a friendly word for every one of us, and we were all glad to think that Mrs Brympton had a pleasant companionable gentleman like that to keep her company when the master was away. Mr Ranford seemed on excellent terms with Mr Brympton too; though I couldn't but wonder that two gentlemen so unlike each other should be so friendly. But then I knew how the real quality can keep their feelings to themselves.

As for Mr Brympton, he came and went, never staying more than a day or two, cursing the dullness and the solitude, grumbling at everything, and (as I soon found out) drinking a deal more than was good for him. After Mrs Brympton left the table he would sit half the night over the old Brympton port and madeira, and once, as I was leaving my mistress's room rather later than usual, I met him coming up the stairs in such a state that I turned sick to think of what some ladies have to endure and hold their tongues about.

The servants said very little about their master; but from what they let drop I could see it had been an unhappy match from the beginning. Mr Brympton was coarse, loud and pleasure-loving; my mistress quiet, retiring, and perhaps a trifle cold. Not that she was not always pleasant-spoken to him: I thought her wonderfully forbearing; but to a gentleman as free as Mr Brympton I dare say she seemed a little offish.

Well, things went on quietly for several weeks. My mistress was kind, my duties were light, and I got on well with the other servants. In short, I had nothing to complain of; yet there was always a weight on me. I can't say why it was so, but I know it was not the loneliness that I felt. I soon got used to that; and being still languid from the fever, I was thankful for the quiet and the good country air. Nevertheless, I was never quite easy in my mind. My mistress, knowing I had been ill, insisted that I should take my walk regular, and often invented errands for me – a yard of ribbon to be fetched from the village, a letter posted or a book returned to Mr Ranford. As soon as I was out of doors my spirits rose, and I looked forward to my walks through the bare moist-smelling woods; but the moment I caught sight of the house again my heart dropped down like a stone in a well. It was not a gloomy house exactly, yet I never entered it but a feeling of gloom came over me.

Mrs Brympton seldom went out in winter; only on the finest days did she walk an hour at noon on the south terrace. Excepting Mr Ranford, we had no visitors but the doctor, who drove over from D— about once a week. He sent for me once or twice to give me some trifling direction about my mistress, and though he never told me what her illness was, I thought, from a waxy look she had now and then of a morning, that it might be the heart that ailed her. The season was soft and unwholesome, and in January we had a long spell of rain. That was a sore trial to me, I own, for I couldn't go out, and sitting over my sewing all day, listening to the drip, drip of the eaves, I grew so nervous that the least sound made me jump. Somehow, the thought of that locked room across the passage began to weigh on me. Once or twice, in the long rainy nights, I fancied I heard noises there; but that was non-sense, of course, and the daylight drove such notions out of my head. Well, one morning Mrs Brympton gave me quite a start of pleasure by telling me she wished me to go to town for some shopping. I hadn't known till then how low my spirits had fallen. I set off in high glee, and my first sight of the crowded streets and the cheerful-looking shops quite took me out of myself. Towards afternoon, however, the noise and confusion began to tire me, and I was actually looking forward to the quiet of Brympton, and thinking how I should enjoy the drive home through the dark woods, when I ran across an old acquaintance, a maid I had once been in service with. We had lost sight of each other for a number of years, and I had to stop and tell her what had happened to me in the interval. When I mentioned where I was living she rolled up her eyes and pulled a long face.

'What! The Mrs Brympton that lives all the year at her place on the Hudson? My dear, you won't stay there three months.'

'Oh, but I don't mind the country,' says I, offended somehow at her tone. 'Since the fever I'm glad to be quiet.'

She shook her head. 'It's not the country I'm thinking of. All I know is she's had four maids in the last six months, and the last one, who was a friend of mine, told me nobody could stay in the house.'

'Did she say why?' I asked.

'No – she wouldn't give me her reason. But she says to me, "Mrs Ansey," she says, "if ever a young woman as you know of thinks of going there, you tell her it's not worth while to unpack her boxes." '

'Is she young and handsome?' said I, thinking of Mr Brympton.

'Not her! She's the kind that mothers engage when they've gay young gentlemen at college.'

Well, though I knew the woman was an idle gossip, the words stuck in my head, and my heart sank lower than ever as I drove up to Brympton in the dusk. There *was* something about the house – I was sure of it now . . .

When I went in to tea I heard that Mr Brympton had arrived, and I saw at a glance that there had been a disturbance of some kind. Mrs Blinder's hand shook so that she could hardly pour the tea, and Mr Wace quoted the most dreadful texts full of brimstone. Nobody said a word to me then, but when I went up to my room Mrs Blinder followed me.

'Oh, my dear,' says she, taking my hand, 'I'm so glad and thankful you've come back to us!'

That struck me, as you may imagine. 'Why,' said I, 'did you think I was leaving for good?'

'No, no, to be sure,' said she, a little confused, 'but I can't a-bear to have madam left alone for a day even.' She pressed my hand hard, and, 'Oh, Miss Hartley,' says she, 'be good to your mistress, as you're a Christian woman.' And with that she hurried away, and left me staring.

A moment later Agnes called me to Mrs Brympton. Hearing Mr Brympton's voice in her room, I went round by the dressing-room, thinking I would lay out her dinner-gown before going in. The dressing-room is a large room with a window over the portico that looks towards the gardens. Mr Brympton's apartments are beyond. When I went in, the door into the bedroom was ajar, and I heard Mr Brympton saying angrily: 'One would suppose he was the only person fit for you to talk to.'

'I don't have many visitors in winter,' Mrs Brympton answered quietly.

'You have *me*!' he flung at her, sneering.

'You are here so seldom,' said she.

'Well – whose fault is that? You make the place about as lively as a family vault –'

With that I rattled the toilet-things, to give my mistress warning and she rose and called me in.

The two dined alone, as usual, and I knew by Mr Wace's manner at supper that things must be going badly. He quoted the prophets something terrible, and worked on the kitchen-maid so that she declared she wouldn't go down alone to put the cold meat in the ice-box. I felt nervous myself, and after I had put my mistress to bed I was half-tempted to go down again and persuade Mrs Blinder to sit up awhile over a game of cards. But I heard her door closing for the night, and so I went on to my own room. The rain had begun again, and the drip, drip, drip seemed to be dropping into my brain. I lay awake listening to it, and turning over what my friend in town had said. What puzzled me was that it was always the maids who left . . .

After a while I slept; but suddenly a loud noise wakened me. My bell had rung. I sat up, terrified by the unusual sound, which seemed to go on jangling through the darkness. My hands shook so that I couldn't find the matches. At length I struck a light and jumped out of bed. I began to think I must have been dreaming; but I looked at the bell against the wall, and there was the little hammer still quivering.

I was just beginning to huddle on my clothes when I heard another sound. This time it was the door of the locked room opposite mine softly opening and closing. I heard the sound distinctly, and it frightened me so that I stood stock still. Then I heard a footstep hurrying down the passage towards the main house. The floor being carpeted, the sound was very faint, but I was quite sure it was a woman's step. I turned cold with the thought of it, and for a minute or two I dursn't breathe or move. Then I came to my senses.

'Alice Hartley,' says I to myself, 'someone left that room just now and ran down the passage ahead of you. The idea isn't pleasant, but you may as well face it. Your mistress has rung for you, and to answer her bell you've got to go the way that other woman has gone.'

Well – I did it. I never walked faster in my life, yet I thought I should never get to the end of the passage or reach Mrs Brympton's room. On the way I heard nothing and saw nothing: all was dark and quiet as the grave. When I reached my mistress's door the silence was so deep that I began to think I must be dreaming, and was half-minded to turn back. Then a panic seized me, and I knocked.

There was no answer, and I knocked again, loudly. To my astonishment the door was opened by Mr Brympton. He started back when he saw me, and in the light of my candle his face looked red and savage.

'You!' he said, in a queer voice. 'How many of you are there, in God's name?'

At that I felt the ground give under me; but I said to myself that he had been drinking, and answered as steadily as I could: 'May I go in, sir? Mrs Brympton has rung for me.'

'You may all go in, for what I care,' says he, and, pushing by me, walked down the hall to his own bedroom. I looked after him as he went, and to my surprise I saw that he walked as straight as a sober man.

I found my mistress lying very weak and still, but she forced a smile when she saw me, and signed to me to pour out some drops for her. After that she lay without speaking, her breath coming quick, and her eyes closed. Suddenly she groped out with her hand, and ' *Emma,*' says she, faintly.

'It's Hartley, madam,' I said. 'Do you want anything?'

She opened her eyes wide and gave me a startled look.

'I was dreaming,' she said. 'You may go, now, Hartley, and thank you kindly. I'm quite well again, you see.' And she turned her face away from me.

THREE

There was no more sleep for me that night, and I was thankful when daylight came.

Soon afterward, Agnes called me to Mrs Brympton. I was afraid she was ill again, for she seldom sent for me before nine, but I found her sitting up in bed, pale and drawn-looking, but quite herself.

'Hartley,' says she quickly, 'will you put on your things at once and go down to the village for me? I want this prescription made up – 'here she hesitated a minute and blushed – 'and I should like you to be back again before Mr Brympton is up.'

'Certainly, madam,' I said.

'And – stay a moment – ' she called me back as if an idea had just struck her – 'while you're waiting for the mixture, you'll have time to go on to Mr Ranford's with this note.'

It was a two-mile walk to the village, and on my way I had time to turn things over in my mind. It struck me as peculiar that my mistress should wish the prescription made up without Mr Brympton's knowledge; and, putting this together with the scene of the night before, and with much else that I had noticed and suspected, I began to wonder if the poor lady was weary of her life, and had come to the mad resolve of ending it. The idea took such hold on me that I reached the village on a run, and dropped breathless into a chair before the chemist's counter. The good man, who was just taking down his shutters, stared at me so hard that it brought me to myself.

'Mr Limmel,' I says, trying to speak indifferent, 'will you run your eye over this, and tell me if it's quite right?'

He put on his spectacles and studied the prescription.

'Why, it's one of Dr Walton's,' says he. 'What should be wrong with it?'

'Well – is it dangerous to take?'

'Dangerous – how do you mean?'

I could have shaken the man for his stupidity.

'I mean – if a person was to take too much of it – by mistake of course – ' says I, my heart in my throat.

'Lord bless you, no. It's only lime-water. You might feed it to a baby by the bottleful.'

I gave a great sigh of relief, and hurried on to Mr Ranford's. But on the way another thought struck me. If there was nothing to conceal about my visit to the chemist's, was it my other errand that Mrs Brympton wished me to keep private? Somehow, that thought frightened me worse than the other. Yet the two gentlemen seemed fast friends, and I would have staked my head on my mistress's goodness. I felt ashamed of my suspicions, and concluded that I was still disturbed by the strange events of the night. I left the note at Mr Ranford's – and, hurrying back to Brympton, slipped in by a side door without being seen, as I thought.

An hour later, however, as I was carrying in my mistress's breakfast, I was stopped in the hall by Mr Brympton.

'What were you doing out so early?' he says, looking hard at me.

'Early – me, sir?' I said, in a tremble.

'Come, come,' he says, an angry red spot coming out on his forehead, 'didn't I see you scuttling home through the shrubbery an hour or more ago?'

I'm a truthful woman by nature, but at that a lie popped out ready-made. 'No, sir, you didn't,' said I, and looked straight back at him.

He shrugged his shoulders and gave a sullen laugh. 'I suppose you think I was drunk last night?' he asked suddenly.

'No, sir, I don't,' I answered, this time truthfully enough.

He turned away with another shrug. 'A pretty notion my servants have of me!' I heard him mutter as he walked off.

Not till I had settled down to my afternoon's sewing did I realise how the events of the night had shaken me. I couldn't pass that locked door without a shiver. I knew I had heard someone come out of it, and walk down the passage ahead of me. I thought of speaking to Mrs Blinder or to Mr Wace, the only two in the house who appeared to have an inkling of what was going on, but I had a feeling that if I questioned them they would deny everything, and that I might learn more by holding my tongue and keeping my eyes open. The idea of spending another night opposite the locked room sickened me, and once I was seized with the notion of packing my trunk and taking the first train to town; but it wasn't in me to throw over a kind mistress in that manner, and I tried to go on with my sewing as if nothing had happened.

I hadn't worked ten minutes before the sewing-machine broke down. It was one I had found in the house, a good machine, but a trifle out of order: Mrs Blinder said it had never been used since Emma Saxon's death. I stopped to see what was wrong, and as I was working at the machine a drawer which I had never been able to open slid forward and a photograph fell out. I picked it up and sat looking at it in amaze. It was a woman's likeness, and I knew I had seen the face somewhere – the eyes had an asking look that I had felt on me before. And suddenly I remembered the pale woman in the passage.

I stood up, cold all over, and ran out of the room. My heart seemed to be thumping in the top of my head, and I felt as if I should never get away from the look in those eyes. I went straight to Mrs Blinder. She was taking her afternoon nap, and sat up with a jump when I came in.

'Mrs Blinder,' said I, 'who is that?' And I held out the photograph.

She rubbed her eyes and stared.

'Why, Emma Saxon,' says she. 'Where did you find it?'

I looked hard at her for a minute. 'Mrs Blinder,' I said, 'I've seen that face before.'

Mrs Blinder got up and walked over to the looking-glass. 'Dear me! I must have been asleep,' she says. 'My front is all over one ear. And now do run along, Miss Hartley, dear, for I hear the clock striking four, and I must go down this very minute and put on the Virginia ham for Mr Brympton's dinner.'

FOUR

To all appearances, things went on as usual for a week or two. The only difference was that Mr Brympton stayed on, instead of going off as he usually did, and that Mr Ranford never showed himself. I heard Mr Brympton remark on this one afternoon when he was sitting in my mistress's room before dinner.

'Where's Ranford?' says he. 'He hasn't been near the house for a week. Does he keep away because I'm here?'

Mrs Brympton spoke so low that I couldn't catch her answer.

'Well,' he went on, 'two's company and three's trumpery; I'm sorry to be in Ranford's way, and I suppose I shall have to take myself off again in a day or two and give him a show.' And he laughed at his own joke.

The very next day, as it happened, Mr Ranford called. The footman said the three were very merry over their tea in the library, and Mr Brympton strolled down to the gate with Mr Ranford when he left.

I have said that things went on as usual; and so they did with the rest of the household; but as for myself, I had never been the same since the night my bell had rung. Night after night I used to lie awake, listening for it to ring again, and for the door of the locked room to open stealthily. But the bell never rang, and I heard no sound across the passage. At last the silence began to be more dreadful to me than the most mysterious sounds. I felt that *someone* were cowering there, behind the locked door, watching and listening as I watched and listened, and I could almost have cried out, 'Whoever you are, come out and let me see you face to face, but don't lurk there and spy on me in the darkness!'

Feeling as I did, you may wonder I didn't give warning. Once I very nearly did so; but at the last moment something held me back. Whether it was compassion for my mistress, who had grown more and more dependent on me, or unwillingness to try a new place, or some other feeling that I couldn't put a name to, I lingered on as if spellbound, though every night was dreadful to me, and the days but little better.

For one thing, I didn't like Mrs Brympton's looks. She had never been the same since that night, no more than I had. I thought she would brighten up after Mr Brympton left, but though she seemed easier in her mind, her spirits didn't revive, nor her strength either. She had grown attached to me, and seemed to like to have me about; and Agnes told me one day that, since Emma Saxon's death, I was the only maid her mistress had taken to. This gave me a warm feeling for the poor lady, though after all there was little I could do to help her.

After Mr Brympton's departure, Mr Ranford took to coming again, though less often than formerly. I met him once or twice in the grounds, or in the village, and I couldn't but think there was a change in him too; but I set it down to my disordered fancy.

The weeks passed, and Mr Brympton had now been a month absent. We heard he was cruising with a friend in the West Indies, and Mr Wace said that was a long way off, but though you had the wings of a dove and went to the uttermost parts of the earth, you couldn't get away from the Almighty. Agnes said that as long as he stayed away from Brympton, the Almighty might have him and welcome; and this raised a laugh, though Mrs Blinder tried to look shocked, and Mr Wace said the bears would eat us.

We were all glad to hear that the West Indies were a long way off, and I remember that, in spite of Mr Wace's solemn looks, we had a very merry dinner that day in the hall. I don't know if it was because of my being in better spirits, but I fancied Mrs Brympton looked better too, and seemed more cheerful in her manner. She had been for a walk in the morning, and after luncheon she lay down in her room, and I read aloud to her. When she dismissed me I went to my own room feeling quite bright and happy, and for the first time in weeks walked past the locked door without thinking of it. As I sat down to my work I looked out and saw a few snowflakes falling. The sight was pleasanter than the eternal rain, and I pictured to myself how pretty the bare gardens would look in their white mantle. It seemed to me as if the snow would cover up all the dreariness, indoors as well as out.

The fancy had hardly crossed my mind when I heard a step at my side. I looked up, thinking it was Agnes.

'Well, Agnes – ' said I, and the words froze on my tongue; for there, in the door, stood Emma Saxon.

I don't know how long she stood there. I only know I couldn't stir or take my eyes from her. Afterwards I was terribly frightened, but at the time it wasn't fear I felt, but something deeper and quieter. She looked at me long and long, and her face was just one dumb prayer to me – but how in the world was I to help her? Suddenly she turned, and I heard her walk down the passage. This time I wasn't afraid to follow – I felt that I must know what she wanted. I sprang up and ran out. She was at the other end of the passage, and I expected her to take the turn toward my mistress's room; but instead of that she pushed open the door that led to the backstairs. I followed her down the stairs, and across the passageway to the back door. The kitchen and hall were empty at that hour, the servants being off duty, except for the footman, who was in the pantry. At the door she stood still a moment, with another look at me; then she turned the handle, and stepped out. For a minute I hesitated. Where was she leading me to? The door had closed softly after her, and I opened it and looked out, half-expecting to find that she had disappeared. But I saw her a few yards off, hurrying across the courtyard to the path through the woods. Her figure looked black and lonely in the snow, and for a second my heart failed me and I thought of turning back. But all the while she was drawing me after her; and catching up an old shawl of Mrs Blinder's I ran out into the open.

Emma Saxon was in the wood-path now. She walked on steadily, and I followed at the same pace, till we passed out of the gates and reached the high-road. Then she struck across the open fields to the village. By this time the ground was white, and as she climbed the slope of a bare hill ahead of me I noticed that she left no footprints behind her. At sight of that, my heart shrivelled up within me, and my knees were water. Somehow, it was worse here than indoors. She made the whole countryside seem lonely as the grave, with none but us two in it, and no help in the wide world.

Once I tried to go back; but she turned and looked at me, and it was as if she had dragged me with ropes. After that I followed her like a dog. We came to the village, and she led me through it, past the church and the blacksmith's shop, and down the lane to Mr Ranford's. Mr Ranford's house stands close to the road: a plain old-fashioned building, with a flagged path leading to the door between box-borders. The lane was deserted, and as I turned into it, I saw Emma Saxon pause under the old elm by the gate. And now another fear came over me. I saw that we had reached the end of our journey, and that it was my turn to act. All the way from Brympton I had been asking myself what she wanted of me, but I had followed in a trance, as it were, and not till I saw her stop at Mr Ranford's gate did my brain begin to clear itself. I stood a little way off in the snow, my heart beating fit to strangle me, and my feet frozen to the ground; and she stood under the elm and watched me.

I knew well enough that she hadn't led me there for nothing. I felt there was something I ought to say or do – but how was I to guess what it was? I had never thought harm of my mistress and Mr Ranford, but I was sure now that, from one cause or another, some dreadful thing hung over them. *She* knew what it was; she would tell me if she could; perhaps she would answer if I questioned her.

It turned me faint to think of speaking to her; but I plucked up heart and dragged myself across the few yards between us. As I did so, I heard the house-door open, and saw Mr Ranford approaching. He looked handsome and cheerful, as my mistress had looked that morning, and at sight of him the blood began to flow again in my veins.

'Why, Hartley,' said he, 'what's the matter? I saw you coming down the lane just now, and came out to see if you had taken root in the snow.' He stopped and stared at me. 'What are you looking at?' he says.

I turned towards the elm as he spoke, and his eyes followed me; but there was no one there. The lane was empty as far as the eye could reach.

A sense of helplessness came over me. She was gone, and I had not been able to guess what she wanted. Her last look had pierced me to the marrow; and yet it had not told me! All at once, I felt more desolate than when she had stood there watching me. It seemed as if she had left me all alone to carry the weight of the secret I couldn't guess. The snow went round me in great circles, and the ground fell away from me . . .

A drop of brandy and the warmth of Mr Ranford's fire soon brought me to, and I insisted on being driven back at once to Brympton. It was nearly dark, and I was afraid my mistress might be wanting me. I explained to Mr Ranford that I had been out for a walk and had been taken with a fit of giddiness as I passed his gate. This was true enough; yet I never felt more like a liar than when I said it.

When I dressed Mrs Brympton for dinner she remarked on my pale looks and asked what ailed me. I told her I had a headache, and she said she would not require me again that evening, and advised me to go to bed.

It was a fact that I could scarcely keep on my feet; yet I had no fancy to spend a solitary evening in my room. I sat downstairs in the hall as long as I could hold my head up; but by nine I crept upstairs, too weary to care what happened if I could but get my head on a pillow. The rest of the household went to bed soon afterwards; they kept early hours when the master was away, and before ten I heard Mrs Blinder's door close, and Mr Wace's soon after.

It was a very still night, earth and air all muffled in snow. Once in bed I felt easier, and lay quiet, listening to the strange noises that come out in a house after dark. Once I thought I heard a door open and close again below: it might have been the glass door that led to the gardens. I got up and peered out of the window; but it was in the dark of the moon, and nothing visible outside but the streaking of snow against the panes.

I went back to bed and must have dozed, for I jumped awake to the furious ringing of my bell. Before my head was clear I had sprung out of bed, and was dragging on my clothes. *It is going to happen now*, I heard myself saying; but what I meant I had no notion. My hands seemed to be covered with glue – I thought I should never get into my clothes. At last I opened my door and peered down the passage. As far as my candle-flame carried, I could see nothing unusual ahead of me. I hurried on, breathless; but as I pushed open the baize door leading to the main hall my heart stood still, for there at the head of the stairs was Emma Saxon, peering dreadfully down into the darkness.

For a second I couldn't stir; but my hand slipped from the door, and as it swung shut the figure vanished. At the same instant there came another sound from below stairs – a stealthy mysterious sound, as of a latch-key turning in the house-door. I ran to Mrs Brympton's room and knocked.

There was no answer, and I knocked again. This time I heard someone moving in the room; the bolt slipped back and my mistress stood before me. To my surprise I saw that she had not undressed for the night. She gave me a startled look.

'What is this, Hartley?' she says in a whisper. 'Are you ill? What are you doing here at this hour?'

'I am not ill, madam; but my bell rang.'

At that she turned pale, and seemed about to fall.

'You are mistaken,' she said harshly; 'I didn't ring. You must have been dreaming.' I had never heard her speak in such a tone. 'Go back to bed,' she said, closing the door on me.

But as she spoke I heard sounds again in the hall below: a man's step this time; and the truth leaped out on me.

'Madam,' I said, pushing past her, 'there is someone in the house –'

'Someone – ?'

'Mr Brympton, I think – I hear his step below – '

A dreadful look came over her, and without a word, she dropped flat at my feet. I fell on my knees and tried to lift her: by the way she breathed I saw it was no common faint. But as I raised her head there came quick steps on the stairs and across the hall; the door was flung open, and there stood Mr Brympton, in his travelling-clothes, the snow dripping from him. He drew back with a start as he saw me kneeling by my mistress.

'What the devil is this?' he shouted. He was less high-coloured than usual, and the red spot came out on his forehead.

'Mrs Brympton has fainted, sir,' said I.

He laughed unsteadily and pushed by me. 'It's a pity she didn't choose a more convenient moment. I'm sorry to disturb her, but – '

I raised myself up, aghast at the man's action.

'Sir,' said I, 'are you mad? What are you doing?'

'Going to meet a friend,' said he, and seemed to make for the dressing-room.

At that my heart turned over. I don't know what I thought or feared; but I sprang up and caught him by the sleeve.

'Sir, sir,' said I, 'for pity's sake look to your wife!'

He shook me off furiously.

'It seems that's done for me,' says he, and caught hold of the dressing-room door.

At that moment I heard a slight noise inside. Slight as it was, he heard it too, and tore the door open; but as he did so he dropped back. On the threshold stood Emma Saxon. All was dark behind her, but I saw her plainly, and so did he. He threw up his hands as if to hide his face from her; and when I looked again she was gone.

He stood motionless, as if the strength had run out of him; and in the stillness my mistress suddenly raised herself, and opening her eyes fixed a look on him. Then she fell back, and I saw the death-flutter pass over her . . .

We buried her on the third day, in a driving snowstorm. There were few people in the church, for it was bad weather to come from town, and I've a notion my mistress was one that hadn't many near friends. Mr Ranford was among the last to come, just before they carried her up the aisle. He was in black, of course, being such a friend of the family, and I never saw a gentleman so pale. As he passed me, I noticed that he leaned a trifle on a stick he carried; and I fancy Mr Brympton noticed it too, for the red spot came out sharp on his forehead, and all through the service he kept staring across the church at Mr Ranford, instead of following the prayers as a mourner should.

When it was over and we went out to the graveyard, Mr Ranford had disappeared, and as soon as my poor mistress's body was underground, Mr Brympton jumped into the carriage nearest the gate and drove off without a word to any of us. I heard him call out, 'To the station,' and we servants went back alone to the house.

The Bolted Door

I

Hubert Granice, pacing the length of his pleasant lamp-lit library, paused to compare his watch with the clock on the chimney-piece.

Three minutes to eight.

In exactly three minutes Mr Peter Ascham, of the eminent legal firm of Ascham and Pettilow, would have his punctual hand on the doorbell of the flat. It was a comfort to reflect that Ascham was so punctual – the suspense was beginning to make his host nervous. And the sound of the doorbell would be the beginning of the end – after that there'd be no going back, by God – no going back!

Granice resumed his pacing. Each time he reached the end of the room opposite the door he caught his reflection in the Florentine mirror above the fine old walnut *credence* he had picked up at Dijon – saw himself spare, quick-moving, carefully brushed and dressed, but furrowed, grey about the temples, with a stoop which he corrected by a spasmodic straightening of the shoulders whenever a glass confronted him: a tired middle-aged man, baffled, beaten, worn out.

As he summed himself up thus for the third or fourth time the door opened and he turned with a thrill of relief to greet his guest. But it was only the manservant who entered, advancing silently over the mossy surface of the old Turkey rug.

'Mr Ascham telephones, sir, to say he's unexpectedly detained and can't be here till eight-thirty.'

Granice made a curt gesture of annoyance. It was becoming harder and harder for him to control these reflexes. He turned on his heel, tossing to the servant over his shoulder: 'Very good. Put off dinner.'

Down his spine he felt the man's injured stare. Mr Granice had always been so mild-spoken to his people – no doubt the odd change in his manner had already been noticed and discussed below stairs. And very likely they suspected the cause. He stood drumming on the writing-table till he heard the servant go out; then he threw himself into a chair, propping his elbows on the table and resting his chin on his locked hands.

Another half-hour alone with it!

He wondered irritably what could have detained his guest. Some professional matter, no doubt – the punctilious lawyer would have allowed nothing less to interfere with a dinner engagement, more especially since Granice, in his note, had said: 'I shall want a little business chat afterwards.'

But what professional matter could have come up at that unprofessional hour? Perhaps some other soul in misery had called on the lawyer; and, after all, Granice's note had given no hint of his own need! No doubt Ascham thought he merely wanted to make another change in his will. Since he had come into his little property, ten years earlier, Granice had been perpetually tinkering with his will.

Suddenly another thought pulled him up, sending a flush to his sallow temples. He remembered a word he had tossed to the lawyer some six weeks earlier, at the Century Club. 'Yes – my play's as good as taken. I shall be calling on you soon to go over the contract. Those theatrical chaps are so slippery – I won't trust anybody but you to tie the knot for me!' That, of course, was what Ascham would think he was wanted for. Granice, at the idea, broke into an audible laugh – a queer stage-laugh, like the cackle of a baffled villain in a melodrama. The absurdity, the unnaturalness of the sound abashed him, and he compressed his lips angrily. Would he take to soliloquy next?

He lowered his arms and pulled open the upper drawer of the writing-table. In the right-hand corner lay a thick manuscript, bound in paper folders, and tied with a string beneath which a letter had been slipped. Next to the manuscript was a small revolver. Granice stared a moment at these oddly associated objects; then he took the letter from under the string and slowly began to open it. He had known he should do so from the moment his hand touched the drawer. Whenever his eye fell on that letter some relentless force compelled him to reread it.

It was dated about four weeks back, under the letter-head of 'The Diversity Theatre'.

My dear Mr Granice – I have given the matter my best consideration for the last month, and it's no use – the play won't do. I have talked it over with Miss Melrose – and you know there isn't a gamer artist on our stage – and I regret to tell you she feels just as I do about it. It isn't the poetry that scares her – or me either. We both want to do all we can to help along the poetic drama – we believe the public's ready for it, and we're willing to take a big financial risk in order to be the first to give them what they want. *But we don't believe they could be made to want this.* The fact is, there isn't enough drama in your play to the allowance of poetry – the thing drags all through. You've got a big idea, but it's not out of swaddling clothes.

If this was your first play I'd say: *Try again.* But it has been just the same with all the others you've shown me. And you remember the result of *The Lee Shore*, where you carried all the expenses of production yourself, and we couldn't fill the theatre for a week. Yet *The Lee Shore* was a modern problem play – much easier to swing than blank verse. It isn't as if you hadn't tried all kinds –

Granice folded the letter and put it carefully back into the envelope. Why on earth was he rereading it, when he knew every phrase in it by heart, when for a month past he had seen it, night after night, stand out in letters of flame against the darkness of his sleepless lids?

It has been just the same with all the others you've shown me.

That was the way they dismissed ten years of passionate unremitting work!

You remember the result of The Lee Shore.

Good God – as if he were likely to forget it! He relived it all now in a drowning flash: the persistent rejection of the play, his sudden resolve to put it on at his own cost, to spend ten thousand dollars of his inheritance on testing his chance of success – the fever of preparation, the dry-mouthed agony of the 'first night', the flat fall, the stupid press, his secret rush to Europe to escape the condolence of his friends!

It isn't as if you hadn't tried all kinds.

No – he had tried all kinds: comedy, tragedy, prose and verse, the light curtain-raiser, the short sharp drama, the bourgeois-realistic and the lyrical-romantic – finally deciding that he would no longer 'prostitute his talent' to win popularity, but would impose on the public his own theory of art in the form of five acts of blank verse. Yes, he had offered them everything – and always with the same result.

Ten years of it – ten years of dogged work and unrelieved failure. The ten years from forty to fifty – the best ten years of his life! And if one counted the years before, the silent years of dreams, assimilation, preparation – then call it half a man's lifetime: half a man's lifetime thrown away!

And what was he to do with the remaining half? Well, he had settled that, thank God! He turned and glanced anxiously at the clock. Ten minutes past eight – only ten minutes had been consumed in that stormy rush through his whole past! And he must wait another twenty minutes for Ascham. It was one of the worst symptoms of his case that, in proportion as he had grown to shrink from human company, he dreaded more and more to be alone . . . But why the devil was he waiting for Ascham? Why didn't he cut the knot himself? Since he was so unutterably sick of the whole business, why did he have to call in an outsider to rid him of this nightmare of living?

He opened the drawer again and laid his hand on the revolver. It was a small slim ivory toy – just the instrument for a tired sufferer to give himself a 'hypodermic' with. Granice raised it slowly in one hand, while with the other he felt under the thin hair at the back of his head, between the ear and the nape. He knew just where to place the muzzle: he had once got a young surgeon to show him. And as he found the spot, and lifted the revolver to it, the inevitable phenomenon occurred. The hand that held the weapon began to shake, the tremor communicated itself to his arm, his heart gave a wild leap which sent up a wave of deadly nausea to his throat, he smelt the powder, he sickened at the crash of the bullet through his skull, and a sweat of fear broke out over his forehead and ran down his quivering face . . .

He laid away the revolver with an oath and, pulling out a cologne-scented handkerchief, passed it tremulously over his brow and temples. It was no use – he knew he could never do it in that way. His attempts at self-destruction were as futile as his snatches at fame! He couldn't make himself a real life, and he couldn't get rid of the life he had. And that was why he had sent for Ascham to help him . . .

The lawyer, over the Camembert and Burgundy, began to excuse himself for his delay.

'I didn't like to say anything while your man was about – but the fact is, I was sent for on a rather unusual matter – '

'Oh, it's all right,' said Granice cheerfully. He was beginning to feel the usual reaction that food and company produced. It was not any recovered pleasure in life that he felt, but only a deeper withdrawal into himself. It was easier to go on automatically with the social gestures than to uncover to any human eye the abyss within him.

'My dear fellow, it's sacrilege to keep a dinner waiting – especially the production of an artist like yours.' Mr Ascham sipped his Burgundy luxuriously. 'But the fact is, Mrs Ashgrove sent for me.'

Granice raised his head with a quick movement of surprise. For a moment he was shaken out of his self-absorption.

'*Mrs Ashgrove?*'

Ascham smiled. 'I thought you'd be interested; I know your passion for *causes célèbres*. And this promises to be one. Of course it's out of our line entirely – we never touch criminal cases. But she wanted to consult me as a friend. Ashgrove was a distant connection of my wife's. And, by Jove, it *is* a queer case!' The servant re-entered, and Ascham snapped his lips shut.

Would the gentlemen have their coffee in the dining-room?

'No – serve it in the library,' said Granice, rising. He led the way back to the curtained confidential room. He was really curious to hear what Ascham had to tell him.

While the coffee and cigars were being served he fidgeted about the library, glancing at his letters – the usual meaningless notes and bills – and picking up the evening paper. As he unfolded it a headline caught his eye. ROSE MELROSE WANTS TO PLAY POETRY. THINKS SHE HAS FOUND HER POET.

He read on with a thumping heart – found the name of a young author he had barely heard of, saw the title of a play, a 'poetic drama', dance before his eyes, and dropped the paper, sick, disgusted. It was true, then – she *was* 'game' – it was not the manner but the matter she mistrusted!

Granice turned to the servant, who seemed to be purposely lingering. 'I shan't need you this evening, Flint. I'll lock up myself.'

He fancied the man's acquiescence implied surprise. What was going on, Flint seemed to wonder, that Mr Granice should want him out of the way? Probably he would find a pretext for coming back to see. Granice suddenly felt himself enveloped in a network of espionage.

As the door closed he threw himself into an armchair and leaned forward to take a light from Ascham's cigar.

'Tell me about Mrs Ashgrove,' he said, seeming to himself to speak stiffly, as if his lips were cracked.

'Mrs Ashgrove? Well, there's not much to *tell*.'

'And you couldn't if there were?' Granice smiled.

'Probably not. As a matter of fact, she wanted my advice about her choice of counsel. There was nothing especially confidential in our talk.'

'And what's your impression, now you've seen her?'

'My impression is, very distinctly, *that nothing will ever be known*.'

'Ah – ?' Granice murmured, puffing at his cigar.

'I'm more and more convinced that whoever poisoned Ashgrove knew his business, and will consequently never be found out. That's a capital cigar you've given me.'

'You like it? I get them over from Cuba.' Granice examined his own reflectively. 'Then you believe in the theory that the clever criminals never *are* caught?'

'Of course I do. Look about you – look back for the last dozen years – none of the big murder problems are ever solved.' The lawyer ruminated behind his blue cloud. 'Why, take the instance in your own family: I'd forgotten I had an illustration at hand! Take old Joseph Lenman's murder – do you suppose that will ever be explained?'

As the words dropped from Ascham's lips his host looked slowly about the library, and every object in it stared back at him with a stale unescapable familiarity. How sick he was of looking at that room! It was as dull as the face of a wife one has wearied of. He cleared his throat slowly; then he turned his head to the lawyer and said: 'I could explain the Lenman murder myself.'

Ascham's eye kindled: he shared Granice's interest in criminal cases.

'By Jove! You've had a theory all this time? It's odd you never mentioned it. Go ahead and tell me. There are certain features in the Lenman case not unlike this Ashgrove affair, and your idea may be a help.'

Granice paused and his eye reverted instinctively to the table drawer in which the revolver and the manuscript lay side by side. What if he were to try another appeal to Rose Melrose? Then he looked at the notes and bills on the table, and the horror of taking up again the lifeless routine of life – of performing the same automatic gestures another day – displaced his fleeting vision.

'I haven't a theory. I *know* who murdered Joseph Lenman.'

Ascham settled himself comfortably in his chair, prepared for enjoyment.

'You *know*? Well, who did?' he laughed.

'I did,' said Granice, rising.

He stood before Ascham, and the lawyer lay back staring up at him. Then he broke into another laugh.

'Why, this is glorious! You murdered him, did you? To inherit his money, I suppose? Better and better! Go on, my boy! Unbosom yourself! Tell me all about it! Confession is good for the soul.'

Granice waited till the lawyer had shaken the last peal of laughter from his throat; then he repeated doggedly: 'I murdered him.'

The two men looked at each other for a long moment, and this time Ascham did not laugh.

'Granice!'

'I murdered him – to get his money, as you say.'

There was another pause, and Granice, with a vague underlying sense of amusement, saw his guest's look change from pleasantry to apprehension.

'What's the joke, my dear fellow? I fail to see.'

'It's not a joke. It's the truth. I murdered him.' He had spoken painfully at first, as if there were a knot in his throat; but each time he repeated the words he found they were easier to say.

Ascham laid down his extinct cigar.

'What's the matter? Aren't you well? What on earth are you driving at?'

'I'm perfectly well. But I murdered my cousin, Joseph Lenman, and I want it known that I murdered him.'

'*You want it known?*'

'Yes. That's why I sent for you. I'm sick of living, and when I try to kill myself I funk it.' He spoke quite naturally now, as if the knot in his throat had been untied.

'Good Lord – good Lord,' the lawyer gasped.

'But I suppose,' Granice continued, 'there's no doubt this would be murder in the first degree? I'm sure of the chair if I own up?'

Ascham drew a long breath; then he said slowly: 'Sit down, Granice. Let's talk.'

TWO

Granice told his story simply, connectedly.

He began by a quick survey of his early years – the years of drudgery and privation. His father, a charming man who could never say no, had so signally failed to say it on certain essential occasions that when he died he left an illegitimate family and a mortgaged estate. His lawful kin found themselves hanging over a gulf of debt, and young Granice, to support his mother and sister, had to leave Harvard and bury himself at eighteen in a broker's office. He loathed his work, and he was always poor, always worried and in ill-health. A few years later his mother died, but his sister, an ineffectual neurasthenic, remained on his hands. His own health gave out, and he had to go away for six months, and work harder than ever when he came back. He had no knack for business, no head for figures, no dimmest insight into the mysteries of commerce. He wanted to travel and write – those were his inmost longings. And as the years dragged on, and he neared middle-age without making any more money, or acquiring any firmer health, a sick despair possessed him. He tried writing, but he always came home from the office so tired that his brain could not work. For half the year he did not reach his dim up-town flat till after dark, and could only 'brush up' for dinner, and afterwards lie on the lounge with his pipe, while his sister droned through the evening paper. Sometimes he spent an evening at the theatre; or he dined out, or, more rarely, strayed off with an acquaintance or two in quest of what is known as 'pleasure'. And in summer, when he and Kate went to the seaside for a month, he dozed through the days in utter weariness. Once he fell in love with a charming girl – but what had he to offer her, in God's name? She seemed to like him, but in common decency he had to drop out of the running. Apparently no one replaced him, for she never married, but grew stoutish, greyish, philanthropic – yet how sweet she had been when he first kissed her! One more wasted life, he reflected . . .

But the stage had always been his master-passion. He would have sold his soul for the time and freedom to write plays! It was *in him* – he could not remember when it had not been his deepest-seated instinct. As the years passed it became a morbid, a relentless obsession – yet with every year the material conditions were more and more against it. He felt himself growing middle-aged, and he watched the reflection of the process in his sister's wasted face. At eighteen she had been pretty, and as full of enthusiasm as he. Now she was sour, trivial, insignificant – she had missed her chance of life. And she had no resources, poor creature, was fashioned simply for the primitive functions she had been denied the chance to fulfil! It exasperated him to think of it – and to reflect that even now a little travel, a little health, a little money, might transform her, make her young and desirable . . . The chief fruit of his experience was that there is no such fixed state as age or youth – there is only health as against sickness, wealth as against poverty, and age or youth as the outcome of the lot one draws.

At this point in his narrative Granice stood up, and went to lean against the mantelpiece, looking down at Ascham, who had not moved from his seat, or changed his attitude of rigid fascinated attention.

'Then came the summer when we went to Wrenfield to be near old Lenman – my mother's cousin, as you know. Some of the family always mounted guard over him – generally a niece or so. But that year they were all scattered, and one of the nieces offered to lend us her cottage if we'd relieve her of duty for two months. It was a nuisance for me, of course, for Wrenfield is two hours from town; but my mother, who was a slave to family observances, had always been good to the old man, so it was natural we should be called on – and there was the saving of rent and the good air for Kate. So we went.

'You never knew Joseph Lenman? Well, picture to yourself an amoeba or some primitive organism of that sort, under a Titan's microscope. He was large, undifferentiated, inert – since I could remember him he had done nothing but take his temperature and read the *Churchman*. Oh, and cultivate melons – that was his hobby. Not vulgar, out-of-door melons – his were grown under glass. He had miles of it at Wrenfield – his big kitchen-garden was surrounded by blinking battalions of greenhouses. And in nearly all of them melons were grown – early melons and late, French, English, domestic – dwarf melons and monsters: every shape, colour and variety. They were petted and nursed like children – a staff of trained attendants waited on them. I'm not sure they didn't have a doctor to take their temperature – at any rate the place was full of thermometers. And they didn't sprawl on the ground like ordinary melons; they were trained against the glass like nectarines, and each melon hung in a net which sustained its weight and left it free on all sides to the sun and air . . .

'It used to strike me sometimes that old Lenman was just like one of his own melons – the pale-fleshed English kind. His life, apathetic and motionless, hung in a net of gold, in an equable warm ventilated atmosphere, high above sordid earthly worries. The cardinal rule of his existence was not to let himself be "worried". I remember his advising me to try it myself, one day when I spoke to him about Kate's bad health, and her need of a change. "I never let myself worry," he said complacently. "It's the worst thing for the liver – and you look to me as if you had a liver. Take my advice and be cheerful. You'll make yourself happier and others too." And all he had to do was to write a cheque, and send the poor girl off for a holiday!

'The hardest part of it was that the money half-belonged to us already. The old skin-flint only had it for life, in trust for us and the others. But his life was a good deal sounder than mine or Kate's – and one could picture him taking extra care of it for the joke of keeping us waiting. I always felt that the sight of our hungry eyes was a tonic to him.

'Well, I tried to see if I couldn't reach him through his vanity. I flattered him, feigned a passionate interest in his melons. And he was taken in, and used to discourse on them by the hour. On fine days he was driven to the greenhouses in his pony-chair, and waddled through them, prodding and leering at the fruit, like a fat Turk in his seraglio. When he bragged to me of the expense of growing them I was reminded of a hideous old Lothario bragging of what his pleasures cost. And the resemblance was completed by the fact that he couldn't eat as much as a mouthful of his melons – had lived for years on buttermilk and toast. "But, after all, it's my only hobby – why shouldn't I indulge it?" he said sentimentally. As if I'd ever been able to indulge any of mine! On the keep of those melons Kate and I could have lived like gods . . .

'One day towards the end of the summer, when Kate was too unwell to drag herself up to the big house, she asked me to go and spend the afternoon with cousin Joseph. It was a lovely soft September afternoon – a day to lie under a Roman stone-pine, with one's eyes on the sky, and let the cosmic harmonies rush through one. Perhaps the vision was suggested by the fact that, as I entered cousin Joseph's hideous black walnut library, I passed one of the under-gardeners, a handsome full-throated Italian, who dashed out in such a hurry that he nearly knocked me down. I remember thinking it queer that the fellow, whom I had often seen about the melon-houses, did not bow to me, or even seem to see me.

'Cousin Joseph sat in his usual seat, behind the darkened windows, his fat hands folded on his protuberant waistcoat, the last number of the *Churchman* at his elbow, and near it, on a huge dish, a fat melon – the fattest melon I'd ever seen. As I looked at it I pictured the ecstasy of contemplation from which I must have roused him, and congratulated myself on finding him in such a mood, since I had made up my mind to ask him a favour. Then I noticed that his face, instead of looking as calm as an egg-shell, was distorted and whimpering – and without stopping to greet me he pointed passionately to the melon.

' "Look at it, look at it – did you ever see such a beauty? Such firmness – roundness – such delicious smoothness to the touch?" It was as if he had said "she" instead of "it", and when he put out his senile hand and touched the melon I positively had to look the other way.

'Then he told me what had happened. The Italian under-gardener, who had been specially recommended for the melon-houses – though it was against my cousin's principles to employ a Papist – had been assigned to the care of the monster: for it had revealed itself, early in its existence, as destined to become a monster, to surpass its plumpest, pulpiest sisters, carry off prizes at agricultural shows, and be photographed and celebrated in every gardening paper in the land. The Italian had done well – seemed to have a sense of responsibility. And that very morning he had been ordered to pick the melon, which was to be shown next day at the county fair, and to bring it in for Mr Lenman to gaze on its blonde virginity. But in picking it, what had the damned scoundrelly Jesuit done but drop it – drop it crash on the sharp spout of a watering-pot, so that it received a deep gash in its firm pale rotundity, and was henceforth but a bruised, ruined, fallen melon?

'The old man's rage was fearful in its impotence – he shook, spluttered and strangled with it. He had just had the Italian up and had sacked him on the spot, without wages or character – had threatened to have him arrested if he was ever caught prowling about Wrenfield. "By God, and I'll do it – I'll write to Washington – I'll have the pauper scoundrel deported! I'll show him what money can do!" As likely as not there was some murderous Black-hand business under it – it would be found that the fellow was a member of a "gang". Those Italians would murder you for a quarter. He meant to have the police look into it . . . And then he grew frightened at his own excitement. "But I must calm myself," he said. He took his temperature, rang for his drops, and turned to the *Churchman*. He had been reading an article on Nestorianism when the melon was brought in. He asked me to go on with it, and I read to him for an hour, in the dim close room, with a fat fly buzzing stealthily about the fallen melon.

'All the while one phrase of the old man's buzzed in my brain like the fly about the melon. "*I'll show him what money can do!*" Good heaven! If *I* could but show the old man! If I could make him see his power of giving happiness as a new outlet for his monstrous egotism! I tried to tell him something about my situation and Kate's – spoke of my ill-health, my unsuccessful drudgery, my longing to write, to make myself a name – I stammered out an entreaty for a loan. "I can guarantee to repay you, sir – I've a half-written play as security . . . "

'I shall never forget his glassy stare. His face had grown as smooth as an egg-shell again – his eyes peered over his fat cheeks like sentinels over a slippery rampart.

' "A half-written play – a play of *yours* as security?" He looked at me almost fearfully, as if detecting the first symptoms of insanity. "Do you understand anything of business?" he enquired mildly. I laughed and answered: "No, not much."

'He leaned back with closed lids. "All this excitement has been too much for me," he said. "If you'll excuse me, I'll prepare for my nap." And I stumbled out of the room, blindly, like the Italian.'

Granice moved away from the mantelpiece, and walked across to the tray set out with decanters and soda-water. He poured himself a tall glass of soda-water, emptied it, and glanced at Ascham's dead cigar.

'Better light another,' he suggested.

The lawyer shook his head, and Granice went on with his tale. He told of his mounting obsession – how the murderous impulse had waked in him on the instant of his cousin's refusal, and he had muttered to himself: 'By God, if you won't, I'll make you.' He spoke more tranquilly as the narrative proceeded, as though his rage had died down once the resolve to act on it was taken. He applied his whole mind to the question of how the old man was to be 'disposed of'. Suddenly he remembered the outcry: 'Those Italians will murder you for a quarter!' But no definite project presented itself: he simply waited for an inspiration.

Granice and his sister moved to town a day or two after the incident of the melon. But the cousins, who had returned, kept them informed of the old man's condition. One day, about three weeks later, Granice, on getting home, found Kate excited over a report from Wrenfield. The Italian had been there again – had somehow slipped into the house, made his way up to the library, and 'used threatening language'. The housekeeper found cousin Joseph gasping, the whites of his eyes showing 'something awful'. The doctor was sent for, and the attack warded off; and the police had ordered the Italian from the neighbourhood.

But cousin Joseph, thereafter, languished, had 'nerves', and lost his taste for toast and buttermilk. The doctor called in a colleague, and the consultation amused and excited the old man – he became once more an important figure. The medical men reassured the family – too completely! – and to the patient they recommended a more varied diet: advised him to take whatever 'tempted him'. And so one day, tremulously, prayerfully, he decided on a tiny bit of melon. It was brought up with ceremony, and consumed in the presence of the housekeeper and a hovering cousin; and twenty minutes later he was dead . . .

'But you remember the circumstances,' Granice went on; 'how suspicion turned at once on the Italian? In spite of the hint the police had given him he had been seen hanging about the house since "the scene". It was said that he had tender relations with the kitchen-maid, and the rest seemed easy to explain. But when they looked round to ask him for the explanation he was gone – gone clean out of sight. He had been "warned" to leave Wrenfield, and he had taken the warning so to heart that no one ever laid eyes on him again.'

Granice paused. He had dropped into a chair opposite the lawyer's, and he sat for a moment, his head thrown back, looking about the familiar room. Everything in it had grown grimacing and alien, and each strange insistent object seemed craning forward from its place to hear him.

'It was I who put the stuff in the melon,' he said. 'And I don't want you to think I'm sorry for it. This isn't "remorse", understand. I'm glad the old skinflint is dead – I'm glad the others have their money. But mine's no use to me any more. My sister married miserably, and died. And I've never had what I wanted.'

Ascham continued to stare; then he said: 'What on earth was your object, then?'

'Why, to *get* what I wanted – what I fancied was in reach! I wanted change, rest, *life*, for both of us – wanted, above all, for myself, the chance to write! I travelled, got back my health, and came home to tie myself up to my work. And I've slaved at it steadily for ten years without reward – without the most distant hope of success! Nobody will look at my stuff. And now I'm fifty, and I'm beaten, and I know it.' His chin dropped forward on his breast. 'I want to chuck the whole business,' he ended.

THREE

It was after midnight when Ascham left.

His hand on Granice's shoulder, as he turned to go – 'District Attorney be hanged; see a doctor, see a doctor!' he had cried; and so, with an exaggerated laugh, had pulled on his coat and departed.

Granice turned back into the library. It had never occurred to him that Ascham would not believe his story. For three hours he had explained, elucidated, patiently and painfully gone over every detail – but without once breaking down the iron incredulity of the lawyer's eye.

At first Ascham had feigned to be convinced – but that, as Granice now perceived, was simply to get him to expose himself, to entrap him into contradictions. And when the attempt failed, when Granice triumphantly met and refuted each disconcerting question, the lawyer dropped the mask suddenly, and said with a good-humoured laugh: 'By Jove, Granice you'll write a successful play yet. The way you've worked this all out is a marvel.'

Granice swung about furiously – that last sneer about the play inflamed him. Was all the world in a conspiracy to deride his failure?

'I did it, I did it,' he muttered sullenly, his rage spending itself against the impenetrable surface of the other's mockery; and Ascham answered with a smile: 'Ever read any of those books on hallucination? I've got a fairly good medico-legal library. I could send you one or two if you like . . .'

Left alone, Granice cowered down in the chair before his writing-table. He understood that Ascham thought him off his head.

'Good God – what if they all think me crazy?'

The horror of it broke out over him in a cold sweat – he sat there and shook, his eyes hidden in his icy hands. But gradually, as he began to rehearse his story for the thousandth time, he saw again how incontrovertible it was, and felt sure that any criminal lawyer would believe him.

'That's the trouble – Ascham's not a criminal lawyer. And then he's a friend. What a fool I was to talk to a friend! Even if he did believe me, he'd never let me see it – his instinct would be to cover the whole thing up . . . But in that case – if he *did* believe me – he might think it a kindness to get me shut up in an asylum . . . ' Granice began to tremble again. 'Good heaven! If he should bring in an expert – one of those damned alienists! Ascham and Pettilow can do anything – their word always goes. If Ascham drops a hint that I'd better be shut up, I'll be in a strait-jacket by tomorrow! And he'd do it from the kindest motives – be quite right to do it if he thinks I'm a murderer!'

The vision froze him to his chair. He pressed his fists to his bursting temples and tried to think. For the first time he hoped that Ascham had not believed his story.

'But he did – he did! I can see it now – I noticed what a queer eye he cocked at me. Good God, what shall I do – what shall I do?'

He started up and looked at the clock. Half-past one. What if Ascham should think the case urgent, rout out an alienist, and come back with him? Granice jumped to his feet, and his sudden gesture brushed the morning paper from the table. Mechanically he stooped to pick it up, and the movement started a new train of association.

He sat down again, and reached for the telephone book in the rack by his chair.

'Give me three-o-ten . . . yes.'

The new idea in his mind had revived his flagging energy. He would act – act at once. It was only by thus planning ahead, committing himself to some unavoidable line of conduct, that he could pull himself through the meaningless days. Each time he reached a fresh decision it was like coming out of a foggy weltering sea into a calm harbour with lights. One of the queerest phases of his long agony was the intense relief produced by these momentary lulls.

'That the office of the *Investigator*? Yes? Give me Mr Denver, please . . . Hallo, Denver . . . Yes, Hubert Granice . . . Just caught you? Going straight home? Can I come and see you . . . yes, now . . . have a talk? It's rather urgent . . . yes, might give you some first-rate "copy" . . . All right!' He hung up the receiver with a laugh. It had been a happy thought to call up the editor of the *Investigator* – Robert Denver was the very man he needed . . .

Granice put out the lights in the library – it was odd how the automatic gestures persisted! – went into the hall, put on his hat and overcoat, and let himself out of the flat. In the hall, a sleepy elevator boy blinked at him and then dropped his head on his folded arms. Granice passed out into the street. At the corner of Fifth Avenue he hailed a crawling cab, and called out an up-town address. The long thoroughfare stretched before him, dim and deserted, like an ancient avenue of tombs. But from Denver's house a friendly beam fell on the pavement; and as Granice sprang from his cab the editor's electric turned the corner.

The two men grasped hands, and Denver, feeling for his latch-key, ushered Granice into the brightly-lit hall.

'Disturb me? Not a bit. You might have, at ten tomorrow morning . . . but this is my liveliest hour . . . you know my habits of old.'

Granice had known Robert Denver for fifteen years – watched his rise through all the stages of journalism to the Olympian pinnacle of the *Investigator*'s editorial office. In the thick-set man with grizzling hair there were few traces left of the hungry-eyed young reporter who, on his way home in the small hours, used to 'bob in' on Granice, while the latter sat grinding at his plays. Denver had to pass Granice's flat on the way to his own, and it became a habit, if he saw a light in the window, and Granice's shadow against the blind, to go in, smoke a pipe and discuss the universe.

'Well – this is like old times – a good old habit reversed.' The editor smote his visitor genially on the shoulder. 'Reminds me of the nights when I used to rout you out . . . How's the play, by the way? There *is* a play, I suppose? It's as safe to ask you that as to say to some men: "How's the baby?" '

Denver laughed good-naturedly, and Granice thought how thick and heavy he had grown. It was evident, even to Granice's tortured nerves, that the words had not been uttered in malice – and the fact gave him a new measure of his insignificance. Denver did not even know that he had been a failure! The fact hurt more than Ascham's irony.

'Come in – come in.' The editor led the way into a small cheerful room, where there were cigars and decanters. He pushed an armchair towards his visitor, and dropped into another with a comfortable groan.

'Now, then – help yourself. And let's hear all about it.'

He beamed at Granice over his pipe-bowl, and the latter, lighting his cigar, said to himself: 'Success makes men comfortable, but it makes them stupid.'

Then he turned, and began: 'Denver, I want to tell you – '

The clock ticked rhythmically on the mantelpiece. The room was gradually filled with drifting blue layers of smoke, and through them the editor's face came and went like the moon through a moving sky. Once the hour struck – then the rhythmical ticking began again. The atmosphere grew denser and heavier, and beads of perspiration began to roll from Granice's forehead.

'Do you mind if I open the window?'

'No. It *is* stuffy in here. Wait – I'll do it myself.' Denver pushed down the upper sash, and returned to his chair. 'Well – go on,' he said, filling another pipe. His composure exasperated Granice.

'There's no use in my going on if you don't believe me.'

The editor remained unmoved. 'Who says I don't believe you? And how can I tell till you've finished?'

Granice went on, ashamed of his outburst. 'It was simple enough, as you'll see. From the day the old man said to me, "Those Italians would murder you for a quarter," I dropped everything and just worked at my scheme. It struck me at once that I must find a way of getting to Wrenfield and back in a night – and that led to the idea of a motor. A motor – that never occurred to you? You wonder where I got the money, I suppose. Well, I had a thousand or so put by, and I nosed around till I found what I wanted – a second-hand racer. I knew how to drive a car, and I tried the thing and found it was all right. Times were bad, and I bought it for my price, and stored it away. Where? Why, in one of those no-questions-asked garages where they keep motors that are not for family use. I had a lively cousin who had put me up to that dodge, and I looked about till I found a queer hole where they took in my car like a baby in a foundling asylum . . . Then I practised running to Wrenfield and back in a night. I knew the way pretty well, for I'd done it often with the same lively cousin – and in the small hours, too. The distance is over ninety miles, and on the third trial I did it under two hours. But my arms were so lame that I could hardly get dressed the next morning . . .

'Well, then came the report about the Italian's threats, and I saw I must act at once . . . I meant to break into the old man's room, shoot him, and get away again. It was a big risk, but I thought I could manage it. Then we heard that he was ill – that there'd been a consultation. Perhaps the fates were going to do it for me! Good Lord, if that could only be! . . . '

Granice stopped and wiped his forehead: the open window did not seem to have cooled the room.

'Then came word that he was better; and the day after, when I came up from my office, I found Kate laughing over the news that he was to try a bit of melon. The housekeeper had just telephoned her – all Wrenfield was in a flutter. The doctor himself had picked out the melon, one of the little French ones that are hardly bigger than a large tomato – and the patient was to eat it at his breakfast the next morning.

'In a flash I saw my chance. It was a bare chance, no more. But I knew the ways of the house – I was sure the melon would be brought in overnight and put in the pantry ice-box. If there were only one melon in the ice-box I could be fairly sure it was the one I wanted. Melons didn't lie around loose in that house – every one was known, numbered, catalogued. The old man was beset by the dread that the servants would eat them, and he took a hundred mean precautions to prevent it. Yes, I felt pretty sure of my melon . . . and poisoning was much safer than shooting. It would have been the devil and all to get into the old man's bedroom without his rousing the house; but I ought to be able to break into the pantry without much trouble.

'It was a cloudy night, too – everything served me. I dined quietly, and sat down at my desk. Kate had one of her usual headaches, and went to bed early. As soon as she was gone I slipped out. I had got together a sort of disguise – red beard and queer-looking ulster. I shoved them into a bag, and went round to the garage. There was no one there but a half-drunken machinist whom I'd never seen before. That served me, too. They were always changing machinists, and this new fellow didn't even bother to ask if the car belonged to me. It was a very easy-going place . . .

'Well, I jumped in, ran up Broadway, and let the car go as soon as I was out of Harlem. Dark as it was, I could trust myself to strike a sharp pace. In the shadow of a wood I stopped a second and got into the beard and ulster. Then away again – it was just eleven-thirty when I got to Wrenfield.

'I left the car in a dark lane behind the Lenman place, and slipped through the kitchen-garden. The melon-houses winked at me through the dark – I remember thinking that they knew what I wanted to know . . . By the stable a dog came out growling – but he nosed me out, jumped on me, and went back . . . The house was as dark as the grave. I knew everybody went to bed by ten. But there might be a prowling servant – the kitchen-maid might have come down to let in her Italian. I had to risk that, of course. I crept around by the back door and hid in the shrubbery. Then I listened. It was all as silent as death. I crossed over to the house, pried open the pantry window and climbed in. I had a little electric lamp in my pocket, and shielding it with my cap I groped my way to the ice-box, opened it – and there was the little French melon . . . only one.

'I stopped to listen – I was quite cool. Then I pulled out my bottle of stuff and my syringe, and gave each section of the melon a hypodermic. It was all done inside of three minutes – at ten minutes to twelve I was back in the car. I got out of the lane as quietly as I could, struck a back road that skirted the village, and let the car out as soon as I was beyond the last houses. I only stopped once on the way in, to drop the beard and ulster into a pond. I had a big stone ready to weight them with and they went down plump, like a dead body – and at two o'clock I was back at my desk.'

Granice stopped speaking and looked across the smoke-fumes at his listener; but Denver's face remained inscrutable.

At length he said: 'Why did you want to tell me this?'

The question startled Granice. He was about to explain, as he had explained to Ascham; but suddenly it occurred to him that if his motive had not seemed convincing to the lawyer it would carry much less weight with Denver. Both were successful men, and success does not understand the subtle agony of failure. Granice cast about for another reason.

'Why, I – the thing haunts me . . . remorse, I suppose you'd call it . . . '

Denver struck the ashes from his empty pipe.

'Remorse? Bosh!' he said energetically.

Granice's heart sank. 'You don't believe in – *remorse?*'

'Not an atom: in the man of action. The mere fact of your talking of remorse proves to me that you're not the man to have planned and put through such a job.'

Granice groaned. 'Well – I lied to you about remorse. I've never felt any.'

Denver's lips tightened sceptically about his freshly-filled pipe. 'What was your motive, then? You must have had one.'

'I'll tell you – ' And Granice began again to rehearse the story of his failure, of his loathing for life. 'Don't say you don't believe me this time . . . that this isn't a real reason!' he stammered out piteously as he ended.

Denver meditated. 'No, I won't say that. I've seen too many queer things. There's always a reason for wanting to get out of life – the wonder is that we find so many for staying in!'

Granice's heart grew light. 'Then you *do* believe me?' he faltered.

'Believe that you're sick of the job? Yes. And that you haven't the nerve to pull the trigger? Oh, yes – that's easy enough, too. But all that doesn't make you a murderer – though I don't say it proves you could never have been one.'

'I *have* been one, Denver – I swear to you.'

'Perhaps.' He meditated. 'Just tell me one or two things.'

'Oh, go ahead. You won't stump me!' Granice heard himself say with a laugh.

'Well – how did you make all those trial trips without exciting your sister's curiosity? I knew your night habits pretty well at that time, remember. You were very seldom out late. Didn't the change in your ways surprise her?'

'No; because she was away at the time. She went to pay several visits in the country soon after we came back from Wrenfield, and was only in town for a night or two before – before I did the job.'

'And that night she went to bed early with a headache?'

'Yes – blinding. She didn't know anything when she had that kind. And her room was at the back of the flat.'

Denver again meditated. 'And when you got back – she didn't hear you? You got in without her knowing it?'

'Yes. I went straight to my work – took it up at the word where I'd left off – *why, Denver, don't you remember?*' Granice suddenly, passionately interjected.

'Remember – ?'

'Yes; how you found me – when you looked in that morning, between two and three . . . your usual hour . . . ?'

'Yes,' the editor nodded.

Granice gave a short laugh. 'In my old coat – with my pipe: looked as if I'd been working all night, didn't I? Well, I hadn't been in my chair ten minutes!'

Denver uncrossed his legs and then crossed them again. 'I didn't know whether *you* remembered that.'

'What?'

'My coming in that particular night – or morning.'

Granice swung round in his chair. 'Why, man alive! That's why I'm here now. Because it was you who spoke for me at the inquest, when they looked round to see what all the old man's heirs had been doing that night – you who testified to having dropped in and found me at my desk as usual . . . I thought *that* would appeal to your journalistic sense if nothing else would!'

Denver smiled. 'Oh, my journalistic sense is still susceptible enough – and the idea's picturesque, I grant you: asking the man who proved your alibi to establish your guilt.'

'That's it – that's it!' Granice's laugh had a ring of triumph.

'Well, but how about the other chap's testimony – I mean that young doctor: what was his name? Ned Ranney. Don't you remember my testifying that I'd met him at the elevated station, and told him I was on my way to smoke a pipe with you, and his saying: "All right; you'll find him in. I passed the house two hours ago, and saw his shadow against the blind, as usual." And the lady with the toothache in the flat across the way: she corroborated his statement, you remember.'

'Yes; I remember.'

'Well, then?'

'Simple enough. Before starting I rigged up a kind of mannikin with old coats and a cushion – something to cast a shadow on the blind. All you fellows were used to seeing my shadow there in the small hours – I counted on that, and knew you'd take any vague outline as mine.'

'Simple enough, as you say. But the woman with the toothache saw the shadow move – you remember she said she saw you sink forward, as if you'd fallen asleep.'

'Yes; and she was right. It *did* move. I suppose some extra-heavy dray must have jolted by the flimsy building – at any rate, something gave my mannikin a jar, and when I came back he had sunk forward, half over the table.'

There was a long silence between the two men. Granice, with a throbbing heart, watched Denver refill his pipe. The editor, at any rate, did not sneer and flout him. After all, journalism gave a deeper insight than the law into the fantastic possibilities of life, prepared one better to allow for the incalculableness of human impulses.

'Well?' Granice faltered out.

Denver stood up with a shrug. 'Look here, man – what's wrong with you? Make a clean breast of it! Nerves gone to smash? I'd like to take you to see a chap I know – an ex-prize-fighter – who's a wonder at pulling fellows in your state out of their hole – '

'Oh, oh – ' Granice broke in. He stood up also, and the two men eyed each other. 'You don't believe me, then?'

'This yarn – how can I? There wasn't a flaw in your alibi.'

'But haven't I filled it full of them now?'

Denver shook his head. 'I might think so if I hadn't happened to know that you *wanted* to. There's the hitch, don't you see?'

Granice groaned. 'No, I didn't. You mean my wanting to be found guilty – ?'

'Of course! If somebody else had accused you, the story might have been worth looking into. As it is, a child could have invented it. It doesn't do much credit to your ingenuity.'

Granice turned sullenly toward the door. What was the use of arguing? But on the threshold a sudden impulse drew him back. 'Look here, Denver – I dare say you're right. But will you do just one thing to prove it? Put my statement in the *Investigator*, just as I've made it. Ridicule it as much as you like. Only give the other fellows a chance at it – men who don't know anything about me. Set them talking and looking about. I don't care a damn whether *you* believe me – what I want is to convince the Grand Jury! I oughtn't to have come to a man who knows me – your cursed incredulity is infectious. I don't put my case well, because I know in advance it's discredited, and I almost end by not believing it myself. That's why I can't convince *you*. It's a vicious circle.' He laid a hand on Denver's arm. 'Send a stenographer, and put my statement in the paper.'

But Denver did not warm to the idea. 'My dear fellow, you seem to forget that all the evidence was pretty thoroughly sifted at the time, every possible clue followed up. The public would have been ready enough then to believe that you murdered old Lenman – you or anybody else. All they wanted was a murderer – the most improbable would have served. But your alibi was too confoundedly complete. And nothing you've told me has shaken it.' Denver laid his cool hand over the other's burning fingers. 'Look here, old fellow, go home and work up a better case – then come in and submit it to the *Investigator*.'

FOUR

The perspiration was rolling off Granice's forehead. Every few minutes he had to draw out his handkerchief and wipe the moisture from his haggard face.

For an hour and a half he had been talking steadily, putting his case to the District Attorney. Luckily he had a speaking acquaintance with Allonby, and had obtained, without much difficulty, a private audience on the very day after his talk with Robert Denver. In the interval between he had hurried home, got out of his evening clothes, and gone forth again at once into the dreary dawn. His fear of Ascham and the alienist made it impossible for him to remain in his rooms. And it seemed to him that the only way of averting that hideous peril was by establishing, in some sane impartial mind, the proof of his guilt. Even if he had not been so incurably sick of life, the electric chair seemed now the only alternative to the strait-jacket.

As he paused to wipe his forehead he saw the District Attorney glance at his watch. The gesture was significant, and Granice lifted an appealing hand. 'I don't expect you to believe me now – but can't you put me under arrest, and have the thing looked into?'

Allonby smiled faintly under his heavy greyish moustache. He had a ruddy face, full and jovial, in which his keen professional eyes seemed to keep watch over impulses not strictly professional.

'Well, I don't know that we need lock you up just yet. But of course I'm bound to look into your statement – '

Granice rose with an exquisite sense of relief. Surely Allonby wouldn't have said that if he hadn't believed him!

'That's all right. Then I needn't detain you. I can be found at any time at my apartment.' He gave the address.

The District Attorney smiled again, more openly. 'What do you say to leaving it for an hour or two this evening? I'm giving a little supper at Rector's – quiet little affair, you understand: just Miss Melrose – I think you know her – and a friend or two; and if you'll join us . . . '

Granice stumbled out of the office without knowing what reply he had made.

He waited for four days – four days of concentrated horror. During the first twenty-four hours the fear of Ascham's alienist dogged him; and as that subsided, it was replaced by the exasperating sense that his avowal had made no impression on the District Attorney. Evidently, if he had been going to look into the case, Allonby would have been heard from before now . . . And that mocking invitation to supper showed clearly enough how little the story had impressed him!

Granice was overcome by the futility of any further attempt to inculpate himself. He was chained to life – a 'prisoner of consciousness'. Where was it he had read the phrase? Well, he was learning what it meant. In the glaring night-hours, when his brain seemed ablaze, he was visited by a sense of his fixed identity, of his irreducible, inexpungable *selfness*, keener, more insidious, more unescapable, than any sensation he had ever known. He had not guessed that the mind was capable of such intricacies of self-realization, of penetrating so deep into its own dark windings. Often he woke from his brief snatches of sleep with the feeling that something material was clinging to him, was on his hands and face, and in his throat – and as his brain cleared he understood that it was the sense of his own loathed personality that stuck to him like some thick viscous substance.

Then, in the first morning hours, he would rise and look out of his window at the awakening activities of the street – at the street-cleaners, the ash-cart drivers, and the other dingy workers flitting hurriedly by through the sallow winter light. Oh, to be one of them – any of them – to take his chance in any of their skins! They were the toilers – the men whose lot was pitied – the victims wept over and ranted about by altruists and economists; and how gladly he would have taken up the load of any one of them, if only he might have shaken off his own! But, no – the iron circle of consciousness held them too: each one was handcuffed to his own hideous ego. Why wish to be any one man rather than another? The only absolute good was not to be . . . And Flint, coming in to draw his bath, would ask if he preferred his eggs scrambled or poached that morning?

On the fifth day he wrote a long urgent letter to Allonby; and for the succeeding two days he had the occupation of waiting for an answer. He hardly stirred from his rooms, in his fear of missing the letter by a moment; but would the District Attorney write, or send a representative: a policeman, a 'secret agent', or some other mysterious emissary of the law?

On the third morning Flint, stepping softly – as if, confound it! his master were ill – entered the library where Granice sat behind an unread news-paper, and proferred a card on a tray.

Granice read the name – J. B. Hewson – and underneath, in pencil, 'From the District Attorney's office'. He started up with a thumping heart, and signed an assent to the servant.

Mr Hewson was a slight sallow nondescript man of about fifty – the kind of man of whom one is sure to see a specimen in any crowd. 'Just the type of the successful detective,' Granice reflected as he shook hands with his visitor.

And it was in that character that Mr Hewson briefly introduced himself. He had been sent by the District Attorney to have 'a quiet talk' with Mr Granice – to ask him to repeat the statement he had made about the Lenman murder.

His manner was so quiet, so reasonable and receptive, that Granice's self-confidence returned. Here was a sensible man – a man who knew his business – it would be easy enough to make *him* see through that ridiculous alibi! Granice offered Mr Hewson a cigar, and lighting one himself – to prove his coolness – began again to tell his story.

He was conscious, as he proceeded, of telling it better than ever before. Practice helped, no doubt; and his listener's detached, impartial attitude helped still more. He could see that Hewson, at least, had not decided in advance to disbelieve him, and the sense of being trusted made him more lucid and more consecutive. Yes, this time his words would certainly carry conviction . . .

FIVE

Despairingly, Granice gazed up and down the shabby street. Beside him stood a young man with bright prominent eyes, a smooth but not too smoothly-shaven face and an Irish smile. The young man's nimble glance followed Granice's.

'Sure of the number, are you?' he asked briskly.

'Oh, yes – it was 104.'

'Well, then, the new building has swallowed it up – that's certain.'

He tilted his head back and surveyed the half-finished front of a brick-and-limestone flat-house that reared its flimsy elegance above a row of tottering tenements and stables.

'Dead sure?' he repeated.

'Yes,' said Granice, discouraged. 'And even if I hadn't been, I know the garage was just opposite Leffler's over there.' He pointed across the street to a tumble-down stable with a blotched sign on which the words 'Livery and Boarding' were still faintly discernible.

The young man dashed across to the opposite pavement. 'Well, that's something – may get a clue there. Leffler's – same name there, anyhow. You remember that name?'

'Yes – distinctly.'

Granice had felt a return of confidence since he had enlisted the interest of the *Explorer's* 'smartest' reporter. If there were moments when he hardly believed his own story, there were others when it seemed impossible that everyone should not believe it; and young Peter McCarren, peering, listening, questioning, jotting down notes, inspired him with an exquisite sense of security. McCarren had fastened on the case at once, 'like a leech', as he phrased it – jumped at it, thrilled to it, and settled down to 'draw the last drop of fact from it, and not let go till he had'. No one else had treated

Granice in that way – even Allonby's detective had not taken a single note. And though a week had elapsed since the visit of that authorised official, nothing had been heard from the District Attorney's office: Allonby had apparently dropped the matter again. But McCarren wasn't going to drop it – not he! He positively hung on Granice's footsteps. They had spent the greater part of the previous day together, and now they were off again, running down clues.

But at Leffler's they got none, after all. Leffler's was no longer a stable. It was condemned to demolition, and in the respite between sentence and execution it had become a vague place of storage, a hospital for broken-down carriages and carts, presided over by a blear-eyed old woman who knew nothing of Flood's garage across the way – did not even remember what had stood there before the new flat-house began to rise.

'Well – we may run Leffler down somewhere; I've seen harder jobs done,' said McCarren, cheerfully noting down the name.

As they walked back towards Sixth Avenue he added, in a less sanguine tone: 'I'd undertake now to put the thing through if you could only put me on the track of that cyanide.'

Granice's heart sank. Yes – there was the weak spot; he had felt it from the first! But he still hoped to convince McCarren that his case was strong enough without it; and he urged the reporter to come back to his rooms and sum up the facts with him again.

'Sorry, Mr Granice, but I'm due at the office now. Besides, it'd be no use till I get some fresh stuff to work on. Suppose I call you up tomorrow or next day?'

He plunged into a trolley and left Granice gazing desolately after him.

Two days later he reappeared at the apartment, a shade less jaunty in demeanor.

'Well, Mr Granice, the stars in their courses are against you, as the bard says. Can't get a trace of Flood, or of Leffler either. And you say you bought the motor through Flood, and sold it through him, too?'

'Yes,' said Granice wearily.

'Who bought it, do you know?'

Granice wrinkled his brows. 'Why, Flood – yes, Flood himself. I sold it back to him three months later.'

'Flood? The devil! And I've ransacked the town for Flood. That kind of business disappears as if the earth had swallowed it.'

Granice, discouraged, kept silence.

'That brings us back to the poison,' McCarren continued, his note-book out. 'Just go over that again, will you?'

And Granice went over it again. It had all been so simple at the time – and he had been so clever in covering up his traces! As soon as he decided on poison he looked about for an acquaintance who manufactured chemicals;

and there was Jim Dawes, a Harvard classmate, in the dyeing business – just the man. But at the last moment it occurred to him that suspicion might turn towards so obvious an opportunity, and he decided on a more tortuous course. Another friend, Carrick Venn, a student of medicine whom irremediable ill-health had kept from the practice of his profession, amused his leisure with experiments in physics, for the exercise of which he had set up a simple laboratory. Granice had the habit of dropping in to smoke a cigar with him on Sunday afternoons, and the friends generally sat in Venn's workshop, at the back of the old family house in Stuyvesant Square. Off this workshop was the cupboard of supplies, with its row of deadly bottles. Carrick Venn was an original, a man of restless curious tastes, and his place, on a Sunday, was often full of visitors: a cheerful crowd of journalists, scribblers, painters, experimenters in divers forms of expression. Coming and going among so many, it was easy enough to pass unperceived; and one afternoon Granice, arriving before Venn had returned home, found himself alone in the workshop, and quickly slipping into the cupboard, transferred the drug to his pocket.

But that had happened ten years ago; and Venn, poor fellow, was long since dead of his dragging ailment. His old father was dead, too, the house in Stuyvesant Square had been turned into a boarding-house, and the shifting life of New York had passed its rapid sponge over every trace of their obscure little history. Even the optimistic McCarren seemed to acknowledge the hopelessness of seeking for proof in that direction.

'And there's the third door slammed in our faces.' He shut his note-book, and throwing back his head, rested his bright inquisitive eyes on Granice's furrowed face.

'Look here, Mr Granice – you see the weak spot, don't you?'

The other made a despairing motion. 'I see so many!'

'Yes: but the one that weakens all the others. Why the deuce do you want this thing known? Why do you want to put your head into the noose?'

Granice looked at him hopelessly, trying to take the measure of his quick light irreverent mind. No one so full of cheerful animal life would believe in the craving for death as a sufficient motive; and Granice racked his brain for one more convincing. But suddenly he saw the reporter's face soften, and melt to a naïve sentimentalism.

'Mr Granice – has the memory of it always haunted you?'

Granice stared a moment, and then leapt at the opening. 'That's it – the memory of it . . . always . . . '

McCarren nodded vehemently. 'Dogged your steps, eh? Wouldn't let you sleep? The time came when you *had* to make a clean breast of it?'

'I had to. Can't you understand?'

The reporter struck his fist on the table. 'God, sir! I don't suppose there's a human being with a drop of warm blood in him that can't picture the deadly horrors of remorse – '

The Celtic imagination was aflame, and Granice mutely thanked him for the word. What neither Ascham nor Denver would accept as a conceivable motive the Irish reporter seized on as the most adequate; and, as he said, once one could find a convincing motive, the difficulties of the case became so many incentives to effort.

'Remorse – *remorse*,' he repeated, rolling the word under his tongue with an accent that was a clue to the psychology of the popular drama; and Granice, perversely, said to himself: 'If I could only have struck that note I should have been running in six theatres at once.'

He saw that from that moment McCarren's professional zeal would be fanned by emotional curiosity; and he profited by the fact to propose that they should dine together, and go on afterwards to some music-hall or theatre. It was becoming necessary to Granice to feel himself an object of preoccupation, to find himself in another mind. He took a kind of grey penumbral pleasure in riveting McCarren's attention on his case; and to feign the grimaces of moral anguish became a passionately engrossing game. He had not entered a theatre for months; but he sat out the meaningless performance in rigid tolerance, sustained by the sense of the reporter's observation.

Between the acts, McCarren amused him with anecdotes about the audience: he knew everyone by sight, and could lift the curtain from every physiognomy. Granice listened indulgently. He had lost all interest in his kind, but he knew that he was himself the real centre of McCarren's attention, and that every word the latter spoke had an indirect bearing on his own problem.

'See that fellow over there – the little dried-up man in the third row, pulling his moustache? *His* memoirs would be worth publishing,' McCarren said suddenly in the last *entr'acte*.

Granice, following his glance, recognised the detective from Allonby's office. For a moment he had the thrilling sense that he was being shadowed.

'Caesar, if *he* could talk – !' McCarren continued. 'Know who he is, of course? Dr John B. Stell, the biggest alienist in the country – '

Granice, with a start, bent again between the heads in front of him. '*That* man – the fourth from the aisle? You're mistaken. That's not Dr Stell.'

McCarren laughed. 'Well, I guess I've been in court enough to know Stell when I see him. He testifies in nearly all the big cases where they plead insanity.'

A cold shiver ran down Granice's spine, but he repeated obstinately: 'That's not Dr Stell.'

'Not Stell? Why, man, I *know* him. Look – here he comes. If it isn't Stell, he won't speak to me.'

The little dried-up man was moving slowly up the aisle. As he neared McCarren he made a slight gesture of recognition.

'How'do, Doctor Stell? Pretty slim show, ain't it?' the reporter cheerfully flung out at him. And Mr J. B. Hewson, with a nod of amicable assent, passed on.

Granice sat benumbed. He knew he had not been mistaken – the man who had just passed was the same man whom Allonby had sent to see him: a physician disguised as a detective. Allonby, then, had thought him insane, like the others – had regarded his confession as the maundering of a maniac. The discovery froze Granice with horror – he seemed to see the madhouse gaping for him.

'Isn't there a man a good deal like him – a detective named J. B. Hewson?'

But he knew in advance what McCarren's answer would be. 'Hewson? J. B. Hewson? Never heard of him. But that was J. B. Stell fast enough – I guess he can be trusted to know himself, and you saw he answered to his name.'

SIX

Some days passed before Granice could obtain a word with the District Attorney: he began to think that Allonby avoided him.

But when they were face to face Allonby's jovial countenance showed no sign of embarrassment. He waved his visitor to a chair, and leaned across his desk with the encouraging smile of a consulting physician.

Granice broke out at once: 'That detective you sent me the other day – '

Allonby raised a deprecating hand.

' – I know: it was Stell the alienist. Why did you do that, Allonby?'

The other's face did not lose its composure. 'Because I looked up your story first – and there's nothing in it.'

'Nothing in it?' Granice furiously interposed.

'Absolutely nothing. If there is, why the deuce don't you bring me proofs? I know you've been talking to Peter Ascham, and to Denver, and to that little ferret McCarren of the *Explorer*. Have any of them been able to make out a case for you? No. Well, what am I to do?'

Granice's lips began to tremble. 'Why did you play me that trick?'

'About Stell? I had to, my dear fellow: it's part of my business. Stell *is* a detective, if you come to that – every doctor is.'

The trembling of Granice's lips increased, communicating itself in a long quiver to his facial muscles. He forced a laugh through his dry throat. 'Well – and what did he detect?'

'In you? Oh, he thinks it's overwork – overwork and too much smoking. If you look in on him someday at his office he'll show you the record of hundreds of cases like yours, and advise you what treatment to follow. It's one of the commonest forms of hallucination. Have a cigar, all the same.'

'But, Allonby, I killed that man!'

The District Attorney's large hand, outstretched on his desk, had an almost imperceptible gesture, and a moment later, as if an answer to the call of an electric bell, a clerk looked in from the outer office.

'Sorry, my dear fellow – lot of people waiting. Drop in on Stell some morning,' Allonby said, shaking hands.

McCarren had to own himself beaten: there was absolutely no flaw in the alibi. And since his duty to his journal obviously forbade his wasting time on insoluble mysteries, he ceased to frequent Granice, who dropped back into a deeper isolation. For a day or two after his visit to Allonby he continued to live in dread of Dr Stell. Why might not Allonby have deceived him as to the alienist's diagnosis? What if he were really being shadowed, not by a police agent but by a mad-doctor? To have the truth out, he suddenly determined to call on Dr Stell.

The physician received him kindly, and reverted without embarrassment to the conditions of their previous meeting. 'We have to do that occasionally, Mr Granice; it's one of our methods. And you had given Allonby a fright.'

Granice was silent. He would have liked to reaffirm his guilt, to produce the fresh arguments which had occurred to him since his last talk with the physician; but he feared his eagerness might be taken for a symptom of derangement, and he affected to smile away Dr Stell's allusion.

'You think, then, it's a case of brain-fag – nothing more?'

'Nothing more. And I should advise you to knock off tobacco. You smoke a good deal, don't you?'

He developed his treatment, recommending massage, gymnastics, travel, or any form of diversion that did not – that in short –

Granice interrupted him impatiently. 'Oh, I loathe all that – and I'm sick of travelling.'

'H'm. Then some larger interest – politics, reform, philanthropy? Something to take you out of yourself.'

'Yes. I understand,' said Granice wearily.

'Above all, don't lose heart. I see hundreds of cases like yours,' the doctor added cheerfully from the threshold.

On the doorstep Granice stood still and laughed. Hundreds of cases like his – the case of a man who had committed a murder, who confessed his guilt, and whom no one would believe! Why, there had never been a case like it in the world. What a good figure Stell would have made in a play: the great alienist who couldn't read a man's mind any better than that!

Granice saw huge comic opportunities in the type.

But as he walked away, his fears dispelled, the sense of listlessness returned on him. For the first time since his avowal to Peter Ascham he found himself without an occupation, and understood that he had been carried through the past weeks only by the necessity of constant action. Now his life had once more become a stagnant backwater, and as he stood on the street corner watching the tides of traffic sweep by, he asked himself despairingly how much longer he could endure to float about in the sluggish circle of his consciousness.

The thought of self-destruction recurred to him; but again his flesh recoiled. He yearned for death from other hands, but he could never take it from his own. And, aside from his insuperable physical reluctance, another motive restrained him. He was possessed by the dogged desire to establish the truth of his story. He refused to be swept aside as an irresponsible dreamer – even if he had to kill himself in the end, he would not do so before proving to society that he had deserved death from it.

He began to write long letters to the papers; but after the first had been published and commented on, public curiosity was quelled by a brief statement from the District Attorney's office, and the rest of his communications remained unprinted. Ascham came to see him, and begged him to travel. Robert Denver dropped in, and tried to joke him out of his delusion; till Granice, mistrustful of their motives, began to dread the reappearance of Dr Stell, and set a guard on his lips. But the words he kept back engendered others and still others in his brain. His inner self became a humming factory of arguments, and he spent long hours reciting and writing down elaborate statements of his crime, which he constantly retouched and developed. Then gradually his activity languished under the lack of an audience, the sense of being buried beneath deepening drifts of indifference. In a passion of resentment he swore that he would prove himself a murderer, even if he had to commit another crime to do it; and for a sleepless night or two the thought flamed red on his darkness. But daylight dispelled it. The determining impulse was lacking and he hated too promiscuously to choose his victim . . . So he was thrown back on the unavailing struggle to impose the truth of his story. As fast as one channel closed on him he tried to pierce another through the sliding sands of incredulity. But every issue seemed blocked, and the whole human race leagued together to cheat one man of the right to die.

Thus viewed, the situation became so monstrous that he lost his last shred of self-restraint in contemplating it. What if he were really the victim of some mocking experiment, the centre of a ring of holiday-makers jeering at a poor creature in its blind dashes against the solid walls of consciousness? But, no – men were not so uniformly cruel: there were flaws in the close surface of their indifference, cracks of weakness and pity here and there . . .

Granice began to think that his mistake lay in having appealed to persons more or less familiar with his past, and to whom the visible conformities of his life seemed a final disproof of its one fierce secret deviation. The general tendency was to take for the whole of life the slit seen between the blinders of habit: and in his walk down that narrow vista Granice cut a correct enough figure. To a vision free to follow his whole orbit his story would be more intelligible: it would be easier to convince a chance idler in the street than the trained intelligence hampered by a sense of his antecedents. This idea shot up in him with the tropic luxuriance of each new seed of thought, and he began to walk the streets, and to frequent out-of-the-way chop-houses and bars in his search for the impartial stranger to whom he should disclose himself.

At first every face looked encouragement; but at the crucial moment he always held back. So much was at stake, and it was so essential that his first choice should be decisive. He dreaded stupidity, timidity, intolerance. The imaginative eye, the furrowed brow, were what he sought. He must reveal himself only to a heart versed in the tortuous motions of the human will; and he began to hate the dull benevolence of the average face. Once or twice, obscurely, allusively, he made a beginning – once sitting down at a man's side in a basement chop-house, another day approaching a lounger on an east-side wharf. But in both cases the premonition of failure checked him on the brink of avowal. His dread of being taken for a man in the clutch of a fixed idea gave him an unnatural keenness in reading the expression of his interlocutors, and he had provided himself in advance with a series of verbal alternatives, trap-doors of evasion from the first dart of ridicule or suspicion.

He passed the greater part of the day in the streets, coming home at irregular hours, dreading the silence and orderliness of his apartment, and the critical scrutiny of Flint. His real life was spent in a world so remote from this familiar setting that he sometimes had the mysterious sense of a living metempsychosis, a furtive passage from one identity to another – yet the other as unescapably himself!

One humiliation he was spared: the desire to live never revived in him. Not for a moment was he tempted to a shabby pact with existing conditions. He wanted to die, wanted it with the fixed unwavering desire which alone attains its end. And still the end eluded him! It would not always, of course – he had full faith in the dark star of his destiny. And he could prove it best by repeating his story, persistently and indefatigably, pouring it into indifferent ears, hammering it into dull brains, till at last it kindled a spark, and some one of the careless millions paused, listened, believed . . .

It was a mild March day, and he had been loitering on the west-side docks, looking at faces. He was becoming an expert in physiognomies: his eagerness no longer made rash darts and awkward recoils. He knew now the face he needed, as clearly as if it had come to him in a vision; and not till he found it would he speak. As he walked eastward through the shabby reeking streets he had a premonition that he should find it that morning. Perhaps it was the promise of spring in the air – certainly he felt calmer than for many days . . .

He turned into Washington Square, struck across it obliquely, and walked up University Place. Its heterogeneous passers always allured him – they were less hurried than in Broadway, less enclosed and classified than in Fifth Avenue. He walked slowly, watching for his face.

At Union Square he felt a sudden relapse into discouragement, like a votary who has watched too long for a sign from the altar. Perhaps, after all, he should never find his face . . . The air was languid, and he felt tired. He walked between the bald grass-plots and the twisted trees, making for an empty seat. Presently he passed a bench on which a girl sat alone, and something as definite as the twitch of a cord made him stop before her. He had never dreamed of telling his story to a girl, had hardly looked at the women's faces as they passed. His case was man's work: how could a woman help him? But this girl's face was extraordinary – quiet and wide as a clear evening sky. It suggested a hundred images of space, distance, mystery, like ships he had seen, as a boy, quietly berthed by a familiar wharf, but with the breath of far seas and strange harbours in their shrouds . . . Certainly this girl would understand. He went up to her quietly, lifting his hat, observing the forms – wishing her to see at once that he was 'a gentleman'.

'I am a stranger to you,' he began, sitting down beside her, 'but your face is so extremely intelligent that I feel . . . I feel it is the face I've waited for . . . looked for everywhere; and I want to tell you – '

The girl's eyes widened: she rose to her feet. She was escaping him!

In his dismay he ran a few steps after her, and caught her roughly by the arm.

'Here – wait – listen! Oh, don't scream, you fool!' he shouted out.

He felt a hand on his own arm; turned and confronted a policeman. Instantly he understood that he was being arrested, and something hard within him was loosened and ran to tears.

'Ah, you know – you *know* I'm guilty!'

He was conscious that a crowd was forming, and that the girl's frightened face had disappeared. But what did he care about her face? It was the policeman who had really understood him. He turned and followed, the crowd at his heels . . .

SEVEN

In the charming place in which he found himself there were so many sympathetic faces that he felt more than ever convinced of the certainty of making himself heard.

It was a bad blow, at first, to find that he had not been arrested for murder; but Ascham, who had come to him at once, explained that he needed rest, and the time to 'review' his statements; it appeared that reiteration had made them a little confused and contradictory. To this end he had willingly acquiesced in his removal to a large quiet establishment, with an open space and trees about it, where he had found a number of intelligent companions, some, like himself, engaged in preparing or reviewing statements of their cases, and others ready to lend an interested ear to his own recital.

For a time he was content to let himself go on the tranquil current of this existence; but although his auditors gave him for the most part an encouraging attention, which, in some, went the length of really brilliant and helpful suggestions, he gradually felt a recurrence of his old doubts. Either his hearers were not sincere, or else they had less power to aid him than they boasted. His interminable conferences resulted in nothing, and as the benefit of the long rest made itself felt, it produced an increased mental lucidity which rendered inaction more and more unbearable. At length he discovered that on certain days visitors from the outer world were admitted to his retreat; and he wrote out long and logically constructed relations of his crime, and furtively slipped them into the hands of these messengers of hope.

This occupation gave him a fresh lease of patience, and he now lived only to watch for the visitors' days, and scan the faces that swept by him like stars seen and lost in the rifts of a hurrying sky.

Mostly, these faces were strange and less intelligent than those of his companions. But they represented his last means of access to the world, a kind of subterranean channel on which he could set his 'statements' afloat, like paper boats which the mysterious current might sweep out into the open seas of life.

One day, however, his attention was arrested by a familiar contour, a pair of bright prominent eyes, and a chin insufficiently shaved. He sprang up and stood in the path of Peter McCarren.

The journalist looked at him doubtfully, then held out his hand with a startled deprecating, '*Why –* ?'

'You didn't know me? I'm so changed?' Granice faltered, feeling the rebound of the other's wonder.

'Why, no; but you're looking quieter – smoothed out,' McCarren smiled.

'Yes: that's what I'm here for – to rest. And I've taken the opportunity to write out a clearer statement – '

Granice's hand shook so that he could hardly draw the folded paper from his pocket. As he did so he noticed that the reporter was accompanied by a tall man with grave compassionate eyes. It came to Granice in a wild thrill of conviction that this was the face he had waited for . . .

'Perhaps your friend – he *is* your friend? – would glance over it – or I could put the case in a few words if you have time?' Granice's voice shook like his hand. If this chance escaped him he felt that his last hope was gone. McCarren and the stranger looked at each other, and the former glanced at his watch.

'I'm sorry we can't stay and talk it over now, Mr Granice; but my friend has an engagement, and we're rather pressed – '

Granice continued to proffer the paper. 'I'm sorry – I think I could have explained. But you'll take this, at any rate?'

The stranger looked at him gently. 'Certainly – I'll take it.' He had his hand out. 'Goodbye.'

'Goodbye,' Granice echoed.

He stood watching the two men move away from him through the long light hall; and as he watched them a tear ran down his face. But as soon as they were out of sight he turned and walked hastily towards his room, beginning to hope again, already planning a new statement.

Outside the building the two men stood still, and the journalist's companion looked up curiously at the long monotonous rows of barred windows.

'So that was Granice?'

'Yes – that was Granice, poor devil,' said McCarren.

'Strange case! I suppose there's never been one just like it? He's still absolutely convinced that he committed that murder?'

'Absolutely. Yes.'

The stranger reflected. 'And there was no conceivable ground for the idea? No one could make out how it started? A quiet conventional sort of fellow like that – where do you suppose he got such a delusion? Did you ever get the least clue to it?'

McCarren stood still, his hands in his pockets, his head cocked up in contemplation of the barred windows. Then he turned his bright hard gaze on his companion.

'That was the queer part of it. I've never spoken of it – but I *did* get a clue.'

'By Jove! That's interesting. What was it?'

McCarren formed his red lips into a whistle. 'Why – that it wasn't a delusion.'

He produced his effect – the other turned on him with a pallid stare.

'He murdered the man all right. I tumbled on the truth by the merest accident, when I'd pretty nearly chucked the whole job.'

'He murdered him – murdered his cousin?'

'Sure as you live. Only don't split on me. It's about the queerest business I ever ran into . . . *Do about it?* Why, what was I to do? I couldn't hang the poor devil, could I? Lord, but I was glad when they collared him, and had him stowed away safe in there!'

The tall man listened with a grave face, grasping Granice's statement in his hand.

'Here – take this; it makes me sick,' he said abruptly, thrusting the paper at the reporter; and the two men turned and walked in silence to the gates.

JOHN TAYLOR WOOD

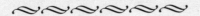

John Taylor Wood (1830–1904), Confederate naval officer, merchant and insurance broker. He grew up at a series of army posts in the American Midwest. In 1847 he entered the United States Navy and when the Civil War erupted won fame as a gunnery officer on board the *Virginia*, which fought to a draw with the *Monitor* in the first confrontation ever between armoured warships, in 1862. During the next three years Wood engaged in a number of daring and celebrated operations against the Union, notably the famous escape of the *Tallahassee* from Halifax, Nova Scotia. Having become something of a hero, when the rebellion collapsed in 1865, he returned to Halifax where he set up as a wholesale merchant, speculated and prospered. Unfortunately, he could not escape the effects of the economic downturn in the mid 1870s, and around 1886 he lost most of his property. Nevertheless, sustained by an 1874 appointment to the Halifax Pilot Commission, he remained a prominent and active member of society, and his death in 1904 was front-page news in Halifax. Although Wood died an American citizen the erstwhile Confederate patriot was a hero for Edwardian Nova Scotia, where his memory has been kept very much alive.

Escape of General Breckinridge

As one of the aides of President Jefferson Davis, I left Richmond with him and his cabinet on 2 April 1865, the night of evacuation, and accompanied him through Virginia, the Carolinas and Georgia, until his capture. Except Lieutenant Barnwell, I was the only one of the party who escaped. After our surprise, I was guarded by a trooper, a German, who had appropriated my horse and most of my belongings. I determined, if possible, to escape; but after witnessing Mr Davis's unsuccessful attempt, I was doubtful of success. However, I consulted him, and he advised me to try. Taking my guard aside, I asked him, by signs (for he could speak little or no English), to accompany me outside the picket-line to the swamp, showing him at the same time a twenty-dollar gold piece. He took it, tried the weight of it in his hands, and put it between his teeth. Fully satisfied that it was not spurious, he escorted me with his carbine to the stream, the banks of which were lined with a few straggling alder bushes and thick saw-grass. I motioned him to return to camp, only a few rods distant. He shook his head, saying, 'Nein, nein.' I gave him another twenty-dollar gold piece; he chinked them together, and held up two fingers. I turned my pockets inside out, and then, satisfied that I had no more, he left me.

Creeping a little farther into the swamp, I lay concealed for about three hours in the most painful position, sometimes moving a few yards almost *ventre à terre* to escape notice; for I was within hearing of the camps on each side of the stream, and often when the soldiers came down for water, or to water their horses, I was within a few yards of them. Some two hours or more passed thus before the party moved. The wagons left first, then the bugles sounded, and the President started on one of his carriage-horses, followed by his staff and a squadron of the enemy. Shortly after their departure I saw someone leading two abandoned horses into the swamp, and recognised Lieutenant Barnwell of our escort. Secreting the horses, we picked up from the debris of the camp parts of two saddles and bridles, and with some patching and tying fitted out our horses, as sad and war-worn animals as ever man bestrode. Though hungry and tired, we gave the remains of the camp provisions to a Mr Fenn for dinner. He recommended us to Widow Paulk's, ten miles distant, an old lady rich in cattle alone.

The day after my escape, I met Judah P. Benjamin as M. Bonfals, a French gentleman travelling for information, in a light wagon, with Colonel Leovie, who acted as interpreter. With goggles on, his beard grown, a hat well over his face, and a large cloak hiding his figure, no one would have recognised him as the late Secretary of State of the Confederacy. I told him of the capture of Mr Davis and his party, and made an engagement to meet him near Madison, Florida, and there decide upon our future movements. He was anxious to push on, and left us to follow more leisurely, passing as paroled soldiers returning home. For the next three days we travelled as fast as our poor horses would permit, leading or driving them; for even if they had been strong enough, their backs were in such a condition that we could not ride. We held on to them simply in the hope that we might be able to dispose of them or exchange them to advantage; but we finally were forced to abandon one.

On the 13th we passed through Valdosta, the first place since leaving Washington, in upper Georgia, in which we were able to purchase anything. Here I secured two hickory shirts and a pair of socks, a most welcome addition to my outfit; for, except what I stood in, I had left all my baggage behind. Near Valdosta we found Mr Osborne Barnwell, an uncle of my young friend, a refugee from the coast of South Carolina, where he had lost a beautiful estate, surrounded with all the comforts and elegances which wealth and a refined taste could offer. Here in the pine forests, as far as possible from the paths of war, and almost outside of civilisation, he had brought his family of ladies and children, and with the aid of his servants, most of whom had followed him, had built with a few tools a rough log cabin with six or eight rooms, but without nails, screws, bolts or glass – almost as primitive a building as Robinson Crusoe's. But, in spite of all drawbacks, the ingenuity and deft hands of the ladies had given to the premises an air of comfort and refinement that was most refreshing. Here I rested two days, enjoying the company of this charming family, with whom Lieutenant Barnwell remained. On the 15th I crossed into Florida, and rode to General Finnegan's, near Madison. Here I met General Breckinridge, the late Secretary of War of the Confederacy, alias Colonel Cabell, and his aide, Colonel Wilson – a pleasant encounter for both parties. Mr Benjamin had been in the neighbourhood, but, hearing that the enemy were in Madison, had gone off at a tangent. We were fully posted as to the different routes to the seaboard by General Finnegan, and discussed with him the most feasible way of leaving the country. I inclined to the eastern coast, and this was decided on. I exchanged my remaining horse with General Finnegan for a better, giving him fifty dollars to boot. Leaving Madison, we crossed the Suwanee River at Moody's Ferry, and took the old St Augustine Road, but seldom travelled in late years as it leads through a pine wilderness and there is one stretch of twenty miles with only water of bad quality, at the Diable Sinks. I rode out of my way some fifteen miles to Mr Yulee's, formerly senator of the United States, and afterward Confederate senator, hoping to meet Mr Benjamin; but he was too wily to be found at the house of a friend. Mr Yulee was absent on my arrival, but Mrs Yulee, a charming lady, and one of a noted family of beautiful women, welcomed me heartily. Mr Yulee returned during the night from Jacksonville, and gave me the first news of what was going on in the world that I had had for nearly a month, including the information that Mr Davis and party had reached Hilton Head on their way north.

Another day's ride brought us to the house of the brothers William and Samuel Owens, two wealthy and hospitable gentlemen, near Orange Lake. Here I rejoined General Breckinridge, and we were advised to secure the services and experience of Captain Dickinson. We sent to Waldo for him, and a most valuable friend he proved. During the war he had rendered notable services; among others he had surprised and captured the United States gunboat *Columbine* on the St John's River, one of whose small boats he had retained and kept concealed near the banks of the river. This boat with two of his best men he now put at our disposal, with orders to meet us on the upper St John.

We now passed through a much more interesting country than the two or three hundred miles of pines we had just traversed. It was better watered, the forests were more diversified with varied species, occasionally thickets or hummocks were met with, and later these gave place to swamps and ever-glades with a tropical vegetation. The road led by Silver Spring, the clear and crystal waters of which show at the depth of hundreds of feet almost as distinctly as though seen through air.

We travelled incognito, known only to good friends, who sent us stage by stage from one to another, and by all we were welcomed most kindly. Besides those mentioned, I recall with gratitude the names of Judge Dawkins, Mr Mann, Colonel Summers, Major Stork, all of whom overwhelmed us with kindness, offering us of everything they had. Of money they were as bare as ourselves, for Confederate currency had disappeared as suddenly as snow before a warm sun, and greenbacks were as yet unknown. Before leaving our friends, we laid in a three weeks' supply of stores; for we could not depend upon obtaining any further south.

On May 25 we struck the St John's River at Fort Butler, opposite Volusia, where we met Russell and O'Toole, two of Dickinson's command, in charge of the boat; and two most valuable and trustworthy comrades they proved to be, either in camp or in the boat, as hunters or fishermen. The boat was a man-of-war's small four-oared gig; her outfit was scanty, but what was necessary we rapidly improvised. Here General Breckinridge and I gave our horses to our companions, and thus ended my long ride of a thousand miles from Virginia.

Stowing our supplies away, we bade goodbye to our friends and started up the river with a fair wind. Our party consisted of General Breckinridge; his aide, Colonel Wilson of Kentucky; the general's servant, Tom, who had been with him all through the war; besides Russell, O'Toole and I – six in all. With our stores, arms, etc., it was a tight fit to get into the boat; there was no room to lie down or to stretch. At night we landed, and, like old campaigners, were soon comfortable. But at midnight the rain came down in bucketfuls, and continued till nearly morning; and, notwithstanding every effort, a large portion of our supplies were soaked and rendered worthless, and, what was worse, some of our powder shared the same fate.

Morning broke on a thoroughly drenched and unhappy company; but a little rum and water, with a corn-dodger and the rising sun, soon stirred us, and with a fair wind we made a good day's run – some thirty-five miles. Except the ruins of two huts, there was no sign that a human being had ever visited these waters; for the war and the occasional visit of a gunboat had driven off the few settlers. The river gradually became narrower and more tortuous as we approached its head waters. The banks are generally low, with a few sandy elevations, thickly wooded or swampy. Occasionally we passed a small opening, or savanna, on which were sometimes feeding a herd of wild cattle and deer; at the latter we had several potshots, all wide. Alligators, as immovable as the logs on which they rested, could be counted by hundreds, and of all sizes up to twelve or fifteen feet. Occasionally, as we passed uncomfortably near, we could not resist, even with our scant supply of ammunition, giving them a little cold lead between the head and shoulders, the only vulnerable place. With a fair wind we sailed the twelve miles across Lake Monroe, a pretty sheet of water, the deserted huts of Enterprise and Mellonville on each side. Above the lake the river became still narrower and more tortuous, dividing sometimes into numerous branches, most of which proved to be mere *culs-de-sac*. The long moss, reaching from the overhanging branches to the water, gave to the surroundings a most weird and funereal aspect.

On May 29 we reached Lake Harney, whence we determined to make the portage to Indian River. O'Toole was sent to look for some means of moving our boat. He returned next day with two small black bulls yoked to a pair of wheels such as are used by lumbermen. Their owner was a compound of Caucasian, African and Indian, with the shrewdness of the white, the good temper of the negro, and the indolence of the red man. He was at first exorbitant in his demands; but a little money, some tobacco, and a spare fowling-piece made him happy, and he was ready to let us drive his beasts to the end of the peninsula. It required some skill to mount the boat securely on the wheels and to guard against any upsets or collisions, for our escape depended upon carrying it safely across.

The next morning we made an early start. Our course was an easterly one, through a roadless, flat, sandy pine-barren, with an occasional thicket and swamp. From the word go trouble with the bulls began. Their owner seemed to think that in furnishing them he had fulfilled his part of the contract. They would neither 'gee' nor 'haw'; if one started ahead, the other would go astern. If by accident they started ahead together, they would certainly bring up with their heads on each side of a tree. Occasionally they would lie down in a pool to get rid of the flies, and only by the most vigorous prodding could they be induced to move.

Paul, the owner, would loiter in the rear, but was always on hand when we halted for meals. Finally we told him, 'No work, no grub; no drive bulls, no tobacco.' This roused him to help us. Two days were thus occupied in covering eighteen miles. It would have been less labour to have tied the beasts, put them into the boat, and hauled it across the portage. The weather was intensely hot, and our time was made miserable by day with sand-flies, and by night with mosquitoes.

The waters of Indian River were a most welcome sight, and we hoped that most of our troubles were over. Paul and his bulls of Bashan were gladly dismissed to the wilderness. Our first care was to make good any defects in our boat: some leaks were stopped by a little calking and pitching. Already our supply of provisions began to give us anxiety: only bacon and sweet potatoes remained. The meal was wet and worthless, and, what was worse, all our salt had dissolved. However, with the waters alive with fish, and some game on shore, we hoped to pull through.

We reached Indian River, or lagoon, opposite Cape Canaveral. It extends along nearly the entire eastern coast of Florida, varying in width from three to six miles, and is separated from the Atlantic by a narrow sand ridge, which is pierced at different points by shifting inlets. It is very shallow, so much so that we were obliged to haul our boat out nearly half a mile before she would float, and the water is teeming with stingarees, swordfish, crabs, etc. But once afloat, we headed to the southward with a fair wind.

For four days we continued to make good progress, taking advantage of every fair wind by night as well as by day. Here, as on the St John's River, the same scene of desolation as far as human beings were concerned was presented. We passed a few deserted cabins, around which we were able to obtain a few coconuts and watermelons, a most welcome addition to our slim commissariat. Unfortunately, oranges were not in season. Whenever the breeze left us the heat was almost suffocating; there was no escape from it. If we landed, and sought any shade, the mosquitoes would drive us at once to the glare of the sun. When sleeping on shore, the best protection was to bury ourselves in the sand, with cap drawn down over the head (my buckskin gauntlets proved invaluable); if in the boat, to wrap the sail or tarpaulin around us. Besides this plague, sand-flies, gnats, swamp-flies, ants and other insects abounded. The little black ant is especially bold and warlike. If, in making our beds in the sand, we disturbed one of their hives, they would rally in thousands to the attack, and the only safety was in a hasty shake and change of residence. Passing Indian River inlet, the river broadens, and there is a thirty-mile straight-away course to Gilbert's Bar, or Old Inlet, now closed; then begin the Jupiter Narrows, where the channel is crooked, narrow, and often almost closed by the dense growth of mangroves, juniper, saw-grass, etc., making a jungle that only a water-snake could penetrate. Several times we lost our reckoning, and had to retreat and take a fresh start; an entire day was lost in these Everglades, which extend across the entire peninsula. Finally, by good luck, we stumbled on a short 'haulover' to the sea, and determined at once to take advantage of it, and to run our boat across and launch her in the Atlantic. A short half-mile over the sand-dunes, and we were clear of the swamps and marshes of Indian River, and were revelling in the Atlantic, free, at least for a time, from mosquitoes, which had punctured and bled us for the last three weeks.

On Sunday, June 4, we passed Jupiter Inlet, with nothing in sight. The lighthouse had been destroyed the first year of the war. From this point we had determined to cross Florida Channel to the Bahamas, about eighty miles; but the wind was ahead, and we could do nothing but work slowly to the southward, waiting for a slant. It was of course a desperate venture to cross this distance in a small open boat, which even a moderate sea would swamp. Our provisions now became a very serious question. As I have said, we had lost all the meal, and the sweet potatoes, our next mainstay, were sufficient only for two days more. We had but little more ammunition than was necessary for our revolvers, and these we might be called upon to use at any time. Very fortunately for us, it was the time of the year when the green turtle deposits its eggs. Russell and O'Toole were old beachcombers, and had hunted eggs before. Sharpening a stick, they pressed it into the sand as they walked along, and wherever it entered easily they would dig. After some hours' search we were successful in finding a nest which had not been destroyed, and I do not think prospectors were ever more gladdened by the sight of 'the yellow' than we were at our find. The green turtle's egg is about the size of a walnut, with a white skin like parchment that you can tear, but not break. The yolk will cook hard, but the longer you boil the egg the softer the white becomes. The flavour is not unpleasant, and for the first two days we enjoyed them; but then we were glad to vary the fare with a few shellfish and even with snails.

From Cape Canaveral to Cape Florida the coast trends nearly north and south in a straight line, so that we could see at a long distance anything going up or down the shore. Some distance to the southward of Jupiter Inlet we saw a steamer coming down, running close to the beach to avoid the three-and four-knot current of the stream. From her yards and general appearance I soon made her out to be a cruiser, so we hauled our boat well up on the sands, turned it over on its side, and went back among the palmettos. When abreast of us and not more than half a mile off, with colours flying, we could see the officer of the deck and others closely scanning the shore. We were in hopes they would look upon our boat as flotsam and jetsam, of which there was more or less strewn upon the beach. To our great relief, the cruiser passed us, and when she was two miles or more to the southward we ventured out and approached the boat, but the sharp lookout saw us, and, to our astonishment, the steamer came swinging about, and headed up the coast. The question at once arose, What was the best course to pursue? The General thought we had better take to the bush again, and leave the boat, hoping they would not disturb it. Colonel Wilson agreed with his chief. I told him that since we had been seen, the enemy would certainly destroy or carry off the boat, and the loss meant, if not starvation, at least privation, and no hope of escaping from the country. Besides, the mosquitoes would suck us as dry as Egyptian mummies. I proposed that we should meet them halfway, in company with Russell and O'Toole, who were paroled men and fortunately had their papers with them, and I offered to row off and see what was wanted. He agreed, and, launching our boat and throwing in two buckets of eggs, we pulled out. By this time the steamer was abreast of us, and had lowered a boat which met us halfway. I had one oar, and O'Toole the other. To the usual hail I paid no attention except to stop rowing. A ten-oared cutter with a smart-looking crew dashed alongside. The sheen was not yet off the lace and buttons of the youngster in charge. With revolver in hand he asked us who we were, where we came from, and where we were going. 'Cap'n,' said I, 'please put away that pistol – I don't like the looks of it – and I'll tell you all about us. We've been rebs and there ain't no use saying we weren't; but it's all up now, and we got home too late to put in a crop, so we just made up our minds to come down shore and see if we couldn't find something. It's all right, cap'n; we've got our papers. Want to see 'em? Got 'em fixed up at Jacksonville.' O'Toole and Russell handed him their paroles, which he said were all right. He asked for mine. I turned my pockets out, looked in my hat, and said: 'I must 'ave dropped mine in camp, but 'tis just the same as theirn.' He asked who was ashore. I told him, 'There's more of we-uns b'iling some turtle-eggs for dinner. Cap'n, I'd like to swap some eggs for tobacco or bread.' His crew soon produced from the slack of their frocks pieces of plug, which they passed on board in exchange for our eggs. I told the youngster if he'd come to camp we'd give him as many as he could eat. Our hospitality was declined. Among other questions he asked if there were any batteries on shore – a battery on a beach where there was not a white man within a hundred miles! 'Up oars – let go forward – let fall – give 'way!' were all familiar orders; but never before had they sounded so welcome. As they shoved off, the coxswain said to the youngster, 'That looks like a man-of-war's gig, sir'; but he paid no attention to him. We pulled leisurely ashore, watching the cruiser. The boat went up to the davits at a run, and she started to the southward again. The General was very much relieved, for it was a narrow escape.

The wind still holding to the southward and eastward, we could work only slowly to the southward, against wind and current. At times we suffered greatly for want of water; our usual resource was to dig for it, but often it was so brackish and warm that when extreme thirst forced its use the consequences were violent pains and retchings. One morning we saw a few wigwams ashore, and pulled in at once and landed. It was a party of Seminoles who had come out of the Everglades like the bears to gather eggs. They received us kindly, and we devoured ravenously the remnants of their breakfast of fish and *kountee*. Only the old chief spoke a little English. Not more than two or three hundred of this once powerful and warlike tribe remain in Florida; they occupy some islands in this endless swamp to the southward of Lake Okeechobee. They have but little intercourse with the whites, and come out on the coast only at certain seasons to fish. We were very anxious to obtain some provisions from them, but excepting *kountee* they had nothing to spare. This is an esculent resembling arrowroot, which they dig, pulverise and use as flour. Cooked in the ashes, it makes a palatable but tough cake, which we enjoyed after our long abstinence from bread. The old chief took advantage of our eagerness for supplies, and determined to replenish his powder-horn. Nothing else would do; not even an old coat, or fish-hooks, or a cavalry sabre would tempt him. Powder only he would have for their long, heavy small-bore rifles with flintlocks, such as Davy Crockett used. We reluctantly divided with him our very scant supply in exchange for some of their flour. We parted good friends, after smoking the pipe of peace.

On the 7th, off New River Inlet, we discovered a small sail standing to the northward. The breeze was very light, so we downed our sail, got out our oars, and gave chase. The stranger stood out to seaward, and endeavoured to escape; but slowly we overhauled her, and finally a shot caused her mainsail to drop. As we pulled alongside I saw from the dress of the crew of three that they were man-of-war's men, and divined that they were deserters. They were thoroughly frightened at first, for our appearance was not calculated to impress them favourably. To our questions they returned evasive answers or were silent, and finally asked by what authority we had overhauled them. We told them that the war was not over so far as we were concerned; that they were our prisoners, and their boat our prize; that they were both deserters and pirates, the punishment of which was death; but that under the circumstances we would not surrender them to the first cruiser we met, but would take their paroles and exchange boats. To this they strenuously objected. They were well armed, and although we outnumbered them five to three (not counting Tom), still, if they could get the first bead on us the chances were about equal. They were desperate, and not disposed to surrender their boat without a tussle. The General and I stepped into their boat, and ordered the spokesman and leader to go forward. He hesitated a moment, and two revolvers looked him in the face. Sullenly he obeyed our orders. The General said, 'Wilson, disarm that man.' The Colonel, with pistol in hand, told him to hold up his hands. He did so while the Colonel drew from his belt a navy revolver and a sheath-knife. The other two made no further show of resistance, but handed us their arms. The crew disposed of, I made an examination of our capture. Unfortunately, her supply of provisions was very small – only some 'salt-horse' and hardtack, with a breaker of fresh water, and we exchanged part of them for some of our *kountee* and turtles' eggs. But it was in our new boat that we were particularly fortunate: sloop-rigged, not much longer than our gig, but with more beam and plenty of freeboard, decked over to the mast, and well found in sails and rigging. After our experience in a boat the gunwale of which was not more than eighteen inches out of water, we felt that we had a craft able to cross the Atlantic. Our prisoners, submitting to the inevitable, soon made themselves at home in their new boat, became more communicative, and wanted some information as to the best course by which to reach Jacksonville or Savannah. We were glad to give them the benefit of our experience, and on parting handed them their knives and two revolvers, for which they were very thankful.

Later we were abreast of Green Turtle Key, with wind light and ahead; still, with all these drawbacks, we were able to make some progress. Our new craft worked and sailed well, after a little addition of ballast. Before leaving the coast, we found it would be necessary to call at Fort Dallas or some other point for supplies. It was running a great risk, for we did not know whom we should find there, whether friend or foe. But without at least four or five days' rations of some kind, it would not be safe to attempt the passage across the Gulf Stream. However, before venturing to do so, we determined to try to replenish our larder with eggs. Landing on the beach, we hunted industriously for some hours, literally scratching for a living; but the ground had evidently been most effectually gone over before, as the tracks of bears proved. A few onions, washed from some passing vessel, were eagerly devoured. We scanned the washings along the strand in vain for anything that would satisfy hunger. Nothing remained but to make the venture of stopping at the fort. This fort, like many others, was established during the Seminole war, and at its close was abandoned. It is near the mouth of the Miami River, a small stream which serves as an outlet to the overflow of the Everglades. Its banks are crowded to the water's edge with tropical verdure, with many flowering plants and creepers, all the colours of which are reflected in its clear waters. The old barracks were in sight as we slowly worked our way against the current. Located in a small clearing, with coconut trees in the foreground, the white buildings made, with a backing of deep green, a very pretty picture. We approached cautiously, not knowing with what reception we should meet. As we neared the small wharf, we found waiting some twenty or thirty men, of all colours, from the pale Yankee to the ebony Congo, all armed: a more motley and villainous-looking crew never trod the deck of one of Captain Kidd's ships. We saw at once with whom we had to deal – deserters from the army and navy of both sides, with a mixture of Spaniards and Cubans, outlaws and renegades. A burly villain, towering head and shoulders above his companions, and whose shaggy black head scorned any covering, hailed us in broken English, and asked who we were. Wreckers, I replied; that we left our vessel outside, and had come in for water and provisions. He asked where we had left our vessel, and her name, evidently suspicious, which was not surprising, for our appearance was certainly against us. Our headgear was unique: the General wore a straw hat that napped over his head like the ears of an elephant; Colonel Wilson, an old cavalry cap that had lost its visor; another, a turban made of some number 4 duck canvas; and all were in our shirt-sleeves, the colours of which were as varied as Joseph's coat. I told him we had left her to the northward a few miles, that a gunboat had spoken us a few hours before, and had overhauled our papers, and had found them all right. After a noisy powwow we were told to land, that our papers might be examined. I said no, but if a canoe were sent off, I would let one of our men go on shore and buy what we wanted. I was determined not to trust our boat within a hundred yards of the shore. Finally a canoe paddled by two negroes came off, and said no one but the captain would be permitted to land. O'Toole volunteered to go, but the boatmen would not take him, evidently having had their orders. I told them to tell their chief that we had intended to spend a few pieces of gold with them, but since he would not permit it, we would go elsewhere for supplies. We got out our sweeps, and moved slowly down the river, a light breeze helping us. The canoe returned to the shore, and soon some fifteen or twenty men crowded into four or five canoes and dugouts, and started for us. We prepared for action, determined to give them a warm reception. Even Tom looked after his carbine, putting on a fresh cap.

Though outnumbered three to one, still we were well under cover in our boat, and could rake each canoe as it came up. We determined to take all the chances, and to open fire as soon as they came within range. I told Russell to try a shot at one some distance ahead of the others. He broke two paddles on one side and hit one man, not a bad beginning. This canoe dropped to the rear at once; the occupants of the others opened fire, but their shooting was wild from the motions of their small craft. The General tried and missed; Tom thought he could do better than his master, and made a good line shot, but short. The General advised husbanding our ammunition until they came within easy range. Waiting a little while, Russell and the Colonel fired together, and the bowman in the nearest canoe rolled over, nearly upsetting her. They were now evidently convinced that we were in earnest, and, after giving us an ineffectual volley, paddled together to hold a council of war. Soon a single canoe with three men started for us with a white flag. We hove to, and waited for them to approach. When within hail, I asked what was wanted.

A white man, standing in the stern, with two negroes paddling, replied: 'What did you fire on us for? We are friends.'

'Friends do not give chase to friends.'

'We wanted to find out who you are.'

'I told you who we are; and if you are friends, sell us some provisions.'

'Come on shore, and you can get what you want.'

Our wants were urgent, and it was necessary, if possible, to make some terms with them; but it would not be safe to venture near their lair again. We told them that if they would bring us some supplies we would wait, and pay them well in gold. The promise of gold served as a bait to secure some concession. After some parleying it was agreed that O'Toole should go on shore in their canoe, be allowed to purchase some provisions, and return in two hours. The buccaneer thought the time too short, but I insisted that if O'Toole were not brought back in two hours, I would speak the first gunboat I met, and return with her and have their nest of freebooters broken up. Time was important, for we had noticed soon after we had started down the river a black column of smoke ascending from near the fort, undoubtedly a signal to some of their craft in the vicinity to return, for I felt convinced that they had other craft besides canoes at their disposal; hence their anxiety to detain us. O'Toole was told to be as dumb as an oyster as to ourselves, but wide awake as to the designs of our dubious friends. The General gave him five eagles for his purchase, tribute-money. He jumped into the canoe, and all returned to the fort. We dropped anchor underfoot to await his return, keeping a sharp lookout for any strange sail. The two hours passed in pleasant surmises as to what he would bring off; another half-hour passed, and no sign of his return; and we began to despair of our anticipated feast, and of O'Toole, a bright young Irishman, whose good qualities had endeared him to us all. The anchor was up, and slowly with a light breeze we drew away from the river, debating what should be our next move. The fort was shut in by a projecting point, and three or four miles had passed when the welcome sight of a canoe astern made us heave to. It was O'Toole with two negroes, a bag of hard bread, two hams, some rusty salt pork, sweet potatoes, fruit and, most important of all, two breakers of water and a keg of New England rum. While O'Toole gave us his experience, a ham was cut, and a slice between two of hardtack, washed down with a jorum of rum and water, with a dessert of oranges and bananas, was a feast to us more enjoyable than any ever eaten at Delmonico's or the Café Riche. On his arrival on shore, our ambassador had been taken to the quarters of Major Valdez, who claimed to be an officer of the Federals, and by him he was thoroughly cross-examined. He had heard of the breaking up of the Confederacy, but not of the capture of Mr Davis, and was evidently sceptical of our story as to being wreckers, and connected us in some way with the losing party, either as persons of note or a party escaping with treasure. However, O'Toole baffled all his queries, and was proof against both blandishments and threats. He learned what he had expected, that they were looking for the return of a schooner; hence the smoke signal, and the anxiety to detain us as long as possible. It was only when he saw us leaving, after waiting over two hours, that the major permitted him to make a few purchases and rejoin us.

Night, coming on, found us inside of Key Biscayne, the beginning of the system of innumerable keys, or small islands, extending from this point to the Tortugos, nearly two hundred miles east and west, at the extremity of the peninsula. Of coral formation, as soon as it is built up to the surface of the water it crumbles under the action of the sea and sun. Sea-fowl rest upon it, dropping the seed of some marine plants, or the hard mangrove is washed ashore on it and its all-embracing roots soon spread in every direction; so are formed these keys. Darkness and shoal water warned us to anchor. We passed an unhappy night fighting mosquitoes. As the sun rose, we saw to the eastward a schooner of thirty or forty tons standing down towards us with a light wind; no doubt it was one from the fort sent in pursuit. Up anchor, up sail, out sweeps, and we headed down Biscayne Bay, a shoal sheet of water between the reefs and mainland. The wind rose with the sun, and, being to windward, the schooner had the benefit of it first, and was fast overhauling us. The water was shoaling, which I was not sorry to see, for our draft must have been from two to three feet less than that of our pursuer, and we recognised that our best chance of escape was by drawing him into shoal water, while keeping afloat ourselves. By the colour and break of the water I saw that we were approaching a part of the bay where the shoals appeared to extend nearly across, with narrow channels between them like the furrows in a ploughed field, with occasional openings from one channel into another. Some of the shoals were just awash, others bare. Ahead was a reef on which there appeared but very little water. I could see no opening into the channel beyond. To attempt to haul by the wind on either tack would bring us in a few minutes under fire of the schooner now coming up hand over hand. I ordered the ballast to be thrown overboard, and determined, as our only chance, to attempt to force her over the reef. She was headed for what looked like a little breakwater on our port bow. As the ballast went overboard we watched the bottom anxiously; the water shoaled rapidly, and the grating of the keel over the coral, with that peculiar tremor most unpleasant to a seaman under any circumstances, told us our danger. As the last of the ballast went overboard she forged ahead, and then brought up. Together we went overboard, and sank to our waists in the black, pasty mud, through which at intervals branches of rotten coral projected, which only served to make the bottom more treacherous and difficult to work on. Relieved of a half-ton of our weight, our sloop forged ahead three or four lengths, and then brought up again. We pushed her forward some distance, but as the water lessened, notwithstanding our efforts, she stopped.

Looking astern, we saw the schooner coming up wing and wing, not more than a mile distant. Certainly the prospect was blue; but one chance was left, to sacrifice everything in the boat. Without hesitation, overboard went the provisions except a few biscuits; the oars were made fast to the main-sheet alongside, and a breaker of water, the anchor and chain, all spare rope, indeed everything that weighed a pound, was dropped alongside, and then, three on each side, our shoulders under the boat's bilges, at the word we lifted together, and foot by foot moved her forward. Sometimes the water would deepen a little and relieve us; again it would shoal. Between the coral-branches we would sink at times to our necks in the slime and water, our limbs lacerated with the sharp projecting points. Fortunately, the wind helped us; keeping all sail on, thus for more than a hundred yards we toiled, until the water deepened and the reef was passed. Wet, foul, bleeding, with hardly strength enough to climb into the boat, we were safe at last for a time. As we cleared the shoal, the schooner hauled by the wind, and opened fire from a nine- or twelve-pounder; but we were at long range, and the firing was wild. With a fair wind we soon opened the distance between us.

General Breckinridge, thoroughly used up, threw himself down in the bottom of the boat; at which Tom, always on the lookout for his master's comfort, said, 'Marse John, s'pose you take a little rum and water.' This proposal stirred us all. The general rose, saying, 'Yes, indeed, Tom, I will; but where is the rum?' supposing it had been sacrificed with everything else.

'I sees you pitchin' eberyt'ing away; I jes put this jug in hyar, 'ca'se I 'lowed you'd want some.'

Opening a looker in the transom, he took out the jug. Never was a potion more grateful; we were faint and thirsty, and it acted like a charm, and, bringing up on another reef, we were ready for another tussle. Fortunately, this proved only a short lift. In the meantime the schooner had passed through the first reef by an opening, as her skipper was undoubtedly familiar with these waters. Still another shoal was ahead; instead of again lifting our sloop over it, I hauled by the wind, and stood for what looked like an opening to the eastward. Our pursuers were on the opposite tack and fast approaching; a reef intervened, and when abeam, distant about half a mile, they opened fire both with their small arms and boat-gun. The second shot from the latter was well directed; it grazed our mast and carried away the luff of the mainsail. Several Minié balls struck on our sides without penetrating; we did not reply, and kept under cover. When abreast of a break in the reef, we up helm, and again went off before the wind. The schooner was now satisfied that she could not overhaul us, and stood off to the northward.

Free from our enemy, we were now able to take stock of our supplies and determine what to do. Our provisions consisted of about ten pounds of hard bread, a twenty-gallon breaker of water, two thirds full, and three gallons of rum. Really a fatality appeared to follow us as regards our commissariat. Beginning with our first drenching on the St John's, every successive supply had been lost, and now what we had bought with so much trouble yesterday, the sellers compelled us to sacrifice today. But our first care was to ballast the sloop, for without it she was so crank as to be unseaworthy. This was not an easy task; the shore of all the keys, as well as that of the mainland in sight, was low and swampy, and covered to the water's edge with a dense growth of mangroves. What made matters worse, we were without any ground-tackle.

At night we were up to Elliott's Key, and anchored by making fast to a sweep shoved into the muddy bottom like a shad-pole. When the wind went down, the mosquitoes came off in clouds. We wrapped ourselves in the sails from head to feet, with only our nostrils exposed. At daylight we started again to the westward, looking for a dry spot where we might land, get ballast, and possibly some supplies. A few palm trees rising from the man-groves indicated a spot where we might find a little *terra firma*. Going in as near as was prudent, we waded ashore, and found a small patch of sand and coral elevated a few feet above the everlasting swamp. Some six or eight cocoa palms rose to the height of forty or fifty feet, and under their umbrella-like tops we could see the bunches of green fruit. It was a question how to get at it. Without saying a word, Tom went on board the boat, brought off a piece of canvas, cut a strip a yard long, tied the ends together, and made two holes for his big toes. The canvas, stretched between his feet, embraced the rough bark so that he rapidly ascended. He threw down the green nuts, and cutting through the thick shell, we found about half a pint of milk. The general suggested a little milk-punch. All the trees were stripped, and what we did not use we saved for sea-stores.

To ballast our sloop was our next care. The jib was unbent, the sheet and head were brought together and made into a sack. This was filled with sand, and, slung on an oar, was shouldered by two and carried on board.

Leaving us so engaged, the General started to try to knock over some of the numerous water-fowl in sight. He returned in an hour thoroughly used up from his struggles in the swamp, but with two pelicans and a white crane. In the stomach of one of the first were a dozen or more mullet, from six to nine inches in length which had evidently just been swallowed. We cleaned them, and wrapping them in palmetto-leaves, roasted them in the ashes, and they proved delicious. Tom took the birds in hand, and as he was an old campaigner, who had cooked everything from a stalled ox to a crow, we had faith in his ability to make them palatable. He tried to pick them, but soon abandoned it, and skinned them. We looked on anxiously, ready after our first course of fish for something more substantial. He broiled them, and with a flourish laid one before the General on a clean leaf, saying, 'I's 'feared, Marse John, it's tough as an old Muscovy drake.'

'Let me try it, Tom.'

After some exertion he cut off a mouthful, while we anxiously awaited the verdict. Without a word he rose and disappeared into the bushes. Returning in a few minutes, he told Tom to remove the game. His tone and expression satisfied us that pelican would not keep us from starving. The Colonel thought the crane might be better, but a taste satisfied us that it was no improvement.

Hungry and tired, it was nearly night before we were ready to move; and, warned by our sanguinary experience of the previous night, we determined to haul off from the shore as far as possible, and get outside the range of the mosquitoes. It was now necessary to determine upon our future course. We had abandoned all hope of reaching the Bahamas, and the nearest foreign shore was that of Cuba, distant across the Gulf Stream from our present position about two hundred miles, or three or four days' sail, with the winds we might expect at this season. With the strictest economy our provisions would not last so long. However, nearly a month in the swamps and among the keys of Florida, in the month of June, had prepared us to face almost any risk to escape from those shores, and it was determined to start in the morning for Cuba. Well out in the bay we hove to, and passed a fairly comfortable night; next day early we started for Caesar's Canal, a passage between Elliott's Key and Key Largo. The channel was crooked and puzzling, leading through a labyrinth of mangrove islets, around which the current of the Gulf Stream was running like a sluice; we repeatedly got aground, when we would jump overboard and push off. So we worked all day before we were clear of the keys and outside among the reefs, which extend three or four miles beyond. Waiting again for daylight, we threaded our way through them, and with a light breeze from the eastward steered south, thankful to feel again the pulsating motion of the ocean.

Several sail and one steamer were in sight during the day, but all at a distance. Constant exposure had tanned us the colour of mahogany, and our legs and feet were swollen and blistered from being so much in the salt water, and the action of the hot sun on them made them excessively painful. Fortunately, but little exertion was now necessary, and our only relief was in lying still, with an impromptu awning over us. General Breckinridge took charge of the water and rum, doling it out at regular intervals, a tot at a time, determined to make it last as long as possible.

Towards evening the wind was hardly strong enough to enable us to hold our own against the stream. At ten, Carysfort Light was abeam, and soon after a dark bank of clouds rising in the eastern sky betokened a change of wind and weather. Everything was made snug and lashed securely, with two reefs in the mainsail, and the bonnet taken off the jib. I knew from experience what we might expect from summer squalls in the straits of Florida. I took the helm, the General the sheet, Colonel Wilson was stationed by the halyards, Russell and O'Toole were prepared to bail. Tom, thoroughly demoralised, was already sitting in the bottom of the boat, between the general's knees. The sky was soon completely overcast with dark lowering clouds; the darkness, which could almost be felt, was broken every few minutes by lurid streaks of lightning chasing one another through black abysses. Fitful gusts of wind were the heralds of the coming blast. Great drops of rain fell like the scattering fire of a skirmish-line, and with a roar like a thousand trumpets we heard the blast coming, giving us time only to lower everything and get the stern of the boat to it, for our only chance was to run with the storm until the rough edge was taken off, and then heave to. I cried, 'All hands down!' as the gale struck us with the force of a thunderbolt, carrying a wall of white water with it which burst over us like a cataract. I thought we were swamped as I clung desperately to the tiller, though thrown violently against the boom. But after the shock, our brave little boat, though half filled, rose and shook herself like a spaniel. The mast bent like a whip-stick, and I expected to see it blown out of her, but, gathering way, we flew with the wind. The surface was lashed into foam as white as the driven snow. The lightning and artillery of the heavens were incessant, blinding, and deafening; involuntarily we bowed our heads, utterly helpless. Soon the heavens were opened, and the floods came down like a waterspout. I knew then that the worst of it had passed, and though one fierce squall succeeded another, each one was tamer. The deluge, too, helped to beat down the sea. To give an order was impossible, for I could not be heard; I could only, during the flashes, make signs to

Russell and O'Toole to bail. Tying themselves and their buckets to the thwarts, they went to work and soon relieved her of a heavy load.

From the general direction of the wind I knew without compass or any other guide that we were running to the westward, and, I feared, were gradually approaching the dreaded reefs, where in such a sea our boat would have been reduced to matchwood in a little while. Therefore, without waiting for the wind or sea to moderate, I determined to heave to, hazardous as it was to attempt anything of the kind. Giving the Colonel the helm, I lashed the end of the gaff to the boom, and then loosed enough of the mainsail to goose-wing it, or make a leg-of-mutton sail of it. Then watching for a lull or a smooth time, I told him to put the helm a-starboard and let her come to on the port tack, head to the southward, and at the same time I hoisted the sail. She came by the wind quickly without shipping a drop of water, but as I was securing the halyards the Colonel gave her too much helm, bringing the wind on the other bow, the boom flew round and knocked my feet from under me, and overboard I went. Fortunately, her way was deadened, and as I came up I seized the sheet, and with the General's assistance scrambled on board. For twelve hours or more I did not trust the helm to anyone. The storm passed over to the westward with many a departing growl and threat. But the wind still blew hoarsely from the eastward with frequent gusts against the stream, making a heavy, sharp sea. In the trough of it the boat was becalmed, but as she rose on the crest of the waves even the little sail set was as much as she could stand up under, and she had to be nursed carefully; for if she had fallen off, one breaker would have swamped us, or any accident to sail or spar would have been fatal: but like a gull on the waters, our brave little craft rose and breasted every billow.

By noon the next day the weather had moderated sufficiently to make more sail, and the sea went down at the same time. Then, hungry and thirsty, Tom was thought of. During the gale he had remained in the bottom of the boat as motionless as a log. As he was roused up, he asked: 'Marse John, whar is you, and whar is you goin'? 'Fore de Lord, I never want to see a boat again.'

'Come, Tom, get us something to drink, and see if there is anything left to eat,' said the General. But Tom was helpless.

The General served out a small ration of water and rum, every drop of which was precious. Our small store of bread was found soaked, but, laid in the sun, it partly dried, and was, if not palatable, at least a relief to hungry men.

During the next few days the weather was moderate, and we stood to the southward; several sail were in sight, but at a distance. We were anxious to speak one even at some risk, for our supplies were down to a pint of rum in water each day under a tropical sun, with two water-soaked biscuits. On the afternoon of the second day a brig drifted slowly down towards us; we made signals that we wished to speak her, and, getting out our sweeps, pulled for her. As we neared her, the captain hailed and ordered us to keep off. I replied that we were shipwrecked men, and only wanted some provisions. As we rounded to under his stern, we could see that he had all his crew of seven or eight men at quarters. He stood on the taff-rail with a revolver in hand, his two mates with muskets, the cook with a huge tormentor and the crew with handspikes.

'I tell you again, keep off, or I'll let fly.'

'Captain, we won't go on board if you will give us some provisions; we are starving.'

'Keep off, I tell you. Boys, make ready.'

One of the mates drew a bead on me; our eyes met in a line over the sights on the barrel. I held up my right hand.

'Will you fire on an unarmed man? Captain, you are no sailor, or you would not refuse to help shipwrecked men.'

'How do I know who you are? And I've got no grub to spare.'

'Here is a passenger who is able to pay you,' said I, pointing to the General.

'Yes; I will pay for anything you let us have.'

The captain now held a consultation with his officers, and then said: 'I'll give you some water and bread. I've got nothing else. But you must not come alongside.'

A small keg, or breaker, was thrown overboard and picked up, with a bag of fifteen or twenty pounds of hardtack. This was the reception given us by the brig *Neptune* of Bangor. But when the time and place are considered, we cannot wonder at the captain's precautions, for a more piratical-looking party than we never sailed the Spanish main. General Breckinridge, bronzed the colour of mahogany, unshaven, with long mustache, wearing a blue flannel shirt open at the neck, exposing his broad chest, with an old slouch hat, was a typical buccaneer. Thankful for what we had received, we parted company. Doubtless the captain reported on his arrival home a blood-curdling story of his encounter with pirates off the coast of Cuba.

'Marse John, I thought the war was done. Why didn't you tell dem folks who you was?' queried Tom. The General told Tom they were Yankees, and would not believe us. 'Is dar any Yankees whar you goin'? – 'ca'se if dar is, we best go back to old Kentucky.' He was made easy on this point, and, with an increase in our larder, became quite perky. A change in the colour of the water showed us that we were on soundings, and had crossed the Stream, and soon after we came in sight of some rocky islets, which I recognised as Double-Headed Shot Keys, thus fixing our position; for our chart, with the rest of our belongings, had disappeared, or had been destroyed by water, and as the heavens, by day and night, were our only guide, our navigation was necessarily very uncertain. For the next thirty miles our course to the southward took us over Salt Key Bank, where the soundings varied from three to five fathoms, but so clear was the water that it was hard to believe that the coral, the shells, and the marine flowers were not within arm's reach. Fishes of all sizes and colours darted by us in every direction. The bottom of the bank was a constantly varying kaleidoscope of beauty. But to starving men, with not a mouthful in our grasp, this display of food was tantalising. Russell, who was an expert swimmer, volunteered to dive for some conchs and shellfish; oysters there were none. Asking us to keep a sharp lookout on the surface of the water for sharks, which generally swim with the dorsal fin exposed, he went down and brought up a couple of live conchs about the size of a man's fist. Breaking the shell, we drew the quivering body out. Without its coat it looked like a huge grub, and not more inviting. The General asked Tom to try it.

'Glory, Marse John, I'm mighty hungry, nebber so hungry sense we been in de almy, and I'm just ready for ole mule, pole-cat or anyt'ing 'cept dis worm.'

After repeated efforts to dissect it we agreed with Tom, and found it not more edible than a pickled football. However, Russell, diving again, brought up bivalves with a very thin shell and beautiful colours, in shape like a large pea-pod. These we found tolerable; they served to satisfy in some small degree our craving for food. The only drawback was that eating them produced great thirst, which is much more difficult to bear than hunger. We found partial relief in keeping our heads and bodies wet with salt water.

On the sixth day from the Florida coast we crossed Nicholas Channel with fair wind. Soon after we made the Cuban coast, and stood to the westward, hoping to sight something which would determine our position. After a run of some hours just outside of the coral-reefs, we sighted in the distance some vessels at anchor. As we approached, a large town was visible at the head of the bay, which proved to be Cardenas. We offered prayful thanks for our wonderful escape, and anchored just off the custom-house, and waited some time for the health officer to give us *pratique*. But as no one came off in answer to our signals, I went on shore to report at the custom-house. It was some time before I could make them comprehend that we were from Florida, and anxious to land. Their astonishment was great at the size of our boat, and they could hardly believe we had crossed in it. Our arrival produced as much sensation as would that of a liner. We might have been filibusters in disguise. The Governor-General had to be telegraphed to; numerous papers were made out and signed; a register was made out for the sloop *No Name*; then we had to make a visit to the Governor before we were allowed to go to a hotel to get something to eat. After a cup of coffee and a light meal I had a warm bath, and donned some clean linen which our friends provided.

We were overwhelmed with attentions, and when the Governor-General telegraphed that General Breckinridge was to be treated as one holding his position and rank, the officials became as obsequious as they had been overbearing and suspicious. The next day one of the Governor-General's aides-de-camp arrived from Havana, with an invitation for the General and the party to visit him, which we accepted, and after two days' rest took the train for the capital. A special car was placed at our disposal, and on our arrival the General was received with all the honours. We were driven to the palace, had a long interview, and dined with Governor-General Concha. The transition from a small open boat at sea, naked and starving, to the luxuries and comforts of civilised life was as sudden as it was welcome and thoroughly appreciated.

At Havana our party separated. General Breckinridge and Colonel Wilson have since crossed the great river; Russell and O'Toole returned to Florida. I should be glad to know what has become of faithful Tom.

WALTER WOOD

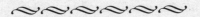

Walter Wood introduces the following account thus in his book *In the Line of Battle*, from which the story of Trooper Potts is taken:

As part of the operations in Gallipoli, it was decided to bombard and attack a very strongly fortified Turkish position near Suvla Bay – a sector stretching from Hill 70 to Hill 112. The frontal attack was a desperate enterprise, as the Turks had dug themselves in up to the neck in two lines of trenches of exceptional strength. The attack was made on the afternoon of 21 August 1915, after a bombardment by battleships and heavy land batteries. It was in the course of this advance that the teller of this story, Trooper Frederick William Owen Potts, of the 1/1st Berkshire Yeomanry (Territorial Force), was struck down, and later performed the unparalleled act for which he was awarded the Victoria Cross. For nearly fifty hours Trooper Potts remained under the Turkish trenches with a severely wounded and helpless comrade, 'although he could have returned to safety,' says the official record. Finally the trooper, in the extraordinary manner which he now describes, saved his comrade's life. Trooper Potts was only twenty-two years old at the time, and the first Yeoman to win the most coveted of all distinctions.

How Trooper Potts won the VC on Burnt Hill

I saw a good deal of the Turks before we came to grips with them near Suvla Bay. I had gone out to Egypt with my regiment, the Berkshire Yeomanry, and for about four months we were doing garrison work and escort work for Turks who had been captured in Gallipoli and the Dardanelles and sent as prisoners of war to Egypt. Our place was not far from Cairo. I was greatly struck by the size and physique of the Turks. There were some very fine big men among them – in fact, I should think the average height was close on six feet.

We had taken our horses out to Egypt with us, and all our work in that country was done with them; but as the weeks went by, and no call came to us for active service, we became disappointed, and got into the way of singing a song which the poet of the regiment had specially composed, and of which the finish of every verse was the line: 'The men that nobody wants' – this meaning that there was no use for us as cavalry in the fighting area. But when the four months had gone, the order suddenly came for us to go to Gallipoli. By that time we had got acclimatised, a point we appreciated later, as the heat was intense and the flies were very troublesome.

From Alexandria we sailed in a transport, which occupied four days in reaching Gallipoli. Here we were transhipped to trawlers and barges, and immediately found ourselves in the thick of one of the most tremendous bombardments the world has ever known. Battleships were firing their big guns, which made a terrific noise, and there was other continual firing of every known sort. We were very lucky in our landing, because we escaped some of the heaviest of the gunfire. The Turks could see us, though we had no sight of them, and whenever a cluster of us was spotted, a shell came crashing over. Thus we had our baptism of fire at the very start.

We were in extraordinarily difficult country, and whatever we needed in the way of food and drink we had to carry with us – even the water. Immense numbers of tins had been filled from the Nile and taken to Gallipoli in barges, and this was the water we used for drinking purposes, as well as water which was condensed from the sea, and kept in big tanks on the shore. Every drop of water we needed had to be fetched from the shore, and this work proved about the hardest and most dangerous of any we had to do after landing and taking up our position on a hill. Several of our chaps were knocked over in this water-fetching work.

While we were at this place we were employed in making roads from

Suvla Bay to Anzac, and hard work it was, because the country was all rocks. We had landed light, without blankets or waterproofs, so that we felt the intense cold of the nights very much.

We had a week of this sort of thing, under fire all the time. I think it was on a Sunday we landed, and a week later we heard that we were to take part in the attack on Hill 70 or, as we called it, because of its appearance, Burnt Hill. There were immense quantities of a horrible sort of scrub on it, and a great deal of this stuff had been fired and charred by gunfire. I little knew then how close and long an acquaintance I was to make with the scrub on Hill 70.

It was about five o'clock in the evening when the great news came. We were to be ready at seven, and ready we were, glad to be in it. We did not know much, but we understood that we were to take our places in some reserve trenches. Night comes quickly in those regions, and when the day had gone we moved round to Anzac, marching along the roads which we had partially made. We reached Anzac at about two o'clock in the morning, in pitch darkness.

We had a pick and two shovels to four men, and took it in turns to carry them. Each man also carried two hundred rounds of ammunition, so that we were pretty well laden. When we reached Anzac Cove we moved right in under the cliffs, which go sheer down to the sea; but there is practically no tide, so that the beach is safe. The only way to reach the shore was to go in single file down a narrow, twisting pathway.

We were on the beach till about two o'clock in the afternoon, when we were ordered to be ready with our packs, and we went up the cliffs, again in single file, forming up when we reached the top. Then we went a mile or so along the road we had marched over the night before – all part of the scheme of operations, I take it. Then we cut across to our right and saw a plain called Salt Lake, where we watched a division going into action under heavy shrapnel fire.

We were now in the thick of the awful country which I was to know so well. The surface was all sand and shrubs, and the great peculiarity of the shrubs was that they were very much like our holly trees at home, though the leaves were not so big, but far more prickly. These shrubs were about three feet high, and they were everywhere; but they did not provide any real cover. There were also immense numbers of long creepers and grass, and a lot of dust and dirt. The heat was fearful, so that you can easily understand how hard it was to get along when we were on the move. These obstacles proved disastrous to many of our chaps when they got into the zone of fire, for the shrapnel set the shrubs ablaze. This meant that many a brave fellow who was hit during the fighting on Hill 70 fell among the burning furze and was burned to death where he lay.

As we were waiting for our turn, we could see the other chaps picking their way through this burning stuff, and charging on towards the Turkish trenches. When our own turn came, the scrub was burning less fiercely, and to some extent we were able to choose our way and avoid the blazing patches. We ran whenever we got the chance, making short rushes; but when we got into the real zone of fire, we never stopped until we were under the protection of Chocolate Hill.

For half an hour we rested at the foot of this hill. From our position we could not see the Turks, who were entrenched over the top; but their snipers were out and bothering us a good deal. It was impossible to see these snipers, because they hid themselves most cunningly in the bushes, and had their faces and rifles painted the same colour as the surrounding objects. However, we levelled up matters by sending out our own sniping parties.

We were on the move again as soon as we had got our breath back. We still understood, as we moved to the left of Chocolate Hill, that we were going to occupy reserve trenches. We went through a field of ripe wheat. About two yards in front of me was a mate of mine, Reginald West. I saw him struck in the thigh by a sniper's bullet, which went in as big as a pea, and came out the size of a five-shilling piece. It was an explosive bullet, one of many that were used against us by the Turks, under their German masters. In a sense West was lucky, because when he was struck down he fell right on the edge of a dug-out, and I heard one of the men shout, 'Roll over, mate! Roll over! You'll drop right in here!' And he did.

The rest of us went on, though in the advance we lost a number of men. Some were killed outright; some were killed by shells and bullets after they had fallen wounded; and some had to lie where they had fallen and do the best they could. We pushed ahead till we struck Hill 70 again.

When we got to the reserve trenches I asked a chap how far away the Turks were, and he answered, 'About a thousand yards,' but I don't think it was as much as that.

Now we began to ascend Hill 70 in short spurts, halting from time to time. We had fairly good cover, because the scrub was not on fire, though several parts had been burnt out. During one of these halts we were ordered to fix bayonets.

We had found shelter in a bit of a gully, and were pretty well mixed up with other regiments – the Borders, Dorsets, and so on. We first got the idea that we were going to charge from an officer near us; but he was knocked out – with a broken arm, I believe – before the charge came off. He was just giving us the wheeze about the coming charge when a bullet struck him.

How did the charge begin? Well, an officer shouted, as far as I can recollect, 'Come on, lads! We'll give 'em beans!' That is not exactly according to drill-books and regulations as I know them; but it was enough. It let the boys loose, and they simply leapt forward and went for the Turkish trenches. It was not to be my good fortune to get into them, however; in fact, I did not get very far after the order to charge was given.

I had gone perhaps twenty or thirty yards when I was knocked off my feet. I knew I was hit. I had a sort of burning sensation; but whether I was hit in the act of jumping, or whether I jumped because I was hit, I do not know. What I *do* know is that I went up in the air, came down again, and lay where I fell. I knew that I had been shot at the top of the left thigh, the bullet going clean through and just missing the artery and the groin by an eighth of an inch, as the doctor told me later.

Utterly helpless, I lay there for about three-quarters of an hour, while the boys rushed round me and scattered in the charge. This happened about a quarter of a mile from the top of the hill. I propped myself up on my arm and watched the boys charging.

I heard later, from a man who was with me in hospital at Malta – he had been struck deaf and dumb for the time being, among other things – that the boys got into the Turkish third trench and that the Turks bolted. He told me that when they reached this third trench there were only seventeen Berkshire boys left to hold it. The enemy seemed to get wind of this; then it looked as if all the Turkish army was going for the seventeen, and they had no alternative but to clear out.

After the charge I saw this handful come back down the hill, quite close to where I was lying. I had fallen in a sort of little thicket, a cluster of the awful scrub which was like holly, but much worse. I was thankful for it, however, because it gave me a bit of shelter and hid me from view.

I had been lying there about half an hour when I heard a noise near me and saw that a poor, wounded chap, a trooper of the Berkshires, was crawling towards me. I recognised him as a fellow-townsman.

'Is that you, Andrews?' I asked.

He simply answered, 'Yes.' That was all he could get out.

'I'm jolly pleased you've come,' I said, and Andrews crawled as close as he could get, and we lay there, perfectly still, for about ten minutes. Andrews had been shot through the groin, a very dangerous wound, and he was suffering terribly and losing a great deal of blood.

We had been together for a few minutes when another trooper – a stranger to me – crawled up to our hiding-place. He had a wound in the leg. We were so cramped for space under the thicket that Andrews had to shift as best he could to make room for the newcomer. That simple act of mercy saved his life, for the stranger had not been with us more than ten minutes when a bullet went through both his legs and mortally wounded him. He kept on crying for water; but we had not a drop among the three of us, and could not do anything to quench his awful thirst.

That fearful afternoon passed slowly, with its grizzling heat and constant fighting, and the night came suddenly. The night hours brought us neither comfort nor security, for a full moon shone, making the countryside as light as day. The cold was intense. The stranger was practically unconscious and kept moving about, which made our position worse, because every time he moved the Turks banged at us.

I was lying absolutely as flat as I could, with my face buried in the dirt, for the bullets were peppering the ground all around us, and one of them actually grazed my left ear – you can see the scar it made, just over the top. This wound covered my face with blood. Was I scared or frightened? I can honestly say that I was not. I had got beyond that stage, and almost as a matter of course I calmly noted the details of everything that happened.

Throughout the whole of that unspeakable night this poor Bucks Hussar chap hung on. He kept muttering, 'Water! Water!' But we could not give him any. When the end came he simply lay down and died right away, and his dead body stayed with us, for we could neither get away nor move him.

During the whole of the next day we lay in our hiding-place, suffering indescribably. The sun, thirst, hunger and our wounds all added to our pain. In our desperation we picked bits off the stalks of the shrubs and tried to suck them; but we got no relief in that way.

The whole of the day went somehow – with such slowness that it seemed as if it would never end. It was impossible to sleep – fighting was going on all the time, and the noise was terrific. We could not see anything of our boys, and we knew that it was impossible for any stretcher-bearers to get through to us, because we were a long way up the hill and no stretcher-bearers could venture out under such terrible fire.

Night came again at last, and Andrews and myself decided to shift, if it was humanly possible to do so, because it was certain death from thirst and hunger to remain where we were, even if we escaped from bullets. So I began to move away by crawling, and Andrews followed as best he could. I would crawl a little way and wait till Andrews, poor fellow, could crawl up to me again. We wriggled like snakes, absolutely flat on the ground and with our faces buried in the stifling dirt.

We managed to wriggle about three hundred yards that night – as near as I can judge. Starting at about a quarter past six, as soon as the day was done, it was about three in the morning when we decided to rest, so that if we had really done three hundred yards we had crawled at the rate of only thirty-three yards an hour!

A great number of rifles were lying about – weapons which had been cast aside in the charge, or had belonged to fallen soldiers; but most of them were quite out of working order, because they were clogged up with dust and dirt. I tried many of them, and at last found one that seemed to be in good working order, and to my joy I came across about fifty rounds of ammunition. Another serviceable rifle was found, so that Andrews and myself were filled with a new hope.

'We'll die like Britons, at any rate,' said Andrews. 'We'll give a good account of ourselves before we go!' And I agreed with him.

We were now some distance from the Turks, and I was terribly anxious to shoot at them; but Andrews was more cautious. 'If you fire they'll discover us, and we shall be done for,' he said. Then we shook hands fervently, because we both believed that this was the last of us, and I know that in thought we both went back to our very early days and offered up our silent prayers to God.

We had managed to crawl to a bit of shelter which was given by some burnt-out scrub, and here we tried to snatch some sleep, for we were both worn out. We went to sleep, for the simple reason that we could not keep awake; but I suddenly awoke, because the cold was intense and I was nearly frozen. Luckily there were a lot of empty sandbags lying about, and I got two or three of these and put them on top of us; but they were really no protection from the bitter air.

Occasionally we made a move, and for the first time we were able to get some water; but only by taking the water-bottles from the poor chaps who had been knocked out. Then we crept back to our shelter, finding immense relief from drinking the water we had got, though it was quite warm and was, I fancy, from the Nile.

We slept, or tried to sleep, there for the rest of that night, and stayed in the place till next morning. We must have been in what is called 'dead ground', a region which cannot be seen or touched by either side, and so it proved to be, for in the early morning there was a real battle, and the bullets were singing right over our heads.

'There's more lead flying about than there was yesterday,' said Andrews; and really some of the bullets were splashing quite close to us – within six feet, I think, though there were not many that came so near.

Andrews was bleeding terribly – every time he moved he bled; but I did the best I could for him with my iodine – I dressed him with mine, and he dressed me with his, and splendid stuff it is. Though we had nothing to eat we did not really feel hungry now – we were past the eating stage. I was very lucky in having four cigarettes and some matches, and I risked a smoke, the sweetest I ever had in my life.

Again we stuck the awful day through.

I was terribly anxious to move and get out of it all at any cost; but still Andrews was very cautious. 'No, we won't try till it gets dark,' he said. I felt that he was right, and so we waited, as patiently as we could, for the night. Three or four yards from us was an inviting-looking bush, and we crawled towards it, thinking it would help us to get away and give us shelter; but at the end of our adventure we discovered that we had done no more than crawl to the bush, crawl round it, and get back to our original hiding-place; so we decided to give up the attempt to get away just then.

When the third night on the hill came we were fairly desperate, knowing that something would have to be done if we meant to live, and that certain death awaited us where we were. We had nothing to eat, and the only drink was the water, which was frightful stuff. But though it was, we were thankful to have it. The water was warm, because of the heat, and was about the colour of wine.

We did not for a moment suppose that we should live to reach the British lines, which we believed to be not far away; but we risked everything on the effort, and in the moonlight we began to wriggle off. We had managed to get no more than half a dozen yards when Andrews had to give it up. I myself, though I was the stronger and better of the two, could scarcely crawl. Every movement was a torture and a misery, because of the thorns that stuck into us from the horrible scrub.

We had kept the sandbags, and with my help Andrews managed to get them over his arms and up to his shoulders. I fastened them with the pieces of string they have, and these gave him a good deal of protection, though the thorns got through and punished us cruelly. I was picking them out of my hands for three weeks afterwards.

Having crawled these half-dozen yards, we gave up the attempt altogether, and did not know what to do. We could see a cluster of trees not far away, about a hundred yards, and there was one that looked fairly tall.

'If we can get to that tree,' said Andrews, 'I could lie there, if I had some water, and perhaps you could strike some of our chaps and bring help.' I had little hope from such an effort as that. Then Andrews unselfishly urged me to look after myself; but, of course, I would not dream of leaving him. I offered to carry him, and I tried, but I was far too weak.

What in the world was to be done? How were we to get out of this deadly place? There seemed no earthly hope of escape – when, literally, like an inspiration, we thought we saw a way out.

Just near us was an ordinary entrenching shovel, which had been dropped or had belonged to some poor chap who had fallen – I can't say which, but there it was. I crawled up and got hold of it, and before we quite knew what was happening, Andrews was resting on it, and I was doing my best to drag him out of danger.

I cannot say whose idea this was, but it is quite likely that Andrews thought of it first. He sat on the shovel as best he could – he was not fastened to it – with his legs crossed, the wounded leg over the sound one, and he put his hands back and clasped my wrists as I sat on the ground behind and hauled away at the handle. Several times he came off, or the shovel fetched away, and I soon saw that it would be impossible to get him away in this fashion.

When we began to move the Turks opened fire on us; but I hardly cared now about the risk of being shot, and for the first time since I had been wounded I stood up and dragged desperately at the shovel, with Andrews on it. I managed to get over half a dozen yards, then I was forced to lie down and rest. Andrews needed a rest just as badly as I did, for he was utterly shaken and suffered greatly.

We started again as soon as we had the strength, and for more than three mortal hours we made this strange journey down the hillside; and at last, with real thankfulness, we reached the bottom and came to a bit of a wood. Sweet beyond expression it was to feel that I could walk upright, and that I was near the British lines. This knowledge came to me suddenly when there rang through the night the command: 'Halt!'

I obeyed – glorious it was to hear that challenge in my native tongue, after what we had gone through. Then this good English sentry said, 'Come up and be recognised!' not quite according to the regulation challenge, but good enough – and he had seen us quite clearly in the moonshine.

Up I went, and found myself face to face with the sentry, whose rifle was presented ready for use, and whose bayonet gleamed in the cold light.

'What are you doing?' said the sentry. 'Are you burying the dead?'

I saw that he was sentry over a trench, and I went to the top of it and leaned over the parapet and said, 'Can you give me a hand?'

'What's up?' said the sentry, who did not seem to realise what had actually happened – and how could he, in such a strange affair?

'I've got a chap out here wounded,' I told him, 'and I've dragged him down the hill on a shovel.'

The sentry seemed to understand like a flash. He walked up to the trench, and when I had made myself clear, three or four chaps bustled round and got a blanket, and I led them to the spot where I had left Andrews lying on the ground. We lifted him off the shovel, put him on the blanket, and carried him to the trench. These men were, I think, Inniskilling Fusiliers, and they did everything for us that human kindness could suggest. They gave me some run and bully beef and biscuit, and it was about the most delightful meal I ever had in my life, because I was famishing and I was safe, with Andrews, after those dreadful hours on the hillside, which seemed as if they would never end.

When we had rested and pulled round a bit, we were put on stretchers and carried to the nearest dressing-station. Afterwards we were sent to Malta, where Andrews was for a long time in hospital.

The granting of the Victoria Cross for what I had done came as a complete surprise to me, because it never struck me that I had done more than any other British soldier would have done for a comrade.

I never lost heart during the time I was lying on Hill 70. All the old things came clearly up in my mind, and many an old prayer was uttered, Andrews joining in. We never lost hope that some way out of our peril would be found – and it seemed as if our prayers had been answered by giving us this inspiration of the shovel.

EDWIN T. WOODHALL

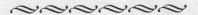

Edwin Thomas Woodhall (1886–1941) had a basic military training in his teens and fulfilled a long held ambition when in 1906, aged twenty, he joined the London Metropolitan Police Force. Woodhall worked his way through the ranks and departments and held posts in several of the specialist areas of policing: Special Political Branch, MI5, Secret Intelligence Police and Protective Surveillance. His work with the Special Political Branch led to a meeting with Lenin at a Nihilist gathering in London's East End. The culmination of his distinguished military and espionage work was during the First World War when he single-handedly captured Percy Topliss, the 'Monocled Mutineer'. Woodhall eventually left the Secret Service to found a detective agency. He had more than forty books published, mainly based on famous crimes; he also appeared in a Peter Lorre film in the 1930s, narrating the prologue. Although his scripts fetched thousands of pounds and his output had been prodigious, he died penniless.

Secret Service Days

ONE

When war broke out my only brother and I both joined up. It seemed strange that I should go safely through some of the fiercest engagements, yet that my brother should be killed in his first attack. His name can be seen on the beautiful Cenotaph between St Lawrence and Ramsgate – 'Samuel Woodhall, age forty-one, killed in action'.

The first shots between the Germans and English, when they came face to face as enemies for the first time in modern history, took place at twenty minutes to one on the afternoon of Sunday, 24 August 1914, and from that period onward to the 6 September my brigade was constantly in action.

An incident of 1914 days which will remain impressed upon my memory concerns the two late field marshals of the British army – the Earl of Ypres and Earl Haig, then Sir John French and Sir Douglas Haig.

It was on the fifth day of our retirement, in face of the German hordes, amidst terrific heat and dust, when, with a few men of my brigade, I went into a large yard of a deserted farm for the purpose of filling water-bottles.

To our astonishment we saw the Union Jack, and in a large dust-covered car the Commander-in-Chief. Standing close by, and in deep silence, was a group of officers who, irrespective of the white dust covering them from head to foot, were obviously of high staff rank.

Their faces, like those of the troops staggering by outside, were grime-covered, unshaven and haggard, with eyes sunken and hollow from want of sleep.

We instinctively turned to go back to the road outside, when one beckoned me towards him, and, as I came near, I at once recognised the handsome features of Sir Douglas Haig, 1st Army Commander.

'What do you boys want?' he asked in lowered tones.

Saluting, I replied: 'Only water, sir, if there's any to be got.'

'Yes,' he answered. 'There's a pump round there. Take what you want, but, for the love of heaven, get it quietly. Make no noise – your Commander-in-Chief has been asleep for five minutes – the first he has had for nearly four days.'

As I passed by on my way to the pump I saw Sir John French lying back in the corner of his car – asleep.

To others, as well as myself, the incident conveyed all that our leaders had to endure. The strain on the men was terrible, but who can fully realise the ordeal which these great soldiers passed in the darkest hours of our nation's history?

I served with my regiment from Mons to the Marne, from the Aisne to Flanders, and in 1915, by the instructions of my commanding officer, Sir Philip Robinson, DSO, KCB, MVO, was transferred to the counter-espionage department of the Intelligence Department, Secret Service. This meant a position of responsibility and opportunity for adventure, which was all to my liking.

It does not need much imagination on the part of anyone who was present in France in those days to picture how arduous was our work in the Intelligence Department.

The country was teeming with German hirelings and spies of all kinds. We had to keep constant vigilance for mysterious lights, pigeon-flying, suspects in British and French uniform, and scrutinise and enquire into the credentials of all civilian labourers working behind the lines. The tricks, resources and ramifications of the German Secret Service were legion.

For instance, on one occasion a French soldier in uniform on leave came into the town of Estaires with his aged father. Questioned as to what they were doing behind the British lines, in the zone of the armies, they produced their *laisser-passer* and said that they wished to visit their former home to see if they could discover a small hoard of money hidden during the first onrush of the German armies.

The Town Major, or British Assistant Provost-Marshal, accepted their version and gave them the necessary authority to proceed to their native village, a shell-blasted derelict place inhabited only by British Artillery observation officers, and within incessant gunfire of the German lines, also in the immediate rear of the British and Canadian section of trenches. I happened to call upon the Town Mayor that day, having just come through on a commission from the 3rd Corps Army Headquarters. In fact, as I alighted from my Triumph motor cycle, our friend and his aged parent came out of his office.

I knocked at his door, saluted and entered. He knew me.

'Good-morning, sergeant,' he said.

'Good-morning, sir,' I answered. 'Anything my way today?'

'No.' he replied. 'One or two lights at night; but the Town Guard saw to that.'

We continued to talk, and I asked him quite casually who were the old man and his son. When he told me, I was suspicious at once. In fact, right throughout my Secret Service days I fostered a dual nature, for I suspected, in the exigencies of my work, everything and everybody until satisfied.

'You'll excuse me, sir,' I said, 'but I think you have exceeded your duty. I shall report this incident to Army Headquarters.'

I did not wait for his reply, but dashed off out and on to my bike.

It did not take me long to overtake them, and dismounting I saluted the French soldier and said: 'Pardon, I am a sergeant of the English Military Police. Show me your military book!'

He explained that he had come on leave; in fact, repeated exactly what the major had previously told me, and everything appeared to be in order, but, just to be on the safe side, they were closely watched – so much so that though they were afterwards found to be 'suspect' by the French authorities, they did not, on that occasion, attempt to carry out their scheme, whatever it was, and had to stick to their assumed role. The result of my report to headquarters was a transfer of the Town Major and an immediate tightening up all round, the Army Brigade and Divisional Provosts-Marshal being the only authorities to visa and issue permits of any description.

With regard to the Allied Secret Service, I state emphatically it was far superior to that of the German.

In real military Secret Service work there is only one set of people who can be relied on, and they are the military spies who act out of purely patriotic motives, and whom I would term, for the want of a better definition, 'national spies'.

The French displayed much daring, resource and intrepid bravery in work of this description, and to quote Colonel W. Nicolai (Chief of the German Secret Service) will, I think, be the best example of what I am trying to convey:

In 1915 nine 'air spies' – four in uniform – and five aeroplanes fell into our hands. Attempts to pick up the spies again were watched. The French aeroplanes would fly at the arranged time over the landing-place, kept under observation by German counter-espionage agents. But the airmen in such cases flew at a considerable height, because the sign agreed upon that the coast was clear was not given. In no case was it definitely ascertained that an 'air spy' was really taken off again.

Some were caught far behind the front in Eastern Belgium. They were instructed that if they reached Holland they were to report to the French Consul, who would see to their return to France.

Some of them had instructions to destroy railway lines and bridges in the rear of the German army, especially in those parts of the front in which a German attack was expected or an Allied offensive was to take place.

Regarding successful enterprises of this nature nothing can be ascertained.

The usefulness of air spies lay mainly in the information they sent by their carrier pigeons.

This method of obtaining information could not be resorted to by the German military authorities. No enemy prisoners of war were found who would undertake work of this nature against their own country.

In respect of bravery displayed by the enemy, they were our equal, but they suffered from being in enemy territory, with inhabitants favourable to the Allies. They tried our methods, but I do not think, from a military point of view, they had the success of the Allies.

I recall seeing the shattered body of a spy near Albert in 1916. He had been dropped from an enemy aeroplane during the night, but his parachute had failed to act. He had given his life for the Fatherland with fortitude as did our own brave men for their cause.

We certainly had much trouble in those days with some French and Belgian civilians working in the pay of the enemy.

Lieutenant E. H. King, Intelligence Officer of my brigade arrested a man named Debacker-Polydore, of Croix de Bac, in the act of cutting our telegraph wires with a pair of insulated pliers.

He was tried by the French Civil and Military Authorities, found guilty, and shot as a spy on the 11 November 1914.

These, it is perhaps needless to say, being inhabitants of the parts in which they operated, were far more difficult to deal with than were German members of the Huns' Secret Service who had crossed the lines for the purpose of espionage. I do not think many got back. In fact, towards 1917, our Intelligence Department had become so efficient that it was almost an impossibility for any civilian in the zone of the armies to move without his every movement being accounted for and recorded.

Pigeons upon both sides played quite an important part during the war. The Germans often used them to send into various secret homing lofts in the Allied territories, or, on the other hand, back to different parts of the occupied territories in Germany.

I have dealt with cases of enemy pigeons in many parts of the British line, some having alighted by reason of mating instinct, exhaustion or wounds.

Dogs, also, were used by both sides, and in cases of attack could be trained to advantage. Some of these dumb animals showed remarkable intelligence, and conveyed, backwards and forwards, repeatedly in the face of death, very valuable information.

Paddy, the dear little mongrel dog whose life-story at some future time I intend to write, is only one of the many dumb Secret Service Agents that worked for the belligerents upon both sides during the war.

In the first months of hostilities innocent civilians became entangled in the machinations of spies without knowing it, as witness the case of the old lady of Fleurbaix.

In the early days of the war I had occasion to be in the neighbourhood of this village, and, owing to my duty, had been keeping watch at certain crossroads for something entirely different from that which I am about to relate.

On two evenings I saw an old peasant woman pass me at about the same time, so, on the third evening, I considered it strange.

On the fourth evening I kept out of sight, but observed that the old lady passed just as before and in the same direction. Having decided to keep watch and satisfy myself about her, I discovered that she invariably entered a partly-ruined church at about seven in the evening, always carrying a little basket.

Evening after evening I discovered this performance to be a regular thing, so I decided to act. She entered the church, went straight to a door in the tower, and began to mount the shell-smashed stairs. Up she went, muttering and mumbling in Flemish, and at last she reached the top storey.

She had no idea that I was close behind her, and when I confronted her she was in the act of handing provisions from her basket to an officer in British uniform.

For a moment I was nonplussed, but, realising that I must go on, I demanded to know who he was, and what he was doing there under such peculiar circumstances.

With great indignation, he replied: 'What do you "vont" to know for?'

That was enough. I whipped out my revolver and covered him. He asked if I had gone crazy, and threatened all sorts of punishments; and I must admit he nearly bluffed me – but that little word 'vont' for 'want' was, I instinctively knew, the mark of the Teuton,

His statement was that he was attached to a local battery and was then on duty as observation officer.

Determined to see it through, I made him precede me downstairs and asked him to accompany me to his commanding officer.

It was then that the truth came out.

He was a German officer, though speaking English almost perfectly. He had been for ten days in the tower and had communicated the movements of our troops by means of a field-telephone, purposely left by the Germans when driven out of the village. When it appeared that he could bluff no longer, he became quite candid.

'You were lucky,' he said. 'In another six hours I should have been back across the lines.'

He smiled as he added: 'The fortune of war!'

The poor old woman was quite an innocent factor. She had been asked by this officer during one of his night expeditions to bring him a daily supply of food, and, thinking him British, and entirely ignorant of military law, she had complied.

The spy, it transpired, had been the manager of a well-known London hotel, and had been recalled to the German flag in July 1914.

I never knew how he ended, but I do not think we shot him. He was taken away by car for interrogation, and, I believe, interned.

My last impression of him was seated in a large Rolls-Royce car between two armed officers *en route* for an unknown destination. As the car moved off, his fine blue eyes met mine.

I smiled and saluted. Yes! a brave man. But he was a spy against my country.

On 22 November 1916, in full view of thousands of mud-grimed soldiers, who watched the combat from their trenches, took place one of the most deadly aerial combats of the war.

It was between Manfred von Richthofen, Germany's crack ace, and Captain Hawker, at that time the most daring and intrepid English airman in the Royal Flying Corps.

Both men, respectively, had a long list of enemy deaths upon their escutcheons of fame and both, as great belligerent champions, were destined one day to meet.

It was a duel between two highly-experienced enemy leaders for the recognised supremacy. Like two fighting eagles, they circled and manoeuvred around each other to gain the vital advantage, and the memory of this sight will remain with me for all time.

With a strong pair of glasses I watched from a forward artillery officer's observation post near Albert the last encircling aerial evolution of the English plane.

By this time Hawker had driven Richthofen well over the German lines towards Bapaume, and from what I could gather, they were going around and around each other in swift and ever-narrowing circles, both playing for the position of target with their machine-guns.

To this day I can never account for it. Perhaps it was some curious optical illusion – but it seemed to happen in a second – suddenly the German red Fokker was behind the English plane, spitting machine-gun fire fifty yards from the tail of Hawker's machine.

With a roaring glide I saw the English machine race earthward toward the German lines – and that was the last seen of one of the greatest English airmen.

Let me add in passing that Baron Manfred von Richthofen, whom I saw upon many occasions in aerial combat with the Allies, has been admitted to be the greatest aerial 'ace' of the world.

Up to the day of his death, 21 April 1918, near the lines of the Thirty-third Australian Field Battery, 5th Division, between Sailley-le-Sec, not far from Corbie, on the Somme, he had brought down no fewer than eighty Allied aeroplanes.

He took his toll of English, French and Americans, among whose names are to be found Hawker, Ball, McCudden, Immelmaan, Guynemer, Lugberry and Quintin Roosevelt.

A well-known American journalist, Mr Floyd Gibbon, attributes the death of Richthofen to the machine-gun fire of Captain Roy Brown, who came up behind while the German was pursuing another English airman named Lieutenant May.

May, with Richthofen roaring behind him, was racing from death with no ammunition. He was planing down in a race towards the British trenches. Near the Australian lines the machines could not have been more than a hundred yards apart – and some of the 'Diggers' were firing on the red Fokker of the German.

Suddenly Captain Brown, from out of the blue as it were, and behind Richthofen, swooped down – and up – releasing as he did so a deadly volley into the cockpit of the Fokker beneath.

Officially, the Royal Flying Corps claim the Red Knight of Germany's death – but to this day the surviving witnesses of the 5th Australian Division claim that a shot from one of their men had already killed the Baron before Captain Brown swooped down upon him from behind.

In a large marquee tent the body of Richthofen lay in state behind the British lines for two or three days prior to its interment.

Thousands of officers from all parts of the Allied front came to see the remains of this daring German airman.

In burying him with full military honours, the British paid the highest tribute possible to the memory of a gallant foe.

Another recollection of the war – and one of the most treasured – goes back to the period when the heir-apparent, our beloved Prince of Wales [later to become Edward VIII], was attached to the General Staff in France.

His known contempt for danger and his habit of 'looking for trouble' were a constant source of anxiety to the high officers responsible for his safety.

The method of guarding the Prince was for his 'shadower' to assume various roles which would render him inconspicuous. Mine usually was that of a dispatch rider.

Often it was quite impossible to keep him in sight, and there were many times when Headquarters received a nasty shock because the Prince was missing.

On one occasion it was suddenly realised that the Prince had not been seen for some time, and, although enquiries were immediately instituted, nobody seemed to know where he had gone.

The first knowledge that I had of the trouble was when I was approached by several staff officers in a long communication trench. They were breathless with hurrying, and were obviously in a state of great anxiety.

One of them recognised me, and a look of relief came over his face as he said: 'Oh, here's the Intelligence Police chap; perhaps he can tell us something.'

I could and I did. I had been trailing the Prince for hours, and at the time during which Headquarters were in a mortal funk lest something should have happened to him, the Prince was in the corner of a machine-gun emplacement, talking to a young lieutenant, some sergeants and a big bunch of interested Tommies.

Can it be wondered that he is so beloved by us all?

He said: 'I found my manhood in France,' and never was a truer and more sincere speech uttered. First and foremost he is a man and a prince afterwards.

It was not long after this that there occurred an incident which might have robbed the throne of its heir.

I was waiting for him to set out on one of his daily pilgrimages when suddenly I saw a high-powered car drive up to the headquarters at Merville. It was clear that he was going up the line, and it was equally clear that he would be going at a pace with which it would be impossible for me to keep up on my bike, good engine though it had.

I hung on as long as I possibly could, but at length lost sight of the car altogether.

However, I carried on until I got well into the danger zone, and the German artillery were putting over some very heavy stuff. I pulled up and made some enquiries of a few Tommies, and through this medium I managed to pick up the trail of the Prince and set off in the direction where he had been last seen. It was in the artillery area and in the very heart of a shell-blasted region.

At that moment a terrible roar and crash indicated the explosion of a shell on a derelict farm about four hundred yards to my front, and I hurried on.

Suddenly, I came upon the Prince standing near to a wall, looking shaky and distinctly pale. And small wonder. It appears that he had left his car in what he considered to be a place of comparative shelter – that is to say, he had left it protected by a thick wall that had been left standing.

He had gone out a little way, and, on his return, was horrified to find that both the wall and the car had been blown to atoms.

A few seconds earlier, and he would have been killed.

More than once (he got to know me and spoke to me often) I have detected a gleam of amusement in his eyes when he caught sight of me. I have seen him glance round at me with a little smile as much as to say: 'So you still insist on shadowing me. Right, old chap! I'll give you a run for your money. By the time I've finished with you and my walk across country, you'll be glad to get back on that old motor bike of yours!'

TWO

Later on in the war I was transferred to Boulogne, Paris, and Le Havre, and at the last-named place not only met with adventures, but came into contact with a number of interesting persons and became acquainted with numerous secrets of espionage. Of the latter I could tell many stories which I am not at liberty to set down at the moment.

My main duties at Le Havre were at the Gare des Voyageurs, the main arrival and departure station for Rouen and Paris. I was attached to the French Commissaire Special, and my primary duties consisted of examination of all persons travelling with British passports, while the French detectives were responsible for all passports of other nationalities.

By certain prearranged visas or markings, I knew who were suspect and who were otherwise. The code was known to all members of the Intelligence Police, and although specific instructions were issued in regard to such, each Intelligence Police member acted on his own initiative and responsibility in determining his line of action in any unforeseen contingency.

The French Detective Chief, or Commissaire Special, was, during my tenure of office, one Monsieur Caserne, under whom were about a dozen or so detectives of various ranks and grades.

Working with them all – these French officials – with their respective personalities, temperaments and mannerisms, remains one of my great experiences, and the memory of certain individuals lingers tenderly in my mind. In the presence of any known superior or anyone they deemed of importance I was Le Serjent Woodhall. I fraternised with superiors and subordinates and was secretly designated 'Monsieur Ted', my Christian name. This, coming from a body of Frenchmen, who, at least, are sticklers for etiquette, showed their friendly appraisement of their foreign comrade.

All travellers to and from Paris, or crossing either way the French, Spanish, Swiss or Italian frontiers, via Southampton and Le Havre, came through my hands, and many and numerous were the strange duties, incidents and irregularities which cropped up.

Ambassadors, diplomatic couriers, King's messengers, special messengers, naval and military attachés and officers of high rank, big commercial magnates – in fact, all, from the highest to the lowest, passed through my hands.

I handled, through my control barrier, the passports and special papers of many distinguished people. On one occasion the late Field Marshal Lord Kitchener, in mufti, came through, as also did Mr Winston Churchill. Of course, no control was necessary in the case of such persons of national importance. Facility of progress was the order in that case.

The late Master of Elibank, Lord Murray, came through, and our recognition was mutual. I saw him to his compartment and we had a long chat with each other. He spoke of the old election days when I was attached to Mr David Lloyd George, and recounted many instances which caused us both amusement. His death a few years ago removed a distinguished man from public affairs.

Joe Childs, jockey to King George V, came through my control on his way from France to England, prior to joining up in the fighting forces. I recall him quite vividly, a charming, quiet and gentlemanly little fellow. We had many laughs together during his sojourn in Le Havre – and if his eyes meet these lines he will smile at a certain incident known only to him and me!

One day there was handed into my custody at the Gare des Voyageurs a man whom I will call 'A'.

He had been arrested by the French when crossing from Spain into France but, being an Englishman, had been sent to us to deal with.

At the time of his arrest his passports were in a muddle. I believe he had foolishly been trying to alter them himself. It was also learnt that he had been trying to get into communication with his wife, who was then in Brussels. His own actions had brought suspicion upon him and the case looked very grave.

When handed over to me he was in a dishevelled state, looked absolutely worn out and emaciated; his clothes were dirty and torn, he had no collar or hat, and was, in fact, a pitiable object. I could see that under normal conditions he was a superior type of man.

As he was handed into my custody by the detective of the French Sûreté Générale, his relief was great. His first words were: 'Thank God, I am in English hands at last!'

It was my duty to bring him over to England and hand him to the authorities at Southampton. This I did, being locked in the cabin with him on the steamer, and, during the trip, he told me much of what he had been through.

Brutally treated, he had been convinced that the French intended to shoot him. In England he had a square deal, eventually joined the forces and served with distinction.

Today he occupies a high position in the journalistic and photographic world.

In the heights round about Le Havre were many encampments of German prisoners, guarded and maintained in some cases by the French.

But the majority of detachments were under English control.

Nearly all the prisoners worked on the quays, loading and unloading the many ocean-going vessels arriving and departing with cargoes. The particular detachment of prisoners to which I refer was comprised of the Prussian Cavalry Guard, from which complement several successful escapes took place in spite of the strongest guard and the utmost vigilance exercised.

Collusion was suspected, and the French Military, to whom this detachment belonged, applied for secret assistance. I was deputed for the commission, and my instructions were to trace the source from which its prisoners got their instructions and assistance.

In conjunction with the French Mobile Sûreté Général I took on my new task; in fact, I lost my identity. From a Sergeant of Intelligence my new role was as follows: A *réformé Anglais* (English discharged soldier) living in Paris, married to a French woman and working as a civilian labourer under the French people.

My first job was to get into the detachment under observation. This I did by applying for a position as crane-driver, realising that in this capacity I should have a better opportunity of watching without being suspected. Along the quayside there were many Belgian and French civilian labourers who, under the instructions of French officers, assisted the German prisoners in their tasks: of course, all under military guard.

My luck was in. I was taken as a crane-driver by the French civilian fore–man on the strength of my *permis de sejour* (authority of local residence) and duly installed.

Naturally, I was instructed by a French crane-driver in the mysteries of an electrically driven crane, which on the first day caused great amusement to the Germans and very nearly terminated my tenure on this earth.

My driving cabin was entered eight feet from the ground, by an iron ladder. The crane itself, being electrically controlled, had a huge arm shooting out from its centre with a large chain running up and down into the holds of any vessels or barges.

It also went round from left to right on an immense circular base. Also it could be moved on metal lines in the same direction if and when the case necessitated it.

I remember there was a switch to make the crane swing round – left to left, right to right – and a lever which you plugged in to hoist and drop the chain, and another lever to send the whole crane along.

I soon picked up the principle and bade fair to become an excellent crane-driver. The only thing that needed dexterity of touch was the crane when it went round. Too much current would swing it instantly round and if – as it was that day – unloading heavy stuff, in this particular instance it was iron plates, the crane could be easily thrown off the cog wheels of its circular base on which it revolved by the swinging momentum of its load.

The afternoon was wearing on as I hoisted and dropped my tons of iron from shore to hold. I had just got the signal from the German officer to hoist from the ground to the ship, which was done, and as the iron load stood out on the end of the suspending chain slowly revolving in mid-air over the heads of the prisoners beneath, my eyes caught a slight movement on the part of a civilian and a German officer prisoner.

At the same time as I saw the movement – a swift passage of something which looked like paper – the civilian's eyes looked up and met mine! For the moment I thought he had detected me, and, in order to cover up any suspicion on his part I accidentally 'yanked' round the switch instead of the lever to lower the load into the hold.

Instantly the crane swung round, and just as quickly I switched back into neutral. The cabin rocked, men flew in all directions and I had a momentary glimpse of about ten tons of iron swinging madly backwards and forwards at the end of my chain hoist.

I shut my eyes, for had it swung off its base, a fifty-ton crane, including its driver, would have been precipitated into about thirty feet of water in the dock.

The crane stopped. I had switched off all current, more by luck than judgement. From below I could see the German prisoners, some laughing, others looking in amazement, and, above all, the voice of the French civilian foreman shouting out. 'Nom de Dieu! Nom de Dieu! Quelle affaire. Quelle affaire.'

The foreman yelled to me to come out, which I did – and he promptly cursed me in his best French, and, to use an Americanism, I was fired!

Ignominiously as I was treated, my purpose was served. I knew my man and in due course proceeded to track him. As he left work I shadowed him home, and left the rest to my French detective colleague.

As a result of my efforts I was informed that through the instrumentality of this particular Belgian labourer – a pure 'hireling' – a huge scheme organised from Berlin through Geneva and Paris was discovered by the French Sûreté Général.

At any rate during the whole period afterwards not another German escaped. The French saw to that! What became of the man I discovered handing over his message, I never knew. The French moved silently, but sometimes with deadly effect.

Upon another occasion I was loaned to the Admiralty. The trouble this time was a mysterious light seen by some of our naval patrol boats outside the port of Le Havre.

It was alleged to be a clear flash to sea in the form of a Morse code, and it was conjectured that some enemy agent was signalling to a hidden submarine.

Therefore, one afternoon, off I went by the ferry from Le Havre to Honfleur, that beautiful old-world town situated in the Commune of Calvados on the mouth of the Siene and opposite to Le Havre.

My orders were to report to the Senior Naval Commander, who at that time had a shore billet on the heights overlooking the Siene and the English Channel. He was a splendid specimen of typical naval officer.

We discussed the question of the light and he admitted that it seemed too strange to be believed, in view of all the precautions taken by the French and English authorities.

I decided to stay for a few nights and investigate. Near to his bungalow, and on the top of the hill looking out to sea, was a small farm occupied by an old woman whose two sons were serving in the French army. Her sole means of support were several cows which she turned out for grazing in the fields around her homestead. Assisting the old lady was an individual of apparently feeble intellect.

As the lights, which appeared every evening just after sundown, seemed, according to the information, to come from this direction, I was at a loss to understand.

On the third day I asked the commander if the light had still been seen, and he assured me that it had. So I decided to watch the farm. It was getting near nightfall when I observed the half-witted man come out of the cottage. The cows were outside lowing to enter their shed for the night.

Judge my astonishment when I beheld the old lady leave the farm door and enter the cowshed. Swinging in her hand was a lighted hurricane lamp. I watched her enter the shed and busy herself with the cattle, all the time passing and repassing with the lamp. Suddenly the mystery of the light was solved!

Turning round I could perceive that from the little farm the view out to sea was absolutely uninterrupted.

I reported accordingly, and the experiment was tried. Next evening at nightfall from out at sea keen eyes were watching – but the light was never seen again, because the commander had informed the local gendarme, with the result that when the old lady required a light she took good care to see that it was not exposed to view.

There was absolutely no ulterior motive, the old lady in rural simplicity never realising her actions. When informed that an exposed light on a high eminence looking out to sea might give cause for much official perturbation, she quite innocently replied that it had been her custom for many years and this was the first time any complaint had ever been made against her!

We left the local gendarme to reprimand her, and there ended an episode which, like many more of a similar nature, turned out to be quite harmless in its foundation.

In 1917 I was transferred from the Intelligence Police to the Military Police at Etaples to assist in the rounding-up of deserters. I arrived at a period when this tremendous base depot, the largest reinforcement camp in France, situated about twenty miles or so from Boulogne, was settling down to comparative quietness. Some time previously a first detachment of WAACs had arrived.

The Military Police at that time was comprised of a peculiarly assorted body of men, tact and experience apparently being the least-sought-for qualification.

It would appear that a quarrel took place one night between a Tommy and a lance-corporal of the Military Police. The subject was one of the WAACs. The row occurred through jealousy and terminated fatally, the Tommy being shot – I believe accidentally – in the struggle.

Immediately the news flew round the huge camp, and the troops rose *en masse.*

'The Military Police! The Red-Caps! Down with 'em!'

And nothing would have prevented a terrible riot had it not been for the presence of mind and wonderful tact displayed by several members of the Headquarters General Staff.

For days the trouble seethed, but in the end it simmered down to normal.

From this time onwards the Military Police was improved by the introduction into its ranks of non-commissioned officers made up mostly of policemen from all parts of the United Kingdom.